The World
of the Short Story

THE
World
OF THE
Short Story

A Twentieth Century Collection

Selected and edited by

Clifton Fadiman

WINGS BOOKS
New York • Avenel, New Jersey

Copyright © 1986 by Clifton Fadiman

This 1990 edition is published by Wings Books, distributed
by Outlet Book Company, Inc., a Random House Company,
40 Engelhard Avenue, Avenel, New Jersey 07001,
by arrangement with Houghton Mifflin Company

Printed and bound in the United States of America

Library of Congress Cataloging in Publication Data

The World of the short story: a 20th century collection /
   selected and edited by Clifton Fadiman.
        p.   cm.
     ISBN 0-517-03400-X
        1. Short stories.   2. Fiction—20th century.
I. Fadiman, Clifton, 1904—
PN6120.2W67   1990   90-38295
                                                      CIP

8   7   6   5   4   3   2

*The editor is grateful for help and counsel
contributed by Anne Fadiman, Robie Macauley,
Alice van Straalen, and Siu Zimmerman.*

Contents

Foreword

This book was designed to place before the reader a generous selection of our century's finest short stories, drawn (as it turned out) from sixteen countries.

Reading or rereading many hundreds of stories, I asked myself two main questions. First, how good is this of its kind? Second, regardless of kind, at how deep a level of feeling and insight is the writer operating? What it boils down to is that in my judgment each story had to be both interesting and of high literary merit. These simple criteria are subjective. I have not tried to "represent" all the countries that produce short stories. An anthology of enjoyable reading should not be the literary equivalent of the United Nations General Assembly.

About three-quarters of the contents is by writers using the English language. That is partly because no honest anthologist can or should resist the normal pressures of his own culture, and partly because I believe that the outstanding work in the field has come from England, Ireland, Canada, English-speaking South Africa, and the United States.

No anthology can avoid being a covert personal statement. The reader or critic may well issue a counterstatement by declaring that he does not like some or perhaps any of the selections. But to go beyond that, to prescribe precisely what the contents *should* have been, is hardly useful. Better that he become an anthologist himself.

This collection is intended not for theoreticians or historians of the short story but for the curious, intelligent reader. That reader may notice the omission of several classic and justly honored names — Sherwood Anderson, Erskine Caldwell, Walter de la Mare, to mention three at random. With the limited space at my disposal, and with respect to members of an older generation, I had to ask myself the question, Does the writer, however important his contribution to the history and art of the short story, still speak to us with the urgency that once animated his voice? If the answer seemed doubtful or negative, I reluctantly omitted him or her.

The fact is that there is more mortality built into a good short story than into a novel of equal literary value. If Sherwood Anderson fades on my ear (though this may not be true for others) it should be remembered that in fifty years or fewer such fine contemporary talents as Trevor and Updike may be equally diminished. Not many short stories resist the tooth of time: there is only one "The Dead," one "A Simple Heart," one "Death of Ivan Ilyich." And, as I name these classic titles, I realize also that all these are quite long — novellas rather than short stories.

Thus one of the greatest names of our century, Thomas Mann, is not here represented. Of the novella he is a master, but I have not felt, after many rereadings, that his shorter tales afford a true measure of his genius. The same is true of Joseph Conrad and the greatly admired Isak Dinesen, but in her case I must not disguise my sense that what once seemed so startling now often sounds mannered, even at times pretentious.

One other notable omission: J. D. Salinger. My only excuse for not representing a talent so original and so enduring in its appeal is that permission to reprint him was not granted.

The stories are arranged by the birth dates of the authors, from early to late. The device, as convenient as any other, is not intended to illustrate the "evolution" of the short story: fiction is not a branch of biology. It does, however, throw into some relief the alterations the form has undergone in our century, the thematic terrains it has abandoned or invaded, the emergence of new styles — or perhaps merely fashions.

The aleatoric mode, I think, is the most pleasantly suited to the reading of an anthology. But the chronological approach, if we care to adopt it, does help us to recognize, as by lightning flashes and in a way denied to formal history books, certain shifts in our perception of reality since World War I. As human beings and as writers Somerset Maugham and Donald Barthelme have basically common interests. But the ways in which they interpret their transient and fugitive worlds, the words and rhythms they choose for the purpose of fixing them on paper — these stand in bewildering contrast or even in opposition.

Thus any collection like this one reinforces our sense of the short story's mutations over the years, as well as of the manner in which fiction glancingly reflects changes in our view of the real world. There is an excellent annual anthology called *Prize Stories: The O. Henry Awards*. Its readers will seek in vain any story even remotely recalling O. Henry or O. Henry's attitude toward life.

As we read our way from between the wars to our own day we begin to recognize in concrete examples the short story's many transformations, the new pathways upon which it has adventured. These have all been clearly pointed out by critics. We note at once that the "modern" story, perhaps taking its cue from the French Symbolists, compels the reader to do some of the work. It relies on suggestion, on implication. Its form (here, of course, Hemingway is the master and before him Chekhov) is determined by what it leaves out. Thus in a way we ourselves write — that is, we imagine — what the ancient masters — a Scott, a Mérimée, a Poe — supplied for us.

Many of the earlier stories in these pages give the reader the sense of closure. An episode or a character is developed in the course of a beginning, a middle, and an end. Some of the later stories reject the notion of closure. Experience is an unfinished business, fragmentary, disjointed. Of the first school John O'Hara and Irwin Shaw are perhaps fair examples, as Ann Beattie is of the second.

Serial narrative, though never abandoned, begins to give ground to broken or distorted sequences; extreme states of mind engage many writers; "magic realism" and other visionary approaches compete with more traditional techniques; Poe's "single effect" doctrine loses its appeal, often replaced by a dynamic of ambiguity; humor darkens; the simple concern with telling a tale is with some writers qualified by the concept of the short story as an experimental laboratory; and, perhaps most important, women exert upon the form a more decisive (and salutary) influence than ever before.

At this writing the short story, as has been generally remarked, is enjoying a boom in both quality and quantity. No one is quite sure why this should be so. Along with others, V. S. Pritchett theorizes that "it is the glancing form of fiction that seems to be right for the nervousness and restlessness of modern life." Along somewhat the same melancholy lines Frank O'Connor reflects that, as compared with the novel, the short story expresses "an intense awareness of human loneliness."

However that may be, it is apparent that the short story has come a long way since the French critic Jules Lemaître described Maupassant as "an almost irreproachable writer in a genre that is not." The genre today is no longer, as T. O Beachcroft once considered it, "at best a very modest art." At its highest level (and I think many of the following pages offer fair evidence) it meets the challenge laid down by Kay Boyle: "to invest a brief sequence of events with reverberating human significance by means of style, selection and ordering of detail, and — most important of all — to present the whole action in such a way that it is at once a parable and a slice of life, at once symbolic and real, both a valid picture of some phase of experience, and a sudden illumination of one of the perennial moral and psychological paradoxes which lie at the heart of *la condition humaine.*"

CLIFTON FADIMAN

The World
of the Short Story

Max Beerbohm
1872–1956

Beerbohm, an Englishman, was a second-order essayist, a superb caricaturist, an outstanding play critic, a master of tour de force in fiction, a delightful raconteur in person and on the radio, and the greatest parodist in our language.

His life stands in quaint, almost archaic contrast to many American literary careers of our day. It was long, pleasant, rather quiet, modestly productive. More to the point, it was perfectly comprehended by him. He calculated exactly the dimensions of his talents. He knew his limitations, worked perfectly within them, never tried to fool either the public or himself by attempting anything to which his exquisite sensibility and not unduly powerful intelligence were not suited. He was not a great man. But he was a great success.

His stories, though written in our century, exude a whiff of the nineties. Nonetheless, they have the perdurability that attaches to any work, particularly a smallish one, in which artifice is unblushing but absolute. Beerbohm himself thought his two best stories were "Enoch Soames" and "A. V. Laider." Of these I have chosen the less familiar and also, I think, the better.

A. V. Laider

1914.

I unpacked my things and went down to await luncheon.

It was good to be here again in this little old sleepy hostel by the sea. Hostel I say, though it spelt itself without an s and even placed a circumflex above the o. It made no other pretension. It was very cosy indeed.

I had been here just a year before, in mid-February, after an attack of influenza. And now I had returned, after an attack of influenza. Nothing was changed. It had been raining when I left, and the waiter — there was but a single, a very old waiter — had told me it was only a shower. That waiter was still here, not a day older. And the shower had not ceased.

Steadfastly it fell on to the sands, steadfastly into the iron-grey sea. I stood looking out at it from the windows of the hall, admiring it very much. There seemed to be little else to do. What little there was I did. I mastered the contents of a blue hand-bill which, pinned to the wall just beneath the framed engraving of Queen Victoria's Coronation, gave token of a concert that was to be held — or rather, was to have been held some weeks ago — in the Town Hall, for the benefit of the Life-Boat Fund. I looked at the barometer, tapped it, was not the wiser. I glanced at a pamphlet about Our Dying Industries (a theme on which Mr. Joseph Chamberlain was at that time trying to alarm us). I wandered to the letter-board.

These letter-boards always fascinate me. Usually some two or three of the envelopes stuck into the cross-garterings have a certain newness and freshness. They seem sure they will yet be claimed. Why not? Why *shouldn't* John Doe, Esq., or Mrs. Richard Roe, turn up at any moment? I do not know. I can only say that nothing in the world seems to me more unlikely. Thus it is that these young bright envelopes touch my heart even more than do their dusty and sallow seniors. Sour resignation is less touching than impatience for what will not be, than the eagerness that has to wane and wither. Soured beyond measure these old envelopes are. They are not nearly so nice as they should be to the young ones. They lose no chance of sneering and discouraging. Such dialogues as this are only too frequent:

A VERY YOUNG ENVELOPE. Something in me whispers that he will come to-day!

A VERY OLD ENVELOPE. He? Well, that's good! Ha, ha, ha! Why didn't he come last week, when *you* came? What reason have you for supposing he'll ever come *now?* It isn't as if he were a frequenter of the place. He's never been here. His name is utterly unknown here. You don't suppose he's coming on the chance of finding *you?*

A. V. Y. E. It may seem silly, but — something in me whispers —

A. V. O. E. Something in *you?* One has only to look at you to see there's nothing in you but a note scribbled to him by a cousin. Look at *me!* There are three sheets, closely written, in *me.* The lady to whom I am addressed —

A. V. Y. E. Yes, sir, yes; you told me all about her yesterday.

A. V. O. E. And I shall do so to-day and tomorrow and every day and all day long. That young lady was a widow. She stayed here many times. She was delicate, and the air suited her. She was poor, and the tariff was just within her means. She was lonely, and had need of love. I have in me for her a passionate avowal and strictly honourable proposal, written to her, after many rough copies, by a gentleman who had made her acquaintance under this very roof. He was rich, he was charming, he was in the prime of life. He had asked if he might write to her. She had flutteringly granted his request. He posted me to her the day after his return to London. I looked forward to being torn open by her. I was very sure she would wear me and my contents next to her bosom. She was gone. She had left no address. She never returned . . . This I tell you, and shall continue to tell you, not because I want any of your callow sympathy — no, *thank* you! — but that you may judge how much less than slight are the chances that you yourself —

But my reader has overheard these dialogues as often as I. He wants to know what was odd about this particular letter-board before which I was standing. At first glance I saw nothing odd about it. But presently I distinguished a handwriting that was vaguely familiar. It was mine. I stared, I wondered. There is always a slight shock in seeing an envelope of one's own after it has gone through the post. It looks as if it had gone through so much. But this was the first time I had ever seen an envelope of mine eating its heart out in bondage on a letter-board. This was outrageous. This was hardly to be believed. Sheer kindness had impelled me to write to "A. V. Laider, Esq.," and this was the result! I hadn't minded receiving no answer. Only now, indeed, did I remember that I hadn't received one. In multitudinous London the memory of A. V. Laider and his trouble had soon passed from my mind. But — well, what a lesson not to go out of one's way to write to casual acquaintances!

My envelope seemed not to recognise me as its writer. Its gaze was the more piteous for being blank. Even so had I once been gazed at by a dog that I had lost and, after many days, found in the Battersea Home. "I don't know who you are, but, whoever you are, claim me, take me out of this!" That was my dog's appeal. This was the appeal of my envelope.

I raised my hand to the letter-board, meaning to effect a swift and lawless rescue, but paused at sound of a footstep behind me. The old waiter had come to tell me that my luncheon was ready. I followed him out of the hall, not, however, without a bright glance across my shoulder to reassure the little captive that I should come back.

I had the sharp appetite of the convalescent, and this the sea-air had whetted already to a finer edge. In touch with a dozen oysters, and with stout, I soon shed away the unreasoning anger I had felt against A. V. Laider. I became merely sorry for him that he had not received a letter which might perhaps have comforted him. In touch with cutlets, I felt how sorely he had needed comfort. And anon, by the big bright fireside of that small dark smoking-room where, a year ago, on the last evening of my stay here, he and I had at length spoken to each other, I reviewed in detail the tragic experience he had told me: and I fairly revelled in reminiscent sympathy with him . . .

A. V. LAIDER — I had looked him up in the visitors' book on the night of his arrival. I myself had arrived the day before, and had been rather sorry there was no one else staying here. A convalescent by the sea likes to have some one to observe, to wonder about, at meal-time. I was glad when, on my second evening, I found seated at the table opposite to mine another guest. I was the gladder because he was just the right kind of guest. He was enigmatic. By this I mean that he did not look soldierly nor financial nor artistic nor anything definite at all. He offered a clean slate for speculation. And thank heaven! he evidently wasn't going to spoil the fun by engaging me in conversation later on. A decently unsociable man, anxious to be left alone.

The heartiness of his appetite, in contrast with his extreme fragility of aspect and limpness of demeanour, assured me that he, too, had just had influenza. I liked him for that. Now and again our eyes met and were instantly parted. We managed, as a rule, to observe each other indirectly. I was sure it was not merely because he had been ill that he looked interesting. Nor did it seem to me that a spiritual melancholy, though I imagined him sad at the best of times, was his sole asset. I conjectured that he was clever. I thought he might also be imaginative. At first glance I had mistrusted him. A shock of white hair, combined with a young face and dark eyebrows, does somehow make a man look like a charlatan. But it is foolish to be guided by an accident of colour. I had soon rejected my first impression of my fellow-diner. I found him very sympathetic.

Anywhere but in England it would be impossible for two solitary men, howsoever much reduced by influenza, to spend five or six days in the same hostel and not exchange a single word. That is one of the charms of England. Had Laider and I been born and bred in any other land we should have become acquainted before the end of our first evening in the small smoking-room, and have found ourselves irrevocably committed to go on talking to each other throughout the rest of our visit. We might, it is true, have happened to like each other more than any one we had ever met. This off-chance may have occurred to us both. But it counted for nothing as against the certain surrender of quietude and liberty. We slightly bowed to each other as we entered or left the dining-room or smoking-room, and as we met on the widespread sands or in the shop that had a small and faded circulating library. That was all. Our mutual aloofness was a positive bond between us.

Had he been much older than I, the responsibility for our silence would of course have been his alone. But he was not, I judged, more than five or six years ahead of me, and thus I might without impropriety have taken it on myself to perform that hard and perilous feat which English people call, with a shiver, "breaking the ice." He had reason, therefore, to be as grateful to me as I to him. Each of us, not the less frankly because silently, recognised his obligation to the other. And when, on the last evening of my stay, the ice actually was broken no ill-will rose between us: neither of us was to blame.

It was a Sunday evening. I had been out for a long last walk and had come in very late to dinner. Laider left his table almost immediately after I sat down to mine. When I entered the smoking-room I found him reading a weekly review which I had bought the day before. It was a crisis. He could not silently offer, nor could I have silently accepted, sixpence. It was a crisis. We faced it like men. He made, by word of mouth, a graceful apology. Verbally, not by signs, I besought him to go on reading. But this, of course, was a vain counsel of perfection. The social code forced us to talk now. We obeyed it like men. To reassure him that our position was not so desperate as it might seem, I took the earliest opportunity to mention that I was going away early next morning. In the tone of his "Oh, are you?" he tried bravely to imply that he was sorry, even now, to hear that. In a way, perhaps, he really was sorry. We had got on so well together, he and I. Nothing could efface the memory of that. Nay, we seemed to be hitting it off even now. Influenza was not our sole theme. We passed from that to the aforesaid weekly review, and to a correspondence that was raging therein on Faith and Reason.

This correspondence had now reached its fourth and penultimate stage — its Australian stage. It is hard to see why these correspondences spring up; one only knows that they do spring up, suddenly, like street crowds. There comes, it would seem, a moment when the whole English-speaking race is unconsciously bursting to have its say about some one thing — the split infinitive, or the habits of migratory birds, or faith and reason, or what-not. Whatever weekly review happens at such a moment to contain a reference, however remote, to the theme in question reaps the storm. Gusts of letters blow in from all corners of the British Isles. These are presently reinforced by Canada in full blast. A few weeks later the Anglo-Indians weigh in. In due course we have the help of our Australian cousins. By that time, however, we of the Mother Country have got our second wind, and so determined are we to make the most of it that at last even the Editor suddenly loses patience and says "This correspondence must now cease. — Ed." and wonders why on earth he ever allowed anything so tedious and idiotic to begin.

I pointed out to Laider one of the Australian letters that had especially pleased me in the current issue. It was from "A Melbourne Man," and was of the abrupt kind which declares that "all your correspondents have been groping in the dark" and then settles the whole matter in one short sharp flash. The flash in this instance was "Reason is faith, faith reason — that is all we know on earth and all we need to know." The writer then inclosed his card and was, etc., "A Melbourne Man." I said to Laider how very restful it was, after influenza, to read anything that meant nothing whatsoever. Laider was inclined to take the letter more seriously than I, and to be mildly metaphysical. I said that for me faith and reason were two separate things, and (as I am no good at metaphysics, however mild) I offered a definite example, to coax the talk on to ground where I should be safe. "Palmistry, for example," I said. "Deep down in my heart I believe in palmistry."

Laider turned in his chair. "You believe in palmistry?"

I hesitated. "Yes, somehow I do. Why? I haven't the slightest notion. I can give myself all sorts of reasons for laughing it to scorn. My common sense utterly rejects it. Of course the shape of the hand means something — is more or less an index of character. But the idea that my past and future are neatly mapped out on my palms —" I shrugged my shoulders.

"You don't like that idea?" asked Laider in his gentle, rather academic voice.

"I only say it's a grotesque idea."

"Yet you do believe in it?"

"I've a grotesque belief in it, yes."

"Are you sure your reason for calling this idea 'grotesque' isn't merely that you dislike it?"

"Well," I said, with the thrilling hope that he was a companion in absurdity, "doesn't it seem grotesque to you?"

"It seems strange."

"You believe in it?"

"Oh, absolutely."

"Hurrah!"

He smiled at my pleasure, and I, at the risk of re-entanglement in metaphysics, claimed him as standing shoulder to shoulder with me against "A Melbourne Man." This claim he gently disputed. "You may think me very prosaic," he said, "but I can't believe without evidence."

"Well, I'm equally prosaic and equally at a disadvantage: I can't take my own belief as evidence, and I've no other evidence to go on."

He asked me if I had ever made a study of palmistry. I said I had read one of Desbarolles' books years ago, and one of Heron-Allen's. But, he asked, had I tried to test them by the lines on my own hands or on the hands of my friends? I confessed that my actual practice in palmistry had been of a merely passive kind — the prompt extension of my palm to any one who would be so good as to "read" it and truckle for a few minutes to my egoism. (I hoped Laider might do this.)

"Then, I almost wonder," he said, with his sad smile, "that you haven't lost your belief, after all the nonsense you must have heard. There are so many young girls who go in for palmistry. I am sure all the five foolish virgins were 'awfully keen on it' and used to say 'You can be led, but not driven,' and 'You are likely to have a serious illness between the ages of forty and forty-five,' and 'You are by nature rather lazy, but can be very energetic by fits and starts.' And most of the professionals, I'm told, are as silly as the young girls."

For the honour of the profession, I named three practitioners whom I had found really good at reading character. He asked whether any of them had been right about past events. I confessed that, as a matter of fact, all three of them had been right in the main. This seemed to amuse him. He asked whether any of them had predicted anything which had since come true. I confessed that all three had predicted that I should do several things which I had since done rather unexpectedly. He asked if I didn't accept this as at any rate a scrap of evidence. I said I could only regard it as a fluke — a rather remarkable fluke.

The superiority of his sad smile was beginning to get on my nerves. I wanted him to see that he was as absurd as I. "Suppose," I said, "suppose for sake of argument that you and I are nothing but helpless automata created to do just this and that, and to have just that and this done to us. Suppose in fact, we *haven't* any free will whatsoever. Is it likely or conceivable that the Power that fashioned us would take the trouble to jot down in cipher on our hands just what was in store for us?"

Laider did not answer this question, he did but annoyingly ask me another. "You believe in free will?"

"Yes, of course. I'll be hanged if I'm an automaton."

"And you believe in free will just as in palmistry — without any reason?"

"Oh no. Everything points to our having free will."

"Everything? What, for instance?"

This rather cornered me. I dodged out, as lightly as I could, by saying "I suppose *you* would say it was written in my hand that I should be a believer in free will."

"Ah, I've no doubt it is."

I held out my palms. But, to my great disappointment, he looked quickly away from them. He had ceased to smile. There was agitation in his voice as he explained that he never looked at people's hands now.

"Never now — never again." He shook his head as though to beat off some memory.

I was much embarrassed by my indiscretion. I hastened to tide over the awkward moment by saying that if *I* could read hands I wouldn't, for fear of the awful things I might see there.

"Awful things, yes," he whispered, nodding at the fire.

"Not," I said in self-defense, "that there's anything very awful, so far as I know, to be read in *my* hands."

He turned his gaze from the fire to me. "You aren't a murderer, for example?"

"Oh, no," I replied, with a nervous laugh.

"*I* am."

This was a more than awkward, it was a painful, moment for me; and I am afraid I must have started or winced, for he instantly begged my pardon. "I don't know," he exclaimed, "why I said it. I'm usually a very reticent man. But sometimes —" He pressed his brow. "What you must think of me!"

I begged him to dismiss the matter from his mind.

"It's very good of you to say that; but — I've placed myself as well as you in a false position. I ask you to believe that I'm not the sort of man who is 'wanted' or ever was 'wanted' by the police. I should be bowed out of any police-station at which I gave myself up. I'm not a murderer in any bald sense of the word. No."

My face must have perceptibly brightened, for "Ah," he said, "don't imagine I'm not a murderer at all. Morally, I am." He looked at the clock. I pointed out that the night was young. He assured me that his story was not a long one. I assured him that I hoped it was. He said I was very kind. I denied this. He warned me that what he had to tell might rather tend to stiffen my unwilling faith in palmistry, and to shake my opposite and cherished faith in free will. I said "Never mind." He stretched his hands pensively toward the fire. I settled myself back in my chair.

"My hands," he said, staring at the backs of them, "are the hands of a very weak man. I dare say you know enough of palmistry to see that for yourself. You notice the slightness of the thumbs and of the two 'little' fingers. They are the hands of a weak and over-sensitive man — a man without confidence, a man who would certainly waver in an emergency. Rather Hamlet-ish hands," he mused. "And I'm like Hamlet in other respects, too: I'm no fool, and I've rather a noble disposition, and I'm unlucky. But Hamlet was luckier than I in one thing: he was a murderer by accident, whereas the murders that I committed one day fourteen years ago — for I must tell you it wasn't one murder, but many murders that I committed — were all of them due to the wretched inherent weakness of my own wretched self.

"I was twenty-six — no, twenty-seven years old, and rather a nondescript person, as I am now. I was supposed to have been called to the

Bar. In fact, I believe I *had* been called to the Bar. I hadn't listened to the call. I never intended to practise, and I never did practise. I only wanted an excuse in the eyes of the world for existing. I suppose the nearest I have ever come to practising is now at this moment: I am defending a murderer. My father had left me well enough provided with money. I was able to go my own desultory way, riding my hobbies where I would. I had a good stableful of hobbies. Palmistry was one of them. I was rather ashamed of this one. It seemed to me absurd, as it seems to you. Like you, though, I believed in it. Unlike you, I had done more than merely read a book or so about it. I had read innumerable books about it. I had taken casts of all my friends' hands. I had tested and tested again the points at which Desbarolles dissented from the gipsies, and — well, enough that I had gone into it all rather thoroughly, and was as sound a palmist as a man may be without giving his whole life to palmistry.

"One of the first things I had seen in my own hand, as soon as I had learned to read it, was that at about the age of twenty-six I should have a narrow escape from death — from a violent death. There was a clean break in the life-line, and a square joining it — the protective square, you know. The markings were precisely the same in both hands. It was to be the narrowest escape possible. And I wasn't going to escape without injury, either. That is what bothered me. There was a faint line connecting the break in the life-line with a star on the line of health. Against that star was another square. I was to recover from the injury, whatever it might be. Still, I didn't exactly look forward to it. Soon after I had reached the age of twenty-five, I began to feel uncomfortable. The thing might be going to happen at any moment. In palmistry, you know, it is impossible to pin an event down hard and fast to one year. This particular event was to be when I was *about* twenty-six; it mightn't be till I was twenty-seven; it might be while I was only twenty-five.

"And I used to tell myself that it mightn't be at all. My reason rebelled against the whole notion of palmistry, just as yours does. I despised my faith in the thing, just as you despise yours. I used to try not to be so ridiculously careful as I was whenever I crossed a street. I lived in London at that time. Motor-cars had not yet come in, but — what hours, all told, I must have spent standing on curbs, very circumspect, very lamentable! It was a pity, I suppose, that I had no definite occupation — something to take me out of myself. I was one of the victims of private means. There came a time when I drove in four-wheelers rather than in hansoms, and was doubtful of four-wheelers. Oh, I assure you, I was very lamentable indeed.

"If a railway-journey could be avoided, I avoided it. My uncle had a place in Hampshire. I was very fond of him and of his wife. Theirs was the only house I ever went to stay in now. I was there for a week in November, not long after my twenty-seventh birthday. There were other people staying there, and at the end of the week we all travelled back to London together. There were six of us in the carriage: Colonel Elbourn and his wife, and their daughter, a girl of seventeen; and another married couple, the Blakes. I had been at Winchester with Blake, but had hardly seen him since that time. He was in the Indian Civil, and was home on leave. He was sailing for India next week. His wife was to remain in England for some months, and then join him out there. They had been married five years. She was now just twenty-four years old. He told me that this was her age.

"The Elbourns I had never met before. They were charming people. We had all been very happy together. The only trouble had been that on the last night, at dinner, my uncle asked me if I still went in for 'the gipsy business,' as he always called it; and of course the three ladies were immensely excited, and implored me to 'do' their hands. I told them it was all nonsense, I said I had forgotten all I once knew, I made various excuses; and the matter dropped. It was quite true that I had given up reading hands. I avoided anything that might remind me of what was in my own hands. And so, next morning, it was a great bore to me when, soon after the train started, Mrs. Elbourn said it would be 'too cruel' of me if I refused to do their hands now. Her daughter and Mrs. Blake also said it would be 'brutal'; and they were all taking off their gloves, and — well, of course I had to give in.

"I went to work methodically on Mrs. Elbourn's hands, in the usual way, you know, first sketching the character from the backs of them; and there was the usual hush, broken by the usual little noises — grunts of assent from the husband, cooings of recognition from the daughter. Presently I asked to see the palms, and from them I filled in the details of Mrs. Elbourn's character before going on to the events in her life. But while I talked I was calculating how old Mrs. Elbourn might be. In my first glance at her palms I had seen that she could not have been less than twenty-five when she married. The daughter was seventeen. Suppose the daughter had been born a year later — how old would the mother be? Forty-three, yes. Not less than that, poor woman!"

Laider looked at me. "Why 'poor woman,' you wonder? Well, in that first glance I had seen other things than her marriage-line. I had seen a very complete break in the lines of life and of fate. I had seen violent death there. At what age? Not later, not possibly *later*, than forty-three. While I talked to her about the things that had happened in her girlhood, the back of my brain was hard at work on those marks of catastrophe. I was horribly wondering that she was still alive. It was impossible that between her and that catastrophe there could be more than a few short months. And all the time I was talking; and I suppose I acquitted myself well, for I remember that when I ceased I had a sort of ovation from the Elbourns.

"It was a relief to turn to another pair of hands. Mrs. Blake was an amusing young creature, and her hands were very characteristic, and prettily odd in form. I allowed myself to be rather whimsical about her nature, and, having begun in that vein, I went on in it — somehow — even after she had turned her palms. In those palms were reduplicated the signs I had seen in Mrs. Elbourn's. It was as though they had been copied neatly out. The only difference was in the placing of them; and it was this difference that was the most horrible point. The fatal age in Mrs. Blake's hands was — not past, no, for here *she* was. But she might have died when she was twenty-one. Twenty-three seemed to be the utmost span. She was twenty-four, you know.

"I have said that I am a weak man. And you will have good proof of that directly. Yet I showed a certain amount of strength that day — yes, even on that day which has humiliated and saddened the rest of my life. Neither my face nor my voice betrayed me when in the palms of Dorothy Elbourn I was again confronted with those same signs. She was all for knowing the future, poor child! I believe I told her all manner of things that were to be. And she had no future — none, none in *this* world — except —

"And then, while I talked, there came to me suddenly a suspicion. I wondered it hadn't come before. You guess what it was? It made me feel very cold and strange. I went on talking. But, also, I went on — quite separately — thinking. The suspicion wasn't a certainty. This mother and daughter were always together. What was to befall the one might anywhere — anywhere — befall the other. But a like fate, in an equally near future, was in store for that other lady. The coincidence was curious, very. Here we all were together — here; they and I — I who was narrowly to escape, so soon now, what they, so soon now, were to suffer. Oh, there was an inference to be drawn. Not a *sure* inference, I told myself. And always I was talking, talking, and the train was swinging and swaying noisily along — to what? It was a fast train. Our carriage was near the engine. I was talking loudly. Full well I had known what I should see in the Colonel's hands. I told myself I had not known. I told myself that even now the thing I dreaded was not sure to be. Don't think I was dreading it for myself. I wasn't so 'lamentable' as all that — now. It was only of them that I thought — only for them. I hurried over the Colonel's character and career; I was perfunctory. It was Blake's hands that I wanted. *They* were the hands that mattered. If *they* had the marks — Remember, Blake was to start for India in the coming week, his wife was to remain in England. They would be apart. Therefore —

"And the marks were there. And I did nothing — nothing but hold forth on the subtleties of Blake's character. There was a thing for me to do. I wanted to do it. I wanted to spring to the window and pull the communication-cord. Quite a simple thing to do. Nothing easier than to stop a train. You just give a sharp pull, and the train slows down, comes to a standstill. And the Guard appears at your window. You explain to the Guard.

"Nothing easier than to tell him there is going to be a collision. Noth-

ing easier than to insist that you and your friends and every other pas-
senger in the train must get out at once ... There *are* easier things than
this? Things that need less courage than this? Some of *them* I could have
done, I daresay. This thing I was going to do. Oh, I was determined that
I would do it — directly.

"I had said all I had to say about Blake's hands. I had brought my
entertainment to an end. I had been thanked and complimented all
round. I was quite at liberty. I was going to do what I had to do. I was
determined, yes.

"We were near the outskirts of London. The air was grey, thickening;
and Dorothy Elbourn had said, 'Oh, this horrible old London! I suppose
there's the same old fog!' And presently I heard her father saying something about 'prevention' and 'a short act of Parliament' and 'anthracite.'
And I sat and listened and agreed and —"

Laider closed his eyes. He passed his hand slowly through the air.

"I had a racking headache. And when I said so, I was told not to talk.
I was in bed, and the nurses were always telling me not to talk. I was in
a hospital. I knew that. But I didn't know why I was there. One day I
thought I should like to know why, and so I asked. I was feeling much
better now. They told me, by degrees, that I had had concussion of the
brain. I had been brought there unconscious, and had remained unconscious for forty-eight hours. I had been in an accident — a railway accident. This seemed to me odd. I had arrived quite safely at my uncle's
place, and I had no memory of any journey since that. In cases of concussion, you know, it's not uncommon for the patient to forget all that
happened just before the accident; there may be a blank of several hours.
So it was in my case. One day my uncle was allowed to come and see
me. And somehow, suddenly, at sight of him, the blank was filled in. I
remembered, in a flash, everything. I was quite calm, though. Or I made
myself seem so, for I wanted to know how the collision had happened.
My uncle told me that the engine-driver had failed to see a signal because of the fog, and our train had crashed into a goods-train. I didn't
ask him about the people who were with me. You see, there was no need
to ask. Very gently my uncle began to tell me, but — I had begun to talk
strangely, I suppose. I remember the frightened look of my uncle's face,
and the nurse scolding him in whispers.

"After that, all a blur. It seems that I became very ill indeed, wasn't
expected to live.

"However, I live."

There was a long silence. Laider did not look at me, nor I at him. The
fire was burning low, and he watched it.

At length he spoke. "You despise me. Naturally. I despise myself."

"No, I don't despise you; but —"

"You blame me." I did not meet his gaze. "You blame me," he
repeated.

"Yes."

"And there, if I may say so, you are a little unjust. It isn't my fault that I was born weak."

"But a man may conquer weakness."

"Yes, if he is endowed with the strength for that."

His fatalism drew from me a gesture of disgust. "Do you really mean," I asked, "that because you didn't pull that cord, you *couldn't* have pulled it?"

"Yes."

"And it's written in your hands that you couldn't?"

He looked at the palms of his hands. "They are the hands of a very weak man," he said.

"A man so weak that he cannot believe in the possibility of free will for himself or for any one?"

"They are the hands of an intelligent man, who can weigh evidence and see things as they are."

"But answer me: Was it fore-ordained that you should not pull that cord?"

"It was fore-ordained."

"And was it actually marked in your hands that you were not going to pull it?"

"Ah, well, you see, it's rather the things one *is* going to do that are actually marked. The things one *isn't* going to do — the innumerable negative things — how could one expect *them* to be marked?"

"But the consequences of what one leaves undone may be positive?"

"Horribly positive," he winced. "My hand is the hand of a man who has suffered a great deal in later life."

"And was it the hand of a man *destined* to suffer?"

"Oh, yes. I thought I told you that."

There was a pause.

"Well," I said, with awkward sympathy, "I suppose all hands are the hands of people destined to suffer."

"Not of people destined to suffer so much as *I* have suffered — as I still suffer."

The insistence of his self-pity chilled me, and I harked back to a question he had not straightly answered. "Tell me: Was it marked in your hands that you were not going to pull that cord?"

Again he looked at his hands, and then, having pressed them for a moment to his face, "It was marked very clearly," he answered, "in *their* hands."

Two or three days after this colloquy there had occurred to me in London an idea — an ingenious and comfortable doubt. How was Laider to be sure that his brain, recovering from concussion, had *remembered* what happened in the course of that railway-journey? How was he to know that his brain hadn't simply, in its abeyance, *invented* all this for him? It might be that he had never seen those signs in those hands. Assuredly, here was a bright loop-hole. I had forthwith written to Laider, pointing it out.

This was the letter which now, at my second visit, I had found miserably pent on the letter-board. I remembered my promise to rescue it. I arose from the retaining fireside, stretched my arms, yawned, and went forth to fulfil my Christian purpose. There was no one in the hall. The "shower" had at length ceased. The sun had positively come out, and the front door had been thrown open in its honour. Everything along the sea-front was beautifully gleaming, drying, shimmering. But I was not to be diverted from my errand. I went to the letter-board. And — my letter was not there! Resourceful and plucky little thing — it had escaped! I did hope it would not be captured and brought back. Perhaps the alarm had already been raised by the tolling of that great bell which warns the inhabitants for miles around that a letter has broken loose from the letter-board. I had a vision of my envelope skimming wildly along the coast-line, pursued by the old but active waiter and a breathless pack of local worthies. I saw it out-distancing them all, dodging past coast-guards, doubling on its tracks, leaping breakwaters, unluckily injuring itself, losing speed, and at last, in a splendour of desperation, taking to the open sea. But suddenly I had another idea. Perhaps Laider had returned?

He had. I espied afar on the sands a form that was recognisably, by the listless droop of it, his. I was glad and sorry — rather glad, because he completed the scene of last year; and very sorry because this time we should be at each other's mercy: no restful silence and liberty, for either of us, this time. Perhaps he had been told I was here, and had gone out to avoid me while he yet could. Oh weak, weak! Why palter? I put on my hat and coat, and marched out to meet him.

"Influenza, of course?" we asked simultaneously.

There is a limit to the time which one man may spend in talking to another about his own influenza; and presently, as we paced the sands, I felt that Laider had passed this limit. I wondered that he didn't break off and thank me now for my letter. He must have read it. He ought to have thanked me for it at once. It was a very good letter, a remarkable letter. But surely he wasn't waiting to answer it by post? His silence about it gave me the absurd sense of having taken a liberty, confound him! He was evidently ill at ease while he talked. But it wasn't for me to help him out of his difficulty, whatever that might be. It was for him to remove the strain imposed on myself.

Abruptly, after a long pause, he did now manage to say, "It was — very good of you to — to write me that letter." He told me he had only just got it, and he drifted away into otiose explanations of this fact. I thought he might at least say it was a remarkable letter; and you can imagine my annoyance when he said, after another interval, "I was very much touched indeed." I had wished to be convincing, not touching. I can't bear to be called touching.

"Don't you," I asked, "think it *is* quite possible that your brain invented all those memories of what — what happened before that accident?"

He drew a sharp sigh. "You make me feel very guilty."

"That's exactly what I tried to make you *not* feel!"

"I know, yes. That's why I feel so guilty."

We had paused in our walk. He stood nervously prodding the hard wet sand with his walking-stick. "In a way," he said, "your theory was quite right. But — it didn't go far enough. It's not only possible, it's a fact, that I didn't see those signs in those hands. I never examined those hands. They weren't there. *I* wasn't there. I haven't an uncle in Hampshire, even. I never had."

I, too, prodded the sand. "Well," I said at length, "I do feel rather a fool."

"I've no right even to beg your pardon, but —"

"Oh, I'm not vexed. Only — I rather wish you hadn't told me this."

"I wish I hadn't had to. It was your kindness, you see, that forced me. By trying to take an imaginary load off my conscience, you laid a very real one on it."

"I'm sorry. But you, of your own free will, you know, exposed your conscience to me last year. I don't yet quite understand why you did that."

"No, of course not. I don't deserve that you should. But I think you will. May I explain? I'm afraid I've talked a great deal already about my influenza, and I shan't be able to keep it out of my explanation. Well, my weakest point — I told you this last year, but it happens to be perfectly true that my weakest point — is my will. Influenza, as you know, fastens unerringly on one's weakest point. It doesn't attempt to undermine my imagination. That would be a forlorn hope. I have, alas! a very strong imagination. At ordinary times my imagination allows itself to be governed by my will. My will keeps it in check by constant nagging. But when my will isn't strong enough even to nag, then my imagination stampedes. I become even as a little child. I tell myself the most preposterous fables, and — the trouble is — I can't help telling them to my friends. Until I've thoroughly shaken off influenza, I'm not fit company for any one. I perfectly realise this, and I have the good sense to go right away till I'm quite well again. I come here usually. It seems absurd, but I must confess I was sorry last year when we fell into conversation. I knew I should very soon be letting myself go, or rather, very soon be swept away. Perhaps I ought to have warned you; but — I'm a rather shy man. And then you mentioned the subject of palmistry. You said you believed in it. I wondered at that. I had once read Desbarolles' book about it, but I am bound to say I thought the whole thing very great nonsense indeed."

"Then," I gasped, "it isn't even true that you believe in palmistry?"

"Oh, no. But I wasn't able to tell you that. You had begun by saying that you believed in palmistry, and then you proceeded to scoff at it. While you scoffed I saw myself as a man with a terribly good reason for *not* scoffing; and in a flash I saw the terribly good reason; I had the whole story — at least I had the broad outlines of it — clear before me."

"You hadn't ever thought of it before?" He shook his head. My eyes beamed. "The whole thing was a sheer improvisation?"

"Yes," said Laider, humbly, "I am as bad as all that. I don't say that all the details of the story I told you that evening were filled in at the very instant of its conception. I was filling them in while we talked about palmistry in general, and while I was waiting for the moment when my story would come in most effectively. And I've no doubt I added some extra touches in the course of the actual telling. Don't imagine that I took the slightest pleasure in deceiving you. It's only my will, not my conscience, that is weakened after influenza. I simply can't help telling what I've made up, and telling it to the best of my ability. But I'm thoroughly ashamed all the time."

"Not of your ability, surely?"

"Yes, of that, too," he said with his sad smile. "I always feel that I'm not doing justice to my idea."

"You are too stern a critic, believe me."

"It is very kind of you to say that. You are very kind altogether. Had I known that you were so essentially a man of the world — in the best sense of that term — I shouldn't have so much dreaded seeing you just now and having to confess to you. But I'm not going to take advantage of your urbanity and your easy-going ways. I hope that some day we may meet somewhere when I haven't had influenza and am a not wholly undesirable acquaintance. As it is, I refuse to let you associate with me. I am an older man than you, and so I may without impertinence warn you against having anything to do with me."

I deprecated this advice, of course; but for a man of weakened will, he showed great firmness. "You," he said, "in your heart of hearts, don't want to have to walk and talk continually with a person who might at any moment try to bamboozle you with some ridiculous tale. And I, for my part, don't want to degrade myself by trying to bamboozle any one — especially one whom I have taught to see through me. Let the two talks we have had be as though they had not been. Let us bow to each other, as last year, but let that be all. Let us follow in all things the precedent of last year."

With a smile that was almost gay he turned on his heel, and moved away with a step that was almost brisk. I was a little disconcerted. But I was also more than a little glad. The restfulness of silence, the charm of liberty — these things were not, after all, forfeit. My heart thanked Laider for that; and throughout the week I loyally seconded him in the system he had laid down for us. All was as it had been last year. We did not smile to each other, we merely bowed, when we entered or left the dining-room or smoking-room, and when we met on the widespread sands or in that shop which had a small and faded, but circulating, library.

Once or twice in the course of the week it did occur to me that perhaps Laider had told the simple truth at our first interview and an ingenious lie at our second. I frowned at this possibility. The idea of any one wishing to be quit of *me* was most distasteful. However, I was to find reassurance. On the last evening of my stay, I suggested, in the small smoking-room, that he and I should, as sticklers for precedent, converse. We did so, very pleasantly. And after a while I happened to say that I had seen this afternoon a great number of sea-gulls flying close to the shore.

"Sea-gulls?" said Laider, turning in his chair.

"Yes. And I don't think I had ever realised how extraordinarily beautiful they are when their wings catch the light."

"Beautiful?" Laider threw a quick glance at me and away from me. "You think them beautiful?"

"Surely."

"Well, perhaps they are, yes; I suppose they are. But — I don't like seeing them. They always remind me of something — rather an awful thing — that once happened to me . . ."

It was a very awful thing indeed.

COLETTE
1873–1954

The day Colette died, the worst thunderstorm in sixty-seven years hit Paris. Her last conscious act was to gesture toward the lightning and cry out, "Look! Look!" The words suggest the essence of her genius.

At eighty-one Colette was a legendary figure. A Grand Officer of the Legion of Honor, president of the Goncourt Academy, she would, to crown her career, receive a state funeral — unexampled honors for a French woman. A veteran of three marriages (the last a happy one), music hall performer, journalist, autobiographer, novelist, short story writer, deeply versed in the natural world of plants, flowers and animals, a connoisseur of more than a single variety of love, in the best sense a woman of the world, she ranked as one of the most vivid personalities of her time. During the final years of a long, crowded life, unable to stir from her Palais-Royal apartment, she reigned, surrounded by her beloved cats, as an object of wonder and pilgrimage.

Few have treated more revealingly at least one great theme, that of sexual love. She was most comfortable with the novella (Chéri, La Fin de Chéri, Gigi, Mitsou), but she excelled also in a kind of post-Maupassant short story, tender, sensual, witty, completely French, completely feminine.

"The Other Wife" is a deft, wry trifle, a small triumph of observation ("Look! Look!"). As with an O. Henry story, everything erupts in the last few words, indeed in the very last word. But her sensibility works on a plane quite different from his.

The Other Wife

"TABLE FOR TWO? This way, Monsieur, Madame, there is still a table next to the window, if Madame and Monsieur would like a view of the bay."

Alice followed the maître d'.

"Oh, yes. Come on, Marc, it'll be like having lunch on a boat on the water . . ."

Her husband caught her by passing his arm under hers. "We'll be more comfortable over there."

"There? In the middle of all those people? I'd much rather . . ."

"Alice, please."

He tightened his grip in such a meaningful way that she turned around. "What's the matter?"

"Shh . . ." he said softly, looking at her intently, and led her toward the table in the middle.

"What is it, Marc?"

"I'll tell you, darling. Let me order lunch first. Would you like the shrimp? Or the eggs in aspic?"

"Whatever you like, you know that."

They smiled at one another, wasting the precious time of an overworked maître d', stricken with a kind of nervous dance, who was standing next to them, perspiring.

"The shrimp," said Marc. "Then the eggs and bacon. And the cold chicken with a romaine salad. *Fromage blanc?* The house specialty? We'll go with the specialty. Two strong coffees. My chauffeur will be having lunch also, we'll be leaving again at two o'clock. Some cider? No, I don't trust it . . . Dry champagne."

He sighed as if he had just moved an armoire, gazed at the colorless midday sea, at the pearly white sky, then at his wife, whom he found lovely in her little Mercury hat with its large, hanging veil.

"You're looking well, darling. And all this blue water makes your eyes look green, imagine that! And you've put on weight since you've been traveling . . . It's nice up to a point, but only up to a point!"

Her firm, round breasts rose proudly as she leaned over the table.

"Why did you keep me from taking that place next to the window?"

Marc Seguy never considered lying. "Because you were about to sit next to someone I know."

"Someone I don't know?"

"My ex-wife."

She couldn't think of anything to say and opened her blue eyes wider.

"So what, darling? It'll happen again. It's not important."

The words came back to Alice and she asked, in order, the inevitable questions. "Did she see you? Could she see that you saw her? Will you point her out to me?"

"Don't look now, please, she must be watching us . . . The lady with brown hair, no hat, she must be staying in this hotel. By herself, behind those children in red . . ."

"Yes. I see."

Hidden behind some broad-brimmed beach hats, Alice was able to look at the woman who, fifteen months ago, had still been her husband's wife.

"Incompatibility," Marc said. "Oh, I mean . . . total incompatibility! We divorced like well-bred people, almost like friends, quietly, quickly. And then I fell in love with you, and you really wanted to be happy with me. How lucky we are that our happiness doesn't involve any guilty parties or victims!"

The woman in white, whose smooth, lustrous hair reflected the light from the sea in azure patches, was smoking a cigarette with her eyes half closed. Alice turned back toward her husband, took some shrimp and butter, and ate calmly. After a moment's silence she asked: "Why didn't you ever tell me that she had blue eyes, too?"

"Well, I never thought about it!"

He kissed the hand she was extending toward the bread basket and she blushed with pleasure. Dusky and ample, she might have seemed somewhat coarse, but the changeable blue of her eyes and her wavy, golden hair made her look like a frail and sentimental blonde. She vowed overwhelming gratitude to her husband. Immodest without knowing it, everything about her bore the overly conspicuous marks of extreme happiness.

They ate and drank heartily, and each thought the other had forgotten the woman in white. Now and then, however, Alice laughed too loudly, and Marc was careful about his posture, holding his shoulders back, his head up. They waited quite a long time for their coffee, in silence. An incandescent river, the straggled reflection of the invisible sun overhead, shifted slowly across the sea and shone with a blinding brilliance.

"She's still there, you know," Alice whispered.

"Is she making you uncomfortable? Would you like to have coffee somewhere else?"

"No, not at all! She's the one who must be uncomfortable! Besides, she doesn't exactly seem to be having a wild time, if you could see her . . ."

"I don't have to. I know that look of hers."

"Oh, was she like that?"

He exhaled his cigarette smoke through his nostrils and knitted his eyebrows. "Like that? No. To tell you honestly, she wasn't happy with me."

"Oh, really now!"

"The way you indulge me is so charming, darling . . . It's crazy . . . You're an angel . . . You love me . . . I'm so proud when I see those eyes of yours. Yes, those eyes . . . She . . . I just didn't know how to make her happy, that's all. I didn't know how."

"She's just difficult!"

Alice fanned herself irritably, and cast brief glances at the woman in white, who was smoking, her head resting against the back of the cane chair, her eyes closed with an air of satisfied lassitude.

Marc shrugged his shoulders modestly.

"That's the right word," he admitted. "What can you do? You have to feel sorry for people who are never satisfied. But we're satisfied . . . Aren't we, darling?"

She did not answer. She was looking furtively, and closely, at her husband's face, ruddy and regular; at his thick hair, threaded here and there with white silk; at his short, well-cared-for hands; and doubtful for the first time, she asked herself, "What more did she want from him?"

And as they were leaving, while Marc was paying the bill and asking for the chauffeur and about the route, she kept looking, with envy and curiosity, at the woman in white, this dissatisfied, this difficult, this superior . . .

SOMERSET MAUGHAM
1874–1965

A reviewer in the London Sunday Telegraph *once called Maugham "the best short story writer of the twentieth century." Today such a judgment elicits a smile, perhaps even a snort. At the moment Maugham is in the literary doghouse, a sad old dog, his teeth worn, hardly a bark in him.*

Yes, he is quite out of sync. We suspect the "well made" story, reflexively associating it with dishonesty. We are all for the open-ended, the inconclusive, and here is Maugham closing his fictions with an almost audible click. His point is always so clear the reader's intelligence may feel insulted. Maugham, poor chap, never bothers to load his work with more meaning than the traffic will bear. Finally, he thinks a story should entertain. Anyone can understand why Maugham's stories are now listed among the penny stocks of modern literature.

Still, for his best tales a fair case can be made. In them he achieves his aims: "lucidity, simplicity and euphony." These qualities may not be the highest, but they should not be disregarded either. It is true, as he is careful to admit, that his work lacks "the intimacy, the broad human touch and the animal serenity which the greatest writers alone can give." But it does offer its modest attractions: worldliness without vulgarity; whatever charm exhales from a thoroughgoing skepticism; shrewd if never penetrating observation of recognizable men and women, subjected to the reflective, ironic scrutiny of a cultivated clubman.

"The Facts of Life" is superficial without being trivial. It makes its neat and valid point with an elegant twist of the wrist. I hope the reader will not object to its cheerful conclusion. After all, there are plenty of items in this collection to satisfy the keenest appetite for unhappiness.

The Facts of Life

It was Henry Garnet's habit on leaving the city of an afternoon to drop in at his club and play bridge before going home to dinner. He was a pleasant man to play with. He knew the game well and you could be sure that he would make the best of his cards. He was a good loser; and when he won was more inclined to ascribe his success to his luck than to his skill. He was indulgent, and if his partner made a mistake could be trusted to find an excuse for him. It was surprising then on this occasion to hear him telling his partner with unnecessary sharpness that he had never seen a hand worse played; and it was more surprising still to see him not only make a grave error himself, an error of which you would never have thought him capable, but when his partner, not unwilling to get a little of his own back, pointed it out, insist against all reason and with considerable heat that he was perfectly right. But they were all old friends, the men he was playing with, and none of them took his ill-humor very seriously. Henry Garnet was a broker, a partner in a firm of repute, and it occurred to one of them that something had gone wrong with some stock he was interested in.

"How's the market to-day?" he asked.

"Booming. Even the suckers are making money."

It was evident that stocks and shares had nothing to do with Henry Garnet's vexation; but something was the matter; that was evident too. He was a hearty fellow, who enjoyed excellent health; he had plenty of money; he was fond of his wife and devoted to his children. As a rule he had high spirits, and he laughed easily at the nonsense they were apt to talk while they played; but to-day he sat glum and silent. His brows were crossly puckered and there was a sulky look about his mouth. Presently, to ease the tension, one of the others mentioned a subject upon which they all knew Henry Garnet was glad to speak.

"How's your boy, Henry? I see he's done pretty well in the tournament."

Henry Garnet's frown grew darker.

"He's done no better than I expected him to."

"When does he come back from Monte?"

"He got back last night."

"Did he enjoy himself?"

"I suppose so; all I know is that he made a damned fool of himself."

"Oh. How?"

"I'd rather not talk about it if you don't mind."

The three men looked at him with curiosity. Henry Garnet scowled at the green baize.

"Sorry, old boy. Your call."

The game proceeded in a strained silence. Garnet got his bid, and when he played his cards so badly that he went three down not a word was said. Another rubber was begun and in the second game Garnet denied a suit.

"Having none?" his partner asked him.

Garnet's irritability was such that he did not even reply, and when at the end of the hand it appeared that he had revoked, and that his revoke cost the rubber, it was not to be expected that his partner should let his carelessness go without remark.

"What the devil's the matter with you, Henry?" he said. "You're playing like a fool."

Garnet was disconcerted. He did not so much mind losing a big rubber himself, but he was sore that his inattention should have made his partner lose too. He pulled himself together.

"I'd better not play any more. I thought a few rubbers would calm me, but the fact is I can't give my mind to the game. To tell you the truth I'm in a hell of a temper."

They all burst out laughing.

"You don't have to tell us that, old boy. It's obvious."

Garnet gave them a rueful smile.

"Well, I bet you'd be in a temper if what's happened to me had happened to you. As a matter of fact I'm in a damned awkward situation, and if any of you fellows can give me any advice how to deal with it I'd be grateful."

"Let's have a drink and you tell us all about it. With a K.C., a Home Office official and an eminent surgeon . . . if we can't tell you how to deal with a situation, nobody can."

The K.C. got up and rang the bell for a waiter.

"It's about that damned boy of mine," said Henry Garnet.

Drinks were ordered and brought. And this is the story that Henry Garnet told them.

The boy of whom he spoke was his only son. His name was Nicholas and of course he was called Nicky. He was eighteen. The Garnets had two daughters besides, one of sixteen and the other of twelve, but however unreasonable it seemed, for a father is generally supposed to like his daughters best, and though he did all he could not to show his preference, there was no doubt that the greater share of Henry Garnet's affection was given to his son. He was kind, in a chaffing, casual way, to his daughters, and gave them handsome presents on their birthdays and at Christmas; but he doted on Nicky. Nothing was too good for him.

He thought the world of him. He could hardly take his eyes off him. You could not blame him, for Nicky was a son that any parent might have been proud of. He was six foot two, lithe but muscular, with broad shoulders and a slim waist, and he held himself gallantly erect; he had a charming head, well placed on the shoulders, with pale brown hair that waved slightly, blue eyes with long dark lashes under well-marked eyebrows, a full red mouth and a tanned, clean skin. When he smiled he showed very regular and very white teeth. He was not shy, but there was a modesty in his demeanour that was attractive. In social intercourse he was easy, polite and quietly gay. He was the offspring of nice, healthy, decent parents, he had been well brought up in a good home, he had been sent to a good school, and the general result was as engaging a specimen of young manhood as you were likely to find in a long time. You felt that he was as honest, open and virtuous as he looked. He had never given his parents a moment's uneasiness. As a child he was seldom ill and never naughty. As a boy he did everything that was expected of him. His school reports were excellent. He was wonderfully popular, and he ended his career, with a creditable number of prizes, as head of the school and captain of the football team. But this was not all. At the age of fourteen Nicky had developed an unexpected gift for lawn tennis. This was a game that his father not only was fond of, but played very well, and when he discerned in the boy the promise of a tennis-player he fostered it. During the holidays he had him taught by the best professionals and by the time he was sixteen he had won a number of tournaments for boys of his age. He could beat his father so badly that only parental affection reconciled the older player to the poor show he put up. At eighteen Nicky went to Cambridge and Henry Garnet conceived the ambition that before he was through with the university he should play for it. Nicky had all the qualifications for becoming a great tennis-player. He was tall, he had a long reach, he was quick on his feet and his timing was perfect. He realised instinctively where the ball was coming and, seemingly without hurry, was there to take it. He had a powerful serve, with a nasty break that made it difficult to return, and his forehand drive, low, long and accurate, was deadly. He was not so good on the backhand and his volleying was wild, but all through the summer before he went to Cambridge Henry Garnet made him work on these points under the best teacher in England. At the back of his mind, though he did not even mention it to Nicky, he cherished a further ambition, to see his son play at Wimbledon, and who could tell, perhaps be chosen to represent his country in the Davis Cup. A great lump came into Henry Garnet's throat as he saw in fancy his son leap over the net to shake hands with the American champion whom he had just defeated, and walk off the court to the deafening plaudits of the multitude.

As an assiduous frequenter of Wimbledon Henry Garnet had a good many friends in the tennis world, and one evening he found himself at a City dinner sitting next to one of them, a Colonel Brabazon, and in due course began talking to him of Nicky and what chance there might be of his being chosen to play for his university during the following season.

"Why don't you let him go down to Monte Carlo and play in the spring tournament there?" said the Colonel suddenly.

"Oh, I don't think he's good enough for that. He's not nineteen yet, he only went up to Cambridge last October; he wouldn't stand a chance against all those cracks."

"Of course, Austin and von Cramm and so on would knock spots off him, but he might snatch a game or two; and if he got up against some of the smaller fry there's no reason why he shouldn't win two or three matches. He's never been up against any of the first-rate players and it would be wonderful practice for him. He'd learn a lot more than he'll ever learn in the seaside tournaments you enter him for."

"I wouldn't dream of it. I'm not going to let him leave Cambridge in the middle of a term. I've always impressed upon him that tennis is only a game and it mustn't interfere with work."

Colonel Brabazon asked Garnet when the term ended.

"That's all right. He'd only have to cut about three days. Surely that could be arranged. You see, two of the men we were depending on have let us down, and we're in a hole. We want to send as good a team as we can. The Germans are sending their best players and so are the Americans."

"Nothing doing, old boy. In the first place Nicky's not good enough, and secondly, I don't fancy the idea of sending a kid like that to Monte Carlo without anyone to look after him. If I could get away myself I might think of it, but that's out of the question."

"I shall be there. I'm going as the non-playing captain of the English team. I'll keep an eye on him."

"You'll be busy, and besides, it's not a responsibility I'd like to ask you to take. He's never been abroad in his life, and to tell you the truth, I shouldn't have a moment's peace all the time he was there."

They left it at that and presently Henry Garnet went home. He was so flattered by Colonel Brabazon's suggestion that he could not help telling his wife.

"Fancy his thinking Nicky's as good as that. He told me he'd seen him play and his style was fine. He only wants more practice to get into the first flight. We shall see the kid playing in the semi-finals at Wimbledon yet, old girl."

To his surprise Mrs. Garnet was not so much opposed to the notion as he would have expected.

"After all the boy's eighteen. Nicky's never got into mischief yet and there's no reason to suppose he will now."

"There's his work to be considered; don't forget that. I think it would be a very bad precedent to let him cut the end of term."

"But what can three days matter? It seems a shame to rob him of a chance like that. I'm sure he'd jump at it if you asked him."

"Well, I'm not going to. I haven't sent him to Cambridge just to play tennis. I know he's steady, but it's silly to put temptation in his way. He's much too young to go to Monte Carlo by himself." .

"You say he won't have a chance against these crack players, but you can't tell."

Henry Garnet sighed a little. On the way home in the car it had struck him that Austin's health was uncertain and that von Cramm had his off-days. Supposing, just for the sake of argument, that Nicky had a bit of luck like that — then there would be no doubt that he would be chosen to play for Cambridge. But of course that was all nonsense.

"Nothing doing, my dear. I've made up my mind and I'm not going to change it."

Mrs. Garnet held her peace. But next day she wrote to Nicky, telling him wha: had happened, and suggested to him what she would do in his place if, wanting to go, he wished to get his father's consent. A day or two later Henry Garnet received a letter from his son. He was bubbling over with excitement. He had seen his tutor, who was a tennis-player himself, and the Provost of his college, who happened to know Colonel Brabazon, and no objection would be made to his leaving before the end of term; they both thought it an opportunity that shouldn't be missed. He didn't see what harm he could come to, and if only, just this once, his father would stretch a point, well, next term, he promised faithfully, he'd work like blazes. It was a very pretty letter. Mrs. Garnet watched her husband read it at the breakfast table; she was undisturbed by the frown on his face. He threw it over to her.

"I don't know why you thought it necessary to tell Nicky something I told you in confidence. It's too bad of you. Now you've thoroughly unsettled him."

"I'm sorry. I thought it would please him to know that Colonel Brabazon had such a high opinion of him. I don't see why one should only tell people the disagreeable things that are said about them. Of course I made it quite clear that there could be no question of his going."

"You've put me in an odious position. If there's anything I hate it's for the boy to look upon me as a spoil-sport and a tyrant."

"Oh, he'll never do that. He may think you rather silly and unreasonable, but I'm sure he'll understand that it's only for his own good that you're being so unkind."

"Christ," said Henry Garnet.

His wife had a great inclination to laugh. She knew the battle was won. Dear, oh dear, how easy it was to get men to do what you wanted. For appearance' sake Henry Garnet held out for forty-eight hours, but then he yielded, and a fortnight later Nicky came to London. He was to start for Monte Carlo next morning, and after dinner, when Mrs. Garnet and her elder daughter had left them, Henry took the opportunity to give his son some good advice.

"I don't feel quite comfortable about letting you go off to a place like Monte Carlo at your age practically by yourself," he finished, "but there it is and I can only hope you'll be sensible. I don't want to play the heavy father, but there are three things especially that I want to warn you against: one is gambling, don't gamble; the second is money, don't lend anyone money; and the third is women, don't have anything to do with women. If you don't do any of those three things you can't come to much harm, so remember them well."

"All right, father," Nicky smiled.

"That's my last word to you. I know the world pretty well and believe me, my advice is sound."

"I won't forget it. I promise you."

"That's a good chap. Now let's go up and join the ladies."

Nicky beat neither Austin nor von Cramm in the Monte Carlo tournament, but he did not disgrace himself. He snatched an unexpected victory over a Spanish player and gave one of the Austrians a closer match than anyone had thought possible. In the mixed doubles he got into the semi-finals. His charm conquered everyone and he vastly enjoyed himself. It was generally allowed that he showed promise, and Colonel Brabazon told him that when he was a little older and had had more practice with first-class players he would be a credit to his father. The tournament came to an end and the day following he was to fly back to London. Anxious to play his best he had lived very carefully, smoking little and drinking nothing, and going to bed early; but on his last evening he thought he would like to see something of the life in Monte Carlo of which he had heard so much. An official dinner was given to the tennis-players and after dinner with the rest of them he went into the Sporting Club. It was the first time he had been there. Monte Carlo was very full and the rooms were crowded. Nicky had never before seen roulette played except in the pictures; in a maze he stopped at the first table he came to; chips of different sizes were scattered over the green cloth in what looked like a hopeless muddle; the croupier gave the wheel a sharp turn and with a flick threw in the little white ball. After what seemed an endless time the ball stopped and another croupier with a broad, indifferent gesture raked in the chips of those who had lost.

Presently Nicky wandered over to where they were playing *trente et quarante,* but he couldn't understand what it was all about and he thought it dull. He saw a crowd in another room and sauntered in. A big game of baccara was in progress and he was immediately conscious of the tension. The players were protected from the thronging bystanders by a brass rail; they sat round the table, nine on each side, with the dealer in the middle and the croupier facing him. Big money was changing hands. The dealer was a member of the Greek Syndicate. Nicky looked at his impassive face. His eyes were watchful, but his expression never changed whether he won or lost. It was a terrifying, strangely impressive sight. It gave Nicky, who had been thriftily brought up, a peculiar thrill to see someone risk a thousand pounds on the turn of a card and when he lost make a little joke and laugh. It was all terribly exciting. An acquaintance came up to him.

"Been doing any good?" he asked.

"I haven't been playing."

"Wise of you. Rotten game. Come and have a drink."

"All right."

While they were having it Nicky told his friend that this was the first time he had ever been in the rooms.

"Oh, but you must have one little flutter before you go. It's idiotic to leave Monte without having tried your luck. After all it won't hurt you to lose a hundred francs or so."

"I don't suppose it will, but my father wasn't any too keen on my coming at all and one of the three things he particularly advised me not to do was to gamble."

But when Nicky left his companion he strolled back to one of the tables where they were playing roulette. He stood for a while looking at the losers' money being raked-in by the croupier and the money that was won paid out to the winners. It was impossible to deny that it was thrilling. His friend was right, it did seem silly to leave Monte without putting something on the table just once. It would be an experience, and at his age you had to have all the experience you could get. He reflected that he hadn't promised his father not to gamble, he'd promised him not to forget his advice. It wasn't quite the same, was it? He took a hundred-franc note out of his pocket and rather shyly put it on number eighteen. He chose it because that was his age. With a wildly beating heart he watched the wheel turn; the little white ball whizzed about like a small demon of mischief; the wheel went round more slowly, the little white ball hesitated, it seemed about to stop, it went on again; Nicky could hardly believe his eyes when it fell into number eighteen. A lot of chips were passed over to him and his hands trembled as he took them. It seemed to amount to a lot of money. He was so confused that he never thought of putting anything on the following round; in fact he had no intention of playing any more, once was enough; and he was surprised when eighteen again came up. There was only one chip on it.

"By George, you've won again," said a man who was standing near to him.

"Me? I hadn't got anything on."

"Yes, you had. Your original stake. They always leave it on unless you ask for it back. Didn't you know?"

Another packet of chips was handed over to him. Nicky's head reeled. He counted his gains: seven thousand francs. A queer sense of power seized him; he felt wonderfully clever. This was the easiest way of making money that he had ever heard of. His frank, charming face was wreathed in smiles. His bright eyes met those of a woman standing by his side. She smiled.

"You're in luck," she said.

She spoke English, but with a foreign accent.

"I can hardly believe it. It's the first time I've ever played."

"That explains it. Lend me a thousand francs, will you? I've lost everything I've got. I'll give it you back in half an hour."

"All right."

She took a large red chip from his pile and with a word of thanks disappeared. The man who had spoken to him before grunted.

"You'll never see that again."

Nicky was dashed. His father had particularly advised him not to lend anyone money. What a silly thing to do! And to somebody he'd never seen in his life. But the fact was, he felt at that moment such a love for the human race that it had never occurred to him to refuse. And that big red chip, it was almost impossible to realise that it had any value. Oh well, it didn't matter, he still had six thousand francs, he'd just try his luck once or twice more and if he didn't win he'd go home. He put a chip on sixteen, which was his elder sister's age, but it didn't come up; then on twelve, which was his younger sister's, and that didn't come up either; he tried various numbers at random, but without success. It was funny, he seemed to have lost his knack. He thought he would try just once more and then stop; he won. He had made up all his losses and had something over. At the end of an hour, after various ups and downs, having experienced such thrills as he had never known in his life, he found himself with so many chips that they would hardly go in his pockets. He decided to go. He went to the changers' office and he gasped when twenty thousand-franc notes were spread out before him. He had never had so much money in his life. He put it in his pocket and was turning away when the woman to whom he had lent the thousand francs came up to him.

"I've been looking for you everywhere," she said. "I was afraid you'd gone. I was in a fever, I didn't know what you'd think of me. Here's your thousand francs and thank you so much for the loan."

Nicky, blushing scarlet, stared at her with amazement. How he had misjudged her! His father had said, don't gamble; well, he had, and he'd made twenty thousand francs; and his father had said, don't lend anyone money; well, he had, he'd lent quite a lot to a total stranger, and she'd returned it. The fact was that he wasn't nearly such a fool as his father thought: he'd had an instinct that he could lend her the money with safety, and you see, his instinct was right. But he was so obviously taken aback that the little lady was forced to laugh.

"What is the matter with you?" she asked.

"To tell you the truth I never expected to see the money back."

"What did you take me for? Did you think I was a — cocotte?"

Nicky reddened to the roots of his wavy hair.

"No, of course not."

"Do I look like one?"

"Not a bit."

She was dressed very quietly, in black, with a string of gold beads round her neck; her simple frock showed off a neat, slight figure; she had a pretty little face and a trim head. She was made up, but not excessively, and Nicky supposed that she was not more than three or four years older than himself. She gave him a friendly smile.

"My husband is in the administration in Morocco, and I've come to Monte Carlo for a few weeks because he thought I wanted a change."

"I was just going," said Nicky because he couldn't think of anything else to say.

"Already!"

"Well, I've got to get up early to-morrow. I'm going back to London by air."

"Of course. The tournament ended to-day, didn't it? I saw you play, you know, two or three times."

"Did you? I don't know why you should have noticed me."

"You've got a beautiful style. And you looked very sweet in your shorts."

Nicky was not an immodest youth, but it did cross his mind that perhaps she had borrowed that thousand francs in order to scrape acquaintance with him.

"Do you ever go to the Knickerbocker?" she asked.

"No. I never have."

"Oh, but you mustn't leave Monte Carlo without having been there. Why don't you come and dance a little? To tell you the truth, I'm starving with hunger and I should adore some bacon and eggs."

Nicky remembered his father's advice not to have anything to do with women, but this was different; you had only to look at the pretty little thing to know at once that she was perfectly respectable. Her husband was in what corresponded, he supposed, to the Civil Service. His father and mother had friends who were Civil Servants and they and their wives sometimes came to dinner. It was true that the wives were neither so young nor so pretty as this one, but she was just as ladylike as they were. And after winning twenty thousand francs he thought it wouldn't be a bad idea to have a little fun.

"I'd love to go with you," he said. "But you won't mind if I don't stay very long. I've left instructions at my hotel that I'm to be called at seven."

"We'll leave as soon as ever you like."

Nicky found it very pleasant at the Knickerbocker. He ate his bacon and eggs with appetite. They shared a bottle of champagne. They danced, and the little lady told him he danced beautifully. He knew he danced pretty well, and of course she was easy to dance with. As light as a feather. She laid her cheek against his and when their eyes met there was in hers a smile that made his heart go pit-a-pat. A coloured woman sang in a throaty, sensual voice. The floor was crowded.

"Have you ever been told that you're very good-looking?" she asked.

"I don't think so," he laughed. "Gosh," he thought, "I believe she's fallen for me."

Nicky was not such a fool as to be unaware that women often liked him, and when she made that remark he pressed her to him a little more closely. She closed her eyes and a faint sigh escaped her lips.

"I suppose it wouldn't be quite nice if I kissed you before all these people," he said.

"What do you think they would take me for?"

It began to grow late and Nicky said that really he thought he ought to be going.

"I shall go too," she said. "Will you drop me at my hotel on your way?"

Nicky paid the bill. He was rather surprised at its amount, but with all that money he had in his pocket he could afford not to care, and they got into a taxi. She snuggled up to him and he kissed her. She seemed to like it.

"By Jove," he thought, "I wonder if there's anything doing."

It was true that she was a married woman, but her husband was in Morocco, and it certainly did look as if she'd fallen for him. Good and proper. It was true also that his father had warned him to have nothing to do with women, but, he reflected again, he hadn't actually promised he wouldn't, he'd only promised not to forget his advice. Well, he hadn't; he was bearing it in mind that very minute. But circumstances alter cases. She was a sweet little thing; it seemed silly to miss the chance of an adventure when it was handed to you like that on a tray. When they reached the hotel he paid off the taxi.

"I'll walk home," he said. "The air will do me good after the stuffy atmosphere of that place."

"Come up a moment," she said. "I'd like to show you the photo of my little boy."

"Oh, have you got a little boy?" he exclaimed, a trifle dashed.

"Yes, a sweet little boy."

He walked upstairs after her. He didn't in the least want to see the photograph of her little boy, but he thought it only civil to pretend he did. He was afraid he'd made a fool of himself; it occurred to him that she was taking him up to look at the photograph in order to show him in a nice way that he'd made a mistake. He'd told her he was eighteen.

"I suppose she thinks I'm just a kid."

He began to wish he hadn't spent all that money on champagne at the night-club.

But she didn't show him the photograph of her little boy after all. They had no sooner got into her room than she turned to him, flung her arms round his neck, and kissed him full on the lips. He had never in all his life been kissed so passionately.

"Darling," she said.

For a brief moment his father's advice once more crossed Nicky's mind and then he forgot it.

Nicky was a light sleeper and the least sound was apt to wake him. Two or three hours later he awoke and for a moment could not imagine where he was. The room was not quite dark, for the door of the bath-room was ajar, and the light in it had been left on. Suddenly he was conscious that someone was moving about the room. Then he remembered. He saw that it was his little friend, and he was on the point of speaking when something in the way she was behaving stopped him. She was walking very cautiously, as though she were afraid of waking him; she stopped once or twice and looked over at the bed. He wondered what she was after. He soon saw. She went over to the chair on which he had placed his clothes and once more looked in his direction. She waited for what seemed to him an interminable time. The silence was so intense that Nicky thought he could hear his own heart beating. Then, very slowly, very quietly, she took up his coat, slipped her hand into the inside pocket and drew out all those beautiful thousand-franc notes that Nicky had been so proud to win. She put the coat back and placed some other clothes on it so that it should look as though it had not been disturbed, then, with the bundle of notes in her hand, for an appreciable time stood once more stock-still. Nicky had repressed an instinctive impulse to jump up and grab her, it was partly surprise that had kept him quiet, partly the notion that he was in a strange hotel, in a foreign country, and if he made a row he didn't know what might happen. She looked at him. His eyes were partly closed and he was sure that she thought he was asleep. In the silence she could hardly fail to hear his regular breathing. When she had reassured herself that her movements had not disturbed him she stepped, with infinite caution, across the room. On a small table in the window a cineraria was growing in a pot. Nicky watched her now with his eyes wide open. The plant was evidently placed quite loosely in the pot, for taking it by the stalks she lifted it out; she put the banknotes in the bottom of the pot and replaced the plant. It was an excellent hiding-place. No one could have guessed that anything was concealed under that richly-flowering plant. She pressed the earth down with her fingers and then, very slowly, taking care not to make the smallest noise, crept across the room, and slipped back into bed.

"Chéri," she said, in a caressing voice.

Nicky breathed steadily, like a man immersed in deep sleep. The little lady turned over on her side and disposed herself to slumber. But though Nicky lay so still his thoughts worked busily. He was extremely indignant at the scene he had just witnessed, and to himself he spoke his thoughts with vigour.

"She's nothing but a damned tart. She and her dear little boy and her husband in Morocco. My eye! She's a rotten thief, that's what she is. Took me for a mug. If she thinks she's going to get away with anything like that, she's mistaken."

He had already made up his mind what he was going to do with the money he had so cleverly won. He had long wanted a car of his own, and had thought it rather mean of his father not to have given him one. After all, a feller doesn't always want to drive about in the family bus. Well, he'd just teach the old man a lesson and buy one himself. For twenty thousand francs, two hundred pounds roughly, he could get a very decent second-hand car. He meant to get the money back, but just then he didn't quite know how. He didn't like the idea of kicking up a row, he was a stranger, in an hotel he knew nothing of; it might very well be that the beastly woman had friends there, he didn't mind facing anyone in a fair fight, but he'd look pretty foolish if someone pulled a gun on him. He reflected besides, very sensibly, that he had no proof the money was his. If it came to a showdown and she swore it was hers, he might very easily find himself hauled off to a police-station. He really didn't know what to do. Presently by her regular breathing he knew that the little lady was asleep. She must have fallen asleep with an easy mind, for she had done her job without a hitch. It infuriated Nicky that she should rest so peacefully while he lay awake worried to death. Suddenly an idea occurred to him. It was such a good one that it was only by the exercise of all his self-control that he prevented himself from jumping out of bed and carrying it out at once. Two could play at her game. She'd stolen his money; well, he'd steal it back again, and they'd be all square. He made up his mind to wait quite quietly until he was sure that deceitful woman was sound asleep. He waited for what seemed to him a very long time. She did not stir. Her breathing was as regular as a child's.

"Darling," he said at last.

No answer. No movement. She was dead to the world. Very slowly, pausing after every movement, very silently, he slipped out of bed. He stood still for a while, looking at her to see whether he had disturbed her. Her breathing was as regular as before. During the time he was waiting he had taken note carefully of the furniture in the room so that in crossing it he should not knock against a chair or a table and make a noise. He took a couple of steps and waited, he took a couple of steps more; he was very light on his feet and made no sound as he walked; he took fully five minutes to get to the window, and here he waited again. He started, for the bed slightly creaked, but it was only because the sleeper turned in her sleep. He forced himself to wait till he had counted one hundred. She was sleeping like a log. With infinite care he seized the cineraria by the stalks and gently pulled it out of the pot; he put his other hand in, his heart beat nineteen to the dozen as his fingers touched the notes, his hand closed on them and he slowly drew them out. He replaced the plant and in his turn carefully pressed down the earth. While he was doing all this he had kept one eye on the form lying in the bed. It remained still. After another pause he crept softly to the chair on which his clothes were lying. He first put the bundle of notes in his coat pocket and then proceeded to dress. It took him a good quarter of an hour, because he could afford to make no sound. He had been wearing a soft shirt with his dinner jacket, and he congratulated himself on this, because it was easier to put on silently than a stiff one. He had some difficulty in tying his tie without a looking-glass, but he very wisely reflected that it didn't really matter if it wasn't tied very well. His spirits were rising. The whole thing now began to seem rather a lark. At length he was completely dressed except for his shoes, which he took in his hand; he thought he would put them on when he got into the passage. Now he had to cross the room to get to the door. He reached it so quietly that he could not have disturbed the lightest sleeper. But the door had to be unlocked. He turned the key very slowly; it creaked.

"Who's that?"

The little woman suddenly sat up in bed. Nicky's heart jumped to his mouth. He made a great effort to keep his head.

"It's only me. It's six o'clock and I've got to go. I was trying not to wake you."

"Oh, I forgot."

She sank back on to the pillow.

"Now that you're awake I'll put on my shoes."

He sat down on the edge of the bed and did this.

"Don't make a noise when you go out. The hotel people don't like it. Oh, I'm so sleepy."

"You go right off to sleep again."

"Kiss me before you go." He bent down and kissed her. "You're a sweet boy and a wonderful lover. *Bon voyage.*"

Nicky did not feel quite safe till he got out of the hotel. The dawn had broken. The sky was unclouded, and in the harbour the yachts and the fishing-boats lay motionless on the still water. On the quay fishermen were getting ready to start on their day's work. The streets were deserted. Nicky took a long breath of the sweet morning air. He felt alert and well. He also felt as pleased as Punch. With a swinging stride, his shoulders well thrown back, he walked up the hill and along the gardens in front of the Casino — the flowers in that clear light had a dewy brilliance that was delicious — till he came to his hotel. Here the day had already begun. In the hall porters with mufflers round their necks and berets on their heads were busy sweeping. Nicky went up to his room and had a hot bath. He lay in it and thought with satisfaction that he was not such a mug as some people might think. After his bath he did his exercises, dressed, packed and went down to breakfast. He had a grand appetite. No continental breakfast for him! He had grapefruit, porridge, bacon and eggs, rolls fresh from the oven, so crisp and delicious they melted in your mouth, marmalade and three cups of coffee. Though feeling perfectly well before, he felt better after that. He lit the pipe he had recently learnt to smoke, paid his bill and stepped into the car that was waiting to take him to the aerodrome on the other side of Cannes. The road as far as Nice ran over the hills and below him was the blue sea and the coast-line. He couldn't help thinking it damned pretty. They passed through Nice, so gay and friendly in the early morning, and presently they came to a long stretch of straight road that ran by the sea. Nicky had paid his bill, not with the money he had won the night before, but with the money his father had given him; he had changed a thousand francs to pay for supper at the Knickerbocker, but that deceitful little woman had returned him the thousand francs he had lent her, so that he still had twenty thousand-franc notes in his pocket. He thought he would like to have a look at them. He had so nearly lost them that they had a double value for him. He took them out of his hip-pocket into which for safety's sake he had stuffed them when he put on the suit he was travelling in, and counted them one by one. Something very strange had happened to them. Instead of there being twenty notes as there should have been there were twenty-six. He couldn't understand it at all. He counted them twice more. There was no doubt about it; somehow or other he had twenty-six thousand francs instead of the twenty he should have had. He couldn't make it out. He asked himself if it was possible that he had won more at the Sporting Club than he had realised. But no, that was out of the question; he distinctly remembered the man at the desk laying the notes out in four rows of five, and he had counted them himself. Suddenly the explanation occurred to him; when he had put his hand into the flower-pot, after taking out the cineraria, he had grabbed everything he felt there. The flower-pot was the little hussy's money-box and he had taken out not only his own money, but her savings as well. Nicky leant back in the car and burst into a roar of laughter. It was the funniest thing he had ever heard in his life. And when he thought of her going to the flower-pot some time later in the morning when she awoke, expecting to find the money she had so cleverly got away with, and finding, not only that it wasn't there, but that her own had gone too, he laughed more than ever. And so far as he was concerned there was nothing to do about it; he neither knew her name, nor the name of the hotel to which she had taken him. He couldn't return her money even if he wanted to.

"It serves her damned well right," he said.

This then was the story that Henry Garnet told his friends over the bridge-table, for the night before, after dinner when his wife and daughter had left them to their port, Nicky had narrated it in full.

"And you know what infuriated me is that he's so damned pleased with himself. Talk of a cat swallowing a canary. And d'you know what he said to me when he'd finished? He looked at me with those innocent eyes of his and said: 'You know, father, I can't help thinking there was something wrong about the advice you gave me. You said, don't gamble; well, I did, and I made a packet; you said, don't lend money; well, I did, and I got it back; and you said, don't have anything to do with women; well, I did, and I made six thousand francs on the deal.'"

It didn't make it any better for Henry Garnet that his three companions burst out laughing.

"It's all very well for you fellows to laugh, but you know, I'm in a damned awkward position. The boy looked up to me, he respected me, he took whatever I said as gospel truth, and now, I saw it in his eyes, he just looks upon me as a drivelling old fool. It's no good my saying one swallow doesn't make a summer; he doesn't see that it was just a fluke, he thinks the whole thing was due to his own cleverness. It may ruin him."

"You do look a bit of a damned fool, old man," said one of the others. "There's no denying that, is there?"

"I know I do, and I don't like it. It's so dashed unfair. Fate has no right to play one tricks like that. After all, you must admit that my advice was good."

"Very good."

"And the wretched boy ought to have burnt his fingers. Well, he hasn't. You're all men of the world, you tell me how I'm to deal with the situation now."

But they none of them could.

"Well, Henry, if I were you I wouldn't worry," said the lawyer. "My belief is that your boy's born lucky, and in the long run that's better than to be born clever or rich."

A. E. COPPARD
1878–1957

Born the son of a tailor and a housemaid, self-educated, A. E. Coppard lived a life of semiobscurity for many years in a small cottage in Essex. He was forty-three when his first story collection, Adam and Eve and Pinch Me, appeared. Good judges, such as Ford Madox Ford, soon recognized his rare talent, that of a true tale teller with no large statements to make. On the whole, however, he remained (perhaps in part by reason of his humble origins) outside English literary society, receiving no honors and very little money up to his death at seventy-nine. If you would like to learn more about him, read his almost certainly autobiographical "My Hundredth Tale."

"It is my feeling," he wrote, "that the closer the modern short story conforms to the ancient tradition of being spoken at you, rather than being read at you, the more acceptable it becomes." At his best (he wrote too many tales and some are forced) he moves us as does a perfect folktale or a ballad of long ago. He uncovered the queerly pied quality of human life in quite unimportant people: shop girls, gypsies, higglers, sailors, tailors, tramps, and country folk whose speech is thick with the rough poetry of sheepcote and hedgerow. A few of his tales of the supernatural work; others do not. Though Thomas Hardy must have influenced him, he belonged to no school and exerted very little influence on his generation of English storytellers. Coppard was an oddity. At his best he was an oddity who was also an artist.

"Dusky Ruth" is a sad, enchanting love lyric done into prose. Perhaps its magic lies in the fact that it tells of one of those erotic adventures, beautiful yet incomplete, that every man in his hidden heart would like to have had and to be able, many years afterward, to remember.

Dusky Ruth

AT THE CLOSE of an April day, chilly and wet, the traveller came to a
country town. In the Cotswolds, though the towns are small and sweet
and the inns snug, the general habit of the land is bleak and bare. He
had newly come upon upland roads so void of human affairs, so lonely,
that they might have been made for some forgotten uses by departed
men, and left to the unwitting passage of such strangers as himself. Even
the unending walls, built of old rough laminated rock, that detailed the
far-spreading fields, had grown very old again in their courses; there
were dabs of darkness, buttons of moss, and fossils on every stone. He
had passed a few neighbourhoods, sometimes at the crook of a stream,
or at the cross of debouching roads, where old habitations, their gan-
grenated thatch riddled with bird holes, had been not so much erected
as just spattered about the places. Beyond these signs an odd lark or
blackbird, the ruckle of partridges, or the nifty gallop of a hare had been
the only mitigation of the living loneliness that was almost as profound
by day as by night. But the traveller had a care for such times and places.
There are men who love to gaze with the mind at things that can never
be seen, feel at least the throb of a beauty that will never be known, and
hear over immense bleak reaches the echo of that which is no celestial
music, but only their own hearts' vain cries; and though his garments
clung to him like clay it was with deliberate questing step that the traveller trod the single street of the town, and at last entered the inn, shuffling his shoes in the doorway for a moment and striking the raindrops
from his hat. Then he turned into a small smoking-room. Leather-lined
benches, much worn, were fixed to the wall under the window and in
other odd corners and nooks behind mahogany tables. One wall was
furnished with all the congenial gear of a bar, but without any interven-
ing counter. Opposite, a bright fire was burning, and a neatly dressed
young woman sat before it in a Windsor chair, staring at the flames.
There was no other inmate of the room, and as he entered, the girl rose
up and greeted him. He found that he could be accommodated for the
night, and in a few moments his hat and scarf were removed and placed
inside the fender, his wet overcoat was taken to the kitchen, the landlord, an old fellow, was lending him a roomy pair of slippers, and a maid
was setting supper in an adjoining room.

He sat while this was doing and talked to the barmaid. She had a beautiful but rather mournful face as it was lit by the firelight, and when her glance was turned away from it her eyes had a piercing brightness. Friendly and well spoken as she was, the melancholy in her aspect was noticeable — perhaps it was the dim room, or the wet day, or the long hours ministering a multitude of cocktails to thirsty gallantry.

When he went to his supper he found cheering food and drink, with pleasant garniture of silver and mahogany. There were no other visitors, he was to be alone; blinds were drawn, lamps lit, and the fire at his back was comforting. So he sat long about his meal until a white-faced maid came to clear the table, discoursing to him about country things as she busied about the room. It was a long, narrow room, with a sideboard and the door at one end and the fireplace at the other. A bookshelf, almost devoid of books, contained a number of plates; the long wall that faced the windows was almost destitute of pictures, but there were hung upon it, for some inscrutable but doubtless sufficient reason, many dish-covers, solidly shaped, of the kind held in such mysterious regard and known as "willow pattern"; one was even hung upon the face of a map. Two musty prints were mixed with them, presentments of horses having a stilted extravagant physique and bestridden by images of inhuman and incommunicable dignity, clothed in whiskers, coloured jackets, and tight white breeches.

He took down the books from the shelf, but his interest was speedily exhausted, and the almanacs, the county directory, and various guidebooks were exchanged for the *Cotswold Chronicle*. With this, having drawn the deep chair to the hearth, he whiled away the time. The newspaper amused him with its advertisements of stock shows, farm auctions, travelling quacks and conjurers, and there was a lengthy account of the execution of a local felon, one Timothy Bridger, who had murdered an infant in some shameful circumstances. This dazzling crescendo proved rather trying to the traveller; he threw down the paper.

The town was all as quiet as the hills, and he could hear no sounds in the house. He got up and went across the hall to the smoke-room. The door was shut, but there was light within, and he entered. The girl sat there much as he had seen her on his arrival, still alone, with feet on fender. He shut the door behind him, sat down, and crossing his legs puffed at his pipe, admired the snug little room and the pretty figure of the girl, which he could do without embarrassment, as her meditative head, slightly bowed, was turned away from him. He could see something of her, too, in the mirror at the bar, which repeated also the agreeable contours of bottles of coloured wines and rich liqueurs — so entrancing in form and aspect that they seemed destined to charming histories, even in disuse — and those of familiar outline containing mere spirits or small beer, for which are reserved the harsher destinies of base oils, horse medicines, disinfectants, and cold tea. There were coloured glasses for bitter wines, white glasses for sweet, a tiny leaden sink beneath them, and the four black handles of the beer engines.

The girl wore a light blouse of silk, a short skirt of black velvet, and a pair of very thin silk stockings that showed the flesh of instep and shin so plainly that he could see they were reddened by the warmth of the fire. She had on a pair of dainty cloth shoes with high heels, but what was wonderful about her was the heap of rich black hair piled at the back of her head and shadowing the dusky neck. He sat puffing his pipe and letting the loud tick of the clock fill the quiet room. She did not stir and he could move no muscle. It was as if he had been willed to come there and wait silently. That, he felt now, had been his desire all the evening; and here, in her presence, he was more strangely stirred in a few short minutes than by any event he could remember.

In youth he had viewed women as futile, pitiable things that grew long hair, wore stays and garters, and prayed incomprehensible prayers. Viewing them in the stalls of the theatre from his vantage-point in the gallery, he always disliked the articulation of their naked shoulders. But still, there was a god in the sky, a god with flowing hair and exquisite eyes, whose one stride with an ardour grandly rendered took him across the whole round hemisphere to which his buoyant limbs were bound like spokes to the eternal rim and axle, his bright hair burning in the pity of the sunsets and tossing in the anger of the dawns.

Master traveller had indeed come into this room to be with this woman, and she as surely desired him, and for all its accidental occasion it was as if he, walking the ways of the world, had suddenly come upon what, what so imaginable with all permitted reverence as, well, just a shrine; and he, admirably humble, bowed the instant head.

Were there no other people within? The clock indicated a few minutes to nine. He sat on, still as stone, and the woman might have been of wax for all the movement or sound she made. There was allurement in the air between them; he had forborne his smoking, the pipe grew cold between his teeth. He waited for a look from her, a movement to break the trance of silence. No footfall in street or house, no voice in the inn but the clock, beating away as if pronouncing a doom. Suddenly it rasped out nine large notes, a bell in the town repeated them dolefully, and a cuckoo no farther than the kitchen mocked them with three times three. After that came the weak steps of the old landlord along the hall, the slam of doors, the clatter of lock and bolt, and then the silence returning unendurably upon them.

He rose and stood behind her; he touched the black hair. She made no movement or sign. He pulled out two or three combs and, dropping them into her lap, let the whole mass tumble about his hands. It had a curious harsh touch in the unravelling, but was so full and shining; black as a rook's wings it was. He slid his palms through it. His fingers searched it and fought with its fine strangeness; into his mind there travelled a serious thought, stilling his wayward fancy — this was no wayward fancy, but a rite accomplishing itself! *(Run, run, silly man, y'are lost!)* But having got so far, he burnt his boats, leaned over, and drew her face back to him. And at that, seizing his wrists, she gave him back ardour for ardour, pressing his hands to her bosom, while the kiss was sealed and sealed again. Then she sprang up and picking his scarf and hat from the fender said:

"I have been drying them for you, but the hat has shrunk a bit, I'm sure — I tried it on."

He took them from her and put them behind him; he leaned lightly back upon the table, holding it with both his hands behind him; he could not speak.

"Aren't you going to thank me for drying them?" she asked, picking her combs from the rug and repinning her hair.

"I wonder why we did that?" he asked, shamedly.

"It is what I'm thinking too," she said.

"You were so beautiful about — about it, you know."

She made no rejoinder, but continued to bind her hair, looking brightly at him under her brows. When she had finished she went close to him.

"Will that do?"

"I'll take it down again."

"No, no, the old man or the old woman will be coming in."

"What of that?" he said, taking her into his arms. "Tell me your name."

She shook her head, but she returned his kisses and stroked his hair and shoulders with beautifully melting gestures.

"What is your name? I want to call you by your name," he said. "I can't keep calling you Lovely Woman, Lovely Woman."

Again she shook her head and was dumb.

"I'll call you Ruth, then, Dusky Ruth, Ruth of the black, beautiful hair."

"That is a nice-sounding name — I knew a deaf and dumb girl named Ruth; she went to Nottingham and married an organ-grinder — but I should like it for my name."

"Then I give it to you."

"Mine is so ugly."

"What is it?"

Again the shaken head and the burning caress.

"Then you shall be Ruth; will you keep that name?"

"Yes, if you give me the name I will keep it for you."

Time had indeed taken them by the forelock, and they looked upon a ruddled world.

"I stake my one talent," he said jestingly, "and behold it returns me fortyfold; I feel like the boy who catches three mice with one piece of cheese."

At ten o'clock the girl said:

"I must go and see how *they* are getting on," and she went to the door.

"Are we keeping them up?"

She nodded.

"Are you tired?"

"No, I am not tired." She looked at him doubtfully.

"We ought not to stay in here; go into the coffee room and I'll come there in a few minutes."

"Right," he whispered gaily, "we'll sit up all night."

She stood at the door for him to pass out, and he crossed the hall to the other room. It was in darkness except for the flash of the fire. Standing at the hearth he lit a match for the lamp, but paused at the globe; then he extinguished the match.

"No, it's better to sit in the firelight."

He heard voices at the other end of the house that seemed to have a chiding note in them.

"Lord," he thought, "is she getting into a row?"

Then her steps came echoing over the stone floor of the hall; she opened the door and stood there with a lighted candle in her hand; he stood at the other end of the room, smiling.

"Good night," she said.

"Oh no, no! come along," he protested, but not moving from the hearth.

"Got to go to bed," she answered.

"Are they angry with you?"

"No."

"Well, then, come over here and sit down."

"Got to go to bed," she said again, but she had meanwhile put her candlestick upon the little sideboard and was trimming the wick with a burnt match.

"Oh, come along, just half an hour," he protested. She did not answer, but went on prodding the wick of the candle.

"Ten minutes, then," he said, still not going towards her.

"Five minutes," he begged.

She shook her head and, picking up the candlestick, turned to the door. He did not move, he just called her name: "Ruth!"

She came back then, put down the candlestick, and tiptoed across the room until he met her. The bliss of the embrace was so poignant that he was almost glad when she stood up again and said with affected steadiness, though he heard the tremor in her voice:

"I must get you your candle."

She brought one from the hall, set it on the table in front of him, and struck the match.

"What is my number?" he asked.

"Number-six room," she answered, prodding the wick vaguely with her match, while a slip of white wax dropped over the shoulder of the new candle. "Number six . . . next to mine."

The match burnt out; she said abruptly: "Good night," took up her own candle, and left him there.

In a few moments he ascended the stairs and went into his room. He fastened the door, removed his coat, collar, and slippers, but the rack of passion had seized him and he moved about with no inclination to sleep. He sat down, but there was no medium of distraction. He tried to read the newspaper that he had carried up with him, and without realizing a single phrase he forced himself to read again the whole account of the execution of the miscreant Bridger. When he had finished this he carefully folded the paper and stood up, listening. He went to the parting wall and tapped thereon with his fingertips. He waited half a minute, one minute, two minutes; there was no answering sign. He tapped again, more loudly, with his knuckles, but there was no response, and he tapped many times. He opened his door as noiselessly as possible; along the dark passage there were slips of light under the other doors, the one next his own, and the one beyond that. He stood in the corridor listening to the rumble of old voices in the farther room, the old man and his wife going to their rest. Holding his breath fearfully, he stepped to *her* door and tapped gently upon it. There was no answer, but he could somehow divine her awareness of him; he tapped again; she moved to the door and whispered: "No, no, go away." He turned the handle, the door was locked.

"Let me in," he pleaded. He knew she was standing there an inch or two beyond him.

"Hush," she called softly. "Go away, the old woman has ears like a fox."

He stood silent for a moment.

"Unlock it," he urged; but he got no further reply, and feeling foolish and baffled he moved back to his own room, cast his clothes from him, doused the candle and crept into the bed with soul as wild as a storm-swept forest, his heart beating a vagrant summons. The room filled with strange heat, there was no composure for mind or limb, nothing but flaming visions and furious embraces.

"Morality . . . what is it but agreement with your own soul?"

So he lay for two hours — the clocks chimed twelve — listening with foolish persistency for *her* step along the corridor, fancying every light sound — and the night was full of them — was her hand upon the door.

Suddenly, then — and it seemed as if his very heart would abash the house with its thunder — he could hear distinctly someone knocking on the wall. He got quickly from his bed and stood at his door, listening. Again the knocking was heard, and having half-clothed himself he crept into the passage, which was now in utter darkness, trailing his hand along the wall until he felt her door; it was standing open. He entered her room and closed the door behind him. There was not the faintest gleam of light, he could see nothing. He whispered: "Ruth!" and she was standing there. She touched him, but not speaking. He put out his hands, and they met round her neck; her hair was flowing in its great wave about her; he put his lips to her face and found that her eyes were streaming with tears, salt and strange and disturbing. In the close darkness he put his arms about her with no thought but to comfort her; one hand had plunged through the long harsh tresses and the other across her hips before he realized that she was ungowned; then he was aware of the softness of her breasts and the cold naked sleekness of her shoulders. But she was crying there, crying silently with great tears, her strange sorrow stifling his desire.

"Ruth, Ruth, my beautiful dear!" he murmured soothingly. He felt for the bed with one hand, and turning back the quilt and sheets, he lifted her in as easily as a mother does her child, replaced the bedding, and, in his clothes, he lay stretched beside her, comforting her. They lay so, innocent as children, for an hour, when she seemed to have gone to sleep. He rose then and went silently to his room, full of weariness.

In the morning he breakfasted without seeing her, but as he had business in the world that gave him just an hour longer at the inn before he left it for good and all, he went into the smoke-room and found her. She greeted him with curious gaze, but merrily enough, for there were other men there now — farmers, a butcher, a registrar, an old, old man. The hour passed, but not these men, and at length he donned his coat, took up his stick, and said good-bye. Her shining glances followed him to the door, and from the window as far as they could view him.

HORACIO QUIROGA
1878–1937

In a way Quiroga recalls our own Edgar Poe and Ambrose Bierce. Apart from their morbidity which he shares, he contributes his own regionalist concern with the primitive lives of the inhabitants of Uruguay, where he was born, and Argentina, where he spent most of his life.

His death obsession was no literary affectation, no gesture of fashionable decadence. His best friend died of an accidental gunshot wound; his father, stepfather, wife, and at last he himself were suicides. Illness and depression dogged his unhappy life from beginning to end.

In Quiroga the death theme frequently plays itself out against a background of inimical natural forces, often including animals. The tone is almost always dark.

The cuento that follows is one of his most famous. Many writers have been challenged by the problem of conveying the sensations of a human being consciously facing death. Here it is successfully and implacably handled, with an absurdist irony that makes us aware of Quiroga's reputation as an authentic modernist.

The Dead Man

WITH HIS MACHETE the man had just finished clearing the fifth lane of the banana grove. Two lanes remained, but, since only chirca trees and jungle mallow were flourishing there, the task still before him was relatively minor. Consequently the man cast a satisfied glance at the brush he had cleared out and started to cross the wire fence so he could stretch out for a while in the grama grass.

But as he lowered the barbed wire to cross through, his foot slipped on a strip of bark hanging loose from the fence post, and in the same instant he dropped his machete. As he was falling, the man had a dim, distant impression that his machete was not lying flat on the ground.

Now he was stretched out on the grass, resting on his right side just the way he liked. His mouth, which had flown open, had closed again. He was as he had wanted to be, his knees doubled and his left hand over his breast. Except that behind his forearm, immediately below his belt, the handle and half the blade of his machete protruded from his shirt; the remainder was not visible.

The man tried to move his head — in vain. He peered out of the corner of his eye at the machete, still damp from the sweat of his hand. He had a mental picture of the extension and the trajectory of the machete in his belly, and coldly, mathematically, and inexorably he knew with certainty that he had reached the end of his existence.

Death. One often thinks in the course of his life that one day, after years, months, weeks, and days of preparation, he will arrive in his turn upon the threshold of death. It is mortal law, accepted and foreseen; so much so that we are in the habit of allowing ourselves to be agreeably transported by our imaginations to that moment, supreme among all moments, in which we breathe our last breath.

But between the present and that dying breath, what dreams, what reverses, what hopes and dramas we imagine for ourselves in our lives! A vigorous existence holds so much in store for us before our elimination from the human scene! Is this our consolation, the pleasure and the reason of our musings on death? Death is so distant, and so unpredictable is that life we still must live.

Still . . . ? Still not two seconds passed: the sun is at exactly the same altitude; the shadows have not advanced one millimeter. Abruptly, the long-term digressions have just been resolved for the man lying there; he is dying.

Dead. One might consider him dead in his comfortable position.

But the man opens his eyes and looks around. How much time has passed? What cataclysm has overtaken the world? What disturbance of nature does this horrible event connote?

He is going to die. Coldly, fatally, and unavoidably, he is going to die.

The man resists — such an unforeseen horror! And he thinks: it's a nightmare; that's what it is! What has changed? Nothing. And he looks: isn't that banana grove *his* banana grove? Doesn't he come every morning to clear it out? Who knows it as well as he? He sees the grove so perfectly, thinned out, the broad leaves bared to the sun. There are the leaves, so near, frayed by the wind. But now they are not moving . . . It is the calm of midday; soon it will be twelve o'clock.

Through the banana trees, high up, the man on the hard ground sees the red roof of his house. To the left, a glimpse of the scrub trees and the wild cinnamon. That's all he can see, but he knows very well that behind his back is the road to the new port and that in the direction of his head, down below, the Paraná, wide as a lake, lies sleeping in the valley. Everything, everything, exactly as always: the burning sun, the vibrant air, the loneliness, the motionless banana trees, the wire fence with the tall, very thick posts that soon will have to be replaced . . .

Dead! But is it possible? Isn't this one of many days on which he has left his house at dawn with his machete in his hand? And isn't his horse, his mare with the star on her forehead, right there just four meters away, gingerly nosing the barbed wire?

But yes! Someone is whistling . . . He can't see because his back is to the road, but he feels the vibration of the horse's hooves on the little bridge . . . It is the boy who goes by toward the new port every morning at 11:30. And always whistling . . . From the bark-stripped post he can almost touch with his boot the live-thicket fence that separates the grove from the road; it is fifteen meters. He knows it perfectly well, because he himself had measured the distance when he put up the fence.

So what is happening, then? Is this or isn't it an ordinary midday like so many others in Misiones, in his bushland, on his pasture, in his cleared-out banana grove? No doubt! Short grass, and hills, silence, leaden sun . . .

Nothing, nothing has changed. Only he is different. For two minutes now his person, his living personality, has had no connection with the cleared land he himself spaded up during five consecutive months, nor with the grove, work of his hands alone. Nor with his family. He has been uprooted, brusquely, naturally, because of a slippery piece of bark and a machete in the belly. Two minutes: he is dying.

The man, very weary, lying on his right side in the grama grass, still resists admitting a phenomenon of such transcendency in the face of the normal, and monotonous, aspect of the boy who has just crossed the bridge as he does every day.

But it isn't possible that he could have slipped! The handle of his machete (it's worn down now; soon it will have to be changed for another) was grasped just right between his left hand and the barbed wire. After ten years in the woods, he knows very well how you manage a bush machete. He is only very weary from the morning's work and is resting a little as usual.

The proof? But he himself planted this grama grass that is poking between his lips in squares of land a meter apart! And that is his banana grove and that his starred mare snorting cautiously by the barbed wire! The horse sees him perfectly; he knows she doesn't dare come around the corner of the fence since he himself is lying almost at the foot of the post. The man distinguishes her very well, and he sees the dark threads of sweat on her crupper and withers. The sun is as heavy as lead, and the calm is great; not a fringe of the banana trees is moving. Every day he has seen the same things.

. . . Very weary, but he's just resting. Several minutes must have passed now . . . And at a quarter to twelve, from up there, from his house with the red roof, his wife and two children will set out for the grove to look for him for lunch. He always hears, before anything else, the voice of his smaller son who tries to break away from his mother's hand: "Pah-pah! Pah-pah!"

Isn't that it . . . ? Of course, he hears it now! It's time. That's just what he hears, the voice of his son . . .

What a nightmare! But, of course, it's just one of many days, ordinary as any other! Excessive light, yellowish shadows, oven-still heat that raises sweat on the motionless horse next to the forbidden banana grove.

. . . Very, very tired, but that's all. How many times, at midday like this, on his way to the house, has he crossed this clearing that was a thicket when he came, and virgin bush before that? He was always tired, slowly returning home with his machete dangling from his left hand.

But still he can move away in his mind if he wants; he can, if he wants, abandon his body for an instant and look at the ordinary everyday landscape from the flood ditch he himself built — the stiff grama grass in the field of volcanic rock, the banana grove and its red sand, the wire fence fading out of sight in the distance as it slopes downward toward the road. And, farther still, the cleared land, the work of his own hands. And at the foot of a bark-stripped post, thrown on his right side, his legs drawn up, exactly like any other day, he can see himself, a sunny little heap on the grama grass — resting, because he is very tired.

But the horse, striped with sweat, cautiously motionless at a corner of the fence, also sees the man on the ground and doesn't dare enter the banana grove, as she would like to. With the voices nearby now — "Pah-pah!" — for a long, long while, the mare turns her motionless ears toward the heap on the ground and finally, quieted, decides to pass between the post and the fallen man — who has rested now.

Franz Kafka
1883–1924

It is a minor circumstance that this collection, by its nature stressing no single view of the human predicament, should include so many writers who seem to have felt a little touch of Kafka in the night: Cortázar, Oates, García Márquez, Helprin, Barthelme, Borges, Singer. After Joyce's, his is perhaps the deepest influence on twentieth-century imaginative prose. W. H. Auden goes so far as to think him "the author who comes nearest to bearing the same relation to our age as Dante, Shakespeare and Goethe bore to theirs."

Which is odd. Kafka, who lived in Prague and wrote in German, was a soul set apart, cut off from normal human happiness. The gap between his strange sensibility and that of most of us would seem unbridgeable. It has turned out otherwise. His obsession with "the inexplicable" connects with some deep-layered response in ourselves.

One obvious explanation — true, but not the truest — is that he fore-felt our time, what he called "the most unhappy of ages." Ernst Pawel, in his fine biography The Nightmare of Reason, speaks of the head torturer in the following story as "a prescient portrait of Adolf Eichmann, drawn from life." The Trial (begun in 1914) and The Castle (written in 1922) are prefiguring metaphors of the bureaucratic state, whether slave or free. Kafka, had he lived, would not have been surprised to hear that among the six million Jewish victims of the German murder machine were his three sisters.

But he is far more than a greater Jules Verne, and what he is does not lend itself to critical exegesis. Each reader will react in his own secret way to Kafka's chill, visionary narratives, detached from the reportable world, composed in simple, unrhetorical language, forever revolving around his own guilts and agonies and oedipal conflicts, yet always evoking the underworld of our own least-acknowledged fears and bafflements.

"In the Penal Colony" ranks among the most horrifying of Kafka's tales. It is about the power of power itself, about the necessity to maintain at any cost the integrity of the "marvelous piece of apparatus." One draws back from the temptation to match this nightmare against ours. After all, what could Kafka have known of the thermonuclear age, our own worldwide penal colony, our own marvelous piece of apparatus? He conceived his engine of death in October 1914, more than seventy years ago.

In the Penal Colony

"IT'S A REMARKABLE piece of apparatus," said the officer to the explorer and surveyed with a certain air of admiration the apparatus which was after all quite familiar to him. The explorer seemed to have accepted merely out of politeness the Commandant's invitation to witness the execution of a soldier condemned to death for disobedience and insulting behavior to a superior. Nor did the colony itself betray much interest in this execution. At least, in the small sandy valley, a deep hollow surrounded on all sides by naked crags, there was no one present save the officer, the explorer, the condemned man, who was a stupid-looking wide-mouthed creature with bewildered hair and face, and the soldier who held the heavy chain controlling the small chains locked on the prisoner's ankles, wrists and neck, chains which were themselves attached to each other by communicating links. In any case, the condemned man looked so like a submissive dog that one might have thought he could be left to run free on the surrounding hills and would only need to be whistled for when the execution was due to begin.

The explorer did not much care about the apparatus and walked up and down behind the prisoner with almost visible indifference while the officer made the last adjustments, now creeping beneath the structure, which was bedded deep in the earth, now climbing a ladder to inspect its upper parts. These were tasks that might well have been left to a mechanic, but the officer performed them with great zeal, whether because he was a devoted admirer of the apparatus or because of other reasons the work could be entrusted to no one else. "Ready now!" he called at last and climbed down from the ladder. He looked uncommonly limp, breathed with his mouth wide open and had tucked two fine ladies' handkerchiefs under the collar of his uniform. "These uniforms are too heavy for the tropics, surely," said the explorer, instead of making some inquiry about the apparatus, as the officer had expected. "Of course," said the officer, washing his oily and greasy hands in a bucket of water that stood ready, "but they mean home to us; we don't want to forget about home. Now just have a look at this machine," he added at once, simultaneously drying his hands on a towel and indicating the apparatus. "Up till now a few things still had to be set by hand, but from this moment it works all by itself." The explorer nodded and followed him. The officer, anxious to secure himself against all contingencies, said: "Things sometimes go wrong, of course; I hope that nothing goes wrong today, but we have to allow for the possibility. The machinery should go on working continuously for twelve hours. But if anything does go wrong it will only be some small matter that can be set right at once.

"Won't you take a seat?" he asked finally, drawing a cane chair out from among a heap of them and offering it to the explorer, who could not refuse it. He was now sitting at the edge of a pit, into which he glanced for a fleeting moment. It was not very deep. On one side of the pit the excavated soil had been piled up in a rampart, on the other side of it stood the apparatus. "I don't know," said the officer, "if the Commandant has already explained this apparatus to you." The explorer waved one hand vaguely; the officer asked for nothing better, since now he could explain the apparatus himself. "This apparatus," he said, taking hold of a crank handle and leaning against it, "was invented by our former Commandant. I assisted at the very earliest experiments and had a share in all the work until its completion. But the credit of inventing it belongs to him alone. Have you ever heard of our former Commandant? No? Well, it isn't saying too much if I tell you that the organization of the whole penal colony is his work. We who were his friends knew even before he died that the organization of the colony was so perfect that his successor, even with a thousand new schemes in his head, would find it impossible to alter anything, at least for many years to come. And our prophecy has come true; the new Commandant has had to acknowledge its truth. A pity you never met the old Commandant! — But," the officer interrupted himself, "I am rambling on, and here stands his apparatus before us. It consists, as you see, of three parts. In the course of time each of these parts has acquired a kind of popular nickname. The lower one is called the 'Bed,' the upper one the 'Designer,' and this one here in the middle that moves up and down is called the 'Harrow.'" "The Harrow?" asked the explorer. He had not been listening very attentively, the glare of the sun in the shadeless valley was altogether too strong, it was difficult to collect one's thoughts. All the more did he admire the officer, who in spite of his tight-fitting full-dress uniform coat, amply befrogged and weighed down by epaulettes, was pursuing his subject with such enthusiasm and, besides talking, was still tightening a screw here and there with a spanner. As for the soldier, he seemed to be in much the same condition as the explorer. He had wound the prisoner's chain round both his wrists, propped himself on his rifle, let his head hang and was paying no attention to anything. That did not surprise the explorer, for the officer was speaking French, and certainly neither the soldier nor the prisoner understood a word of French. It was all the more remarkable, therefore, that the prisoner was none the less making an effort to follow the officer's explanations. With a kind of drowsy persistence he directed his gaze wherever the officer pointed a finger, and at the interruption of the explorer's question he, too, as well as the officer, looked around.

"Yes, the Harrow," said the officer, "a good name for it. The needles are set in like the teeth of a harrow and the whole thing works something like a harrow, although its action is limited to one place and contrived with much more artistic skill. Anyhow, you'll soon understand it. On the Bed here the condemned man is laid — I'm going to describe the apparatus first before I set it in motion. Then you'll be able to follow the proceedings better. Besides, one of the cogwheels in the Designer is badly worn; it creaks a lot when it's working; you can hardly hear yourself speak; spare parts, unfortunately, are difficult to get here. — Well, here is the Bed, as I told you. It is completely covered with a layer of cotton wool; you'll find out why later. On this cotton wool the condemned man is laid, face down, quite naked, of course; here are straps for the hands, here for the feet, and here for the neck, to bind him fast. Here at the head of the bed, where the man, as I said, first lays down his face, is this little gag of felt, which can be easily regulated to go straight into his mouth. It is meant to keep him from screaming and biting his tongue. Of course the man is forced to take the felt into his mouth, for otherwise his neck would be broken by the strap." "Is that cotton wool?" asked the explorer, bending forward. "Yes, certainly," said the officer, with a smile. "Feel it for yourself." He took the explorer's hand and guided it over the bed. "It's specially prepared cotton wool; that's why it looks so different; I'll tell you presently what it's for." The explorer already felt a dawning interest in the apparatus; he sheltered his eyes from the sun with one hand and gazed up at the structure. It was a huge affair. The Bed and the Designer were of the same size and looked like two dark wooden chests. The Designer hung about two meters above the Bed; each of them was bound at the corners with four rods of brass that almost flashed out rays in the sunlight. Between the chests shuttled the Harrow on a ribbon of steel.

The officer had scarcely noticed the explorer's previous indifference, but he was now well aware of his dawning interest; so he stopped explaining in order to leave a space of time for quiet observation. The condemned man imitated the explorer; since he could not use a hand to shelter his eyes he gazed upwards without shade.

"Well, the man lies down," said the explorer, leaning back in his chair and crossing his legs.

"Yes," said the officer, pushing his cap back a little and passing one hand over his heated face, "now listen! Both the Bed and the Designer have an electric battery each; the Bed needs one for itself, the Designer for the Harrow. As soon as the man is strapped down, the Bed is set in motion. It quivers in minute, very rapid vibrations, both from side to side and up and down. You will have seen similar apparatus in hospitals; but in our Bed the movements are all precisely calculated; you see, they have to correspond very exactly to the movements of the Harrow. And the Harrow is the instrument for the actual execution of the sentence."

"And how does the sentence run?" asked the explorer.

You don't know that either?" said the officer in amazement, and bit his lips. "Forgive me if my explanations seem rather incoherent. I do beg your pardon. You see, the Commandant always used to do the explaining; but the new Commandant shirks this duty; yet that such an important visitor" — the explorer tried to deprecate the honor with both hands; the officer, however, insisted — "that such an important visitor should not even be told about the kind of sentence we pass is a new development, which — " He was just on the point of using strong language but checked himself and said only: "I was not informed, it is not my fault. In any case, I am certainly the best person to explain our procedure, since I have here" — he patted his breast pocket — "the relevant drawings made by our former Commandant."

"The Commandant's own drawings?" asked the explorer. "Did he combine everything in himself, then? Was he soldier, judge, mechanic, chemist and draughtsman?"

"Indeed he was," said the officer, nodding assent, with a remote, glassy look. Then he inspected his hands critically; they did not seem clean enough to him for touching the drawings; so he went over to the bucket and washed them again. They he drew out a small leather wallet and said: "Our sentence does not sound severe. Whatever commandment the prisoner has disobeyed is written upon his body by the Harrow. This prisoner, for instance" — the officer indicated the man — "will have written on his body: HONOR THY SUPERIORS!"

The explorer glanced at the man; he stood, as the officer pointed him out, with bent head, apparently listening with all his ears in an effort to catch what was being said. Yet the movement of his blubber lips, closely pressed together, showed clearly that he could not understand a word. Many questions were troubling the explorer, but at the sight of the prisoner he asked only: "Does he know his sentence?" "No," said the officer, eager to go on with his exposition, but the explorer interrupted him: "He doesn't know the sentence that has been passed on him?" "No," said the officer again, pausing a moment as if to let the explorer elaborate his question, and then said: "There would be no point in telling him. He'll learn it on his body." The explorer intended to make no answer, but he felt the prisoner's gaze turned on him; it seemed to ask if he approved such goings on. So he bent forward again, having already leaned back in his chair, and put another question: "But surely he knows that he has been sentenced?" "Nor that either," said the officer, smiling at the explorer as if expecting him to make further surprising remarks. "No," said the explorer, wiping his forehead, "then he can't know either whether his defense was effective?" "He has had no chance of putting up a defense," said the officer, turning his eyes away as if speaking to himself and so sparing the explorer the shame of hearing self-evident matters explained. "But he must have had some chance of defending himself," said the explorer, and rose from his seat.

The officer realized that he was in danger of having his exposition of the apparatus held up for a long time; so he went up to the explorer, took him by the arm, waved a hand towards the condemned man, who was standing very straight now that he had so obviously become the center of attention — the soldier had also given the chain a jerk — and said: "This is how the matter stands. I have been appointed judge in this penal colony. Despite my youth. For I was the former Commandant's assistant in all penal matters and know more about the apparatus than anyone. My guiding principle is this: Guilt is never to be doubted. Other courts cannot follow that principle, for they consist of several opinions and have higher courts to scrutinize them. That is not the case here, or at least, it was not the case in the former Commandant's time. The new man has certainly shown some inclination to interfere with my judgments, but so far I have succeeded in fending him off and will go on succeeding. You wanted to have the case explained; it is quite simple, like all of them. A captain reported to me this morning that this man, who had been assigned to him as a servant and sleeps before his door, had been asleep on duty. It is his duty, you see, to get up every time the hour strikes and salute the captain's door. Not an exacting duty, and very necessary, since he has to be a sentry as well as a servant, and must be alert in both functions. Last night the captain wanted to see if the man was doing his duty. He opened the door as the clock struck two and there was his man curled up asleep. He took his riding whip and lashed him across the face. Instead of getting up and begging pardon, the man caught hold of his master's legs, shook him and cried: 'Throw that whip away or I'll eat you alive.' — That's the evidence. The captain came to me an hour ago, I wrote down his statement and appended the sentence to it. Then I had the man put in chains. That was all quite simple. If I had first called the man before me and interrogated him, things would have got into a confused tangle. He would have told lies, and had I exposed these lies he would have backed them up with more lies, and so on and so forth. As it is, I've got him and I won't let him go. — Is that quite clear now? But we're wasting time, the execution should be beginning and I haven't finished explaining the apparatus yet." He pressed the explorer back into his chair, went up again to the apparatus and began: "As you see, the shape of the Harrow corresponds to the human form; here is the harrow for the torso, here are the harrows for the legs. For the head there is only this one small spike. Is that quite clear?" He bent amiably forward towards the explorer, eager to provide the most comprehensive explanations.

The explorer considered the Harrow with a frown. The explanation of the judicial procedure had not satisfied him. He had to remind himself that this was in any case a penal colony where extraordinary measures were needed and that military discipline must be enforced to the last. He also felt that some hope might be set on the new Commandant, who was apparently of a mind to bring in, although gradually, a new kind of procedure which the officer's narrow mind was incapable of understanding. This train of thought prompted his next question: "Will the Commandant attend the execution?" "It is not certain," said the officer, wincing at the direct question, and his friendly expression darkened. "That is just why we have to lose no time. Much as I dislike it, I shall have to cut my explanations short. But of course tomorrow, when the apparatus has been cleaned — its one drawback is that it gets so messy — I can recapitulate all the details. For the present, then, only the essentials. — When the man lies down on the Bed and it begins to vibrate, the Harrow is lowered onto his body. It regulates itself automatically so that the needles barely touch his skin; once contact is made the steel ribbon stiffens immediately into a rigid band. And then the performance begins. An ignorant onlooker would see no difference between one punishment and another. The Harrow appears to do its work with uniform regularity. As it quivers, its points pierce the skin of the body which is itself quivering from the vibration of the Bed. So that the actual progress of the sentence can be watched, the Harrow is made of glass. Getting the needles fixed in the glass was a technical problem, but after many experiments we overcame the difficulty. No trouble was too great for us to take, you see. And now anyone can look through the glass and watch the inscription taking form on the body. Wouldn't you care to come a little nearer and have a look at the needles?"

The explorer got up slowly, walked across and bent over the Harrow. "You see," said the officer, "there are two kinds of needles arranged in multiple patterns. Each long needle has a short one beside it. The long needle does the writing, and the short needle sprays a jet of water to wash away the blood and keep the inscription clear. Blood and water together are then conducted here through small runnels into this main runnel and down a waste pipe into the pit." With his finger the officer traced the exact course taken by the blood and water. To make the picture as vivid as possible he held both hands below the outlet of the waste pipe as if to catch the outflow, and when he did this the explorer drew back his head and feeling behind him with one hand sought to return to his chair. To his horror he found that the condemned man too had obeyed the officer's invitation to examine the Harrow at close quarters and had followed him. He had pulled forward the sleepy soldier with the chain and was bending over the glass. One could see that his uncertain eyes were trying to perceive what the two gentlemen had been looking at, but since he had not understood the explanation he could not make head or tail of it. He was peering this way and that way. He kept running his eyes along the glass. The explorer wanted to drive him away, since what he was doing was probably culpable. But the officer firmly restrained the explorer with one hand and with the other took a clod of earth from the rampart and threw it at the soldier. He opened his eyes with a jerk, saw what the condemned man had dared to do, let his rifle fall, dug his heels into the ground, dragged his prisoner back so that he stumbled and fell immediately, and then stood looking down at him, watching him struggling and rattling in his chains. "Set him on his feet!" yelled the officer, for he noticed that the explorer's attention was being too much distracted by the prisoner. In fact he was even leaning right across the Harrow, without taking any notice of it, intent only on finding out what was happening to the prisoner. "Be careful with him!" cried the officer again. He ran round the apparatus, himself caught the condemned man under the shoulders and with the soldier's help got him up on his feet, which kept slithering from under him.

"Now I know all about it," said the explorer as the officer came back to him. "All except the most important thing," he answered, seizing the explorer's arm and pointing upwards: "In the Designer are all the cogwheels that control the movements of the Harrow, and this machinery is regulated according to the inscription demanded by the sentence. I am still using the guiding plans drawn by the former Commandant. Here they are" — he extracted some sheets from the leather wallet — "but I'm sorry I can't let you handle them; they are my most precious possessions. Just take a seat and I'll hold them in front of you like this, then you'll be able to see everything quite well." He spread out the first sheet of paper. The explorer would have liked to say something appreciative, but all he could see was a labyrinth of lines crossing and re-crossing each other, which covered the paper so thickly that it was difficult to discern the blank spaces between them. "Read it," said the officer. "I can't," said the explorer. "Yet it's clear enough," said the officer. "It's very ingenious," said the explorer evasively, "but I can't make it out." "Yes," said the officer with a laugh, putting the paper away again, "it's no calligraphy for school children. It needs to be studied closely. I'm quite sure that in the end you would understand it too. Of course the script can't be a simple one; it's not supposed to kill a man straight off, but only after an interval of, on an average, twelve hours; the turning point is reckoned to come at the sixth hour. So there have to be lots and lots of flourishes around the actual script; the script itself runs round the body only in a narrow girdle; the rest of the body is reserved for the embellishments. Can you appreciate now the work accomplished by the Harrow and the whole apparatus? — Just watch it!" He ran up the ladder, turned a wheel, called down: "Look out, keep to one side!" and everything started working. If the wheel had not creaked, it would have been marvelous. The officer, as if surprised by the noise of the wheel, shook his fist at it, then spread out his arms in excuse to the explorer and climbed down rapidly to peer at the working of the machine from below. Something perceptible to no one save himself was still not in order; he clambered up again, did something with both hands in the interior of the Designer, then slid down one of the rods, instead of using the ladder, so as to get down quicker, and with the full force of his lungs, to make himself heard at all in the noise, yelled in the explorer's ear: "Can you follow it? The Harrow is beginning to write; when it finishes the first draft of the inscription on the man's back, the layer of cotton wool begins to roll and slowly turns the body over, to give the Harrow fresh space for writing. Meanwhile the raw part that has been written on lies on the cotton wool, which is specially prepared to staunch the bleeding and so makes all ready for a new deepening of the script. Then these teeth at the edge of the Harrow, as the body turns further round, tear the cotton wool away from the wounds, throw it into the pit, and there is more work for the Harrow. So it keeps on writing deeper and deeper for the whole twelve hours. The first six hours the condemned man stays alive almost as before, he suffers only pain. After two hours the felt gag is taken away, for he has no longer strength to scream. Here, into this electrically heated basin at the head of the bed, some warm rice pap is poured, from which the man, if he feels like it, can take as much as his tongue can lap. Not one of them ever misses the chance. I can remember none, and my experience is extensive. Only about the sixth hour does the man lose all desire to eat. I usually kneel down here at that moment and observe what happens. The man rarely swallows his last mouthful, he only rolls it round his mouth and spits it out into the pit. I have to duck just then or he would spit it in my face. But how quiet he grows at just about the sixth hour! Enlightenment comes to the most dull-witted. It begins around the eyes. From there it radiates. A moment that might tempt one to get under the Harrow oneself. Nothing more happens than that the man begins to understand the inscription, he purses his mouth as if he were listening. You have seen how difficult it is to decipher the script with one's eyes; but our man deciphers it with his wounds. To be sure, that is a hard task; he needs six hours to accomplish it. By that time the Harrow has pierced him quite through and casts him into the pit, where he pitches down upon the blood and water and the cotton wool. Then the judgment has been fulfilled, and we, the soldier and I, bury him."

The explorer had inclined his ear to the officer and with his hands in his jacket pockets watched the machine at work. The condemned man watched it too, but uncomprehendingly. He bent forward a little and was intent on the moving needles when the soldier, at a sign from the officer, slashed through his shirt and trousers from behind with a knife, so that they fell off; he tried to catch at his falling clothes to cover his nakedness, but the soldier lifted him into the air and shook the last remnants from him. The officer stopped the machine, and in the sudden silence the condemned man was laid under the Harrow. The chains were loosened and the straps fastened on instead; in the first moment that seemed almost a relief to the prisoner. And now the Harrow was adjusted a little lower, since he was a thin man. When the needle points touched him a shudder ran over his skin; while the soldier was busy strapping his right hand, he flung out his left hand blindly; but it happened to be in the direction towards where the explorer was standing. The officer kept watching the explorer sideways, as if seeking to read from his face the impression made on him by the execution, which had been at least cursorily explained to him.

The wrist strap broke; probably the soldier had drawn it too tight. The officer had to intervene, the soldier held up the broken piece of strap to show him. So the officer went over to him and said, his face still turned towards the explorer: "This is a very complex machine, it can't be helped that things are breaking or giving way here and there; but one must not thereby allow oneself to be diverted in one's general judgment. In any case, this strap is easily made good; I shall simply use a chain; the delicacy of the vibrations for the right arm will of course be a little impaired." And while he fastened the chains, he added: "The resources for maintaining the machine are now very much reduced. Under the former Commandant I had free access to a sum of money set aside entirely for this purpose. There was a store, too, in which spare parts were kept for repairs of all kinds. I confess I have been almost prodigal with them, I mean in the past, not now as the new Commandant pretends, always looking for an excuse to attack our old way of doing things. Now he has taken charge of the machine money himself, and if I send for a new strap they ask for the broken old strap as evidence, and the new strap takes ten days to appear and then is of shoddy material and not much good. But how I am supposed to work the machine without a strap, that's something nobody bothers about."

The explorer thought to himself: It's always a ticklish matter to intervene decisively in other people's affairs. He was neither a member of the penal colony nor a citizen of the state to which it belonged. Were he to denounce this execution or actually try to stop it, they could say to him: You are a foreigner, mind your own business. He could make no answer to that, unless he were to add that he was amazed at himself in this connection, for he traveled only as an observer, with no intention at all of altering other people's methods of administering justice. Yet here he found himself strongly tempted. The injustice of the procedure and the inhumanity of the execution were undeniable. No one could suppose that he had any selfish interest in the matter, for the condemned man was a complete stranger, not a fellow countryman or even at all sympathetic to him. The explorer himself had recommendations from high quarters, had been received here with great courtesy, and the very fact that he had been invited to attend the execution seemed to suggest that his views would be welcome. And this was all the more likely since the

Commandant, as he had heard only too plainly, was no upholder of the procedure and maintained an attitude almost of hostility to the officer.

At that moment the explorer heard the officer cry out in rage. He had just, with considerable difficulty, forced the felt gag into the condemned man's mouth when the man in an irresistible access of nausea shut his eyes and vomited. Hastily the officer snatched him away from the gag and tried to hold his head over the pit; but it was too late, the vomit was running all over the machine. "It's all the fault of that Commandant!" cried the officer, senselessly shaking the brass rods in front, "the machine is befouled like a pigsty." With trembling hands he indicated to the explorer what had happened. "Have I not tried for hours at a time to get the Commandant to understand that the prisoner must fast for a whole day before the execution? But our new, mild doctrine thinks otherwise. The Commandant's ladies stuff the man with sugar candy before he's led off. He has lived on stinking fish his whole life long and now he has to eat sugar candy! But it could still be possible, I should have nothing to say against it, but why won't they get me a new felt gag, which I have been begging for the last three months. How should a man not feel sick when he takes a felt gag into his mouth which more than a hundred men have already slobbered and gnawed in their dying moments?"

The condemned man had laid his head down and looked peaceful; the soldier was busy trying to clean the machine with the prisoner's shirt. The officer advanced towards the explorer, who in some vague presentiment fell back a pace, but the officer seized him by the hand, and drew him to one side. "I should like to exchange a few words with you in confidence," he said, "may I?" "Of course," said the explorer, and listened with downcast eyes.

"This procedure and method of execution, which you are now having the opportunity to admire, has at the moment no longer any open adherents in our colony. I am its sole advocate, and at the same time the sole advocate of the old Commandant's tradition. I can no longer reckon on any further extension of the method; it takes all my energy to maintain it as it is. During the old Commandant's lifetime the colony was full of his adherents; his strength of conviction I still have in some measure, but not an atom of his power; consequently the adherents have skulked out of sight, there are still many of them but none of them will admit it. If you were to go into the teahouse today, on execution day, and listen to what is being said, you would perhaps hear only ambiguous remarks. These would all be made by adherents, but under the present Commandant and his present doctrines they are of no use to me. And now I ask you: because of this Commandant and the women who influence him, is such a piece of work, the work of a lifetime" — he pointed to the machine — "to perish? Ought one to let that happen? Even if one has only come as a stranger to our island for a few days? But there's no time to lose, an attack of some kind is impending on my function as judge;

conferences are already being held in the Commandant's office from which I am excluded; even your coming here today seems to me a significant move; they are cowards and use you as a screen, you, a stranger. — How different an execution was in the old days! A whole day before the ceremony the valley was packed with people; they all came only to look on; early in the morning the Commandant appeared with his ladies; fanfares roused the whole camp; I reported that everything was in readiness; the assembled company — no high official dared to absent himself — arranged itself round the machine; this pile of cane chairs is a miserable survival from that epoch. The machine was freshly cleaned and glittering, I got new spare parts for almost every execution. Before hundreds of spectators — all of them standing on tiptoe as far as the heights there — the condemned man was laid under the Harrow by the Commandant himself. What is left today for a common soldier to do was then my task, the task of the presiding judge, and was an honor for me. And then the execution began! No discordant noise spoilt the working of the machine. Many did not care to watch it but lay with closed eyes in the sand; they all knew: Now Justice is being done. In the silence one heard nothing but the condemned man's sighs, half muffled by the felt gag. Nowadays the machine can no longer wring from anyone a sigh louder than the felt gag can stifle; but in those days the writing needles let drop an acid fluid, which we're no longer permitted to use. Well, and then came the sixth hour! It was impossible to grant all the requests to be allowed to watch it from near by. The Commandant in his wisdom ordained that the children should have the preference; I, of course, because of my office had the privilege of always being at hand; often enough I would be squatting there with a small child in either arm. How we all absorbed the look of transfiguration on the face of the sufferer, how we bathed our cheeks in the radiance of that justice, achieved at last and fading so quickly! What times these were, my comrade!" The officer had obviously forgotten whom he was addressing; he had embraced the explorer and laid his head on his shoulder. The explorer was deeply embarrassed, impatiently he stared over the officer's head. The soldier had finished his cleaning job and was now pouring rice pap from a pot into the basin. As soon as the condemned man, who seemed to have recovered entirely, noticed this action he began to reach for the rice with his tongue. The soldier kept pushing him away, since the rice pap was certainly meant for a later hour, yet it was just as unfitting that the soldier himself should thrust his dirty hands into the basin and eat out of it before the other's avid face.

The officer quickly pulled himself together. "I didn't want to upset you," he said. "I know it is impossible to make those days credible now. Anyhow, the machine is still working and it is still effective in itself. It is effective in itself even though it stands alone in this valley. And the corpse still falls at the last into the pit with an incomprehensibly gentle wafting motion, even although there are no hundreds of people swarming round like flies as formerly. In those days we had to put a strong fence round the pit; it has long since been torn down."

The explorer wanted to withdraw his face from the officer and looked round him at random. The officer thought he was surveying the valley's desolation; so he seized him by the hands, turned him round to meet his eyes, and asked: "Do you realize the shame of it?"

But the explorer said nothing. The officer left him alone for a little; with legs apart, hands on hips, he stood very still, gazing at the ground. Then he smiled encouragingly at the explorer and said: "I was quite near you yesterday when the Commandant gave you the invitation. I heard him giving it. I know the Commandant. I divined at once what he was after. Although he is powerful enough to take measures against me, he doesn't dare to do it yet, but he certainly means to use your verdict against me, the verdict of an illustrious foreigner. He has calculated it carefully: this is your second day on the island, you did not know the old Commandant and his ways, you are conditioned by European ways of thought, perhaps you object on principle to capital punishment in general and to such mechanical instruments of death in particular, besides you will see that the execution has no support from the public, a shabby ceremony — carried out with a machine already somewhat old and worn — now, taking all that into consideration, would it not be likely (so thinks the Commandant) that you might disapprove of my methods? And if you disapprove, you wouldn't conceal the fact (I'm still speaking from the Commandant's point of view), for you are a man to feel confidence in your own well-tried conclusions. True, you have seen and learned to appreciate the peculiarities of many peoples, and so you would not be likely to take a strong line against our proceedings, as you might do in your own country. But the Commandant has no need of that. A casual, even an unguarded remark will be enough. It doesn't even need to represent what you really think, so long as it can be used speciously to serve his purpose. He will try to prompt you with sly questions, of that I am certain. And his ladies will sit around you and prick up their ears; you might be saying something like this: 'In our country we have a different criminal procedure,' or 'In our country the prisoner is interrogated before he is sentenced,' or 'We haven't used torture since the Middle Ages.' All these statements are as true as they seem natural to you, harmless remarks that pass no judgment on my methods. But how would the Commandant react to them? I can see him, our good Commandant, pushing his chair away immediately and rushing onto the balcony, I can see his ladies streaming out after him, I can hear his voice — the ladies call it a voice of thunder — well, and this is what he says: 'A famous Western investigator, sent out to study criminal procedure in all the countries of the world, has just said that our old tradition of administering justice is inhuman. Such a verdict from such a personality makes it impossible for me to countenance these methods any longer. Therefore from this very day I ordain . . .' and so on. You may want to interpose that you never said any such thing, that you never called my methods inhumane; on the contrary your profound experience leads you to believe they are most humane and most in consonance with human dignity, and you admire the machine greatly — but it will be too late; you won't even get onto the balcony, crowded as it will be with ladies; you may try to draw attention to yourself; you may want to scream out; but a lady's hand will close your lips — and I and the work of the old Commandant will be done for."

The explorer had to suppress a smile; so easy, then, was the task he had felt to be so difficult. He said evasively: "You overestimate my influence; the Commandant has read my letters of recommendation, he knows that I am no expert in criminal procedure. If I were to give an opinion, it would be as a private individual, an opinion no more influential than that of any ordinary person, and in any case much less influential than that of the Commandant, who, I am given to understand, has very extensive powers in this penal colony. If his attitude to your procedure is as definitely hostile as you believe, then I fear the end of your tradition is at hand, even without any humble assistance from me."

Had it dawned on the officer at last? No, he still did not understand. He shook his head emphatically, glanced briefly round at the condemned man and the soldier, who both flinched away from the rice, came close up to the explorer and without looking at his face but fixing his eye on some spot on his coat said in a lower voice than before: "You don't know the Commandant; you feel yourself — forgive the expression — a kind of outsider so far as all of us are concerned; yet, believe me, your influence cannot be rated too highly. I was simply delighted when I heard that you were to attend the execution all by yourself. The Commandant arranged it to aim a blow at me, but I shall turn it to my advantage. Without being distracted by lying whispers and contemptuous glances — which could not have been avoided had a crowd of people attended the execution — you have heard my explanations, seen the machine and are now in course of watching the execution. You have doubtless already formed your own judgment; if you still have some small uncertainties the sight of the execution will resolve them. And now I make this request to you: help me against the Commandant!"

The explorer would not let him go on. "How could I do that?" he cried. "It's quite impossible. I can neither help nor hinder you."

"Yes, you can," the officer said. The explorer saw with a certain apprehension that the officer had clenched his fists. "Yes, you can," repeated the officer, still more insistently. "I have a plan that is bound to succeed. You believe your influence is insufficient. I know that it is sufficient. But even granted that you are right, is it not necessary, for the sake of preserving this tradition, to try even what might prove insufficient? Listen to my plan, then. The first thing necessary for you to carry it out is to be as reticent as possible today regarding your verdict on these proceedings. Unless you are asked a direct question you must say nothing at all; but what you do say must be brief and general; let it be remarked that you would prefer not to discuss the matter, that you are out of patience with it, that if you are to let yourself go you would use strong language. I don't ask you to tell any lies; by no means; you should only give curt answers, such as: 'Yes, I saw the execution,' or 'Yes, I had it explained to me.' Just that, nothing more. There are grounds enough for any impatience you betray, although not such as will occur to the Commandant. Of course, he will mistake your meaning and interpret it to please himself. That's what my plan depends on. Tomorrow in the Commandant's office there is to be a large conference of all the high administrative officials, the Commandant presiding. Of course the Commandant is the kind of man to have turned these conferences into public spectacles. He has had a gallery built that is always packed with spectators. I am compelled to take part in the conferences, but they make me sick with disgust. Now, whatever happens, you will certainly be invited to this conference; if you behave today as I suggest the invitation will become an urgent request. But if for some mysterious reason you're not invited, you'll have to ask for an invitation; there's no doubt of your getting it then. So tomorrow you're sitting in the Commandant's box with the ladies. He keeps looking up to make sure you're there. After various trivial and ridiculous matters, brought in merely to impress the audience — mostly harbor works, nothing but harbor works! — our judicial procedure comes up for discussion too. If the Commandant doesn't introduce it, or not soon enough, I'll see that it's mentioned. I'll stand up and report that today's execution has taken place. Quite briefly, only a statement. Such a statement is not usual, but I shall make it. The Commandant thanks me, as always, with an amiable smile, and then he can't restrain himself, he seizes the excellent opportunity. 'It has just been reported,' he will say, or words to that effect, 'that an execution has taken place. I should like merely to add that this execution was witnessed by the famous explorer who has, as you all know, honored our colony so greatly by his visit to us. His presence at today's session of our conference also contributes to the importance of this occasion. Should we not now ask the famous explorer to give us his verdict on our traditional mode of execution and the procedure that leads up to it?' Of course there is loud applause, general agreement, I am more insistent than anyone. The Commandant bows to you and says: 'Then in the name of the assembled company, I put the question to you.' And now you advance to the front of the box. Lay your hands where everyone can see them, or the ladies will catch them and press your fingers. — And then at last you can speak out. I don't know how I'm going to endure the tension of waiting for that moment. Don't put any restraint on yourself when you make your speech, publish the truth aloud, lean over the front of the box, shout, yes, indeed, shout your verdict, your unshakable conviction, at the Commandant. Yet perhaps you wouldn't care to do that, it's not in keeping with your character, in your country perhaps people do these things differently, well, that's all right too, that will be quite as effective, don't even stand up, just say a few words, even in a whisper, so that only the officials beneath you will hear them, that will be quite enough, you don't even need to mention the lack of public support for the execution, the creaking wheel, the broken strap, the filthy gag of felt, no, I'll take all that upon me, and, believe me, if my indictment doesn't drive him out of the conference hall, it will force him to his knees to make the acknowledgment: Old Commandant, I humble myself before you. — That is my plan; you will help me to carry it out? But of course you are willing, what is more, you must." And the officer seized the explorer by both arms and gazed, breathing heavily, into his face. He had shouted the last sentence so loudly that even the soldier and the condemned man were startled into attending; they had not understood a word but they stopped eating and looked over at the explorer, chewing their previous mouthfuls.

From the very beginning the explorer had no doubt about what answer he must give; in his lifetime he had experienced too much to have any uncertainty here; he was fundamentally honorable and unafraid. And yet now, facing the soldier and the condemned man, he did hesitate, for as long as it took to draw one breath. At last, however, he said, as he had to: "No." The officer blinked several times but did not turn his eyes away. "Would you like me to explain?" asked the explorer. The officer nodded wordlessly. "I do not approve of your procedure," said the explorer then, "even before you took me into your confidence — of course I shall never in any circumstances betray your confidence — I was already wondering whether it would be my duty to intervene and whether my intervention would have the slightest chance of success. I realized to whom I ought to turn: to the Commandant, of course. You have made that fact even clearer, but without having strengthened my resolution; on the contrary, your sincere conviction has touched me, even though it cannot influence my judgment."

The officer remained mute, turned to the machine, caught hold of a brass rod, and then, leaning back a little, gazed at the Designer as if to assure himself that all was in order. The soldier and the condemned man seemed to have come to some understanding; the condemned man was making signs to the soldier, difficult though his movements were because of the tight straps; the soldier was bending down to him; the condemned man whispered something and the soldier nodded.

The explorer followed the officer and said: "You don't know yet what I mean to do. I shall tell the Commandant what I think of the procedure, certainly, but not at a public conference, only in private; nor shall I stay here long enough to attend any conference; I am going away early to-morrow morning, or at least embarking on my ship."

It did not look as if the officer had been listening. "So you did not find the procedure convincing," he said to himself and smiled, as an old man smiles at childish nonsense and yet pursues his own meditations behind the smile.

"Then the time has come," he said at last, and suddenly looked at the explorer with bright eyes that held some challenge, some appeal for co-operation. "The time for what?" asked the explorer uneasily, but got no answer.

"You are free," said the officer to the condemned man in the native tongue. The man did not believe it at first. "Yes, you are set free," said the officer. For the first time the condemned man's face woke to real animation. Was it true? Was it only a caprice of the officer's that might change again? Had the foreign explorer begged him off? What was it? One could read these questions on his face. But not for long. Whatever it might be, he wanted to be really free if he might, and he began to struggle so far as the Harrow permitted him.

"You'll burst my straps," cried the officer. "Lie still! We'll soon loosen them." And signing the soldier to help him, he set about doing so. The condemned man laughed wordlessly to himself, now he turned his face left towards the officer, now right towards the soldier, nor did he forget the explorer.

"Draw him out," ordered the officer. Because of the Harrow this had to be done with some care. The condemned man had already torn him-self a little in the back through his impatience.

From now on, however, the officer paid hardly any attention to him. He went up to the explorer, pulled out the small leather wallet again, turned over the papers in it, found the one he wanted and showed it to the explorer. "Read it," he said. "I can't," said the explorer, "I told you before that I can't make out these scripts." "Try taking a close look at it," said the officer and came quite near to the explorer so that they might read it together. But when even that proved useless, he outlined the script with his little finger, holding it high above the paper as if the surface dared not be sullied by touch, in order to help the explorer to follow the script in that way. The explorer did make an effort, meaning to please the officer in this respect at least, but he was quite unable to follow. Now the officer began to spell it, letter by letter, and then read out the words. " 'BE JUST!' is what is written there," he said. "Surely you can read it now." The explorer bent so close to the paper that the officer feared he might touch it and drew it farther away; the explorer made no remark, yet it was clear that he still could not decipher it. " 'BE JUST!' is what is written there," said the officer once more. "Maybe," said the explorer, "I am prepared to believe you." "Well, then," said the officer, at least partly satisfied, and climbed up the ladder with the paper; very carefully he laid it inside the Designer and seemed to be changing the disposition of all the cogwheels; it was a troublesome piece of work and must have involved wheels that were extremely small, for sometimes the officer's head vanished altogether from sight inside the Designer, so precisely did he have to regulate the machinery.

The explorer, down below, watched the labor uninterruptedly, his neck grew stiff and his eyes smarted from the glare of sunshine over the sky. The soldier and the condemned man were now busy together. The man's shirt and trousers, which were already lying in the pit, were fished out by the point of the soldier's bayonet. The shirt was abominably dirty and its owner washed it in the bucket of water. When he put on the shirt and trousers both he and the soldier could not help guffawing, for the garments were of course slit up behind. Perhaps the condemned man felt it incumbent on him to amuse the soldier, he turned round and round in his slashed garments before the soldier, who squatted on the ground beating his knees with mirth. All the same, they presently controlled their mirth out of respect for the gentlemen.

When the officer had at length finished his task aloft, he surveyed the machinery in all its details once more, with a smile, but this time shut the lid of the Designer, which had stayed open till now, climbed down, looked into the pit and then at the condemned man, noting with satisfaction that the clothing had been taken out, then went over to wash his hands in the water bucket, perceived too late that it was disgustingly dirty, was unhappy because he could not wash his hands, in the end thrust them into the sand — this alternative did not please him, but he had to put up with it — then stood upright and began to unbutton his uniform jacket. As he did this, the two ladies' handkerchiefs he had tucked under his collar fell into his hands. "Here are your handkerchiefs," he said, and threw them to the condemned man. And to the explorer he said in explanation: "A gift from the ladies."

In spite of the obvious haste with which he was discarding first his uniform jacket and then all his clothing, he handled each garment with loving care, he even ran his fingers caressingly over the silver lace on the jacket and shook a tassel into place. This loving care was certainly out of keeping with the fact that as soon as he had a garment off he flung it at once with a kind of unwilling jerk into the pit. The last thing left to him was his short sword with the sword belt. He drew it out of the scabbard, broke it, then gathered all together, the bits of the sword, the scabbard and the belt, and flung them so violently down that they clattered into the pit.

Now he stood naked there. The explorer bit his lips and said nothing. He knew very well what was going to happen, but he had no right to obstruct the officer in anything. If the judicial procedure which the officer cherished were really so near its end — possibly as a result of his own intervention, as to which he felt himself pledged — then the officer was doing the right thing; in his place the explorer would not have acted otherwise.

The soldier and the condemned man did not understand at first what was happening; at first they were not even looking on. The condemned man was gleeful at having got the handkerchiefs back, but he was not allowed to enjoy them for long, since the soldier snatched them with a sudden, unexpected grab. Now the condemned man in turn was trying to twitch them from under the belt where the soldier had tucked them, but the soldier was on his guard. So they were wrestling, half in jest. Only when the officer stood quite naked was their attention caught. The condemned man especially seemed struck with the notion that some great change was impending. What had happened to him was now going to happen to the officer. Perhaps even to the very end. Apparently the foreign explorer had given the order for it. So this was revenge. Although he himself had not suffered to the end, he was to be revenged to the end. A broad, silent grin now appeared on his face and stayed there all the rest of the time.

The officer, however, had turned to the machine. It had been clear enough previously that he understood the machine well, but now it was almost staggering to see how he managed it and how it obeyed him. His hand had only to approach the Harrow for it to rise and sink several times till it was adjusted to the right position for receiving him; he touched only the edge of the Bed and already it was vibrating; the felt gag came to meet his mouth, one could see that the officer was really reluctant to take it but he shrank from it only a moment, soon he submitted and received it. Everything was ready, only the straps hung down at the sides, yet they were obviously unnecessary, the officer did not need to be fastened down. Then the condemned man noticed the loose straps, in his opinion the execution was incomplete unless the straps were buckled, he gestured eagerly to the soldier and they ran together to strap the officer down. The latter had already stretched out one foot to push the lever that started the Designer; he saw the two men coming up; so he drew his foot back and let himself be buckled in. But now he could not reach the lever; neither the soldier nor the condemned man would be able to find it, and the explorer was determined not to lift a finger. It was not necessary; as soon as the straps were fastened the machine began to work; the Bed vibrated, the needles flickered above the skin, the Harrow rose and fell. The explorer had been staring at it quite a while before he remembered that a wheel in the Designer should have been creaking; but everything was quiet, not even the slightest hum could be heard.

Because it was working so silently the machine simply escaped one's attention. The explorer observed the soldier and the condemned man. The latter was the more animated of the two, everything in the machine interested him, now he was bending down and now stretching up on tiptoe, his forefinger was extended all the time pointing out details to the soldier. This annoyed the explorer. He was resolved to stay till the end, but he could not bear the sight of these two. "Go back home," he said. The soldier would have been willing enough, but the condemned man took the order as a punishment. With clasped hands he implored to be allowed to stay, and when the explorer shook his head and would not relent, he even went down on his knees. The explorer saw that it was no use merely giving orders; he was on the point of going over and driving them away. At that moment he heard a noise above him in the Designer. He looked up. Was that cogwheel going to make trouble after all? But it was something quite different. Slowly the lid of the Designer rose up and then clicked wide open. The teeth of a cogwheel showed themselves and rose higher, soon the whole wheel was visible; it was as if some enormous force were squeezing the Designer so that there was no longer room for the wheel; the wheel moved up till it came to the very edge of the Designer, fell down, rolled along the sand a little on its rim and then lay flat. But a second wheel was already rising after it, followed by many others, large and small and indistinguishably minute, the same thing happened to all of them, at every moment one imagined the Designer must now really be empty, but another complex of numerous wheels was already rising into sight, falling down, trundling along the sand and lying flat. This phenomenon made the condemned man completely forget the explorer's command, the cogwheels fascinated him, he was always trying to catch one and at the same time urging the soldier to help, but always drew back his hand in alarm, for another wheel always came hopping along which, at least on its first advance, scared him off.

The explorer, on the other hand, felt greatly troubled; the machine was obviously going to pieces; its silent working was a delusion; he had a feeling that he must now stand by the officer, since the officer was no longer able to look after himself. But while the tumbling cogwheels absorbed his whole attention he had forgotten to keep an eye on the rest of the machine; now that the last cogwheel had left the Designer, however, he bent over the Harrow and had a new and still more unpleasant surprise. The Harrow was not writing, it was only jabbing, and the bed was not turning the body over but only bringing it up quivering against the needles. The explorer wanted to do something, if possible, to bring the whole machine to a standstill, for this was no exquisite torture such as the officer desired, this was plain murder. He stretched out his hands. But at that moment the Harrow rose with the body spitted on it and moved to the side, as it usually did only when the twelfth hour had come. Blood was flowing in a hundred streams, not mingled with water, the water jets too had failed to function. And now the last action failed to fulfil itself, the body did not drop off the long needles, streaming with blood it went on hanging over the pit without falling into it. The Harrow tried to move back to its old position, but as if it had itself noticed that it had not yet got rid of its burden it stuck after all where it was, over the pit. "Come and help!" cried the explorer to the other two, and himself seized the officer's feet. He wanted to push against the feet while the others seized the head from the opposite side and so the officer might be slowly eased off the needles. But the other two could not make up their minds to come; the condemned man actually turned away; the explorer had to go over to them and force them into position at the officer's head. And here, almost against his will, he had to look at the face of the corpse. It was as it had been in life; no sign was visible of the promised redemption; what the others had found in the machine the officer had not found; the lips were firmly pressed together, the eyes were open, with the same expression as in life, the look was calm and convinced, through the forehead went the point of the great iron spike.

As the explorer, with the soldier and the condemned man behind him, reached the first houses of the colony, the soldier pointed to one of them and said: "There is the teahouse."

In the ground floor of the house was a deep, low, cavernous space, its walls and ceiling blackened with smoke. It was open to the road all along its length. Although this teahouse was very little different from the other houses of the colony, which were all very dilapidated, even up to the Commandant's palatial headquarters, it made on the explorer the impression of a historic tradition of some kind, and he felt the power of past days. He went near to it, followed by his companions, right up between the empty tables which stood in the street before it, and breathed the cool, heavy air that came from the interior. "The old man's buried here," said the soldier. "The priest wouldn't let him lie in the churchyard. Nobody knew where to bury him for a while, but in the end they buried him here. The officer never told you about that, for sure, because of course that's what he was most ashamed of. He even tried several times to dig the old man up by night, but he was always chased away." "Where is the grave?" asked the explorer, who found it impossible to believe the soldier. At once both of them, the soldier and the condemned man, ran before him pointing with outstretched hands in the direction where the grave should be. They led the explorer right up to the back wall, where guests were sitting at a few tables. They were apparently dock laborers, strong men with short, glistening, full black beards. None had a jacket, their shirts were torn, they were poor, humble creatures. As the explorer drew near, some of them got up, pressed close to the wall, and stared at him. "It's a foreigner," ran the whisper around him. "He wants to see the grave." They pushed one of the tables aside, and under it there was really a gravestone. It was a simple stone, low enough to be covered by a table. There was an inscription on it in very small letters, the explorer had to kneel down to read it. This was what it said: "Here rests the old Commandant. His adherents, who now must be nameless, have dug this grave and set up this stone. There is a prophecy that after a certain number of years the Commandant will rise again and lead his adherents from this house to recover the colony. Have faith and wait!" When the explorer had read this and risen to his feet he saw all the bystanders around him smiling, as if they too had read the inscription, had found it ridiculous and were expecting him to agree with them. The explorer ignored this, distributed a few coins among them, waiting till the table was pushed over the grave again, quitted the teahouse and made for the harbor.

The soldier and the condemned man had found some acquaintances in the teahouse, who detained them. But they must have soon shaken them off, for the explorer was only halfway down the long flight of steps leading to the boats when they came rushing after him. Probably they wanted to force him at the last minute to take them with him. While he was bargaining below with a ferryman to row him to the steamer, the two of them came headlong down the steps, in silence, for they did not dare to shout. But by the time they reached the foot of the steps the explorer was already in the boat, and the ferryman was just casting off from the shore. They could have jumped into the boat, but the explorer lifted a heavy knotted rope from the floor boards, threatened them with it and so kept them from attempting the leap.

D. H. Lawrence
1885–1930

Schoolteacher, novelist, poet, essayist, short story writer, marvelous letter writer, literary critic, dramatist, painter, traveler, controversialist, prophet, dreamer of utopias — this son of a Nottingham coal miner died of tuberculosis at forty-four, having lived a life of burning intensity, stupefying productivity, and pathetic adversity. Some find distasteful the hectoring, moralistic, and insistent personality that informs much of his work. Others, including many professional critics, rank him among the greatest of English novelists.

When Lawrence writes of animals and inanimate nature he is supreme. He appears to have less sympathy for those human beings, quite numerous, who do not happen to share his views on women, love, the middle classes, and the proper conduct of life in general.

Like many other readers, I feel his best short stories, and in particular certain longer ones, offer more satisfaction than do his best novels, beautiful as these often are in patches. The briefer form tolerates less of the Lawrentian sprawl and repetitiveness, lends itself less easily to self-exposure and pulpiteering. Such stories as "Tickets, Please," "The Rockinghorse Winner," "The Daughters of the Vicar," "The Woman Who Rode Away," "The Horse Dealer's Daughter," "The Man Who Loved Islands," "A Sick Collier," "The Shadow in the Rose Garden" — these are as remarkable in range as they are absolute in effect.

So, too, is "Odour of Chrysanthemums." Though not his first published story, it was surely the first important one. When Ford Madox Ford printed it in the June 1911 issue of his English Review he decided he had caught a genius. Though it could not have been written had Lawrence been born of different parents, the autobiographical element is suffused rather than imposed. The central symbol (in fiction Lawrence early worked out the devices of the French Symbolist poets) perfectly bears its heavy weight of meaning. One of literature's recurrent themes, "the utter isolation of the human soul," is here clothed in unforgettable realistic detail as Lawrence registers the pitiless self-discovery sometimes brought about only through the death of another.

Odour of Chrysanthemums

THE SMALL locomotive engine, Number 4, came clanking, stumbling down from Selston with seven full wagons. It appeared round the corner with loud threats of speed, but the colt that it startled from among the gorse, which still flickered indistinctly in the raw afternoon, out-distanced it at a canter. A woman, walking up the railway line to Underwood, drew back into the hedge, held her basket aside, and watched the footplate of the engine advancing. The trucks thumped heavily past, one by one, with slow inevitable movement, as she stood insignificantly trapped between the jolting black wagons and the hedge; then they curved away towards the coppice where the withered oak leaves dropped noiselessly, while the birds, pulling at the scarlet hips beside the track, made off into the dusk that had already crept into the spinney. In the open, the smoke from the engine sank and cleaved to the rough grass. The fields were dreary and forsaken, and in the marshy strip that led to the whimsey, a reedy pit-pond, the fowls had already abandoned their run among the alders, to roost in the tarred fowl-house. The pit-bank loomed up beyond the pond, flames like red sores licking its ashy sides, in the afternoon's stagnant light. Just beyond rose the tapering chimneys and the clumsy black headstocks of Brinsley Colliery. The two wheels were spinning fast up against the sky, and the winding engine rapped out its little spasms. The miners were being turned up.

The engine whistled as it came into the wide bay of railway lines beside the colliery, where rows of trucks stood in harbour.

Miners, single, trailing and in groups, passed like shadows diverging home. At the edge of the ribbed level of sidings squat a low cottage, three steps down from the cinder track. A large bony vine clutched at the house, as if to claw down the tiled roof. Round the bricked yard grew a few wintry primroses. Beyond, the long garden sloped down to a bush-covered brook course. There were some twiggy apple trees, winter-crack trees, and ragged cabbages. Beside the path hung dishevelled pink chrysanthemums, like pink cloths hung on bushes. A woman came stooping out of the felt-covered fowl-house, half-way down the garden. She closed and padlocked the door, then drew herself erect, having brushed some bits from her white apron.

She was a tall woman of imperious mien, handsome, with definite black eyebrows. Her smooth black hair was parted exactly. For a few moments she stood steadily watching the miners as they passed along the railway: then she turned towards the brook course. Her face was calm and set, her mouth was closed with disillusionment. After a moment she called:

"John!" There was no answer. She waited, and then said distinctly:

"Where are you?"

"Here!" replied a child's sulky voice from among the bushes. The woman looked piercingly through the dusk.

"Are you at that brook?" she asked sternly.

For answer the child showed himself before the raspberry-canes that rose like whips. He was a small, sturdy boy of five. He stood quite still, defiantly.

"Oh!" said the mother, conciliated. "I thought you were down at that wet brook — and you remember what I told you —"

The boy did not move or answer.

"Come, come on in," she said more gently, "it's getting dark. There's your grandfather's engine coming down the line!"

The lad advanced slowly, with resentful, taciturn movement. He was dressed in trousers and waistcoat of cloth that was too thick and hard for the size of the garments. They were evidently cut down from a man's clothes.

As they went slowly towards the house he tore at the ragged wisps of chrysanthemums and dropped the petals in handfuls along the path.

"Don't do that — it does look nasty," said his mother. He refrained, and she, suddenly pitiful, broke off a twig with three or four wan flowers and held them against her face. When mother and son reached the yard her hand hesitated, and instead of laying the flower aside, she pushed it in her apron-band. The mother and son stood at the foot of the three steps looking across the bay of lines at the passing home of the miners. The trundle of the small train was imminent. Suddenly the engine loomed past the house and came to a stop opposite the gate.

The engine-driver, a short man with round grey beard, leaned out of the cab high above the woman.

"Have you got a cup of tea?" he said in a cheery, hearty fashion.

It was her father. She went in, saying she would mash. Directly, she returned.

"I didn't come to see you on Sunday," began the little grey-bearded man.

"I didn't expect you," said his daughter.

The engine-driver winced; then, reassuming his cheery, airy manner, he said:

"Oh, have you heard then? Well, and what do you think —?"

"I think it is soon enough," she replied.

At her brief censure the little man made an impatient gesture, and said coaxingly, yet with dangerous coldness:

"Well, what's a man to do? It's no sort of life for a man of my years, to sit at my own hearth like a stranger. And if I'm going to marry again it may as well be soon as late — what does it matter to anybody?"

The woman did not reply, but turned and went into the house. The man in the engine-cab stood assertive, till she returned with a cup of tea and a piece of bread and butter on a plate. She went up the steps and stood near the footplate of the hissing engine.

"You needn't 'a' brought me bread an' butter," said her father. "But a cup of tea" — he sipped appreciatively — "it's very nice." He sipped for a moment or two, then: "I hear as Walter's got another bout on," he said.

"When hasn't he?" said the woman bitterly.

"I heerd tell of him in the Lord Nelson braggin' as he was going to spend that b—— afore he went: half a sovereign that was."

"When?" asked the woman.

"A' Sat'day night — I know that's true."

"Very likely," she laughed bitterly. "He gives me twenty-three shillings."

"Aye, it's a nice thing, when a man can do nothing with his money but make a beast of himself!" said the grey-whiskered man. The woman turned her head away. Her father swallowed the last of his tea and handed her the cup.

"Aye," he sighed, wiping his mouth. "It's a settler, it is —"

He put his hand on the lever. The little engine strained and groaned, and the train rumbled towards the crossing. The woman again looked across the metals. Darkness was settling over the spaces of the railway and trucks: the miners, in grey sombre groups, were still passing home. The winding engine pulsed hurriedly, with brief pauses. Elizabeth Bates looked at the dreary flow of men, then she went indoors. Her husband did not come.

The kitchen was small and full of firelight; red coals piled glowing up the chimney mouth. All the life of the room seemed in the white, warm hearth and the steel fender reflecting the red fire. The cloth was laid for tea; cups glinted in the shadows. At the back, where the lowest stairs protruded into the room, the boy sat struggling with a knife and a piece of white wood. He was almost hidden in the shadow. It was half-past four. They had but to await the father's coming to begin tea. As the mother watched her son's sullen little struggle with the wood, she saw herself in his silence and pertinacity; she saw the father in her child's indifference to all but himself. She seemed to be occupied by her husband. He had probably gone past his home, slunk past his own door, to drink before he came in, while his dinner spoiled and wasted in waiting. She glanced at the clock, then took the potatoes to strain them in the yard. The garden and fields beyond the brook were closed in uncertain darkness. When she rose with the saucepan, leaving the drain steaming into the night behind her, she saw the yellow lamps were lit along the high road that went up the hill away beyond the space of the railway lines and the field.

Then again she watched the men trooping home, fewer now and fewer.

Indoors the fire was sinking and the room was dark red. The woman put her saucepan on the hob, and set a batter-pudding near the mouth of the oven. Then she stood unmoving. Directly, gratefully, came quick young steps to the door. Someone hung on the latch a moment, then a little girl entered and began pulling off her outdoor things, dragging a mass of curls, just ripening from gold to brown, over her eyes with her hat.

Her mother chid her for coming late from school, and said she would have to keep her at home the dark winter days.

"Why, mother, it's hardly a bit dark yet. The lamp's not lighted, and my father's not home."

"No, he isn't. But it's a quarter to five! Did you see anything of him?"

The child became serious. She looked at her mother with large, wistful blue eyes.

"No, mother, I've never seen him. Why? Has he come up an' gone past, to Old Brinsley? He hasn't, mother, 'cos I never saw him."

"He'd watch that," said the mother bitterly, "he'd take care as you didn't see him. But you may depend upon it, he's seated in the Prince o' Wales. He wouldn't be this late."

The girl looked at her mother piteously.

"Let's have our teas, mother, should we?" said she.

The mother called John to table. She opened the door once more and looked out across the darkness of the lines. All was deserted: she could not hear the winding-engines.

"Perhaps," she said to herself, "he's stopped to get some ripping done."

They sat down to tea. John, at the end of the table near the door, was almost lost in the darkness. Their faces were hidden from each other. The girl crouched against the fender slowly moving a thick piece of bread before the fire. The lad, his face a dusky mark on the shadow, sat watching her who was transfigured in the red glow.

"I do think it's beautiful to look in the fire," said the child.

"Do you?" said her mother. "Why?"

"It's so red, and full of little caves — and it feels so nice, and you can fair smell it."

"It'll want mending directly," replied her mother, "and then if your father comes he'll carry on and say there never is a fire when a man comes home sweating from the pit. A public-house is always warm enough."

There was silence till the boy said complainingly: "Make haste, our Annie."

"Well, I am doing! I can't make the fire do it no faster, can I?"

"She keeps wafflin' it about so's to make 'er slow," grumbled the boy.

"Don't have such an evil imagination, child," replied the mother.

Soon the room was busy in the darkness with the crisp sound of crunching. The mother ate very little. She drank her tea determinedly, and sat thinking. When she rose her anger was evident in the stern unbending of her head. She looked at the pudding in the fender, and broke out:

"It is a scandalous thing as a man can't even come home to his dinner! If it's crozzled up to a cinder I don't see why I should care. Past his very door he goes to get to a public-house, and here I sit with his dinner waiting for him —"

She went out. As she dropped piece after piece of coal on the red fire, the shadows fell on the walls, till the room was almost in total darkness.

"I canna see," grumbled the invisible John. In spite of herself, the mother laughed.

"You know the way to your mouth," she said. She set the dust-pan outside the door. When she came again like a shadow on the hearth, the lad repeated, complaining sulkily:

"I canna see."

"Good gracious!" cried the mother irritably, "you're as bad as your father if it's a bit dusk!"

Nevertheless, she took a paper spill from a sheaf on the mantelpiece and proceeded to light the lamp that hung from the ceiling in the middle of the room. As she reached up, her figure displayed itself just rounding with maternity.

"Oh, mother —!" exclaimed the girl.

"What?" said the woman, suspended in the act of putting the lamp-glass over the flame. The copper reflector shone handsomely on her, as she stood with uplifted arm, turning to face her daughter.

"You've got a flower in your apron!" said the child, in a little rapture at this unusual event.

"Goodness me!" exclaimed the woman, relieved. "One would think the house was afire." She replaced the glass and waited a moment before turning up the wick. A pale shadow was seen floating vaguely on the floor.

"Let me smell!" said the child, still rapturously, coming forward and putting her face to her mother's waist.

"Go along, silly!" said the mother, turning up the lamp. The light revealed their suspense so that the woman felt it almost unbearable. Annie was still bending at her waist. Irritably, the mother took the flowers out from her apron-band.

"Oh, mother — don't take them out!" Annie cried, catching her hand and trying to replace the sprig.

"Such nonsense!" said the mother, turning away. The child put the pale chrysanthemums to her lips, murmuring:

"Don't they smell beautiful!"

Her mother gave a short laugh.

"No," she said, "not to me. It was chrysanthemums when I married him, and chrysanthemums when you were born, and the first time they ever brought him home drunk, he'd got brown chrysanthemums in his button-hole."

She looked at the children. Their eyes and their parted lips were wondering. The mother sat rocking in silence for some time. Then she looked at the clock.

"Twenty minutes to six!" In a tone of fine bitter carelessness she continued: "Eh, he'll not come now till they bring him. There he'll stick! But he needn't come rolling in here in his pit-dirt, for *I* won't wash him. He can lie on the floor — Eh, what a fool I've been, what a fool! And this is what I came here for, to this dirty hole, rats and all, for him to slink past his very door. Twice last week — he's begun now —"

She silenced herself, and rose to clear the table.

While for an hour or more the children played, subduedly intent, fertile of imagination, united in fear of the mother's wrath, and in dread of their father's home-coming, Mrs. Bates sat in her rocking-chair making a "singlet" of thick cream-coloured flannel, which gave a dull wounded sound as she tore off the grey edge. She worked at her sewing with energy, listening to the children, and her anger wearied itself, lay down to rest, opening its eyes from time to time and steadily watching, its ears raised to listen. Sometimes even her anger quailed and shrank, and the mother suspended her sewing, tracing the footsteps that thudded along the sleepers outside; she would lift her head sharply to bid the children "hush," but she recovered herself in time, and the footsteps went past the gate, and the children were not flung out of their play-world.

But at last Annie sighed, and gave in. She glanced at her wagon of slippers, and loathed the game. She turned plaintively to her mother.

"Mother!" — but she was inarticulate.

John crept out like a frog from under the sofa. His mother glanced up.

"Yes," she said, "just look at those shirt-sleeves!"

The boy held them out to survey them, saying nothing. Then somebody called in a hoarse voice away down the line, and suspense bristled in the room, till two people had gone by outside, talking.

"It is time for bed," said the mother.

"My father hasn't come," wailed Annie plaintively. But her mother was primed with courage.

"Never mind. They'll bring him when he does come — like a log." She meant there would be no scene. "And he may sleep on the floor till he wakes himself. I know he'll not go to work to-morrow after this!"

The children had their hands and faces wiped with a flannel. They were very quiet. When they had put on their night-dresses, they said their prayers, the boy mumbling. The mother looked down at them, at the brown silken bush of intertwining curls in the nape of the girl's neck, at the little black head of the lad, and her heart burst with anger at their father, who caused all three such distress. The children hid their faces in her skirts for comfort.

When Mrs. Bates came down, the room was strangely empty, with a tension of expectancy. She took up her sewing and stitched for some time without raising her head. Meantime her anger was tinged with fear.

II

The clock struck eight and she rose suddenly, dropping her sewing on her chair. She went to the stair-foot door, opened it, listening. Then she went out, locking the door behind her.

Something scuffled in the yard, and she started, though she knew it was only the rats with which the place was over-run. The night was very dark. In the great bay of railway lines, bulked with trucks, there was no trace of light, only away back she could see a few yellow lamps at the pit-top, and the red smear of the burning pit-bank on the night. She hurried along the edge of the track, then, crossing the converging lines, came to the stile by the white gates, whence she emerged on the road. Then the fear which had led her shrank. People were walking up to New Brinsley; she saw the lights in the houses; twenty yards farther on were the broad windows of the Prince of Wales, very warm and bright, and the loud voices of men could be heard distinctly. What a fool she had been to imagine that anything had happened to him! He was merely drinking over there at the Prince of Wales. She faltered. She had never yet been to fetch him, and she never would go. So she continued her walk towards the long straggling line of houses, standing back on the highway. She entered a passage between the dwellings.

"Mr. Rigley? — Yes! Did you want him? No, he's not in at this minute."

The raw-boned woman leaned forward from her dark scullery and peered at the other, upon whom fell a dim light through the blind of the kitchen window.

"Is it Mrs. Bates?" she asked in a tone tinged with respect.

"Yes. I wondered if your Master was at home. Mine hasn't come yet."

"'Asn't 'e! Oh, Jack's been 'ome an' 'ad 'is dinner an' gone out. 'E's just gone for 'alf an hour afore bed-time. Did you call at the Prince of Wales?"

"No —"

"No, you didn't like —! It's not very nice." The other woman was indulgent. There was an awkward pause. "Jack never said nothink about — about your Master," she said.

"No! — I expect he's stuck in there!"

Elizabeth Bates said this bitterly, and with recklessness. She knew that the woman across the yard was standing at her door listening, but she did not care. As she turned:

"Stop a minute! I'll just go an' ask Jack if 'e knows anythink," said Mrs. Rigley.

"Oh no — I wouldn't like to put —!"

"Yes, I will, if you'll just step inside an' see as th' childer doesn't come downstairs and set theirselves afire."

Elizabeth Bates, murmuring a remonstrance, stepped inside. The other woman apologised for the state of the room.

The kitchen needed apology. There were little frocks and trousers and childish undergarments on the squab and on the floor, and a litter of playthings everywhere. On the black American cloth of the table were pieces of bread and cake, crusts, slops, and a teapot with cold tea.

"Eh, ours is just as bad," said Elizabeth Bates, looking at the woman, not at the house. Mrs. Rigley put a shawl over her head and hurried out, saying:

"I shanna be a minute."

The other sat, noting with faint disapproval the general untidiness of the room. Then she fell to counting the shoes of various sizes scattered over the floor. There were twelve. She sighed and said to herself: "No wonder!" — glancing at the litter. There came the scratching of two pairs of feet on the yard, and the Rigleys entered. Elizabeth Bates rose. Rigley was a big man, with very large bones. His head looked particularly bony. Across his temple was a blue scar, caused by a wound got in the pit, a wound in which the coal-dust remained blue like tattooing.

"'Asna 'e come whoam yit?" asked the man, without any form of greeting, but with deference and sympathy. "I couldna say wheer he is — 'e's non ower theer!" — he jerked his head to signify the Prince of Wales.

"'E's 'appen gone up to th' Yew," said Mrs. Rigley.

There was another pause. Rigley had evidently something to get off his mind:

"Ah left 'im finishin' a stint," he began. "Loose-all 'ad bin gone about ten minutes when we com'n away, an' I shouted: 'Are ter comin', Walt?' an' 'e said: 'Go on, Ah shanna be but a'ef a minnit,' so we com'n ter th' bottom, me an' Bowers, thinkin' as 'e wor just behint, an' 'ud come up i' th' next bantle —"

He stood perplexed, as if answering a charge of deserting his mate. Elizabeth Bates, now again certain of disaster, hastened to reassure him:

"I expect 'e's gone up to th' Yew Tree, as you say. It's not the first time.

I've fretted myself into a fever before now. He'll come home when they carry him."

"Ay, isn't it too bad!" deplored the other woman.

"I'll just step up to Dick's an' see if 'e *is* theer," offered the man, afraid of appearing alarmed, afraid of taking liberties.

"Oh, I wouldn't think of bothering you that far," said Elizabeth Bates, with emphasis, but he knew she was glad of his offer.

As they stumbled up the entry, Elizabeth Bates heard Rigley's wife run across the yard and open her neighbour's door. At this, suddenly all the blood in her body seemed to switch away from her heart.

"Mind!" warned Rigley. "Ah've said many a time as Ah'd fill up them ruts in this entry, sumb'dy 'll be breakin' their legs yit."

She recovered herself and walked quickly along with the miner.

"I don't like leaving the children in bed, and nobody in the house," she said.

"No, you dunna!" he replied courteously. They were soon at the gate of the cottage.

"Well, I shanna be many minnits. Dunna you be frettin' now, 'e'll be all right," said the butty.

"Thank you very much, Mr. Rigley," she replied.

"You're welcome!" he stammered, moving away. "I shanna be many mi....its."

The house was quiet. Elizabeth Bates took off her hat and shawl, and rolled back the rug. When she had finished, she sat down. It was a few minutes past nine. She was startled by the rapid chuff of the winding-engine at the pit, and the sharp whirr of the brakes on the rope as it descended. Again she felt the painful sweep of her blood, and she put her hand to her side, saying aloud: "Good gracious! — it's only the nine o'clock deputy going down," rebuking herself.

She sat still, listening. Half an hour of this, and she was wearied out.

"What am I working myself up like this for?" she said pitiably to herself, "I s'll only be doing myself some damage."

She took out her sewing again.

At a quarter to ten there were footsteps. One person! She watched for the door to open. It was an elderly woman, in a black bonnet and a black woollen shawl — his mother. She was about sixty years old, pale, with blue eyes, and her face all wrinkled and lamentable. She shut the door and turned to her daughter-in-law peevishly.

"Eh, Lizzie, whatever shall we do, whatever shall we do!" she cried.

Elizabeth drew back a little, sharply.

"What is it, mother?" she said.

The elder woman seated herself on the sofa.

"I don't know, child, I can't tell you!" — she shook her head slowly. Elizabeth sat watching her, anxious and vexed.

"I don't know," replied the grandmother, sighing very deeply. "There's no end to my troubles, there isn't. The things I've gone through, I'm sure it's enough —!" She wept without wiping her eyes, the tears running.

"But, mother," interrupted Elizabeth, "what do you mean? What is it?"

The grandmother slowly wiped her eyes. The fountains of her tears were stopped by Elizabeth's directness. She wiped her eyes slowly.

"Poor child! Eh, you poor thing!" she moaned. "I don't know what we're going to do, I don't — and you as you are — it's a thing, it is indeed!"

Elizabeth waited.

"Is he dead?" she asked, and at the words her heart swung violently, though she felt a slight flush of shame at the ultimate extravagance of the question. Her words sufficiently frightened the old lady, almost brought her to herself.

"Don't say so, Elizabeth! We'll hope it's not as bad as that; no, may the Lord spare us that, Elizabeth. Jack Rigley came just as I was sittin' down to a glass afore going to bed, an' 'e said: ''Appen you'll go down th' line, Mrs. Bates. Walt's had an accident. 'Appen you'll go an' sit wi' 'er till we can get him home.' I hadn't time to ask him a word afore he was gone. An' I put my bonnet on an' come straight down, Lizzie. I thought to myself: 'Eh, that poor blessed child, if anybody should come an' tell her of a sudden, there's no knowin' what'll 'appen to 'er.' You mustn't let it upset you, Lizzie — or you know what to expect. How long is it, six months — or is it five, Lizzie? Ay!" — the old woman shook her head — "time slips on, it slips on! Ay!"

Elizabeth's thoughts were busy elsewhere. If he was killed — would she be able to manage on the little pension and what she could earn? — she counted up rapidly. If he was hurt — they wouldn't take him to the hospital — how tiresome he would be to nurse! — but perhaps she'd be able to get him away from the drink and his hateful ways. She would — while he was ill. The tears offered to come to her eyes at the picture. But what sentimental luxury was this she was beginning? She turned to consider the children. At any rate she was absolutely necessary for them. They were her business.

"Ay!" repeated the old woman, "it seems but a week or two since he brought me his first wages. Ay — he was a good lad, Elizabeth, he was, in his way. I don't know why he got to be such a trouble, I don't. He was a happy lad at home, only full of spirits. But there's no mistake he's been a handful of trouble, he has! I hope the Lord'll spare him to mend his ways. I hope so, I hope so. You've had a sight o' trouble with him, Elizabeth, you have indeed. But he was a jolly enough lad wi' me, he was, I can assure you. I don't know how it is . . . "

The old woman continued to muse aloud, a monotonous irritating sound, while Elizabeth thought concentratedly, startled once, when she heard the winding-engine chuff quickly, and the brakes skirr with a shriek. Then she heard the engine more slowly, and the brakes made no sound. The old woman did not notice. Elizabeth waited in suspense. The mother-in-law talked, with lapses into silence.

"But he wasn't your son, Lizzie, an' it makes a difference. Whatever he was, I remember him when he was little, an' I learned to understand him and to make allowances. You've got to make allowances for them —"

It was half-past ten, and the old woman was saying: "But it's trouble from beginning to end; you're never too old for trouble, never too old for that —" when the gate banged back, and there were heavy feet on the steps.

"I'll go, Lizzie, let me go," cried the old woman, rising. But Elizabeth was at the door. It was a man in pit-clothes.

"They're bringin' 'im, Missis," he said. Elizabeth's heart halted a moment. Then it surged on again, almost suffocating her.

"Is he — is it bad?" she asked.

The man turned away, looking at the darkness:

"The doctor says 'e'd been dead hours. 'E saw 'im i' th' lamp-cabin."

The old woman, who stood just behind Elizabeth, dropped into a chair, and folded her hands, crying: "Oh, my boy, my boy!"

"Hush!" said Elizabeth, with a sharp twitch of a frown. "Be still, mother, don't waken th' children: I wouldn't have them down for anything!"

The old woman moaned softly, rocking herself. The man was drawing away. Elizabeth took a step forward.

"How was it?" she asked.

"Well, I couldn't say for sure," the man replied, very ill at ease. "'E wor finishin' a stint an' th' butties 'ad gone, an' a lot o' stuff come down atop 'n 'im."

"And crushed him?" cried the widow, with a shudder.

"No," said the man, "it fell at th' back of 'im. 'E wor under th' face, an' it niver touched 'im. It shut 'im in. It seems 'e wor smothered."

Elizabeth shrank back. She heard the old woman behind her cry:

"What? — what did 'e say it was?"

The man replied, more loudly: "'E wor smothered!"

Then the old woman wailed aloud, and this relieved Elizabeth.

"Oh, mother," she said, putting her hand on the old woman, "don't waken th' children, don't waken th' children."

She wept a little, unknowing, while the old mother rocked herself and moaned. Elizabeth remembered that they were bringing him home, and she must be ready. "They'll lay him in the parlour," she said to herself, standing a moment pale and perplexed.

Then she lighted a candle and went into the tiny room. The air was cold and damp, but she could not make a fire, there was no fireplace. She set down the candle and looked round. The candlelight glittered on the lustre-glasses, on the two vases that held some of the pink chrysan-themums, and on the dark mahogany. There was a cold, deathly smell of chrysanthemums in the room. Elizabeth stood looking at the flowers. She turned away, and calculated whether there would be room to lay him on the floor, between the couch and the chiffonier. She pushed the chairs aside. There would be room to lay him down and to step round him. Then she fetched the old red tablecloth, and another old cloth, spreading them down to save her bit of carpet. She shivered on leaving the parlour; so, from the dresser drawer she took a clean shirt and put it at the fire to air. All the time her mother-in-law was rocking herself in the chair and moaning.

"You'll have to move from there, mother," said Elizabeth. "They'll be bringing him in. Come in the rocker."

The old mother rose mechanically, and seated herself by the fire, con-tinuing to lament. Elizabeth went into the pantry for another candle, and there, in the little pent-house under the naked tiles, she heard them coming. She stood still in the pantry doorway, listening. She heard them pass the end of the house, and come awkwardly down the three steps, a jumble of shuffling footsteps and muttering voices. The old woman was silent. The men were in the yard.

Then Elizabeth heard Matthews, the manager of the pit, say: "You go in first, Jim. Mind!"

The door came open, and the two women saw a collier backing into the room, holding one end of a stretcher, on which they could see the nailed pit-boots of the dead man. The two carriers halted, the man at the head stooping to the lintel of the door.

"Wheer will you have him?" asked the manager, a short, white-bearded man.

Elizabeth roused herself and came from the pantry carrying the un-lighted candle.

"In the parlour," she said.

"In there, Jim!" pointed the manager, and the carriers backed round into the tiny room. The coat with which they had covered the body fell off as they awkwardly turned through the two doorways, and the women saw their man, naked to the waist, lying stripped for work. The old woman began to moan in a low voice of horror.

"Lay th' stretcher at th' side," snapped the manager, "an' put 'im on th' cloths. Mind now, mind! Look you now—!"

One of the men had knocked off a vase of chrysanthemums. He stared awkwardly, then they set down the stretcher. Elizabeth did not look at her husband. As soon as she could get in the room, she went and picked up the broken vase and the flowers.

"Wait a minute!" she said.

The three men waited in silence while she mopped up the water with a duster.

"Eh, what a job, what a job, to be sure!" the manager was saying, rubbing his brow with trouble and perplexity. "Never knew such a thing in my life, never! He'd no business to ha' been left. I never knew such a thing in my life! Fell over him clean as a whistle, an' shut him in. Not four foot of space, there wasn't — yet it scarce bruised him."

He looked down at the dead man, lying prone, half naked, all grimed with coal-dust.

"''Sphyxiated,' the doctor said. It *is* the most terrible job I've ever known. Seems as if it was done o' purpose. Clean over him, an' shut 'im in, like a mouse-trap" — he made a sharp, descending gesture with his hand.

The colliers standing by jerked aside their heads in hopeless comment.

The horror of the thing bristled upon them all.

Then they heard the girl's voice upstairs calling shrilly: "Mother, mother — who is it? Mother, who is it?"

Elizabeth hurried to the foot of the stairs and opened the door:

"Go to sleep!" she commanded sharply. "What are you shouting about? Go to sleep at once — there's nothing —"

Then she began to mount the stairs. They could hear her on the boards, and on the plaster floor of the little bedroom. They could hear her distinctly:

"What's the matter now? — what's the matter with you, silly thing?" — her voice was much agitated, with an unreal gentleness.

"I thought it was some men come," said the plaintive voice of the child. "Has he come?"

"Yes, they've brought him. There's nothing to make a fuss about. Go to sleep now, like a good child."

They could hear her voice in the bedroom, they waited whilst she covered the children under the bedclothes.

"Is he drunk?" asked the girl, timidly, faintly.

"No! No — he's not! He — he's asleep."

"Is he asleep downstairs?"

"Yes — and don't make a noise."

There was silence for a moment, then the men heard the frightened child again:

"What's that noise?"

"It's nothing, I tell you, what are you bothering for?"

The noise was the grandmother moaning. She was oblivious of everything, sitting on her chair rocking and moaning. The manager put his hand on her arm and bade her "Sh — sh!!"

The old woman opened her eyes and looked at him. She was shocked by this interruption, and seemed to wonder.

"What time is it?" the plaintive thin voice of the child, sinking back unhappily into sleep, asked this last question.

"Ten o'clock," answered the mother more softly. Then she must have bent down and kissed the children.

Matthews beckoned to the men to come away. They put on their caps and took up the stretcher. Stepping over the body, they tiptoed out of the house. None of them spoke till they were far from the wakeful children.

When Elizabeth came down she found her mother alone on the parlour floor, leaning over the dead man, the tears dropping on him.

"We must lay him out," the wife said. She put on the kettle, then returning knelt at the feet, and began to unfasten the knotted leather laces. The room was clammy and dim with only one candle, so that she had to bend her face almost to the floor. At last she got off the heavy boots and put them away.

"You must help me now," she whispered to the old woman. Together they stripped the man.

When they arose, saw him lying in the naïve dignity of death, the women stood arrested in fear and respect. For a few moments they remained still, looking down, the old mother whimpering. Elizabeth felt countermanded. She saw him, how utterly inviolable he lay in himself. She had nothing to do with him. She could not accept it. Stooping, she laid her hand on him, in claim. He was still warm, for the mine was hot where he had died. His mother had his face between her hands, and was murmuring incoherently. The old tears fell in succession as drops from wet leaves; the mother was not weeping, merely her tears flowed. Elizabeth embraced the body of her husband, with cheek and lips. She seemed to be listening, inquiring, trying to get some connection. But she could not. She was driven away. He was impregnable.

She rose, went into the kitchen, where she poured warm water into a bowl, brought soap and flannel and a soft towel.

"I must wash him," she said.

Then the old mother rose stiffly, and watched Elizabeth as she carefully washed his face, carefully brushing the big blond moustache from his mouth with the flannel. She was afraid with a bottomless fear, so she ministered to him. The old woman, jealous, said:

"Let me wipe him!" — and she kneeled on the other side drying slowly as Elizabeth washed, her big black bonnet sometimes brushing the dark head of her daughter-in-law. They worked thus in silence for a long time. They never forgot it was death, and the touch of the man's dead body gave them strange emotions, different in each of the women; a great dread possessed them both, the mother felt the lie was given to her womb, she was denied; the wife felt the utter isolation of the human soul, the child within her was a weight apart from her.

At last it was finished. He was a man of handsome body, and his face showed no traces of drink. He was blond, full-fleshed, with fine limbs. But he was dead.

"Bless him," whispered his mother, looking always at his face, and speaking out of sheer terror. "Dear lad — bless him!" She spoke in a faint, sibilant ecstasy of fear and mother love.

Elizabeth sank down again to the floor, and put her face against his neck, and trembled and shuddered. But she had to draw away again. He was dead, and her living flesh had no place against his. A great dread and weariness held her: she was so unavailing. Her life was gone like this.

"White as milk he is, clear as a twelve-month baby, bless him, the darling!" the old mother murmured to herself. "Not a mark on him, clear and clean and white, beautiful as ever a child was made," she murmured with pride. Elizabeth kept her face hidden.

"He went peaceful, Lizzie — peaceful as sleep. Isn't he beautiful, the lamb? Ay — he must ha' made his peace, Lizzie. 'Appen he made it all right, Lizzie, shut in there. He'd have time. He wouldn't look like this if he hadn't made his peace. The lamb, the dear lamb. Eh, but he had a hearty laugh. I loved to hear it. He had the heartiest laugh, Lizzie, as a lad —"

Elizabeth looked up. The man's mouth was fallen back, slightly open under the cover of the moustache. The eyes, half shut, did not show glazed in the obscurity. Life with its smoky burning gone from him, had left him apart and utterly alien to her. And she knew what a stranger he was to her. In her womb was ice of fear, because of this separate stranger with whom she had been living as one flesh. Was this what it all meant — utter, intact separateness, obscured by heat of living? In dread she turned her face away. The fact was too deadly. There had been nothing between them, and yet they had come together, exchanging their nakedness repeatedly. Each time he had taken her, they had been two isolated beings, far apart as now. He was no more responsible than she. The child was like ice in her womb. For as she looked at the dead man, her mind, cold and detached, said clearly: "Who am I? What have I been doing? I have been fighting a husband who did not exist. *He* existed all the time. What wrong have I done? What was that I have been living with? There lies the reality, this man." And her soul died in her for fear: she knew she had never seen him, he had never seen her, they had met in the dark and had fought in the dark, not knowing whom they met nor whom they fought. And now she saw, and turned silent in seeing. For she had been wrong. She had said he was something he was not; she had felt familiar with him. Whereas he was apart all the while, living as she never lived, feeling as she never felt.

In fear and shame she looked at his naked body, that she had known falsely. And he was the father of her children. Her soul was torn from her body and stood apart. She looked at his naked body and was ashamed, as if she had denied it. After all, it was itself. It seemed awful to her. She looked at his face, and she turned her own face to the wall. For his look was other than hers, his way was not her way. She had denied him what he was — she saw it now. She had refused him as himself. And this had been her life, and his life. She was grateful to death, which restored the truth. And she knew she was not dead.

And all the while her heart was bursting with grief and pity for him. What had he suffered? What stretch of horror for this helpless man! She was rigid with agony. She had not been able to help him. He had been cruelly injured, this naked man, this other being, and she could make no reparation. There were the children — but the children belonged to life. This dead man had nothing to do with them. He and she were only channels through which life had flowed to issue in the children. She was a mother — but how awful she knew it now to have been a wife. And he, dead now, how awful he must have felt it to be a husband. She felt that in the next world he would be a stranger to her. If they met there, in the beyond, they would only be ashamed of what had been before. The children had come, for some mysterious reason, out of both of them. But the children did not unite them. Now he was dead, she knew how eternally he was apart from her, how eternally he had nothing more to do with her. She saw this episode of her life closed. They had denied each other in life. Now he had withdrawn. An anguish came over her. It was finished then: it had become hopeless between them long before he died. Yet he had been her husband. But how little!

"Have you got his shirt, 'Lizabeth?"

Elizabeth turned without answering, though she strove to weep and behave as her mother-in-law expected. But she could not, she was silenced. She went into the kitchen and returned with the garment.

"It is aired," she said, grasping the cotton shirt here and there to try. She was almost ashamed to handle him; what right had she or anyone to lay hands on him; but her touch was humble on his body. It was hard work to clothe him. He was so heavy and inert. A terrible dread gripped her all the while: that he could be so heavy and utterly inert, unresponsive, apart. The horror of the distance between them was almost too much for her — it was so infinite a gap she must look across.

At last it was finished. They covered him with a sheet and left him lying, with his face bound. And she fastened the door of the little parlour, lest the children should see what was lying there. Then, with peace sunk heavy on her heart, she went about making tidy the kitchen. She knew she submitted to life, which was her immediate master. But from death, her ultimate master, she winced with fear and shame.

KATHERINE MANSFIELD
1888–1923

We might classify Katherine Mansfield as a New Zealand writer rather than an English one. Some of her finest stories summon up and transform her New Zealand childhood. Though hardly twenty-one when she removed to England, her talent, once hailed as genius, originated in her family memories. It was the shock of losing her beloved brother Leslie in World War I that somehow liberated these memories and permitted her to transcend the narrow outlook marking her early work.

In 1918 she married the writer John Middleton Murry, became for a time part of the febrile literary environment dominated by D. H. Lawrence, led a difficult, discontinuous life, and, while a member of the cultist Fontainebleau community exploited by the charlatan Gurdjieff, died of tuberculosis.

During the last couple of decades her stock has declined. The modernist movement she helped to define has been taken over by greater names: Joyce, Eliot, Woolf, Lawrence. She has been accused, sometimes justly, not merely of being inspired by Chekhov but of too crassly imitating him. Nor has her reputation been helped by the excessive claims Murry and others made for her.

If, however, we consider the rather featureless state of the English short story in 1920, when Bliss and Other Stories *appeared, it is hard to gainsay her contribution. She demonstrated great delicacy of feeling, a notable ability to reconstruct the world of childhood, the courage to ignore conventional narrative patterns, and often an unconcessive realism perhaps stimulated by a constant sense of her own mortality. After her brother's death she made a resolute entry in her notebook: "But all must be told with a sense of mystery, a radiance, an afterglow . . ." This her finest work has.*

"The Fly" points to a harder strain in her nature. Coldly it acknowledges that our ostensibly deepest emotions may be shallow and transient. It asks a disturbing question: Do we unconsciously on occasion annul our own pain by inflicting it on other creatures?

The Fly

"Y'ARE VERY SNUG in here," piped old Mr. Woodifield, and he peered out of the great, green leather armchair by his friend the boss's desk as a baby peers out of its pram. His talk was over; it was time for him to be off. But he did not want to go. Since he had retired, since his . . . stroke, the wife and the girls kept him boxed up in the house every day of the week except Tuesday. On Tuesday he was dressed up and brushed and allowed to cut back to the City for the day. Though what he did there the wife and girls couldn't imagine. Made a nuisance of himself to his friends, they supposed . . . Well, perhaps so. All the same, we cling to our last pleasures as the tree clings to its last leaves. So there sat old Woodifield, smoking a cigar and staring almost greedily at the boss, who rolled in his office chair, stout, rosy, five years older than he, and still going strong, still at the helm. It did one good to see him.

Wistfully, admiringly, the old voice added, "It's snug in here, upon my word!"

"Yes, it's comfortable enough," agreed the boss, and he flipped the *Financial Times* with a paper-knife. As a matter of fact he was proud of his room; he liked to have it admired, especially by old Woodifield. It gave him a feeling of deep, solid satisfaction to be planted there in the midst of it in full view of that frail old figure in the muffler.

"I've had it done up lately," he explained, as he had explained for the past — how many? — weeks. "New carpet," and he pointed to the bright red carpet with a pattern of large white rings. "New furniture," and he nodded towards the massive bookcase and the table with legs like twisted treacle. "Electric heating!" He waved almost exultantly towards the five transparent, pearly sausages glowing so softly in the tilted copper pan.

But he did not draw old Woodifield's attention to the photograph over the table of a grave-looking boy in uniform standing in one of those spectral photographers' parks with photographers' storm-clouds behind him. It was not new. It had been there for over six years.

"There was something I wanted to tell you," said old Woodifield, and his eyes grew dim remembering. "Now what was it? I had it in my mind when I started out this morning." His hands began to tremble, and patches of red showed above his beard.

Poor old chap, he's on his last pins, thought the boss. And, feeling kindly, he winked at the old man, and said jokingly, "I tell you what. I've got a little drop of something here that'll do you good before you go out into the cold again. It's beautiful stuff. It wouldn't hurt a child." He took a key off his watch-chain, unlocked a cupboard below his desk, and drew forth a dark, squat bottle. "That's the medicine," said he. "And the man from whom I got it told me on the strict Q.T. it came from the cellars at Windsor Cassel."

Old Woodifield's mouth fell open at the sight. He couldn't have looked more surprised if the boss had produced a rabbit.

"It's whisky, ain't it?" he piped, feebly.

The boss turned the bottle and lovingly showed him the label. Whisky it was.

"D'you know," said he, peering up at the boss wonderingly, "they won't let me touch it at home." And he looked as though he was going to cry.

"Ah, that's where we know a bit more than the ladies," cried the boss, swooping across for two tumblers that stood on the table with the water-bottle, and pouring a generous finger into each. "Drink it down. It'll do you good. And don't put any water with it. It's sacrilege to tamper with stuff like this. Ah!" He tossed off his, pulled out his handkerchief, hastily wiped his moustaches, and cocked an eye at old Woodifield, who was rolling his in his chaps.

The old man swallowed, was silent a moment, and then said faintly, "It's nutty!"

But it warmed him; it crept into his chill old brain — he remembered.

"That was it," he said, heaving himself out of his chair. "I thought you'd like to know. The girls were in Belgium last week having a look at poor Reggie's grave, and they happened to come across your boy's. They're quite near each other, it seems."

Old Woodifield paused, but the boss made no reply. Only a quiver in his eyelids showed that he heard.

"The girls were delighted with the way the place is kept," piped the old voice. "Beautifully looked after. Couldn't be better if they were at home. You've not been across, have yer?"

"No, no!" For various reasons the boss had not been across.

"There's miles of it," quavered old Woodifield, "and it's all as neat as a garden. Flowers growing on all the graves. Nice broad paths." It was plain from his voice how much he liked a nice broad path.

The pause came again. Then the old man brightened wonderfully.

"D'you know what the hotel made the girls pay for a pot of jam?" he piped. "Ten francs! Robbery, I call it. It was a little pot, so Gertrude says, no bigger than a half-crown. And she hadn't taken more than a spoonful when they charged her ten francs. Gertrude brought the pot away with her to teach 'em a lesson. Quite right, too; it's trading on our feelings. They think because we're over there having a look around we're ready to pay anything. That's what it is." And he turned towards the door.

"Quite right, quite right!" cried the boss, though what was quite right he hadn't the least idea. He came round by his desk, followed the shuffling footsteps to the door, and saw the old fellow out. Woodifield was gone.

For a long moment the boss stayed, staring at nothing, while the grey-haired office messenger, watching him, dodged in and out of his cubbyhole like a dog that expects to be taken for a run. Then: "I'll see nobody for half an hour, Macey," said the boss. "Understand? Nobody at all."

"Very good, sir."

The door shut, the firm heavy steps recrossed the bright carpet, the fat body plumped down in the spring chair, and leaning forward, the boss covered his face with his hands. He wanted, he intended, he had arranged to weep . . .

It had been a terrible shock to him when old Woodifield sprang that remark upon him about the boy's grave. It was exactly as though the earth had opened and he had seen the boy lying there with Woodifield's girls staring down at him. For it was strange. Although over six years had passed away, the boss never thought of the boy except as lying unchanged, unblemished in his uniform, asleep for ever. "My son!" groaned the boss. But no tears came yet. In the past, in the first months and even years after the boy's death, he had only to say those words to be overcome by such grief that nothing short of a violent fit of weeping could relieve him. Time, he had declared then, he had told everybody, could make no difference. Other men perhaps might recover, might live their loss down, but not he. How was it possible? His boy was an only son. Ever since his birth the boss had worked at building up this business for him; it had no other meaning if it was not for the boy. Life itself had come to have no other meaning. How on earth could he have slaved, denied himself, kept going all those years without the promise for ever before him of the boy's stepping into his shoes and carrying on where he left off?

And that promise had been so near being fulfilled. The boy had been in the office learning the ropes for a year before the war. Every morning they had started off together; they had come back by the same train. And what congratulations he had received as the boy's father! No wonder; he had taken to it marvellously. As to his popularity with the staff, every man jack of them down to old Macey couldn't make enough of the boy. And he wasn't in the least spoilt. No, he was just his bright, natural self, with the right word for everybody, with that boyish look and his habit of saying, "Simply splendid!"

But all that was over and done with as though it never had been. The day had come when Macey had handed him the telegram that brought the whole place crashing about his head. "Deeply regret to inform you . . . " And he had left the office a broken man, with his life in ruins.

Six years ago, six years . . . How quickly time passed! It might have happened yesterday. The boss took his hands from his face; he was puzzled. Something seemed to be wrong with him. He wasn't feeling as he wanted to feel. He decided to get up and have a look at the boy's photograph. But it wasn't a favorite photograph of his; the expression was unnatural. It was cold, even stern-looking. The boy had never looked like that.

At that moment the boss noticed that a fly had fallen into his broad inkpot, and was trying feebly but desperately to clamber out again. Help! help! said those struggling legs. But the sides of the inkpot were wet and slippery; it fell back again and began to swim. The boss took up a pen, picked the fly out of the ink, and shook it on to a piece of blotting-paper. For a fraction of a second it lay still on the dark patch that oozed round it. Then the front legs waved, took hold, and, pulling its small sodden body up it began the immense task of cleaning the ink from its wings. Over and under, over and under, went a leg along a wing, as the stone goes over and under the scythe. Then there was a pause, while the fly, seeming to stand on the tips of its toes, tried to expand first one wing and then the other. It succeeded at last, and, sitting down, it began, like a minute cat, to clean its face. Now one could imagine that the little front legs rubbed against each other lightly, joyfully. The horrible danger was over; it had escaped; it was ready for life again.

But just then the boss had an idea. He plunged his pen back into the ink, leaned his thick wrist on the blotting paper, and as the fly tried its wings down came a great heavy blot. What would it make of that? What indeed! The little beggar seemed absolutely cowed, stunned, and afraid to move because of what would happen next. But then, as if painfully, it dragged itself forward. The front legs waved, caught hold, and, more slowly this time, the task began from the beginning.

He's a plucky little devil, thought the boss, and he felt a real admiration for the fly's courage. That was the way to tackle things; that was the right spirit. Never say die; it was only a question of . . . But the fly had again finished its laborious task, and the boss had just time to refill his pen, to shake fair and square on the new-cleaned body yet another dark drop. What about it this time? A painful moment of suspense followed. But behold, the front legs were again waving; the boss felt a rush of relief. He leaned over the fly and said to it tenderly, "You artful little b . . . " And he actually had the brilliant notion of breathing on it to help the drying process. All the same, there was something timid and weak about its efforts now, and the boss decided that this time should be the last, as he dipped the pen into the inkpot.

It was. The last blot on the soaked blotting-paper, and the draggled fly lay in it and did not stir. The back legs were stuck to the body; the front legs were not to be seen.

"Come on," said the boss. "Look sharp!" And he stirred it with his pen — in vain. Nothing happened or was likely to happen. The fly was dead.

The boss lifted the corpse on the end of the paper-knife and flung it into the waste-paper basket. But such a grinding feeling of wretchedness seized him that he felt positively frightened. He started forward and pressed the bell for Macey.

"Bring me some fresh blotting-paper," he said, sternly, "and look sharp about it." And while the old dog padded away he fell to wondering what it was he had been thinking about before. What was it? It was . . . He took out his handkerchief and passed it inside his collar. For the life of him he could not remember.

KATHERINE ANNE PORTER
1890–1980

Katherine Anne Porter, a direct descendant of Daniel Boone, lived to be ninety. Her production, in the light of this circumstance, appears small: one flawed novel, Ship of Fools, *published when she was seventy-two and which made her a million dollars; a collection of articles; a book on the Sacco-Vanzetti case; and a modest total of novellas and short stories, many of them patently autobiographical. The latter have evoked, for the precision of their style and their evocative imagery, the admiration, almost the adoration, of many professional critics. She is, as is often said, a writer's writer.*

Porter's native Texas plays an important part in her recollective fictions, but she differs from the post-Faulkner school of Southern novelists in her greater cosmopolitanism, a certain worldliness, even a coolness of approach to human character. I have chosen one of her native-soil stories. It has simplicity, poignancy, a stoic frontier acceptance of lives lived with all the odds against them.

He

LIFE WAS VERY HARD for the Whipples. It was hard to feed all the hungry mouths, it was hard to keep the children in flannels during the winter, short as it was: "God knows what would become of us if we lived north," they would say: keeping them decently clean was hard. "It looks like our luck won't never let up on us," said Mr. Whipple, but Mrs. Whipple was all for taking what was sent and calling it good, anyhow when the neighbors were in earshot. "Don't ever let a soul hear us complain," she kept saying to her husband. She couldn't stand to be pitied. "No, not if it comes to it that we have to live in a wagon and pick cotton around the country," she said, "nobody's going to get a chance to look down on us."

Mrs. Whipple loved her second son, the simple-minded one, better than she loved the other two children put together. She was forever saying so, and when she talked with certain of her neighbors, she would even throw in her husband and her mother for good measure.

"You needn't keep on saying it around," said Mr. Whipple, "you'll make people think nobody else has any feelings about Him but you."

"It's natural for a mother," Mrs. Whipple would remind him. "You know yourself it's more natural for a mother to be that way. People don't expect so much of fathers, some way."

This didn't keep the neighbors from talking plainly among themselves. "A Lord's pure mercy if He should die," they said. "It's the sins of the fathers," they agreed among themselves. "There's bad blood and bad doings somewhere, you can bet on that." This behind the Whipples' backs. To their faces everybody said, "He's not so bad off. He'll be all right yet. Look how He grows!"

Mrs. Whipple hated to talk about it, she tried to keep her mind off it, but every time anybody set foot in the house, the subject always came up, and she had to talk about Him first, before she could get on to anything else. It seemed to ease her mind. "I wouldn't have anything happen to Him for all the world, but it just looks like I can't keep Him out of mischief. He's so strong and active, He's always into everything; He was like that since He could walk. It's actually funny sometimes, the way He can do anything; it's laughable to see Him up to His tricks. Emly has more accidents; I'm forever tying up her bruises, and Adna can't fall a foot without cracking a bone. But He can do anything and not get a scratch. The preacher said such a nice thing once when he was here. He said, and I'll remember it to my dying day, 'The innocent walk with God — that's why He don't get hurt.'" Whenever Mrs. Whipple repeated these words, she always felt a warm pool spread in her breast, and the tears would fill her eyes, and then she could talk about something else.

He did grow and He never got hurt. A plank blew off the chicken house and struck Him on the head and He never seemed to know it. He had learned a few words, and after this He forgot them. He didn't whine for food as the other children did, but waited until it was given Him; He ate squatting in the corner, smacking and mumbling. Rolls of fat covered Him like an overcoat, and He could carry twice as much wood and water as Adna. Emly had a cold in the head most of the time — "she takes that after me," said Mrs. Whipple — so in bad weather they gave her the extra blanket off His cot. He never seemed to mind the cold.

Just the same, Mrs. Whipple's life was a torment for fear something might happen to Him. He climbed the peach trees much better than Adna and went skittering along the branches like a monkey, just a regular monkey. "Oh, Mrs. Whipple, you hadn't ought to let Him do that. He'll lose His balance sometime. He can't rightly know what He's doing."

Mrs. Whipple almost screamed out at the neighbor. "He *does* know what He's doing! He's as able as any other child! Come down out of there, you!" When He finally reached the ground she could hardly keep her hands off Him for acting like that before people, a grin all over His face and her worried sick about Him all the time.

"It's the neighbors," said Mrs. Whipple to her husband. "Oh, I do mortally wish they would keep out of our business. I can't afford to let Him do anything for fear they'll come nosing around about it. Look at the bees, now. Adna can't handle them, they sting him up so; I haven't got time to do everything, and now I don't dare let Him. But if He gets a sting He don't really mind."

"It's just because He ain't got sense enough to be scared of anything," said Mr. Whipple.

"You ought to be ashamed of yourself," said Mrs. Whipple, "talking that way about your own child. Who's to take up for Him if we don't, I'd like to know? He sees a lot that goes on, He listens to things all the time. And anything I tell Him to do He does it. Don't never let anybody hear you say such things. They'd think you favored the other children over Him."

"Well, now I don't, and you know it, and what's the use of getting all worked up about it? You always think the worst of everything. Just let Him alone, He'll get along somehow. He gets plenty to eat and wear, don't He?" Mr. Whipple suddenly felt tired out. "Anyhow, it can't be helped now."

Mrs. Whipple felt tired too, she complained in a tired voice. "What's done can't never be undone, I know that as good as anybody; but He's my child, and I'm not going to have people say anything. I get sick of people coming around saying things all the time."

In the early fall Mrs. Whipple got a letter from her brother saying he and his wife and two children were coming over for a little visit next Sunday week. "Put the big pot in the little one," he wrote at the end. Mrs. Whipple read this part out loud twice, she was so pleased. Her brother was a great one for saying funny things. "We'll just show him that's no joke," she said, "we'll just butcher one of the sucking pigs."

"It's a waste and I don't hold with waste the way we are now," said Mr. Whipple. "That pig'll be worth money by Christmas."

"It's a shame and a pity we can't have a decent meal's vittles once in a while when my own family comes to see us," said Mrs. Whipple. "I'd hate for his wife to go back and say there wasn't a thing in the house to eat. My God, it's better than buying up a great chance of meat in town. There's where you'd spend the money!"

"All right, do it yourself then," said Mr. Whipple. "Christamighty, no wonder we can't get ahead!"

The question was how to get the little pig away from his ma, a great fighter, worse than a Jersey cow. Adna wouldn't try it: "That sow'd rip my insides out all over the pen." "All right, old fraidy," said Mrs. Whipple, "*He's* not scared. Watch *Him* do it." And she laughed as though it was all a good joke and gave Him a little push towards the pen. He sneaked up and snatched the pig right away from the teat and galloped back and was over the fence with the sow raging at His heels. The little black squirming thing was screeching like a baby in a tantrum, stiffening its back and stretching its mouth to the ears. Mrs. Whipple took the pig with her face stiff and sliced its throat with one stroke. When He saw the blood He gave a great jolting breath and ran away. "But He'll forget and eat plenty, just the same," thought Mrs. Whipple. Whenever she was thinking, her lips moved making words. "He'd eat it all if I didn't stop Him. He'd eat up every mouthful from the other two if I'd let Him."

She felt badly about it. He was ten years old now and a third again as large as Adna, who was going on fourteen. "It's a shame, a shame," she kept saying under her breath, "and Adna with so much brains!"

She kept on feeling badly about all sorts of things. In the first place it was the man's work to butcher; the sight of the pig scraped pink and naked made her sick. He was too fat and soft and pitiful-looking. It was simply a shame the way things had to happen. By the time she had finished it up, she almost wished her brother would stay at home.

Early Sunday morning Mrs. Whipple dropped everything to get Him all cleaned up. In an hour He was dirty again, with crawling under fences after a possum, and straddling along the rafters of the barn looking for eggs in the hayloft. "My Lord, look at you now after all my trying! And here's Adna and Emly staying so quiet. I get tired trying to keep you decent. Get off that shirt and put on another, people will say I don't half dress you!" And she boxed Him on the ears, hard. He blinked and blinked and rubbed His head, and His face hurt Mrs. Whipple's feelings. Her knees began to tremble, she had to sit down while she buttoned His shirt. "I'm just all gone before the day starts."

The brother came with his plump healthy wife and two great roaring hungry boys. They had a grand dinner, with the pig roasted to a crackling in the middle of the table, full of dressing, a pickled peach in his mouth and plenty of gravy for the sweet potatoes.

"This looks like prosperity all right," said the brother; "you're going to have to roll me home like I was a barrel when I'm done."

Everybody laughed out loud; it was fine to hear them laughing all at once around the table. Mrs. Whipple felt warm and good about it. "Oh, we've got six more of these; I say it's as little as we can do when you come to see us so seldom."

He wouldn't come into the dining room, and Mrs. Whipple passed it off very well. "He's timider than my other two," she said, "He'll just have to get used to you. There isn't everybody He'll make up with, you know how it is with some children, even cousins." Nobody said anything out of the way.

"Just like my Alfy here," said the brother's wife. "I sometimes got to lick him to make him shake hands with his own grandmammy."

So that was over, and Mrs. Whipple loaded up a big plate for Him first, before everybody."I always say He ain't to be slighted, no matter who else goes without," she said, and carried it to Him herself.

"He can chin Himself on the top of the door," said Emly, helping along.

"That's fine, He's getting along fine," said the brother.

They went away after supper. Mrs. Whipple rounded up the dishes, and sent the children to bed and sat down and unlaced her shoes. "You see?" she said to Mr. Whipple. "That's the way my whole family is. Nice and considerate about everything. No out-of-the-way remarks — they *have* got refinement. I get awfully sick of people's remarks. Wasn't that pig good?"

Mr. Whipple said, "Yes, we're out three hundred pounds of pork, that's all. It's easy to be polite when you come to eat. Who knows what they had in their minds all along?"

"Yes, that's like you," said Mrs. Whipple. "I don't expect anything else from you. You'll be telling me next that my own brother will be saying around that we made Him eat in the kitchen! Oh, my God!" She rocked her head in her hands, a hard pain started in the very middle of her forehead. "Now it's all spoiled, and everything was so nice and easy. All right, you don't like them and you never did — all right, they'll not come here again soon, never you mind! But they *can't* say He wasn't dressed every lick as good as Adna — oh, honest, sometimes I wish I was dead!"

"I wish you'd let up," said Mr. Whipple. "It's bad enough as it is."

It was a hard winter. It seemed to Mrs. Whipple that they hadn't ever known anything but hard times, and now to cap it all a winter like this. The crops were about half of what they had a right to expect; after the cotton was in it didn't do much more than cover the grocery bill. They swapped off one of the plow horses, and got cheated, for the new one died of the heaves. Mrs. Whipple kept thinking all the time it was terrible to have a man you couldn't depend on not to get cheated. They cut down on everything, but Mrs. Whipple kept saying there are things you can't cut down on, and they cost money. It took a lot of warm clothes for Adna and Emly, who walked four miles to school during the three-months session. "He sets around the fire a lot, He won't need so much," said Mr. Whipple. "That's so," said Mrs. Whipple, "and when He does the outdoor chores He can wear your tarpaullion coat. I can't do no better, that's all."

In February He was taken sick, and lay curled up under His blanket looking very blue in the face and acting as if He would choke. Mr. and Mrs. Whipple did everything they could for Him for two days, and then they were scared and sent for the doctor. The doctor told them they must keep Him warm and give Him plenty of milk and eggs. "He isn't as stout as He looks, I'm afraid," said the doctor. "You've got to watch them when they're like that. You must put more cover onto Him, too."

"I just took off His big blanket to wash," said Mrs. Whipple, ashamed. "I can't stand dirt."

"Well, you'd better put it back on the minute it's dry," said the doctor, "or He'll have pneumonia."

Mr. and Mrs. Whipple took a blanket off their own bed and put His cot in by the fire. "They can't say we didn't do everything for Him," she said, "even to sleeping cold ourselves on His account."

When the winter broke He seemed to be well again, but He walked as if His feet hurt Him. He was able to run a cotton planter during the season.

"I got it all fixed up with Jim Ferguson about breeding the cow next time," said Mr. Whipple. "I'll pasture the bull this summer and give Jim some fodder in the fall. That's better than paying out money when you haven't got it."

"I hope you didn't say such a thing before Jim Ferguson," said Mrs. Whipple. "You oughtn't to let him know we're so down as all that."

"Godamighty, that ain't saying we're down. A man is got to look ahead sometimes. He can lead the bull over today. I need Adna on the place."

At first Mrs. Whipple felt easy in her mind about sending Him for the bull. Adna was too jumpy and couldn't be trusted. You've got to be steady around animals. After He was gone she started thinking, and after a while she could hardly bear it any longer. She stood in the lane and watched for Him. It was nearly three miles to go and a hot day, but He oughtn't to be so long about it. She shaded her eyes and stared until colored bubbles floated in her eyeballs. It was just like everything else in life, she must always worry and never know a moment's peace about anything. After a long time she saw Him turn into the side lane, limping. He came on very slowly, leading the big hulk of an animal by a ring in the nose, twirling a little stick in His hand, never looking back or sideways, but coming on like a sleepwalker with His eyes half shut.

Mrs. Whipple was scared sick of bulls; she had heard awful stories about how they followed on quietly enough, and then suddenly pitched on with a bellow and pawed and gored a body to pieces. Any second now that black monster would come down on Him, my God, He'd never have sense enough to run.

She mustn't make a sound nor a move; she mustn't get the bull started. The bull heaved his head aside and horned the air at a fly. Her voice burst out of her in a shriek, and she screamed at Him to come on, for God's sake. He didn't seem to hear her clamor, but kept on twirling His switch and limping on, and the bull lumbered along behind him as gently as a calf. Mrs. Whipple stopped calling and ran towards the house, praying under her breath: "Lord, don't let anything happen to Him. Lord, you *know* people will say we oughtn't to have sent Him. You *know* they'll say we didn't take care of Him. Oh, get Him home, safe home, safe home, and I'll look out for Him better! Amen."

She watched from the window while He led the beast in, and tied him up in the barn. It was no use trying to keep up, Mrs. Whipple couldn't bear another thing. She sat down and rocked and cried with her apron over her head.

From year to year the Whipples were growing poorer and poorer. The place just seemed to run down of itself, no matter how hard they worked. "We're losing our hold," said Mrs. Whipple. "Why can't we do like other people and watch for our best chances? They'll be calling us poor white trash next."

"When I get to be sixteen I'm going to leave," said Adna. "I'm going to get a job in Powell's grocery store. There's money in that. No more farm for me."

"I'm going to be a schoolteacher," said Emly. "But I've got to finish the eighth grade, anyhow. Then I can live in town. I don't see any chances here."

"Emly takes after my family," said Mrs. Whipple. "Ambitious every last one of them, and they don't take second place for anybody."

When fall came Emly got a chance to wait on table in the railroad eating-house in the town near by, and it seemed such a shame not to take it when the wages were good and she could get her food too, that Mrs. Whipple decided to let her take it, and not bother with school until the next session. "You've got plenty of time," she said. "You're young and smart as a whip."

With Adna gone too, Mr. Whipple tried to run the farm with just Him to help. He seemed to get along fine, doing His work and part of Adna's without noticing it. They did well enough until Christmas time, when one morning He slipped on the ice coming up from the barn. Instead of getting up He thrashed round and round, and when Mr. Whipple got to Him, He was having some sort of fit.

They brought Him inside and tried to make Him sit up, but He blubbered and rolled, so they put Him to bed and Mr. Whipple rode to town for the doctor. All the way there and back he worried about where the money was to come from: it sure did look like he had about all the troubles he could carry.

From then on He stayed in bed. His legs swelled up double their size, and the fits kept coming back. After four months, the doctor said, "It's no use, I think you'd better put Him in the County Home for treatment right away. I'll see about it for you. He'll have good care there and be off your hands."

"We don't begrudge Him any care, and I won't let Him out of my sight," said Mrs. Whipple. "I won't have it said I sent my sick child off among strangers."

"I know how you feel," said the doctor. "You can't tell me anything about that, Mrs. Whipple. I've got a boy of my own. But you'd better listen to me. I can't do anything more for Him, that's the truth."

Mr. and Mrs. Whipple talked it over a long time that night after they went to bed. "It's just charity," said Mrs. Whipple, "that's what we've come to, charity! I certainly never looked for this."

"We pay taxes to help support the place just like everybody else," said Mr. Whipple, "and I don't call that taking charity. I think it would be fine to have Him where He'd get the best of everything . . . and besides, I can't keep up with these doctor bills any longer."

"Maybe that's why the doctor wants us to send Him — he's scared he won't get his money," said Mrs. Whipple.

"Don't talk like that," said Mr. Whipple, feeling pretty sick, "or we won't be able to send Him."

"Oh, but we won't keep Him there long," said Mrs. Whipple. "Soon's He's better, we'll bring Him right back home."

"The doctor has told you and told you time and again He can't ever get better, and you might as well stop talking," said Mr. Whipple.

"Doctors don't know everything," said Mrs. Whipple, feeling almost happy. "But anyhow, in the summer Emly can come home for a vacation, and Adna can get down for Sundays: we'll all work together and get on our feet again, and the children will feel they've got a place to come to."

All at once she saw it full summer again, with the garden going fine, and new white roller shades up all over the house, and Adna and Emly home, so full of life, all of them happy together. Oh, it could happen, things would ease up on them.

They didn't talk before Him much, but they never knew just how much He understood. Finally the doctor set the day and a neighbor who owned a double-seated carryall offered to drive them over. The hospital would have sent an ambulance, but Mrs. Whipple couldn't stand to see Him going away looking so sick as all that. They wrapped Him in blankets, and the neighbor and Mr. Whipple lifted Him into the back seat of the carryall beside Mrs. Whipple, who had on her black shirt waist. She couldn't stand to go looking like charity.

"You'll be all right, I guess I'll stay behind," said Mr. Whipple. "It don't look like everybody ought to leave the place at once."

"Besides, it ain't as if He was going to stay forever," said Mrs. Whipple to the neighbor. "This is only for a little while."

They started away, Mrs. Whipple holding to the edges of the blankets to keep Him from sagging sideways. He sat there blinking and blinking. He worked His hands out and began rubbing His nose with His knuckles, and then with the end of the blanket. Mrs. Whipple couldn't believe what she saw; He was scrubbing away big tears that rolled out of the corners of His eyes. He sniveled and made a gulping noise. Mrs. Whipple kept saying, "Oh, honey, you don't feel so bad, do you? You don't feel so bad, do you?" for He seemed to be accusing her of something. Maybe He remembered that time she boxed His ears, maybe He had been scared that day with the bull, maybe He had slept cold and couldn't tell her about it; maybe He knew they were sending Him away for good and all because they were too poor to keep Him. Whatever it was, Mrs. Whipple couldn't bear to think of it. She began to cry, frightfully, and wrapped her arms tight around Him. His head rolled on her shoulder: she had loved Him as much as she possibly could, there were Adna and Emly who had to be thought of too, there was nothing she could do to make up to Him for His life. Oh, what a mortal pity He was ever born.

They came in sight of the hospital, with the neighbor driving very fast, not daring to look behind him.

Ivo Andrić

1892–1975

Awarded the Nobel Prize for literature in 1961, Andrić was born in Trav-
nik, Bosnia (now Yugoslavia). As a young man he was involved in the na-
tionalist movement highlighted by the assassination of Archduke Franz Fer-
dinand at Sarajevo. After World War I he spent three years in prison. He
then began a career as a Yugoslav diplomat, rising to the post of ambassador
to Berlin in 1939.

   Essayist, short story writer, and novelist, Andrić is probably best known
to us for his epic novels The Bridge on the Drina *and* Bosnian Chronicle.
The story "Thirst," steeped in the dark tragedy of the Balkan experience,
turns on a conflict between the imperatives of compassion and pleasure. It
demonstrates the power that still lives in the pre-Hemingway approach to
narrative. Recognizably Slavic, it is slow, explicit, shadowed by a stoic
compassion.

Thirst

IMMEDIATELY AFTER the Austrian occupation, a gendarmerie barracks was set up in Sokoc, a village on a high plateau. Its commander had brought with him a beautiful blonde wife from somewhere in the far-off world. She had large blue eyes that looked as though they were made of glass and, with her fragile beauty, her European clothes and possessions, she looked like a small luxury object some traveler might have lost as he passed over this mountain on his journey from one city to another.

The village had not yet recovered from its surprise and the young bride had not quite finished arranging her bridal room, full of cushions, embroidery, and ribbons, when bandits were reported in the district. As a result, a detachment of *Streifkorps* soon arrived at the barracks and the personnel was doubled thereby.

The commander began to spend whole days and nights out on duty, planning and directing the patrols. Bewildered and a little frightened by what was happening, the young bride passed the time with certain of the village women, in hopes of feeling less lonely. But she was always waiting. Sleep and food no longer refreshed or strengthened her; every feeling was drained by her constant anxiety. The village women pleaded with her and urged her to eat, while eating and drinking heartily themselves. At night some of them would come to talk, telling her anecdotes and stories in order to help her fall asleep. But in the end the women, tired out with their tales, would fall asleep and the young wife lying in bed would stare at them as they slept on the red rug, herself sleepless and oppressed by the heavy smells of milk and wool that rose from their bodies.

When, after several days of such waiting, the commander would arrive home, she could not even then feel much comfort and relief. He would return exhausted from tramping through forests and from sleepless nights, unshaven, spattered with mud, and soaking wet. Two boys would have to struggle to remove his sodden boots, pulling away some of the skin from his bruised and swollen legs as they did so. He would sit dejected and worried by the failure of his campaign, absent-minded, but at the same time planning new moves. The look of his face would be worn and haggard; the sun had burned it and the mountain wind had cracked his lips. During that short respite at home, his wife would tend to him as if he were wounded, but in three or four days he would be dressed and booted again at dawn, ready to set off with his men into the mountains. Again all her thoughts would be prayers; that the outlaws would be captured and that this terrible kind of life would come to an end.

The prayers came true one day. Lazar Zelenović, the chief and the shrewdest of the outlaws, was captured. The word went round the barracks and the village, and opinion was that it would now be much easier to capture or scatter the rest.

Lazar was caught by chance, by a patrol that had been tracking one of his men. It came about this way: two months before, when Lazar had first come from Hercegovina, he had been wounded by a bullet in the chest. To give himself time to recover, he and some of his men had built a shelter of dry branches, driftwood, and mud under the lee of a huge fallen log and alongside one of the mountain streams. Thus he was protected from observation from the paths that ran higher along the river line, and in this hole he lived. He lay there all day, bathing the wound in his chest with river water while the patrols searched everywhere among the cliffs and crags for him. If he'd had better luck, a better hiding place, and if the weather had not turned hot so early in the season, Lazar could have recovered. But, as it was, the heat made the wound septic. He protected himself as best he could against the flies and mosquitoes, but the wound continued to fester and the inflammation spread. His fever grew.

This was Lazar's state when one of the younger men decided to bring him a little wax and brandy as a cure. The patrol happened to sight the boy just as he was leaving a shepherd's hut to set off into the mountains. But, after he had nearly reached the stream, the boy looked back and glimpsed some of the *Streifkorps* men on his trail. He got away easily among the undergrowth along the river.

At the first signal, the commander had left his horse in a field and had gone on, running ahead of his men. As he came through the trees toward the river, he suddenly caught his foot against something and fell up to his waist in mud and slime. Just as he was beginning, with some trouble, to extricate himself to go on in further pursuit, he caught the terrible smell of Lazar's wound and he noticed the low shelter against the log. He pulled himself from the mud and approached carefully; through the opening in the heaped-up branches he could see part of a sheepskin. He thought that he had run across the hiding-place of the man he had just been following.

To deceive the hidden outlaw, the commander called back orders to the *Streifkorps* patrol: "He must have gone further down river. Double time after him and I'll follow along. I've hurt my leg on these thorns." While he was shouting this, he signaled with one hand for the men to be silent, and with the other he motioned for them to move up around him. When three of them were there, they suddenly launched themselves into the hiding-place and seized the brigand from behind, like a badger in his hole. Lazar had a long rifle and a knife, but he did not fight back. He could barely move.

They fettered his hands with a chain and tied his feet with a rope. They carried him out like a log, over the steep pathless slope to the field where the commander's horse was waiting. As they walked, they felt stifled by the stench from him and when they laid him down on the grass they saw the great red wound on his chest. A certain Zhivan from Gorazhde, serving as spy and informant for the *Streifkorps*, recognized Lazar at once. They came from the same village; they had both celebrated the same saint's day, the day of St. John.

The commander was not sure. He asked Zhivan to confirm again that this really was Lazar. They all bent to look at the prisoner.

Zhivan said, "It's you, Lazar!"

"You know me better than I know you."

"You know me too, Lazar. Of course you do."

"Even if I'd never known you, now I'd know what and who you are. Everybody in the villages, Serb or Turk, from here to Gorazhde, would recognize you. A half-witted kid looking at us for the first time would say: the one who is lying there tied-up and wounded is Lazar and that miserable thing leaning over him is Zhivan."

The outlaw, in his fever, seemed to have a need to talk. Zhivan wanted to defend his reputation, and who knows how long they might have argued if the commander hadn't stopped them in order to ask Lazar some questions. Lazar fell silent. He would not answer to anything about his comrades. The commander grew stern. He gave orders to the sergeant major that Zhivan should not be allowed a single drop of water, no matter how much he begged, until he was ready to speak about this.

While they were making a rough stretcher, the young commander sat alone at a little distance, trying to rest and collect his thoughts. He leaned his elbow on one knee and his forehead on his palm, staring at the fresh green of the mountainsides that rolled away in the distance like great waves of a static sea. He wanted to think about his success, the reputation he would get, about being at home again with his wife. But no real thoughts would form. He felt only the leaden fatigue that the traveler through night and heavy snow feels, and like that traveler he knew that he must keep himself awake. He stood up and gave the order to move.

Now they were nine in all. The stretcher was clumsy and there were many knots. One of the *Streifkorps* men went up to it and threw his overcoat onto the form of the wounded man. He did this in an odd way, turning as he let go, as if he were throwing the coat into an abyss. They went slowly. The sun was scorching. The commander at first rode behind the stretcher but he found the smell from the wound so terrible that he made his horse go on ahead. Late in the afternoon when they came down into the Glasinac valley they were able to commandeer a cart and oxen from a peasant. And so before sunset they made their way across the plain to Sokoc. They might have been men coming back from a hunt if the bundle of their prey had not looked and smelled so strange.

In the field that fronted the barracks the village women and children gathered to watch, the commander's wife among them. At first she waited only to see her husband again and gave no thought to the outlaw. But, as the women talked more and more about the prisoner, as they told more and more fantastic tales of him, and as the small procession moved over the plain toward them — slow and spaced out like a funeral — she began to feel another kind of anticipation and a sense of fear. They arrived at last. With some noise and commotion the men opened up the left side of the main gate, something that was ordinarily done only for the cartloads of wood or hay. The procession moved up to the doors of the barracks. There the commander dismounted, landing heavily on the ground with the movements of a man exhausted. Then his wife felt the bristly several-days' growth of beard against her face, and she smelled again the compound odor of sweat, earth, and rain which he always carried with him from these nights and days on duty.

While the commander was giving orders, his wife glanced at the outlaw, who was lying bound to the stretcher and perfectly still. Only his head was slightly raised on a block of wood and a little straw. He looked at nobody. She smelled the acute stench which seemed like that of a wounded wild animal.

When he had given the necessary orders, the commander took his wife by the arm and led her into the house in order that she should not see them untying and removing the prisoner. After he had washed and changed into clean clothes, he went out again to see how Lazar had been secured. The temporary prison was nothing more than the cellar under the commander's house. It was not satisfactory because the door — which had an iron grille in the upper part — was hardly very stout and had only a simple lock. Therefore a guard had to be placed on the improvised cell at night.

The commander ate some food and talked for a long time with his wife. At first he spoke of trifles. He was animated and gay, like a child. He was enormously pleased with the outcome. He had captured the chief and most dangerous of the outlaws after five months of search and frustration, after five months of unwarranted reprimands from his superior officer in Rogatica and from Command Headquarters in Sarajevo. Now he would find out from Lazar where the other outlaws were hiding and the names of their collaborators in the countryside. The commander thought he could finish his job, set his heart at rest, and at last enjoy the recognition of success.

"And if he won't betray them?" asked his wife anxiously.

"He will . . . He must," answered the commander and would not talk any more of it.

The commander was sleepy. He felt an awful weight of fatigue stronger than the pride of his victory, than his hunger, than his desire for his wife. The freshness of the bed made him feel dizzy. He struggled to keep on talking to show that he was not really so tired, but the words caught in his mouth and the intervals between words became longer. In mid-sentence he fell asleep, his left hand resting on the small, white, rounded shoulder of his wife.

She did not want to sleep, though. She felt contented and excited — but at the same time frightened and sad. For a long time she watched the sleeping man beside her, the right side of his face sunk in the soft feather pillow, his cracked lips slightly parted as if he were trying to drink that pillow. Between our wakeful selves and the sleeper beside us there always forms a great, cold distance. It is made of non-understanding, a strange sense of desertion, and deathly loneliness.

The young wife tried to go to sleep herself. But she was jolted out of her first slumber by the noise of the changing of the guard in front of the cellar door. As if she had not slept or thought of anything else since the return, her mind was on the idea of the outlaw.

Zhivan, the spy and Lazar's compatriot, was on guard. She realized that it was not so much the sound of the guard changing that had awakened her as the sound of Lazar's voice calling for water. Now he was asking something again.

"Which of you is on duty?"

Silence.

"Is it you, Zhivan?"

"Yes. Shut up."

"How can I shut up, damn you, when I'm dying of thirst and fever? Give me a little water, Zhivan, in the name of our patron St. John — don't let me perish here like vermin."

Zhivan pretended not to hear, in hopes that the prisoner would get tired of pleading. But the low, hoarse voice came again.

"If you have any idea of what suffering and captivity are, don't refuse me, Zhivan, in the name of your children."

"Don't swear by the name of my children! I've got orders and this is my duty. Shut up. You'll wake the commander."

"Let him rot. He's worse than a Turk to torture me with thirst on top of all my bad luck. Go on, shove me a little water if you're a man."

She discovered, from some further muffled conversation, that her husband had denied water for Lazar in order to force him to betray his men. The prisoner was tortured by violent thirst and fever, but evidently he found some relief in swearing, in stringing together wild words and curses, and in repeating the word "water." For a few moments he would be silent, then he would let out a deep sigh, then he would utter a stream of words.

"Zhivan, Zhivan, curse you a hundred times for this torture. Give me a little water and you can kill me then — with good luck to you in this world and the other."

But Zhivan had stopped answering.

"Zhivan, Zhivan! I implore you. I'm burning . . . "

Nothing. The burnt-out last quarter of the moon came late into the sky. Zhivan stood in the shadow, and when he spoke again his voice was muted. Lazar yelled to the commander.

"Commander, don't torture me any more, for Christ's sake, when it's no use."

The silence seemed greater after his voice. In that silence, the outlaw would suddenly give a hoarse grunt and a heavy groan, no longer knowing what he said.

"Foul dogs suck your blood forever and never get enough! Let our blood choke you. Commander, where are you, damn your guts."

The last words came in a stifled tone from his parched throat. Again Zhivan told him to be still and promised that he'd call the commander at first light. The commander would surely give him water if only Lazar told them what they asked. He had to be patient until then. But the prisoner would forget, and in a few moments he would scream again.

"In God's name, Zhivan, water . . . I'm burning." And he would repeat the word a hundred times, the fever and his uneasy breathing changing his voice, now loud, now low.

She sat on the edge of her bed and listened to all this, unconscious of herself and where she was, lost completely in the new horrors she heard in the outlaw's voice.

When she was a child in her parents' house there were nights when she could not sleep. They came, usually, in the spring or the autumn, and in those hours she would listen the whole night through to troubled, monotonous voices that came to her from the dark outside: the wind honing on the edge of the chimney or banging the forgotten garden gate. The child lying there had given these sounds a human quality, imagining that they were living beings in trouble in the night, struggling, howling, moaning. Our childhoods are often repeated farther on in life. How wonderful if it were only childhood again, with nothing but the innocent terror that awoke the little girl — here in this remote village, here in her marriage bed. If the voice of the dying man were only the wind swinging a gate.

But it was not the wind on the chimney or the sound of hinges, though it came at the same regular intervals; it was unmistakably the human voice coming through dry open lips over the burnt tongue. "Water, water, water."

When Zhivan was relieved by another guard, the prisoner's cries did not stop, yet they became lower and more exhausted. The young wife continued to sit in the dark of her room, riveted, listened to every sound from below, ceaselessly thinking the same thought. How could she grasp and understand the life of these people? She saw only that some of them were outlaws and some of them were gendarmerie and that these were two faces of the same disaster. She saw that they would hunt each other mercilessly and that she would stay here between the two, hopeless with grief and pity.

There had been a great deal of talk about Lazar in Sokoc and she had heard all the tales of his cruelty: the way he tortured the villagers who would not submit to him, how he ambushed the gendarmes, leaving them dead and naked in the road. She knew that they were only taking their revenge now. But could revenge last forever? It seemed as if they were all staggering over some precipice and that they would all fall on just such a night into darkness, blood, thirst, and unknown horrors.

At times she had thought of waking the sleeping man on the bed and asking him to disperse all this nightmare with one word, one smile. But she did not stir nor did she wake him. She stayed motionless and alone with the voice from the cellar. She thought, too, of the prayers she had learned in childhood. But those protections were for a vanished life and they were helpless now. She resigned herself to the idea that the calling voice would forever plead and call to her, while the one who was sleeping here beside her would sleep on silently forever.

The night weighed, denser and heavier. It was no longer one in the chain of days, but a desert of dark time in which the last living man on earth was crying for help without hope and without the relief of one merciful drop of water. In the whole of God's great world, with all its rivers, rains, and dews there was no longer even one teardrop of water left nor a living hand to carry it. The waters had dried up and men had rotted away. There remained in the universe just the one weak rush-light of her own senses as the only witness of it all.

At last the daybreak came. Disbelieving, she watched the wall turn slowly white, just as it had on mornings before this, and she saw the day, first gray and then russet, take possession of the room. Objects separated and took their own forms again.

She strained her ears and she could still hear the outlaw's voice, but it seemed to come from a further distance. There was no longer a cursing but a hoarse, occasional groan. It was as if she guessed rather than actually hearing it.

The young wife had no strength to move. Stiff, bent, with her head in her hands, she did not even notice when the commander awoke.

The man opened his rested eyes and his glance fell on the bent shoulders and white neck of his wife. Then, after the first sleepy uncertainty, something like a warm wave spread through his body, a joyful sense of reality. He wanted to call to his wife, to shout her name. But he changed his mind. Smiling, he silently raised himself a little, leaning on his left arm. Then, still without a word, he suddenly clasped her shoulders and pulled her to him.

She struggled against him briefly and vainly. The quick embrace seemed terrible to her and, at the same time, she could not resist. It seemed impossible and blasphemous to betray, so silently and easily, the night world in which she had moments ago been living and suffering. She wanted to tell him that it couldn't be, that she could not be dragged thus into everyday life, that there were heavy and dreadful things that she must make him understand. The bitter words welled, but she could not pronounce a single one. She twisted her body, but he did not realize this as a sign of resistance. She tried to push him from her, but her movement had not half the strength of her bitterness nor the speed of her thoughts. The warmth of that live, rested, wakeful body weighed on her like a burden. The bones and muscles of her own body began to yield, like an obedient machine. Her mouth was sealed by his. She felt him like a huge stone to which she was tied; they were falling headlong together.

She sank, drowning in the familiar passion, while all of the thought of last night's human darkness rose like bubbles to the surface and vanished.

The ornamented room suddenly filled with the ardent light of day.

Isaac Babel
1894–1941

Babel, born in Odessa, is believed to have died in a Siberian concentration camp. His end is obscure: it may have been the result of typhus or he may have been shot. In 1975 he was "rehabilitated," restoring his good name to the communist ranks.

As a young man he served in the czarist army, joining the Bolsheviks in 1917. He worked with the Cheka and then became a supply officer with Budenny's notorious Cossack band. This was a formative experience — that of a nonviolent, imaginative Jew in conflict with, adjusting to, perhaps even absorbing some of, a mindless, anti-Semitic military ethos. It generated his finest volume of stories, Red Cavalry *(1929), from which "My First Goose" is taken. In connection with that experience a sentence of Babel's is always quoted. A story called "After the Battle" ends with the narrator "imploring fate to grant me the simplest of proficiencies — the ability to kill my fellow man." The words, in which are hidden some irony but more sincerity, light up the internal struggle that nurtured Babel's original genius.*

"My First Goose," spare, laconic, seemingly impersonal, might be casually described as an initiation story, turning on the desire of the outsider to pass the test that will permit him to become an insider. That it is, but also much more. It suggests the violence that attracts and repels, the joy and also the brutality of male comradeship. Its narrator seems merely to be recounting a wartime episode, whereas in fact he crams irony into almost every line. Babel makes fifteen hundred words do a lot of work. He learned much from his masters, Flaubert and Maupassant. To us he seems something like a Russian Hemingway.

My First Goose

SAVITSKY, Commander of the VI Division, rose when he saw me, and I wondered at the beauty of his giant's body. He rose, the purple of his riding breeches and the crimson of his little tilted cap and the decorations stuck on his chest cleaving the hut as a standard cleaves the sky. A smell of scent and the sickly sweet freshness of soap emanated from him. His long legs were like girls sheathed to the neck in shining riding boots.

He smiled at me, struck his riding whip on the table, and drew toward him an order that the Chief of Staff had just finished dictating. It was an order for Ivan Chesnokov to advance on Chugunov-Dobryvodka with the regiment entrusted to him, to make contact with the enemy and destroy the same.

"For which destruction," the Commander began to write, smearing the whole sheet, "I make this same Chesnokov entirely responsible, up to and including the supreme penalty, and will if necessary strike him down on the spot; which you, Chesnokov, who have been working with me at the front for some months now, cannot doubt."

The Commander signed the order with a flourish, tossed it to his orderlies and turned upon me gray eyes that danced with merriment.

I handed him a paper with my appointment to the Staff of the Division.

"Put it down in the Order of the Day," said the Commander. "Put him down for every satisfaction save the front one. Can you read and write?"

"Yes, I can read and write," I replied, envying the flower and iron of that youthfulness. "I graduated in law from St. Petersburg University."

"Oh, are you one of those grinds?" he laughed. "Specs on your nose, too! What a nasty little object! They've sent you along without making any enquiries; and this is a hot place for specs. Think you'll get on with us?"

"I'll get on all right," I answered, and went off to the village with the quartermaster to find a billet for the night.

The quartermaster carried my trunk on his shoulder. Before us stretched the village street. The dying sun, round and yellow as a pumpkin, was giving up its roseate ghost to the skies.

We went up to a hut painted over with garlands. The quartermaster stopped, and said suddenly, with a guilty smile:

"Nuisance with specs. Can't do anything to stop it, either. Not a life for the brainy type here. But you go and mess up a lady, and a good lady too, and you'll have the boys patting you on the back."

He hesitated, my little trunk on his shoulder; then he came quite close to me, only to dart away again despairingly and run to the nearest yard. Cossacks were sitting there, shaving one another.

"Here, you soldiers," said the quartermaster, setting my little trunk down on the ground. "Comrade Savitsky's orders are that you're to take this chap in your billets, so no nonsense about it, because the chap's been through a lot in the learning line."

The quartermaster, purple in the face, left us without looking back. I raised my hand to my cap and saluted the Cossacks. A lad with long straight flaxen hair and the handsome face of the Ryazan Cossacks went over to my little trunk and tossed it out at the gate. Then he turned his back on me and with remarkable skill emitted a series of shameful noises.

"To your guns — number double-zero!" an older Cossack shouted at him, and burst out laughing. "Running fire!"

His guileless art exhausted, the lad made off. Then, crawling over the ground, I began to gather together the manuscripts and tattered garments that had fallen out of the trunk. I gathered them up and carried them to the other end of the yard. Near the hut, on a brick stove, stood a cauldron in which pork was cooking. The steam that rose from it was like the far-off smoke of home in the village, and it mingled hunger with desperate loneliness in my head. Then I covered my little broken trunk with hay, turning it into a pillow, and lay down on the ground to read in *Pravda* Lenin's speech at the Second Congress of the Comintern. The sun fell upon me from behind the toothed hillocks, the Cossacks trod on my feet, the lad made fun of me untiringly, the beloved lines came toward me along a thorny path and could not reach me. Then I put aside the paper and went out to the landlady, who was spinning on the porch.

"Landlady," I said, "I've got to eat."

The old woman raised to me the diffused whites of her purblind eyes and lowered them again.

"Comrade," she said, after a pause, "what with all this going on, I want to go and hang myself."

"Christ!" I muttered, and pushed the old woman in the chest with my fist. "You don't suppose I'm going to go into explanations with you, do you?"

And turning around I saw somebody's sword lying within reach. A severe-looking goose was waddling about the yard, inoffensively preening its feathers. I overtook it and pressed it to the ground. Its head cracked beneath my boot, cracked and emptied itself. The white neck lay stretched out in the dung, the wings twitched.

"Christ!" I said, digging into the goose with my sword. "Go and cook it for me, landlady."

Her blind eyes and glasses glistening, the old woman picked up the slaughtered bird, wrapped it in her apron, and started to bear it off toward the kitchen.

"Comrade," she said to me, after a while, "I want to go and hang myself." And she closed the door behind her.

The Cossacks in the yard were already sitting around their cauldron. They sat motionless, stiff as heathen priests at a sacrifice, and had not looked at the goose.

"The lad's all right," one of them said, winking and scooping up the cabbage soup with his spoon.

The Cossacks commenced their supper with all the elegance and restraint of peasants who respect one another. And I wiped the sword with sand, went out at the gate, and came in again, depressed. Already the moon hung above the yard like a cheap earring.

"Hey, you," suddenly said Surovkov, an older Cossack. "Sit down and feed with us till your goose is done."

He produced a spare spoon from his boot and handed it to me. We supped up the cabbage soup they had made, and ate the pork.

"What's in the newspaper?" asked the flaxen-haired lad, making room for me.

"Lenin writes in the paper," I said, pulling out *Pravda*. "Lenin writes that there's a shortage of everything."

And loudly, like a triumphant man hard of hearing, I read Lenin's speech out to the Cossacks.

Evening wrapped about me the quickening moisture of its twilight sheets; evening laid a mother's hand upon my burning forehead. I read on and rejoiced, spying out exultingly the secret curve of Lenin's straight line.

"Truth tickles everyone's nostrils," said Surovkov, when I had come to the end. "The question is, how's it to be pulled from the heap. But he goes and strikes at it straight off like a hen pecking at a grain!"

This remark about Lenin was made by Surovkov, platoon commander of the Staff Squadron; after which we lay down to sleep in the hayloft. We slept, all six of us, beneath a wooden roof that let in the stars, warming one another, our legs intermingled. I dreamed: and in my dreams saw women. But my heart, stained with bloodshed, grated and brimmed over.

James Thurber
1894–1961

Thurber's best and funniest prose work (his drawings, of course, are even funnier) is My Life and Hard Times, *a now classic memoir of his family's odd doings in Columbus, Ohio, early in the century. I suspect that his beautifully skewed genius must have touched up what he offers, deadpan, as exact recollection. Technically, however, it is nonfiction; otherwise I would have extracted one of its chapters to represent our finest humorist since Mark Twain.*

Thurber's sheaf of regular short stories includes some parodies worthy of Max Beerbohm; witty-wicked small brilliancies in the Saki tradition; neatly plotted variations on one of his favorite themes, the war between men and women; narrative character studies of eccentrics for whom he felt a natural affinity; and a couple of satires on the literary temperament. Though few in number, at least one has become a permanent part of our mental landscape, "The Secret Life of Walter Mitty."

Like "Mitty," "The Greatest Man in the World" *satisfies certain unconscious longings that lie doggo in many of us. Some of our current celebrities, especially politicos but also athletes and entertainers (Nobel Prize winners never get to be heroes), seem to be begging for the Smurch treatment. In this story Thurber provides a pattern for one of our dearest daydreams.*

The Greatest Man in the World

LOOKING BACK on it now, from the vantage point of 1950, one can only marvel that it hadn't happened long before it did. The United States of America had been, ever since Kitty Hawk, blindly constructing the elaborate petard by which, sooner or later, it must be hoist. It was inevitable that some day there would come roaring out of the skies a national hero of insufficient intelligence, background, and character successfully to endure the mounting orgies of glory prepared for aviators who stayed up a long time or flew a great distance. Both Lindbergh and Byrd, fortunately for national decorum and international amity, had been gentlemen; so had our other famous aviators. They wore their laurels gracefully, withstood the awful weather of publicity, married excellent women, usually of fine family, and quietly retired to private life and the enjoyment of their varying fortunes. No untoward incidents, on a worldwide scale, marred the perfection of their conduct on the perilous heights of fame. The exception to the rule was, however, bound to occur and it did, in July, 1937, when Jack ("Pal") Smurch, erstwhile mechanic's helper in a small garage in Westfield, Iowa, flew a second-hand, single-motored Bresthaven Dragon-Fly III monoplane all the way around the world, without stopping.

Never before in the history of aviation had such a flight as Smurch's ever been dreamed of. No one had even taken seriously the weird floating auxiliary gas tanks, invention of the mad New Hampshire professor of astronomy, Dr. Charles Lewis Gresham, upon which Smurch placed full reliance. When the garage worker, a slightly built, surly, unprepossessing young man of twenty-two, appeared at Roosevelt Field in early July, 1937, slowly chewing a great quid of scrap tobacco, and announced, "Nobody ain't seen no flyin' yet," the newspapers touched briefly and satirically upon his projected twenty-five-thousand-mile flight. Aeronautical and automotive experts dismissed the idea curtly, implying that it was a hoax, a publicity stunt. The rusty, battered, second-hand plane wouldn't go. The Gresham auxiliary tanks wouldn't work. It was simply a cheap joke.

Smurch, however, after calling on a girl in Brooklyn who worked in the flap-folding department of a large paper-box factory, a girl whom he later described as his "sweet patootie," climbed nonchalantly into his ridiculous plane at dawn of the memorable seventh of July, 1937, spit a curve of tobacco juice into the still air, and took off, carrying with him only a gallon of bootleg gin and six pounds of salami.

When the garage boy thundered out over the ocean the papers were forced to record, in all seriousness, that a mad, unknown young man — his name was variously misspelled — had actually set out upon a preposterous attempt to span the world in a rickety, one-engined contraption, trusting to the long-distance refuelling device of a crazy schoolmaster. When, nine days later, without having stopped once, the tiny plane appeared above San Francisco Bay, headed for New York, spluttering and choking, to be sure, but still magnificently and miraculously aloft, the headlines, which long since had crowded everything else off the front page — even the shooting of the Governor of Illinois by the Vileti gang — swelled to unprecedented size, and the news stories began to run to twenty-five and thirty colums. It was noticeable, however, that the accounts of the epoch-making flight touched rather lightly upon the aviator himself. This was not because facts about the hero as a man were too meagre, but because they were too complete.

Reporters, who had been rushed out to Iowa when Smurch's plane was first sighted over the little French coast town of Serly-le-Mer, to dig up the story of the great man's life, had promptly discovered that the story of his life could not be printed. His mother, a sullen short-order cook in a shack restaurant on the edge of a tourists' camping ground near Westfield, met all inquiries as to her son with an angry, "Ah, the hell with him; I hope he drowns." His father appeared to be in jail somewhere for stealing spotlights and laprobes from tourists' automobiles; his young brother, a weak-minded lad, had but recently escaped from the Preston, Iowa, Reformatory and was already wanted in several Western towns for the theft of money-order blanks from post offices. These alarming discoveries were still piling up at the very time that Pal Smurch, the greatest hero of the twentieth century, blear-eyed, dead for sleep, half-starved, was piloting his crazy junk-heap high above the region in which the lamentable story of his private life was being unearthed, headed for New York and a greater glory than any man of his time had ever known.

The necessity for printing some account in the papers of the young man's career and personality had led to a remarkable predicament. It was of course impossible to reveal the facts, for a tremendous popular feeling in favor of the young hero had sprung up, like a grass fire, when he was halfway across Europe on his flight around the globe. He was, therefore, described as a modest chap, taciturn, blond, popular with his friends, popular with girls. The only available snapshot of Smurch, taken at the wheel of a phony automobile in a cheap photo studio at an amusement park, was touched up so that the little vulgarian looked quite handsome. His twisted leer was smoothed into a pleasant smile.

The truth was, in this way, kept from the youth's ecstatic compatriots; they did not dream that the Smurch family was despised and feared by its neighbors in the obscure Iowa town, nor that the hero himself, because of numerous unsavory exploits, had come to be regarded in Westfield as a nuisance and a menace. He had, the reporters discovered, once knifed the principal of his high school — not mortally, to be sure, but he had knifed him; and on another occasion, surprised in the act of stealing an altar-cloth from a church, he had bashed the sacristan over the head with a pot of Easter lilies; for each of these offences he had served a sentence in the reformatory.

Inwardly, the authorities, both in New York and in Washington, prayed that an understanding Providence might, however awful such a thing seemed, bring disaster to the rusty, battered plane and its illustrious pilot, whose unheard-of flight had aroused the civilized world to hosannas of hysterical praise. The authorities were convinced that the character of the renowned aviator was such that the limelight of adulation was bound to reveal him to all the world as a congenital hooligan mentally and morally unequipped to cope with his own prodigious fame. "I trust," said the Secretary of State, at one of many secret Cabinet meetings called to consider the national dilemma, "I trust that his mother's prayer will be answered," by which he referred to Mrs. Emma Smurch's wish that her son might be drowned. It was, however, too late for that — Smurch had leaped the Atlantic and then the Pacific as if they were millponds. At three minutes after two o'clock on the afternoon of July 17, 1937, the garage boy brought his idiotic plane into Roosevelt Field for a perfect three-point landing.

It had, of course, been out of the question to arrange a modest little reception for the greatest flier in the history of the world. He was received at Roosevelt Field with such elaborate and pretentious ceremonies as rocked the world. Fortunately, however, the worn and spent hero promptly swooned, had to be removed bodily from his plane, and was spirited from the field without having opened his mouth once. Thus he did not jeopardize the dignity of this first reception, a reception illumined by the presence of the Secretaries of War and the Navy, Mayor Michael J. Moriarity of New York, the Premier of Canada, Governors Fanniman, Groves, McFeely, and Critchfield, and a brilliant array of European diplomats. Smurch did not, in fact, come to in time to take part in the gigantic hullabaloo arranged at City Hall for the next day. He was rushed to a secluded nursing home and confined to bed. It was nine days before he was able to get up, or to be more exact, before he was permitted to get up. Meanwhile the greatest minds in the country, in solemn assembly, had arranged a secret conference of city, state, and government officials, which Smurch was to attend for the purpose of being instructed in the ethics and behavior of heroism.

On the day that the little mechanic was finally allowed to get up and dress and, for the first time in two weeks, took a great chew of tobacco, he was permitted to receive the newspapermen — this by way of testing him out. Smurch did not wait for questions. "Youse guys," he said — and the *Times* man winced — "youse guys can tell the cock-eyed world dat I put it over on Lindbergh, see? Yeh — an' made an ass o' them two frogs." The "two frogs" was a reference to a pair of gallant French fliers who, in attempting a flight only halfway round the world, had, two weeks before, unhappily been lost at sea. The *Times* man was bold enough, at this point, to sketch out for Smurch the accepted formula for interviews in cases of this kind; he explained that there should be no arrogant statements belittling the achievements of other heroes, particularly heroes of foreign nations. "Ah, the hell with that," said Smurch. "I did it, see? I did it, an' I'm talkin' about it." And he did talk about it.

None of this extraordinary interview was, of course, printed. On the contrary, the newspapers, already under the disciplined direction of a secret directorate created for the occasion and composed of statesmen and editors, gave out to a panting and restless world that "Jacky," as he had been arbitrarily nicknamed, would consent to say only that he was very happy and that anyone could have done what he did. "My achievement has been, I fear, slightly exaggerated," the *Times* man's article had him protest, with a modest smile. These newspaper stories were kept from the hero, a restriction which did not serve to abate the rising malevolence of his temper. The situation was, indeed, extremely grave, for Pal Smurch was, as he kept insisting, "rarin' to go." He could not much longer be kept from a nation clamorous to lionize him. It was the most desperate crisis the United States of America had faced since the sinking of the *Lusitania*.

On the afternoon of the twenty-seventh of July, Smurch was spirited away to a conference-room in which were gathered mayors, governors, government officials, behaviorist psychologists, and editors. He gave them each a limp, moist paw and a brief unlovely grin. "Hah ya?" he said. When Smurch was seated, the Mayor of New York arose and, with obvious pessimism, attempted to explain what he must say and how he must act when presented to the world, ending his talk with a high tribute to the hero's courage and integrity. The Mayor was followed by Governor Fanniman of New York, who, after a touching declaration of faith, introduced Cameron Spottiswood, Second Secretary of the American Embassy in Paris, the gentleman selected to coach Smurch in the amenities of public ceremonies. Sitting in a chair, with a soiled yellow tie in his hand and his shirt open at the throat, unshaved, smoking a rolled cigarette, Jack Smurch listened with a leer on his lips. "I get ya, I get ya," he cut in, nastily. "Ya want me to ack like a softy, huh? Ya want me to ack like that — — baby-faced Lindbergh, huh? Well, nuts to that, see?" Everyone took in his breath sharply; it was a sigh and a hiss. "Mr.

Lindbergh," began a United States Senator, purple with rage, "and Mr. Byrd —" Smurch, who was paring his nails with a jackknife, cut in again. "Byrd!" he exclaimed. "Aw fa God's sake, dat big —" Somebody shut off his blasphemies with a sharp word. A newcomer had entered the room. Everyone stood up except Smurch, who, still busy with his nails, did not even glance up. "Mr. Smurch," said someone sternly, "the President of the United States!" It had been thought that the presence of the Chief Executive might have a chastening effect upon the young hero, and the former had been, thanks to the remarkable cooperation of the press, secretly brought to the obscure conference-room.

A great, painful silence fell. Smurch looked up, waved a hand at the President. "How ya comin'?" he asked, and began rolling a fresh cigarette. The silence deepened. Someone coughed in a strained way. "Geez, it's hot, ain't it?" said Smurch. He loosened two more shirt buttons, revealing a hairy chest and the tattooed word "Sadie" enclosed in a stencilled heart. The great and important men in the room, faced by the most serious crisis in recent American history, exchanged worried frowns. Nobody seemed to know how to proceed. "Come awn, come awn," said Smurch. "Let's get the hell out of here! When do I start cuttin' in on de parties, huh? And what's they goin' to be *in* it?" He rubbed a thumb and forefinger together meaningly. "Money!" exclaimed a state senator, shocked, pale. "Yeh, money," said Pal, flipping his cigarette out of a window. "An' big money." He began rolling a fresh cigarette. "Big money," he repeated, frowning over the rice paper. He tilted back in his chair, and leered at each gentleman, separately, the leer of an animal that knows its power, the leer of a leopard loose in a bird-and-dog shop. "Aw fa God's sake, let's get some place where it's cooler," he said. "I been cooped up plenty for three weeks!"

Smurch stood up and walked over to an open window, where he stood staring down into the street, nine floors below. The faint shouting of newsboys floated up to him. He made out his name. "Hot dog!" he cried, grinning, ecstatic. He leaned out over the sill. "You tell 'em, babies!" he shouted down. "Hot diggity dog!" In the tense little knot of men standing behind him, a quick, mad impulse flared up. An unspoken word of appeal, of command, seemed to ring through the room. Yet it was deadly silent. Charles K. L. Brand, secretary to the Mayor of New York City, happened to be standing nearest Smurch; he looked inquiringly at the President of the United States. The President, pale, grim, nodded shortly. Brand, a tall, powerfully built man, once a tackle at Rutgers, stepped forward, seized the greatest man in the world by his left shoulder and the seat of his pants, and pushed him out the window.

"My God, he's fallen out the window!" cried a quick-witted editor.

"Get me out of here!" cried the President. Several men sprang to his side and he was hurriedly escorted out of a door toward a side-entrance of the building. The editor of the Associated Press took charge, being used to such things. Crisply he ordered certain men to leave, others to stay; quickly he outlined a story which all the papers were to agree on, sent two men to the street to handle that end of the tragedy, commanded a Senator to sob and two Congressmen to go to pieces nervously. In a word, he skillfully set the stage for the gigantic task that was to follow, the task of breaking to a grief-stricken world the sad story of the untimely, accidental death of its most illustrious and spectacular figure.

The funeral was, as you know, the most elaborate, the finest, the solemnest, and the saddest ever held in the United States of America. The monument in Arlington Cemetery, with its clean white shaft of marble and the simple device of a tiny plane carved on its base, is a place for pilgrims, in deep reverence, to visit. The nations of the world paid lofty tributes to little Jacky Smurch, America's greatest hero. At a given hour there were two minutes of silence throughout the nation. Even the inhabitants of the small, bewildered town of Westfield, Iowa, observed this touching ceremony; agents of the Department of Justice saw to that. One of them was especially assigned to stand grimly in the doorway of a little shack restaurant on the edge of the tourists' camping ground just outside the town. There, under his stern scrutiny, Mrs. Emma Smurch bowed her head above two hamburger steaks sizzling on her grill — bowed her head and turned away, so that the Secret Service man could not see the twisted, strangely familiar, leer on her lips.

ANÍBAL MONTEIRO MACHADO
1895–1964

A Brazilian, Machado was trained to the law and appointed public prose-
cutor in a town in Minas Gerais. This position he held for only about a
year. He once remarked, "I always felt like taking the accused for a cup of
coffee."

He later taught literature in a high school in Rio de Janeiro. He held
various public offices, wrote stories, essays, and two plays, one based on
the following story. A novel was published posthumously.

Humor, not strikingly characteristic of the Latin American renaissance,
animates this tale in which a faithful piano is the protagonist. But the story
also illustrates on a small scale that curious blend of traditional naturalism
and sheer oddity known as "magic realism" and familiar to us in writers
like García Márquez and Isabel Allende. The ending, one reluctantly admits,
reminds us rather of O. Henry.

The Piano

"ROSÁLIA!" shouted João de Oliveira to his wife, who was upstairs. "I told the guy to get out. What a nerve! He laughed at it. He said it wasn't worth even five hundred cruzeiros."

"It's an old trick," she replied. "He wants to get it for nothing and then sell it to somebody else. That's how these fellows get rich."

But Rosália and Sara looked somewhat alarmed as they came downstairs. The family approached the old piano respectfully, as if to console it after the insult.

"We'll get a good price for it, you'll see," asserted Oliveira, gazing at the piano with a mixture of affection and apprehension. "They don't make them like this any more."

"Put an ad in the paper," said Rosália, "and they'll come flocking. The house will be like *this* with people." She joined the tips of the fingers of her right hand in customary token of an immense crowd. "It's a pity to have to give it up."

"Ah, it's a love of a piano!" said João. "Just looking at it you think you hear music." He caressed its oaken case.

"Well, come on, João. Let's put the ad in."

It had to be sold so that the little parlor could be made into a bedroom for Sara and her intended, a lieutenant in the artillery. Besides, the price would pay for her trousseau.

Three mornings later, the piano was adorned with flowers for the sacrifice, and the house was ready to receive prospective buyers.

The first to arrive were a lady and her daughter. The girl opened the piano and played a few chords.

"It's no good at all, Mama."

The lady stood up, looked at it, and noticed that the ivory was missing from some of the keys. She took her daughter by the hand and walked out, muttering as she went: "Think of coming all this distance to look at a piece of junk."

The Oliveira family had no time to feel resentment, for three new candidates appeared, all at the same time: an elderly lady who smelled like a rich widow, a young girl wearing glasses and carrying a music portfolio, and a redheaded man in a worn, wrinkled suit.

"I was here ahead of you," said the young girl to the old lady. "It doesn't really matter. I only came because my mother wanted me to.

There must be plenty of others for sale. But I'd just like to say that I was ringing the doorbell while you were still getting off the bus. We came in together but I got here first."

This rivalry for priority pleased the Oliveiras. They thought it wise, however, to break up the argument, so they smiled at everyone and offered them all coffee. The young girl went over to the piano, while the redheaded man stood at a distance and evaluated it with a cool eye. At this moment a lady entered holding a schoolgirl by the hand. They sat down distrustfully.

Suddenly the young girl began to play, and the whole room hung on the notes that she extracted from the keyboard. Off-pitch, metallic, horrible notes. The Oliveiras anxiously studied the faces of their visitors. The redheaded man remained utterly impassive. The others glanced at one another as if seeking a common understanding. The newly arrived lady made a wry face. The perfumed old lady seemed more tolerant and looked indulgently at the old piano case.

It was a jury trial and the piano was the accused. The young girl continued to play, as if she were wringing a confession from it. The timbre suggested that of a decrepit, cracked-voiced soprano with stomach trouble. Some of the notes did not play at all. Doli joined in with her barking, a bitch's well-considered verdict. A smile passed around the room. No one was laughing, however. The girl seemed to be playing now out of pure malice, hammering at the dead keys and emphasizing the cacophony. It was a dreadful situation.

"There's something you ought to know about this piano," explained João de Oliveira. "It's very sensitive to the weather, it changes a great deal with variations in temperature."

The young girl stopped abruptly. She rose, put on some lipstick, and picked up her music portfolio.

"I don't know how you had'the nerve to advertise this horror," she said, speaking to João but looking disdainfully at Rosália as if she had been the horror.

And she left.

João said nothing for a moment. After all, the insult had been directed at the old piano, not at him. Nevertheless, he felt constrained to declare that it was a genuine antique.

"They don't make them like this any more," he said emphatically. "They just don't make them."

There was a long silence. The status of the piano had reached its nadir. Finally the redheaded man spoke: "What are you asking for it?"

In view of what had happened, João de Oliveira lowered substantially the price he had had in mind.

"Five contos," he said timidly.

He looked at everyone to see the effect. There was a silent response. Oliveira felt cold. Was the price monstrously high? Only the old lady showed any delicacy at all: she said she would think it over. But, through her veil of mercy, João perceived her decision.

As they all were leaving, a man about to enter stepped out of their way.

"Did you come about the piano?" asked one of them. "Well, you'll . . ."

But Oliveira interrupted.

"Come in," he said cheerfully. "It's right here. Lots of people have been looking at it."

The man was middle-aged, with a shock of grayish hair. He lifted the lid of the piano and examined the instrument at length. "Probably a music teacher," thought João.

The man did not ask the price. "Thank you," he said and left.

The house was empty again. Sara returned to her room. Rosália and João looked at each other in disappointment.

"Nobody understands its value," commented João sadly. "If I can't get a decent price for it, I'd rather not sell it at all."

"But what about Sara's trousseau?" said Rosália.

"I'll borrow the money."

"You'd never be able to pay it back out of your salary."

"We'll postpone the marriage."

"They love each other, João. They'll want to get married no matter what, trousseau or no trousseau."

At this moment, Sara could be heard shouting from her room that she could not possibly get married without two new slips and so forth.

"The thing is," Rosália went on, "this house is about the size of a matchbox. Where can we put the newlyweds? We'll have to give up the piano to make room for them. Nobody nowadays has enough room."

Sara's voice was heard again: "No, don't sell the piano. It's so pretty . . ."

"It's also so silent," interrupted her mother. "You never play it any more. All you ever play is the victrola."

She went to her daughter's room to speak further with her. Strange that Sara should talk like that. Rosália put the dilemma flatly: "A husband or a piano. Choose."

"Oh, a husband!" replied Sara with voluptuous conviction. "Of course."

She hugged her pillow.

"So . . . ?"

"You're always against it, Rosália," shouted João de Oliveira.

"Against what?"

"Our piano."

"Oh, João, how can you say such a thing!"

The next day, as soon as he got back from work, João de Oliveira asked about the piano.

"Did any people answer the ad, Rosália?"

Yes, there had been several telephone calls for information about the piano, and an old man had come and looked at it. Also, the redheaded man had come again.

"Did any of them say anything about buying it?" asked João.

"No. But the two men who came to the house looked at it a long time."

"They did? Did they look at it with interest? With admiration?"

"It's hard to say."

"Yes, they admired it," said Sara. "Especially the old man. He almost ate it with his eyes."

João de Oliveira was touched. It was no longer a matter of price. He just wanted his piano to be treated with consideration and respect, that's all. Maybe it wasn't worth a lot of money but it certainly deserved some courteous attention. He was sorry he hadn't been there, but what his daughter told him of the old man's respectful attitude consoled him for the contumely of the day before. That man must understand the soul of antique furniture.

"Did he leave his address, Sara? No? Oh, well . . . he'll probably be back."

He rose from his chair and walked around the old instrument. He smiled at it lovingly.

"My piano," he said softly. He ran his hand over the varnished wood as if he were caressing an animal.

No candidate the next day. Only a voice with a foreign accent asking if it was new. Rosália replied that it wasn't but that they had taken such good care of it that it almost looked like new.

"Tomorrow is Saturday," thought Oliveira. "There's bound to be a lot of people."

There were two, a man and a little girl, and they came in a limousine. The man looked at the modest house of the Oliveira family and considered it useless to go in. Nevertheless, he went to the door and asked the make and age of the piano.

"Thank you. There's no need for me to see it," he replied to João's insistence that he look at it. "I thought it would be a fairly new piano. Good luck . . ."

And he went away.

João was grief-stricken. Ever since he had inherited the piano he had prized it dearly. He had never thought he would have to part with it. Worst of all, no one appreciated it, no one understood its value.

No one, except possibly the fellow who came the next Wednesday. He praised the piano in the most enthusiastic terms, said it was marvelous, and refused to buy. He said that if he paid so low a price for it he would feel he was stealing it, and that João and Rosália were virtually committing a crime in letting this precious thing get out of their hands. Oliveira did not exactly understand.

"Does he mean what he says?" he asked Rosália.

"I think he's just trying to be funny," she replied.

"I don't know. Maybe not."

Rosália was the first to lose hope. Her main concern now, when her husband came home from work, was to alleviate his suffering.

"How many today?"

"Nobody. Two telephone calls. They didn't give their names but they said they'd probably come and look at it."

Her voice was calm, soothing.

"How about the redheaded fellow?"

"I'm sure he'll be back."

For several days no one came or telephoned. João de Oliveira's feelings may be compared to those of a man who sees his friend miss a train: he is sad for his friend's sake and he is happy because he will continue for a time to have the pleasure of his company. João sat down near the piano and enjoyed these last moments with it. He admired its dignity. He confided his thoughts to it. Three generations had played it. How many people it had induced to dream or to dance! All this had passed away, but the piano remained. It was the only piece of furniture that bespoke the presence of his forebears. It was sort of eternal. It and the old oratory upstairs.

"Sara, come and play that little piece by Chopin. See if you remember it."

"I couldn't Papa. The piano sounds terrible."

"Don't say that," Rosália whispered. "Can't you see how your father feels?"

Whenever Sara's eyes lit on the piano, they transformed it into a nuptial bed in which she and the lieutenant were kissing and hugging.

For days and days no prospective buyer appeared. Nothing but an occasional telephone call from the redheaded man, as if he had been a doctor verifying the progress of a terminal case. The advertisement was withdrawn.

"Well, João, what are we going to do about it?"

"What are we going to do about what, Rosália?"

"The piano!"

"I'm not going to sell it," João shouted. "These leeches don't give a damn about the piano; they just want a bargain. I'd rather give it away to someone who'll take good care of it, who knows what it represents."

He was walking back and forth agitatedly. Suddenly the expression of his face changed.

"Listen, Rosália. Let's phone our relatives in Tijuca."

Rosália understood his purpose and was pleased.

"Hello! Is Messias there? He went out? Oh, is this Cousin Miquita? Look . . . I want to give you our piano as a present . . . Yes, as a present . . . No, it's not a joke . . . Really . . . Right . . . Exactly . . . So it won't go out of the family . . . Fine. Have it picked up here sometime soon . . . You're welcome. I'm glad to do it . . ."

After he had hung up he turned to his wife.

"You know what? She didn't believe me at first. She thought it was All Fools' Day."

Rosália was delighted. João walked over to the old piano as if to confer with it about what he had just done.

"My conscience is clear," he thought. "You will not be rejected. You will stay in the family, with people of the same blood. My children's children will know and respect you; you will play for them. I'm sure you understand and won't be angry with us."

"When will they come for it?" interrupted Rosália, eager to get the room ready for the bridal couple.

The next day Messias telephones his relatives in Ipanema. Did they really mean to give him a piano? It was too much. He was grateful but they really shouldn't. When his wife told him, he could hardly believe it.

"No, it's true, Messias. You know, our house is about as big as a nutshell. We can't keep the piano here, and João doesn't want it to fall into the hands of strangers. If you people have it, it's almost the same as if it were still with us. Are you going to send for it soon?"

Several days went by. No moving van came. Mrs. and Mrs. Oliveira thought the silence of their relatives in Tijuca extremely odd.

"Something's wrong. Telephone them, Rosália."

Cousin Miquita answered. She was embarrassed. The moving men asked a fortune for the job.

"I guess it's the gasoline shortage . . . Wait a few more days. Messias will arrange something. We're delighted about getting the piano. We think of nothing else, Rosália."

This last sentence struck a false note, thought Rosália. After a week, João de Oliveira telephoned again.

"Do you want it or don't you, Messias?"

"João, you can't imagine how terrible we feel about this," came the stammered reply. "You give us a fine present and we can't accept it. They're asking an arm and a leg to move it here. And, anyway, we really have no room for it. We haven't even got enough room for the stuff we have now. We should have thought of this before. Miquita feels awful about it."

"In short, you don't want the piano."

"We want it . . . But we don't . . . we can't . . ."

João de Oliveira hung up. He was beginning to understand.

"You see, Rosália. We can't even give the piano away. We can't even give it away."

"What can you do, João! Everything ends up with nobody wanting it."

After a few minutes of silent despondence, they were aroused by Sara, who interspersed her sobs with words of bitter desperation. Her mother comforted her.

"Don't worry, child. It'll be all right. We'll sell it for whatever we can get."

"I want it out right away, Mama. In a few days I'm to be married and my room isn't even ready yet. None of our things are in here. Only that terrible piano ruining my life, that piano that nobody wants."

"Speak softly, dear. Your father can hear you."

"I want him to hear me," she cried, with another sob. She wiped her eyes.

João de Oliveira slept little that night. He was meditating about life. His thoughts were confused and generally melancholy. They induced in him a fierce rage against both life and the piano. He left the house early and went to a nearby bar, where he talked with several men.

"What is my husband doing in a place like that?" Rosália asked herself. João was never a drinker.

Oliveira came back accompanied by a shabbily dressed Negro and two husky Portuguese in work clothes. He showed them the piano. They hefted it and said they doubted if they could handle it, just the three of them.

Rosália and Sara looked on in amazement.

"Have you found a buyer?" asked Rosália.

"No, wife. Nobody will buy this piano."

"You're giving it away?"

"No, wife. Nobody wants it even for free."

"Then what are you doing, João? What in the world are you doing?"

João's eyes watered but his face hardened.

"I'm going to throw it the ocean."

"Oh, no, Papa!" exclaimed Sara. "That's crazy!"

The Oliveiras could not see the ocean from their windows, but they could smell it and hear it, for they were only three blocks from the avenue that ran along the beach.

The men were waiting, talking among themselves.

"What a courageous thing to do, João!" said his wife. "But shouldn't we talk it over first? Is there no other way out? People will think it funny, throwing a piano into the water."

"What else can we do, Rosália? Lots of ships go to the bottom of the ocean. Some of them have pianos on board."

This irrefutable logic silenced his wife. João seemed to take heart.

"Okay, you fellows," he cried. "Up with it! Let's go!"

One of the Portuguese came forward and said humbly, on behalf of his colleagues and himself, that they couldn't do it. They hoped he would excuse them, but it would hurt their conscience to throw something like that in the sea. It almost seemed like a crime.

"Boss, why don't you put an ad in the paper? The piano is in such good condition."

"Yes, I know," replied Oliveira ironically. "You may go."

The men left. For a moment the Negro entertained the idea that he might take the piano for himself. He stared at it. He was fascinated by the idea of owning something, and a fine, luxurious thing at that. It was a dream that could become an immediate reality. But where would he take it? He had no house.

Rosália rested her head on her husband's shoulder and fought back the tears.

"Ah, João, what a decision you have made!"

"But if nobody wants it, and if it can't stay here . . ."

"I know, João. But I can't help feeling sad. It's always been with us. Doesn't it seem cruel, after all these years, to throw it in the ocean? Look at it, standing there, knowing nothing about what's going to happen to it. It's been there almost twenty years, in that corner, never doing any harm . . ."

"We must try to avoid sentimentality, Rosália."

She looked at him with admiration.

"All right, João. Do what you must."

Groups of Negro boys, ragged but happy, start out from the huts at Pinto and Latolandia where they live and stroll through the wealthy neighborhoods. One can always find them begging nickels for ice cream, gazing in rapture at the posters outside the movie houses, or rolling on the sand in Leblon.

That morning a southwester was whipping the Atlantic into a fury. The piano, needless to say, remained as tranquil as ever. And imposing in the severity of its lines.

Preparations for the departure were under way. João de Oliveira asked his wife and daughter to remove the parts that might possibly be useful. Accordingly, the bronze candlesticks were taken off, then the pedals and metal ornaments, and finally the oak top.

"Ugh!" exclaimed Sara. "It looks so different."

Without mentioning it to his family, João de Oliveira had recruited a bunch of Negro boys. They were waiting impatiently outside the door. Oliveira now told them to come in, the strongest ones first.

It was twenty after four in the afternoon when the funeral cortege started out. A small crowd on the sidewalk made way for it. The piano moved slowly and irregularly. Some people came up to observe it more closely. Rosália and her daughter contemplated it sadly from the porch, their arms around each other's shoulders. They could not bring themselves to accompany it. The cook was wiping her eyes on her apron.

"Which way?" asked the Negro boys when the procession reached the corner. They were all trying to hold the piano at the same time, with the result that it almost fell.

"Which way?" they repeated.

"To the sea!" cried João de Oliveira. And with the grand gesture of a naval commander he pointed toward the Atlantic.

"To the sea! To the sea!" echoed the boys in chorus.

They began to understand that the piano was going to be destroyed, and this knowledge excited them. They laughed and talked animatedly among themselves. The hubbub inspired the little bitch Doli to leap in the air and bark furiously.

The balconies of the houses were crowded, chiefly with young girls.

"Mother of heaven!" they exclaimed. "What is it?" And, incredulously, "A piano!"

"It came from ninety-nine," cried a Negro urchin, running from house to house to inform the families.

"Why, that's where Sara lives."

An acquaintance ran out to learn the facts from Oliveira himself.

"What's wrong, João?"

"Nothing's wrong. I know what I'm doing. Just everybody keep out of the way."

"But why don't you sell it?"

"I'll sell it, all right. I'll sell it to the Atlantic Ocean. See it there? The ocean . . ."

With the air of a somewhat flustered executioner, he resumed his command.

"More to the left, fellows . . . Careful, don't let it drop . . . Just the big boys now, everybody else let go."

From time to time one of the boys would put his arm inside the piano and run his hand along the strings. The sound was a sort of death rattle.

A lady on a balcony shouted at João, "Would you sell it?"

"No, madam, it's not for sale. I'll give it away. You want it?"

The lady reddened, felt offended, and went into her house. João made his offer more general.

"Anyone around here want a piano?"

At number forty-three a family of Polish refugees accepted. They were astounded, but they accepted.

"Then it's yours," shouted João de Oliveira.

The Polish family came down and stood around the piano.

"We'll take it, all right . . . But . . . our house is very small. Give us a couple of days to get ready for it."

"Now or never!" replied Oliveira. "Here it is, right outside your house. You don't want it? Okay, fellows, let's go."

The piano moved closer and closer to the sea. It swayed like a dead cockroach carried by ants.

João de Oliveira distinguished only a few of the exclamations coming from the doors, windows, and balconies of the houses.

"This is the craziest thing I ever heard of," someone shouted from a balcony.

"Crazy?" replied João de Oliveira, looking up at the speaker. "Okay then you take it. Take it . . ."

Farther on, the scene was repeated. Everyone thought it was a crazy thing to do and everyone wanted the piano; but as soon as the owner offered immediate possession, there was just embarrassed silence. After all, who is prepared to receive a piano at a moment's notice?

João de Oliveira proceeded resolutely, accompanied by a buzz of comments and lamentations. He decided to make no more replies.

A group of motorcycle policemen stopped the procession and surrounded the old piano. João de Oliveira gave a detailed explanation. They asked to see his documents. He went back to the house and got them. He thought the requirement natural enough, for the nation was at war. But he resented having had to give an explanation, for he was acting pursuant to a personal decision for which he was accountable to no one outside the family. He certainly had a right to throw away his own property. This thought reawakened his affection for the instrument. Placing his hand on the piano as if on the forehead of a deceased friend, he felt deeply moved and began to discourse on its life.

"It's an antique, one of the oldest pianos in Brazil."

It had belonged to his grandparents, who had been in the service of the Empire.

"It was a fine piano, you may believe me. Famous musicians played on it. They say that Chopin preferred it over all others. But what does this matter? No one appreciates it any more. Times have changed . . . Sara, my daughter, is getting married. She'll live with us. The house is small. What can I do? No one wants it. This is the only way out."

And he nodded toward the sea.

The Negro boys were growing impatient with the interruptions. They were eager to see the piano sink beneath the waves. Almost as impatient as these improvised movers, were the people who had joined the procession, including delivery men, messenger boys, a few women, and a great many children.

The police examined the interior of the piano but found nothing suspicious. They returned Oliveira's papers and suggested that he hurry so that traffic would not be impeded.

A photographer asked some of the people to form a group and snapped their picture. João de Oliveira was on the left side in a pose expressing sadness. Then he became annoyed with all these interruptions that prolonged the agony of his piano.

Night fell rapidly. A policeman observed that after six o'clock they would not be permitted to go on. They would have to wait till the next day.

The Negro boys dispersed. They were to be paid later, at Oliveira's house. People were amazed that evening at the number of young Negroes strolling around with small, ivory-plated pieces of wood in their hands.

The piano remained there on the street where they had left it, keeled over against the curb. A ridiculous position. Young men and women on their evening promenade soon surrounded it and made comments.

When he got home, João de Oliveira found some of Sara's girl friends there, eagerly questioning her about the piano.

It was still dark when João and his wife awoke to the loud sound of rain. Wind, rain, and the roar of the surf. They lit the light and looked at each other.

"I was thinking about the piano, Rosália."

"So was I, João. Poor thing! Out in the rain there . . . and it's so cold!"

"The water must be getting into the works and ruining everything . . . the felt, the strings. It's terrible, isn't it, Rosália?"

"We did an ungrateful thing, João."

"I don't even like to think about it, Rosália."

João de Oliveira looked out the window. Flashes of lightning illuminated the trees, revealing branches swaying wildly in the wind. João went back to bed and slept fitfully. He awoke again and told his wife that he had been listening to the piano.

"I heard everything that was ever played on it. Many different hands. My grandmother's hands, my mother's, yours, my aunt's, Sara's. More than twenty hands, more than a hundred white fingers were pressing the keys. I never heard such pretty music. It was sublime, Rosália. The dead hands sometimes played better than the live ones. Lots of young girls from earlier generations were standing around the piano, listening. Couples who later got married were sitting nearby, holding hands. I don't know why, but after a while they all looked at me — with contempt. Suddenly the hands left the piano, but it kept on playing. The Funeral March. Then the piano shut by itself . . . There was a torrent of water. The piano let itself get swept along . . . toward the ocean. I shouted to it but it wouldn't listen to me. It seemed to be offended, Rosália, and it just kept on going . . . I stood there in the street, all alone. I began to cry . . ."

João de Oliveira was breathing hard. The mysterious concert had left him in a state of emotion. He felt remorseful.

The rain stopped. As soon as it was light, João went out to round up the Negro boys. All he wanted now was to get the thing over with as quickly as possible.

The wind was still strong, and the ocean growled as if it were digesting the storm of the night before. The boys came, but in smaller numbers than before. Several grown men were among them. João de Oliveira, in a hoarse voice, assumed command again.

On the beach the piano moved more slowly. Finally the long tongues of the waves began to lick it.

Some families stood on the sidewalk, watching the spectacle. Oliveira's crew carried and pushed the piano far enough for the surf to take charge and drag it out to sea. Two enormous waves broke over it without effect. The third made it tremble. The fourth carried it away forever.

João de Oliveira stood there, knee deep in water, with his mouth open. The sea seemed enormously silent. No one could tell that he was crying, for the tears on his cheeks were indistinguishable from the drops of spray.

Far off, he saw Sara with her head resting on the lieutenant's shoulder. Doli was with her, her snout expressing inquiry and incipient dismay; she had always slept next to the piano. João was glad that Rosália had not come.

Many people appeared later on the beach, asking one another what had happened. It seemed at first that an entire Polish family had drowned. Subsequently, it was learned that only one person had drowned. Some said it was a child. Others insisted that it was a lady who had had an unhappy love affair. Only later was it generally known that the person who had drowned was a piano.

People posted themselves at their windows to watch João de Oliveira come back from the beach.

"That's the man!" someone announced.

Oliveira walked slowly, staring at the ground. Everyone felt respect for him.

"It's gone, Rosália," he said as he entered the house. "It has passed the point of no return."

"Before we talk about it, João, go change your clothes."

"Our piano will never come back, Rosália."

"Of course it won't come back. That's why you threw it in the sea."

"Who knows," said Sara. "Maybe it'll be washed up on a beach somewhere."

"Let's not think about it any more. It's over. It's finished. Sara, it's time you did your room."

There was a pause, after which João resumed his lamentation.

"I saw the waves swallow it."

"Enough, my husband. Enough!"

"It came back to the surface twice."

"It's all over! Let's not think about it anymore."

"I didn't mention it to anybody so they wouldn't think I went crazy . . . though they're beginning to think I'm crazy anyway . . . The fact is, I'm probably the most rational man in the whole neighborhood . . . But a little while ago I clearly heard the piano play the Funeral March."

"That was in your dream last night," Rosália reminded him.

"No, it was there by the sea, in broad daylight. Didn't you hear it, Sara? Right afterward, it was covered all with foam, and the music stopped."

He nodded his head, expressing hopelessness before the inevitable. He was talking as if to himself.

"It must be far away by now. Under the water, moving along past strange sights. The wrecks of ships. Submarines. Fishes. Until yesterday it had never left this room . . . Years from now it will be washed up on some island in an ocean on the other side of the world. And when Sara, Rosália, and I are dead, it will still remember the music it made in this house."

He left the room. Sara, alone, looked at the place where the piano had been. Again, she pictured the conjugal bed there, but this time she felt a little guilty.

Her thoughts were interrupted by a knock at the door. A fellow came in with an official notice. Some unidentified person had told the police that a secret radio was hidden in the piano and that her father had wanted to get rid of it. He was to appear at the district police station and answer questions. Well, it was the sort of thing you had to expect in wartime. Nothing anyone could do about it.

Oliveira spent the rest of the day at the police station. He came home late.

"What a life, Rosália!" he said as he fell dejected into the armchair. "What a life! We can't even throw away things that belong to us."

João felt oppressed, stifled. He meditated awhile and then spoke again.

"Have you ever noticed, Rosália, how people hate to get rid of old things? How they cling to them?"

"Not only old things," replied Rosália. "Old ideas too."

Doli was sniffing the area where the piano had been. She wailed a little and fell asleep.

The doorbell rang. A man entered and drew some papers from a briefcase. He said he came from the Port Captain's office.

"Are you João de Oliveira?"

"Yes, I am João de Oliveira."

"What did you cast in the sea this morning?"

Oliveira was stupefied.

"Out here we're not in that port, my dear sir. It's ocean."

"Are you going to give me a vocabulary lesson, Mr. Oliveira?"

The man repeated his previous question and explained that regulations now forbade the placing of objects in or on the sea without a license.

"Have you a license?"

Oliveira humbly asked whether what he had done was in any way offensive or bad.

"That's not the question. Don't you know that we're at war? That our coasts must be protected? That the Nazis are always watching for an opportunity?"

"But it was just a piano, sir."

"It's still a violation. Anyway, was it really a piano? Are you absolutely sure?"

"I think I am," João blurted, looking at his daughter and his wife. "Wasn't it a piano, Rosália? Wasn't it, Sara?"

"Where's your head, João?" exclaimed Rosália. "You know it was a piano."

Her husband's doubt surprised everyone. He seemed to be musing.

"I thought a person could throw anything in the ocean that he wanted to."

"No, indeed! That's all we need . . ."

João arose. He looked delirious.

"Suppose I want to throw myself in the sea. Can I?"

"It all depends," replied the man from the Port Captain's office.

"Depends on whom? On me and nobody else! I'm a free man. My life belongs to me."

"Much less than you think," said the man.

Sara broke into the smile with which she always greeted the lieutenant, who had just come in. She ran to kiss him.

"See our room, darling. It looks good now, doesn't it?"

"Yes, real good. Where are you going to put the new one?"

"The new one?"

"Yes. Aren't you going to get another?"

Sara and her mother exchanged glances of amazement.

"I'm crazy for a piano," said Sara's fiancé. "You have no idea how it relaxes me. All day long I have to hear guns shooting. A little soft music in the evening . . ."

Sara had a fit of coughing. João de Oliveira went out the door. He felt suffocated; he needed to breathe.

Who else would come out of the night and make new demands of him? How could he have known that a piano hidden from the world, living in quiet anonymity, was really an object of public concern? Why hadn't he just left it where it was?

It was miles away now, traveling . . . Far away, riding the southern seas . . . And free. More so than he or Sara or Rosália. It was he, João de Oliveira, who now felt abandoned. For himself and for his family. It wasn't their piano any more. It was a creature loose in the world. Full of life and pride, moving boldly through the seven seas. Sounding forth. Embraced by all the waters of the world. Free to go where it wished, to do what it wished.

Beneath the trees in front of the house, the Negro boys were waiting for their second day's pay. They had worked hard. It was so dark that he could scarcely distinguish their shaved heads. In the midst of them he saw a vaguely familiar form. The person opened the garden gate and asked permission to enter.

With some difficulty João recognized the redheaded man, but he was wholly unprepared for what the man was about to say:

"I've come back about the piano. I think I can make you a reasonable offer."

F. Scott Fitzgerald
1896–1940

The Fitzgerald industry has put obstacles in the way of reading him. The aura of the Jazz Age, the sadness and glitter of his overpublicized career, have become so much a part of our national legendry as to obscure the work itself. As an English critic, A. T. K. Crozier of the University of Sussex, puts it: "It is hard not to think that everything he wrote was a mythic rehearsal of his own sense of exclusion."

For his enjoyment to be pure, the reader must go back to one of the tenets of what used to be called the New Criticism. Emptying his mind of all biographical considerations, he must stick to a careful scrutiny of the text itself and give himself over to Fitzgerald's art, not to Fitzgerald. Unless this is done, his pleasure becomes confused, alloyed with the dubious satisfaction that comes of matching the words against the life of the writer of the words.

Most of Fitzgerald's short stories, written to pay the bills, are ephemeral. At least three seem to me admirable: the extraordinary "May Day," unfortunately too long for inclusion here; "Crazy Sunday," a funny, brilliant, acid etching of Hollywood in its palmy days; and reprinted here, "Babylon Revisited."

Reading this tale, which mingles Fitzgerald's familiar nostalgia, romanticism, and bitterness, we must try to forget that it indirectly reflects his difficult relationship with his daughter and his wife, Zelda, that it hides a sorrowful assessment of his triumph and decline, and that at its heart lies the problem of the alcoholism that helped to ruin him. When read without these preconceptions, it stands up beautifully as a controlled study of one of the inexorable demands life frequently makes on us. "The big party's over now," remarks one of the characters. How does one pay for the past?

Babylon Revisited

"AND WHERE'S MR. CAMPBELL?" Charlie asked.

"Gone to Switzerland. Mr. Campbell's a pretty sick man, Mr. Wales."

"I'm sorry to hear that. And George Hardt?" Charlie inquired.

"Back in America, gone to work."

"And where is the Snow Bird?"

"He was in here last week. Anyway, his friend, Mr. Schaeffer, is in Paris."

Two familiar names from the long list of a year and a half ago. Charlie scribbled an address in his notebook and tore out the page.

"If you see Mr. Schaeffer, give him this," he said. "It's my brother-in-law's address. I haven't settled on a hotel yet."

He was not really disappointed to find Paris was so empty. But the stillness in the Ritz bar was strange and portentous. It was not an American bar any more — he felt polite in it, and not as if he owned it. It had gone back into France. He felt the stillness from the moment he got out of the taxi and saw the doorman, usually in a frenzy of activity at this hour, gossiping with a *chasseur* by the servants' entrance.

Passing through the corridor, he heard only a single, bored voice in the once-clamorous women's room. When he turned into the bar he traveled the twenty feet of green carpet with his eyes fixed straight ahead by old habit; and then, with his foot firmly on the rail, he turned and surveyed the room, encountering only a single pair of eyes that fluttered up from a newspaper in the corner. Charlie asked for the head barman, Paul, who in the latter days of the bull market had come to work in his own custom-built car — disembarking, however, with due nicety at the nearest corner. But Paul was at his country house today and Alix giving him information.

"No, no more," Charlie said, "I'm going slow these days."

Alix congratulated him: "You were going pretty strong a couple of years ago."

"I'll stick to it all right," Charlie assured him. "I've stuck to it for over a year and a half now."

"How do you find conditions in America?"

"I haven't been to America for months. I'm in business in Prague, representing a couple of concerns there. They don't know about me down there."

Alix smiled.

"Remember the night of George Hardt's bachelor dinner here?" said Charlie. "By the way, what's become of Claude Fessenden?"

Alix lowered his voice confidentially: "He's in Paris, but he doesn't come here any more. Paul doesn't allow it. He ran up a bill of thirty thousand francs, charging all his drinks and his lunches, and usually his dinner, for more than a year. And when Paul finally told him he had to pay, he gave him a bad check."

Alix shook his head sadly.

"I don't understand it, such a dandy fellow. Now he's all bloated up —" He made a plump apple of his hands.

Charlie watched a group of strident queens installing themselves in a corner.

"Nothing affects them," he thought. "Stocks rise and fall, people loaf or work, but they go on forever." The place oppressed him. He called for the dice and shook with Alix for the drink.

"Here for long, Mr. Wales?"

"I'm here for four or five days to see my little girl."

"Oh-h! You have a little girl?"

Outside, the fire-red, gas-blue, ghost-green signs shone smokily through the tranquil rain. It was late afternoon and the streets were in movement; the *bistros* gleamed. At the corner of the Boulevard des Capucines he took a taxi. The Place de la Concorde moved by in pink majesty; they crossed the logical Seine, and Charlie felt the sudden provincial quality of the Left Bank.

Charlie directed his taxi to the Avenue de l'Opera, which was out of his way. But he wanted to see the blue hour spread over the magnificent façade, and imagine that the cab horns, playing endlessly the first few bars of *Le Plus que Lent*, were the trumpets of the Second Empire. They were closing the iron grill in front of Brentano's Book-store, and people were already at dinner behind the trim little bourgeois hedge of Duval's. He had never eaten at a really cheap restaurant in Paris. Five-course dinner, four francs fifty, eighteen cents, wine included. For some odd reason he wished that he had.

As they rolled on to the Left Bank and he felt its sudden provincialism, he thought, "I spoiled this city for myself. I didn't realize it, but the days came along one after another, and then two years were gone, and everything was gone, and I was gone."

He was thirty-five, and good to look at. The Irish mobility of his face was sobered by a deep wrinkle between his eyes. As he rang his brother-in-law's bell in the Rue Palatine, the wrinkle deepened till it pulled down his brows; he felt a cramping sensation in his belly. From behind the maid who opened the door darted a lovely little girl of nine who shrieked "Daddy!" and flew up, struggling like a fish, into his arms. She pulled his head around by one ear and set her cheek against his.

"My old pie," he said.

"Oh, daddy, daddy, daddy, daddy, dads, dads, dads!"

She drew him into the salon, where the family waited, a boy and girl his daughter's age, his sister-in-law and her husband. He greeted Marion with his voice pitched carefully to avoid either feigned enthusiasm or dislike, but her response was more frankly tepid, though she minimized her expression of unalterable distrust by directing her regard toward his child. The two men clasped hands in a friendly way and Lincoln Peters rested his for a moment on Charlie's shoulder.

The room was warm and comfortably American. The three children moved intimately about, playing through the yellow oblongs that led to other rooms; the cheer of six o'clock spoke in the eager smacks of the fire and the sounds of French activity in the kitchen. But Charlie did not relax; his heart sat up rigidly in his body and he drew confidence from his daughter, who from time to time came close to him, holding in her arms the doll he had brought.

"Really extremely well," he declared in answer to Lincoln's question. "There's a lot of business there that isn't moving at all, but we're doing even better than ever. In fact, damn well. I'm bringing my sister over from America next month to keep house for me. My income last year was bigger than it was when I had money. You see, the Czechs —"

His boasting was for a specific purpose; but after a moment, seeing a faint restiveness in Lincoln's eye, he changed the subject:

"Those are fine children of yours, well brought up, good manners."

"We think Honoria's a great little girl too."

Marion Peters came back from the kitchen. She was a tall woman with worried eyes, who had once possessed a fresh American loveliness. Charlie had never been sensitive to it and was always surprised when people spoke of how pretty she had been. From the first there had been an instinctive antipathy between them.

"Well, how do you find Honoria?" she asked.

"Wonderful. I was astonished how much she's grown in ten months. All the children are looking well."

"We haven't had a doctor for a year. How do you like being back in Paris?"

"It seems very funny to see so few Americans around."

"I'm delighted," Marion said vehemently. "Now at least you can go into a store without their assuming you're a millionaire. We've suffered like everybody, but on the whole it's a good deal pleasanter."

"But it was nice while it lasted," Charlie said. "We were a sort of royalty, almost infallible, with a sort of magic around us. In the bar this afternoon" — he stumbled, seeing his mistake — "there wasn't a man I knew."

She looked at him keenly. "I should think you'd have had enough of bars."

"I only stayed a minute. I take one drink every afternoon, and no more."

"Don't you want a cocktail before dinner?" Lincoln asked.

"I take only one drink every afternoon, and I've had that."

"I hope you keep to it," said Marion.

Her dislike was evident in the coldness with which she spoke, but Charlie only smiled; he had larger plans. Her very aggressiveness gave him an advantage, and he knew enough to wait. He wanted them to initiate the discussion of what they knew had brought him to Paris.

At dinner he couldn't decide whether Honoria was most like him or her mother. Fortunate if she didn't combine the traits of both that had brought them to disaster. A great wave of protectiveness went over him. He thought he knew what to do for her. He believed in character; he wanted to jump back a whole generation and trust in character again as the eternally valuable element. Everything else wore out.

He left soon after dinner, but not to go home. He was curious to see Paris by night with clearer and more judicious eyes than those of other days. He bought a *strapontin* for the Casino and watched Josephine Baker go through her chocolate arabesques.

After an hour he left and strolled toward Montmartre, up the Rue Pigalle into the Place Blanche. The rain had stopped and there were a few people in evening clothes disembarking from taxis in front of cabarets, and *cocottes* prowling singly or in pairs, and many Negroes. He passed a lighted door from which issued music, and stopped with the sense of familiarity; it was Bricktop's, where he had parted with so many hours and so much money. A few doors farther on he found another ancient rendezvous and incautiously put his head inside. Immediately an eager orchestra burst into sound, a pair of professional dancers leaped to their feet and a maître de'hôtel swooped toward him, crying, "Crowd just arriving, sir!" But he withdrew quickly.

"You have to be damn drunk," he thought.

Zelli's was closed, the bleak and sinister cheap hotels surrounding it were dark; up in the Rue Blanche there was more light and a local, colloquial French crowd. The Poet's Cave had disappeared, but the two great mouths of the Café of Heaven and the Café of Hell still yawned — even devoured, as he watched, the meager contents of a tourist bus — a German, a Japanese, and an American couple who glanced at him with frightened eyes.

So much for the effort and ingenuity of Montmartre. All the catering to vice and waste was on an utterly childish scale, and he suddenly realized the meaning of the word "dissipate" — to dissipate into thin air; to make nothing out of something. In the little hours of the night every move from place to place was an enormous human jump, an increase of paying for the privilege of slower and slower motion.

He remembered thousand-franc notes given to an orchestra for playing a single number, hundred-franc notes tossed to a doorman for calling a cab.

But it hadn't been given for nothing.

It had been given, even the most wildly squandered sum, as an offering to destiny that he might not remember the things most worth remembering, the things that now he would always remember — his child taken from his control, his wife escaped to a grave in Vermont.

In the glare of a *brasserie* a woman spoke to him. He bought her some eggs and coffee, and then, eluding her encouraging stare, gave her a twenty-franc note and took a taxi to his hotel.

II

He woke upon a fine fall day — football weather. The depression of yesterday was gone and he liked the people on the streets. At noon he sat opposite Honoria at Le Grand Vatel, the only restaurant he could think of not reminiscent of champagne dinners and long luncheons that began at two and ended in a blurred and vague twilight.

"Now, how about vegetables? Oughtn't you to have some vegetables?"

"Well, yes."

"Here's *épinards* and *chou-fleur* and carrots and *haricots*."

"I'd like *chou-fleur*."

"Wouldn't you like to have two vegetables?"

"I usually only have one at lunch."

The waiter was pretending to be inordinately fond of children. *"Qu'elle est mignonne la petite! Elle parle exactement comme une Française."*

"How about dessert? Shall we wait and see?"

The waiter disappeared. Honoria looked at her father expectantly.

"What are we going to do?"

"First, we're going to that toy store in the Rue Saint-Honoré and buy you anything you like. And then we're going to the vaudeville at the Empire."

She hesitated. "I like it about the vaudeville, but not the toy store."

"Why not?"

"Well, you brought me this doll." She had it with her. "And I've got lots of things. And we're not rich any more, are we?"

"We never were. But today you are to have anything you want."

"All right," she agreed resignedly.

When there had been her mother and a French nurse he had been inclined to be strict; now he extended himself, reached out for a new tolerance; he must be both parents to her and not shut any of her out of communication.

"I want to get to know you," he said gravely. "First let me introduce myself. My name is Charles J. Wales, of Prague."

"Oh, daddy!" her voice cracked with laughter.

"And who are you, please?" he persisted, and she accepted a rôle immediately: "Honoria Wales, Rue Palatine, Paris."

"Married or single?"

"No, not married. Single."

He indicated the doll. "But I see you have a child, madame."

Unwilling to disinherit it, she took it to her heart and thought quickly: "Yes, I've been married, but I'm not married now. My husband is dead."

He went on quickly, "And the child's name?"

"Simone. That's after my best friend at school."

"I'm very pleased that you're doing so well at school."

"I'm third this month," she boasted. "Elsie" — that was her cousin — "is only about eighteenth, and Richard is about at the bottom."

"You like Richard and Elsie, don't you?"

"Oh, yes. I like Richard quite well and I like her all right."

Cautiously and casually he asked: "And Aunt Marion and Uncle Lincoln — which do you like best?"

"Oh, Uncle Lincoln, I guess."

He was increasingly aware of her presence. As they came in, a murmur ". . . adorable" followed them, and now the people at the next table bent all their silences upon her, staring as if she were something no more conscious than a flower.

"Why don't I live with you?" she asked suddenly. "Because mamma's dead?"

"You must stay here and learn more French. It would have been hard for daddy to take care of you so well."

"I don't really need much taking care of any more. I do everything for myself."

Going out of the restaurant, a man and a woman unexpectedly hailed him.

"Well, the old Wales!"

"Hello there, Lorraine . . . Dunc."

Sudden ghosts out of the past: Duncan Schaeffer, a friend from college. Lorraine Quarrles, a lovely, pale blonde of thirty; one of a crowd who had helped them make months into days in the lavish times of three years ago.

"My husband couldn't come this year," she said, in answer to his question. "We're poor as hell. So he gave me two hundred a month and told me I could do my worst on that . . . This is your little girl?"

"What about coming back and sitting down?" Duncan asked.

"Can't do it." He was glad for an excuse. As always, he felt Lorraine's passionate, provocative attraction, but his own rhythm was different now.

"Well, how about dinner?" she asked.

"I'm not free. Give me your address and let me call you."

"Charlie, I believe you're sober," she said judicially. "I honestly believe he's sober, Dunc. Pinch him and see if he's sober."

Charlie indicated Honoria with his head. They both laughed.

"What's your address?" said Duncan skeptically.

He hesitated, unwilling to give the name of his hotel.

"I'm not settled yet. I'd better call you. We're going to see the vaude-ville at the Empire."

"There! That's what I want to do," Lorraine said. "I want to see some clowns and acrobats and jugglers. That's just what we'll do, Dunc."

"We've got to do an errand first," said Charlie. "Perhaps we'll see you there."

"All right, you snob . . . Good-by, beautiful little girl."

"Good-by."

Honoria bobbed politely.

Somehow, an unwelcome encounter. They liked him because he was functioning, because he was serious; they wanted to see him, because he was stronger than they were now, because they wanted to draw a certain sustenance from his strength.

At the Empire, Honoria proudly refused to sit upon her father's folded coat. She was already an individual with a code of her own, and Charlie was more and more absorbed by the desire of putting a little of himself into her before she crystallized utterly. It was hopeless to try to know her in so short a time.

Between the acts they came upon Duncan and Lorraine in the lobby where the band was playing.

"Have a drink?"

"All right, but not up at the bar. We'll take a table."

"The perfect father."

Listening abstractedly to Lorraine, Charlie watched Honoria's eyes leave their table, and he followed them wistfully about the room, wondering what they saw. He met her glance and she smiled.

"I liked that lemonade," she said.

What had she said? What had he expected? Going home in a taxi afterward, he pulled her over until her head rested against his chest.

"Darling, do you ever think about your mother?"

"Yes, sometimes," she answered vaguely.

"I don't want you to forget her. Have you got a picture of her?"

"Yes. I think so. Anyhow, Aunt Marion has. Why don't you want me to forget her?"

"She loved you very much."

"I loved her too."

They were silent for a moment.

"Daddy, I want to come and live with you," she said suddenly.

His heart leaped; he had wanted it to come like this.

"Aren't you perfectly happy?"

"Yes, but I love you better than anybody. And you love me better than anybody, don't you, now that mummy's dead?"

"Of course I do. But you won't always like me best, honey. You'll grow up and meet somebody your own age and go marry him and forget you ever had a daddy."

"Yes, that's true," she agreed tranquilly.

He didn't go in. He was coming back at nine o'clock and he wanted to keep himself fresh and new for the thing he must say then.

"When you're safe inside, just show yourself in that window."

"All right. Good-by, dads, dads, dads, dads."

He waited in the dark street until she appeared, all warm and glowing, in the window above and kissed her fingers out into the night.

III

They were waiting, Marion sat behind the coffee service in a dignified black dinner dress that just faintly suggested mourning. Lincoln was walking up and down with the animation of one who had already been talking. They were as anxious as he to get into the question. He opened it almost immediately:

"I suppose you know what I want to see you about — why I really came to Paris."

Marion played with the black stars on her necklace and frowned.

"I'm awfully anxious to have a home," he continued. "And I'm awfully anxious to have Honoria in it. I appreciate your taking in Honoria for her mother's sake, but things have changed now" — he hesitated and then continued more forcibly — "changed radically with me, and I want to ask you to reconsider the matter. It would be silly for me to deny that about three years ago I was acting badly —"

Marion looked up at him with hard eyes.

"— but all that's over. As I told you. I haven't had more than a drink a day for over a year, and I take that drink deliberately, so that the idea of alcohol won't get too big in my imagination. You see the idea?"

"No," said Marion succinctly.

"It's a sort of stunt I set myself. It keeps the matter in proportion."

"I get you," said Lincoln. "You don't want to admit it's got any attraction for you."

"Something like that. Sometimes I forget and don't take it. But I try to take it. Anyhow, I couldn't afford to drink in my position. The people I represent are more than satisfied with what I've done, and I'm bringing my sister over from Burlington to keep house for me, and I want awfully to have Honoria too. You know that even when her mother and I weren't getting along well we never let anything that happened touch Honoria. I know she's fond of me and I know I'm able to take care of her and — well, there you are. How do you feel about it?"

He knew that now he would have to take a beating. It would last an hour or two hours, and it would be difficult, but if he modulated his inevitable resentment to the chastened attitude of the reformed sinner, he might win his point in the end.

Keep your temper, he told himself. You don't want to be justified. You want Honoria.

Lincoln spoke first: "We've been talking it over ever since we got your letter last month. We're happy to have Honoria here. She's a dear little thing, and we're glad to be able to help her, but of course that isn't the question —"

Marion interrupted suddenly. "How long are you going to stay sober, Charlie?" she asked.

"Permanently, I hope."

"How can anybody count on that?"

"You know I never did drink heavily until I gave up business and came over here with nothing to do. Then Helen and I began to run around with —"

"Please leave Helen out of it. I can't bear to hear you talk about her like that."

He stared at her grimly; he had never been certain how fond of each other the sisters were in life.

"My drinking only lasted about a year and a half — from the time we came over until I — collapsed."

"It was time enough."

"It was time enough," he agreed.

"My duty is entirely to Helen," she said. "I try to think what she would have wanted me to do. Frankly, from the night you did that terrible thing you haven't really existed for me. I can't help that. She was my sister."

"Yes."

"When she was dying she asked me to look out for Honoria. If you hadn't been in a sanitarium then, it might have helped matters."

He had no answer.

"I'll never in my life be able to forget the morning when Helen knocked at my door, soaked to the skin and shivering, and said you'd locked her out."

Charlie gripped the sides of the chair. This was more difficult than he expected; he wanted to launch out into a long expostulation and explanation, but he only said: "The night I locked her out —" and she interrupted, "I don't feel up to going over that again."

After a moment's silence Lincoln said: "We're getting off the subject. You want Marion to set aside her legal guardianship and give you Honoria. I think the main point for her is whether she has confidence in you or not."

"I don't blame Marion," Charlie said slowly, "but I think she can have entire confidence in me. I had a good record up to three years ago. Of course, it's within human possibilities I might go wrong any time. But if we wait much longer I'll lose Honoria's childhood and my chance for a home." He shook his head, "I'll simply lose her, don't you see?"

"Yes, I see," said Lincoln.

"Why didn't you think of all this before?" Marion asked.

"I suppose I did, from time to time, but Helen and I were getting along badly. When I consented to the guardianship, I was flat on my back in a sanitarium and the market had cleaned me out. I knew I'd acted badly, and I thought if it would bring any peace to Helen, I'd agree to anything. But now it's different. I'm functioning, I'm behaving damn well, so far as —"

"Please don't swear at me," Marion said.

He looked at her, startled. With each remark the force of her dislike became more and more apparent. She had built up all her fear of life into one wall and faced it toward him. This trivial reproof was possibly the result of some trouble with the cook several hours before. Charlie became increasingly alarmed at leaving Honoria in this atmosphere of hostility against himself; sooner or later it would come out, in a word here, a shake of the head there, and some of that distrust would be irrevocably implanted in Honoria. But he pulled his temper down out of his face and shut it up inside him; he had won a point, for Lincoln realized the absurdity of Marion's remark and asked her lightly since when she had objected to the word "damn."

"Another thing," Charlie said: "I'm able to give her certain advantages now. I'm going to take a French governess to Prague with me. I've got a lease on a new apartment —"

He stopped, realizing that he was blundering. They couldn't be expected to accept with equanimity the fact that his income was again twice as large as their own.

"I suppose you can give her more luxuries than we can," said Marion. "When you were throwing away money we were living along watching every ten francs . . . I suppose you'll start doing it again."

"Oh, no," he said. "I've learned. I worked hard for ten years, you know — until I got lucky in the market, like so many people. Terribly lucky. It didn't seem any use working any more, so I quit. It won't happen again."

There was a long silence. All of them felt their nerves straining, and for the first time in a year Charlie wanted a drink. He was sure now that Lincoln Peters wanted him to have his child.

Marion shuddered suddenly; part of her saw that Charlie's feet were planted on the earth now, and her own maternal feeling recognized the naturalness of his desire; but she had lived for a long time with a prejudice — a prejudice founded on a curious disbelief in her sister's happiness, and which, in the shock of one terrible night, had turned to hatred for him. It had all happened at a point in her life where the discouragement of ill health and adverse circumstances made it necessary for her to believe in tangible villainy and a tangible villain.

"I can't help what I think!" she cried out suddenly. "How much you were responsible for Helen's death, I don't know. It's something you'll have to square with your own conscience."

An electric current of agony surged through him; for a moment he was almost on his feet, an unuttered sound echoing in his throat. He hung on to himself for a moment, another moment.

"Hold on there," said Lincoln uncomfortably. "I never thought you were responsible for that."

"Helen died of heart trouble," Charlie said dully.

"Yes, heart trouble." Marion spoke as if the phrase had another meaning for her.

Then, in the flatness that followed her outburst, she saw him plainly and she knew he had somehow arrived at control over the situation. Glancing at her husband, she found no help from him, and as abruptly as if it were a matter of no importance, she threw up the sponge.

"Do what you like!" she cried, springing up from her chair. "She's your child. I'm not the person to stand in your way. I think if it were my child I'd rather see her —" She managed to check herself. "You two decide it. I can't stand this. I'm sick. I'm going to bed."

She hurried from the room; after a moment Lincoln said:

"This has been a hard day for her. You know how strongly she feels —" His voice was almost apologetic: "When a woman gets an idea in her head."

"Of course."

"It's going to be all right. I think she sees now that you — can provide for the child, and so we can't very well stand in your way or Honoria's way."

"Thank you, Lincoln."

"I'd better go along and see how she is."

"I'm going."

He was still trembling when he reached the street, but a walk down the Rue Bonaparte to the quais set him up, and as he crossed the Seine, fresh and new by the quai lamps, he felt exultant. But back in his room he couldn't sleep. The image of Helen haunted him. Helen whom he had loved so until they had senselessly begun to abuse each other's love, tear it into shreds. On that terrible February night that Marion remembered so vividly, a slow quarrel had gone on for hours. There was a scene at the Florida, and then he attempted to take her home, and then she kissed young Webb at a table; after that there was what she had hysterically said. When he arrived home alone he turned the key in the lock in wild anger. How could he know she would arrive an hour later alone, that there would be a snowstorm in which she wandered about in slippers, too confused to find a taxi? Then the aftermath, her escaping pneumonia by a miracle, and all the attendant horror. They were "reconciled," but that was the beginning of the end, and Marion, who had seen with her own eyes and who imagined it to be one of many scenes from her sister's martyrdom, never forgot.

Going over it again brought Helen nearer, and in the white, soft light that steals upon half sleep near monring he found himself talking to her again. She said that he was perfectly right about Honoria and that she wanted Honoria to be with him. She said she was glad he was being good and doing better. She said a lot of other things — very friendly things — but she was in a swing in a white dress, and swinging faster and faster all the time, so that at the end he could not hear clearly all that she said.

IV

He woke up feeling happy. The door of the world was open again. He made plans, vistas, futures for Honoria and himself, but suddenly he grew sad, remembering all the plans he and Helen had made. She had not planned to die. The present was the thing — work to do and some-one to love. But not to love too much, for he knew the injury that a father can do to a daughter or a mother to a son by attaching them too closely: afterward, out in the world, the child would seek in the marriage partner the same blind tenderness and, failing probably to find it, turn against love and life.

It was another bright, crisp day. He called Lincoln Peters at the bank where he worked and asked if he could count on taking Honoria when he left for Prague. Lincoln agreed that there was no reason for delay. One thing — the legal guardianship. Marion wanted to retain that a while longer. She was upset by the whole matter, and it would oil things if she felt that the situation was still in her control for another year. Charlie agreed, wanting only the tangible, visible child.

Then the question of a governess. Charles sat in a gloomy agency and talked to a cross Béarnaise and to a buxom Breton peasant, neither of whom he could have endured. There were others whom he would see tomorrow.

He lunched with Lincoln Peters at Griffons, trying to keep down his exultation.

"There's nothing quite like your own child," Lincoln said. "But you understand how Marion feels too."

"She's forgotten how hard I worked for seven years there," Charlie said. "She just remembers one night."

"There's another thing." Lincoln hesitated. "While you and Helen were tearing around Europe throwing money away, we were just getting along. I didn't touch any of the prosperity because I never got ahead enough to carry anything but my insurance. I think Marion felt there was some kind of injustice in it — you not even working toward the end, and getting richer and richer."

"It went just as quick as it came," said Charlie.

"Yes, a lot of it stayed in the hands of *chasseurs* and saxophone players and maîtres d'hôtel — well, the big party's over now. I just said that to explain Marion's feeling about those crazy years. If you drop in about six o'clock tonight before Marion's too tired, we'll settle the details on the spot."

Back at his hotel, Charlie found a *pneumatique* that had been redirected from the Ritz bar where Charlie had left his address for the purpose of finding a certain man.

> Dear Charlie:
> You were so strange when we saw you the other day that I wondered if I did something to offend you. If so, I'm not conscious of it. In fact, I have thought about you too much for the last year, and it's always been in the back of my mind that I might see you if I came over here. We *did* have such good times that crazy spring, like the night you and I stole the butcher's tricycle, and the time we tried to call on the president and you had the old derby rim and the wire cane. Everybody seems so old lately, but I don't feel old a bit. Couldn't we get together some time today for old time's sake? I've got a vile hang-over for the moment, but will be feeling better this afternoon and will look for you about five in the sweat-shop at the Ritz.
>
> Always devotedly,
Lorraine

His first feeling was one of awe that he had actually, in his mature years, stolen a tricycle and pedalled Lorraine all over the Étoile between the small hours and dawn. In retrospect it was a nightmare. Locking out Helen didn't fit in with any other act of his life, but the tricycle incident did — it was one of many. How many weeks or months of dissipation to arrive at that condition of utter irresponsibility?

He tried to picture how Lorraine had appeared to him then — very attractive; Helen was unhappy about it, though she said nothing. Yesterday, in the restaurant, Lorraine had seemed trite, blurred, worn away. He emphatically did not want to see her, and he was glad Alix had not given away his hotel address. It was a relief to think, instead, of Honoria, to think of Sundays spent with her and of saying good morning to her and of knowing she was there in his house at night, drawing her breath in the darkness.

At five he took a taxi and bought presents for all the Peters — a piquant cloth doll, a box of Roman soldiers, flowers for Marion, big linen handkerchiefs for Lincoln.

He saw, when he arrived in the apartment, that Marion had accepted the inevitable. She greeted him now as though he were a recalcitrant member of the family, rather than a menacing outsider. Honoria had been told she was going; Charlie was glad to see that her tact made her conceal her excessive happiness. Only on his lap did she whisper her delight and the question "When?" before she slipped away with the other children.

He and Marion were alone for a minute in the room, and on an impulse he spoke out boldly:

"Family quarrels are bitter things. They don't go according to any rules. They're not like aches or wounds; they're more like splits in the skin that won't heal because there's not enough material. I wish you and I could be on better terms."

"Some things are hard to forget," she answered. "It's a question of confidence." There was no answer to this and presently she asked, "When do you propose to take her?"

"As soon as I can get a governess. I hoped the day after tomorrow."

"That's impossible. I've got to get her things in shape. Not before Saturday."

He yielded. Coming back into the room, Lincoln offered him a drink. "I'll take my daily whisky," he said.

It was warm here, it was a home, people together by a fire. The children felt very safe and important; the mother and father were serious, watchful. They had things to do for the children more important than his visit here. A spoonful of medicine was, after all, more important than the strained relations between Marion and himself. They were not dull people, but they were very much in the grip of life and circumstances. He wondered if he couldn't do something to get Lincoln out of his rut at the bank.

A long peal at the door-bell; the *bonne à tout faire* passed through and went down the corridor. The door opened upon another long ring, and then voices, and the three in the salon looked up expectantly; Lincoln moved to bring the corridor within his range of vision, and Marion rose. Then the maid came back along the corridor, closely followed by the voices, which developed under the light into Duncan Schaeffer and Lorraine Quarrles.

They were gay, they were hilarious, they were roaring with laughter. For a moment Charlie was astounded, unable to understand how they ferreted out the Peters' address.

"Ah-h-h!" Duncan wagged his finger roguishly at Charlie. "Ah-h-h!"

They both slid down another cascade of laughter. Anxious and at a loss, Charlie shook hands with them quickly and presented them to Lincoln and Marion. Marion nodded, scarcely speaking. She had drawn back a step toward the fire; her little girl stood beside her, and Marion put an arm about her shoulder.

With growing annoyance at the intrusion, Charlie waited for them to explain themselves. After some concentration Duncan said:

"We came to invite you out to dinner. Lorraine and I insist that all this chi-chi, cagy business 'bout your address got to stop."

Charlie came closer to them, as if to force them backward down the corridor.

"Sorry, but I can't. Tell me where you'll be and I'll phone you in half an hour."

This made no impression. Lorraine sat down suddenly on the side of a chair, and focusing her eyes on Richard, cried, "Oh, what a nice little boy! Come here, little boy." Richard glanced at his mother, but did not move. With a perceptible shrug of her shoulders, Lorraine turned back to Charlie:

"Come and dine. Sure your cousins won' mine. See you so sel'om. Or solemn."

"I can't," said Charlie sharply. "You two have dinner and I'll phone you."

Her voice became suddenly unpleasant. "All right, we'll go. But I remember once when you hammered on my door at four A.M. I was enough of a good sport to give you a drink. Come on, Dunc."

Still in slow motion, with blurred, angry faces, with uncertain feet, they retired along the corridor.

"Good night," Charlie said.

"Good night!" responded Lorraine emphatically.

When he went back into the salon Marion had not moved, only now her son was standing in the circle of her other arm. Lincoln was still swinging Honoria back and forth like a pendulum from side to side.

"What an outrage!" Charlie broke out. "What an absolute outrage!"

Neither of them answered. Charlie dropped into an armchair, picked up his drink, set it down again and said:

"People I haven't seen for two years having the colossal nerve —"

He broke off. Marion had made the sound "Oh!" in one swift, furious breath, turned her body from him with a jerk and left the room.

Lincoln set down Honoria carefully.

"You children go in and start your soup," he said, and when they obeyed, he said to Charlie:

"Marion's not well and she can't stand shocks. That kind of people make her really physically sick."

"I didn't tell them to come here. They wormed your name out of somebody. They deliberately —"

"Well, it's too bad. It doesn't help matters. Excuse me a minute."

Left alone, Charlie sat tense in his chair. In the next room he could hear the children eating, talking in monosyllables, already oblivious to the scene between their elders. He heard a murmur of conversation from a farther room and then the ticking bell of a telephone receiver picked up, and in a panic he moved to the other side of the room and out of earshot.

In a minute Lincoln came back. "Look here, Charlie. I think we'd better call off dinner for tonight. Marion's in bad shape."

"Is she angry with me?"

"Sort of," he said, almost roughly. "She's not strong and —"

"You mean she's changed her mind about Honoria?"

"She's pretty bitter right now. I don't know. You phone me at the bank tomorrow."

"I wish you'd explain to her I never dreamed these people would come here. I'm just as sore as you are."

"I couldn't explain anything to her now."

Charlie got up. He took his coat and hat and started down the corridor. Then he opened the door of the dining room and said in a strange voice, "Good night, children."

Honoria rose and ran around the table to hug him.

"Good night, sweetheart," he said vaguely, and then trying to make his voice more tender, trying to conciliate something, "Good night, dear children."

V

Charlie went directly to the Ritz bar with the furious idea of finding Lorraine and Duncan, but they were not there, and he realized that in any case there was nothing he could do. He had not touched his drink at the Peters', and now he ordered a whisky-and-soda. Paul came over to say hello.

"It's a great change," he said sadly. "We do about half the business we did. So many fellows I hear about back in the States lost everything, maybe not in the first crash, but then in the second. Your friend George Hardt lost every cent, I hear. Are you back in the States?"

"No, I'm in business in Prague."

"I heard that you lost a lot in the crash."

"I did," and he added grimly, "but I lost everything I wanted in the boom."

"Selling short."

"Something like that."

Again the memory of those days swept over him like a nightmare — the people they had met travelling; then people who couldn't add a row of figures or speak a coherent sentence. The little man Helen had consented to dance with at the ship's party, who had insulted her ten feet from the table; the women and girls carried screaming with drink or drugs out of public places —

— The men who locked their wives out in the snow, because the snow of twenty-nine wasn't real snow. If you didn't want it to be snow, you just paid some money.

He went to the phone and called the Peters' apartment; Lincoln answered.

"I called up because this thing is on my mind. Has Marion said anything definite?"

"Marion's sick," Lincoln answered shortly. "I know this thing isn't altogether your fault, but I can't have her go to pieces about it. I'm afraid we'll have to let it slide for six months; I can't take the chance of working her up to this state again."

"I see."

"I'm sorry, Charlie."

He went back to his table. His whisky glass was empty, but he shook his head when Alix looked at it questioningly. There wasn't much he could do now except send Honoria some things; he would send her a lot of things tomorrow. He thought rather angrily that this was just money — he had given so many people money . . .

"No, no more," he said to another waiter. "What do I owe you?"

He would come back some day; they couldn't make him pay forever. But he wanted his child, and nothing was much good now, beside that fact. He wasn't young any more, with a lot of nice thoughts and dreams to have by himself. He was absolutely sure Helen wouldn't have wanted him to be so alone.

WILLIAM FAULKNER
1897–1962

Winner of the Nobel Prize for literature in 1950 and considered by many reputable critics among the greatest of American novelists, Faulkner calls for no commentary in these pages.

From his widely admired stories I have chosen one that achieves its effect with what is, for Faulkner, relative straightforwardness. "That Evening Sun" is a tale of terror told from the limited viewpoint of a child. The melodrama is muted, perfectly controlled.

That Evening Sun

MONDAY IS NO DIFFERENT from any other weekday in Jefferson now.
The streets are paved now, and the telephone and electric companies are
cutting down more and more of the shade trees — the water oaks, the
maples and locusts and elms — to make room for iron poles bearing
clusters of bloated and ghostly and bloodless grapes, and we have a city
laundry which makes the rounds on Monday morning, gathering the
bundles of clothes into bright-colored, specially-made motor cars: the
soiled wearing of a whole week now flees apparitionlike behind alert
and irritable electric horns, with a long diminishing noise of rubber and
asphalt like tearing silk, and even the Negro women who still take in
white people's washing after the old custom, fetch and deliver it in
automobiles.

But fifteen years ago, on Monday morning the quiet, dusty, shady
streets would be full of Negro women with, balanced on their steady,
turbaned heads, bundles of clothes tied up in sheets, almost as large as
cotton bales, carried so without touch of hand between the kitchen door
of the white house and the blackened washpot beside a cabin door in
Negro Hollow.

Nancy would set her bundle on the top of her head, then upon the
bundle in turn she would set the black straw sailor hat which she wore
winter and summer. She was tall, with a high, sad face sunken a little
where her teeth were missing. Sometimes we would go a part of the day
down the lane and across the pasture with her, to watch the balanced
bundle and the hat that never bobbed nor wavered, even when she
walked down into the ditch and up the other side and stooped through
the fence. She would go down on her hands and knees and crawl
through the gap, her head rigid, uptilted, the bundle steady as a rock or
a balloon, and rise to her feet again and go on.

Sometimes the husbands of the washing women would fetch and deliver the clothes, but Jesus never did that for Nancy, even before father
told him to stay away from our house, even when Dilsey was sick and
Nancy would come to cook for us.

And then about half the time we'd have to go down the lane to Nancy's cabin and tell her to come on and cook breakfast. We would stop
at the ditch, because father told us to not have anything to do with Jesus
— he was a short black man, with a razor scar down his face — and we

would throw rocks at Nancy's house until she came to the door, leaning her head around it without any clothes on.

"What yawl mean, chunking my house?" Nancy said. "What you little devils mean?"

"Father says for you to come on and get breakfast," Caddy said. "Father says it's over a half an hour now, and you've got to come this minute."

"I aint studying no breakfast," Nancy said. "I going to get my sleep out."

"I bet you're drunk," Jason said. "Father says you're drunk. Are you drunk, Nancy?"

"Who says I is?" Nancy said. "I got to get my sleep out. I aint studying no breakfast."

So after a while we quit chunking the cabin and went back home. When she finally came, it was too late for me to go to school. So we thought it was whisky until that day they arrested her again and they were taking her to jail and they passed Mr. Stovall. He was the cashier in the bank and a deacon in the Baptist church, and Nancy began to say:

"When you going to pay me, white man? When you going to pay me, white man? It's been three times now since you paid me a cent —" Mr. Stovall knocked her down, but she kept on saying, "When you going to pay me, white man? It's been three times now since —" until Mr. Stovall kicked her in the mouth with his heel and the marshal caught Mr. Stovall back, and Nancy lying in the street, laughing. She turned her head and spat out some blood and teeth and said, "It's been three times now since he paid me a cent."

That was how she lost her teeth, and all that day they told about Nancy and Mr. Stovall, and all that night the ones that passed the jail could hear Nancy singing and yelling. They could see her hands holding to the window bars, and a lot of them stopped along the fence, listening to her and to the jailer trying to make her stop. She didn't shut up until almost daylight, when the jailer began to hear a bumping and scraping upstairs and he went up there and found Nancy hanging from the window bar. He said that it was cocaine and not whisky, because no nigger would try to commit suicide unless he was full of cocaine, because a nigger full of cocaine wasn't a nigger any longer.

The jailer cut her down and revived her; then he beat her, whipped her. She had hung herself with her dress. She had fixed it all right, but when they arrested her she didn't have on anything except a dress and so she didn't have anything to tie her hands with and she couldn't make her hands let go of the window ledge. So the jailer heard the noise and ran up there and found Nancy hanging from the window, stark naked, her belly already swelling out a little, like a little balloon.

When Dilsey was sick in her cabin and Nancy was cooking for us, we could see her apron swelling out; that was before father told Jesus to stay away from the house. Jesus was in the kitchen, sitting behind the stove, with his razor scar on his black face like a piece of dirty string. He said it was a watermelon that Nancy had under her dress.

"It never come off of your vine, though," Nancy said.

"Off of what vine?" Caddy said.

"I can cut down the vine it did come off of," Jesus said.

"What makes you want to talk like that before these chillen?" Nancy said. "Whyn't you go on to work? You done et. You want Mr. Jason to catch you hanging around his kitchen, talking that way before these chillen?"

"Talking what way?" Caddy said. "What vine?"

"I cant hang around white man's kitchen," Jesus said. "But white man can hang around mine. White man can come in my house, but I cant stop him. When white man want to come in my house, I aint got no house. I cant stop him, but he cant kick me outen it. He cant do that."

Dilsey was still sick in her cabin. Father told Jesus to stay off our place. Dilsey was still sick. It was a long time. We were in the library after supper.

"Isn't Nancy through in the kitchen yet?" mother said. "It seems to me that she has had plenty of time to have finished the dishes."

"Let Quentin go and see," father said. "Go and see if Nancy is through, Quentin. Tell her she can go on home."

I went to the kitchen. Nancy was through. The dishes were put away and the fire was out. Nancy was sitting in a chair, close to the cold stove. She looked at me.

"Mother wants to know if you are through," I said.

"Yes," Nancy said. She looked at me. "I done finished." She looked at me.

"What is it?" I said. "What is it?"

"I aint nothing but a nigger," Nancy said. "It aint none of my fault."

She looked at me, sitting in the chair before the cold stove, the sailor hat on her head. I went back to the library. It was the cold stove and all, when you think of a kitchen being warm and busy and cheerful. And with a cold stove and the dishes all put away, and nobody wanting to eat at that hour.

"Is she through?" mother said.

"Yessum," I said.

"What is she doing?" mother said.

"She's not doing anything. She's through."

"I'll go and see," father said.

"Maybe she's waiting for Jesus to come and take her home," Caddy said.

"Jesus is gone," I said. Nancy told us how one morning she woke up and Jesus was gone.

"He quit me," Nancy said. "Done gone to Memphis, I reckon. Dodging them city *po*-lice for a while, I reckon."

"And a good riddance," father said. "I hope he stays there."

"Nancy's scaired of the dark," Jason said.

"So are you," Caddy said.

"I'm not," Jason said.

"Scairy cat," Caddy said.

"I'm not," Jason said.

"You, Candace!" mother said. Father came back.

"I am going to walk down the lane with Nancy," he said. "She says that Jesus is back."

"Has she seen him?" mother said.

"No. Some Negro sent her word that he was back in town. I wont be long."

"You'll leave me alone, to take Nancy home?" mother said. "Is her safety more precious to you than mine?"

"I wont be long," father said.

"You'll leave these children unprotected, with that Negro about?"

"I'm going too," Caddy said. "Let me go, Father."

"What would he do with them, if he were unfortunate enough to have them?" father said.

"I want to go, too," Jason said.

"Jason!" mother said. She was speaking to father. You could tell that by the way she said the name. Like she believed that all day father had been trying to think of doing the thing she wouldn't like the most, and that she knew all the time that after a while he would think of it. I stayed quiet, because father and I both knew that mother would want him to make me stay with her if she just thought of it in time. So father didn't look at me. I was the oldest. I was nine and Caddy was seven and Jason was five.

"Nonsense," father said. "We wont be long."

Nancy had her hat on. We came to the lane. "Jesus always been good to me," Nancy said. "Whenever he had two dollars, one of them was mine." We walked in the lane. "If I can just get through the lane," Nancy said, "I be all right then."

The lane was always dark. "This is where Jason got scaired on Hallowe'en," Caddy said.

"I didn't," Jason said.

"Cant Aunt Rachel do anything with him?" father said. Aunt Rachel was old. She lived in a cabin beyond Nancy's, by herself. She had white hair and she smoked a pipe in the door, all day long; she didn't work any more. They said she was Jesus' mother. Sometimes she said she was and sometimes she said she wasn't any kin to Jesus.

"Yes, you did," Caddy said. "You were scairder than Frony. You were scairder than T.P. even. Scairder than niggers."

"Cant nobody do nothing with him," Nancy said. "He say I done woke up the devil in him and aint but one thing going to lay it down again."

"Well, he's gone now," father said. "There's nothing for you to be afraid of now. And if you'd just let white men alone."

"Let what white men alone?" Caddy said. "How let them alone?"

"He aint gone nowhere," Nancy said. "I can feel him. I can feel him now, in this lane. He hearing us talk, every word, hid somewhere, waiting. I aint seen him, and I aint going to see him again but once more, with that razor in his mouth. That razor on that string down his back, inside his shirt. And then I aint going to be even surprised."

"I wasn't scaired," Jason said.

"If you'd behave yourself, you'd have kept out of this," father said. "But it's all right now. He's probably in St. Louis now. Probably got another wife by now and forgot all about you."

"If he has, I better not find out about it," Nancy said. "I'd stand right over them, and every time he wropped her, I'd cut that arm off. I'd cut his head off and I'd slit her belly and I'd shove —"

"Hush," father said.

"Slit whose belly, Nancy?" Caddy said.

"I wasn't scaired," Jason said. "I'd walk right down this lane by myself."

"Yah," Caddy said. "You wouldn't dare to put your foot down in it if we were not here too."

II

Dilsey was still sick, so we took Nancy home every night until mother said, "How much longer is this going on? I to be left alone in this big house while you take home a frightened Negro?"

We fixed a pallet in the kitchen for Nancy. One night we waked up, hearing the sound. It was not singing and it was not crying, coming up the dark stairs. There was a light in mother's room and we heard father going down the hall, down the back stairs, and Caddy and I went into the hall. The floor was cold. Our toes curled away from it while we listened to the sound. It was like singing and it wasn't like singing, like the sounds that Negroes make.

Then it stopped and we heard father going down the back stairs, and we went to the head of the stairs. Then the sound began again, in the stairway, not loud, and we could see Nancy's eyes halfway up the stairs, against the wall. They looked like cat's eyes do, like a big cat against the wall, watching us. When we came down the steps to where she was, she quit making the sound again, and we stood there until father came back up from the kitchen, with his pistol in his hand. He went back down with Nancy and they came back with Nancy's pallet.

We spread the pallet in our room. After the light in mother's room went off, we could see Nancy's eyes again. "Nancy," Caddy whispered, "are you asleep, Nancy?"

Nancy whispered something. It was oh or no, I dont know which. Like nobody had made it, like it came from nowhere and went nowhere, until it was like Nancy was not there at all; that I had looked so hard at her eyes on the stairs that they had got printed on my eyeballs, like the sun does when you have closed your eyes and there is no sun. "Jesus," Nancy whispered. "Jesus."

"Was it Jesus?" Caddy said. "Did he try to come into the kitchen?"

"Jesus," Nancy said. Like this: Jeeeeeeeeeeeeeeeeesus, until the sound went out, like a match or a candle does.

"It's the other Jesus she means," I said.

"Can you see us, Nancy?" Caddy whispered. "Can you see our eyes too?"

"I aint nothing but a nigger," Nancy said. "God knows. God knows."

"What did you see down there in the kitchen?" Caddy whispered. "What tried to get in?"

"God knows," Nancy said. We could see her eyes. "God knows."

Dilsey got well. She cooked dinner. "You'd better stay in bed a day or two longer," father said.

"What for?" Dilsey said. "If I had been a day later, this place would be to rack and ruin. Get on out of here now, and let me get my kitchen straight again."

Dilsey cooked supper too. And that night, just before dark, Nancy came into the kitchen.

"How do you know he's back?" Dilsey said. "You aint seen him."

"Jesus is a nigger," Jason said.

"I can feel him," Nancy said. "I can feel him laying yonder in the ditch."

"Tonight?" Dilsey said. "Is he there tonight?"

"Dilsey's a nigger too," Jason said.

"You try to eat something," Dilsey said.

"I dont want nothing," Nancy said.

"I aint a nigger," Jason said.

"Drink some coffee," Dilsey said. She poured a cup of coffee for Nancy. "Do you know he's out there tonight? How come you know it's tonight?"

"I know," Nancy said. "He's there, waiting. I know. I done lived with him too long. I know what he is fixing to do 'fore he know it himself."

"Drink some coffee," Dilsey said. Nancy held the cup to her mouth and blew into the cup. Her mouth pursed out like a spreading adder's, like a rubber mouth, like she had blown all the color out of her lips with blowing the coffee.

"I aint a nigger," Jason said. "Are you a nigger, Nancy?"

"I hellborn, child," Nancy said. "I wont be nothing soon. I going back where I come from soon."

III

She began to drink the coffee. While she was drinking, holding the cup in both hands, she began to make the sound again. She made the sound into the cup and the coffee sploshed out onto her hands and her dress. Her eyes looked at us and she sat there, her elbows on her knees, holding the cup in both hands, looking at us across the wet cup, making the sound. "Look at Nancy," Jason said. "Nancy cant cook for us now. Dilsey's got well now."

"You hush up," Dilsey said. Nancy held the cup in both hands, looking at us, making the sound, like there were two of them: one looking at us and the other making the sound. "Whyn't you let Mr. Jason telefoam the marshal?" Dilsey said. Nancy stopped then, holding the cup in her long brown hands. She tried to drink some coffee again, but it sploshed out of the cup, onto her hands and her dress, and she put the cup down. Jason watched her.

"I cant swallow it," Nancy said. "I swallows but it wont go down me."

"You go down to the cabin," Dilsey said. "Frony will fix you a pallet and I'll be there soon."

"Wont no nigger stop him," Nancy said.

"I aint a nigger," Jason said. "Am I, Dilsey?"

"I reckon not," Dilsey said. She looked at Nancy. "I dont reckon so. What you going to do, then?"

Nancy looked at us. Her eyes went fast, like she was afraid there wasn't time to look, without hardly moving at all. She looked at us, at all three of us at one time. "You member that night I stayed in yawls' room?" she said. She told them about how we waked up early the next morning, and played. We had to play quiet, on her pallet, until father woke up and it was time to get breakfast. "Go and ask your maw to let me stay here tonight," Nancy said. "I wont need no pallet. We can play some more."

Caddy asked mother. Jason went too. "I cant have Negroes sleeping in the bedrooms," mother said. Jason cried. He cried until mother said he couldn't have any dessert for three days if he didn't stop. Then Jason said he would stop if Dilsey would make a chocolate cake. Father was there.

"Why dont you do something about it?" mother said. "What do we have officers for?"

"Why is Nancy afraid of Jesus?" Caddy said. "Are you afraid of father, mother?"

"What could the officers do?" father said. "If Nancy hasn't seen him, how could the officers find him?"

"Then why is she afraid?" mother said.

"She says he is there. She says she knows he is there tonight."

"Yet we pay taxes," mother said. "I must wait here alone in the big house while you take a Negro woman home."

"You know that I am not lying outside with a razor," father said.

"I'll stop if Dilsey will make a chocolate cake," Jason said. Mother told us to go out and father said he didn't know if Jason would get a chocolate cake or not, but he knew what Jason was going to get in about a minute. We went back to the kitchen and told Nancy.

"Father said for you to go home and lock the door, and you'll be all right," Caddy said. "All right from what, Nancy? Is Jesus mad at you?" Nancy was holding the coffee cup in her hands again, her elbows on her knees and her hands holding the cup between her knees. She was looking into the cup. "What have you done that made Jesus mad?" Caddy said. Nancy let the cup go. It didn't break on the floor, but the coffee spilled out, and Nancy sat there with her hands still making the shape of the cup. She began to make the sound again, not loud. Not singing and not unsinging. We watched her.

"Here," Dilsey said. "You quit that, now. You get aholt of yourself. You wait here. I going to get Versh to walk home with you." Dilsey went out.

We looked at Nancy. Her shoulders kept shaking, but she quit making the sound. We watched her. "What's Jesus going to do to you?" Caddy said. "He went away."

Nancy looked at us. "We had fun that night I stayed in yawls' room, didn't we?"

"I didn't," Jason said. "I didn't have any fun."

"You were asleep in mother's room," Caddy said. "You were not there."

"Let's go down to my house and have some more fun," Nancy said.

"Mother wont let us," I said. "It's too late now."

"Dont bother her," Nancy said. "We can tell her in the morning. She wont mind."

"She wouldn't let us," I said.

"Dont ask her now," Nancy said. "Dont bother her now."

"She didn't say we couldn't go," Caddy said.

"We didn't ask," I said.

"If you go, I'll tell," Jason said.

"We'll have fun," Nancy said. "They wont mind, just to my house. I been working for yawl a long time. They wont mind."

"I'm not afraid to go," Caddy said. "Jason is the one that's afraid. He'll tell."

"I'm not," Jason said.

"Yes, you are," Caddy said. "You'll tell."

"I wont tell," Jason said. "I'm not afraid."

"Jason aint afraid to go with me," Nancy said. "Is you, Jason?"

"Jason is going to tell," Caddy said. The lane was dark. We passed the pasture gate. "I bet if something was to jump out from behind that gate, Jason would holler."

"I wouldn't," Jason said. We walked down the lane. Nancy was talking loud.

"What are you talking so loud for, Nancy?" Caddy said.

"Who; me?" Nancy said. "Listen at Quentin and Caddy and Jason saying I'm talking loud."

"You talk like there was five of us here," Caddy said. "You talk like father was here too."

"Who; me talking loud, Mr. Jason?" Nancy said.

"Nancy called Jason 'Mister,'" Caddy said.

"Listen how Caddy and Quentin and Jason talk," Nancy said.

"We're not talking loud," Caddy said. "You're the one that's talking like father —"

"Hush," Nancy said; "hush, Mr. Jason."

"Nancy called Jason 'Mister' aguh —"

"Hush," Nancy said. She was talking loud when we crossed the ditch and stooped through the fence where she used to stoop through with the clothes on her head. Then we came to her house. We were going fast then. She opened the door. The smell of the house was like the lamp and the smell of Nancy was like the wick, like they were waiting for one another to begin to smell. She lit the lamp and closed the door and put the bar up. Then she quit talking loud, looking at us.

"What're we going to do?" Caddy said.

"What do yawl want to do?" Nancy said.

"You said we would have some fun," Caddy said.

There was something about Nancy's house; something you could smell besides Nancy and the house. Jason smelled it, even. "I dont want to stay here," he said. "I want to go home."

"Go home, then," Caddy said.

"I dont want to go by myself," Jason said.

"We're going to have some fun," Nancy said.

"How?" Caddy said.

Nancy stood by the door. She was looking at us, only it was like she had emptied her eyes, like she had quit using them. "What do you want to do?" she said.

"Tell us a story," Caddy said. "Can you tell a story?"

"Yes," Nancy said.

"Tell it," Caddy said. We looked at Nancy. "You dont know any stories."

"Yes," Nancy said. "Yes, I do."

She came and sat in a chair before the hearth. There was a little fire there. Nancy built it up, when it was already hot inside. She built a good blaze. She told a story. She talked like her eyes looked, like her eyes watching us and her voice talking to us did not belong to her. Like she was living somewhere else, waiting somewhere else. She was outside the cabin. Her voice was inside and the shape of her, the Nancy that could stoop under a barbed wire fence with a bundle of clothes balanced on her head as though without weight, like a balloon, was there. But that was all. "And so this here queen come walking up to the ditch, where the bad man was hiding. She was walking up to the ditch, and she say, 'If I can just get past this here ditch,' was what she say . . ."

"What ditch?" Caddy said. "A ditch like that one out there? Why did a queen want to go into a ditch?"

"To get to her house," Nancy said. She looked at us. "She had to cross the ditch to get into her house quick and bar the door."

"Why did she want to go home and bar the door?" Caddy said.

IV

Nancy looked at us. She quit talking. She looked at us. Jason's legs stuck straight out of his pants where he sat on Nancy's lap. "I dont think that's a good story," he said. "I want to go home."

"Maybe we had better," Caddy said. She got up from the floor. "I bet they are looking for us right now." She went toward the door.

"No," Nancy said. "Dont open it." She got up quick and passed Caddy. She didn't touch the door, the wooden bar.

"Why not?" Caddy said.

"Come back to the lamp," Nancy said. "We'll have fun. You dont have to go."

"We ought to go," Caddy said. "Unless we have a lot of fun." She and Nancy came back to the fire, the lamp.

"I want to go home," Jason said. "I'm going to tell."

"I know another story," Nancy said. She stood close to the lamp. She looked at Caddy, like when your eyes look up at a stick balanced on your nose. She had to look down to see Caddy, but her eyes looked like that, like when you are balancing a stick.

"I wont listen to it," Jason said. "I'll bang on the floor."

"It's a good one," Nancy said. "It's better than the other one."

"What's it about?" Caddy said. Nancy was standing by the lamp. Her hand was on the lamp, against the light, long and brown.

"Your hand is on that hot globe," Caddy said. "Dont it feel hot to your hand?"

Nancy looked at her hand on the lamp chimney. She took her hand away, slow. She stood there, looking at Caddy, wringing her long hand as though it were tied to her wrist with a string.

"Let's do something else," Caddy said.

"I want to go home," Jason said.

"I got some popcorn," Nancy said. She looked at Caddy and then at Jason and then at me and then at Caddy again. "I got some popcorn."

"I dont like popcorn," Jason said. "I'd rather have candy."

Nancy looked at Jason. "You can hold the popper." She was still wringing her hand; it was long and limp and brown.

"All right," Jason said. "I'll stay a while if I can do that. Caddy cant hold it. I'll want to go home again if Caddy holds the popper."

Nancy built up the fire. "Look at Nancy putting her hands in the fire," Caddy said. "What's the matter with you, Nancy?"

"I got popcorn," Nancy said. "I got some." She took the popper from under the bed. It was broken. Jason began to cry.

"Now we cant have any popcorn," he said.

"We ought to go home, anyway," Caddy said. "Come on, Quentin."

"Wait," Nancy said; "wait. I can fix it. Dont you want to help me fix it?"

"I dont think I want any," Caddy said. "It's too late now."

"You help me, Jason," Nancy said. "Dont you want to help me?"

"No," Jason said. "I want to go home."

"Hush," Nancy said; "hush. Watch. Watch me. I can fix it so Jason can hold it and pop the corn." She got a piece of wire and fixed the popper.

"It wont hold good," Caddy said.

"Yes, it will," Nancy said. "Yawl watch. Yawl help me shell some corn."

The popcorn was under the bed too. We shelled it into the popper and Nancy helped Jason hold the popper over the fire.

"It's not popping," Jason said. "I want to go home."

"You wait," Nancy said. "It'll begin to pop. We'll have fun then." She was sitting close to the fire. The lamp was turned up so high it was beginning to smoke.

"Why dont you turn it down some?" I said.

"It's all right," Nancy said. "I'll clean it. Yawl wait. The popcorn will start in a minute."

"I dont believe it's going to start," Caddy said. "We ought to start home, anyway. They'll be worried."

"No," Nancy said. "It's going to pop. Dilsey will tell um yawl with me. I been working for yawl long time. They wont mind if yawl at my house. You wait, now. It'll start popping any minute now."

Then Jason got some smoke in his eyes and he began to cry. He dropped the popper into the fire. Nancy got a wet rag and wiped Jason's face, but he didn't stop crying.

"Hush," she said. "Hush." But he didn't hush. Caddy took the popper out of the fire.

"It's burned up," she said. "You'll have to get some more popcorn, Nancy."

"Did you put all of it in?" Nancy said.

"Yes," Caddy said. Nancy looked at Caddy. Then she took the popper and opened it and poured the cinders into her apron and began to sort the grains, her hands long and brown, and we watching her.

"Haven't you got any more?" Caddy said.

"Yes," Nancy said; "yes. Look. This here aint burnt. All we need to do is —"

"I want to go home," Jason said. "I'm going to tell."

"Hush," Caddy said. We all listened. Nancy's head was already turned toward the barred door, her eyes filled with red lamplight. "Somebody is coming," Caddy said.

Then Nancy began to make that sound again, not loud, sitting there above the fire, her long hands dangling between her knees; all of a sudden water began to come out on her face in big drops, running down her face, carrying in each one a little turning ball of firelight like a spark until it dropped off her chin. "She's not crying," I said.

"I aint crying," Nancy said. Her eyes were closed. "I aint crying. Who is it?"

"I don't know," Caddy said. She went to the door and looked out. "We've got to go now," she said. "Here comes father."

"I'm going to tell," Jason said. "Yawl made me come."

The water still ran down Nancy's face. She turned in her chair. "Listen. Tell him. Tell him we going to have fun. Tell him I take good care of yawl until in the morning. Tell him to let me come home with yawl and sleep on the floor. Tell him I wont need no pallet. We'll have fun. You member last time how we had so much fun?"

"I didn't have fun," Jason said. "You hurt me. You put smoke in my eyes. I'm going to tell."

V

Father came in. He looked at us. Nancy did not get up.

"Tell him," she said.

"Caddy made us come down here," Jason said. "I didn't want to."

Father came to the fire. Nancy looked up at him. "Cant you go to Aunt Rachel's and stay?" he said. Nancy looked up at father, her hands between her knees. "He's not here," father said. "I would have seen him. There's not a soul in sight."

"He in the ditch," Nancy said. "He waiting in the ditch yonder."

"Nonsense," father said. He looked at Nancy. "Do you know he's there?"

"I got the sign," Nancy said.

"What sign?"

"I got it. It was on the table when I come in. It was a hogbone, with blood meat still on it, laying by the lamp. He's out there. When yawl walk out that door, I gone."

"Gone where, Nancy?" Caddy said.

"I'm not a tattletale," Jason said.

"Nonsense," father said.

"He out there," Nancy said. "He looking through that window this minute, waiting for yawl to go. Then I gone."

"Nonsense," father said. "Lock up your house and we'll take you on to Aunt Rachel's."

"'Twont do no good," Nancy said. She didn't look at father now, but he looked down at her, at her long, limp, moving hands. "Putting it off wont do no good."

"Then what do you want to do?" father said.

"I dont know," Nancy said. "I cant do nothing. Just put it off. And that dont do no good. I reckon it belong to me. I reckon what I going to get aint no more than mine."

"Get what?" Caddy said. "What's yours?"

"Nothing," father said. "You all must get to bed."

"Caddy made me come," Jason said.

"Go on to Aunt Rachel's," father said.

"It wont do no good," Nancy said. She sat before the fire, her elbows on her knees, her long hands between her knees. "When even your own kitchen wouldn't do no good. When even if I was sleeping on the floor in the room with your chillen, and the next morning there I am, and blood —"

"Hush," father said. "Lock the door and put out the lamp and go to bed."

"I scaired of the dark," Nancy said. "I scaired for it to happen in the dark."

"You mean you're going to sit right here with the lamp lighted?" father said. Then Nancy began to make the sound again, sitting before the fire, her long hands between her knees. "Ah, damnation," father said. "Come along, chillen. It's past bedtime."

"When yawl go home, I gone," Nancy said. She talked quieter now, and her face looked quiet, like her hands. "Anyway, I got my coffin money saved up with Mr. Lovelady." Mr. Lovelady was a short, dirty man who collected the Negro insurance, coming around to the cabins or the kitchens every Saturday morning, to collect fifteen cents. He and his wife lived at the hotel. One morning his wife committed suicide. They had a child, a little girl. He and the child went away. After a week or two he came back alone. We would see him going along the lanes and the back streets on Saturday mornings.

"Nonsense," father said. "You'll be the first thing I'll see in the kitchen tomorrow morning."

"You'll see what you'll see, I reckon," Nancy said. "But it will take the Lord to say what that will be."

VI

We left her sitting before the fire.

"Come and put the bar up," father said. But she didn't move. She didn't look at us again, sitting quietly there between the lamp and the fire. From some distance down the lane we could look back and see her through the open door.

"What, Father?" Caddy said. "What's going to happen?"

"Nothing," father said. Jason was on father's back, so Jason was the tallest of all of us. We went down into the ditch. I looked at it, quiet. I couldn't see much where the moonlight and the shadows tangled.

"If Jesus is hid here, he can see us, cant he?" Caddy said.

"He's not there," father said. "He went away a long time ago."

"You made me come," Jason said, high; against the sky it looked like father had two heads, a little one and a big one. "I didn't want to."

We went up out of the ditch. We could still see Nancy's house and the open door, but we couldn't see Nancy now, sitting before the fire with the door open, because she was tired. "I just done got tired," she said. "I just a nigger. It aint no fault of mine."

But we could hear her, because she began just after we came up out of the ditch, the sound that was not singing and not unsinging. "Who will do our washing now, Father?" I said.

"I'm not a nigger," Jason said, high and close above father's head.

"You're worse," Caddy said, "you are a tattletale. If something was to jump out, you'd be scairder than a nigger."

"I wouldn't," Jason said.

"You'd cry," Caddy said.

"Caddy," father said.

"I wouldn't!" Jason said.

"Scairy cat," Caddy said.

"Candace!" father said.

Jorge Luis Borges
1899–1986

Born in Buenos Aires of Spanish and English parentage, Borges exemplifies the staying power of antirealist fiction in our time. From age fifty-six he was totally blind. This did not hinder him from pursuing a magnificent career as poet, critic, delver into arcane fields of scholarship, and artificer of speculative universes.

Fantastic is too shallow an adjective to fit his "fictions." They work (or play) with profound enigmas — those of time, infinity, identity, the nature of reality, the dream life that flows into and fuses with our conscious existence. For Borges's art "the hallucinatory nature of the world" is a requisite.

In addition to these central interests, "Tlön" displays the vein of mingled sober and invented scholarship that pervades so much of his work, infusing humor and irony. At first "Tlön" hardly seems a story at all, but rather a deadpan account of an imaginary planet, in the tradition of Lucian and Swift. Soon, however, we begin to feel it as an intricate, detailed metaphor, suggesting all potential impingements of the imagination on what we term reality. And this metaphor, for all its calculated tone of academic exposition, turns out to be a true narrative, a progression through a labyrinth, every sentence directed toward the climax: "The world will be Tlön."

Tlön, Uqbar, Orbis Tertius

I

I OWE the discovery of Uqbar to the conjunction of a mirror and an encyclopedia. The mirror troubled the depths of a corridor in a country house on Gaona Street in Ramos Mejía; the encyclopedia is fallaciously called *The Anglo-American Cyclopaedia* (New York, 1917) and is a literal but delinquent reprint of the *Encyclopaedia Britannica* of 1902. The event took place some five years ago. Bioy Casares had had dinner with me that evening and we became lengthily engaged in a vast polemic concerning the composition of a novel in the first person, whose narrator would omit or disfigure the facts and indulge in various contradictions which would permit a few readers — very few readers — to perceive an atrocious or banal reality. From the remote depths of the corridor, the mirror spied upon us. We discovered (such a discovery is inevitable in the late hours of the night) that mirrors have something monstrous about them. Then Bioy Casares recalled that one of the heresiarchs of Uqbar had declared that mirrors and copulation are abominable, because they increase the number of men. I asked him the origin of this memorable observation and he answered that it was reproduced in *The Anglo-American Cyclopaedia,* in its article on Uqbar. The house (which we had rented furnished) had a set of this work. On the last pages of Volume XLVI we found an article on Upsala; on the first pages of Volume XLVII, one on Ural-Altaic Languages, but not a word about Uqbar. Bioy, a bit taken aback, consulted the volumes of the index. In vain he exhausted all of the imaginable spellings: Ukbar, Ucbar, Ooqbar, Ookbar, Oukbahr . . . Before leaving, he told me that it was a region of Iraq or of Asia Minor. I must confess that I agreed with some discomfort. I conjectured that this undocumented country and it anonymous heresiarch were a fiction devised by Bioy's modesty in order to justify a statement. The fruitless examination of one of Justus Perthes' atlases fortified my doubt.

The following day, Bioy called me from Buenos Aires. He told me he had before him the article on Uqbar, in Volume XLVI of the encyclopedia. The heresiarch's name was not forthcoming, but there was a note on his doctrine, formulated in words almost identical to those he had repeated, though perhaps literarily inferior. He had recalled: *Copulation and mirrors are abominable.* The text of the encyclopedia said: *For one*

of those gnostics, the visible universe was an illusion (or more precisely)
a sophism. Mirrors and fatherhood are abominable because they multi-
ply and disseminate that universe. I told him, in all truthfulness, that I
should like to see that article. A few days later he brought it. This surprised me, since the scrupulous cartographical indices of Ritter's *Erd-*
kunde were plentifully ignorant of the name Uqbar.

The tome Bioy brought was, in fact, Volume XLVI of the *Anglo-Amer-*
ican Cyclopaedia. On the half-title page and the spine, the alphabetical
marking (Tor-Ups) was that of our copy, but, instead of 917, it contained
921 pages. These four additional pages made up the article on Uqbar,
which (as the reader will have noticed) was not indicated by the alphabetical marking. We later determined that there was no other difference
between the volumes. Both of them (as I believe I have indicated) are
reprints of the tenth *Encyclopaedia Britannica.* Bioy had acquired his
copy at some sale or other.

We read the article with some care. The passage recalled by Bioy was
perhaps the only surprising one. The rest of it seemed very plausible,
quite in keeping with the general tone of the work and (as is natural) a
bit boring. Reading it over again, we discovered beneath its rigorous
prose a fundamental vagueness. Of the fourteen names which figured in
the geographical part, we only recognized three — Khorasan, Armenia,
Erzerum — interpolated in the text in an ambiguous way. Of the historical names, only one: the impostor magician Smerdis, invoked more as
a metaphor. The note seemed to fix the boundaries of Uqbar, but its
nebulous reference points were rivers and craters and mountain ranges
of that same region. We read, for example, that the lowlands of Tsai
Khaldun and the Axa Delta marked the southern frontier and that on
the islands of the delta wild horses procreate. All this, on the first part
of page 918. In the historical section (page 920) we learned that as a
result of the religious persecutions of the thirteenth century, the orthodox believers sought refuge on these islands, where to this day their
obelisks remain and where it is not uncommon to unearth their stone
mirrors. The section on Language and Literature was brief. Only one
trait is worthy of recollection: it noted that the literature of Uqbar was
one of fantasy and that its epics and legends never referred to reality,
but to the two imaginary regions of Mlejnas and Tlön . . . The bibliog-
raphy enumerated four volumes which we have not yet found, though
the third — Silas Haslam: *History of the Land Called Uqbar,* 1874 —
figures in the catalogues of Bernard Quaritch's book shop.[1] The first,
Lesbare und lesenswerthe Bemerkungen über das Land Ukkbar in
Klein-Asien, dates from 1641 and is the work of Johannes Valentinus
Andreä. This fact is significant; a few years later, I came upon that name
in the unsuspected pages of De Quincey (*Writings,* Volume XIII) and
learned that it belonged to a German theologian who, in the early sev-

---

[1] Haslam has also published *A General History of Labyrinths.*

enteenth century, described the imaginary community of Rosae Crucis
— a community that others founded later, in imitation of what he had
prefigured.

That night we visited the National Library. In vain we exhausted atlases, catalogues, annuals of geographical societies, travelers' and historians' memoirs: no one had ever been in Uqbar. Neither did the general index of Bioy's encyclopedia register that name. The following day,
Carlos Mastronardi (to whom I had related the matter) noticed the black
and gold covers of the *Anglo-American Cyclopaedia* in a bookshop on
Corrientes and Talcahuano . . . He entered and examined Volume XLVI.
Of course, he did not find the slightest indication of Uqbar.

II

Some limited and waning memory of Herbert Ashe, an engineer of the
southern railways, persists in the hotel at Adrogué, amongst the effusive
honeysuckles and in the illusory depths of the mirrors. In his lifetime,
he suffered from unreality, as do so many Englishmen; once dead, he is
not even the ghost he was then. He was tall and listless and his tired
rectangular beard had once been red. I understand he was a widower,
without children. Every few years he would go to England, to visit (I
judge from some photographs he showed us) a sundial and a few oaks.
He and my father had entered into one of those close (the adjective is
excessive) English friendships that begin by excluding confidences and
very soon dispense with dialogue. They used to carry out an exchange
of books and newspapers and engage in taciturn chess games . . . I remember him in the hotel corridor, with a mathematics book in his hand,
sometimes looking at the irrecoverable colors of the sky. One afternoon,
we spoke of the duodecimal system of numbering (in which twelve is
written as 10). Ashe said that he was converting some kind of tables
from the duodecimal to the sexagesimal system (in which sixty is written
as 10). He added that the task had been entrusted to him by a Norwe-
gian, in Rio Grande do Sul. We had known him for eight years and he
had never mentioned his sojourn in that region . . . We talked of country
life, of the *capangas,* of the Brazilian etymology of the word *gaucho*
(which some old Uruguayans still pronounce *gaúcho*) and nothing more
was said — may God forgive me — of duodecimal functions. In September of 1937 (we were not at the hotel), Herbert Ashe died of a ruptured
aneurysm. A few days before, he had received a sealed and certified
package from Brazil. It was a book in large octavo. Ashe left it at the
bar, where — months later — I found it. I began to leaf through it and
experienced an astonished and airy feeling of vertigo which I shall not

describe, for this is not the story of my emotions but of Uqbar and Tlön and Orbis Tertius. On one of the nights of Islam called the Night of Nights, the secret doors of heaven open wide and the water in the jars becomes sweeter; if those doors opened, I would not feel what I felt that afternoon. The book was written in English and contained 1001 pages. On the yellow leather back I read these curious words which were repeated on the title page: *A First Encyclopaedia of Tlön. Vol. XI. Hlaer to Jangr.* There was no indication of date or place. On the first page and on a leaf of silk paper that covered one of the color plates there was stamped a blue oval with this inscription: *Orbis Tertius.* Two years before I had discovered, in a volume of a certain pirated encyclopedia, a superficial description of a nonexistent country; now chance afforded me something more precious and arduous. Now I held in my hands a vast methodical fragment of an unknown planet's entire history, with its architecture and its playing cards, with the dread of its mythologies and the murmur of its languages, with its emperors and its seas, with its minerals and its birds and its fish, with its algebra and its fire, with its theological and metaphysical controversy. And all of it articulated, coherent, with no visible doctrinal intent or tone of parody.

In the "Eleventh Volume" which I have mentioned, there are allusions to preceding and succeeding volumes. In an article in the *N. R. F.* which is now classic, Néstor Ibarra has denied the existence of those companion volumes; Ezequiel Martínez Estrada and Drieu La Rochelle have refuted that doubt, perhaps victoriously. The fact is that up to now the most diligent inquiries have been fruitless. In vain we have upended the libraries of the two Americas and of Europe. Alfonso Reyes, tired of these subordinate sleuthing procedures, proposes that we should all undertake the task of reconstructing the many and weighty tomes that are lacking: *ex ungue leonem.* He calculates, half in earnest and half jokingly, that a generation of *tlönistas* should be sufficent. This venturesome computation brings us back to the fundamental problem: Who are the inventors of Tlön? The plural is inevitable, because the hypothesis of a lone inventor — an infinite Leibniz laboring away darkly and modestly — has been unanimously discounted. It is conjectured that this brave new world is the work of a secret society of astronomers, biologists, engineers, metaphysicians, poets, chemists, algebraists, moralists, painters, geometers . . . directed by an obscure man of genius. Individuals mastering these diverse disciplines are abundant, but not so those capable of inventiveness and less so those capable of subordinating that inventiveness to a rigorous and systematic plan. This plan is so vast that each writer's contribution is infinitesimal. At first it was believed that Tlön was a mere chaos, an irresponsible license of the imagination; now it is known that it is a cosmos and that the intimate laws which govern it have been formulated, at least provisionally. Let it suffice for me to recall that the apparent contradictions of the Eleventh Volume are the fundamental basis for the proof that the other volumes exist, so lucid and exact is the order observed in it. The popular magazines, with pardonable excess, have spread news of the zoology and topography of Tlön; I think its transparent tigers and towers of blood perhaps do not merit the continued attention of *all* men. I shall venture to request a few minutes to expound its concept of the universe.

Hume noted for all time that Berkeley's arguments did not admit the slightest refutation nor did they cause the slightest conviction. This dictum is entirely correct in its application to the earth, but entirely false in Tlön. The nations of this planet are congenitally idealist. Their language and the derivations of their language — religion, letters, metaphysics — all presuppose idealism. The world for them is not a concourse of objects in space; it is a heterogeneous series of independent acts. It is successive and temporal, not spatial. There are no nouns in Tlön's conjectural *Ursprache*, from which the "present" languages and the dialects are derived: there are impersonal verbs, modified by monosyllabic suffixes (or prefixes) with an adverbial value. For example: there is no word corresponding to the word "moon," but there is a verb which in English would be "to moon" or "to moonate." "The moon rose above the river" is *hlör u fang axaxaxas mlö,* or literally: "upward behind the onstreaming it mooned."

The preceding applies to the languages of the southern hemisphere. In those of the northern hemisphere (on whose *Ursprache* there is very little data in the Eleventh Volume) the prime unit is not the verb, but the monosyllabic adjective. The noun is formed by an accumulation of adjectives. They do not say "moon," but rather "round airy-light on dark" or "pale-orange-of-the-sky" or any other such combination. In the example selected the mass of adjectives refers to a real object, but this is purely fortuitous. The literature of this hemisphere (like Meinong's subsistent world) abounds in ideal objects, which are convoked and dissolved in a moment, according to poetic needs. At times they are determined by mere simultaneity. There are objects composed of two terms, one of visual and another of auditory character: the color of the rising sun and the faraway cry of a bird. There are objects of many terms: the sun and the water on a swimmer's chest, the vague tremulous rose color we see with our eyes closed, the sensation of being carried along by a river and also by sleep. These second-degree objects can be combined with others; through the use of certain abbreviations, the process is practically infinite. There are famous poems made up of one enormous word. This word forms a *poetic object* created by the author. The fact that no one believes in the reality of nouns paradoxically causes their number to be unending. The languages of Tlön's northern hemisphere contain all the nouns of the Indo-European languages — and many others as well.

It is no exaggeration to state that the classic culture of Tlön comprises only one discipline: psychology. All others are subordinated to it. I have said that the men of this planet conceive the universe as a series of mental processes which do not develop in space but successively in time. Spinoza ascribes to his inexhaustible divinity the attributes of extension and thought; no one in Tlön would understand the juxtaposition of the first (which is typical only of certain states) and the second — which is a perfect synonym of the cosmos. In other words, they do not conceive that the spatial persists in time. The perception of a cloud of smoke on the horizon and then of the burning field and then of the half-extinguished cigarette that produced the blaze is considered an example of association of ideas.

This monism or complete idealism invalidates all science. If we explain (or judge) a fact, we connect it with another; such linking, in Tlön, is a later state of the subject which cannot affect or illuminate the previous state. Every mental state is irreducible: the mere fact of naming it — i.e., of classifying it — implies a falsification. From which it can be deduced that there are no sciences on Tlön, not even reasoning. The paradoxical truth is that they do exist, and in almost uncountable number. The same thing happens with philosophies as happens with nouns in the northern hemisphere. The fact that every philosophy is by definition a dialectical game, a *Philosophie des Als Ob,* has caused them to multiply. There is an abundance of incredible systems of pleasing design or sensational type. The metaphysicians of Tlön do not seek for the truth or even for verisimilitude, but rather for the astounding. They judge that metaphysics is a branch of fantastic literature. They know that a system is nothing more than the subordination of all aspects of the universe to any one such aspect. Even the phrase "all aspects" is rejectable, for it supposes the impossible addition of the present and of all past moments. Neither is it licit to use the plural "past moments," since it supposes another impossible operation . . . One of the schools of Tlön goes so far as to negate time: it reasons that the present is indefinite, that the future has no reality other than as a present hope, that the past has no reality other than as a present memory.[1] Another school declares that *all time* has already transpired and that our life is only the crepuscular and no doubt falsified and mutilated memory or reflection of an irrecoverable process. Another, that the history of the universe — and in it our lives and the most tenuous detail of our lives — is the scripture produced by a subordinate god in order to communicate with a demon. Another, that the universe is comparable to those cryptographs in which not all the symbols are valid and that only what happens every three hundred nights is true. Another, that while we sleep here, we are awake elsewhere and that in this way every man is two men.

---

[1] Russell (*The Analysis of Mind,* 1921, page 159) supposes that the planet has been created a few minutes ago, furnished with a humanity that "remembers" an illusory past.

Amongst the doctrines of Tlön, none has merited the scandalous reception accorded to materialism. Some thinkers have formulated it with less clarity than fervor, as one might put forth a paradox. In order to facilitate the comprehension of this inconceivable thesis, a heresiarch of the eleventh century[1] devised the sophism of the nine copper coins, whose scandalous renown is in Tlön equivalent to that of the Eleatic paradoxes. There are many versions of this "specious reasoning," which vary the number of coins and the number of discoveries; the following is the most common:

On Tuesday, X crosses a deserted road and loses nine copper coins. On Thursday, Y finds in the road four coins, somewhat rusted by Wednesday's rain. On Friday, Z discovers three coins in the road. On Friday morning, X finds two coins in the corridor of his house. The heresiarch would deduce from this story the reality — i.e., the continuity — of the nine coins which were recovered. *It is absurd* (he affirmed) *to imagine that four of the coins have not existed between Tuesday and Thursday, three between Tuesday and Friday afternoon, two between Tuesday and Friday morning. It is logical to think that they have existed — at least in some secret way, hidden from the comprehension of men — at every moment of those three periods.*

The language of Tlön resists the formulation of this paradox; most people did not even understand it. The defenders of common sense at first did no more than negate the veracity of the anecdote. They repeated that it was a verbal fallacy, based on the rash application of two neologisms not authorized by usage and alien to all rigorous thought: the verbs "find" and "lose," which beg the question, because they presuppose the identity of the first and of the last nine coins. They recalled that all nouns (man, coin, Thursday, Wednesday, rain) have only a metaphorical value. They denounced the treacherous circumstance "somewhat rusted by Wednesday's rain," which presupposes what is trying to be demonstrated: the persistence of the four coins from Tuesday to Thursday. They explained that *equality* is one thing and *identity* another, and formulated a kind of *reductio ad absurdum:* the hypothetical case of nine men who on nine successive nights suffer a severe pain. Would it not be ridiculous — they questioned — to pretend that this pain is one and the same?[2] They said that the heresiarch was prompted only by the blasphemous intention of attributing the divine category of *being* to some simple coins and that at times he negated plurality and at other times did

---

[1] A century, according to the duodecimal system, signifies a period of a hundred and forty-four years.

[2] Today, one of the churches of Tlön Platonically maintains that a certain pain, a certain greenish tint of yellow, a certain temperature, a certain sound, are the only reality. All men, in the vertiginous moment of coitus, are the same man. All men who repeat a line from Shakespeare *are* William Shakespeare.

not. They argued: if equality implies identity, one would also have to admit that the nine coins are one.

Unbelievably, these refutations were not definitive. A hundred years after the problem was stated, a thinker no less brilliant than the heresiarch but of orthodox tradition formulated a very daring hypothesis. This happy conjecture affirmed that there is only one subject, that this indivisible subject is every being in the universe and that these beings are the organs and masks of the divinity. X is Y and is Z. Z discovers three coins because he remembers that X lost them; X finds two in the corridor because he remembers that the others have been found . . . The Eleventh Volume suggests that three prime reasons determined the complete victory of this idealist pantheism. The first, its repudiation of solipsism; the second, the possibility of preserving the psychological basis of the sciences; the third, the possibility of preserving the cult of the gods. Schopenhauer (the passionate and lucid Schopenhauer) formulates a very similar doctrine in the first volume of *Parerga und Paralipomena*.

The geometry of Tlön comprises two somewhat different disciplines: the visual and the tactile. The latter corresponds to our own geometry and is subordinated to the first. The basis of visual geometry is the surface, not the point. This geometry disregards parallel lines and declares that man in his movement modifies the forms which surround him. The basis of its arithmetic is the notion of indefinite numbers. They emphasize the importance of the concepts of greater and lesser, which our mathematicians symbolize as $>$ and $<$. They maintain that the operation of counting modifies quantities and converts them from indefinite into definite sums. The fact that several individuals who count the same quantity should obtain the same result is, for the psychologists, an example of association of ideas or of a good exercise of memory. We already know that in Tlön the subject of knowledge is one and eternal.

In literary practices the idea of a single subject is also all-powerful. It is uncommon for books to be signed. The concept of plagiarism does not exist: it has been established that all works are the creation of one author, who is atemporal and anonymous. The critics often invent authors: they select two dissimilar works — the *Tao Te Ching* and the *1001 Nights*, say — attribute them to the same writer and then determine most scrupulously the psychology of this interesting *homme de lettres* . . .

Their books are also different. Works of fiction contain a single plot, with all its imaginable permutations. Those of a philosophical nature invariably include both the thesis and the antithesis, the rigorous pro and con of a doctrine. A book which does not contain its counterbook is considered incomplete.

Centuries and centuries of idealism have not failed to influence reality. In the most ancient regions of Tlön, the duplication of lost objects is not infrequent. Two persons look for a pencil; the first finds it and says nothing; the second finds a second pencil, no less real, but closer to his expectations. These secondary objects are called *hrönir* and are, though awkward in form, somewhat longer. Until recently, the *hrönir* were the accidental products of distraction and forgetfulness. It seems unbelievable that their methodical production dates back scarcely a hundred years, but this is what the Eleventh Volume tells us. The first efforts were unsuccessful. However, the *modus operandi* merits description. The director of one of the state prisons told his inmates that there were certain tombs in an ancient river bed and promised freedom to whoever might make an important discovery. During the months preceding the excavation the inmates were shown photographs of what they were to find. This first effort proved that expectation and anxiety can be inhibitory; a week's work with pick and shovel did not manage to unearth anything in the way of a *hrön* except a rusty wheel of a period posterior to the experiment. But this was kept in secret and the process was repeated later in four schools. In three of them the failure was almost complete; in the fourth (whose director died accidentally during the first excavations) the students unearthed — or produced — a gold mask, an archaic sword, two or three clay urns and the moldy and mutilated torso of a king whose chest bore an inscription which it has not yet been possible to decipher. Thus was discovered the unreliability of witnesses who knew of the experimental nature of the search . . . Mass investigations produce contradictory objects; now individual and almost improvised jobs are preferred. The methodical fabrication of *hrönir* (says the Eleventh Volume) has performed prodigious services for archaeologists. It has made possible the interrogation and even the modification of the past, which is now no less plastic and docile than the future. Curiously, the *hrönir* of second and third degree — the *hrönir* derived from another *hrön,* those derived from the *hrön* of a *hrön* — exaggerate the aberrations of the initial one; those of fifth degree are almost uniform; those of ninth degree become confused with those of the second; in those of the eleventh there is a purity of line not found in the original. The process is cyclical: the *hrön* of twelfth degree begins to fall off in quality. Stranger and more pure than any *hrön* is, at times, the *ur:* the object produced through suggestion, educed by hope. The great golden mask I have mentioned is an illustrious example.

Things become duplicated in Tlön, they also tend to become effaced and lose their details when they are forgotten. A classic example is the doorway which survived so long as it was visited by a beggar and disappeared at his death. At times some birds, a horse, have saved the ruins of an amphitheater.

Postscript (1947). I reproduce the preceding article just as it appeared in the *Anthology of Fantastic Literature* (1940), with no omission other than that of a few metaphors and a kind of sarcastic summary which now seems frivolous. So many things have happened since then . . . I shall do no more than recall them here.

In March of 1941 a letter written by Gunnar Erfjord was discovered in a book by Hinton which had belonged to Herbert Ashe. The envelope bore a cancellation from Ouro Preto; the letter completely elucidated the mystery of Tlön. Its text corroborated the hypotheses of Martínez Estrada. One night in Lucerne or in London, in the early seventeenth century, the splendid history has its beginning. A secret and benevolent society (amongst whose members were Dalgarno and later George Berkeley) arose to invent a country. Its vague initial program included "hermetic studies," philanthropy and the cabala. From this first period dates the curious book by Andreä. After a few years of secret conclaves and premature syntheses it was understood that one generation was not sufficient to give articulate form to a country. They resolved that each of the masters should elect a disciple who would continue his work. This hereditary arrangement prevailed; after an interval of two centuries the persecuted fraternity sprang up again in America. In 1824, in Memphis (Tennessee), one of its affiliates conferred with the ascetic millionaire Ezra Buckley. The latter, somewhat disdainfully, let him speak — and laughed at the plan's modest scope. He told the agent that in America it was absurd to invent a country and proposed the invention of a planet. To this gigantic idea he added another, a product of his nihilism:[1] that of keeping the enormous enterprise secret. At that time the twenty volumes of the *Encyclopaedia Britannica* were circulating in the United States; Buckley suggested that a methodical encyclopedia of the imaginary planet be written. He was to leave them his mountains of gold, his navigable rivers, his pasture lands roamed by cattle and buffalo, his Negroes, his brothels and his dollars, on one condition: "The work will make no pact with the impostor Jesus Christ." Buckley did not believe in God, but he wanted to demonstrate to this nonexistent God that mortal man was capable of conceiving a world. Buckley was poisoned in Baton Rouge in 1828; in 1914 the society delivered to its collaborators, some three hundred in number, the last volume of the First Encyclopedia of Tlön. The edition was a secret one; its forty volumes (the vastest undertaking ever carried out by man) would be the basis for another more detailed edition, written not in English but in one of the languages of Tlön. This revision of an illusory world, was called, provisionally, *Orbis Tertius* and one of its modest demiurgi was Herbert Ashe, whether as an agent of Gunnar Erfjord or as an affiliate, I do not know. His having received a copy of the Eleventh Volume would seem to favor the latter assumption. But what about the others?

In 1942 events became more intense. I recall one of the first of these with particular clarity and it seems that I perceived then something of

---

[1]Buckley was a freethinker, a fatalist and a defender of slavery.

its premonitory character. It happened in an apartment on Laprida Street, facing a high and light balcony which looked out toward the sunset. Princess Faucigny Lucinge had received her silverware from Poitiers. From the vast depths of a box embellished with foreign stamps, delicate immobile objects emerged: silver from Utrecht and Paris covered with hard heraldic fauna, and a samovar. Amongst them — with the perceptible and tenuous tremor of a sleeping bird — a compass vibrated mysteriously. The Princess did not recognize it. Its blue needle longed for magnetic north; its metal case was concave in shape; the letters around its edge corresponded to one of the alphabets of Tlön. Such was the first intrusion of this fantastic world into the world of reality.

I am still troubled by a stroke of chance which made me the witness of the second intrusion as well. It happened some months later, at a country store owned by a Brazilian in Cuchilla Negra. Amorim and I were returning from Sant' Anna. The River Tacuarembó had flooded and we were obliged to sample (and endure) the proprietor's rudimentary hospitality. He provided us with some creaking cots in a large room cluttered with barrels and hides. We went to bed, but were kept from sleeping until dawn by the drunken ravings of an unseen neighbor, who intermingled inextricable insults with snatches of *milongas* — or rather with snatches of the same *milonga*. As might be supposed, we attributed this insistent uproar to the store owner's fiery cane liquor. By daybreak, the man was dead in the hallway. The roughness of his voice had deceived us: he was only a youth. In his delirium a few coins had fallen from his belt, along with a cone of bright metal, the size of a die. In vain a boy tried to pick up this cone. A man was scarcely able to raise it from the ground. I held it in my hand for a few minutes; I remember that its weight was intolerable and that after it was removed, the feeling of oppressiveness remained. I also remember the exact circle it pressed into my palm. This sensation of a very small and at the same time extremely heavy object produced a disagreeable impression of repugnance and fear. One of the local men suggested we throw it into the swollen river; Amorim acquired it for a few pesos. No one knew anything about the dead man, except that "he came from the border." These small, very heavy cones (made from a metal which is not of this world) are images of the divinity in certain regions of Tlön.

Here I bring the personal part of my narrative to a close. The rest is in the memory (if not in the hopes or fears) of all my readers. Let it suffice for me to recall or mention the following facts, with a mere brevity of words which the reflective recollection of all will enrich or amplify. Around 1944, a person doing research for the newspaper *The American* (of Nashville, Tennessee) brought to light in a Memphis library the forty volumes of the First Encyclopedia of Tlön. Even today there is a controversy over whether this discovery was accidental or whether it was permitted by the directors of the still nebulous *Orbis Tertius*. The latter is most likely. Some of the incredible aspects of the Eleventh Volume (for example, the multiplication of the *hrönir*) have been eliminated or attenuated in the Memphis copies; it is reasonable to imagine that these omissions follow the plan of exhibiting a world which is not too incompatible with the real world. The dissemination of objects from Tlön over different countries would complement this plan . . . [1] The fact is that the international press infinitely proclaimed the "find." Manuals, anthologies, summaries, literal versions, authorized re-editions and pirated editions of the Greatest Work of Man flooded and still flood the earth. Almost immediately, reality yielded on more than one account. The truth is that it longed to yield. Ten years ago any symmetry with a semblance of order — dialectical materialism, anti-Semitism, Nazism — was sufficient to entrance the minds of men. How could one do other than submit to Tlön, to the minute and vast evidence of an orderly planet? It is useless to answer that reality is also orderly. Perhaps it is, but in accordance with divine laws — I translate: inhuman laws — which we never quite grasp. Tlön is surely a labyrinth, but it is a labyrinth devised by men, a labyrinth destined to be deciphered by men.

The contact and the habit of Tlön have disintegrated this world. Enchanted by its rigor, humanity forgets over and again that it is a rigor of chess masters, not of angels. Already the schools have been invaded by the (conjectural) "primitive language" of Tlön; already the teaching of its harmonious history (filled with moving episodes) has wiped out the one which governed in my childhood; already a fictitious past occupies in our memories the place of another, a past of which we know nothing with certainty — not even that it is false. Numismatology, pharmacology and archaeology have been reformed. I understand that biology and mathematics also await their avatars . . . A scattered dynasty of solitary men has changed the face of the world. Their task continues. If our forecasts are not in error, a hundred years from now someone will discover the hundred volumes of the Second Encyclopedia of Tlön.

Then English and French and mere Spanish will disappear from the globe. The world will be Tlön. I pay no attention to all this and go on revising, in the still days at the Adrogué hotel, an uncertain Quevedian translation (which I do not intend to publish) of Browne's *Urn Burial*.

---

[1] There remains, of course, the problem of the *material* of some objects.

ELIZABETH BOWEN
1899–1973

While in the main it is proper to say that Henry James founded no school, his influence on Elizabeth Bowen, always auspicious, is commonly noted by critics. Like him, she dealt intimately with upper-middle-class gentry, in her case often Anglo-Irish. Like him, she was drawn to the observation of the subtlest of human relationships. Like him, she elaborated a style, though far less mandarin, reflecting the finely bred sensibility of her characters.

Yet she remained her own woman. Her voice is unmistakable, whether we hear it in her novels (such as The Death of the Heart and The Hotel), such memoirs as Bowen's Court, or her many short stories, seventy-nine in all.

The short story, as she saw it, "allows for what is crazy about humanity: obstinacies, inordinate heroisms, 'immortal longings.' " "Mysterious Kôr," one of the finest of her wartime tales, proceeds from this inclination of her mind. Two young women and a young man respond in different ways to the stark human fact of loneliness and to their own small immortal longings set against "the war's total of unlived lives." I suppose Kôr, the ghost city, to be of the same family as James's Great Good Place, the abiding place of the imagination, all that war would destroy.

Delicate, almost tremulous in its rhythm, "Mysterious Kôr," if we listen to it carefully, says more about life during the Blitz than the most explicit reportage.

Mysterious Kôr

FULL MOONLIGHT drenched the city and searched it; there was not a niche left to stand in. The effect was remorseless: London looked like the moon's capital — shallow, cratered, extinct. It was late, but not yet midnight; now the buses had stopped the polished roads and streets in this region sent for minutes together a ghostly unbroken reflection up. The soaring new flats and the crouching old shops and houses looked equally brittle under the moon, which blazed in windows that looked its way. The futility of the black-out became laughable: from the sky, presumably, you could see every slate in the roofs, every whited kerb, every contour of the naked winter flowerbeds in the park; and the lake, with its shining twists and tree-darkened islands would be a landmark for miles, yes, miles, overhead.

However, the sky, in whose glassiness floated no clouds but only opaque balloons, remained glassy-silent. The Germans no longer came by the full moon. Something more immaterial seemed to threaten, and to be keeping people at home. This day between days, this extra tax, was perhaps more than senses and nerves could bear. People stayed indoors with a fervour that could be felt: the buildings strained with battened-down human life, but not a beam, not a voice, not a note from a radio escaped. Now and then under streets and buildings the earth rumbled: the Underground sounded loudest at this time.

Outside the now gateless gates of the park, the road coming downhill from the north-west turned south and became a street, down whose perspective the traffic lights went through their unmeaning performance of changing colour. From the promontory of pavement outside the gates you saw at once up the road and down the street: from behind where you stood, between the gateposts, appeared the lesser strangeness of grass and water and trees. At this point, at this moment, three French soldiers, directed to a hostel they could not find, stopped singing to listen derisively to the waterbirds wakened up by the moon. Next, two wardens coming off duty emerged from their post and crossed the road diagonally, each with an elbow cupped inside a slung-on tin hat. The wardens turned their faces, mauve in the moonlight, towards the Frenchmen with no expression at all. The two sets of steps died in opposite directions, and, the birds subsiding, nothing was heard or seen until, a little way down the street, a trickle of people came out of the Underground, around the anti-panic brick wall. These all disappeared quickly, in an abashed way, or as though dissolved in the street by some white acid, but for a girl and a soldier who, by their way of walking, seemed to have no destination but each other and to be not quite certain even of that. Blotted into one shadow he tall, she little, these two proceeded towards the park. They looked in, but did not go in; they stood there debating without speaking. Then, as though a command from the street behind them had been received by their synchronized bodies, they faced round to look back the way they had come.

His look up the height of a building made his head drop back, and she saw his eyeballs glitter. She slid her hand from his sleeve, stepped to the edge of the pavement and said: "Mysterious Kôr."

"What is?" he said, not quite collecting himself.

"This is —

> 'Mysterious Kôr thy walls forsaken stand,
> Thy lonely towers beneath a lonely moon —'
>
> — this is Kôr."

"Why," he said, "it's years since I've thought of that."

She said: "I think of it all the time —

> 'Not in the waste beyond the swamps and sand,
> The fever-haunted forest and lagoon,
> Mysterious Kôr thy walls —'

— a completely forsaken city, as high as cliffs and as white as bones, with no history —"

"But something must once have happened: why had it been forsaken?"

"How could anyone tell you when there's nobody there?"

"Nobody there since how long?"

"Thousands of years."

"In that case, it would have fallen down."

"No, not Kôr," she said with immediate authority. "Kôr's altogether different; it's very strong; there is not a crack in it anywhere for a weed to grow in; the corners of stones and the monuments might have been cut yesterday, and the stairs and arches are built to support themselves."

"You know all about it," he said, looking at her.

"I know, I know all about it."

"What, since you read that book?"

"Oh, I didn't get much from that; I just got the name. I knew that must be the right name; it's like a cry."

"Most like the cry of a crow to me." He reflected, then said: "But the poem begins with 'Not' — 'Not in the waste beyond the swamps and sand —' And it goes on, as I remember, to prove Kôr's not really anywhere. When even a poem says there's no such place —"

"What it tries to say doesn't matter: I see what it makes me see. Anyhow, that was written some time ago, at that time when they thought they had got everything taped, because the whole world had been explored, even the middle of Africa. Every thing and place had been found and marked on some map; so what wasn't marked on any map couldn't be there at all. So *they* thought: that was why he wrote the poem. '*The world is disenchanted,*' it goes on. That was what set me off hating civilization."

"Well, cheer up," he said; "there isn't much of it left."

"Oh, yes, I cheered up some time ago. This war shows we've by no means come to the end. If you can blow whole places out of existence, you can blow whole places into it. I don't see why not. They say we can't say what's come out since the bombing started. By the time we've come to the end, Kôr may be the one city left: the abiding city. I should laugh."

"No, you wouldn't," he said sharply. "*You* wouldn't — at least, I hope not. I hope you don't know what you're saying — does the moon make you funny?"

"Don't be cross about Kôr; please don't, Arthur," she said.

"I thought girls thought about people."

"What, these days?" she said. "Think about people? How can anyone think about people if they've got any heart? I don't know how other girls manage: I always think about Kôr."

"Not about me?" he said. When she did not at once answer, he turned her hand over, in anguish, inside his grasp. "Because I'm not there when you want me — is that my fault?"

"But to think about Kôr *is* to think about you and me."

"In that dead place?"

"No, ours — we'd be alone here."

Tightening his thumb on her palm while he thought this over, he looked behind them, around them, above them — even up at the sky. He said finally: "But we're alone here."

"That was why I said 'Mysterious Kôr.' "

"What, you mean we're there now, that here's there, that now's then? . . . *I* don't mind," he added, letting out as a laugh the sigh he had been holding in for some time. "You ought to know the place, and for all I could tell you we might be anywhere: I often do have it, this funny feeling, the first minute or two when I've come up out of the Underground. Well, well: join the Army and see the world." He nodded towards the perspective of traffic lights and said, a shade craftily: "What are those, then?"

Having caught the quickest possible breath, she replied: "Inexhaustible gases; they bored through to them and lit them as they came up; by changing colour they show the changing of minutes; in Kôr there is no sort of other time."

"You've got the moon, though: that can't help making months."

"Oh, and the sun, of course; but those two could do what they liked; we should not have to calculate when they'd come or go."

"We might not have to," he said, "but I bet I should."

"I should not mind what you did, so long as you never said, 'What next?'"

"I don't know about 'next,' but I do know what we'd do first."

"What, Arthur?"

"Populate Kôr."

She said: "I suppose it would be all right if our children were to marry each other?"

But her voice faded out; she had been reminded that they were homeless on this his first night of leave. They were, that was to say, in London without any hope of any place of their own. Pepita shared a two-roomed flatlet with a girl friend, in a by-street off the Regent's Park Road, and towards this they must make their half-hearted way. Arthur was to have the sitting-room divan, usually occupied by Pepita, while she herself had half of her girl friend's bed. There was really no room for a third, and least of all for a man, in those small rooms packed with furniture and the two girls' belongings: Pepita tried to be grateful for her friend Callie's forbearance — but how could she be, when it had not occurred to Callie that she would do better to be away tonight? She was more slow-witted than narrow-minded — but Pepita felt she owed a kind of ruin to her. Callie, not yet known to be home later than ten, would be now waiting up, in her house-coat, to welcome Arthur. That would mean three-sided chat, drinking cocoa, then turning in: that would be that, and that would be all. That was London, this war — they were lucky to have a roof — London, full enough before the Americans came. Not a place: they would even grudge you sharing a grave — that was what even married couples complained. Whereas in Kôr . . .

In Kôr . . . Like glass, the illusion shattered: a car hummed like a hornet towards them, veered, showed its scarlet tail-light, streaked away up the road. A woman edged round a front door and along the area railings timidly called her cat; meanwhile a clock near, then another set further back in the dazzling distance, set about striking midnight. Pepita, feeling Arthur release her arm with an abruptness that was the inverse of passion, shivered; whereat he asked brusquely: "Cold? Well, which way? — we'd better be getting on."

Callie was no longer waiting up. Hours ago she had set out the three cups and saucers, the tins of cocoa and household milk and, on the gas-ring, brought the kettle to just short of the boil. She had turned open Arthur's bed, the living-room divan, in the neat inviting way she had learnt at home — then, with a modest impulse, replaced the cover. She had, as Pepita foresaw, been wearing her cretonne housecoat, the nearest thing to a hostess gown that she had; she had already brushed her hair for the night, rebraided it, bound the braids in a coronet round her head. Both lights and the wireless had been on, to make the room both look and sound gay: all alone, she had come to that peak moment at which company should arrive — but so seldom does. From then on she felt welcome beginning to wither in her, a flower of the heart that had bloomed too early. There she had sat like an image, facing the three cold cups, on the edge of the bed to be occupied by an unknown man.

Callie's innocence and her still unsought-out state had brought her to take a proprietary pride in Arthur; this was all the stronger, perhaps, because they had not yet met. Sharing the flat with Pepita, this last year, she had been content with reflecting the heat of love. It was not, surprisingly, that Pepita seemed very happy — there were times when she was palpably on the rack, and this was not what Callie could understand. "Surely you owe it to Arthur," she would then say, "to keep cheerful? So long as you love each other —" Callie's calm brow glowed — one might say that it glowed in place of her friend's; she became the guardian of that ideality which for Pepita was constantly lost to view. It was true, with the sudden prospect of Arthur's leave, things had come nearer to earth: he became a proposition, and she would have been as glad if he could have slept somewhere else. Physically shy, a brotherless virgin, Callie shrank from sharing this flat with a young man. In this flat you could hear everything: what was once a three-windowed Victorian drawing-room had been partitioned, by very thin walls, into kitchenette, living-room, Callie's bedroom. The living-room was in the centre; the two others open off it. What was once the conservatory, half a flight down, was now converted into a draughty bathroom, shared with somebody else on the girl's floor. The flat, for these days, was cheap — even so, it was Callie, earning more than Pepita, who paid the greater part of the rent: it thus became up to her, more or less, to express good will as to Arthur's making a third. "Why, it will be lovely to have him here," Callie said. Pepita accepted the good will without much grace — but then, had she ever much grace to spare? — she was as restlessly secretive, as self-centred, as a little half-grown black cat. Next came a puzzling moment: Pepita seemed to be hinting that Callie should fix herself up somewhere else. "But where would I go?" Callie marvelled when this was at last borne in on her. "You know what London's like now. And, anyway" — here she laughed, but hers was a forehead that coloured as easily as it glowed — "it wouldn't be proper, would it, me going off and leaving just you and Arthur; I don't know what your mother would say to me. No, we may be a little squashed, but we'll make things ever so homey. I shall not mind playing gooseberry, really, dear."

But the hominess by now was evaporating, as Pepita and Arthur still and still did not come. At half-past ten, in obedience to the rule of the house, Callie was obliged to turn off the wireless, whereupon silence out of the stepless street began seeping into the slighted room. Callie recollected the fuel target and turned off her dear little table lamp, gaily painted with spots to make it look like a toadstool, thereby leaving only the hanging light. She laid her hand on the kettle, to find it gone cold again and sigh for the wasted gas if not for her wasted thought. Where are they? Cold crept up her out of the kettle; she went to bed.

Callie's bed lay along the wall under the window: she did not like sleeping so close up under glass, but the clearance that must be left for the opening of door and cupboards made this the only possible place. Now she got in and lay rigidly on the bed's inner side, under the hanging hems of the window curtains, training her limbs not to stray to what would be Pepita's half. This sharing of her bed with another body would not be the least of her sacrifice to the lovers' love; tonight would be the first night — or at least, since she was an infant — that Callie had slept with anyone. Child of a sheltered middle-class household, she had kept physical distances all her life. Already repugnance and shyness ran through her limbs; she was preyed upon by some more obscure trouble than the expectation that she might not sleep. As to *that,* Pepita was restless; her tossings on the divan, her broken-off exclamations and blurred pleas had been to be heard, most nights, through the dividing wall.

Callie knew, as though from a vision, that Arthur would sleep soundly, with assurance and majesty. Did they not all say, too, that a soldier sleeps like a log? With awe she pictured, asleep, the face that she had not yet, awake, seen — Arthur's man's eyelids, cheekbones and set mouth turned up to the darkened ceiling. Wanting to savour darkness herself, Callie reached out and put off her bedside lamp.

At once she knew that something was happening — outdoors, in the street, the whole of London, the world. An advance, an extraordinary movement was silently taking place; blue-white beams overflowed from it, silting, dropping round the edges of the muffling black-out curtains. When, starting up, she knocked a fold of the curtain, a beam like a mouse ran across her bed. A searchlight, the most powerful of all time, might have been turned full and steady upon her defended window; finding flaws in the black-out stuff, it made veins and stars. Once gained by this idea of pressure she could not lie down again; she sat tautly, drawn-up knees touching her breasts, and asked herself if there were anything she should do. She parted the curtains, opened them slowly wider, looked out — and was face to face with the moon.

Below the moon, the houses opposite her window blazed back in transparent shadow; and something — was it a coin or a ring? — glittered half-way across the chalk-white street. Light marched in past her face, and she turned to see where it went: out stood the curves and garlands of the great white marble Victorian mantelpiece of that lost drawing-room; out stood, in the photographs turned her way, the thoughts with which her parents had faced the camera, and the humble puzzlement of her two dogs at home. Of silver brocade, just faintly purpled with roses, became her housecoat hanging over the chair. And the moon did more: it exonerated and beautified the lateness of the lovers' return. No wonder, she said herself, no wonder — if this was the world they walked in, if this was whom they were with. Having drunk in the white explanation, Callie lay down again. Her half of the bed was in shadow, but she allowed one hand to lie, blanched, in what would be Pepita's place. She lay and looked at the hand until it was no longer her own.

Callie woke to the sound of Pepita's key in the latch. But no voices? What had happened? Then she heard Arthur's step. She heard his unslung equipment dropped with a weary, dull sound, and the plonk of his tin hat on a wooden chair. "Sssh-sssh!" Pepita exclaimed, "she *might* be asleep!"

Then at last Arthur's voice: "But I thought you said —"

"I'm not asleep; I'm just coming!" Callie called out with rapture, leaping out from her form in shadow into the moonlight, zipping on her enchanted house-coat over her nightdress, kicking her shoes on, and pinning in place, with a trembling firmness, her plaits in their coronet round her head. Between these movements of hers she heard not another sound. Had she only dreamed they were there? Her heart beat: she stepped through the living-room, shutting her door behind her.

Pepita and Arthur stood the other side of the table; they gave the impression of being lined up. Their faces, at different levels — for Pepita's rough, dark head came only an inch above Arthur's khaki shoulder — were alike in abstention from any kind of expression; as though, spiritually, they both still refused to be here. Their features looked faint, weathered — was this the work of the moon? Pepita said at once: "I suppose we are very late?"

"I don't wonder," Callie said, "on this lovely night."

Arthur had not raised his eyes; he was looking at the three cups. Pepita now suddenly jogged his elbow, saying, "Arthur, wake up; say something; this is Callie — well, Callie, this is Arthur, of course."

"Why, yes of course this is Arthur," returned Callie, whose candid eyes since she entered had not left Arthur's face. Perceiving that Arthur did not know what to do, she advanced round the table to shake hands with him. He looked up, she looked down, for the first time: she rather beheld than felt his red-brown grip on what still seemed her glove of moonlight. "Welcome, Arthur," she said. "I'm so glad to meet you at last. I hope you will be comfortable in the flat."

"It's been kind of you," he said after consideration.

"Please do not feel that," said Callie. "This is Pepita's home, too, and we both hope — don't we, Pepita? — that you'll regard it as yours. Please feel free to do just as you like. I am sorry it is so small."

"Oh, I don't know," Arthur said, as though hypnotized; "it seems a nice little place."

Pepita, meanwhile, glowered and turned away.

Arthur continued to wonder, though he had once been told, how these two unalike girls had come to set up together — Pepita so small, except for her too-big head, compact of childish brusqueness and of unchildish passion, and Callie, so sedate, waxy and tall — an unlit candle. Yes, she was like one of those candles on sale outside a church; there could be something votive even in her demeanour. She was unconscious that her good manners, those of an old fashioned country doctor's daughter, were putting the other two at a disadvantage. He found himself touched by the grave good faith with which Callie was wearing that tartish house-coat, about which her face kept the glaze of sleep; and, as she knelt to relight the gas-ring under the kettle, he marked the strong, delicate arch of one bare foot, disappearing into the arty green shoe. Pepita was now too near him ever again to be seen as he now saw Callie — in a sense, he never *had* seen Pepita for the first time: she had not been, and still sometimes was not, his type. No, he had not thought of her twice; he had not remembered her until he began to remember her with passion. You might say he had not seen Pepita coming: their love had been a collision in the dark.

Callie, determined to get this over, knelt back and said: "Would Arthur like to wash his hands?" When they had heard him stumble down the half-flight of stairs, she said to Pepita: "Yes, I was so glad you had the moon."

"Why?" said Pepita. She added: "There was too much of it."

"You're tired. Arthur looks tired, too."

"How would you know? He's used to marching about. But it's all this having no place to go."

"But, Pepita, you —"

But at this point Arthur came back: from the door he noticed the wireless, and went direct to it. "Nothing much on now, I suppose?" he doubtfully said.

"No; you see it's past midnight; we're off the air. And, anyway, in this house they don't like the wireless late. By the same token," went on Callie, friendly smiling, "I'm afraid I must ask you, Arthur, to take your boots off, unless, of course, you mean to stay sitting down. The people below us —"

Pepita flung off, saying something under her breath, but Arthur, remarking, "No, I don't mind," both sat down and began to take off his boots. Pausing, glancing to left and right at the divan's fresh cotton spread, he said: "It's all right is it, for me to sit on this?"

"That's my bed," said Pepita. "You are to sleep in it."

Callie then made the cocoa, after which they turned in. Preliminary trips to the bathroom having been worked out, Callie was first to retire, shutting the door behind her so that Pepita and Arthur might kiss each other good night. When Pepita joined her, it was without knocking: Pepita stood still in the moon and began to tug off her clothes. Glancing with hate at the bed, she asked: "Which side?"

"I expect you'd like the outside."

"What are you standing about for?"

"I don't really know: as I'm inside I'd better get in first."

"Then why not get in?"

When they had settled rigidly, side by side, Callie asked: "Do you think Arthur's got all he wants?"

Pepita jerked her head up. "We can't sleep in all this moon."

"Why, you don't believe the moon does things, actually?"

"Well, it couldn't hope to make some of us *much* more screwy."

Callie closed the curtains, then said: "What do you mean? And — didn't you hear? — I asked if Arthur's got all he wants."

"That's what I meant — have you got a screw loose, really?"

"Pepita, I won't stay here if you're going to be like this."

"In that case, you had better go in with Arthur."

"What about me?" Arthur loudly said through the wall. "I can hear practically all you girls are saying."

They were both startled — rather that than abashed. Arthur, alone in there, had thrown off the ligatures of his social manner: his voice held the whole authority of his sex — he was impatient, sleepy, and he belonged to no one.

"Sorry," the girls said in unison. Then Pepita laughed soundlessly, making their bed shake, till to stop herself she bit the back of her hand, and this movement made her elbow strike Callie's cheek. "Sorry," she had to whisper. No answer: Pepita fingered her elbow and found, yes, it was quite true, it was wet. "Look, shut up crying, Callie: what have I done?"

Callie rolled right round, in order to press her forehead closely under the window, into the curtains, against the wall. Her weeping continued to be soundless: now and then, unable to reach her handkerchief, she staunched her eyes with a curtain, disturbing slivers of moon. Pepita gave up marvelling, and soon slept: at least there is something in being dog-tired.

A clock struck four as Callie woke up again — but something else had made her open her swollen eyelids. Arthur, stumbling about on his padded feet, could be heard next door attempting to make no noise. Inevitably, he bumped the edge of the table. Callie sat up: by her side Pepita lay like a mummy rolled half over, in forbidding, tenacious sleep. Arthur groaned. Callie caught a breath, climbed lightly over Pepita, felt for her torch on the mantelpiece, stopped to listen again. Arthur groaned again: Callie, with movements soundless as they were certain, opened the door and slipped through to the living-room. "What's the matter?" she whispered. "Are you ill?"

"No; I just got a cigarette. Did I wake you up?"

"But you groaned."

"I'm sorry; I'd no idea."

"But do you often?"

"I've no idea, really, I tell you," Arthur repeated. The air of the room was dense with his presence, overhung by tobacco. He must be sitting on the edge of his bed, wrapped up in his overcoat — she could smell the coat, and each time he pulled on the cigarette his features appeared down there, in the fleeting, dull reddish glow. "Where are you?" he said. "Show a light."

Her nervous touch on her torch, like a reflex to what he said, made it flicker up for a second. "I am just by the door; Pepita's asleep; I'd better go back to bed."

"Listen. Do you two get on each other's nerves?"

"Not till tonight," said Callie, watching the uncertain swoops of the cigarette as he reached across to the ashtray on the edge of the table. Shifting her bare feet patiently, she added: "You don't see us as we usually are."

"She's a girl who shows things in funny ways — I expect she feels bad at our putting you out like this — I know I do. But then we'd got no choice, had we?"

"It is really I who am putting you out," said Callie.

"Well, that can't be helped either, can it? You had the right to stay in your own place. If there'd been more time, we might have gone to the country, though I still don't see where we'd have gone there. It's one harder when you're not married, unless you've got the money. Smoke?"

"No, thank you. Well, if you're all right, I'll go back to bed."

"I'm glad she's asleep — funny the way she sleeps, isn't it? You can't help wondering where she is. You haven't got a boy, have you, just at present?"

"No. I've never had one."

"I'm not sure in one way that you're not better off. I can see there's not so much in it for a girl these days. It makes me feel cruel the way I unsettle her: I don't know how much it's me myself or how much it's something the matter that I can't help. How are any of us to know how things could have been? They forget war's not just only war; it's years out of people's lives that they've never had before and won't have again. Do you think she's fanciful?"

"Who, Pepita?"

"It's enough to make her — tonight was the pay-off. We couldn't get near any movies or any place for sitting; you had to fight into the bars, and she hates the staring in bars, and with all that milling about, every street we went, they kept on knocking her even off my arm. So then we took the tube to that park down there, but the place was as bad as daylight, let alone it was cold. We hadn't the nerve — well, that's nothing to do with you."

"I don't mind."

"Or else you don't understand. So we began to play — we were off in Kôr."

"Core of what?"

"Mysterious Kôr — ghost city."

"Where?"

"You may ask. But I could have sworn she saw it, and from the way she saw it I saw it, too. A game's a game, but what's a hallucination? You begin by laughing, then it gets in you and you can't laugh it off. I tell you, I woke up just now not knowing where I'd been; and I had to get up and feel round this table before I even knew where I was. It wasn't till then that I thought of a cigarette. Now I see why she sleeps like that, if that's where she goes."

"But she is just as often restless; I often hear her."

"Then she doesn't always make it. Perhaps it takes me, in some way — Well, I can't see any harm: when two people have got no place, why not want Kôr, as a start? There are no restrictions on wanting, at any rate."

"But, oh, Arthur, can't wanting want what's human?"

He yawned. "To be human's to be at a dead loss." Stopping yawning, he ground out his cigarette: the china tray skidded at the edge of the table. "Bring that light here a moment — that is, will you? I think I've messed ash all over these sheets of hers."

Callie advanced with the torch alight, but at arm's length: now and then her thumb made the beam wobble. She watched the lit-up inside of Arthur's hand as he brushed the sheet; and once he looked up to see her white-nightgowned figure curving above and away from him, behind the arc of light. "What's that swinging?"

"One of my plaits of hair. Shall I open the window wider?"

"What, to let the smoke out? Go on. And how's your moon?"

"Mine?" Marvelling over this, as the first sign that Arthur remembered that she was Callie, she uncovered the window, pushed up the sash, then after a minute said: "Not so strong."

Indeed, the moon's power over London and the imagination had now declined. The siege of light had relaxed; the search was over; the street had a look of survival and no more. Whatever had glittered there, coin or ring, was now invisible or had gone. To Callie it seemed likely that there would never be such a moon again; and on the whole she felt this was for the best. Feeling air reach in like a tired arm round her body, she dropped the curtains against it and returned to her own room.

Back by her bed, she listened: Pepita's breathing still had the regular sound of sleep. At the other side of the wall the divan creaked as Arthur stretched himself out again. Having felt ahead of her lightly, to make sure her half was empty, Callie climbed over Pepita and got in. A certain amount of warmth had travelled between the sheets from Pepita's flank, and in this Callie extended her sword-cold body: she tried to compose her limbs; even they quivered after Arthur's words in the dark, words *to* the dark. The loss of her own mysterious expectation, of her love for love, was a small thing beside the war's total of unlived lives. Suddenly Pepita flung out one hand: its back knocked Callie lightly across the face.

Pepita had now turned over and lay with her face up. The hand that had struck Callie must have lain over the other, which grasped the pyjama collar. Her eyes, in the dark, might have been either shut or open, but nothing made her frown more or less steadily: it became certain, after another moment, that Pepita's act of justice had been unconscious. She lay still, as she had lain, in an avid dream, of which Arthur had been the source, of which Arthur was not the end. With him she looked this way, that way, down the wide, void, pure streets, between statues, pillars and shadows, through archways and colonnades. With him she went up the stairs down which nothing but moon came; with him trod the ermine dust of the endless halls, stood on terraces, mounted the extreme tower, looked down on the statued squares, the wide, void, pure streets. He was the password, but not the answer: it was to Kôr's finality that she turned.

VLADIMIR NABOKOV
1899–1977

Nabokov's fictions, as with those of many moderns (such as John Barth), are often self-referential. His novels, memoirs, and short stories explore their own medium while of course doing other things as well. His aristocratic art floats on a current of experiments with language. Our enjoyment of it is quickened if we can join him in his subtle games.

The noble Russian family into which Nabokov was born lost everything in the revolution in 1919. The tragedy was compounded when in 1922 his father, a liberal, was assassinated by a rightist. The themes of loss and assassination were to emerge in Nabokov's later work.

He spent his life as an exile, always adjusting with the equanimity of the well bred, in Cambridge, England, where he took a degree; in Germany and France; in the United States, where he taught Russian and European literature at Cornell University; and finally in a hotel in Montreux, Switzerland. Whether thought of as a Russian or an American writer, he is recognized, except by the Soviets, as a master. In 1955 Lolita brought him fame and fortune, but, for all its brilliance, it is probably surpassed by The Gift, the ineffably intricate Pale Fire, and his most ambitious work, Ada.

Nabokov's short stories reflect several of his pervasive themes: memory's magic mirror, the world of exile, the distortions by which experience is transmuted into art. "First Love" is probably more autobiographical than most of his shorter works, more loosely structured, a memoir rather than a tale. But how admirable is the delicate joining of the two episodes, that of the railway journey and that of Colette. Indulging in few linguistic acrobatics, Nabokov triumphs as he condenses the lyric excitement of childhood in the face of first experience.

First Love

IN THE EARLY YEARS of this century, a travel agency on Nevski Avenue displayed a three-foot-long model of an oak-brown international sleeping car. In delicate verisimilitude it completely outranked the painted tin of my clockwork trains. Unfortunately it was not for sale. One could make out the blue upholstery inside, the embossed leather lining of the compartment walls, their polished panels, inset mirrors, tulip-shaped reading lamps, and other maddening details. Spacious windows alternated with narrower ones, single or geminate, and some of these were of frosted glass. In a few of the compartments, the beds had been made.

The then great and glamorous Nord Express (it was never the same after World War One when its elegant brown became a nouveau-riche blue), consisting solely of such international cars and running but twice a week, connected St. Petersburg with Paris. I would have said: directly with Paris, had passengers not been obliged to change from one train to a superficially similar one at the Russo-German frontier (Verzhbolovo-Eydtkuhnen), where the ample and lazy Russian sixty-and-a-half-inch gauge was replaced by the fifty-six-and-a-half-inch standard of Europe and coal succeeded birch logs.

In the far end of my mind I can unravel, I think, at least five such journeys to Paris, with the Riviera or Biarritz as their ultimate destination. In 1909, the year I now single out, our party consisted of eleven people and one dachshund. Wearing gloves and a traveling cap, my father sat reading a book in the compartment he shared with our tutor. My brother and I were separated from them by a washroom. My mother and her maid, Natasha, occupied a compartment adjacent to ours. Next came my two small sisters, their English governess, Miss Lavington, and a Russian nurse. The odd one of our party, my father's valet, Osip (whom, a decade later, the pedantic Bolsheviks were to shoot, because he appropriated our bicycles instead of turning them over to the nation), had a stranger for a companion.

Historically and artistically, the year had started with a political cartoon in *Punch:* goddess England bending over goddess Italy, on whose head one of Messina's bricks has landed — probably, the worst picture *any* earthquake has ever inspired. In April of that year, Peary had reached the North Pole. In May, Shalyapin had sung in Paris. In June, bothered by rumors of new and better Zeppelins, the United States War Department had told reporters of plans for an aerial Navy. In July, Blériot had flown from Calais to Dover (with a little additional loop when he lost his bearings). It was late August now. The firs and marshes of Northwestern Russia sped by, and on the following day gave way to German pine-woods and heather.

At a collapsible table, my mother and I played a card game called *durachki*. Although it was still broad daylight, our cards, a glass, and on a different plane the locks of a suitcase were reflected in the window. Through forest and field, and in sudden ravines, and among scuttling cottages, those discarnate gamblers kept steadily playing on for steadily sparkling stakes. It was a long, very long game: on this gray winter morning, in the looking glass of my bright hotel room, I see shining the same, the very same, locks of that now seventy-year-old valise, a highish, heavyish *nécessaire de voyage* of pigskin, with "H.N." elaborately interwoven in thick silver under a similar coronet, which had been bought in 1897 for my mother's wedding trip to Florence. In 1917 it transported from St. Petersburg to the Crimea and then to London a handful of jewels. Around 1930, it lost to a pawnbroker its expensive receptacles of crystal and silver leaving empty the cunningly contrived leathern holders on the inside of the lid. But that loss has been amply recouped during the thirty years it then traveled with me — from Prague to Paris, from St. Nazaire to New York and through the mirrors of more than two hundred motel rooms and rented houses, in forty-six states. The fact that of our Russian heritage the hardiest survivor proved to be a traveling bag is both logical and emblematic.

"*Ne budet-li, tï ved' ustal* [Haven't you had enough, aren't you tired]?" my mother would ask, and then would be lost in thought as she slowly shuffled the cards. The door of the compartment was open and I could see the corridor window, where the wires — six thin black wires — were doing their best to slant up, to ascend skywards, despite the lightning blows dealt them by one telegraph pole after another; but just as all six, in a triumphant swoop of pathetic elation, were about to reach the top of the window, a particularly vicious blow would bring them down, as low as they had ever been, and they would have to start all over again.

When, on such journeys as these, the train changed its pace to a dignified amble and all but grazed housefronts and shop signs, as we passed through some big German town, I used to feel a twofold excitement, which terminal stations could not provide. I saw a city, with its toylike trams, linden trees, and brick walls enter the compartment, hobnob with the mirrors, and fill to the brim the windows on the corridor side. This informal contact between train and city was one part of the thrill. The other was putting myself in the place of some passerby who, I imagined,

was moved as I would be moved myself to see the long, romantic, au-
burn cars, with their intervestibular connecting curtains as black as bat
wings and their metal lettering copper-bright in the low sun, unhurriedly
negotiate an iron bridge across an everyday thoroughfare and then turn,
with all windows suddenly ablaze, around a last block of houses.

There were drawbacks to those optical amalgamations. The wide-
windowed dining car, a vista of chaste bottles of mineral water, miter-
folded napkins, and dummy chocolate bars (whose wrappers — Cailler,
Kohler, and so forth — enclosed nothing but wood), would be perceived
at first as a cool haven beyond a consecution of reeling blue corridors;
but as the meal progressed toward its fatal last course, and more and
more dreadfully one equilibrist with a full tray would back against our
table to let another equilibrist pass with another full tray, I would keep
catching the car in the act of being recklessly sheathed, lurching waiters
and all, in the landscape, while the landscape itself went through a complex system of motion, the day-time moon stubbornly keeping abreast
of one's plate, the distant meadows opening fanwise, the near trees
sweeping up on invisible swings toward the track, a parallel rail line all
at once committing suicide by anastomosis, a bank of nictitating grass
rising, rising, rising, until the little witness of mixed velocities was made
to disgorge his portion of *omelette aux confitures de fraises*.

It was at night, however, that the *Compagnie Internationale des Wa-
gons-Lits et des Grands Express Européens* lived up to the magic of its
name. From my bed under my brother's bunk (Was he asleep? Was he
there at all?), in the semidarkness of our compartment, I watched things,
and parts of things, and shadows, and sections of shadows cautiously
moving about and getting nowhere. The woodwork gently creaked and
crackled. Near the door that led to the toilet, a dim garment on a peg
and, higher up, the tassel of the blue, bivalved night light swung rhythmically. It was hard to correlate those halting approaches, that hooded
stealth, with the headlong rush of the outside night, which I knew *was*
rushing by, spark-streaked, illegible.

I would put myself to sleep by the simple act of identifying myself
with the engine driver. A sense of drowsy well-being invaded my veins
as soon as I had everything nicely arranged — the carefree passengers in
their rooms enjoying the ride I was giving them, smoking, exchanging
knowing smiles, nodding, dozing; the waiters and cooks and train
guards (whom I had to place somewhere) carousing in the diner; and
myself, goggled and begrimed, peering out of the engine cab at the tapering track, at the ruby or emerald point in the black distance. And
then, in my sleep, I would see something totally different — a glass marble rolling under a grand piano or a toy engine lying on its side with its
wheels still working gamely.

A change in the speed of the train sometimes interrupted the current
of my sleep. Slow lights were stalking by; each, in passing, investigated

the same chink, and then a luminous compass measured the shadows. Presently, the train stopped with a long-drawn Westinghousian sigh. Something (my brother's spectacles, as it proved next day) fell from above. It was marvelously exciting to move to the foot of one's bed, with part of the bedclothes following, in order to undo cautiously the catch of the window shade, which could be made to slide only halfway up, impeded as it was by the edge of the upper berth.

Like moons around Jupiter, pale moths revolved about a lone lamp. A dismembered newspaper stirred on a bench. Somewhere on the train one could hear muffled voices, somebody's comfortable cough. There was nothing particularly interesting in the portion of station platform before me, and still I could not tear myself away from it until it departed of its own accord.

Next morning, wet fields with misshapen willows along the radius of a ditch or a row of poplars afar, traversed by a horizontal band of milky-white mist, told one that the train was spinning through Belgium. It reached Paris at 4 P.M., and even if the stay was only an overnight one, I had always time to purchase something — say, a little brass *Tour Eiffel*, rather roughly coated with silver paint — before we boarded, at noon on the following day, the Sud-Express, which, on its way to Madrid, dropped us around 10 P.M. at the La Négresse station of Biarritz, a few miles from the Spanish frontier.

2

Biarritz still retained its quiddity in those days. Dusty blackberry bushes and weedy *terrains à vendre* bordered the road that led to our villa. The Carlton was still being built. Some thirty-six years had to elapse before Brigadier General Samuel McCroskey would occupy the royal suite of the Hôtel du Palais, which stands on the site of a former palace, where, in the sixties, that incredibly agile medium, Daniel Home, is said to have been caught stroking with his bare foot (in imitation of a ghost hand) the kind, trustful face of Empress Eugénie. On the promenade near the Casino, an elderly flower girl, with carbon eyebrows and a painted smile, nimbly slipped the plump torus of a carnation into the buttonhole of an intercepted stroller whose left jowl accentuated its royal fold as he glanced down sideways at the coy insertion of the flower.

The rich-hued Oak Eggars questing amid the brush were quite unlike ours (which did not breed on oak, anyway), and here the Speckled Woods haunted not woods, but hedges and had tawny, not pale-yellow-ish, spots. Cleopatra, a tropical-looking, lemon-and-orange Brimstone, languorously flopping about in gardens, had been a sensation in 1907 and was still a pleasure to net.

Along the back line of the *plage,* various seaside chairs and stools supported the parents of straw-hatted children who were playing in front on the sand. I could be seen on my knees trying to set a found comb aflame by means of a magnifying glass. Men sported white trousers that to the eye of today would look as if they had comically shrunk in the washing; ladies wore, that particular season, light coats with silk-faced lapels, hats with big crowns and wide brims, dense embroidered white veils, frill-fronted blouses, frills at their wrists, frills on their parasols. The breeze salted one's lips. At a tremendous pace a stray Clouded Yellow came dashing across the palpitating *plage.*

Additional movement and sound were provided by venders hawking *cacahuètes,* sugared violets, pistachio ice cream of a heavenly green, cachou pellets, and huge convex pieces of dry, gritty, waferlike stuff that came from a red barrel. With a distinctness that no later superpositions have dimmed, I see that waffleman stomp along through deep mealy sand, with the heavy cask on his bent back. When called, he would sling it off his shoulder by a twist of its strap, bang it down on the sand in a Tower of Pisa position, wipe his face with his sleeve, and proceed to manipulate a kind of arrow-and-dial arrangement with numbers on the lid of the cask. The arrow rasped and whirred around. Luck was supposed to fix the size of a sou's worth of wafer. The bigger the piece, the more I was sorry for him.

The process of bathing took place on another part of the beach. Professional bathers, burly Basques in black bathing suits, were there to help ladies and children enjoy the terrors of the surf. Such a *baigneur* would place the *client* with his back to the incoming wave and hold him by the hand as the rising, rotating mass of foamy, green water violently descended from behind, knocking one off one's feet with one mighty wallop. After a dozen of these tumbles, the *baigneur,* glistening like a seal, would lead his panting, shivering, moistly snuffling charge landward, to the flat foreshore, where an unforgettable old woman with gray hairs on her chin promptly chose a bathing robe from several hanging on a clothesline. In the security of a little cabin, one would be helped by yet another attendant to peel off one's soggy, sand-heavy bathing suit. It would plop onto the boards, and, still shivering, one would step out of it and trample on its bluish, diffuse stripes. The cabin smelled of pine. The attendant, a hunchback with beaming wrinkles, brought a basin of steaming-hot water, in which one immersed one's feet. From him I learned, and have preserved ever since in a glass cell of my memory, that "butterfly" in the Basque language is *misericoletea* — or at least it sounded so (among the seven words I have found in dictionaries the closest approach is *micheletea*).

3

On the browner and wetter part of the *plage,* that part which at low
tide yielded the best mud for castles, I found myself digging, one day,
side by side with a little French girl called Colette.

She would be ten in November, I had been ten in April. Attention was
drawn to a jagged bit of violet mussel shell upon which she had stepped
with the bare sole of her narrow long-toed foot. No, I was not English.
Her greenish eyes seemed flecked with the overflow of the freckles that
covered her sharp-featured face. She wore what might now be termed a
playsuit, consisting of a blue jersey with rolled-up sleeves and blue knitted shorts. I had taken her at first for a boy and then had been puzzled
by the bracelet on her thin wrist and the cork-screw brown curls dangling from under her sailor cap.

She spoke in birdlike bursts of rapid twitter, mixing governess English
and Parisian French. Two years before, on the same *plage,* I had been
much attached to Zina, the lovely, sun-tanned, bad-tempered little
daughter of a Serbian naturopath — she had, I remember (absurdly, for
she and I were only eight at the time), a *grain de beauté* on her apricot
skin just below the heart, and there was a horrible collection of chamber
pots, full and half-full, and one with surface bubbles, on the floor of the
hall in her family's boardinghouse lodgings which I visited early one
morning to be given by her, as she was being dressed, a dead humming-
bird moth found by the cat. But when I met Colette, I knew at once that
this was the real thing. Colette seemed to me so much stranger than all
my other chance playmates at Biarritz! I somehow acquired the feeling
that she was less happy than I, less loved. A bruise on her delicate,
downy forearm gave rise to awful conjectures. "He pinches as bad as
my mummy," she said, speaking of a crab. I evolved various schemes to
save her from her parents, who were *"des bourgeois de Paris"* as I heard
somebody tell my mother with a slight shrug. I interpreted the disdain
in my own fashion, as I knew that those people had come all the way
from Paris in their blue-and-yellow limousine (a fashionable adventure
in those days) but had drably sent Colette with her dog and governess
by an ordinary coach-train. The dog was a female fox terrier with bells
on her collar and a most waggly behind. From sheer exuberance, she
would lap up salt water out of Colette's toy pail. I remembered the sail,
the sunset, and the lighthouse pictured on that pail, but I cannot recall
the dog's name, and this bothers me.

During the two months of our stay at Biarritz, my passion for Colette
all but surpassed my passion for Cleopatra. Since my parents were not
keen to meet hers, I saw her only on the beach; but I thought of her
constantly. If I noticed she had been crying, I felt a surge of helpless
anguish that brought tears to my own eyes. I could not destroy the mosquitoes that had left their bites on her frail neck, but I could, and did,

have a successful fistfight with a red-haired boy who had been rude to her. She used to give me warm handfuls of hard candy. One day, as we were bending together over a starfish, and Colette's ringlets were tickling my ear, she suddenly turned toward me and kissed me on the cheek. So great was my emotion that all I could think of saying was, "You little monkey."

I had a gold coin that I assumed would pay for our elopement. Where did I want to take her? Spain? America? The mountains above Pau? *"Là-bas, là-bas, dans la montagne,"* as I had heard Carmen sing at the opera. One strange night, I lay awake, listening to the recurrent thud of the ocean and planning our flight. The ocean seemed to rise and grope in the darkness and then heavily fall on its face.

Of our actual getaway, I have little to report. My memory retains a glimpse of her obediently putting on rope-soled canvas shoes, on the lee side of a flapping tent, while I stuffed a folding butterfly net into a brown-paper bag. The next glimpse is of our evading pursuit by entering a pitch-dark *cinéma* near the Casino (which, of course, was absolutely out of bounds). There we sat, holding hands across the dog, which now and then gently jingled in Colette's lap, and were shown a jerky, drizzly, but highly exciting bullfight at St. Sebástian. My final glimpse is of myself being led along the promenade by Linderovski. His long legs move with a kind of ominous briskness and I can see the muscles of his grimly set jaw working under the tight skin. My bespectacled brother, aged nine, whom he happens to hold with his other hand, keeps trotting out forward to peer at me with awed curiosity, like a little owl.

Among the trivial souvenirs acquired at Biarritz before leaving, my favorite was not the small bull of black stone and not the sonorous sea shell but something which now seems almost symbolic — a meerschaum penholder with a tiny peephole of crystal in its ornamental part. One held it quite close to one's eye, screwing up the other, and when one had got rid of the shimmer of one's own lashes, a miraculous photographic view of the bay and of the line of cliffs ending in a lighthouse could be seen inside.

And now a delightful thing happens. The process of recreating that penholder and the microcosm in its eyelet stimulates my memory to a last effort. I try again to recall the name of Colette's dog — and, triumphantly, along those remote beaches, over the glassy evening sands of the past, where each footprint slowly fills up with sunset water, here it comes, here it comes, echoing and vibrating: Floss, Floss, Floss!

Colette was back in Paris by the time we stopped there for a day before continuing our homeward journey; and there, in a fawn park under a cold blue sky, I saw her (by arrangement between our mentors, I believe) for the last time. She carried a hoop and a short stick to drive it with, and everything about her was extremely proper and stylish in an autumnal, Parisian, *tenue-de-ville-pour-fillettes* way. She took from her governess and slipped into my brother's hand a farewell present, a box of sugar-coated almonds, meant, I knew, solely for me; and instantly she was off, tap-tapping her glinting hoop through light and shade, around and around a fountain choked with dead leaves, near which I stood. The leaves mingle in my memory with the leather of her shoes and gloves, and there was, I remember, some detail in her attire (perhaps a ribbon on her Scottish cap, or the pattern of her stockings) that reminded me then of the rainbow spiral in a glass marble. I still seem to be holding that wisp of iridescence, not knowing exactly where to fit it, while she runs with her hoop ever faster around me and finally dissolves among the slender shadows cast on the graveled path by the interlaced arches of its low looped fence.

Ernest Hemingway
1899–1961

As with Fitzgerald, Hemingway's personality so imposed itself upon the consciousness of his era as to create some difficulty for the reader anxious to approach his work without prejudgments. But the difficulty is less frustrating than in Fitzgerald's case. Hemingway was far more complex, he had more to offer, he could more effectively distance himself from his work. Besides, he was simply more talented.

This courageous, generous, mean egotist showed true humility only toward his art. That was enough; it made possible the discipline that lay behind the well-deserved Nobel Prize in 1954. When he shot himself in 1961, he had said all he had to say. That, too, was enough; he had helped to turn American prose around, to "make it new."

As time winnows things out, it seems more and more probable that he will be preserved by his short stories, including many early ones. A reading of "My Old Man," even for the tenth time, calls forth, freshly and inevitably, precisely what Hemingway slaved for: "the sequence of motion and fact which made the emotion." We unconsciously supply all the canny omissions, we respond almost reflexively to the pressures Hemingway's invisible hand exerts. He says: "When I have an idea, I turn down the flame, as if it were a little alcohol stove, as low as it will go. Then it explodes and that is my idea."

In about six thousand necessary words, "My Old Man" almost incidentally (but of course Hemingway is never incidental) evokes and then compels us to internalize one of his worlds, that of the racetrack. Yet beyond and underneath this it is a love story, about a love that, as always in Hemingway, must encounter and then bear the pain of risk, the intimidation of loss.

My Old Man

I GUESS looking at it, now, my old man was cut out for a fat guy, one of those regular little roly fat guys you see around, but he sure never got that way, except a little toward the last, and then it wasn't his fault, he was riding over the jumps only and he could afford to carry plenty of weight then. I remember the way he'd pull on a rubber shirt over a couple of jerseys and a big sweat shirt over that, and get me to run with him in the forenoon in the hot sun. He'd have, maybe, taken a trial trip with one of Razzo's skins early in the morning after just getting in from Torino at four o'clock in the morning and beating it out to the stables in a cab and then with the dew all over everything and the sun just starting to get going, I'd help him pull off his boots and he'd get into a pair of sneakers and all these sweaters and we'd start out.

"Come on, kid," he'd say, stepping up and down on his toes in front of the jock's dressing room, "let's get moving."

Then we'd start off jogging around the infield once, maybe, with him ahead, running nice, and then turn out the gate and along one of those roads with all the trees along both sides of them that run out from San Siro. I'd go ahead of him when we hit the road and I could run pretty good and I'd look around and he'd be jogging easy just behind me and after a little while I'd look around again and he'd begun to sweat. Sweating heavy and he'd just be dogging it along with his eyes on my back, but when he'd catch me looking at him he'd grin and say, "Sweating plenty?" When my old man grinned, nobody could help but grin too. We'd keep right on running out toward the mountains and then my old man would yell, "Hey, Joe!" and I'd look back and he'd be sitting under a tree with a towel he'd had around his waist wrapped around his neck.

I'd come back and sit down beside him and he'd pull a rope out of his pocket and start skipping rope out in the sun with the sweat pouring off his face and him skipping rope out in the white dust with the rope going cloppetty, cloppetty, clop, clop, clop, and the sun hotter, and him working harder up and down a patch of the road. Say, it was a treat to see my old man skip rope, too. He could whirr it fast or lop it slow and fancy. Say, you ought to have seen wops look at us sometimes, when they'd come by, going into town walking along with big white steers hauling the cart. They sure looked as though they thought the old man was nuts. He'd start the rope whirring till they'd stop dead still and watch him, then give the steers a cluck and a poke with the goad and get going again.

When I'd sit watching him working out in the hot sun I sure felt fond of him. He sure was fun and he done his work so hard and he'd finish up with a regular whirring that'd drive the sweat out on his face like water and then sling the rope at the tree and come over and sit down with me and lean back against the tree with the towel and a sweater wrapped around his neck.

"Sure is hell keeping it down, Joe," he'd say and lean back and shut his eyes and breathe long and deep, "it ain't like when you're a kid." Then he'd get up and before he started to cool we'd jog along back to the stables. That's the way it was keeping down to weight. He was worried all the time. Most jocks can just about ride off all they want to. A jock loses about a kilo every time he rides, but my old man was sort of dried out and he couldn't keep down his kilos without all that running.

I remember once at San Siro, Regoli, a little wop, that was riding for Buzoni, came out across the paddock going to the bar for something cool; and flicking his boots with his whip, after he'd just weighed in and my old man had just weighed in too, and came out with the saddle under his arm looking red-faced and tired and too big for his silks and he stood there looking at young Regoli standing up to the outdoors bar, cool and kid-looking, and I said, "What's the matter, Dad?" cause I thought maybe Regoli had bumped him or something and he just looked at Regoli and said, "Oh, to hell with it," and went on to the dressing room.

Well, it would have been all right, maybe, if we'd stayed in Milan and ridden at Milan and Torino, 'cause if there ever were any easy courses, it's those two. "Pianola, Joe," my old man said when he dismounted in the winning stall after what the wops thought was a hell of steeplechase. I asked him once. "This course rides itself. It's the pace you're going at, that makes riding the jumps dangerous, Joe. We ain't going any pace here, and they ain't really bad jumps either. But it's the pace always — not the jumps — that makes the trouble."

San Siro was the swellest course I'd ever seen but the old man said it was a dog's life. Going back and forth between Mirafiore and San Siro and riding just about every day in the week with a train ride every other night.

I was nuts about the horses, too. There's something about it, when they come out and go up the track to the post. Sort of dancy and tight looking with the jock keeping a tight hold on them and maybe easing off a little and letting them run a little going up. Then once they were at the barrier it got me worse than anything. Especially at San Siro with that big green infield and the mountains way off and the fat wop starter with his big whip and the jocks fiddling them around and then the barrier snapping up and that bell going off and them all getting off in a bunch and then commencing to string out. You know the way a bunch of skins gets off. If you're up in the stand with a pair of glasses all you see is them plunging off and then that bell goes off and it seems like it rings for a thousand years and then they come sweeping round the turn. There wasn't ever anything like it for me.

But my old man said one day, in the dressing room, when he was getting into his street clothes, "None of these things are horses, Joe. They'd kill that bunch of skates for their hides and hoofs up at Paris." That was the day he'd won the Premio Commercio with Lantorna shooting her out of the field the last hundred meters like pulling a cork out of a bottle.

It was right after the Premio Commercio that we pulled out and left Italy. My old man and Holbrook and a fat wop in a straw hat that kept wiping his face with a handkerchief were having an argument at a table in the Galleria. They were all talking French and the two of them was after my old man about something. Finally he didn't say anything any more but just sat there and looked at Holbrook, and the two of them kept after him, first one talking and then the other, and the fat wop always butting in on Holbrook.

"You go out and buy me a *Sportsman,* will you, Joe?" my old man said, and handed me a couple of soldi without looking away from Holbrook.

So I went out of the Galleria and walked over to in front of the Scala and bought a paper, and came back and stood a little way away because I didn't want to butt in and my old man was sitting back in his chair looking down at his coffee and fooling with a spoon and Holbrook and the big wop were standing and the big wop was wiping his face and shaking his head. And I came up and my old man acted just as though the two of them weren't standing there and said, "Want an ice, Joe?" Holbrook looked down at my old man and said slow and careful, "You son of a bitch," and he and the fat wop went out through the tables.

My old man sat there and sort of smiled at me, but his face was white and he looked sick as hell and I was scared and felt sick inside because I knew something had happened and I didn't see how anybody could call my old man a son of a bitch, and get away with it. My old man opened up the *Sportsman* and studied the handicaps for a while and then he said, "You got to take a lot of things in this world, Joe." And three days later we left Milan for good on the Turin train for Paris, after an auction sale out in front of Turner's stables of everything we couldn't get into a trunk and a suit case.

We got into Paris early in the morning in a long, dirty station the old man told me was the Gare de Lyon. Paris was an awful big town after Milan. Seems like in Milan everybody is going somewhere and all the trams run somewhere and there ain't any sort of a mix-up, but Paris is all balled up and they never do straighten it out. I got to like it, though, part of it, anyway, and say, it's got the best race courses in the world.

Seems as though that were the thing that keeps it all going and about the only thing you can figure on is that every day the buses will be going out to whatever track they're running at, going right out through everything to the track. I never really got to know Paris well, because I just came in about once or twice a week with the old man from Maisons and he always sat at the Café de la Paix on the Opera side with the rest of the gang from Maisons and I guess that's one of the busiest parts of the town. But, say, it is funny that a big town like Paris wouldn't have a Galleria, isn't it?

Well, we went out to live at Maisons-Lafitte, where just about everybody lives except the gang at Chantilly, with a Mrs. Meyers that runs a boarding house. Maisons is about the swellest place to live I've ever seen in all my life. The town ain't so much, but there's a lake and a swell forest that we used to go off bumming in all day, a couple of us kids, and my old man made me a sling shot and we got a lot of things with it but the best one was a magpie. Young Dick Atkinson shot a rabbit with it one day and we put it under a tree and were all sitting around and Dick had some cigarettes and all of a sudden the rabbit jumped up and beat it into the brush and we chased it but we couldn't find it. Gee, we had fun at Maisons. Mrs. Meyers used to give me lunch in the morning and I'd be gone all day. I learned to talk French quick. It's an easy language.

As soon as we got to Maisons, my old man wrote to Milan for his license and he was pretty worried till it came. He used to sit around the Café de Paris in Maisons with the gang, there were lots of guys he'd known when he rode up at Paris, before the war, lived at Maisons, and there's a lot of time to sit around because the work around a racing stable, for the jocks, that is, is all cleaned up by nine o'clock in the morning. They take the first bunch of skins out to gallop them at 5.30 in the morning and they work the second lot at 8 o'clock. That means getting up early all right and going to bed early, too. If a jock's riding for somebody too, he can't go boozing around because the trainer always has an eye on him if he's a kid and if he ain't a kid he's always got an eye on himself. So mostly if a jock ain't working he sits around the Café de Paris with the gang and they can all sit around about two or three hours in front of some drink like a vermouth and seltz and they talk and tell stories and shoot pool and it's sort of like a club or the Galleria in Milan. Only it ain't really like the Galleria because there everybody is going by all the time and there's everybody around at the tables.

Well, my old man got his license all right. They sent it through to him without a word and he rode a couple of times. Amiens, up country and that sort of thing, but he didn't seem to get any engagement. Everybody liked him and whenever I'd come into the Café in the forenoon I'd find somebody drinking with him because my old man wasn't tight like most of these jockies that have got the first dollar they made riding at the

World's Fair in St. Louis in nineteen ought four. That's what my old man would say when he'd kid George Burns. But it seemed like everybody steered clear of giving my old man any mounts.

We went out to wherever they were running every day with the car from Maisons and that was the most fun of all. I was glad when the horses came back from Deauville and the summer. Even though it meant no more bumming in the woods, 'cause then we'd ride to Enghien or Tremblay or St. Cloud and watch them from the trainers' and jockeys' stand. I sure learned about racing from going out with that gang and the fun of it was going every day.

I remember once out at St. Cloud. It was a big two hundred thousand franc race with seven entries and Kzar a big favorite. I went around to the paddock to see the horses with my old man and you never saw such horses. This Kzar is a great big yellow horse that looks like just nothing but run. I never saw such a horse. He was being led around the paddocks with his head down and when he went by me I felt all hollow inside he was so beautiful. There never was such a wonderful, lean, running built horse. And he went around the paddock putting his feet just so and quiet and careful and moving easy like he knew just what he had to do and not jerking and standing up on his legs and getting wild eyed like you see these selling platers with a shot of dope in them. The crowd was so thick I couldn't see him again except just his legs going by and some yellow and my old man started out through the crowd and I followed him over to the jock's dressing room back in the trees and there was a big crowd around there, too, but the man at the door in a derby nodded to my old man and we got in and everybody was sitting around at getting dressed and pulling shirts over their heads and pulling boots on and it all smelled hot and sweaty and linimenty and outside was the crowd looking in.

The old man went over and sat down beside George Gardner that was getting into his pants and said, "What's the dope, George?" just in an ordinary tone of voice 'cause there ain't any use him feeling around because George either can tell him or he can't tell him.

"He won't win," George says very low, leaning over and buttoning the bottom of his breeches.

"Who will?" my old man says, leaning over close so nobody can hear.

"Kircubbin," George says, "and if he does, save me a couple of tickets."

My old man says something in a regular voice to George and George says, "Don't ever bet on anything I tell you," kidding like, and we beat it out and through all the crowd that was looking in, over to the 100 franc mutuel machine. But I knew something big was up because George is Kzar's jockey. On the way he gets one of the yellow odds-sheets with the starting prices on and Kzar is only paying 5 for 10, Cefisidote is next at 3 to 1 and fifth down the list this Kircubbin at 8 to 1. My old man bets five thousand on Kircubbin to win and puts on a thousand to place and we went around back of the grandstand to go up the stairs and get a place to watch the race.

We were jammed in tight and first a man in a long coat with a gray tall hat and a whip folded up in his hand came out and then one after another the horses, with the jocks up and a stable boy holding the bridle on each side and walking along, followed the old guy. That big yellow horse Kzar came first. He didn't look so big when you first looked at him until you saw the length of his legs and the whole way he's built and the way he moves. Gosh, I never saw such a horse. George Gardner was riding him and they moved along slow, back of the old guy in the gray tall hat that walked along like he was a ring master in a circus. Back of Kzar, moving along smooth and yellow in the sun, was a good looking black with a nice head with Tommy Archibald riding him; and after the black was a string of five more horses all moving along slow in a procession past the grandstand and the pesage. My old man said the black was Kircubbin and I took a good look at him and he was a nice-looking horse, all right, but nothing like Kzar.

Everybody cheered Kzar when he went by and he sure was one swell looking horse. The procession of them went around on the other side past the pelouse and then back up to the near end of the course and the circus master had the stable boys turn them loose one after another so they could gallop by the stands on their way up to the post and let everybody have a good look at them. They weren't at the post hardly any time at all when the gong started and you could see them way off across the infield all in a bunch starting on the first swing like a lot of little toy horses. I was watching them through the glasses and Kzar was running well back, with one of the bays making the pace. They swept down and around and came pounding past and Kzar was way back when they passed us and this Kircubbin horse in front and going smooth. Gee, it's awful when they go by you and then you have to watch them go farther away and get smaller and smaller and then all bunched up on the turns and then come around towards into the stretch and you feel like swearing and goddamming worse and worse. Finally they made the last turn and came into the straightaway with this Kircubbin horse way out in front. Everybody was looking funny and saying "Kzar" in sort of a sick way and them pounding nearer down the stretch, and then something came out of the pack right into my glasses like a horse-headed yellow streak and everybody began to yell "Kzar" as though they were crazy. Kzar came on faster than I'd ever seen anything in my life and pulled up on Kircubbin that was going fast as any black horse could go with the jock flogging hell out of him with the gad and they were right dead neck and neck for a second but Kzar seemed going about twice as fast with those great jumps and that head out — but it was while they were neck and neck that they passed the winning post and when the numbers went up in the slots the first one was 2 and that meant that Kircubbin had won.

I felt all trembly and funny inside, and then we were all jammed in with the people going downstairs to stand in front of the board where they'd post what Kircubbin paid. Honest, watching the race I'd forgot how much my old man had bet on Kircubbin. I'd wanted Kzar to win so damned bad. But now it was all over it was swell to know we had the winner.

"Wasn't it a swell race, Dad?" I said to him.

He looked at me sort of funny with his derby on the back of his head. "George Gardner's a swell jockey, all right," he said. "It sure took a great jock to keep that Kzar horse from winning."

Of course I knew it was funny all the time. But my old man saying that right out like that sure took the kick all out of it for me and I didn't get the real kick back again ever, even when they posted the numbers upon the board and the bell rang to pay off and we saw that Kircubbin paid 67.50 for 10. All round people were saying, "Poor Kzar! Poor Kzar!" And I thought, I wish I were a jockey and could have rode him instead of that son of a bitch. And that was funny, thinking of George Gardner as a son of a bitch because I'd always liked him and besides he'd given us the winner, but I guess that's what he is, all right.

My old man had a big lot of money after that race and he took to coming into Paris oftener. If they raced at Tremblay he'd have them drop him in town on their way back to Maisons and he and I'd sit out in front of the Café de la Paix and watch the people go by. It's funny sitting there. There's streams of people going by and all sorts of guys come up and want to sell you things, and I loved to sit there with my old man. That was when we'd have the most fun. Guys would come by selling funny rabbits that jumped if you squeezed a bulb and they'd come up to us and my old man would kid with them. He could talk French just like English and all those kind of guys knew him 'cause you can always tell a jockey — and then we always sat at the same table and they got used to seeing us there. There were guys selling matrimonial papers and girls selling rubber eggs that when you squeezed them a rooster came out of them and one old wormy-looking guy that went by with post-cards of Paris, showing them to everybody, and, of course, nobody ever bought any, and then he would come back and show the under side of the pack and they would all be smutty post-cards and lots of people would dig down and buy them.

Gee, I remember the funny people that used to go by. Girls around supper time looking for somebody to take them out to eat and they'd speak to my old man and he'd make some joke at them in French and they'd pat me on the head and go on. Once there was an American woman sitting with her kid daughter at the next table to us and they were both eating ices and I kept looking at the girl and she was awfully good looking and I smiled at her and she smiled at me but that was all that ever came of it because I looked for her mother and her every day and I made up ways that I was going to speak to her and I wondered if

I got to know her if her mother would let me take her out to Auteuil or Tremblay but I never saw either of them again. Anyway, I guess it wouldn't have been any good, anyway, because looking back on it I remember the way I thought out would be best to speak to her was to say, "Pardon me, but perhaps I can give you a winner at Enghien today?" and, after all, maybe she would have thought I was a tout instead of really trying to give her a winner.

We'd sit at the Café de la Paix, my old man and me, and we had a big drag with the waiter because my old man drank whisky and it cost five francs, and that meant a good tip when the saucers were counted up. My old man was drinking more than I'd ever seen him, but he wasn't riding at all now and besides he said that whisky kept his weight down. But I noticed he was putting it on, all right, just the same. He'd busted away from his old gang out at Maisons and seemed to like just sitting around on the boulevard with me. But he was dropping money every day at the track. He'd feel sort of doleful after the last race, if he'd lost on the day, until we'd get to our table and he'd have his first whisky and then he'd be fine.

He'd be reading the *Paris-Sport* and he'd look over at me and say, "Where's your girl, Joe?" to kid me on account I had told him about the girl that day at the next table. And I'd get red, but I liked being kidded about her. It gave me a good feeling. "Keep your eye peeled for her, Joe," he'd say, "she'll be back."

He'd ask me questions about things and some of the things I'd say he'd laugh. And then he'd get started talking about things. About riding down in Egypt, or at St. Moritz on the ice before my mother died, and about during the war when they had regular races down in the south of France without any purses, or betting or crowd or anything just to keep the breed up. Regular races with the jocks riding hell out of the horses. Gee, I could listen to my old man talk by the hour, especially when he'd had a couple or so of drinks. He'd tell me about when he was a boy in Kentucky and going coon hunting, and the old days in the States before everything went on the bum there. And he'd say, "Joe, when we've got a decent stake, you're going back there to the States and go to school."

"What've I got to go back there to go to school for when everything's on the bum there?" I'd ask him.

"That's different," he'd say and get the waiter over and pay the pile of saucers and we'd get a taxi to the Gare St. Lazare and get on the train out to Maisons.

One day at Auteuil, after a selling steeplechase, my old man bought in the winner for 30,000 francs. He had to bid a little to get him but the stable let the horse go finally and my old man had his permit and his colors in a week. Gee, I felt proud when my old man was an owner. He fixed it up for stable space with Charles Drake and cut out coming in to Paris, and started his running and sweating out again, and him and I were the whole stable gang. Our horse's name was Gilford, he was Irish bred and a nice, sweet jumper. My old man figured that training him and riding him, himself, he was a good investment. I was proud of everything and I thought Gilford was as good a horse as Kzar. He was a good, solid jumper, a bay, with plenty of speed on the flat, if you asked him for it, and he was a nice-looking horse, too.

Gee, I was fond of him. The first time he started with my old man up, he finished third in a 2500 meter hurdle race and when my old man got off him, all sweating and happy in the place stall, and went in to weigh, I felt as proud of him as though it was the first race he'd ever placed in. You see, when a guy ain't been riding for a long time, you can't make yourself really believe that he has ever rode. The whole thing was different now, 'cause down in Milan, even big races never seemed to make any difference to my old man, if he won he wasn't ever excited or anything, and now it was so I couldn't hardly sleep the night before a race and I knew my old man was excited, too, even if he didn't show it. Riding for yourself makes an awful difference.

Second time Gilford and my old man started, was a rainy Sunday at Auteuil, in the Prix du Marat, a 4500 meter steeplechase. As soon as he'd gone out I beat it up in the stand with the new glasses my old man had bought for me to watch them. They started way over at the far end of the course and there was some trouble at the barrier. Something with goggle blinders on was making a great fuss and rearing around and busted the barrier once, but I could see my old man in our black jacket, with a white cross and a black cap, sitting up on Gilford, and patting him with his hand. Then they were off in a jump and out of sight behind the trees and the gong going for dear life and the pari-mutuel wickets rattling down. Gosh, I was so excited, I was afraid to look at them, but I fixed the glasses on the place where they would come out back of the trees and then out they came with the old black jacket going third and they all sailing over the jump like birds. Then they went out of sight again and then they came pounding out and down the hill and all going nice and sweet and easy and taking the fence smooth in a bunch, and moving away from us all solid. Looked as though you could walk across on their backs they were all so bunched and going so smooth. Then they bellied over the big double Bullfinch and something came down. I couldn't see who it was, but in a minute the horse was up and galloping free and the field, all bunched still, sweeping around the long left turn into the straightaway. They jumped the stone wall and came jammed down the stretch toward the big water-jump right in front of the stands. I saw them coming and hollered at my old man as he went by, and he was leading by about a length and riding way out, and light as a monkey, and they were racing for the water-jump. They took off over the big hedge of the water-jump in a pack and then there was a crash, and two horses pulled sideways out off it, and kept on going, and three others were piled up. I couldn't see my old man anywhere. One horse kneed himself up and the jock had hold of the bridle and mounted and went slamming on after the place money. The other horse was up and away by himself, jerking his head and galloping with the bridle rein hanging and the jock staggered over to one side of the track against the fence. Then Gilford rolled over to one side off my old man and got up and started to run on three legs with his front off hoof dangling and there was my old man laying there on the grass flat out with his face up and blood all over the side of his head. I ran down the stand and bumped into a jam of people and got to the rail and a cop grabbed me and held me and two big stretcher-bearers were going out after my old man and around on the other side of the course I saw three horses, strung way out, coming out of the trees and taking the jump.

My old man was dead when they brought him in and while a doctor was listening to his heart with a thing plugged in his ears, I heard a shot up the track that meant they'd killed Gilford. I lay down beside my old man, when they carried the stretcher into the hospital room, and hung onto the stretcher and cried and cried, and he looked so white and gone and so awfully dead, and I couldn't help feeling that if my old man was dead maybe they didn't need to have shot Gilford. His hoof might have got well. I don't know. I loved my old man so much.

Then a couple of guys came in and one of them patted me on the back and then went over and looked at my old man and then pulled a sheet off the cot and spread it over him; and the other was telephoning in French for them to send the ambulance to take him out to Maisons. And I couldn't stop crying, crying and choking, sort of, and George Gardner came in and sat down beside me on the floor and put his arm around me and says, "Come on, Joe, old boy. Get up and we'll go out and wait for the ambulance."

George and I went out to the gate and I was trying to stop bawling and George wiped off my face with his handkerchief and we were standing back a little ways while the crowd was going out of the gate and a couple of guys stopped near us while we were waiting for the crowd to get through the gate and one of them was counting a bunch of mutuel tickets and he said, "Well, Butler got his, all right."

The other guy said, "I don't give a good goddam if he did, the crook. He had it coming to him on the stuff he's pulled."

"I'll say he had," said the other guy, and tore the bunch of tickets in two.

And George Gardner looked at me to see if I'd heard and I had all right and he said, "Don't you listen to what those bums said, Joe. Your old man was one swell guy."

But I don't know. Seems like when they get started they don't leave a guy nothing.

E. B. WHITE
1899–1985

E. B. White was not a short story professional. Primarily an essayist and social commentator, he was also a graceful writer of light verse and the author of children's books, two of which — Charlotte's Web *and* Stuart Little — *are considered classics. Fiction was not his forte; "The Door" is singularly, tantalizingly uncharacteristic of the accepted image of E. B. White as the elegant, witty embodiment of* The New Yorker's *outlook on the world.*

The kind and degree of one's own frustration, one's own perception of problems "incapable of solution," will determine the effect on each reader of this nightmare of a story. Ostensibly a study in madness, it suggests itself also as a kind of judgment on our time in general. Whatever is unreal in the world about us, whatever resists our bewildered, ratlike attempts to find the right door, seems to be clothed, in these distorted, chilling sentences, in suitably haunting metaphors. The "unspeakably bright imploring look of the frustrated" can trouble one's dreams.

E. B. White never again wrote anything like "The Door." Nobody has done so.

The Door

EVERYTHING (he kept saying) is something it isn't. And everybody is always somewhere else. Maybe it was the city, being in the city, that made him feel how queer everything was and that it was something else. Maybe (he kept thinking) it was the names of the things. The names were tex and frequently koid. Or they were flex and oid, or they were duroid (sani) or flexsan (duro), but everything was glass (but not quite glass) and the thing that you touched (the surface, washable, crease-resistant) was rubber, only it wasn't quite rubber and you didn't quite touch it but almost. The wall, which was glass but thrutex, turned out on being approached not to be a wall, it was something else, it was an opening or doorway — and the doorway (through which he saw himself approaching) turned out to be something else, it was a wall. And what he had eaten not having agreed with him.

He was in a washable house, but he wasn't sure. Now about those rats, he kept saying to himself. He meant the rats that the Professor had driven crazy by forcing them to deal with problems which were beyond the scope of rats, the insoluble problems. He meant the rats that had been trained to jump at the square card with the circle in the middle, and the card (because it was something it wasn't) would give way and let the rat into a place where the food was, but then one day it would be a trick played on the rat, and the card would be changed, and the rat would jump but the card wouldn't give way, and it was an impossible situation (for a rat) and the rat would go insane and into its eyes would come the unspeakably bright imploring look of the frustrated, and after the convulsions were over and the frantic racing around, then the passive stage would set in and the willingness to let anything be done to it, even if it was something else.

He didn't know which door (or wall) or opening in the house to jump at, to get through, because one was an opening that wasn't a door (it was a void, or koid) and the other was a wall that wasn't an opening, it was a sanitary cupboard of the same color. He caught a glimpse of his eyes staring into his eyes, in the thrutex, and in them was the expression he had seen in the picture of the rats — weary after convulsions and the frantic racing around, when they were willing and did not mind having anything done to them. More and more (he kept saying) I am confronted by a problem which is incapable of solution (for this time even if he chose the right door, there would be no food behind it) and that is what madness is, and things seeming different from what they are. He heard, in the house where he was, in the city to which he had gone (as toward a door which might, or might not, give way), a noise — not a loud noise but more of a low prefabricated humming. It came from a place in the base of the wall (or stat) where the flue carrying the filterable air was, and not far from the Minipiano, which was made of the same material nail-brushes are made of, and which was under the stairs. "This, too, has been tested," she said, pointing, but not at it, "and found viable." It wasn't a loud noise, he kept thinking, sorry that he had seen his eyes, even though it was through his own eyes that he had seen them.

First will come the convulsions (he said), then the exhaustion, then the willingness to let anything be done. "And you better believe it *will* be."

All his life he had been confronted by situations which were incapable of being solved, and there was a deliberateness behind all this, behind this changing of the card (or door), because they would always wait till you had learned to jump at the certain card (or door) — the one with the circle — and then they would change it on you. There have been so many doors changed on me, he said, in the last twenty years, but it is now becoming clear that it is an impossible situation, and the question is whether to jump again, even though they ruffle you in the rump with a blast of air — to make you jump. He wished he wasn't standing by the Minipiano. First they would teach you the prayers and the Psalms, and that would be the right door (the one with the circle), and the long sweet words with the holy sound, and that would be the one to jump at to get where the food was. Then one day you jumped and it didn't give way, so that all you got was the bump on the nose, and the first bewilderment, the first young bewilderment.

I don't know whether to tell her about the door they substituted or not, he said, the one with the equation on it and the picture of the amoeba reproducing itself by division. Or the one with the photostatic copy of the check for thirty-two dollars and fifty cents. But the jumping was so long ago, although the bump is . . . how those old wounds hurt! Being crazy this way wouldn't be so bad if only, if only. If only when you put your foot forward to take a step, the ground wouldn't come up to meet your foot the way it does. And the same way in the street (only I may never get back to the street unless I jump at the right door), the curb coming up to meet your foot, anticipating ever so delicately the weight of the body, which is somewhere else. "We could take your name," she said, "and send it to you." And it wouldn't be so bad if only you could read a sentence all the way through without jumping (your eye) to something else on the same page; and then (he kept thinking) there was that man out in Jersey, the one who started to chop his trees down, one by one, the man who began talking about how he would take his house to pieces, brick by brick, because he faced a problem incapable of solution, probably, so he began to hack at the trees in the yard, began to pluck with trembling fingers at the bricks in the house. Even if a house is not washable, it is worth taking down. It is not till later that the exhaustion sets in.

But it is inevitable that they will keep changing the doors on you, he said, because that is what they are for; and the thing is to get used to it and not let it unsettle the mind. But that would mean not jumping, and you can't. Nobody can not jump. There will be no not-jumping. Among rats, perhaps, but among people never. Everybody has to keep jumping at a door (the one with the circle on it) because that is the way everybody is, specially some people. You wouldn't want me, standing here, to tell you, would you, about my friend the poet (deceased) who said, "My heart has followed all my days something I cannot name"? (It had the circle on it.) And like many poets, although few so beloved, he is gone. It killed him, the jumping. First, of course, there were the preliminary bouts, the convulsions, and the calm and the willingness.

I remember the door with the picture of the girl on it (only it was spring), her arms outstretched in loveliness, her dress (it was the one with the circle on it) uncaught, beginning the slow, clear, blinding cascade — and I guess we would all like to try that door again, for it seemed like the way and for a while it was the way, the door would open and you would go through winged and exalted (like any rat) and the food would be there, the way the Professor had it arranged, everything O.K., and you had chosen the right door for the world was young. The time they changed that door on me, my nose bled for a hundred hours — how do you like that, Madam? Or would you prefer to show me further through this so strange house, or you could take my name and send it to me, for although my heart has followed all my days something I cannot name, I am tired of the jumping and I do not know which way to go, Madam, and I am not even sure that I am not tried beyond the endurance of man (rat, if you will) and have taken leave of sanity. What are you following these days, old friend, after your recovery from the last bump? What is the name, or is it something you cannot name? The rats have a name for it by this time, perhaps, but I don't know what they call it. I call it plexikoid and it comes in sheets, something like insulating board, unattainable and ugli-proof.

And there was the man out in Jersey, because I keep thinking about his terrible necessity and the passion and trouble he had gone to all those years in the indescribable abundance of a householder's detail, building the estate and the planting of the trees and in spring the lawn-dressing and in fall the bulbs for the spring burgeoning, and the watering of the grass on the long light evenings in summer and the gravel for the driveway (all had to be thought out, planned) and the decorative borders, probably, the perennials and the bug spray, and the building of the house from plans of the architect, first the sills, then the studs, then the full corn in the ear, the floors laid on the floor timbers, smoothed, and then the carpets upon the smooth floors and the curtains and the rods therefor. And then, almost without warning, he would be jumping at the same old door and it wouldn't give: they had changed it on him, making life no longer supportable under the elms in the elm shade, under the maples in the maple shade.

"Here you have the maximum of openness in a small room."

It was impossible to say (maybe it was the city) what made him feel the way he did, and I am not the only one either, he kept thinking — ask any doctor if I am. The doctors, they know how many there are, they even know where the trouble is only they don't like to tell you about the prefrontal lobe because that means making a hole in your skull and removing the work of centuries. It took so long coming, this lobe, so many, many years. (Is it something you read in the paper, perhaps?) And now, the strain being so great, the door having been changed by the Professor once too often . . . but it only means a whiff of ether, a few deft strokes, and the higher animal becomes a little easier in his mind and more like the lower one. From now on, you see, that's the way it will be, the ones with the small prefrontal lobes will win because the other ones are hurt too much by this incessant bumping. They can stand just so much, eh, Doctor? (And what is that, pray, that you have in your hand?) Still, you never can tell, eh, Madam?

He crossed (carefully) the room, the thick carpet under him softly, and went toward the door carefully, which was glass and he could see himself in it, and which, at his approach, opened to allow him to pass through; and beyond he half expected to find one of the old doors that he had known, perhaps the one with the circle, the one with the girl her arms outstretched in loveliness and beauty before him. But he saw instead a moving stairway, and descended in light (he kept thinking) to the street below and to the other people. As he stepped off, the ground came up slightly, to meet his foot.

SEAN O'FAOLAIN

1900–

The note of political disillusionment, indeed the critical note in general, sounds more emphatically in O'Faolain than it does in his fellow realist and Cork man Frank O'Connor. Without Ireland he could not live; but without his quarrel with Ireland he could not live either. He differs also from O'Connor in the somewhat greater geographical and class range of his vast output of short fiction. His muse, like Proust's, is memory, though he works with particles of recollection rather than with intricately connected whole patterns. What he values most is the "secret, self-deceiving ambiguities" of character.

Perhaps Ireland is a favorable seminary for writers because it is home to so many repressions against which the artist can fruitfully react. That is one reading of O'Faolain. Akin to it is the recurrent theme of loneliness; perhaps the Irish as a race have felt lonely for centuries.

"All Ireland lives in a dream," says O'Faolain, and the story that follows, one of his most successful as well as ambitious, has a dreamlike quality. One perceptive reader felt that, like the lake itself, which bears so rich a burden of metaphor, it is "shrouded in the most wonderfully mystical mist." It is about two passions, one of faith, the other of flesh. A character in another story says, "The stamp of the Church is on you. 'Tis on all of us." In "Lovers of the Lake" the intricacies of the Church's hold on the Irish are played against the passion felt by two complex human beings, and to masterly effect.

As with O'Connor it is hard to select, amid O'Faolain's almost innumerable stories, his finest. Surely this is a contender.

Lovers of the Lake

"THEY MIGHT WEAR WHITES," she had said, as she stood sipping her tea and looking down at the suburban tennis players in the square. And then, turning her head in that swift movement that always reminded him of a jackdaw: "By the way, Bobby, will you drive me up to Lough Derg next week?"

He replied amiably from the lazy deeps of her armchair.

"Certainly! What part? Killaloe? But is there a good hotel there?"

"I mean the other Lough Derg. I want to do the pilgrimage."

For a second he looked at her in surprise and then burst into laughter; then he looked at her peeringly.

"Jenny! Are you serious?"

"Of course."

"Do you mean that place with the island where they go around on their bare feet on sharp stones, and starve for days, and sit up all night ologroaning and ologoaning?" He got out of the chair, went over to the cigarette box on the bookshelves, and, with his back to her, said coldly, "Are you going religious on me?"

She walked over to him swiftly, turned him about, smiled her smile that was whiter than the whites of her eyes, and lowered her head appealingly on one side. When this produced no effect she said:

"Bobby! I'm always praising you to my friends as a man who takes things as they come. So few men do. Never looking beyond the day. Doing things on the spur of the moment. It's why I like you so much. Other men are always weighing up, and considering and arguing. I've built you up as a sort of magnificent, wild, brainless tomcat. Are you going to let me down now?"

After a while he had looked at his watch and said:

"All right, then. I'll try and fix up a few days free next week. I must drop into the hospital now. But I warn you, Jenny, I've noticed this Holy Joe streak in you before. You'll do it once too often."

She patted his cheek, kissed him sedately, said, "You are a good boy," and saw him out with a loving smile.

They enjoyed that swift morning drive to the Shannon's shore. He suspected nothing when she refused to join him in a drink at Carrick. Leaning on the counter they had joked with the barmaid like any husband

and wife off on a motoring holiday. As they rolled smoothly around the northern shore of Lough Gill he had suddenly felt so happy that he had stroked her purple glove and winked at her. The lough was vacant under the midday sun, its vast expanse of stillness broken only by a jumping fish or by its eyelash fringe of reeds. He did not suspect anything when she sent him off to lunch by himself in Sligo, saying that she had to visit an old nun she knew in the convent. So far the journey had been to him no more than one of her caprices; until a yellow signpost marked TO BUNDORAN made them aware that her destination and their parting was near, for she said:

"What are you proposing to do until Wednesday?"

"I hadn't given it a thought."

"Don't go off and forget all about me, darling. You know you're to pick me up on Wednesday about midday?"

After a silence he grumbled:

"You're making me feel a hell of a bastard, Jenny."

"Why on earth?"

"All this penitential stuff is because of me, isn't it?"

"Don't be silly. It's just something I thought up all by myself out of my own clever little head."

He drove on for several miles without speaking. She looked sideways, with amusement, at his ruddy, healthy, hockey-player face glimmering under the peak of his checked cap. The brushes at his temples were getting white. Everything about him bespoke the distinguished Dublin surgeon on holiday: his pale-green shirt, his darker-green tie, his double-breasted waistcoat, his driving gloves with the palms made of woven cord. She looked pensively towards the sea. He growled:

"I may as well tell you this much, Jenny, if you were my wife I wouldn't stand for any of this nonsense."

So their minds had travelled to the same thought? But if she were his wife the question would never have arisen. She knew by the sudden rise of speed that he was in one of his tempers, so that when he pulled into the grass verge, switched off, and turned towards her she was not taken by surprise. A sea gull moaned high overhead. She lifted her grey eyes to his, and smiled, waiting for the attack.

"Jenny, would you mind telling me exactly what all this is about? I mean, why are you doing this fal-lal at this particular time?"

"I always wanted to do this pilgrimage. So it naturally follows that I would do it sometime, doesn't it?"

"Perhaps. But why, for instance, this month and not last month?"

"The island wasn't open to pilgrims last month."

"Why didn't you go last year instead of this year?"

"You know we went to Austria last year."

"Why not the year before last?"

"I don't know. And stop bullying me. It is just a thing that everybody wants to do sometime. It is a special sort of Irish thing, like Lourdes, or Fatima, or Lisieux. Everybody who knows about it feels drawn to it. If you were a practising Catholic you'd understand."

"I understand quite well," he snapped. "I know perfectly well that people go on pilgrimages all over the world. Spain. France. Mexico. I shouldn't be surprised if they go on them in Russia. What I am asking you is what has cropped up to produce this extra-special performance just *now?*"

"And I tell you I don't know. The impulse came over me suddenly last Sunday looking at those boys and girls playing tennis. For no reason. It just came. I said to myself, 'All right, go now!' I felt that if I didn't do it on the impulse I'd never do it at all. Are you asking me for a rational explanation? I haven't got one. I'm not clever and intelligent like you, darling."

"You're as clever as a bag of cats."

She laughed at him.

"I do love you, Bobby, when you are cross. Like a small boy."

"Why didn't you ask George to drive you?"

She sat up straight.

"I don't want my husband to know anything whatever about this. Please don't mention a word of it to him."

He grinned at his small victory, considered the scythe of her jawbone, looked at the shining darkness of her hair, and restarted the car.

"All the same," he said after a mile, "there must be some reason. Or call it a cause if you don't like the word reason. And I'd give a lot to know what it is."

After another mile:

"Of course, I might as well be talking to that old dolmen over there as be asking a woman why she does anything. And if she knew she wouldn't tell you."

After another mile:

"Mind you, I believe all this is just a symptom of something else. Never forget, my girl, that I'm a doctor. I'm trained to interpret symptoms. If a woman comes to me with a pain . . ."

"Oh, yes, if a woman comes to Surgeon Robert James Flannery with a pain he says to her, 'Never mind, that's only a pain.' My God! If a woman has a pain she has a bloody pain!"

He said quietly:

"Have you a pain?"

"Oh, do shut up! The only pain I have is in my tummy. I'm ravenous."

"I'm sorry. Didn't they give you a good lunch at the convent?"

"I took no lunch; you have to arrive at the island fasting. That's the rule."

"Do you mean to say you've had nothing at all to eat since breakfast?"

"I had no breakfast."

"What will you get to eat when you arrive on the island?"

"Nothing. Or next to nothing. Everybody has to fast on the island the whole time. Sometime before night I might get a cup of black tea, or hot water with pepper and salt in it. I believe it's one of their lighthearted jokes to call it soup."

Their speed shot up at once to sixty-five. He drove through Bundoran's siesta hour like the chariot of the Apocalypse. Nearing Ballyshannon they slowed down to a pleasant, humming fifty.

"Jenny!"

"Yes?"

"Are you tired of me?"

"Is this more of you and your symptoms?"

He stopped the car again.

"Please answer my question."

She laid her purple-gloved hand on his clenched fist.

"Look, darling! We've known one another for six years. You know that like any good little Catholic girl I go to my duties every Easter and every Christmas. Once or twice I've told you so. You've growled and grumbled a bit, but you never made any fuss about it. What are you suddenly worrying about now?"

"Because all that was just routine. Like the French or the Italians. Good Lord, I'm not bigoted. There's no harm in going to church now and again. I do it myself on state occasions, or if I'm staying in some house where they'd be upset if I didn't. But this sort of lunacy isn't routine!"

She slewed her head swiftly away from his angry eyes. A child in a pink pinafore with shoulder frills was driving two black cows through a gap.

"It was never routine. It's the one thing I have to hang on to in an otherwise meaningless existence. No children. A husband I'm not in love with. And I can't marry you."

She slewed back to him. He slewed away to look up the long empty road before them. He slewed back; he made as if to speak; he slewed away impatiently again.

"No?" she interpreted. "It isn't any use, is it? It's my problem, not yours. Or if it is yours you've solved it long ago by saying it's all a lot of damned nonsense."

"And how have you solved it?" he asked sardonically.

"Have you any cause to complain of how I've solved it? Oh, I'm not defending myself. I'm a fraud, I'm a crook, I admit it. You are more honest than I am. You don't believe in anything. But it's the truth that all I have is you and . . ."

"And what?"

"It sounds so blasphemous I can't say it."

"Say it!"

"All I have is you, and God."

He took out his cigarette case and took one. She took one. When he lit hers their eyes met. He said, very softly, looking up the empty road:

"Poor Jenny! I wish you'd talked like this to me before. It is, after all, as you say, your own affair. But what I can't get over is that this thing you're doing is so utterly extravagant. To go off to an island, in the middle of a lake, in the mountains, with a lot of Crawthumpers of every age and sex, and no sex, and peel off your stockings and your shoes, and go limping about on your bare feet on a lot of sharp stones, and kneel in the mud, psalming and beating your breast like a criminal, and drink nothing for three days but salt water . . . it's not like you. It's a side of you I've never known before. The only possible explanation for it must be that something is happening inside in you that I've never seen happen before!"

She spread her hands in despair. He chucked away his cigarette and restarted the car. They drove on in silence. A mist began to speckle the windscreen. They turned off the main road into sunless hills, all brown as hay. The next time he glanced at her she was making up her face; her mouth rolling the lipstick into her lips; her eyes rolling around the mirror. He said:

"You're going to have a nice picnic if the weather breaks."

She glanced out apprehensively.

"It won't be fun."

A sudden flog of rain lashed into the windscreen. The sky had turned its bucket upside down. He said:

"Even if it's raining do you still have to keep walking around on those damn stones?"

"Yes."

"You'll get double pneumonia."

"Don't worry, darling. It's called Saint Patrick's Purgatory. He will look after me."

That remark started a squabble that lasted until they drew up beside the lake. Other cars stood about like stranded boats. Other pilgrims stood by the boat slip, waiting for the ferry, their backs hunched to the wind, their clothes ruffled like the fur of cattle. She looked out across the lough at the creeping worms of foam.

He looked about him sullenly at the waiting pilgrims, a green bus, two taxi-loads of people waiting for the rain to stop. They were not his kind of people at all, and he said so.

"That," she smiled, "is what comes of being a surgeon. You don't meet people, you meet organs. Didn't you once tell me that when you are operating you never look at the patient's face?"

He grunted. Confused and hairy-looking clouds combed themselves on the ridges of the hills. The lake was crumpled and grey, except for those yellow worms of foam blown across it in parallel lines. To the south a cold patch of light made it all look far more dreary. She stared out towards the island and said:

"It's not at all like what I expected."

"And what the hell did you expect? Capri?"

"I thought of an old island, with old grey ruins, and old holly trees and rhododendrons down to the water, a place where old monks would live."

They saw tall buildings like modern hotels rising by the island's shore, an octagonal basilica big enough for a city, four or five bare, slated houses, a long shed like a ballroom. There was one tree. Another bus drew up beside them and people peered out through the wiped glass.

"Oh, God!" she groaned. "I hope this isn't going to be like Lourdes."

"And what, pray, is wrong with Lourdes when it's at home?"

"Commercialized. I simply can't believe that this island was the most famous pilgrimage of the Middle Ages. On the rim of the known world. It must have been like going off to Jerusalem or coming home brown from the sun with a cockle in your hat from Galilee."

He put on a vulgar Yukon voice:

"Thar's gold somewhere in them thar hills. It looks to me like a damn good financial proposition for somebody."

She glared at him. The downpour had slackened. Soon it almost ceased. Gurgles of streams. A sound of pervasive drip. From the back seat she took a small red canvas bag marked T.W.A.

"You will collect me on Wednesday about noon, won't you?"

He looked at her grimly. She looked every one of her forty-one years. The skin of her neck was corrugated. In five years' time she would begin to have jowls.

"Have a good time," he said, and slammed in the gears, and drove away.

The big, lumbering ferryboat was approaching, its prow slapping the corrugated waves. There were three men to each oar. It began to spit rain again. With about a hundred and fifty men and women, of every age and, so far as she could see, of every class, she clambered aboard. They pushed out and slowly they made the crossing, huddling together from the wind and rain. The boat nosed into its cleft and unloaded. She had a sensation of dark water, wet cement, houses, and a great number of people; and that she would have given gold for a cup of hot tea. Beyond the four or five white-washed houses — she guessed that they had been the only buildings on the island before trains and buses made the pilgrimage popular — and beyond the cement paths, she came on the remains of the natural island: a knoll, some warm grass, the tree, and the roots of the old hermits' cells across whose teeth of stone bare-footed pilgrims were already treading on one another's heels. Most of these barefooted people wore mackintoshes. They not only stumbled on one another's heels; they kneeled on one another's toes and tails; for the island was crowded — she thought there must be nearly two thousand people on it. They were packed between the two modern hostels and the big church. She saw a priest in sou'wester and gum boots. A nun waiting for the new arrivals at the door of the women's hostel took her name and address, and gave her the number of her cubicle. She went upstairs to it, laid her red bag on the cot, sat beside it, unfastened her garters, took off her shoes, unpeeled her nylons, and without transition became yet another anonymous pilgrim. As she went out among the pilgrims already praying in the rain she felt only a sense of shame as if she were specially singled out under the microscope of the sky. The wet ground was cold.

A fat old woman in black, rich-breasted, grey-haired, took her kindly by the arm and said in a warm, Kerry voice: "You're shivering, you poor creature! Hould hard now. Sure, when we have the first station done they'll be giving us the ould cup of black tay."

And laughed at the folly of this longing for the tea. She winced when she stepped on the gritty concrete of the terrace surrounding the basilica, built out on piles over the lake. A young man smiled sympathetically, seeing that she was a delicate subject for the rigours before her: he was dressed like a clerk, with three pens in his breast pocket, and he wore a Total Abstinence badge.

"Saint's Island they call it," he smiled. "Some people think it should be called Divil's Island."

She disliked his kindness — she had never in her life asked for pity from anybody, but she soon found that the island floated on kindness. Everything and everybody about her seemed to say, "We are all sinners here, wretched creatures barely worthy of mercy." She felt the abasement of the doomed. She was among people who had surrendered all personal identity, all pride. It was like being in a concentration camp.

The fat old Kerrywoman was explaining to her what the routine was, and as she listened she realized how long her stay would really be. In prospect it had seemed so short: come on Monday afternoon, leave on Wednesday at noon; it had seemed no more than one complete day and two bits of nights. She had not foreseen that immediately after arriving she must remain out of doors until the darkness fell, walking the rounds of the stones, praying, kneeling, for about five hours. And even then she would get no respite, for she must stay awake all night praying in the basilica. It was then that she would begin the second long day, as long and slow as the night; and on the third day she would still be walking those rounds until mid-day. She would be without food, even when she would have left the island, until the midnight of that third day.

"Yerrah, but sure," the old woman cackled happily, "they say that fasting is good for the stomach."

She began to think of "they."

They had thought all this up. They had seen how much could be done with simple prayers. For when she began to tot up the number of Pater-nosters and Aves that she must say she had to stop at the two thousandth. And these reiterated prayers must be said while walking on the stones, or kneeling in the mud, or standing upright with her two arms extended. This was the posture she disliked most. Every time she came to do it, her face to the lake, her arms spread, the queue listening to her renouncing her sins, she had to force herself to the posture and the words. The first time she did it, with the mist blowing into her eyes, her arms out like a crucifix, her lips said the words but her heart cursed herself for coming so unprepared, for coming at all. Before she had completed her first circuit — four times around each one of six cells — one ankle and one toe was bleeding. She was then permitted to ask for the cup of black tea. She received it sullenly, as a prisoner might receive his bread and water.

She wished after that first circuit to start again and complete a second — the six cells, and the seven other ordeals at other points of the island — and so be done for the day. But she found that "they" had invented something else: she must merge with the whole anonymous mass of pilgrims for mass prayer in the church.

A slur of wet feet; patter of rain on leaded windows; smells of bog water and damp clothing; the thousand voices responding to the incantations. At her right a young girl of about seventeen was uttering heartfelt responses. On her left an old man in his sixties gave them out loudly. On all sides, before her, behind her, the same passionate exchange of energy, while all she felt was a crust hardening about her heart, and she thought, in despair, "I have no more feeling than a stone!" And she thought, looking about her, that tonight this vigil would go on for hour after hour until the dark, leaded windows coloured again in the morning light. She leaned her face in her palms and whispered, "O God, please let me out of myself!" The waves of voices beat and rumbled in her ears as in an empty shell.

She was carried out on the general sliding whispering of the bare feet into the last gleanings of the daylight to begin her second circuit. In the porch she cowered back from the rain. It was settling into a filthy night. She was thrust forward by the crowd, flowed with its force to the iron cross by the shingle's edge. She took her place in the queue and then with the night wind pasting her hair across her face she raised her arms and once again renounced the world, the flesh, and the Devil. She did four circles of the church on the gritty concrete. She circled the first cell's stones. She completed the second circle. Her prayers were become numb by now. She stumbled, muttering them, up and down the third steeply sloped cell, or bed. She was a drowned cat and one knee was bleeding. At the fourth cell she saw him.

He was standing about six yards away looking at her. He wore a white raincoat buttoned tight about his throat. His feet were bare. His hair was streaked down his forehead as if he had been swimming. She stumbled towards him and dragged him by the arm down to the edge of the boat slip.

"What are you doing here?" she cried furiously. "Why did you follow me?"

He looked down at her calmly:

"Why shouldn't I be here?"

"Because you don't believe in it! You've just followed me to sneer at me, to mock at me! Or from sheer vulgar curiosity!"

"No," he said, without raising his voice. "I've come to see just what it is that you believe in. I want to know all about you. I want to know why you came here. I don't want you to do anything or have anything that I can't do or can't know. And as for believing — we all believe in something."

Dusk was closing in on the island and the lake. She had to peer into his face to catch his expression.

"But I've known you for years and you've never shown any sign of believing in anything but microscopes and microbes and symptoms. It's absurd, you couldn't be serious about anything like this. I'm beginning to hate you!"

"Are you?" he said, so softly that she had to lean near him to hear him over the slapping of the waves against the boat slip. A slow rift in the clouds let down a star; by its light she saw his smile.

"Yes!" she cried, so loudly that he swept out a hand and gripped her by the arm. Then he took her other arm and said gently:

"I don't think you should have come here, Jenny. You're only tearing yourself to bits. There are some places where some people should never go, things some people should never try to do — however good they may be for others. I know why you came here. You feel you ought to get rid of me, but you haven't the guts to do it, so you come up here into the mountains to get your druids to work it by magic. All right! I'm going to ask them to help you."

He laughed and let her go, giving her a slight impulse away from him.

"Ask? You will *ask?* Do you mean to tell me that you have said as much as one single, solitary prayer on this island?"

"Yes," he said casually, "I have."

She scorned him.

"Are you trying to tell me, Bobby, that you are doing this pilgrimage?"

"I haven't fasted. I didn't know about that. And, anyway, I probably won't. I've got my pockets stuffed with two pounds of the best chocolates I could buy in Bundoran. I don't suppose I'll even stay up all night like the rest of you. The place is so crowded that I don't suppose anybody will notice me if I curl up in some corner of the boathouse. I heard somebody saying that people had to sleep there last night. But you never know — I might — I just might stay awake. If I do, it will remind me of going to midnight Mass with my father when I was a kid. Or going to retreats, when we used all hold up a lighted candle and renounce the Devil.

"It was a queer sensation standing up there by the lake and saying

those words all over again. Do you know, I thought I'd completely forgotten them!"

"The next thing you're going to say is that you believe in the Devil!
You fraud!"

"Oh, there's no trouble about believing in that old gentleman. There
isn't a doctor in the world who doesn't, though he will give him another
name. And on a wet night, in a place like this, you could believe in a lot
of things. No, my girl, what I find it hard to believe in is the flesh and
the world. They are good things. Do you think I'm ever going to believe
that your body and my body are evil? And you don't either! And you
are certainly never going to renounce the world, because you are tied to
it hand and foot!"

"That's not true!"

His voice cut her like a whip:

"Then why do you go on living with your husband?"

She stammered feebly. He cut at her again:

"You do it because he's rich, and you like comfort, and you like being
a 'somebody.'"

With a switch of her head she brushed past him. She did not see him
again that night.

The night world turned imperceptibly. In the church, for hour after hour,
the voices obstinately beat back the responses. She sank under the hum
of the prayer wheel, the lust for sleep, her own despairs. Was he among
the crowd? Or asleep in a corner of the boatshed? She saw his flatly
domed fingers, a surgeon's hand, so strong, so sensitive. She gasped at
the sensual image she had evoked.

The moon touched a black window with colour. After an age it had
stolen to another. Heads drooped. Neighbours poked one another
awake with a smile. Many of them had risen from the benches in order
to keep themselves awake and were circling the aisles in a loose procession of slurring feet, responding as they moved. Exhaustion began to
work on her mind. Objects began to disconnect, become isolated each
within its own outline — now it was the pulpit, now a statue, now a
crucifix. Each object took on the vividness of a hallucination. The crucifix detached itself from the wall and leaned towards her, and for a long
while she saw nothing but the heavy pendent body, the staring eyes, so
that when the old man at her side let his head sink over on her shoulder
and then woke up with a start she felt him no more than if they were
two fishes touching in the sea. Bit by bit the incantations drew her in;
sounds came from her mouth; prayers flowed between her and those
troubled eyes that fixed hers. She swam into an ecstasy as rare as one of
those perfect dances of her youth when she used to swing in a whirl of
music, a swirl of bodies, a circling of lights, floated out of her mortal
frame, alone in the arms that embraced her.

Suddenly it all exploded. One of the four respites of the night had halted the prayers. The massed pilgrims relaxed. She looked blearily about her, no longer disjunct. Her guts rumbled. She looked at the old man beside her. She smiled at him and he at her.

"My poor old knees are crucified," he grinned.

"You should have the skirts," she grinned back.

They were all going out to stretch in the cool, and now dry, air, or to snatch a smoke. The amber windows of the church shivered in a pool of water. A hearty-voiced young woman leaning on the balustrade lit a match for her. The match hissed into the invisible lake lapping below.

"The ould fag," said the young woman, dragging deep on her cigarette, "is a great comfort. 'Tis as good as a man."

"I wonder," she said, "what would Saint Patrick think if he saw women smoking on his island?"

"He'd beat the living lights out of the lot of us."

She laughed aloud. She must tell him that . . . She began to wander through the dark crowds in search of him. He had said something that wasn't true and she would answer him. She went through the crowds down to the boat slip. He was standing there, looking out into the dark as if he had not stirred since she saw him there before midnight. For a moment she regarded him, frightened by the force of the love that gushed into her. Then she approached him.

"Well, Mr. Worldly Wiseman? Enjoying your boathouse bed?"

"I'm doing the vigil," he said smugly.

"You sound almighty pleased with yourself."

He spoke eagerly now:

"Jenny, we mustn't quarrel. We must understand one another. And understand this place. I'm just beginning to. An island. In a remote lake. Among the mountains. Nighttime. No sleep. Hunger. The conditions of the desert. I was right in what I said to you. Can't you see how the old hermits who used to live here could swim off into a trance in which nothing existed but themselves and their visions? I told you a man can renounce what he calls the Devil, but not the flesh, not the world. They thought, like you, that they could throw away the flesh and the world, but they were using the flesh to achieve one of the rarest experiences in the world! Don't you see it?"

"Experiences! The next thing you'll be talking about is symptoms."

"Well, surely, you must have observed?" He peered at the luminous dial of his watch. "I should say that about four o'clock we will probably begin to experience a definite sense of dissociation. After that a positive alienation . . ."

She turned furiously from him. She came back to say:

"I would much prefer, Bobby, if you would have the decency to go away in the morning. I can find my own way home. I hope we don't meet again on this island. Or out of it!"

"The magic working?" he laughed.

After that she made a deliberate effort of the mind to mean and to feel every separate word of the prayers — which is a great foolishness since prayers are not poems to be read or even understood; they are an instinct; to dance would be as wise. She thought that if she could not feel what she said how could she mean it, and so she tried to savour every word, and, from trying to mean each word, lagged behind the rest, sank into herself, and ceased to pray. After the second respite she prayed only to keep awake. As the first cold pallor of morning came into the windows her heart rose again. But the eastern hills are high here and the morning holds off stubbornly. It is the worst hour of the vigil, when the body ebbs, the prayers sink to a drone, and the night seems to have begun all over again.

At the last respite she emerged to see pale tents of blue on the hills. The slow cumulus clouds cast a sheen on the water. There is no sound. No birds sing. At this hour the pilgrims are too awed or too exhausted to speak, so that the island reverts to its ancient silence in spite of the crowds.

By the end of the last bout she was calm like the morning lake. She longed for the cup of black tea. She was unaware of her companions. She did not think of him. She was unaware of herself. She no more thought of God than a slave thinks of his master, and after she had drunk her tea she sat in the morning sun outside the women's hostel like an old blind woman who has nothing in life to wait for but sleep.

The long day expired as dimly as the vapour rising from the water. The heat became morbid. One is said to be free on this second day to converse, to think, to write, to read, to do anything at all that one pleases except the one thing everybody wants to do — to sleep. She did nothing but watch the clouds, or listen to the gentle muttering of the lake. Before noon she heard some departing pilgrims singing a hymn as the great ferryboats pushed off. She heard their voices without longing; she did not even desire food. When she met him she was without rancour.

"Still here?" she said, and when he nodded: "Sleepy?"

"Sleepy."

"Too many chocolates, probably."

"I didn't eat them. I took them out of my pockets one by one as I leaned over the balustrade and guessed what centre each had — coffee, marshmallow, nut, toffee, cream — and dropped it in with a little splash to the holy fishes."

She looked up at him gravely.

"Are you really trying to join in this pilgrimage?"

"Botching it. I'm behindhand with my rounds. I have to do five circuits between today and tomorrow. I may never get them done. Still, something is better than nothing."

"You dear fool!"

If he had not walked away then she would have had to; such a gush of affection came over her at the thought of what he was doing, and why he was doing it — stupidly, just like a man; sceptically, just like a man; not admitting it to himself, just like a man; for all sorts of damn-fool rational reasons, just like a man; and not at all for the only reason that she knew was his real reason: because she was doing it, which meant that he loved her. She sat back, and closed her eyes, and the tears of chagrin oozed between her lids as she felt her womb stir with desire of him.

When they met again it was late afternoon.

"Done four rounds," he said so cheerfully that he maddened her.

"It's not golf, Bobby, damn you!"

"I should jolly well think not. I may tell you my feet are in such a condition I won't be able to play golf for a week. Look!"

She did not look. She took his arm and led him to the quietest corner she could find.

"Bobby, I am going to confess something to you. I've been thinking about it all day trying to get it clear. I know now why I came here. I came because I know inside in me that some day our apple will have to fall off the tree. I'm forty. You are nearly fifty. It will have to happen. I came here because I thought it right to admit that some day, if it has to be, I am willing to give you up."

He began to shake all over with laughter.

"What the hell are you laughing at?" she moaned.

"When women begin to reason! Listen, wasn't there a chap one time who said, 'O God, please make me chaste, but not just yet'?"

"What I am saying is 'now,' if it has to be, if it can be, if I can make it be. I suppose," she said wildly, "I'm really asking for a miracle, that my husband would die, or that you'd die, or something like that that would make it all come right!"

He burst into such a peal of laughter that she looked around her apprehensively. A few people near them also happened to be laughing over something and looked at them indulgently.

"Do you realize, Bobby, that when I go to confession here I will have to tell all about us, and I will have to promise to give you up?"

"Yes, darling, and you won't mean a single word of it."

"But I always mean it!"

He stared at her as if he were pushing curtains aside in her.

"Always? Do you mean you've been saying it for six years?"

"I mean it when I say it. Then I get weak. I can't help it, Bobby. You know that!" She saw the contempt in his eyes and began to talk rapidly, twisting her marriage ring madly around her finger. He kept staring into her eyes like a man staring down the long perspective of a railway line waiting for the engine to appear. "So you see why there wasn't any sense in asking me yesterday why I come now and not at some other time, because with me there isn't any other time, it's always *now*, I meet you *now*, and I love you *now*, and I think it's not right *now*, and then I think, 'No, not *now*,' and then I say I'll give you up *now*, and I mean it every time until we meet again, and it begins all over again, and there's never any end to it until some day I can say, 'Yes, I used to know him once, but not now,' and then it will be a *now* where there won't be any other *now* any more because there'll be nothing to live for."

The tears were leaking down her face. He sighed:

"Dear me! You have got yourself into a mess, haven't you?"

"O God, the promises and the promises! I wish the world would end tonight and we'd both die together!"

He gave her his big damp handkerchief. She wiped her eyes and blew her nose and said:

"You don't mean to go to confession, do you?"

He chuckled sourly.

"And promise? I must go and finish a round of pious golf. I'm afraid, old girl, you just want to get me into the same mess as yourself. No, thank you. You must solve your own problems in your own way, and I in mine."

That was the last time she spoke to him that day.

She went back to the balustrade where she had smoked with the hearty girl in the early hours of the morning. She was there again. She wore a scarlet beret. She was smoking again. She began to talk, and the talk flowed from her without stop. She had fine broad shoulders, a big mobile mouth, and a pair of wild goat's eyes. After a while it became clear that the woman was beside herself with terror. She suddenly let it all out in a gush of exhaled smoke.

"Do you know why I'm hanging around here? Because I ought to go into confession and I'm in dread of it. He'll tear me alive. He'll murder me. It's not easy for a girl like me, I can promise you!"

"You must have terrible sins to tell?" she smiled comfortingly.

"He'll slaughter me, I'm telling you."

"What is it? Boys?"

The two goat's eyes dilated with fear and joy. Her hands shook like a drunkard's.

"I can't keep away from them. I wish to God I never came here."

"But how silly! It's only a human thing. I'm sure half the people here have the same tale to tell. It's an old story, child, the priests are sick of hearing it."

"Oh, don't be talking! Let me alone! I'm criminal, I tell yeh! And there are things you can't explain to a priest. My God, you can hardly explain 'em to a doctor!"

"You're married?" — looking at her ring.

"Poor Tom! I have him wore out. He took me to a doctor one time to know would anything cure me. The old foolah took me temperature and gave me a book like a bus guide about when it's safe and when it isn't safe to make love, the ould eedjut! I was pregnant again before Christmas. Six years married and I have six kids; nobody could stand that gait o'going. And I'm only twenty-four. Am I to have a baby every year of my life? I'd give me right hand this minute for a double whiskey."

"Look, you poor child! We are all in the same old ferryboat here. What about me?"

"You?"

"It's not men with me, it's worse."

"Worse? In God's name, what's worse than men?"

The girl looked all over her, followed her arm down to her hand, to her third finger.

"One man."

The tawny eyes swivelled back to her face and immediately understood.

"Are you very fond of him?" she asked gently, and taking the unspoken answer said, still more pityingly, "You can't give him up?"

"It's six years now and I haven't been able to give him up."

The girl's eyes roved sadly over the lake as if she were surveying a lake of human unhappiness. Then she threw her butt into the water and her red beret disappeared into the maw of the church porch.

She saw him twice before the dusk thickened and the day grew cold again with the early sunset. He was sitting directly opposite her before the men's hostel, smoking, staring at the ground between his legs. They sat facing one another. They were separated by their identities, joined by their love. She glimpsed him only once after that, at the hour when the sky and the hills merge, an outline passing across the lake. Soon after she had permission to go to her cubicle. Immediately she lay down she spiralled to the bottom of a deep lake of sleep.

She awoke refreshed and unburthened. She had received the island's gift: its sense of remoteness from the world, almost a sensation of the world's death. It is the source of the island's kindness. Nobody is just matter, poor to be exploited by rich, weak to be exploited by the strong; in mutual generosity each recognizes the other only as a form of soul; it is a brief, harsh Utopia of equality in nakedness. The bare feet are a symbol of that nakedness unknown in the world they have left.

The happiness to which she awoke was dimmed a little by a conversation she had with an Englishman over breakfast — the usual black tea and a piece of oaten bread. He was a city man who had arrived the day before, been up all night while she slept. He had not yet shaved; he was about sixty-two or three; small and tubby, his eyes perpetually wide and unfocusing behind pince-nez glasses.

"That's right," he said, answering her question. "I'm from England.

Liverpool. I cross by the night boat and get here the next afternoon. Quite convenient, really. I've come here every year for the last twenty-two years, apart from the war years. I come on account of my wife."

"Is she ill?"

"She died twenty-two years ago. No, it's not what you might think — I'm not praying for her. She was a good woman, but, well, you see, I wasn't very kind to her. I don't mean I quarrelled with her, or drank, or was unfaithful. I never gambled. I've never smoked in my life." His hands made a faint movement that was meant to express a whole life, all the confusion and trouble of his soul. "It's just that I wasn't kind. I didn't make her happy."

"Isn't that," she said, to comfort him, "a very private feeling? I mean, it's not in the Ten Commandments that thou shalt make thy wife happy."

He did not smile. He made the same faint movement with his fingers.

"Oh, I don't know! What's love if it doesn't do that? I mean to say, it is something godly to love another human being, isn't it? I mean, what does 'godly' mean if it doesn't mean giving up everything for another? It isn't human to love, you know. It's foolish, it's a folly, a divine folly. It's beyond all reason, all limits. I didn't rise to it," he concluded sadly.

She looked at him, and thought, "A little fat man, a clerk in some Liverpool office all his life, married to some mousy little woman, thinking about love as if he were some sort of Greek mystic."

"It's often," she said lamely, "more difficult to love one's husband, or one's wife, as the case may be, than to love one's neighbour."

"Oh, much!" he agreed without a smile. "Much! Much more difficult!"

At which she was overcome by the thought that inside ourselves we have no room without a secret door; no solid self that has not a ghost inside it trying to escape. If I leave Bobby I still have George. If I leave George I still have myself, and whatever I find in myself. She patted the little man's hand and left him, fearing that if she let him talk on even his one little piece of sincerity would prove to be a fantasy, and in the room that he had found behind his own room she would open other doors leading to other obsessions. He had told her something true about her own imperfection, and about the nature of love, and she wanted to share it while it was still true. But she could not find him, and there was still one more circuit to do before the ferryboat left. She did meet Goat's Eyes. The girl clutched her with tears magnifying her yellow-and-green irises and gasped joyously:

"I found a lamb of a priest. A saint anointed! He was as gentle! 'What's your husband earning?' says he. 'Four pounds ten a week, Father,' says I. 'And six children?' says he. 'You poor woman,' says he, 'you don't need to come here at all. Your Purgatory is at home.' He laid all the blame on poor Tom. And, God forgive me, I let him do it. 'Bring him here to me,' says he, 'and I'll cool him for you.' God bless the poor innocent priest, I wish I knew as little about marriage as he does. But," and she broke into a wail, "sure he has me ruined altogether now. He's after making me so fond of poor Tommy I think I'll never get home soon enough to go to bed with him." And in a vast flood of tears of joy, of relief, and of fresh misery: "I wish I was a bloomin' nun!"

It was not until they were all waiting at the ferryboat that she saw him. She managed to sit beside him in the boat. He touched her hand and winked. She smiled back at him. The bugler blew his bugle. A tardy traveller came racing out of the men's hostel. The boatload cheered him, the bugler helped him aboard with a joke about people who can't be persuaded to stop praying, and there was a general chaff about people who have a lot to pray about, and then somebody raised the parting hymn, and the rowers began to push the heavy oars, and singing they were slowly rowed across the summer lake back to the world.

They were driving back out of the hills by the road they had come, both silent. At last she could hold in her question no longer:

"Did you go, Bobby?"

Meaning: had he, after all his years of silence, of rebellion, of disbelief, made his peace with God at the price of a compact against her. He replied gently:

"Did I probe your secrets all these years?"

She took the rebuke humbly, and for several miles they drove on in silence. They were close, their shoulders touched, but between them there stood that impenetrable wall of identity that segregates every human being in a private world of self. Feeling it she realized at last that it is only in places like the lake-island that the barriers of self break down. The tubby little clerk from Liverpool had been right. Only when love desires nothing but renunciation, total surrender, does self surpass self. Everybody who ever entered the island left the world of self behind for a few hours, exchanged it for what the little man had called a divine folly. It was possible only for a few hours — unless one had the courage, or the folly, to renounce the world altogether. Then another thought came to her. In the world there might also be escape from the world.

"Do you think, Bobby, that when people are in love they can give up everything for one another?"

"No," he said flatly. "Except perhaps in the first raptures?"

"If I had a child I think I could sacrifice anything for it. Even my life."

"Yes," he agreed. "It has been known to happen."

And she looked at him sadly, knowing that they would never be able to marry, and even if she did that she would never have children. And yet, if they could have married, there was a lake . . .

"Do you know what I'm planning at this moment?" he asked breezily. She asked without interest what it was.

"Well, I'm simply planning the meal we're going to eat tonight in Galway, at midnight."

"At midnight? Then we're going on with this pilgrimage? Are we?"

"Don't *you* want to? It was your idea in the beginning."

"All right. And what are we going to do until midnight? I've never known time to be so long."

"I'm going to spend the day fishing behind Glencar. That will kill the hungry day. After that, until midnight, we'll take the longest possible road around Connemara. Then would you have any objections to mountain trout cooked in milk, stuffed roast kid with fresh peas and spuds in their jackets, apple pie and whipped cream, with a cool Pouilly Fuissé, a cosy 1929 claret, West of Ireland Pont l'Évêque, finishing up with Gaelic coffee and two Otards? Much more in your line, if I know anything about you, than your silly old black tea and hot salt water."

"I admit I like the things of the flesh."

"You live for them!"

He had said it so gently, so affectionately that, half in dismay, half with amusement, she could not help remembering Goat's Eyes, racing home as fast as the bus would carry her to make love to her Tommy. After that they hardly spoke at all, and then only of casual things such as a castle beside the road, the sun on the edging sea, a tinker's caravan, an opening view. It was early afternoon as they entered the deep valley at Glencar and he probed in second gear for an attractive length of stream, found one and started eagerly to put his rod together. He began to walk up against the dazzling bubble of water and within an hour was out of sight. She stretched herself out on a rug on the bank and fell sound asleep.

It was nearly four o'clock before she woke up, stiff and thirsty. She drank from a pool in the stream, and for an hour she sat alone by the pool, looking into its peat-brown depth, as vacantly contented as a tinker's wife to live for the moment, to let time wind and unwind everything. It was five o'clock before she saw him approaching, plodding in his flopping waders, with four trout on a rush stalk. He threw the fish at her feet and himself beside them.

"I nearly ate them raw," he said.

"Let's cook them and eat them," she said fiercely.

He looked at her for a moment, then got up and began to gather dry twigs, found Monday's newspaper in the car — it looked like a paper of years ago — and started the fire. She watched while he fed it. When it was big enough in its fall to have made a hot bed of embers he roasted two of the trout across the hook of his gaff, and she smelled the crisping flesh and sighed. At last he laid them, browned and crackly, on the grass by her hand. She took one by its crusted tail, smelled it, looked at him, and slung it furiously into the heart of the fire. He gave a sniff-laugh and did the same with his.

"Copy cat!" she said.

"Let's get the hell out of here," he said, jumping up. "Carry the kit, will you?"

She rose, collected the gear, and followed him saying:

"I feel like an Arab wife. 'Carry the pack. Go here. Go there.' "

They climbed out of the glens on to the flat moorland of the Easky peninsula where the evening light was a cold ochre gleaming across the green bogland that was streaked with all the weedy colours of a strand at ebb. At Ballina she suggested that they should have tea.

"It will be a pleasant change of diet!" he said.

When they had found a café and she was ordering the tea he said to the waitress:

"And bring lots of hot buttered toast."

"This," she said, as she poured out the tea and held up the milk jug questioningly, "is a new technique of seduction. Milk?"

"Are you having milk?"

"No."

"No, then."

"Some nice hot buttered toast?"

"Are you having toast?" he demanded.

"Why the bloody hell should it be up to me to decide?"

"I asked you a polite question," he said rudely.

"No."

"No!"

They looked at one another as they sipped the black tea like two people who are falling head over heels into hatred of one another.

"Could you possibly tell me," he said presently, "why I bother my head with a fool of a woman like you?"

"I can only suppose, Bobby, that it is because we are in love with one another."

"I can only suppose so," he growled. "Let's get on!"

They took the longest way round he could find on the map, west into County Mayo, across between the lake at Pontoon, over the level bogland to Castlebar. Here the mountains walled in the bogland plain with cobalt air — in the fading light the land was losing all solidity. Clouds like soapsuds rose and rose over the edges of the mountains until they glowed as if there was a fire of embers behind the blue ranges. In Castlebar he pulled up by the post office and telephoned to the hotel at Salthill for dinner and two rooms. When he came out he saw a poster in a shop window and said:

"Why don't we go to the pictures? It will kill a couple of hours."

"By rights," she said, "you ought to be driving me home to Dublin."

"If you wish me to I will."

"Would you if I asked you?"

"Do you want me to?"

"I suppose it's rather late now, isn't it?"

"Not at all. Fast going we could be there about one o'clock. Shall we?"

"It wouldn't help. George is away. I'd have to bring you in and give you something to eat, and . . . Let's go to the blasted movies!"

The film was *Charley's Aunt*. They watched its slapstick gloomily. When they came out, after nine o'clock, there was still a vestigial light in the sky. They drove on and on, westward still, prolonging the light, prolonging the drive, holding off the night's decision. Before Killary they paused at a black-faced lake, got out, and stood beside its quarried beauty. Nothing along its stony beach but a few wind-torn rushes.

"I could eat you," he said.

She replied that only lovers and cannibals talk like that.

They dawdled past the long fiord of Killary where young people on holiday sat outside the hotel, their drinks on the trestled tables. In Clifden the street was empty, people already climbing to bed, as the lights in the upper windows showed. They branched off on the long coastal road where the sparse whitewashed cottages were whiter than the foam of waves that barely suggested sea. At another darker strand they halted, but now they saw no foam at all and divined the sea only by its invisible whispering, or when a star touched a wave. Midnight was now only an hour away.

Their headlights sent rocks and rabbits into movement. The heather streamed past them like kangaroos. It was well past eleven as they poured along the lonely land by Galway Bay. Neither of them had spoken for an hour. As they drove into Salthill there was nobody abroad. Galway was dark. Only the porch light of the hotel showed that it was alive. When he turned off the engine the only sound at first was the crinkle of contracting metal as the engine began to cool. Then to their right they heard the lisping bay. The panel button lit the dashboard clock.

"A quarter to," he said, leaning back. She neither spoke nor stirred. "Jenny!" he said sharply.

She turned her head slowly and by the dashboard light he saw her white smile.

"Yes, darling?"

"Worn out?" he asked, and patted her knee.

She vibrated her whole body so that the seat shook, and stretched her arms about her head, and lowering them let her head fall on his shoulder, and sighed happily, and said:

"What I want is a good long drink of anything on earth except tea."

These homing twelve o'clockers from Lough Derg are well known in every hotel all over the west of Ireland. Revelry is the reward of penance. The porter welcomed them as if they were heroes returned from a war. As he led them to their rooms he praised them, he sympathized with them, he patted them up and he patted them down, he assured them that the ritual grill was at that moment sizzling over the fire, he proffered them hot baths, and he told them where to discover the bar. "Ye will discover it . . ." was his phrase. The wording was exact, for the bar's gaiety was muffled by dim lighting, drawn blinds, locked doors. In the overheated room he took off his jacket and loosened his tie. They had to win a corner of the counter, and his order was for two highballs with ice in them. Within two minutes they were at home with the crowd. The island might never have existed if the barmaid, who knew where they had come from, had not laughed: "I suppose ye'll ate like lions?"

After supper they relished the bar once more, sipping slowly now, so refreshed that they could have started on the road again without distaste or regret. As they sipped they gradually became aware of a soft strumming and drumming near at hand, and were told that there was a dance on in the hotel next door. He raised his eyebrows to her. She laughed and nodded.

They gave it up at three o'clock and walked out into the warm-cool of the early summer morning. Gently tipsy, gently tired they walked to the little promenade. They leaned on the railing and he put his arm about her waist, and she put hers around his, and they gazed at the moon silently raking its path across the sea towards Aran. They had come, she knew, to the decisive moment. He said:

"They have a fine night for it tonight on the island."

"A better night than we had," she said tremulously.

After another spell of wave fall and silence he said:

"Do you know what I'm thinking, Jenny? I'm thinking that I wouldn't mind going back there again next year. Maybe I might do it properly the next time?"

"The next time?" she whispered, and all her body began to dissolve and, closing her eyes, she leaned against him. He, too, closed his eyes, and all his body became as rigid as a steel girder that flutters in a storm. Slowly they opened their love-drunk eyes, and stood looking long over the brightness and blackness of the sea. Then, gently, ever so gently, with a gentleness that terrified her he said:

"Shall we go in, my sweet?"

She did not stir. She did not speak. Slowly turning to him she lifted her eyes to him pleadingly.

"No, Bobby, please, not yet."

"Not yet?"

"Not tonight!"

He looked down at her, and drew his arms about her. They kissed passionately. She knew what that kiss implied. Their mouths parted. Hand in hand they walked slowly back to the hotel, to their separate rooms.

V. S. PRITCHETT
1900–

V. S. Pritchett (Sir Victor since 1975) has in his long career established himself not only as one of the half dozen finest short story writers now using
English but as a travel writer, biographer, autobiographer and, notably, literary critic. In all these fields his distinguishing qualities are sanity, a high
intelligence that never loses reader-contact, and a natural kinship with a
large variety of humankind. The critic Frank Kermode has called him "the
finest English writer alive"; if this is true, it is mainly his short stories that
should have won him the accolade.

   Pritchett writes: "By the 1930's I had at any rate discovered my voice and
that my native bent was to the designs of comedy and its ironies. For me
comedy has a militant, tragic edge, even when I've proceeded to the purely
comic or to farce." This is his unchanging general approach, but it does not
suggest the dazzling variety of figures and situations to which that approach
so perfectly addresses itself. He reminds one of Keats's notion of the poet:
"he has no identity — he is continually informing — and filling some other
body."

   Pritchett seems to be on intimate terms with all classes and subclasses of
English people, being exceptionally knowledgeable about trades and voca-
tions, the manner in which ordinary men and women earn their daily bread.
He exerts his surest touch with the lower middle class, in whom he is sure
to find (like Dickens, with whom he is often compared) the most surprising
yet convincing oddities and subtleties of character. As a whole his stories
compose a magnificent dramatization of a bromide: people are not what
they seem.

   Against a background of the antique business (one of the dozens he seems
to know all about) "The Camberwell Beauty" examines, in a characteristic
seriocomic vein, the curious nature of lust. "The heart of the trade is lust,"
remarks the narrator and then proceeds to tell us a story in which the lust
for an armoire or a piece of Meissen is curiously merged with a passion for
a girl: "Pliny had got something I wanted."

The Camberwell Beauty

AUGUST'S? On the Bath road? Twice-Five August — of course I knew August: ivory man. And the woman who lived with him — her name was Price. She's dead. He went out of business years ago. He's probably dead too. I was in the trade only three or four years but I soon knew every antique dealer in the South of England. I used to go to all the sales. Name another. Naseley of Close Place? Jades, Asiatics, never touched India. Alsop of Ramsey? Ephemera. Marbright, High Street, Boxley? Georgian silver. Fox? Are you referring to Fox of Denton or Fox of Camden — William Morris, art nouveau — or the Fox Brothers in the Portobello Road? — the eldest stuttered. They had an uncle in Brighton who went mad looking for old Waterford. Hindmith? No, he was just a copier. Ah now, Pliny! He was a very different cup of tea: Caughley ware. (Coalport took it over in 1821.) I am speaking of specialties: furniture is the bread and butter of the trade. It keeps a man going while his mind is on his specialty, and within that specialty there is one object he broods on from one year to the next, most of his life: the thing a man would commit murder to get his hands on if he had the nerve, but I have never heard of a dealer who had. Theft perhaps. A stagnant lot. But if he does get hold of that thing he will never let it go or certainly not to a customer — dealers only really like dealing among themselves — but every other dealer in the trade knows he's got it. So they sit in their shops reading the catalogues and watching one another. Fox broods on something Alsop has. Alsop has his eye on Pliny and Pliny puts his hands to one of his big red ears when he hears the name of August. At the heart of the trade is lust, but a lust that is a dream paralysed by itself. So paralysed that the only release, the only hope, as everyone knows, is disaster: a bankruptcy, a divorce, a court case, a burglary, trouble with the police, a death. Perhaps then the grip on some piece of treasure will weaken and fall into the watcher's hands and even if it goes elsewhere he will go on dreaming about it.

What was it that Pliny, Gentleman Pliny, wanted of a man like August, who was not much better than a country junk dealer? When I opened up in London I thought it was a particular Staffordshire figure, but Pliny was far above that. These figures fetch very little, though one or two are hard to find: "The Burning of Cranmer," for example. Very few were made; it never sold and the firm dropped it. I was young and eager and one day when a collector, a scholarly man, as dry as a stick, came to my shop and told me he had a complete collection except for this piece, I said in my innocent way: "You've come to the right man. I'm fairly certain I can get it for you — at a price." This was a lie; but I was astonished to see the old man look at me with contempt, then light up like a fire, and when he left, look back furtively at me: he had betrayed his lust.

You rarely see an antique shop standing on its own; there are always three or four together watching each other. I asked the advice of the man next door who ran a small boatyard on the canal in his spare time and he said, "Try Pliny down the Green: he knows everyone." I went "over the water," to Pliny; he was closed, but I did find him at last at a sale room. Pliny was marking his catalogue and waiting for the next lot to come up and he said to me in a scornful way, slapping a young man down, "August's got it." I saw him wink at the man next to him as I left.

I had bought myself a small red car that annoyed the older dealers and I drove down the other side of Steepleton on the Bath road. August's was one of four shops opposite the Lion Hotel on the main road at the end of the town where the country begins again, and there I got my first lesson. The shop was closed. I went across to the bar of the hotel, and August was there, a fat man of fifty in wide trousers and a drip to his nose who was paying for drinks from a bunch of dirty notes in his jacket pocket and dropping them on the floor. He was drunk and very offended when I picked a couple up and gave them to him. He'd just come back from Newbury races. I humoured him but he kept rolling about and turning his back to me half the time and so I blurted out, "I've just been over at the shop. You've got some Staffordshire, I hear."

He stood still and looked me up and down and the beer swelled in him.

"Who may you be?" he said with all the pomposity of drink. I told him. I said right out, "Staffordshire. 'Cranmer's Burning.' " His face went dead and the colour of liver.

"So is London," he said, and turned away to the bar.

"I'm told you might have it. I've got a collector," I said.

"Give this lad a glass of water," said August to the barmaid. "He's on fire."

There is nothing more to say about the evening or the many other visits I made to August's except that it has a moral to it and that I had to help August over to his shop, where an enormous woman much taller than he in a black dress and a little girl of fourteen or so were at the door waiting for him. The girl looked frightened and ran a few yards from the door as August and his woman collided belly to belly.

"Come back," called the woman.

The child crept back. And to me the woman said, "We're closed," and having got the two inside, shut the door in my face.

The moral is this: if "The Burning of Cranmer" was August's treasure, it was hopeless to try and get it before he had time to guess what mine was. It was clear to him I was too new to the trade to have one. And in fact I don't think he had the piece. Years later, I found my collector had left his collection complete to a private museum in Leicester when he died. He had obtained what he craved: a small immortality in being memorable for his relation to a minor work of art.

I know what happened at August's that night. In time his woman, Mrs. Price, bellowed it to me, for her confidences could be heard down the street. August flopped on his bed, and while he was sleeping off the drink she got the bundles of notes out of his pockets and counted them. She always did this after his racing days. If he had lost she woke him up and shouted at him; if he had made a profit she kept quiet and hid it under her clothes in a chest of drawers. I went down from London again and again, but August was not there.

Most of the time these shops are closed. You rattle the door handle; no reply. Look through the window, and each object inside stands gleaming with something like a smile of malice, especially on porcelain and glass. The furniture states placidly that it has been in better houses than you will ever have, the brass speaks of vanished servants. Everything speaks of the dead hands that have touched it; even the dust is like the dust of vanished families. In the shabby places — and August's was shabby — the dealer is like a toadstool that has grown out of the unwanted. There was only one attractive object in August's shop — as I say, he went in for ivories, and on a table at the back was a set of white and red chessmen set out on a board partly concealed by a screen. I was tapping my feet impatiently and looking through the window when I was astonished to see two of the chessmen had moved; then I saw a hand, a long, thin work-reddened hand appear from behind the screen and move one of the pieces back. Life in the place! I rattled the door handle again and the child came from behind the screen. She had a head loaded with heavy black hair to her shoulders and a white heart-shaped face and wore a skimpy dress with small pink flowers on it. She was so thin that she looked as if she would blow away in fright out of the shop, but instead, pausing on tiptoe, she swallowed with appetite: her sharp eyes had seen my red car outside the place. She looked back cautiously at the inner door of the shop and then ran to unlock the door. I went in.

"What are you up to?" I said. "Playing chess?"

"I'm teaching my children," she said, putting up her chin like a child of five. "Do you want to buy something?"

At once Mrs. Price was there, shouting, "Isabel, I told you not to open the door. Go back into the room."

Mrs. Price went to the chessboard and put the pieces back in their places.

"She's a child," said Mrs. Price, accusing me.

And when she said this, Mrs. Price blew herself out to a larger size; then her sullen face went blank and babyish as if she had travelled out of herself for a beautiful moment. Then her brows levelled and she became sullen.

"Mr. August's out," she said.

"It is about a piece of Staffordshire," I said. "He mentioned it to me. When will he be in?"

"He's in and out. No good asking. He doesn't know himself."

"I'll try again."

"If you like."

There was nothing to be got out of Mrs. Price.

In my opinion, the antique trade is not one for a woman, unless she is on her own. Give a woman a shop and she wants to sell something: even the little girl at August's wanted to sell. It's instinct. It's an excitement. Mrs. Price, August's woman, was living with a man exactly like the others in the trade; he hated customers and hated parting with anything. By middle age these women have dead blank faces, they look with resentment and indifference at what is choking their shops; their eyes go smaller and smaller as the chances of getting rid of it become rarer and rarer and they are defeated. Kept out of the deals their husbands have among themselves, they see even their natural love of intrigue frustrated. This was the case of Mrs. Price, who must have been handsome in a big-boned way when she was young, but who had swollen into a drudge. What allured the men did not allure her at all. The trade feeds on illusions. If you go after Georgian silver you catch the illusion, while you are bidding, that you are related to the rich families who owned it. You acquire imaginary ancestors. Or, like Pliny with the piece of Meissen he never got his hands on, you drift into German history and become a secret curator of the Victoria and Albert Museum — a place he often visited. August's lust for "the ivories" gave to his horse-racing mind a private Oriental side: he dreamt of rajahs, sultans, harems, and lavish gamblers, which, in a man as vulgar as he was, came out in sad reality as a taste for country girls and the company of bookies. Illusions lead to furtiveness in everyday life and to sudden temptations: the trade is close to larceny, to situations where you don't ask where something has come from, especially for a man like August, whose dreams had landed him in low company. He had started at the bottom, and very early he "received" and got twelve months for it. This frightened him. He took up with Mrs. Price, and though he resented it, she had made a fairly honest man of him. August was to be *her* work of art.

But he did not make an honest woman of her. No one disapproved of this except herself. Her very size, growing year by year, was an assertion of virtue. Everyone took her side in her public quarrels with him. And as if to make herself more respectable, she had taken in her sister's little girl when the sister died: the mother had been in Music Hall. Mrs. Price petted and prinked the little thing. When August became a failure as a work of art, Mrs. Price turned to the child. Even August was charmed by her when she jumped on his knee and danced about showing him her new clothes. A little actress, as everyone said — exquisite.

It took me a long time to give up the belief that August had the Cranmer piece, and as I know now, he hadn't got it; but at last I did see I was wasting my time and settled into the routine of the business. I sometimes saw August at country sales, and at one outside Marlborough something ridiculous happened. It was a big sale and went on till late in the afternoon and he had been drinking; after lunch the auctioneer had put up a china cabinet and the bidding was strong. Some outsider was bidding against the dealers, a thing that made them close their faces with moral indignation: the instinctive hatred of customers united them. Drink always stirred August morally; he was a rather despised figure and he was, I suppose, determined to speak for all. He entered the bidding. Up went the price: 50,5,60,5,70,5,80,5,90. The outsiders were a young couple with a dog.

"Ninety, ninety?" called the auctioneer.

August could not stand it. "Twice-five," he shouted.

There is not much full-throated laughter at sales: it is usually shoppish and dusty. But the crowd in this room looked round at August and shouted with a laughter that burst the gloom of trade. He was put out for a second and then saw his excitement had made him famous. The laughter went on: the wonder had for a whole minute stopped the sale. "Twice-five!" He was slapped on the back. At sixty-four the man who had never had a nickname had been christened. He looked round him. I saw a smile cross his face and double the pomposity that beer had put into him and he redoubled it that evening at the nearest pub. I went off to my car, and Alsop of Ramsey, the ephemera man who had picked up some Victorian programs, followed me and said out of the side of his mouth, "More trouble tonight at August's."

And then to change the subject and speaking for every dealer south of the Trent, he offered serious news. "Pliny's mother's dead — Pliny of the Green."

The voice had all the shifty meaning of the trade. I was too simple to grasp the force of this confidence. It surprised me in the following weeks to hear people repeat the news, "Pliny's mother's dead," in so many voices, from the loving-memory-and-deepest-sympathy manner as much suited to old clothes, old furniture, and human beings indiscriminately as to the flat statement that an event of business importance had occurred in my eventless trade. I was in it for the money and so, I suppose, were all the rest — how else could they live? — but I seemed to be surrounded by a dreamy freemasonry who thought of it in a different secretive way.

On a wet morning the following spring I was passing through Salisbury on market day and stopped in the square to see if there was anything worth picking up at the stalls there. It was mostly junk, though I did find a pretty Victorian teapot — no mark, I agree — with a chip in the spout for a few shillings, because the fever of the trade never quite leaves one even on dull days. (I sold the pot five years later for eight pounds when prices started to go mad.) I went into one of the pubs on the square — I forget its name — and I was surprised to see Marbright and Alsop there and, sitting near the window, Mrs. Price. August was getting drinks at the bar.

Alsop said to me, "Pliny's here. I passed him a minute ago."

Marbright said, "He was standing in Woolworth's doorway. I asked him to come and have one, but he wouldn't."

"It's hit him hard, his mother going," Marbright said. "What's he doing here? Queen Mary's dead."

It was an old joke that Gentleman Pliny had never been the same since the old Queen had come to his shop some time back — everyone knew what she was for picking up things. He only opened on Sundays now and a wealthy crowd came there in their big cars — a new trend, as Alsop said. August brought the drinks and stood near, for Mrs. Price spread herself on the bench and never left much room for anyone else to sit down. He looked restless and glum.

"Where will Pliny be without his mother," Mrs. Price moaned into her glass and, putting it down, glowered at August. She had been drinking a good deal.

August ignored her and said, sneering, "He kept her locked up." There is always a lot of talking about "locking up" in the trade; people's minds go to their keys.

"It was a kindness," Mrs. August said, "after the burglars got in at Sampson's, three men in a van loading it up in broad daylight. Any woman of her age would be frightened."

"It was nothing to do with the burglary," said August, always sensitive when crime was mentioned. "She was getting soft in the head. He caught her giving his stuff away when she was left on her own. She was past it."

Mrs. Price was a woman who didn't like to be contradicted.

"He's a gentleman," said Mrs. Price, accusing August. "He was good to his mother. He took her out every Sunday night of his life. She liked a glass of stout on Sundays."

This was true, though Mrs. Price had not been to London for years and had never seen this event; but all agreed. We live on myths.

"It was her kidneys," moaned Mrs. Price; one outsize woman was mourning another, seeing a fate.

"I suppose that's why he didn't get married, looking after her," said Marbright.

"Pliny! Get married! Don't make me laugh," said August with a defiant recklessness that seemed to surprise even himself. "The last Saturday in every month like a clock striking he was round the pubs in Brixton with old Lal Drake."

And now, as if frightened by what he said, he swanked his way out of the side door of the pub on his way to the gents'.

We lowered our eyes. There are myths, but there are facts. They all knew — even I had heard — that what August said was true, but it was not a thing a sensible man would say in front of Mrs. Price. And — mind you — Pliny standing a few doors down the street. But Mrs. Price stayed calm among the thoughts in her mind.

"That's a lie," she said peacefully, though she was eyeing the door waiting for August to come back.

"I knew his father," said Alsop. We were soon laughing about the ancient Pliny, the Bermondsey boy who began with a barrow shouting "Old iron" in the streets, a man who never drank, never had a bank account — didn't trust banks — who belted his son while his mother "educated him up" — she was a tall woman and the boy grew up like her, tall with a long arching nose and those big red ears that looked as though his parents had pulled him now this way, now that, in their fight over him. She had been a housekeeper in a big house and she had made a son who looked like an old family butler, Cockney to the bone, but almost a gentleman. Except, as Alsop said, his way of blowing his nose like a foghorn on the Thames, but sharp as his father. Marbright said you could see the father's life in the store at the back of the shop: it was piled high with what had made the father's money — every kind of old-fashioned stuff.

"Enough to furnish two or three hotels," Alsop said. Mrs. Price nodded.

"Wardrobes, tables . . ." she said.

"A museum," said Marbright. "Helmets, swords. Two fourposters the last time I was there."

"Ironwork. Brass," nodded Mrs. Price mournfully.

"Must date back to the Crimean War," said Marbright.

"And it was all left to Pliny."

There was a general sigh.

"And he doesn't touch it. Rubbish, he calls it. He turned his back on it. Only goes in for the best. Hepplewhite, marquetries, his consoles, Regency."

There was a pause.

"And," I said, "his Meissen."

They looked at me as if I were a criminal. They glanced at one another as if asking whether they should call the police. I was either a thief or I had publicly stripped them of all their clothes. I had publicly announced Pliny's lust.

Although Mrs. Price had joined in the conversation, it was in the manner of someone talking in her sleep, for when this silence came she woke up and said in a startled voice, "Lal Drake." And screwing up her fists she got up, and pausing to get ready for a rush, she heaved herself fast to the door by which August had left for the gents' down the alley a quarter of an hour before.

"The other door, missis," someone shouted. But she was through it.

"Drink up," we said and went out by the front door. I was the last and had a look down the side alley and there I saw a sight: August with a hand doing up his fly buttons and the other arm protecting his face. Mrs. Price was hitting out at him and shouting. The language!

"You dirty sod. I knew it. The girl told me." She was shouting. She saw me, stopped hitting and rushed at me in tears and shouted back at him. "The filthy old man."

August saw his chance and got out of the alley and made for the cars in the square. She let me go, to shout after him. We were all there, and in Woolworth's doorway was Pliny. Rain was still falling and he looked wet and all the more alone for being wet. I walked off, and, I suppose, seeing me go and herself being alone and giddy in her rage she looked all round and turned her temper on me. "The girl has got to go," she shouted.

Then she came to her senses.

"Where is August?" August had got to his car and was driving out of the square. She could do nothing. Then she saw Pliny. She ran from me to Pliny, from Pliny to me.

"He's going after the girl," she screamed.

We calmed her down and it was I who drove her home. (This was when she told me, as the wipers went up and down on the windshield, that she and August were not married.) Her tears were like the hissing water we splashed through on the road. "I'm worried for the child. I told her, 'Keep your door locked.' I see it's locked every night. I'm afraid I'll forget and won't hear him if I've had a couple. She's a kid. She doesn't know anything." I understood that the face I had always thought was empty was really filled with the one person she loved: Isabel.

August was not there when we got to their shop. Mrs. Price went in, and big as she was, she did not knock anything over.

"Isabel?" she called.

The girl was in the scullery and came out with a wet plate that dripped on the carpet. In two years she had changed. She was wearing an old dress and an apron, but also a pair of silver high-heeled evening shoes. She had become the slut of the house and her pale skin looked dirty.

"You're dripping that thing everywhere. What have you got those shoes on for? Where did you get them?"

"Uncle Harry, for Christmas," she said. She called August "Uncle Harry." She tried to look jaunty, as if she had put all her hope in life into those silly evening shoes.

"All right," said Mrs. Price weakly, looking at me to keep quiet and say nothing.

Isabel took off her apron when she saw me. I don't know whether she remembered me. She was still pale, but had the shapeliness of a small young woman. Her eyes looked restlessly and uncertainly at both of us; her chin was firmer but it trembled. She was smiling too, and because I was there and the girl might see an ally in me, Mrs. Price looked with half kindness at Isabel. But when I got up to go, the girl looked at me as if she would follow me out the door. Mrs. Price got up fast to bar the way. She stood on the doorstep of the shop watching me get into the car, puffing with the inability to say "Thank you" or "Good-bye." If the girl was a child, Mrs. Price was ten times a child, and both of them standing on the doorstep were like children who don't want anyone to go away.

I drove off, and for a few miles I thought about Mrs. Price and the girl, but once settled into the long drive to London, the thought of Pliny supplanted them. I had been caught up in the fever of the trade. Pliny's mother was dead. What was going to happen to Pliny and all that part of the business Pliny had inherited from his father, the stuff he despised and had not troubled himself with very much in his mother's time? I ought to go "over the water" — as we say in London — to have a look at it sometime.

In a few days I went there; I found the idea had occurred to many others. The shop was on one of the main bus routes in South London, a speckled early Victorian place with an ugly red-brick store behind it. Pliny's father had had an eye for a cosy but useful bit of property. Its windows had square panes (1810) and to my surprise the place was open and I could see people inside. There was Pliny with his nose which looked servile rather than distinguished, wearing a long biscuit-coloured tweed jacket with leather pads at the elbows like a Cockney sportsman. There, too, was August with his wet eyes and drinker's shame, Mrs. Price swelling over him in her best clothes, and the girl. They had come up from the country and August had had his boots cleaned. The girl was in her best, too, and was standing apart touching things in the shop and on the point of merriment, looking with wonder at Pliny's ears. He often seemed to be talking at her when he was talking to Mrs. Price. I said, "Hullo! Up from the country? What are you doing here?"

Mrs. Price was so large that she had to turn her whole body and place her belly in front of everyone who spoke to her.

"Seeing to his teeth," she said, nodding at August, and from years of habit, August turned, too, when his wife turned, in case it was just as well not to miss one of her pronouncements, whatever else he might dodge. One side of August's jaw was swollen. Then Mrs. Price slowly turned her whole body to face Pliny again. They were talking about his mother's death. Mrs. Price was greedy, as one stout woman thinking of another, for a melancholy tour of the late mother's organs. The face of the girl looked prettily wise and holidayfied because the heavy curls of her hair hung close to her face. She looked out of the window, restless and longing to get away while her elders went on talking, but she was too listless to do so. Then she would look again at Pliny's large ears with a child's pleasure in anything strange: they gave him a dog-like appearance, and if the Augusts had not been there, I think she would have jumped at him mischievously to touch them but remembered in time that she had lately grown into a young lady. When she saw him looking at her she turned her back and began writing in the dust on a little table standing next to a cabinet which had a small jug in it. She was writing her name in the dust I S A B . . . And then stopped. She turned round suddenly because she saw I had been watching.

"Is that old Meissen?" she called out, pointing to the jug in the cabinet. They stopped talking. It was comic to see her pretending, for my benefit, that she knew all about porcelain.

"Cor! Old Meissen!" said August, pulling his racing newspaper out of his jacket pocket with excitement, and Mrs. Price fondly swung her big handbag; all laughed loudly — a laugh of lust and knowledge. They knew, or thought they knew, that Pliny had a genuine Meissen piece somewhere, probably upstairs where he lived. The girl was pleased to have made them laugh at her; she had been noticed.

Pliny said decently, "No, dear. That's Caughley. Would you like to see it?"

He walked to the cabinet and took the jug down and put it on a table.

"Got the leopard?" said August knowingly. Pliny showed the mark of the leopard on the base of the jug and put it down again. It was a pretty, shapely jug with a spray of branches and in the branches a pair of pheasants were perching, done in transfer. The girl scared us all by picking it up in both hands, but it was charming to see her holding it up and studying it.

"Careful," said Mrs. Price.

"She's all right," said Pliny. Then — it alarmed us — she wriggled with laughter.

"What a funny face," she said.

Under the lip of the jug was the small face of an old man with a long nose looking sly and wicked.

"They used to put a face under the lip," Pliny said.

"That's right," said August.

The girl held it out at arm's length, and looking from the jug to Pliny, she said, "It's like you, Mr. Pliny."

"Isabel!" said Mrs. Price. "That's rude."

"But it is," said Isabel. "Isn't it?" She was asking me. Pliny grinned. We were all relieved to see him take the jug from her and put it back in the cabinet.

"It belonged to my mother," he said. "I keep it there."

Pliny said to me, despising me because I had said nothing and because I was a stranger, "Go into the back and have a look round if you want to. The light's on."

I left the shop and went down the steps into the long storeroom, where the whitewashed walls were grey with dust. There was an alligator hanging by a nail near the steps, a couple of cavalry helmets and a dirty drum that must have been there since the Crimean War. I went down into streets of stacked-up furniture. I felt I was walking into an inhuman crypt or, worse still, one of those charnel houses or ossuaries I had seen pictures of in one of my father's books when I was a boy. Large as the store was, it was lit by a single electric light bulb hanging from a girder in the roof, and the yellow light was deathly. The notion of "picking up" anything at Pliny's depressed me, so that I was left with a horror of the trade I had joined. Yet feelings of this kind are never simple. After half an hour I left the shop.

I understood before that day was over and I was back in the room over my own place that what had made me more wretched was the wound of a sharp joy. First, the sight of the girl leaving her name unfinished in the dust had made my heart jump; then when she held the vase in her hands I had felt the thrill of a revelation: until then I had never settled what I should go in for, but now I saw it. Why not collect Caughley? That was it. Caughley: it was one of those inspirations that excite one so that every sight in the world changes — even houses, buses, streets, and people are transfigured and become unreal as desire carries one away — and then, cruelly, it passes and one is left exhausted. The total impossibility of an impatient young man like myself collecting Caughley, which hadn't been made since 1821, became brutally clear. Too late for Staffordshire, too late for Dresden, too late for Caughley and all the beautiful things. I was savage for lack of money. The following day I went to the Victoria and Albert and there I saw other far more beautiful things enshrined and inaccessible. I gazed with wonder. My longing for possession held me, and then I was elevated to a state of worship, as if they were idols, holy and never to be touched. Then I remembered the girl's hands and a violent daydream passed through my head: it lasted only a second or two, but in that time I smashed the glass case, grabbed a treasure, and bolted with it. It frightened me that such an idea could have occurred to me. I left the museum and I turned against my occupation, against Marbright, Alsop and, above all, Pliny and August, and it broke my heart to think of that pretty girl living among such people and drifting into the shabbiness of the trade. I S A B — half a name, written by a living finger in dust.

One has these brief sensations when one is young. They pass and one does nothing about them. There is nothing remarkable about Caughley — except that you can't get it. I did not collect Caughley for a simple reason: I had to collect my wits. The plain truth is that I was incompetent. I had only to look at my bank account. I had bought too much.

At the end of the year it seemed like the bankruptcy court unless I had a stroke of luck. Talk of trouble making the trade move: I was trouble myself; dealers could smell it coming and came sniffing into my shop — and at the end of the year I sold up for what I could get. It would have been better if I could have waited for a year or two when the boom began. For some reason I kept the teapot I had bought in Salisbury to remind me of wasted time. In its humble way it was pretty.

In the next six months I changed. I had to. I pocketed my pride and got a dull job at an auctioneer's; at least it took me out of the office when I got out keys and showed people round. The firm dealt in house property and developments. The word "develop" took hold of me. The firm was a large one and sometimes "developed" far outside London. I was told to go and inspect some of the least important bits of property that were coming into the market. One day a row of shops in Steepleton came up for sale. I said I knew them. They were on the London road opposite the Lion Hotel at the end of the town. My boss was always impressed by topography and the names of hotels and sent me down there. The shops were in the row where August and one or two others had had their business, six of them.

What a change! The Lion had been repainted; the little shops seemed to have got smaller. In my time the countryside had begun at the end of the row. Now builders' scaffolding was standing in the fields beyond. I looked for August's. A cheap café had taken over his place. He had gone. The mirror man who lived next door was still there but had gone into beads and fancy art jewellery. His window was full of hanging knick-knacks and mobiles.

"It's the tourist trade now," he said. He looked ill.

"What happened to August?"

He studied me for a moment and said, "Closed down," and I could get no more out of him. I crossed the street to the Lion. Little by little, a sentence at a time in a long slow suspicious evening, I got news of August from the barmaid as she went back and forth serving customers, speaking in a low voice, her eye on the new proprietor in case the next sentence that came out of her might be bad for custom. The sentences were spoken like sentences from a judge summing up, bit by bit. August had got two years for receiving stolen goods; the woman — "She wasn't his wife" — had been knocked down by a car as she was coming out of the bar at night — "not that she drank, not really drank; her weight, really" — and then came the final sentence that brought back to me the alerting heat and fever of the trade's secrets: "There was always trouble over there. It started when the girl ran away."

"Isabel?" I said.

"I dunno — the girl."

I stood outside the hotel and looked to the east and then to the west.

It was one of those quarters of an hour on a main road when, for some reason, there is no traffic coming either way. I looked at the now far-off fields where the February wind was scything over the grass, turning it into waves of silver as it passed over them. I thought of Isab . . . running with a case in her hand, three years ago. Which way? Where do girls run to? Sad.

I went back to London. There are girls in London too, you know. I grew a beard, reddish; it went with the red car, which I had managed to keep. I could afford to take a girl down to the south coast now and then. Sometimes we came back by the Brixton road, sometimes through Camberwell, and when we did this I often slowed down at Pliny's and told the girls, "That man's sitting on a gold mine." They never believed it or, at least, only one did. She said: "Does he sell rings? Let us have a look."

"They're closed," I said. "They're always closed."

"I want to look," she said, so we stopped and got out.

We looked into the dark window — it was Saturday night — and we could see nothing, and as we stared we heard a loud noise coming, it seemed, from the place next door or from down the drive-in at the side of Pliny's shop, a sound like someone beating boxes or bathtubs at first until I got what it was: drums. Someone blew a bugle, a terrible squeaky sound. There was heavy traffic on the street, but the bugle seemed to split it in half.

"Boys' Brigade, practicing for Sunday," I said. We stood laughing with our hands to our ears as we stared into the dark. All I could make out was something white on a table at the back of the shop. Slowly I saw it was a set of chessmen. Chess, ivories, August — perhaps Pliny had got August's chessmen.

"What a din!" said the girl. I said no more to her, for in my mind there was the long-forgotten picture of Isabel's finger on the pieces, at Steepleton.

When I've got time, I thought, I will run over to Pliny's; perhaps he will know what happened to the girl.

And I did go there again, one afternoon, on my own. Still closed. I rattled the door handle. There was no answer. I went to a baker's next door, then to a butcher's, then to a pub. The same story. "He only opens on Sundays" or "He's at a sale." Then to a tobacconist's. I said it was funny to leave a shop empty like that, full of valuable stuff. The tobacconist became suspicious.

"There's someone there, all right. His wife's there."

"No, she's not," his wife said. "They've gone off to a sale. I saw them." She took the hint.

"No one in charge to serve customers," she said.

I said I'd seen a chessboard that interested me and the tobacconist said: "It's dying out. I used to play."

"I didn't know he got married," I said.

"He's got beautiful things," said his wife. "Come on Sunday."

Pliny married! That made me grin. The only women in his life I had ever heard of were his mother and the gossip about Lal Drake. Perhaps he had made an honest woman of *her*. I went back for one last look at the chessmen and, sure enough, as the tobacconist's wife had hinted, someone *had* been left in charge, for I saw a figure pass through the inner door of the shop. The watcher was watched. Almost at once I heard the tap and roll of a kettledrum; I put my ear to the letter box and distinctly heard a boy's voice shouting orders. Children! All the drumming I had heard on Saturday had come from Pliny's — a whole family drumming. Think of Pliny married to a widow with kids: he had not had time to get his own. I took back what I had thought of him and Lal Drake. I went off for an hour to inspect a house that was being sold on Camberwell Green, and stopped once more at Pliny's on the way back, on the chance of catching him, and I went to the window. Standing in the middle of the shop was Isabel.

Her shining black hair went to her shoulders. She was wearing a red dress with a schoolgirlish white collar to it. If I had not known her by her heart-shaped face and her full childish lips, I would have known her by her tiptoe way of standing like an actress just about to sing a song or do a dance when she comes forward on the stage. She looked at me daringly. It was the way, I remembered, she had looked at everyone. She did not know me. I went to the door and tipped the handle. It did not open. I saw her watching the handle move. I went on rattling. She straightened and shook her head, pushing back her hair. She did not go away: she was amused by my efforts. I went back to the window of the shop and asked to come in. She could not hear, of course. My mouth was opening and shutting foolishly. That amused her even more. I pointed to something in the window, signalling that I was interested in it. She shook her head again. I tried pointing to other things: a cabinet, an embroidered fire screen, a jar three feet high. At each one she shook her head. It was like a guessing game. I was smiling, even laughing, to persuade her. I put my hands to my chest and pretended to beg like a dog. She laughed at this and looked behind, as if calling to someone. If Pliny wasn't there, his wife might be, or the children, so I pointed up-wards and made a movement of my hands, imitating someone turning a key in a lock. I was signalling "Go and get the key from Mrs. Pliny," and I stepped back and looked up at a window above the shop. When I did this, Isabel was frightened; she went away shouting to someone. And that was the end of it; she did not come back.

I went away thinking, Well, that is a strange thing! What ideas people put into your head and you build fancies yourself: that woman in the bar at Steepleton telling me Isabel had run away and I imagining her running in those poor evening shoes I'd once seen, in the rain down the Bath road, when — what was more natural in a trade where they all live with their hands in one another's pockets — Pliny had married, and they had taken the girl on at the shop. It was a comfort to think of. I hadn't realized how much I had worried about what would happen to a naïve girl like Isabel when the break-up came. Alone in the world! How silly. I thought, One of these Sundays I'll go up there and hear the whole story. And I did.

There was no one there except Pliny and his rich Sunday customers. I even went into the store at the back, looked everywhere. No sign of Isabel. The only female was a woman in a shabby black dress and not wearing a hat who was talking to a man testing the door of a wardrobe, making it squeak, while the woman looked on without interest, in the manner of a dealer's wife: obviously the new Mrs. Pliny. She turned to make way for another couple waiting to look at it. I nearly knocked over a stack of cane chairs as I got past.

If there was no sign of Isabel, the sight of Pliny shocked me. He had been a dead man, permanently dead as wood, even clumsy in his big servile bones, though shrewd. Now he had come to life in the strangest, excited way — much older to look at, thinner and frantic as he looked about him this way and that. He seemed to be possessed by a demon. He talked loudly to people in the shop and was suspicious when he was not talking. He was frightened, abrupt, rude. Pliny married! Marriage had wrecked him or he was making too much money; he looked like a man expecting to be robbed. He recognized me at once. I had felt him watching me from the steps going down to the store. As I came back to the steps to speak to him he spoke to me first — distinctly, in a loud voice, "I don't want any of August's men here, see?"

I went red in the face. "What do you mean?" I said.

"You heard me," he said. "You know what he got."

Wells of Hungerford was standing near, pretending not to listen. Pliny was telling the trade that I was in with August — publicly accusing me of being a fence. I controlled my temper.

"August doesn't interest me," I said. "I'm in property. Marsh, Help, and Hitchcock. I sold his place, the whole street."

And I walked past him looking at a few things as I left.

I was in a passion. The dirty swine — all right when his mother kept an eye on him, the poor old woman, but now he'd gone mad. And that poor girl! I went to the tobacconist's for the Sunday paper in a dream, put down my money and took it without a word and was almost out the door when the wife called out, "Did you find him? Did you get what you wanted?" A friendly London voice. I tapped the side of my head.

"You're telling me," the wife said. "Well, he has to watch everything now. Marrying a young girl like that, it stands to reason," she said in a melancholy voice.

"Wears him out, at his age," suggested the tobacconist.

"Stop the dirty talk, Alfred," said the wife.

"You mean he married the *girl?*" I said. "Who's the big woman without a hat — in the store?"

"What big woman is that?" asked the tobacconist's wife. "He's married to the girl. Who else do you think — there's no one else."

The wife's face went as blank as a tombstone in the sly London way.

"She's done well for herself," said the tobacconist. "Keeps her locked up like his mother, wasn't I right?"

"He worships her," said the woman.

I went home to my flat. I was nauseated. The thought of Isabel in bed with that dressed-up servant, with his wet eyes, his big raw ears, and his breath smelling of onions! Innocent? No, as the woman said, "She has done well for herself." Happy with him too. I remembered her pretty face laughing in the shop. What else could you expect, after August and Mrs. Price.

The anger I felt with Pliny grew to a rage, but by the time I was in my own flat, Pliny vanished from the picture in my mind. I was filled with passion for the girl. The fever of the trade had come alive in me: Pliny had got something I wanted. I could think of nothing but her, just as I remember the look August gave Pliny when the girl asked if the jug was Meissen. I could see her holding the jug at arm's length, laughing at the old man's face under the lip. And I could see that Pliny was not mad: what was making him frantic was possessing the girl.

I kept away from Pliny's. I tried to drive the vision out of my mind, but I could not forget it. I became cunning. Whenever my job allowed it — and even when it didn't — I started passing the time of day with any dealer I had known, picked up news of the sales, studied catalogues, tried to find out which ones Pliny would go to. She might be with him. I actually went to Newbury but he was not there. Bath he couldn't miss and, sure enough, he was there and she wasn't. It was ten in the morning and the sale had just started.

I ran off and got into my car. I drove as fast as I could the hundred miles back to London and cursed the lunchtime traffic. I got to Pliny's shop and rang the bell. Once, then several long rings. At once the drum started beating and went on as if troops were marching. People passing in the street paused to listen too. I stood back from the window and I saw a movement at a curtain upstairs. The drumming was still going on, and when I bent to listen at the letter box I could hear the sound become deafening and often very near and then there was a blast from the bugle. It was a misty day south of the river, and for some reason or other I was fingering the grey window and started writing her name, I S A B . . . hopelessly, but hoping that perhaps she might come near enough to see. The drumming stopped. I waited and waited and then I saw an extraordinary sight: Isabel herself in the dull-red dress, but with a lancer's helmet on her head and a side drum on its straps hanging from her shoulders and the drumsticks in her hand. She was standing upright like a boy playing soldiers, her chin up and puzzling at the sight of the letters ꓭ A Ƨ I on the window. When she saw me she was confused. She immediately gave two or three taps to the drum and then bent almost double with laughter. Then she put on a straight face and played the game of pointing to one thing after another in the shop. Every time I shook my head, until at last I pointed to her. This pleased her. Then I shouted through the letter box, "I want to come in."

"Come in," she said. "It's open." The door had been open all the time: I had not thought of trying it. I went inside.

"I thought you were locked in."

She did not answer but wagged her head from side to side.

"Sometimes I lock myself in," she said. "There are bad people about, August's men."

She said this with an air of great importance, but her face became ugly as she said it. She took off the helmet and put down the drum.

"So I beat the drum when Mr. Pliny is away," she said. She called him Mr. Pliny.

"What good does that do?"

"It is so quiet when Mr. Pliny is away. I don't do it when he's here. It frightens August's men away."

"It's as good as telling them you are alone here," I said. "That's why I came. I heard the drum and the bugle."

"Did you?" she said eagerly. "Was it loud?"

"Very loud."

She gave a deep sigh of delight.

"You see!" she said, nodding her head complacently.

"Who taught you to blow the bugle?" I said.

"My mother did," she said. "She did it on the stage. Mr. Pliny — you know, when Mr. Pliny fetched me in his motor car — I forgot it. He had to go back and get it. I was too frightened."

"Isab . . ." I said.

She blushed. She remembered.

"I might be one of August's men," I said.

"No, you're not. I know who you are," she said. "Mr. Pliny's away for the day but that doesn't matter. I am in charge. Is there something you were looking for?"

The child had gone when she put the drum aside. She became serious and practical: Mrs. Pliny! I was confused by my mistake in not knowing the door was open and she busied herself about the shop. She knew what she was doing and I felt very foolish.

"Is there something special?" she said. "Look around." She had become a confident woman. I no longer felt there was anything strange about her. I drifted to look at the chessmen and I could not pretend to myself that they interested me, but I did ask her the price. She said she would look it up and went to a desk where Pliny kept his papers, and after going through some lists of figures which were all in code she named the sum. It was enormous — something like two hundred and seventy-five pounds — and I said "What!" in astonishment. She put the list back on the desk and said firmly, "My husband paid two hundred and sixty pounds for it last Sunday. It was carved by Dubois. There are only two more like it. It was the last thing he did in 1785."

(I found out afterwards this was nonsense.)

She said this in Pliny's voice; it was exactly the sort of casual sentence he would have used. She looked expressionless and not at all surprised when I said, "Valuable," and moved away.

I meant, of course, that she was valuable, and in fact her mystery having gone, she seemed conscious of being valuable and important herself, the queen and owner of everything in the shop, efficiently in charge of her husband's things. The cabinet in the corner, she said, in an off-hand way, as I went to look at it, had been sold to an Australian. "We are waiting for the packers." We! Not to feel less knowing than she was, I looked round for some small thing to buy from her. There were several small things, like a cup and saucer, a little china tray, a christening mug. I picked things up and put them down listlessly, and from being indifferent she became eager and watched me. The self-important, serious expression she had had vanished, she became childish suddenly, and anxious: she was eager to sell something. I found a little china figure on a shelf.

"How much is this?" I said. It was Dresden: the real thing. She took it and looked at the label. I knew it was far beyond my purse and I asked her the price in the bored hopeless voice one puts on.

"I'll have to look it up," she said.

She went to the desk again and looked very calculating and thoughtful and then said, as if naming an enormous sum, "Two pounds."

"It can't be," I said.

She looked sad as I put it back on the shelf and she went back to the desk. Then she said, "I tell you what I'll do. It's got a defect. You can have it for thirty-five shillings."

I picked it up again. There was no defect in it. I could feel the huge wave of temptation that comes to one in the trade, the sense of the incredible chance, the lust that makes one shudder first and then breaks over one so that one is possessed, though even at that last moment, one plays at delay in a breathless pause now that one is certain of one's desire.

I said, "I'll give you thirty bob for it."

Young Mrs. Pliny raised her head and her brown eyes became brilliant with naïve joy.

"All right," she said.

The sight of her wrapping the figure, packing it in a box and taking the money so entranced me, that I didn't realize what she was doing or what I had done. I wasn't thinking of the figure at all; I was thinking of her. We shook hands. Hers were cold and she waved from the shop door when I left. And when I got to the end of the street and found myself holding the box I wondered why I had bought it. I didn't want it. I had felt the thrill of the thief and I was so ashamed that I once or twice thought of dropping it into a litter box. I even thought of going back and returning it to her and saying to her, "I didn't want it. It was a joke. I wanted you. Why did you marry an awful old man like Pliny?" And those stories of Pliny going off once a month in the old days, in his mother's time, to Lal Drake, that old whore in Brixton, came back to me. I didn't even unpack the figure but put it on the mantelpiece in my room, then on the top shelf of a cupboard which I rarely used. I didn't want to see it. And when in the next months — or even years — I happened to see it, I remembered her talking about the bad people, August's men.

But though I kept away from Pliny's on Sundays, I could not resist going back to the street and eventually to the shop — just for the sight of her.

And after several misses I did see her in the shop. It was locked. When I saw her she stared at me with fear and made no signals and quickly disappeared — I suppose, into the room at the back. I crossed the main road and looked at the upper part of the house. She was upstairs, standing at a window. So I went back across the street and tried to signal, but of course she could only see my mouth moving. I was obsessed by the way I had cheated her. My visits were a siege, for the door was never open now. I did see her once through the window and this time I had taken the box and offered it to her in dumb show. That did have an effect. I saw she was looking very pale, her eyes ringed and tired, and whether she saw I was remorseful or not I couldn't tell, but she made a rebuking yet defiant face. Another day I went and she looked terrified. She pointed and pointed to the door, but as I eagerly stepped towards it she shook her head and raised a hand to forbid me. I did not understand until, soon, I saw Pliny walking about the shop. I moved off. People in the neighbourhood must often have seen me standing there and the tobacconist I went to gave me a look that suggested he knew what was going on.

Then, on one of my vigils, I saw a doctor go to the side door down the goods entrance and feared she was ill, but the butcher told me it was Pliny. His wife, they said, had been nursing him. He ought to convalesce somewhere. "A nice place by the sea. But he won't. It would do his wife good. The young girl has worn herself out looking after him. Shut up all day with him." And the tobacconist said what his wife had said a long time back. "Like his poor mother. He kept *her* locked in too. Sunday evening's the only time she's out. It's all wrong."

I got sick of myself. I didn't notice the time I was wasting, for one day passed like a smear of grey into another and I wished I could drag myself away from the district, especially now that Pliny was always there. At last one Saturday I fought hard against a habit so useless and I had the courage to drive past the place for once and not park my car up the street. I drove on, taking side streets (which I knew, nevertheless, would lead me back), but I made a mistake with the one-ways and got on the main Brixton road and was heading north to freedom from myself.

It was astonishing to be free. It was seven o'clock in the evening, and to celebrate I went into a big pub where they had singers on Saturday nights; it was already filling up with people. How normal, how cheerful they were, a crowd of them, drinking, shouting and talking: the human race! I got a drink and chose a quiet place in a corner and I was taking my first mouthful of the beer, saying to myself: "Here's to yourself, my boy," as though I had just met myself as I used to be. And then, with the glass still at my lips, I saw in a crowd at the other end of the bar Pliny, with his back half turned. I recognized him by his jug-handle ears, his white hair, and the stoop of a tall man. He was not in his dressy clothes but in a shabby suit that made him seem disguised. He was listening to a woman with a large handbag who had bright blond hair and a big red mouth; she was telling him a joke and she banged him in the stomach with her bag and laughed. Someone near me said, "Lal's on the job early this evening." Lal Drake. All the old stories about Pliny and his woman came back to me and how old Castle of Westbury said that Pliny's mother had told him, when she was saying what a good son he was to her, that the one and only time he had been seen with a woman he had come home and told her and put his head in her lap and cried "like a child" and promised on the Bible he'd never do such a thing again. Castle swore this was true.

I put down my beer and got out of the pub fast without finishing it. Not because I was afraid of Pliny. Oh, no! I drove straight back to Pliny's shop. I rang the bell. The drum started beating a few taps and then a window upstairs opened.

"What do you want?" said Isabel in a whisper.

"I want to see you. Open the door."

"It's locked."

"Get the key."

She considered me for a long time.

"I haven't got one," she said, still in a low voice, so hard to hear that she had to say it twice.

"Where have you been?" she said.

We stared at each other's white faces in the dark. She had missed me!

"You've got a key. You must have," I said. "Somewhere. What about the back door?"

She leaned on the window, her arms on the sill. She was studying my clothes.

"I have got something for you," I said. This changed her. She leaned forward, trying to see more of me in the dark. She was curious. Today I understand what I did not understand then: she was looking me over minutely, inch by inch — what she could see of me in the sodium light of the street lamp — not because I was strange or unusual but because I was not. She had been shut up either alone or with Pliny without seeing another soul for so long. He was treating her like one of his collector's pieces, like the Meissen August had said he kept hidden upstairs. She closed the window. I stood there wretched and impatient. I went down the goods entrance ready to kick the side door down, break a window, climb in somehow. The side door had no letter box or glass panes, no handle even. I stood in front of it and suddenly it was opened. She was standing there.

"You're *not* locked in," I said.

She was holding a key.

"I found it," she said.

I saw she was telling a lie.

"Just now?"

"No. I know where he hides it," she said, lowering her frank eyes.

It was a heavy key with an old piece of frayed used-up string on it.

"Mr. Pliny does not like me to show people things," she said. "He has gone to see his sister in Brixton. She is very ill. I can't show you anything."

She recited these words as if she had learned them by heart. It was wonderful to stand so near to her in the dark.

"Can I come in?" I said.

"What do you want?" she said cautiously.

"You," I said.

She raised her chin.

"Are you one of August's men?" she said.

"You know I'm not. I haven't seen August for years."

"Mr. Pliny says you are. He said I was never to speak to you again. August was horrible."

"The last I heard he was in prison."

"Yes," she said. "He steals." This seemed to please her: she forgave him that easily. Then she put her head out of the doorway as if to see if August were waiting behind me.

"He does something else too," she said.

I remembered the violent quarrel between August and poor Mrs. Price when she was drunk in Salisbury — the quarrel about Isabel.

"You ran away," I said.

She shook her head.

"I didn't run away. Mr. Pliny fetched me," she said and nodded primly, "in his car. I told you."

Then she said, "Where is the present you were bringing me?"

"It isn't a present," I said. "It's the little figure I bought from you. You didn't charge me enough. Let me in. I want to explain."

I couldn't bring myself to tell her that I had taken advantage of her ignorance, so I said, "I found out afterwards that it was worth much more than I paid you. I want to give it back to you."

She gave a small jump towards me. "Oh, please, please," she said and took me by the hand. "Where is it?"

"Let me come in," I said, "and I will tell you. I haven't got it with me. I'll bring it tomorrow — no, not tomorrow — Monday."

"Oh, please," she pleaded. "Mr. Pliny was so angry with me for selling it. He'd never been angry with me before. It was terrible. It was awful."

It had never occurred to me that Pliny would even know she had sold the piece; but now I remembered the passions of the trade and the stored-up lust that seems to pass between things and men like Pliny. He wouldn't forgive. He would be savage.

"Did he do something to you? He didn't hit you, did he?"

Isabel did not answer.

"What did he do?"

I remembered how frantic Pliny had been and how violent he had sounded when he told me to get out of his shop.

"He cried," she said. "He cried and he cried. He went down on his knees and he would not stop crying. I was wicked to sell it. I am the most precious thing he has. Please bring it. It will make him better."

"Is he still angry?"

"It has made him ill," she said.

"Let me come in," I said.

"Will you promise?"

"I swear I'll bring it," I said.

"For a minute," she said, "but not in the shop."

I followed her down a dark passage into the store and was so close that I could smell her hair.

Pliny crying! At first I took this to be one of Isabel's fancies. Then I thought of tall, clumsy, servant-like Pliny — expert at sales with his long-nosed face pouring out water like a pump — acting repentant, remorseful, agonized like an animal to a pretty girl. Why? Just because she had sold something? Isabel loved to sell things. He must have had some other reason. I remembered Castle of Westbury's story. What had he done to the girl? Only a cruel man could have gone in for such an orgy of self-love. He had the long face on which tears would be a blackmail. He would be like a horse crying because it had lost a race.

Yet those tears were memorable to Isabel and she so firmly called him "Mr. Pliny." In bed, did she still call him "Mr. Pliny"? I have often thought since that she did: it would have given her a power — perhaps cowed him.

At night the cold, whitewashed storeroom was silent under the light of its single bulb and the place was mostly in shadow; only the tops of stacked furniture stood out in the yellow light, some of them like buildings. The foundations of the stacks were tables or chests, desks on which chairs or small cabinets were piled. We walked down alleys between the stacks. It was like walking through a dead, silent city, abandoned by everyone who once lived there. There was the sour smell of upholstery; in one part there was a sort of plaza where two large dining tables stood with their chairs set around and a pile of dessert plates on them. Isabel was walking confidently. She stopped by a dressing table with a mirror on it next to a group of wardrobes and turning round to face it, she said proudly, "Mr. Pliny gave it all to me. And the shop."

"All of this?"

"When he stopped crying," she said.

And then she turned about and we faced the wardrobes. There were six or seven, one in rosewood and an ugly yellow one, and they were so arranged here that they made a sort of alcove or room. The wardrobe at the corner of the alley was very heavy and leaned so that its doors were open in a manner of such empty hopelessness, showing its empty shelves, that it made me uneasy. Someone might have just taken his clothes from it in a hurry, perhaps that very minute, and gone off. He might be watching us. It was the wardrobe with the squeaking door which I had seen the customer open while the woman (whom I had thought to be Mrs. Pliny) stood by. Each piece of furniture seemed to watch — even the small things, like an umbrella stand or a tray left on a table. Isabel walked into the alcove, and there was a greenish-grey sofa with a screwed-up paper bag of toffees on it and on the floor beside it I saw, of all things, the lancer's helmet and the side drum and the bugle. The yellow light scarcely lit this corner.

"There's your drum," I said.

"This is my house," she said, gaily now. "Do you like it? When Mr. Pliny is away I come here in case August's men come . . ."

She looked at me doubtfully when she mentioned that name again.

"And you beat the drum to drive them away?" I said.

"Yes," she said stoutly.

I could not make out whether she was playing the artless child or not, yet she was a woman of twenty-five at least. I was bewildered.

"You are frightened here on your own, aren't you?"

"No, I am not. It's nice."

Then she said very firmly, "You will come here on Monday and give me the box back?"

I said, "I will if you'll let me kiss you. I love you, Isabel."

"Mr. Pliny loves me too," she said.

"Isab . . ." I said. That did move her.

I put my arm round her waist and she let me draw her to me. It was strange to hold her because I could feel her ribs, but her body was so limp and feeble that, loving her as I did, I was shocked and pulled her tightly against me. She turned her head weakly so that I could only kiss her cheek and see only one of her eyes, and I could not make out whether she was enticing me, simply curious about my embrace, or drooping in it without heart.

"You *are* one of August's men," she said, getting away from me. "He used to try and get into my bed. After that, I locked my door."

"Isabel," I said, "I am in love with you. I think you love me. Why did you marry a horrible old man like Pliny?"

"Mr. Pliny is not horrible," she said. "I love him. He never comes to my room."

"Then he doesn't love you," I said. "Leaving you locked up here. And you don't love him."

She listened in the manner of someone wanting to please, waiting for me to stop.

"He is not a real husband, a real lover," I said.

"Yes, he is," she said proudly. "He takes my clothes off before I go to bed. He likes to look at me. I am the most precious thing he has."

"That isn't love, Isabel," I said.

"It is," she said with warmth. "You don't love me. You cheated me. Mr. Pliny said so. And you don't want to look at me. You don't think I'm precious."

I went to take her in my arms again and held her.

"I love you. I want you. You are beautiful. I didn't cheat you. Pliny is cheating you, not me," I said. "He is not with his sister. He's in bed with a woman in Brixton. I saw them in a pub. Everyone knows it."

"No, he is not. I *know* he is not. He doesn't like it. He promised his mother," she said.

The voice in which she said this was not her playful voice: the girl vanished and a woman had taken her place — not a distressed woman, not a contemptuous or a disappointed one.

"He worships me," she said, and in the squalid store of dead junk she seemed to be illumined by the simple knowledge of her own value and looked at my love as if it were nothing at all.

I looked at the sofa and was so mad that I thought of grabbing her and pulling her down there. What made me hesitate was the crumpled bag of toffees on it. I was as nonplussed and perhaps as impotent as Pliny must have been. In that moment of hesitation she picked up her bugle, and standing in the aisle, she blew it hard, her cheeks going out full, and the noise and echoes seemed to make the shadows jump. I have never heard a bugle call that scared me so much. It killed my desire.

"I told you not to come in," she said. "Go away."

And she walked into the aisle between the furniture, swinging her key to the door.

"Come back," I said as I followed her.

I saw her face in the dressing-table mirror we had passed before, then I saw my own face, red and sweating on the upper lip and my mouth helplessly open. And then in the mirror I saw another face following mine — Pliny's. Pliny must have seen me in the pub.

In that oblong frame of mahogany with its line of yellow inlay, Pliny's head looked winged by his ears and he was coming at me, his head down, his mouth with its yellowing teeth open under the moustache and his eyes stained in the bad light. He looked like an animal. The mirror concentrated him, and before I could do more than half turn he had jumped in a clumsy way at me and jammed one of my shoulders against a tallboy.

"What are you doing here?" he shouted.

The shouts echoed over the store.

"I warned you. I'll get the police on you. You leave my wife alone. Get out. You thought you'd get her on her own and swindle her again."

I hated to touch a white-haired man, but in pain I shoved him back hard. We were, as I have said, close to the wardrobe, and he staggered back so far that he hit the shelves and the door swung towards him, so that he was half out of my sight for a second. I kicked the door hard with my left foot and it swung to and hit him in the face. He jumped out with blood on his nose. But I had had time to topple the pile of little cane chairs into the alleyway between us. Isabel saw this and ran round the block of furniture and reached him, and when I saw her she was standing with the bugle raised like a weapon in her hand to defend the old man from me. He was wiping his face. She looked triumphant.

"Don't you touch Mr. Pliny," she shouted at me. "He's ill."

He *was* ill. He staggered. I pushed my way through the fallen chairs and I picked up one and said, "Pliny, sit down on this." Pliny with the bleeding face glared and she forced him to sit down. He was panting. And then a new voice joined us: the tobacconist came down the alley.

"I heard the bugle," he said. "Anything wrong? Oh, Gawd, look at his face. What happened, Pliny? Mrs. Pliny, you all right?" And then he saw me. All the native shadiness of the London streets, all the gossip of the neighbourhood, came into his face.

"I said to my wife," he said, "something's wrong at Pliny's."

"I came to offer Mr. Pliny a piece of Dresden," I said, "but he was out at Brixton seeing his sister, his wife said. He came back and thought I'd broken in and hit himself on the wardrobe."

"You oughtn't to leave Mrs. Pliny alone with all this valuable stock, Mr. Pliny. Saturday night too," the tobacconist said.

Tears had started rolling down Pliny's cheeks very suddenly when I mentioned Brixton and he looked at me and the tobacconist in panic.

"I'm not interested in Dresden," he managed to say.

Isabel dabbed his face and sent the tobacconist for a glass of water.

"No, dear, you're not," said Isabel.

And to me she said, "We're not interested."

That was the end. I found myself walking in the street. How unreal people looked in the sodium light.

KAY BOYLE

1903–

Of all members of the Hemingway generation Kay Boyle may be the most undervalued. Sensitive critics, such as David Daiches, have acclaimed her as "one of the finest short story writers of our time." But she has never become a "name," an impressive point of reference, like Fitzgerald. Yet when I match the entire body of her work in the short story against his, she seems the more serious, the more moving artist.

Her expatriate experience in the twenties and thirties (vividly recalled in the revised version of Being Geniuses Together) and the tragedy of Europe from 1933 to 1950 supply her raw material. She has been close, uncomfortably close, to history. Though that history informs her stories, it is so beautifully distanced that what emerges, at her best, is the human tragicomedy remaining after the captains and the kings have departed.

Yet in the deepest sense her voice is political, enlisted in the enduring cause of human rights and of the emotionally dispossessed. Brief and unpretentious, "Men" perfectly expresses, however indirectly, her sense of the unremitting conflict between those whose eyes are open to "the actual living world of natural ritual" and those who are blind to it.

Men

THE BARON had been set to work with the others on a road that lay in the Isère valley, running side by side with the river with only a row of trees standing tall and almost lifeless-seeming in between. He was a strong man and he liked the air he breathed and the unaccustomed action of the work after the months of being closed away. It was in the early spring, and the war not over yet, so there was still the movement of troops to be seen as there had been all winter and the passage of camouflaged liaison cars and lorries on the roads. It was then, in March, that the French had got the idea that there should be no more railway crossings to hold up the military traffic, and that bridges should be built instead to carry the thoroughfares up over the rails. So they took the men that they couldn't do anything else with and put them to work on the roads in the south and in the north and in all parts of the country, as if this sudden hastening of animate and inanimate material from place to place could alter the look of history in the end.

The railway line came across the Isère from the direction of Italy, from Modane, and cut across the highroad, but it was such a little line that the Baron could not see the sense in what they had to do. Only an occasional freight train moved idly along it, so it seemed it could not offer much interference. But still the powers that were had decided to hoist the highroad up over the rails, and the group of foreigners had been sent out into the bleak retarded springtime of the valley, perhaps fifty or more of them, to hack at the black surface of the road and the still hard soil around the condemned trees. The sky was heavy, as if there were snow yet to fall from it, and the flat shallow river that passed so close to them as they worked was cold, metallic, deathly, like a needle of ice that pierced their hearts. A little ahead of them, perhaps half a kilometer or less, there was a house to be seen on the field and swamp side of the road: a humble, rather dilapidated little house with a low-pitched roof fading between the tree trunks into a piece with the road's and the valley's flawless imitation of November. It was only when the Baron turned his head and looked the other way, up toward the mountains and saw the snow lying miraculously fair and high on their crests, that he believed again in the actual living world of natural ritual: of moon and sun, men and women, and the changes of the seasons instead of in this phantom and twilit rendering of fixed despair.

The Baron was twenty-eight that year, and from the look of him he came from a cold-stoned, dour-climated, castle country which might have been Scotland just as readily as Austria. He was tall and big-boned, with a longish, weather-flushed face, and shy, strained, rather prominent green eyes. If you were seeking for other things to place him than what women would call handsome you might not have seen that he was at first, and yet that too was there. Anyone knowing the German statuary of the Renaissance would have recognized him at once: Theodoric, King of the Ostrogoths, or Emperor Rudolph of Habsburg, or even Arthur of England somehow taken out of his century and his armor and put to work digging a roadbed in sight of the Alps. His hair might have been light except for the amount of water it needed to slap it, like a school-boy's, into place; and his nose was fine enough for any member of royalty to have worn with pride. But it was his laugh, just after you had decided he was too reserved or grave for that, which it did you good to hear. Dostoevsky has written that one can know a man from his laugh, and that if you like a man's laugh before you know anything of him, you may say he is a good man. It was perhaps this laugh, so pure and hearty, so entirely without venom, which made the others come close to him and allow their hearts to open just a little, like men spreading their cold fingers before a flame.

But if the Baron looked now and again at the mountains, the other men had had enough of scenery: it was the house they liked to look toward down the road. The seven months they had spent in internment had altered their eyesight for them so that the little house appeared singularly sweet and touching to them; it had a homely, nearly familiar look to them all as if they had seen it somewhere before in another country. There was one man among them who was a Spaniard who couldn't take his eyes from it, and he would stand there putting his black hair back off his forehead with his fingers, letting the shovel fall idle between his narrow legs. He had something like a red stocking knotted around his neck because his throat was sore, and the ends of it hung down in front inside his raveling jersey. To him the house half a kilometer away seemed like his own house, the size of it and the shape, if only the sun had been out to give it the color of plaster, and if the doorway had had a beaded curtain hanging in it to keep the flies of another climate from getting in, and if the roof had been flat, and if there had been melons and gourds ripening on the step. Otherwise, it was exactly like his house in Pastrana, seen through the Spanish tree stems, at the end of town. Even the Baron made a rather foolish remark about it that first day. He said that the side of it which was turned toward them, with the two windows and the shape of a door and the dark headdress of the sloping roof, looked to him like a woman's head; and then he burst out laughing.

"*Regardez,* my house," the Spaniard said, and he showed his bad young teeth as he smiled. He spoke the words in French, but with a strange, untamed accent which gave them another sound. "Chicken cooking in tomatoes, and the woman waiting," he said. "That's where I go to sleep tonight, in a bed too. Nobody's going to get any of it but me."

He stood there, slouched thin and dark on the road, drawing his dark-skinned narrow hand under his nose to wipe the bead of cold off while the others went on hacking at this doomed portion of the highway, their backs bent, their heads down, digging the public and unhallowed grave. He might have been saying these words to any of the men working there around him, to the Hungarian doctor who had glanced once or twice down the road and believed there was a certain portion of the wall of the house, the tilt of the right side of the roof or the placing of the windows, which made it peculiarly his, better and closer than memory to him; or spoken them to the Czech tailor who had a wife and two children waiting in Avignon for nothing better than the cards he could send them twice in the month saying his leg was better or wasn't better or that he limped still (he, too, who had looked down the road and thought for an instant that he saw their faces at the windows of home, and the color of flowers on this side of the glass). But they all knew well enough that the Spaniard had spoken to the Baron and that he was tittering his rather vulgar girlish laughter for the Baron to hear; for it was the Baron, the strongest and the hardest worker among them, who seemed to keep night and day the patience to give ear and interest to what anybody had to say.

"*Regardez,* my house," the Spaniard said, croaking because of the soreness in his throat, and the Baron did not stop working while he said:

"It's a very good reproduction of a *Schloss*. Allow me to compliment you on your taste. It's exactly what I myself would have chosen." He straightened up for a moment and looked down the speechless, colorless road to the humble little house in the trees. "I like the turrets," he said. "Strikingly medieval," and he made a rather awkward gesture toward the slanting-roofed cottage, covered with tiles or corrugated tin or whatever material they could not tell from here. "And the way you've repeated the armorial bearings in red on the shutters, quite in keeping with the earliest German baroque. If I might make one or two suggestions," he said, saying it earnestly as he leaned again and struck the pick into the stone-clogged soil, "I'd have the iron deer moved back from the bridle path and placed a little more centrally on the lawns where they'd show to better advantage and at the same time do away with any possibility of the hunt taking fright." He spoke French a little heavily and carefully, but with the vocabulary of one who has read the words a long time and knows them well, although he has not had the habit of speaking them aloud. "I take it the banqueting hall overlooks the river," he said, hacking at the hard, alien earth and stone. "If so, I should have the statues placed nearer to that magnificent fountain which plays in the vicinity of the grottoes, and thus disengage the view of the façade."

The sentry was coming down the line toward them, a young man in uniform with a gun on his shoulder, callow and harmless enough looking, but at the sight of him coming the Spaniard picked up his shovel and seemed to set to work again.

"So if I didn't go back the same direction as you tonight," he went on saying in a low, almost wistful voice to the Austrian's strong bowed back, "you'd know where I'd gone. You'd know this time I decided to go to my house. I decided to go home."

The Baron could hear the scrape of the other man's spade as it struck on rock, and then the patter of the loose soil on soil as he flung the shovelful out on the road. In another moment the sentry's shoes had passed them, and without turning his head the Baron said:

"What is the name of the place you come from?" as a teacher might ask it of a child, or a doctor ask exactly where the pain might be.

"Pastrana," said the Spaniard. "Between Teruel and Madrid," and the sound of it laid such a languor on his blood that he must put the spade aside again and look down the road. "Pastrana," he repeated, and he leaned on the shovel and wiped his nose slowly and absently with the ends of the stocking or scarf that was knotted around his neck. "Pas-tra-na," he said again, pronouncing it lingeringly.

"That would be a long way," said the Baron, and as he worked he saw the geographical picture of it, the line of the coast from Marseille to Castellon and the journey inland in the heat. And now the Spaniard spoke to him in winning, playful slyness.

"Maybe just half a kilometer. Just over there," he said, tittering like a vulgar girl as he looked down the road. "I can smell something. I can smell the olive oil heating on the coals."

Still the Baron did not look around, but he knew well enough that the Spaniard was looking toward the house clamped fast between the tree trunks in the cold.

"That isn't Pastrana," he said. "You've made a mistake. That's Schloss Weidlingau. They're having venison and kraut for supper."

"No," said the Spaniard, the young but already corrupted teeth showing between his lips again as he spoke. "I can even say how the woman looks —"

"Ah, the woman," said the Austrian. For a moment he felt the thing stifling his heart, and then they both began laughing without warning, the Spaniard behind him laughing in quick high foolish gasps as he leaned on his shovel, and the Austrian in pure loud guffaws of blank and terrible despair.

Every day that they came out from the camp to work on the road brought them a little closer to the house, and day by day now it seemed to have become some sort of goal, almost an actual destination to them.

They never saw smoke coming from its chimney, nor light in its windows, and toward evening they waited almost in grief for that cold quick rush of valley darkness which would engulf it with gloom beneath the trees. In the mornings, while their hearts were fresh still, they had the inexplicable feeling that once they had come abreast the house, work must somehow cease of itself, that merely reaching it must be the end, the signal for them to fling down their shovels and picks, as absurd as if the actual announcement of an armistice had been made. It might have been that the war itself and its issue had been waiting all winter for this little group of foreigners to come up the road by the river to where the house stood before the word of respite could be given.

During the final days, as they approached it, the Spaniard would be seized with sudden insane transports of joy and would fling his hair back and sing wildly to the trees; and as he worked the Hungarian doctor's eyes would fill incomprehensibly with tears. The others were nervous, ill at ease among themselves, like animals when the wind is changing: their heads lifting quickly from their work at the sound of a car or a lorry coming out of the distance, as if it might be the purveyor of the message to them, and their speech would be suddenly heated against one another when, keeping to the still unbroken side of the road, it would pass them by. The strings of army mules and soldiers who trailed past once or twice in the day, picking their way across the destroyed ground, seemed at one moment objects of humor to them, the mules' ears and lips and even the sketchily clad soldiers ludicrous to the Baron and the Spaniard, and the next moment they recognized them in hopelessness as the delegates of some final and inexpressible tragedy. Perhaps they had really come to believe that once they reached the place where the house stood the fighting would have to cease, the conflict stop forever, although what they felt or what they thought they could not find the words to say.

The Baron listened to the Czech speaking of home as he worked near him, for some reason speaking of the iron fencing which had stood around the garden of the tailoring shop as if it were an emblem of freedom rather than injunction, and as he broke the ground with his pick and listened to the other man speaking, the same pure vision of justice and freedom and peace was in the Baron's thoughts: that of freed men returning miraculously to their salvaged countries and their peoples, but in some way it seemed to have grown clearer, sharper, even more painful to him, as if the realization of it now that they approached the house could not be far.

One day at noon they came so close to it that they saw the scrawny, tough-footed chickens in the enclosure that stood, fowl-picked-clean, behind the house. It was at two, just after the midday rest, that the sergeant took it into his head to send two men on before the others to start getting the branded willow out. He picked the Baron for his size and his reliability, and the Spaniard because he seemed to be doing nothing but lounging there with the shovel in his hands.

"You two go on ahead and get to work on the tree," the sergeant said, and he looked at the width of the Baron's shoulders, and in something nearer to contempt at the Baron's absurdly noble and vulnerable face. "You'll have a day's gain on the others, so by the time they're up with you you'll have it out," he said.

So it was in this way that the Austrian and the Spaniard happened to be the first to walk up the still untouched road and pass the house. The others paused a moment in their work and watched them go: the big, strong, blondish young man in the corduroy breeches and the French-cut shabby jacket with his wrists hanging naked from the sleeves, and the delicate-boned, gypsy-dark one with a red string knotted around his throat, carrying their pick and shovel straight past the house to the tree that stood on the other side. But even now that they had passed it, nothing happened, nothing altered in the air, and the other foreigners of the road gang stood there as if stricken with disappointment an instant, and then the sentry moved down the line and they lifted their implements and savagely attacked the soil. It was only when the Austrian and the Spaniard had reached the other side of the house that they saw what none of the others could: they saw the girl standing in the doorway looking out over the marshy fields that lay on this side of the road. She was simply standing quietly and innocently there, and at first she did not seem to see them. But when the Spaniard said: "Blood of God, there's a woman," she turned her head and looked at them where they had halted by the tree.

"Get on with the work," said the Austrian, but however immune his voice was when he said it, he had to turn his shaking heart away.

What she looked like it was never possible to say after. She was merely a young girl, perhaps seventeen, perhaps a little older, wearing some kind of fresh, clean dress, a blue one, or maybe a white one, who came down the one step from the doorway of the house and walked partway across the clean-picked, barren yard toward where the Baron had already thrust his shovel into the soil.

"What are you going to do?" she said. "Are you going to take the tree down?" Or, "You're not going to take that tree down, are you?"

The Spaniard gave a sly little sideways glance at the Baron, who had not moved from his place by the tree, and then his quick dark furtive hand went up to the string of red around his neck and his fingers undid it and slid it down, out of sight, inside the jersey's raveling wool.

"You're not going to take the tree down, are you?" the girl said, and all the time she walked toward them saying this the Baron was repeating to himself: *This isn't it, of course, this isn't the thing we were waiting for.* She was almost at the edge of the road, almost visible now to the others working beyond, and suddenly the Baron knew that for the sake of every woman they had not seen in months he must stop her from coming further. He threw his head back on his neck and he turned around, and again he thought: *This isn't it, of course;* so afraid he was that she would be different from what he wanted her to be.

"Yes, Mademoiselle," he said in his heavy, rather awkward French. "That is what we have to do, Mademoiselle. We have to take it down." He was facing her, drawing his hand back over his hair as a boy might do, but he could not bring himself really to look at her, only at the light, perhaps cotton, perhaps something else, but wondrously clean stuff of her dress. "Please, if you would go back there, back by the house," he said, and as he walked toward her she took first one step and then three or four backwards in obedience before him. "If you would not go out on the road, please, but let me tell you there by the house, then I could explain to you, Mademoiselle," he said.

He had put himself between her and the sight of the Spaniard who had not moved from his place by the tree, shielding her it might be from the Spaniard's dreams of love as from what the Hungarian or the Czech or any man might remember of her night after continent night in sleepless, frustrated memory. She was standing near to him, her hands and her bare arms hanging in her dress, her look moving curiously but without any quality of fear in it across his face. Even now that he looked at her, the Baron could find no human judgment of light or dark, pretty or not, to bring to her; he could not say what the color of her hair or mouth or skin was, or what the sound of her voice was like, although he had listened to her speak. He knew from the fact that her face must be lifted to his that she was shorter than he, but apart from this there was nothing, no physical sign or mark, to distinguish her from a thousand women — only the endowment of womanly purity which lay like a lovely garment on her flesh.

"Let me tell you, Mademoiselle," he said a little wildly. "Let me explain to you that we are altering the road here. There are certain changes which have to be made in preparation for the bridge which will go up over the railway line."

She did not move, she did not seem to hear him even, but her glance moved clearly and innocently, transparent in its curiosity as a child's eyes, over his cheeks and mouth and hair.

"I'm not from this part of the country either," she said, and she stood looking at him. "I've been evacuated from the north with my little brother. What language do they speak where you come from?" she said.

The breath caught in the Baron's throat, and he waited a moment. As he looked at her even his heart seemed stilled in his breast. At first he believed he would lie, and then he knew he could not, for it was no longer merely this, merely a girl in a clean dress putting a question to a stranger working in sweat and filth and hardness on the road. It may have been music like this, he thought, which the middle-aged, the older men heard playing when they had drunk too much in camp on Saturday nights in the winter and begun to weep among themselves, and to babble their wives' names, or their mothers', or their children's, though if they had families any longer no one ever knew. The Baron's ears had been deaf so long to everything except the cries of men calling out at night that he could scarcely hear it and scarcely credit it now that he heard: the voice of ineffable and nearly forgotten tenderness finding the questions to put to him at last.

"I speak German," he said to her, his hands thrust down in his breeches' pockets as he spoke. "They speak German in my country."

"German," the girl repeated. She said it gently, trying it out, almost as if it were a word she did not know the actual meaning of. "But you don't look like a German," she said, and the Baron said quickly, eagerly to her:

"No, Mademoiselle, the truth is that I am not a German. It is only that my country and Germany have that language in common." He took one hand out of his pocket and made a gesture toward the road. "You see, I am working now for the French," he said.

She looked at him another moment in silence, standing before him pure-skinned and guileless and young. And then she went on with a child's exact, curious persistence:

"But why do you do this work? It's funny work for you to be doing. Why don't you do some other kind of work?"

"Because we are not allowed to choose," said the Baron, and as he said it he felt the color come into his face. He might have stood there a little longer in uneasy silence, half ashamed, half shy, seeking to look beyond her and even beyond himself upon the spectacle of his own disastrous fate, had not his pride and his humor suddenly delivered him and he looked as if he were about to start laughing out loud. "That is, this isn't our war, at least to fight in, the one you read about in the papers," he said. "We're rather special people, all of us, very much enlightened, educated, scholars even, so obviously they couldn't put us into the trenches with ordinary men. Therefore they gave us our own battlefield," he said. He jerked his head in the direction of the road, and his mouth was smiling. "A very pleasant, peaceful one with a nice view of the river, only they can't decide what sort of uniforms to put on us yet or what grades to give us —"

All this, from the very beginning, may have taken no more than a minute or two, but when the Baron looked back on it the conversation seemed to him to have been marvelously complete and varied, as if they had talked profoundly and for an incalculable length of time. He had scarcely finished speaking when he saw that there were tears in her eyes, but her voice did not alter and her chin did not tremble as she said:

"Because you are prisoners. I thought you were prisoners when I saw the sentry walking up and down there all week with a gun."

"Yes, Mademoiselle," said the Baron quietly. "That is true. But our sentences are all for the same crime and for the same period of years, which somehow divides the burden among us." -

"I am sorry for you, I am sorry for you," the girl said, and she stood looking at him and slowly moving her head. It seemed she might put out her hand and touch his arm but she did not; instead she said: "It is not warm out here. Come into the house before the sentry passes again and I will give you a little glass of cognac. It will do you good," and because it was her voice that said it even the liquor's fiery, bitter little word sounded cooler and purer to him than any water she might have drawn from the faucet and offered him to drink.

"Yes," he said helplessly. "Thank you, Mademoiselle, I will," and as he followed her in over the step he heard the Spaniard's whistle, long, low, derisive, coming after him from underneath the tree.

She said two or three things more: she said she could make real lace and she showed him the hook and the spool of linen thread while he drank the cognac down in one quick jerk; and she asked him how long he had been away from home and how long since he had seen his people, and he answered that it was two years now, and, standing hooking the nickel needle through the thread, she said to him:

"But afterwards it will be all right and you can go back to them. After France has won the war it will be all right," and the Baron said quickly:

"Of course it will be all right then. It will be all right after France has won the war."

He stood tall and young, outsized and weather-hardened, in the little room near the stove, his hands in his pockets, the blondish pieces of his hair beginning to stand up of themselves. There he hesitated in the low-roofed kitchen that seemed too small for him, looking strangely and intently at her and trying to speak. He was trying to say that for a long time now he had come to believe it was not the loss of home, not the loss of country or freedom even, not even the loss of identity that was defeating them, but that it was something else, it was something else, but he could not find the name to give it. He wished to say that it was something as good and as necessary as the air they breathed that had been taken from them and not replaced: not the emotion of love or pity, but perhaps the flesh of these things, and he stood there silent, watching her hook the needle into the thread and draw the new loop through. He wanted to say: "Sometimes lying awake at night in camp among the others I scarcely believe in country or home or freedom or even in humanity any more, that all this is a fool's dream, all less than nothing to us. It is something else that has perished for us, that thing you gave us by walking out of the door and coming across the yard to us," but he could not say it out.

In another minute or two he was back on the roadside again with the taste of the cognac still in his mouth, and the fluid of tenderness pouring softly in him. Even with the shovel in his hands and his back bent, he moved still in the strangely perfect substance of the dream. It was only when the Spaniard, smiting the earth beside him with the pick's beak, said: "What about us? What about the rest of us? What do we get out of it?" that he started awake and stared about him in bewilderment.

"Out of what?" he said, and even as the Spaniard said the words he saw the sentry coming. It was not the exact meaning he heard, for hearing and sight and action had merged singularly into one. The shovel had fallen and his hand had lifted and struck hard across the Spaniard's mouth at the same instant that the sentry came toward them, his gun lowered, up the broken road.

MORLEY CALLAGHAN
1903–

Callaghan's overpublicized friendship with Hemingway and his links with the between-the-wars expatriate group have not worked entirely to his advantage. It is in the light of this background that he has been too often viewed. He is not a second-order Hemingway but an authentic Canadian voice. Like Hemingway, he tends to handle seamy characters in lowlife situations. But that's a poor reason for refusing to judge him on his own terms.

A quiet, uninsistent writer in the mainstream realistic tradition, he is not really much influenced by the Hemingway techniques of condensation and omission. Perhaps his major achievement lies in his effect on Canadian literature. He helped to redirect its rather uncertain course. He brought to life, particularly for American readers, a whole city, Toronto. To him the brilliant post-Callaghan group of Canadians — Robertson Davies, Mordecai Richler, Alice Munro, Margaret Atwood — owe much.

"A Cap for Steve" is a simple story about simple people. It deals, however, with large themes: boyhood, paternity, trust, loyalty, and the traps in which ordinary lives may be caught. Its unforced "happy" ending moves us. It is honest.

A Cap for Steve

DAVE DIAMOND, a poor man, a carpenter's assistant, was a small, wiry, quick-tempered individual who had learned how to make every dollar count in his home. His wife, Anna, had been sick a lot, and his twelve-year-old son, Steve, had to be kept in school. Steve, a big-eyed, shy kid, ought to have known the value of money as well as Dave did. It had been ground into him.

But the boy was crazy about baseball, and after school, when he could have been working as a delivery boy or selling papers, he played ball with the kids. His failure to appreciate that the family needed a few extra dollars disgusted Dave. Around the house he wouldn't let Steve talk about baseball, and he scowled when he saw him hurrying off with his glove after dinner.

When the Phillies came to town to play an exhibition game with the home team and Steve pleaded to be taken to the ball park, Dave, of course, was outraged. Steve knew they couldn't afford it. But he had got his mother on his side. Finally Dave made a bargain with them. He said that if Steve came home after school and worked hard helping to make some kitchen shelves he would take him that night to the ball park.

Steve worked hard, but Dave was still resentful. They had to coax him to put on his good suit. When they started out Steve held aloof, feeling guilty, and they walked down the street like strangers; then Dave glanced at Steve's face and, half-ashamed, took his arm more cheerfully.

As the game went on, Dave had to listen to Steve's recitation of the batting average of every Philly that stepped up to the plate; the time the boy must have wasted learning these averages began to appal him. He showed it so plainly that Steve felt guilty again and was silent.

After the game Dave let Steve drag him onto the field to keep him company while he tried to get some autographs from the Philly players, who were being hemmed in by gangs of kids blocking the way to the club-house. But Steve, who was shy, let the other kids block him off from the players. Steve would push his way in, get blocked out, and come back to stand mournfully beside Dave. And Dave grew impatient. He was wasting valuable time. He wanted to get home; Steve knew it and was worried.

Then the big, blond Philly outfielder, Eddie Condon, who had been held up by a gang of kids tugging at his arm and thrusting their score cards at him, broke loose and made a run for the club-house. He was jostled, and his blue cap with the red peak, tilted far back on his head, fell off. It fell at Steve's feet, and Steve stooped quickly and grabbed it. "Okay, son," the outfielder called, turning back. But Steve, holding the hat in both hands, only stared at him.

"Give him his cap, Steve," Dave said, smiling apologetically at the big outfielder who towered over them. But Steve drew the hat closer to his chest. In an awed trance he looked up at big Eddie Condon. It was an embarrassing moment. All the other kids were watching. Some shouted. "Give him his cap."

"My cap, son," Eddie Condon said, his hand out.

"Hey, Steve," Dave said, and he gave him a shake. But he had to jerk the cap out of Steve's hands.

"Here you are," he said.

The outfielder, noticing Steve's white, worshipping face and pleading eyes, grinned and then shrugged. "Aw, let him keep it," he said.

"No, Mister Condon, you don't need to do that," Steve protested.

"It's happened before. Forget it," Eddie Condon said, and he trotted away to the club-house.

Dave handed the cap to Steve; envious kids circled around them and Steve said, "He said I could keep it, Dad. You heard him, didn't you?"

"Yeah, I heard him," Dave admitted. The wonder in Steve's face made him smile. He took the boy by the arm and they hurried off the field.

On the way home Dave couldn't get him to talk about the game; he couldn't get him to take his eyes off the cap. Steve could hardly believe in his own happiness. "See," he said suddenly, and he showed Dave that Eddie Condon's name was printed on the sweat-band. Then he went on dreaming. Finally he put the cap on his head and turned to Dave with a slow, proud smile. The cap was away too big for him; it fell down over his ears. "Never mind," Dave said. "You can get your mother to take a tuck in the back."

When they got home Dave was tired and his wife didn't understand the cap's importance, and they couldn't get Steve to go to bed. He swaggered around wearing the cap and looking in the mirror every ten minutes. He took the cap to bed with him.

Dave and his wife had a cup of coffee in the kitchen, and Dave told her again how they had got the cap. They agreed that their boy must have an attractive quality that showed in his face, and that Eddie Condon must have been drawn to him — why else would he have singled Steve out from all the kids?

But Dave got tired of the fuss Steve made over that cap and of the way he wore it from the time he got up in the morning until the time he went to bed. Some kid was always coming in, wanting to try on the cap. It was childish, Dave said, for Steve to go around assuming that the cap made him important in the neighbourhood, and to keep telling them how he had become a leader in the park a few blocks away where he played ball in the evenings. And Dave wouldn't stand for Steve's keeping the cap on while he was eating. He was always scolding his wife for accepting Steve's explanation that he'd forgotten he had it on. Just the same, it was remarkable what a little thing like a ball cap could do for a kid, Dave admitted to his wife as he smiled to himself.

One night Steve was late coming home from the park. Dave didn't realize how late it was until he put down his newspaper and watched his wife at the window. Her restlessness got on his nerves. "See what comes from encouraging the boy to hang around with those park loafers," he said. "I don't encourage him," she protested. "You do," he insisted irritably, for he was really worried now. A gang hung around the park until midnight. It was a bad park. It was true that on one side there was a good district with fine, expensive apartment houses, but the kids from that neighbourhood left the park to the kids from the poorer homes. When his wife went out and walked down to the corner it was his turn to wait and worry and watch at the open window. Each waiting moment tortured him. At last he heard his wife's voice and Steve's voice, and he relaxed and sighed; then he remembered his duty and rushed angrily to meet them.

"I'll fix you, Steve, once and for all," he said. "I'll show you you can't start coming into the house at midnight."

"Hold your horses, Dave," his wife said. "Can't you see the state he's in?" Steve looked utterly exhausted and beaten.

"What's the matter?" Dave asked quickly.

"I lost my cap," Steve whispered; he walked past his father and threw himself on the couch in the living-room and lay with his face hidden.

"Now, don't scold him, Dave," his wife said.

"Scold him. Who's scolding him?" Dave asked, indignantly. "It's his cap, not mine. If it's not worth his while to hang on to it, why should I scold him?" But he was implying resentfully that he alone recognized the cap's value.

"So you are scolding him," his wife said. "It's his cap. Not yours. What happened, Steve?"

Steve told them he had been playing ball and he found that when he ran the bases the cap fell off; it was still too big despite the tuck his mother had taken in the band. So the next time he came to bat he tucked the cap in his hip pocket. Someone had lifted it, he was sure.

"And he didn't even know whether it was still in his pocket," Dave said sarcastically.

"I wasn't careless, Dad," Steve said. For the last three hours he had been wandering around to the homes of the kids who had been in the park at the time; he wanted to go on, but he was too tired. Dave knew the boy was apologizing to him, but he didn't know why it made him angry.

"If he didn't hang on to it, it's not worth worrying about now," he said, and he sounded offended.

After that night they knew that Steve didn't go to the park to play ball; he went to look for the cap. It irritated Dave to see him sit around listlessly, or walk in circles, trying to force his memory to find a particular incident which would suddenly recall to him the moment when the cap had been taken. It was no attitude for a growing, healthy boy to take, Dave complained. He told Steve firmly once and for all that he didn't want to hear any more about the cap.

One night, two weeks later, Dave was walking home with Steve from the shoemaker's. It was a hot night. When they passed an ice-cream parlour Steve slowed down. "I guess I couldn't have a soda, could I?" Steve said. "Nothing doing," Dave said firmly. "Come on now," he added as Steve hung back, looking in the window.

"Dad, look!" Steve cried suddenly, pointing at the window. "My cap! There's my cap! He's coming out!"

A well-dressed boy was leaving the ice-cream parlour; he had on a blue ball cap with a red peak, just like Steve's cap. "Hey, you!" Steve cried, and he rushed at the boy, his small face fierce and his eyes wild. Before the boy could back away Steve had snatched the cap from his head. "That's my cap!" he shouted.

"What's this?" the bigger boy said. "Hey, give me my cap or I'll give you a poke on the nose."

Dave was surprised that his own shy boy did not back away. He watched him clutch the cap in his left hand, half crying with excitement as he put his head down and drew back his right fist: he was willing to fight. And Dave was proud of him.

"Wait, now," Dave said. "Take it easy, son," he said to the other boy, who refused to back away.

"My boy says it's his cap," Dave said.

"Well, he's crazy. It's my cap."

"I was with him when he got this cap. When the Phillies played here. It's a Philly cap."

"Eddie Condon gave it to me," Steve said. "And you stole it from me, you jerk."

"Don't call me a jerk, you little squirt. I never saw you before in my life."

"Look," Steve said, pointing to the printing on the cap's sweatband. "It's Eddie Condon's cap. See? See, Dad?"

"Yeah. You're right, Son. Ever see this boy before, Steve?"

"No," Steve said reluctantly.

The other boy realized he might lose the cap. "I bought it from a guy," he said. "I paid him. My father knows I paid him." He said he got the cap at the ball park. He groped for some magically impressive words and suddenly found them. "You'll have to speak to my father," he said.

"Sure, I'll speak to your father," Dave said. "What's your name? Where do you live?"

"My name's Hudson. I live about ten minutes away on the other side of the park." The boy appraised Dave, who wasn't any bigger than he was and who wore a faded blue windbreaker and no tie. "My father is a lawyer," he said boldly. "He wouldn't let me keep the cap if he didn't think I should."

"Is that a fact?" Dave asked belligerently. "Well, we'll see. Come on. Let's go." And he got between the two boys and they walked along the street. They didn't talk to each other. Dave knew the Hudson boy was waiting to get to the protection of his home, and Steve knew it, too, and he looked up apprehensively at Dave. And Dave, reaching for his hand, squeezed it encouragingly and strode along, cocky and belligerent, knowing that Steve relied on him.

The Hudson boy lived in that row of fine apartment houses on the other side of the park. At the entrance to one of these houses Dave tried not to hang back and show he was impressed, because he could feel Steve hanging back. When they got into the small elevator Dave didn't know why he took off his hat. In the carpeted hall on the fourth floor the Hudson boy said, "Just a minute," and entered his own apartment. Dave and Steve were left alone in the corridor, knowing that the other boy was preparing his father for the encounter. Steve looked anxiously at his father, and Dave said, "Don't worry, Son," and he added resolutely, "No one's putting anything over on us."

A tall balding man in a brown velvet smoking-jacket suddenly opened the door. Dave had never seen a man wearing one of those jackets, although he had seen them in department-store windows. "Good evening," he said, making a deprecatory gesture at the cap Steve still clutched tightly in his left hand. "My boy didn't get your name. My name is Hudson."

"Mine's Diamond."

"Come on in," Mr. Hudson said, putting out his hand and laughing good-naturedly. He led Dave and Steve into his living-room. "What's this about that cap?" he asked. "The way kids can get excited about a cap. Well, it's understandable, isn't it?"

"So it is," Dave said, moving closer to Steve, who was awed by the broadloom rug and the fine furniture. He wanted to show Steve he was at ease himself, and he wished Mr. Hudson wouldn't be so polite. That meant Dave had to be polite and affable, too, and it was hard to manage when he was standing in the middle of the floor in his old windbreaker.

"Sit down, Mr. Diamond," Mr. Hudson said. Dave took Steve's arm and sat him down beside him on the chesterfield. The Hudson boy watched his father. And Dave looked at Steve and saw that he wouldn't face Mr. Hudson or the other boy; he kept looking up at Dave, putting all his faith in him.

"Well, Mr. Diamond, from what I gathered from my boy, you're able to prove this cap belonged to your boy."

"That's a fact," Dave said.

"Mr. Diamond, you'll have to believe my boy bought that cap from some kid in good faith."

"I don't doubt it," Dave said. "But no kid can sell something that doesn't belong to him. You know that's a fact, Mr. Hudson."

"Yes, that's a fact," Mr. Hudson agreed. "But that cap means a lot to my boy, Mr. Diamond."

"It means a lot to my boy, too, Mr. Hudson."

"Sure it does. But supposing we called in a policeman. You know what he'd say? He'd ask you if you were willing to pay my boy what he paid for the cap. That's usually the way it works out," Mr. Hudson said, friendly and smiling, as he eyed Dave shrewdly.

"But that's not right. It's not justice," Dave protested. "Not when it's my boy's cap."

"I know it isn't right. But that's what they do."

"All right. What did you say your boy paid for the cap?" Dave said reluctantly.

"Two dollars."

"Two dollars!" Dave repeated. Mr. Hudson's smile was still kindly, but his eyes were shrewd, and Dave knew the lawyer was counting on his not having the two dollars; Mr. Hudson thought he had Dave sized up; he had looked at him and decided he was broke. Dave's pride was hurt, and he turned to Steve. What he saw in Steve's face was more powerful than the hurt to his pride: it was the memory of how difficult it had been to get an extra nickel, the talk he heard about the cost of food, the worry in his mother's face as she tried to make ends meet, and the bewildered embarrassment that he was here in a rich man's home, forcing his father to confess that he couldn't afford to spend two dollars. Then Dave grew angry and reckless. "I'll give you the two dollars," he said.

Steve looked at the Hudson boy and grinned brightly. The Hudson boy watched his father.

"I suppose that's fair enough," Mr. Hudson said. "A cap like this can be worth a lot to a kid. You know how it is. Your boy might want to sell — I mean be satisfied. Would he take five dollars for it?"

"Five dollars?" Dave repeated. "Is it worth five dollars, Steve?" he asked uncertainly.

Steve shook his head and looked frightened.

"No, thanks, Mr. Hudson," Dave said firmly.

"I'll tell you what I'll do," Mr. Hudson said. "I'll give you ten dollars. The cap has a sentimental value for my boy, a Philly cap, a big-leaguer's cap. It's only worth about a buck and a half really," he added. But Dave shook his head again. Mr. Hudson frowned. He looked at his own boy with indulgent concern, but now he was embarrassed. "I'll tell you what I'll do," he said. "This cap — well, it's worth as much as a day at the circus to my boy. Your boy should be recompensed. I want to be fair. Here's twenty dollars," and he held out two ten-dollar bills to Dave.

That much money for a cap, Dave thought, and his eyes brightened. But he knew what the cap had meant to Steve; to deprive him of it now that it was within his reach would be unbearable. All the things he needed in his life gathered around him; his wife was there, saying he couldn't afford to reject the offer, he had no right to do it; and he turned to Steve to see if Steve thought it wonderful that the cap could bring them twenty dollars.

"What do you say, Steve?" he asked uneasily.

"I don't know," Steve said. He was in a trance. When Dave smiled, Steve smiled too, and Dave believed that Steve was as impressed as he was, only more bewildered, and maybe even more aware that they could not possibly turn away that much money for a ball cap.

"Well, here you are," Mr. Hudson said, and he put the two bills in Steve's hand. "It's a lot of money. But I guess you had a right to expect as much."

With a dazed, fixed smile Steve handed the money slowly to his father, and his face was white.

Laughing jovially, Mr. Hudson led them to the door. His own boy followed a few paces behind.

In the elevator Dave took the bills out of his pocket. "See, Stevie," he whispered eagerly. "That windbreaker you wanted! And ten dollars for your bank! Won't Mother be surprised?"

"Yeah," Steve whispered, the little smile still on his face. But Dave had to turn away quickly so their eyes wouldn't meet, for he saw that it was a scared smile.

Outside, Dave said, "Here, you carry the money home, Steve. You show it to your mother."

"No, you keep it," Steve said, and then there was nothing to say. They walked in silence.

"It's a lot of money," Dave said finally. When Steve didn't answer him, he added angrily, "I turned to you, Steve. I asked you, didn't I?"

"That man knew how much his boy wanted that cap," Steve said.

"Sure. But he recognized how much it was worth to us."

"No, you let him take it away from us," Steve blurted.

"That's unfair," Dave said. "Don't dare say that to me."

"I don't want to be like you," Steve muttered, and he darted across the road and walked along on the other side of the street.

"It's unfair," Dave said angrily, only now he didn't mean that Steve was unfair, he meant that what had happened in the prosperous Hudson home was unfair, and he didn't know quite why. He had been trapped, not just by Mr. Hudson, but by his own life. Across the road Steve was hurrying along with his head down, wanting to be alone. They walked most of the way home on opposite sides of the street, until Dave could stand it no longer. "Steve," he called, crossing the street. "It was very unfair. I mean, for you to say . . ." but Steve started to run. Dave walked as fast as he could and Steve was getting beyond him, and he felt enraged and suddenly he yelled, "Steve!" and he started to chase his son. He wanted to get hold of Steve and pound him, and he didn't know why. He gained on him, he gasped for breath and he almost got him by the shoulder. Turning, Steve saw his father's face in the street light and was terrified; he circled away, got to the house, and rushed in, yelling, "Mother!"

"Son, Son!" she cried, rushing from the kitchen. As soon as she threw her arms around Steve, shielding him, Dave's anger left him and he felt stupid. He walked past them into the kitchen.

"What happened?" she asked anxiously. "Have you both gone crazy? What did you do, Steve?"

"Nothing," he said sullenly.

"What did your father do?"

"We found the boy with my ball cap, and he let the boy's father take it from us."

"No, no," Dave protested. "Nobody pushed us around. The man didn't put anything over us." He felt tired and his face was burning. He told what had happened; then he slowly took the two ten-dollar bills out of his wallet and tossed them on the table and looked up guiltily at his wife.

It hurt him that she didn't pick up the money, and that she didn't rebuke him. "It is a lot of money, Son," she said slowly. "Your father was only trying to do what he knew was right, and it'll work out, and you'll understand." She was soothing Steve, but Dave knew she felt that she needed to be gentle with him, too, and he was ashamed.

When she went with Steve to his bedroom, Dave sat by himself. His son had contempt for him, he thought. His son, for the first time, had seen how easy it was for another man to handle him, and he had judged him and had wanted to walk alone on the other side of the street. He looked at the money and he hated the sight of it.

His wife returned to the kitchen, made a cup of tea, talked soothingly, and said it was incredible that he had forced the Hudson man to pay him twenty dollars for the cap, but all Dave could think of was Steve was scared of me.

Finally, he got up and went into Steve's room. The room was in darkness, but he could see the outline of Steve's body on the bed, and he sat down beside him and whispered, "Look, Son, it was a mistake. I know why. People like us — in circumstances where money can scare us. No, no," he said, feeling ashamed and shaking his head apologetically; he was taking the wrong way of showing the boy they were together; he was covering up his own failure. For the failure had been his, and it had come out of being so separated from his son that he had been blind to what was beyond the price in a boy's life. He longed now to show Steve he could be with him from day to day. His hand went out hesitantly to Steve's shoulder. "Steve, look," he said eagerly. "The trouble was I didn't realize how much I enjoyed it that night at the ball park. If I had watched you playing for your own team — the kids around here say you could be a great pitcher. We could take that money and buy a new pitcher's glove for you, and a catcher's mitt. Steve, Steve, are you listening? I could catch you, work with you in the lane. Maybe I could be your coach . . . watch you become a great pitcher." In the half-darkness he could see the boy's pale face turn to him.

Steve, who had never heard his father talk like this, was shy and wondering. All he knew was that his father, for the first time, wanted to be with him in his hopes and adventures. He said, "I guess you do know how important that cap was." His hand went out to his father's arm. "With that man the cap was — well it was just something he could buy, eh Dad?" Dave gripped his son's hand hard. The wonderful generosity of childhood — the price a boy was willing to pay to be able to count on his father's admiration and approval — made him feel humble, then strangely exalted.

FRANK O'CONNOR
1903–1966

No single story O'Connor ever wrote is a masterpiece. His stories as a whole are his masterpiece, a body of immensely satisfying work in the realistic mode. From George Moore to Julia O'Faolain the Irish have displayed a strong affinity for the short story, so strong that with Joyce it flowered in genius. But perhaps the fullest, the liveliest, certainly the most heart-warming picture of twentieth-century Ireland, at least on its lower- and middle-class levels, is found in O'Connor.

Not only did he possess the right eye and ear — especially ear — but somehow he held in harmonious balance a rich assortment of feelings about his countrymen and countrywomen: love, skepticism, amusement, irony, admiration, compassion. He was neither profound (he could never have written "The Dead") nor innovative in technique. But once caught up in his world, the captivated reader will be willing to settle for the pervasive humaneness that is his hallmark.

The staples of Irish fiction are poverty, religion, sexual puritanism, revolutionary politics, liquor, and talk. O'Connor works with all these, but especially talk. The key to his art, as he once wrote, is "voices in his head," and so perfectly does he render these voices that soon they begin to sound in our heads too.

It's hard to single out any one O'Connor story. He is here represented by a quite slight, unambitious little affair. But in its few pages it mirrors many qualities of his mind and temperament. Among them are (pre-eminently) his humor, but also his delight in conversation; his keen, unsentimental sense of the part drink plays in the Irish experience; his constant awareness of the Irish character as one formed outside the mainstream of European culture; and his feeling, rooted in his poverty-stricken early years, for the innocence and wisdom of childhood.

The Drunkard

IT WAS a terrible blow to Father when Mr. Dooley on the terrace died. Mr. Dooley was a commercial traveller with two sons in the Dominicans and a car of his own, so socially he was miles ahead of us, but he had no false pride. Mr. Dooley was an intellectual, and, like all intellectuals the thing he loved best was conversation, and in his own limited way Father was a well-read man and could appreciate an intelligent talker. Mr. Dooley was remarkably intelligent. Between business acquaintances and clerical contacts, there was very little he didn't know about what went on in town, and evening after evening he crossed the road to our gate to explain to Father the news behind the news. He had a low, palavering voice and a knowing smile, and Father would listen in astonishment, giving him a conversational lead now and again, and then stump triumphantly in to Mother with his face aglow and ask: "Do you know what Mr. Dooley is after telling me?" Ever since, when somebody has given me some bit of information off the record I have found myself on the point of asking: "Was it Mr. Dooley told you that?"

Till I actually saw him laid out in his brown shroud with the rosary beads entwined between his waxy fingers I did not take the report of his death seriously. Even then I felt there must be a catch and that some summer evening Mr. Dooley must reappear at our gate to give us the lowdown on the next world. But Father was very upset, partly because Mr. Dooley was about one age with himself, a thing that always gives a distinctly personal turn to another man's demise; partly because now he would have no one to tell him what dirty work was behind the latest scene at the Corporation. You could count on your fingers the number of men in Blarney Lane who read the papers as Mr. Dooley did, and none of these would have overlooked the fact that Father was only a laboring man. Even Sullivan, the carpenter, a mere nobody, thought he was a cut above Father. It was certainly a solemn event.

"Half past two to the Curragh," Father said meditatively, putting down the paper.

"But you're not thinking of going to the funeral?" Mother asked in alarm.

"'Twould be expected," Father said, scenting opposition. "I wouldn't give it to say to them."

"I think," said Mother with suppressed emotion, "it will be as much as anyone will expect if you go to the chapel with him."

("Going to the chapel," of course, was one thing, because the body was removed after work, but going to a funeral meant the loss of a half-day's pay.)

"The people hardly know us," she added.

"God between us and all harm," Father replied with dignity, "we'd be glad if it was our own turn."

To give Father his due, he was always ready to lose a half day for the sake of an old neighbor. It wasn't so much that he liked funerals as that he was a conscientious man who did as he would be done by; and nothing could have consoled him so much for the prospect of his own death as the assurance of a worthy funeral. And, to give Mother her due, it wasn't the half-day's pay she begrudged, badly as we could afford it.

Drink, you see, was Father's great weakness. He could keep steady for months, even for years, at a stretch, and while he did he was as good as gold. He was first up in the morning and brought the mother a cup of tea in bed, stayed at home in the evenings and read the paper; saved money and bought himself a new blue serge suit and bowler hat. He laughed at the folly of men who, week in week out, left their hard-earned money with the publicans; and sometimes, to pass an idle hour, he took pencil and paper and calculated precisely how much he saved each week through being a teetotaller. Being a natural optimist he sometimes continued this calculation through the whole span of his prospective existence and the total was breathtaking. He would die worth hundreds.

If I had only known it, this was a bad sign; a sign he was becoming stuffed up with spiritual pride and imagining himself better than his neighbors. Sooner or later, the spiritual pride grew till it called for some form of celebration. Then he took a drink — not whiskey, of course; nothing like that — just a glass of some harmless drink like lager beer. That was the end of Father. By the time he had taken the first he already realized that he had made a fool of himself, took a second to forget it and a third to forget that he couldn't forget, and at last came home reeling drunk. From this on it was "The Drunkard's Progress," as in the moral prints. Next day he stayed in from work with a sick head while Mother went off to make his excuses at the works, and inside a fortnight he was poor and savage and despondent again. Once he began he drank steadily through everything down to the kitchen clock. Mother and I knew all the phases and dreaded all the dangers. Funerals were one.

"I have to go to Dunphy's to do a half-day's work," said Mother in distress. "Who's to look after Larry?"

"I'll look after Larry," Father said graciously. "The little walk will do him good."

There was no more to be said, though we all knew I didn't need anyone to look after me, and that I could quite well have stayed at home and looked after Sonny, but I was being attached to the party to act as a brake on Father. As a brake I had never achieved anything, but Mother still had great faith in me.

Next day, when I got home from school, Father was there before me and made a cup of tea for both of us. He was very good at tea, but too heavy in the hand for anything else; the way he cut bread was shocking. Afterwards, we went down the hill to the church, Father wearing his best blue serge and a bowler cocked to one side of his head with the least suggestion of the masher. To his great joy he discovered Peter Crowley among the mourners. Peter was another danger signal, as I knew well from certain experiences after Mass on Sunday morning; a mean man, as Mother said, who only went to funerals for the free drinks he could get at them. It turned out that he hadn't even known Mr. Dooley! But Father had a sort of contemptuous regard for him as one of the foolish people who wasted their good money in public-houses when they could be saving it. Very little of his own money Peter Crowley wasted!

It was an excellent funeral from Father's point of view. He had it all well studied before we set off after the hearse in the afternoon sunlight.

"Five carriages!" he exclaimed. "Five carriages and sixteen covered cars! There's one alderman, two councillors and 'tis unknown how many priests. I didn't see a funeral like this from the road since Willie Mack, the publican, died."

"Ah, he was well liked," said Crowley in his husky voice.

"My goodness, don't I know that?" snapped Father. "Wasn't the man my best friend? Two nights before he died — only two nights — he was over telling me the goings-on about the housing contract. Them fellows in the Corporation are night and day robbers. But even I never imagined he was as well connected as that."

Father was stepping out like a boy, pleased with everything: the other mourners, and the fine houses along Sunday's Well. I knew the danger signals were there in full force: a sunny day, a fine funeral, and a distinguished company of clerics and public men were bringing out all the natural vanity and flightiness of Father's character. It was with something like genuine pleasure that he saw his old friend lowered into the grave; with the sense of having performed a duty and the pleasant awareness that however much he would miss poor Mr. Dooley in the long summer evenings, it was he and not poor Mr. Dooley who would do the missing.

"We'll be making tracks before they break up," he whispered to Crowley as the gravediggers tossed in the first shovelfuls of clay, and away he went, hopping like a goat from grassy hump to hump. The drivers, who were probably in the same state as himself, though without months of abstinence to put an edge on it, looked up hopefully.

"Are they nearly finished, Mick?" bawled one.

"All over now bar the last prayers," trumpeted Father in the tone of one who brings news of great rejoicing.

The carriages passed us in a lather of dust several hundred yards from the public-house, and Father, whose feet gave him trouble in hot weather, quickened his pace, looking nervously over his shoulder for any sign of the main body of mourners crossing the hill. In a crowd like that a man might be kept waiting.

When we did reach the pub the carriages were drawn up outside, and solemn men in black ties were cautiously bringing out consolation to mysterious females whose hands reached out modestly from behind the drawn blinds of the coaches. Inside the pub there were only the drivers and a couple of shawly women. I felt if I was to act as a brake at all, this was the time, so I pulled Father by the coattails.

"Dadda, can't we go home now?" I asked.

"Two minutes now," he said, beaming affectionately. "Just a bottle of lemonade and we'll go home."

This was a bribe, and I knew it, but I was always a child of weak character. Father ordered lemonade and two pints. I was thirsty and swallowed my drink at once. But that wasn't Father's way. He had long months of abstinence behind him and an eternity of pleasure before. He took out his pipe, blew through it, filled it, and then lit it with loud pops, his eyes bulging above it. After that he deliberately turned his back on the pint, leaned one elbow on the counter in the attitude of a man who did not know there was a pint behind him, and deliberately brushed the tobacco from his palms. He had settled down for the evening. He was steadily working through all the important funerals he had ever attended. The carriages departed and the minor mourners drifted in till the pub was half full.

"Dadda," I said, pulling his coat again, "can't we go home now?"

"Ah, your mother won't be in for a long time yet," he said benevolently enough. "Run out in the road and play, can't you?"

It struck me as very cool, the way grown-ups assumed that you could play all by yourself on a strange road. I began to get bored as I had so often been bored before. I knew Father was quite capable of lingering there till nightfall. I knew I might have to bring him home, blind drunk, down Blarney Lane, with all the old women at their doors, saying: "Mick Delaney is on it again." I knew that my mother would be half crazy with anxiety; that next day Father wouldn't go out to work; and before the end of the week she would be running down to the pawn with the clock under her shawl. I could never get over the lonesomeness of the kitchen without a clock.

I was still thirsty. I found if I stood on tiptoe I could just reach Father's glass, and the idea occurred to me that it would be interesting to know what the contents were like. He had his back to it and wouldn't notice. I took down the glass and sipped cautiously. It was a terrible disappointment. I was astonished that he could even drink such stuff. It looked as if he had never tried lemonade.

I should have advised him about lemonade but he was holding forth himself in great style. I heard him say that bands were a great addition to a funeral. He put his arms in the position of someone holding a rifle in reverse and hummed a few bars of Chopin's Funeral March. Crowley nodded reverently. I took a longer drink and began to see that porter might have its advantages. I felt pleasantly elevated and philosophic. Father hummed a few bars of the Dead March in *Saul*. It was a nice pub and a very fine funeral, and I felt sure that poor Mr. Dooley in Heaven must be highly gratified. At the same time I thought they might have given him a band. As Father said, bands were a great addition.

But the wonderful thing about porter was the way it made you stand aside, or rather float aloft like a cherub rolling on a cloud, and watch yourself with your legs crossed, leaning against a bar counter, not worrying about trifles but thinking deep, serious, grown-up thoughts about life and death. Looking at yourself like that, you couldn't help thinking after a while how funny you looked, and suddenly you got embarrassed and wanted to giggle. But by the time I had finished the pint, that phase too had passed; I found it hard to put back the glass, the counter seemed to have grown so high. Melancholia was supervening again.

"Well," Father said reverently, reaching behind him for his drink, "God rest the poor man's soul, wherever he is!" He stopped, looked first at the glass, and then at the people round him. "Hello," he said in a fairly good-humored tone, as if he were prepared to consider it a joke, even if it was in bad taste, "who was at this?"

There was silence for a moment while the publican and the old women looked first at Father and then at his glass.

"There was no one at it, my good man," one of the women said with an offended air. "Is it robbers you think we are?"

"Ah, there's no one here would do a thing like that, Mick," said the publican in a shocked tone.

"Well, someone did it," said Father, his smile beginning to wear off.

"If they did, they were them that were nearer it," said the woman darkly, giving me a dirty look; and at the same moment the truth began to dawn on Father. I suppose I must have looked a bit starry-eyed. He bent and shook me.

"Are you all right, Larry?" he asked in alarm.

Peter Crowley looked down at me and grinned.

"Could you beat that?" he exclaimed in a husky voice.

I could, and without difficulty. I started to get sick. Father jumped back in holy terror that I might spoil his good suit, and hastily opened the back door.

"Run! run! run!" he shouted.

I saw the sunlit wall outside with the ivy overhanging it, and ran. The intention was good but the performance was exaggerated, because I lurched right into the wall, hurting it badly, as it seemed to me. Being always very polite, I said "Pardon" before the second bout came on me.

Father, still concerned for his suit, came up behind and cautiously held me while I got sick.

"That's a good boy!" he said encouragingly. "You'll be grand when you get that up."

Begor, I was not grand! Grand was the last thing I was. I gave one unmerciful wail out of me as he steered me back to the pub and put me sitting on the bench near the shawlies. They drew themselves up with an offended air, still sore at the suggestion that they had drunk his pint.

"God help us!" moaned one, looking pityingly at me, "isn't it the likes of them would be fathers?"

"Mick," said the publican in alarm, spraying sawdust on my tracks, "that child isn't supposed to be in here at all. You'd better take him home quick in case a bobby would see him."

"Merciful God!" whimpered Father, raising his eyes to Heaven and clapping his hands silently as he only did when distraught, "what misfortune was on me? Or what will his mother say? . . . If women might stop at home and look after their children themselves!" he added in a snarl for the benefit of the shawlies. "Are them carriages all gone, Bill?"

"The carriages are finished long ago, Mick," replied the publican.

"I'll take him home," Father said despairingly . . . "I'll never bring you out again," he threatened me. "Here," he added, giving me a clean handkerchief from his breast pocket, "put that over your eye."

The blood on the handkerchief was the first indication I got that I was cut, and instantly my temple began to throb and I set up another howl.

"Whisht, whisht, whisht!" Father said testily, steering me out the door. "One'd think you were killed. That's nothing. We'll wash it when we get home."

"Steady now, old scout!" Crowley said, taking the other side of me. "You'll be all right in a minute."

I never met two men who knew less about the effects of drink. The first breath of fresh air and the warmth of the sun made me groggier than ever and I pitched and rolled between wind and tide till Father started to whimper again.

"God Almighty, and the whole road out! What misfortune was on me didn't stop at my work! Can't you walk straight?"

I couldn't. I saw plain enough that, coaxed by the sunlight, every woman old and young in Blarney Lane was leaning over her half-door or sitting on her doorstep. They all stopped gabbling to gape at the strange spectacle of two sober, middle-aged men bringing home a drunken small boy with a cut over his eye. Father, torn between the shamefast desire to get me home as quick as he could, and the neighborly need to explain that it wasn't his fault, finally halted outside Mrs. Roche's. There was a gang of old women outside a door at the opposite side of the road. I didn't like the look of them from the first. They seemed altogether too interested in me. I leaned against the wall of Mrs. Roche's cottage with my hands in my trouser pockets, thinking mournfully of poor Mr. Dooley in his cold grave on the Curragh, who would never walk down the road again, and, with great feeling, I began to sing a favorite song of Father's.

> *"Though lost to Mononia and cold in the grave*
> *He returns to Kincora no more."*

"Wisha, the poor child!" Mrs. Roche said. "Haven't he a lovely voice, God bless him!"

That was what I thought myself, so I was the more surprised when Father said "Whisht!" and raised a threatening finger at me. He didn't seem to realize the appropriateness of the song, so I sang louder than ever.

"Whisht, I tell you!" he snapped, and then tried to work up a smile for Mrs. Roche's benefit. "We're nearly home now. I'll carry you the rest of the way."

But, drunk and all as I was, I knew better than to be carried home ignominiously like that.

"Now," I said severely, "can't you leave me alone? I can walk all right. 'Tis only my head. All I want is a rest."

"But you can rest at home in bed," he said viciously, trying to pick me up, and I knew by the flush on his face that he was very vexed.

"Ah, Jasus," I said crossly, "what do I want to go home for? Why the hell can't you leave me alone?"

For some reason the gang of old women at the other side of the road thought this very funny. They nearly split their sides over it. A gassy fury began to expand in me at the thought that a fellow couldn't have a drop taken without the whole neighborhood coming out to make game of him.

"Who are ye laughing at?" I shouted, clenching my fists at them. "I'll make ye laugh at the other side of yeer faces if ye don't let me pass."

They seemed to think this funnier still; I had never seen such ill-mannered people.

"Go away, ye bloody bitches!" I said.

"Whisht, whisht, whisht, I tell you!" snarled Father, abandoning all pretense of amusement and dragging me along behind him by the hand. I was maddened by the women's shrieks of laughter. I was maddened by Father's bullying. I tried to dig in my heels but he was too powerful for me, and I could only see the women by looking back over my shoulder.

"Take care or I'll come back and show ye!" I shouted. "I'll teach ye to let decent people pass. Fitter for ye to stop at home and wash yeer dirty faces."

"'Twill be all over the road," whimpered Father. "Never again, never again, not if I lived to be a thousand!"

To this day I don't know whether he was forswearing me or the drink.

By way of a song suitable to my heroic mood I bawled "The Boys of Wexford," as he dragged me in home. Crowley, knowing he was not safe, made off and Father undressed me and put me to bed. I couldn't sleep because of the whirling in my head. It was very unpleasant, and I got sick again. Father came in with a wet cloth and mopped up after me. I lay in a fever, listening to him chopping sticks to start a fire. After that I heard him lay the table.

Suddenly the front door banged open and Mother stormed in with Sonny in her arms, not her usual gentle, timid self, but a wild, raging woman. It was clear that she had heard it all from the neighbors.

"Mick Delaney," she cried hysterically, "what did you do to my son?"

"Whisht, woman, whisht, whisht!" he hissed, dancing from one foot to the other. "Do you want the whole road to hear?"

"Ah," she said with a horrifying laugh, "the road knows all about it by this time. The road knows the way you filled your unfortunate innocent child with drink to make sport for you and that other rotten, filthy brute."

"But I gave him no drink," he shouted, aghast at the horrifying interpretation the neighbors had chosen to give his misfortune. "He took it while my back was turned. What the hell do you think I am?"

"Ah," she replied bitterly, "everyone knows what you are now. God forgive you, wasting our hard-earned few ha'pence on drink, and bringing up your child to be a drunken corner-boy like yourself."

Then she swept into the bedroom and threw herself on her knees by the bed. She moaned when she saw the gash over my eye. In the kitchen Sonny set up a loud bawl on his own, and a moment later Father appeared in the bedroom door with his cap over his eyes, wearing an expression of the most intense self-pity.

"That's a nice way to talk to me after all I went through," he whined. "That's a nice accusation, that I was drinking. Not one drop of drink crossed my lips the whole day. How could it when he drank it all? I'm the one that ought to be pitied, with my day ruined on me, and I after being made a show for the whole road."

But next morning, when he got up and went out quietly to work with his dinner-basket, Mother threw herself on me in the bed and kissed me. It seemed it was all my doing, and I was being given a holiday till my eye got better.

"My brave little man!" she said with her eyes shining. "It was God did it you were there. You were his guardian angel."

GRAHAM GREENE
1904–

Graham Greene handles his multifaceted talent with such seeming ease that one sometimes forgets how good he can be at his best. He has written novels (some deeply reflective, some "entertainments"), short stories, stage plays, screenplays, book and film criticism, literary essays, memoirs, travel books.

In 1926 he converted to Roman Catholicism, a spiritual shift reflected (never without rich ambiguity) in his finest novels: The Power and the Glory, The Heart of the Matter, The End of the Affair, A Burnt-Out Case. *In these books the Greene quiddity is elusive. He somehow composes a constant awareness of evil, an almost tormented sense of God, and a worldly wisdom that verges on world-weariness.*

His reputation (he should have been a Nobelist long ago) will not rest on his short stories. He thinks of himself as "a novelist who has happened to write short stories," just as he thinks of Maupassant and Pritchett as short story writers who have happened to write novels. Greene is always professionally skillful, somewhat in the Somerset Maugham manner, a manner curiously English and one that Americans do not seem able to assume. Many of his stories are contrived, some cruel, a few shallow.

These last adjectives do not apply to "Cheap in August." It mutates a well-worn theme, that of the middle-aged woman, vaguely frustrated, in quest of a "holiday affair." The civilized Mary Watson and the broken, wrecked old man appear grotesquely ill-matched. In the end they seem less so. At the heart of the matter Greene first conceals, then reveals two of his specialties: failure and fear. Told with characteristic casualness, the story reverberates.

Cheap in August

IT WAS CHEAP in August: the essential sun, the coral reefs, the bamboo bar and the calypsos — they were all of them at cut prices, like the slightly soiled slips in a bargain-sale. Groups arrived periodically from Philadelphia in the manner of school-treats and departed with less *bruit*, after an exact exhausting week, when the picnic was over. Perhaps for twenty-four hours the swimming-pool and the bar were almost deserted, and then another school-treat would arrive, this time from St. Louis. Everyone knew everyone else; they had bussed together to an airport, they had flown together, together they had faced an alien customs; they would separate during the day and greet each other noisily and happily after dark, exchanging impressions of "shooting the rapids," the botanic gardens, the Spanish fort. "We are doing that tomorrow."

Mary Watson wrote to her husband in Europe, "I had to get away for a bit and it's so cheap in August." They had been married ten years and they had only been separated three times. He wrote to her every day and the letters arrived twice a week in little bundles. She arranged them like newspapers by the date and read them in the correct order. They were tender and precise; what with his research, with preparing lectures and writing letters, he had little time to *see* Europe — he insisted on calling it "your Europe" as though to assure her that he had not forgotten the sacrifice which she must have made by marrying an American professor from New England, but sometimes little criticisms of "her Europe" escaped him: the food was too rich, cigarettes too expensive, wine too often served and milk very difficult to obtain at lunch-time — which might indicate that, after all, she ought not to exaggerate her sacrifice. Perhaps it would have been a good thing if James Thomson, who was his special study at the moment, had written *The Seasons* in America — an American fall, she had to admit, was more beautiful than an English autumn.

Mary Watson wrote to him every other day, but sometimes a postcard only, and she was apt to forget if she had repeated the postcard. She wrote in the shade of the bamboo bar where she could see everyone who passed on the way to the swimming-pool. She wrote truthfully, "It's so cheap in August; the hotel is not half full, and the heat and the humidity are very tiring. But, of course, it's a change." She had no wish to appear extravagant; the salary, which to her European eyes had seemed astronomically large for a professor of literature, had long dwindled to its proper proportions, relative to the price of steaks and salads — she must justify with a little enthusiasm the money she was spending in his absence. So she wrote also about the flowers in the botanic gardens — she had ventured that far on one occasion — and with less truth of the beneficial changes wrought by the sun and the lazy life on her friend Margaret who from "her England" had written and demanded her company: a Margaret, she admitted frankly to herself, who was not visible to any eye but the eye of faith. But then Charlie had complete faith. Even good qualities become with the erosion of time a reproach. After ten years of being happily married, she thought, one undervalues security and tranquillity.

She read Charlie's letters with great attention. She longed to find in them one ambiguity, one evasion, one time-gap which he had ill-explained. Even an unusually strong expression of love would have pleased her, for its strength might have been there to counterweigh a sense of guilt. But she couldn't deceive herself that there was any sense of guilt in Charlie's facile flowing informative script. She calculated that if he had been one of the poets he was now so closely studying, he would have completed already a standard-sized epic during his first two months in "her Europe," and the letters, after all, were only a spare-time occupation. They filled up the vacant hours, and certainly they could have left no room for any other occupation. "It is ten o'clock at night, it is raining outside and the temperature is rather cool for August, not above fifty-six degrees. When I have said good-night to you, my dear one, I shall go happily to bed with the thought of you. I have a long day tomorrow at the museum and dinner in the evening with the Henry Wilkinsons who are passing through on their way from Athens — you remember the Henry Wilkinsons, don't you?" (Didn't she just?) She had wondered whether, when Charlie returned, she might perhaps detect some small unfamiliar note in his love-making which would indicate that a stranger had passed that way. Now she disbelieved in the possibility, and anyway the evidence would arrive too late — it was no good to her now that she might be justified later. She wanted her justification immediately, a justification not alas! for any act that she had committed but only for an intention, for the intention of betraying Charlie, of having, like so many of her friends, a holiday affair (the idea had come to her immediately the dean's wife had said, "It's so cheap in Jamaica in August").

The trouble was that, after three weeks of calypsos in the humid evenings, the rum punches (for which she could no longer disguise from herself a repugnance), the warm Martinis, the interminable red snappers, and tomatoes with everything, there had been no affair, not even the hint of one. She had discovered with disappointment the essential morality of a holiday resort in the cheap season; there were no opportunities for infidelity, only for writing postcards — with great brilliant blue skies and seas — to Charlie. Once a woman from St. Louis had taken too obvious pity on her, when she sat alone in the bar writing postcards, and invited her to join their party which was about to visit the botanic gardens — "We are an awfully jolly bunch," she had said with a big turnip smile. Mary exaggerated her English accent to repel her better and said that she didn't much care for flowers. It had shocked the woman as deeply as if she had said she did not care for television. From the motion of the heads at the other end of the bar, the agitated clinking of the Coca-Cola glasses, she could tell that her words were being repeated from one to another. Afterwards, until the jolly bunch had taken the airport limousine on the way back to St. Louis, she was aware of averted heads. She was English, she had taken a superior attitude to flowers, and as she preferred even warm Martinis to Coca-Cola, she was probably in their eyes an alcoholic.

It was a feature common to most of these jolly bunches that they contained no male attachment, and perhaps that was why the attempt to look attractive was completely abandoned. Huge buttocks were exposed in their full horror in tight large-patterned Bermuda shorts. Heads were bound in scarves to cover rollers which were not removed even by lunch-time — they stuck out like small mole-hills. Daily she watched the bums lurch by like hippos on the way to the water. Only in the evening would the women change from the monstrous shorts into monstrous cotton frocks, covered with mauve or scarlet flowers, in order to take dinner on the terrace where formality was demanded in the book of rules, and the few men who appeared were forced to wear jackets and ties though the thermometer stood at close on eighty degrees after sunset. The market in femininity being such, how could one hope to see any male foragers? Only old and broken husbands were sometimes to be seen towed towards an Issa store advertising free-port prices.

She had been encouraged during the first week by the sight of three men with crew-cuts who went past the bar towards the swimming-pool wearing male bikinis. They were far too young for her, but in her present mood she would have welcomed altruistically the sight of another's romance. Romance is said to be contagious, and if in the candle-lit evenings the "informal" coffee tavern had contained a few young amorous couples, who could say what men of maturer years might not eventually arrive to catch the infection? But her hopes dwindled. The young men came and went without a glance at the Bermuda shorts or the pinned hair. Why should they stay? They were certainly more beautiful than any girl there and they knew it.

By nine o'clock most evenings Mary Watson was on her way to bed. A few evenings of calypsos, of quaint false impromptus and the hideous jangle of rattles, had been enough. Outside the closed windows of the hotel annexe the boxes of the air-conditioners made a continuous rumble in the starred and palmy night like overfed hotel guests. Her room was full of dried air which bore no more resemblance to fresh air than the dried figs to the newly picked fruit. When she looked in the glass to brush her hair she often regretted her lack of charity to the jolly bunch from St. Louis. It was true she did not wear Bermuda shorts nor coil her hair in rollers, but her hair was streaky nonetheless with heat and the mirror reflected more plainly than it seemed to do at home her thirty-nine years. If she had not paid in advance for a four-weeks *pension* on her individual round-trip tour, with tickets exchangeable for a variety of excursions, she would have turned tail and returned to the campus. Next year, she thought, when I am forty, I must feel grateful that I have preserved the love of a good man.

She was a woman given to self-analysis, and perhaps because it is a great deal easier to direct questions to a particular face rather than to a void (one has the right to expect some kind of a response even from eyes one sees many times a day in a compact), she posed the questions to herself with a belligerent direct stare into the looking-glass. She was an honest woman, and for that reason the questions were all the cruder. She would say to herself, I have slept with no one other than Charlie (she wouldn't admit as sexual experiences the small exciting half-way points that she had reached before marriage); why am I now seeking to find a strange body, which will probably give me less pleasure than the body I already know? It had been more than a month before Charlie brought her real pleasure. Pleasure, she had learnt, grew with habit, so that if it were not really pleasure that she now looked for, what was it? The answer could only be the unfamiliar. She had friends, even on the respectable campus, who had admitted to her, in the frank admirable American way, their adventures. These had usually been in Europe — a momentary marital absence had given opportunity for a momentary excitement, and then with what a sigh of relief they had found themselves safely at home. All the same they felt afterwards that they had enlarged their experience; they understood something that their husbands did not really understand — the real character of a Frenchman, an Italian, even — there were such cases — of an Englishman.

Mary Watson was painfully aware, as an Englishwoman, that her experience was confined to one American. They all, on the campus, believed her to be European, but all she knew was confined to one man and he was a citizen of Boston who had no curiosity for the great Western regions. In a sense she was more American by choice than he was by birth. Perhaps she was less European even than the wife of the Professor of Romance Languages, who had confided to her that once — overwhelmingly — in Antibes . . . it had happened only once because the sabbatical year was over . . . her husband was up in Paris checking manuscripts before they flew home . . .

Had she herself, Mary Watson sometimes wondered, been just such a European adventure which Charlie mistakenly had domesticated? (She couldn't pretend to be a tigress in a cage, but they kept smaller creatures in cages, white mice, love-birds.) And, to be fair, Charlie too was her adventure, her American adventure, the kind of man whom at twenty-seven she had not before encountered in frowsy London. Henry James had described the type, and at that moment in her history she had been reading a great deal of Henry James: "A man of intellect whose body was not much to him and its senses and appetites not importunate." All the same for a while she had made the appetites importunate.

That was her private conquest of the American continent, and when the Professor's wife had spoken of the dancer of Antibes (no, that was a Roman inscription — the man had been a *marchand de vin*) she had thought, The lover I know and admire is American and I am proud of it. But afterwards came the thought: American or New England? Yet to know a country must one know every region sexually?

It was absurd at thirty-nine not to be content. She had her man. The book on James Thomson would be published by the University Press, and Charlie had the intention afterwards of making a revolutionary break from the romantic poetry of the eighteenth century into a study of the American image in European literature — it was to be called *The Double Reflection:* the effect of Fenimore Cooper on the European scene: the image of America presented by Mrs. Trollope — the details were not yet worked out. The study might possibly end with the first arrival of Dylan Thomas on the shores of America — at the Cunard quay or at Idlewild? That was a point for later research. She examined herself again closely in the glass — the new decade of the forties stared frankly back at her — an Englander who had become a New Englander. After all she hadn't travelled very far — Kent to Connecticut. This was not just the physical restlessness of middle age, she argued; it was the universal desire to see a little bit further, before one surrendered to old age and the blank certitude of death.

2

Next day she picked up her courage and went as far as the swimming-pool. A strong wind blew and whipped up the waves in the almost land-girt harbour — the hurricane season would soon be here. All the world creaked around her: the wooden struts of the shabby harbour, the jalousies of the small hopeless houses which looked as though they had been knocked together from a make-it-yourself kit, the branches of the palms — a long, weary, worn-out creaking. Even the water of the swimming-pool imitated in miniature the waves of the harbour.

She was glad that she was alone in the swimming-pool, at least for all practical purposes alone, for the old man splashing water over himself, like an elephant, in the shallow end hardly counted. He was a solitary elephant and not one of the hippo band. They would have called her with merry cries to join them — and it's difficult to be stand-offish in a swimming-pool which is common to all as a table is not. They might even in their resentment have ducked her — pretending like schoolchildren that it was all a merry game; there was nothing she put beyond those thick thighs, whether they were encased in bikinis or Bermuda shorts. As she floated in the pool her ears were alert for their approach. At the first sound she would get well away from the water, but today they were probably making an excursion to Tower Isle on the other side of the island, or had they done that yesterday? Only the old man watched her, pouring water over his head to keep away sunstroke. She was safely alone, which was the next best thing to the adventure she had come here to find. All the same, as she sat on the rim of the pool, and let the sun and wind dry her, she realized the extent of her solitude. She had spoken to no one but black waiters and Syrian receptionists for more than two weeks. Soon, she thought, I shall even begin to miss Charlie — it would be an ignoble finish to what she had intended to be an adventure.

A voice from the water said to her, "My name's Hickslaughter — Henry Hickslaughter." She couldn't have sworn to the name in court, but that was how it had sounded at the time and he never repeated it. She looked down at a polished mahogany crown surrounded by white hair; perhaps he resembled Neptune more than an elephant. Neptune was always outsize, and as he had pulled himself a little out of the water to speak, she could see the rolls of fat folding over the blue bathing-slip, with tough hair lying like weeds along the ditches. She replied with amusement, "My name is Watson. Mary Watson."

"You're English?"

"My husband's American," she said in extenuation.

"I haven't seen him around, have I?"

"He's in England," she said with a small sigh, for the geographical and national situation seemed too complicated for casual explanation.

"You like it here?" he asked and lifting a hand-cup of water he distributed it over his bald head.

"So so."

"Got the time on you?"

She looked in her bag and told him, "Eleven fifteen."

"I've had my half hour," he said and trod heavily away towards the ladder at the shallow end.

An hour later, staring at her lukewarm Martini with its great green unappetizing olive, she saw him looming down at her from the other end of the bamboo bar. He wore an ordinary shirt open at the neck and a brown leather belt; his type of shoes in her childhood had been known as co-respondent, but one seldom saw them today. She wondered what Charlie would think of her pick-up; unquestionably she had landed him, rather as an angler struggling with a heavy catch finds that he has hooked nothing better than an old boot. She was no angler; she didn't know whether a boot would put an ordinary hook out of action altogether, but she knew that *her* hook could be irremediably damaged. No one would approach her if she were in his company. She drained the Martini in one gulp and even attacked the olive so as to have no excuse to linger in the bar.

"Would you do me the honour," Mr. Hickslaughter asked, "of having a drink with me?" His manner was completely changed; on dry land he seemed unsure of himself and spoke with an old-fashioned propriety.

"I'm afraid I've only just finished one. I have to be off." Inside the gross form she thought she saw a tousled child with disappointed eyes. "I'm having lunch early today." She got up and added rather stupidly, for the bar was quite empty, "You can have my table."

"I don't need a drink that much," he said solemnly. "I was just after company." She knew that he was watching her as she moved to the adjoining coffee tavern, and she thought with guilt, at least I've got the old boot off the hook. She refused the shrimp cocktail with tomato ketchup and fell back as was usual with her on a grapefruit, with grilled trout to follow. "Please no tomato with the trout," she implored, but the black waiter obviously didn't understand her. While she waited she began with amusement to picture a scene between Charlie and Mr. Hickslaughter, who happened for the purpose of her story to be crossing the campus. "This is Henry Hickslaughter, Charlie. We used to go bathing together when I was in Jamaica." Charlie, who always wore English clothes, was very tall, very thin, very concave. It was a satisfaction to know that he would never lose his figure — his nerves would see to that and his extreme sensibility. He hated anything gross; there was no grossness in *The Seasons,* not even in the lines on spring.

She heard slow footsteps coming up behind her and panicked. "May I share your table?" Mr. Hickslaughter asked. He had recovered his terrestrial politeness, but only so far as speech was concerned, for he sat firmly down without waiting for her reply. The chair was too small for him; his thighs overlapped like a double mattress on a single bed. He began to study the menu.

"They copy American food; it's worse than the reality," Mary Watson said.

"You don't like American food?"

"Tomatoes even with the trout!"

"Tomatoes? Oh, you mean tomatoes," he said, correcting her accent. "I'm very fond of tomatoes myself."

"And fresh pineapple in the salad."

"There's a lot of vitamins in fresh pineapple." Almost as if he wished to emphasize their disagreement, he ordered shrimp cocktail, grilled trout and a sweet salad. Of course, when her trout arrived, the tomatoes were there. "You can have mine if you want to," she said and he accepted with pleasure. "You are very kind. You are really very kind." He held out his plate like Oliver Twist.

She began to feel oddly at ease with the old man. She would have been less at ease, she was certain, with a possible adventure: she would have been wondering about her effect on him, while now she could be sure that she gave him pleasure — with the tomatoes. He was perhaps less the old anonymous boot than an old shoe comfortable to wear. And curiously enough, in spite of his first approach and in spite of his correcting her over the pronunciation of tomatoes, it was not really an old American shoe of which she was reminded. Charlie wore English clothes over his English figure, he studied English eighteenth-century literature, his book would be published in England by the Cambridge University Press who would buy sheets, but she had the impression that he was far more fashioned as an American shoe than Hickslaughter. Even Charlie, whose manners were perfect, if they had met for the first time today at the swimming-pool, would have interrogated her more closely. Interrogation had always seemed to her a principal part of American social life — an inheritance perhaps from the Indian smoke-fires: "Where are you from? Do you know the so and so's? Have you been to the botanic gardens?" It came over her that Mr. Hickslaughter, if that were really his name, was perhaps an American reject — not necessarily more flawed than the pottery rejects of famous firms you find in bargain-basements.

She found herself questioning *him*, with circumlocutions, while he savoured the tomatoes. "I was born in London. I couldn't have been born much more than six hundred miles from there without drowning, could I? But you belong to a continent thousands of miles wide and long. Where were you born?" (She remembered a character in a Western movie directed by John Ford who asked, "Where do you hail from, stranger?" The question was more frankly put than hers.)

He said, "St. Louis."

"Oh, then there are lots of your people here — you are not alone." She felt a slight disappointment that he might belong to the jolly bunch.

"I'm alone," he said. "Room 63." It was in her own corridor on the third floor of the annexe. He spoke firmly as though he were imparting information for future use. "Five doors down from you."

"Oh."

"I saw you come out your first day."

"I never noticed you."

"I keep to myself unless I see someone I like."

"Didn't you see anyone you liked from St. Louis?"

"I'm not all that fond of St. Louis, and St. Louis can do without me. I'm not a favourite son."

"Do you come here often?"

"In August. It's cheap in August." He kept on surprising her. First there was his lack of local patriotism, and now his frankness about money or rather about the lack of it, a frankness that could almost be classed as an un-American activity.

"Yes."

"I have to go where it's reasonable," he said, as though he were exposing his bad hand to a partner at gin.

"You've retired?"

"Well — I've been retired." He added, "You ought to take salad . . . It's good for you."

"I feel quite well without it."

"You could do with more weight." He added appraisingly, "A couple of pounds." She was tempted to tell him that he could do with less. They had both seen each other exposed.

"Were you in business?" She was being driven to interrogate. He hadn't asked her a personal question since his first at the pool.

"In a way," he said. She had a sense that he was supremely uninterested in his own doings; she was certainly discovering an America which she had not known existed.

She said, "Well, if you'll excuse me . . ."

"Aren't you taking any dessert?"

"No, I'm a light luncher."

"It's all included in the price. You ought to eat some fruit." He was looking at her under his white eyebrows with an air of disappointment which touched her.

"I don't care much for fruit and I want a nap. I always have a nap in the afternoon."

Perhaps, after all, she thought, as she moved away through the formal dining-room, he is disappointed only because I'm not taking full advantage of the cheap rate.

She passed his room going to her own: the door was open and a big white-haired mammy was making the bed. The room was exactly like her own; the same pair of double beds, the same wardrobe, the same dressing-table in the same position, the same heavy breathing of the air-conditioner. In her own room she looked in vain for the thermos of iced water; then she rang the bell and waited for several minutes. You couldn't expect good service in August. She went down the passage; Mr. Hickslaughter's door was still open and she went in to find the maid. The door of the bathroom was open too and a wet cloth lay on the tiles.

How bare the bedroom was. At least she had taken the trouble to add a few flowers, a photograph and half a dozen books on a bedside table which gave her room a lived-in air. Beside his bed there was only a literary digest lying open and face down; she turned it over to see what he was reading — as she might have expected it was something to do with calories and proteins. He had begun writing a letter at his dressing-table and with the simple unscrupulousness of an intellectual she began to read it with her ears cocked for any sound in the passage.

"Dear Joe," she read, "the draft was two weeks late last month and I was in real difficulties. I had to borrow from a Syrian who runs a tourist junk-shop in Curaçao and pay him interest. You owe me a hundred dollars for the interest. It's your own fault. Mum never gave us lessons on how to live with an empty stomach. Please add it to the next draft and be sure to do that, you wouldn't want me coming back to collect. I'll be here till the end of August. It's cheap in August, and a man gets tired of nothing but Dutch, Dutch, Dutch. Give my love to Sis."

The letter broke off unfinished. Anyway she would have had no opportunity to read more because someone was approaching down the passage. She went to the door in time to see Mr. Hickslaughter on the threshold. He said, "You looking for me?"

"I was looking for the maid. She was in here a minute ago."

"Come in and sit down."

He looked through the bathroom door and then at the room in general. Perhaps it was only an uneasy conscience which made her think that his eyes strayed a moment to the unfinished letter.

"She's forgotten my iced water."

"You can have mine if it's filled." He shook his thermos and handed it to her.

"Thanks a lot."

"When you've had your sleep . . ." he began and looked away from her. Was he looking at the letter?

"Yes?"

"We might have a drink."

She was, in a sense, trapped. She said, "Yes."

"Give me a ring when you wake up."

"Yes." She said nervously, "Have a good sleep yourself."

"Oh, I don't sleep." He didn't wait for her to leave the room before turning away, swinging that great elephantine backside of his towards her. She had walked into a trap baited with a flask of iced water, and in her room she drank the water gingerly as though it might have a flavour different from hers.

3

She found it difficult to sleep: the old fat man had become an individual since she had read his letter. She couldn't help comparing his style with

Charlie's. "When I have said good-night to you, my dear one, I shall go happily to bed with the thought of you." In Mr. Hickslaughter's there was an ambiguity, a hint of menace. Was it possible that the old man could be dangerous?

At half past five she rang up room 63. It was not the kind of adventure she had planned, but it was an adventure nonetheless. "I'm awake," she said.

"You coming for a drink?" he asked.

"I'll meet you in the bar."

"Not the bar," he said. "Not at the prices they charge for bourbon. I've got all we need here." She felt as though she were being brought back to the scene of the crime, and she needed a little courage to knock on the door.

He had everything prepared: a bottle of Old Walker, a bucket of ice, two bottles of soda. Like books, drinks can make a room inhabited. She saw him as a man fighting in his own fashion against the sense of solitude.

"Siddown," he said, "make yourself comfortable," like a character in a movie. He began to pour out two highballs.

She said, "I've got an awful sense of guilt. I did come in here for iced water, but I was curious too. I read your letter."

"I knew someone had touched it," he said.

"I'm sorry."

"Who cares? It was only to my brother."

"I had no business . . ."

"Look," he said, "if I came into your room and found a letter open I'd read it, wouldn't I? Only your letter would be more interesting."

"Why?"

"I don't write love letters. Never did and I'm too old now." He sat down on a bed — she had the only easy chair. His belly hung in heavy folds under his sports-shirt, and his flies were a little open. Why was it always fat men who left them unbuttoned? He said, "This is good bourbon," taking a drain of it. "What does your husband do?" he asked — it was his first personal question since the pool and it took her by surprise.

"He writes about literature. Eighteenth-century poetry," she added, rather inanely under the circumstances.

"Oh."

"What did you do? I mean when you worked."

"This and that."

"And now?"

"I watch what goes on. Sometimes I talk to someone like you. Well, no, I don't suppose I've ever talked to anyone like you before." It might have seemed a compliment if he had not added, "A professor's wife."

"And you read the *Digest*?"

"Ye-eh. They make books too long — I haven't the patience. Eighteenth-century poetry. So they wrote poetry back in those days, did they?"

She said, "Yes," not sure whether or not he was mocking her.

"There was a poem I liked at school. The only one that ever stuck in my head. By Longfellow, I think. You ever read Longfellow?"

"Not really. They don't read him much in school any longer."

"Something about 'Spanish sailors with bearded lips and something and mystery of the ships and the something of the sea.' It hasn't stuck all that well, but I suppose I learned it sixty years ago and even more. Those were the days."

"The 1900s?"

"No, no. I meant pirates, Kidd and Bluebeard and those fellows. This was their stamping ground, wasn't it? The Caribbean. It makes you kind of sick to see those women going around in their shorts here." His tongue had been tingled into activity by the bourbon.

It occurred to her that she had never really been curious about another human being; she had been in love with Charlie, but he hadn't aroused her curiosity except sexually, and she had satisfied that only too quickly. She asked him, "Do you love your sister?"

"Yes, of course, why? How do you know I've got a sister?"

"And Joe?"

"You certainly read my letter. Oh, he's O.K."

"O.K.?"

"Well, you know how it is with brothers. I'm the eldest in my family. There was one that died. My sister's twenty years younger than I am. Joe's got the means. He looks after her."

"You haven't got the means?"

"I had the means. I wasn't good at managing them though. We aren't here to talk about myself."

"I'm curious. That's why I read your letter."

"You? Curious about me?"

"It could be, couldn't it?"

She had confused him, and now that she had the upper hand, she felt that she was out of the trap; she was free, she could come and go as she pleased, and if she chose to stay a little longer, it was her own choice.

"Have another bourbon?" he said. "But you're English. Maybe you'd prefer Scotch?"

"Better not mix."

"No." He poured her another glass. He said, "I was wondering — sometimes I want to get away from this joint for a little while. What about having dinner down the road?"

"It would be stupid," she said. "We've both paid our *pension* here, haven't we? And it would be the same dinner in the end. Red snapper. Tomatoes."

"I don't know what you have against tomatoes." But he did not deny the good sense of her economic reasoning: he was the first unsuccessful American she had ever had a drink with. One must have seen them in the street . . . But even the young men who came to the house were not yet unsuccessful. The Professor of Romance Languages had perhaps hoped to be head of a university — success is relative, but it remains success.

He poured out another glass. She said, "I'm drinking all your bourbon."

"It's in a good cause."

She was a little drunk by now and things — which only *seemed* relevant — came to her mind. She said, "That thing of Longfellow's. It went on — something about 'the thoughts of youth are long, long thoughts.' I must have read it somewhere. That was the refrain, wasn't it?"

"Maybe. I don't remember."

"Did you want to be a pirate when you were a boy?"

He gave an almost happy grin. He said, "I succeeded. That's what Joe called me once — 'pirate.' "

"But you haven't any buried treasure?"

He said, "He knows me well enough not to send me a hundred dollars. But if he feels scared enough that I'll come back — he might send fifty. And the interest was only twenty-five. He's not mean, but he's stupid."

"How?"

"He ought to know I wouldn't go back. I wouldn't do one thing to hurt Sis."

"Would it be any good if I asked you to have dinner with me?"

"No. It wouldn't be right." In some ways he was obviously very conservative. "It's as you said — you don't want to go throwing money about." When the bottle of Old Walker was half empty, he said, "You'd better have some food even if it is red snapper and tomatoes."

"Is your name really Hickslaughter?"

"Something like that."

They went downstairs, following rather carefully in each other's footsteps like ducks. In the formal restaurant open to all the heat of the evening, the men sat and sweated in their jackets and ties. They passed, the two of them, through the bamboo bar into the coffee tavern, which was lit by candles that increased the heat. Two young men with crewcuts sat at the next table — they weren't the same young men she had seen before, but they came out of the same series. One of them said, "I'm not denying that he has a certain style, but even if you *adore* Tennessee Williams . . ."

"Why did he call you a pirate?"

"It was just one of those things."

When it came to the decision there seemed nothing to choose except red snapper and tomatoes, and again she offered him her tomatoes; perhaps he had grown to expect it and already she was chained by custom.

He was an old man, he had made no pass which she could reasonably reject — how could a man of his age make a pass to a woman of hers? — and yet all the same she had a sense that she had landed on a conveyor belt . . . The future was not in her hands, and she was a little scared. She would have been more frightened if it had not been for her unusual consumption of bourbon.

"It was good bourbon," she commented for something to say, and immediately regretted it. It gave him an opening.

"We'll have another glass before bed."

"I think I've drunk enough."

"A good bourbon won't hurt you. You'll sleep well."

"I always sleep well." It was a lie — the kind of unimportant lie one tells a husband or a lover in order to keep some privacy. The young man who had been talking about Tennessee Williams rose from his table. He was very tall and thin and he wore a skin-tight black sweater; his small elegant buttocks were outlined in skin-tight trousers. It was easy to imagine him a degree more naked. Would he have looked at her, she wondered, with interest if she had not been sitting there in the company of a fat old man so horribly clothed? It was unlikely; his body was not designed for a woman's caress.

"I don't."

"You don't what?"

"I don't sleep well." The unexpected self-disclosure after all his reticences came as a shock. It was as though he had put out one of his square brick-like hands and pulled her to him. He had been aloof, he had evaded her personal questions, he had lulled her into a sense of security, but now every time she opened her mouth, she seemed doomed to commit an error, to invite him nearer. Even her harmless remark about the bourbon . . . She said stupidly, "Perhaps it's the change of climate."

"What change of climate?"

"Between here and . . . and . . ."

"Curaçao? I guess there's no great difference. I don't sleep there either."

"I've got some very good pills . . ." she said rashly.

"I thought you said you slept well."

"Oh, there are always times. It's sometimes just a question of digestion."

"Yes, digestion. You're right there. A bourbon will be good for that. If you've finished dinner . . ."

She looked across the coffee tavern to the bamboo bar, where the young man stood *déhanché,* holding a glass of crème-de-menthe between his face and his companion's like an exotically coloured monocle.

Mr. Hickslaughter said in a shocked voice, "You don't care for that type, do you?"

"They're often good conversationalists."

"Oh, conversation . . . If that's what you want." It was as though she had expressed an un-American liking for snails or frogs' legs.

"Shall we have our bourbon in the bar? It's a little cooler tonight."

"And pay and listen to their chatter? No, we'll go upstairs."

He swung back again in the direction of old-fashioned courtesy and came behind her to pull her chair — even Charlie was not so polite, but was it politeness or the determination to block her way of escape to the bar?

They entered the lift together. The black attendant had a radio turned on, and from the small brown box came the voice of a preacher talking about the Blood of the Lamb. Perhaps it was a Sunday, and that would explain the temporary void around them — between one jolly bunch and another. They stepped out into the empty corridor like undesirables marooned. The boy followed them out and sat down upon a chair beside the elevator to wait for another signal, while the voice continued to talk about the Blood of the Lamb. What was she afraid of? Mr. Hickslaughter began to unlock his door. He was much older than her father would have been if he had been still alive; he could be her grandfather — the excuse, 'What will the boy think?' was inadmissible — it was even shocking, for his manner had never ceased to be correct. He might be old, but what right had she to think of him as "dirty"?

"Damn the hotel key . . ." he said. "It won't open."

She turned the handle for him. "The door wasn't locked."

"I can sure do with a bourbon after those nancies . . ."

But now she had her excuse ready on the lips. "I've had one too many already, I'm afraid. I've got to sleep it off." She put her hand on his arm. "Thank you so much . . . It was a lovely evening." She was aware how insulting her English accent sounded as she walked quickly down the corridor leaving it behind her like a mocking presence, mocking all the things she liked best in him: his ambiguous character, his memory of Longfellow, his having to make ends meet.

She looked back when she reached her room: he was standing in the passage as though he couldn't make up his mind to go in. She was reminded of an old man whom she had passed one day on the campus leaning on his broom among the unswept autumn leaves.

4

In her room she picked up a book and tried to read. It was Thomson's *Seasons*. She had carried it with her, so that she could understand any reference to his work that Charlie might make in a letter. This was the first time she had opened it, and she was not held:

> And now the mounting Sun dispels the Fog:
> The rigid Hoar-Frost melts before his Beam;
> And hung on every Spray, on every Blade
> Of Grass, the myriad Dew-Drops twinkle round.

If she could be so cowardly, she thought, with a harmless old man like that, how could she have faced the real decisiveness of an adventure? One was not, at her age, "swept off the feet." Charlie had been proved just as sadly right to trust her as she was right to trust Charlie. Now with the difference in time he would be leaving the Museum, or rather, if this were a Sunday as the Blood of the Lamb seemed to indicate, he would probably have just quit writing in his hotel room. After a successful day's work he always resembled an advertisement for a new shaving-cream: a kind of glow . . . She found it irritating, like living with a halo. Even his voice had a different timbre and he would call her "old girl" and pat her bottom patronizingly. She preferred him when he was touchy with failure: only temporary failure, of course, the failure of an idea which hadn't worked out, the touchiness of a child's disappointment at a party which has not come up to his expectations, not the failure of the old man — the rusted framework of a ship transfixed once and for all upon the rock where it had struck.

She felt ignoble. What earthly risk could the old man represent to justify refusing him half an hour's companionship? He could no more assault her than the boat could detach itself from the rock and steam out to sea for the Fortunate Islands. She pictured him sitting alone with his half-empty bottle of bourbon seeking unconsciousness. Or was he perhaps finishing the crude blackmailing letter to his brother? What a story she would make of it one day, she thought with self-disgust as she took off her dress, her evening with a blackmailer and "pirate."

There was one thing she could do for him: she could give him her bottle of pills. She put on her dressing-gown and retrod the corridor, room by room, until she arrived at 63. His voice told her to come in. She opened the door and in the light of the bedside lamp saw him sitting on the edge of the bed wearing a crumpled pair of cotton pyjamas with broad mauve stripes. She began, 'I've brought you . . .' and then she saw to her amazement that he had been crying. His eyes were red and the evening darkness of his cheeks sparkled with points like dew. She had only once before seen a man cry — Charlie, when the University Press had decided against his first volume of literary essays.

"I thought you were the maid," he said. "I rang for her."

"What did you want?"

"I thought she might take a glass of bourbon," he said.

"Did you want so much . . . ? I'll take a glass." The bottle was still on the dressing-table where they had left it and the two glasses — she identified hers by the smear of lipstick. "Here you are," she said, "drink it up. It will make you sleep."

He said, "I'm not an alcoholic."

"Of course you aren't."

She sat on the bed beside him and took his left hand in hers. It was cracked and dry and she wanted to clean back the cuticle until she remembered that was something she did for Charlie.

"I wanted company," he said.

"I'm here."

"You'd better turn off the bell-light or the maid will come."

"She'll never know what she missed in the way of Old Walker."

When she returned from the door he was lying back against the pillows in an odd twisted position, and she thought again of the ship broken-backed upon the rocks. She tried to pick up his feet to lay them on the bed, but they were like heavy stones at the bottom of a quarry.

"Lie down," she said, "you'll never be sleepy that way. What do you do for company in Curaçao?"

"I manage," he said.

"You've finished the bourbon. Let me put out the lights."

"It's no good pretending to you," he said.

"Pretending?"

"I'm afraid of the dark."

She thought, I'll smile later when I think of who it was I feared. She said, "Do the old pirates you fought come back to haunt you?"

"I've done some bad things," he said, "in my time."

"Haven't we all?"

"Nothing extraditable," he explained as though that were an extenuation.

"If you take one of my pills . . ."

"You won't go — not yet?"

"No, no. I'll stay till you're sleepy."

"I've been wanting to talk to you for days."

"I'm glad you did."

"Would you believe it — I hadn't got the nerve." If she had shut her eyes it might have been a very young man speaking. "I don't know your sort."

"Don't you have my sort in Curaçao?"

"No."

"You haven't taken the pill yet."

"I'm afraid of not waking up."

"Have you so much to do tomorrow?"

"I mean ever." He put out his hand and touched her knee, searchingly, without sensuality, as if he needed support from the bone. "I'll tell you what's wrong. You're a stranger, so I can tell you. I'm afraid of dying, with nobody around, in the dark."

"Are you ill?"

"I wouldn't know. I don't see doctors. I don't like doctors."

"But why should you think . . .?"

"I'm over seventy. The Bible age. It could happen any day now."

"You'll live to a hundred," she said with an odd conviction.

"Then I'll have to live with my fear the hell of a long time."

"Was that why you were crying?"

"No. I thought you were going to stay awhile, and then suddenly you went. I guess I was disappointed."

"Are you never alone in Curaçao?"

"I pay not to be alone."

"As you'd have paid the maid?"

"Ye-eh. Sort of."

It was as though she were discovering for the first time the interior of the enormous continent on which she had elected to live. America had been Charlie, it had been New England; through books and movies she had been aware of the wonders of nature like some great cineramic film with Lowell Thomas cheapening the Painted Desert and the Grand Canyon with his clichés. There had been no mystery anywhere from Miami to Niagara Falls, from Cape Cod to the Pacific Palisades; tomatoes were served on every plate and Coca-Cola in every glass. Nobody anywhere admitted failure or fear; they were like sins "hushed up" — worse perhaps than sins, for sins have glamour — they were bad taste. But here, stretched on the bed, dressed in striped pyjamas which Brooks Brothers would have disowned, failure and fear talked to her without shame, and in an American accent. It was as though she were living in the remote future, after God knew what catastrophe.

She said, "I wasn't for sale? There was only the Old Walker to tempt me."

He raised his antique Neptune head a little way from the pillow and said, "I'm not afraid of death. Not sudden death. Believe me, I've looked for it here and there. It's the certain-sure business, closing in on you, like tax-inspectors . . ."

She said, "Sleep now."

"I can't."

"Yes, you can."

"If you'd stay with me awhile . . ."

"I'll stay with you. Relax." She lay down on the bed beside him on the outside of the sheet. In a few minutes he was deeply asleep and she turned off the light. He grunted several times and spoke only once, when he said, "You've got me wrong," and after that he became for a little while like a dead man in his immobility and his silence, so that during that period she fell asleep. When she woke she was aware from his breathing that he was awake too. He was lying away from her so that their bodies wouldn't touch. She put out her hand and felt no repulsion at all at his excitement. It was as though she had spent many nights beside him in the one bed, and when he made love to her, silently and abruptly in the darkness, she gave a sigh of satisfaction. There was no guilt; she would be going back in a few days, resigned and tender, to Charlie and Charlie's loving skill, and she wept a little, but not seriously, at the temporary nature of this meeting.

"What's wrong?" he asked.

"Nothing. Nothing. I wish I could stay."

"Stay a little longer. Stay till it's light." That would not be very long. Already they could distinguish the grey masses of the furniture standing around them like Caribbean tombs.

"Oh yes, I'll stay till it's light. That wasn't what I meant." His body began to slip out of her, and it was as though he were carrying away her unknown child, away in the direction of Curaçao, and she tried to hold him back, the fat old frightened man whom she almost loved.

He said, "I never had this in mind."

"I know. Don't say it. I understand."

"I guess after all we've got a lot in common," he said, and she agreed in order to quieten him. He was fast asleep by the time the light came back, so she got off the bed without waking him and went to her room. She locked the door and began with resolution to pack her bag: it was time for her to leave, it was time for term to start again. She wondered afterwards, when she thought of him, what it was they could have had in common, except the fact, of course, that for both of them Jamaica was cheap in August.

Isaac Bashevis Singer
1904—

Isaac Singer uses a dying language, Yiddish. (As Singer puts it, "Yiddish has been in trouble for the last five hundred years and will still be in trouble for the next thousand.") He draws his subject matter from an obliterated culture, the orthodox Polish shtetl Jewry of almost a century ago. No leading writer of our day is so blithely unconcerned with his own time. None so coolly ignores every literary innovation, every experimental technique traceable since Flaubert. Experts in such matters can keep themselves busy, if not happy, accounting for the paradox that he enjoys a worldwide readership and in 1978 won the Nobel Prize for literature.

Singer has written some remarkable stories about contemporary Jews in America, but the bulk of his work deals with a dead Eastern European world that at will he galvanizes into life. His energy derives not merely from the richness and precision of his youthful memories, but from his conviction that a culture is not necessarily of interest simply because it happens to be a going concern. One of his characters reaches the conclusion that "modern man was as fanatic in his non-belief as ancient man had been in his faith." And so he writes about his Chassidic fanatics with the assurance of Ann Beattie writing about today's yuppies.

Singer's disregard of the present-day is deepened by his conviction that all history must be understood in relation to another universe of supernatural presences, angels, demons, dybbuks. The fool Gimpel says, "The world is entirely an imaginary world, but it is only once removed from the real world." The dybbuk Getsl, who enters poor Liebe Yentl's body in "The Dead Fiddler," warns us that "reality itself hangs by a thread." Another Singer character, Herman Gumbiner, believes that "so-called inanimate objects had their own whims and caprices."

Singer, a rabbi's son, writes about Orthodox Jews, but he is less a religious writer than a supernaturalist writer. His tales, mingling the erotic, the comic, the antirationalistic and the magical, are not created from an altitude. He tells them as Homer must have told his, in all faith and credence. Or at least that is what he makes us feel.

The Dead Fiddler

I

IN THE TOWN of Shidlovtse, which lies between Radom and Kielce, not far from the Mountains of the Holy Cross, there lived a man by the name of Reb Sheftel Vengrover. This Reb Sheftel was supposedly a grain merchant, but all the buying and selling was done by his wife, Zise Feige. She bought wheat, corn, barley, and buckwheat from the landowners and the peasants and sent it to Warsaw. She also had some of the grain milled and sold the flour to stores and bakeries. Zise Feige owned a granary and had an assistant, Zalkind, who helped her in the business and did all the work that required a man's hand; he carried sacks, looked after the horses, and served as coachman whenever Zise Feige drove out to a fair or went to visit a landowner.

Reb Sheftel held to the belief that the Torah is the worthiest merchandise of all. He rose at dawn and went to the study house to pore over the Gemara, the Annotations and Commentaries, the Midrash, and the Zohar. In the evenings, he would read a lesson from the Mishnah with the Mishnah Society. Reb Sheftel also devoted himself to community affairs and was an ardent Radzymin Hasid.

Reb Sheftel was not much taller than a midget, but he had the longest beard in Shidlovtse and the surrounding district. His beard reached down to his knees and seemed to contain every color: red, yellow, even the color of hay. At Tishe b'Av, when the mischiefmakers pelted everyone with burs, Reb Sheftel's beard would be full of them. At first Zise Feige had tried to pull them out, but Reb Sheftel would not allow it, for she pulled out the hairs of the beard too, and a man's beard is a mark of his Jewishness and a reminder that he was created in the image of God. The burs remained in his beard until they dropped out by themselves. Reb Sheftel did not curl his sidelocks, considering this a frivolous custom. They hung down to his shoulders. A tuft of hair grew on his nose. As he studied, he smoked a long pipe.

When Reb Sheftel stood at the lectern in the synagogue in his prayer shawl and phlacteries, he looked like one of the ancients. He had a high forehead, and under shaggy eyebrows, eyes that combined the sharp glance of a scholar with the humility of a God-fearing man. Reb Sheftel imposed a variety of penances upon himself. He drank no milk unless he had been present at the milking. He ate no meat except on the Sabbath and on holidays and only if he had examined the slaughtering knife in advance. It was told of him that on the eve of Passover he ordered that the cat wear socklets on its feet, lest it bring into the house the smallest crumb of unleavened bread. Every night, he faithfully performed the midnight prayers. People said that although he had inherited his grain business from his father and grandfather he still could not distinguish between rye and wheat.

Zise Feige was a head taller than her husband and in her younger days had been famous for her good looks. The landlords who sold her grain showered her with compliments, but a good Jewish woman pays no attention to idle talk. Zise Feige loved her husband and considered it an honor to help him serve the Almighty.

She had borne nine children, but only three remained: a married son, Jedidiah, who took board with his father-in-law in Wlodowa; a boy, Tsadock Meyer, who was still in cheder; and a grown daughter, Liebe Yentl. Liebe Yentl had been engaged and about to be married, but her fiancé, Ozer, caught a cold and died. This Ozer had a reputation as a prodigy and a scholar. His father was the president of the community in Opola. Although Liebe Yentl had seen Ozer only during the signing of the betrothal papers, she wept bitterly when she heard the bad news. Almost at once she was besieged with marriage offers, for she was already a ripe girl of seventeen, but Zise Feige felt that it was best to wait until she got over her misfortune.

Liebe Yentl's betrothed, Ozer, departed this world just after Passover. Now it was already the month of Heshvan. Sukkoth is usually followed by rains and snow, but this fall was a mild one. The sun shone. The sky was blue, as after Pentecost. The peasants in the villages complained that the winter crops were beginning to sprout in the fields, which could lead to crop failure. People feared that the warm weather might bring epidemics. In the meantime, grain prices rose by three groschen on the pood, and Zise Feige had higher profits. As was the custom between man and wife, she gave Reb Sheftel an accounting of the week's earnings every Sabbath evening, and he immediately deducted a share — for the study house, the prayer house, the mending of sacred books, for the inmates of the poorhouse, and for itinerant beggars. There was no lack of need for charity.

Since Zise Feige had a servant girl, Dunya, and was herself a fine housekeeper, Liebe Yentl paid little attention to household matters. She had her own room, where she would often sit, reading storybooks. She copied letters from the letter book. When she had read through all the storybooks, she secretly took to borrowing from her father's bookcase. She was also good at sewing and embroidery. She was fond of fine clothes. Liebe Yentl inherited her mother's beauty, but her red hair came from her father's side. Like her father's beard, her hair was uncommonly long — down to her loins. Since the mishap with Ozer, her face, always pale, had grown paler still and more delicate. Her eyes were green.

Reb Sheftel paid little attention to his daughter. He merely prayed to the Lord to send her the right husband. But Zise Feige saw that the girl was growing up as wild as a weed. Her head was full of whims and fancies. She did not allow herring or radishes to be mentioned in her presence. She averted her eyes from slaughtered fowl and from meat on the salting board or in the soaking dish. If she found a fly in her groats, she would eat nothing for the rest of the day. She had no friends in Shidlovtse. She complained that the girls of the town were common and backward; as soon as they were married, they became careless and slovenly. Whenever she had to go among people, she fasted the day before, for fear that she might vomit. Although she was beautiful, clever, and learned, it always seemed to her that people were laughing and pointing at her.

Zise Feige wanted many times to talk to her husband about the troubles she was having with their daughter, but she was reluctant to divert him from his studies. Besides, he might not understand a woman's problems. He had a rule for everything. On the few occasions when Zise Feige had tried to tell him of her fears, his only reply was, "When, God willing, she gets married, she will forget all this foolishness."

After the calamity with Ozer, Liebe Yentl fell ill from grieving. She did not sleep nights. Her mother heard her sobbing in the dark. She was constantly going for a drink of water. She drank whole dippers full, and Zise Feige could not imagine how her stomach could hold so much water. As though, God forbid, a fire were raging inside her, consuming everything.

Sometimes, Liebe Yentl spoke to her mother like one who was altogether unsettled. Zise Feige thought to herself that it was fortunate the girl avoided people. But how long can anything remain a secret? It was already whispered in town that Liebe Yentl was not all there. She played with the cat. She took solitary walks down the Gentile street that led to the cemetery. When anyone addressed her, she turned pale and her answers were quite beside the point. Some people thought that she was deaf. Others hinted that Liebe Yentl might be dabbling in magic. She had been seen on a moonlit night walking in the pasture across the bridge and bending down every now and then to pick flowers or herbs. Women spat to ward off evil when they spoke of her. "Poor thing, unlucky and sick besides."

II

Liebe Yentl was about to become betrothed again, this time to a young man from Zawiercia. Reb Sheftel had sent an examiner to the prospective bridegroom, and he came back with the report that Shmelke Motl was a scholar. The betrothal contract was drawn up, ready to be signed.

The examiner's wife, Traine, who had visited Zawiercia with her husband (they had a daughter there), told Zise Feige that Shmelke Motl was small and dark. He did not look like much, but he had the head of a genius. Because he was an orphan, the householders provided his meals; he ate at a different home every day of the week. Liebe Yentl listened without a word.

When Traine had gone, Zise Feige brought in her daughter's supper — buckwheat and pot roast with gravy. But Liebe Yentl did not touch the food. She rocked over the plate as though it were a prayer book. Soon afterwards, she retired to her room. Zise Feige sighed and also went to bed. Reb Sheftel had gone to sleep early, for he had to rise for midnight prayers. The house was quiet. Only the cricket sang its night song behind the oven.

Suddenly Zise Feige was wide awake. From Liebe Yentl's room came a muffled gasping, as though someone were choking there. Zise Feige ran into her daughter's room. In the bright moonlight she saw the girl sitting on her bed, her hair disheveled, her face chalk-white, struggling to keep down her sobs. Zise Feige cried out, "My daughter, what is wrong? Woe is me!" She ran to the kitchen, lit a candle, and returned to Liebe Yentl, bringing a cup of water to splash at her if, God forbid, the girl should faint.

But at this moment a man's voice broke from Liebe Yentl's lips. "No need to revive me, Zise Feige," the voice called out. "I'm not in the habit of fainting. You'd better fetch me a drop of vodka."

Zise Feige stood petrified with horror. The water spilled over from the cup.

Reb Sheftel had also wakened. He washed his hands hastily, put on his bathrobe and slippers, and came into his daughter's room.

The man's voice greeted him. "A good awakening to you, Reb Sheftel. Let me have a schnapps — my throat's parched. Or Slivovitz — anything will do, so long as I wet my whistle."

Man and wife knew at once what had happened: a dybbuk had entered Liebe Yentl. Reb Sheftel asked with a shudder: "Who are you? What do you want?"

"Who I am you wouldn't know," the dybbuk answered. "You're a scholar in Shidlovtse, and I'm a fiddler from Pinchev. You squeeze the bench, and I squeezed the wenches. You're still around in the Imaginary World, and I'm past everything. I've kicked the bucket and have already had my taste of what comes after. I've had it cold and hot, and now I'm back on the sinful earth — there's no place for me either in heaven or in hell. Tonight I started out flying to Pinchev, but I lost my way and got to Shidlovtse instead — I'm a musician, not a coachman. One thing I do know, though — my throat's itchy."

Zise Feige was seized by a fit of trembling. The candle in her hand shook so badly it singed Reb Sheftel's beard. She wanted to scream, to call for help, but her voice stuck in her throat. Her knees buckled, and she had to lean against the wall to keep from falling.

Reb Sheftel pulled at his sidelock as he addressed the dybbuk. "What is your name?"

"Getsl."

"Why did you choose to enter my daughter?" he asked in desperation.

"Why not? She's a good-looking girl. I hate the ugly ones — always have, always will." With that, the dybbuk began to shout ribaldries and obscenities, both in ordinary Yiddish and in musician's slang. "Don't make me wait, Feige dear," he called out finally. "Bring me a cup of cheer. I'm dry as a bone. I've got an itching in my gullet, a twitching in my gut."

"Good people, help!" Zise Feige wailed. She dropped the candle and Reb Sheftel picked it up, for it could easily have set the wooden house on fire.

Though it was late, the townsfolk came running. There are people everywhere with something bothering them; they cannot sleep nights. Tevye the night watchman thought a fire had broken out and ran through the street, knocking at the shutters with his stick. It was not long before Reb Sheftel's house was packed.

Liebe Yentl's eyes goggled, her mouth twisted like an epileptic's, and a voice boomed out of her that could not have come from a woman's throat. "Will you bring me a glass of liquor or won't you? What the devil are you waiting for?"

"And what if we don't?" asked Zeinvl the butcher, who was on his way home from the slaughterhouse.

"If you don't, I'll lay you all wide open, you pious hypocrites. And the secrets of your wives — may they burn up with hives."

"Get him liquor! Give him a drink!" voices cried on every side.

Reb Sheftel's son, Tsadock Meyer, a boy of eleven, had also been awakened by the commotion. He knew where his father kept the brandy that he drank on the Sabbath, after the fish. He opened the cupboard, poured out a glass, and brought it to his sister. Reb Sheftel leaned against the chest of drawers, for his legs were giving way. Zise Feige fell into a chair. Neighbors sprinkled her with vinegar against fainting.

Liebe Yentl stretched out her hand, took the glass, and tossed it down. Those who stood nearby could not believe their eyes. The girl didn't even twitch a muscle.

The dybbuk said, "You call that liquor? Water, that's what it is — hey, fellow, bring me the bottle!"

"Don't let her have it! Don't let her have it!" Zise Feige cried. "She'll poison herself, God help us!"

The dybbuk gave a laugh and a snort. "Don't worry, Zise Feige, nothing can kill me again. So far as I'm concerned, your brandy is weaker than candy."

"You won't get a drink until you tell us who you are and how you got in here," Zeinvl the butcher said. Since no one else dared to address the spirit, Zeinvl took it upon himself to be the spokesman.

"What does the meatman want here?" the dybbuk asked. "Go on back to your gizzards and guts!"

"Tell us who you are!"

"Do I have to repeat it? I am Getsl the fiddler from Pinchev. I was fond of things nobody else hates, and when I cashed in, the imps went to work on me. I couldn't get into paradise, and hell was too hot for my taste. The devils were the death of me. So at night, when the watchman dropped off, I made myself scarce. I meant to go to my wife, may she rot alive, but it was dark on the way and I got to Shidlovtse instead. I looked through the wall and saw this girl. My heart jumped in my chest and I crawled into her breast."

"How long do you intend to stay?"

"Forever and a day."

Reb Sheftel was almost speechless with terror, but he remembered God and recovered. He called out, "Evil spirit, I command you to leave the body of my innocent daughter and go where men do not walk and beasts do not tread. If you don't, you shall be driven out by Holy Names, by excommunication, by the blowing of the ram's horn."

"In another minute you'll have me scared!" the dybbuk taunted. "You think you're so strong because your beard's long?"

"Impudent wretch, betrayer of Israel!" Reb Sheftel cried in anger.

"Better an open rake than a sanctimonious fake," the dybbuk answered. "you may have the Shidlovtse schlemiels fooled, but Getsl the fiddler of Pinchev has been around. I'm telling you. Bring me the bottle or I'll make you crawl."

There was an uproar at the door. Someone had wakened the rabbi, and he came with Bendit the beadle. Bendit carried a stick, a ram's horn, and the *Book of the Angel Raziel.*

III

Once in the bedroom, the rabbi, Reb Yeruchim, ordered the ram's horn to be blown. He had the beadle pile hot coals into a brazier, then he poured incense on the coals. As the smoke of the herbs filled the room, he commanded the evil one with holy oaths from the Zohar, *The Book of Creation,* and other books of the Cabala to leave the body of the woman Liebe Yentl, daughter of Zise Feige. But the unholy spirit defied everyone. Instead of leaving, he played out a succession of dances, marches, hops — just with the lips. He boomed like a bass viol, he jingled like a cymbal, he whistled like a flute, and drummed like a drum.

The page is too short for a recital of all that the dybbuk did and said that night and the nights that followed — his brazen tricks, his blasphemies against the Lord, the insults he hurled at the townsfolk, the boasts of all the lecheries he had committed, the mockery, the outbursts of laughing and of crying, the stream of quotations from the Torah and wedding jester's jokes, and all of it in singsong and in rhyme.

The dybbuk made himself heard only after dark. During the day Liebe Yentl lay exhausted in bed and evidently did not remember what went on at night. She thought that she was sick and occasionally begged her mother to call the doctor or to give her some medicine. Most of the time she dozed, with her eyes and her lips shut tight.

Since the incantations and the amulets of the Shidlovtse rabbi were of no avail, Reb Sheftel went to seek the advice of the Radzymin rabbi. On the very morning he left, the mild weather gave way to wind and snow. The roads were snowed in and it was difficult to reach Radzymin, even in a sleigh. Weeks went by, and no news came from Reb Sheftel. Zise Feige was so hard hit by the calamity that she fell ill, and her assistant Zalkind had to take over the whole business.

Winter nights are long, and idlers look for ways to while away the time. Soon after twilight, they would gather at Zise Feige's house to hear the dybbuk's talk and to marvel at his antics. Zise Feige forbade them to annoy her daughter, but the curiosity of the townspeople was so great that they would break the door open and enter.

The dybbuk knew everyone and had words for each man according to his position and conduct. Most of the time he heaped mud and ashes upon the respected leaders of the community and their wives. He told each one exactly what he was: a miser or a swindler, a sycophant or a beggar, a slattern or a snob, an idler or a grabber. With the horse traders he talked about horses, and with the butchers about oxen. He reminded Chaim the miller that he had hung a weight under the scale on which he weighed the flour milled for the peasants. He questioned Yukele the thief about his latest theft. His jests and his jibes provoked both astonishment and laughter. Even the older folks could not keep from smiling. The dybbuk knew things that no stranger could have known, and it became clear to the visitors that they were dealing with a soul from which nothing could be hidden, for it saw through all their secrets. Although the evil spirit put everyone to shame, each man was willing to suffer his own humiliation for the sake of seeing others humbled.

When the dybbuk tired of exposing the sins of the townsfolk, he would turn to recitals of his own misdeeds. Not an evening passed without revelations of new vices. The dybbuk called everything by its name,

denying nothing. When he was asked whether he regretted his abominations, he said with a laugh: "And if I did, could anything be changed?
Everything is recorded up above. For eating a single wormy plum, you
get six hundred and eighty-nine lashes. For a single moment of lust,
you're rolled for a week on a bed of nails." Between one jest and another,
he would sing and bleat and play out tunes so skillfully that no one
living could vie with him.

One evening the teacher's wife came running to the rabbi and reported
that people were dancing to the dybbuk's music. The rabbi put on his
robe and his hat and hurried to the house. Yes, the men and women
danced together in Zise Feige's kitchen. The rabbi berated them and
warned that they were committing a sacrilege. He sternly forbade Zise
Feige to allow the rabble into her house. But Zise Feige lay sick in bed,
and her boy, Tsadock Meyer, was staying with relatives. As soon as the
rabbi left, the idlers resumed their dancing — a scissors dance, a quarrel
dance, a cossack, a water dance. It went on till midnight, when the dybbuk gave out a snore, and Liebe Yentl fell asleep.

A few days later there was a new rumor in town: a second dybbuk
had entered Liebe Yentl, this time a female one. Once more an avid
crowd packed the house. And, indeed, a woman's voice now came from
Liebe Yentl — not her own gentle voice but the hoarse croaking of a
shrew. People asked the new dybbuk who she was, and she told them
that her name was Beyle Tslove and that she came from the town of
Plock, where she had been a barmaid in a tavern and had later become
a whore.

Beyle Tslove spoke differently from Getsl the fiddler, with the flat ac-
cents of her region and a mixture of Germanized words unknown in
Shidlovtse. Beyle Tslove's language made even the butchers and the
combers of pigs' bristles blush. She sang ribald songs and soldiers' dit-
ties. She said she had wandered for eighty years in waste places. She had
been reincarnated as a cat, a turkey, a snake, and a locust. For a long
time her soul resided in a turtle. When someone mentioned Getsl the
fiddler and asked whether she knew him and whether she knew that he
was also lodged in the same woman, she answered, "I neither know him
nor want to know him."

"Why not? Have you turned virtuous all of a sudden?" Zeinvl the
butcher asked her.

"Who wants a dead fiddler?"

The people began to call to Getsl the fiddler, urging him to speak up.
They wanted to hear the two dybbuks talk to each other. But Getsl the
fiddler was silent.

Beyle Tslove said, "I see no Getsl here."

"Maybe he's hiding?" someone said.

"Where? I can smell a man a mile away."

In the midst of this excitement, Reb Sheftel returned. He looked older and even smaller than before. His beard was streaked with gray. He had brought talismans and amulets from Radzymin, to hang in the corners of the room and around his daughter's neck.

People expected the dybbuk to resist and fight the amulets, as evil spirits do when touched by a sacred object. But Beyle Tslove was silent while the amulets were hung around Liebe Yentl's neck. Then she asked, "What's this? Sacred toilet paper?"

"These are Holy Names from the Radzymin rabbi!" Reb Sheftel cried out. "If you do not leave my daughter at once, not a spur shall be left of you!"

"Tell the Radzymin rabbi that I spit at his amulets," the woman said brazenly.

"Harlot! Fiend! Harridan!" Reb Sheftel screamed.

"What's he bellowing for, that Short Friday? Some man — nothing but bone and beard!"

Reb Sheftel had brought with him blessed six-groschen coins, a piece of charmed amber, and several other magical objects that the Evil Host is known to shun. But Beyle Tslove, it seemed, was afraid of nothing. She mocked Reb Sheftel and told him she would come at night and tie an elflock in his beard.

That night Reb Sheftel recited the Shema of the Holy Isaac Luria. He slept in his fringed garment with *The Book of Creation* and a knife under his pillow — like a woman in childbirth. But in the middle of the night he woke and felt invisible fingers on his face. An unseen hand was burrowing in his beard. Reb Sheftel wanted to scream, but the hand covered his mouth. In the morning Reb Sheftel got up with his whole beard full of tangled braids, gummy as if stuck together with glue.

Although it was a fearful matter, the Worka Hasidim, who were bitter opponents of the Radzymin rabbi, celebrated that day with honey cake and brandy in their study house. Now they had proof that the Radzymin rabbi did not know the Cabala. The followers of the Worka rabbi had advised Reb Sheftel to make a journey to Worka, but he ignored them, and now they had their revenge.

IV

One evening, as Beyle Tslove was boasting of her former beauty and of all the men who had run after her, the fiddler of Pinchev suddenly raised his voice. "What were they so steamed up about?" he asked her mockingly. "Were you the only female in Plock?"

For a while all was quiet. It looked as though Beyle Tslove had lost her tongue. Then she gave a hoarse laugh. "So he's here — the scraper! Where were you hiding? In the gall?"

"If you're blind, I can be dumb. Go on, Grandma, keep jabbering. Your story had a gray beard when I was still in my diapers. In your place, I'd take such tall tales to the fools of Chelm. In Shidlovtse there are two or three clever men, too."

"A wise guy, eh?" Beyle Tslove said. "Let me tell you something. A live fiddle-scraper's no prize — and when it comes to a dead one! Go back, if you forgive me, to your resting place. They miss you in the Pinchev cemetery. The corpses who pray at night need another skeleton to make up their quorum."

The people who heard the two dybbuks quarrel were so stunned that they forgot to laugh. Now a man's voice came from Liebe Yentl, now a woman's. The Pinchev fiddler's "r"s were soft, the Plock harlot's hard.

Liebe Yentl herself rested against two pillows, her face pale, her hair down, her eyes closed. No one rightly saw her move her lips, though the room was full of people watching. Zise Feige was unable to keep them out, and there was no one to help her. Reb Sheftel no longer came home at night; he slept in the study house. Dunya the servant girl had left her job in the middle of the year. Zalkind, Zise Feige's assistant, went home in the evenings to his wife and children. People wandered in and out of the house as if it did not belong to anyone. Whenever one of the respectable members of the community came to upbraid the merry gang for ridiculing a stricken girl, the two dybbuks hurled curses and insults at him. The dybbuks gave the townspeople new nicknames: Reitse the busybody, Mindl glutton, Yekl tough, Dvoshe the strumpet. On several occasions, Gentiles and members of the local gentry came to see the wonder, and the dybbuks bantered with them in Polish. A landowner said in a tavern afterwards that the best theater in Warsaw could not compete with the scenes played out by the two dead rascals in Shidlovtse.

After a while, Reb Sheftel, who had been unbending in his loyalty to the Radzymin rabbi, gave in and went to see the rabbi of Worka; perhaps he might help.

The two dybbuks, meanwhile, were carrying on their word duel. It is generally thought that women will get the better of men where the tongue is concerned, but the Pinchev fiddler was a match for the Plock whore. The fiddler cried repeatedly that it was beneath his dignity to wrangle with a harlot — a maid with a certificate of rape — but the hoodlums egged him on. "Answer her! Don't let her have the last word!" They whistled, hooted, clapped their hands, stamped their feet.

The battle of wits gradually turned into storytelling. Beyle Tslove related that her mother, a pious and virtuous woman, had borne her husband, a Hasid and a loafer, eight children, all of them girls. When Beyle Tslove made her appearance in the world, her father was so chagrined that he left home. By trickery, he collected the signatures of a hundred rabbis, permitting him to remarry, and her mother became an abandoned wife. To support the family, she went to market every morning to sell hot beans to the yeshiva students. A wicked tutor, with a goat's beard and sidelocks down to his shoulders, came to teach Beyle Tslove to pray, but he raped her. She was not yet eight years old. When Beyle Tslove went on to tell how she had become a barmaid, how the peasants had pinched and cursed her and pulled her hair, and how a bawd, pretending to be a pious woman, had lured her to a distant city and brought her into a brothel, the girls who were listening burst into tears. The young men, too, dabbed their eyes.

Getsl the fiddler questioned her. Who were the guests? How much did they pay? How much did she have to give the procurers and what was left for her to live on? Had she ever gone to bed with a Turk or a blackamoor?

Beyle Tslove answered all the questions. The young rakes had tormented her in their ways, and the old lechers had wearied her with their demands. The bawd took away her last groschen and locked the bread in the cupboard. The pimp whipped her with a wet strap and stuck needles into her buttocks. From fasting and homesickness she contracted consumption and ended by spitting out her lungs at the poorhouse. And because she had been buried behind the fence, without Kaddish, she was immediately seized by multitudes of demons, imps, mockers, and Babuks. The Angel Dumah asked her the verse that went with her name, and when she could not answer he split her grave with a fiery rod. She begged to be allowed into hell, for there the punishment lasts only twelve months, but the Unholy Ones dragged her off to waste places and deserts. She said that in the desert she had come upon a pit that was the door to Gehenna. Day and night, the screams of sinners who were being punished there came from the pit. She was carried to the Congealed Sea, where sailing ships, wrecked by storms, were held immobile, with dead crews and captains turned to stone. Beyle Tslove had also flown to a land inhabited by giants with two heads and single eyes in their foreheads. Few females were born there, and every woman had six husbands.

Getsl the fiddler also began to talk about the events of his life. He told of incidents at the weddings and balls of the gentry where he had played, and of what happened later, in the hereafter. He said that evildoers did not repent, even in the Nether Regions. Although they had already learned the truth of things, their souls still pursued their lusts. Gamblers played with invisible cards, thieves stole, swindlers swindled, and fornicators indulged in their abominations.

The townsfolk who heard the two were amazed, and Zeinvl the butcher asked, "How can anyone sin when he is rotting in the earth?"

Getsl explained that it was, anyway, the soul and not the body that enjoyed sin. This was why the soul was punished. Besides, there were bodies of all kinds — of smoke, of spiderwebs, of shadow — and they could be used for a while, until the Angels of Destruction tore them to pieces. There were castles, inns, and ruins in the deserts and abysses, which provided hiding places from Judgment, and also Avenging Angels who could be bribed with promises or even with the kind of money that has no substance but is used in the taverns and brothels of the Nether World.

When one of the idlers cried out that this was unbelievable, Getsl called on Beyle Tslove to attest to the truth of his words. "Tell us, Beyle Tslove, what did you really do all these years? Did you recite psalms, or did you wander through swamps and wastes, consorting with demons, Zmoras, and Malachais?"

Instead of replying, Beyle Tslove giggled and coughed. "I can't speak — my mouth's dry."

"Yes, let's have a drop," Getsl chimed in, and when somebody brought over a tumbler of brandy, Liebe Yentl downed it like water. She did not open her eyes or even wince. It was clear to everybody that she was entirely in the sway of the dybbuks within her.

When Zeinvl the butcher realized that the two dybbuks had made peace, he asked, "Why don't you two become man and wife? You'd make a good pair."

"And what are we to do after the wedding?" Beyle Tslove answered. "Pray from the same prayer book?"

"You'll do what all married couples do."

"With what? We're past all doing. Anyway, there's no time — we won't be staying here much longer."

"Why not? Liebe Yentl is still young."

"The Worka rabbi is not the Radzymin schlemiel," Beyle Tslove said. "Asmodeus himself is afraid of his talismans."

"The Worka rabbi can kiss me you know where," Getsl boasted. "But I'm not about to become a bridegroom."

"The match isn't good enough for you?" Beyle Tslove cried. "If you knew who wanted to marry me, you'd croak a second time."

"If she's cursing me now, what can I expect later?" Getsl joked. "Besides, she's old enough to be my great-grandmother — seventy years older than I am, anyway you figure it."

"Numskull. I was twenty-seven years old when I kicked in, and I can't get any older. And how old are you, bottle-bum? Close to sixty, if you're a day."

"May you get as many carbuncles on your bloated flesh as the years I was short of fifty."

"Just give me the flesh, I won't argue over the carbuncles."

The two kept up their wrangling and the crowd kept up its urging until finally the dybbuks consented. Those who have not heard the dead bride and groom haggle about the dowry, the trousseau, the presents, will never know what unholy spirits are capable of.

Beyle Tslove said that she had long since paid for all her transgressions and was therefore as pure as a virgin. "Is there such a thing as a virgin, anyway?" she argued. "Every soul has lodged countless times both in men and in women. There are no more new souls in Heaven. A soul is cleansed in a caldron, like dishes before Passover. It is purified and sent back to earth. Yesterday's beggar is today's magnate. A rabbi's wife becomes a coachman. A horse thief returns as a community elder. A slaughterer comes back as an ox. So what's all the fuss about? Everything is kneaded of the same dough — cat and mouse, bear hunter and bear, old man and infant." Beyle Tslove herself had in previous incarnations been a grain merchant, a dairymaid, a rabbi's wife, a teacher of the Talmud.

"Do you remember any Talmud?" Getsl asked.

"If the Angel of Forgetfulness had not tweaked me on the nose, I would surely remember."

"What do you say to my bride?" Getsl bantered. "A whittled tongue. She could convince a stone. If my wife in Pinchev knew what I was exchanging her for, she'd drown herself in a bucket of slops."

"Your wife filled her bed before you were cold . . ."

The strange news spread throughout the town: tomorrow there would be a wedding at Reb Sheftel's house; Getsl the fiddler and Beyle Tslove would become man and wife.

v

When the rabbi heard of the goings on, he issued a proscription forbidding anyone to attend the black wedding. He sent Bendit the beadle to stand guard at the door of Reb Sheftel's house and allow no one to enter. That night, however, there was a heavy snowfall, and by morning it turned bitterly cold. The wind had blown up great drifts and whistled in all the chimneys. Bendit was shrouded in white from head to foot and looked like a snowman made by children. His wife came after him and took him home, half frozen. As soon as dusk began to fall, the rabble gathered at Reb Sheftel's house. Some brought bottles of vodka or brandy; others, dried mutton and honey cake.

As usual, Liebe Yentl had slept all day and did not waken even when the ailing Zise Feige poured a few spoonfuls of broth into her mouth. But once darkness came, the girl sat up. There was such a crush in the house that people could not move.

Zeinvl the butcher took charge. "Bride, did you fast on your wedding day?"

"The way the dead eat, that's how they look," Beyle Tslove replied with a proverb.

"And you, bridegroom, are you ready?"

"Let her first deliver the dowry."

"You can take all I have — a pinch of dust, a moldy crust . . ."

Getsl proved that evening that he was not only an expert musician but could also serve as rabbi, cantor, and wedding jester. First he played a sad tune and recited "God Is Full of Mercy" for the bride and groom. Then he played a merry tune, accompanying it with appropriate jests. He admonished the bride to be a faithful wife, to dress and adorn herself, and to take good care of her household. He warned the couple to be mindful of the day of death, and sang to them:

> Weep, bride, weep and moan,
> Dead men fear to be alone.
> In the Sling, beneath the tide,
> A groom is waiting for his bride.
> Corpse and corpse, wraith and wraith,
> Every demon seeks a mate.
> Angel Dumah, devil, Shed,
> A coffin is a bridal bed.

Although it was a mock wedding, many a tear fell from the women's eyes. The men sighed. Everything proceeded according to custom. Getsl preached, sang, played. The guests could actually hear the weeping of a fiddle, the piping of a clarinet, the bleating of a trumpet, the wailing of a bagpipe. Getsl pretended to cover the bride with the veil and played a melody appropriate to the veiling ceremony. After the wedding march he recited the words of "Thou Art Sanctified," which accompany the giving of the ring. He delivered the bridegroom's oration, and announced the wedding presents: a shrouded mirror, a little sack of earth from the Holy Land, a burial cleansing spoon, a stopped clock. When the spirits of the guests seemed to droop, Getsl struck up a kozotsky. They tried to dance, but there was scarcely room to take a step. They swayed and gesticulated.

Beyle Tslove suddenly began to wail. "Oy, Getsl!"

"What, my dove!"

"Why couldn't this be real? We weren't born dead!"

"Pooh! Reality itself hangs by a thread."

"It's not a game to me, you fool."

"Whatever it is, let's drink and keep cool. May we rejoice and do well until all the fires are extinguished in hell."

A glass of wine was brought, and Liebe Yentl emptied it to the last drop. Then she dashed it against the wall, and Getsl began to recite in the singsong of the cheder boys:

> *Such is Noah's way,*
> *Wash your tears away.*
> *Take a drink instead,*
> *The living and the dead.*
> *Wine will make you strong,*
> *Eternity is long.*

Zise Feige could not endure any more. She rose from her sickbed, wrapped herself in a shawl, and shuffled into her daughter's room in her slippers. She tried to push through the crowd. "Beasts," she cried. "You are torturing my child!"

Beyle Tslove screamed at her, "Don't you worry, old sourpuss! Better a rotten fiddler than a creep from Zawiercia!"

VI

In the middle of the night there were sounds of steps and shouts outside the door. Reb Sheftel had come home from Worka, bringing a bagful of new amulets, charms, and talismans. The Hasidim of the Worka rabbi entered with him, ready to drive out the rabble. They swung their sashes, crying, "Get out, you scum!"

Several young fellows tried to fight off the Worka Hasidim, but the Shidlovtse crowd was tired from standing so long, and they soon began to file out the door. Getsl called after them, "Brothers, don't let the holy schlemiels get you! Give them a taste of your fists! Hey, you, big shot!"

"Cowards! Bastards! Mice!" Beyle Tslove screeched.

A few of the Worka Hasidim got a punch or two, but after a while the riffraff slunk off. The Hasidim burst into the room, panting and threatening the dybbuks with excommunication.

The warden of the Worka synagogue, Reb Avigdor Yavrover, ran up to Liebe Yentl's bed and tried to hang a charm around her neck, but the girl pulled off his hat and skullcap with her right hand, and with her left she seized him by the beard. The other Hasidim tried to pull him away, but Liebe Yentl thrashed out in all directions. She kicked, bit, and scratched. One man got a slap on the cheek, another had his sidelock pulled, a third got a mouthful of spittle on his face, a fourth a punch in the ribs. In order to frighten off the pious, she cried that she was in her unclean days. Then she tore off her shift and exhibited her shame. Those who did not avert their eyes remarked that her belly was distended like a drum. On the right and the left were two bumps as big as heads, and it was clear that the spirits were there. Getsl roared like a lion, howled like a wolf, hissed like a snake. He called the Worka rabbi a eunuch, a clown, a baboon, insulted all the holy sages, and blasphemed against God.

Reb Sheftel sank to the floor and sat there like a mourner. He covered his eyes with both hands and rocked himself as over a corpse. Zise Feige snatched a broom and tried to drive away the men who swarmed around her daughter, but she was dragged aside and fell to the ground. Two neighboring women helped her to get up. Her bonnet fell off, exposing her shaven head with its gray stubble. She raised two fists and screamed, sobbing, "Torturers, you're killing my child! Lord in Heaven, send Pharaoh's curses upon them!"

Finally, several of the younger Hasidim caught Liebe Yentl's hands and feet and tied her to the bed with their sashes. Then they slipped the Worka rabbi's amulets around her neck.

Getsl, who had fallen silent during the struggle, spoke up. "Tell your miracle worker his charms are tripe."

"Wretch, you're in Hell, and you still deny?" Reb Avigdor Yavrover thundered.

"Hell's full of your kind."

"Dog, rascal, degenerate!"

"Why are you cursing, you louses?" Beyle Tslove yelled. "Is it our fault that your holy idiot hands out phony talismans? You'd better leave the girl alone. We aren't doing her any harm. Her good is our good. We're also Jews, remember — not Tartars. Our souls have stood on Mount Sinai, too. If we erred in life, we've paid our debt, with interest."

"Strumpet, hussy, slut, out with you!" one of the Hasidim cried.

"I'll go when I feel like it."

"Todres, blow the ram's horn — a long blast!"

The ram's horn filled the night with its eerie wail.

Beyle Tslove laughed and jeered. "Blow hot, blow cold, who cares!"

"A broken trill now!"

"Don't you have enough breaks under your rupture bands?" Getsl jeered.

"Satan, Amalekite, apostate!"

Hours went by, but the dybbuks remained obdurate. Some of the Worka Hasidim went home. Others leaned against the wall, ready to do battle until the end of their strength. The hoodlums who had run away returned with sticks and knives. The Hasidim of the Radzymin rabbi had heard the news that the Worka talismans had failed, and they came to gloat.

Reb Sheftel rose from the floor and in his anguish began to plead with the dybbuks. "If you are Jews, you should have Jewish hearts. Look what has become of my innocent daughter, lying bound like a sheep prepared for slaughter. My wife is sick. I myself am ready to drop. My business is falling apart. How long will you torture us? Even a murderer has a spark of pity."

"Nobody pities us."

"I'll see to it that you get forgiveness. It says in the Bible, 'His banished be not expelled from Him.' No Jewish soul is rejected forever."

"What will you do for us?" asked Getsl. "Help us moan?"

"I will recite psalms and read the Mishnah for you. I will give alms. I will say Kaddish for you for a full twelve months."

"I'm not one of your peasants. You can't fool me."

"I have never fooled anyone."

"Swear that you will keep your word!" Getsl commanded.

"What's the matter, Getsl? You anxious to leave me already?" Beyle Tslove asked with a laugh.

Getsl yawned. "I'm sorry for the old folks."

"You want to leave me a deserted wife the very first night?"

"Come along if you can."

"Where to? Behind the Mountains of Darkness?"

"Wherever our eyes take us."

"You mean sockets, comedian!"

"Swear, Reb Sheftel, that you will keep all your promises," Getsl the fiddler repeated. "Make a holy vow. If you break your word, I'll be back with the whole Evil Host and scatter your bones to the four winds."

"Don't swear, Reb Sheftel, don't swear!" the Hasidim cried. "Such a vow is a desecretion of the Name!"

"Swear, my husband, swear. If you don't, we shall all perish."

Reb Sheftel put his hand on his beard. "Dead souls, I swear that I will faithfully fulfill all that I take upon myself. I will study the Mishnah for you. I will say Kaddish for twelve months. Tell me when you died, and I will burn memorial candles for you. If there are no headstones on your graves, I will journey to the cemeteries and have them erected."

"Our graves have been leveled long since. Come, Beyle Tslove, let's go. Dawn is rising over Pinchev."

"Imp, you made a fool of a Jewish daughter all for nothing!" Beyle Tslove reproached him.

"Hey, men, move aside!" Getsl cried. "Or I shall enter one of you!"

There was such a crush that, though the door stood open, no one could get out. Hats and skullcaps fell off. Caftans caught on nails and ripped. A muffled cry rose from the crowd. Several Hasidim fell, and others trampled them. Liebe Yentl's mouth opened wide and there was a shot as from a pistol. Her eyes rolled and she fell back on the pillow, white as death. A stench swept across the room — a foul breath of the grave. Zise Feige stumbled on weak legs toward her daughter and untied her. The girl's belly was now flat and shrunken like the belly of a woman after childbirth.

Reb Sheftel attested afterward that two balls of fire came out of Liebe Yentl's nostrils and flew to the window. A pane split open, and the two sinful souls returned through the crack to the World of Delusion.

VII

For weeks after the dybbuks had left her, Liebe Yentl lay sick. The doctor applied cups and leeches; he bled her, but Liebe Yentl never opened her eyes. The woman from the Society of Tenders of the Sick who sat with the girl at night related that she heard sad melodies outside the window, and Getsl's voice begging her to remove the amulets from the girl's neck and let him in. The woman also heard Beyle Tslove's giggling.

Gradually Liebe Yentl began to recover, but she had almost stopped speaking. She sat in bed and stared at the window. Winter was over. Swallows returned from the warm countries and were building a nest under the eaves. From her bed Liebe Yentl could see the roof of the synagogue, where a pair of storks were repairing last year's nest.

Reb Sheftel and Zise Feige feared that Liebe Yentl would no longer be accepted in marriage, but Shmelke Motl wrote from Zawiercia that he would keep to his agreement if the dowry were raised by one third. Reb Sheftel and Zise Feige consented at once. After Pentecost, Shmelke Motl made his appearance at the Shidlovtse prayer house — no taller than a cheder boy but with a large head on a thin neck and tightly twisted sidelocks that stood up like a pair of horns. He had thick eyebrows and dark eyes that looked down at the tip of his nose. As soon as he entered the study house, he took out a Gemara and sat down to study. He sat there, swaying and mumbling, until he was taken to the ceremony of betrothal.

Reb Sheftel invited only a selected few to the engagement meal, for during the time that his daughter had been possessed by the dybbuks he had made many enemies both among the Radzymin Hasidim and among those of Worka. According to custom, the men sat at one table, the women at another. The bridegroom delivered an impromptu sermon on the subject of the Stoned Ox. Such sermons usually last half an hour, but two hours went by and the groom still talked on in his high, grating voice, accompanying his words with wild gestures. He grimaced as though gripped with pain, pulled at a sidelock, scratched his chin, which was just beginning to sprout a beard, grasped the lobe of his ear. From time to time his lips stretched in a smile, revealing blackened teeth, pointed as nails.

Liebe Yentl never once took her eyes from him. The women tried to talk to her; they urged her to taste the cookies, the jam, the mead. But Liebe Yentl bit her lips and stared.

The guests began to cough and fidget, hinting in various ways that it was time to bring the oration to an end, and finally the bridegroom broke off his sermon. The betrothal contract was brought to him, but he did not sign it at once. First he read the page from beginning to end. He was evidently nearsighted, for he brought the paper right up to his nose. Then he began to bargain. "The prayer shawl should have silver braid."

"It will have any braid you wish," Reb Sheftel agreed.

"Write it in."

It was written in on the margin. The groom read on, and demanded, "I want a Talmud printed in Slovita."

"Very well, it will be from Slovita."

"Write it in."

After much haggling and writing in, the groom signed the contract: Shmelke Motl son of the late Catriel Godl. The letters of the signature were as tiny as flyspecks.

When Reb Sheftel brought the contract over to Liebe Yentl and handed her the pen, she said in a clear voice, "I will not sign."

"Daughter, you shame me!"

"I will not live with him."

Zise Feige began to pinch her wrinkled cheeks. "People, go home!" she called out. She snuffed the candles in the candlesticks. Some of the women wept with the disgraced mother; others berated the bride. But the girl answered no one. Before long, the house was dark and empty. The servant went out to close the shutters.

Reb Sheftel usually prayed at the synagogue with the first quorum, but that morning he did not show himself at the holy place. Zise Feige did not go out to do her shopping. The door of Reb Sheftel's house stood locked; the windows were shuttered. Shmelke Motl returned at once to Zawiercia.

After a time Reb Sheftel went back to praying at the synagogue, and Zise Feige went again to market with her basket. But Liebe Yentl no longer came out into the street. People thought that her parents had sent her away somewhere, but Liebe Yentl was at home. She kept to her room and refused to speak to anyone. When her mother brought her a plate of soup, she first knocked at the door as though they were gentry. Liebe Yentl scarcely touched the food, and Zise Feige sent it to the poorhouse.

For some months the matchmakers still came with offers, but since a dybbuk had spoken from her and she had shamed a bridegroom Liebe Yentl could no longer make a proper match. Reb Sheftel tried to obtain a pardon from the young man in Zawiercia, but he had gone away to some yeshiva in Lithuania. There was a rumor that he had hanged himself with his sash. Then it became clear that Liebe Yentl would remain an old maid. Her younger brother, Tsadock Meyer, had in the meantime grown up and got married to a girl from Bendin.

Reb Sheftel was the first to die. This happened on a Thursday night in winter. Reb Sheftel had risen for midnight prayers. He stood at the reading desk, with ash on his head, reciting a lament on the Destruction of the Temple. A beggar was spending that night at the prayer house. About three o'clock in the morning, the man awakened and put some potatoes into the stove to bake. Suddenly he heard a thud. He stood up and saw Reb Sheftel on the floor. He sprinkled him with water from the pitcher, but the soul had already departed.

The townspeople mourned Reb Sheftel. The body was not taken home but lay in the prayer house with candles at its head until the time of burial. The rabbi and some of the town's scholars delivered eulogies. On Friday, Liebe Yentl escorted the coffin with her mother. Liebe Yentl was wrapped in a black shawl from head to toe; only a part of her face showed, white as the snow in the cemetery. The two sons lived far from Shidlovtse, and the funeral could not be postponed till after the Sabbath; it is a dishonor for a corpse to wait too long for burial. Reb Sheftel was put to rest near the grave of the old rabbi. It is known that those who are buried on Friday after noon do not suffer the pressure of the grave, for the Angel Dumah puts away his fiery rod on the eve of the Sabbath.

Zise Feige lingered a few years more, but she was fading day by day. Her body bent like a candle. In her last year she no longer attended to the business, relying entirely on her assistant, Zalkind. She began to rise at dawn to pray at the women's synagogue, and she often went to the cemetery and prostrated herself on Reb Sheftel's grave. She died as suddenly as her husband. It happened during evening prayer on Yom Kippur. Zise Feige had stood all day, weeping, at the railing that divided the women's section from the men's in the prayer house. Her neighbors, seeing her waxen-yellow face, urged her to break her fast, for human life takes precedence over all laws, but Zise Feige refused. When the cantor intoned, "The gates of Heaven open," Zise Feige took from her bosom a vial of aromatic drops, which are a remedy against faintness. But the vial slipped from her hand and she fell forward onto the reading desk. There was an outcry and women ran for the doctor, but Zise Feige had already passed into the True World. Her last words were: "My daughter . . ."

This time the funeral was delayed until the arrival of the two sons. They sat in mourning with their sister. But Liebe Yentl avoided all strangers. Those who came to pray with the mourners and to comfort them found only Jedidiah and Tsadock Meyer. Liebe Yentl would lock herself away in her room.

Nothing was left of Reb Sheftel's wealth. People muttered that the assistant had pocketed the money, but it could not be proved. Reb Sheftel and Zise Feige had kept no books. All the accounting had been done with a piece of chalk on the wall of a wardrobe. After the seven days of mourning, the sons called Zalkind to the rabbi's court, but he offered to swear before the Holy Scrolls and black candles that he had not touched a groschen of his employers' money. The rabbi forbade such an oath. He said that a man who could break the commandment "Thou Shalt Not Steal" could also violate the commandment "Thou Shalt Not Take the Name of Thy God the Lord in Vain."

After the judgment, the two sons went home. Liebe Yentl remained with the servant. Zalkind took over the business and merely sent Liebe Yentl two gulden a week for food. Soon he refused to give even that and sent only a few groschen. The servant woman left and went to work elsewhere.

Now that Liebe Yentl no longer had a servant, she was compelled to show herself in the street, but she never came out during the day. She would leave the house only after dark, waiting until the streets were empty and the stores without other customers. She would appear suddenly, as though from nowhere. The storekeepers were afraid of her. Dogs barked at her from Christian yards.

Summer and winter she was wrapped from head to toe in a long shawl. She would enter the store and forget what she wanted to buy. She often gave more money than was asked, as though she no longer remembered how to count. A few times she was seen entering the Gentile tavern to buy vodka. Tevye the night watchman had heard Liebe Yentl pacing the house at night, talking to herself.

Zise Feige's good friends tried repeatedly to see the girl, but the door was always bolted. Liebe Yentl never came to the synagogue on holidays to pray for the souls of the deceased. During the months of Nisan and Elul, she never went to visit the graves of her parents. She did not bake Sabbath bread on Fridays, did not set roasts overnight in the oven, and probably did not bless the candles. She did not come to the women's synagogue even on the High Holy Days.

People began to forget Liebe Yentl — as if she were dead — but she lived on. At times, smoke rose from her chimney. Late at night, she was sometimes seen going to the well for a pail of water. Those who caught sight of her swore that she did not look a day older. Her face was becoming even more pale, her hair redder and longer. It was said that Liebe Yentl played with cats. Some whispered that she had dealings with a demon. Others thought that the dybbuk had returned to her. Zalkind still delivered a measure of flour to the house every Thursday, leaving it in the larder in the entrance hall. He also provided Liebe Yentl with firewood.

There had formerly been several other Jewish households on the street, but gradually the owners had sold to Gentiles. A hog butcher had moved into one house and built a high fence around it. Another house was occupied by a deaf old widow who spent her days spinning flax, guarded by a blind dog at her feet.

Years went by. One early morning in Elul, when the rabbi was sitting in his study writing commentary and drinking tea from a samovar, Tevye the night watchman knocked at his door. He told the rabbi that he had seen Liebe Yentl on the road leading to Radom. The girl wore a long white dress; she had no kerchief on her head and walked barefoot. She was accompanied by a man with long hair, carrying a violin case. The full moon shone brightly. Tevye wanted to call out, but since the figures cast no shadow he was seized with fear. When he looked again, the pair had vanished.

The rabbi ordered Tevye to wait until the worshippers assembled for morning prayer in the synagogue. Then Tevye told the people of the apparition, and two men — a driver and a butcher — went to Reb Sheftel's house. They knocked, but no one answered. They broke open the door and found Liebe Yentl dead. She lay in the middle of the room among piles of garbage, in a long shift, barefoot, her red hair loose. It was obvious that she had not been among the living for many days — perhaps a week or even more. The women of the Burial Society hastily carried off the corpse to the hut for the cleansing of the dead. When the shroud-makers opened the wardrobe, a cloud of moths flew out, filling the house like a swarm of locusts. All the clothes were eaten, all the linens moldy and decayed.

Since Liebe Yentl had not taken her own life and since she had exhibited all the signs of madness, the rabbi permitted her to be buried next to her parents. Half the town followed the body to the cemetery. The brothers were notified and came later to sell the house and order a stone for their sister's grave.

It was clear to everyone that the man who had appeared with Liebe Yentl on the road to Radom was the dead fiddler of Pinchev. Dunya, Zise Feige's former servant, told the women that Liebe Yentl had not been able to forget her dead bridegroom Ozer and that Ozer had become a dybbuk in order to prevent the marriage to Shmelke Motl. But where would Ozer, a scholar and the son of a rich man, have learned to play music and to perform like a wedding jester? And why would he appear on the Radom road in the guise of a fiddler? And where was he going with the dead Liebe Yentl that night? And what had become of Beyle Tslove? Heaven and earth have sworn that the truth shall remain forever hidden.

More years went by, but the dead fiddler was not forgotten. He was heard playing at night in the cold synagogue. His fiddle sang faintly in the bathhouse, the poorhouse, the cemetery. It was said in town that he came to weddings. Sometimes, at the end of a wedding after the Shidlovtse band had stopped playing, people still heard a few lingering notes, and they knew that it was the dead fiddler.

In autumn, when leaves fell and winds blew from the Mountains of the Holy Cross, a low melody was often heard in the chimneys, thin as a hair and mournful as the world. Even children would hear it, and they would ask, "Mama, who is playing?" And the mother would answer, "Sleep, child. It's the dead fiddler."

JOHN O'HARA
1905–1970

"John O'Hara once told me [Irwin Shaw] he could have dinner, with several drinks, and go home and start and finish a story, and a very good one, indeed, before going to bed." He wrote more than three hundred stories, two hundred and thirty-five appearing in The New Yorker. This prolificacy has been unfairly held against him, for much may be said for an imagination that, presented with a situation, a person, a voice overheard, or even an object, can at will create a fiction that rarely depends on conventional formulas or mere machinery.

Too much also has been made of O'Hara's obsession with marks of status, details of dress, peculiarities of speech, the paraphernalia of wealth. He may over-notice such matters; it is more to the point that he did notice them, and in such detail that his work as a whole gives us a remarkably convincing sense of a dozen American subcultures of his period, from that of the underworld to that of the most exclusive country clubs.

It is only by reading all of O'Hara's stories — a career in itself — that one sees good reason to re-evaluate him. It is only then that his remarkable insight into the America he knew — far more extraordinary, it seems to me, than Fitzgerald's — becomes clear. His small snobberies, his echoes of Hemingway, his occasionally unbalanced misanthropy, even the fluency that bothered so many critical readers — all this suddenly seems to matter little when weighed against the dimensions of his achievement.

"Flight" is not a typical O'Hara story. It is not hard or bitter; it goes far beyond the snapshot, the vignette, the capturing of a moment. In a few pages it encloses a large part of a whole life, a life of failure in some respects, of triumph in others. The metaphor of flight, established at the outset, is beautifully sustained to the end. Here O'Hara abandons his more characteristic naturalism and uses to beautiful effect the dream and the broken current of recollection. Nothing brittle here, or merely photographic. One risks the cliché: call it Chekhovian.

Flight

FOR THE LONGEST fraction of a second, while both feet were off the icy road, Charles Kinsmith was exhilarated. Then he hit the ground with a jolting, humiliating abruptness and for a full minute he remained in a sitting position. Physically and spiritually he was so shocked that he could not get up. But he was so anxious not to be seen in his plight that he summoned all his resources and slowly, cautiously, tentatively got to a kneeling and to a standing position, and walking flatfooted he made his way home.

"That you, Charles?" his wife called from the sitting-room.

"It's me," he said, and muttered to himself, "somewhat the worse for wear." He hung up his coat and hat and put away his stick.

"Wasn't it slippery out there?" she said, without looking up from her darning.

"Very," he said.

"How far did you go?" she said.

"About a half a mile, horizontally, and four feet perpendicularly."

She put her darning in her lap and took off her glasses. "Now let me figure that out. Horizontally is this way, and perpendicularly is up. Did you take a spill?"

"I took a spill. I went up in the air, both feet out from under me, and came down *bang!* on my coccyx bone."

"You poor *thing,*" she said. "Did it shake you up? Why don't you have a drink?"

"I'm thinking of having a drink," he said.

"You didn't hit your head or anything, I hope?"

"No need to be alarmed. I'm suffering excruciating pain but nothing's broken."

"You *are* in pain?"

"Of course I'm in pain, woman. Most men would be making a big thing of this, but I happen to be brave."

"Yes, I think you're brave. I really do think so," she said. "At least you don't complain as much as most men. I'll get you a drink. What do you want?"

"A straight bourbon, with a water chaser," he said.

"You weren't wearing any rubbers, were you?" she said.

"The only thing that would have kept me from taking a spill was if

I'd been wearing my creepers. Those ice creepers. But inasmuch as I don't know where I put them, I didn't have them on. I haven't had them on for four or five years. Nor have I taken a spill in that time."

"We're getting on," she said. She placed the water tumbler on the table beside him and handed him the glass of bourbon.

"We're not getting on. We're there," he said. "Thanks."

"I believe I'll have one myself."

"It's too early for you to start drinking now," he said.

"It is a little early, but I just thought you wouldn't want to drink alone."

"This is a medicinal drink."

"Well, I've had a bit of a shock, too," she said.

"Oh? What happened to you?"

"Nothing happened to me, but I don't like to think of you slipping on the ice."

"Then in that case, have a drink."

"No, I guess not. It is too early," she said. "Have your drink and then go upstairs and take a real hot tub. With some Epsom salts in it, if we have any. If we haven't, I know we have some ordinary table salt. Does it hurt now?"

"Yes. It's going to hurt for two or three days. I probably won't be able to get out of bed tomorrow."

"It might be a good idea to call Dr. Gray," she said.

"I'll see how I feel after I've had my bath. If I can't go on enduring this excruciating agony, we can send for Jimmy Gray. He'll surely respond with his usual promptness, along about half past eleven."

"Not if I tell him you're in pain," she said. "He'll come right away, if he possibly can, or he'll send someone else."

"The bourbon is having a good effect."

"That's good," she said. "It may be the best thing for you."

"Four or five of these and I'll be feeling no pain," he said.

"If you're planning to have four or five, have them in the bedroom, because I couldn't possibly get you upstairs."

"Let's take the bottle upstairs and forget about dinner, forget about everything," he said.

"You sure you didn't strike your head?" she said.

"I know the difference between my head and my coccyx bone," he said.

"I'll give you another bourbon and you can take it upstairs with you. Do you want me to run your tub?"

"All right," he said.

She refilled his glass and handed it to him, and he took a sip and started to get to his feet. It was not easy, and he grunted, but he stood full height.

"Shall I assist you?" she said.

"You make it sound like a Boy Scout with an old lady crossing the street. No thanks, I'll make it. You carry my drink and run my tub while I get undressed."

"I can't be sure whether you're serious or not," she said.

"I'm not sure myself, if the truth be known," he said. "Actually I'm not in any great pain, but I got shaken up."

"Yes, that can be as bad as a real injury," she said.

"It *is* a real injury. What are you talking about? What's worse at our age than getting bounced around and unable to get to your feet? I went through positive hell out there."

"You did? How long were you there?" she said.

"Lying there? I must have been lying there — at least a hundred and twenty seconds, every second seeming like a small eternity. But then I finally struggled manfully to my feet, risking another fall, another outrage to my dignity, and not to mention the peril to my fragile bones. But I drew myself up to my full height and marched bravely, triumphantly home. The indomitable spirit of Charles David Kinsmith. Then with scarcely a mention of the whole episode, so's not to disturb the composure of his excitable, loving spouse, he partakes of a small whiskey and a small sip of another, and is now about to mount the stairs to the second-story bedchamber, divest himself of raiment, and gingerly lower himself into the soothing waters of a hot bath."

"What I like about you is your stoical courage."

"That's right. The stiff upper lip, we call it. Never let on when disaster strikes. Suffer in silence."

"Suffer in silence, that's it," she said. "All right, let's go upstairs. You go first and I'll follow."

"In case I shouldn't be too steady on my pins?" he said. "You'll be there to catch me?"

"Yes, my dear," she said.

In the hallway, as they passed the umbrella stand, he pointed a finger at his walking stick. "A hell of a lot of help *you* were," he said. "When the chips are down, a wife is more dependable than a walking stick any day."

"Thank you, dear," she said.

"You are, you know. I'd much rather have you than a cane."

"Would you?"

"I really would," he said.

"Keep moving, don't stop," she said.

"Do you ever think of me as an old stick?"

"No, not so far," she said.

"I should hope not," he said. "After all, I rescued you from those humble surroundings — not humble, prosaic. And introduced you into the fascinating world of the theater. If you'd married the man your parents chose for you, would you ever have met Freddie Lonsdale? Ina

Claire? Arthur Hopkins? Miriam Hopkins? Peggy Hopkins Joyce? Robert Benchley?"

"I don't think I ever met Peggy Hopkins Joyce," she said.

"You always say that, but you did. She was at Antibes in 1925."

"She was, but I wasn't. We didn't go there till 1926."

"The year that we were there, she was there. You took an instant dislike to her."

"That wasn't Peggy Hopkins Joyce. That was Geraldine St. John."

"The English girl. Are you sure?"

"You'll never get it out of your head that it wasn't Peggy Joyce, but it wasn't. It was Geraldine St. John."

"She wasn't even an actress," he said.

"I'll look and see if there's any Epsom salts," she said. "She had been an actress, though."

"No, she *wanted* to be an actress. She was thinking of becoming one."

"Well, whichever it was, she had some reason for buttering you up."

"She wasn't buttering me up," he said. "She was doing her best to seduce me. I was so darned attractive in those days, you must have gone through hell. But fortunately I was a man of strong character, and very much in love with you. I think of all the women that went on the make for me, and how resolutely I spurned them."

"There's only a half a boxful of Epsom salts. Do you think that'll be enough?"

"Oh, sure. Five pounds to a box. Two and a half pounds ought to be enough. The important thing is to have the water hot. The Epsom salts don't make that much difference. It's the heat of the water." He was naked.

"Turn around," she said. "Where did you hit yourself?"

"Isn't there a bruise?"

"Not on the coccyx bone. There's a red mark here, on the left hip, but the skin isn't broken. Do you want me to put something on it? Why don't I wait till you've had your tub, and then I'll use some rubbing alcohol on it. Your clothing protected you, softened the impact."

"If I don't get in the tub you'll be a quivering mass of frustrated passion."

"I know," she said. "Shall I bring your drink in the bathroom?"

"Trying to get me drunk, too. That's what Geraldine St. John tried to do, but it got her nowhere. Absolutely nowhere."

"I'm relieved to know it, after all these years," she said.

He put a foot in the water, and took it out immediately.

"Too hot?" she said.

"Just put your hand in and see," he said.

"I'll take your word for it. Turn on the cold."

"Is that the way it's done?" he said.

"You wanted it hot."

"It's a good thing I didn't put both feet in."

She turned on the cold water, knelt on the floor and made a whirlpool with a scrubbing brush. "Don't catch cold," she said. "Put something on."

"You don't have to look."

"I know, but put on your bathrobe anyway," she said.

"Don't get it too cold."

"I'm going to make it medium temperature and then you can change it to suit yourself, once you get in. It really isn't terribly hot, you know. Your feet were cold, but I think you can stand it now."

"How do you know my feet were cold?"

"Because they're always cold, and you've been out in the snow into the bargain," she said.

Now he put one foot, then the other, in the water and lowered himself into the tub.

"How is it?" she said.

"It'll be all right. Thanks."

"I'm going to fill the hot-water bottle. I suggest you go right to bed after your bath. It's been a shock and sleep is the best thing for it. I'll leave your drink in the bedroom."

"Where are you going?"

"I think I'll go down and put the meat back in the deep freeze. I want you to soak in the hot tub for at least a half an hour, and then go right to bed. We'll wait and see how you feel around nine o'clock. If you're still asleep, fine. If not, we can have dinner then."

"All right," he said.

As he lay in the tub, changing the water from time to time, he could hear her moving about in the small house. She came in once at the end of fifteen minutes. "You all right?" she said.

"Completely relaxed," he said.

"Take another fifteen minutes. I've got the heating pad in your bed. I'll turn it on when you've finished your soak. I don't want to put it on too soon."

"It's automatic," he said.

"I know, but I don't trust those things," she said, and went out again.

This time he noticed no thoughts, and though he did not close his eyes, he could not account for a period of five or six minutes and there was no doubt that he had in effect been asleep.

"Are you done to a crisp?" he heard her say.

"Do you realize that it's twenty years for Rex?"

"On the ninth of March," she said.

"The hardest thing to believe is that if he'd lived, we'd have a middle-aged son. He'd be forty-three years old. I'll never be able to stretch my imagination that far, that you and I would have a son forty-three. Forty-three. There's no use kidding ourselves, forty-three isn't young."

"I don't think we kid ourselves very much," she said. "I think you've had enough warm water. How does your back feel?"

"I'll know when I get up," he said.

"Here, I'll give you a hand."

"No, I want to get up normally, use the usual muscles. That's the only way to tell." He got out of the tub, and she held up a bath towel for him. "Feel all right."

"Dry yourself and I'll turn on the heating pad," she said.

"Don't you want to talk about Rex?" he said.

"Not at the moment, no. I want to get you into a warm bed and let you have at least an hour's sleep. Some shut-eye."

"Some what?" he said.

"Some shut-eye," she said.

"I wonder if you realize who the first person was that we ever heard use that expression," he said.

"Shut-eye? Was it Rex?"

"No, it wasn't Rex. It was someone very different from Rex. It was Paul Vincent."

"How can you be so sure of that?"

"Because I'm a playwright, and I listen to what people say."

"But that far back?"

"It was one of the first things I ever heard him say, and he was the first one I ever heard say it," he said. He buttoned up his pajamas.

"I don't think I'll open the window," she said. "I'll come up in an hour or so and open it if you're asleep."

"You don't want to talk about either one of them, Rex or Paul Vincent," he said.

"Do you?" she said.

"I have no objection to talking about Rex," he said. "We don't much, any more. Actually we never did. I think we've always hoped that he might still be alive."

"I never had any such hope. Two of his friends saw his plane go down in smoke, and one of them saw it fall into the ocean. There was no reason to hope. You only tortured yourself by hoping. How did you get started thinking about him now?"

"Some of my best ideas come to me in the bathtub. Just like Archimedes. Remember, 'Eureka!'?"

"Vaguely," she said. "So vaguely that I would have said it was Socrates."

"It was Archimedes. Archimedes," he said.

"He discovered something while taking a bath, but I don't remember what. And I certainly don't know what it had to do with Rex."

"It had nothing to do with Rex, but *I* made a discovery. Two discoveries, actually. One, that I can think of him without pain. And two, that it's much better to remember him as we do than as a middle-aged man of forty-three."

"Assuming he'd die at forty-three, which I don't assume."

"No, assuming that we'll die whenever we do, and that he'd have gone on living, to forty-five, or fifty, or whatever we are when we cash in. When I die, just before I die, one of my last thoughts will be of my son as he was the last time we saw him. Young, strong, brave, gay. And handsome. He was just old enough to be truly handsome. Nobody looks like that when they're forty-three. It's gone at thirty, at the latest. We never saw him when he had to wear reading glasses, or starting to get thick through the middle. I wouldn't want Rex to wear arch supports, or have a receding hair-line. Would you?"

"Yes."

"I wonder. You'd want him alive. But he might have bored you, you know. He would have married a nice girl, in all likelihood. They'd have produced three or four children, the way most of his generation have done, and you and I wouldn't count for much. I gave very little thought to my father and mother after you and I were married."

"Rex never would have bored me," she said. "Are you all tucked in?"

"All tucked in, and all tuckered out," he said. "I think I'll sleep."

"I won't wake you. I'll let you sleep as long as you can. Shall I leave the drink?"

"No, you might as well take it with you," he said. The bedclothes were all the way up to his chin; only his head showed. "Emily, I want to ask you a question."

"Yes, and I'm sure I know what it is," she said.

"Well, did you?"

"Did I what?" she said.

"If you know what the question is, why don't you answer it?"

"Because I could be wrong," she said.

"Did you sleep with Paul Vincent?" he said.

"That's what I thought you were going to ask me. The answer is no."

"The answer has always been no," he said.

"Are you hoping that some day I'll change no to yes?"

"No, but yes would be easier to believe than no."

"Well, I didn't, so go to sleep," she said.

"Why didn't you? You were sore as hell at me about the St. John girl."

"Yes I was, but I wasn't going to make a fool of myself just because you were making a fool of yourself."

"How did I make a fool of myself? She was the one that was acting foolish."

"You were as bad as she was, in a different way. Talking with an English accent."

"My God, you should have heard yourself, parroting Paul Vincent and that lingo of his. He couldn't say sleep, he had to say shut-eye. What were some of the other quaint expressions he used? He never said hands. He said lunch-hooks."

"I don't remember that at all," she said.

"You and the rest of you, you with your gentle upbringing. You all thought he was fascinating because he talked that way. Lunch-hooks. Shut-eye. Puddle-jumper. And none of it was original, although you all thought it was. It all came from cartoonists and the theatrical publications."

"Next time you go for a walk in the snow, wear your creepers," she said. "You seem to have shaken up a lot of old memories."

"I seem to have," he said.

"Do you want this light on?" she said.

"No thanks."

"I'll be in to see how you're getting along," she said . . .

Twice in the next three hours she visited the room, and on the second visit she opened the windows. Both times he was asleep, helpless against an attacker, and the captive of his unwanted dreams, which were seldom nightmarish but always full of complicated problems and dilemmas. Sometimes he would wake up in the night and turn the light on and scribble a few words that were the key to involved plots for plays. In the morning, when he was having his coffee, he would study his notes to himself and be unable to make any sense out of them. "Beautifully logical plot, a well-constructed, logical three-act play," he would say. But he had not written a play in at least ten years. They did not need the money. Back in the Twenties and Thirties he had had two big hits and two moderate successes that together had made him close to a million dollars. Bob Abercrombie had invested the money for him, and his capital was now past the million mark. She, Emily Kinsmith, had an income of her own. "A good thing, too," he would say. "I could never make a living in the theater today. Actually I shouldn't even call myself a playwright any more. I'd have just as much right to call myself a wrestler. I wrestled in college and got a minor letter. But it's almost as long since I've written a play as it is since I helped beat M.I.T. on the mat."

"Except that I have a feeling you were better known as a playwright than as a wrestler."

"You tell that to one of the new managers," he said.

They lived the year round in the house that had once been their summer cottage, out beyond East Hampton on Long Island. A drama critic on *Newsweek* once referred to him as the late Charles Kinsmith, and he spent a day composing several letters of correction, none of which he mailed. "After all, how can I be sure he isn't right?" said Charles. Someone at the Dramatists Guild, an associate professor at the University of Michigan, and a woman at the Pasadena Playhouse wrote to the magazine to set it straight. Excerpts of their letters were printed. Several East Hampton friends said they too had written, but their letters were not published. "Probably because they never actually got written," said Charles.

"Well, you know how people are," said Emily.

"Oh, yes. I know how people are," said Charles.

Just before Christmas they would go to New York on a Monday and stay until Thursday afternoon. "That gives us a chance to see four plays, including one matinee. But last year we were driven to going to a musical comedy. There just weren't four plays I wanted to see. I don't want to see a play in which a man kisses a man. I know it happens. It happens not far from here, every weekend all summer long. It happened when I was in college. I don't even mind plays about homosexuals. But you can do a play about homosexuals without having one character kiss the other on the mouth. The minute you succumb to that temptation, you admit you haven't got much of a play. You have a little shocker, and that's all. I've had adultery in four or five of my plays, but there's never been a bed on the set. *That* would have been quite a temptation to some of my actors and actresses, and I may have been unconsciously guided by prudence. Think of the magnetic attraction a bed would have had for Lita Pastorius, for instance. If we'd had a bed on the set she wouldn't have been able to take her eyes off it. But knowing that there was an imaginary bed offstage, she gave a very convincing performance. The actors have to imagine things as well as the audience, you know. One time we had George Fleming's glass filled with a real Martini and he just drank it down without any enjoyment. It was an experiment. He said himself he preferred plain water onstage. With plain water, he could act. But he was so used to real Martinis in real life that when we gave him one in the play, he didn't react. He was supposed to say, 'This is a fine cocktail,' and it was. I mixed it. But he read the line so unconvincingly that we went back to plain water, and I want to tell you that when an actor turns down a free drink it's something to think about," he said.

East Hampton was far enough away from New York to provide excuses for Charles to stay in the country. To take the morning train he would have to rise at five o'clock; by motor the trip was tiresome and long, through the business sections of the Suffolk County villages and the monotonous parkways of Nassau. In emergencies — which were rare — he could charter an airplane, an expense that he could justify only in rather extreme cases. "What constitutes an extreme case?" he would say. "Well, an actor's funeral, if the actor was in one of my plays and I was still speaking to him, or her, at the end of the run. Or a favorite waiter, if I hear about his funeral in time. The trouble there, of course, is that I seldom knew their last names and I don't always hear about their dying. I go to a restaurant and find out months later. I used to go to critics' funerals, but the critics that reviewed my plays are no longer around. Benchley. Hammond. Mantle. Anderson. Gabriel. Woollcott. I didn't feel I had to go to Nathan's funeral. He was never really a critic. Some funerals mean staying in town overnight. Personal friends. But I find that I haven't nearly as many personal friends as I once did. One of my ushers died last year in Chicago and I didn't know about it till I read it in the alumni magazine. Nothing in the New York papers. On the other hand, when my tailor died there was quite a lengthy obit in both papers, in which I was mentioned as one of his customers. I didn't go to his funeral. He'd been overcharging me for years because he knew damn well I was too lazy to break in someone else. A lot of men my age have stopped having things custom-made. We buy off the rack when we buy at all. It's too depressing to be reminded that a really good suit or pair of shoes will outlast you. My present dinner jacket is thirty-two years old, and I guess that tells as well as anything else could how much we go out in the evening. Every four or five years I buy one of those white linen dinner jackets for the summer festivities. The summer festivities consist of sixteen dinner parties and four appearances at the John Drew Theater. I'm quite accurate about the dinner parties. I counted up by checking through old appointment books of Emily's. It comes out to exactly sixteen a summer, as guest and host. At that it's too many, but between Thanksgiving and Memorial Day there are hardly any. Since the War there's been a tendency for people to keep their houses open all winter, and come down for long weekends. But the entertaining then isn't as elaborate. You don't have to see people unless you really want to. Emily can always pretend I'm working — and I am. I'm writing the libretto of an opera. As soon as you tell people you're writing the libretto of an *opera* they think twice about disturbing you. But it has to be an opera. An opera takes years. Sometimes they ask me if it was commissioned, and I tell them it was certainly not commissioned by the Met, and look wise. Implying that it's a secret project. If they ask me the name of the composer I tell them that *is* a secret. They ask me if it's going to be modern and I make a little joke. 'Not by the time it's finished,' I tell them. It'll never be finished, because it's never been started, but it's been very useful to me for ten years or more, and I've had a great many letters about it. If I were a little more unscrupulous I could have made some money on it. One of the television companies wanted to pay me $10,000 for an option on it. That put me momentarily in a spot, but I wriggled out of it. I said if they were willing to pay me $50,000, I'd listen. I heard no more from them. It was somehow reassuring to learn that they wouldn't go to fifty. I wouldn't like to think that things have gotten so out of hand that a television company would pay me $50,000 for an *option* on an unwritten opera. I sold one of my plays to the movies for $50,000 in 1930, and I thought they must be out of their minds. They weren't though. I see it on television now and then, sometimes the first cast. Not to mention an entirely different story, but it always has to say, 'Based on the play by Charles Kinsmith.' I want to say, '*What* play by Charles Kinsmith,' but Emily's never gotten used to my habit of talking to the radio set or the television. She pretends to think I'm batty. She doesn't mind my talking out loud when I'm actually writing dialog. She could see a reason for that. But muttering things at the TV set shows a lack of restraint that she pretends not to understand. She comes of a tight-lipped Yankee family. Ethan Frome-Calvin Coolidge types. My family were so poor that talk was practically our only form of entertainment. Nobody paid much attention to what anyone else said, but we jawed away from morning to night. It was really like talking to yourself in our house. Two brothers and two sisters and my father and mother, all gabbing at once. Bedlam. And yet we somehow managed to maintain communications. It took me about two years to learn that Emily's family weren't being so taciturn because I was a stranger. It was their way. They came to the table to eat, and they ate everything that was put on their plates, by the old man. He never asked anyone if they *wanted* cauliflower, or turnips. If that's what there was, that's what you got, and you damn well ate it. In silence, preferably. When I finally caught on, and didn't try to make conversation, everybody was more relaxed. Emily's mother said one day, 'Charles, didn't you like your turnips?' and I said, 'Nope.' That was all. But from then on whenever I had a meal at their house they didn't serve turnips. Emily hated turnips, too, but she'd never been asked. She was very well brought up, from a future husband's point of view. Her family never asked her what she wanted, never asked her what she thought. Consequently she was very appreciative of common politeness on the part of outsiders, and if anyone was actually kind to her, or treated her with uncommon respect, or *loved* her — she was extremely appreciative. When I first met her I didn't know any of these things about her family life. She was a classmate of one of my sisters at Wellesley. Not a particularly close friend, but a classmate, and I was introduced to her at their commencement, along with a dozen other girls. As far as I was concerned, Emily was all there was. Dark and shy in her long white dress, then later when she was wearing her mortarboard it wasn't on quite straight. It gave her accidentally a *dash,* although it was unintentional. Is there anything more unfeminine than a girl in a riding habit, with a stiff white stock and her hat on the top of her head? And yet is there anything more feminine? Yes, there is. It's a girl in cap and gown. If she's strongly feminine, it'll come through in spite of the attire, in both cases. Emily and my sister and I rode together on the New York train. I wasn't getting much out of her conversationally, but I knew she liked me, and I was determined to see more of her. Then when we got back to New York we were met by her grandmother's chauffeur, Emile, in black leather puttees and breeches and a tunic that buttoned up to the throat. That was totally unexpected. I'd somehow got the impression that Emily was in better circumstances than we were, but not much better. I'd pictured her father as the insurance man in a small town in Connecticut, because I knew she lived in a small town in Connecticut and that her father was in the insurance business. She'd told me that much. But when I saw that chauffeur I began to wonder. She offered to give us a lift to my aunt's house in Brooklyn, and before my sister could refuse, I accepted. I wanted to find out all I could. Her grandmother's car removed any doubt I had about Emily's financial status. It was a big Renault limousine, with the radiator in the middle of the hood. Ugly as could be, but the effect was overwhelming. It wasn't a new car, even then, but it'd been well taken care of, and I'd never been inside a limousine before. We weren't sure how to get to Brooklyn by car, but Emile knew. In those days a lot of people like Emily's grandmother lived in Brooklyn, and he'd been there oftener than we had. My uncle was a clergyman, pastor of a Dutch Reformed church on Brooklyn Heights, and Emile had actually taken people to weddings there. Emily insisted on going with us — she was postponing her meeting with her grandmother, she told me later. She was terrified of her grandmother, who was her mother's mother. Old Mrs. Van Rhyne disliked Yankees and had never altogether approved of her daughter's marriage to Emily's father. The fact that he had made a big success in the insurance business didn't cut much ice with her. This was all to come out much later, but apparently Mrs. Van Rhyne felt that Mr. Williams had all the Yankee virtues and none of the vices. He was shrewd and thrifty and dependable, but he wouldn't take a drink or look at another woman. Your true Yankee does both. I know. I went to Dartmouth for four years, and all my preconceived notions of Puritan New Englanders went up the flue. Those Green Mountain Boys and State-of-Mainers are very fond of liquor and pussy, no matter what you hear to the contrary. Mrs. Van Rhyne didn't *advocate* adultery and boozing, but she was a handsome woman herself and accustomed to flattering attentions by the male sex. She also liked her little nip. And remember that car, that big green French monster, and that dapper French chauffeur. Most of her contemporaries had Pierce-Arrows and ex-coachmen, usually Irish or English. She had style, and she didn't want her daughter to go through life as a frump. Unfortunately, Mrs. Williams *was* a frump, and Mr. Williams was just what she wanted. A reaction, obviously to the pleasure-loving Mrs. Van Rhyne. I never knew Mr. Van Rhyne. He had passed out of the picture by the time I came along, but I gathered from bits and pieces that I was able to pick up that he was as much in favor of ease and elegance as she was. He never did a tap of work. He went to Columbia for two years and then to Oxford, but Mrs. Van Rhyne was always rather evasive about his Oxford career. I was curious, and I thought of writing to Oxford to try to find out if he ever actually became a member of that university. Then I decided that would be spying, so I never wrote. The Van Rhyne money was in real estate. They owned solid blocks of it in the West Seventies and Eighties, and all they had to do was sit there and watch it triple in value. Theodore Van Rhyne died before he was forty, but people remembered him as a real sybarite. Whenever his name came up they'd always get that look, that tolerant smile that they had when anybody'd mention Edward VII. If you lead a completely useless life, but do it with style and die young enough, you're quite likely to be remembered with more affection than the man who has a record of accomplishment. But the secret is to die young enough. If you think you're going to live to a ripe old age, it's better to pile up a record of accomplishment of some sort. It may be bridge-building, or money-making, or butterfly-collecting, but it has to be something. People don't like to see longevity wasted on a do-nothing. And as a rule, it isn't. Do-nothings don't usually last very long. The first twenty years of a man's life are a struggle, getting through the childhood diseases and accidents, and the sex revolution that begins around eleven or twelve in most boys, and the constant readjustments in relations with your parents. Those first twenty years are anything but do-nothing years. It's the next twenty that determine whether a man is a do-nothing or an accomplisher. He knows what he wants to do, even if it's nothing, and he sets a timer in himself that will go off when his energy is used up. I'm convinced that most people really know just about how long they're going to last, and they guide their lives and expend their resources accordingly. Emily's grandfather, for instance, told Mrs. Van Rhyne that when their daughter got married he wanted his brother Curtis and not his brother William to give her away. Clearly indicating that he didn't expect to be there, and he wasn't. But Emily's mother was only about ten years old at the time. He knew. If you ask a man when he's going to die, he won't be able to tell you, but he knows. I know when I'm going to die, but it isn't going to be from this fall."

"*Charles! Charles!* Wake up, darling," said Emily Kinsmith.

He opened his eyes. She was sitting on the edge of the bed and holding his hand in her two. "You were groaning," she said. "I think it was a nightmare."

"No, I don't remember any nightmare," he said.

"Does your back hurt?" she said. "Maybe that was it."

He pulled himself up to a sitting position. "My back does hurt a little," he said. "But not while I'm lying still. Only when I move."

"You must have been turning in your sleep."

"Maybe," he said. "How long have I been asleep?"

"Oh, about an hour and a half. I came in a couple of times to see how you were."

"How was I?"

"Dead to the world," she said.

"I've been that for a long time. *Newsweek* said so."

"Was it *Newsweek*? I thought it was *Time*."

"You thought it was time what?"

"I thought it was *Time* that had you in the obituary column."

"Oh, I thought you meant it was time I woke up," he said.

"No, you sleep as long as you like."

"I don't want to sleep any more."

"You want to have dinner?" she said.

"I want to talk," he said.

"All right," she said. She fixed the pillows behind him. "Shall I get you a glass of water?"

"Yes, my mouth is dry."

She got him a tumbler of water and handed it to him. He sipped it slowly. "Do you know how it feels to be a bird? I don't think birds appreciate what they have. For just a fraction of a second, the tiniest fraction of a fraction of a second, I knew how it felt to be a bird today."

"When you had your fall," she said.

"Yes. When my feet left the ground, both feet, and before I came down on my behind. It wasn't like jumping. I've jumped from the top of a barn into a pile of straw and enjoyed it. But that was voluntary. This was something over which I had no control. Suddenly I was given the gift of flight. But being a member of the human species, a descendant of Pithecanthropus erectus, I couldn't adapt myself to the new situation. Nevertheless I had the experience of being air-borne today, and I'm thinking of trying it again. The question is, how? I can't go up on the roof and jump off. I have to wait until Nature gives me the gift again. But I must say it was exhilarating."

"Is that what you were dreaming about?" she said.

"I wasn't dreaming about anything, Emily," he said.

"You most certainly were," she said. "You were groaning and muttering —"

"But I wasn't dreaming. I was talking to somebody."

"But you were sound asleep, talking to somebody or not talking to somebody. Who *was* it you were talking to?"

"I have no idea. Nobody in particular," he said.

"Me?"

"No. Nobody I ever knew. Nobody that I could identify in any way. I mean I don't know whether it was a man or a woman, young or old, white or black. I haven't the faintest idea who I was talking to, but that's what I was doing."

"Another form of nightmare," she said. "Can you remember what you were telling this person?"

"Yes, I was telling him about us. About you, and your grandmother and grandfather. The Van Rhynes, I mean. I told him about Emile."

"Emile who?"

"Your grandmother's chauffeur," he said.

"Emile Blanc. What else did you tell him — and I notice you say *him,* so it must have been a man you were talking to."

"I think it probably was a man, but not anyone I know. There's a possibility that it was someone that never existed, a combination of two people. Paul Vincent and Geraldine St. John. They were the last people I thought of before falling asleep."

"No, we were talking about Rex."

"That's true, we were. Do you suppose I could have been talking to Rex? Yes, that's quite possible. Not our Rex, not our boy as we knew him, but a Rex Kinsmith in his forties. A stranger to you and me. Yes, I could have been telling this Rex Kinsmith all about you and me. Mostly about you. Very little about me. Hardly anything about me."

"It might be a good idea if you got out of bed and had something to eat. You could watch television for a while and then go back to bed and you won't have the same dream."

"I'm not sure I don't want the same dream. But now that I know who I was talking to — I think it *was* this Rex Kinsmith — I doubt if I'll pick up the dream where it left off. Then I didn't know who I was talking to, but now I would know."

"Yes, that would change it. You probably will never have the dream again, now that you've figured out who it was."

"Oh, I'm not so sure about that," he said. "I can very easily imagine going to sleep again and starting right out by thinking of this Rex Kinsmith, and addressing him directly."

"That's just the opposite of what you said before," she said.

"No, not quite. This time I'd be starting a new dream, not the old one, and I wouldn't have any doubts as to who I was talking to."

"Oh, well now we're getting into a different thing. Communication with the dead. Did this person ever answer you while you were talking to him?"

"No. Never said anything at all," he said.

"I wish you'd put on your flannel bathrobe and come downstairs and have something to eat. I don't like this conversation very much. You know I don't believe in an after-life. This idea that you were talking to Rex after he'd been dead all these years, but according to your recollection he went on living and is now in his forties."

"I think so, yes," he said.

"Well, you see that's where I part company with you right away. He was killed when he was twenty-three, and I don't know *anybody* that believes you go on growing after you die. Even the most religious people believe that a baby that dies is a baby through all eternity, and a man that lives to be eighty stays eighty."

"You have a point," he said. "Nevertheless I could have created a Rex Kinsmith, like a character in one of my plays, and made him seem so real to my subconscious mind that he becomes a figure that I could talk to."

"Here, put this on," she said, handing him his bathrobe. "And you'd better put on some socks or you'll catch cold."

He held out his hand for the robe, took hold of it, and let it fall on the bedclothes. "I can't, Emily," he said.

"I'll help you."

"You can't either. I can't move."

"What do you mean, you can't move?"

"Just what I say. I think I'm paralyzed."

"No, Charles. You're not paralyzed. You were able to pull yourself up on your pillow."

"Have you got a pin? Stick a pin in my leg. I want to see if I can feel it."

"I don't have to stick you with a pin. I'll pinch you."

"All right," he said.

She put her hand under the bedclothes, and held it there.

"See? I didn't feel anything," he said.

"No, because I haven't touched you," she said.

"Well, touch me," he said. "Are you afraid?"

They looked at each other, eye to eye.

"Have you touched me yet?" he said.

"No."

"Then touch me now, please. I have to know," he said.

She took her hand out from under the bedclothes.

"What?" he said.

She nodded. "I pinched your calf, I even bent your toe back."

"I am paralyzed?" he said.

"Yes," she said.

"It's probably temporary," he said. "I knew I hurt myself taking that spill. You'd better call Jimmy Gray. Call him at home, he'll be having dinner. *And don't worry*. It's only temporary. One of those pinched-nerve things."

"Of course it is," she said.

"I'm just glad I didn't break my hip. That's what happens so often to people our age. That can be real hell, they say. Call Jimmy, and I'll talk to him."

She looked in the directory and dialed the bedside telephone. "This is Mrs. Charles Kinsmith on Jagger Lane. Could I speak to Dr. Gray, please? It's urgent."

"Let me talk to him," said Charles.

She shook her head. "I see. Well, will you please tell him to call me right away? Mrs. Charles Kinsmith, Amagansett 8-5564." She replaced the telephone. "The answering service. I wonder if I ought to try another doctor."

"No," he said.

"Are you in pain?" she said.

"Not really," he said. "More than before, across my back, but none in my legs."

"Is it all right if I lie on the bed beside you?"

"I wish you would," he said.

"I'd give you something to stop the pain, but I don't know what would be the right thing. I don't want to give you the wrong thing."

"Well, you never have," he said.

She smiled at him. "Haven't I, dear?"

"Never," he said.

"Are you falling asleep?"

"Hmm?"

"I think you're falling asleep," she said.

He did not answer, and she stared at him. He quivered, shuddered, and expired. She got on the bed and lay beside him. "Take me with you," she said. "Can you hear me, boy? Please take me with you?"

Until Jimmy Gray called there was nothing to be done; no right thing, no wrong thing, and life is divided between the right things and the wrong things. "Isn't it, Charles?" she said. "You know it is. You knew it a minute ago." Now the telephone rang and she reached for it.

"Hello? Yes, is this you, Jimmy? It's Charles. He just went down in flames. He was flying like a bird, and he went down in flames. No, you can't talk to him. He's right here, but he's dead," she said. She hung up. "I wonder what's next," she said. "You know, Charles. What's next?"

Robert Penn Warren

1905 – 1989

One of the most distinguished, prize-medal-and-fellowship-laden novelists and poets of the older generation, Warren is remarkable among American writers for his ability to change and develop. Born in Kentucky, he began his career as a convinced Southern agrarian, then was greatly influenced by the New Criticism of the thirties and forties. His novels and more particularly his poetry reflect a constantly broadening outlook. His early regionalism has become infused with more general philosophical concerns.

Warren's most successful novel, based on the career of Huey Long, is *All the King's Men.* But a greater power to endure may be found in his verse and a few of his short stories.

Often drawn from the backwoods Tennessee of three generations ago, his tales tend to show, perhaps inevitably, the influence of Faulkner. "Blackberry Winter," often singled out as Warren's finest story, is so frequently anthologized that I have chosen the less familiar "The Patented Gate and the Mean Hamburger." It's a fair example of Southern ultrablack tragicomedy, with every genre touch laid on neatly and unobtrusively. That intensities of passion lie back of the seeming impassivity of the poor white is one of the truths with which the Southern school starts. Here the axiom is skillfully developed.

The Patented Gate and
the Mean Hamburger

YOU HAVE SEEN HIM a thousand times. You have seen him standing on the street corner on Saturday afternoon, in the little county-seat towns. He wears blue jean pants, or overalls washed to a pale pastel blue like the color of sky after a shower in spring, but because it is Saturday he has on a wool coat, an old one, perhaps the coat left from the suit he got married in a long time back. His long wrist bones hang out from the sleeves of the coat, the tendons showing along the bone like the dry twist of grapevine still corded on the stove-length of a hickory sapling you would find in his wood box beside his cookstove among the split chunks of gum and red oak. The big hands, with the knotted, cracked joints and the square, horn-thick nails, hang loose off the wrist bone like clumsy, home-made tools hung on the wall of a shed after work. If it is summer, he wears a straw hat with a wide brim, the straw fraying loose around the edge. If it is winter, he wears a felt hat, black once, but now weathered with streaks of dark gray and dull purple in the sunlight. His face is long and bony, the jawbone long under the drawn-in cheeks. The flesh along the jawbone is nicked in a couple of places where the unaccustomed razor has been drawn over the leather-coarse skin. A tiny bit of blood crusts brown where the nick is. The color of the face is red, a dull red like the red clay mud or clay dust which clings to the bottom of his pants and to the cast-iron-looking brogans on his feet, or a red like the color of a piece of hewed cedar which has been left in the weather. The face does not look alive. It seems to be molded from the clay or hewed from the cedar. When the jaw moves, once, with its deliberate, massive motion on the quid of tobacco, you are still not convinced. That motion is but the cunning triumph of a mechanism concealed within.

But you see the eyes. You see that the eyes are alive. They are pale blue or gray, set back under the deep brows and thorny eyebrows. They are not wide, but are squinched up like eyes accustomed to wind or sun or to measuring the stroke of the ax or to fixing the object over the rifle sights. When you pass, you see that the eyes are alive and are warily and dispassionately estimating you from the ambush of the thorny brows. Then you pass on, and he stands there in that stillness which is his gift.

With him may be standing two or three others like himself, but they are still, too. They do not talk. The young men, who will be like these men when they get to be fifty or sixty, are down at the beer parlor, carousing and laughing with a high, whickering laugh. But the men on the corner are long past all that. They are past many things. They have endured and will endure in their silence and wisdom. They will stand on the street corner and reject the world which passes under their level gaze as a rabble passes under the guns of a rocky citadel around whose base a slatternly town has assembled.

I had seen Jeff York a thousand times, or near, standing like that on the street corner in town, while the people flowed past him, under the distant and wary and dispassionate eyes in ambush. He would be waiting for his wife and the three towheaded children who were walking around the town looking into store windows and at the people. After a while they would come back to him, and then, wordlessly, he would lead them to the store where they always did their trading. He would go first, marching with a steady bent-kneed stride, setting the cast-iron brogans down deliberately on the cement; then his wife, a small woman with covert, sidewise, curious glances for the world, would follow, and behind her the towheads bunched together in a dazed, glory-struck way. In the store, when their turn came, Jeff York would move to the counter, accept the clerk's greeting, and then bend down from his height to catch the whispered directions of his wife. He would straighten up and say, "Gimme a sack of flahr, if'n you please." Then when the sack of flour had been brought, he would lean again to his wife for the next item. When the stuff had all been bought and paid for with the grease-thick, wadded dollar bills which he took from an old leather coin purse with a metal catch to it, he would heave it all together into his arms and march out, his wife and towheads behind him and his eyes fixed level over the heads of the crowd. He would march down the street and around to the hitching lot where the wagons were, and put his stuff into his wagon and cover it with an old quilt to wait till he got ready to drive out to his place.

For Jeff York had a place. That was what made him different from the other men who looked like him and with whom he stood on the street corner on Saturday afternoon. They were croppers, but he, Jeff York, had a place. But he stood with them because his father had stood with their fathers and his grandfathers with their grandfathers, or with men like their fathers and grandfathers, in other towns, in settlements in the mountains, in towns beyond the mountains. They were the great-great-great-grandsons of men who, half woodsmen and half farmers, had been shoved into the sand hills, into the limestone hills, into the barrens, two hundred, two hundred and fifty years before and had learned there the way to grabble a life out of the sand and the stone. And when the soil had leached away into the sand or burnt off the stone, they went on west, walking with the bent-kneed stride over the mountains, their eyes squinching warily in the gaunt faces, the rifle over the crooked arm, hunting a new place.

But there was a curse on them. They only knew the life they knew, and that life did not belong to the fat bottom lands, where the cane was head-tall, and to the grassy meadows and the rich swale. So they passed those places by and hunted for the place which was like home and where they could pick up the old life, with the same feel in the bones and the squirrel's bark sounding the same after first light. They had walked a long way, to the sand hills of Alabama, to the red country of North Mississippi and Louisiana, to the Barrens of Tennessee, to the Knobs of Kentucky and the scrub country of West Kentucky, to the Ozarks. Some of them had stopped in Cobb County, Tennessee, in the hilly eastern part of the county, and had built their cabins and dug up the ground for the corn patch. But the land had washed away there, too, and in the end they had come down out of the high land into the bottoms — for half of Cobb County is a rich, swelling country — where the corn was good and the tobacco unfurled a leaf like a yard of green velvet and the white houses stood among the cedars and tulip trees and maples. But they were not to live in the white houses with the limestone chimneys set strong at the end of each gable. No, they were to live in the shacks on the back of the farms, or in cabins not much different from the cabins they had once lived in two hundred years before over the mountains or, later, in the hills of Cobb County. But the shacks and the cabins now stood on somebody else's ground, and the curse which they had brought with them over the mountain trail, more precious than the bullet mold or grandma's quilt, the curse which was the very feeling in the bones and the habit in the hand, had come full circle.

Jeff York was one of those men, but he had broken the curse. It had taken him more than thirty years to do it, from the time when he was nothing but a big boy until he was fifty. It had taken him from sun to sun, year in and year out, and all the sweat in his body, and all the power of rejection he could muster, until the very act of rejection had become a kind of pleasure, a dark, secret, savage dissipation, like an obsessing vice. But those years had given him his place, sixty acres with a house and barn.

When he bought the place, it was not very good. The land was run-down from years of neglect and abuse. But Jeff York put brush in the gullies to stop the wash and planted clover on the run-down fields. He mended the fences, rod by rod. He patched the roof on the little house and propped up the porch, buying the lumber and shingles almost piece by piece and one by one as he could spare the sweat-bright and grease-slick quarters and half-dollars out of his leather purse. Then he painted the house. He painted it white, for he knew that that was the color you painted a house sitting back from the road with its couple of maples, beyond the clover field.

Last, he put up the gate. It was a patented gate, the kind you can ride up to and open by pulling on a pull rope without getting off your horse or out of your buggy or wagon. It had a high pair of posts, well braced and with a high crossbar between, and the bars for the opening mechanism extending on each side. It was painted white, too. Jeff was even prouder of the gate than he was of the place. Lewis Simmons, who lived next to Jeff's place, swore he had seen Jeff come out after dark on a mule and ride in and out of that gate, back and forth, just for the pleasure of pulling on the rope and making the mechanism work. The gate was the seal Jeff York had put on all the years of sweat and rejection. He could sit on his porch on a Sunday afternoon in summer, before milking time, and look down the rise, down the winding dirty track, to the white gate beyond the clover, and know what he needed to know about all the years passed.

Meanwhile Jeff York had married and had had the three towheads. His wife was twenty years or so younger than he, a small, dark woman, who walked with her head bowed a little and from that humble and unprovoking posture stole sidewise, secret glances at the world from eyes which were brown or black — you never could tell which because you never remembered having looked her straight in the eye — and which were surprisingly bright in that sidewise, secret flicker, like the eyes of a small, cunning bird which surprise you from the brush. When they came to town she moved along the street, with a child in her arms or later with the three trailing behind her, and stole her looks at the world. She wore a calico dress, dun-colored, which hung loose to conceal whatever shape her thin body had, and in winter over the dress a brown wool coat with a scrap of fur at the collar which looked like some tattered growth of fungus feeding on old wood. She wore black high-heeled shoes, slippers of some kind, which she kept polished and which surprised you under that dress and coat. In the slippers she moved with a slightly limping, stealthy gait, almost sliding them along the pavement, as though she had not fully mastered the complicated trick required to use them properly. You knew that she wore them only when she came to town, that she carried them wrapped up in a piece of newspaper until their wagon had reached the first house on the outskirts of town, and that, on the way back, at the same point, she would take them off and wrap them up again and hold the bundle in her lap until she got home. If the weather happened to be bad, or if it was winter, she would have a pair of old brogans under the wagon seat.

It was not that Jeff York was a hard man and kept his wife in clothes that were as bad as those worn by the poorest of the women of the croppers. In fact, some of the cropper women, poor or not, black or white, managed to buy dresses with some color in them and proper hats, and went to the moving picture show on Saturday afternoon. But Jeff still owed a little money on his place, less than two hundred dollars, which he had had to borrow to rebuild his barn after it was struck by lightning. He had, in fact, never been entirely out of debt. He had lost a mule which had got out on the highway and been hit by a truck. That had set him back. One of his towheads had been sickly for a couple of winters. He had not been in deep, but he was not a man, with all those years of rejection behind him, to forget the meaning of those years. He was good enough to his family. Nobody ever said the contrary. But he was good to them in terms of all the years he had lived through. He did what he could afford. He bought the towheads a ten-cent bag of colored candy every Saturday afternoon for them to suck on during the ride home in the wagon, and the last thing before they left town, he always took the lot of them over to the dogwagon to get hamburgers and orange pop.

The towheads were crazy about hamburgers. And so was his wife, for that matter. You could tell it, even if she didn't say anything, for she would lift her bowed-forward head a little, and her face would brighten, and she would run her tongue out to wet her lips just as the plate with the hamburger would be set on the counter before her. But all those folks, like Jeff York and his family, like hamburgers, with pickle and onions and mustard and tomato catsup, the whole works. It is something different. They stay out in the country and eat hog-meat, when they can get it, and greens and corn bread and potatoes, and nothing but a pinch of salt to brighten it on the tongue, and when they get to town and get hold of beef and wheat bread and all the stuff to jack up the flavor, they have to swallow to keep the mouth from flooding before they even take the first bite.

So the last thing every Saturday, Jeff York would take his family over to Slick Hardin's Dew Drop Inn Diner and give them the treat. The diner was built like a railway coach, but it was set on a concrete foundation on a lot just off the main street of town. At each end the concrete was painted to show wheels. Slick Hardin kept the grass just in front of the place pretty well mowed and one or two summers he even had a couple of flower beds in the middle of that shirttail-size lawn. Slick had a good business. For a few years he had been a prelim fighter over in Nashville and had got his name in the papers a few times. So he was a kind of hero, with the air of romance about him. He had been born, however, right in town and, as soon as he had found out he wasn't ever going to be good enough to be a real fighter, he had come back home and started the dogwagon, the first one ever in town. He was a slick-skinned fellow, about thirty-five, prematurely bald, with his head slick all over. He had big eyes, pale blue and slick looking like agates. When he said something that he thought smart, he would roll his eyes around, slick in his head like marbles, to see who was laughing. Then he'd wink. He had done very well with his business, for despite the fact that he had picked up city ways and a lot of city talk, he still remembered enough to deal with the country people, and they were the ones who brought the dimes in. People who lived right there in town, except for school kids in the afternoon and the young toughs from the pool room or men on the night shift down at the railroad, didn't often get around to the dogwagon.

Slick Hardin was perhaps trying to be smart when he said what he did to Mrs. York. Perhaps he had forgotten, just for that moment, that people like Jeff York and his wife didn't like to be kidded, at least not in that way. He said what he did, and then grinned and rolled his eyes around to see if some of the other people present were thinking it was funny.

Mrs. York was sitting on a stool in front of the counter, flanked on one side by Jeff York and on the other by the three towheads. She had just sat down to wait for the hamburger — there were several orders in ahead of the York order — and had been watching in her sidewise fashion every move of Slick Hardin's hands as he patted the pink meat onto the hot slab and wiped the split buns over the greasy iron to make them ready to receive it. She always watched him like that, and when the hamburger was set before her she would wet her lips with her tongue.

That day Slick set the hamburger down in front of Mrs. York, and said, "Anybody likes hamburger much as you, Mrs. York, ought to git him a hamburger stand."

Mrs. York flushed up, and didn't say anything, staring at her plate. Slick rolled his eyes to see how it was going over, and somebody down the counter snickered. Slick looked back at the Yorks, and if he had not been so encouraged by the snicker he might, when he saw Jeff York's face, have hesitated before going on with his kidding. People like Jeff York are touchous, and they are especially touchous about the womenfolks, and you do not make jokes with or about their womenfolks unless it is perfectly plain that the joke is a very special kind of friendly joke. The snicker down the counter had defined the joke as not entirely friendly. Jeff was looking at Slick, and something was growing slowly in that hewed-cedar face, and back in the gray eyes in the ambush of thorny brows.

But Slick did not notice. The snicker had encouraged him, and so he said, "Yeah, if I liked them hamburgers much as you, I'd buy me a hamburger stand. Fact, I'm selling this one. You want to buy it?"

There was another snicker, louder, and Jeff York, whose hamburger had been about half way to his mouth for another bite, laid it down deliberately on his plate. But whatever might have happened at that moment did not happen. It did not happen because Mrs. York lifted her flushed face, looked straight at Slick Hardin, swallowed hard to get down a piece of the hamburger or to master her nerve, and said in a sharp, strained voice, "You sellen this place?"

There was complete silence. Nobody had expected her to say anything. The chances were she had never said a word in that diner in the couple of hundred times she had been in it. She had come in with Jeff York and, when a stool had come vacant, had sat down, and Jeff had said, "Gimme five hamburgers, if'n you please, and make 'em well done, and five bottles of orange pop." Then, after the eating was over, he had always laid down seventy-five cents on the counter — that is, after there were five hamburger-eaters in the family — and walked out, putting his brogans down slow, and his wife and kids following without a word. But now she spoke up and asked the question, in that strained, artificial voice, and everybody, including her husband, looked at her with surprise.

As soon as he could take it in, Slick Hardin replied, "Yeah, I'm selling it."

She swallowed hard again, but this time it could not have been hamburger, and demanded, "What you asken fer hit?"

Slick looked at her in the new silence, half shrugged, a little contemptuously, and said, "Fourteen hundred and fifty dollars."

She looked back at him, while the blood ebbed from her face. "Hit's a lot of money," she said in a flat tone, and returned her gaze to the hamburger on her plate.

"Lady," Slick said defensively, "I got that much money tied up here. Look at that there stove. It is a Heat Master and they cost. Them coffee urns, now. Money can't buy no better. And this here lot, lady, the diner sets on. Anybody knows I got that much money tied up here. I got more. This lot cost me more'n . . ." He suddenly realized that she was not listening to him. And he must have realized, too, that she didn't have a dime in the world and couldn't buy his diner, and that he was making a fool of himself, defending his price. He stopped abruptly, shrugged his shoulders, and then swung his wide gaze down the counter to pick out somebody to wink to.

But before he got the wink off, Jeff York had said, "Mr. Hardin."

Slick looked at him and asked, "Yeah?"

"She didn't mean no harm," Jeff York said. "She didn't mean to be messen in yore business."

Slick shrugged. "Ain't no skin off my nose," he said. "Ain't no secret I'm selling out. My price ain't no secret neither."

Mrs. York bowed her head over her plate. She was chewing a mouthful of her hamburger with a slow, abstracted motion of her jaw, and you knew that it was flavorless on her tongue.

That was, of course, on a Saturday. On Thursday afternoon of the next week Slick was in the diner alone. It was the slack time, right in the middle of the afternoon. Slick, as he told it later, was wiping off the stove and wasn't noticing. He was sort of whistling to himself, he said. He had a way of whistling soft through his teeth. But he wasn't whistling loud, he said, not so loud he wouldn't have heard the door open or the steps if she hadn't come gum-shoeing in on him to stand there waiting in the middle of the floor until he turned round and was so surprised he nearly had heart failure. He had thought he was there alone, and there she was, watching every move he was making, like a cat watching a goldfish swim in a bowl.

"Howdy-do," he said, when he got his breath back.

"This place still fer sale?" she asked him.

"Yeah, lady," he said.

"What you asken fer hit?"

"Lady, I done told you," Slick replied, "fourteen hundred and fifty dollars."

"Hit's a heap of money," she said.

Slick started to tell her how much money he had tied up there, but before he had got going, she had turned and slipped out of the door.

"Yeah," Slick said later to the men who came into the diner, "me like a fool starting to tell her how much money I got tied up here when I knowed she didn't have a dime. That woman's crazy. She must've walked that five or six miles in here just to ask me something she already knowed the answer to. And then turned right round and walked out. But I am selling me this place. I'm tired of slinging hash to them hicks. I got me some connections over in Nashville and I'm gonna open me a place over there. A cigar stand and about three pool tables and maybe some beer. I'll have me a sort of club in the back. You know, member-ship cards to git in, where the boys will play a little game. Just sociable. I got good connections over in Nashville. I'm selling this place. But that woman, she ain't got a dime. She ain't gonna buy it."

But she did.

On Saturday Jeff York led his family over to the diner. They ate ham-burgers without a word and marched out. After they had gone, Slick said, "Looks like she ain't going to make the invest-mint. Gonna buy a block of bank stock instead." Then he rolled his eyes, located a brother down the counter, and winked.

It was almost the end of the next week before it happened. What had been going on inside the white house out on Jeff York's place nobody knew or was to know. Perhaps she just starved him out, just not doing the cooking or burning everything. Perhaps she just quit attending to the children properly and he had to come back tired from work and take care of them. Perhaps she just lay in bed at night and talked and talked to him, asking him to buy it, nagging him all night long, while he would fall asleep and then wake up with a start to hear her voice still going on. Or perhaps she just turned her face away from him and wouldn't let him touch her. He was a lot older than she, and she was probably the only woman he had ever had. He had been too ridden by his dream and his passion for rejection during all the years before to lay even a finger on a woman. So she had him there. Because he was a lot older and because he had never had another woman. But perhaps she used none of these methods. She was a small, dark, cunning woman, with a sidewise look from her lowered face, and she could have thought up ways of her own, no doubt.

Whatever she thought up, it worked. On Friday morning Jeff York went to the bank. He wanted to mortgage his place, he told Todd Sullivan, the president. He wanted fourteen hundred and fifty dollars, he said. Todd Sullivan would not let him have it. He already owed the bank one hundred and sixty dollars and the best he could get on a mortgage was eleven hundred dollars. That was in 1935 and then farmland wasn't worth much and half the land in the country was mortgaged anyway. Jeff York sat in the chair by Todd Sullivan's desk and didn't say anything. Eleven hundred dollars would not do him any good. Take off the hundred and sixty he owed and it wouldn't be but a little over nine hundred dollars clear to him. He sat there quietly for a minute, apparently turning that fact over in his head. Then Todd Sullivan asked him, "How much you say you need?"

Jeff York told him.

"What you want it for?" Todd Sullivan asked.

He told him that.

"I tell you," Todd Sullivan said, "I don't want to stand in the way of a man bettering himself. Never did. That diner ought to be a good proposition, all right, and I don't want to stand in your way if you want to come to town and better yourself. It will be a step up from that farm for you, and I like a man has got ambition. The bank can't lend you the money, not on that piece of property. But I tell you what I'll do. I'll buy your place. I got me some walking horses I'm keeping out on my father's place. But I could use me a little place of my own. For my horses. I'll give you seventeen hundred for it. Cash."

Jeff York did not say anything to that. He looked slow at Todd Sullivan as though he did not understand.

"Seventeen hundred," the banker repeated. "That's a good figure. For these times."

Jeff was not looking at him now. He was looking out the window, across the alleyway — Todd Sullivan's office was in the back of the bank. The banker, telling about it later when the doings of Jeff York had become for a moment a matter of interest, said, "I thought he hadn't even heard me. He looked like he was half asleep or something. I coughed to sort of wake him up. You know the way you do. I didn't want to rush him. You can't rush those people, you know. But I couldn't sit there all day. I had offered him a fair price."

It was, as a matter of fact, a fair price for the times, when the bottom was out of everything in the section.

Jeff York took it. He took the seventeen hundred dollars and bought the dogwagon with it, and rented a little house on the edge of town and moved in with his wife and the towheads. The first day after they got settled, Jeff York and his wife went over to the diner to get instructions from Slick about running the place. He showed Mrs. York all about how to work the coffee machine and the stove, and how to make up the sandwiches, and how to clean the place up after herself. She fried up hamburgers for all of them, herself, her husband, and Slick Hardin, for practice, and they ate the hamburgers while a couple of hangers-on watched them. "Lady," Slick said, for he had money in his pocket and was heading out for Nashville on the seven o'clock train that night, and was feeling expansive, "lady, you sure fling a mean hamburger."

He wiped the last crumbs and mustard off his lips, got his valise from behind the door, and said, "Lady, git in there and pitch. I hope you make a million hamburgers." Then he stepped out into the bright fall sunshine and walked away whistling up the street, whistling through his teeth and rolling his eyes as thought there were somebody to wink to. That was the last anybody in town ever saw of Slick Hardin.

The next day, Jeff York worked all day down at the diner. He was scrubbing up the place inside and cleaning up the trash which had accumulated behind it. He burned all the trash. Then he gave the place a good coat of paint outside, white paint. That took him two days. Then he touched up the counter inside with varnish. He straightened up the sign out front, which had begun to sag a little. He had that place looking spick and span.

Then on the fifth day after they got settled — it was Sunday — he took a walk in the country. It was along toward sundown when he started out, not late, as a matter of fact, for by October the days are shortening up. He walked out the Curtisville pike and out the cut-off leading to his farm. When he entered the cut-off, about a mile from his own place, it was still light enough for the Bowdoins, who had a filling station at the corner, to see him plain when he passed.

The next time anybody saw him was on Monday morning about six o'clock. A man taking milk into town saw him. He was hanging from the main cross bar of the white patented gate. He had jumped off the gate. But he had propped the thing open so there wouldn't be any chance of clambering back up on it if his neck didn't break when he jumped and he should happen to change his mind.

But that was an unnecessary precaution, as it developed. Dr. Stauffer said that his neck was broken very clean. "A man who can break a neck as clean as that could make a living at it," Dr. Stauffer said. And added, "If he's damned sure it ain't ever his own neck."

Mrs. York was much cut up by her husband's death. People were sympathetic and helpful, and out of a mixture of sympathy and curiosity she got a good starting trade at the diner. And the trade kept right on. She got so she didn't hang her head and look sidewise at you and the world. She would look straight at you. She got so she could walk in high heels without giving the impression that it was a trick she was learning. She wasn't a bad-looking woman, as a matter of fact, once she had caught on how to fix herself up a little. The railroad men and the pool hall gang liked to hang out there and kid with her. Also, they said, she flung a mean hamburger.

DINO BUZZATI

1906–1972

In Europe Buzzati is more highly reputed than he is here. For several decades he worked on Milan's great newspaper, Corriere della Sera, *as editor, reporter, correspondent, and feature writer. During this period he produced plays, novels, short stories, and paintings. In 1958 he was awarded the Strega prize for literature.*

Buzzati is often compared to Kafka (he wrote an interesting travel piece about Kafka's Prague) and also to Borges, but can hardly claim to be on their level. American readers may sense a kinship with Barthelme or, to go back in time, with Hawthorne — if an absurdist can also be a moralist. Italians may think of Italo Calvino. The English may feel he belongs with such masters of the macabre as John Collier, Roald Dahl, and even Saki, though he lacks the latter's lightness of touch.

In the composition of his witty, sometimes cruel, often nihilistic tales of the fantastic and arabesque, Buzzati reflects his conditioning as a reporter: "The effectiveness of a fantastic story will depend on its being told in the most simple and practical terms." The method is quite unlike that of Poe, who aims to transport us into the entirely hallucinatory. Many of Buzzati's seemingly surrealist inventions uncomfortably nudge us toward a contemplation of the bizarre, but perfectly real, pressures of our own day. Thus the Voltairean trifle that follows may appear quite timely. After all, we are the first generation in history that may experience the end of the world, or at least the end of us.

The End of the World

ONE MORNING about ten o'clock an immense fist appeared in the sky above the city. Then it slowly unclenched and remained this way, immobile, like an enormous canopy of ruin. It looked like rock, but it was not rock; it looked like flesh but it wasn't; it even seemed made of cloud, but cloud it was not. It was God, and the end of the world. A murmuring, which here became a moan, there a shout, spread through the districts of the city, until it grew into a single voice, united and terrible, rising shrilly like a trumpet.

Luisa and Pietro were in a small square, warmed by the early sun, enclosed by strange places and partly by gardens. But in the sky, at an immeasurable height, hung the hand. Windows were thrown open amid fearful cries, while the initial shout of the city gradually subsided, and half-dressed young women looked out to watch the apocalypse. People left their houses, many of them breaking into a run. They felt the need to move, to do something, anything, but they didn't know where to turn. Luisa burst into uncontrollable tears: "I knew it," she stammered between sobs, "I knew it had to end this way . . . never when you were in church, never when you were praying . . . I didn't give a damn, didn't care at all, and now . . . I felt it had to happen this way! . . ." What could Pietro do to console her? Even he began to cry like a baby. Most of the people were in tears too, especially the women. Only two friars, spry little old men, went along as happily as if they were on their way to a party. "Now it's all over for the smart ones!" they joyfully exclaimed, proceeding at a brisk pace, turning toward the most notable passersby. "You're not so smart anymore, eh? We're the smart ones now!" they sneered. "Always mocked, always considered dunces — now we'll see who the smart ones are!" Cheerful as schoolboys, they passed through the middle of the growing crowd, which glared at them without daring to make any resistance. Minutes after they had disappeared down an alley, a man instinctively rushed in pursuit of them, as if a precious opportunity had been allowed to slip away. "By God!" he shouted, beating his forehead, "and to think they could have confessed us." "Damn it!" someone else quickly added, "What idiots we've been! They turn up right under our noses and we let them get away!" But who could ever catch up with the sprightly friars?

In the meantime women and evil men who had previously been arrogant were returning from churches, cursing, disappointed, and discouraged. The more clever confessors had vanished — it was reported — probably bought up by the most influential people and the powerful industrialists. It was very strange, but money amazingly preserved its certain prestige even though it was the end of the world; it was estimated that maybe a few minutes, or hours, or even several days were still left, but who knew. As for the rest of the available confessors, such a frightening throng formed in the churches that they were not even considered. It was said that serious incidents occurred precisely because of the extreme overcrowding, and that swindlers dressed as priests were even offering to make house calls to hear confessions for exorbitant prices. On the other hand, young couples hurriedly withdrew to make love one last time, stretching out on the grass in gardens without the slightest pretense of restraint. The hand, meanwhile, had turned an ashen color, even though the sun was shining, and as a result it was more frightening. The rumor that the catastrophe was imminent began to circulate; a few people were certain they would not see noon.

Just then a young priest was seen on the small, elegant balcony of a palace, a little higher than street level (it was reached by two fan-shaped flights of stairs). With his head sunk between his shoulders, he rushed as if he were afraid to leave. It was strange to see a priest at that hour, in that sumptuous house peopled by courtesans. "A priest! A priest!" was being shouted somewhere. With lightning speed the people succeeded in stopping him before he could get away. "Confess us, confess us!" they cried at him. He paled, was dragged to a pretty sort of niche which jutted out from the balcony like a covered pulpit; it seemed especially made for this purpose. Dozens of men and women immediately bunched together, creating an uproar, surging from below, clambering up the ornamental projections, clinging to the columns and the edge of the bannister; after all, it wasn't very high.

The priest began to hear confessions. Very quickly he listened to breathless secrets from unknown people (who at this point were not concerned with whether the others could hear them). Before they finished, he traced a small sign of the cross with his right hand, absolved them, and immediately turned toward the next sinner. But there were so many of them. The priest looked around in a daze, measuring the rising sea of sins that were to be erased. With great effort Luisa and Pietro also came beneath him, got their turns, managed to be heard. "I never go to Mass, I tell lies," the young girl shouted hurriedly in a frenzy of humiliation, afraid that she wouldn't make it in time, "and then any sin you want . . . add all of them, really . . . and I don't say this because I'm frightened that all these people are here, believe me, it's only that I desire to be near God, I swear to you . . . ," and the priest was convinced of her sincerity. "*Ego te absolvo* . . . ," he murmured and turned to listen to Pietro.

Now an inexpressible longing arose among men. One asked: "How much time until the universal judgment?" Another, a well-informed man, looked at his watch. "Ten minutes," he said authoritatively. The priest heard the man and suddenly tried to leave. But, insatiable, the people held him. He looked feverish. It was clear that the wave of confessions came to him as no more than a confused murmur devoid of sense; he made signs of the cross one after another, repeated *Ego te absolvo* mechanically.

"Eight minutes!" warned a man's voice from the crowd. The priest literally trembled, he stamped his feet on the marble like a child throwing a tantrum. "And me? What about me?" he began to implore, desperate. They cheated him of his soul's salvation, those cursed people; the Devil take them, however many they were. But how would he deliver himself? How provide for himself? He was on the brink of tears. "And me? Me?" he asked of a thousand postulants, voracious of Paradise. Yet no one paid any attention to him.

EUDORA WELTY
1909—

Eudora Welty was born in Jackson, Mississippi, has lived there most of her life, and writes stories and novels penetrated only in a minor way by rumors from beyond the Delta country. But her world suffices. As Jane Austen taught us long ago, the nonparochial mind can make do with a parish.

She differs from other writers of the Southern school in at least two related respects. She is not oppressed by the tragic weight of the Southern past, and, for all her realism, her tone is in general not as dark as that of Faulkner and some of his followers.

Henry James has been called the historian of fine consciences. Though Eudora Welty has other strings to her bow, she may be called the historian of relatively unevolved consciences, recording the ways of the inhabitants of the bend in the road, the anonymous and unacknowledged.

Two of her preoccupying themes, loneliness and the redemptive power of love, fuse in the story that follows, one of her earliest. It is neither coldly detached nor judgmental, merely gravely contemplative. Bowman, like many of her characters, wishes passionately to connect, to establish relationships that will make him more human. In a double sense he dies of heart failure.

Death of a Traveling Salesman

R. J. BOWMAN, who for fourteen years had traveled for a shoe company through Mississippi, drove his Ford along a rutted dirt path. It was a long day! The time did not seem to clear the noon hurdle and settle into soft afternoon. The sun, keeping its strength here even in winter, stayed at the top of the sky, and every time Bowman stuck his head out of the dusty car to stare up the road, it seemed to reach a long arm down and push against the top of his head, right through his hat — like the practical joke of an old drummer, long on the road. It made him feel all the more angry and helpless. He was feverish, and he was not quite sure of the way.

This was his first day back on the road after a long siege of influenza. He had had very high fever, and dreams, and had become weakened and pale, enough to tell the difference in the mirror, and he could not think clearly ... All afternoon, in the midst of his anger, and for no reason, he had thought of his dead grandmother. She had been a comfortable soul. Once more Bowman wished he could fall into the big feather bed that had been in her room ... Then he forgot her again.

This desolate hill country! And he seemed to be going the wrong way — it was as if he were going back, far back. There was not a house in sight ... There was no use wishing he were back in bed, though. By paying the hotel doctor his bill he had proved his recovery. He had not even been sorry when the pretty trained nurse said good-bye. He did not like illness, he distrusted it, as he distrusted the road without signposts. It angered him. He had given the nurse a really expensive bracelet, just because she was packing up her bag and leaving.

But now — what if in fourteen years on the road he had never been ill before and never had an accident? His record was broken, and he had even begun almost to question it ... He had gradually put up at better hotels, in the bigger towns, but weren't they all, eternally, stuffy in summer and drafty in winter? Women? He could only remember little rooms within little rooms, like a nest of Chinese paper boxes, and if he thought of one woman he saw the worn loneliness that the furniture of that room seemed built of. And he himself — he was a man who always wore rather wide-brimmed black hats, and in the wavy hotel mirrors had looked something like a bullfighter, as he paused for that inevitable instant on the landing, walking downstairs to supper ... He leaned out of the car again, and once more the sun pushed at his head.

Bowman had wanted to reach Beulah by dark, to go to bed and sleep off his fatigue. As he remembered, Beulah was fifty miles away from the last town, on a graveled road. This was only a cow trail. How had he ever come to such a place? One hand wiped the sweat from his face, and he drove on.

He had made the Beulah trip before. But he had never seen this hill or this petering-out path before — or that cloud, he thought shyly, looking up and then down quickly — any more than he had seen this day before. Why did he not admit he was simply lost and had been for miles? . . . He was not in the habit of asking the way of strangers, and these people never knew where the very roads they lived on went to; but then he had not even been close enough to anyone to call out. People standing in the fields now and then, or on top of the haystacks, had been too far away, looking like leaning sticks or weeds, turning a little at the solitary rattle of his car across their countryside, watching the pale sobered winter dust where it chunked out behind like big squashes down the road. The stares of these distant people had followed him solidly like a wall, impenetrable, behind which they turned back after he had passed.

The cloud floated there to one side like the bolster on his grandmother's bed. It went over a cabin on the edge of a hill, where two bare chinaberry trees clutched at the sky. He drove through a heap of dead oak leaves, his wheels stirring their weightless sides to make a silvery melancholy whistle as the car passed through their bed. No car had been along this way ahead of him. Then he saw that he was on the edge of a ravine that fell away, a red erosion, and that this was indeed the road's end.

He pulled the brake. But it did not hold, though he put all his strength into it. The car, tipped toward the edge, rolled a little. Without doubt, it was going over the bank.

He got out quietly, as though some mischief had been done him and he had his dignity to remember. He lifted his bag and sample case out, set them down, and stood back and watched the car roll over the edge. He heard something — not the crash he was listening for, but a slow, unuproarious crackle. Rather distastefully he went to look over, and he saw that his car had fallen into a tangle of immense grapevines as thick as his arm, which caught it and held it, rocked it like a grotesque child in a dark cradle, and then, as he watched, concerned somehow that he was not still inside it, released it gently to the ground.

He sighed.

Where am I? he wondered with a shock. Why didn't I do something? All his anger seemed to have drifted away from him. There was the house, back on the hill. He took a bag in each hand and with almost childlike willingness went toward it. But his breathing came with difficulty, and he had to stop to rest.

· · ·

It was a shotgun house, two rooms and an open passage between, perched on the hill. The whole cabin slanted a little under the heavy heaped-up vine that covered the roof, light and green, as though forgotten from summer. A woman stood in the passage.

He stopped still. Then all of a sudden his heart began to behave strangely. Like a rocket set off, it began to leap and expand into uneven patterns of beats which showered into his brain, and he could not think. But in scattering and falling it made no noise. It shot up with great power, almost elation, and fell gently, like acrobats into nets. It began to pound profoundly, then waited irresponsibly, hitting in some sort of inward mockery first at his ribs, then against his eyes, then under his shoulder blades, and against the roof of his mouth when he tried to say, "Good afternoon, madam." But he could not hear his heart — it was as quiet as ashes falling. This was rather comforting; still it was shocking to Bowman to feel his heart beating at all.

Stock-still in his confusion, he dropped his bags, which seemed to drift in slow bulks gracefully through the air and to cushion themselves on the gray prostrate grass near the doorstep.

As for the woman standing there, he saw at once that she was old. Since she could not possibly hear his heart, he ignored the pounding and now looked at her carefully, and yet in his distraction dreamily, with his mouth open.

She had been cleaning the lamp, and held it, half blackened, half clear, in front of her. He saw her with the dark passage behind her. She was a big woman with a weather-beaten but unwrinkled face; her lips were held tightly together, and her eyes looked with a curious dulled brightness into his. He looked at her shoes, which were like bundles. If it were summer she would be barefoot . . . Bowman, who automatically judged a woman's age on sight, set her age at fifty. She wore a formless garment of some gray coarse material, rough-dried from a washing, from which her arms appeared pink and unexpectedly round. When she never said a word, and sustained her quiet pose of holding the lamp, he was convinced of the strength in her body.

"Good afternoon, madam," he said.

She stared on, whether at him or at the air around him he could not tell, but after a moment she lowered her eyes to show that she would listen to whatever he had to say.

"I wonder if you would be interested —" He tried once more. "An accident — my car . . ."

Her voice emerged low and remote, like a sound across a lake. "Sonny he ain't here."

"Sonny?"

"Sonny ain't here now."

Her son — a fellow able to bring my car up, he decided in blurred relief. He pointed down the hill. "My car's in the bottom of the ditch. I'll need help."

"Sonny ain't here, but he'll be here."

She was becoming clearer to him and her voice stronger, and Bowman saw that she was stupid.

He was hardly surprised at the deepening postponement and tedium of his journey. He took a breath, and heard his voice speaking over the silent blows of his heart. "I was sick. I am not strong yet . . . May I come in?"

He stooped and laid his big black hat over the handle on his bag. It was a humble motion, almost a bow, that instantly struck him as absurd and betraying of all his weakness. He looked up at the woman, the wind blowing his hair. He might have continued for a long time in this unfamiliar attitude; he had never been a patient man, but when he was sick he had learned to sink submissively into the pillows, to wait for his medicine. He waited on the woman.

Then she, looking at him with blue eyes, turned and held open the door, and after a moment Bowman, as if convinced in his action, stood erect and followed her in.

Inside, the darkness of the house touched him like a professional hand, the doctor's. The woman set the half-cleaned lamp on a table in the center of the room and pointed, also like a professional person, a guide, to a chair with a yellow cowhide seat. She herself crouched on the hearth, drawing her knees up under the shapeless dress.

At first he felt hopefully secure. His heart was quieter. The room was enclosed in the gloom of yellow pine boards. He could see the other room, with the foot of an iron bed showing, across the passage. The bed had been made up with a red-and-yellow pieced quilt that looked like a map or a picture, a little like his grandmother's girlhood painting of Rome burning.

He had ached for coolness, but in this room it was cold. He stared at the hearth with dead coals lying on it and iron pots in the corners. The hearth and smoked chimney were of the stone he had seen ribbing the hills, mostly slate. Why is there no fire? he wondered.

And it was so still. The silence of the fields seemed to enter and move familiarly through the house. The wind used the open hall. He felt that he was in a mysterious, quiet, cool danger. It was necessary to do what? . . . To talk.

"I have a nice line of women's low-priced shoes . . ." he said.

But the woman answered, "Sonny'll be here. He's strong. Sonny'll move your car."

"Where is he now?"

"Farms for Mr. Redmond."

Mr. Redmond. Mr. Redmond. That was someone he would never have to encounter, and he was glad. Somehow the name did not appeal to him . . . In a flare of touchiness and anxiety, Bowman wished to avoid even mention of unknown men and their unknown farms.

"Do you two live here alone?" He was surprised to hear his old voice, chatty, confidential, inflected for selling shoes, asking a question like that — a thing he did not even want to know.

"Yes. We are alone."

He was surprised at the way she answered. She had taken a long time to say that. She had nodded her head in a deep way too. Had she wished to affect him with some sort of premonition? he wondered unhappily. Or was it only that she would not help him, after all, by talking with him? For he was not strong enough to receive the impact of unfamiliar things without a little talk to break their fall. He had lived a month in which nothing had happened except in his head and his body — an almost inaudible life of heartbeats and dreams that came back, a life of fever and privacy, a delicate life which had left him weak to the point of — what? Of begging. The pulse in his palm leapt like a trout in a brook.

He wondered over and over why the woman did not go ahead with cleaning the lamp. What prompted her to stay there across the room, silently bestowing her presence upon him? He saw that with her it was not a time for doing little tasks. Her face was grave; she was feeling how right she was. Perhaps it was only politeness. In docility he held his eyes stiffly wide; they fixed themselves on the woman's clasped hands as though she held the cord they were strung on.

Then, "Sonny's coming," she said.

He himself had not heard anything, but there came a man passing the window and then plunging in at the door, with two hounds beside him. Sonny was a big enough man, with his belt slung low about his hips. He looked at least thirty. He had a hot, red face that was yet full of silence. He wore muddy blue pants and an old military coat stained and patched. World War? Bowman wondered. Great God, it was a Confederate coat. On the back of his light hair he had a wide filthy black hat which seemed to insult Bowman's own. He pushed down the dogs from his chest. He was strong, with dignity and heaviness in his way of moving . . . There was the resemblance to his mother.

They stood side by side . . . He must account again for his presence here.

"Sonny, this man, he had his car to run off over the prec'pice an' wants to know if you will git it out for him," the woman said after a few minutes.

Bowman could not even state his case.

Sonny's eyes lay upon him.

He knew he should offer explanations and show money — at least appear either penitent or authoritative. But all he could do was to shrug slightly.

Sonny brushed by him going to the window, followed by the eager dogs, and looked out. There was effort even in the way he was looking, as if he could throw his sight out like a rope. Without turning Bowman felt that his own eyes could have seen nothing: it was too far.

"Got me a mule out there an' got me a block an' tackle," said Sonny meaningfully. "I *could* catch me my mule an' git me my ropes, an' before long I'd git your car out the ravine."

He looked completely around the room, as if in meditation, his eyes roving in their own distance. Then he pressed his lips firmly and yet shyly together, and with the dogs ahead of him this time, he lowered his head and strode out. The hard earth sounded, cupping to his powerful way of walking — almost a stagger.

Mischievously, at the suggestion of those sounds, Bowman's heart leapt again. It seemed to walk about inside him.

"Sonny's goin' to do it," the woman said. She said it again, singing it almost, like a song. She was sitting in her place by the hearth.

Without looking out, he heard some shouts and the dogs barking and the pounding of hoofs in short runs on the hill. In a few minutes Sonny passed under the window with a rope, and there was a brown mule with quivering, shining, purple-looking ears. The mule actually looked in the window. Under its eyelashes it turned target-like eyes into his. Bowman averted his head and saw the woman looking serenely back at the mule, with only satisfaction in her face.

She sang a little more, under her breath. It occurred to him, and it seemed quite marvelous, that she was not really talking to him, but rather following the thing that came about with words that were unconscious and part of her looking.

So he said nothing, and this time when he did not reply he felt a curious and strong emotion, not fear, rise up in him.

This time, when his heart leapt, something — his soul — seemed to leap too, like a little colt invited out of a pen. He stared at the woman while the frantic nimbleness of his feeling made his head sway. He could not move; there was nothing he could do, unless perhaps he might embrace this woman who sat there growing old and shapeless before him.

But he wanted to leap up, to say to her, I have been sick and I found out then, only then, how lonely I am. Is it too late? My heart puts up a struggle inside me, and you may have heard it, protesting against emptiness . . . It should be full, he would rush on to tell her, thinking of his heart now as a deep lake, it should be holding love like other hearts. It should be flooded with love. There would be a warm spring day . . . Come and stand in my heart, whoever you are, and a whole river would cover your feet and rise higher and take your knees in whirlpools, and draw you down to itself, your whole body, your heart too.

But he moved a trembling hand across his eyes, and looked at the placid crouching woman across the room. She was still as a statue. He felt ashamed and exhausted by the thought that he might, in one more moment, have tried by simple words and embraces to communicate some strange thing — something which seemed always to have just escaped him . . .

Sunlight touched the furthest pot on the hearth. It was late afternoon. This time tomorrow he would be somewhere on a good graveled road, driving his car past things that happened to people, quicker than their happening. Seeing ahead to the next day, he was glad, and knew that this was no time to embrace an old woman. He could feel in his pounding temples the readying of his blood for motion and for hurrying away.

"Sonny's hitched up your car by now," said the woman. "He'll git it out the ravine right shortly."

"Fine!" he cried with his customary enthusiasm.

Yet it seemed a long time that they waited. It began to get dark. Bowman was cramped in his chair. Any man should know enough to get up and walk around while he waited. There was something like guilt in such stillness and silence.

But instead of getting up, he listened . . . His breathing restrained, his eyes powerless in the growing dark, he listened uneasily for a warning sound, forgetting in wariness what it would be. Before long he heard something — soft, continuous, insinuating.

"What's that noise?" he asked, his voice jumping into the dark. Then wildly he was afraid it would be his heart beating so plainly in the quiet room, and she would tell him so.

"You might hear the stream," she said grudgingly.

Her voice was closer. She was standing by the table. He wondered why she did not light the lamp. She stood there in the dark and did not light it.

Bowman would never speak to her now, for the time was past. I'll sleep in the dark, he thought, in his bewilderment pitying himself.

Heavily she moved on to the window. Her arm, vaguely white, rose straight from her full side and she pointed out into the darkness.

"That white speck's Sonny," she said, talking to herself.

He turned unwillingly and peered over her shoulder; he hesitated to rise and stand beside her. His eyes searched the dusky air. The white speck floated smoothly toward her finger, like a leaf on a river, growing whiter in the dark. It was as if she had shown him something secret, part of her life, but had offered no explanation. He looked away. He was moved almost to tears, feeling for no reason that she had made a silent declaration equivalent to his own. His hand waited upon his chest.

Then a step shook the house, and Sonny was in the room. Bowman felt how the woman left him there and went to the other man's side.

"I done got your car out, mister," said Sonny's voice in the dark. "She's settin' a-waitin' in the road, turned to go back where she come from."

"Fine!" said Bowman, projecting his own voice to loudness. "I'm surely much obliged — I could never have done it myself — I was sick . . ."

"I could do it easy," said Sonny.

Bowman could feel them both waiting in the dark, and he could hear the dogs panting out in the yard, waiting to bark when he should go. He felt strangely helpless and resentful. Now that he could go, he longed to stay. Of what was he being deprived? His chest was rudely shaken by the violence of his heart. These people cherished something here that he could not see, they withheld some ancient promise of food and warmth and light. Between them they had a conspiracy. He thought of the way she had moved away from him and gone to Sonny, she had flowed toward him. He was shaking with cold, he was tired, and it was not fair. Humbly and yet angrily he stuck his hand into his pocket.

"Of course I'm going to pay you for everything —"

"We don't take money for such," said Sonny's voice belligerently.

"I want to pay. But do something more . . . Let me stay — tonight . . ." He took another step toward them. If only they could see him, they would know his sincerity, his real need! His voice went on, "I'm not very strong yet, I'm not able to walk far, even back to my car, maybe, I don't know — I don't know exactly where I am —"

He stopped. He felt as if he might burst into tears. What would they think of him!

Sonny came over and put his hands on him. Bowman felt them pass (they were professional too) across his chest, over his hips. He could feel Sonny's eyes upon him in the dark.

"You ain't no revenuer come sneakin' here, mister, ain't got no gun?"

To this end of nowhere! And yet *he* had come. He made a grave answer. "No."

"You can stay."

"Sonny," said the woman, "you'll have to borry some fire."

"I'll go git it from Redmond's," said Sonny.

"What?" Bowman strained to hear their words to each other.

"Our fire, it's out, and Sonny's got to borry some, because it's dark an' cold," she said.

"But matches — I have matches —"

"We don't have no need for 'em," she said proudly. "Sonny's goin' after his own fire."

"I'm goin' to Redmond's," said Sonny with an air of importance, and he went out.

After they had waited a while, Bowman looked out the window and saw a light moving over the hill. It spread itself out like a little fan. It zigzagged along the field, darting and swift, not like Sonny at all . . . Soon enough, Sonny staggered in, holding a burning stick behind him in tongs, fire flowing in his wake, blazing light into the corners of the room.

"We'll make a fire now," the woman said, taking the brand.

When that was done she lit the lamp. It showed its dark and light.

The whole room turned golden-yellow like some sort of flower, and the walls smelled of it and seemed to tremble with the quiet rushing of the fire and the waving of the burning lampwick in its funnel of light.

The woman moved among the iron pots. With the tongs she dropped hot coals on top of the iron lids. They made a set of soft vibrations, like the sound of a bell far away.

She looked up and over at Bowman, but he could not answer. He was trembling . . .

"Have a drink, mister?" Sonny asked. He had brought in a chair from the other room and sat astride it with his folded arms across the back. Now we are all visible to one another, Bowman thought, and cried, "Yes, sir, you bet, thanks!"

"Come after me and do just what I do," said Sonny.,

It was another excursion into the dark. They went through the hall, out to the back of the house, past a shed and a hooded well. They came to a wilderness of thicket.

"Down on your knees," said Sonny.

"What?" Sweat broke out on his forehead.

He understood when Sonny began to crawl through a sort of tunnel that the bushes made over the ground. He followed, startled in spite of himself when a twig or a thorn touched him gently without making a sound, clinging to him and finally letting him go.

Sonny stopped crawling and, crouched on his knees, began to dig with both his hands into the dirt. Bowman shyly struck matches and made a light. In a few minutes Sonny pulled up a jug. He poured out some of the whisky into a bottle from his coat pocket, and buried the jug again. "You never know who's liable to knock at your door," he said, and laughed. "Start back," he said, almost formally. "Ain't no need for us to drink outdoors, like hogs."

At the table by the fire, sitting opposite each other in their chairs, Sonny and Bowman took drinks out of the bottle, passing it across. The dogs slept; one of them was having a dream.

"This is good," said Bowman. "This is what I needed." It was just as though he were drinking the fire off the hearth.

"He makes it," said the woman with quiet pride.

She was pushing the coals off the pots, and the smells of corn bread and coffee circled the room. She set everything on the table before the men, with a bone-handled knife stuck into one of the potatoes, splitting out its golden fiber. Then she stood for a minute looking at them, tall and full above them where they sat. She leaned a little toward them.

"You all can eat now," she said, and suddenly smiled.

Bowman had just happened to be looking at her. He set his cup back on the table in unbelieving protest. A pain pressed at his eyes. He saw that she was not an old woman. She was young, still young. He could think of no number of years for her. She was the same age as Sonny, and she belonged to him. She stood with the deep dark corner of the room behind her, the shifting yellow light scattering over her head and her gray formless dress, trembling over her tall body when it bent over them in its sudden communication. She was young. Her teeth were shining and her eyes glowed. She turned and walked slowly and heavily out of the room, and he heard her sit down on the cot and then lie down. The pattern on the quilt moved.

"She's goin' to have a baby," said Sonny, popping a bite into his mouth.

Bowman could not speak. He was shocked with knowing what was really in this house. A marriage, a fruitful marriage. That simple thing. Anyone could have had that.

Somehow he felt unable to be indignant or protest, although some sort of joke had certainly been played upon him. There was nothing remote or mysterious here — only something private. The only secret was the ancient communication between two people. But the memory of the woman's waiting silently by the cold hearth, of the man's stubborn journey a mile away to get fire, and how they finally brought out their food and drink and filled the room proudly with all they had to show, was suddenly too clear and too enormous within him for response . . .

"You ain't as hungry as you look," said Sonny.

The woman came out of the bedroom as soon as the men had finished, and ate her supper while her husband stared peacefully into the fire.

Then they put the dogs out, with the food that was left.

"I think I'd better sleep here by the fire, on the floor," said Bowman.

He felt that he had been cheated, and that he could afford now to be generous. Ill though he was, he was not going to ask them for their bed. He was through with asking favors in this house, now that he understood what was there.

"Sure, mister."

But he had not known yet how slowly he understood. They had not meant to give him their bed. After a little interval they both rose and looking at him gravely went into the other room.

He lay stretched by the fire until it grew low and dying. He watched every tongue of blaze lick out and vanish. "There will be special reduced prices on all footwear during the month of January," he found himself repeating quietly, and then he lay with his lips tight shut.

How many noises the night had! He heard the stream running, the fire dying, and he was sure now that he heard his heart beating, too, the sound it made under his ribs. He heard breathing, round and deep, of the man and his wife in the room across the passage. And that was all. But emotion swelled patiently within him, and he wished that the child were his.

He must get back to where he had been before. He stood weakly before the red coals and put on his overcoat. It felt too heavy on his shoulders. As he started out he looked and saw that the woman had never got through with cleaning the lamp. On some impulse he put all the money from his billfold under its fluted glass base, almost ostentatiously.

Ashamed, shrugging a little, and then shivering, he took his bags and went out. The cold of the air seemed to lift him bodily. The moon was in the sky.

On the slope he began to run, he could not help it. Just as he reached the road, where his car seemed to sit in the moonlight like a boat, his heart began to give off tremendous explosions like a rifle, bang bang bang.

He sank in fright onto the road, his bags falling about him. He felt as if all this had happened before. He covered his heart with both hands to keep anyone from hearing the noise it made.

But nobody heard it.

JOHN CHEEVER
1912–1982

Of old Massachusetts stock, Cheever, in his early novels The Wapshot
Chronicle *and* The Wapshot Scandal, *used as materials his family tradition
and experience. His short stories, however, generally draw on the outwardly
comfortable yet precariously balanced middle-class world of New York's
suburbia, as well as on the more fashionable enclaves of the great city itself.
Though Cheever won both a Pulitzer Prize and a National Medal for Literature, the sad fact remains that his high reputation is largely posthumous.
As time passes, it may be that his sixty-one tales may come to be ranked,
after Hemingway's work and along with John O'Hara's, as the finest examples of the modern American short story.*

*At first glance Cheever's interests seem so restricted that they arouse
doubts as to his lasting appeal. He takes little account of large social movements, contemporary historic events, the world of the poor, of ethnic minorities, indeed of any world lying beyond a sixty-mile radius of New York
(with an occasional stop in Rome). His stories have no "ideas." Yet, on
careful reading, all this seems to matter little. Kipling's Indian tales, the best
of them, still speak to us though the society they reflect is as dead as Nine-
veh. So with Cheever. Like Kipling, he is preserved by personality. The exact
dimensions of his terrain do not matter. What does matter is the odd, unique
angle of his penetrating glance. Add to this his Ancient Mariner's power,
rare in our time, to glue us to his narrative, plus a perfect command of an
ironical, economical, and elegant prose style.*

*"The Five-Forty-Eight" is one of several Cheever stories successfully
transferred to television. It is about a disturbed woman. No, it is not at all
about a disturbed woman but about love, the sort of human being who can
feel it and the sort who never will.*

The Five-Forty-Eight

WHEN BLAKE stepped out of the elevator, he saw her. A few people, mostly men waiting for girls, stood in the lobby watching the elevator doors. She was among them. As he saw her, her face took on a look of such loathing and purpose that he realized she had been waiting for him. He did not approach her. She had no legitimate business with him. They had nothing to say. He turned and walked toward the glass doors at the end of the lobby, feeling that faint guilt and bewilderment we experience when we bypass some old friend or classmate who seems threadbare, or sick, or miserable in some other way. It was five-eighteen by the clock in the Western Union office. He could catch the express. As he waited his turn at the revolving doors, he saw that it was still raining. It had been raining all day, and he noticed now how much louder the rain made the noises of the street. Outside, he started walking briskly east toward Madison Avenue. Traffic was tied up, and horns were blowing urgently on a crosstown street in the distance. The sidewalk was crowded. He wondered what she had hoped to gain by a glimpse of him coming out of the office building at the end of the day. Then he wondered if she was following him.

Walking in the city, we seldom turn and look back. The habit restrained Blake. He listened for a minute — foolishly — as he walked, as if he could distinguish her footsteps from the worlds of sound in the city at the end of a rainy day. Then he noticed, ahead of him on the other side of the street, a break in the wall of buildings. Something had been torn down; something was being put up, but the steel structure had only just risen above the sidewalk fence and daylight poured through the gap. Blake stopped opposite here and looked into a store window. It was a decorator's or an auctioneer's. The window was arranged like a room in which people live and entertain their friends. There were cups on the coffee table, magazines to read, and flowers in the vases, but the flowers were dead and the cups were empty and the guests had not come. In the plate glass, Blake saw a clear reflection of himself and the crowds that were passing, like shadows, at his back. Then he saw her image — so close to him that it shocked him. She was standing only a foot or two behind him. He could have turned then and asked her what she wanted, but instead of recognizing her, he shied away abruptly from the reflection of her contorted face and went along the street. She might be meaning to do him harm — she might be meaning to kill him.

The suddenness with which he moved when he saw the reflection of her face tipped the water out of his hat brim in such a way that some of it ran down his neck. It felt unpleasantly like the sweat of fear. Then the cold water falling into his face and onto his bare hands, the rancid smell of the wet gutters and paving, the knowledge that his feet were beginning to get wet and that he might catch cold — all the common discomforts of walking in the rain — seemed to heighten the menace of his pursuer and to give him a morbid consciousness of his own physicalness and of the ease with which he could be hurt. He could see ahead of him the corner of Madison Avenue, where the lights were brighter. He felt that if he could get to Madison Avenue he would be all right. At the corner, there was a bakery shop with two entrances, and he went in by the door on the crosstown street, bought a coffee ring, like any other commuter, and went out the Madison Avenue door. As he started down Madison Avenue, he saw her waiting for him by a hut where newspapers were sold.

She was not clever. She would be easy to shake. He could get into a taxi by one door and leave by the other. He could speak to a policeman. He could run — although he was afraid that if he did run, it might precipitate the violence he now felt sure she had planned. He was approaching a part of the city that he knew well and where the maze of street-level and underground passages, elevator banks, and crowded lobbies made it easy for a man to lose a pursuer. The thought of this, and a whiff of sugary warmth from the coffee ring, cheered him. It was absurd to imagine being harmed on a crowded street. She was foolish, misled, lonely perhaps — that was all it could amount to. He was an insignificant man, and there was no point in anyone's following him from his office to the station. He knew no secrets of any consequence. The reports in his briefcase had no bearing on war, peace, the dope traffic, the hydrogen bomb, or any of the other international skulduggeries that he associated with pursuers, men in trench coats, and wet sidewalks. Then he saw ahead of him the door of a men's bar. Oh, it was so simple!

He ordered a Gibson and shouldered his way in between two other men at the bar, so that if she should be watching from the window she would lose sight of him. The place was crowded with commuters putting down a drink before the ride home. They had brought in on their clothes — on their shoes and umbrellas — the rancid smell of the wet dusk outside, but Blake began to relax as soon as he tasted his Gibson and looked around at the common, mostly not-young faces that surrounded him and that were worried, if they were worried at all, about tax rates and who would be put in charge of merchandising. He tried to remember her name — Miss Dent, Miss Bent, Miss Lent — and he was surprised to find that he could not remember it, although he was proud of the retentiveness and reach of his memory and it had only been six months ago.

Personnel had sent her up one afternoon — he was looking for a secretary. He saw a dark woman — in her twenties, perhaps — who was slender and shy. Her dress was simple, her figure was not much, one of her stockings was crooked, but her voice was soft and he had been willing to try her out. After she had been working for him a few days, she told him that she had been in the hospital for eight months and that it had been hard after this for her to find work, and she wanted to thank him for giving her a chance. Her hair was dark, her eyes were dark; she left with him a pleasant impression of darkness. As he got to know her better, he felt that she was oversensitive and, as a consequence, lonely. Once, when she was speaking to him of what she imagined his life to be — full of friendships, money, and a large and loving family — he had thought he recognized a peculiar feeling of deprivation. She seemed to imagine the lives of the rest of the world to be more brilliant than they were. Once, she had put a rose on his desk, and he had dropped it into the wastebasket. "I don't like roses," he told her.

She had been competent, punctual, and a good typist, and he had found only one thing in her that he could object to — her handwriting. He could not associate the crudeness of her handwriting with her appearance. He would have expected her to write a rounded backhand, and in her writing there were intermittent traces of this, mixed with clumsy printing. Her writing gave him the feeling that she had been the victim of some inner — some emotional — conflict that had in its violence broken the continuity of the lines she was able to make on paper. When she had been working for him three weeks — no longer — they stayed late one night and he offered, after work, to buy her a drink. "If you really want a drink," she said, "I have some whiskey at my place."

She lived in a room that seemed to him like a closet. There were suit boxes and hatboxes piled in a corner, and although the room seemed hardly big enough to hold the bed, the dresser, and the chair he sat in, there was an upright piano against one wall, with a book of Beethoven sonatas on the rack. She gave him a drink and said that she was going to put on something more comfortable. He urged her to; that was, after all, what he had come for. If he had any qualms, they would have been practical. Her diffidence, the feeling of deprivation in her point of view, promised to protect him from any consequences. Most of the many women he had known had been picked for their lack of self-esteem.

When he put on his clothes again, an hour or so later, she was weeping. He felt too contented and warm and sleepy to worry much about her tears. As he was dressing, he noticed on the dresser a note she had written to a cleaning woman. The only light came from the bathroom — the door was ajar — and in this half light the hideously scrawled letters again seemed entirely wrong for her, and as if they must be the handwriting of some other and very gross woman. The next day, he did what he felt was the only sensible thing. When she was out for lunch, he called personnel and asked them to fire her. Then he took the afternoon off. A few days later, she came to the office, asking to see him. He told the switchboard girl not to let her in. He had not seen her again until this evening.

Blake drank a second Gibson and saw by the clock that he had missed the express. He would get the local — the five-forty-eight. When he left the bar the sky was still light; it was still raining. He looked carefully up and down the street and saw that the poor woman had gone. Once or twice, he looked over his shoulder, walking to the station, but he seemed to be safe. He was still not quite himself, he realized, because he had left his coffee ring at the bar, and he was not a man who forgot things. This lapse of memory pained him.

He bought a paper. The local was only half full when he boarded it, and he got a seat on the river side and took off his raincoat. He was a slender man with brown hair — undistinguished in every way, unless you could have divined in his pallor or his gray eyes his unpleasant tastes. He dressed — like the rest of us — as if he admitted the existence of sumptuary laws. His raincoat was the pale buff color of a mushroom. His hat was dark brown; so was his suit. Except for the few bright threads in his necktie, there was a scrupulous lack of color in his clothing that seemed protective.

He looked around the car for neighbors. Mrs. Compton was several seats in front of him, to the right. She smiled, but her smile was fleeting. It died swiftly and horribly. Mr. Watkins was directly in front of Blake. Mr. Watkins needed a haircut, and he had broken the sumptuary laws; he was wearing a corduroy jacket. He and Blake had quarreled, so they did not speak.

The swift death of Mrs. Compton's smile did not affect Blake at all. The Comptons lived in the house next to the Blakes, and Mrs. Compton had never understood the importance of minding her own business. Louise Blake took her troubles to Mrs. Compton, Blake knew, and instead of discouraging her crying jags, Mrs. Compton had come to imagine herself a sort of confessor and had developed a lively curiosity about the Blakes' intimate affairs. She had probably been given an account of their most recent quarrel. Blake had come home one night, overworked and tired, and had found that Louise had done nothing about getting supper. He had gone into the kitchen, followed by Louise, and had pointed out to her that the date was the fifth. He had drawn a circle around the date on the kitchen calendar. "One week is the twelfth," he had said. "Two weeks will be the nineteenth." He drew a circle around the nineteenth. "I'm not going to speak to you for two weeks," he had said. "That will be the nineteenth." She had wept, she had protested, but it had been eight or ten years since she had been able to touch him with her entreaties. Louise had got old. Now the lines in her face were ineradicable, and when she clapped her glasses onto her nose to read the evening paper, she looked to him like an unpleasant stranger. The physical charms that had been her only attraction were gone. It had been nine years since Blake had built a bookshelf in the doorway that connected their rooms and had fitted into the bookshelf wooden doors that could be locked, since he did not want the children to see his books. But their prolonged estrangement didn't seem remarkable to Blake. He had quarreled with his wife, but so did every other man born of woman. It was human nature. In any place where you can hear their voices — a hotel courtyard, an air shaft, a street on a summer evening — you will hear harsh words.

The hard feeling between Blake and Mr. Watkins also had to do with Blake's family, but it was not as serious or as troublesome as what lay behind Mrs. Compton's fleeting smile. The Watkinses rented. Mr. Watkins broke the sumptuary laws day after day — he once went to the eight-fourteen in a pair of sandals — and he made his living as a commercial artist. Blake's oldest son — Charlie was fourteen — had made friends with the Watkins boy. He had spent a lot of time in the sloppy rented house where the Watkinses lived. The friendship had affected his manners and his neatness. Then he had begun to take some meals with the Watkinses, and to spend Saturday nights there. When he had moved most of his possessions over to the Watkinses' and had begun to spend more than half his nights there, Blake had been forced to act. He had spoken not to Charlie but to Mr. Watkins, and had, of necessity, said a number of things that must have sounded critical. Mr. Watkins' long and dirty hair and his corduroy jacket reassured Blake that he had been in the right.

But Mrs. Compton's dying smile and Mr. Watkins' dirty hair did not lessen the pleasure Blake took in setting himself in an uncomfortable seat on the five-forty-eight deep underground. The coach was old and smelled oddly like a bomb shelter in which whole families had spent the night. The light that spread from the ceiling down onto their heads and shoulders was dim. The filth on the window glass was streaked with rain from some other journey, and clouds of rank pipe and cigarette smoke had begun to rise from behind each newspaper, but it was a scene that meant to Blake that he was on a safe path, and after his brush with danger he even felt a little warmth toward Mrs. Compton and Mr. Watkins.

The train traveled up from underground into the weak daylight, and the slums and the city reminded Blake vaguely of the woman who had followed him. To avoid speculation or remorse about her, he turned his attention to the evening paper. Out of the corner of his eye he could see the landscape. It was industrial and, at that hour, sad. There were machine sheds and warehouses, and above these he saw a break in the clouds — a piece of yellow light. "Mr. Blake," someone said. He looked up. It was she. She was standing there holding one hand on the back of the seat to steady herself in the swaying coach. He remembered her name then — Miss Dent. "Hello, Miss Dent," he said.

"Do you mind if I sit here?"

"I guess not."

"Thank you. It's very kind of you. I don't like to inconvenience you like this. I don't want to . . ." He had been frightened when he looked up and saw her, but her timid voice rapidly reassured him. He shifted his hams — that futile and reflexive gesture of hospitality — and she sat down. She sighed. He smelled her wet clothing. She wore a formless black hat with a cheap crest stitched onto it. Her coat was thin cloth, he saw, and she wore gloves and carried a large pocketbook.

"Are you living out in this direction now, Miss Dent?"

"No."

She opened her purse and reached for the handkerchief. She had begun to cry. He turned his head to see if anyone in the car was looking, but no one was. He had sat beside a thousand passengers on the evening train. He had noticed their clothes, the holes in their gloves; and if they fell asleep and mumbled he had wondered what their worries were. He had classified almost all of them briefly before he buried his nose in the paper. He had marked them as rich, poor, brilliant or dull, neighbors or strangers, but no one of the thousand had ever wept. When she opened her purse, he remembered her perfume. It had clung to his skin the night he went to her place for a drink.

"I've been very sick," she said. "This is the first time I've been out of bed in two weeks. I've been terribly sick."

"I'm sorry that you've been sick, Miss Dent," he said in a voice loud enough to be heard by Mr. Watkins and Mrs. Compton. "Where are you working now?"

"What?"

"Where are you working now?"

"Oh, don't make me laugh," she said softly.

"I don't understand."

"You poisoned their minds."

He straightened his neck and braced his shoulders. These wrenching movements expressed a brief — and hopeless — longing to be in some other place. She meant trouble. He took a breath. He looked with deep feeling at the half-filled, half-lighted coach to affirm his sense of actuality, of a world in which there was not very much bad trouble after all. He was conscious of her heavy breathing and the smell of her rain-soaked coat. The train stopped. A nun and a man in overalls got off. When it started again, Blake put on his hat and reached for his raincoat.

"Where are you going?" she said.

"I'm going to the next car."

"Oh, no," she said. "No, no, no." She put her white face so close to his ear that he could feel her warm breath on his cheek. "Don't do that," she whispered. "Don't try and escape me. I have a pistol and I'll have to kill you and I don't want to. All I want to do is to talk with you. Don't move or I'll kill you. Don't, don't, don't!"

Blake sat back abruptly in his seat. If he had wanted to stand and shout for help, he would not have been able to. His tongue had swelled to twice its size, and when he tried to move it, it stuck horribly to the roof of his mouth. His legs were limp. All he could think of to do then was to wait for his heart to stop its hysterical beating, so that he could judge the extent of his danger. She was sitting a little sidewise, and in her pocketbook was the pistol, aimed at his belly.

"You understand me now, don't you?" she said. "You understand that I'm serious?" He tried to speak but he was still mute. He nodded his head. "Now we'll sit quietly for a little while," she said. "I got so excited that my thoughts are all confused. We'll sit quietly for a little while, until I can get my thoughts in order again."

Help would come, Blake thought. It was only a question of minutes. Someone, noticing the look on his face or her peculiar posture, would stop and interfere, and it would all be over. All he had to do was to wait until someone noticed his predicament. Out of the window he saw the river and the sky. The rain clouds were rolling down like a shutter, and while he watched, a streak of orange light on the horizon became brilliant. Its brilliance spread — he could see it move — across the waves until it raked the banks of the river with a dim firelight. Then it was put out. Help would come in a minute, he thought. Help would come before they stopped again; but the train stopped, there were some comings and goings, and Blake still lived on, at the mercy of the woman beside him. The possibility that help might not come was one that he could not face. The possibility that his predicament was not noticeable, that Mrs. Compton would guess that he was taking a poor relation out to dinner at Shady Hill, was something he would think about later. Then the saliva came back into his mouth and he was able to speak.

"Miss Dent?"

"Yes."

"What do you want?"

"I want to talk to you."

"You can come to my office."

"Oh, no. I went there every day for two weeks."

"You could make an appointment."

"No," she said. "I think we can talk here. I wrote you a letter but I've been too sick to go out and mail it. I've put down all my thoughts. I like to travel. I like trains. One of my troubles has always been that I could never afford to travel. I suppose you see this scenery every night and don't notice it any more, but it's nice for someone who's been in bed a long time. They say that He's not in the river and the hills but I think He is. 'Where shall wisdom be found?' it says. 'Where is the place of understanding? The depth saith it is not in me; the sea saith it is not with me. Destruction and death say we have heard the force with our ears.'

"Oh, I know what you're thinking," she said. "You're thinking that I'm crazy, and I have been very sick again but I'm going to be better. It's going to make me better to talk with you. I was in the hospital all the time before I came to work for you but they never tried to cure me, they only wanted to take away my self-respect. I haven't had any work now for three months. Even if I did have to kill you, they wouldn't be able to do anything to me except put me back in the hospital, so you see I'm not afraid. But let's sit quietly for a little while longer. I have to be calm."

The train continued its halting progress up the bank of the river, and Blake tried to force himself to make some plans for escape, but the immediate threat to his life made this difficult, and instead of planning sensibly, he thought of the many ways in which he could have avoided her in the first place. As soon as he had felt these regrets, he realized their futility. It was like regretting his lack of suspicion when she first mentioned her months in the hospital. It was like regretting his failure to have been warned by her shyness, her diffidence, and the handwriting that looked like the marks of a claw. There was no way of rectifying his mistakes, and he felt — for perhaps the first time in his mature life — the full force of regret. Out of the window, he saw some men fishing on the nearly dark river, and then a ramshackle boat club that seemed to have been nailed together out of scraps of wood that had been washed up on the shore.

Mr. Watkins had fallen asleep. He was snoring. Mrs. Compton read her paper. The train creaked, slowed, and halted infirmly at another station. Blake could see the southbound platform, where a few passengers were waiting to go into the city. There was a workman with a lunch pail, a dressed-up woman, and a woman with a suitcase. They stood apart from one another. Some advertisements were posed on the wall behind them. There was a picture of a couple drinking a toast in wine, a picture of a Cat's Paw rubber heel, and a picture of a Hawaiian dancer. Their cheerful intent seemed to go no farther than the puddles of water on the platform and to expire there. The platform and the people on it looked lonely. The train drew away from the station into the scattered lights of a slum and then into the darkness of the country and the river.

"I want you to read my letter before we get to Shady Hill," she said. "It's on the seat. Pick it up. I would have mailed it to you, but I've been too sick to go out. I haven't gone out for two weeks. I haven't had any work for three months. I haven't spoken to anybody but the landlady. Please read my letter."

He picked up the letter from the seat where she had put it. The cheap paper felt abhorrent and filthy to his fingers. It was folded and refolded. "Dear Husband," she had written, in that crazy, wandering hand, "they say that human love leads us to divine love, but is this true? I dream about you every night. I have such terrible desires. I have always had a gift for dreams. I dreamed on Tuesday of a volcano erupting with blood. When I was in the hospital they said they wanted to cure me but they only wanted to take away my self-respect. They only wanted me to dream about sewing and basketwork but I protected my gift for dreams. I'm clairvoyant. I can tell when the telephone is going to ring. I've never had a true friend in my whole life . . ."

The train stopped again. There was another platform, another picture of the couple drinking a toast, the rubber heel, and the Hawaiian dancer. Suddenly she pressed her face close to Blake's again and whispered in his ear. "I know what you're thinking. I can see it in your face. You're thinking you can get away from me in Shady Hill, aren't you? Oh, I've been planning this for weeks. It's all I've had to think about. I won't harm you if you'll let me talk. I've been thinking about devils. I mean, if there are devils in the world, if there are people in the world who represent evil, is it our duty to exterminate them? I know that you always prey on weak people. I can tell. Oh, sometimes I think I ought to kill you. Sometimes I think you're the only obstacle between me and my happiness. Sometimes . . ."

She touched Blake with the pistol. He felt the muzzle against his belly. The bullet, at that distance, would make a small hole where it entered, but it would rip out of his back a place as big as a soccer ball. He remembered the unburied dead he seen in the war. The memory came in a rush; entrails, eyes, shattered bone, ordure, and other filth.

"All I've ever wanted in life is a little love," she said. She lightened the pressure of the gun. Mr. Watkins still slept. Mrs. Compton was sitting calmly with her hands folded in her lap. The coach rocked gently, and the coats and mushroom-colored raincoats that hung between the windows swayed a little as the car moved. Blake's elbow was on the window sill and his left shoe was on the guard above the steampipe. The car smelled like some dismal classroom. The passengers seemed asleep and apart, and Blake felt that he might never escape the smell of heat and wet clothing and the dimness of the light. He tried to summon the calculated self-deceptions with which he sometimes cheered himself, but he was left without any energy for hope of self-deception.

The conductor put his head in the door and said, "Shady Hill, next, Shady Hill."

"Now," she said. "Now you get out ahead of me."

Mr. Watkins waked suddenly, put on his coat and hat, and smiled at Mrs. Compton, who was gathering her parcels to her in a series of maternal gestures. They went to the door. Blake joined them, but neither of them spoke to him or seemed to notice the woman at his back. The conductor threw open the door, and Blake saw on the platform of the next car a few other neighbors who had missed the express, waiting patiently and tiredly in the wan light for their trip to end. He raised his head to see through the open door the abandoned mansion out of town, a NO TRESPASSING sign nailed to a tree, and then the oil tanks. The concrete abutments of the bridge passed, so close to the open door that he could have touched them. Then he saw the first of the lampposts on the northbound platform, the sign SHADY HILL in black and gold, and the little lawn and flower bed kept up by the Improvement Association, and then the cab stand and a corner of the old-fashioned depot. It was raining again; it was pouring. He could hear the splash of water and see the lights reflected in puddles and in the shining pavement, and the idle sound of splashing and dripping formed in his mind a conception of shelter, so light and strange that it seemed to belong to a time of his life that he could not remember.

He went down the steps with her at his back. A dozen or so cars were waiting by the station with their motors running. A few people got off from each of the other coaches; he recognized most of them, but none of them offered to give him a ride. They walked separately or in pairs — purposefully out of the rain to the shelter of the platform, where the car horns called to them. It was time to go home, time for a drink, time for love, time for supper, and he could see the lights on the hill — lights by which children were being bathed, meat cooked, dishes washed — shining in the rain. One by one, the cars picked up the heads of families, until there were only four left. Two of the stranded passengers drove off in the only taxi the village had. "I'm sorry, darling," a woman said tenderly to her husband when she drove up a few minutes later. "All our clocks are slow." The last man looked at his watch, looked at the rain, and then walked off into it, and Blake saw him go as if they had some reason to say goodbye — not as we say goodbye to friends after a party but as we say goodbye when we are faced with an inexorable and unwanted parting of the spirit and the heart. The man's footsteps sounded as he crossed the parking lot to the sidewalk, and then they were lost. In the station, a telephone began to ring. The ringing was loud, evenly spaced, and unanswered. Someone wanted to know about the next train to Albany, but Mr. Flanagan, the stationmaster, had gone home an hour ago. He had turned on all his lights before he went away. They burned in the empty waiting room. They burned, tin-shaded, at intervals up and down the platform and with the peculiar sadness of dim and purposeless lights. They lighted the Hawaiian dancer, the couple drinking a toast, the rubber heel.

"I've never been here before," she said. "I thought it would look different. I didn't think it would look so shabby. Let's get out of the light. Go over there."

His legs felt sore. All his strength was gone. "Go on," she said.

North of the station there were a freight house and a coalyard and an inlet where the butcher and the baker and the man who ran the service station moored the dinghies, from which they fished on Sundays, sunk now to the gunwales with the rain. As he walked toward the freight house, he saw a movement on the ground and heard a scraping sound, and then he saw a rat take its head out of a paper bag and regard him. The rat seized the bag in its teeth and dragged it into a culvert.

"Stop," she said. "Turn around. Oh, I ought to feel sorry for you. Look at your poor face. But you don't know what I've been through. I'm afraid to go out in the daylight. I'm afraid the blue sky will fall down on me. I'm like poor Chicken-Licken. I only feel like myself when it begins to get dark. But still and all I'm better than you. I still have good dreams sometimes. I dream about picnics and heaven and the brotherhood of man, and about castles in the moonlight and a river with willow trees all along the edge of it and foreign cities, and after all I know more about love than you."

He heard from off the dark river the drone of an outboard motor, a sound that drew slowly behind it across the dark water such a burden of clear, sweet memories of gone summers and gone pleasures that it made his flesh crawl, and he thought of dark in the mountains and the children singing. "They never wanted to cure me," she said. "They . . ." The noise of a train coming down from the north drowned out her voice, but she went on talking. The noise filled his ears, and the windows where people ate, drank, slept, and read flew past. When the train had passed beyond the bridge, the noise grew distant, and he heard her screaming at him, "*Kneel down!* Kneel down! Do what I say. *Kneel down!*"

He got to his knees. He bent his head. "There," she said. "You see, if you do what I say, I won't harm you, because I really don't want to harm you, I want to help you, but when I see your face it sometimes seems to me that I can't help you. Sometimes it seems to me that if I were good and loving and sane — oh, much better than I am — sometimes it seems to me that if I were all these things and young and beautiful, too, and if I called to show you the right way, you wouldn't heed me. Oh, I'm better than you, I'm better than you, and I shouln't waste my time or spoil my life like this. Put your face in the dirt. *Put your face in the dirt!* Do what I say. Put your face in the dirt."

He fell forward in the filth. The coal skinned his face. He stretched out on the ground, weeping. "Now I feel better," she said. "Now I can wash my hands of you, I can wash my hands of all this, because you see there is some kindness, some saneness in me that I can find and use. I can wash my hands." Then he heard her footsteps go away from him, over the rubble. He heard the clearer and more distant sound they made on the hard surface of the platform. He heard them diminish. He raised his head. He saw her climb the stairs of the wooden footbridge and cross it and go down to the other platform, where her figure in the dim light looked small, common, and harmless. He raised himself out of the dust — warily at first, until he saw by her attitude, her looks, that she had forgotten him; that she had completed what she had wanted to do, and that he was safe. He got to his feet and picked up his hat from the ground where it had fallen and walked home.

MARY LAVIN

1912—

*Though no one could write stories more Irish than hers, Mary Lavin did
not see Ireland until she was ten. At that time she moved from her birthplace, East Walpole, Massachusetts, to her parents' native land. She was
educated at Loreto Convent and University College, both of Dublin. After
her first husband's death she and her three daughters worked their County
Meath farm; her familiarity with rural life is reflected in many of her tales,
collected in several volumes.*

In the preface to her Selected Stories *she writes: "I . . . wish that I could
break up the two long novels I have written into the few short stories they
ought to have been." The statement reflects one's sense that the short story
is the form most ideally suited to the Irish imaginative genius. This circumstance is in past ascribed to the oral tradition so integral to Irish life. The
mass of Irish men and women prize language as much as the mass of Americans misprize it. It is for them the natural form in which personality may
express itself.*

*V. S. Pritchett thinks Mary Lavin "a great short story writer." Certainly
she is a fine one. Without relying too heavily on the three staple themes —
religion, politics, and strong drink — she deals, always with a moral ele-
vation that reminds one of George Eliot, with manifold variations of Irish
experience. "The Living" is rooted in Irish language rhythms, Irish pieties,
and Irish mercurial emotion. But it deals with common matters — life and
death. These "terrible, terrible words" are seen as they impinge, all mixed
up, on the confused but alert consciousness of a small boy. The assumption
of this unusual viewpoint lends a certain transfixing truth to "The Living."*

The Living

"HOW MANY dead people do you know?" said Mickser suddenly.

Immediately, painfully, I felt my answer would show me once more his inferior.

"Do you mean ghosts?" I said slowly, to gain time.

"No," said Mickser, "I mean corpses."

"But don't they get buried?" I cried.

"They're not buried for three days," said Mickser, scathingly. "They have to be scrubbed and laid out and waked. You're not allowed to keep them any longer than that, though, because their eyes go like this," and he put up his hands to his eyes and drew down the lower lids to show the inner lids swimming with watery blood. "They rot," he explained, succinctly.

"Mind would you fall!" said I, hastily, thinking he might let go his eyelids if he had to steady himself on the gate post.

We were sitting one on each pier of the big gate posts at the school-house that was down on the main road. We were supposed to be sitting there watching the cars coming home from the Carlow and Kerry foot-ball finals. But it wasn't much fun. As Mickser said, it was only the family man that came home straight after a match. The real followers, by which he meant the enthusiasts, didn't come home till near night; or near morning, maybe! And they were the only ones it was any sport to watch.

"Those ones have no drink taken," said Mickser, contemptuously, of the cars that were going past at the time. "It's great sport when the drunks are coming home. Passing each other out on the roads; on the corners, mind! But your mammy wouldn't let you stay out long enough for that."

It was only too true. It was a wonder she let me down to the road at all. You'd think she knew there'd be no fun in it. She had a terrible dread of fun, my mammy. She always saw danger in it.

"You can go down to the schoolhouse and look at the cars coming home if you're careful. And mind yourself!" she said to me. "Keep well in from the road! And wait a minute. Don't sit up on that high wall the way I saw you doing once."

That was why we were up on the gate posts, although they were much higher than the wall.

"Gate posts isn't walls," said Mickser, definitely.

That was Mickser all over. You could count on him to get you out of anything. But he could get you into anything too! You never knew where a word would lead you with him. This talk about dead people seemed safe enough though.

"How many do you know, Mickser?" I asked, fearful, but fascinated.

"Oh, I couldn't count them," said Mickser, loftily. "I bet you don't know any at all."

"My grandfather's dead."

"How long is he dead?"

"He died the year I was born," I said. "On the very day after," I added, importantly, having heard it told by my mother to many people.

"Bah!" said Mickser. "You can't count him. If you could, then you could count your great-grandfather and your great-great-grandfather and your great-great-great-grandfather and —" but he stopped enumerating them suddenly as a more vivid denunciation of my foolishness occurred to him. "Isn't the ground full of dead people that nobody knew?" He pointed down below us to where, through the nettles, the clay under the wall showed black and sour. "If you took up a spade this minute," he said, "and began digging down there, or anywhere you liked, you'd be no time digging till you'd come on bones; somebody's bones! Oh no!" He shook his head. "You can't count people you didn't *see* dead, like my Uncle Bat, that was sitting up eating a boiled egg one minute, and lying back dead the next minute. He's the best one on my list though," he added, magnanimously. "I saw him alive *and* dead. But most of them I only saw dead, like my two aunts that died within a week of each other. Everyone said it was a pity if they had to go it couldn't have been closer together, so we could have made the one wake of it. But if they did I might have to count them as one. What do you think?" He didn't wait for an answer. "How many is that?" he asked. "How many have I now?"

"Only three," I said, and my heart rose. He mightn't be able to think of any more.

Not a chance of it. He looked at me severely. He was a bit of a mind reader as well as everything else. "I want to pick out the good ones for first," he said.

That overwhelmed me altogether.

"Ah sure, Mickser," I said, frankly and fairly, "you needn't strain yourself thinking of good ones for me, because I never saw one at all. One of my aunts died a year ago all right, and they had to take me to the funeral because they had no one to leave me with, but they wouldn't let me into the house till the funeral was ready to move off. They took it in turns to sit out in the car with me."

"And what was that for?" said Mickser, looking blankly at me.

"I don't know," I said, in a grieved voice, but after a bit, in fairness to my mother and father, I felt obliged to hazard a reason for their behavior. Maybe they thought I'd be dreaming of it in my sleep!

"Not that it did much good keeping me outside," I said, "because I dreamt about it all the same. I kept them up till morning, nightmaring about coffins and hearses!"

"Did you?" said Mickser, genuinely interested, but baffled too, I could see. "Coffins and hearses," he reflected. "What was there about them to have you nightmaring? It's corpses that give people the creeps." He looked at me with further interest, with curiosity. "I wonder what way you'd take on if you saw a corpse!" he said. And then suddenly he snapped his fingers together. "I have it!" he said. "There's a wake in a cottage the other side of the town."

"Mind would you fall," I cried, urgently this time, because there looked to be every danger of it with the way he was hopping about with excitement.

"Do you know the cottage I mean? It's at the level crossing. Do you know the woman in it, the one that opens and shuts the railway gates? Well, her son is dead. Did you know that? Did you ever see him?"

"A big fellow with red hair, is it?"

"That's the one," he cried. "She used to have him sitting outside the cottage most days on a chair in the sun. He was a class of delicate" — deftly Mickser tapped his own pate. "Up here," he said. "Did you know that? Well, he's dead now anyway. He died this morning. Isn't it a bit of luck I was put in mind of it?"

"This is your chance of having one corpse, anyway, for your list. But we'd want to get there quick," he said, taking one jump down off the gate-pier, into the nettles and all without minding them any more than if he were a dog. "We'll have to get down there before the crowds. They'll be glad to see us no matter who we are, if we're the first to come. They're always glad to see the first signs of people arriving, after the cleaning and scrubbing they've been at all night. And they love to see children above all — at first, that is to say. 'Look who we have here,' they say," he mimicked, in a voice that nearly made myself fall off the pier. " 'Bless their little hearts,' " he went on. " 'Come in, child,' they say, and they lead you inside, telling each other that there's no prayers like the prayers of a child. Up they bring you straight to the bed, and down they put you kneeling beside it where you can get a good gawk at everything. Oh, but it's a different story altogether, I can tell you, if you leave it till late in the evening. They've got wise to things by then, and you haven't a chance of getting inside the door. 'Out of this with you, you little brats.' That's all you'd hear then. 'This is no place for children — out of it, quick!' They'd take the yard brush to you if you didn't get yourself out of sight double quick. So we'd better go up there immediately. What are you waiting for?"

I was hanging back for more reasons than one.

"I was told to stay here," I said.

"You were told not to be climbing too," said Mickser, as keen as a lawyer. "So you can't say you were doing what you were told, anyway.

Not but that it's doing all you're told to do that has you the way you are this day, knowing nothing about anything. Come on out of that, and I'll show you a bit of what's going on round you, or if you don't, I'd dread to think how you'll end up in the finish. Sure fathers and mothers are the worst people in the world to depend on for finding out the least thing. They're all out for keeping us back. I've proved that many a time with my own ones. And there's yourself!" he cried. "To think they wouldn't let you see your own aunt laid out! I know it wouldn't be me that would be done out of a thing like that. And what's more, you oughtn't to put up with it either. You ought to tell them there'd be no nightmaring or carrying on about corpses if you were let get used to them like me. Are you coming, or are you not?"

It was a sweet, mild afternoon as we set out for the edge of the town to where the level crossing was, and the small slated house to one side of it. It was very familiar to me when I was a bit smaller and my mother used to take me for a walk out of the town into the country air. We often had to wait for the gates to be opened for us, although the train would have thundered past.

"What is the delay?" my mother would ask impatiently.

"I have to wait for the signals, ma'am," the woman in charge would say. "You can pass through the wicket gate if you like, ma'am, but that's none of my responsibility."

"Oh, we're in no hurry," my mother would say hastily, no doubt to give me good example.

But there was no need. I had heard Mickser say he put a half-penny on the line one day and the train made a penny out of it. I had no fancy for being flattened out to the size of a man. And anyway, I used to be very curious about the big, white-faced boy that used to be sitting in the little bit of garden outside the house on a chair; a chair brought out of the parlor, not one you'd leave outside like we had in the garden at home.

"Does she take it in at night?" I asked.

"Of course she does," said my mother, in a shocked voice, but she must have thought I meant the boy. "Please don't stare," she'd say to me. "Why do I always have to tell you the same thing fifty times?"

Only when the gates were opened, and we were crossing over the rails, would she let on to see him for her part. It was always the same.

"How is he today?" she'd ask the woman.

And the woman's answer was always the same too.

"Poorly." At times, but rarely, she'd add a few words. "It's a great cross to me, but I suppose God knows what He's doing."

"We must hope so anyway," my mother would say hastily, and she'd step over the rails more quickly till we were on the other side. "How is it," she'd say testily to me, "those gates are always shut no matter what time of the day we want to pass?"

And now here, today, for the first time in my life, the railway gates were wide open.

"Do you think they might have forgot to close them on account of the wake?" I said, hanging back nervously as Mickser dashed over the shining tracks.

He stood in the middle of the line and looked back at me.

"God knows it's high time someone took you in hand," he said. "You're nothing but an old babby. What harm would it be if they did forget? Haven't you eyes? Haven't you ears? And if it comes to that, haven't you legs? Come on out of that!" But he slowed down himself and looked up and down the line.

"We're the first here," he said, when we got to the cottage. "They're not finished yet," he said, expertly sizing up the look of the little house.

To me it was like as if it had been washed down from top to bottom like I was washed down myself every Saturday night, and not only the house, but the bit of garden outside it was the same, neatened and tidied, and the big stones that I used to remark around the flower beds keeping back the clay from the grass, were whitewashed every one of them! It was a treat: the stones bright white and the clay bright black with not one weed to be seen out of all the weeds there used to be everywhere. But the chair wasn't out!

"We're too early, maybe." Suddenly Mickser sidestepped over to the window that was to the left of the door. I couldn't see near so well as him, being behind him, but I saw enough to open my mouth. Between white counterpanes and white tablecloths and white mantlecloths and white doilies, the place was got up like the chapel at Lady Day. And, in the middle of it all, like the high altar, was a big bed with a counterpane as white and glossy as marble and —

But Mickser didn't let me see any more. He pulled me away.

"I don't think they're ready yet," he said. He seemed to be losing courage just as I was getting mine. He put his hands in his pockets and sauntered toward the door.

"There now, what did I tell you," he cried, as we only missed getting drenched to the skin by a big basin of slops that was sloshed out the door at that minute. "Did you ever go down the line? he asked suddenly. And I knew he'd let up altogether on going to the wake.

"I'm not allowed to walk on the line," I said. Anyway, I was bent on seeing the bed better, and what was on it. "Let me get a look in the window anyway." I skipped back over the flower bed and pasted my face to the glass.

What did I expect to see? I don't know. Not the full-grown man that was carved out on the bed, hard as stone, all but his red hair. The hair was real looking, like the hair on a doll.

"Eh Mickser. Could you give me a leg-up on the window sill?" I cried, getting more and more curious and excited.

"Are you pots?" said Mickser. "If they came out and caught you up on that windowsill you'd be clouted out of here with one of those stones," and he kicked at one of the big white stones, leaving the black track of his boot on it.

"A true word if ever there was one!" said a voice at that moment, and a thin bit of a woman in black came round the gable end with her sleeves rolled up and no smile on her, I can tell you. "Out of here with you!" she shouted. "This is no place for you!" Just the very thing Mickser said wouldn't be said to us.

But before we had time to get out of the flower bed, another woman came running out of the front door — the woman herself that used to have charge of the crossing gates.

"It's not right to send anyone from the door of a dead-house," she said, dully.

"Hush now; they're only gossoons," said the other one.

"He was only a gossoon too," said our woman. "Only a child. That's what the priest said to me many a time. Not that he ever had any child-hood, any real childhood." She lost the dull look for a minute; a lively look came into her face. "Isn't that strange," she said, "I never thought of it before, but he was like an old man when he ought to have been a babby; and he was nothing but a babby when he ought to have been a man. I did my best, but it was no use. And you can't do everything, isn't that true? He'd have liked to have other children to keep him company, but they wouldn't understand."

We weren't sure if it was to us or the other woman she was talking. I wanted to say that I'd have kept him company, but that I didn't know if my mother would allow me. And as that didn't sound very polite, I said nothing. It was good I did, because I think it was to the other woman she was talking.

"There now! there now!" said the other one. "Isn't it better God took him before yourself anyway?"

"I used to pray He would," said the woman, "but now I'm not so sure. Wasn't it the unnatural thing to have to pray for anyway? Don't all women pray for the opposite; to die before them and not be a burden on them, and wasn't it a hard thing to have to bring them into the world only to pray for them to be taken out of it? Oh, it's little you know about it, and if there was a woman standing here in front of me, and she had the same story, I'd say the same thing to her. Isn't it little anyone knows about what goes on inside another person?"

She was getting a bit wild looking, and the other woman began drag-ging at her to get her back into the house. "Hush now, you'll feel differ-ent when time goes on."

"Will I?" said the mother, looking wonderingly at the other one. "That's what's said to everyone, but is it true? I'll feel different, maybe, sometimes when I look at the clock and have to pull off my apron and run out to throw back the gates. I'll feel different, maybe, when some woman stops to have a word with me, or when I have to take the jug and go down the road for a sup of milk. But in the middle of the night, or first thing when the jackdaws start talking in the chimney and wake me out of my sleep, will I feel different then? And what if I do forget?" she cried, suddenly pulling her arm free from the other woman. "I'll have nothing at all then! It will be like as if I never had him at all." She put her hand up to her head at that and began brushing her hair back from her forehead.

Stepping behind her back, the woman that wanted to be rid of us, started making signs at us to make off with ourselves, but it was too late. The dead man's mother started forward and caught us by the hands.

"We must make the most of every minute we have him," she cried. "Come inside and see him." She pushed us in the doorway. "Kneel down and say a prayer for him," she commanded, pushing us down on our knees, but her voice was wonderfully gentle now where it had been wild. "He was never able to pray for himself," she said, softly, "but God must listen to the prayers of children if He listens to nothing else. I used to long for him to be able to say one little prayer, and I was always trying to teach him, but he couldn't learn. When he'd be sitting out in the sun on his chair, I used to show him the flowers and tell him God made them. And do you know all he'd say?" — she gave a little laugh before she told us — " 'Who's that fellow?' he'd say! And he'd look round to see if He was behind him! But the priest said God wouldn't heed him; he said he'd make allowances for him. I sometimes think God must have a lot to put up with no more than ourselves. That's why we've no right to complain against Him."

But I wasn't listening. When she put us kneeling down, I put up my hands to my face and I started to say my prayers, but after a minute or two I opened my fingers and took a look out through them at the man on the bed. I was a bit confused. Why was she saying he was a child? He was a man if ever I saw one! Just then the woman swooped down on me. She saw me looking at him. I thought she might be mad with me, but it was the opposite.

"If only he could see you here now beside him," she said. She leaned across me and began to stroke his hands. And she began to talk to him, instead of to us. "Here's two nice little boys come to see you!" she said, and then her eyes got very bright and wild again. "He never had another child come into the house to see him in all his life. He never had another child as much as put out a hand and touch him, isn't that a lonely thing to think?"

It was indeed, I thought. I wonder would it be any use me shaking hands with him now, I thought. And it might be she saw the thought in my eyes.

"Would it be asking too much of you to stroke his hand?" she said, and then, as if she settled it in her own mind that it wouldn't be asking much at all, she got very excited. "Stand up like good boys," she said, "and stroke his hands. Then I won't feel he's going down into his grave so altogether unnatural. No; wait a minute," she cried, and she got another idea, and she delved her hand into her pocket. "How would you like to comb his hair?" she cried.

I was nearer to the head of the bed than Mickser, but Mickser was nearer to her than me, and I couldn't be sure which of us she meant. I wanted above all to be polite, but for that again I didn't want to put myself forward in any way. I stood up in any case so as to be ready if it was me she meant. She was taking a few big red hairs off the comb. Mickser stood up too, but it was only to give me a shove out of his way.

"Let me out of here!" he shouted, and pushing the woman and me to either side of him, he bolted for the door. The next minute he was flying across the lines.

And me after him. I told you I wanted to be polite to the people, the dead one included, but after all it was Mickser brought me, and it wouldn't be very polite to him to stay on after him. Not that he showed any appreciation, but I thought maybe there was something wrong with him: he was very white in the face when I caught up with him.

I was full of talk.

"Well! I have one for my list anyway, now," I said, cheerfully.

"I suppose you have," he said, kind of grudgingly, I thought, and then he nearly spoiled it all on me. "That one oughtn't to count by rights," he said. "He wasn't all in it when he was alive; he was sort of dead all along!" He tapped his pate again like he did the first time. "Up here!" he added.

I thought about that for a minute. "He looked all in it there on the bed!" I said.

But Mickser didn't seem to take well to talking about him at all. "I've had enough of corpses."

You don't know how sorry I was to hear that, and I wondering when we'd get a chance to go to another wake.

"You're not done with them altogether, are you, Mickser?"

"I am," said Mickser, flatly. "Come on back to the main road. The cars are coming along good-o now. Can't you hear them? Some of those boyos have a few jars in them, I'd say, in spite of the wives." He looked expertly into the sky. "There'll maybe be a fog later on, and in that case the lot will be coming home early; the drunks and all! Come on!"

"Ah, you can go and watch them yourself," I said. "I'm going home."

The truth was I was too excited to sit on any wall for long. I wanted to go home because there were a few things I'd like to find out from my mother, if I could bring the talk around to the topic of corpses without letting on where I got the information I had already.

As I ran off from Mickser across the fields for home, I felt that I was a new man. The next time there was a funeral I felt sure there would be no need to leave me sitting out in a car. I felt sure they would all notice a change in me when I went into the house.

"Wipe your feet, son," my mother cried out to me through the open door of the kitchen, the minute I came in sight. She was often scrubbing the floor. "Not that you'd be the only one to put tracks all over the place," she said, and I could see what she meant, because there, in the middle of the floor, was my brother's old bike, upended, with the wheels in the air, resting on its saddle, and he busy mending a puncture. Or was it my father she meant? Because he was sitting the other side of the fire with his feet in a basin of water.

It must have been my father she meant, because she lit on him just then. "This is no place for washing your feet," she said. "There's a fire inside in the parlor. Why don't you go in there and wash them? I haven't got room to turn around with you all."

"The parlor is no place for washing feet," said my father, quietly, and he pointed to the bike in the middle of the floor. "When that fellow's done with that bike you'll be glad to have a bit of water on the floor to swish out the mess he'll have made. Why don't you make him take it out in the yard?"

My mother sighed. She was always sighing, but they weren't the kind of sighs you'd heed. They were caused by something we'd done on her, all right, but they were sighs of patience, if you know what I mean, and not complaint.

"It's a bit cold outside," she said. But she turned to me. "Here, you, son," she said, and she picked up my satchel and shoved it under my arm. "Let you set a good example and go into the parlor and do your homework there by the nice fire."

But I wasn't going into the empty parlor.

"Dear *knows!*" she said. "I don't know why I waste my time lighting that fire every day and none of you ever set foot in there until it's nearly night. I only wish I could go in and sit by it. Then I'd leave you the kitchen and welcome."

But I think she knew well that if she was to go in there that minute, it wouldn't be many minutes more till we'd all be in there along with her, myself and my satchel, and my father with his feet in the basin, and the old bike as well if it could be squeezed in at all between the piano and the chiffonier and those other big useless pieces of furniture that were kept in there out of the way.

"Ah sure, aren't we all right here," said my father, "where we can be looking at you?"

"You must have very little worth looking at if you want to be looking at me," said my mother, in a sort of voice I knew well that sounded cross but couldn't be, because she always stretched up when she spoke like that, so she'd see into the little mirror on the mantel shelf and she always smiled at what she saw in the glass. And well she might. She always looked pretty, my mother, but she used to look best of all when we were all around her in the kitchen, annoying her and making her cheeks red with the fuss of keeping us in order.

"Mind would you catch your finger in the spokes of that wheel!" she cried just then to my brother.

"Mind would you catch your hair in it, my girl," said Father, because as the kettle boiled and the little kitchen got full of steam, her hair used to loosen and lop around her face like a young girl's. And he caught a hold of her as if to pull her back from the bike.

"Let go of me," she cried. "Will you never get sense?"

"I hope not," said my father, "and what is more, I don't want you to get too much either."

"Oh, go on with you and your old talk, before the boys and all," she cried, and then she tried harder to drag herself free.

"She's not as strong as her tongue would have us believe, boys," said my father, tightening his hold. And then he laughed. "You'll never be the man I am!" he said, and this time it was my mother herself that giggled, although I didn't see anything specially funny in it.

And that very minute, in the middle of tricking and laughing, my father's face changed and it was like as if he wasn't holding her for fun at all, but the way he'd hold us if he had something against us.

"You're feeling all right these days, aren't you?" he cried. "You'd tell me if you weren't, wouldn't you?" And then, suddenly, he let her go, and put his hands up to his head. "Oh, my God, what would I do if anything happened to you!" he said.

"Such talk!" said my mother again, but her voice sounded different too, and although she was free she didn't ask to move away, but stood there beside him, with such a sad look on her face I suddenly wanted to cry.

And all I had wanted to ask her about the poor fellow at the level crossing came back into my mind. But I didn't feel like asking her then at all. And do you know what came into my mind? It was the words of the prayers we said every night.

". . . the living and the dead . . ." Over and over we'd said them, night after night, and I never paid any heed. But I suddenly felt that they were terrible, terrible words, and if we were to be kneeling down at that moment saying them, I couldn't bear it: I'd start nightmaring, there and then, in the middle of them all, with the lamps lit, and it not dark.

But the kettle began to spit on the range, and my mother ran over and lifted it back from the blaze.

"How about us taking our tea in the parlor?" she cried. "All of us. The kitchen is no fitter than the backyard with you!"

And in the excitement, I forgot all about the living and the dead. For a time.

WILLIAM SANSOM

1912–1970

Over a thirty-five-year period William Sansom wrote some half dozen novels, travel books, a biography of Proust, and five volumes of short stories. His work has had little impact on the American reading public, and although greatly admired by good judges in his native Britain, perhaps not a great deal more there. Not having read them, I cannot speak for his novels, but his short stories deserve far more recognition than they have won.

In her introduction to his collected best work Elizabeth Bowen identifies the core of his curious talent: "The substance of a Sansom story is sensation." The broad human touch of a Pritchett or a Trevor is not his. His aim is to render a scene, a moment, a predicament by transferring to the reader's imagination what his own almost painfully alert five senses have perceived. He works most effectively with visual images: "I am a painter manqué."

He seems to have been drawn in large part to situations involving terror or the bizarre or the agonizing approach of some inevitable calamity. His best-known story, "The Wall," derives from his World War II experience in London as a member of the Auxiliary Fire Service. It is simply an account of the fall of a blazing building as some firefighters try to handle the conflagration. It sounds like the sort of challenge daily presented to a newspaper reporter, but Sansom makes out of it something Poe or Bierce would have been proud to sign.

Sansom is a master of slow motion, gaining his effects by pure concentration on the moment or even fraction of a moment. In "The Vertical Ladder" we are, like poor Flegg, pinned on the ladder forever, to all eternity. We are compelled to suffer a nightmare occurring in the real world. That is all he is concerned to create, but he creates it completely.

The Vertical Ladder

As HE FELT the first watery eggs of sweat moistening the palms of his hands, as with every rung higher his body seemed to weigh more heavily, this young man Flegg regretted in sudden desperation but still in vain, the irresponsible events that had thrust him up into his present precarious climb. Here he was, isolated on a vertical iron ladder flat to the side of a gasometer and bound to climb higher and higher until he should reach the vertiginous skyward summit.

How could he ever have wished this on himself? How easy it had been to laugh away his cautionary fears on the firm ground . . . now he would give the very hands that clung to the ladder for a safe conduct to solid earth.

It had been a strong spring day, abruptly as warm as midsummer. The sun flooded the parks and streets with sudden heat — Flegg and his friends had felt stifled in their thick winter clothes. The green glare of the new leaves everywhere struck the eye too fiercely, the air seemed almost sticky from the exhalations of buds and swelling resins. Cold winter senses were overcome — the girls had complained of headaches — and their thoughts had grown confused and uncomfortable as the wool underneath against their skins. They had wandered out from the park by a back gate, into an area of back streets.

The houses there were small and old, some of them already falling into disrepair; short streets, cobbles, narrow pavements, and the only shops a tobacconist or a desolate corner oil-shop to colour the grey — it was the outcrop of some industrial undertaking beyond. At first these quiet, almost deserted streets had seemed more restful than the park; but soon a dusty air of peeling plaster and powdering brick, the dark windows and the dry stone steps, the very dryness altogether had proved more wearying than before, so that when suddenly the houses ended and the ground opened to reveal the yards of a disused gasworks, Flegg and his friends had welcomed the green of nettles and milkwort that grew among the scrap-iron and broken brick.

They walked out into the wasteland, the two girls and Flegg and the other two boys, and stood presently before the old gasometer itself. Among the ruined sheds this was the only erection still whole, it still predominated over the yards, towering high above other buildings for hundreds of feet around. So they threw bricks against its rusted sides.

The rust flew off in flakes and the iron rang dully. Flegg, who wished to excel in the eyes of the dark-haired girl, began throwing his bricks higher than the others, at the same time lobbing them, to suggest that he knew something of grenade-throwing, claiming for himself vicariously the glamour of a uniform. He felt the girl's eyes follow his shoulders, his shoulders broadened. She had black eyes, unshadowed beneath short wide-awake lids, as bright as a boy's eyes; her lips pouted with difficulty over a scramble of irregular teeth, so that it often looked as if she were laughing; she always frowned — and Flegg liked her earnest, purposeful expression. Altogether she seemed a wide-awake girl who would be the first to appreciate an active sort of a man. Now she frowned and shouted: "Bet you can't climb as high as you can throw!"

Then there began one of those uneasy jokes, innocent at first, that taken seriously can accumulate an hysterical accumulation of spite. Everyone recognizes this underlying unpleasantness, it is plainly felt; but just because of this the joke must at all costs be pressed forward, one becomes frightened, one laughs all the louder, pressing to drown the embarrassments of danger and guilt. The third boy had instantly shouted: "Course he can't, he can't climb no higher than himself."

Flegg turned round scoffing, so that the girl had quickly shouted again, laughing shrilly and pointing upwards. Already all five of them felt uneasy. Then in quick succession, all in a few seconds, the third boy had repeated: "Course he bloody can't." Flegg had said: "Climb to the top of anything." The other boy had said: "Climb to the top of my aunt Fanny." The girl had said: "Climb to the top of the gasworks then."

Flegg had said: "That's nothing." And the girl, pressing on then as she had to, suddenly introduced the inevitable detail that made these suppositions into fact: "Go on then, climb it. Here — tie my hanky on the top. Tie my flag to the top."

Even then Flegg had a second's chance. It occurred to him instantly that he could laugh it off; but an hysterical emphasis now possessed the girl's face — she was dancing up and down and clapping her hands insistently — and this confused Flegg. He began stuttering after the right words. But the words refused to come. At all costs he had to cover his stuttering. So: "Off we go then!" he had said. And he had turned to the gasometer.

It was not, after all, so very high. It was hardly a full-sized gasometer, its trellised iron top-rail would have stood level with the roof-coping of a five- or six-storey tenement. Until then Flegg had only seen the gasometer as a rough mass of iron, but now every detail sprang into abrupt definition. He studied it intently, alertly considering its size and every feature of stability, the brown rusted iron sheeting smeared here and there with red lead, a curious buckling that sometimes deflated its curved bulk as though a vacuum were collapsing it from within, and the ladders scaling the sides flush with the sheeting. The grid of girders, a complexity of struts, the bolting.

There were two ladders, one a Jacob's ladder, clamped fast to the side, another that was more of a staircase, zigzagging up the belly of the gas-ometer in easy gradients and provided with a safety rail. This must have been erected later as a substitute for the Jacob's ladder, which demanded an unnecessarily stringent climb and was now in fact in disuse, for some twenty feet of its lower rungs had been worn away; however, there was apparently some painting in progress, for a wooden painter's ladder had been propped beneath with its head reaching to the undamaged bottom of the vertical ladder — the ascent was thus serviceable again. Flegg looked quickly at the foot of the wooden ladder — was it well grounded? — and then at the head farther up — was this secure? — and then up to the top, screwing his eyes to note any fault in the iron rungs reaching immediately and indistinctly, like the dizzying strata of a zip, to the summit platform.

Flegg, rapidly assessing these structures, never stopped sauntering for-ward. He was committed, and so while deliberately sauntering to appear thus the more at ease, he knew that he must never hesitate. The two boys and his own girl kept up a chorus of encouraging abuse. "How I climbed Mount Everest," they shouted. "He'll come down quicker'n he went up." "Mind you don't bang your head on a harp, Sir Galahad." But the second girl had remained quiet throughout; she was already frightened, sensing instantly that the guilt for some tragedy was hers alone — although she had never in fact opened her mouth. Now she chewed passionately on gum that kept her jaws firm and circling.

Suddenly the chorus rose shriller. Flegg had veered slightly towards the safer staircase. His eyes had naturally questioned this along with the rest of the gasometer, and almost unconsciously his footsteps had veered in the direction of his eyes; then this instinct had emerged into full con-sciousness — perhaps he could use the staircase, no one had actually instanced the Jacob's ladder, there might yet be a chance? But the quick eyes behind him had seen, and immediately the chorus rose: "No you don't!" "Not up those sissy stairs!" Flegg switched his course by only the fraction that turned him again to the perpendicular ladder. "Who's talking about stairs?" he shouted back.

Behind him they still kept up a din, still kept him up to pitch, worrying at him viciously. "Look at him, he doesn't know which way to go — he's like a ruddy duck's uncle without an aunt."

So that Flegg realized finally that there was no alternative. He had to climb the gasometer by the vertical ladder. And as soon as this was fi-nally settled, the doubt cleared from his mind. He braced his shoulders and suddenly found himself really making light of the job. After all, he thought, it isn't so high? Why should I worry? Hundreds of men climb such ladders each day, no one falls, the ladders are clamped as safe as houses? He began to smile within himself at his earlier perturbations. Added to this, the girl now ran up to him and handed him her handker-chief. As her black eyes frowned a smile at him, he saw that her expression no longer held its vicious laughing scorn, but now instead had grown softer, with a look of real encouragement and even admiration. "Here's your flag," she said. And then she even added: "Tell you what — you don't really have to go! I'll believe you!" But this came too late. Flegg had accepted the climb, it was fact, and already he felt something of an exhilarating glow of glory. He took the handkerchief, blew the girl a dramatic kiss, and started up the lowest rungs of the ladder at a run.

This painter's ladder was placed at a comfortable slant. But nevertheless Flegg had only climbed some ten feet — what might have corresponded to the top of a first-floor window — when he began to slow up, he stopped running and gripped harder at the rungs above and placed his feet more firmly on the unseen bars below. Although he had not yet measured his distance from the ground, somehow he sensed distinctly that he was already unnaturally high, with nothing but air and a precarious skeleton of wooden bars between him and the receding ground. He felt independent of solid support; yet, according to his eyes, which stared straight forward at the iron sheeting beyond, he might have been still standing on the lowest rungs by the ground. The sensation of height infected him strongly, it had become an urgent necessity to maintain a balance, each muscle of his body became unnaturally alert. This was not an unpleasant feeling, he almost enjoyed a new athletic command of every precarious movement. He climbed then methodically until he reached the ladderhead and the first of the perpendicular iron rungs.

Here for a moment Flegg had paused. He had rested his knees up against the last three steps of the safely slanting wooden ladder, he had grasped the two side supports of the rusted iron that led so straightly upwards. His knees then clung to the motherly wood, his hands felt the iron cold and gritty. The rust powdered off and smeared him with its red dust; one large scrap flaked off and fell on to his face as he looked upwards. He wanted to brush this away from his eye, but the impulse was, to his surprise, much less powerful than the vice-like will that clutched his hands to the iron support. His hand remained firmly gripping the iron, he had to shake off the rust-flake with a jerk of his head. Even then this sharp movement nearly unbalanced him, and his stomach gulped coldly with sudden shock. He settled his knees more firmly against the wood, and though he forced himself to laugh at this sudden fear, so that in some measure his poise did really return, nevertheless he did not alter the awkward knock-kneed position of his legs patently clinging for safety. With all this he had scarcely paused. Now he pulled at the staunchions of the iron ladder, they were as firm as if they had been driven into rock.

He looked up, following the dizzying rise of the rungs to the skyline. From this angle flat against the iron sheeting, the gasometer appeared higher than before. The blue sky seemed to descend and almost touch it. The redness of the rust dissolved into a deepening grey shadow, the distant curved summit loomed over black and high. Although it was immensely stable, as seen in rounded perspective from a few yards away, there against the side it appeared top heavy, so that this huge segment of sheet iron seemed to have lost the support of its invisible complement behind, the support that was now unseen and therefore unfelt, and Flegg imagined despite himself that the entire erection had become unsteady, that quite possibly the gasometer might suddenly blow over like a gigantic top-heavy sail. He lowered his eyes quickly and concentrated on the hands before him. He began to climb.

From beneath there still rose a few cries from the boys. But the girl had stopped shouting — probably she was following Flegg's every step with admiring eyes. He imagined again her frown and her peculiarly pouting mouth, and from this image drew new strength with which he clutched the rungs more eagerly. But now he noticed that the cries had begun to ring with an unpleasant new echo, as though they were already far off. And Flegg could not so easily distinguish their words. Even at this height he seemed to have penetrated into a distinct stratum of separate air, for it was certainly cooler, and for the first time that day he felt the light fanning of a wind. He looked down. His friends appeared shockingly small. Their bodies had disappeared and he saw only their upturned faces. He wanted to wave, to demonstrate in some way a carefree attitude; but then instantly he felt frustrated as his hands refused to unlock their grip. He turned to the rungs again with the smile dying on his lips.

He swallowed uneasily and continued to tread slowly upwards, hand after hand, foot after foot. He had climbed ten rungs of the iron ladder when his hands first began to feel moist, when suddenly, as though a catastrophe had overtaken him not gradually but in one overpowering second, he realized that he was afraid; incontrovertibly. He could cover it no longer, he admitted it all over his body. His hands gripped with pitiable eagerness, they were now alert to a point of shivering, as though the nerves inside them had been forced taut for so long that now they had burst beyond their strained tegument; his feet no longer trod firmly on the rungs beneath, but first stepped for their place timorously, then glued themselves to the iron. In this way his body lost much of its poise; these nerves and muscles in his two legs and two arms seemed to work independently, no longer integrated with the rhythm of his body, but moving with the dangerous unwilled jerk of crippled limbs.

His body hung slack away from the ladder, with nothing beneath it but a thirty foot drop to the ground; only his hands and feet were fed with the security of an attachment, most of him lay off the ladder, hanging in space; his arms revolted at the strain of their familiar angle, as though they were flies' feet denying all natural laws. For the first time, as the fear took hold of him, he felt that what he had attempted was impossible. He could never achieve the top. If at this height of only thirty feet, as it were three storeys of a building, he felt afraid — what would he feel at sixty feet? Yet . . . he trod heavily up. He was afraid, but not desperate. He dreaded each step, yet forced himself to believe that at some time it would be over, it could not take long.

A memory crossed his mind. It occurred to him vividly, then flashed away, for his eyes and mind were continually concentrated on the rusted iron bars and the white knuckles of his hands. But for an instant he remembered waking up long ago in the nursery and seeing that the windows were light, as if they reflected a coldness of moonlight. Only they were not so much lit by light as by a sensation of space. The windows seemed to echo with space. He had crawled out of bed and climbed on to a chair that stood beneath the window. It was as he had thought. Outside there was space, nothing else, a limitless area of space; yet this was not unnatural, for soon his logical eyes had supplied for what had at first appeared an impossible infinity the later image of a perfectly reasonable flood. A vast plain of still water continued as far as his eyes could see. The tennis courts and the houses beyond had disappeared; they were quite submerged, flat motionless water spread out immeasurably to the distant arced horizon all around. It lapped silently at the sides of the house, and in the light of an unseen moon winked and washed darkly, concealing great beasts of mystery beneath its black calm surface. This water attracted him, he wished to jump into it from the window and immerse himself in it and allow his head to sink slowly under. However he was perched up too high. He felt, alone at the window, infinitely high, so that the flood seemed to lie in miniature at a great distance below, as later in life when he was ill he had seen the objects of his bedroom grow small and infinitely remote in the fevered reflection behind his eyes. Isolated at the little window he had been frightened by the emptiness surrounding him, only the sky and the water and the marooned stone wall of the house; he had been terrified yet drawn down by dread and desire.

Then a battleship had sailed by. He had woken up, saved by the appearance of the battleship. And now on the ladder he had a sudden hope that something as large and stable would intervene again to help him.

But ten rungs farther up he began to sweat more violently than ever. His hands streamed with wet rust, the flesh inside his thighs blenched. Another flake of rust fell on his forehead; this time it stuck in the wetness. He felt physically exhausted. Fear was draining his strength and the precarious position of his body demanded an awkward physical effort. From his outstretched arms suspended most of the weight of his body. Each stressed muscle ached. His body weighed more heavily at each step upwards, it sagged beneath his arms like a leaden sack. His legs no longer provided their adequate support; it seemed as though they needed every pull of their muscle to force themselves, as independent limbs, close to the ladder. The wind blew faster. It dragged now at his coat, it blew its space about him, it echoed silently a lonely spaciousness. "Don't look down," the blood whispered in his temples, "Don't look down, for God's sake, DON'T LOOK DOWN."

Three-quarters up the gasometer, and fifty feet from the ground, Flegg grew desperate. Every other consideration suddenly left him. He wanted only to reach the ground as quickly as possible, only that. Nothing else mattered. He stopped climbing and clung to the ladder panting. Very slowly, lowering his eyes carefully so that he could raise them instantly if he saw too much, he looked down a rung, and another past his armpit, past his waist — and focused them on the ground beneath. He looked quickly up again.

He pressed himself to the ladder. Tears started in his eyes. For a moment they reeled red with giddiness. He closed them, shutting out everything. Then instantly opened them, afraid that something might happen. He must watch his hands, watch the bars, watch the rusted iron sheeting itself; no movement should escape him; the struts might come creaking loose, the whole edifice might sway over; although a fading reason told him that the gasometer had remained firm for years and was still as steady as a cliff, his horrified senses suspected that this was the one moment in the building's life when a wind would blow that was too strong for it, some defective strut would snap, the whole edifice would heel over and go crashing to the ground. This image became so clear that he could see the sheets of iron buckling and folding like cloth as the huge weight sank to the earth.

The ground had receded horribly, the drop now appeared terrifying, out of all proportion to this height he had reached. From the ground such a height would have appeared unnoteworthy. But now looking down the distance seemed to have doubled. Each object familiar to his everyday eyes — his friends, the lamp-posts, a brick wall, the kerb, a drain — all these had grown infinitely small. His senses demanded that these objects should be of a certain accustomed size. Alternatively, the world of chimneys and attic windows and roof-coping would grow unpleasantly giant as his pavement-bred eyes approached. Even now the iron sheeting that stretched to either side and above and below seemed to have grown, he was lost among such huge smooth dimensions, grown smaller himself and clinging now like a child lost on some monstrous desert of red rust.

These unfamiliarities shocked his nerves more than the danger of falling. The sense of isolation was overpowering. All things were suddenly alien. Yet exposed on the iron spaces, with the unending winds blowing aerially round him, among such free things — he felt shut in! Trembling and panting so that he stifled himself with the shortness of his own breath, he took the first step downwards . . .

A commotion began below. A confusion of cries came drifting up to him. Above all he could hear the single voice of the girl who had so far kept quiet. She was screaming high, a shrill scream that rose in the air incisively like a gull's shriek. "Put it back, put it back, put it back!" the scream seemed to say. So that Flegg, thinking that these cries were to warn him of some new danger apparent only from the ground — Flegg gripped himself into the ladder and looked down again. He glanced down for a fractional second — but in that time saw enough. He saw that the quiet girl was screaming and pointing to the base of the iron ladder. He saw the others crowding round her, gesticulating. He saw that she really had been crying, "Put it back!" And he realized now what the words meant — someone had removed the painter's ladder.

It lay clearly on the ground, outlined white like a child's drawing of a ladder. The boys must have seen his first step downwards, and then, from fun or from spite they had removed his only means of retreat. He remembered that from the base of the iron ladder to the ground the drop fell twenty feet. He considered quickly descending and appealing from the bottom of the ladder; but foresaw that for precious minutes they would jeer and argue, refusing to replace the ladder, and he felt then that he could never risk these minutes, unnerved, with his strength failing. Besides, he had already noticed that the whole group of them were wandering off. The boys were driving the quiet girl away, now more concerned with her than with Flegg. The quiet girl's sense of guilt had been brought to a head by the removal of the ladder. Now she was hysterically terrified. She was yelling to them to put the ladder back. She — only she, the passive one — sensed the terror that awaited them all. But her screams defeated their own purpose. They had altogether distracted the attention of the others; now it was fun to provoke more screams, to encourage this new distraction — and they forgot about Flegg far up and beyond them. They were wandering away. They were abandoning him, casually unconcerned that he was alone and helpless up in his wide prison of rust. His heart cried out for them to stay. He forgot their scorn in new and terrible torments of self-pity. An uneasy feeling lumped his throat, his eyes smarted with dry tears.

But they were wandering away. There was no retreat. They did not even know he was in difficulties. So Flegg had no option but to climb higher. Desperately he tried to shake off his fear, he actually shook his head. Then he stared hard at the rungs immediately facing his eyes, and tried to imagine that he was not high up at all. He lifted himself tentatively by one rung, then by another, and in this way dragged himself higher and higher . . . until he must have been some ten rungs from the top, over the fifth storey of a house, with now perhaps only one more storey to climb. He imagined that he might then be approaching the summit platform, and to measure this last distance he looked up.

He looked up and heaved. He felt for the first time panicked beyond desperation, wildly violently loose. He almost let go. His senses screamed to let go, yet his hands refused to open. He was stretched on a rack made by these hands that would not unlock their grip and by the panic desire to drop. The nerves left his hands so that they might have been dried bones of fingers gripped round the rungs, hooks of bone fixed perhaps strongly enough to cling on, or perhaps at some moment of pressure to uncurl their vertebrae and straighten to a drop. His insteps pricked with cold cramp. The sweat sickened him. His loins seemed to empty themselves. His trousers ran wet. He shivered, grew giddy, and flung himself froglike on to the ladder.

The sight of the top of the gasometer had proved endemically more frightful than the appearance of the drop beneath. There lay about it a sense of material danger, not of the risk of falling, but of something removed and unhuman — a sense of appalling isolation. It echoed its elemental iron aloofness, a wind blew round it that had never known the warmth of flesh nor the softness of green fibres. Its blind eyes were raised above the world. It was like the eyeless iron vizor of an ancient god, it touched against the sky having risen in awful perpendicular to this isolation, solitary as the grey gannet cliffs that mark the end of the northern world. It was immeasurably old, outside the connotation of time; it was nothing human, only washed by the high weather, echoing with wind, visited never and silently alone.

And in this summit Flegg measured clearly the full distance of his climb. This close skyline emphasized the whirling space beneath him. He clearly saw a man fall through this space, spread-eagling to smash with the sickening force of a locomotive on the stone beneath. The man turned slowly in the air, yet his thoughts raced faster than he fell.

Flegg, clutching his body close to the rust, made small weeping sounds through his mouth. Shivering, shuddering, he began to tread up again, working his knees and elbows outward like a frog, so that his stomach could feel the firm rungs. Were they firm? His ears filled with a hot roaring, he hurried himself, he began to scramble up, wrenching at his last strength, whispering urgent meaningless words to himself like the swift whispers that close in on a nightmare. A huge weight pulled him, dragging him to drop. He climbed higher. He reached the top rung — and found his face staring still at a wall of red rust. He looked, with wild terror. It was the top rung! the ladder had ended! Yet — no platform . . . the real top rungs were missing . . . the platform jutted five impassable feet above . . . Flegg stared dumbly, circling his head like a lost animal . . . then he jammed his legs in the lower rungs and his arms past the elbows to the armpits in through the top rungs and there he hung shivering and past knowing what more he could ever do . . .

Irwin Shaw
1913–1984

In the course of his long, prolific, and successful career as a novelist, play-wright, and short story writer, reviewers constantly described Irwin Shaw not as an artist but as a craftsman. We may accept the judgment but only if we add that his craft was, like that of his contemporary John O'Hara, of the very first order. He does not know how to be unreadable. So varied in tone, theme, and background are his stories, so professional in their audi-ence-sense, that even on a second or third reading the best of them stand up well. Several, such as "Sailor off the Bremen," "The Girls in Their Summer Dresses," and "Act of Faith," continue to show up in anthologies decades after they were written. Not a bad test.

During World War II Picasso, living in German-occupied Paris, was not popular with the Gestapo. One German officer, investigating his apartment, noticed a photograph of Guernica on the table. "Did you do that?" he asked. "No, you did," said Picasso.

In this sense the Germans wrote several stories in this volume. One of their finest productions is "Medal from Jerusalem."

Medal from Jerusalem

"THE QUESTION that haunts me," Schneider was saying in his high, soft voice, "is, my jazz, is it real jazz or is it merely European jazz?" He was leaning against the bar of the Patio restaurant between Tel Aviv and Jaffa, which used to be the old German consulate, and speaking to Lieutenant Mitchell Gunnison in short, gaspy bursts of talk, smiling a little sadly and a little archly at Mitchell, and occasionally touching his sleeve lightly with the tips of his fingers. "I mean," he said, "I know it's good enough for Palestine, but in America what would they say about a pianist like me?"

"Well," said Gunnison gravely, "I'd say they'd think it was real jazz." He was young and he spoke slowly and he seemed to think very hard before he answered a question.

"You don't know," Schneider said, sighing, "how you've encouraged me. I listen to the records, of course, but they're old, and you never know what actually is going on in America and, after all, we all know there *is* no other jazz, no place, and with a war like this, and God knows how long it's going to last, a musician gets out of touch. And once you are out of touch, you might as well die. Just die."

"You have nothing to worry about," Mitchell said. "You'll be a sensation in America."

"If I ever get there." Schneider smiled sadly and shrugged a little. "Anyway, you must come tomorrow. I'm working on a new arrangement with the drummer. A rhumba, Viennese style. It's ridiculous, but I think you'll like it."

"I'm sorry," Mitchell said. "I won't be here tomorrow."

"Then next night," said Schneider.

"I won't be here then, either," Mitchell said. "I'm going tomorrow. Leave's up."

There was a little silence and Schneider looked down at the bar and flicked his beer glass with his fingernail, making a frail musical sound in the dark oak barroom. "Some more fighting?" Schneider asked.

"A little more fighting." Mitchell nodded soberly.

"You fly, no doubt," said Schneider. "I have no wish to intrude on military information, but the wings on the chest . . ."

"I'm a navigator." Mitchell smiled at him.

"It must be an interesting profession. Measuring the distance between one star and another star." Schneider finished his beer slowly. "Well *sho-lom aleichem* . . . That's good luck. Or, to be more exact, peace be with you."

"Thank you," Mitchell said.

"Hebrew," said Schneider. "I'm ashamed to talk Hebrew to anybody who knows it. The accent, they tell me, is frightful. But you don't mind, do you?"

"No," said Mitchell. He turned to the bartender. "Mr. Abrams," he said, "another beer please, for Mr. Schneider."

"No, no." Schneider waved his hands in protest. "The artist should not drink before the performance. After . . . Another matter . . . Ah," he said, bowing elaborately, "*Fräulein,* we are enchanted."

Mitchell turned around. Ruth was standing there, looking a little hurried and out of breath, but smiling, and as pretty as ever in a light cotton dress, with her skin burned dark by the sun and her eyes full of welcome and pleasure at seeing him.

"I was afraid," she said, coming over to him and taking his hand, "I was afraid you were going to be angry and leave."

"I wasn't going to leave," Mitchell said. "Not until they closed the doors on me and threw me out."

"I am delighted." Ruth laughed and squeezed his arm. "I am so absolutely delighted."

"My presence," Schneider said, bowing, "I no longer consider necessary. A hundred thanks for the beer, Lieutenant. Now I play or Mr. Abrams will start complaining he is not getting his money's worth out of me. Listen, carefully, if it is not too much of a bore, to my version of 'Stardust.' "

"We'll listen very carefully," Mitchell said.

Schneider went outside to the patio, and a moment later preliminary erratic runs and fragments of melody came floating into the bar as he warmed up for the night's work.

"So." Ruth faced him, looking at him with an expression that was half ownership, half amusement. "So. What have we been doing all day?"

"Well," Mitchell started, "we . . ."

"You are the most beautiful lieutenant in the American Army," Ruth said, grinning.

"Well, we went swimming," Mitchell said, pleased and embarrassed, pretending she'd said nothing. "And we hung around on the beach. And we flew a couple of barroom missions. Gin and grapefruit juice."

"Isn't Palestinian grapefruit wonderful?" Ruth asked loyally.

"Sensational," Mitchell said. "Nothing like it in America."

"You're such a liar." Ruth leaned over and kissed him lightly.

"There was an Eighth Air Force pilot down from England," Mitchell said, "and he told us how tough it was over Wilhelmshaven and we told the lies about Ploesti and then it was time to shave and come to see you."

"What did you think while you were shaving? Were you sad because you had to leave your interesting friends and see me?"

"Broken-hearted," Mitchell said.

"You've got such a nice, skinny face." Ruth touched the line of his jaw. "You're as pretty as an English lieutenant. I'm not fond of the English, but they have the prettiest lieutenants of any army."

"We send our pretty ones to the Pacific," said Mitchell. "Guadalcanal. We preserve them for American womanhood."

Ruth signaled Mr. Abrams for a drink. "I was in Jerusalem today. I told my boss I was sick and went there. It's so bad — we never got to see Jerusalem together."

"Some other time," Mitchell said. "I'll come back and we'll see Jerusalem."

"Don't lie to me," Ruth said, seriously. "Please don't lie. You won't come back. You won't see me again. Absolutely no lies, please."

Mitchell felt very young. He felt there was something to be said, and an older man would know how to say it, but he felt dumb and bereaved and clumsy, and it must have showed on his face as he peered at his glass, because Ruth laughed and touched his lips with her fingers and said, "You have such a tragic face for an American. Where do you come from in America?"

"Vermont," Mitchell said.

"Has everybody got a face like yours in Vermont?"

"Everybody."

"I will visit there," Ruth drained her glass, "at some later date."

"I'll give you my address," Mitchell said.

"Of course," said Ruth politely. "You must write it down some time."

They went out into the patio and sat down at a table on the old flagstones under a palm tree, with the blue blackout lights shining dimly over the uniforms and pale dresses, and the moon riding over the Mediterranean and casting flickering shadows over the dancers who now claimed the spot where the German consul had lived well in days gone by. Mitchell ordered champagne because it was his last night. It was Syrian champagne, but not bad, and to both of them it gave an air of festivity and importance to the evening, as it rocked in its silver bucket of ice. Eric, the waiter with the limp, ceremoniously took Ruth's ration tickets, and Schneider, seated with the drummer across the patio, with the drum dimly lit from inside by an orange light of which Schneider was very proud, played "Summertime" because he had decided that was the song Mitchell liked best. The old song, played trickily and well in the soft, echoing patio, somehow sounded, by some ineradicable stamp in Schneider's blood, like Carolina and Vienna and the Balkans, with here and there chords of an old Hebrew chant, quite just and indigenous here between the heavy stone walls on the edge of the Sinai desert.

"I'm jealous of him," said Ruth, speaking over the edge of her glass.

"Who?"

"Schneider."

"Why?" Mitchell asked.

"Because of the way he looks at you. He's crazy about you. Has he asked you to come to tea with him and his mother?"

"Yes," said Mitchell, trying not to smile.

"I'll tear his eyes out," Ruth said. "I'm jealous of anybody who looks at you that way. The girls back in Vermont and those Red Cross girls."

"You have nothing to worry about," Mitchell said. "Nobody looks at me that way. Not even Schneider or you."

"That's the nicest thing about you," Ruth said. "You don't know anything. I'm so used to men who know just how many steps out of bed each look a woman gives them measures. I must visit America after the war . . ."

"Where will you really go?" Mitchell asked. "Back to Berlin?"

"No." Ruth stared reflectively down at her plate. "No, not back to Berlin. Never back to Berlin. The Germans have made clear their feeling about me. A little thing like a war will not change them. The lamb does not go back to the slaughterhouse. Anyway, I have nobody there. There was a young man . . ." She leaned over and picked up the bottle and absently poured for Mitchell and herself. "I don't know what happened to him. Stalingrad, maybe, Alamein . . . who knows?"

Four men came into the patio and walked through the brief illumination of the blue lights. Three of them were Arabs in European dress, and the fourth was a man in the uniform of the American Army with the civilian technical adviser patch on his shoulder. They stopped at the table. The three Arabs bowed a little, ceremoniously, to Ruth, and the American said, "I thought you were sick."

"This is Mr. Carver," Ruth said to Mitchell, with a wave to the American. "He's my boss."

"Hi, Lieutenant," said Carver. He was a big, fat man, with a weary, puffy, intelligent face. He turned back to Ruth. "I thought you were sick," he repeated in a pleasant, loud, slightly drunken voice.

"I was sick," Ruth said, cheerfully. "I had a miraculous recovery."

"The American Army," Carver said, "expects every civilian worker to do her duty."

"Tomorrow," said Ruth. "Now please go away with your friends. The lieutenant and I are having an intimate talk."

"Lieutenant . . ." It was one of the Arabs, the shortest of the three, a slight, dark man, with a round face and liquid, veiled eyes. "My name is Ali Khazen. Permit me to introduce myself, as no one here seems to remember his manners well enough to do so."

Mitchell stood up. "Mitchell Gunnison," he said, putting out his hand.

"Forgive me," Carver said. "I'm suffering from drink. This is Sayed Taif . . ." He indicated the tallest of the Arabs, a middle-aged man with a severe, handsome, tight-lipped face. Mitchell shook hands with him.

"He doesn't like Americans," Carver said loudly. "He's the leading journalist of the local Arab world and he writes for thirty-five papers in the United States and he doesn't like Americans."

"What was that?" Taif asked politely, inclining his head in a reserved, small gesture.

"Also, he's deaf," said Carver. "Most useful equipment for any journalist."

Nobody bothered to introduce the third Arab, who stood a little to one side, watching Taif with a fierce, admiring stare, like a boxer dog at his master's feet.

"Why don't you all go away and eat your dinner?" Ruth said.

"Lieutenant," Carver said, ignoring her, "take the advice of a veteran of the Middle East. Do not become involved with Palestine."

"He's not becoming involved with Palestine," Ruth said. "He's becoming involved with me."

"Beware Palestine." Carver weaved a little as he spoke. "The human race is doomed in Palestine. For thousands of years. They chop down the forests, burn down the cities, wipe out the inhabitants. This is no place for an American.,"

"You drink too much, Mr. Carver," Ruth said.

"Nevertheless," Carver shook his big head heavily, "it is no accident that they picked this place to crucify Christ. You couldn't pick a better place to crucify Christ if you scoured the maps of the world for five hundred years. I'm a Quaker myself, from the city of Philadelphia, Pennsylvania, and all I see here is the blood of bleeding humanity. When this war is over I'm going back to Philadelphia and wait until I pick up the morning newspaper and read that everybody in Palestine has exterminated everybody else in Palestine the night before." He walked unsteadily over to Ruth's chair and bent over and peered intently into her face. "Beautiful girl," he said, "beautiful, forlorn girl." He straightened up. "Gunnison, I admonish you, as an officer and gentleman, do not harm one hair on this beautiful girl's head."

"Every hair," Mitchell said, gravely, "is safe with me."

"If you must drink," Ruth said to Carver sharply, "why don't you do it with Americans? Why do you have to go around with bandits and murderers like these?" She waved her hand toward the Arabs. The journalist smiled, his handsome face frosty and amused in the wavering light.

"Impartiality," Carver boomed. "American impartiality. We are famous for it. We are nobody's friend and nobody's enemy. We merely build airfields and pipelines. Impartially. Tomorrow I lunch with the President of the Jewish Agency."

Ruth turned to the journalist. "Taif," she said, loudly, "I read your last piece."

"Ah, yes," he said, his voice a little dead and without timbre. "Did you like it?"

"You'll be responsible for the death of thousands of Jews," said Ruth.

"Ah, thank you," he said. He smiled. "It is my fondest hope." He turned to Mitchell. "Naturally, Lieutenant," he said, "our charming little Ruth is biased in the matter. It is necessary to give the Arab side of the proposition." He began to speak more seriously, with a severe, oratorical emphasis, like an evangelical preacher. "The world is dazzled by the Jewish accomplishment in Palestine. Fine, clean cities, with plumbing. Industries. Where once was desert, now the rose and the olive bloom. Et cetera."

"Taif, old boy," Carver pulled at his arm, "let's eat and you can lecture the lieutenant some other time."

"No, if you please." The journalist pulled his arm politely away from Carver's hand. "I welcome the opportunity to talk to our American friends. You see, my good Lieutenant, you may be very pleased with the factory and the plumbing, and perhaps, even, from one point of view, they may be good things. But they have nothing to do with the Arab. Perhaps the Arab prefers the desert as it was. The Arab has his own culture . . ."

"When I hear the word 'culture,' " Carver said, "I reach for my pistol. What famous American said that?"

"To Americans and Europeans," the journalist went on, in his sing-song, dead voice, "the culture of the Arab perhaps seems backward and dreadful. But, forgive us, the Arab prefers it. The virtues which are particularly Arab are kept alive by primitive living. They die among the plumbing."

"Now," said Ruth, "we have heard a new one. Kill the Jew because he brings the shower bath."

The journalist smiled indulgently at Ruth, as at a clever child. "Personally," he said, "I have nothing against the Jews. I swear that I do not wish to harm a single Jew living in Palestine today. But I will fight to the death to keep even one more Jew from entering the country. This is an Arab state, and it must remain an Arab state."

"Gunnison," Carver said, "aren't you glad you came?"

"Six million Jews have died in Europe," Ruth said, her voice harsh and passionate, and surprising to Mitchell. "Where do you want the survivors to go?" She and the journalist had forgotten the rest of them and were locked with each other across the table.

The journalist shrugged and looked for a moment up above the palm fronds at the dark sky. "That," he said, "is a question for the world to decide. Why must the poor Arab have the whole decision? We've taken in much more than our share. If the rest of the world really wants to see the Jewish race survive let them take them in. America, Britain, Russia . . . I do not notice those large countries taking in great masses of Jews."

"There are no great masses," Ruth said. "There is only a handful."

Taif shrugged. "Even so. The truth may be, perhaps," he paused, a little doubtfully, reminding Mitchell of an old Latin teacher in a class in Cicero, shrewdly hesitating for effect, before telling the class whether the word in question was in the ablative or dative absolute, "the truth may be that the rest of the world really wants to see the Jewish race die out." He turned and smiled warmly at Mitchell. "It is an interesting supposition, Lieutenant. It might be most interesting to examine it before talking any more about Palestine." He walked over to Ruth and leaned over and kissed her fleetingly on the forehead. "Good night, little Ruth," he said, and went to a table across the patio, with the silent, adoring Arab behind him.

"If I see you with that man once more," Ruth spoke to the man who had introduced himself to Mitchell, and who had remained standing at their table, "I'll never talk to you again."

The Arab looked swiftly at Mitchell, a veiled, probing flick of the eyes, and said something to Ruth in Arabic.

"No," said Ruth, her voice clipped and sharp. "Definitely no."

The Arab bowed slightly, put out his hand to Mitchell and, as they shook hands, said, "Very pleasant meeting you, Lieutenant," and went off to join his friends at their table.

"*Thé dansants* in old Tel Aviv," said Carver. "Bring the kiddies. Good night." He waddled over to the other table.

"Ruth," Mitchell started to talk.

"Lieutenant Gunnison . . ." It was the soft, apologetic voice of Schneider at his elbow. "I am so anxious for your opinion. What did you think of 'Stardust'?"

Mitchell turned slowly from staring at Ruth, who was sitting tense and upright in her chair. "Great, Schneider," Mitchell said. "I thought it was sensational."

Schneider beamed with pleasure. "You are too kind," he said. "I will play you 'Summertime' once more."

"Thanks a lot," said Mitchell. He put out his hand and covered Ruth's, lying on the table. "You all right?" he asked.

She smiled up at him. "Sure," she said. "I am an admirer of abstract political discussions." Her face grew serious. "Do you want to know what Khazen asked when he spoke to me in Arabic?"

"Not if you don't want to tell me."

"I want to tell you." Ruth absently caressed his fingers. "He asked me if I would meet him later."

"Yes," said Mitchell.

"I told him no."

"I heard you." Mitchell grinned at her. "They probably heard you in Cairo."

"I didn't want you to feel disturbed or doubtful," Ruth said, "your last night."

"I feel fine," Mitchell said.

"I've been going with him for four years." She played for a moment with the food on the plate that the waiter had put before her. "When I came here in the beginning I was frightened and lonely and he was very decent. He's a contractor for the Americans and British and he's made a fortune during the war. But when Rommel was outside Alexandria he and his friends used to celebrate in secret. I can't stand him any more. I tell him when I take up with other men. But he hangs on. Ah, finally, I suppose he'll get me to marry him. I'm not strong enough any more." She looked up at Mitchell and tried to smile. "Don't be shocked, darling," she said. "Americans can't understand how tired the human race can get." She stood up suddenly. "Let's dance."

They went onto the floor and Schneider broke into "Summertime" when he saw them and smiled fondly at them as they danced. She danced very well, lightly and passionately, and Mitchell knew as he danced that he was going to remember this for a long time, at odd moments, swinging away from targets with the flak falling off behind him, and later, if he made it, in the snowy hills of his home state, the light, soft pressure of the bright cotton dress, the dark, curved, delicate face below his, the hushed sound of their feet on the old floor under the palms, the clever, rich music of the piano under the small blue lights strung out from the stone building. There were a million things that crowded his throat that he wanted to tell her, and there was no way of saying them. He kissed her cheek as the music ended, and she glanced up at him, and smiled and said, "There, that's better," and they were laughing by the time they got back to their table.

He paid the bill and they went out, saying good night to Schneider, not looking back at the table where Carver and the three Arabs sat, but hearing Carver's deep voice rolling through the music and the darkness, calling, "Does anyone want an airfield? I'll build it for him. Does anyone want a crown of thorns? I'll build it for him."

There was an old carriage waiting outside the restaurant, its driver dozing and its lights dimmed, and they climbed in and sat close together as the driver clucked to the horse and they rattled slowly back toward town. The breeze had gone down as it did at nine o'clock every night, and there was a small, warm breath of salt off the Mediterranean and every once in a while a jeep rushed past in a whistle of American wind, with its slits of cat's-eye lights cutting a darting, frail, skidding pattern in the darkness, making the creakings and rustlings of the old carriage older and dearer and more private as they sat there holding on to each other in silence.

They got off a block from where Ruth lived because the people from whom she rented her room were intensely moral and did not approve of their boarder going out with soldiers. They walked past the corner where the Italian bombers had killed a hundred and thirty people on a

Friday morning the year before, and turned into Ruth's street. From a darkened window came the sound of someone practicing the third movement of the Brahms violin concerto, and Mitchell couldn't help smiling and realizing that one of his strongest memories of Tel Aviv would be the strains of Tchaikovsky and Brahms and Beethoven coming through the opened windows on every street of the town, as the furiously cultured inhabitants practiced runs and cadenzas with never-ending zeal.

All the houses were blacked out, but there was a tiny sliver of light along one of the windows in the third-floor apartment in which Ruth lived, and they stopped in dismay when they saw it.

"She's up," Ruth said.

"Doesn't she ever sleep?" Mitchell asked angrily.

Ruth giggled and kissed him. "She can't stay up forever," Ruth said. "We'll take a little walk and by the time we get back she'll be asleep."

Mitchell took her arm and they walked slowly down toward the sea. Soldiers and whores and fat, placid couples strolled on the concrete walk along the beach, and the Mediterranean heaved gently under the moon and broke in small white rolls of foam against the beach, with a steady, foreign grumble, not like the roar of the Atlantic on the cold northern beaches of home. From a café a hundred yards away came the sound of a string quartet playing a Strauss waltz as though Vienna had never been taken, the waltz never lost to the enemy.

Mitchell and Ruth went down the steps to the beach. A weaving British lance-corporal, coming up the steps with a girl, stiffened and saluted rigidly, his hand quivering with respect for authority, and Mitchell saluted back, and Ruth giggled.

"What're you laughing at?" Mitchell asked, when they had passed the lance-corporal.

"I laugh," Ruth said, "every time I see you salute."

"Why?"

"I don't know why. I just laugh. Forgive me." She took off her shoes and walked barefoot in the sand up to the water's edge. The sea swept softly in from Gibraltar and Tunis and Cyrene and Alexandria and lapped at her toes.

"The Mediterranean," Ruth said. "I hate the Mediterranean."

"What's the matter with it?" Mitchell stared out at the flickering silver path of the moon over the water.

"I was on it," Ruth said, "for thirty-three days. In the hold of a Greek steamer that used to carry cement. Maybe I oughtn't to tell you things like that. You're a tired boy who's been sent here to have a good time so he can go back and fight well . . ."

"You tell me anything you want to tell me," Mitchell said. "I'll fight all right."

"Should I tell you about Berlin, too? Do you want to hear about Berlin?" Ruth's voice was hard and cold, and somehow a little sardonic, not at all like her voice as he had heard it in the whole week he had known her. The meeting with the journalist at the restaurant had started something stirring within her, something that he hadn't seen before, and he felt that before he left he should see that side of her too.

"Tell me about Berlin," Mitchell said.,

"I worked for a newspaper," Ruth said, her toes digging lightly in the sand, "even after the Nazis came in, and I was in love with the man who wrote the Economics column and he was in love with me . . ."

"Economics?" Mitchell was puzzled.

"The stock exchange. The prophecies and excuses."

"Oh," said Mitchell, trying to picture what a man who wrote stock-exchange tips in Berlin in 1934 would look like.

"He was very gay," Ruth said. "Very young, but elegant, with checkered vests, and he wore a monocle and he lost all his money at the races. His name was Joachim. He used to take me to the races and to the cafés and it used to drive my mother crazy, because if they ever found out I was a Jewish girl out with a Gentile man, they would have sentenced me to death for polluting the blood stream of the German nation. They'd have sent him to a concentration camp, too, but he was always easy and laughing, and he said, 'The important thing is to be brave,' and we were never questioned, and I went to every night club in Berlin, even nights that Goering and Goebbels were in the same room.

"My father was taken to a concentration camp and we decided it was time for me to leave, and Joachim got together all the money he could lay his hands on and gave it to me and I went to Vienna. I was supposed to go to Palestine, if I could, and send for my mother, and for my father, too, if he ever got out of the concentration camp. There was an office in Vienna, and it was filled with refugees from all over Germany, and we collected money to buy transportation and bribe the nations of the world to let some of us in. I slept in the bathtub and talked to sailors and thieves and murderers and crooked shipowners, and finally we got a Greek steamer that was supposed to put in at Genoa and pick us up if we managed to get there. We gave the man 75,000 dollars in cash in advance because that's the only way he would do it, and somehow we got the Austrian government and the Italian government to look the other way, at a price, and they piled us into freight cars, eight hundred of us, and locked us in, men, women and children, lying one on top of another, and the trip took a week and a day to Genoa, and when we got there the ship never arrived. The Greek took the 75,000 dollars and disappeared. There are all kinds of Greeks, and I have nothing against them, but this was a bad one. Then the Italian government sent us back to Vienna and six people committed suicide because they couldn't bear it, and we started in all over again."

Mitchell stared out at the dark line of the sea where it blended in the western distance with the purple of the sky. He tried to think of what it would have been like for his sister and mother if they had been locked into freight cars at Rutland and forced to travel for eight days up to Quebec, say, to wait for an illegal ship to an unknown country. His mother was tall and white-haired and unruffled and pleasant, and his sister was cool and pretty and had some irritating superior mannerisms that she had picked up when she had been foolishly sent for a year to a fancy girls' finishing school in Maryland.

"Let's start home," Ruth said. "If my landlady's still up, we'll shoot her."

They turned their backs on the quiet, white churn of the waves and walked, hand in hand, across the heavy sand of the beach toward the black pile of the buildings of the city.

"Well," Mitchell said, "I want to hear the rest of it."

"No, you don't," Ruth said. "Forgive me for telling you so much. It's too dreary."

"I want to hear," Mitchell said. In the week he had known Ruth, she had been gay and light-hearted, and had helped him to forget the planes spinning out of control and the dying men lying in their frozen blood on the tangled wires and broken aluminum of the Liberator floors, and now he felt as though he owed it to himself and to Ruth to take back with him some of her agony, too, not only the laughter and the tender jokes and the self-effacing merriment. Suddenly, tonight, she had become terribly dear to him, and he felt responsible to her in a way he had never felt responsible to a girl before.

"Tell me," he said.

Ruth shrugged. "Back in Vienna," she said, "we did it all over again. It took two months and the police caught a lot of us, and it meant hiding and running most of the time, but we collected the money again, and we found ourselves another Greek, and this time he turned out to be honest. Or at least as honest as people were to Jews without passports in those days in Europe. We got down to Genoa in only five days this time, and we boarded the steamer at night and they locked the hatch doors on us after we had paid every cent of the money in advance, and we set sail before dawn. The steamer had been built in 1887." They were at the edge of the beach now, and Ruth leaned on Mitchell's shoulder as she put on her shoes. "Nobody can have any idea," Ruth said, as they went up the steps to the concrete walk above, "of what dirt is like until he has been locked into the hold of a fifty-year-old Greek ship with 700 people for over a month. People died every day, and the ship captain would let a rabbi and three other people up on deck at night to perform the burial service and dump the body overboard. The only thing we got to eat was biscuit and canned beef, and there were always worms in everything, even the water we got to drink, and everybody got sores all over their bodies, and the old people got too weak to move and the children wept all day, and the relatives of the people who died screamed a good deal of the time, and it is impossible to tell anyone who was not on that boat what it smelled like, in the middle of the summer in the Mediterranean, with a ventilating system that had been installed in Salonika in 1903."

They turned off the beach walk and climbed slowly up the hill toward the center of the town, past the clean, white, very modernistic apartment houses with gardens and fountains and balconies that faced the sea.

"We were supposed to be let off in Turkey." Ruth went on, her voice almost without inflection and emotion, as though she were reciting from a ledger the business accounts of an importing firm for the year 1850. "And we had given the Greek money to pay off every officer of the port, but something went wrong and we had to put out to sea again, and we started toward Palestine, although the British had patrols along every mile of coastline. But there was no place else to go. People started to get hallucinations about food, and the sailors would sell a sandwich or a lemon for twenty dollars or a bowl of soup for a gold candlestick. And three of the girls couldn't stand it any more and allowed themselves to be taken up every night to be used by the sailors in exchange for regular meals. It was hard to blame them, but they were cursed by the older people as they walked through the crowd each night toward the ladder, and once a Polish woman with two small daughters knocked one of the girls down with an iron pin and tried to stab her with a kitchen knife she had in her bag."

They turned into Ruth's street and looked up at the window just in time to see the thin edge of light under the blind disappear. They stopped and leaned against a stucco fence in front of a plain, shining white house with cactus plants and a fig tree in the front yard.

"We were on that ship for thirty-five days," Ruth said, "and we came to the coast of Palestine between Haifa and Rehovoth, at night, and maybe someone had been bribed, and maybe it was just lucky, but people were waiting for us in rowboats and in eight hours we were all off. There was one woman, who looked as strong as anyone, a solid, sensible-looking woman, and she seemed cheerful and healthy when she got into the little boat with me, but she suddenly died ten feet off the coast, when the water was so shallow a child could have stepped out and walked ashore. Luckily, it was a dark night, and there were no patrols, and we were taken in cars to a movie theater in a little town near Haifa and put inside. The theater had been playing Betty Grable in *Campus Confessions,* a musical picture, and there were signs with her in tights and ostrich plumes all over it, and the management had written all over the posters, 'Closed This Week for Repairs.' "

"I saw the picture," Mitchell said. He had seen it one night in Cambridge, and he remembered how some of the boys in the audience had whistled when Miss Grable had kissed the leading man.

"We were all told to keep absolutely quiet," Ruth said, "because the British had patrols going through every town. They must have known something, because that week three men high up in the police force were suspended and investigated. It wasn't so hard to keep the older people quiet, but it was awful with the children, and one man really proposed that a little girl who kept crying all day be strangled for the good of the others. We sat there for a week, whispering, making a noise like thousands of mice in a cupboard, and each night cars would come and some people would be taken away to a collective farm somewhere in the hills. Finally, my turn came and I stayed on that farm for two years, working in the fields and teaching children how to read and write German.

"After two years, the British gave you papers, if you managed to dodge them all that time, and I got my papers and started to work for a canning factory outside Tel Aviv. My father was let out of concentration camp in 1938, but his ship was turned back at Haifa, and he was put back in concentration camp in Germany, and for all I know he's still there now, although he's probably dead.

"Joachim wrote me, and my mother, from Berlin. They became good friends once I was gone, and he brought her food, and on Friday nights would come and watch her light the candles. My mother wrote me he told her he had a girl, but he was dissatisfied, he guessed he'd gotten the taste for Jewish girls." Ruth smiled slightly, thinking of the boy with the checkered vest and the monocle many years ago, and Mitchell wondered if he had dropped a bomb near the market-analyzer somewhere in Africa, or in Sicily or Italy.

"He helped my mother get out of Germany," Ruth went on, staring up at the window of her home, which was now secure and dark. "She came out in a Portuguese boat, and I heard she was coming and I was on the shore at Haifa Harbor when it came in. But the British wouldn't let it dock, and after six days they insisted that it turn back, and there were thousands of people on the shore, relatives and friends of the people on that boat, and the worst sound I've ever heard in the world was the sound those people on the shore made when the boat turned around and started to steam toward the Haifa breakwater. But the boat never got out of the harbor." Ruth paused and licked her lips, and spoke very matter-of-factly. "There was an explosion. We saw the puff of dirty black smoke first, then a long time later we heard the noise, and people on shore were screaming and laughing and crying. Then there was fire and the boat started to go down, and everybody grabbed at any kind of boat they could find and started out toward the steamer, and there were people who couldn't find boats who just jumped into the water, clothes and all, and started to swim, and nobody ever found out how many people drowned that way, because bodies were washed in to shore for three weeks afterward. My mother was drowned and five hundred other people on the boat, but seven hundred were saved, and then the British had to let them in, and I suppose that's what the people who set the bomb figured would happen. Some people would die, but some would be saved. If the boat went back to Europe, everybody would be killed. Of course, they bungled it somewhat, and they didn't figure on the fire, and they thought the boat would sink more slowly and only a few people would be killed, but even so it was a pretty fair bargain." Ruth lit a cigarette calmly and held the light for Mitchell. "My mother was washed up a week later, and at least her grave is in Palestine. I couldn't tell my father she was dead, so when I wrote to him in concentration camp, I forged letters from my mother, because I had a lot of her letters and I learned how to make good copies. Even now, through the Red Cross, I write him notes in my mother's handwriting, and if he's alive he thinks my mother is living on a farm with a family near Rehovoth."

Ruth pulled at her cigarette and inhaled deeply and in the increased glow Mitchell looked at her and thought again, as he'd thought so many times before, that it was a wonderful and terrible thing that the human race covered its scars so completely, so that Ruth, standing there, with the torture and smuggling and burning and drowning and hiding and dying behind her, looked, with her lipstick and fluffy, cleverly combed hair, and her soft, fragile, print dress, like any one of a thousand girls at a dance in America, with nothing more behind them than a weekly allowance from father, and two proms a season at New Haven or Cambridge.

"Ah," Ruth said, throwing her cigarette away, "she must be asleep by now. Come." She smiled at him, dry-eyed and pleasant, and took his hand, and they walked quietly up through the dim hallways to the apartment in which she lived. She opened the door silently and waved him in, her finger to her lips, and when they were safely in her room, with the door locked behind them, she giggled like a child who has pulled some sly trick on the grown-up world, then kissed him hungrily in the dark room, and whispered, "Mitchell, Mitchell," making the name somehow foreign and tender by the way she said it.

He held her tight, but she pulled away. "Not yet, Lieutenant," she said, grinning, "not yet." She put on a light and went over to a chest of drawers in a corner and started to rummage under some scarves. "I have something for you. Sit down and wait, like a polite boy."

Mitchell sat on the low daybed, blinking in the light. The room was small and painted white and very clean. There was a large piece of Egyptian batik in red and dark green on the wall over the bed and there were three photographs on a dressing table. Mitchell looked at the photographs — a round, smiling woman, with a healthy, simple face, Ruth's mother, the picture taken long before the morning when the ship went down in Haifa Harbor. The other two photographs were of men. There was a man who looked like Ruth, obviously her father, a studious, humorous, rather weak face, with frail, delicate bones and shy, childish eyes. And there was the young man in the checkered vest, slender and laughing and proud of himself, with the monocle in his eye like a burlesque of a German general or a British actor.

"Here." Ruth came over to him and sat down beside him. She had a soft chamois bag, and there was a little rich clinking as she put it in his hand. "To take with you," she said.

Mitchell slowly opened the bag. A heavy silver medal on a chain, glittering dully in the lamplight, fell into his hand. Ruth was crouched on her knees on the couch beside him, looking anxiously at his face to see if her present would meet with favor. Mitchell turned it over. It was a Saint Christopher, old and irregular, of heavy silver, with the Saint awkward and angular and archaic and very religious in the loving workmanship of a silversmith who had died a long time before.

"It's for voyages," Ruth said, hurriedly. "For a navigator, I thought, it might be quite — quite useful . . ." She smiled uncertainly at him. "Of course," she said, "it is not in my religion, but I don't think it would do any harm to give it to you. That's why I went to Jerusalem. Something like this, something holy, might have a tendency to be more effective if it comes from Jerusalem, don't you think?"

"Of course," Mitchell said. "It's bound to be."

"Will you wear it?" Ruth glanced quickly and shyly at him, sitting there, dangling the medal on its chain.

"All the time," Mitchell said. "Day and night, every mission, every jeep-ride, year in, year out."

"May I put it on for you?"

Mitchell opened his collar and gave the medal to Ruth. She stood up and he bowed his head and she slipped it on, then leaned over and kissed the back of his neck where the chain lay against the flesh.

She stepped back. "Now," she said matter-of-factly. "There we are." She went over to the lamp. "We don't need this any more." She put the light out and went over to the window and threw back the blackout blinds, and a faint breeze carrying salt and the scent of gardens came into the room. She stood at the window, looking out, and Mitchell got up and crossed over to her, feeling the unfamiliar cool jewelry of the medal dangling against his chest. He stood behind her, silently, holding her lightly, looking out over the city. The white buildings shone in the heavy moonlight machined and modern and Biblical all at once, and from the west came the faint sound of the sea. Mitchell wanted to tell her that he would remember her, remember everything about her, her drowned mother and imprisoned father, her old, courageous lover, drinking champagne with her at the Nazi cafés; he wanted to tell her that he would remember the dealings with the Greek sailor and the hold of the ship that had been built in 1887 and the dying Jews buying a lemon with a gold candlestick; he wanted to tell her that flying over the Germans in Europe or watching the first snow fall at Stowe he would remember the small boat grating on the sand in the darkness outside Rehovoth and the week in the closed movie theater with the British patrols outside; he wanted to tell her that the terror and courage would not be forgotten, but he didn't know how to say it, and besides, being honest with himself, he knew it would be difficult to remember, and finally, back in Vermont, it would blur and cloud over and seem unreal as a story in a child's book, read many years ago and now almost forgotten. He held her more tightly, but he said nothing.

"There he is," Ruth said, her voice casual and unimpressed. "See him standing down there next to the house with the picket gate . . ."

Mitchell looked over Ruth's shoulder. Down on the street, thirty yards from the entrance of Ruth's house, was a small dark figure, almost completely lost in shadow.

"Ali Khazen," Ruth said. "He comes and waits outside my window. Ah . . ." she sighed, "I suppose finally he'll kill me."

She turned away from the window and led him back to the couch across the strip of moonlight that divided the room. She looked up at him gravely, then suddenly pushed him gently down to the couch and fell beside him, holding on to him. She held him and kissed his cheek and chuckled a little. "Now, Lieutenant," she said, "tell me about Vermont."

JULIO CORTÁZAR •
1914–1984

Poet, novelist, short story writer, translator of Poe, and a pretty good jazz saxophonist, Cortázar, though born in Brussels, lived near and in Buenos Aires until 1951. He then removed to Paris, his home to the time of his death. Politically anti-Peronist, his revolutionary spirit expressed itself more characteristically in literature. Indeed his novel Hopscotch, which first made his reputation, is an indirect attack not only on the conventional novel but on convention itself. Influenced by surrealism and other French vanguard movements, Cortázar became a leading figure as Latin American "magic realism" proceeded to triumph in the sixties and seventies.

He manipulates a simultaneous disintegration of language and conscious-ness to create fiction that is experimental, ambiguous, hallucinatory, often absurdist, and on occasion self-consciously "modern." His work in prose may be compared with that of René Magritte in painting.

One of his more straightforward efforts, "The Southern Thruway," sim-ply dazzles. The Mexican writer and diplomat Carlos Fuentes calls it a "marvelous story," and that it is, though it seems to deal with the banality of a traffic jam. It may be an ironical metaphor for the bottleneck in which our civilization seems stuck. It may be talking in microcosm about the social contract, about how communities form and succeed and fail. It is certainly a diverting, disturbing commentary on the gifts of technology.

Shortly after Cortázar's death, life decided to imitate art. The newspapers and the airwaves were full of reports of a superjam on the highway leading from the French Alps into Italy. Homage to a dead writer, suggests Fuentes.

The Southern Thruway

Sweltering motorists do not seem to have a history . . . As a reality a traffic
jam is impressive, but it doesn't say much.
— *Arrigo Benedetti*, L'Espresso, Rome, 6.21.64

AT FIRST the girl in the Dauphine had insisted on keeping track of the
time, but the engineer in the Peugeot 404 didn't care anymore. Anyone
could look at his watch, but it was as if that time strapped to your right
wrist or the beep beep on the radio were measuring something else —
the time of those who haven't made the blunder of trying to return to
Paris on the southern thruway on a Sunday afternoon and, just past
Fontainebleau, have had to slow down to a crawl, stop, six rows of cars
on either side (everyone knows that on Sundays both sides of the thruway are reserved for those returning to the capital), start the engine,
move three yards, stop, talk with the two nuns in the 2CV on the right,
look in the rear-view mirror at the pale man driving the Caravelle, ironically envy the birdlike contentment of the couple in the Peugeot 203
(behind the girl's Dauphine) playing with their little girl, joking, and
eating cheese, or suffer the exasperated outbursts of the two boys in the
Simca, in front of the Peugeot 404, and even get out at the stops to
explore, not wandering off too far (no one knows when the cars up front
will start moving again, and you have to run back so that those behind
you won't begin their battle of horn blasts and curses), and thus move
up along a Taunus in front of the girl's Dauphine — she is still watching
the time — and exchange a few discouraged or mocking words with the
two men traveling with the little blond boy, whose great joy at this particular moment is running his toy car over the seats and the rear ledge
of the Taunus, or to dare and move up just a bit, since it doesn't seem
the cars up ahead will budge very soon, and observe with some pity the
elderly couple in the ID Citroën that looks like a big purple bathtub with
the little old man and woman swimming around inside, he resting his
arms on the wheel with an air of resigned fatigue, she nibbling on an
apple, fastidious rather than hungry.

By the fourth time he had seen all that, done all that, the engineer
decided not to leave his car again and to just wait for the police to
somehow dissolve the bottleneck. The August heat mingled with the tire-
level temperature and made immobility increasingly irritating. All was

gasoline fumes, screechy screams from the boys in the Simca, the sun's glare bouncing off glass and chrome frames, and to top it off, the contradictory sensation of being trapped in a jungle of cars made to run. The engineer's 404 occupied the second lane on the right, counting from the median, which meant that he had four cars on his right and seven on his left, although, in fact, he could see distinctly only the eight cars surrounding him and their occupants, whom he was already tired of observing. He had chatted with them all, except for the boys in the Simca, whom he disliked. Between stops the situation had been discussed down to the smallest detail, and the general impression was that, up to Corbeil-Essonnes, they would move more or less slowly, but that between Corbeil and Juvisy things would pick up once the helicopters and motorcycle police managed to break up the worst of the bottleneck. No one doubted that a serious accident had taken place in the area, which could be the only explanation for such an incredible delay. And with that, the government, taxes, road conditions, one topic after another, three yards, another commonplace, five yards, a sententious phrase or a restrained curse.

The two little nuns in the 2CV wanted so much to get to Milly-la-Forêt before eight because they were bringing a basket of greens for the cook. The couple in the Peugeot 203 were particularly interested in not missing the games on television at nine-thirty; the girl in the Dauphine had told the engineer that she didn't care if she got to Paris a little late, she was complaining only as a matter of principle because she thought it was a crime to subject thousands of people to the discomforts of a camel caravan. In the last few hours (it must have been around five, but the heat was unbearable) they had moved about fifty yards according to the engineer's calculations, but one of the men from the Taunus who had come to talk, bringing his little boy with him, pointed ironically to the top of a solitary plane tree, and the girl in the Dauphine remembered that this plane (if it wasn't a chestnut) had been in line with her car for such a long time that she would no longer bother looking at her watch, since all calculations were useless.

Night would never come; the sun's vibrations on the highway and cars pushed vertigo to the edge of nausea. Dark glasses, handkerchiefs moistened with cologne pressed against foreheads, the measures improvised to protect oneself from screaming reflections or from the foul breath expelled by exhaust pipes at every start, were being organized, perfected, and were the object of reflection and commentary. The engineer got out again to stretch his legs, exchanged a few words with the couple (who looked like farmers) traveling in the Ariane in front of the nuns' 2CV. Behind the 2CV was a Volkswagen with a soldier and a girl who looked like newlyweds. The third line toward the edge of the road no longer interested him because he would have had to go dangerously far from the 404; he could distinguish colors, shapes, Mercedes Benz, ID, Lancia,

Skoda, Morris Minor, the whole catalog. To the left, on the opposite side of the road, an unreachable jungle of Renaults, Anglias, Peugeots, Porsches, Volvos. It was so monotonous that finally, after chatting with the two men in the Taunus and unsuccessfully trying to exchange views with the solitary driver of the Caravelle, there was nothing better to do than to go back to the 404 and pick up the same conversation about the time, distances, and the movies with the girl in the Dauphine.

Sometimes a stranger would appear, someone coming from the opposite side of the road or from the outside lanes on the right, who would slip between cars to bring some news, probably false, relayed from car to car along the hot miles. The stranger would savor the impact of his news, the slamming of doors as passengers rushed back to comment on the events; but after a while a horn, or an engine starting up, would drive the stranger away, zigzagging through the cars, rushing to get into his and away from the justified anger of the others. And so, all afternoon, they heard about the crash of a Floride and a 2CV near Corbeil — three dead and one child wounded; the double collision of a Fiat 1500 and a Renault station wagon, which in turn smashed into an Austin full of English tourists; the overturning of an Orly airport bus, teeming with passengers from the Copenhagen flight. The engineer was sure that almost everything was false, although something awful must have happened near Corbeil or even near Paris itself to have paralyzed traffic to such an extent. The farmers in the Ariane, who had a farm near Montereau and knew the region well, told them about another Sunday when traffic had been at a standstill for five hours, but even that much time seemed ludicrous now that the sun, going down on the left side of the road, poured a last avalanche of orange jelly into each car, making metals boil and clouding vision, the treetops behind them never completely disappearing, the shadow barely seen in the distance up ahead never getting near enough so that you could feel the line of cars was moving, even if only a little, even if you had to start and then slam on the breaks and never leave first gear; the dejection of again going from first to neutral, brake, hand brake, stop, and the same thing time and time again.

At one point, tired of inactivity, the engineer decided to take advantage of a particularly endless stop to make a tour of the lanes on the left and, leaving the Dauphine behind he found a DKW, another 2CV, a Fiat 600, and he stopped by a De Soto to chat with an astonished tourist from Washington, D.C. who barely understood French, but had to be at the Place de l'Opéra at eight sharp, you understand, my wife will be awfully anxious, damn it, and they were talking about things in general when a traveling salesman type emerged from the DKW to tell them that someone had come by before saying that a Piper Cub had crashed in the middle of the highway, several dead. The American couldn't give a damn about the Piper Cub, likewise the engineer who, hearing a chorus of horns, rushed back to the 404, passing on the news as he went to the men in the Taunus and the couple in the 203. He saved a more detailed account for the girl in the Dauphine as the cars moved a few slow yards. (Now the Dauphine was slightly behind in relation to the 404, later it would be the opposite; actually, the twelve rows moved as a block, as if an invisible traffic cop at the end of the highway were ordering them to advance in unison, not letting anyone get ahead.) A Piper Cub, Miss, is a small touring plane. Oh. Some nerve crashing right on the thruway on a Sunday afternoon! Really. If only it weren't so hot in these damn cars, if those trees to the right were finally behind us, if the last number in the odometer were finally to fall into its little black hole instead of hanging by its tail, endlessly.

At one point (night was softly falling, the horizon of car tops was turning purple), a big white butterfly landed on the Dauphine's windshield, and the girl and the engineer admired its wings, spread in brief and perfect suspension while it rested; then with acute nostalgia, they watched it fly away over the Taunus and the old couple's ID, head toward the Simca, where a hunter's hand tried vainly to catch it, wing amiably over the Ariane, where the two farmers seemed to be eating something, and finally disappear to the right. At dusk, the line of cars made a first big move of about forty yards; when the engineer looked absently at the odometer, one half of the six had vanished, and the seven was beginning to move down. Almost everybody listened to the radio, and the boys in the Simca had theirs at full blast, singing along with a twist, rocking the car with their gyrations; the nuns were saying their rosaries; the little boy in the Taunus had fallen asleep with his face against the window, the toy car still in his hand. At one point (it was nighttime now), some strangers came with more news, as contradictory as the news already forgotten. It wasn't a Piper, but a glider flown by a general's daughter. It was true that a Renault van had smashed into an Austin, not in Juvisy though, but practically at the gates of Paris. One of the strangers explained to the couple in the 203 that the pavement had caved in around Igny, and five cars had overturned when their front wheels got caught in the cracks. The idea of a natural catastrophe spread all the way to the engineer, who shrugged without a comment. Later, thinking of those first few hours of darkness when they had begun to breathe more easily, he remembered that, at one point, he had stuck his arm out of his window to tap on the Dauphine and wake up the girl; she had fallen asleep, oblivious to a new advance. It was perhaps already midnight when one of the nuns timidly offered him a ham sandwich, assuming that he was hungry. The engineer accepted it (although, in fact, he felt nauseous) and asked if he could share it with the girl in the Dauphine, who accepted and voraciously ate the sandwich and a chocolate bar she got from the traveling salesman in the DKW, her neighbor to the left. A lot of people had stepped out of the stuffy cars, because again it had been hours since the last advance; thirst was prevalent, the bottles of lemonade and even the wine on board were already exhausted. The first to complain was the little girl in the 203, and the soldier and the engineer left their cars to go with her father to get water. In front of the Simca, where the radio seemed to provide ample nourishment, the engineer found a Beaulieu occupied by an older woman with nervous eyes. No, she didn't have any water, but she could give him some candy for the little girl. The couple in the ID consulted each other briefly before the old woman pulled a small can of fruit juice out of her bag. The engineer expressed his gratitude and asked if they were hungry, or if he could be of any service; the old man shook his head, but the old lady seemed to accept his offer silently. Later, the girl from the Dauphine and the engineer explored the rows on the left, without going too far; they came back with a few pastries and gave them to the old lady in the ID, just in time to run back to their own cars under a shower of horn blasts.

Aside from those quick jaunts, there was so little to do that the hours began to blend together, becoming one in the memory; at one point, the engineer thought of striking that day from his appointments book and had to keep from laughing out loud, but later, when the nuns, the men in the Taunus, and the girl in the Dauphine began to make contradictory calculations, he realized it would have been better to keep track of time. The local radio stations stopped transmitting for the day, and only the traveling salesman had a short-wave radio, which insisted on reporting exclusively on the stockmarket. Around three, it seemed as if a tacit agreement had been reached, and the line didn't move until dawn. The boys in the Simca pulled out inflatable beds and lay down by their car; the engineer lowered the back of the front seat of the 404 and offered the cushions to the nuns, who refused them; before lying down for a while, the engineer thought of the girl in the Dauphine, who was still at the wheel, and, pretending it didn't make any difference to him, offered to switch cars with her until dawn, but she refused, claiming that she could sleep fine in any position. For a while, you could hear the boy in the Taunus cry; he was lying on the back seat and probably suffering from the heat. The nuns were still praying when the engineer lay down on the seat and began falling asleep, but his sleep was too close to wakefulness, and he finally awoke sweaty and nervous, not realizing at first where he was. Sitting up straight, he began to perceive confused movements outside, a gliding of shadows between the cars, and then he saw a black bulk disappear toward the edge of the highway; he guessed why, and later he, too, left his car to relieve himself at the edge of the road; there were no hedges or trees, only the starless black fields, something that looked like an abstract wall fencing off the white strip of asphalt with its motionless river of cars. He almost bumped into the farmer from the Ariane, who mumbled something unintelligible; the smell of gasoline over the road now mingled with the more acid presence of man, and the engineer hurried back to his car as soon as he could. The girl in the

Dauphine slept leaning on the steering wheel, a lock of hair in her eyes. Before climbing into the 404, the engineer amused himself by watching her shadow, divining the curve of her slightly puckered lips. On the other side, smoking silently, the man in the DKW was also watching the girl sleep.

In the morning they moved a little, enough to give them hope that by afternoon the route to Paris would open up. At nine, a stranger brought good news: The cracks on the road had been filled, and traffic would soon be back to normal. The boys in the Simca turned on the radio, and one of them climbed on top of the car singing and shouting. The engineer told himself that the news was as false as last night's and that the stranger had taken advantage of the group's happiness to ask for and get an orange from the couple in the Ariane. Later another stranger came and tried the same trick, but got nothing. The heat was beginning to rise, and the people preferred to stay in their cars and wait for the good news to come true. At noon, the little girl in the 203 began crying again, and the girl in the Dauphine went to play with her and made friends with her parents. The 203's had no luck: On the right they had the silent man in the Caravelle, oblivious to everything happening around him, and from their left they had to endure the verbose indignation of the driver of the Floride, for whom the bottleneck was a personal affront. When the little girl complained of thirst again, the engineer decided to talk to the couple in the Ariane, convinced that there were many provisions in that car. To his surprise, the farmers were very friendly; they realized that in a situation like this it was necessary to help one another, and they thought that if someone took charge of the group (the woman made a circular gesture with her hand, encompassing the dozen cars surrounding them), they would have enough to get them to Paris. The idea of appointing himself organizer bothered him, and he chose to call the men from the Taunus for a meeting with the couple in the Ariane. A while later, the rest of the group was consulted one by one. The young soldier in the Volkswagen agreed immediately, and the couple in the 203 offered the few provisions they had left. (The girl in the Dauphine had gotten a glass of pomegranate juice for the little girl, who was now laughing and playing.) One of the Taunus men who went to consult with the boys in the Simca received only mocking consent; the pale man in the Caravelle said it made no difference to him, they could do whatever they wanted. The old couple in the ID and the lady in the Beaulieu reacted with visible joy, as if they felt more protected now. The drivers of the Floride and DKW made no comment, and the American looked at them astonished, saying something about God's will. The engineer found it easy to nominate one of the Taunus men, in whom he had instinctive confidence, as coordinator of all activities. No one would have to go hungry for the time being, but they needed water; the leader, whom the boys in the Simca called Taunus for fun, asked the engineer, the soldier, and one of the boys to explore the zone of highway around them, offering food in exchange for beverages. Taunus, who evidently knew how to command, figured that they should obtain supplies for a maximum of a day and a half, taking the most pessimistic view. In the nuns' 2CV and the farmer's Ariane there were enough supplies for such a period of time and, if the explorers returned with water, all problems would be solved. But only the soldier returned with a full flask, and its owner had demanded food for two people in exchange. The engineer failed to find anyone who could give him water, but his trip allowed him to observe that beyond his group other cells were being organized and were facing similar problems; at a given moment, the driver of an Alfa Romeo refused to speak to him, referring him to the leader of his group five cars behind. Later, the boy from the Simca came back without any water, but Taunus figured they already had enough water for the two children, the old lady in the ID, and the rest of the women. The engineer was telling the girl in the Dauphine about his trip around the periphery (it was one in the afternoon, and the sun kept them in their cars), when she interrupted him with a gesture and pointed to the Simca. In two leaps the engineer reached the car and grabbed the elbow of the boy sprawled in the seat and drinking in great gulps from a flask he had brought back hidden in his jacket. To the boy's angry gesture the engineer responded by increasing the pressure on his arm; the other boy got out of the car and jumped on the engineer, who took two steps back and waited for him, almost with pity. The soldier was already running toward them, and the nuns' shrieks alerted Taunus and his companion. Taunus listened to what had happened, approached the boy with the flask, and slapped him twice. Sobbing, the boy screamed and protested, while the other grumbled without daring to intervene. The engineer took the flask away and gave it to Taunus. Horns began to blare, and everyone returned to his car, but to no avail, since the line moved barely five yards.

At siesta time, under a sun that was even stronger than the day before, one of the nuns took off her coif, and her companion doused her temples with cologne. The women improvised their Samaritan activities little by little, moving from one car to the next, taking care of the children to allow the men more freedom. No one complained, but the jokes were strained, always based on the same word plays, in snobbish skepticism. The greatest humiliation for the girl in the Dauphine and the engineer was to feel sweaty and dirty; the farmers' absolute indifference to the odor that emanated from their armpits moved them to pity. Toward dusk, the engineer looked casually into the rear-view mirror and found, as always, the pale face and tense features of the driver of the Caravelle who, like the fat driver of the Floride, had remained aloof from all the activities. He thought that his features had become sharper and wondered if he were sick. But later on, when he went to talk with the soldier and his wife, he had a chance to look at him more closely and told himself that the man was not sick, that it was something else, a separation, to give it a name. The soldier in the Volkswagen later told him that his wife was afraid of that silent man who never left the wheel and seemed to sleep awake. Conjectures arose; a folklore was created to fight against inactivity. The children in the Taunus and the 203 had become friends, quarreled, and later made up; their parents visited each other, and once in a while the girl in the Dauphine went to see how the old lady in the ID and the woman in the Beaulieu were doing. At dusk, when some gusts of wind swept through, and the sun went behind the clouds in the west, the people were happy, thinking it would get cooler. A few drops fell, coinciding with an extraordinary advance of almost 100 yards; far away, lightning glowed, and it got even hotter. There was so much electricity in the atmosphere that Taunus, with an instinct the engineer silently admired, left the group alone until night, as if he sensed the possible consequences of the heat and fatigue. At eight, the women took charge of distributing the food; it had been decided that the farmer's Ariane should be the general warehouse and the nuns' 2CV a supplementary depot. Taunus had gone in person to confer with the leaders of the four or five neighboring groups; later, with the help of the soldier and the man in the 203, he took an amount of food to the other groups and returned with more water and some wine. It was decided that the boys in the Simca would yield their inflatable beds to the old lady in the ID and the woman in the Beaulieu; the girl in the Dauphine also brought them two plaid blankets, and the engineer offered his car, which he mockingly called the "sleeping car," to whoever might need it. To his surprise, the girl in the Dauphine accepted the offer and that night shared the 404 cushions with one of the nuns; the other nun went to sleep in the 203 with the little girl and her mother, while the husband spent the night on the pavement wrapped in a blanket. The engineer was not sleepy and played dice with Taunus and his mate; at one point, the farmer in the Ariane joined them, and they talked about politics and drank a few shots of brandy that the farmer had turned over to Taunus that morning. The night wasn't bad; it had cooled down, and a few stars shone between the clouds.

Toward morning, they were overcome by sleep, that need to feel covered which came with the half-light of dawn. While Taunus slept beside the boy in the back seat, his friend and the engineer rested up front. Between two images of a dream, the engineer thought he heard screams in the distance and saw a vague glow; the leader of another group came to tell them that thirty cars ahead there had been the beginnings of a fire in an Estafette — someone had tried to boil vegetables on the sly. Taunus joked about the incident as he went from car to car to find out how they had spent the night, but everyone got his message. That morning, the line began to move very early, and there was an excited rush to pick up mattresses and blankets, but, since the same was probably happening all over, almost no one was impatient or blew his horn. Toward noon, they had moved more than fifty yards, and the shadow of a forest could be seen to the right of the highway. They envied those lucky people who at that moment could go to the shoulder of the road and enjoy the shade; maybe there was a brook or a faucet with running water. The girl in the Dauphine closed her eyes and thought of a shower falling down her neck and back, running down her legs; the engineer, observing her out of the corner of his eye, saw two tears streaming down her cheeks.

Taunus, who had moved up to the ID, came back to get the younger women to tend the old lady, who wasn't feeling well. The leader of the third group to the rear had a doctor among his men, and the soldier rushed to get him. The engineer, who had followed with ironical benevolence the efforts the boys in the Simca had been making to be forgiven, thought it was time to give them their chance. With the pieces of a tent the boys covered the windows of the 404, and the "sleeping car" became an ambulance where the old lady could sleep in relative darkness. Her husband lay down beside her, and everyone left them alone with the doctor. Later, the nuns attended to the old lady, who felt much better, and the engineer spent the afternoon as best he could, visiting other cars and resting in Taunus' when the sun bore down too hard; he had to run only three times to his car, where the old couple seemed to sleep, to move it up with the line to the next stop. Night came without their having made it to the forest.

Toward two in the morning, the temperature dropped, and those who had blankets were glad to bundle up. Since the line couldn't move until morning (it was something you felt in the air, that came from the horizon of motionless cars in the night), the engineer sat down to smoke with Taunus and to chat with the farmer in the Ariane and the soldier. Taunus' calculations no longer corresponded to reality, and he said so frankly; something would have to be done in the morning to get more provisions and water. The soldier went to get the leaders of the neighboring groups, who were not sleeping either, and they discussed the problem quietly so as not to wake up the women. The leaders had spoken with the leaders of faraway groups, in a radius of about eighty or 100 cars, and they were sure that the situation was analogous everywhere. The farmer knew the region well and proposed that two or three men from each group go out at dawn to buy provisions from the neighboring farms, while Taunus appointed drivers for the cars left unattended during the expedition. The idea was good, and it was not difficult to collect money from those present; it was decided that the farmer, the soldier, and Taunus' friend would go together, taking all the paper bags, string bags, and flasks available. The other leaders went back to their groups to organize similar expeditions and, at dawn, the situation was explained to the women, and the necessary preparations were made, so that the line could keep moving. The girl in the Dauphine told the engineer that the old lady felt better already and insisted on going back to her ID; at eight, the doctor came and saw no reason why the couple shouldn't return to their car. In any case, Taunus decided that the 404 would be the official ambulance; for fun the boys made a banner with a red cross and put it on the antenna. For a while now, people preferred to leave their cars as little as possible; the temperature continued to drop, and at noon, showers began to fall with lightning in the distance. The farmer's wife rushed to gather water with a funnel and a plastic pitcher, to the special amusement of the boys in the Simca. Watching all this, leaning on his wheel with a book in front of him that he wasn't too interested in, the engineer wondered why the expeditionaries were taking so long; later, Taunus discreetly called him over to his car and, when they got in, told him they had failed. Taunus' friend gave details: The farms were either abandoned or the people refused to sell to them, alleging regulations forbidding the sale to private individuals and suspecting that they were inspectors taking advantage of the circumstances to test them. In spite of everything, they had been able to bring back a small amount of water and some provisions, perhaps stolen by the soldier, who was grinning and not going into details. Of course, the bottleneck couldn't last much longer, but the food they had wasn't the best for the children or the old lady. The doctor, who came around four-thirty to see the sick woman, made a gesture of weariness and exasperation and told Taunus that the same thing was happening in all the neighboring groups. The radio had spoken about emergency measures being taken to clear up the thruway, but aside from a helicopter that appeared briefly at dusk, there was no action to be seen. At any rate, the heat was gradually tapering off, and people seemed to be waiting for night to cover up in their blankets and erase a few more hours of waiting in their sleep. From his car the engineer listened to the conversation between the girl in the Dauphine and the traveling salesman in the DKW, who was telling her jokes that made her laugh halfheartedly. He was surprised to see the lady from the Beaulieu, who never left her car, and got out to see if she needed something, but she only wanted the latest news and went over to talk with the nuns. A nameless tedium weighed upon them at nightfall; people expected more from sleep than from the always contradictory or unfounded news. Taunus' friend discreetly went to get the engineer, the soldier, and the man in the 203. Taunus informed them that the man in the Floride had just deserted; one of the boys in the Simca had seen the car empty and after a while started looking for the man just to kill time. No one knew the fat man in the Floride well. He had complained a lot the first day, but had turned out to be as silent as the driver of the Caravelle. When at five in the morning there was no longer any doubt that Floride, as the boys in the Simca got a kick out of calling him, had deserted, taking a handbag with him and leaving behind another filled with shirts and underwear, Taunus decided that one of the boys would take charge of the abandoned car so as not to immobilize the lane. They were all vaguely annoyed by this desertion in the dark and wondered how far Floride could have gotten in his flight through the fields. Aside from this, it seemed to be the night for big decisions; lying on the seat cushion of his 404, the engineer seemed to hear a moan, but he figured it was coming from the soldier and his wife, which, after all, was understandable in the middle of the night and under such circumstances. But then he thought better and lifted the canvas that covered the rear window; by the light of one of the few stars shining, he saw the ever-present windshield of the Caravelle a yard and a half away, and behind it, as if glued to the glass and slightly slanted, the man's convulsed face. Quietly, he got out the left side so as not to wake up the nuns and approached the Caravelle. Then he looked for Taunus, and the soldier went to get the doctor. Obviously, the man had committed suicide by taking some kind of poison; a few lines scrawled in pencil in his appointments book were enough, plus the letter addressed to one Yvette, someone who had left him in Vierzon. Fortunately, the habit of sleeping in the cars was well established (the nights were so cold now that no one would have thought of staying outside), and few were bothered by others slipping between the cars toward the edges of the thruway to relieve themselves. Taunus called a war council, and the doctor agreed with his proposal. To leave the body on the edge of the road would mean to subject those coming behind to an at least painful surprise; to carry him further out into the fields could provoke a violent reaction from the villagers who, the night before, had threatened and beaten up a boy from another group, out looking for food. The farmer in the Ariane and the traveling salesman had what was needed to hermetically seal the Caravelle's trunk. The girl in the Dauphine joined them just as they were beginning their task, and hung on to the engineer's arm. He quietly explained what had happened and returned her, a little calmer, to her car. Taunus and his men had put the body in the trunk, and the traveling salesman worked with tubes of glue and Scotch tape by the light of the soldier's lantern. Since the woman in the 203 could drive, Taunus decided that her husband would take over the Caravelle, which was on the 203's right; so, in the morning, the little girl in the 203 discovered that her daddy had another car and played for hours at switching cars and putting some of her toys in the Caravelle.

For the first time, it felt cold during the day, and no one thought of taking off his coat. The girl in the Dauphine and the nuns made an inventory of coats available in the group. There were a few sweaters that turned up unexpectedly in the cars, or in some suitcase, a few blankets, a light overcoat or two. A list of priorities was drawn up, and the coats were distributed. Water was again scarce, and Taunus sent three of his men, including the engineer, to try to establish contact with the villagers. While impossible to say why, outside resistance was total. It was enough to step out of the thruway's boundaries for stones to come raining in from somewhere. In the middle of the night, someone threw a sickle that hit the top of the DKW and fell beside the Dauphine. The traveling salesman turned very pale and didn't move from his car, but the American in the De Soto (who was not in Taunus' group, but was appreciated by everyone for his guffaws and good humor) came running, twirled the sickle around and hurled it back with everything he had, shouting curse words. But Taunus did not think it wise to increase the hostility; perhaps it was still possible to make a trip for water.

Nobody kept track anymore of how much they had moved in that day or days; the girl in the Dauphine thought that it was between eighty and two hundred yards; the engineer was not as optimistic, but amused himself by prolonging and confusing his neighbor's calculations, interested in stealing her away from the traveling salesman, who was courting her in his professional manner. That same afternoon, the boy in charge of the Floride came to tell Taunus that a Ford Mercury was offering water at a good price. Taunus refused, but at nightfall one of the nuns asked the engineer for a drink of water for the old lady in the ID, who was suffering in silence, still holding her husband's hand, and being tended alternately by the nuns and the girl in the Dauphine. There was half a bottle of water left, and the women assigned it to the old lady and the woman in the Beaulieu. That same night Taunus paid out of his own pocket for two bottles of water; the Ford Mercury promised to get more the next day, at double the price.

It was difficult to get together and talk, because it was so cold that no one would leave his car except for very pressing reasons. The batteries were beginning to run down, and they couldn't keep the heaters running all the time, so Taunus decided to reserve the two best equipped cars for the sick, should the situation arise. Wrapped in blankets (the boys in the Simca had ripped off the inside covers of their car to make coats and hats for themselves, and others started to imitate them), everyone tried his best to open doors as little as possible to preserve the heat. On one of those freezing nights the engineer heard the girl in the Dauphine sobbing softly. Quietly he opened her door and groped for her in the dark until he felt a wet cheek. Almost without resistance, she let herself be drawn to the 404; the engineer helped her lie down on the back seat, covered her with his only blanket, and then with his overcoat. Darkness was thicker in the ambulance car, its windows covered with the tent's canvas. At one point, the engineer pulled down the two sun visors and hung his shirt and a sweater from them to shut the car off completely. Toward dawn, she whispered in his ear that before starting to cry she thought she saw in the distance, on the right, the lights of a city.

Maybe it was a city, but in the morning mist you couldn't see more than twenty yards away. Curiously, the line moved a lot more that day, perhaps two or three hundred yards. This coincided with new radio flashes. (Hardly anyone listened anymore, with the exception of Taunus, who felt it was his duty to keep up.) The announcers talked emphatically about exceptional measures that would clear the thruway and referred to the weary toil of highway patrolmen and police forces. Suddenly, one of the nuns became delirious. As her companion looked on terrified, and the girl in the Dauphine dabbed her temples with what was left of the cologne, the nun spoke of Armageddon, the Ninth Day, the chain of cinnabar. The doctor came much later, making his way through the snow that had been falling since noon and that was gradually walling the cars in. He regretted the lack of sedatives and advised them to put the nun in a car with good heating. Taunus put her in his own car, and the little boy moved to the Caravelle with his little girl friend from the 203; they played with their toy cars and had a lot of fun, because they were the only ones who didn't go hungry. That day and the following days, it snowed almost continuously, and when the line moved up a few yards, the snow that had accumulated between cars had to be removed by improvised means.

No one would have conceived of being surprised at the way they were getting provisions and water. The only thing Taunus could do was administer the common fund and get as much as possible out of trades. The Ford Mercury and a Porsche came every night to traffic with food; Taunus and the engineer were in charge of distributing it according to the physical state of each one. Incredibly, the old lady in the ID was surviving, although sunken in a stupor that the women diligently fought off. The lady in the Beaulieu, who had been fainting and feeling nauseous a few days before, had recovered with the cold weather and was now one of the most active in helping the nun take care of her companion, still weak and a bit lost. The soldier's wife and 203's were in charge of the two children; the traveling salesman in the DKW, perhaps to console himself for losing Dauphine to the engineer, spent hours telling stories to the children. At night, the groups entered another life, secret and private; doors would open or close to let a frozen figure in or out; no one looked at the others; eyes were as blind as darkness itself. Some kind of happiness endured here and there under dirty blankets, in hands with overgrown fingernails, in bodies smelling of unchanged clothes and of days cramped inside. The girl in the Dauphine had not been mistaken — a city sparkled in the distance, and they were approaching it slowly. In the afternoons, one of the boys in the Simca would climb to the top of the car, relentless lookout wrapped in pieces of seat covers and green burlap. Tired of exploring the futile horizon, he'd look for the thousandth time at the cars surrounding him; somewhat enviously he'd discover Dauphine in 404's car, a hand caressing a neck, the end of a kiss. To play a joke on them, now that he had regained 404's friendship, he'd yell that the line was about to move. Dauphine would have to leave 404 and go to her car, but after a while she'd come back looking for warmth, and the boy in the Simca would have liked so much to bring a girl from another group to his car, but it was unthinkable with this cold and hunger, not to mention that the group up front was openly hostile to Taunus' because of some story about a can of condensed milk, and except for official transactions with Ford Mercury and Porsche, there was no possible contact with other groups. Then the boy in the Simca would sigh unhappily and continue his lookout until the snow and the cold forced him trembling back into his car.

But the cold began to give way and, after a period of rains and winds that enervated a few spirits and increased food supply difficulties, came some cool sunny days when it was again possible to leave your car, pay visits, restore relations with neighboring groups. The leaders had discussed the situation, and peace was finally made with the group ahead. Ford Mercury's sudden disappearance was much talked about, although no one knew what could have happened to him. But Porsche kept coming and controlling the black market. Water and some preserves were never completely lacking, but the group's funds were diminishing, and Taunus and the engineer asked themselves what would happen the day when there was no more money to give Porsche. The possibility of an ambush was brought up, of taking him prisoner and forcing him to reveal the source of his supplies; but the line had advanced a good stretch, and the leaders preferred to wait some more and avoid the risk of ruining it all by a hasty decision. The engineer, who had given into an almost pleasant indifference, was momentarily stunned by the timid news from the girl in the Dauphine, but later he understood that nothing could be done to avoid it, and the idea of having a child by her seemed as natural as the nightly distribution of supplies or the secret trips to the edge of the thruway. Nor could the death of the old lady in the ID surprise anyone. Again it was necessary to work at night, to console her husband, who just couldn't understand, and to keep him company. A fight broke out between the two groups up ahead, and Taunus had to act as mediator and tentatively solve the disagreement. Anything would happen at any moment, without prearranged schedules; the most important things began when nobody expected it anymore, and the least responsible was the first to find out. Standing on the roof of the Simca, the elated lookout had the impression that the horizon had changed (it was dusk; the meager, level light of a yellowish sun was slipping away) and that something unbelievable was happening five hundred, three hundred, two hundred and fifty yards away. He shouted it to 404, and 404 said something to Dauphine, and she dashed to her car, when Taunus, the soldier, and the farmer were already running, and from the roof of the Simca the boy was pointing ahead and endlessly repeating the news as if to convince himself that what he was seeing was true. Then they heard the rumble, as if a heavy but uncontrollable migratory wave were awakening from a long slumber and testing its strength.

Taunus yelled at them to get back to their cars; the Beaulieu, the ID, the Fiat 600, and the De Soto started moving at once. Now the 2CV, the Taunus, the Simca, and the Ariane were beginning to move, and the boy in the Simca, proud of what was to him something of a personal triumph, turned to the 404 and waved his arm, while the 404, the Dauphine, the 2CV, and the DKW in turn started moving. But it all hinged on how long this was going to last, 404 thought almost routinely, as he kept pace with Dauphine and smiled encouragement to her. Behind them, the Volkswagen, the Caravelle, the 203, and the Floride started moving slowly, a stretch in first gear, then second, forever second, but already without having to clutch, as so many times before, with the foot firmly on the accelerator, waiting to move on to third. 404, reaching out to touch Dauphine's hand, barely grazed her fingertips, saw on her face a smile of incredulous hope, and thought that they would make it to Paris and take a bath, go somewhere together, to her house or his to take a bath, eat, bathe endlessly and eat and drink, and that later there would be furniture, a bedroom with furniture and a bathroom with shaving cream to really shave, and toilets, food and toilets and sheets, Paris was a toilet and two sheets and hot water running down his chest and legs, and a nail clipper, and white wine, they would drink white wine before kissing and smell each other's lavender water and cologne before really making love with the lights on, between clean sheets, and bathing again just for fun, to make love and bathe and drink and go to the barber shop, go into the bathroom, caress the sheets and caress each other between the sheets and make love among the suds and lavender water and toothbrushes, before beginning to think about what they were going to do, about the child and all the problems and the future, and all that as long as they didn't stop, just as long as the rows kept on moving, even though you couldn't go to third yet, just moving like that, in second, but moving. With his bumper touching the Simca, 404 leaned back, felt the speed picking up, felt that it was possible to accelerate without bumping into the Simca and that the Simca could accelerate without fear of crashing into Beaulieu, and that behind came the Caravelle and that they all accelerated more and more, and that it was O.K. to move on to third without forcing the engine, and the pace became even, and they all accelerated even more, and 404 looked around with surprise and tenderness, searching for Dauphine's eyes. But, naturally, speeding up like that the lanes could no longer stay parallel. Dauphine had moved almost a yard ahead of 404, and he saw her neck and barely her profile just as she was turning to look at him with surprise, noticing that the 404 was falling further behind. 404 calmed her down with a smile and accelerated abruptly, but he had to brake almost immediately, because he was about to bump the Simca; he blew the horn, and the boy looked at him in the rear-view mirror and made a gesture of helplessness, pointing to the Beaulieu, which was up against him. The Dauphine was three yards ahead, level with the Simca, and the little girl in the 203, now alongside the 404, waved her arms and showed him her doll. A red blot on his right confused 404; instead of the nuns' 2CV or the soldier's Volkswagen, he saw an unknown Chevrolet, and almost immediately the Chevrolet moved ahead followed by a Lancia and a Renault 8. To his left, an ID was gaining on him yard by yard, but before its place was taken by a 403, 404 was still able to make out up ahead the 203 that was already blocking Dauphine. The group was falling apart; it didn't exist anymore. Taunus had to be at least twenty yards away, followed by Dauphine; at the same time, the third row on the left was falling behind since, instead of the traveling salesman's DKW, 404 could see only the rear end of an old black van, perhaps a Citroën or a Peugeot. The cars were in third, gaining or losing ground according to the pace of their lane, and on the side of the thruway trees and some houses in the thick mist and dusk sped by. Later, it was the red lights they all turned on, following the example of those ahead, the night that suddenly closed in on them. From time to time, horns blew, speedometer needles climbed more and more, some lanes were going at forty-five miles an hour, others at forty, some at thirty-five. 404 still hoped that with the gaining and losing of ground he would again catch up with Dauphine, but each minute that slipped by convinced him that it was useless, that the group had dissolved irrevocably, that the everyday meetings would never take place again, the few rituals, the war councils in Taunus' car, Dauphine's caresses in the quiet of night, the children's laughter as they played with their little cars, the nun's face as she said her rosary. When the Simca's brake lights came on, 404 slowed down with an absurd feeling of hope, and as soon as he put on the handbrake he bolted out and ran ahead. Outside of the Simca and the Beaulieu (the Caravelle would be behind him, but he didn't care), he didn't recognize any cars; through strange windows faces he'd never seen before stared at him in surprise and perhaps even outrage. Horns began to blare, and 404 had to go back to his car; the boy in the Simca made a friendly gesture, pointing with encouragement toward Paris. The line got moving again, slowly for a few minutes, and later as if the thruway were completely free. On 404's left was a Taunus, and for a second 404 had the impression that the group was coming together again, that everything was returning to order, that it would be possible to move ahead without destroying anything. But it was a green Taunus, and there was a woman with dark glasses at the wheel who looked straight ahead. There was nothing to do but give in to the pace, adapt mechanically to the speed of the cars around, and not think. His leather jacket must still be in the soldier's Volkswagen. Taunus had the novel he had been reading the first few days. An almost empty bottle of lavender water was in the nuns' 2CV. And he had, there where he touched it at times with his right hand, the teddy bear Dauphine had given him as a pet. He clung absurdly to the idea that at nine-thirty the food would be distributed and the sick would have to be visited, the situation would have to be examined with Taunus and the farmer in the Ariane; then it would be night, Dauphine sneaking into his car, stars or clouds, life. Yes, it had to be like that. All that couldn't have ended forever. Maybe the soldier would get some water, which had been scarce the last few hours; at any rate, you could always count on Porsche, as long as you paid his price. And on the car's antenna the red-cross flag waved madly, and you moved at fifty-five miles an hour toward the lights that kept growing, not knowing why all this hurry, why this mad race in the night among unknown cars, where no one knew anything about the others, where everyone looked straight ahead, only ahead.

BERNARD MALAMUD
1914–1986

Born in Brooklyn, that seedbed of gifted American Jews, Malamud made his living as a teacher and writer. The Magic Barrel (1958), *his first collection of short stories, won a National Book Award; his novel* The Fixer (1966) *gained him another, and a Pulitzer Prize to boot.*

We think of Thomas Mann as a broadly representative German writer, Gide and Balzac as French. In that exact sense perhaps there are no typically American writers. Hawthorne is a New Englander, Faulkner is Deep Southern, and Hemingway a Midwesterner overlaid by cosmopolitanism. Malamud is Brooklyn-Jewish. But, like Hawthorne and Faulkner and Hemingway, he uses regionalism as a kind of idiom with which to convey the ultraparochial. For the most part his is a limited world of poor city Jews. They suffer, they aspire, they are skeptical — and all are seen with an unsentimental tenderness that arcs the gap separating an enclave from the mainstream culture. Whatever our origins, we resonate without difficulty to the vibrations set up by Malamud's funny-sad, often magical sense of the life he knows. "All men are Jews," he once wrote.

"The Jewbird" is a shaggy dog story made to yield rich emotional dividends. In a way it's about anti-Semitism, in another way about Jewish anti-Semitism. But perhaps it is really about one of Malamud's pervading themes: how the experience of suffering changes its face as humor is brought to bear upon it.

The Jewbird

THE WINDOW was open so the skinny bird flew in. Flappity-flap with its frazzled black wings. That's how it goes. It's open, you're in. Closed, you're out and that's your fate. The bird wearily flapped through the open kitchen window of Harry Cohen's top-floor apartment on First Avenue near the lower East River. On a rod on the wall hung an escaped canary cage, its door wide open, but this black-type longbeaked bird — its ruffled head and small dull eyes, crossed a little, making it look like a dissipated crow — landed if not smack on Cohen's thick lamb chop, at least on the table, close by. The frozen foods salesman was sitting at supper with his wife and young son on a hot August evening a year ago. Cohen, a heavy man with hairy chest and beefy shorts; Edie, in skinny yellow shorts and red halter; and their ten-year-old Morris (after her father) — Maurie, they called him, a nice kid though not overly bright — were all in the city after two weeks out, because Cohen's mother was dying. They had been enjoying Kingston, New York, but drove back when Mama got sick in her flat in the Bronx.

"Right on the table," said Cohen, putting down his beer glass and swatting at the bird. "Son of a bitch."

"Harry, take care with your language," Edie said, looking at Maurie, who watched every move.

The bird cawed hoarsely and with a flap of its bedraggled wings — feathers tufted this way and that — rose heavily to the top of the open kitchen door, where it perched staring down.

"Gevalt, a pogrom!"

"It's a talking bird," said Edie in astonishment.

"In Jewish," said Maurie.

"Wise guy," muttered Cohen. He gnawed on his chop, then put down the bone. "So if you can talk, say what's your business. What do you want here?"

"If you can't spare a lamb chop," said the bird, "I'll settle for a piece of herring with a crust of bread. You can't live on your nerve forever."

"This ain't a restaurant," Cohen replied. "All I'm asking is what brings you to this address?"

"The window was open," the bird sighed; adding after a moment, "I'm running. I'm flying but I'm also running."

"From whom?" asked Edie with interest.

"Anti-Semeets."

"Anti-Semites?" they all said.

"That's from who."

"What kind of anti-Semites bother a bird?" Edie asked.

"Any kind," said the bird, "also including eagles, vultures, and hawks. And once in a while some crows will take your eyes out."

"But aren't you a crow?"

"Me? I'm a Jewbird."

Cohen laughed heartily. "What do you mean by that?"

The bird began dovening. He prayed without Book or tallith, but with passion. Edie bowed her head though not Cohen. And Maurie rocked back and forth with the prayer, looking up with one wide-open eye.

When the prayer was done Cohen remarked, "No hat, no phylacteries?"

"I'm an old radical."

"You're sure you're not some kind of a ghost or dybbuk?"

"Not a dybbuk," answered the bird, "though one of my relatives had such an experience once. It's all over now, thanks God. They freed her from a former lover, a crazy jealous man. She's now the mother of two wonderful children."

"Birds?" Cohen asked slyly.

"Why not?"

"What kind of birds?"

"Like me. Jewbirds."

Cohen tipped back in his chair and guffawed. "That's a big laugh. I've heard of a Jewfish but not a Jewbird."

"We're once removed." The bird rested on one skinny leg, then on the other. "Please, could you spare maybe a piece of herring with a small crust of bread?"

Edie got up from the table.

"What are you doing?" Cohen asked her.

"I'll clear the dishes."

Cohen turned to the bird. "So what's your name, if you don't mind saying?"

"Call me Schwartz."

"He might be an old Jew changed into a bird by somebody," said Edie, removing a plate.

"Are you?" asked Harry, lighting a cigar.

"Who knows?" answered Schwartz. "Does God tell us everything?"

Maurie got up on his chair. "What kind of herring?" he asked the bird in excitement.

"Get down, Maurie, or you'll fall," ordered Cohen.

"If you haven't got matjes, I'll take schmaltz," said Schwartz.

"All we have is marinated, with slices of onion — in a jar," said Edie.

"If you'll open for me the jar I'll eat marinated. Do you have also, if you don't mind, a piece of rye bread — the spitz?"

Edie thought she had.

"Feed him out on the balcony," Cohen said. He spoke to the bird. "After that take off."

Schwartz closed both bird eyes. "I'm tired and it's a long way."

"Which direction are you headed, north or south?"

Schwartz, barely lifting his wings, shrugged.

"You don't know where you're going?"

"Where there's charity I'll go."

"Let him stay, papa," said Maurie. "He's only a bird."

"So stay the night," Cohen said, "but no longer."

In the morning Cohen ordered the bird out of the house but Maurie cried, so Schwartz stayed for a while. Maurie was still on vacation from school and his friends were away. He was lonely and Edie enjoyed the fun he had, playing with the bird.

"He's no trouble at all," she told Cohen, "and besides his appetite is very small."

"What'll you do when he makes dirty?"

"He flies across the street in a tree when he makes dirty, and if nobody passes below, who notices?"

"So all right," said Cohen, "but I'm dead set against it. I warn you he ain't gonna stay here long."

"What have you got against the poor bird?"

"Poor bird, my ass. He's a foxy bastard. He thinks he's a Jew."

"What difference does it make what he thinks?"

"A Jewbird, what a chuzpah. One false move and he's out on his drumsticks."

At Cohen's insistence Schwartz lived out on the balcony in a new wooden birdhouse Edie had bought him.

"With many thanks," said Schwartz, "though I would rather have a human roof over my head. You know how it is at my age. I like the warm, the windows, the smell of cooking. I would also be glad to see once in a while the *Jewish Morning Journal* and have now and then a schnapps because it helps my breathing, thanks God. But whatever you give me, you won't hear complaints."

However, when Cohen brought home a bird feeder full of dried corn, Schwartz said, "Impossible."

Cohen was annoyed. "What's the matter, crosseyes, is your life getting too good for you? Are you forgetting what it means to be migratory? I'll bet a helluva lot of crows you happen to be acquainted with, Jews or otherwise, would give their eyeteeth to eat this corn."

Schwartz did not answer. What can you say to a grubber yung?

"Not for my digestion," he later explained to Edie. "Cramps. Herring is better even if it makes you thirsty. At least rainwater don't cost anything." He laughed sadly in breathy caws.

And herring, thanks to Edie, who knew where to shop, was what Schwartz got, with an occasional piece of potato pancake, and even a bit of soupmeat when Cohen wasn't looking.

When school began in September, before Cohen would once again suggest giving the bird the boot, Edie prevailed on him to wait a little while until Maurie adjusted.

"To deprive him right now might hurt his school work, and you know what trouble we had last year."

"So okay, but sooner or later the bird goes. That I promise you."

Schwartz, though nobody had asked him, took on full responsibility for Maurie's performance in school. In return for favors granted, when he was let in for an hour or two at night, he spent most of his time overseeing the boy's lessons. He sat on top of the dresser near Maurie's desk as he laboriously wrote out his homework. Maurie was a restless type and Schwartz gently kept him to his studies. He also listened to him practice his screechy violin, taking a few minutes off now and then to rest his ears in the bathroom. And they afterwards played dominoes. The boy was an indifferent checker player and it was impossible to teach him chess. When he was sick, Schwartz read him comic books though he personally disliked them. But Maurie's work improved in school and even his violin teacher admitted his playing was better. Edie gave Schwartz credit for these improvements though the bird pooh-poohed them.

Yet he was proud there was nothing lower than C minuses on Maurie's report card, and on Edie's insistence celebrated with a little schnapps.

"If he keeps up like this," Cohen said, "I'll get him in an Ivy League college for sure."

"Oh I hope so," sighed Edie.

But Schwartz shook his head. "He's a good boy — you don't have to worry. He won't be a shicker or a wifebeater, God forbid, but a scholar he'll never be, if you know what I mean, although maybe a good mechanic. It's no disgrace in these times."

"If I were you," Cohen said, angered, "I'd keep my big snoot out of other people's private business."

"Harry, please," said Edie.

"My goddamn patience is wearing out. That crosseyes butts into everything."

Though he wasn't exactly a welcome guest in the house, Schwartz gained a few ounces although he did not improve in appearance. He looked bedraggled as ever, his feathers unkempt, as though he had just flown out of a snowstorm. He spent, he admitted, little time taking care of himself. Too much to think about. "Also outside plumbing," he told Edie. Still there was more glow to his eyes so that though Cohen went on calling him crosseyes he said it less emphatically.

Liking his situation, Schwartz tried tactfully to stay out of Cohen's way, but one night when Edie was at the movies and Maurie was taking a hot shower, the frozen foods salesman began a quarrel with the bird.

was, she said, "Be patient, Mr. Schwartz. When the cat gets to know you better he won't try to catch you any more."

"When he stops trying we will both be in Paradise," Schwartz answered. "Do me a favor and get rid of him. He makes my whole life worry. I'm losing feathers like a tree loses leaves."

"I'm awfully sorry but Maurie likes the pussy and sleeps with it."

What could Schwartz do? He worried but came to no decision, being afraid to leave. So he ate the herring garnished with cat food, tried hard not to hear the paper bags bursting like fire crackers outside the birdhouse at night, and lived terror-stricken closer to the ceiling than the floor, as the cat, his tail flicking, endlessly watched him.

Weeks went by. Then on the day after Cohen's mother had died in her flat in the Bronx, when Maurie came home with a zero on an arithmetic test, Cohen, enraged, waited until Edie had taken the boy to his violin lesson, then openly attacked the bird. He chased him with a broom on the balcony and Schwartz frantically flew back and forth, finally escaping into his birdhouse. Cohen triumphantly reached in, and grabbing both skinny legs, dragged the bird out, cawing loudly, his wings wildly beating. He whirled the bird around and around his head. But Schwartz, as he moved in circles, managed to swoop down and catch Cohen's nose in his beak, and hung on for dear life. Cohen cried out in great pain, punched the bird with his fist, and tugging at its legs with all his might, pulled his nose free. Again he swung the yawking Schwartz around until the bird grew dizzy, then with a furious heave, flung him into the night. Schwartz sank like stone into the street. Cohen then tossed the birdhouse and feeder after him, listening at the ledge until they crashed on the sidewalk below. For a full hour, broom in hand, his heart palpitating and nose throbbing with pain, Cohen waited for Schwartz to return but the broken-hearted bird didn't.

That's the end of that dirty bastard, the salesman thought and went in. Edie and Maurie had come home.

"Look," said Cohen, pointing to his bloody nose swollen three times its normal size, "what that sonofabitchy bird did. It's a permanent scar."

"Where is he now?" Edie asked, frightened.

"I threw him out and he flew away. Good riddance."

Nobody said no, though Edie touched a handkerchief to her eyes and Maurie rapidly tried the nine times table and found he knew approximately half.

In the spring when the winter's snow had melted, the boy, moved by a memory, wandered in the neighborhood, looking for Schwartz. He found a dead black bird in a small lot near the river, his two wings broken, neck twisted, and both bird-eyes plucked clean.

"Who did it to you, Mr. Schwartz?" Maurie wept.

"Anti-Semeets," Edie said later.

SAUL BELLOW
1915–

Bellow is an intellectual who does not think and write as nonintellectuals believe intellectuals think and write. He has no program of "ideas," his world is not exclusionary, his language is as open, as vigorous, as colloquial as Mark Twain's. Though much of his work dramatizes the dilemmas, often comic, faced by American Jews, he eludes any such diminishing label as "American-Jewish novelist." The range of his interest is as broad as his sympathies are deep. As a whole his work adds a special luster to the noble word "humanist"; he belongs among the sagest and most philosophic of our novelists. No mistake was made when in 1976 he won the Nobel Prize for literature.

Bellow's powers are most fully displayed in such novels as the picaresque Adventures of Augie March, *the beautifully constructed* Herzog, *and the sad-comic* Mr. Sammler's Planet. *But the collection* Him with His Foot in His Mouth and Other Stories *shows how effective he can be when the scope is more restricted. From it is drawn "A Silver Dish."*

Here Bellow interweaves a number of themes: the intersection, in our loose societal agglomerate, of three religious faiths; the influence of a delightful rascal of a father on a solid bourgeois son; the surprising moral ramifications of an unvirtuous act. A complex story — rueful, ruminative, droll — it is one of Bellow's most knowledgeable studies of American urban life, a territory he has marked as his own.

A Silver Dish

WHAT DO YOU DO about death — in this case, the death of an old father? If you're a modern person, sixty years of age, and a man who's been around, like Woody Selbst, what do you do? Take this matter of mourning, and take it against a contemporary background. How, against a contemporary background, do you mourn an octogenarian father, nearly blind, his heart enlarged, his lungs filling with fluid, who creeps, stumbles, gives off the odors, the moldiness or gassiness, of old men. I *mean!* As Woody put it, be realistic. Think what times these are. The papers daily give it to you — the Lufthansa pilot in Aden is described by the hostages, on his knees, begging the Palestinian terrorists not to execute him, but they shoot him through the head. Later they themselves are killed. And still others shoot others, or shoot themselves. That's what you read in the press, see on the tube, mention at dinner. We know now what goes daily through the whole of the human community, like a global death-peristalsis.

Woody, a businessman in South Chicago, was not an ignorant person. He knew more such phrases than you would expect a tile contractor (offices, lobbies, lavatories) to know. The kind of knowledge he had was not the kind for which you get academic degrees. Although Woody had studied for two years in a seminary, preparing to be a minister. Two years of college during the Depression was more than most high-school graduates could afford. After that, in his own vital, picturesque, original way (Morris, his old man, was also, in his days of nature, vital and picturesque), Woody had read up on many subjects, subscribed to *Science* and other magazines that gave real information, and had taken night courses at De Paul and Northwestern in ecology, criminology, existentialism. Also he had traveled extensively in Japan, Mexico, and Africa, and there was an African experience that was especially relevant to mourning. It was this: on a launch near the Murchison Falls in Uganda, he had seen a buffalo calf seized by a crocodile from the bank of the White Nile. There were giraffes along the tropical river, and hippopotamuses, and baboons, and flamingos and other brilliant birds crossing the bright air in the heat of the morning, when the calf, stepping into the river to drink, was grabbed by the hoof and dragged down. The parent buffaloes couldn't figure it out. Under the water the calf still threshed, fought, churned the mud. Woody, the robust traveler, took this in as he sailed by, and to him it looked as if the parent cattle were asking each other dumbly what had happened. He chose to assume that there was pain in this, he read brute grief into it. On the White Nile, Woody had the impression that he had gone back to the pre-Adamite past, and he brought reflections on this impression home to South Chicago. He brought also a bundle of hashish from Kampala. In this he took a chance with the customs inspectors, banking perhaps on his broad build, frank face, high color. He didn't look like a wrongdoer, a bad guy; he looked like a good guy. But he liked taking chances. Risk was a wonderful stimulus. He threw down his trenchcoat on the customs counter. If the inspectors searched the pockets, he was prepared to say that the coat wasn't his. But he got away with it, and the Thanksgiving turkey was stuffed with hashish. This was much enjoyed. That was practically the last feast at which Pop, who also relished risk or defiance, was present. The hashish Woody had tried to raise in his backyard from the Africa seeds didn't take. But behind his warehouse, where the Lincoln Continental was parked, he kept a patch of marijuana. There was no harm at all in Woody, but he didn't like being entirely within the law. It was simply a question of self-respect.

After that Thanksgiving, Pop gradually sank as if he had a slow leak. This went on for some years. In and out of the hospital, he dwindled, his mind wandered, he couldn't even concentrate enough to complain, except in exceptional moments on the Sundays Woody regularly devoted to him. Morris, an amateur who once was taken seriously by Willie Hoppe, the great pro himself, couldn't execute the simplest billiard shots anymore. He could only conceive shots; he began to theorize about impossible three-cushion combinations. Halina, the Polish woman with whom Morris had lived for over forty years as man and wife, was too old herself now to run to the hospital. So Woody had to do it. There was Woody's mother, too — a Christian convert — needing care; she was over eighty and frequently hospitalized. Everybody had diabetes and pleurisy and arthritis and cataracts and cardiac pacemakers. And everybody had lived by the body, but the body was giving out.

There were Woody's two sisters as well, unmarried, in their fifties, very Christian, very straight, still living with Mama in an entirely Christian bungalow. Woody, who took full responsibility for them all, occasionally had to put one of the girls (they had become sick girls) in a mental institution. Nothing severe. The sisters were wonderful women, both of them gorgeous once, but neither of the poor things was playing with a full deck. And all the factions had to be kept separate — Mama, the Christian convert; the fundamentalist sisters; Pop, who read the Yiddish paper as long as he could still see print; Halina, a good Catholic. Woody, the seminary forty years behind him, described himself as an agnostic. Pop had no more religion than you could find in the Yiddish paper, but he made Woody promise to bury him among Jews, and that was where he lay now, in the Hawaiian shirt Woody had bought for him at the tilers' convention in Honolulu. Woody would allow no undertaker's as-

sistant to dress him, but came to the parlor and buttoned the stiff into
the shirt himself, and the old man went down looking like Ben-Gurion
in a simple wooden coffin, sure to rot fast. That was how Woody wanted
it all. At the graveside, he had taken off and folded his jacket, rolled up
his sleeves on thick freckled biceps, waved back the little tractor standing by, and shoveled the dirt himself. His big face, broad at the bottom,
narrowed upward like a Dutch house. And, his small good lower teeth
taking hold of the upper lip in his exertion, he performed the final duty
of a son. He was very fit, so it must have been emotion, not the shov-
eling, that made him redden so. After the funeral, he went home with
Halina and her son, a decent Polack like his mother, and talented, too
— Mitosh played the organ at hockey and basketball games in the Stadium, which took a smart man because it was a rabble-rousing kind of
occupation — and they had some drinks and comforted the old girl.
Halina was true blue, always one hundred percent for Morris.

Then for the rest of the week Woody was busy, had jobs to run, office
responsibilities, family responsibilities. He lived alone; as did his wife;
as did his mistress: everybody in a separate establishment. Since his wife,
after fifteen years of separation, had not learned to take care of herself,
Woody did her shopping on Fridays, filled her freezer. He had to take
her this week to buy shoes. Also, Friday night he always spent with
Helen — Helen was his wife de facto. Saturday he did his big weekly
shopping. Saturday night he devoted to Mom and his sisters. So he was
too busy to attend to his own feelings except, intermittently, to note to
himself, "First Thursday in the grave." "First Friday, and fine weather."
"First Saturday; he's got to be getting used to it." Under his breath he
occasionally said, "Oh, Pop."

But it was Sunday that hit him, when the bells rang all over South
Chicago — the Ukrainian, Roman Catholic, Greek, Russian, African
Methodist churches, sounding off one after another. Woody had his offices in his warehouse, and there had built an apartment for himself, very
spacious and convenient, in the top story. Because he left every Sunday
morning at seven to spend the day with Pop, he had forgotten by how
many churches Selbst Tile Company was surrounded. He was still in bed
when he heard the bells, and all at once he knew how heartbroken he
was. This sudden big heartache in a man of sixty, a practical, physical,
healthy-minded, and experienced man, was deeply unpleasant. When he
had an unpleasant condition, he believed in taking something for it. So
he thought: What shall I take? There were plenty of remedies available.
His cellar was stocked with cases of Scotch whisky, Polish vodka, Ar-
magnac, Moselle, Burgundy. There were also freezers with steaks and
with game and with Alaskan king crab. He bought with a broad hand
—by the crate and by the dozen. But in the end, when he got out of bed,
he took nothing but a cup of coffee. While the kettle was heating, he
put on his Japanese judo-style suit and sat down to reflect.

Woody was moved when things were *honest*. Bearing beams were honest, undisguised concrete pillars inside high-rise apartments were honest. It was bad to cover up anything. He hated faking. Stone was honest. Metal was honest. These Sunday bells were very straight. They broke loose, they wagged and rocked, and the vibrations and the banging did something for him — cleansed his insides, purified his blood. A bell was a one-way throat, had only one thing to tell you and simply told it. He listened.

He had had some connections with bells and churches. He was after all something of a Christian. Born a Jew, he was a Jew facially, with a hint of Iroquois or Cherokee, but his mother had been converted more than fifty years ago by her brother-in-law, the Reverend Doctor Kovner. Kovner, a rabbinical student who had left the Hebrew Union College in Cincinnati to become a minister and establish a mission, had given Woody a partly Christian upbringing. Now, Pop was on the outs with these fundamentalists. He said that the Jews came to the mission to get coffee, bacon, canned pineapple, day-old bread, and dairy products. And if they had to listen to sermons, that was okay — this was the Depression and you couldn't be too particular — but he knew they sold the bacon.

The Gospels said it plainly: "Salvation is from the Jews."

Backing the Reverend Doctor were wealthy fundamentalists, mainly Swedes, eager to speed up the Second Coming by converting all Jews. The foremost of Kovner's backers was Mrs. Skoglund, who had inherited a large dairy business from her late husband. Woody was under her special protection.

Woody was fourteen years of age when Pop took off with Halina, who worked in his shop, leaving his difficult Christian wife and his converted son and his small daughters. He came to Woody in the backyard one spring day and said, "From now on you're the man of the house." Woody was practicing with a golf club, knocking off the heads of dandelions. Pop came into the yard in his good suit, which was too hot for the weather, and when he took off his fedora the skin of his head was marked with a deep ring and the sweat was sprinkled over his scalp — more drops than hairs. He said, "I'm going to move out." Pop was anxious, but he was set to go — determined. "It's no use. I can't live a life like this." Envisioning the life Pop simply *had* to live, his free life, Woody was able to picture him in the billiard parlor, under the El tracks in a crap game, or playing poker at Brown and Koppel's upstairs. "You're going to be the man of the house," said Pop. "It's okay. I put you all on welfare. I just got back from Wabansia Avenue, from the relief station." Hence the suit and the hat. "They're sending out a caseworker." Then he said, "You got to lend me money to buy gasoline — the caddie money you saved."

Understanding that Pop couldn't get away without his help, Woody turned over to him all he had earned at the Sunset Ridge Country Club in Winnetka. Pop felt that the valuable life lesson he was transmitting was worth far more than these dollars, and whenever he was conning his boy a sort of high-priest expression came down over his bent nose, his ruddy face. The children, who got their finest ideas at the movies, called him Richard Dix. Later, when the comic strip came out, they said he was Dick Tracy.

As Woody now saw it, under the tumbling bells, he had bankrolled his own desertion. Ha ha! He found this delightful; and especially Pop's attitude of "That'll teach you to trust your father." For this was a demonstration on behalf of real life and free instincts, against religion and hypocrisy. But mainly it was aimed against being a fool, the disgrace of foolishness. Pop had it in for the Reverend Doctor Kovner, not because he was an apostate (Pop couldn't have cared less), not because the mission was a racket (he admitted that the Reverend Doctor was personally honest), but because Doctor Kovner behaved foolishly, spoke like a fool, and acted like a fiddler. He tossed his hair like a Paganini (this was Woody's addition; Pop had never even heard of Paganini). Proof that he was not a spiritual leader was that he converted Jewish women by stealing their hearts. "He works up all those broads," said Pop. "He doesn't even know it himself, I swear he doesn't know how he gets them."

From the other side, Kovner often warned Woody, "Your father is a dangerous person. Of course, you love him; you should love him and forgive him, Voodrow, but you are old enough to understand he is leading a life of wice."

It was all petty stuff: Pop's sinning was on a boy level and therefore made a big impression on a boy. And on Mother. Are wives children, or what? Mother often said, "I hope you put that brute in your prayers. Look what he has done to us. But only pray for him, don't see him." But he saw him all the time. Woodrow was leading a double life, sacred and profane. He accepted Jesus Christ as his personal redeemer. Aunt Rebecca took advantage of this. She made him work. He had to work under Aunt Rebecca. He filled in for the janitor at the mission and settlement house. In winter, he had to feed the coal furnace, and on some nights he slept near the furnace room, on the pool table. He also picked the lock of the storeroom. He took canned pineapple and cut bacon from the flitch with his pocketknife. He crammed himself with uncooked bacon. He had a big frame to fill out.

Only now, sipping Melitta coffee, he asked himself: Had he been so hungry? No, he loved being reckless. He was fighting Aunt Rebecca Kovner when he took out his knife and got on a box to reach the bacon. She didn't know, she couldn't prove that Woody, such a frank, strong, positive boy, who looked you in the eye, so direct, was a thief also. But he was also a thief. Whenever she looked at him, he knew that she was seeing his father. In the curve of his nose, the movements of his eyes, the thickness of his body, in his healthy face, she saw that wicked savage Morris.

Morris, you see, had been a street boy in Liverpool — Woody's mother and her sister were British by birth. Morris's Polish family, on their way to America, abandoned him in Liverpool because he had an eye infection and they would all have been sent back from Ellis Island. They stopped awhile in England, but his eyes kept running and they ditched him. They slipped away, and he had to make out alone in Liverpool at the age of twelve. Mother came of better people. Pop, who slept in the cellar of her house, fell in love with her. At sixteen, scabbing during a seamen's strike, he shoveled his way across the Atlantic and jumped ship in Brooklyn. He became an American, and America never knew it. He voted without papers, he drove without a license, he paid no taxes, he cut every corner. Horses, cards, billiards, and women were his lifelong interests, in ascending order. Did he love anyone (he was so busy)? Yes, he loved Halina. He loved his son. To this day, Mother believed that he had loved her most and always wanted to come back. This gave her a chance to act the queen, with her plump wrists and faded Queen Victoria face. "The girls are instructed never to admit him," she said. The Empress of India speaking.

Bell-battered Woodrow's soul was whirling this Sunday morning, indoors and out, to the past, back to his upper corner of the warehouse, laid out with such originality — the bells coming and going, metal on naked metal, until the bell circle expanded over the whole of steel-making, oil-refining, power-producing mid-autumn South Chicago, and all its Croatians, Ukrainians, Greeks, Poles, and respectable blacks heading for their churches to hear Mass or to sing hymns.

Woody himself had been a good hymn singer. He still knew the hymns. He had testified, too. He was often sent by Aunt Rebecca to get up and tell a churchful of Scandihoovians that he, a Jewish lad, accepted Jesus Christ. For this she paid him fifty cents. She made the disbursement. She was the bookkeeper, fiscal chief, general manager of the mission. The Reverend Doctor didn't know a thing about the operation. What the Doctor supplied was the fervor. He was genuine, a wonderful preacher. And what about Woody himself? He also had fervor. He was drawn to the Reverend Doctor. The Reverend Doctor taught him to lift up his eyes, gave him his higher life. Apart from this higher life, the rest was Chicago — the ways of Chicago, which came so natural that nobody thought to question them. So, for instance, in 1933 (what ancient, ancient times!), at the Century of Progress World's Fair, when Woody was a coolie and pulled a rickshaw, wearing a peaked straw hat and trotting with powerful, thick legs, while the brawny red farmers — his boozing passengers — were laughing their heads off and pestered him for whores, he, although a freshman at the seminary, saw nothing wrong, when girls asked him to steer a little business their way, in making dates and accepting tips from both sides. He necked in Grant Park with a powerful girl who had to go home quickly to nurse her baby. Smelling of milk, she rode beside him on the streetcar to the West Side, squeezing his rickshaw puller's thigh and wetting her blouse. This was the Roosevelt Road car. Then, in the apartment where she lived with her mother, he couldn't remember that there were any husbands around. What he did remember was the strong milk odor. Without inconsistency, next morning he did New Testament Greek: The light shineth in darkness — *to fos en te skotia fainei* — and the darkness comprehended it not.

And all the while he trotted between the shafts on the fairgrounds he had one idea, nothing to do with these horny giants having a big time in the city: that the goal, the project, the purpose was (and he couldn't explain why he thought so; all evidence was against it) — God's idea was that this world should be a love world, that it should eventually recover and be entirely a world of love. He wouldn't have said this to a soul, for he could see himself how stupid it was — personal and stupid. Nevertheless, there it was at the center of his feelings. And at the same time, Aunt Rebecca was right when she said to him, strictly private, close to his ear even, "You're a little crook, like your father."

There was some evidence for this, or what stood for evidence to an impatient person like Rebecca. Woody matured quickly — he had to — but how could you expect a boy of seventeen, he wondered, to interpret the viewpoint, the feelings, of a middle-aged woman, and one whose breast had been removed? Morris told him that this happened only to neglected women, and was a sign. Morris said that if titties were not fondled and kissed, they got cancer in protest. It was a cry of the flesh. And this had seemed true to Woody. When his imagination tried the theory on the Reverend Doctor, it worked out — he couldn't see the Reverend Doctor behaving in that way to Aunt Rebecca's breasts! Morris's theory kept Woody looking from bosoms to husbands and from husbands to bosoms. He still did that. It's an exceptionally smart man who isn't marked forever by the sexual theories he hears from his father, and Woody wasn't all that smart. He knew this himself. Personally, he had gone far out of his way to do right by women in this regard. What nature demanded. He and Pop were common, thick men, but there's nobody too gross to have ideas of delicacy.

The Reverend Doctor preached, Rebecca preached, rich Mrs. Skoglund preached from Evanston, Mother preached. Pop also was on a soapbox. Everyone was doing it. Up and down Division Street, under every lamp, almost, speakers were giving out: anarchists, Socialists, Stalinists, single-taxers, Zionists, Tolstoyans, vegetarians, and fundamentalist Christian preachers — you name it. A beef, a hope, a way of life or salvation, a protest. How was it that the accumulated gripes of all the ages took off so when transplanted to America?

And that fine Swedish immigrant Aase (Osie, they pronounced it), who had been the Skoglunds' cook and married the eldest son, to become his rich, religious widow — she supported the Reverend Doctor. In her time she must have been built like a chorus girl. And women seem to have lost the secret of putting up their hair in the high basketry fence of braid she wore. Aase took Woody under her special protection and paid his tuition at the seminary. And Pop said . . . But on this Sunday, at peace as soon as the bells stopped banging, this velvet autumn day when the grass was finest and thickest, silky green: before the first frost, and the blood in your lungs is redder than summer air can make it and smarts with oxygen, as if the iron in your system was hungry for it, and the chill was sticking it to you in every breath . . . Pop, six feet under, would never feel this blissful sting again. The last of the bells still had the bright air streaming with vibrations.

On weekends, the institutional vacancy of decades came back to the warehouse and crept under the door of Woody's apartment. It felt as empty on Sundays as churches were during the week. Before each business day, before the trucks and the crews got started, Woody jogged five miles in his Adidas suit. Not on this day still reserved for Pop, however. Although it was tempting to go out and run off the grief. Being alone hit Woody hard this morning. He thought: Me and the world; the world and me. Meaning that there always was some activity to interpose, an errand or a visit, a picture to paint (he was a creative amateur), a massage, a meal — a shield between himself and that troublesome solitude which used the world as its reservoir. But Pop! Last Tuesday, Woody had gotten into the hospital bed with Pop because he kept pulling out the intravenous needles. Nurses stuck them back, and then Woody astonished them all by climbing into bed to hold the struggling old guy in his arms. "Easy, Morris, Morris, go easy." But Pop still groped feebly for the pipes.

When the tolling stopped, Woody didn't notice that a great lake of quiet had come over his kingdom, the Selbst Tile warehouse. What he heard and saw was an old red Chicago streetcar, one of those trams the color of a stockyard steer. Cars of this type went out before Pearl Harbor — clumsy, big-bellied, with tough rattan seats and brass grips for the standing passengers. Those cars used to make four stops to the mile, and ran with a wallowing motion. They stank of carbolic or ozone and throbbed when the air compressors were being charged. The conductor had his knotted signal cord to pull, and the motorman beat the foot gong with his mad heel.

Woody recognized himself on the Western Avenue line and riding through a blizzard with his father, both in sheepskins and with hands and faces raw, the snow blowing in from the rear platform when the doors opened and getting into the longitudinal cleats of the floor. There wasn't warmth enough inside to melt it. And Western Avenue was the longest car line in the world, the boosters said, as if it was a thing to brag about. Twenty-three miles long, made by a draftsman with a T square, lined with factories, storage buildings, machine shops, used-car lots, trolley barns, gas stations, funeral parlors, six-flats, utility buildings, and junkyards, on and on from the prairies on the south to Evanston on the north. Woodrow and his father were going north to Evanston, to Howard Street, and then some, to see Mrs. Skoglund. At the end of the line they would still have about five blocks to hike. The purpose of the trip? To raise money for Pop. Pop had talked him into this. When they found out, Mother and Aunt Rebecca would be furious, and Woody was afraid, but he couldn't help it.

Morris had come and said, "Son, I'm in trouble. It's bad."

"What's bad, Pop?"

"Halina took money from her husband for me and has to put it back before old Bujak misses it. He could kill her."

"What did she do it for?"

"Son, you know how the bookies collect? They send a goon. They'll break my head open."

"Pop! You know I can't take you to Mrs. Skoglund."

"Why not? You're my kid, aren't you? The old broad wants to adopt you, doesn't she? Shouldn't I get something out of it for my trouble? What am I — outside? And what about Halina? She puts her life on the line, but my own kid says no."

"Oh, Bujak wouldn't hurt her."

"Woody, he'd beat her to death."

Bujak? Uniform in color with his dark-gray work clothes, short in the legs, his whole strength in his tool-and-die-maker's forearms and black fingers; and beat-looking — there was Bujak for you. But, according to Pop, there was big, big violence in Bujak, a regular boiling Bessemer inside his narrow chest. Woody could never see the violence in him. Bujak wanted no trouble. If anything, maybe he was afraid that Morris and Halina would gang up on him and kill him, screaming. But Pop was no desperado murderer. And Halina was a calm, serious woman. Bujak kept his savings in the cellar (banks were going out of business). The worst they did was to take some of his money, intending to put it back. As Woody saw him, Bujak was trying to be sensible. He accepted his sorrow. He set minimum requirements for Halina: cook the meals, clean the house, show respect. But at stealing Bujak might have drawn the line, for money was different, money was vital substance. If they stole his savings he might have had to take action, out of respect for the substance, for himself — self-respect. But you couldn't be sure that Pop hadn't invented the bookie, the goon, the theft — the whole thing. He was capable of it, and you'd be a fool not to suspect him. Morris knew that Mother and Aunt Rebecca had told Mrs. Skoglund how wicked he was. They had painted him for her in poster colors — purple for vice, black for his soul, red for Hell flames: a gambler, smoker, drinker, deserter, screwer of women, and atheist. So Pop was determined to reach her. It was risky for everybody. The Reverend Doctor's operating costs were met by Skoglund Dairies. The widow paid Woody's seminary tuition; she bought dresses for the little sisters.

Woody, now sixty, fleshy and big, like a figure for the victory of American materialism, sunk in his lounge chair, the leather of its armrests softer to his fingertips than a woman's skin, was puzzled and, in his depths, disturbed by certain blots within him, blots of light in his brain, a blot combining pain and amusement in his breast (how did *that* get there?). Intense thought puckered the skin between his eyes with a strain bordering on headache. Why had he let Pop have his way? Why did he agree to meet him that day, in the dim rear of the poolroom?

"But what will you tell Mrs. Skoglund?"

"The old broad? Don't worry, there's plenty to tell her, and it's all true. Ain't I trying to save my little laundry-and-cleaning shop? Isn't the bailiff coming for the fixtures next week?" And Pop rehearsed his pitch on the Western Avenue car. He counted on Woody's health and his freshness. Such a straightforward-looking body was perfect for a con.

Did they still have such winter storms in Chicago as they used to have? Now they somehow seemed less fierce. Blizzards used to come straight down from Ontario, from the Arctic, and drop five feet of snow in an afternoon. Then the rusty green platform cars, with revolving brushes at both ends, came out of the barns to sweep the tracks. Ten or twelve streetcars followed in slow processions, or waited, block after block.

There was a long delay at the gates of Riverview Park, all the amusements covered for the winter, boarded up — the dragon's-back high-rides, the Bobs, the Chute, the Tilt-a-Whirl, all the fun machinery put together by mechanics and electricians, men like Bujak the tool-and-die-maker, good with engines. The blizzard was having it all its own way behind the gates, and you couldn't see far inside; only a few bulbs burned behind the palings. When Woody wiped the vapor from the glass, the wire mesh of the window guards was stuffed solid at eye level with snow. Looking higher, you saw mostly the streaked wind horizontally driving from the north. In the seat ahead, two black coal heavers, both in leather Lindbergh flying helmets, sat with shovels between their legs, returning from a job. They smelled of sweat, burlap sacking, and coal. Mostly dull with black dust, they also sparkled here and there.

There weren't many riders. People weren't leaving the house. This was a day to sit legs stuck out beside the stove, mummified by both the outdoor and the indoor forces. Only a fellow with an angle, like Pop, would go and buck such weather. A storm like this was out of the compass, and you kept the human scale by having a scheme to raise fifty bucks. Fifty soldiers! Real money in 1933.

"That woman is crazy for you," said Pop.

"She's just a good woman, sweet to all of us."

"Who knows what she's got in mind. You're a husky kid. Not such a kid, either."

"She's a religious woman. She really has religion."

"Well, your mother isn't your only parent. She and Rebecca and Kovner aren't going to fill you up with their ideas. I know your mother wants to wipe me out of your life. Unless I take a hand, you won't even understand what life is. Because they don't know — those silly Christers."

"Yes, Pop."

"The girls I can't help. They're too young. I'm sorry about them, but I can't do anything. With you it's different."

He wanted me like himself, an American.

They were stalled in the storm, while the cattle-colored car waited to have the trolley reset in the crazy wind, which boomed, tingled, blasted. At Howard Street they would have to walk straight into it, due north.

"You'll do the talking at first," said Pop.

Woody had the makings of a salesman, a pitchman. He was aware of this when he got to his feet in church to testify before fifty or sixty people. Even though Aunt Rebecca made it worth his while, he moved his own heart when he spoke up about his faith. But occasionally, without notice, his heart went away as he spoke religion and he couldn't find it anywhere. In its absence, sincere behavior got him through. He had to rely for delivery on his face, his voice — on behavior. Then his eyes came closer and closer together. And in this approach of eye to eye he felt the strain of hypocrisy. The twisting of his face threatened to betray him. It took everything he had to keep looking honest. So, since he couldn't bear the cynicism of it, he fell back on mischievousness. Mischief was where Pop came in. Pop passed straight through all those divided fields, gap after gap, and arrived at his side, bent-nosed and broad-faced. In regard to Pop, you thought of neither sincerity nor insincerity. Pop was like the man in the song: he wanted what he wanted when he wanted it. Pop was physical; Pop was digestive, circulatory, sexual. If Pop got serious, he talked to you about washing under the arms or in the crotch or of drying between your toes or of cooking supper, of baked beans and fried onions, of draw poker or of a certain horse in the fifth race at Arlington. Pop was elemental. That was why he gave such relief from religion and paradoxes, and things like that. Now, Mother *thought* she was spiritual, but Woody knew that she was kidding herself. Oh, yes, in the British accent she never gave up she was always talking to God or about Him — please God, God willing, praise God. But she was a big substantial bread-and-butter down-to-earth woman, with down-to-earth duties like feeding the girls, protecting, refining, keeping pure the girls. And those two protected doves grew up so overweight, heavy in the hips and thighs, that their poor heads looked long and slim. And mad. Sweet but cuckoo — Paula cheerfully cuckoo, Joanna depressed and having episodes.

"I'll do my best by you, but you have to promise, Pop, not to get me in Dutch with Mrs. Skoglund."

"You worried because I speak bad English? Embarrassed? I have a mockie accent?"

"It's not that. Kovner has a heavy accent, and she doesn't mind."

"Who the hell are those freaks to look down on me? You're practically a man and your dad has a right to expect help from you. He's in a fix. And you bring him to her house because she's bighearted, and you haven't got anybody else to go to."

"I got you, Pop."

The two coal trimmers stood up at Devon Avenue. One of them wore a woman's coat. Men wore women's clothing in those years, and women men's, when there was no choice. The fur collar was spiky with the wet, and sprinkled with soot. Heavy, they dragged their shovels and got off at the front. The slow car ground on, very slow. It was after four when they reached the end of the line, and somewhere between gray and black, with snow sprouting and whirling under the street lamps. In Howard Street, autos were stalled at all angles and abandoned. The sidewalks were blocked. Woody led the way into Evanston, and Pop followed him up the middle of the street in the furrows made earlier by trucks. For four blocks they bucked the wind and then Woody broke through the drifts to the snowbound mansion, where they both had to push the wrought-iron gate because of the drift behind it. Twenty rooms or more in this dignified house and nobody in them but Mrs. Skoglund and her servant Hjordis, also religious.

As Woody and Pop waited, brushing the slush from their sheepskin collars and Pop wiping his big eyebrows with the ends of his scarf, sweating and freezing, the chains began to rattle and Hjordis uncovered the air holes of the glass storm door by turning a wooden bar. Woody called her "monk-faced." You no longer see women like that, who put no female touch on the face. She came plain, as God made her. She said, "Who is it and what do you want?"

"It's Woodrow Selbst. Hjordis? It's Woody."

"You're not expected."

"No, but we're here."

"What do you want?"

"We came to see Mrs. Skoglund."

"What for do you want to see her?"

"Just tell her we're here."

"I have to tell her what you came for, without calling up first."

"Why don't you say it's Woody with his father, and we wouldn't come in a snowstorm like this if it wasn't important."

The understandable caution of women who live alone. Respectable old-time women, too. There was no such respectability now in those Evanston houses, with their big verandas and deep yards and with a servant like Hjordis, who carried at her belt keys to the pantry and to every closet and every dresser drawer and every padlocked bin in the cellar. And in High Episcopal Christian Science Women's Temperance Evanston, no tradespeople rang at the front door. Only invited guests. And here, after a ten-mile grind through the blizzard, came two tramps from the West Side. To this mansion where a Swedish immigrant lady, herself once a cook and now a philanthropic widow, dreamed, snowbound, while frozen lilac twigs clapped at her storm windows, of a new Jerusalem and a Second Coming and a Resurrection and a Last Judgment. To hasten the Second Coming, and all the rest, you had to reach the hearts of these scheming bums arriving in a snowstorm.

Sure, they let us in.

Then in the heat that swam suddenly up to their mufflered chins Pop and Woody felt the blizzard for what it was; their cheeks were frozen slabs. They stood beat, itching, trickling in the front hall that *was* a hall, with a carved newel post staircase and a big stained-glass window at the top. Picturing Jesus with the Samaritan woman. There was a kind of Gentile closeness to the air. Perhaps when he was with Pop, Woody made more Jewish observations than he would otherwise. Although Pop's most Jewish characteristic was that Yiddish was the only language he could read a paper in. Pop was with Polish Halina, and Mother was with Jesus Christ, and Woody ate uncooked bacon from the flitch. Still, now and then he had a Jewish impression.

Mrs. Skoglund was the cleanest of women — her fingernails, her white neck, her ears — and Pop's sexual hints to Woody all went wrong because she was so intensely clean, and made Woody think of a waterfall, large as she was, and grandly built. Her bust was big. Woody's imagination had investigated this. He thought she kept things tied down tight, very tight. But she lifted both arms once to raise a window and there it was, her bust, beside him, the whole unbindable thing. Her hair was like the raffia you had to soak before you could weave with it in a basket class — pale, pale. Pop, as he took his sheepskin off, was in sweaters, no jacket. His darting looks made him seem crooked. Hardest of all for these Selbsts with their bent noses and big, apparently straightforward faces was to look honest. All the signs of dishonesty played over them. Woody had often puzzled about it. Did it go back to the muscles, was it fundamentally a jaw problem — the projecting angles of the jaws? Or was it the angling that went on in the heart? The girls called Pop Dick Tracy, but Dick Tracy was a good guy. Whom could Pop convince? Here Woody caught a possibility as it flitted by. Precisely because of the way Pop looked, a sensitive person might feel remorse for condemning unfairly or judging unkindly. Just because of a face? Some must have bent over backward. Then he had them. Not Hjordis. She would have put Pop into the street then and there, storm or no storm. Hjordis was religious, but she was wised up, too. She hadn't come over in steerage and worked forty years in Chicago for nothing.

Mrs. Skoglund, Aase (Osie), led the visitors into the front room. This, the biggest room in the house, needed supplementary heating. Because of fifteen-foot ceilings and high windows, Hjordis had kept the parlor stove burning. It was one of those elegant parlor stoves that wore a nickel crown, or miter, and this miter, when you moved it aside, automatically raised the hinge of an iron stove lid. That stove lid underneath the crown was all soot and rust, the same as any other stove lid. Into this hole you tipped the scuttle and the anthracite chestnut rattled down. It made a cake or dome of fire visible through the small isinglass frames. It was a pretty room, three-quarters paneled in wood. The stove was plugged into the flue of the marble fireplace, and there were parquet floors and Axminster carpets and cranberry-colored tufted Victorian upholstery, and a kind of Chinese étagère, inside a cabinet, lined with mirrors and containing silver pitchers, trophies won by Skoglund cows, fancy sugar tongs and cut-glass pitchers and goblets. There were Bibles and pictures of Jesus and the Holy Land and that faint Gentile odor, as if things had been rinsed in a weak vinegar solution.

"Mrs. Skoglund, I brought my dad to you. I don't think you ever met him," said Woody.

"Yes, Missus, that's me, Selbst."

Pop stood short but masterful in the sweaters, and his belly sticking out, not soft but hard. He was a man of the hard-bellied type. Nobody intimidated Pop. He never presented himself as a beggar. There wasn't a cringe in him anywhere. He let her see at once by the way he said "Missus" that he was independent and that he knew his way around. He communicated that he was able to handle himself with women. Handsome Mrs. Skoglund, carrying a basket woven out of her own hair, was in her fifties — eight, maybe ten years his senior.

"I asked my son to bring me because I know you do the kid a lot of good. It's natural you should know both of his parents."

"Mrs. Skoglund, my dad is in a tight corner and I don't know anybody else to ask for help."

This was all the preliminary Pop wanted. He took over and told the widow his story about the laundry-and-cleaning business and payments overdue, and explained about the fixtures and the attachment notice, and the bailiff's office and what they were going to do to him; and he said, "I'm a small man trying to make a living."

"You don't support your children," said Mrs. Skoglund.

"That's right," said Hjordis.

"I haven't got it. If I had it, wouldn't I give it? There's bread lines and soup lines all over town. Is it just me? What I have I divvy with. I give the kids. A bad father? You think my son would bring me if I was a bad father into your house? He loves his dad, he trusts his dad, he knows his dad is a good dad. Every time I start a little business going I get wiped out. This one is a good little business, if I could hold on to that little business. Three people work for me, I meet a payroll, and three people will be on the street, too, if I close down. Missus, I can sign a note and pay you in two months. I'm a common man, but I'm a hard worker and a fellow you can trust."

Woody was startled when Pop used the word "trust." It was as if from all four corners a Sousa band blew a blast to warn the entire world: "Crook! This is a crook!" But Mrs. Skoglund, on account of her religious preoccupations, was remote. She heard nothing. Although everybody in this part of the world, unless he was crazy, led a practical life, and you'd have nothing to say to anyone, your neighbors would have nothing to say to you, if communications were not of a practical sort, Mrs. Skoglund, with all her money, was unworldly — two-thirds out of this world.

"Give me a chance to show what's in me," said Pop, "and you'll see what I do for my kids."

So Mrs. Skoglund hesitated, and then she said she'd have to go upstairs, she'd have to go to her room and pray on it and ask for guidance — would they sit down and wait. There were two rocking chairs by the stove. Hjordis gave Pop a grim look (a dangerous person) and Woody a blaming one (he brought a dangerous stranger and disrupter to injure two kind Christian ladies). Then she went out with Mrs. Skoglund.

As soon as they left, Pop jumped up from the rocker and said in anger, "What's this with the praying? She has to ask God to lend me fifty bucks?"

Woody said, "It's not you, Pop, it's the way these religious people do."

"No," said Pop. "She'll come back and say that God wouldn't let her."

Woody didn't like that; he thought Pop was being gross and he said, "No, she's sincere. Pop, try to understand: she's emotional, nervous, and sincere, and tries to do right by everybody."

And Pop said, "That servant will talk her out of it. She's a toughie. It's all over her face that we're a couple of chiselers."

"What's the use of us arguing," said Woody. He drew the rocker closer to the stove. His shoes were wet through and would never dry. The blue flames fluttered like a school of fishes in the coal fire. But Pop went over to the Chinese-style cabinet or étagère and tried the handle, and then opened the blade of his penknife and in a second had forced the lock of the curved glass door. He took out a silver dish.

"Pop, what is this?" said Woody.

Pop, cool and level, knew exactly what this was. He relocked the étagère, crossed the carpet, listened. He stuffed the dish under his belt and pushed it down into his trousers. He put the side of his short thick finger to his mouth.

So Woody kept his voice down, but he was all shook up. He went to Pop and took him by the edge of his hand. As he looked into Pop's face, he felt his eyes growing smaller and smaller, as if something were contracting all the skin on his head. They call it hyperventilation when everything feels tight and light and close and dizzy. Hardly breathing, he said, "Put it back, Pop."

Pop said, "It's solid silver; it's worth dough."

"Pop, you said you wouldn't get me in Dutch."

"It's only insurance in case she comes back from praying and tells me no. If she says yes, I'll put it back."

"How?"

"It'll get back. If I don't put it back, you will."

"You picked the lock. I couldn't. I don't know how."

"There's nothing to it."

"We're going to put it back now. Give it here."

"Woody, it's under my fly, inside my underpants. Don't make such a noise about nothing."

"Pop, I can't believe this."

"For cry-ninety-nine, shut your mouth. If I didn't trust you I wouldn't have let you watch me do it. You don't understand a thing. What's with you?"

"Before they come down, Pop, will you dig that dish out of your long johns."

Pop turned stiff on him. He became absolutely military. He said, "Look, I order you!"

Before he knew it, Woody had jumped his father and begun to wrestle with him. It was outrageous to clutch your own father, to put a heel behind him, to force him to the wall. Pop was taken by surprise and said loudly, "You want Halina killed? Kill her! Go on, you be responsible." He began to resist, angry, and they turned about several times, when Woody, with a trick he had learned in a Western movie and used once on the playground, tripped him and they fell to the ground. Woody, who already outweighed the old man by twenty pounds, was on top. They landed on the floor beside the stove, which stood on a tray of decorated tin to protect the carpet. In this position, pressing Pop's hard belly, Woody recognized that to have wrestled him to the floor counted for nothing. It was impossible to thrust his hand under Pop's belt to recover the dish. And now Pop had turned furious, as a father has every right to be when his son is violent with him, and he freed his hand and hit Woody in the face. He hit him three or four times in midface. Then Woody dug his head into Pop's shoulder and held tight only to keep from being struck and began to say in his ear, "Jesus, Pop, for Christ sake remember where you are. Those women will be back!" But Pop brought up his short knee and fought and butted him with his chin and rattled Woody's teeth. Woody thought the old man was about to bite him. And because he was a seminarian, he thought: Like an unclean spirit. And held tight. Gradually Pop stopped threshing and struggling. His eyes stuck out and his mouth was open, sullen. Like a stout fish. Woody released him and gave him a hand up. He was then overcome with many many bad feelings of a sort he knew the old man never suffered. Never, never. Pop never had these groveling emotions. There was his whole superiority. Pop had no such feelings. He was like a horseman from Central Asia, a bandit from China. It was Mother, from Liverpool, who had the refinement, the English manners. It was the preaching Reverend Doctor in his black suit. You have refinements, and all they do is oppress you? The hell with that.

The long door opened and Mrs. Skoglund stepped in, saying, "Did I imagine, or did something shake the house?"

"I was lifting the scuttle to put coal on the fire and it fell out of my hand. I'm sorry I was so clumsy," said Woody.

Pop was too huffy to speak. With his eyes big and sore and the thin hair down over his forehead, you could see by the tightness of his belly how angrily he was fetching his breath, though his mouth was shut.

"I prayed," said Mrs. Skoglund.

"I hope it came out well," said Woody.

"Well, I don't do anything without guidance, but the answer was yes, and I feel right about it now. So if you'll wait, I'll go to my office and write a check. I asked Hjordis to bring you a cup of coffee. Coming in such a storm."

And Pop, consistently a terrible little man, as soon as she shut the door, said, "A check? Hell with a check. Get me the greenbacks."

"They don't keep money in the house. You can cash it in her bank tomorrow. But if they miss that dish, Pop, they'll stop the check, and then where are you?"

As Pop was reaching below the belt, Hjordis brought in the tray. She was very sharp with him. She said, "Is this a place to adjust clothing, Mister? A men's washroom?"

"Well, which way is the toilet, then?" said Pop.

She had served the coffee in the seamiest mugs in the pantry, and she bumped down the tray and led Pop down the corridor, standing guard at the bathroom door so that he shouldn't wander about the house.

Mrs. Skoglund called Woody to her office and after she had given him the folded check said that they should pray together for Morris. So once more he was on his knees, under rows and rows of musty marbled-cardboard files, by the glass lamp by the edge of the desk, the shade with flounced edges, like the candy dish. Mrs. Skoglund, in her Scandinavian accent — an emotional contralto — raising her voice to Jesus-uh Christ-uh, as the wind lashed the trees, kicked the side of the house, and drove the snow seething on the windowpanes, to send light-uh, give guidance-uh, put a new heart-uh in Pop's bosom. Woody asked God only to make Pop put the dish back. He kept Mrs. Skoglund on her knees as long as possible. Then he thanked her, shining with candor (as much as he knew how), for her Christian generosity and he said, "I know that Hjordis has a cousin who works at the Evanston YMCA. Could she please phone him and try to get us a room tonight so that we don't have to fight the blizzard all the way back? We're almost as close to the Y as to the car line. Maybe the cars have even stopped running."

Suspicious Hjordis, coming when Mrs. Skoglund called to her, was burning now. First they barged in, made themselves at home, asked for money, had to have coffee, probably left gonorrhea on the toilet seat. Hjordis, Woody remembered, was a woman who wiped the doorknobs with rubbing alcohol after guests had left. Nevertheless, she telephoned the Y and got them a room with two cots for six bits.

Pop had plenty of time, therefore, to reopen the étagère, lined with reflecting glass or German silver (something exquisitely delicate and tricky), and as soon as the two Selbsts had said thank you and goodbye and were in midstreet again up to the knees in snow, Woody said, "Well, I covered for you. Is that thing back?"

"Of course it is," said Pop.

They fought their way to the small Y building, shut up in wire grille and resembling a police station — about the same dimensions. It was locked, but they made a racket on the grille, and a small black man let them in and shuffled them upstairs to a cement corridor with low doors. It was like the small-mammal house in Lincoln Park. He said there was nothing to eat, so they took off their wet pants, wrapped themselves tightly in the khaki army blankets, and passed out on their cots.

First thing in the morning, they went to the Evanston National Bank and got the fifty dollars. Not without difficulties. The teller went to call Mrs. Skoglund and was absent a long time from the wicket. "Where the hell has he gone?" said Pop.

But when the fellow came back, he said, "How do you want it?"

Pop said, "Singles." He told Woody, "Bujak stashes it in one-dollar bills."

But by now Woody no longer believed Halina had stolen the old man's money.

Then they went into the street, where the snow-removal crews were at work. The sun shone broad, broad, out of the morning blue, and all Chicago would be releasing itself from the temporary beauty of those vast drifts.

"You shouldn't have jumped me last night, Sonny."

"I know, Pop, but you promised you wouldn't get me in Dutch."

"Well, it's okay. We can forget it, seeing you stood by me."

Only, Pop had taken the silver dish. Of course he had, and in a few days Mrs. Skoglund and Hjordis knew it, and later in the week they were all waiting for Woody in Kovner's office at the settlement house. The group included the Reverend Doctor Crabbie, head of the seminary, and Woody, who had been flying along, level and smooth, was shot down in flames. He told them he was innocent. Even as he was falling, he warned that they were wronging him. He denied that he or Pop had touched Mrs. Skoglund's property. The missing object — he didn't even know what it was — had probably been misplaced, and they would be very sorry on the day it turned up. After the others were done with him, Dr. Crabbie said that until he was able to tell the truth he would be suspended from the seminary, where his work had been unsatisfactory anyway. Aunt Rebecca took him aside and said to him, "You are a little crook, like your father. The door is closed to you here."

To this Pop's comment was "So what, kid?"

"Pop, you shouldn't have done it."

"No? Well, I don't give a care, if you want to know. You can have the dish if you want to go back and square yourself with all those hypocrites."

"I didn't like doing Mrs. Skoglund in the eye, she was so kind to us."

"Kind?"

"Kind."

"Kind has a price tag."

Well, there was no winning such arguments with Pop. But they debated it in various moods and from various elevations and perspectives for forty years and more, as their intimacy changed, developed, matured.

"Why did you do it, Pop? For the money? What did you do with the fifty bucks?" Woody, decades later, asked him that.

"I settled with the bookie, and the rest I put in the business."

"You tried a few more horses."

"I maybe did. But it was a double, Woody. I didn't hurt myself, and at the same time did you a favor."

"It was for me?"

"It was too strange of a life. That life wasn't *you*, Woody. All those women . . . Kovner was no man, he was an inbetween. Suppose they made you a minister? Some Christian minister! First of all, you wouldn't have been able to stand it, and second, they would throw you out sooner or later."

"Maybe so."

"And you wouldn't have converted the Jews, which was the main thing they wanted."

"And what a time to bother the Jews," Woody said. "At least *I* didn't bug them."

Pop had carried him back to his side of the line, blood of his blood, the same thick body walls, the same coarse grain. Not cut out for a spiritual life. Simply not up to it.

Pop was no worse than Woody, and Woody was no better than Pop. Pop wanted no relation to theory, and yet he was always pointing Woody toward a position — a jolly, hearty, natural, likable, unprincipled position. If Woody had a weakness, it was to be unselfish. This worked to Pop's advantage, but he criticized Woody for it, nevertheless. "You take too much on yourself," Pop was always saying. And it's true that Woody gave Pop his heart because Pop was so selfish. It's usually the selfish people who are loved the most. They do what you deny yourself, and you love them for it. You give them your heart.

Remembering the pawn ticket for the silver dish, Woody startled himself with a laugh so sudden that it made him cough. Pop said to him after his expulsion from the seminary and banishment from the settlement house, "You want in again? Here's the ticket. I hocked that thing. It wasn't so valuable as I thought."

"What did they give?"

"Twelve-fifty was all I could get. But if you want it you'll have to raise the dough yourself, because I haven't got it anymore."

"You must have been sweating in the bank when the teller went to call Mrs. Skoglund about the check."

"I was a little nervous," said Pop. "But I didn't think they could miss the thing so soon."

That theft was part of Pop's war with Mother. With Mother, and Aunt Rebecca, and the Reverend Doctor. Pop took his stand on realism. Mother represented forces of religion and hypochondria. In four decades, the fighting never stopped. In the course of time, Mother and the girls turned into welfare personalities and lost their individual outlines. Ah, the poor things, they became dependents and cranks. In the meantime, Woody, the sinful man, was their dutiful and loving son and brother. He maintained the bungalow — this took in roofing, pointing, wiring, insulation, air-conditioning — and he paid for heat and light and food, and dressed them all out of Sears, Roebuck and Wieboldt's, and bought them a TV, which they watched as devoutly as they prayed. Paula took courses to learn skills like macramé-making and needlepoint, and sometimes got a little job as recreational worker in a nursing home. But she wasn't steady enough to keep it. Wicked Pop spent most of his life removing stains from people's clothing. He and Halina in the last years ran a Cleanomat in West Rogers Park — a so-so business resembling a Laundromat — which gave him leisure for billiards, the horses, rummy and pinochle. Every morning he went behind the partition to check out the filters of the cleaning equipment. He found amusing things that had been thrown into the vats with the clothing — sometimes, when he got lucky, a locket chain or a brooch. And when he had fortified the cleaning fluid, pouring all that blue and pink stuff in from plastic jugs, he read the *Forward* over a second cup of coffee, and went out, leaving Halina in charge. When they needed help with the rent, Woody gave it.

After the new Disney World was opened in Florida, Woody treated all his dependents to a holiday. He sent them down in separate batches, of course. Halina enjoyed this more than anybody else. She couldn't stop talking about the address given by an Abraham Lincoln automaton. "Wonderful, how he stood up and moved his hands, and his mouth. So real! And how beautiful he talked." Of them all, Halina was the soundest, the most human, the most honest. Now that Pop was gone, Woody and Halina's son, Mitosh, the organist at the Stadium, took care of her needs over and above Social Security, splitting expenses. In Pop's opinion, insurance was a racket. He left Halina nothing but some out-of-date equipment.

Woody treated himself, too. Once a year, and sometimes oftener, he left his business to run itself, arranged with the trust department at the bank to take care of his gang, and went off. He did that in style, imaginatively, expensively. In Japan, he wasted little time on Tokyo. He spent three weeks in Kyoto and stayed at the Tawaraya Inn, dating from the seventeenth century or so. There he slept on the floor, the Japanese way, and bathed in scalding water. He saw the dirtiest strip show on earth, as well as the holy places and the temple gardens. He visited also Istanbul, Jerusalem, Delphi, and went to Burma and Uganda and Kenya on safari, on democratic terms with drivers, Bedouins, bazaar merchants. Open, lavish, familiar, fleshier and fleshier but (he jogged, he lifted weights) still muscular — in his naked person beginning to resemble a Renaissance courtier in full costume — becoming ruddier every year, an outdoor type with freckles on his back and spots across the flaming forehead and the honest nose. In Addis Ababa he took an Ethiopian beauty to his room from the street and washed her, getting into the shower with her to soap her with his broad, kindly hands. In Kenya he taught certain American obscenities to a black woman so that she could shout them out during the act. On the Nile, below Murchison Falls, those fever trees rose huge from the mud, and hippos on the sandbars belched at the passing launch, hostile. One of them danced on his spit of sand, springing from the ground and coming down heavy, on all fours. There, Woody saw the buffalo calf disappear, snatched by the crocodile.

Mother, soon to follow Pop, was being lightheaded these days. In company, she spoke of Woody as her boy — "What do you think of my Sonny?" — as though he was ten years old. She was silly with him, her behavior was frivolous, almost flirtatious. She just didn't seem to know the facts. And behind her all the others, like kids at the playground, were waiting their turn to go down the slide: one on each step, and moving toward the top.

Over Woody's residence and place of business there had gathered a pool of silence of the same perimeter as the church bells while they were ringing, and he mourned under it, this melancholy morning of sun and autumn. Doing a life survey, taking a deliberate look at the gross side of his case — of the other side as well, what there was of it. But if this heartache continued, he'd go out and run it off. A three-mile jog — five, if necessary. And you'd think that this jogging was an entirely physical activity, wouldn't you? But there was something else in it. Because, when he was a seminarian, between the shafts of his World's Fair rickshaw, he used to receive, pulling along (capable and stable), his religious experiences while he trotted. Maybe it was all a single experience repeated. He felt truth coming to him from the sun. He received a communication that was also light and warmth. It made him very remote from his horny Wisconsin passengers, those farmers whose whoops and whore cries he could hardly hear when he was in one of his states. And again out of the flaming of the sun would come to him a secret certainty that the goal set for this earth was that it should be filled with good, saturated with it. After everything preposterous, after dog had eaten dog, after the crocodile death had pulled everyone into his mud. It wouldn't conclude as Mrs. Skoglund, bribing him to round up the Jews and hasten the Second Coming, imagined it, but in another way. This was his clumsy intuition.

It went no further. Subsequently, he proceeded through life as life seemed to want him to do it.

There remained one thing more this morning, which was explicitly physical, occurring first as a sensation in his arms and against his breast and, from the pressure, passing into him and going into his breast.

It was like this: When he came into the hospital room and saw Pop with the sides of his bed raised, like a crib, and Pop, so very feeble, and writhing, and toothless, like a baby, and the dirt already cast onto his face, into the wrinkles — Pop wanted to pluck out the intravenous needles and he was piping his weak death noise. The gauze patches taped over the needles were soiled with dark blood. Then Woody took off his shoes, lowered the side of the bed, and climbed in and held him in his arms to soothe and still him. As if he were Pop's father, he said to him, "Now, Pop. Pop." Then it was like the wrestle in Mrs. Skoglund's parlor, when Pop turned angry like an unclean spirit and Woody tried to appease him, and warn him, saying, "Those women will be back!" Beside the coal stove, when Pop hit Woody in the teeth with his head and then became sullen, like a stout fish. But this struggle in the hospital was weak — so weak! In his great pity, Woody held Pop, who was fluttering and shivering. From those people, Pop had told him, you'll never find out what life is, because they don't know what it is. Yes, Pop — well, what is it, Pop? Hard to comprehend that Pop, who was dug in for eighty-three years and had done all he could to stay, should now want nothing but to free himself. How could Woody allow the old man to pull the intravenous needles out? Willful Pop, he wanted what he wanted when he wanted it. But what he wanted at the very last Woody failed to follow, it was such a switch.

After a time, Pop's resistance ended. He subsided and subsided. He rested against his son, his small body curled there. Nurses came and looked. They disapproved, but Woody, who couldn't spare a hand to wave them out, motioned with his head toward the door. Pop, whom Woody thought he had stilled, only had found a better way to get around him. Loss of heat was the way he did it. His heat was leaving him. As can happen with small animals while you hold them in your hand, Woody presently felt him cooling. Then, as Woody did his best to restrain him, and thought he was succeeding, Pop divided himself. And when he was separated from his warmth, he slipped into death. And there was his elderly, large, muscular son, still holding and pressing him when there was nothing anymore to press. You could never pin down that self-willed man. When he was ready to make his move, he made it — always on his own terms. And always, always, something up his sleeve. That was how he was.

JEAN STAFFORD

1915–1979

Born in California, Jean Stafford was educated in Colorado and Germany. She married writers of high distinction — the poet Robert Lowell, then the brilliant A. J. Liebling. Her life with Lowell may be reflected in several knife-edged satiric studies of the literary temperament, notably "An Influx of Poets." In 1944 she published her first novel, Boston Adventure, *announcing the advent of a writer both assured and original. Though widely anthologized, her short stories, elegant in form and reverberant with personality, are still undervalued.*

A beneficent part of our nature acts to make us forget pain. Usually we can recall the fact of pain but not the raw truth of it. Thus, though in imaginative literature we can find many treatments of operations and of hospital episodes in general, there are few of pain itself, an experience most human beings are bound to encounter in their lives.

"The Interior Castle" cuts and digs ruthlessly into the sensation of physical pain and its nightmare effect on the mind. It is a tour de force of empathic writing, for pain is a private possession, unshareable, therefore ostensibly uncommunicable. Pansy Vanneman's case is made more difficult to describe because her anguish is complicated by the terror of violation, the violation of her brain. I can think of no other short story that manipulates so frightening a theme with such mastery.

The Interior Castle

PANSY VANNEMAN, injured in an automobile accident, often woke up before dawn when the night noises of the hospital still came, in hushed hurry, through her half-open door. By day, when the nurses talked audibly with the internes, laughed without inhibition, and took no pains to soften their footsteps on the resounding composition floors, the routine of the hospital seemed as bland and commonplace as that of a bank or a factory. But in the dark hours, the whispering and the quickly stilled clatter of glasses and basins, the moans of patients whose morphine was wearing off, the soft squeak of a stretcher as it rolled past on its way from the emergency ward — these suggested agony and death. Thus, on the first morning, Pansy had faltered to consciousness long before daylight and had found herself in a ward from every bed of which, it seemed to her, came the bewildered protest of someone about to die. A caged light burned on the floor beside the bed next to hers. Her neighbor was dying and a priest was administering Extreme Unction. He was stout and elderly and he suffered from asthma so that the struggle of his breathing, so close to her, was the basic pattern and all the other sounds were superimposed upon it. Two middle-aged men in overcoats knelt on the floor beside the high bed. In a foreign tongue, the half-gone woman babbled against the hissing and sighing of the Latin prayers. She played with her rosary as if it were a toy; she tried, and failed, to put it into her mouth.

Pansy felt horror, but she felt no pity. An hour or so later, when the white ceiling lights were turned on and everything — faces, counterpanes, and the hands that groped upon them — was transformed into a uniform gray sordor, the woman was wheeled away in her bed to die somewhere else, in privacy. Pansy did not quite take this in, although she stared for a long time at the new, empty bed that had replaced the other.

The next morning, when she again woke up before the light, this time in a private room, she recalled the woman with such sorrow that she might have been a friend. Simultaneously, she mourned the driver of the taxicab in which she had been injured, for he had died at about noon the day before. She had been told this as she lay on a stretcher in the corridor, waiting to be taken to the X-ray room; an interne, passing by, had paused and smiled down at her and had said, "Your cab driver is dead. You were lucky."

Six weeks after the accident, she woke one morning just as daylight was showing on the windows as a murky smear. It was a minute or two before she realized why she was so reluctant to be awake, why her uneasiness amounted almost to alarm. Then she remembered that her nose was to be operated on today. She lay straight and motionless under the seersucker counterpane. Her blood-red eyes in her darned face stared through the window and saw a frozen river and leafless elm trees and a grizzled esplanade where dogs danced on the ends of leashes, their bundled-up owners stumbling after them, half blind with sleepiness and cold. Warm as the hospital room was, it did not prevent Pansy from knowing, as keenly as though she were one of the walkers, how very cold it was outside. Each twig of a nearby tree was stark. Cold red brick buildings nudged the low-lying sky which was pale and inert like a punctured sac.

In six weeks, the scene had varied little: there was promise in the skies neither of sun nor of snow; no red sunsets marked these days. The trees could neither die nor leaf out again. Pansy could not remember another season in her life so constant, when the very minutes themselves were suffused with the winter pallor as they dropped from the moon-faced clock in the corridor. In the same way, her room accomplished no alterations from day to day. On the glass-topped bureau stood two potted plants telegraphed by faraway well-wishers. They did not fade, and if a leaf turned brown and fell, it soon was replaced; so did the blossoms renew themselves. The roots, like the skies and like the bare trees, seemed zealously determined to maintain a status quo. The bedside table, covered every day with a clean white towel, though the one removed was always immaculate, was furnished sparsely with a water glass, a bent drinking tube, a sweating pitcher, and a stack of paper handkerchiefs. There were a few letters in the drawer, a hairbrush, a pencil, and some postal cards on which, from time to time, she wrote brief messages to relatives and friends: "Dr. Nash says that my reflexes are shipshape (*sic*) and Dr. Rivers says the frontal fracture has all but healed and that the occipital is coming along nicely. Dr. Nicholas, the nose doctor, promises to operate as soon as Dr. Rivers gives him the go-ahead sign (*sic*)."

The bed itself was never rumpled. Once fretful and now convalescent, Miss Vanneman might have been expected to toss or to turn the pillows or to unmoor the counterpane; but hour after hour and day after day she lay at full length and would not even suffer the nurses to raise the headpiece of the adjustable bed. So perfect and stubborn was her body's immobility that it was as if the room and the landscape, mortified by the ice, were extensions of herself. Her resolute quiescence and her disinclination to talk, the one seeming somehow to proceed from the other, resembled, so the nurses said, a final coma. And they observed, in pitying indignation, that she might as *well* be dead for all the interest she took in life. Among themselves they scolded her for what they thought a moral weakness: an automobile accident, no matter how serious, was not reason enough for anyone to give up the will to live or to be happy. She had not — to come down bluntly to the facts — had the decency to be grateful that it was the driver of the cab and not she who had died. (And how dreadfully the man had died!) She was twenty-five years old and she came from a distant city. These were really the only facts known about her. Evidently she had not been here long, for she had no visitors, a lack which was at first sadly moving to the nurses but which became to them a source of unreasonable annoyance: had anyone the right to live so one-dimensionally? It was impossible to laugh at her, for she said nothing absurd; her demands could not be complained of because they did not exist; she could not be hated for a sharp tongue nor for a supercilious one; she could not be admired for bravery or for wit or for interest in her fellow creatures. She was believed to be a frightful snob.

Pansy, for her part, took a secret and mischievous pleasure in the bewilderment of her attendants and the more they courted her with offers of magazines, crossword puzzles, and a radio that she could rent from the hospital, the farther she retired from them into herself and into the world which she had created in her long hours here and which no one could ever penetrate nor imagine. Sometimes she did not even answer the nurses' questions; as they rubbed her back with alcohol and steadily discoursed, she was as remote from them as if she were miles away. She did not think that she lived on a higher plane than that of the nurses and the doctors but that she lived on a different one and that at this particular time — this time of exploration and habituation — she had no extra strength to spend on making herself known to them. All she had been before and all the memories she might have brought out to disturb the monotony of, say, the morning bath, and all that the past meant to the future when she would leave the hospital, were of no present consequence to her. Not even in her thoughts did she employ more than a minimum of memory. And when she did remember, it was in flat pictures, rigorously independent of one another: she saw her thin, poetic mother who grew thinner and more poetic in her canvas deck chair at Saranac reading *Lalla Rookh*. She saw herself in an inappropriate pink hat drinking iced tea in a garden so oppressive with the smell of phlox that the tea itself tasted of it. She recalled an afternoon in autumn in Vermont when she had heard three dogs' voices in the north woods and she could tell, by the characteristic minor key struck three times at intervals, like bells from several churches, that they had treed something: the eastern sky was pink and the trees on the horizon looked like some eccentric vascular system meticulously drawn on colored paper.

What Pansy thought of all the time was her own brain. Not only the brain as the seat of consciousness, but the physical organ itself which she envisaged, romantically, now as a jewel, now as a flower, now as a light in a glass, now as an envelope of rosy vellum containing other envelopes, one within the other, diminishing infinitely. It was always pink and always fragile, always deeply interior and invaluable. She believed that she had reached the innermost chamber of knowledge and that perhaps her knowledge was the same as the saint's achievement of pure love. It was only convention, she thought, that made one say "sacred heart" and not "sacred brain."

Often, but never articulately, the color pink troubled her and the picture of herself in the wrong hat hung steadfastly before her mind's eye. None of the other girls had worn hats, and since autumn had come early that year, they were dressed in green and rusty brown and dark yellow. Poor Pansy wore a white eyelet frock with a lacing of black ribbon around the square neck. When she came through the arch, overhung with bittersweet, and saw that they had not yet heard her, she almost turned back, but Mr. Oliver was there and she was in love with him. She was in love with him though he was ten years older than she and had never shown any interest in her beyond asking her once, quite fatuously but in an intimate voice, if the yodeling of the little boy who peddled clams did not make her wish to visit Switzerland. Actually, there was more to this question than met the eye, for some days later Pansy learned that Mr. Oliver, who was immensely rich, kept an apartment in Geneva. In the garden that day, he spoke to her only once. He said, "My dear, you look exactly like something out of Katherine Mansfield," and immediately turned and within her hearing asked Beatrice Sherburne to dine with him that night at the Country Club. Afterward, Pansy went down to the sea and threw the beautiful hat onto the full tide and saw it vanish in the wake of a trawler. Therefore, when she heard the clam boy coming down the road, she locked the door and when the knocking had stopped and her mother called down from her chaise longue, "Who was it, dearie?" she replied, "A salesman."

It was only the fact that the hat had been pink that worried her. The rest of the memory was trivial, for she knew that she could never again love anything as ecstatically as she loved the spirit of Pansy Vanneman, enclosed within her head.

But her study was not without distraction, and she fought two adversaries: pain and Dr. Nicholas. Against Dr. Nicholas, she defended herself valorously and in fear; but pain, the pain, that is, that was independent of his instruments, she sometimes forced upon herself adventurously like a child scaring himself in a graveyard.

Dr. Nicholas greatly admired her crushed and splintered nose which he daily probed and peered at, exclaiming that he had never seen anything like it. His shapely hands ached for their knives; he was impatient with the skull-fracture man's cautious delay. He spoke of "our" nose and said "we" would be a new person when we could breathe again. His own nose was magnificent. Not even his own brilliant surgery could have improved upon it nor could a first-rate sculptor have duplicated its direct downward line which permitted only the least curvature inward toward the end; or the delicately rounded lateral declivities; or the thin-walled, perfectly matched nostrils.

Miss Vanneman did not doubt his humaneness or his talent — he was a celebrated man — but she questioned whether he had imagination. Immediately beyond the prongs of his speculum lay her treasure whose price he, no more than the nurses, could estimate. She believed he could not destroy it, but she feared that he might maim it: might leave a scratch on one of the brilliant facets of the jewel, bruise a petal of the flower, smudge the glass where the light burned, blot the envelopes, and that then she would die or would go mad. While she did not question that in either eventuality her brain would after a time redeem its original impeccability, she did not quite yet wish to enter upon either kind of eternity, for she was not certain that she could carry with her her knowledge as well as its receptacle.

Blunderer that he was, Dr. Nicholas was an honorable enemy, not like the demon, pain, which skulked in a thousand guises within her head, and which often she recklessly willed to attack her and then drove back in terror. After the rout, sweat streamed from her face and soaked the neck of the coarse hospital shirt. To be sure, it came usually of its own accord, running like a wild fire through all the convolutions to fill with flame the small sockets and ravines and then, at last, to withdraw, leaving behind a throbbing and an echo. On these occasions, she was as helpless as a tree in a wind. But at the other times when, by closing her eyes and rolling up the eyeballs in such a way that she fancied she looked directly on the place where her brain was, the pain woke sluggishly and came toward her at a snail's pace. Then, bit by bit, it gained speed. Sometimes it faltered back, subsided altogether, and then it rushed like a tidal wave driven by a hurricane, lashing and roaring until she lifted her hands from the counterpane, crushed her broken teeth into her swollen lip, stared in panic at the soothing walls with her ruby eyes, stretched out her legs until she felt their bones must snap. Each cove, each narrow inlet, every living bay was flooded and the frail brain, a little hat-shaped boat, was washed from its mooring and set adrift. The skull was as vast as the world and the brain was as small as a seashell.

Then came calm weather and the safe journey home. She kept vigil for a while, though, and did not close her eyes, but gazing serenely at the trees, conceived of the pain as the guardian of her treasure who would not let her see it; that was why she was handled so savagely whenever she turned her eyes inward. Once this watch was interrupted: by chance she looked into the corridor and saw a shaggy mop slink past the door, followed by a senile porter. A pair of ancient eyes, as rheumy as an old dog's, stared uncritically in at her and a toothless mouth formed a brutish word. She was so surprised that she immediately closed her eyes to shut out the shape of the word and the pain dug up the unmapped regions of her head with mattocks, ludicrously huge. It was the familiar pain, but this time, even as she endured it, she observed with detachment that its effect upon her was less than that of its contents, the by-products, for example, of temporal confusion and the bizarre mis-application of the style of one sensation to another. At the moment, for example, although her brain reiterated to her that *it* was being assailed, she was stroking her right wrist with her left hand as though to assuage the ache, long since dispelled, of the sprain in the joint. Some minutes after she had opened her eyes and left off soothing her wrist, she lay rigid, experiencing the sequel to the pain, an ideal terror. For, as before on several occasions, she was overwhelmed with the knowledge that the pain had been consummated in the vessel of her mind and for the moment the vessel was unbeautiful: she thought, quailing, of those plastic folds as palpable as the fingers of locked hands containing in their very cells, their fissures, their repulsive hemispheres, the mind, the soul, the inscrutable intelligence.

The porter, then, like the pink hat and like her mother and the hounds' voices, loitered with her.

Dr. Nicholas came at nine o'clock to prepare her for the operation. With him came an entourage of white-frocked acolytes, and one of them wheeled in a wagon on which lay knives and scissors and pincers, cans of swabs and gauze. In the midst of these was a bowl of liquid whose rich purple color made it seem strange like the brew of an alchemist.

"All set?" the surgeon asked her, smiling. "A little nervous, what? I don't blame you. I've often said I'd rather break a leg than have a sub-mucous resection." Pansy thought for a moment he was going to touch his nose. His approach to her was roundabout. He moved through the yellow light shed by the globe in the ceiling which gave his forehead a liquid gloss; he paused by the bureau and touched a blossom of the cyclamen; he looked out the window and said, to no one and to all, "I couldn't start my car this morning. Came in a cab." Then he came forward. As he came, he removed a speculum from the pocket of his short-sleeved coat and like a cat, inquiring of the nature of a surface with its paws, he put out his hand toward her and drew it back, gently mur-muring, "You must not be afraid, my dear. There is no danger, you know. Do you think for a minute I would operate if there were?"

Dr. Nicholas, young, brilliant, and handsome, was an aristocrat, a husband, a father, a clubman, a Christian, a kind counselor, and a trustee of his preparatory school. Like many of the medical profession, even those whose specialty was centered on the organ of the basest sense, he interested himself in the psychology of his patients: in several in-stances, for example, he had found that severe attacks of sinusitis were coincident with emotional crises. Miss Vanneman more than ordinarily captured his fancy since her skull had been fractured and her behavior throughout had been so extraordinary that he felt he was observing at first hand some of the results of shock, that incommensurable element, which frequently were too subtle to see. There was, for example, the matter of her complete passivity during a lumbar puncture, reports of which were written down in her history and were enlarged upon for him by Dr. Rivers' interne who had been in charge. Except for a tremor in her throat and a deepening of pallor, there were no signs at all that she was aware of what was happening to her. She made no sound, did not close her eyes nor clench her fists. She had had several punctures; her only reaction had been to the very first one, the morning after she had been brought in. When the interne explained to her that he was going to drain off cerebrospinal fluid which was pressing against her brain, she exclaimed, "My God!" but it was not an exclamation of fear. The young man had been unable to name what it was he had heard in her voice; he could only say that it had not been fear as he had observed it in other patients.

Dr. Nicholas wondered about her. There was no way of guessing whether she had always had a nature of so tolerant and undemanding a complexion. It gave him a melancholy pleasure to think that before her accident she had been high-spirited and loquacious; he was moved to think that perhaps she had been a beauty and that when she had first seen her face in the looking glass she had lost all joy in herself. It was very difficult to tell what the face had been, for it was so bruised and swollen, so hacked-up and lopsided. The black stitches the length of the nose, across the saddle, across the cheekbone, showed that there would be unsightly scars. He had ventured once to give her the name of a plastic surgeon but she had only replied with a vague, refusing smile. He had hoisted a manly shoulder and said, "You're the doctor."

Much as he pondered, coming to no conclusions, about what went on inside that pitiable skull, he was, of course, far more interested in the nose, deranged so badly that it would require his topmost skill to restore its functions to it. He would be obliged not only to make a submucous resection, a simple run-of-the-mill operation, but to remove the vomer, always a delicate task but further complicated in this case by the proximity of the bone to the frontal fracture line which conceivably was not entirely closed. If it were not and he operated too soon and if a cold germ then found its way into the opening, his patient would be carried off by meningitis in the twinkling of an eye. He wondered if she knew in what potential danger she lay; he desired to assure her that he had brought his craft to its nearest perfection and that she had nothing to fear of him, but feeling that she was perhaps both ignorant and unimaginative and that such consolation would create a fear rather than dispel one, he held his tongue and came nearer to the bed.

Watching him, Pansy could already feel the prongs of his pliers opening her nostrils for the insertion of his fine probers. The pain he caused her with his instruments was of a different kind from that she felt unaided: it was a naked, clean, and vivid pain that made her faint and ill and made her wish to die. Once she had fainted as he ruthlessly explored and after she was brought around, he continued until he had finished his investigation. The memory of this outrage had afterward several times made her cry.

This morning she looked at him and listened to him with hatred. Fixing her eyes upon the middle of his high, protuberant brow, she imagined the clutter behind it and she despised its obtuse imperfection. In his bland unawareness, this nobody, this nose-bigot, was about to play with fire and she wished him ill.

He said, "I can't blame you. No, I expect you're not looking forward to our little party. But you'll be glad to be able to breathe again."

He stationed his lieutenants. The interne stood opposite him on the left side of the bed. The surgical nurse wheeled the wagon within easy reach of his hands and stood beside it. Another nurse stood at the foot of the bed. A third drew the shades at the windows and attached a blinding light that shone down on the patient hotly, and then she left the room, softly closing the door. Pansy stared at the silver ribbon tied in a great bow round the green crepe paper of one of the flowerpots. It made her realize for the first time that one of the days she had lain here had been Christmas, but she had no time to consider this strange and thrilling fact, for Dr. Nicholas was genially explaining his anesthetic. He would soak packs of gauze in the purple fluid, a cocaine solution, and he would place them in her nostrils, leaving them there for an hour. He warned her that the packing would be disagreeable (he did not say "painful") but that it would be well worth a few minutes of discomfort not to be in the least sick after the operation. He asked her if she were ready and when she nodded her head, he adjusted the mirror on his forehead and began.

At the first touch of his speculum, Pansy's fingers mechanically bent to the palms of her hands and she stiffened. He said, "A pack, Miss Kennedy," and Pansy closed her eyes. There was a rush of plunging pain as he drove the sodden gobbet of gauze high up into her nose and something bitter burned in her throat so that she retched. The doctor paused a moment and the surgical nurse wiped Pansy's mouth. He returned to her with another pack, pushing it with his bodkin doggedly until it lodged against the first. Stop! Stop! cried all her nerves, wailing along the surface of her skin. The coats that covered them were torn off and they shuddered like naked people screaming, Stop! Stop! But Dr. Nicholas did not hear. Time and again he came back with a fresh pack and did not pause at all until one nostril was finished. She opened her eyes and saw him wipe the sweat off his forehead and saw the dark interne bending over her, fascinated. Miss Kennedy bathed her temples in ice water and Dr. Nicholas said, "There. It won't be much longer. I'll tell them to send you some coffee, though I'm afraid you won't be able to taste it. Ever drink coffee with chicory in it? I have no use for it."

She snatched at his irrelevancy and, though she had never tasted chicory, she said severely, "I love it."

Dr. Nicholas chuckled. "De gustibus. Ready? A pack, Miss Kennedy."

The second nostril was harder to pack since the other side was now distended and this passage was anyhow much narrower, as narrow, he had once remarked, as that in the nose of an infant. In such pain as passed all language and even the farthest fetched analogies, she turned her eyes inward, thinking that under the obscuring cloak of the surgeon's pain she could see her brain without the knowledge of its keeper. But Dr. Nicholas and his aides would give her no peace. They surrounded her with their murmuring and their foot-shuffling and the rustling of their starched uniforms, and her eyelids continually flew back in embarrassment and mistrust. She was claimed entirely by this present, meaningless pain and suddenly and sharply she forgot what she had meant to do. She was aware of nothing but her ascent to the summit of something; what it was she did not know, whether it was a tower or a peak or Jacob's ladder. Now she was an abstract word, now she was a theorem of geometry, now she was a kite flying, a top spinning, a prism flashing, a kaleidoscope turning.

But none of the others in the room could see inside and when the surgeon was finished, the nurse at the foot of the bed said, "Now you must take a look in the mirror. It's simply too comical." And they all laughed intimately like old, fast friends. She smiled politely and looked at her reflection: over the gruesomely fattened snout, her scarlet eyes stared in fixed reproach upon her upturned lips, gray with bruises. But even in its smile of betrayal, the mouth itself was puzzled: it reminded her that something had been left behind, but she could not recall what it was. She was hollowed out and was as dry as a white bone.

They strapped her ankles to the operating table and put leather nooses round her wrists. Over her head was a mirror with a thousand facets in which she saw a thousand travesties of her face. At her right side was the table, shrouded in white, where lay the glittering blades of the many knives, thrusting out fitful rays of light. All the cloth was frosty; everything was white or silver and as cold as snow. Dr. Nicholas, a tall snowman with silver eyes and silver fingernails, came into the room soundlessly, for he walked on layers and layers of snow that deadened his footsteps; behind him came the interne, a smaller snowman, less impressively proportioned. At the foot of the table, a snow figure put her frozen hands upon Pansy's helpless feet. The doctor plucked the packs from the cold, numb nose. His laugh was like a cry on a bitter, still night: "I will show you now," he called across the expanse of snow, "that you can feel nothing." The pincers bit at nothing, snapped at the air and cracked a nerveless icicle. Pansy called back and heard her own voice echo: "I feel nothing."

Here the walls were gray, not tan. Suddenly the face of the nurse at the foot of the table broke apart and Pansy first thought it was in grief. But it was a smile and she said, "Did you enjoy your coffee?" Down the gray corridors of the maze, the words rippled, ran like mice, birds, broken beads: Did you enjoy your coffee? your coffee? your coffee? Similarly once in another room that also had gray walls, the same voice had said, "Shall I give her some whisky?" She was overcome with gratitude that this young woman (how pretty she was with her white hair and her white face and her china-blue eyes!) had been with her that first night and was with her now.

In the great stillness of the winter, the operation began. The knives carved snow. Pansy was happy. She had been given a hypnotic just before they came to fetch her and she would have gone to sleep had she not enjoyed so much this trickery of Dr. Nicholas' whom now she tenderly loved.

There was a clock in the operating room and from time to time she looked at it. An hour passed. The snowman's face was melting; drops of water hung from his fine nose, but his silver eyes were as bright as ever. Her love was returned, she knew: he loved her nose exactly as she loved his knives. She looked at her face in the domed mirror and saw how the blood had streaked her lily-white cheeks and had stained her shroud. She returned to the private song: Did you enjoy your coffee? your coffee?

At the half-hour, a murmur, anguine and slumbrous, came to her and only when she had repeated the words twice did they engrave their meaning upon her. Dr. Nicholas said, "Stand back now, nurse. I'm at this girl's brain and I don't want my elbow jogged." Instantly Pansy was alive. Her strapped ankles arched angrily; her wrists strained against their bracelets. She jerked her head and she felt the pain flare; she had made the knife slip.

"Be still!" cried the surgeon. "Be quiet, please!"

He had made her remember what it was she had lost when he had rammed his gauze into her nose: she bustled like a housewife to shut the door. She thought, I must hurry before the robbers come. It would be like the time Mother left the cellar door open and the robber came and took, of all things, the terrarium.

Dr. Nicholas was whispering to her. He said, in the voice of a lover, "If you can stand it five minutes more, I can perform the second operation now and you won't have to go through this again. What do you say?"

She did not reply. It took her several seconds to remember why it was her mother had set such store by the terrarium and then it came to her that the bishop's widow had brought her an herb from Palestine to put in it.

The interne said, "You don't want to have your nose packed again, do you?"

The surgical nurse said, "She's a good patient, isn't she, sir?"

"Never had a better," replied Dr. Nicholas. "But don't call me 'sir.' You must be a Canadian to call me 'sir.' "

The nurse at the foot of the bed said, "I'll order some more coffee for you."

"How about it, Miss Vanneman?" said the doctor. "Shall I go ahead?"

She debated. Once she had finally fled the hospital and fled Dr. Nicholas, nothing could compel her to come back. Still, she knew that the time would come when she could no longer live in seclusion, she must go into the world again and must be equipped to live in it; she banally acknowledged that she must be able to breathe. And finally, though the world to which she would return remained unreal, she gave the surgeon her permission.

He had now to penetrate regions that were not anesthetized and this he told her frankly, but he said that there was no danger at all. He apologized for the slip of the tongue he had made: in point of fact, he had not been near her brain, it was only a figure of speech. He began. The knives ground and carved and curried and scoured the wounds they made; the scissors clipped hard gristle and the scalpels chipped off bone. It was as if a tangle of tiny nerves were being cut dexterously, one by one; the pain writhed spirally and came to her who was a pink bird and sat on the top of a cone. The pain was a pyramid made of a diamond; it was an intense light; it was the hottest fire, the coldest chill, the highest peak, the fastest force, the furthest reach, the newest time. It possessed nothing of her but its one infinitestimal scene: beyond the screen as thin as gossamer, the brain trembled for its life, hearing the knives hunting like wolves outside, sniffing and snapping. Mercy! Mercy! cried the scalped nerves.

At last, miraculously, she turned her eyes inward tranquilly. Dr. Nicholas had said, "The worst is over. I am going to work on the floor of your noise," and at his signal she closed her eyes and this time and this time alone she saw her brain lying in a shell-pink satin case. It was a pink pearl, no bigger than a needle's eye, but it was so beautiful and so pure that its smallness made no difference. Anyhow, as she watched, it grew. It grew larger and larger until it was an enormous bubble that contained the surgeon and the whole room within its rosy luster. In a long-ago summer, she had often been absorbed by the spectacle of flocks of yellow birds that visited a cedar tree and she remembered that everything that summer had been some shade of yellow. One year of childhood, her mother had frequently taken her to have tea with an aged schoolmistress upon whose mantelpiece there was a herd of ivory elephants; that had been the white year. There was a green spring when early in April she had seen a grass snake on a boulder, but the very summer that followed was violet, for vetch took her mother's garden. She saw a swatch of blue tulle lying in a raffia basket on the front porch of Uncle Marion's brown house. Never before had the world been pink, whatever else it had been. Or had it been, one other time? She could not be sure and she did not care. Of one thing she was certain: never had the world enclosed her before and never had the quiet been so smooth.

For only a moment the busybodies left her to her ecstasy and then, impatient and gossiping, they forced their way inside, slashed at her resisting trance with questions and congratulations, with statements of fact and jokes. "Later," she said to them dumbly. "Later on, perhaps. I am busy now." But their voices would not go away. They touched her, too, washing her face with cloths so cold they stung, stroking her wrists with firm, antiseptic fingers. The surgeon, squeezing her arm with avuncular pride, said, "Good girl," as if she were a bright dog that had retrieved a bone. Her silent mind abused him: "You are a thief," it said, "you are heartless and you should be put to death." But he was leaving, adjusting his coat with an air of vainglory, and the interne, abject with admiration, followed him from the operating room, smiling like a silly boy.

Shortly after they took her back to her room, the weather changed, not for the better. Momentarily the sun emerged from its concealing murk, but in a few minutes the snow came with a wind that promised a blizzard. There was great pain, but since it could not serve her, she rejected it and she lay as if in a hammock in a pause of bitterness. She closed her eyes, shutting herself up within her treasureless head.

CARSON MCCULLERS

1917–1967

Born in Columbus, Georgia, Carson McCullers is usually slotted as Southern Gothic. Thus she takes a place along with the founding father Poe, the
acknowledged master Faulkner, and such talents as Eudora Welty and Flannery O'Connor. Insofar as the accordion term "Gothic" suggests the fear-
some, the monstrous, and the macabre, it probably applies to McCullers.
Insofar as it is limited by such adjectives, it does not. Somewhat truer is her
own formula: "I suppose my central theme is the theme of spiritual
isolation."

At twenty-three she scored an immediate success with her novel signifi-
cantly titled The Heart Is a Lonely Hunter. She adapted her A Member of
the Wedding into what became a stage hit; it was later made into a film.
The Ballad of the Sad Café, the novella that is probably her finest work,
was dramatized by Edward Albee. To these professional triumphs her personal life stood in sad contrast. From her twenty-ninth year she was paralyzed on her left side and thereafter lived with pain.

Her isolate characters are often emotionally maimed or physically hand-
icapped. One is a hunchbacked dwarf, another a deaf-mute, still another a
thirteen-year-old motherless girl. But whatever draws her to the abnormal,
even the freakish, is often, though not always, balanced by a redeeming
intensity, a feeling for the lost, the outsider, a feeling sure to emerge in any
culture that ostensibly idolizes "progress" and pure energy.

"Madame Zilensky" is about a kind of madness and also about music (as
a young woman Carson McCullers studied music in New York City). An
engimatic tale, not without its special humor, it illustrates the author's
preoccupation with grotesques who touch the heart.

Madame Zilensky and
the King of Finland

To MR. BROOK, the head of the music department at Ryder College, was due all the credit for getting Madame Zilensky on the faculty. The college considered itself fortunate; her reputation was impressive, both as a composer and as a pedagogue. Mr. Brook took on himself the responsibility of finding a house for Madame Zilensky, a comfortable place with a garden, which was convenient to the college and next to the apartment house where he himself lived.

No one in Westbridge had known Madame Zilensky before she came. Mr. Brook had seen her pictures in musical journals, and once he had written to her about the authenticity of a certain Buxtehude manuscript. Also, when it was being settled that she was to join the faculty, they had exchanged a few cables and letters on practical affairs. She wrote in a clear, square hand, and the only thing out of the ordinary in these letters was the fact that they contained an occasional reference to objects and persons altogether unknown to Mr. Brook, such as "the yellow cat in Lisbon" or "poor Heinrich." These lapses Mr. Brook put down to the confusion of getting herself and her family out of Europe.

Mr. Brook was a somewhat pastel person; years of Mozart minuets, of explanations about diminished sevenths and minor triads, had given him a watchful vocational patience. For the most part, he kept to himself. He loathed academic fiddle-faddle and committees. Years before, when the music department had decided to gang together and spend the summer in Salzburg, Mr. Brook sneaked out of the arrangement at the last moment and took a solitary trip to Peru. He had a few eccentricities himself and was tolerant of the peculiarities of others; indeed, he rather relished the ridiculous. Often, when confronted with some grave and incongruous situation, he would feel a little inside tickle, which stiffened his long, mild face and sharpened the light in his gray eyes.

Mr. Brook met Madame Zilensky at the Westbridge station a week before the beginning of the fall semester. He recognized her instantly. She was a tall, straight woman with a pale and haggard face. Her eyes were deeply shadowed and she wore her dark, ragged hair pushed back from her forehead. She had large, delicate hands, which were very grubby. About her person as a whole there was something noble and abstract that made Mr. Brook draw back for a moment and stand nervously undoing his cuff links. In spite of her clothes — a long, black skirt and a broken-down old leather jacket — she made an impression of vague elegance. With Madame Zilensky were three children, boys between the ages of ten and six, all blond, blank-eyed, and beautiful. There was one other person, an old woman who turned out later to be the Finnish servant.

This was the group he found at the station. The only luggage they had with them was two immense boxes of manuscripts, the rest of their paraphernalia having been forgotten in the station at Springfield when they changed trains. That is the sort of thing that can happen to anyone. When Mr. Brook got them all into a taxi, he thought the worst difficulties were over, but Madame Zilensky suddenly tried to scramble over his knees and get out of the door.

"My God!" she said. "I left my — how do you say? — my tick-tick-tick —"

"Your watch?" asked Mr. Brook.

"Oh no!" she said vehemently. "You know, my tick-tick-tick," and she waved her forefinger from side to side, pendulum fashion.

"Tick-tick," said Mr. Brook, putting his hands to his forehead and closing his eyes. "Could you possibly mean a metronome?"

"Yes! Yes! I think I must have lost it there where we changed trains."

Mr. Brook managed to quiet her. He even said, with a kind of dazed gallantry, that he would get her another one the next day. But at the time he was bound to admit to himself that there was something curious about this panic over a metronome when there was all the rest of the lost luggage to consider.

The Zelinsky ménage moved into the house next door, and on the surface everything was all right. The boys were quiet children. Their names were Sigmund, Boris, and Sammy. They were always together and they followed each other around Indian file, Sigmund usually the first. Among themselves they spoke a desperate-sounding family Esperanto made up of Russian, French, Finnish, German, and English; when other people were around, they were strangely silent. It was not any one thing that the Zilenskys did or said that made Mr. Brook uneasy. There were just little incidents. For example, something about the Zilensky children subconsciously bothered him when they were in a house, and finally he realized that what troubled him was the fact that the Zilensky boys never walked on a rug; they skirted it single file on the bare floor, and if a room was carpeted, they stood in the doorway and did not go inside. Another thing was this: Weeks passed and Madame Zilensky seemed to make no effort to get settled or to furnish the house with anything more than a table and some beds. The front door was left open day and night, and soon the house began to take on a queer, bleak look like that of a place abandoned for years.

The college had every reason to be satisfied with Madame Zilensky.

She taught with a fierce insistence. She could become deeply indignant if some Mary Owens or Bernadine Smith would not clean up her Scarlatti trills. She got hold of four pianos for her college studio and set four dazed students to playing Bach fugues together. The racket that came from her end of the department was extraordinary, but Madame Zilensky did not seem to have a nerve in her, and if pure will and effort can get over a musical idea, then Ryder College could not have done better. At night Madame Zilensky worked on her twelfth symphony. She seemed never to sleep; no matter what time of night Mr. Brook happened to look out of his sitting-room window, the light in her studio was always on. No, it was not because of any professional consideration that Mr. Brook became so dubious.

It was in late October when he felt for the first time that something was unmistakably wrong. He had lunched with Madame Zilensky and had enjoyed himself, as she had given him a very detailed account of an African safari she had made in 1928. Later in the afternoon she stopped in at his office and stood rather abstractly in the doorway.

Mr. Brook looked up from his desk and asked, "Is there anything you want?"

"No, thank you," said Madame Zilensky. She had a low, beautiful, sombre voice. "I was only just wondering. You recall the metronome. Do you think perhaps that I might have left it with that French?"

"Who?" asked Mr. Brook.

"Why, that French I was married to," she answered.

"Frenchman," Mr. Brook said mildly. He tried to imagine the husband of Madame Zilensky, but his mind refused. He muttered half to himself, "The father of the children."

"But no," said Madame Zilensky with decision. "The father of Sammy."

Mr. Brook had a swift prescience. His deepest instincts warned him to say nothing further. Still, his respect for order, his conscience, demanded that he ask, "And the father of the other two?"

Madame Zilensky put her hand to the back of her head and ruffled up her short, cropped hair. Her face was dreamy, and for several moments she did not answer. Then she said gently, "Boris is of a Pole who played the piccolo."

"And Sigmund?" he asked. Mr. Brook looked over his orderly desk, with the stack of corrected papers, the three sharpened pencils, the ivory-elephant paperweight. When he glanced up at Madame Zilensky, she was obviously thinking hard. She gazed around at the corners of the room, her brows lowered and her jaw moving from side to side. At last she said, "We were discussing the father of Sigmund?"

"Why, no," said Mr. Brook. "There is no need to do that."

Madame Zilensky answered in a voice both dignified and final. "He was a fellow-countryman."

Mr. Brook really did not care one way or the other. He had no prejudices; people could marry seventeen times and have Chinese children so far as he was concerned. But there was something about this conversation with Madame Zilensky that bothered him. Suddenly he understood. The children didn't look at all like Madame Zilensky, but they looked exactly like each other, and as they all had different fathers, Mr. Brook thought the resemblance astonishing.

But Madame Zilensky had finished with the subject. She zipped up her leather jacket and turned away.

"That is exactly where I left it," she said, with a quick nod. "*Chez* that French."

Affairs in the music department were running smoothly. Mr. Brook did not have any serious embarrassments to deal with, such as the harp teacher last year who had finally eloped with a garage mechanic. There was only this nagging apprehension about Madame Zilensky. He could not make out what was wrong in his relations with her or why his feelings were so mixed. To begin with, she was a great globe-trotter, and her conversations were incongruously seasoned with references to far-fetched places. She would go along for days without opening her mouth, prowling through the corridor with her hands in the pockets of her jacket and her face locked in meditation. Then suddenly she would buttonhole Mr. Brook and launch out on a long, volatile monologue, her eyes reckless and bright and her voice warm with eagerness. She would talk about anything or nothing at all. Yet, without exception, there was something queer, in a slanted sort of way, about every episode she ever mentioned. If she spoke of taking Sammy to the barbershop, the impression she created was just as foreign as if she were telling of an afternoon in Bagdad. Mr. Brook could not make it out.

The truth came to him very suddenly, and the truth made everything perfectly clear, or at least clarified the situation. Mr. Brook had come home early and lighted a fire in the little grate in his sitting room. He felt comfortable and at peace that evening. He sat before the fire in his stocking feet, with a volume of William Blake on the table by his side, and he had poured himself a half-glass of apricot brandy. At ten o'clock he was drowsing cozily before the fire, his mind full of cloudy phrases of Mahler and floating half-thoughts. Then all at once, out of this delicate stupor, four words came to his mind: "The King of Finland." The words seemed familiar, but for the first moment he could not place them. Then all at once he tracked them down. He had been walking across the campus that afternoon when Madame Zilensky stopped him and began some preposterous rigmarole, to which he had only half listened; he was thinking about the stack of canons turned in by his counterpoint class. Now the words, the inflections of her voice, came back to him with insidious exactitude. Madame Zilensky had started off with the following remark: "One day, when I was standing in front of a *pâtisserie*, the King of Finland came by in a sled."

Mr. Brook jerked himself up straight in his chair and put down his glass of brandy. The woman was a pathological liar. Almost every word she uttered outside of class was an untruth. If she worked all night, she would go out of her way to tell you she spent the evening at the cinema. If she ate lunch at the Old Tavern, she would be sure to mention that she had lunched with her children at home. The woman was simply a pathological liar, and that accounted for everything.

Mr. Brook cracked his knuckles and got up from his chair. His first reaction was one of exasperation. That day after day Madame Zilensky would have the gall to sit there in his office and deluge him with her outrageous falsehoods! Mr. Brook was intensely provoked. He walked up and down the room, then he went into his kitchenette and made himself a sardine sandwich.

An hour later, as he sat before the fire, his irritation had changed to a scholarly and thoughtful wonder. What he must do, he told himself, was to regard the whole situation impersonally and look on Madame Zilensky as a doctor looks on a sick patient. Her lies were of the guileless sort. She did not dissimulate with any intention to deceive, and the untruths she told were never used to any possible advantage. That was the maddening thing; there was simply no motive behind it all.

Mr. Brook finished off the rest of the brandy. And slowly, when it was almost midnight, a further understanding came to him. The reason for the lies of Madame Zilensky was painful and plain. All her life long Madame Zilensky had worked — at the piano, teaching, and writing those beautiful and immense twelve symphonies. Day and night she had drudged and struggled and thrown her soul into her work, and there was not much of her left over for anything else. Being human, she suffered from this lack and did what she could to make up for it. If she passed the evening bent over a table in the library and later declared that she had spent that time playing cards, it was as though she had managed to do both those things. Through the lies, she lived vicariously. The lies doubled the little of her existence that was left over from work and augmented the little rag end of her personal life.

Mr. Brook looked into the fire, and the face of Madame Zilensky was in his mind — a severe face, with dark, weary eyes and delicately disciplined mouth. He was conscious of a warmth in his chest, and a feeling of pity, protectiveness, and dreadful understanding. For a while he was in a state of lovely confusion.

Later on he brushed his teeth and got into his pajamas. He must be practical. What did this clear up? That French, the Pole with the piccolo, Bagdad? And the children, Sigmund, Boris, and Sammy — who were they? Were they really her children after all, or had she simply rounded them up from somewhere? Mr. Brook polished his spectacles and put them on the table by his bed. He must come to an immediate understanding with her. Otherwise, there would exist in the department a situation which could become most problematical. It was two o'clock. He glanced out of his window and saw that the light in Madame Zilensky's workroom was still on. Mr. Brook got into bed, made terrible faces in the dark, and tried to plan what he would say next day.

Mr. Brook was in his office by eight o'clock. He sat hunched up behind his desk, ready to trap Madame Zilensky as she passed down the corridor. He did not have to wait long, and as soon as he heard her footsteps he called out her name.

Madame Zilensky stood in the doorway. She looked vague and jaded. "How are you? I had such a fine night's rest," she said.

"Pray be seated, if you please," said Mr. Brook. "I would like a word with you."

Madame Zilensky put aside her portfolio and leaned back wearily in the armchair across from him. "Yes?" she asked.

"Yesterday you spoke to me as I was walking across the campus," he said slowly. "And if I am not mistaken, I believe you said something about a pastry shop and the King of Finland. Is that correct?"

Madame Zilensky turned her head to one side and stared retrospectively at a corner of the window sill.

"Something about a pastry shop," he repeated.

Her tired face brightened. "But of course," she said eagerly. "I told you about the time I was standing in front of this shop and the King of Finland —"

"Madame Zilensky!" Mr. Brook cried. "There *is* no King of Finland."

Madame Zilensky looked absolutely blank. Then, after an instant, she started off again. "I was standing in front of Bjarne's *pâtisserie* when I turned away from the cakes and suddenly saw the King of Finland —"

"Madame Zilensky, I just told you that there is no King of Finland."

"In Helsingfors," she started off again desperately, and again he let her get as far as the King, and then no further.

"Finland is a democracy," he said. "You could not possibly have seen the King of Finland. Therefore, what you have just said is an untruth. A pure untruth."

Never afterward could Mr. Brook forget the face of Madame Zilensky at that moment. In her eyes there was astonishment, dismay, and a sort of cornered horror. She had the look of one who watches his whole interior world split open and disintegrate.

"It is a pity," said Mr. Brook with real sympathy.

But Madame Zilensky pulled herself together. She raised her chin and said coldly, "I am a Finn."

"That I do not question," answered Mr. Brook. On second thought, he did question it a little.

"I was born in Finland and I am a Finnish citizen."

"That may very well be," said Mr. Brook in a rising voice.

"In the war," she continued passionately, "I rode a motorcycle and was a messenger."

"Your patriotism does not enter into it."

"Just because I am getting out the first papers —"

"Madame Zilensky!" said Mr. Brook. His hands grasped the edge of the desk. "That is only an irrelevant issue. The point is that you maintained and testified that you saw — that you saw —" But he could not finish. Her face stopped him. She was deadly pale and there were shadows around her mouth. Her eyes were wide open, doomed, and proud. And Mr. Brook felt suddenly like a murderer. A great commotion of feelings — understanding, remorse, and unreasonable love — made him cover his face with his hands. He could not speak until this agitation in his insides quieted down, and then he said very faintly, "Yes. Of course. The King of Finland. And was he nice?"

An hour later, Mr. Brook sat looking out of the window of his office. The trees along the quiet Westbridge street were almost bare, and the gray buildings of the college had a calm, sad look. As he idly took in the familiar scene, he noticed the Drakes' old Airedale waddling along down the street. It was a thing he had watched a hundred times before, so what was it that struck him as strange? Then he realized with a kind of cold surprise that the old dog was running along backward. Mr. Brook watched the Airedale until he was out of sight, then resumed his work on the canons which had been turned in by the class in counterpoint.

Peter Taylor

1917–

Though as Southern as they come, Peter Taylor's quiet, unaggressive approach to his material sets him somewhat apart from other writers of that school. He has staked out his own territory — the patrician class that some might call simply nice people and some, less sympathetically, the country club set. Their hitherto dominant culture, beginning to falter during the Depression, was further disrupted by the crucial 1954 Supreme Court segregation decision. Taylor is that class's interpreter.

His voice is quite his own. In its polite, understated intonations one can detect irony, affection, detachment, and melancholy as he anatomizes the society into which he was born. His tempo is leisurely, as is true of most Southern writers, their feeling for narrative being rooted in talk, in yarns, in tribal memories constantly modulated and transformed. Their talent does not lie in concentration or the build-up of suspense, but in the notation of the subtleties, often the trivialities, of clan, family, and class relationships.

Beneath the ostensible, specific subjects of many of his stories is Taylor's more general concern with the erosion of nineteenth-century codes of middle- and upper-class conduct under the pressures of the new South. In the story "Guests" the successful lawyer Edmund Harper is making a sick call on his old Cousin Johnny, who had refused to enter the modern world: ". . . the old ways, the old life, where people had real grandfathers and real children, and where love was something that could endure the light of day — something real, not merely a hand one holds in the dark so that sleep will come. Our trouble was, Cousin Johnny, we were lost without our old realities."

In the story that follows, the narrator, his flabby character precisely reflected in his rambling conversational style, is one of the lost. Not until his unutterably sad final phrase does he become fully conscious of how lost he really is.

The Gift of the Prodigal

THERE'S RICKY down in the washed river gravel of my driveway. I had my yardman out raking it before 7 A.M. — the driveway. It looks nearly perfect. Ricky also looks nearly perfect down there. He looks extremely got up and cleaned up, as though he had been carefully raked over and smoothed out. He is wearing a three-piece linen suit, which my other son, you may be sure, wouldn't be seen wearing on any occasion. And he has on an expensive striped shirt, open at the collar. No tie, of course. His thick head of hair, parted and slicked down, is just the same tan color as the gravel. Hair and gravel seem equally clean and in order. The fact is, Ricky looks this morning as though he belongs nowhere else in the world but out there in that smooth spread of washed river gravel (which will be mussed up again before noon, of course — I'm resigned to it), looks as though he feels perfectly at home in that driveway of mine that was so expensive to install and that requires so much upkeep.

Since one can't see his freckles from where I stand at this second-story window, his skin looks very fair — almost transparent. (Ricky just misses being a real redhead, and so never lets himself get suntanned. Bright sunlight tends to give him skin cancers.) From the window directly above him, I am able to get the full effect of his outfit. He looks very masculine standing down there, which is no doubt the impression his formfitting clothes are meant to give. And Ricky *is* very masculine, no matter what else he is or isn't. Peering down from up here, I mark particularly that where his collar stands open, and with several shirt buttons left carelessly or carefully undone, you can see a triangle of darker hair glistening on his chest. It isn't hard to imagine just how recently he has stepped out of the shower. In a word, he is looking what he considers his very best. And this says to me that Ricky is coming to me *for* something, or *because of* something.

His little sports car is parked in the turnaround behind this house, which I've built since he and the other children grew up and since their mother died. I know of course that, for them, coming here to see me can never really be like coming home. For Rick it must be like going to see any other old fellow who might happen to be his boss and who is ailing and is staying away from the office for a few days. As soon as I saw him down there, though, I knew something was really seriously wrong. From here I could easily recognize the expression on his face. He has a way, when he is concerned about something, of knitting his eyebrows and at the same time opening his eyes very wide, as though his eyes are about to pop out of his head and his eyebrows are trying to hold them in. It's a look that used to give him away even as a child when he was in trouble at school. If his mother and I saw that expression on his face, we would know that we were apt to be rung up by one of his teachers in a day or so or maybe have a house call from one of them.

Momentarily Ricky massages his face with his big right hand, as if to wipe away the expression. And clearly now he is headed for the side door that opens on the driveway. But before actually coming over to the door he has stopped in one spot and keeps shuffling his suede shoes about, roughing up the smooth gravel, like a young bull in a pen. I almost call out to him not to *do* that, not to muss up my gravel, which even his car wheels haven't disturbed — or not so much as he is doing with his suede shoes. I *almost* call out to him. But of course I don't really. For Ricky is a man twenty-nine years old, with two divorces already and no doubt another coming up soon. He's been through all that, besides a series of live-ins between marriages that I don't generally speak of, even.

For some time before coming on into the house, Ricky remains there in that spot in the driveway. While he stands there, it occurs to me that he may actually be looking the place over, as though he'd never noticed what this house is like until now. The old place on Wertland Street, where he and the other children grew up, didn't have half the style and convenience of this one. It had more room, but the room was mostly in pantries and hallways, with front stairs and back stairs and third-floor servants' quarters in an age when no servant would be caught dead living up there in the attic — or staying anywhere else on the place, for that matter. I am not unaware, of course, how much better that old house on Wertland was than this one. You couldn't have replaced it for twice what I've poured into this compact and well-appointed habitation out here in Farmington. But its neighborhood had gone bad. Nearly all of Charlottesville proper has, as a matter of fact, either gone commercial or been absorbed by the university. You can no longer live within the shadow of Mr. Jefferson's Academical Village. And our old Wertland Street house is now a funeral parlor. Which is what it ought to have been five years before I left it. From the day my wife, Cary, died, the place seemed like a tomb. I wandered up and down the stairs and all around, from room to room, sometimes greeting myself in one of Cary's looking glasses, doing so out of loneliness or out of thinking *that* couldn't be *me* still in my dressing gown and slippers at midday, or fully dressed — necktie and all — at 3 A.M. I knew well enough it was time to sell. And, besides, I wanted to have the experience at last of making something new. You see, we never built a house of our own, Cary and I. We always bought instead of building, wishing to be in an established neighborhood, you know, where there were good day schools for the girls (it was before St. Anne's moved to the suburbs), where there were streetcars and buses for the servants, or, better still, an easy walk for them to Ridge Street.

My scheme for building a new house after Cary died seemed a harebrained idea to my three older children. They tried to talk me out of it. They said I was only doing it out of idleness. They'd laugh and say I'd chosen a rather expensive form of entertainment for myself in my old age. That's what they *said*. That wasn't all they *thought*, however. But I never held against them what they thought. All motherless children — regardless of age — have such thoughts. They had in mind that I'd got notions of marrying again. Me! Why, I've never looked at another woman since the day I married. Not to this very hour. At any rate, one night when we were having dinner and they were telling me how they worried about me, and making it plainer than usual what they thought my plans for the future were or might be, Ricky spoke up — Ricky who never gave a thought in his life to what happened to anybody except himself — and he came out with just what was on the others' minds. "What if you should take a notion to marry again?" he asked. And I began shaking my head before the words were out of his mouth, as did all the others. It was an unthinkable thought for them as well as for me. "Why not?" Ricky persisted, happy of course that he was making everybody uncomfortable. "Worse things have happened, you know. And I nominate the handsome Mrs. Capers as a likely candidate for bride."

I *think* he was referring to a certain low sort of woman who had recently moved into the old neighborhood. You could depend upon Rick to know about her and know her name. As he spoke he winked at me. Presently he crammed his wide mouth full of food, and as he chewed he made a point of drawing back his lips and showing his somewhat over-large and overly white front teeth. He continued to look straight at me as he chewed, but looking with only one eye, keeping the eye he'd winked at me squinched up tight. He looked for all the world like some old tomcat who's found a nasty morsel he likes the taste of and is not going to let go of. I willingly would have knocked him out of his chair for what he'd said, even more for that common look he was giving me. I knew he knew as well as the others that I'd never looked at any woman besides his mother.

Yet I laughed with the others as soon as I realized they were laughing. You don't let a fellow like Ricky know he's got your goat — especially when he's your own son, and has been in one bad scrape after another ever since he's been grown, and seems always just waiting for a chance to get back at you for something censorious you may have said to him while trying to help him out of one of his escapades. Since Cary died, I've tried mostly just to keep lines of communication open with him. I think that's the thing she would have wanted of me — that is, not to shut Rick out, to keep him talking. Cary used to say to me, "You may be the only person he can talk to about the women he gets involved with. He can't talk to me about such things." Cary always thought it was the women he had most on his mind and who got him into scrapes. I never used to think so. Anyway, I believe that Cary would have wished above all else for me to keep lines open with Rick, would have wanted it even more than she would have wanted me to go ahead in whatever way I chose with schemes for a new house for my old age.

The house was *our* plan originally, you see, hers and mine. It was something we never told the children about. There seemed no reason why we should. Not talking about it except between ourselves was part of the pleasure of it, somehow. And that night when Ricky came out with the speculation about my possibly marrying again, I didn't tell him or the others that actually I had already sold the Wertland Street house and already had blueprints for the new house here in Farmington locked away in my desk drawer, and even a contractor all set to break ground.

Well, my new house was finished the following spring. By that time all the children, excepting Rick, had developed a real enthusiasm for it. (Rick didn't give a damn one way or the other, of course.) They helped me dispose of all the superfluous furniture in the old house. The girls even saw to the details of moving and saw to it that I got comfortably settled in. They wanted me to be happy out here. And soon enough they saw I was. There was no more they could do for me now than there had been in recent years. They had their good marriages to look after (that's what Cary would have wished for them), and they saw to it that I wasn't left out of whatever of their activities I wanted to be in on. In a word, they went on with their busy lives, and my own life seemed busy enough for any man my age.

What has vexed the other children, though, during the five years since I built my house, is their brother Ricky's continuing to come to me at almost regular intervals with new ordeals of one kind or another that he's been going through. They have thought he ought not to burden me with his outrageous and sometimes sordid affairs. I think they have especially resented his troubling me here at home. I still go to the office, you see, two or three days a week — just whenever I feel like it or when I'm not playing golf or bridge or am not off on a little trip to Sarasota (I stay at the same inn Cary and I used to go to). And so I've always seen Ricky quite regularly at the office. He's had every chance to talk to me there. But the fact is Rick was never one for bringing his personal problems to the office. He has always brought them home.

Even since I've moved, he has always come *here,* to the house, when he's really wanted to talk to me about something. I don't know whether it's the two servants I still keep or some of the young neighbors hereabouts who tell them, but somehow the other children always know when Ricky has been here. And they of course can put two and two

together. It will come out over Sunday dinner at one of their houses or
at the Club — in one of those little private dining rooms. It is all right
if we eat in the big dining room, where everybody else is. I know I'm
safe there. But as soon as I see they've reserved a private room I know
they want to talk about Ricky's latest escapade. They will begin by making veiled references to it among themselves. But at last it is I who am
certain to let the cat out of the bag. For I can't resist joining in when
they get onto Rick, as they all know very well I won't be able to. You
see, often they will have the details wrong — maybe they get them wrong
on purpose — and I feel obliged to straighten them out. Then one of
them will turn to me, pretending shocked surprise: "How ever did you
know about it? Has *he* been bringing his troubles to *you* again? At his
age you'd think he'd be ashamed to! Someone ought to remind him he's
a grown man now!" At that point one of the girls is apt to rest her hand
on mine. As they go on, I can hear the love for me in their voices and
see it in their eyes. I know then what a lucky man I am. I want to say to
them that their affection makes up for all the unhappiness Ricky causes
me. But I have never been one to make speeches like that. Whenever I
have managed to say such things, I have somehow always felt like a
hypocrite afterward. Anyway, the talk will go on for a while till I remember a bridge game I have an appointment for in the Club lounge,
at two o'clock. Or I recall that my golf foursome is waiting for me in
the locker room.

I've never tried to defend Rick from the others. The things he does are
really quite indefensible. Sometimes I've even found myself giving details
about some escapade of his that the others didn't already know and are
genuinely shocked to hear — especially coming from me. He was in a
shooting once that everybody in Farmington and in the whole county
set knew about — or knew about, that is, in a general way, though
without knowing the very thing that would finally make it a public scandal. It's an ugly story, I warn you, as, indeed, nearly all of Ricky's stories
are.

He had caught another fellow in bed with a young married woman
with whom he himself was running around. Of course it was a scandalous business, all of it. But the girl, as Rick described her to me afterward,
was a real beauty of a certain type and, according to Rick, as smart as
a whip. Rick even showed me her picture, though I hadn't asked to see
it, naturally. She had a tight little mouth, and eyes that — even in that
wallet-sized picture — burned themselves into your memory. She was
the sort of intense and reckless-looking girl that Ricky has always gone
for. I've sometimes looked at pictures of his other girls, too, when he
wanted to show them to me. And of course I know what his wives have
looked like. All three of his wives have been from good families. For,
bad as he is, Ricky is not the sort of fellow who would embarrass the
rest of us by *marrying* some slut. Yet even his wives have tended to dress

themselves in a way that my own daughters wouldn't. They have dressed, that is to say, in clothes that seemed designed to call attention to their female forms and not, as with my daughters, to call attention to the station and the affluence of their husbands. Being the timid sort of man I am, I used to find myself whenever I talked with his wife — whichever one — carefully looking out the window or looking across the room, away from her, at some inanimate object or other over there or out there. My wife, Cary, used to say that Ricky had bad luck in his wives, that each of them turned out to have just as roving an eye as Ricky himself. I can't say for certain whether this was true for each of them in the beginning or whether it was something Ricky managed to teach them all.

Anyway, the case of the young married woman in whose bed — or apartment — Ricky found that other fellow came near to causing Ricky more trouble than any of his other escapades. The fellow ran out of the apartment, with Rick chasing him into the corridor and down the corridor to a door of an outside stairway. It was not here in Farmington, you see, but out on Barracks Road, where so many of Rick's friends are — in a development that's been put up on the very edge of where the horse farms begin. The fellow scurried down the outside stairs and across a parking lot toward some pastureland beyond. And Rick, as he said, couldn't resist taking a shot at him from that upstairs stoop where he had abandoned the chase. He took aim just when the fellow reached the first pasture fence and was about to climb over. Afterward, Rick said that it was simply too good to miss. But Rick rarely misses a target when he takes aim. He hit the fellow with a load of rat shot right in the seat of the pants.

I'll never know how Rick happened to have the gun with him. He told me that he was deeply in love with the young woman and would have married her if her husband had been willing to give her a divorce. The other children maintain to this day that it was the husband Rick meant to threaten with the gun, but the husband was out of town and Rick lost his head when he found that other fellow there in his place. Anyhow, the story got all over town. I suppose Ricky himself helped to spread it. He thought it all awfully funny at first. But before it was over, the matter came near to getting into the courts and into the paper. And that was because there was something else involved, which the other children and the people in the Barracks Road set didn't know about and I did. In fact, it was something that I worried about from the beginning. You see, Rick naturally took that fellow he'd blasted with the rat shot to a doctor — a young doctor friend of theirs — who removed the shot. But, being a friend, the doctor didn't report the incident. A certain member of our judiciary heard the details and thought perhaps the matter needed looking into. We were months getting it straightened out. Ricky went out of town for a while, and the young doctor ended by having to move away permanently — to Richmond or Norfolk, I think. I only give this incident in such detail in order to show the sort of low company Ricky has always kept, even when he seemed to be among our own sort.

His troubles haven't all involved women, though. Or not primarily. And that's what I used to tell Cary. Like so many people in Charlottesville, Rick has always had a weakness for horses. For a while he fancied himself a polo player. He bought a polo pony and got cheated on it. He bought it at a stable where he kept another horse he owned — bought it from the man who ran the stable. After a day or so, he found that the animal was a worthless, worn-out nag. It couldn't even last through the first chukker, which was humiliating of course for Ricky. He daren't try to take it onto the field again. It had been all doped up when he bought it. Ricky was outraged. Instead of simply trying to get his money back, he wanted to have his revenge upon the man and make an even bigger fool of *him*. He persuaded a friend to dress himself up in a turtleneck sweater and a pair of yellow jodhpurs and pretend just to be passing by the stall in the same stable where the polo pony was still kept. His friend played the role, you see, of someone only just taking up the game and who thought he *had* to have that particular pony. He asked the man whose animal it was, and before he could get an answer he offered more than twice the price that Rick had paid. He even put the offer into writing — using an assumed name, of course. He said he was from up in Maryland and would return in two days' time. Naturally, the stableman telephoned Ricky as soon as the stranger in jodhpurs had left the stable. He said he had discovered, to his chagrin, that the pony was not in as good condition as he had thought it was. And he said that in order that there be no bad feelings between them he was willing to buy it back for the price Ricky had paid.

Ricky went over that night and collected his money. But when the stranger didn't reappear and couldn't be traced, the stableman of course knew what had happened. Rick didn't return to the stable during the following several days. I suppose, being Ricky, he was busy spreading the story all over town. His brother and sisters got wind of it. And I did soon enough. On Sunday night, two thugs and some woman Ricky knew but would never identify — not even to me — came to his house and persuaded him to go out and sit in their car with them in front of his house. And there they beat him brutally. He had to be in the hospital for five or six days. They broke his right arm, and one of them — maybe it was the woman — was trying to bite off the lobe of his left ear when Ricky's current wife, who had been out to some party without the favor of his company, pulled into the driveway beside the house. The assailants shoved poor Ricky, bruised and bleeding and with his arm broken, out onto the sidewalk. And then of course they sped away down the street in their rented car. Ricky's wife and the male friend who was with her got the license number, but the car had been rented under an assumed name — the same name, actually, as some kind of joke, I suppose, that Ricky's friend in jodhpurs had used with the stablekeeper.

Since Ricky insisted that he could not possibly recognize his two male assailants in a lineup, and since he refused to identify the woman, there was little that could be done about his actual beating. I don't know that he ever confessed to anyone but me that he knew the woman. It was easy enough for me to imagine what *she* looked like. Though I would not have admitted it to Ricky or to anyone else, I would now and then during the following weeks see a woman of a certain type on the streets downtown — with one of those tight little mouths and with burning eyes — and imagine that she might be the very one. All we were ever able to do about the miserable fracas was to see to it finally that that stable was put out of business and that the man himself had to go elsewhere (he went down into North Carolina) to ply his trade.

There is one other scrape of Ricky's that I must mention, because it remains particularly vivid for me. The nature and the paraphernalia of this one will seem even more old-fashioned than those of the other incidents. Maybe that's why it sticks in my mind so. It's something that might have happened to any number of rough fellows I knew when I was coming along.

Ricky, not surprising to say, likes to gamble. From the time he was a young boy he would often try to inveigle one of the other children into making wagers with him on how overdone his steak was at dinner. He always liked it very rare and when his serving came he would hold up a bite on his fork and, for a decision on the bet, would ask everyone what shade of brown the meat was. He made all the suggestions of color himself. And one night his suggestions got so coarse and vile his mother had to send him from the dining room and not let him have a bite of supper. Sometimes he would try to get the other children to bet with him on the exact number of minutes the parson's sermon would last on Sunday or how many times the preacher would use the word "Hell" or "damnation" or "adultery." Since he has got grown, it's the races, of course, he likes — horse races, it goes without saying, but also such low-life affairs as dog races and auto races. What catches his fancy above all else, though, are the chicken fights we have always had in our part of the country. And a few years ago he bought himself a little farm a dozen miles or so south of town where he could raise his own game chickens. I saw nothing wrong with that at the time. Then he built an octagonal barn down there, with a pit in it where he could hold the fights. I worried a little when he did that. But we've always had cockfights hereabouts. The birds are beautiful creatures, really, though they have no brains, of course. The fight itself is a real spectacle and no worse than some other things people enjoy. At Ricky's urging, I even went down to two or three fights at his place. I didn't bet, because I knew the stakes were very high. (Besides, it's the betting that's illegal.) And I didn't tell the other children about my going. But this was after Cary was dead, you see, and I thought maybe she would have liked my going for Ricky's sake, though she would never have acknowledged it. Pretty soon, sizable crowds began attending the fights on weekend nights. Cars would be parked all over Ricky's front pasture and all around the yard of the tenant house. He might as well have put up a sign down at the gate where his farm road came off the highway.

The point is, everyone knew that the cockfights went on. And one of his most regular customers and biggest bettors was one of the county sheriff's right-hand men. I'm afraid Rick must have bragged about that in advertising his fights to friends — friends who would otherwise have been a little timid about coming. And during the fights he would move about among the crowd, winking at people and saying to them under his breath, "The deputy's here tonight." I suppose it was his way of reassuring them that everything was all right. I don't know whether or not his spreading the word so widely had anything to do with the raid, but nevertheless the deputy was present the night the federal officers came stealing up the farm road, with their car lights off and with search warrants in their pockets. And it was the deputy who first got wind of the federal officers' approach. He had one of his sidekicks posted outside the barn. Maybe he had somebody watching out there every night that he came. Maybe all along he had had a plan for his escape in such an emergency. Rick thought so afterward. Anyhow, the deputy's man outside knew at once what those cars moving up the lane with their lights off meant. The deputy got the word before anyone else, but, depend upon Ricky, he saw the first move the deputy made to leave. And he was not going to have it. He took out after him.

The deputy's watchman was prepared to stay on and take his chances. (He wasn't even a patrolman. He probably only worked in the office.) I imagine he was prepared to spend a night in jail if necessary, and pay whatever fine there might be, because his presence could explain one of the sheriff's cars' being parked in the pasture. But the deputy himself took off through the backwoods on Ricky's property and toward a county road on the back of the place. Ricky, as I've said, was not going to have that. Since the cockfight was on his farm, he knew there was no way out of trouble for himself. But he thought it couldn't, at least, do him any harm to have the deputy caught along with everybody else. Moreover, the deputy had lost considerable amounts of money there at the pit in recent weeks and had insinuated to Ricky that he suspected some of the cocks had been tampered with. (I, personally, don't believe Ricky would stand for that.) Ricky couldn't be sure there wasn't some collusion between the deputy and the feds. He saw the deputy's man catch the deputy's eye from the barn doorway and observed the deputy's departure. He was right after him. He overtook him just before he reached the woods. Fortunately, the deputy wasn't armed. (Ricky allowed no one to bring a gun inside the barn.) And fortunately Ricky wasn't armed, either, that night. They scuffled a little near the gate to the woods lot. The deputy, being a man twice Rick's age, was no match for him and was soon overpowered. Ricky dragged him back to the barn, himself resisting — as he later testified — all efforts at bribery on the deputy's part, and turned in both himself and his captive to the federal officers.

Extricating Ricky from that affair and setting matters aright was a long and complicated undertaking. The worst of it really began for Ricky after the court proceedings were finished and all fines were paid (there were no jail terms for anyone), because from his last appearance in the federal courthouse Ricky could drive his car scarcely one block through that suburb where he lives without receiving a traffic ticket of some kind. There may not have been anything crooked about it, for Ricky is a wild sort of driver at best. But, anyhow, within a short time his driving license was revoked for the period of a year. Giving up driving was a great inconvenience for him and a humiliation. All we could do about the deputy, who, Ricky felt sure, had connived with the federal officers, was to get him out of his job after the next election.

The outcome of the court proceedings was that Rick's fines were very heavy. Moreover, efforts were made to confiscate all the livestock on his farm, as well as the farm machinery. But he was saved from the confiscation by a special circumstance, which, however, turned out to produce for him only a sort of Pyrrhic victory. It turned out, you see, that the farm was not in Ricky's name but in that of his young tenant farmer's wife. I never saw her, or didn't know it if I did. Afterward, I used to try to recall if I hadn't seen some such young woman when I was down watching the cockfights — one who would have fitted the picture in my mind. My imagination played tricks on me, though. I would think I remembered the face or figure of some young girl I'd seen there who could conceivably be the one. But then suddenly I'd recall another and think possibly it might be she who had the title to Ricky's farm. I never could be sure.

When Ricky appeared outside my window just now, I'd already had a very bad morning. The bursitis in my right shoulder had waked me before dawn. At last I got up and dressed, which was an ordeal in itself. (My right hip was hurting somewhat, too.) When finally the cook came in, she wanted to give me a massage before she began fixing breakfast even. Cary would never have allowed her to make that mistake. A massage, you see, is the worst thing you can do for my sort of bursitis. What I wanted was some breakfast. And I knew it would take Meg three quarters of an hour to put breakfast on the table. And so I managed to get out of my clothes again and ease myself into a hot bath, groaning so loud all the while that Meg came up to the door twice and asked if I was all right. I told her just to go and get my breakfast ready. After breakfast, I waited till a decent hour and then telephoned one of my golf foursome to tell him I couldn't play today. It's this damp fall weather that does us in worst. All you can do is sit and think how you've got the whole winter before you and wonder if you'll be able to get yourself off to someplace like Sarasota.

While I sat at a front window, waiting for the postman (he never brings anything but circulars and catalogs on Saturday; besides, all my serious mail goes to the office and is opened by someone else), I found myself thinking of all the things I couldn't do and all the people who are dead and that I mustn't think about. I tried to do a little better — that is, to think of something cheerful. There was lots I *could* be cheerful about, wasn't there? At least three of my children were certain to telephone today — all but Ricky, and it was sure to be bad news if he did! And a couple of the grandchildren would likely call, too. Then tomorrow I'd be going to lunch with some of them if I felt up to it. Suddenly I thought of the pills I was supposed to have taken before breakfast and had forgotten to: the Inderal and the potassium and the hydrochlorothiazide. I began to get up from my chair and then I settled down again. It didn't really matter. There was no ailment I had that could really be counted on to be fatal if I missed one day's dosage. And then I wholeheartedly embraced the old subject, the old speculation: How many days like this one, how many years like this one lay ahead for me? And finally, irresistibly, I descended to lower depths still, thinking of past times not with any relish but remembering how in past times I had always *told* myself I'd someday look back with pleasure on what would seem good old days, which was an indication itself that they hadn't somehow been good enough — not good enough, that is, to stand on their own as an end in themselves. If the old days were so damned good, why had I had to think always how good they would someday seem in retrospect? I had just reached the part where I think there was nothing *wrong* with them and that I ought to be satisfied, had just reached that point at which I recall that I loved and was loved by my wife, that I love and am loved by my children, that it's not them or my life but *me* there's something wrong with! — had just reached that inevitable syllogism that I always come to, when I was distracted by the arrival of Saturday morning's late mail delivery. It was brought in, it was handed to me by a pair of black hands, and of course it had nothing in it. But I took it upstairs to my sitting room. (So that even the servant wouldn't see there was nothing worth having in it.) I had just closed my door and got out my pills when I heard Ricky's car turn into the gravel driveway.

He was driving so slowly that his car wheels hardly disturbed the gravel. That in itself was an ominous phenomenon. He was approaching slowly and quietly. He didn't want me to know ahead of time what there was in store for me. My first impulse was to lock my door and refuse to admit him. I simply did not feel up to Rick this morning! But I said to myself, "That's something I've never done, though maybe ought to have done years ago no matter what Cary said. He's sure to send my blood pressure soaring." I thought of picking up the telephone and phoning one of the other children to come and protect me from this monster of a son and from whatever sort of trouble he was now in.

But it was just then that I caught my first glimpse of him down in the driveway. I had the illusion that he was admiring the place. And then of course I was at once disillusioned. He was only hesitating down there because he dreaded seeing me. But he was telling himself he *had* to see me. There would be no other solution to his problem but to see his old man. I knew what he was thinking by the gesture he was making with his left hand. It's strange how you get the notion that your children are like you just because they have the same facial features and the same gestures when talking to themselves. None of it means a thing! It's only an illusion. Even now I find myself making gestures with my hands when I'm talking to myself that I used to notice my own father making some-times when we were out walking together and neither of us had spoken a word for half an hour or so. It used to get on my nerves when I saw Father do it, throwing out his hand almost imperceptibly, with his long fingers spread apart. I don't know why it got on my nerves so. But, anyhow, I never dreamed that I could inherit such a gesture — or much less that one of my sons would. And yet there Ricky is, down in the driveway, making the same gesture precisely. And there never were three men with more different characters than my father and me and my youngest child. I watch Ricky make the gesture several times while standing in the driveway. And now suddenly he turns as if to go back to his car. I step away from the window, hoping he hasn't seen me and will go on off. But having once seen him down there, I can't, of course, do that. I have to receive him and hear him out. I open the sash and call down to him, "Come on up, Ricky."

He looks up at me, smiles guiltily, and shrugs. Then he comes on in the side entrance. As he moves through the house and up the stairs, I try to calm myself. I gaze down at the roughed-up gravel where his suede shoes did their damage and tell myself it isn't so bad and even manage to smile at my own old-maidishness. Presently, he comes into the sitting room. We greet each other with the usual handshake. I can smell his shaving lotion. Or maybe it is something he puts on his hair. We go over and sit down by the fireplace, where there is a fire laid but not lit in this season, of course. He begins by talking about everything under the sun except what is on his mind. This is standard procedure in our talks at such times. Finally, he begins looking into the fireplace as though the fire were lit and as though he were watching low-burning flames. I barely keep myself from smiling when he says, "I've got a little problem — not so damned little, in fact. It's a matter that's got out of hand."

And then I say, "I supposed as much."

You can't give Ricky an inch at these times, you see. Else he'll take advantage of you. Pretty soon he'll have shifted the whole burden of how he's to be extricated onto your shoulders. I wait for him to continue, and he is about to, I think. But before he can get started he turns his eyes away from the dry logs and the unlit kindling and begins looking about the room, just as he looked about the premises outside. It occurs to me again that he seems to be observing my place for the very first time. But I don't suppose he really is. His mind is, as usual, on himself. Then all at once his eyes do obviously come to focus on something over my shoulder. He runs his tongue up under his upper lip and then under his lower lip, as though he were cleaning his teeth. I, involuntarily almost, look over my shoulder. There on the library table behind me, on what I call my desk, are my cut-glass tumbler and three bottles of pills — my hydrochlorothiazide, my Inderal, and my potassium. Somehow I failed to put them back in my desk drawer earlier. I was so distracted by my morbid thoughts when I came upstairs that I forgot to stick them away in the place where I keep them out of sight from everybody. (I don't even like for the servants to see what and how much medicine I take.) Without a word passing between us, and despite the pains in my shoulder and hip, I push myself up out of my chair and sweep the bottles, and the tumbler, too, into the desk drawer. I keep my back to Ricky for a minute or so till I can overcome the grimacing I never can repress when these pains strike. Suddenly, though, I do turn back to him and find he has come to his feet. I pay no special attention to that. I ease myself back into my chair saying, "Yes, Ricky." Making my voice rather hard, I say, "You've got a problem?" He looks at me coldly, without a trace of the sympathy any one of the other children would have shown — knowing, that is, as he surely does, that I am having pains of some description. And he speaks to me as though I were a total stranger toward whom he feels nothing but is just barely human enough to wish not to torture. "Man," he says — the idea of his addressing *me* that way! — "Man, you've got problems enough of your own. Even the world's greatest snotface can see that. One thing sure, you don't need to hear *my* crap."

I am on my feet so quick you wouldn't think I have a pain in my body. "Don't you use that gutter language with me, Ricky!" I say. "You weren't brought up in some slum over beyond Vinegar Hill!" He only turns and looks into the fireplace again. If there were a fire going I reckon he would have spat in it at this point. Then he looks back at me, running his tongue over his teeth again. And then, without any apology or so much as a by-your-leave, he heads for the door. "Come back here, Ricky!" I command. "Don't you dare leave the room!" Still moving toward the closed door, he glances back over his shoulder at me, with a wide, hard grin on his face, showing his mouthful of white teeth, as though my command were the funniest thing he has ever heard. At the door, he puts his big right hand on the glass knob, covering it entirely. Then he twists hs upper body, his torso, around — seemingly just from the hips — to face me. And simultaneously he brings up his left hand and scratches that triangle of dark hair where his shirt is open. It is like some kind of dirty gesture he is making. I say to myself, "He really is like something not quite human. For all the jams and scrapes he's been in, he's never suffered any second thoughts or known the meaning of remorse. I ought to have let him hang," I say to myself, "by his own beautiful locks."

But almost simultaneously what I hear myself saying aloud is "Please don't go, Rick. Don't go yet, son." Yes, I am pleading with him, and I mean what I say with my whole heart. He still has his right hand on the doorknob and has given it a full turn. Our eyes meet across the room, directly, as they never have before in the whole of Ricky's life or mine. I think neither of us could tell anyone what it is he sees in the other's eyes, unless it is a need beyond any description either of us is capable of.

Presently Rick says, "You don't need to hear my crap."

And I hear my bewildered voice saying, "I do . . . I do." And "Don't go, Rick, my boy." My eyes have even misted over. But I still meet his eyes across the now too silent room. He looks at me in the most compassionate way imaginable. I don't think any child of mine has ever looked at me so before. Or perhaps it isn't really with compassion he is viewing me but with the sudden, gratifying knowledge that it is not, after all, such a one-sided business, the business between us. He keeps his right hand on the doorknob a few seconds longer. Then I hear the latch click and know he has let go. Meanwhile, I observe his left hand making that familiar gesture, his fingers splayed, his hand tilting back and forth. I am out of my chair by now. I go to the desk and bring out two Danlys cigars from another desk drawer, which I keep locked. He is there ready to receive my offering when I turn around. He accepts the cigar without smiling, and I give it without smiling, too. Seated opposite each other again, each of us lights his own.

And then Ricky begins. What will it be this time, I think. I am wild with anticipation. Whatever it will be, I know it is all anyone in the world can give me now — perhaps the most anyone has ever been able to give a man like me. As Ricky begins, I try to think of all the good things the other children have done for me through the years and of their affection, and of my wife's. But it seems this was all there ever was. I forget my pains and my pills, and the canceled golf game, and the meaningless mail that morning. I find I can scarcely sit still in my chair for wanting Ricky to get on with it. Has he been brandishing his pistol again? Or dragging the sheriff's deputy across a field at midnight? And does he have in his wallet perhaps a picture of some other girl with a tight little mouth, and eyes that burn? Will his outrageous story include her? And perhaps explain it, leaving her a blessed mystery? As Ricky begins, I find myself listening not merely with fixed attention but with my whole being . . . I hear him beginning. I am listening. I am listening gratefully to all he will tell me about himself, about any life that is not my own.

DORIS LESSING

1919–

Born in Iran, Doris Lessing was brought to Southern Rhodesia at the age of six. In 1949 she removed to England, where she has since lived. Her early work, especially the novel Children of Violence, *registers her South African experience. She has been concerned with many forms of liberation — racial, economic, sexual — but, like her fellow South African Nadine Gordimer, bursts the bonds of protest literature.*

One critic has called her "the great realist writer of our time." Although her recent work in the novel form has been in the domain of philosophical fantasy, her latest book, The Good Terrorist, *marks a return to realism. She is a feminist whose persuasive power lies in her refusal to evade her gender, to write as a "human being." Candidly female, her short stories are generally realistic, occupied with a cool appraisal of the male-female relationship, and in the finest sense worldly.*

For thousands of years women have been quietly amused by a perennial masculine type: he who fancies himself as a seducer, preens himself on his understanding of women, knows how to "handle" them. In "One off the Short List" Doris Lessing artfully develops the theme's comic possibilities. But the subtle interplay between Graham Spence and Barbara Coles also turns on something not at all comic. From outset to end Barbara's attitude to Spence flows from a contempt (or perhaps merely an indifference) deeper than the sexual. She and her colleagues are artists, or at least craftsmen, bound by "a democracy of respect for each other's work." Spence's stance toward women is connected with his secret view of himself. As he has lost pride in himself as a man, so has he lost pride in himself as a responsible professional writer. This story is as moral as it is amusing. Its characters are value systems made flesh.

One off the Short List

WHEN HE HAD first seen Barbara Coles, some years before, he only noticed her because someone said: "That's Johnson's new girl." He certainly had not used of her the private erotic formula: *Yes, that one.* He even wondered what Johnson saw in her. She won't last long, he remembered thinking as he watched Johnson, a handsome man, but rather flushed with drink, flirting with some unknown girl while Barbara stood by a wall looking on. He thought she had a sullen expression.

She was a pale girl, not slim, for her frame was generous, but her figure could pass as good. Her straight yellow hair was parted on one side in a way that struck him as gauche. He did not notice what she wore. But her eyes were all right, he remembered: large, and solidly green, square-looking because of some trick of the flesh at their corners. Emeraldlike eyes in the face of a schoolgirl, or young schoolmistress who was watching her lover flirt and would later sulk about it.

Her name sometimes cropped up in the papers. She was a stage decorator, a designer, something on those lines.

Then a Sunday newspaper had a competition for stage design and she won it. Barbara Coles was one of the "names' in the theatre, and her photograph was seen about. It was always serious. He remembered having thought her sullen.

One night he saw her across the room at a party. She was talking with a well-known actor. Her yellow hair was still done on one side, but now it looked sophisticated. She wore an emerald ring on her right hand that seemed deliberately to invite comparison with her eyes. He walked over and said: "We have met before, Graham Spence." He noted, with discomfort, that he sounded abrupt. "I'm sorry, I don't remember, but how do you do?" she said, smiling. And continued her conversation.

He hung around a bit, but soon she went off with a group of people she was inviting to her home for a drink. She did not invite Graham. There was about her an assurance, a carelessness, that he recognised as the signature of success. It was then, watching her laugh as she went off with her friends, that he used the formula: *Yes, that one.* And he went home to his wife with enjoyable expectation, as if his date with Barbara Coles were already arranged.

His marriage was twenty years old. At first it had been stormy, painful, tragic — full of partings, betrayals and sweet reconciliations. It had taken him at least a decade to realise that there was nothing remarkable about this marriage that he had lived through with such surprise of the mind and the senses. On the contrary, the marriages of most of the people he knew, whether they were first, second, or third attempts, were just the same. His had run true to form even to the serious love affair with the young girl for whose sake he had *almost* divorced his wife — yet at the last moment had changed his mind, letting the girl down so that he must have her for always (not unpleasurably) on his conscience. It was with humiliation that he had understood that this drama was not at all the unique thing he had imagined. It was nothing more than the experience of everyone in his circle. And presumably in everybody else's circle too?

Anyway, round about the tenth year of his marriage he had seen a good many things clearly, a certain kind of emotional adventure went from his life, and the marriage itself changed.

His wife had married a poor youth with a great future as a writer. Sacrifices had been made, chiefly by her, for that future. He was neither unaware of them, nor ungrateful; in fact he felt permanently guilty about it. He at last published a decently successful book, then a second, which now, thank God, no one remembered. He had drifted into radio, television, book reviewing.

He understood he was not going to make it; that he had become — not a hack, no one could call him that — but a member of that army of people who live by their wits on the fringes of the arts. The moment of realisation was when he was in a pub one lunchtime near the B.B.C. where he often dropped in to meet others like himself: he understood that was why he went there — they *were* like him. Just as that melodramatic marriage had turned out to be like everyone else's — except that it had been shared with one woman instead of with two or three — so it had turned out that his unique talent, his struggles as a writer had led him here, to this pub and the half-dozen pubs like it, where all the men in sight had the same history. They all had their novel, their play, their book of poems, a moment of fame, to their credit. Yet here they were, running television programmes about which they were cynical (to each other or to their wives) or writing reviews about other people's books. Yes, that's what he had become, an impresario of other people's talent. These two moments of clarity, about his marriage and about his talent, had roughly coincided; and (perhaps not by chance) had coincided with his wife's decision to leave him for a man younger than himself who had a future, she said, as a playwright. Well, he had talked her out of it. For her part, she had to understand he was not going to be the T. S. Eliot or Graham Greene of our time — but after all, how many were? She must finally understand this, for he could no longer bear her awful bitterness. For his part, he must stop coming home drunk at five in the morning, and starting a new romantic affair every six months which he took so seriously that he made her miserable because of her implied deficiencies. In short he was to be a good husband. (He had always been a dutiful father.) And she a good wife. And so it was: the marriage became stable, as they say.

The formula: *Yes, that one* no longer implied a necessarily sexual relationship. In its more mature form, it was far from being something he was ashamed of. On the contrary, it expressed a humorous respect for what he was, for his real talents and flair, which had turned out to be not artistic after all, but to do with emotional life, hard-earned experience. It expressed an ironical dignity, a proving to himself not only: I can be honest about myself, but also: I have earned the best in *that* field whenever I want it.

He watched the field for the women who were well known in the arts, or in politics; looked out for photographs, listened for bits of gossip. He made a point of going to see them act, or dance, or orate. He built up a not unshrewd picture of them. He would either quietly pull strings to meet a woman or — more often, for there was a gambler's pleasure in waiting — bide his time until he met her in the natural course of events, which was bound to happen sooner or later. He would be seen out with her a few times in public, which was in order, since his work meant he had to entertain well-known people, male and female. His wife always knew, he told her. He might have a brief affair with this woman, but more often than not it was the appearance of an affair. Not that he didn't get pleasure from other people envying him — he would make a point, for instance, of taking this woman into the pubs where his male colleagues went. It was that his real pleasure came when he saw her surprise at how well she was understood by him. He enjoyed the atmosphere he was able to set up between an intelligent woman and himself: a humorous complicity which had in it much that was unspoken, and which almost made sex irrelevant.

Onto the list of women with whom he planned to have this relationship went Barbara Coles. There was no hurry. Next week, next month, next year, they would meet at a party. The world of well-known people in London is a small one. Big and little fishes, they drift around, nose each other, flirt their fins, wriggle off again. When he bumped into Barbara Coles, it would be time to decide whether or not to sleep with her.

Meanwhile he listened. But he didn't discover much. She had a husband and children, but the husband seemed to be in the background. The children were charming and well brought up, like everyone else's children. She had affairs, they said; but while several men he met sounded familiar with her, it was hard to determine whether they had slept with her, because none directly boasted of her. She was spoken of in terms of her friends, her work, her house, a party she had given, a job she had found someone. She was liked, she was respected, and Graham Spence's self-esteem was flattered because he had chosen her. He looked forward to saying in just the same tone: "Barbara Coles asked me what I thought about the set and I told her quite frankly . . ."

Then by chance he met a young man who did boast about Barbara Coles; he claimed to have had the great love affair with her, and recently at that; and he spoke of it as something generally known. Graham realised how much he had already become involved with her in his imagination because of how perturbed he was now, on account of the character of this youth, Jack Kennaway. He had recently become successful as a magazine editor — one of those young men who, not as rare as one might suppose in the big cities, are successful from sheer impertinence, effrontery. Without much talent or taste, yet he had the charm of his effrontery. "Yes, I'm going to succeed, because I've decided to; yes, I may be stupid, but not so stupid that I don't know my deficiencies. Yes, I'm going to be successful because you people with integrity, et cetera, et cetera, simply don't believe in the possibility of people like me. You are too cowardly to stop me. Yes, I've taken your measure and I'm going to succeed because I've got the courage not only to be unscrupulous but to be quite frank about it. And besides, you admire me; you must, or otherwise you'd stop me . . ." Well, that was young Jack Kennaway, and he shocked Graham. He was a tall, languishing young man, handsome in a dark melting way, and, it was quite clear, he was either asexual or homosexual. And this youth boasted of the favours of Barbara Coles; boasted, indeed, of her love. Either she was a raving neurotic with a taste for neurotics; or Jack Kennaway was a most accomplished liar; or she slept with anyone. Graham was intrigued. He took Jack Kennaway out to dinner in order to hear him talk about Barbara Coles. There was no doubt the two were pretty close — all those dinners, theatres, weekends in the country — Graham Spence felt he had put his finger on the secret pulse of Barbara Coles; and it was intolerable that he must wait to meet her; he decided to arrange it.

It became unnecessary. She was in the news again, with a run of luck. She had done a successful historical play, and immediately afterwards a modern play, and then a hit musical. In all three, the sets were remarked on. Graham saw some interviews in newspapers and on television. These all centered around the theme of her being able to deal easily with so many different styles of theatre; but the real point was, of course, that she was a woman, which naturally added piquancy to the thing. And now Graham Spence was asked to do a half-hour radio interview with her. He planned the questions he would ask her with care, drawing on what people had said of her, but above all on his instinct and experience with women. The interview was to be at nine-thirty at night; he was to pick her up at six from the theatre where she was currently at work, so that there would be time, as the letter from the B.B.C. had put it, "for you and Miss Coles to get to know each other."

At six he was at the stage door, but a message from Miss Coles said she was not quite ready, could he wait a little. He hung about, then went to the pub opposite for a quick one, but still no Miss Coles. So he made his way backstage, directed by voices, hammering, laughter. It was badly lit, and the group of people at work did not see him. The director, James Poynter, had his arm around Barbara's shoulders. He was newly well known, a carelessly goodlooking young man reputed to be intelligent. Barbara Coles wore a dark blue overall, and her flat hair fell over her face so that she kept pushing it back with the hand that had the emerald on it. These two stood close, side by side. Three young men, stagehands, were on the other side of a trestle which had sketches and drawings on it. They were studying some sketches. Barbara said, in a voice warm with energy: "Well, so I thought if we did *this* — do you see, James? What do you think, Steven?" "Well, love," said the young man she called Steven, "I see your idea, but I wonder if . . ." "I think you're right, Babs," said the director. "Look," said Barbara, holding one of the sketches toward Steven, "look, let me show you." They all leaned forward, the five of them, absorbed in the business.

Suddenly Graham couldn't stand it. He understood he was shaken to his depths. He went off-stage, and stood with his back against a wall in the dingy passage that led to the dressing rooms. His eyes were filled with tears. He was seeing what a long way he had come from the crude, uncompromising, admirable young egomaniac he had been when he was twenty. That group of people there — working, joking, arguing, yes, that's what he hadn't known for years. What bound them was the democracy of respect for each other's work, a confidence in themselves and in each other. They looked like people banded together against a world which they — no, not despised, but which they measured, understood, would fight to the death, out of respect for what *they* stood for, for what *it* stood for. It was a long time since he felt part of that balance. And he understood that he had seen Barbara Coles when she was most herself, at ease with a group of people she worked with. It was then, with the tears drying on his eyelids, which felt old and ironic, that he decided he would sleep with Barbara Coles. It was a necessity for him. He went back through the door onto the stage, burning with this single determination.

The five were still together. Barbara had a length of blue gleaming stuff which she was draping over the shoulder of Steven, the stagehand. He was showing it off, and the others watched. "What do you think, James?" she asked the director. "We've got that sort of dirty green, and I thought . . ." "Well," said James, not sure at all, "well, Babs, well . . ."

Now Graham went forward so that he stood beside Barbara, and said: "I'm Graham Spence, we've met before." For the second time she smiled socially and said: "Oh, I'm sorry, I don't remember." Graham nodded at James, whom he had known, or at least had met off and on, for years. But it was obvious James didn't remember him either.

"From the B.B.C.," said Graham to Barbara, again sounding abrupt, against his will. "Oh I'm sorry, I'm so sorry, I forgot all about it. I've got to be interviewed," she said to the group. "Mr. Spence is a journalist." Graham allowed himself a small smile ironical of the word "journalist," but she was not looking at him. She was going on with her work. "We should decide tonight," she said. "Steven's right." "Yes, I am right," said the stagehand. "She's right, James, we need that blue with that sludge-green everywhere." "James," said Barbara, "James, what's wrong with it? You haven't said." She moved forward to James, passing Graham. Remembering him again, she became contrite. "I'm sorry," she said, "we can none of us agree. Well, look" — she turned to Graham — "you advise us, we've got so involved with it that . . ." At which James laughed, and so did the stagehands. "No, Babs," said James, "of course Mr. Spence can't advise. He's just this moment come in. We've got to decide. Well I'll give you till tomorrow morning. Time to go home, it must be six by now."

"It's nearly seven," said Graham, taking command.

"It isn't!" said Barbara, dramatic. "My God, how terrible, how appalling, how could I have done such a thing . . ." She was laughing at herself. "Well, you'll have to forgive me, Mr. Spence, because you haven't got any alternative."

They began laughing again: this was clearly a group joke. And now Graham took his chance. He said firmly, as if he were her director, in fact copying James Poynter's manner with her: "No, Miss Coles, I won't forgive you, I've been kicking my heels for nearly an hour." She grimaced, then laughed and accepted it. James said: "There, Babs, that's how you ought to be treated. We spoil you." He kissed her on the cheek, she kissed him on both his, the stagehands moved off. "Have a good evening, Babs," said James, going, and nodding to Graham. Who stood concealing his pleasure with difficulty. He knew, because he had had the courage to be firm, indeed, peremptory, with Barbara, that he had saved himself hours of maneuvering. Several drinks, a dinner — perhaps two or three evenings of drinks and dinners — had been saved because he was now on this footing with Barbara Coles, a man who could say: No, I won't forgive you, you've kept me waiting.

She said: "I've just got to . . ." and went ahead of him. In the passage she hung her overall on a peg. She was thinking, it seemed, of something else, but seeing him watching her, she smiled at him, companionably: he realised with triumph it was the sort of smile she would offer one of the stagehands, or even James. She said again: "Just one second . . ." and went to the stage-door office. She and the stage doorman conferred. There was some problem. Graham said, taking another chance: "What's the trouble, can I help?" — as if he could help, as if he expected to be able to. "Well . . ." she said, frowning. Then, to the man: "No, it'll be all right. Goodnight." She came to Graham. "We've got ourselves into a bit of a fuss because half the set's in Liverpool and half's here and — but it will sort itself out." She stood, at ease, chatting to him, one colleague to another. All this was admirable, he felt; but there would be a bad moment when they emerged from the special atmosphere of the theatre into the street. He took another decision, grasped her arm firmly, and said: "We're going to have a drink before we do anything at all, it's a terrible evening out." Her arm felt resistant, but remained within his. It was raining outside, luckily. He directed her, authoritative: "No, not that pub, there's a nicer one around the corner." "Oh, but I like this pub," said Barbara, "we always use it."

Of course you do, he said to himself. But in that pub there would be the stagehands, and probably James, and he'd lose contact with her. He'd become a *journalist* again. He took her firmly out of danger around two corners, into a pub he picked at random. A quick look around — no, they weren't there. At least, if there were people from the theatre, she showed no sign. She asked for a beer. He ordered her a double Scotch, which she accepted. Then, having won a dozen preliminary rounds already, he took time to think. Something was bothering him — what? Yes, it was what he had observed backstage, Barbara and James Poynter. Was she having an affair with him? Because if so, it would all be much more difficult. He made himself see the two of them together, and thought with a jealousy surprisingly strong: *Yes, that's it.* Meantime he sat looking at her, seeing himself look at her, *a man gazing in calm appreciation at a woman:* waiting for her to feel it and respond. She was examining the pub. Her white woollen suit was belted, and had a not unprovocative suggestion of being a uniform. Her flat yellow hair, hastily pushed back after work, was untidy. Her clear white skin, without any colour, made her look tired. Not very exciting, at the moment, thought Graham, but maintaining his appreciative pose for when she would turn and see it. He knew what she would see: he was relying not only on the "warm, kindly" beam of his gaze, for this was merely a reinforcement of the impression he knew he made. He had black hair, a little greyed. His clothes were loose and bulky — masculine. His eyes were humorous and appreciative. He was not, never had been, concerned to lessen the impression of being settled, dependable: the husband and father. On the contrary, he knew women found it reassuring.

When she at last turned, she said, almost apologetic: "Would you mind if we sat down? I've been lugging great things around all day." She had spotted two empty chairs in a corner. So had he, but rejected them, because there were other people at the table. "But my dear, of course!" They took the chairs, and then Barbara said: "If you'll excuse me a moment." She had remembered she needed makeup. He watched her go off, annoyed with himself. She was tired; and he could have understood, protected, sheltered. He realised that in the other pub, with the people she had worked with all day, she would not have thought: I must make myself up, I must be on show. That was for outsiders. She had not, until now, considered Graham an outsider, because of his taking his chance to seem one of the working group in the theatre; but now he had thrown this opportunity away. She returned armoured. Her hair was sleek, no longer defenceless. And she had made up her eyes. Her eyebrows were untouched, pale gold streaks above the brilliant green eyes whose lashes were blackened. Rather good, he thought, the contrast. Yes, but the moment had gone when he could say: Did you know you had a smudge on your cheek? Or — my dear girl — pushing her hair back with the edge of a brotherly hand. In fact, unless he was careful, he'd be back at starting point.

He remarked: "That emerald is very cunning," smiling into her eyes.

She smiled politely, and said: "It's not cunning, it's an accident; it was my grandmother's." She flirted her hand lightly by her face, though, smiling. But that was something she had done before, to a compliment she had had before, and often. It was all social, she had become social entirely. She remarked: "Didn't you say it was half past nine we had to record?"

"My dear Barbara, we've got two hours. We'll have another drink or two, then I'll ask you a couple of questions, then we'll drop down to the studio and get it over, and then we'll have a comfortable supper."

"I'd rather eat now, if you don't mind. I had no lunch, and I'm really hungry."

"But my dear, of course." He was angry. Just as he had been surprised by his real jealousy over James, so now he was thrown off balance by his anger: he had been counting on the long quiet dinner afterwards to establish intimacy. "Finish your drink and I'll take you to Nott's." Nott's was expensive. He glanced at her assessingly as he mentioned it. She said: "I wonder if you know Butler's? It's good and it's rather close." Butler's was good, and it was cheap, and he gave her a good mark for liking it. But Nott's it was going to be. "My dear, we'll get into a taxi and be at Nott's in a moment, don't worry."

She obediently got to her feet: the way she did it made him understand how badly he had slipped. She was saying to herself: Very well, he's like that, then all right, I'll do what he wants and get it over with . . .

Swallowing his own drink, he followed her, and took her arm in the pub doorway. It was polite within his. Outside it drizzled. No taxi. He was having bad luck now. They talked in silence to the end of the street. There Barbara glanced into a side street where a sign said: BUTLER'S. Not to remind him of it, on the contrary, she concealed the glance. And here she was, entirely at his disposal; they might never have shared the comradely moment in the theatre.

They walked half a mile to Nott's. No taxis. She made conversation: this was, he saw, to cover any embarrassment he might feel because of a half-mile walk through rain when she was tired. She was talking about some theory to do with the theatre, with designs for theatre building. He heard himself saying, and repeatedly: "Yes, yes, yes." He thought about Nott's, how to get things right when they reached Nott's. There he took the headwaiter aside, gave him a pound, and instructions. They were put in a corner. Large Scotches appeared. The menus were spread. "And now, my dear," he said, "I apologise for dragging you here, but I hope you'll think it's worth it."

"Oh, it's charming, I've always liked it. It's just that . . ." She stopped herself saying: It's such a long way. She smiled at him, raising her glass, and said: "It's one of my very favourite places, and I'm glad you dragged me here." Her voice was flat with tiredness. All this was appalling; he knew it; and he sat thinking how to retrieve his position. Meanwhile she fingered the menu. The headwaiter took the order, but Graham made a gesture which said: Wait a moment. He wanted the Scotch to take effect before she ate. But she saw his silent order; and, without annoyance or reproach, leaned forward to say, sounding patient: "Graham, please, I've got to eat; you don't want me drunk when you interview me, do you?"

"They are bringing it as fast as they can," he said, making it sound as if she were greedy. He looked neither at the headwaiter nor at Barbara. He noted in himself, as he slipped further and further away from contact with her, a cold determination growing in him — one apart from, apparently, any conscious act of will — that come what may, if it took all night, he'd be in her bed before morning. And now, seeing the small pale face, with the enormous green eyes, it was for the first time that he imagined her in his arms. Although he had said: *Yes, that one,* weeks ago, it was only now that he imagined her as a sensual experience. Now he did, so strongly that he could only glance at her, and then away towards the waiters who were bringing food.

"Thank the Lord," said Barbara, and all at once her voice was gay and intimate. "Thank heavens. Thank every power that is . . ." She was making fun of her own exaggeration; and, as he saw, because she wanted to put him at his ease after his boorishness over delaying the food. (She hadn't been taken in, he saw, humiliated, disliking her.) "Thank all the gods of Nott's," she went on, "because if I hadn't eaten inside five minutes I'd have died, I tell you." With which she picked up her knife and fork and began on her steak. He poured wine, smiling with her, thinking that *this* moment of closeness he would not throw away. He watched her frank hunger as she ate, and thought: Sensual — it's strange I hadn't wondered whether she would be or not.

"Now," she said, sitting back, having taken the edge off her hunger, "let's get to work."

He said: "I've thought it over very carefully — how to present you. The first thing seems to me, we must get away from that old chestnut: Miss Coles, how extraordinary for a woman to be so versatile in her work . . . I hope you agree?" This was his trump card. He had noted, when he had seen her on television, her polite smile when this note was struck. (The smile he had seen so often tonight.) This smile said: All right, if you *have* to be stupid, what can I do?

Now she laughed and said: "What a relief. I was afraid you were going to do the same thing."

"Good, now you eat and I'll talk."

In his carefully prepared monologue he spoke of the different styles of theatre she had shown herself mistress of, but not directly: he was flattering her on the breadth of her experience; the complexity of her character, as shown in her work. She ate, steadily, her face showing nothing. At last she asked: "And how did you plan to introduce this?"

He had meant to spring that on her as a surprise, something like: Miss Coles, a surprisingly young woman for what she has accomplished (she was thirty? thirty-two?) and a very attractive one . . . Perhaps I can give you an idea of what she's like if I say she could be taken for the film star Marie Carletta . . . The Carletta was a strong earthy blonde, known to be intellectual. He now saw he could not possibly say this: he could imagine her cool look if he did. She said: "Do you mind if we get away from all that — my manifold talents, et cetera . . ." He felt himself stiffen with annoyance, particularly because this was not an accusation; he saw she did not think him worth one. She had assessed him: This is the kind of man who uses this kind of flattery and therefore . . . It made him angrier that she did not even trouble to say: Why did you do exactly what you promised you wouldn't? She was being invincibly polite, trying to conceal her patience with his stupidity.

"After all," she was saying, "it is a stage designer's job to design what comes up. Would anyone take, let's say, Johnnie Cranmore" (another stage designer) "onto the air or television and say: "How very versatile you are because you did that musical about Java last month and a modern play about Irish labourers this?"

He battered down his anger. "My dear Barbara, I'm sorry. I didn't realise that what I said would sound just like the mixture as before. So what shall we talk about?"

"What I was saying as we walked to the restaurant: can we get away from the personal stuff?"

Now he almost panicked. Then, thank God, he laughed from nervousness, for she laughed and said: "You didn't hear one word I said."

"No, I didn't. I was frightened you were going to be furious because I made you walk so far when you were tired."

They laughed together, back to where they had been in the theatre. He leaned over, took her hand, kissed it. He said: "Tell me again." He thought: Damn, now she's going to be earnest and intellectual.

But he understood he had been stupid. He had forgotten himself at twenty — or, for that matter, at thirty; forgotten one could live inside an idea, a set of ideas, with enthusiasm. For in talking about her ideas (also the ideas of the people she worked with) for a new theatre, a new style of theatre, she was as she had been with her colleagues over the sketches or the blue material. She was easy, informal, almost chattering. This was how, he remembered, one talked about ideas that were a breath of life. The ideas, he thought, were intelligent enough; and he would agree with them, with her, if he believed it mattered a damn one way or another, if any of these enthusiasms mattered a damn. But at least he now had the key; he knew what to do. At the end of not more than half an hour, they were again two professionals, talking about ideas they shared, for he remembered caring about all this himself once. *When? How many years ago was it that he had been able to care?*

At last he said: "My dear Barbara, do you realise the impossible position you're putting me in? Margaret Ruyen who runs this programme is determined to do you personally; the poor woman hasn't got a serious thought in her head."

Barbara frowned. He put his hand on hers, teasing her for the frown: "No, wait, trust me, we'll circumvent her." She smiled. In fact Margaret Ruyen had left it all to him, had said nothing about Miss Coles.

"They aren't very bright — the brass," he said. "Well, never mind: we'll work out what we want, do it, and it'll be a *fait accompli.*"

"Thank you, what a relief. How lucky I was to be given you to interview me." She was relaxed now, because of the whisky, the food, the wine, above all because of this new complicity against Margaret Ruyen. It would all be easy. They worked out five or six questions, over coffee, and took a taxi through rain to the studios. He noted that the cold necessity to have her, to make her, to beat her down, had left him. He was even seeing himself, as the evening ended, kissing her on the cheek and going home to his wife. This comradeship was extraordinarily pleasant. It was balm to the wound he had not known he carried until that evening, when he had had to accept the justice of the word "journalist." He felt he could talk forever about the state of the theatre, its finances, the stupidity of the government, the philistinism of . . .

At the studios he was careful to make a joke so that they walked in on the laugh. He was careful that the interview began at once, without conversation with Margaret Ruyen; and that from the moment the green light went on, his voice lost its easy familiarity. He made sure that not one personal note was struck during the interview. Afterwards, Margaret Ruyen, who was pleased, came forward to say so; but he took her aside to say that Miss Coles was tired and needed to be taken home at once: for he knew this must look to Barbara as if he were squaring a producer who had been expecting a different interview. He led Barbara off, her hand held tight in his against his side. "Well," he said, "we've done it, and I don't think she knows what hit her."

"Thank you," she said, "it really was pleasant to talk about something sensible for once."

He kissed her lightly on the mouth. She returned it, / he felt sure that the mood need not slip again, he coula .

"There are two things we can do," he said. "You can come . and have a drink. Or I can drive you home and you can give me a u. I have to go past you."

"Where do you live?"

"Wimbledon." He lived, in fact, at Highgate; but she lived in Fulham. He was taking another chance, but by the time she found out, they would be in a position to laugh over his ruse.

"Good," she said. "You can drop me home then. I have to get up early." He made no comment. In the taxi he took her hand; it was heavy in his, and he asked: "Does James slave-drive you?"

"I didn't realise you knew him — no, he doesn't."

"Well, I don't know him intimately. What's he like to work with?"

"Wonderful," she said at once. "There's no one I enjoy working with more."

Jealousy spurted in him. He could not help himself: "Are you having an affair with him?"

She looked: What's it to do with you? but said: "No, I'm not."

"He's very attractive," he said, with a chuckle of worldly complicity. She said nothing, and he insisted: "If I were a woman I'd have an affair with James."

It seemed she might very well say nothing. But she remarked: "He's married."

His spirits rose in a swoop. It was the first stupid remark she had made. It was a remark of such staggering stupidity that . . . he let out a humouring snort of laughter, put his arm around her, kissed her, said: "My dear little Babs."

She said: "Why Babs?"

"Is that the prerogative of James. And of the stagehands?" he could not prevent himself adding.

"I'm only called that at work." She was stiff inside his arm.

"My dear Barbara, then . . ." He waited for her to enlighten and explain, but she said nothing. Soon she moved out of his arm, on the pretext of lighting a cigarette. He lit it for her. He noted that his determination to lay her, and at all costs, had come back. They were outside her house. He said quickly: "And now, Barbara, you can make me a cup of coffee and give me a brandy." She hesitated; but he was out of the taxi, paying, opening the door for her. The house had no lights on, he noted. He said: "We"ll be very quiet so as not to wake the children."

She turned her head slowly to look at him. She said, flat, replying to his real question: "My husband is away. As for the children, they are visiting friends tonight." She now went ahead of him to the door of the house. It was a small house, in a terrace of small and not very pretty houses. Inside a little, bright, intimate hall, she said: "I'll go and make some coffee. Then, my friend, you must go home because I'm very tired."

The "my friend" struck him deep, because he had become vulnerable during their comradeship. He said, gabbling: "You're annoyed with me — oh, please don't, I'm sorry."

She smiled, from a cool distance. He saw, in the small light from the ceiling, her extraordinary eyes. "Green" eyes are hazel, are brown with green flecks, are even blue. Eyes are chequered, flawed, changing. Hers were solid green, but really, he had never seen anything like them before. They were like very deep water. They were like — well, emeralds, or the absolute clarity of green in the depths of a tree in summer. And now, as she smiled almost perpendicularly up at him, he saw a darkness come over them. Darkness swallowed the clear green. She said: "I'm not in the least annoyed." It was as if she had yawned with boredom. "And now I'll get the things . . . in there." She nodded at a white door and left him. He went into a long, very tidy white room that had a narrow bed in one corner, a table covered with drawings, sketches, pencils. Tacked to the walls with drawing pins were swatches of coloured stuffs. Two small chairs stood near a low round table: an area of comfort in the working room. He was thinking: I wouldn't like it if my wife had a room like this. I wonder what Barbara's husband . . . ? He had not thought of her till now in relation to her husband, or to her children. Hard to imagine her with a frying pan in her hand, or for that matter, cosy in the double bed.

A noise outside: he hastily arranged himself, leaning with one arm on the mantelpiece. She came in with a small tray that had cups, glasses, brandy, coffeepot. She looked abstracted. Graham was on the whole flattered by this: it probably meant she was at ease in his presence. He realised he was a little tight and rather tired. Of course, she was tired too; that was why she was vague. He remembered that earlier that evening he had lost a chance by not using her tiredness. Well now, if he were intelligent . . . She was about to pour coffee. He firmly took the coffeepot out of her hand, and nodded at a chair. Smiling, she obeyed him. "That's better," he said. He poured coffee, poured brandy, and pulled the table towards her. She watched him. Then he took her hand, kissed it, patted it, laid it down gently. Yes, he thought, I did that well.

Now, a problem. He wanted to be closer to her, but she was fitted into a damned silly little chair that had arms. If he were to sit by her on the floor . . . ? But no, for him, the big bulky reassuring man, there could be no casual gestures, no informal postures. Suppose I scoop her out of the chair onto the bed? He drank his coffee as he plotted. Yes, he'd carry her to the bed, but not yet.

"Graham," she said, setting down her cup. She was, he saw with annoyance, looking tolerant. "Graham, in about half an hour I want to be in bed and asleep."

As she said this, she offered him a smile of amusement at this situation — man and woman manoeuvring, the great comic situation. And with part of himself he could have shared it. Almost, he smiled with her, laughed. (Not till days later he exclaimed to himself: Lord what a mistake I made, not to share the joke with her then: that was where I went seriously wrong.) But he could not smile. His face was frozen, with a stiff pride. Not because she had been watching him plot — the amusement she now offered him took the sting out of that — but because of his revived determination that he was going to have his own way, he was going to have her. He was not going home. But he felt that he held a bunch of keys, and did not know which one to choose.

He lifted the second small chair opposite to Barbara, moving aside the coffee table for this purpose. He sat in this chair, leaned forward, took her two hands, and said: "My dear, don't make me go home yet, don't, I beg you." The trouble was, nothing had happened all evening that could be felt to lead up to these words and his tone — simple, dignified, human being pleading with human being for surcease. He saw himself leaning forward, his big hands swallowing her small ones; he saw his face, warm with the appeal. And he realised he had meant the words he used. They were nothing more than what he felt. He wanted to stay with her because she wanted him to, because he was her colleague, a fellow worker in the arts. He needed this desperately. But she was examining him, curious rather than surprised, and from a critical distance. He heard himself saying: "If James were here, I wonder what you'd do?" His voice was aggrieved; he saw the sudden dark descend over her eyes, and she said: "Graham, would you like some more coffee before you go?"

He said; "I've been wanting to meet you for years. I know a good many people who know you."

She leaned forward, poured herself a little more brandy, sat back, holding the glass between her two palms on her chest. An odd gesture: Graham felt that this vessel she was cherishing between her hands was herself. A patient, long-suffering gesture. He thought of various men who had mentioned her. He thought of Jack Kennaway, wavered, panicked, said: "For instance, Jack Kennaway."

And now, at the name, an emotion lit her eyes — what was it? He went on, deliberately testing this emotion, adding to it: "I had dinner with him last week — oh, quite by chance! — and he was talking about you."

"Was he?"

He remembered he had thought her sullen, all those years ago. Now she seemed defensive, and she frowned. He said: "In fact he spent most of the evening talking about you."

She said in short, breathless sentences, which he realised were due to anger: "I can very well imagine what he says. But surely you can't think I enjoy being reminded that . . ." She broke off, resenting him, he saw, because he forced her down on to a level she despised. But it was not his level either: it was all her fault, all hers! He couldn't remember not being in control of a situation with a woman for years. Again he felt like a man teetering on a tightrope. He said, trying to make good use of Jack Kennaway, even at this late hour: "Of course, he's a charming boy, but not a man at all."

She looked at him, silent, guarding her brandy glass against her breasts.

"Unless appearances are totally deceptive, of course." He could not resist probing, even though he knew it was fatal.

She said nothing.

"Do you know you are supposed to have had the great affair with Jack Kennaway?" he exclaimed, making this an amused expostulation against the fools who could believe it.

"So I am told." She set down her glass. "And now," she said, standing up, dismissing him. He lost his head, took a step forward, grabbed her in his arms, and groaned: "Barbara!"

She turned her face this way and that under his kisses. He snatched a diagnostic look at her expression — it was still patient. He placed his lips against her neck, groaned "Barbara" again, and waited. She would have to do something. Fight free, respond, something. She did nothing at all. At last she said: "For the Lord's sake, Graham!" She sounded amused: he was again being offered amusement. But if he shared it with her, it would be the end of this chance to have her. He clamped his mouth over hers, silencing her. She did not fight him off so much as blow him off. Her mouth treated his attacking mouth as a woman blows and laughs in water, puffing off waves or spray with a laugh, turning aside her head. It was a gesture half-annoyance, half-humour. He continued to kiss her while she moved her head and face about under the kisses as if they were small attacking waves.

And so began what, when he looked back on it afterwards, was the most embarrassing experience of his life. Even at the time he hated her for his ineptitude. For he held her there for what must have been nearly half an hour. She was much shorter than he, he had to bend, and his neck ached. He held her rigid, his thighs on either side of hers, her arms clamped to her side in a bear's hug. She was unable to move, except for her head. When his mouth ground hers open and his tongue moved and writhed inside it, she still remained passive. And he could not stop himself. While with his intelligence he watched this ridiculous scene, he was determined to go on, because sooner or later her body must soften in wanting his. And he could not stop because he could not face the horror of the moment when he set her free and she looked at him. And he hated her more, every moment. Catching glimpses of her great green eyes, open and dismal beneath his, he knew he had never disliked anything more than those "jewelled" eyes. They were repulsive to him. It occurred to him at last that even if by now she wanted him, he wouldn't know it, because she was not able to move at all. He cautiously loosened his hold so that she had an inch or so leeway. She remained quite passive. As if, he thought derisively, she had read or been told that the way to incite men maddened by lust was to fight them. He found he was thinking: Stupid cow, so you imagine I find you attractive, do you? You've got the conceit to think that!

The sheer, raving insanity of this thought hit him, opened his arms, his thighs, and lifted his tongue out of her mouth. She stepped back, wiping her mouth with the back of her hand, and stood dazed with incredulity. The embarrassment that lay in wait for him nearly engulfed him, but he let anger postpone it. She said positively apologetic, even, at this moment, humorous: "You're crazy, Graham. What's the matter, are you drunk? You don't seem drunk. You don't even find me attractive."

The blood of hatred went to his head and he gripped her again. Now she had got her face firmly twisted away so that he could not reach her mouth, and she repeated steadily as he kissed the parts of her cheeks and neck that were available to him: "Graham, let me go, do let me go, Graham." She went on saying this; he went on squeezing, grinding, kissing and licking. It might go on all night: it was a sheer contest of wills, nothing else, He thought: It's only a really masculine woman who wouldn't have given in by now out of sheer decency of the flesh! One thing he knew, however: that she would be in that bed, in his arms, and very soon. He let her go, but said: "I'm going to sleep with you tonight, you know that, don't you?"

She leaned with hand on the mantelpiece to steady herself. Her face was colourless, since he had licked all the makeup off. She seemed quite different: small and defenceless with her large mouth pale now, her smudged green eyes fringed with gold. And now, for the first time, he felt what it might have been supposed (certainly by her) he felt hours ago. Seeing the small damp flesh of her face, he felt kinship, intimacy with her, he felt intimacy of the flesh, the affection and good humour of sensuality. He felt she was flesh of his flesh, his sister in the flesh. He felt desire for her, instead of the will to have her; and because of this, was ashamed of the farce he had been playing. Now he desired simply to take her into bed in the affection of his senses.

She said: "What on earth am I supposed to do? Telephone for the police, or what?" He was hurt that she still addressed the man who had ground her into sulky apathy; she was not addressing *him* at all.

She said: "Or scream for the neighbours, is that what you want?"

The gold-fringed eyes were almost black, because of the depth of the shadow of boredom over them. She was bored and weary to the point of falling to the floor, he could see that.

He said: "I'm going to sleep with you."

"But how can you possibly want to?" — a reasonable, a civilised demand addressed to a man who (he could see) she believed would respond to it. She said: "You know I don't want to, and I know you don't really give a damn one way or the other."

He was stung back into being the boor because she had not the intelligence to see that the boor no longer existed; because she could not see that this was a man who wanted her in a way which she must respond to.

There she stood, supporting herself with one hand, looking small and white and exhausted, and utterly incredulous. She was going to turn and walk off out of simple incredulity, he could see that. "Do you think I don't mean it?" he demanded, grinding this out between his teeth. She made a movement — she was on the point of going away. His hand shot out on its own volition and grasped her wrist. She frowned. His other hand grasped her other wrist. His body hove up against hers to start the pressure of a new embrace. Before it could, she said: "Oh Lord, no, I'm not going through all that again. Right, then."

"What do you mean — right, then?" he demanded.

She said: "You're going to sleep with me. O.K. Anything rather than go through that again. Shall we get it over with?"

He grinned, saying in silence: "No darling, oh no you don't, I don't care what words you use, I'm going to have you now and that's all there is to it."

She shrugged. The contempt, the weariness of it, had no effect on him, because he was now again hating her so much that wanting her was like needing to kill something or someone.

She took her clothes off, as if she were going to bed by herself: her jacket, skirt, petticoat. She stood in white bra and panties, a rather solid girl, brown-skinned still from the summer. He felt a flash of affection for the brown girl with her loose yellow hair as she stood naked. She got into bed and lay there, while the green eyes looked at him in civilised appeal: Are you really going through with this? Do you have to? Yes, his eyes said back: I do have to. She shifted her gaze aside, to the wall, saying silently: Well, if you want to take me without any desire at all on my part, then go ahead, if you're not ashamed. He was not ashamed, because he was maintaining the flame of hate for her which he knew quite well was all that stood between him and shame. He took off his clothes, and got into bed beside her. As he did so, knowing he was putting himself in the position of raping a woman who was making it elaborately clear he bored her, his flesh subsided completely, sad, and full of reproach because a few moments ago it was reaching out for his sister whom he could have made happy. He lay on his side by her, secretly at work on himself, while he supported himself across her body on his elbow, using the free hand to manipulate her breasts. He saw that she gritted her teeth against his touch. At least she could not know that after all this fuss he was not potent.

In order to incite himself, he clasped her again. She felt his smallness, writhed free of him, sat up and said: "Lie down."

While she had been lying there, she had been thinking: The only way to get this over with is to make him big again, otherwise I've got to put up with him all night. His hatred of her was giving him a clairvoyance: he knew very well what went on through her mind. She had switched on, with the determination to *get it all over with,* a sensual good humour, a patience. He lay down. She squatted beside him, the light from the ceiling blooming on her brown shoulders, her flat fair hair falling over her face. But she would not look at his face. Like a bored, skilled wife, she was; or like a prostitute. She administered to him, she was setting herself to please him. Yes, he thought, she's sensual, or she could be. Meanwhile she was succeeding in defeating the reluctance of his flesh, which was the tender token of a possible desire for her, by using a cold skill that was the result of her contempt for him. Just as he decided: Right, it's enough, now I shall have her properly, she made him come. It was not a trick, to hurry or cheat him; what defeated him was her transparent thought: Yes, that's what he's worth.

Then, having succeeded, and waited for a moment or two, she stood up, naked, the fringes of gold at her loins and in her armpits speaking to him a language quite different from that of her green, bored eyes. She looked at him and thought, showing it plainly: What sort of man is it who . . . He watched the slight movement of her shoulders: a just-checked shrug. She went out of the room: then the sound of running water. Soon she came back in a white dressing-gown, carrying a yellow towel. She handed him the towel, looking away in politeness as he used it. "Are you going now?" she enquired hopefully, at this point.

"No, I'm not." He believed that now he would have to start fighting her again, but she lay down beside him, not touching him (he could feel the distaste of her flesh for his) and he thought: Very well, my dear, but there's a lot of the night left yet. He said aloud: "I'm going to have you properly tonight." She said nothing, lay silent, yawned. Then she remarked consolingly, and he could have laughed outright from sheer surprise: "Those were hardly conducive circumstances for making love." She was *consoling* him. He hated her for it. A proper little slut: I force her into bed, she doesn't want me, but she still has to make me feel good, like a prostitute. But even while he hated her he responded in kind, from the habit of sexual generosity. "It's because of my admiration for you, because . . . after all, I was holding in my arms one of the thousand women."

A pause. "The thousand?" she enquired, carefully.

"The thousand especial women."

"In Britain or in the world? You choose them for their brains, their beauty — what?"

"Whatever it is that makes them outstanding," he said, offering her a compliment.

"Well," she remarked at last, inciting him to be amused again, "I hope that at least there's a short list you can say I am on, for politeness' sake."

He did not reply for he understood he was sleepy. He was still telling himself that he must stay awake when he was slowly waking and it was morning. It was about eight. Barbara was not there. He thought: My God! What on earth shall I tell my wife? Where was Barbara? He remembered the ridiculous scenes of last night and nearly succumbed to shame. Then he thought, reviving anger: If she didn't sleep beside me here I'll never forgive her ... He sat up, quietly, determined to go through the house until he found her and, having found her, to possess her, when the door opened and she came in. She was fully dressed in a green suit, her hair done, her eyes made up. She carried a tray of coffee, which she set down beside the bed. He was conscious of his big loose hairy body, half uncovered. He said to himself that he was not going to lie in bed, naked, while she was dressed. He said: "Have you got a gown of some kind?" She handed him, without speaking, a towel, and said: "The bathroom's second on the left." She went out. He followed, the towel around him. Everything in this house was gay, intimate — not at all like her efficient working room. He wanted to find out where she had slept, and opened the first door. It was the kitchen, and she was in it, putting a brown earthenware dish into the oven. "The next door," said Barbara. He went hastily past the second door, and opened (he hoped quietly) the third. It was a cupboard full of linen. "This door," said Barbara, behind him.

"So all right then, where did you sleep?"

"What's it to do with you? Upstairs, in my own bed. Now, if you have everything, I'll say goodbye. I want to get to the theatre."

"I'll take you," he said at once.

He saw again the movement of her eyes, the dark swallowing the light in deadly boredom. "I'll take you," he insisted.

"I'd prefer to go by myself," she remarked. Then she smiled: "However, you'll take me. Then you'll make a point of coming right in, so that James and everyone can see — that's what you want to take me for, isn't it?"

He hated her, finally, and quite simply, for her intelligence; that not once had he got away with anything, that she had been watching, since they had met yesterday, every movement of his campaign for her. However, some fate or inner urge over which he had no control made him say sentimentally: "My dear, you must see that I'd like at least to take you to your work."

"Not at all, have it on me," she said, giving him the lie direct. She went past him to the room he had slept in. "I shall be leaving in ten minutes," she said.

He took a shower, fast. When he returned, the workroom was already tidied, the bed made, all signs of the night gone. Also, there were no signs of the coffee she had brought in for him. He did not like to ask for it, for fear of an outright refusal. Besides, she was ready, her coat on, her handbag under her arm. He went, without a word, to the front door, and she came after him, silent.

He could see that every fibre of her body signalled a simple message: Oh God, for the moment when I can be rid of this boor! She was nothing but a slut, he thought.

A taxi came. In it she sat as far away from him as she could. He thought of what he should say to his wife.

Outside the theatre she remarked: "You could drop me here, if you liked." It was not a plea, she was too proud for that. "I'll take you in," he said, and saw her thinking: Very well, I'll go through with it to shame him. He was determined to take her in and hand her over to her colleagues, he was afraid she would give him the slip. But far from playing it down, she seemed determined to play it his way. At the stage door, she said to the doorman: "This is Mr. Spence, Tom — do you remember, Mr. Spence from last night?" "Good morning, Babs," said the man, examining Graham, politely, as he had been ordered to do.

Barbara went to the door to the stage, opened it, held it open for him. He went in first, then held it open for her. Together they walked into the cavernous, littered, badly lit place and she called out: "James, James!" A man's voice called out from the front of the house: "Here, Babs, why are you so late?"

The auditorium opened before them, darkish, silent, save for an early-morning busyness of charwomen. A vacuum cleaner roared, smally, somewhere close. A couple of stagehands stood looking up at a drop which had a design of blue-and-green spirals. James stood with his back to the auditorium, smoking. "You're late, Babs," he said again. He saw Graham behind her, and nodded. Barbara and James kissed. Barbara said, giving allowance to every syllable: "You remember Mr. Spence from last night?" James nodded: How do you do? Barbara stood beside him, and they looked together up at the blue-and-green backdrop. Then Barbara looked again at Graham, asking silently: All right now, isn't that enough? He could see her eyes, sullen with boredom.

He said: "Bye, Babs. Bye, James. I'll ring you, Babs." No response, she ignored him. He walked off slowly, listening for what might be said. For instance: Babs, for God's sake, what are you doing with him? Or she might say: Are you wondering about Graham Spence? Let me explain.

Graham passed the stagehands, who, he could have sworn, didn't recognise him. Then at least he heard James's voice to Barbara: "It's no good, Babs, I know you're enamoured of that particular shade of blue, but do have another look at it, there's a good girl . . ." Graham left the stage, went past the office where the stage doorman sat reading a newspaper. He looked up, nodded, went back to his paper. Graham went to find a taxi, thinking: I'd better think up something convincing, then I'll telephone my wife.

Luckily he had an excuse not to be at home that day, for this evening he had to interview a young man (for television) about his new novel.

TADEUSZ BOROWSKI

1922–1951

On July 1, 1951, the Polish journalist, poet, and short story writer Tadeusz Borowski opened a gas valve and took his own life. He was not yet thirty. The specific reasons for his suicide are unclear. Central Europeans of his generation would place the responsibility on the dark history of their time.

We may be confident, however, that the Soviets and the Germans did all they could to help him to his death. His mother and father had both spent years in Soviet labor camps. The young Borowski led a harried life as part of the Warsaw underground during the German occupation. Caught, he spent two years (from 1943 to 1945) in Auschwitz and Dachau. Borowski survived, less because he was an Aryan than because (as he makes clear in his concentration camp stories) he was not of the stuff of which heroes and saints are made.

Borowski's most lasting work will be found in a little volume of quasi-stories called This Way for the Gas, Ladies and Gentlemen (Penguin Books). No Holocaust literature is as icy as Borowski's. For him the concentration camp is the norm and the world outside is, and will be again, one large concentration camp. "The Supper" is merely an anecdote, part of this normal world. But try to forget it.

The Supper

WE WAITED PATIENTLY for the darkness to fall. The sun had already slipped far beyond the hills. Deepening shadows, permeated with the evening mist, lay over the freshly ploughed hillsides and valleys, still covered with occasional patches of dirty snow; but here and there, along the sagging underbelly of the sky, heavy with rain clouds, you could still see a few rose-coloured streaks of sunlight.

A dark, gusty wind, heavy with the smells of the thawing, sour earth, tossed the clouds about and cut through your body like a blade of ice. A solitary piece of tar-board, torn by a stronger gust, rattled monotonously on a rooftop; a dry but penetrating chill was moving in from the fields. In the valley below, wheels clattered against rails and locomotives whined mournfully. Dusk was falling; our hunger was growing more and more terrible; the traffic along the highway had died down almost completely, only now and then the wind would waft a fragment of conversation, a coachman's call, or the occasional rumble of a cow-drawn cart; the cows dragged their hooves lazily along the gravel. The clatter of wooden sandals on the pavement and the guttural laughter of the peasant girls hurrying to a Saturday night dance at the village were slowly fading in the distance.

The darkness thickened at last and a soft rain began to fall. Several bluish lamps, swaying to and fro on top of high lamp-posts, threw a dim light over the black, tangled tree branches reaching out over the road, the shiny sentry-shack roofs, and the empty pavement that glistened like a wet leather strap. The soldiers marched under the circle of lights and then disappeared again in the dark. The sound of their footsteps on the road was coming nearer.

And then the camp Kommandant's driver threw a searchlight beam on a passage between two blockhouses. Twenty Russian soldiers in camp stripes, their arms tied with barbed-wire behind their backs, were being led out of the washroom and driven down the embankment. The Block Elders lined them up along the pavement facing the crowd that had been standing there for many silent hours, motionless, bareheaded, hungry. In the strong glare, the Russians' bodies stood out incredibly clearly. Every fold, bulge or wrinkle in their clothing; the cracked soles in their worn-out boots; the dry lumps of brown clay stuck to the edges of their trousers; the thick seams along their crotches; the white thread showing on the blue stripe of their prison suits; their sagging buttocks; their stiff hands and bloodless fingers twisted in pain, with drops of dry blood at the joints; their swollen wrists where the skin had started turning blue from the rusty wire cutting into the flesh; their naked elbows, pulled back unnaturally and tied with another piece of wire — all this emerged out of the surrounding blackness as if carved in ice. The elongated shadows of the men fell across the road and the barbed-wire fences glittering with tiny drops of water, and were lost on the hillside covered with dry, rustling grasses.

The Kommandant, a greying, sunburned man, who had come from the village especially for the occasion, crossed the lighted area with a tired but firm step and, stopping at the edge of the darkness, decided that the two rows of Russians were indeed a proper distance apart. From then on matters proceeded quickly, though maybe not quite quickly enough for the freezing body and the empty stomach that had been waiting seventeen hours for a pint of soup, still kept hot perhaps in the kettles at the barracks. "This is a serious matter!" cried a very young Camp Elder, stepping out from behind the Kommandant. He had one hand under the lapel of his "custom made," fitted black jacket, and in the other hand he was holding a willow crop which he kept tapping rhythmically against the top of his high boots.

"These men — they are criminals! I reckon I don't have to explain . . . They are Communists! Herr Kommandant says to tell you that they are going to be punished properly, and what the Herr Kommandant says . . . Well boys, I tell you, you too had better be careful, eh?"

"*Los, los,* we have no time to waste," interrupted the Kommandant, turning to an officer in an unbuttoned top-coat. He was leaning against the fender of his small Skoda automobile and slowly removing his gloves.

"This certainly shouldn't take long," said the officer in the unbuttoned top-coat. He snapped his fingers, a smile at the corner of his mouth.

"*Ja,* and tonight the entire camp will go without dinner!" shouted the young Camp Elder. "The Block Elders will carry the soup back to the kitchen and . . . if even one cup is missing, you'll have to answer to me. Understand, boys?"

A long, deep sigh went through the crowd. Slowly, slowly, the rear rows began pushing forward; the crowd near the road grew denser and a pleasant warmth spread along your back from the breath of the men pressing behind you, preparing to jump forward.

The Kommandant gave a signal and out of the darkness emerged a long line of S.S. men with rifles in their hands. They placed themselves neatly behind the Russians, each behind one man. You could no longer tell that they had returned from the labour Kommandos with us. They had had time to eat, to change to fresh, gala uniforms, and even to have a manicure. Their fingers were clenched tightly around their rifle butts and their fingernails looked neat and pink; apparently they were planning to join the local girls at the village dance. They cocked their rifles sharply, leaned the rifle butts on their hips and pressed the muzzles up against the clean-shaven napes of the Russians.

"Achtung! Bereit, Feuer!" said the Kommandant without raising his voice. The rifles barked, the soldiers jumped back a step to keep from being splattered by the shattered heads. The Russians seemed to quiver on their feet for an instant and then fell to the ground like heavy sacks, splashing the pavement with blood and scattered chunks of brain. Throwing their rifles over their shoulders, the soldiers marched off quickly. The corpses were dragged temporarily under the fence. The Kommandant and his retinue got into the Skoda; it backed up to the gate, snorting loudly.

No sooner was the greying, sunburned Kommandant out of sight than the silent crowd, pressing forward more and more persistently, burst into a shrieking roar, and fell in an avalanche on the blood-spattered pavement, swarming over it noisily. Then, dispersed by the Block Elders and the barracks chiefs called in for help from the camp, they scattered and disappeared one by one inside the blocks. I had been standing some distance away from the place of execution so I could not reach the road. But the following day, when we were again driven out to work, a "Muslimized"* Jew from Estonia who was helping me haul steel bars tried to convince me all day that human brains are, in fact, so tender you can eat them absolutely raw.

---

*"Muslim" was the camp name for a prisoner who had been destroyed physically and spiritually, and who had neither the strength nor the will to go on living — a man ripe for the gas chamber.

MAVIS GALLANT

1922–

Mavis Gallant is one of an increasing number of highly talented contemporary Canadian novelists and short story writers. Starting with a convent at age four, she attended seventeen different schools, then worked for a Montreal newspaper. Most of her adult life, however, has been spent in Europe; she now lives in Paris. Thus she has drawn literary nourishment from two cultures, somewhat in the manner of Henry James. Since his day the international scene has become shabbier, flatter, less elegant and nuanced. It is the gap between her world and James's that lends interest to much of her work.

Her Canadian stories are sharp-edged, at times turning on the two-language problem, at times involving the national sense of inferiority, the worried search for identity. Many of her characters, whether their background is Canadian or European, seem dislocated, engaged (not always with great conviction) in escaping from a restricted environment.

Unsentimental but not cynical, Gallant pins to her pages small souls in seedy pensions, displaced wanderers not quite certain of what to do with their lives, needy expatriates and émigrés. "Going Ashore" shows her art at its most characteristic. Simultaneously touching and pitiless, it portrays a frequently encountered American type, the widow who has been left some money, is used to a total dependence on men, and whose brain power is simply unable to cope with ordinary life. Emma, the hotel child who has had, alas, "the best that money can buy," may become the victim of her mother's pathetic stupidity, or as the final sentences suggest, she may escape to "a new life." Not unfamiliar, the theme is beautifully handled.

Going Ashore

AT TANGIER it was surprisingly cold, even for December. The sea was lead, the sky cloudy and low. Most of the passengers going ashore for the day came to breakfast wrapped in scarves and sweaters. They were, most of them, thin-skinned, elderly people, less concerned with the prospect of travel than with getting through another winter in relative comfort; on bad days, during the long crossing from the West Indies, they had lain in deck chairs, muffled as mummies, looking stricken and deceived. When Emma Ellenger came into the breakfast lounge barelegged, in sandals, wearing a light summer frock, there was a low flurry of protest. Really, Emma's mother should take more care! The child would catch her death.

Feeling the disapproval almost as an emanation, like the salt one breathed in the air, Emma looked around for someone who liked her — Mr. Cowan, or the Munns. There were the Munns, sitting in a corner, frowning over their toast, coffee, and guidebooks. She waved, although they had not yet seen her, threaded her way between the closely spaced tables, and, without waiting to be asked, sat down.

Miss and Mrs. Munn looked up with a single movement. They were daughter and mother, but so identically frizzy, tweedy, and elderly that they might have been twins. Mrs. Munn, the kindly twin, gazed at Emma with benevolent, rather popping brown eyes, and said, "Child, you'll freeze in that little dress. Do tell your mother — now, don't forget to tell her — that the North African winter can be treacherous, very treacherous indeed." She tapped one of the brown paper-covered guidebooks that lay beside her coffee tray. The Munns always went ashore provided with books, maps, and folders telling them what to expect at every port of call. They differed in every imaginable manner from Emma and her mother, who seldom fully understood where they were and who were often daunted and upset (particularly Mrs. Ellenger) if the people they encountered ashore were the wrong color or spoke an unfamiliar language.

"You should wear a thick scarf," Mrs. Munn went on, "and warm stockings." Thinking of the Ellengers' usual wardrobe, she paused, discouraged. "The most important parts of the —" But she stopped again, unable to say "body" before a girl of twelve. "One should keep the throat and the ankles warm," she said, lowering her gaze to her book.

"We can't," Emma said respectfully. "We didn't bring anything for the cruise except summer dresses. My mother thought it would be warm all the time."

"She should have inquired," Miss Munn said. Miss Munn was crisper, taut; often the roles seemed reversed, and it appeared that she, of the two, should have been the mother.

"I guess she didn't think," Emma said, cast down by all the things her mother failed to do. Emma loved the Munns. It was distressing when, as now, they failed to approve of her. They were totally unlike the people she was accustomed to, with their tweeds, their pearls, their strings of fur that bore the claws and muzzles of some small, flattened beast. She had fallen in love with them the first night aboard, during the first dinner out. The Munns and the Ellengers had been seated together, the dining-room steward having thought it a good plan to group, at a table for four, two solitary women and their solitary daughters.

The Munns had been so kind, so interested, asking any number of friendly questions. They wondered how old Emma was, and where Mr. Ellenger might be ("In Heaven," said Emma, casual), and where the Ellengers lived in New York.

"We live all over the place." Emma spoke up proudly. It was evident to her that her mother wasn't planning to say a word. *Somebody* had to be polite. "Most of the time we live in hotels. But last summer we didn't. We lived in an apartment. A big apartment. It wasn't our place. It belongs to this friend of my mother's, Mr. Jimmy Salter, but he was going to be away, and the rent was paid anyway, and we were living there already, so he said — he said —" She saw her mother's face and stopped, bewildered.

"That was nice," said Mrs. Munn, coloring. Her daughter looked down, smiling mysteriously.

Emma's mother said nothing. She lit a cigarette and blew the smoke over the table. She wore a ring, a wedding band, a Mexican necklace, and a number of clashing bracelets. Her hair, which was long and lighter even than Emma's, had been carefully arranged, drawn into a tight chignon and circled with flowers. Clearly it was not for Miss or Mrs. Munn that she had taken such pains; she had expected a different table arrangement, one that included a man. Infinitely obliging, Mrs. Munn wished that one of them were a man. She bit her lip, trying to find a way out of this unexpected social thicket. Turning to Emma, she said, a little wildly, "Do you like school? I mean I see you are not in school. Have you have been ill?"

Emma ill? The idea was so outrageous, so clearly a criticism of Mrs. Ellenger's care, that she was forced, at last, to take notice of this pair of frumps. "There's nothing the matter with my daughter's health," she said a little too loudly. "Emma's never been sick a day. From the time she was born, she's had the best of everything — the best food, the best clothes, the best that money can buy. Emma, isn't that right?"

Emma said yes, hanging her head and wishing her mother would stop.

"Emma was born during the war," Mrs. Ellenger said, dropping her voice. The Munns looked instantly sympathetic. They waited to hear the rest of the story, some romantic misadventure doomed by death or the fevered nature of the epoch itself. Mrs. Munn puckered her forehead, as if already she were prepared to cry. But evidently that part of the story had ceased to be of interest to Emma's mother. "I had a nervous break-down when she was born," Mrs. Ellenger said. "I had plenty of troubles. My God, *troubles!*" Brooding, she suddenly dropped her cigarette into the dregs of her coffee cup. At the sound it made, the two ladies winced. Their glances crossed. Noticing, Emma wondered what her mother had done now. "I never took my troubles out on Emma," Mrs. Ellenger said. "No, Emma had the best, always the best. I brought her up like a little lady. I kept her all in white — white shoes, white blankets, white bunny coats, white hand-knitted angora bonnets. When she started to walk, she had little white rubbers for the rain. I got her a white buggy with white rubber tires. During the *war,* this was. Emma, isn't it true? Didn't you see your pictures, all in white?"

Emma moved her lips.

"It was the very best butter," Miss Munn murmured.

"She shows your care," Mrs. Munn said gently. "She's a lovely girl."

Emma wanted to die. She looked imploringly at her mother, but Mrs. Ellenger rushed on. It was important, deeply important, that everyone understand what a good mother she had been. "Nobody has to worry about Emma's school, either," she said. "I teach her, so nobody has to worry at all. Emma loves to study. She reads all the time. Just before dinner tonight, she was reading. She was reading Shakespeare. Emma, weren't you reading Shakespeare?"

"I had this book," Emma said, so low that her answer was lost. The Munns began to speak about something else, and Emma's mother re-laxed, triumphant.

In truth, Emma had been reading Shakespeare. While they were still unpacking and settling in, she had discovered among their things a bat-tered high school edition of *The Merchant of Venice.* Neither she nor her mother had ever seen it before. It was in the suitcase that contained Mrs. Ellenger's silver evening slippers and Emma's emergency supply of comic books. Emma opened the book and read, "You may do so; but let it be so hasted that supper be ready at the farthest by five of the clock." She closed the book and dropped it. "It must have come from Uncle Jimmy Salter's place," she said. "The maid must have put it in when she helped us pack." "I didn't know he could read," Mrs. Ellenger said. She and Mr. Salter had stopped being friends. "We'll mail it back sometime. It'll be a nice surprise."

Of course, they had never mailed the book. Now, at Tangier, it was still with them, wedged between the comic books and the silver slippers. It had never occurred to Emma's mother to give the book to a steward, or the purser, still less take it ashore during an excursion; the mechanics of wrapping and posting a parcel from a strange port were quite beyond her. The cruise, as far as she was concerned, had become a series of hazards; attempting to dispatch a volume of Shakespeare would have been the last straw. She was happy, or at least not always *un*happy, in a limited area of the ship — the bar, the beauty salon, and her own cabin. As long as she kept to this familiar, hotel-like circuit, there was almost no reason to panic. She had never before been at sea, and although she was not sickened by the motion of the ship, the idea of space, of endless leagues of water, perplexed, then frightened, then, finally, made her ill. It had come to her, during the first, dismal dinner out, that her life as a pretty young woman was finished. There were no men on board — none, at least, that would do — and even if there had been, it was not at all certain that any of them would have desired her. She saw herself flung into an existence that included the Munns, censorious, respectable, prying into one's affairs. At that moment, she had realized what the cruise would mean: She was at sea. She was adrift on an ocean whose immenseness she could not begin to grasp. She was alone, she had no real idea of their route, and it was too late to turn back. Embarking on the cruise had been a gesture, directed against the person Emma called Uncle Jimmy Salter. Like any such gesture, it had to be carried through, particularly since it had been received with total indifference, even relief.

Often, even now, with twenty-four days of the cruise behind and only twenty more to be lived through, the fears she had experienced the first evening would recur: She was at sea, alone. There was no one around to tip stewards, order drinks, plan the nights, make love to her, pay the bills, tell her where she was and what it was all about. How had this happened? However had she mismanaged her life to such a degree? She was still young. She looked at herself in the glass and, covering the dry, darkening skin below her eyes, decided she was still pretty. Perplexed, she went to the beauty salon and had her hair washed by a sympathetic girl, a good listener. Then, drugged with heat, sated with shared confidences, she wandered out to the first-class bar and sat at her own special stool. Here the sympathetic girl was replaced by Eddy, the Eurasian bartender from Hong Kong. Picking up the thread of her life, Mrs. Ellenger talked to Eddy, describing her childhood and her stepmother. She told him about Emma's father, and about the time she and Emma went to California. Talking, she tried to pretend she was in New York and that the environment of the ship was perfectly normal and real. She played with her drink, smiling anxiously at herself in the mirror behind the bar.

Eddy wasn't much of an audience, because he had other things to do, but after a time Mrs. Ellenger became so engrossed in her own recital, repeating and recounting the errors that had brought her to this impasse, that she scarcely noticed at all.

"I was a mere child, Eddy," she said. "A child. What did I know about life?"

"You can learn a lot about life in a job like mine," Eddy said. Because he was half Chinese, Eddy's customers expected him to deliver remarks tinged with Oriental wisdom. As a result, he had got into the habit of saying anything at all as if it were important.

"Well, I got Emma out of it all." Mrs. Ellenger never seemed to hear Eddy's remarks. "I've got my Emma. That's something. She's a big girl, isn't she, Eddy? Would you take her for only twelve? Some people take her for fourteen. They take us for sisters."

"The Dolly Sisters," Eddy said, ensconced on a reputation that had him not only a sage but a scream.

"Well, I never try to pass Emma off as my sister," Mrs. Ellenger went on. "Oh, it's not that I couldn't. I mean enough people have told me. And I was a mere child myself when she was born. But I don't care if they know she's my daughter. I'm *proud* of my Emma. She was born during the war. I kept her all in white . . ."

Her glass slid away, reminding her that she was not in New York but at sea. It was no use. She thought of the sea, of travel, of being alone; the idea grew so enormous and frightening that, at last, there was nothing to do but go straight to her cabin and get into bed, even if it was the middle of the day. Her head ached and so did her wrists. She took off her heavy jewelry and unpinned her hair. The cabin was gray, chintzed, consolingly neutral; it resembled all or any of the hotel rooms she and Emma had shared in the past. She was surrounded by her own disorder, her own scent. There were yesterday's clothes on a chair, trailing, smelling faintly of cigarette smoke. There, on the dressing table, was an abandoned glass of brandy, an unstoppered bottle of cologne.

She rang the service bell and sent someone to look for Emma.

"Oh, Emma, darling," she said when Emma, troubled and apprehensive, came in. "Emma, why did we come on this crazy cruise? I'm so unhappy, Emma."

"I don't know," Emma said. "I don't know why we came at all." Sitting on her own bed, she picked up her doll and played with its hair or its little black shoes. She had outgrown dolls as toys years before, but this doll, which had no name, had moved about with her as long as she could remember. She knew that her mother expected something from this winter voyage, some miracle, but the nature of the miracle was beyond her. They had shopped for the cruise all summer — Emma remembered that — but when she thought of those summer weeks, with Uncle Jimmy Salter away, and her mother sulking and upset, she had an impression of heat and vacancy, as if no one had been contained in the summer season but Mrs. Ellenger and herself. Left to themselves, she and her mother had shopped, they had bought dresses and scarves and blouses and bathing suits and shoes of every possible color. They bought hats to match the dresses and bags to match the shoes. The boxes the new clothes had come in piled up in the living room, spilling tissue.

"Is he coming back?" Emma had asked once.

"I'm not waiting for *him* to make up *his* mind," her mother had said, which was, to Emma, scarcely an answer at all. "I've got my life, too. I mean," she amended, "we have, Emma. We've got a life, too. We'll go away. We'll go on a cruise or something."

"Maybe he'd like that," Emma had said, with such innocent accuracy that her mother, presented with the thought, stared at her, alarmed. "Then he could have the place all to himself."

In November, they joined the cruise. They had come aboard wearing summer dresses, confident in the climate promised by travel posters — the beaches, the blue-painted seas, the painted-yellow suns. Their cabin was full of luggage and flowers. Everything was new — their white bags, the clothes inside them, neatly folded, smelling of shops.

"It's a new life, Emma," said Mrs. Ellenger.

Emma had caught some of the feeling, for at last they were doing something together, alone, with no man, no Uncle Anyone, to interfere. She felt intensely allied to her mother, then and for several days after. But then, when it became certain that the miracle, the new life, had still to emerge, the feeling disappeared. Sometimes she felt it again just before they reached land — some strange and unexplored bit of coast, where anything might happen. The new life was always there, just before them, like a note indefinitely suspended or a wave about to break. It was there, but nothing happened.

All this, Emma sensed without finding words, even in her mind, to give the idea form. When her mother, helpless and lost, asked why they had come, she could only sit on her bed, playing with her doll's shoe, and, embarrassed by the spectacle of such open unhappiness, murmur, "I don't know. I don't know why we came at all."

Answers and explanations belonged to another language, one she had still to acquire. Even now, in Tangier, longing to explain to the Munns about the summer dresses, she knew she had better not begin. She knew that there must be a simple way of putting these things in words, but when Mrs. Munn spoke of going ashore, of the importance of keeping the throat and ankles warm, it was not in Emma's grasp to explain how it had come about that although she and her mother had shopped all summer and had brought with them much more luggage than they needed, it now developed that they had nothing to wear.

"Perhaps we shall see you in Tangier, later today," said Mrs. Munn. "You must warn your mother about Tangier. Tell her to watch her purse."

Emma nodded vigorously. "I'll tell her."

"And tell her to be careful about the food if you lunch ashore," Mrs. Munn said, beginning to gather together her guidebooks. "No salads. No fruit. Only bottled water. Above all, no native restaurants."

"I'll tell her," Emma said again.

After the Munns had departed, she sat for a moment, puzzled. Certainly they would be lunching in Tangier. For the first time, now she remembered something. The day before (or had it been the day before that?) Emma had invited Eddy, the bartender, to meet them in Tangier for lunch. She had extended the invitation with no sense of what it involved, and no real concept of place and time. North Africa was an imaginary place, half desert, half jungle. Then, this morning, she had looked through the porthole above her bed. There was Tangier, humped and yellowish, speckled with houses, under a wintry sky. It was not a jungle but a city, real. Now the two images met and blended. Tangier was a real place, and somewhere in those piled-up city blocks was Eddy, waiting to meet them for lunch.

She got up at once and hurried back to the cabin. The lounge was clearing; the launch, carrying passengers ashore across the short distance that separated them from the harbor, had been shuttling back and forth since nine o'clock.

Emma's mother was up, and — miracle — nearly dressed. She sat at the dressing table, pinning an artificial camellia into her hair. She did not turn around when Emma came in but frowned at herself in the glass, concentrating. Her dress was open at the back. She had been waiting for Emma to come and do it up. Emma sat down on her own bed. In honor of the excursion ashore, she was wearing gloves, a hat, and carrying a purse. Waiting, she sorted over the contents of her purse (a five-dollar bill, a St. Christopher medal, a wad of Kleenex, a comb in a plastic case), pulled on her small round hat, smoothed her gloves, sighed.

Her mother looked small and helpless, struggling with the awkward camellia. Emma never pitied her when she suffered — it was too disgraceful, too alarming — but she sometimes felt sorry for some detail of her person; now she was touched by the thin veined hands fumbling with flower and pins, and the thin shoulder blades that moved like wings. Her pity took the form of exasperation; it made her want to get up and do something crazy and rude — slam a door, say all the forbidden words she could think of. At last, Mrs. Ellenger stood up, nearly ready. But, no, something had gone wrong.

"Emma, I can't go ashore like this," her mother said. She sat down again. "My dress is wrong. My shoes are wrong. Look at my eyes. I look old. Look at my figure. Before I had you, my figure was wonderful. Never have a baby, Emma. Promise me."

"O.K.," Emma said. She seized the moment of pensive distraction — her mother had a dreamy look, which meant she was thinking of her pretty, fêted youth — and fastened her mother's dress. "You look lovely," Emma said rapidly. "You look just beautiful. The Munns said to tell you to dress warm, but it isn't cold. Please, let's go. Please, let's hurry. All the other people have gone. Listen, we're in *Africa*."

"That's what so crazy," Mrs. Ellenger said, as if at last she had discovered the source of all her grievances. "What am I doing in Africa?"

"Bring a scarf for your head," said Emma. "Please, let's go."

They got the last two places in the launch. Mrs. Ellenger bent and shuddered and covered her eyes; the boat was a terrible ordeal, windy and smelling of oil. She felt chilled and vomitous. "Oh, Emma," she moaned.

Emma put an arm about her, reassuring. "It's only a minute," she said. "We're nearly there now. Please look up. Why don't you look? The sun's come out."

"I'm going to be sick," Mrs. Ellenger said.

"No, you're not."

At last they were helped ashore, and stood, brushing their wrinkled skirts, on the edge of Tangier. Emma decided she had better mention Eddy right away.

"Wouldn't it be nice if we sort of ran into Eddy?" she said. "He knows all about Tangier. He's been here before. He could take us around."

"Run into *who?*" Mrs. Ellenger took off the scarf she had worn in the launch, shook it, folded it, and put it in her purse. Just then, a light wind sprang up from the bay. With a little moan, Mrs. Ellenger opened her bag and took out the scarf. She seemed not to know what to do with it, and finally clutched it to her throat. "I'm so cold," she said. "Emma, I've never been so cold in my whole life. Can't we get away from here? Isn't there a taxi or something?"

Some of their fellow passengers were standing a short distance away in a sheeplike huddle, waiting for a guide from a travel bureau to come and fetch them. They were warmly dressed. They carried books, cameras, and maps. Emma suddenly thought of how funny she and her mother must look, alone and baffled, dressed for a summer excursion. Mrs. Ellenger tottered uncertainly on high white heels.

"I think if we just walk up to that big street," Emma said, pointing. "I even see taxis. Don't worry. It'll be all right." Mrs. Ellenger looked back, almost wistfully, to the cruise ship; it was, at least, familiar. "Don't look *that* way," said Emma. "Look where we're going. Look at Africa."

Obediently, Mrs. Ellenger looked at Africa. She saw hotels, an avenue, a row of stubby palms. As Emma had said, there were taxis, one of which, at their signals, rolled out of a rank and drew up before them. Emma urged her mother into the cab and got in after her.

"We might run into Eddy," she said again.

Mrs. Ellenger saw no reason why, on this particular day, she should be forced to think about Eddy. She started to say so, but Emma was giving the driver directions, telling him to take them to the center of town. "But what if we *did* see Eddy?" Emma asked.

"Will you stop that?" Mrs. Ellenger cried. "Will you stop that about Eddy? If we see him, we see him. I guess he's got the same rights ashore as anyone else!"

Emma found this concession faintly reassuring. It did not presage an outright refusal to be with Eddy. She searched her mind for some sympathetic reference to him — the fact, for instance, that he had two children named Wilma and George — but, glancing sidelong at her mother, decided to say nothing more. Mrs. Ellenger had admitted Eddy's rights, a point that could be resurrected later, in case of trouble. They were driving uphill, between houses that looked, Emma thought, neither interesting nor African. It was certainly not the Africa she had imaged the day she invited Eddy — a vista of sand dunes surrounded by jungle, full of camels, lions, trailing vines. It was hard now to remember just why she had asked him, or if, indeed, she really had. It had been morning. The setting was easy to reconstruct. She had been the only person at the bar; she was drinking an elaborate mixture of syrup and fruit concocted by Eddy. Eddy was wiping glasses. He wore a white coat, from the pocket of which emerged the corner of a colored handkerchief. The handkerchief was one of a dozen given him by a kind American lady met on a former cruise; it bore his name, embroidered in a dashing hand. Emma had been sitting, admiring the handkerchief, thinking about the hapless donor ("She found me attractive, et cetera, et cetera," Eddy had once told her, looking resigned) when suddenly Eddy said something about Tangier, the next port, and Emma had imagined the three of them together — herself, her mother, and Eddy.

"My mother wants you to go ashore with us in Africa," she had said, already convinced this was so.

"What do you mean, ashore?" Eddy said. "Take you around, meet you for lunch?" There was nothing unusual in the invitation, as such; Eddy was a great favorite with many of his clients. "It's funny she never mentioned it."

"She forgot," Emma said. "We don't know anyone in Africa, and my mother always likes company."

"I know *that*," Eddy said softly, smiling to himself. With a little shovel, he scooped almonds into glass dishes. "What I mean is your mother actually said" — and here he imitated Mrs. Ellenger, his voice going plaintive and high — " 'I'd just adore having dear Eddy as our guest for lunch.' She actually said that?"

"Oh, Eddy!" Emma had to laugh so hard at the very idea that she doubled up over her drink. Eddy could be so witty when he wanted to be, sending clockwork spiders down the bar, serving drinks in trick glasses that unexpectedly dripped on people's clothes! Sometimes, watching him being funny with favorite customers, she would laugh until her stomach ached.

"I'll tell you what," Eddy said, having weighed the invitation. "I'll meet you *in* Tangier. I can't go ashore with you, I mean — not in the same launch; I have to go with the crew. But I'll meet you there."

"Where'll you meet us?" Emma said. "Should we pick a place?"

"Oh, I'll find you," Eddy said. He set his plates of almonds at spaced intervals along the bar. "Around the center of town. I know where you'll go." He smiled again his secret, superior smile.

They had left it at that. Had Eddy really said the center of town, Emma wondered now, or had she thought that up herself? Had the whole scene, for that matter, taken place, or had she thought that up, too? No, it was real, for, their taxi having deposited them at the Plaza de Francia, Eddy at once detached himself from the crowd on the street and came toward them.

Eddy was dapper. He wore a light suit and a square-shouldered topcoat. He closed their taxi door and smiled at Emma's mother, who was paying the driver.

"Look," Emma said. "Look who's here!"

Emma's mother moved over to a shopwindow and became absorbed in a display of nylon stockings; presented with a *fait accompli,* she withdrew from the scene — turned her back, put on a pair of sunglasses, narrowed her interest to a single stocking draped on a chrome rack. Eddy seemed unaware of tension. He carried several small parcels, his purchases. Jauntily he joined Mrs. Ellenger at the window.

"This is a good place to buy nylons," he said. "In fact, you should stock up on everything you need, because it's tax free. Anything you buy here, you can sell in Spain."

"My daughter and I have everything we require," Mrs. Ellenger said. She walked off and then quickened her step, so that he wouldn't appear to be walking with them.

Emma smiled at Eddy and fell back very slightly, striking a balance between the two. "What did you buy?" she said softly. "Something for Wilma and George?"

"Lots of stuff," said Eddy. "Now, this café right here," he called after Mrs. Ellenger, "would be a good place to sit down. Right here, in the Plaza de Francia, you can see everyone important. They all come here, the high society of two continents."

"Of two continents," Emma said, wishing her mother would pay more attention. She stared at all the people behind the glass café fronts — the office workers drinking coffee before hurrying back to their desks, the tourists from cruise ships like their own.

Mrs. Ellenger stopped. She extended her hand to Emma and said, "My daughter and I have a lot of sightseeing to do, Eddy. I'm sure there are things you want to do, too." She was smiling. The surface of her sunglasses, mirrored, gave back a small, distorted public square, a tiny Eddy, and Emma, anguished, in gloves and hat.

"Oh, Eddy!" Emma cried. She wanted to say something else, to explain that her mother didn't understand, but he vanished, just like that, and moments later she picked out his neat little figure bobbing along in the crowd going downhill, away from the Plaza. "Eddy sort of expected to stay with us," she said.

"So I noticed," said Mrs. Ellenger. They sat down in a café — not the one Eddy had suggested, but a similar café nearby. "One Coca-Cola," she told the waiter, "and one brandy-and-water." She sighed with relief, as if they had been walking for hours.

Their drinks came. Emma saw, by the clock in the middle of the square, that it was half past eleven. It was warm in the sun, as warm as May. Perhaps, after all, they had been right about the summer dresses. Forgetting Eddy, she looked around. This was Tangier, and she, Emma Ellenger, was sitting with the high society of two continents. Outside was a public square, with low buildings, a café across the street, a clock, and, walking past in striped woollen cloaks, Arabs. The Arabs were real; if the glass of the window had not been there, she could have touched them.

"There's sawdust or something in my drink," Mrs. Ellenger said. "It must have come off the ice." Nevertheless, she drank it to the end and ordered another.

"We'll go out soon, won't we?" Emma said, faintly alarmed.

"In a minute."

The waiter brought them a pile of magazines, including a six-month-old *Vogue*. Mrs. Ellenger removed her glasses, looking pleased.

"We'll go soon?" Emma repeated.

There was no reply.

The square swelled with a midday crowd. Sun covered their table until Mrs. Ellenger's glasses became warm to the touch.

"Aren't we going out?" Emma said. "Aren't we going to have anything for lunch?" Her legs ached from sitting still.

"You could have something here," Mrs. Ellenger said, vague.

The waiter brought Emma a sandwich and a glass of milk. Mrs. Ellenger continued to look at *Vogue*. Sometimes passengers from their ship went by. They waved gaily, as if Tangier were the last place they had ever expected to see a familiar face. The Munns passed, walking in step. Emma thumped on the window, but neither of the ladies turned. Something about their solidarity, their sureness of purpose, made her feel lonely and left behind. Soon they would have seen Tangier, while she and her mother might very well sit here until it was time to go back to the ship. She remembered Eddy and wondered what he was doing.

Mrs. Ellenger had come to the end of her reading material. She seemed suddenly to find her drink distasteful. She leaned on her hand, fretful and depressed, as she often was at that hour of the day. She was sorry she had come on the cruise and said so again. The warm ports were cold. She wasn't getting the right things to eat. She was getting so old and ugly that the bartender, having nothing better in view, and thinking she would be glad of anything, had tried to pick her up. What was she doing here, anyway? Her life . . .

"I wish we could have gone with Eddy," Emma said, with a sigh.

"Why, Emma," Mrs. Ellenger said. Her emotions jolted from a familiar track, it took her a moment or so to decide how she felt about this interruption. She thought it over, and became annoyed. "You mean you'd have more fun with that Chink than with me? Is that what you're trying to tell me?"

"It isn't that exactly. I only meant, we *could* have gone with him. He's been here before. Or the Munns, or this other friend of mine, Mr. Cowan. Only, he didn't come ashore today, Mr. Cowan. You shouldn't say 'Chink.' You should say 'Chinese person,' Mr. Cowan told me. Otherwise it offends. You should never offend. You should never say 'Irishman.' You should say 'Irish person.' You should never say 'Jew.' You should say —"

"Some cruise!" said Mrs. Ellenger, who had been listening to this with an expression of astounded shock, as if Emma had been repeating blasphemy. "All I can say is some cruise. Some selected passengers! What else did he tell you? What does he want with a little girl like you, anyway? Did he ever ask you into his stateroom — anything like that?"

"Oh, goodness, no!" Emma said impatiently; so many of her mother's remarks were beside the point. She knew all about not going anywhere with men, not accepting presents, all that kind of thing. "His stateroom's too small even for him. It isn't the one he paid for. He tells the purser all the time, but it doesn't make any difference. That's why he stays in the bar all day."

Indeed, for most of the cruise, Emma's friend had sat in the bar writing a long journal, which he sent home, in installments, for the edification of his analyst. His analyst, Mr. Cowan had told Emma, was to blame for the fact that he had taken the cruise. In revenge, he passed his days writing down all the things at fault with the passengers and the service, hoping to make the analyst sad and guilty. Emma began to explain her own version of this to Mrs. Ellenger, but her mother was no longer listening. She stared straight before her in the brooding, injured way Emma dreaded. Her gaze seemed turned inward, rather than to the street, as if she were concentrating on some terrible grievance and struggling to bring it to words.

"You think I'm not a good mother," she said, still not looking at Emma, or, really, at anything. "That's why you hang around these other people. It's not fair. I'm good to you. Well, am I?"

"Yes," said Emma. She glanced about nervously, wondering if anyone could hear.

"Do you ever need anything?" her mother persisted. "Do you know what happens to a lot of kids like you? They get left in schools, that's what happens. Did I ever do that to you?"

"No."

"I always kept you with me, no matter what anyone said. You mean more to me than anybody, any man. You know that. I'd give up anyone for you. I've even done it."

"I know," Emma said. There was a queer pain in her throat. She had to swallow to make it go away. She felt hot and uncomfortable and had to do something distracting; she took off her hat, rolled her gloves into a ball and put them in her purse.

Mrs. Ellenger sighed. "Well," she said in a different voice, "if we're going to see anything of this town, we'd better move." She paid for their drinks, leaving a large tip on the messy table, littered with ashes and magazines. They left the café and, arm in arm, like Miss and Mrs. Munn, they circled the block, looking into the dreary windows of luggage and furniture stores. Some of the windows had been decorated for Christmas with strings of colored lights. Emma was startled; she had forgotten all about Christmas. It seemed unnatural that there should be signs of it in a place like Tangier. "Do Arabs have Christmas?" she said.

"Everyone does," Mrs. Ellenger said. "Except —" She could not remember the exceptions.

It was growing cool, and her shoes were not right for walking. She looked up and down the street, hoping a taxi would appear, and then, with one of her abrupt, emotional changes, she darted into a souvenir shop that had taken her eye. Emma followed, blinking in the dark. The shop was tiny. There were colored bracelets in a glass case, leather slippers, and piles of silky material. From separate corners of the shop, a man and a woman converged on them.

"I'd like a bracelet for my little girl," Mrs. Ellenger said.

"For Christmas?" said the woman.

"Sort of. Although she gets plenty of presents, all the time. It doesn't have to be anything special."

"What a fortunate girl," the woman said absently, unlocking the case.

Emma was not interested in the bracelet. She turned her back on the case and found herself facing a shelf on which were pottery figures of lions, camels, and tigers. They were fastened to bases marked "*Souvenir de Tanger*," or "*Recuerdo*."

"Those are nice," Emma said, to the man. He wore a fez, and leaned against the counter, staring idly at Mrs. Ellenger. Emma pointed to the tigers. "Do they cost a lot?"

He said something in a language she could not understand. Then, lapsing into a creamy sort of English, "They are special African tigers." He grinned, showing his gums, as if the expression "African tigers" were a joke they shared. "They come from a little village in the mountains. There are interesting old myths connected with them." Emma looked at him blankly. "They are magic," he said.

"There's no such thing," Emma said. Embarrassed for him, she looked away, coloring deeply.

"This one," the man said, picking up a tiger. It was glazed in stripes of orange and black. The seam of the factory mold ran in a faint ridge down its back; the glaze had already begun to crack. "This is a special African tiger," he said. "It is good for ten wishes. Any ten."

"There's no such thing," Emma said again, but she took the tiger from him and held it in her hand, where it seemed to grow warm of its own accord. "Does it cost a lot?"

The man looked over at the case of bracelets and exchanged a swift, silent signal with his partner. Mrs. Ellenger, still talking, was hesitating between two enamelled bracelets.

"Genuine Sahara work," the woman said of the more expensive piece. When Mrs. Ellenger appeared certain to choose it, the woman nodded, and the man said to Emma, "The tiger is a gift. It costs you nothing."

"A present?" She glanced toward her mother, busy counting change. "I'm not allowed to take anything from strange men" rose to her lips. She checked it.

"For Christmas," the man said, still looking amused. "Think of me on Christmas Day, and make a wish."

"Oh, I will," Emma said, suddenly making up her mind. "Thanks. Thanks a lot." She put the tiger in her purse.

"Here, baby, try this on," Mrs. Ellenger said from across the shop. She clasped the bracelet around Emma's wrist. It was too small, and pinched, but everyone exclaimed at how pretty it looked.

"Thank you," Emma said. Clutching her purse, feeling the lump the tiger made, she said, looking toward the man, "Thanks, I love it."

"Be sure to tell your friends," he cried, as if the point of the gift would otherwise be lost.

"Are you happy?" Mrs. Ellenger asked kissing Emma. "Do you really love it? Would you still rather be with Eddy and these other people?" Her arm around Emma, they left the shop. Outside, Mrs. Ellenger walked a few steps, looking piteously at the cars going by. "Oh, God, let there be a taxi," she said. They found one and hailed it, and she collapsed inside, closing her eyes. She had seen as much of Tangier as she wanted. They rushed downhill. Emma, her face pressed against the window, had a blurred impression of houses. Their day, all at once, spun out in reverse; there was the launch, waiting. They embarked and, in a moment, the city, the continent, receded.

Emma thought, confused, Is that all? Is that all of Africa?

But there was no time to protest. Mrs. Ellenger, who had lost her sunglasses, had to be consoled and helped with her scarf. "Oh, thank God!" she said fervently, as she was helped from the launch. "Oh, my God, what a day!" She tottered off to bed, to sleep until dinner.

The ship was nearly empty. Emma lingered on deck, looking back at Tangier. She made a detour, peering into the bar; it was empty and still. A wire screen had been propped against the shelves of bottles. Reluctantly, she made her way to the cabin. Her mother had already gone to sleep. Emma pulled the curtain over the porthole, dimming the light, and picked up her mother's scattered clothes. The new bracelet pinched terribly; when she unclasped it, it left an ugly greenish mark, like a bruise. She rubbed at the mark with soap and then cologne and finally most of it came away. Moving softly, so as not to waken her mother, she put the bracelet in the suitcase that contained her comic books and Uncle Jimmy Salter's *Merchant of Vernice*. Remembering the tiger, she took it out of her purse and slipped it under her pillow.

The bar, suddenly, was full of noise. Most of it was coming from a newly installed loudspeaker. "Oh, little town of Bethlehem," Emma heard, even before she opened the heavy glass doors. Under the music, but equally amplified, were the voices of people arguing, the people who, somewhere on the ship, were trying out the carol recordings. Eddy hadn't yet returned. Crew members, in working clothes, were hanging Christmas decorations. There was a small silver tree over the bar and a larger one, real, being lashed to a pillar. At one of the low tables in front of the bar Mr. Cowan sat reading a travel folder.

"Have a good time?" he asked, looking up. He had to bellow because "Oh, Little Town of Bethlehem" was coming through so loudly. "I've just figured something out," he said, as Emma sat down. "If I take a plane from Madrid, I can be home in sixteen hours."

"Are you going to take it?"

"I don't know," he said, looking disconsolately at the folder. "Madrid isn't a port. I'd have to get off at Gibraltar or Málaga and take a train. And then, what about all my stuff? I'd have to get my trunk shipped. On the other hand," he said, looking earnestly at Emma, talking to her in the grown-up, if mystifying, way she liked, "why should I finish this ghastly cruise just for spite? They brought the mail on today. There was a letter from my wife. She says I'd better forget it and come home for Christmas."

Emma accepted without question the new fact that Mr. Cowan had a wife. Eddy had Wilma and George, the Munns had each other. Everyone she knew had a life, complete, that all but excluded Emma. "Will you go?" she repeated, unsettled by the idea that someone she liked was going away.

"Yes," he said. "I think so. We'll be in Gibraltar tomorrow. I'll get off there. How was Tangier? Anyone try to sell you a black-market Coke?"

"No," Emma said. "My mother bought a bracelet. A man gave me an African tiger."

"What kind of tiger?"

"A toy," said Emma. "A little one."

"Oh. Damn bar's been closed all day," he said, getting up. "Want to walk? Want to go down to the other bar?"

"No, thanks. I have to wait here for somebody," Emma said, and her eyes sought the service door behind the bar through which, at any moment, Eddy might appear. After Mr. Cowan had left, she sat, patient, looking at the folder he had forgotten.

Outside, the December evening drew in. The bar began to fill; passengers drifted in, compared souvenirs, talked in high, excited voices about the journey ashore. It didn't sound as if they'd been in Tangier at all, Emma thought. It sounded like some strange, imagined city, full of hazard and adventure.

". . . so this little Arab boy comes up to me," a man was saying, "and with my wife standing right there, right there beside me, he says —"

"Hush," his wife said, indicating Emma. "Not so loud."

Eddy and Mrs. Ellenger arrived almost simultaneously, coming, of course, through separate doors. Eddy had his white coat on, a fresh colored handkerchief in the pocket. He turned on the lights, took down the wire screen. Mrs. Ellenger had changed her clothes and brushed her hair. She wore a flowered dress, and looked cheerful and composed. "All alone, baby?" she said. "You haven't even changed, or washed your face. Never mind, there's no time now."

Emma looked at the bar, trying in vain to catch Eddy's eye. "Aren't you going to have a drink before dinner?"

"No. I'm hungry. Emma, you look a mess." Still talking, Mrs. Ellenger ushered Emma out to the dining room. Passing the bar, Emma called, "Hey, Eddy, hello," but, except to throw her a puzzling look, he did not respond.

They ate in near silence. Mrs. Ellenger felt rested and hungry, and, in any case, had at no time anything to communicate to the Munns. Miss Munn, between courses, read a book about Spain. She had read aloud the references to Gibraltar, and now turned to the section on Málaga, where they would be in two days. "From the summit of the Gibralfaro," she said, "one has an excellent view of the city and harbor. Two asterisks. At the state-controlled restaurant, refreshments . . ." She looked up and said, to Mrs. Munn, who was listening hard, eyes shut, "That's where we'll have lunch. We can hire a horse and *calesa*. It will kill the morning and part of the afternoon."

Already, they knew all about killing time in Málaga. They had never been there, but it would hold no surprise; they would make no mistakes. It was no use, Emma thought. She and her mother would never be like the Munns. Her mother, she could see, was becoming disturbed by this talk of Gibraltar and Málaga, by the threat of other ventures ashore. Had she not been so concerned with Eddy, she would have tried, helpfully, to lead the talk to something else. However, her apology to Eddy was infinitely more urgent. As soon as she could, she pushed back her chair and hurried out to the bar. Her mother dawdled behind her, fishing in her bag for a cigarette.

Emma sat up on one of the high stools and said, "Eddy, where did you go? What did you do? I'm sorry about the lunch."

At that, he gave her another look, but still said nothing. Mrs. Ellenger arrived and sat down next to Emma. She looked from Emma to Eddy, eyebrows raised.

Don't let her be rude, Emma silently implored an undefined source of assistance. Don't let her be rude to Eddy, and I'll never bother you again. Then, suddenly, she remembered the tiger under the pillow.

There was no reason to worry. Eddy and her mother seemed to understand each other very well. "Get a good lunch, Eddy?" her mother asked.

"Yes. Thanks."

He moved away from them, down the bar, where he was busy entertaining new people, two men and a woman, who had come aboard that day from Tangier. The woman wore harlequin glasses studded with flashing stones. She laughed in a sort of bray at Eddy's antics and his funny remarks. "You can't get mad at him," Emma heard her say to one of the men. "He's like a monkey, if a monkey could talk."

"Eddy, our drinks," Mrs. Ellenger said.

Blank, polite, he poured brandy for Mrs. Ellenger and placed before Emma a bottle of Coca-Cola and a glass. Around the curve of the bar, Emma stared at the noisy woman, Eddy's new favorite, and the two fat old men with her. Mrs. Ellenger sipped her brandy, glancing obliquely in the same direction. She listened to their conversation. Two were husband and wife, the third a friend. They had picked up the cruise because they were fed up with North Africa. They had been traveling for several months. They were tired, and each of them had had a touch of colic.

Emma was sleepy. It was too much, trying to understand Eddy, and the day ashore. She drooped over her drink. Suddenly, beside her, Mrs. Ellenger spoke. "You really shouldn't encourage Eddy like that. He's an awful show-off. He'll dance around like that all night if you laugh enough." She said it with her nicest smile. The new people stared, taking her in. They looked at her dress, her hair, her rings. Something else was said. When Emma took notice once more, one of the two men had shifted stools so he sat halfway between his friends and Emma's mother. Emma heard the introductions: Mr. and Mrs. Frank Timmins. Mr. Boyd Oliver. Mrs. Ellenger. Little Emma Ellenger, my daughter.

"Now, don't tell me that young lady's your daughter," Mr. Boyd Oliver said, turning his back on his friends. He smiled at Emma, and, just because of the smile, she suddenly remembered Uncle Harry Todd, who had given her the complete set of Sue Barton books, and another uncle, whose name she had forgotten, who had taken her to the circus when she was six.

Mr. Oliver leaned toward Mrs. Ellenger. It was difficult to talk; the bar was filling up. She picked up her bag and gloves from the stool next to her own, and Mr. Oliver moved once again. Polite and formal, they agreed that that made talking much easier.

Mr. Oliver said that he was certainly glad to meet them. The Timminses were wonderful friends, but sometimes, traveling like this, he felt like the extra wheel. Did Mrs. Ellenger know what he meant to say?

They were all talking: Mr. Oliver, Eddy, Emma's mother, Mr. and

Mrs. Timmins, the rest of the people who had drifted in. The mood, collectively, was a good one. It had been a wonderful day. They all agreed to that, even Mrs. Ellenger. The carols had started again, the same record. Someone sang with the music: "Yet in thy dark streets shineth the everlasting light . . ."

"I'd take you more for *sisters*," Mr. Oliver said.

"Really?" Mrs. Ellenger said. "Do you really think so? Well, I suppose we are, in a way. I was practically a child myself when she came into the world. But I wouldn't try to pass Emma off as my sister. I'm proud to say she's my daughter. She was born during the war. We only have each other."

"Well," Mr. Oliver said, after thinking this declaration over for a moment or so, "that's the way it should be. You're a brave little person."

Mrs. Ellenger accepted this. He signaled for Eddy, and she turned to Emma. "I think you could go to bed now. It's been a big day for you."

The noise and laughter stopped as Emma said her good nights. She remembered all the names. "Good night, Eddy," she said, at the end, but he was rinsing glasses and seemed not to hear.

Emma could still hear the carols faintly as she undressed. She knelt on her bed for a last look at Tangier; it seemed different again, exotic and remote, with the ring of lights around the shore, the city night sounds drifting over the harbor. She thought, Today I was in Africa . . . But Africa had become unreal. The café, the clock in the square, the shop where they had bought the bracelet, had nothing to do with the Tangier she had imagined or this present view from the ship. Still, the tiger was real: it was under her pillow, proof that she had been to Africa, that she had touched shore. She dropped the curtain, put out the light. To the sound of Christmas music, she went to sleep.

It was late when Mrs. Ellenger came into the cabin. Emma had been asleep for hours, her doll beside her, the tiger under her head. She came out of a confused and troubled dream about a house she had once lived in, somewhere. There were new tenants in the house; when she tried to get in, they sent her away. She smelled her mother's perfume and heard her mother's voice before opening her eyes. Mrs. Ellenger had turned on the light at the dressing table and dropped into the chair before it. She was talking to herself, and sounded fretful. "Where's my cold cream?" she said. "Where'd I put it? Who took it?" She put her hand on the service bell and Emma prayed: It's late. Don't let her ring . . . The entreaty was instantly answered, for Mrs. Ellenger changed her mind and pulled off her earrings. Her hair was all over the place, Emma noticed. She looked all askew, oddly put together. Emma closed her eyes. She could identify, without seeing them, by the sounds, the eau de cologne, the make-up remover, and the lemon cream her mother used at night. Mrs. Ellenger undressed and pulled on the nightgown that had been laid out for her. She went into the bathroom, put on the light, and cleaned

her teeth. Then she came back into the cabin and got into bed with
Emma. She was crying. She lay so close that Emma's face was wet with
her mother's tears and sticky with lemon cream.

"Are you awake?" her mother whispered. "I'm sorry, Emma. I'm so
sorry."

"What for?"

"Nothing," Mrs. Ellenger said. "Do you love your mother?"

"Yes." Emma stirred, turning her face away. She slipped a hand up
and under the pillow. The tiger was still there.

"I can't help it, Emma," her mother whispered. "I can't live like we've
been living on this cruise. I'm not made for it. I don't like being alone. I
need friends." Emma said nothing. Her mother waited, then said, "He'll
go ashore with us tomorrow. It'll be someone to take us around.
Wouldn't you like that?"

"Who's going with us?" Emma said. "The fat old man?"

Her mother had stopped crying. Her voice changed. She said, loud
and matter-of-fact, "He's got a wife someplace. He only told me now, a
minute ago. Why? Why not right at the beginning, in the bar? I'm not
like that. I want something different, a *friend*." The pillow between their
faces was wet. Mrs. Ellenger rubbed her cheek on the cold damp patch.
"Don't ever get married, Emma," she said. "Don't have anything to do
with men. Your father was no good. Jimmy Salter was no good. This
one's no better. He's got a wife and look at how — Promise me you'll
never get married. We should always stick together, you and I. Promise
me we'll always stay together."

"All right," Emma said.

"We'll have fun," Mrs. Ellenger said, pleading. "Didn't we have fun
today, when we were ashore, when I got you the nice bracelet? Next
year, we'll go someplace else. We'll go anywhere you want."

"I don't want to go anywhere," Emma said.

But her mother wasn't listening. Sobbing quietly, she went to sleep.
Her arm across Emma grew heavy and slack. Emma lay still; then she
saw that the bathroom light had been left on. Carefully, carrying the
tiger, she crawled out over the foot of the bed. Before turning out the
light, she looked at the tiger. Already, his coat had begun to flake away.
The ears were chipped. Turning it over, inspecting the damage, she saw,
stamped in blue: "Made in Japan." The man in the shop had been mistaken, then. It was not an African tiger, good for ten wishes, but something quite ordinary.

She put the light out and, in the dim stateroom turning gray with
dawn, she got into her mother's empty bed. Still holding the tiger, she
lay, hearing her mother's low breathing and the unhappy words she muttered out of her sleep.

Mr. Oliver, Emma thought, trying to sort things over, one at a time.
Mr. Oliver would be with them for the rest of the cruise. Tomorrow,

they would go ashore together. "I think you might call Mr. Oliver Uncle Boyd," her mother might say.

Emma's grasp on the tiger relaxed. There was no magic about it; it did not matter, really, where it had come from. There was nothing to be gained by keeping it hidden under a pillow. Still, she had loved it for an afternoon, she would not throw it away or inter it, like the bracelet, in a suitcase. She put it on the table by the bed and said softly, trying out the sound, "I'm too old to call you Uncle Boyd. I'm thirteen next year. I'll call you Boyd or Mr. Oliver, whatever you choose. I'd rather choose Mr. Oliver." What her mother might say then Emma could not imagine. At the moment, she seemed very helpless, very sad, and Emma turned over with her face to the wall. Imagining probable behavior was a terrible strain; this was as far as she could go.

Tomorrow, she thought, Europe began. When she got up, they would be docked in a new harbor, facing the outline of a new, mysterious place. "Gibraltar," she said aloud. Africa was over, this was something else. The cabin grew steadily lighter. Across the cabin, the hinge of the port-hole creaked, the curtain blew in. Lying still, she heard another sound, the rusty cri-cri-cri of sea gulls. That meant they were getting close. She got up, crossed the cabin, and, carefully avoiding the hump of her mother's feet under the blanket, knelt on the end of her bed. She pushed the curtain away. Yes, they were nearly there. She could see the gulls swooping and soaring, and something on the horizon — a shape, a rock, a whole continent untouched and unexplored. A tide of newness came in with the salty air: she thought of new land, new dresses, clean, untouched, unworn. A new life. She knelt, patient, holding the curtain, waiting to see the approach to shore.

NADINE GORDIMER

1923–

Excluding Doris Lessing (now really part of the English literary main-stream), Nadine Gordimer would appear to be the finest writer so far produced by South Africa. Born in a small town outside Johannesburg, she began to write at age nine. In addition to eight novels she has published nine volumes of short stories. Most of her work turns on the tragic dilemma posed by her native country's race problem and on the intricacies and consequences of apartheid. Her attitude is liberal, but her art advances far beyond the literature of protest.

The South African stories, many extremely subtle and powerful, address her central interest — indeed her central passion. Discriminating readers will find them well worth tracking down. But I have chosen a quite uncharacteristic Gordimer story because I admire it; because it throws an odd and, I think, needed light on one of the few unqualifiedly great writers in this collection, Franz Kafka; and because its inclusion gives evidence of what wary anthology readers should always keep in mind: the vagaries of taste.

"Letter from His Father" is an imagined response to the famous "Letter to His Father," full of pent-up bitterness, which Kafka wrote but never sent to the parent who dominated his life. For me old Hermann's letter is just what the publishers say it is: "A funny, irascible and moving diatribe." For me it is just what the Sunday Times *of London said it is: "Full of ingenious ironies about parental loves and differences." Indeed for me it is a kind of accidental, non-Gordimerian, small masterpiece. Or, if not, at least a dazzling tour de force.*

On the other hand, in the New York Times Book Review *of July 29, 1984, the talented novelist Salman Rushdie assessed Gordimer's collection* Something Out There *favorably — with one striking exception. For him "Letter from His Father" was " an unmitigated disaster."*

A comparison of these polar judgments may make a reading of the story more interesting.

Letter from His Father

MY DEAR SON,

You wrote me a letter you never sent.

It wasn't for me — it was for the whole world to read. (You and your instructions that everything should be burned. Hah!) You were never open and frank with me — that's one of the complaints you say I was always making against you. You write it in the letter you didn't want me to read; so what does *that* sound like, eh? But I've read the letter now, I've read it anyway, I've read everything, although you said I put your books on the night-table and never touched them. You know how it is, here where I am: not something that can be explained to anyone who isn't here — they used to talk about secrets going to the grave, but the funny thing is there are no secrets here at all. If there was something you wanted to know, you should have known, if it doesn't let you lie quiet, then you can *have knowledge of it,* from here. Yes, you gave me that much credit, you said I was a true Kafka in "strength . . . eloquence, endurance, a certain way of doing things on a grand scale" and I've not been content just to rot. In that way, I'm still the man I was, the go-getter. Restless. Restless. Taking whatever opportunity I can. There isn't anything, now, you can regard as hidden from me. Whether you say I left it unread on the night-table or whether you weren't man enough, even at the age of thirty-six, to show me a letter that was supposed to be for me.

I write to you after we are both dead. Whereas you don't stir. There won't be any response from you, I know that. You began that letter by saying you were afraid of me — and then you were afraid to let me read it. And now you've escaped altogether. Because without the Kafka will-power you can't reach out from nothing and nowhere. I was going to call it a desert, but where's the sand, where're the camels, where's the sun — I'm still *mensch* enough to crack a joke — you see? Oh excuse me, I forgot — you didn't like my jokes, my fooling around with kids. My poor boy, unfortunately you had no life in you, in all those books and diaries and letters (the ones you posted, to strangers, to women) you said it a hundred times before you put the words in my mouth, in your literary way, in that letter: you yourself were "unfit for life." So death comes, how would you say, quite naturally to you. It's not like that for a man of vigour like I was, I can tell you, and so here I am writing, talking . . . I don't know if there is a word for what this is. Anyway, it's *Hermann Kafka*. I've outlived you here, same as in Prague.

That is what you really accuse me of, you know, for sixty or so pages (I notice the length of that letter varies a bit from language to language, of course it's been translated into everything — I don't know what — Hottentot and Icelandic, Chinese, although you wrote it "for me" in German). I *outlived* you, not for seven years, as an old sick man, after you died, but while you were young and alive. Clear as daylight, from the examples you give of being afraid of me, from the time you were a little boy: you were not afraid, you were envious. At first, when I took you swimming and you say you felt yourself a nothing, puny and weak beside my big, strong, naked body in the change-house — all right, you also say you were proud of such a father, a father with a fine physique . . . And may I remind you that father was taking the trouble and time, the few hours he could get away from the business, to try and make something of that *nebich,* develop his muscles, put some flesh on those poor little bones so he would grow up sturdy? But even before your barmitzvah the normal pride every boy has in his father changed to jealousy, with you. You couldn't be like me, so you decided I wasn't good enough for you: coarse, loud-mouthed, ate "like a pig" (your very words), cut my fingernails at table, cleaned my ears with a toothpick. Oh yes, you can't hide anything from me, now, I've read it all, all the thousands and thousands of words you've used to shame your own family, your own father, before the whole world. And with your gift for words you turn everything inside-out and prove, like a circus magician, it's love, the piece of dirty paper's a beautiful silk flag, you *loved your father too much,* and so — what? *You* tell me. You couldn't be like him? You wanted to be like *him?* The *ghasa,* the shouter, the gobbler? Yes, my son, these "insignificant details" you write down and quickly dismiss — these details hurt. Eternally. After all, you've become immortal through writing, as you insist you did, only about me, "everything was about you, father"; a hundred years after your birth, the Czech Jew, son of Hermann and Julie Kafka, is supposed to be one of the greatest writers who ever lived. Your work will be read as long as there are people to read it. That's what they say everywhere, even the Germans who burned your sisters and my grandchildren in incinerators. Some say you were also some kind of prophet (God knows what you were thinking, shut away in your room while the rest of the family was having a game of cards in the evening); after you died, some countries built camps where the things you made up for that story *In the Penal Colony* were practised, and ever since then there have been countries in different parts of the world where the devil's work that came into your mind is still carried out — I don't want to think about it.

You were not blessed to bring any happiness to this world with your genius, my son. Not at home, either. Well, we had to accept what God gave. Do you ever stop to think whether it wasn't a sorrow for me (never mind — for once — how you felt) that your two brothers, who might have grown up to bring your mother and me joy, died as babies? And you sitting there at meals always with a pale, miserable, glum face, not a word to say for yourself, picking at your food . . . You haven't forgotten that I used to hold up the newspaper so as not to have to see that. You bear a grudge. You've told everybody. But you don't think about what there was in a father's heart. From the beginning. I had to hide it behind a newspaper — anything. For your sake.

Because you were never like any other child. You admit it: however we had tried to bring you up, you say you would have become a "weakly, timid, hesitant person." What small boy doesn't enjoy a bit of a rough-house with his father? But writing at thirty-six years old, you can only remember being frightened when I chased you, in fun, round the table, and your mother, joining in, would snatch you up out of my way while you shrieked. For God's sake, what's so terrible about that? I should have such memories of my childhood! I know you never liked to hear about it, it bored you, you don't spare me the written information that it "wore grooves in your brain," but when *I* was seven years old I had to push my father's barrow from village to village, with open sores on my legs in winter. Nobody gave me delicacies to mess about on my plate; we were glad when we got potatoes. You make a show of me, mimicking how I used to say these things. But wasn't I right when I told you and your sisters — provided for by me, living like fighting-cocks because I stood in the business twelve hours a day — what did you know of such things? What did anyone know, what I suffered as a child? And then it's a sin if I wanted to give my own son a little pleasure I never had.

And that other business you *schlepped* up out of the past — the night I'm supposed to have shut you out on the *pavlatche*. Because of you the whole world knows the Czech word for the kind of balcony we had in Prague! Yes, the whole world knows that story, too. I am famous, too. You made me famous as the father who frightened his child once and for all: for life. Thank you very much. I want to tell you that I don't even remember that incident. I'm not saying it didn't happen, although you always had an imagination such as nobody ever had before or since, eh? But it could only have been the last resort your mother and I turned to — you know that your mother spoilt you, *over-protected* they would call it, now. You couldn't possibly remember how naughty you were at night, what a little tyrant you were, how you thought of every excuse to keep us sleepless. It was all right for you, you could nap during the day, a small child. But I had my business, I had to earn the living, I needed some rest. Pieces of bread, a particular toy you fancied, make wee-wee, another blanket on, a blanket taken off, drinks of water — there was no end to your tricks and whining. I suppose I couldn't stand it any longer.

I feared to do you some harm. (You admit I never beat you, only scared you a little by taking off my braces in preparation to use them on you.) So I put you out of harm's way. That night. Just for a few minutes. It couldn't have been more than a minute. As if your mother would have let you catch cold! God forbid! And you've held it against me all your life. I'm sorry, I have to say it again, that old expression of mine that irritated you so much: I wish I had your worries.

Everything that went wrong for you is my fault. You write it down for sixty pages or so and at the same time you say to me "I believe you are entirely blameless in the matter of our estrangement." I was a "true Kafka," you took after your mother's, the Löwy side etc. — all you inherited from me, according to you, were your bad traits, without having the benefit of my vitality. I was "too strong" for you. You could not help it; I could not help it. So? All you wanted was *for me to admit that,* and we could have lived in peace. You were judge, you were jury, you were accused; you sentenced yourself, first. "At my desk, that is my place. My head in my hands — that is my attitude." (And that's what your poor mother and I had to look at, that was our pride and joy, our only surviving son!) But I was accused, too; you were judge, you were jury in my case, too. Right? By what right? Fancy goods — you despised the family business that fed us all, that paid for your education. What concern was it of yours, the way I treated the shop assistants? You only took an interest so you could judge, judge. It was a mistake to have let you study law. You did nothing with your qualification, your expensive education that I slaved and ruined my health for. Nothing but sentence me. — Now what did I want to say? Oh yes. Look what you wanted me to admit, under the great writer's beautiful words. If something goes wrong, somebody must be to blame, eh? We were not straw dolls, pulled about from above on strings. One of *us* must be to blame. And don't tell me you think it could be you. The stronger is always to blame, isn't that so? I'm not a deep thinker like you, only a dealer in retail fancy goods, but isn't that a law of life? "The effect you had on me was the effect you could not help having." You think I'll believe you're paying me a compliment, forgiving me, when you hand me the worst insult any father could receive? If it's what I am that's to blame, then I'm to blame, to the last drop of my heart's blood and whatever this is that's survived my body, for what *I am,* for being alive and begetting a son! You! Is that it? Because of you *I* should never have lived at all!

You always had a fine genius (never mind your literary one) for working me up. And you knew it was bad for my heart-condition. Now, what does it matter . . . but, as God's my witness, you aggravate me . . . you make me . . .

Well.

All I know is that I am to blame forever. You've seen to that. It's written, and not alone by you. There are plenty of people writing books about Kafka, Franz Kafka. I'm even blamed for the name I handed down, our family name. *Kafka* is Czech for jackdaw, so that's maybe the reason for your animal obsession. *Dafke!* Insect, ape, dog, mouse, stag, what didn't you imagine yourself. They say the beetle story is a great masterpiece, thanks to me — I'm the one who treated you like an inferior species, gave you the inspiration . . . You wake up as a bug, you give a lecture as an ape. Do any of these wonderful scholars think what this meant to me, having a son who didn't have enough self-respect to feel himself a man?

You have such a craze for animals, but may I remind you, when you were staying with Ottla at Zürau you wouldn't even undress in front of a cat she'd brought in to get rid of the mice . . .

Yet you imagined a dragon coming into your room. It said (an educated dragon, *noch*): "Drawn hitherto by your longing . . . I offer myself to you." Your longing, Franz: ugh, for monsters, for perversion. You describe a person (yourself, of course) in some crazy fantasy of living with a horse. Just listen to you, ". . . for a year I lived together with a horse in such ways as, say, a man would live with a girl whom he respects, but by whom he is rejected." You even gave the horse a girl's name, Eleanor. I ask you, is that the kind of story made up by a normal young man? Is it decent that people should read such things, long after you are gone? But it's published, everything is published.

And worst of all, what about the animal in the synagogue. Some sort of rat, weasel, a marten you call it. You tell how it ran all over during prayers, running along the lattice of the women's section and even climbing down to the curtain in front of the Ark of the Covenant. A *schande,* an animal running about during divine service. Even if it's only a story — only you would imagine it. No respect.

You go on for several pages (in that secret letter) about my use of vulgar Yiddish expressions, about my "insignificant scrap of Judaism," which was "purely social" and so meant we couldn't "find each other in Judaism" if in nothing else. This, from you! When you were a youngster and I had to drag you to the Yom Kippur services once a year you were sitting there making up stories about unclean animals approaching the Ark, the most holy object of the Jewish faith. Once you were grown up, you went exactly once to the Altneu synagogue. The people who write books about you say it must have been to please me. I'd be surprised. When you suddenly discovered you were a Jew, after all, of course your Judaism was highly intellectual, nothing in common with the Jewish customs I was taught to observe in my father's *shtetl*, pushing the barrow at the age of seven. Your Judaism was learnt at the Yiddish Theatre. That's a *nice* crowd! Those dirty-living travelling players you took up with at the Savoy Café. Your friend the actor Jizchak Löwy. No relation to your mother's family, thank God. I wouldn't let such a man even meet her. You had the disrespect to bring him into your parents' home, and I saw it was my duty to speak to him in such a way that he wouldn't ever dare to come back again. (Hah! I used to look down from the window and watch him, hanging around in the cold, outside the building, waiting for you.) And the Tschissik woman, that *nafke,* one of his actresses — I've found out you thought you were in love with her, a married woman (if you can call the way those people live a marriage). Apart from Fräulein Bauer you never fancied anything but a low type of woman. I say it again as I did then: if you lie down with dogs, you get up with fleas. You lost your temper (yes, you, this time), you flew into a rage at your father when he told you that. And when I reminded you of my heart-condition, you put yourself in the right again, as usual, you said (I remember like it was yesterday) "I make great efforts to restrain myself." But now I've read your diaries, the dead don't need to creep into your bedroom and read them behind your back (which you accused your mother and me of doing), I've read what you wrote afterwards, that you sensed in me, your father, "as always at such moments of extremity, the existence of a wisdom which I can no more than scent." So you *knew,* while you were defying me, you knew I was right!

The fact is that you were antisemitic, Franz. You were never interested in what was happening to your own people. The hooligans' attacks on Jews in the streets, on houses and shops, that took place while you were growing up — I don't see a word about them in your diaries, your notebooks. You were only *imagining* Jews. Imagining them tortured in places like your *Penal Colony,* maybe. I don't want to think about what that means.

Right, towards the end you studied Hebrew, you and your sister Ottla had some wild dream about going to Palestine. You, hardly able to breathe by then, digging potatoes on a kibbutz! The latest book about you says you were in revolt against the "shopkeeper mentality" of your father's class of Jew; but it was the shopkeeper father, the buttons and buckles, braid, ribbons, ornamental combs, press-studs, hooks-and-eyes, boot laces, photo frames, shoe horns, novelties and notions that earned the bread for you to dream by. You were antisemitic, Franz; if such a thing is possible as for a Jew to cut himself in half. (For you, I suppose, anything is possible.) You told Ottla that to marry that goy Josef Davis was better than marrying ten Jews. When your great friend Brod wrote a book called *The Jewesses* you wrote there were too many of them in it. You saw them like lizards. (Animals again, low animals.) "However happy we are to watch a single lizard on a footpath in Italy, we would be horrified to see hundreds of them crawling over each other in a pickle jar." From where did you get such ideas? Not from your home, that I know.

And look how Jewish you are, in spite of the way you despised us — Jews, your Jewish family! You answer questions with questions. I've discovered that's your style, your famous literary style: your Jewishness.

Did you or did you not write the following story, playlet, wha'd'you-call-it, your friend Brod kept every scribble and you knew he wouldn't burn even a scrap. "Once at a spiritualist seance a new spirit announced its presence, and the following conversation with it took place. The spirit: Excuse me. The spokesman: Who are you? The spirit: Excuse me. The spokesman: What do you want? The spirit: To go away. The spokesman: But you've only just come. The spirit: It's a mistake. The spokesman: No, it isn't a mistake. You've come and you'll stay. The spirit: I've just begun to feel ill. The spokesman: Badly? The spirit: Badly? The spokesman: Physically? The spirit: Physically? The spokes-man: You answer with questions. That will not do. We have ways of punishing you, so I advise you to answer, for then we shall soon dismiss you. The spirit: Soon? The spokesman: Soon. The spirit: In one minute? The spokesman: Don't go on in this miserable way . . ."

Questions without answers. Riddles. You wrote "It is always only in contradiction that I can live. But this doubtless applies to everyone; for living, one dies, dying, one lives." Speak for yourself! So who did you think you were when that whim took you — their prophet, Jesus Christ? What did you *want*? The *goyishe* heavenly hereafter? What did you mean when a lost man, far from his native country, says to someone he meets "I am in your hands" and the other says, "No. You are free and that is why you are lost"? What's the sense in writing about a woman "I lie in wait for her in order not to meet her"? There's only one of your riddles I think I understand, and then only because for forty-two years, God help me, I had to deal with you myself. "A cage went in search of a bird." That's you. The cage, not the bird. I don't know why. Maybe it will come to me. As I say, if a person wants to, he can know everything, here.

All that talk about going away. You called your home (more riddles) "My prison — my fortress." You grumbled — in print, everything ended up in print, my son — that your room was only a passage, a thorough-fare between the livingroom and your parents' bedroom. You com-plained you had to write in pencil because we took away your ink to stop you writing. It was for your own good, your health — already you were a grown man, a qualified lawyer, but you know you couldn't look after yourself. Scribbling away half the night, you'd have been too tired to work properly in the mornings, you'd have lost your position at the Assicurazioni Generali (or was it by then the Arbeiter-Unfall-Versicher-ungs-Anstalt für das Königreich Böhmen, my memory doesn't get any better, here). And I wasn't made of money. I couldn't go on supporting everybody for ever.

You've published every petty disagreement in the family. It was a ter-rible thing, according to you, we didn't want you to go out in bad weather, your poor mother wanted you to wrap up. You with your del-icate health, always sickly — you didn't inherit my constitution, it was only a lifetime of hard work, the business, the family worries that got me, in the end! You recorded that you couldn't go for a walk without your parents making a fuss, but at twenty-eight you were still living at home. Going away. My poor boy. You could hardly get yourself to the next room. You shut yourself up when people came to visit. Always crawling off to bed, sleeping in the day (oh yes, you couldn't sleep at night, not like anybody else), sleeping your life away. You invented *Amerika* instead of having the guts to emigrate, get up off the bed, pack up and go there, make a new life! Even that girl you jilted twice managed it. Did you know Felice is still alive somewhere, there now, in America? She's an old, old woman with great-grandchildren. They didn't get her into the death camps those highly-educated people say you knew about before they happened. America you never went to, Spain you dreamt about . . . your Uncle Alfred was going to find you jobs there, in Madeira, the Azores . . . God knows where else. Grandson of a ritual slaughterer, a *schochet,* that was why you couldn't bear to eat meat, they say, and that made you weak and undecided. So that was my fault, too, because my poor father had to earn a living. When your mother was away from the flat, you'd have starved yourself to death if it hadn't been for me. And what was the result? You resented so much what I provided for you, you went and had your stomach pumped out! Like someone who's been poisoned! And you didn't forget to write it down, either: "My feeling is that disgusting things will come out."

Whatever I did for you was *dreck.* You felt "despised, condemned, beaten down" by me. But you despised *me;* the only difference, I wasn't so easy to beat down, eh? How many times did you try to leave home, and you couldn't go? It's all there in your diaries, in the books they write about you. What about that other masterpiece of yours, *The Judgment.* A father and son quarrelling, and then the son goes and drowns himself, saying "Dear parents, I have always loved you, all the same." The wonderful discovery about that story, you might like to hear, it proves Hermann Kafka most likely didn't want his son to grow up and be a man, any more than his son wanted to manage without his parents' protection. The *meshuggener* who wrote that, may he get rich on it! I wouldn't wish it on him to try living with you, that's all, the way we had to. When your hunchback friend secretly showed your mother a complaining letter of yours, to get you out of your duty of going to the asbestos factory to help your own sister's husband, Brod kept back one thing you wrote. But now it's all published, all, all, all the terrible things you thought about your own flesh and blood. "I hate them all": father, mother, sisters.

You couldn't do without us — without me. You only moved away from us when you were nearly thirty-two, a time when every *man* has a wife and children already, a home of his own.

You were always dependent on someone. Your friend Brod, poor devil. If it hadn't been for the little hunchback, who would know of your existence today? Between the incinerators that finished your sisters and the fire you wanted to burn up your manuscripts, nothing would be left. The kind of men you invented, the Gestapo, confiscated whatever papers of yours there were in Berlin, and no trace of them has ever been found, even by the great Kafka experts who stick their noses into everything. You said you loved Max Brod more than yourself. I can see that. You liked the idea he had of you, that you knew wasn't yourself (you see, sometimes I'm not so *grob,* uneducated, knowing nothing but fancy goods, maybe I got from you some "insights"). Certainly, I wouldn't recognize my own son the way Brod described you: "the aura Kafka gave out of extraordinary strength, something I've never encountered elsewhere, even in meetings with great and famous men . . . the infallible solidity of his insights never tolerated a single lacuna, nor did he ever speak an insignificant word . . . He was life-affirming, ironically tolerant towards the idiocies of the world, and therefore full of sad humour."

I must say, your mother who put up with your faddiness when she came back from a day standing in the business, your sisters who acted in your plays to please you, your father who worked his heart out for his family — we never got the benefit of your tolerance. Your sisters (except Ottla, the one you admit you were a bad influence on, encouraging her to leave the shop and work on a farm like a peasant, to starve herself with you on rabbit-food, to marry that goy) were giggling idiots, so far as you were concerned. Your mother never felt the comfort of her son's strength. You never gave us anything to laugh at, sad or otherwise. And you hardly spoke to me at all, even an insignificant word. Whose fault was it you were that person you describe "strolling about on the island in the pool, where there are neither books nor bridges, hearing the music, but not being heard." You wouldn't cross a road, never mind a bridge, to pass the time of day, to be pleasant to other people, you shut yourself in your room and stuffed your ears with Oropax against the music of life, yes, the sounds of cooking, people coming and going (what were we supposed to do, pass through closed doors?), even the singing of the pet canaries annoyed you, laughter, the occasional family tiff, the bed squeaking where normal married people made love.

What I've just said may surprise. That last bit, I mean. But since I died in 1931 I know the world has changed a lot. People, even fathers and sons, are talking about things that shouldn't be talked about. People aren't ashamed to read anything, even private diaries, even letters. There's no shame, anywhere. With that, too, you were ahead of your time, Franz. You were not ashamed to write in your diary, which your friend Brod would publish — you must have known he would publish everything, make a living out of us — things that have led one of the famous Kafka scholars to *study* the noises in our family flat in Prague. Writing about me: "It would have been out of character for Hermann

Kafka to restrain any noises he felt like making during coupling; it would have been out of character for Kafka, who was ultra-sensitive to noise and had grown up with these noises, to mention the suffering they caused him."

You left behind you for everyone to read that the sight of your parents' pyjamas and nightdress on the bed disgusted you. Let me also speak freely like everyone else. You were made in that bed. That disgusts me: your disgust over a place that should have been holy to you, a place to hold in the highest respect. Yet you are the one who complained about my coarseness when I suggested you ought to find yourself a woman — buy one, hire one — rather than try to prove yourself a man at last, at thirty-six, by marrying some Prague Jewish tart who shook her tits in a thin blouse. Yes, I'm speaking of that Julie Wohryzek, the shoemaker's daughter, your second fiancée. You even had the insolence to throw the remark in my face, in that letter you didn't send, but I've read it anyway, I've read everything now, although you said I put *In the Penal Colony* on the bedside table and never mentioned it again.

I have to talk about another matter we didn't discuss, father and son, while we were both alive — all right, it was my fault, maybe you're right, as I've said, times were different . . . Women. I must bring this up because — my poor boy — marriage was "the greatest terror" of your life. You write that. You say your attempts to explain why you couldn't marry — on these depends the "success" of the whole letter you didn't send. According to you, marrying, founding a family was "the utmost a human being can succeed in doing at all." Yet you couldn't marry. How is any ordinary human being to understand that? You wrote more than a quarter of a million words to Felice Bauer, but you couldn't be a husband to her. You put your parents through the farce of travelling all the way to Berlin for an engagement party (there's the photograph you had taken, the happy couple, in the books they write about you, by the way). The engagement was broken, was on again, off again. Can you wonder? Anyone who goes into a bookshop or library can read what you wrote to your fiancée when your sister Elli gave birth to our first grand-daughter. You felt nothing but nastiness, envy against your brother-in-law because "I'll never have a child." No, not with the Bauer girl, not in a decent marriage, like anybody else's son; but I've found out you had a child, Brod says so, by a woman, Grete Bloch, who was supposed to be the Bauer girl's best friend, who even acted as matchmaker between you! What do you say to that? Maybe it's news to you. I don't know. (That's how irresponsible you were.) They say she went away. Perhaps she never told you.

As for the next one you tried to marry, the one you make such a song and dance over because of my remark about Prague Jewesses and the blouse etc. — for once you came to your senses, and you called off the wedding only two days before it was supposed to take place. Not that I could have influenced you. Since when did you take into consideration what your parents thought? When you told me you wanted to marry the shoemaker's daughter — naturally I was upset. At least the Bauer girl came from a nice family. What I said about the blouse just came out, I'm human, after all. But I was frank with you, man to man. You weren't a youngster anymore. A man doesn't have to marry a nothing who will go with anybody.

I saw what that marriage was about, my poor son. You wanted a woman. Nobody understood that better than I did, believe me, I was normal man enough, eh! There were places in Prague where one could get a woman. (I suppose whatever's happened, there still are, always will be.) I tried to help you; I offered to go along with you myself. I said it in front of your mother, who — yes, as you write you were so shocked to see, was in agreement with me. We wanted so much to help you, even your own mother would go so far as that.

But in that letter you didn't think I'd ever see, you accuse me of humiliating you and I don't know what else. You wanted to marry a tart, but you were insulted at the idea of buying one?

Writing that letter only a few days after you yourself called off your second try at getting married, aged thirty-six, you find that your father, as a man-of-the-world, not only showed "contempt" for you on that occasion, but that when he had spoken to you as a broad-minded father when you were a youngster, he had given you information that set off the whole ridiculous business of your never being able to marry, ever. Already, twenty years before the Julie Wohryzek row, with "a few frank words" (as you put it) your father made you incapable of taking a wife and pushed you down "into the filth as if it were my destiny." You remember some walk with your mother and me on the Josefsplatz when you showed curiosity about, well, men's feelings and women, and I was open and honest with you and told you I could give you advice about where to go so that these things could be done quite safely, without bringing home any disease. You were sixteen years old, physically a man, not a child, eh? Wasn't it time to talk about such things?

Shall I tell you what *I* remember? Once you picked a quarrel with your mother and me because we hadn't educated you sexually — your words. Now you complain because I tried to guide you in these matters. I did — I didn't. Make up your mind. Have it your own way. Whatever I did, you believed it was *because of what I did* that you couldn't bring yourself to marry. When you thought you wanted the Bauer girl, didn't I give in, to please you? Although you were in no financial position to marry, although I had to give your two married sisters financial help, although I had worries enough, a sick man, you'd caused me enough trouble by persuading me to invest in a *mechulah* asbestos factory? Didn't I give in? And when the girl came to Prague to meet your parents and sisters, you wrote, "My family likes her almost more than I'd like it to." So it went as far as that: you couldn't like anything we liked, was that why you couldn't marry her?

A long time ago, a long way ... ah, it all moves away, it's getting faint ... But I haven't finished. Wait.

You say you wrote your letter because you wanted to explain why you couldn't marry. I'm writing this letter because you tried to write it for me. *You would take even that away from your father.* You answered your own letter, before I could. You made what you imagine as my reply part of the letter you wrote me. To save me the trouble ... Brilliant, like they say. With your great gifts as a famous writer, you express it all better than I could. You are there, quickly, with an answer, before I can be. You take the words out of my mouth: while you are accusing yourself, in my name, of being "too clever, obsequious, parasitic and insincere" in blaming your life on me, you are — yet again, one last time! — finally being too clever, obsequious, parasitic and insincere in the trick of stealing your father's chance to defend himself. A genius. What is left to say about you if — how well you know yourself, my boy, it's terrible — you call yourself the kind of vermin that doesn't only sting, but at the same time sucks blood to keep itself alive? And even that isn't the end of the twisting, the cheating. You then confess that this whole "correction," "rejoinder," as you, an expensively educated man, call it, "does not originate" in your father but in you yourself, Franz Kafka. So you see, here's the proof, something *I* know you, with all your brains, can't know *for me:* you say you always wrote about me, it was all about me, your father; but it was all about you. The beetle. The bug that lay on its back waving its legs in the air and couldn't get up to go and see America or the Great Wall of China. You, you, self, self. And in your letter, after you have defended me against yourself, when you finally make the confession — right again, in the right again, always — you take the last word, in proof of your saintliness I could know nothing about, never understand, a businessman, a shopkeeper. That is your "truth" about us you hoped might be able to "make our living and our dying easier."

The way you ended up, Franz. The last woman you found yourself. It wasn't our wish, God knows. Living with that Eastern Jewess, and in sin. We sent you money; that was all we could do. If we'd come to see you, if we'd swallowed our pride, meeting that woman, our presence would only have made you worse. It's there in everything you've written, everything they write about you: everything connected with us made you depressed and ill. We knew she was giving you the wrong food, cooking like a gypsy on a spirit stove. She kept you in an unheated hovel in Berlin ... may God forgive me (Brod has told the world), I had to turn my back on her at your funeral.

Franz ... When you received copies of your book *In the Penal Colony* from Kurt Wolff Verlag that time ... You gave me one and I said "Put it on the night-table." You say I never mentioned it again. Well, don't you understand — I'm not a literary man. I'm telling you now. I read a little bit, a page or two at a time. If you had seen that book, there was a pencil mark every two, three pages, so I would know next time where I left off. It wasn't like the books I knew — I hadn't much time for reading, working like a slave since I was a small boy, I wasn't like you, I couldn't shut myself up in a room with books, when I was young. I would have starved. But you know that. Can't you understand that I was — yes — not too proud — ashamed to let you know I didn't find it easy to understand your kind of writing, it was all strange to me.

Hah! I know I'm no intellectual, but I knew how to live!

Just a moment . . . give me time . . . there's a fading . . . Yes — can you imagine how we felt when Ottla told us you had tuberculosis? Oh how could you bring it over your heart to remind me I once said, in a temper, to a useless assistant coughing all over the shop (you should have had to deal with those lazy *goyim*), he ought to die, the sick dog. Did I know you would get tuberculosis, too? It wasn't our fault your lungs rotted. I tried to expand your chest when you were little, teaching you to swim; you should never have moved out of your own home, the care of your parents, to that rat-hole in the Schönbornpalais. And the hovel in Berlin . . . We had some good times, didn't we? Franz? When we had beer and sausages after the swimming lessons? At least you remembered the beer and sausages, when you were dying.

One more thing. It chokes me, I have to say it. I know you'll never answer. You once wrote "Speech is possible only where one wants to lie." You were too *ultra-sensitive* to speak to us, Franz. You kept silence, with the truth: those playing a game of cards, turning in bed on the other side of the wall — it was the sound of live people you didn't like. Your revenge, that you were too cowardly to take in life, you've taken here. We can't lie peacefully in our graves; dug up, unwrapped from our shrouds by your fame. To desecrate your parents' grave as well as their bed, aren't you ashamed? Aren't you ashamed — now? Well, what's the use of quarrelling. We lie together in the same grave — you, your mother and I. We've ended up as we always should have been, united. Rest in peace, my son. I wish you had let me.

Your father,
Hermann Kafka

TRUMAN CAPOTE
1924–1984

Along with Flannery O'Connor, Carson McCullers, Tennessee Williams, and the larger figure of Faulkner, Truman Capote is often characterized as a practitioner of Southern Gothic, the powerful American tradition rooted in Poe. This academic slotting, while convenient, fixes the attention too narrowly on one aspect of Capote's talent. His "nonfiction novel," In Cold Blood, did actually break new ground. He was a gifted journalist and an intuitive amateur criminal psychologist. Furthermore, he had a Wildean genius that enabled him to create a sometimes garish but often fascinating public persona. This won for him an international reputation that his work, when finally assessed, may not entirely sustain.

Capote was drawn to situations involving moral and mental disintegration, isolation, criminality, sexual deviance, bizarre forms of evil, and the transcendent sense of dubious superiority conferred by wealth and fashion. These he treated with elegance and rather self-conscious artistry.

"Miriam" may be a ghost story. It may also be a good example of the traditional theme of the double. Of this genre Poe's "William Wilson" is an early instance and Conrad's "The Secret Sharer" the greatest. Many readers will feel it is a frightening study of the postures of dominance and submission. "The Man Who Came to Dinner" deals with the same subject on the level of farce. Capote digs deeper. He compels us to look at the manner in which the human will, condensed as pure evil, might well work.

Miriam

FOR SEVERAL YEARS, Mrs. H. T. Miller had lived alone in a pleasant apartment (two rooms with kitchenette) in a remodeled brownstone near the East River. She was a widow: Mr. H. T. Miller had left a reasonable amount of insurance. Her interests were narrow, she had no friends to speak of, and she rarely journeyed farther than the corner grocery. The other people in the house never seemed to notice her: her clothes were matter-of-fact, her hair iron-gray, clipped and casually waved; she did not use cosmetics, her features were plain and inconspicuous, and on her last birthday she was sixty-one. Her activities were seldom spontaneous: she kept the two rooms immaculate, smoked an occasional cigarette, prepared her own meals and tended a canary.

Then she met Miriam. It was snowing that night. Mrs. Miller had finished drying the supper dishes and was thumbing through an afternoon paper when she saw an advertisement of a picture playing at a neighborhood theater. The title sounded good, so she struggled into her beaver coat, laced her galoshes and left the apartment, leaving one light burning in the foyer: she found nothing more disturbing than a sensation of darkness.

The snow was fine, falling gently, not yet making an impression on the pavement. The wind from the river cut only at street crossings. Mrs. Miller hurried, her head bowed, oblivious as a mole burrowing a blind path. She stopped at a drugstore and bought a package of peppermints.

A long line stretched in front of the box office; she took her place at the end. There would be (a tired voice groaned) a short wait for all seats. Mrs. Miller rummaged in her leather handbag till she collected exactly the correct change for admission. The line seemed to be taking its own time and, looking around for some distraction, she suddenly became conscious of a little girl standing under the edge of the marquee.

Her hair was the longest and strangest Mrs. Miller had ever seen: absolutely silver-white, like an albino's. It flowed waist-length in smooth, loose lines. She was thin and fragilely constructed. There was a simple, special elegance in the way she stood with her thumbs in the pockets of a tailored plum-velvet coat.

Mrs. Miller felt oddly excited, and when the little girl glanced toward her, she smiled warmly. The little girl walked over and said, "Would you care to do me a favor?"

"I'd be glad to, if I can," said Mrs. Miller.

"Oh, it's quite easy. I merely want you to buy a ticket for me; they won't let me in otherwise. Here, I have the money." And gracefully she handed Mrs. Miller two dimes and a nickel.

They went into the theater together. An usherette directed them to a lounge; in twenty minutes the picture would be over.

"I feel just like a genuine criminal," said Mrs. Miller gaily, as she sat down. "I mean that sort of thing's against the law, isn't it? I do hope I haven't done the wrong thing. Your mother knows where you are, dear? I mean she does, doesn't she?"

The little girl said nothing. She unbuttoned her coat and folded it across her lap. Her dress underneath was prim and dark blue. A gold chain dangled about her neck, and her fingers, sensitive and musical-looking, toyed with it. Examining her more attentively, Mrs. Miller decided the truly distinctive feature was not her hair, but her eyes; they were hazel, steady, lacking any childlike quality whatsoever and, because of their size, seemed to consume her small face.

Mrs. Miller offered a peppermint. "What's your name, dear?"

"Miriam," she said, as though, in some curious way, it were information already familiar.

"Why, isn't that funny — my name's Miriam, too. And it's not a terribly common name either. Now, don't tell me your last name's Miller!"

"Just Miriam."

"But isn't that funny?"

"Moderately," said Miriam, and rolled the peppermint on her tongue.

Mrs. Miller flushed and shifted uncomfortably. "You have such a large vocabulary for such a little girl."

"Do I?"

"Well, yes," said Mrs. Miller, hastily changing the topic to: "Do you like the movies?"

"I really wouldn't know," said Miriam. "I've never been before."

Women began filling the lounge; the rumble of the newsreel bombs exploded in the distance. Mrs. Miller rose, tucking her purse under her arm. "I guess I'd better be running now if I want to get a seat," she said. "It was nice to have met you."

Miriam nodded ever so slightly.

It snowed all week. Wheels and footsteps moved soundlessly on the street, as if the business of living continued secretly behind a pale but impenetrable curtain. In the falling quiet there was no sky or earth, only snow lifting in the wind, frosting the window glass, chilling the rooms, deadening and hushing the city. At all hours it was necessary to keep a lamp lighted, and Mrs. Miller lost track of the days: Friday was no different from Saturday and on Sunday she went to the grocery: closed, of course.

That evening she scrambled eggs and fixed a bowl of tomato soup. Then, after putting on a flannel robe and cold-creaming her face, she propped herself up in bed with a hot-water bottle under her feet. She was reading the *Times* when the doorbell rang. At first she thought it must be a mistake and whoever it was would go away. But it rang and rang and settled to a persistent buzz. She looked at the clock: a little after eleven; it did not seem possible, she was always asleep by ten.

Climbing out of bed, she trotted barefoot across the living room. "I'm coming, please be patient." The latch was caught; she turned it this way and that way and the bell never paused an instant. "Stop it," she cried. The bolt gave way and she opened the door an inch. "What in heaven's name?"

"Hello," said Miriam.

"Oh . . . why, hello," said Mrs. Miller, stepping hesitantly into the hall. "You're that little girl."

"I thought you'd never answer, but I kept my finger on the button; I knew you were home. Aren't you glad to see me?"

Mrs. Miller did not know what to say. Miriam, she saw, wore the same plum-velvet coat and now she had also a beret to match; her white hair was braided in two shining plaits and looped at the ends with enormous white ribbons.

"Since I've waited so long, you could at least let me in," she said.

"It's awfully late . . ."

Miriam regarded her blankly. "What difference does that make? Let me in. It's cold out here and I have on a silk dress." Then, with a gentle gesture, she urged Mrs. Miller aside and passed into the apartment.

She dropped her coat and beret on a chair. She was indeed wearing a silk dress. White silk. White silk in February. The skirt was beautifully pleated and the sleeves long; it made a faint rustle as she strolled about the room. "I like your place," she said. "I like the rug, blue's my favorite color." She touched a paper rose in a vase on the coffee table. "Imitation," she commented wanly. "How sad. Aren't imitations sad?" She seated herself on the sofa, daintily spreading her skirt.

"What do you want?" asked Mrs. Miller.

"Sit down," said Miriam. "It makes me nervous to see people stand."

Mrs. Miller sank to a hassock. "What do you want?" she repeated.

"You know, I don't think you're glad I came."

For a second time Mrs. Miller was without an answer; her hand motioned vaguely. Miriam giggled and pressed back on a mound of chintz pillows. Mrs. Miller observed that the girl was less pale than she remembered; her cheeks were flushed.

"How did you know where I lived?"

Miriam frowned. "That's no question at all. What's your name? What's mine?"

"But I'm not listed in the phone book."

"Oh, let's talk about something else."

Mrs. Miller said, "Your mother must be insane to let a child like you wander around at all hours of the night — and in such ridiculous clothes. She must be out of her mind."

Miriam got up and moved to a corner where a covered bird cage hung from a ceiling chain. She peeked beneath the cover. "It's a canary," she said. "Would you mind if I woke him? I'd like to hear him sing."

"Leave Tommy alone," said Mrs. Miller, anxiously. "Don't you dare wake him."

"Certainly," said Miriam. "But I don't see why I can't hear him sing." And then, "Have you anything to eat? I'm starving! Even milk and a jam sandwich would be fine."

"Look," said Mrs. Miller, rising from the hassock, "look — if I make some nice sandwiches will you be a good child and run along home? It's past midnight, I'm sure."

"It's snowing," reproached Miriam. "And cold and dark."

"Well, you shouldn't have come here to begin with," said Mrs. Miller, struggling to control her voice. "I can't help the weather. If you want anything to eat you'll have to promise to leave."

Miriam brushed a braid against her cheek. Her eyes were thoughtful, as if weighing the proposition. She turned toward the bird cage. "Very well," she said, "I promise."

How old is she? Ten? Eleven? Mrs. Miller, in the kitchen, unsealed a jar of strawberry preserves and cut four slices of bread. She poured a glass of milk and paused to light a cigarette. *And why has she come?* Her hand shook as she held the match, fascinated, till it burned her finger. The canary was singing; singing as he did in the morning and at no other time. "Miriam," she called, "Miriam, I told you not to disturb Tommy." There was no answer. She called again; all she heard was the canary. She inhaled the cigarette and discovered she had lighted the cork-tip end and — oh, really, she mustn't lose her temper.

She carried the food in on a tray and set it on the coffee table. She saw first that the bird cage still wore its night cover. And Tommy was singing. It gave her a queer sensation. And no one was in the room. Mrs. Miller went through an alcove leading to her bedroom; at the door she caught her breath.

"What are you doing?" she asked.

Miriam glanced up and in her eyes there was a look that was not ordinary. She was standing by the bureau, a jewel case opened before her. For a minute she studied Mrs. Miller, forcing their eyes to meet, and she smiled. "There's nothing good here," she said. "But I like this." Her hand held a cameo brooch. "It's charming."

"Suppose — perhaps you'd better put it back," said Mrs. Miller, feeling suddenly the need of some support. She leaned against the door frame; her head was unbearably heavy; a pressure weighted the rhythm of her heartbeat. The light seemed to flutter defectively. "Please, child — a gift from my husband . . ."

"But it's beautiful and I want it," said Miriam. "*Give it to me.*"

As she stood, striving to shape a sentence which would somehow save the brooch, it came to Mrs. Miller there was no one to whom she might turn; she was alone; a fact that had not been among her thoughts for a long time. Its sheer emphasis was stunning. But here in her own room in the hushed snow-city were evidences she could not ignore or, she knew with startling clarity, resist.

Miriam ate ravenously, and when the sandwiches and milk were gone, her fingers made cobweb movements over the plate, gathering crumbs. The cameo gleamed on her blouse, the blonde profile like a trick reflection of its wearer. "That was very nice," she sighed, "though now an almond cake or a cherry would be ideal. Sweets are lovely, don't you think?"

Mrs. Miller was perched precariously on the hassock, smoking a cigarette. Her hair net had slipped lopsided and loose strands straggled down her face. Her eyes were stupidly concentrated on nothing and her cheeks were mottled in red patches, as though a fierce slap had left permanent marks.

"Is there a candy — a cake?"

Mrs. Miller tapped ash on the rug. Her head swayed slightly as she tried to focus her eyes. "You promised to leave if I made the sandwiches," she said.

"Dear me, did I?"

"It was a promise and I'm tired and I don't feel well at all."

"Mustn't fret," said Miriam. "I'm only teasing."

She picked up her coat, slung it over her arm, and arranged her beret in front of a mirror. Presently she bent close to Mrs. Miller and whispered, "Kiss me good night."

"Please — I'd rather not," said Mrs. Miller.

Miriam lifted a shoulder, arched an eyebrow. "As you like," she said, and went directly to the coffee table, seized the vase containing the paper roses, carried it to where the hard surface of the floor lay bare, and hurled it downward. Glass sprayed in all directions and she stamped her foot on the bouquet.

Then slowly she walked to the door, but before closing it she looked back at Mrs. Miller with a slyly innocent curiosity.

Mrs. Miller spent the next day in bed, rising once to feed the canary and drink a cup of tea; she took her temperature and had none, yet her dreams were feverishly agitated; their unbalanced mood lingered even as she lay staring wide-eyed at the ceiling. One dream threaded through the others like an elusively mysterious theme in a complicated symphony, and the scenes it depicted were sharply outlined, as though sketched by a hand of gifted intensity: a small girl, wearing a bridal gown and a wreath of leaves, led a gray procession down a mountain path, and among them there was unusual silence till a woman at the rear asked, "Where is she taking us?" "No one knows," said an old man marching in front. "But isn't she pretty?" volunteered a third voice. "Isn't she like a frost flower . . . so shining and white?"

Tuesday morning she woke up feeling better; harsh slats of sunlight, slanting through Venetian blinds, shed a disrupting light on her unwholesome fancies. She opened the window to discover a thawed, mild-as-spring day; a sweep of clean new clouds crumpled against a vastly blue, out-of-season sky; and across the low line of roof-tops she could see the river and smoke curving from tug-boat stacks in a warm wind. A great silver truck plowed the snow-banked street, its machine sound humming in the air.

After straightening the apartment, she went to the grocer's, cashed a check and continued to Schrafft's where she ate breakfast and chatted happily with the waitress. Oh, it was a wonderful day — more like a holiday — and it would be so foolish to go home.

She boarded a Lexington Avenue bus and rode up to Eighty-sixth Street; it was here that she had decided to do a little shopping.

She had no idea what she wanted or needed, but she idled along, intent only upon the passers-by, brisk and preoccupied, who gave her a disturbing sense of separateness.

It was while waiting at the corner of Third Avenue that she saw the man: an old man, bowlegged and stooped under an armload of bulging packages; he wore a shabby brown coat and a checkered cap. Suddenly she realized they were exchanging a smile: there was nothing friendly about this smile, it was merely two cold flickers of recognition. But she was certain she had never seen him before.

He was standing next to an El pillar, and as she crossed the street he turned and followed. He kept quite close; from the corner of her eye she watched his reflection wavering on the shopwindows.

Then in the middle of the block she stopped and faced him. He stopped also and cocked his head, grinning. But what could she say? Do? Here, in broad daylight, on Eighty-sixth Street? It was useless and, despising her own helplessness, she quickened her steps.

Now Second Avenue is a dismal street, made from scraps and ends; part cobblestone, part asphalt, part cement; and its atmosphere of desertion is permanent. Mrs. Miller walked five blocks without meeting anyone, and all the while the steady crunch of his footfalls in the snow stayed near. And when she came to a florist's shop, the sound was still with her. She hurried inside and watched through the glass door as the old man passed; he kept his eyes straight ahead and didn't slow his pace, but he did one strange, telling thing: he tipped his cap.

. . .

"Six white ones, did you say?" asked the florist. "Yes," she told him, "white roses." From there she went to a glassware store and selected a vase, presumably a replacement for the one Miriam had broken, though the price was intolerable and the vase itself (she thought) grotesquely vulgar. But a series of unaccountable purchases had begun, as if by prearranged plan: a plan of which she had not the least knowledge or control.

She bought a bag of glazed cherries, and at a place called she Knickerbocker Bakery she paid forty cents for six almond cakes.

Within the last hour the weather had turned cold again; like blurred lenses, winter clouds cast a shade over the sun, and the skeleton of an early dusk colored the sky; a damp mist mixed with the wind and the voices of a few children who romped high on mountains of gutter snow seemed lonely and cheerless. Soon the first flake fell, and when Mrs. Miller reached the brownstone house, snow was falling in a swift screen and foot tracks vanished as they were printed.

The white roses were arranged decoratively in the vase. The glazed cherries shone on a ceramic plate. The almond cakes, dusted with sugar, awaited a hand. The canary fluttered on its swing and picked at a bar of seed.

At precisely five the doorbell rang. Mrs. Miller *knew* who it was. The hem of her housecoat trailed as she crossed the floor. "Is that you?" she called.

"Naturally," said Miriam, the word resounding shrilly from the hall. "Open this door."

"Go away," said Mrs. Miller.

"Please hurry . . . I have a heavy package."

"Go away," said Mrs. Miller. She returned to the living room, lighted a cigarette, sat down and calmly listened to the buzzer; on and on and on. "You might as well leave. I have no intention of letting you in."

Shortly the bell stopped. For possibly ten minutes Mrs. Miller did not move. Then, hearing no sound, she concluded Miriam had gone. She tiptoed to the door and opened it a sliver; Miriam was half-reclining atop a cardboard box with a beautiful French doll cradled in her arms.

"Really, I thought you were never coming," she said peevishly. "Here, help me get this in, it's awfully heavy."

It was not spell-like compulsion that Mrs. Miller felt, but rather a curious passivity; she brought in the box, Miriam the doll. Miriam curled up on the sofa, not troubling to remove her coat or beret, and watched disinterestedly as Mrs. Miller dropped the box and stood trembling, trying to catch her breath.

"Thank you," she said. In the daylight she looked pinched and drawn, her hair less luminous. The French doll she was loving wore an exquisite powdered wig and its idiot glass eyes sought solace in Miriam's. "I have a surprise," she continued. "Look into my box."

Kneeling, Mrs. Miller parted the flaps and lifted out another doll; then a blue dress which she recalled as the one Miriam had worn that first night at the theater; and of the remainder she said, "It's all clothes. Why?"

"Because I've come to live with you," said Miriam, twisting a cherry stem. "Wasn't it nice of you to buy me the cherries . . . ?"

"But you can't! For God's sake go away — go away and leave me alone!"

". . . and the roses and the almond cakes? How really wonderfully generous. You know, these cherries are delicious. The last place I lived was with an old man; he was terribly poor and we never had good things to eat. But I think I'll be happy here." She paused to snuggle her doll closer. "Now, if you'll just show me where to put my things . . ."

Mrs. Miller's face dissolved into a mask of ugly red lines; she began to cry, and it was an unnatural, tearless sort of weeping, as though, not having wept for a long time, she had forgotten how. Carefully she edged backward till she touched the door.

She fumbled through the hall and down the stairs to a landing below. She pounded frantically on the door of the first apartment she came to; a short, red-headed man answered and she pushed past him. "Say, what the hell is this?" he said. "Anything wrong, lover?" asked a young woman who appeared from the kitchen, drying her hands. And it was to her that Mrs. Miller turned.

"Listen," she cried. "I'm ashamed behaving this way but — well, I'm Mrs. H. T. Miller and I live upstairs and . . ." She pressed her hands over her face. "It sounds so absurd . . ."

The woman guided her to a chair, while the man excitedly rattled pocket change. "Yeah?"

"I live upstairs and there's a little girl visiting me, and I suppose that I'm afraid of her. She won't leave and I can't make her and — she's going to do something terrible . She's already stolen my cameo, but she's about to do something worse — something terrible!"

The man asked, "Is she a relative, huh?"

Mrs. Miller shook her head. "I don't know who she is. Her name's Miriam, but I don't know for certain who she is."

"You gotta calm down, honey," said the woman, stroking Mrs. Miller's arm. "Harry here'll tend to this kid. Go on, lover." And Mrs. Miller said, "The door's open — 5A."

After the man left, the woman brought a towel and bathed Mrs. Miller's face. "You're very kind," Mrs. Miller said. "I'm sorry to act like such a fool, only this wicked child . . ."

"Sure, honey," consoled the woman. "Now, you better take it easy."

Mrs. Miller rested her head in the crook of her arm; she was quiet enough to be asleep. The woman turned a radio dial; a piano and a husky voice filled the silence and the woman, tapping her foot, kept excellent time. "Maybe we oughta go up too," she said.

"I don't want to see her again. I don't want to be anywhere near her."

"Uh huh, but what you shoulda done, you shoulda called a cop."

Presently they heard the man on the stairs. He strode into the room frowning and scratching the back of his neck. "Nobody there," he said, honestly embarrassed. "She musta beat it."

"Harry, you're a jerk," announced the woman. "We been sitting here the whole time and we woulda seen . . ." she stopped abruptly, for the man's glance was sharp.

"I looked all over," he said, "and there just ain't nobody there. Nobody, understand?"

"Tell me," said Mrs. Miller, rising, "tell me, did you see a large box? Or a doll?"

"No, ma'am, I didn't."

And the woman, as if delivering a verdict, said, "Well, for cryin out loud . . ."

Mrs. Miller entered her apartment softly; she walked to the center of the room and stood quite still. No, in a sense it had not changed: the roses, the cakes, and the cherries were in place. But this was an empty room, emptier than if the furnishings and familiars were not present, lifeless and petrified as a funeral parlor. The sofa loomed before her with a new strangeness: its vacancy had a meaning that would have been less penetrating and terrible had Miriam been curled on it. She gazed fixedly at the space where she remembered setting the box and, for a moment, the hassock spun desperately. And she looked through the window; surely the river was real, surely snow was falling — but then, one could not be certain witness to anything: Miriam, so vividly *there* — and yet, where was she? Where, where?

As though moving in a dream, she sank to a chair. The room was losing shape; it was dark and getting darker and there was nothing to be done about it; she could not lift her hand to light a lamp.

Suddenly, closing her eyes, she felt an upward surge, like a diver emerging from some deeper, greener depth. In times of terror or immense distress, there are moments when the mind waits, as though for a revelation, while a skein of calm is woven over thought; it is like a sleep, or a supernatural trance; and during this lull one is aware of a force of quiet reasoning: well, what if she had never really known a girl named Miriam? that she had been foolishly frightened on the street? In the end, like everything else, it was of no importance. For the only thing she had lost to Miriam was her identity, but now she knew she had found again the person who lived in this room, who cooked her own meals, who owned a canary, who was someone she could trust and believe in: Mrs. H. T. Miller.

Listening in contentment, she became aware of a double sound: a bureau drawer opening and closing; she seemed to hear it long after completion — opening and closing. Then gradually, the harshness of it was replaced by the murmur of a silk dress and this, delicately faint, was moving nearer and swelling in intensity till the walls trembled with the vibration and the room was caving under a wave of whispers. Mrs. Miller stiffened and opened her eyes to a dull, direct stare.

"Hello," said Miriam.

YUKIO MISHIMA
1925–1970

Mishima's flamboyant career reminds us slightly of Byron's. It also makes us think of the French decadent poets of the last half of the nineteenth century and of Oscar Wilde, for the homosexual theme appears in many of Mishima's novels. He was tormented by hyperaestheticism, by visions of violence and suicide, by hatred of as well as attraction to the westernization of Japan, and by a nationalist obsession. Following an absurd attempt to achieve a reactionary coup d'état, he ritually disemboweled himself and was decapitated by one of his faithful followers. A preview of this tragic death will be found in his famous short story "Patriotism," later made into the film Yukoku *(1960), which he directed and in which he starred.*

"Three Million Yen" exemplifies his absorption in the more outré aspects of sex. The contrasts between the childish innocence of the couple when they visit the fun house and the kinky way in which they are compelled to make a living is neatly drawn. The unpleasant story has high shock value, as have some of his longer works.

Three Million Yen

"WE'RE TO MEET HER AT NINE?" asked Kenzō.

"At nine, she said, in the toy department on the ground floor," replied Kiyoko. "But it's too noisy to talk there, and I told her about the coffee shop on the third floor instead."

"That was a good idea."

The young husband and wife looked up at the neon pagoda atop the New World Building, which they were approaching from the rear.

It was a cloudy, muggy night, of a sort common in the early-summer rainy season. Neon lights painted the low sky in rich colors. The delicate pagoda, flashing on and off in the softer of neon tones, was very beautiful indeed. It was particularly beautiful when, after all the flashing neon tubes had gone out together, they suddenly flashed on again, so soon that the after-image had scarcely disappeared. To be seen from all over Asakusa, the pagoda had replaced Gourd Pond, now filled in, as the main landmark of the Asakusa night.

To Kenzō and Kiyoko the pagoda seemed to encompass in all its purity some grand, inaccessible dream of life. Leaning against the rail of the parking lot, they looked absently up at it for a time.

Kenzō was in an undershirt, cheap trousers, and wooden clogs. His skin was fair but the lines of the shoulders and chest were powerful, and bushes of black hair showed between the mounds of muscle at the armpits. Kiyoko, in a sleeveless dress, always had her own armpits carefully shaved. Kenzō was very fussy. Because they hurt when the hair began to grow again, she had become almost obsessive about keeping them shaved, and there was a faint flush on the white skin.

She had a round little face, the pretty features as though woven of cloth. It reminded one of some earnest, unsmiling little animal. It was a face which a person trusted immediately, but not one on which to read thoughts. On her arm she had a large pink plastic handbag and Kenzō's pale blue sports shirt. Kenzō liked to be empty-handed.

From her modest coiffure and make-up one sensed the frugality of their life. Her eyes were clear and had no time for other men.

They crossed the dark road in front of the parking lot and went into the New World. The big market on the ground floor was filled with myriad-colored mountains of splendid, gleaming, cheap wares, and salesgirls peeped from crevices in the mountains. Cool fluorescent lighting poured over the scene. Behind a grove of antimony models of the

Tokyo Tower was a row of mirrors painted with Tokyo scenes, and in them, as the two passed, were rippling, waving images of the mountain of ties and summer shirts opposite.

"I couldn't stand living in a place with so many mirrors," said Kiyoko. "I'd be embarrassed."

"Nothing to be embarrassed about." Though his manner was gruff, Kenzō was not one to ignore what his wife said, and his answers were generally perceptive. The two had come to the toy department.

"She knows how you love the toy department. That's why she said to meet her here."

Kenzō laughed. He was fond of the trains and automobiles and space missiles, and he always embarrassed Kiyoko, getting an explanation for each one and trying each one out, but never buying. She took his arm and steered him some distance from the counter.

"It's easy to see that you want a boy. Look at the toys you pick."

"I don't care whether it's a boy or a girl. I just wish it would come soon."

"Another two years, that's all."

"Everything according to plan."

They had divided the savings account they were so assiduously building up into several parts, labeled Plan X and Plan Y and Plan Z and the like. Children must come strictly according to plan. However much they might want a child now, it would have to wait until sufficient money for Plan X had accumulated. Seeing the inadvisability, for numerous reasons, of installment buying, they waited until the money for Plan A or Plan B or Plan C had accumulated, and then paid cash for an electric washing machine or refrigerator or a television set. Plan A and Plan B had already been carried out. Plan D required little money, but, since it had as its object a low-priority clothes cupboard, it was always being pushed back. Neither of them was much interested in clothes. What they had they could hang in the closet, and all they really needed was enough to keep them warm in the winter.

They were very cautious when making a large purchase. They collected catalogues and looked at various possibilities and asked the advice of people who had already made the purchase, and, when the time for buying finally came, went off to a wholesaler in Okachimachi.

A child was still more serious. First there had to be a secure livelihood and enough money, more than enough money, to see that the child had surroundings of which a parent need not be ashamed, if not, perhaps, enough to see it all the way to adulthood. Kenzō had already made thorough inquiries with friends who had children, and knew what expenditures for powdered milk could be considered reasonable.

With their own plans so nicely formed, the two had nothing but contempt for the thoughtless, floundering ways of the poor. Children were to be produced according to plan in surroundings ideal for rearing them, and the best days were waiting after a child had arrived. Yet they were sensible enough not to pursue their dreams too far. They kept their eyes on the light immediately before them.

There was nothing that enraged Kenzō more than the view of the young that life in contemporary Japan was without hope. He was not a person given to deep thinking, but he had an almost religious faith that if a man respected nature and was obedient to it, and if he but made an effort for himself, the way would somehow open. The first thing was reverence for nature, founded on connubial affection. The greatest antidote for despair was the faith of a man and woman in each other.

Fortunately, he was in love with Kiyoko. To face the future hopefully, therefore, he had only to follow the conditions laid down by nature. Now and then some other woman made a motion in his direction, but he sensed something unnatural in pleasure for the sake of pleasure. It was better to listen to Kiyoko complaining about the dreadful price these days of vegetables and fish.

The two had made a round of the market and were back at the toy department.

Kenzō's eyes were riveted to the toy before him, a station for flying saucers. On the sheet-metal base the complicated mechanism was painted as if viewed through a window, and a revolving light flashed on and off inside the control tower. The flying saucer, of deep-blue plastic, worked on the old principle of the flying top. The station was apparently suspended in space, for the background of the metal base was covered with stars and clouds, among the former the familiar rings of Saturn.

The bright stars of the summer night were splendid. The painted metal surface was indescribably cool, and it was as if all the discomfort of the muggy night would go if a person but gave himself up to that sky.

Before Kiyoko could stop him, Kenzō had resolutely snapped a spring at one corner of the station.

The saucer went spinning toward the ceiling.

The salesgirl reached out and gave a little cry.

The saucer described a gentle arc toward the pastry counter across the aisle and settled square on the million-yen crackers.

"We're in!" Kenzō ran over to it.

"What do you mean, we're in?" Embarrassed, Kiyoko turned quickly away from the salesgirl and started after him.

"Look. Look where it landed. This means good luck. Not a doubt about it."

The oblong crackers were in the shape of decidedly large banknotes, and the baked-in design, again like a banknote, carried the words "One Million Yen." On the printed label of the cellophane wrapper, the figure of a bald shopkeeper took the place of Prince Shōtoku, who decorates most banknotes. There were three large crackers in each package.

Over the objections of Kiyoko, who thought fifty yen for three crackers ridiculous, Kenzō bought a package to make doubly sure of the good luck. He immediately broke the wrapping, gave a cracker to Kiyoko, and took one himself. The third went into her handbag.

As his strong teeth bit into the cracker, a sweet, slightly bitter taste flowed into his mouth. Kiyoko took a little mouselike bite from her own cracker, almost too large for her grasp.

Kenzō brought the flying saucer back to the toy counter. The salesgirl, out of sorts, looked away as she reached to take it.

Kiyoko had high, arched breasts, and, though she was small, her figure was good. When she walked with Kenzō she seemed to be hiding in his shadow. At street crossings he would take her arm firmly, look to the right and the left, and help her across, pleased at the feel of the rich flesh.

Kenzō liked the pliant strength in a woman who, although she could perfectly well do things for herself, always deferred to her husband. Kiyoko had never read a newspaper, but she had an astonishingly accurate knowledge of her surroundings. When she took a comb in her hand or turned over the leaf of a calendar or folded a summer kimono, it was not as if she were engaged in housework, but rather as if, fresh and alert, she were keeping company with the "things" known as comb and calendar and kimono. She soaked in her world of things as she might soak in a bath.

"There's an indoor amusement park on the fourth floor. We can kill time there," said Kenzō. Kiyoko followed silently into a waiting elevator, but when they reached the fourth floor she tugged at his belt.

"It's a waste of money. Everything seems so cheap, but it's all arranged so that you spend more money than you intend to."

"That's no way to talk. This is our good night, and if you tell yourself it's like a first-run movie it doesn't seem so expensive."

"What's the sense in a first-run movie? If you wait a little while you can see it for half as much."

Her earnestness was most engaging. A brown smudge from the cracker clung to her puckered lips.

"Wipe your mouth," said Kenzō. "You're making a mess of yourself."

Kiyoko looked into a mirror on a near-by pillar and removed the smear with the nail of her little finger. She still had two thirds of a cracker in her hand.

They were at the entrance to "Twenty Thousand Leagues Under the Sea." Jagged rocks reached to the ceiling, and the porthole of a submarine on the sea floor served as the ticket window: forty yen for adults, twenty yen for children.

"But forty yen is too high," said Kiyoko, turning away from the mirror. "You aren't any less hungry after you look at all those cardboard fish, and for forty yen you can get a hundred grams of the best kind of real fish."

"Yesterday they wanted forty for a cut of black snapper. Oh, well. When you're chewing on a million yen you don't talk like a beggar."

The brief debate finished, Kenzō bought the tickets.

"You've let that cracker go to your head."

"But it isn't bad at all. Just right when you're hungry."

"You just ate."

At a landing like a railway platform five or six little boxcars, each large enough for two people, stood at intervals along a track. Three or four other couples were waiting, but the two climbed unabashedly into a car. It was in fact a little tight for two, and Kenzō had to put his arm around his wife's shoulders.

The operator was whistling somewhat disdainfully. Kenzō's powerful arm, on which the sweat had dried, was solid against Kiyoko's naked shoulders and back. Naked skin clung to naked skin like the layers of some intricately folded insect's wing. The car began to shake.

"I'm afraid," said Kiyoko, with the expression of one not in the least afraid.

The cars, each some distance from the rest, plunged into a dark tunnel of rock. Immediately inside there was a sharp curve, and the reverberations were deafening.

A huge shark with shining green scales passed, almost brushing their heads, and Kiyoko ducked away. As she clung to her young husband he gave her a kiss. After the shark had passed, the car ground around a curve in pitch darkness again, but his lips landed unerringly on hers, little fish speared in the dark. The little fish jumped and were still.

The darkness made Kiyoko strangely shy. Only the violent shaking and grinding sustained her. As she slipped deep into the tunnel, her husband's arms around her, she felt naked and flushed crimson. The darkness, dense and impenetrable, had a strength that seemed to render clothes useless. She thought of a dark shed she had secretly played in as a child.

Like a flower springing from the darkness, a red beam of light flashed at them, and Kiyoko cried out once more. It was the wide, gaping mouth of a big angler fish on the ocean floor. Around it, coral fought with the poisonous dark green of seaweed.

Kenzō put his cheek to his wife's — she was still clinging to him — and with the fingers of the arm around her shoulders played with her hair. Compared to the motion of the car the motion of the fingers was slow and deliberate. She knew that he was enjoying the show and enjoying her fright at it as well.

"Will it be over soon? I'm afraid." But her voice was drowned out in the roar.

Once again they were in darkness. Though frightened, Kiyoko had her store of courage. Kenzō's arms were around her, and there was no fright and no shame she could not bear. Because hope had never left them, the state of happiness was for the two of them just such a state of tension.

A big, muddy octopus appeared before them. Once again Kiyoko cried out. Kenzō promptly kissed the nape of her neck. The great tentacles of the octopus filled the cave, and a fierce lightning darted from its eyes.

At the next curve a drowned corpse was standing disconsolately in a seaweed forest.

Finally the light at the far end began to show, the car slowed down, and they were liberated from the unpleasant noise. At the bright platform the uniformed attendant waited to catch the forward handle of the car.

"Is that all?" asked Kenzō.

The man said that it was.

Arching her back, Kiyoko climbed to the platform and whispered in Kenzō's ear: "It makes you feel like a fool, paying forty yen for that."

At the door they compared their crackers. Kiyoko had two thirds left, and Kenzō more than half.

"Just as big as when we came in," said Kenzō. "It was so full of thrills that we didn't have time to eat.

"If you think about it that way, it doesn't seem so bad after all."

Kenzō's eyes were already on the gaudy sign by another door. Electric decorations danced around the word "Magicland," and green and red lights flashed on and off in the startled eyes of a cluster of dwarfs, their domino costumes shining in gold and silver dust. A bit shy about suggesting immediately that they go in, Kenzō leaned against the wall and munched away at his cracker.

"Remember how we crossed the parking lot? The light brought out our shadows on the ground, maybe two feet apart, and a funny idea came to me. I thought to myself how it would be if a little boy's shadow bobbed up and we took it by the hand. And just then a shadow really did break away from ours and come between them."

"No!"

"Then I looked around, and it was someone behind us. A couple of drivers were playing catch, and one of them had dropped the ball and run after it."

"One of these days we really will be out walking, three of us."

"And we'll bring it here." Kenzō motioned toward the sign. "And so we ought to go in and have a look at it first."

Kiyoko said nothing this time as he started for the ticket window.

Possibly because it was a bad time of the day, Magicland was not popular. On both sides of the path as they entered there were flashing banks of artificial flowers. A music box was playing.

"When we build our house this is the way we'll have the path."

"But it's in very bad taste," objected Kiyoko.

How would it feel to go into a house of your own? A building fund had not yet appeared in the plans of the two, but in due course it would. Things they scarcely dreamed of would one day appear in the most natural way imaginable. Usually so prudent, they let their dreams run on this evening, perhaps, as Kiyoko said, because the million-yen crackers had gone to their heads.

Great artificial butterflies were taking honey from the artificial flowers. Some were as big as brief cases, and there were yellow and black spots on their translucent red wings. Tiny bulbs flashed on and off in their protuberant eyes. In the light from below, a soft aura as of sunset in a mist bathed the plastic flowers and grasses. It may have been dust rising from the floor.

The first room they came to, following the arrow, was the leaning room. The floor and all the furnishings leaned so that when one entered upright there was a grating, discordant note to the room.

"Not the sort of house I'd want to live in," said Kenzō, bracing himself against a table on which there were yellow wooden tulips. The words were like a command. He was not himself aware of it, but his decisiveness was that of the privileged one whose hope and well-being refuse to admit outsiders. It was not strange that in the hope there was a scorn for the hopes of others and that no one was allowed to lay a finger on the well-being.

Braced against the leaning table, the determined figure in the undershirt made Kiyoko smile. It was a very domestic scene. Kenzō was like an outraged young man who, having built an extra room on his Sunday holidays, had made a mistake somewhere and ended up with the windows and floors all askew.

"You *could* live in a place like this, though," said Kiyoko. Spreading her arms like a mechanical doll, she leaned forward as the room leaned, and her face approached Kenzō's broad left shoulder at the same angle as the wooden tulips.

His brow wrinkled in a serious young frown, Kenzō smiled. He kissed the cheek that leaned toward him and bit roughly into his million-yen cracker.

By the time they had emerged from the wobbly staircases, the shaking passageways, the log bridges from the railings of which monster heads protruded, and numerous other curious places as well, the heat was too much for them. Kenzō finished his own cracker, took what was left of his wife's between his teeth, and set out in search of a cool evening breeze. Beyond a row of rocking horses a door led out to a balcony.

"What time is it?" asked Kiyoko.

"A quarter to nine. Let's go out and cool off till nine."

"I'm thirsty. The cracker was so dry." She fanned at her perspiring white throat with Kenzō's sports shirt.

"In a minute you can have something to drink."

The night breeze was cool on the wide balcony. Kenzō yawned a wide yawn and leaned against the railing beside his wife. Bare young arms caressed the black railing, wet with the night dew.

"It's much cooler than when we came in."

"Don't be silly," said Kenzō. "It's just higher."

Far below, the black machines of the outdoor amusement park seemed to slumber. The bare seats of the merry-go-round, slightly inclined, were exposed to the dew. Between the iron bars of the aerial observation car, suspended chairs swayed gently in the breeze.

The liveliness of the restaurant to the left was in complete contrast. They had a bird's-eye view into all the corners of the wide expanse inside its walls. Everything was there to look at, as if on a stage: the roofs of the separate cottages, the passages joining them, the ponds and brooks in the garden, the stone lanterns, the interiors of the Japanese rooms, some with serving maids whose kimono sleeves were held up by red cords, others with dancing geisha. The strings of lanterns at the eaves were beautiful, and their white lettering was beautiful too.

The wind carried away the noises of the place, and there was something almost mystically beautiful about it, congealed in delicate detail there at the bottom of the murky summer night.

"I'll bet it's expensive." Kiyoko was once more at her favorite romantic topic.

"Naturally. Only a fool would go there."

"I'll bet they say that cucumbers are a great delicacy, and they charge some fantastic price. How much?"

"Two hundred, maybe." Kenzō took his sports shirt and started to put it on.

Buttoning it for him, Kiyoko continued: "They must think their customers are fools. Why, that's ten times what cucumbers are worth. You can get three of the very best for twenty yen."

"Oh? They're getting cheap."

"The price started going down a week or so ago."

It was five to nine. They went out to look for a stairway to the coffee shop on the third floor. Two of the crackers had disappeared. The other was too large for Kiyoko's very large handbag, and protruded from the unfastened clasp.

The old lady, an impatient person, had arrived early and was waiting. The seats from which the loud jazz orchestra could best be seen were all taken, but there were vacant places where the bandstand was out of sight, beside the potted palm probably rented from some gardener. Sitting alone in a summer kimono, the old lady seemed wholly out of place.

She was a small woman not far past middle age, and she had the clean, well-tended face of the plebeian lowlands. She spoke briskly with many delicate gestures. She was proud of the fact that she got along so nicely with young people.

"You'll be treating me, of course, so I ordered something expensive while I was waiting." Even as she spoke the tall glass arrived, pieces of fruit atop a parfait.

"Now that was generous of you. All we needed was soda water."

Her outstretched little finger taut, the old lady plunged in with her spoon and skillfully brought out the cream beneath. Meanwhile she was talking along at her usual brisk pace.

"It's nice that this place is so noisy and no one can hear us. Tonight we go to Nakano — I think I mentioned it over the phone. An ordinary private house and — can you imagine it? — the customers are house-wives having a class reunion. There's not much that the rich ladies don't know about these days. And I imagine they walk around pretending the idea never entered their heads. Anyway, I told them about you, and they said they had to have you and no one else. They don't want someone who's all beaten up by the years, you know. And I must say that I can't blame them. So I asked a good stiff price and she said it was low and if they were pleased they'd give you a good tip. They haven't any idea what the market rate is, of course. But I want you to do your best, now. I'm sure I don't need to tell you, but if they're pleased we'll get all sorts of rich customers. There aren't many that go as well together as you two do, of course, and I'm not worried, but don't do anything to make me ashamed of you. Well, anyhow, the woman of the house is the wife of some important person or other, and she'll be waiting for us at the coffee shop in front of Nakano station. You know what will happen next. She'll send the taxi through all sorts of back alleys to get us mixed up. I don't imagine she'll blindfold us, but she'll pull us through the back door so we don't have a chance to read the sign on the gate. I won't like it any better than you will, but she has herself to consider, after all. Don't let it bother you. Me? Oh, I'll be doing the usual thing, keeping watch in the hall. I can bluff my way through, I don't care who comes in. Well, maybe we ought to get started. And let me say it again, I want a good performance from you."

It was late in the night, and Kiyoko and Kanzō had left the old lady and were back in Asakusa. They were even more exhausted than usual. Ken-zō's wooden clogs dragged along the street. The billboards in the park were a poisonous black under the cloudy sky.

Simultaneously, they looked up at the New World. The neon pagoda was dark.

"What a rotten bunch. I don't think I've ever seen such a rotten, stuck-up bunch," said Kenzō.

Her eyes on the ground, Kiyoko did not answer.

"Well? Did you ever see a worse bunch of affected old women?"

"No. But what can you do? The pay was good."

"Playing around with money they pry from their husbands. Don't get to be that way when you have money."

"Silly." Kiyoko's smiling face was sharply white in the darkness.

"A really nasty bunch." Kenzō spat in a strong white arc. "How much?"

"This." Kiyoko reached artlessly into her handbag and pulled out some bills.

"Five thousand? We've never made that much before. And the old woman took three thousand. Damn! I'd like to tear it up, that's what I'd like to do. That would really feel good."

Kiyoko took the money back in some consternation. Her finger touched the last of the million-yen crackers.

"Tear this up in its place," she said softly.

Kenzō took the cracker, wadded the cellophane wrapper, and threw it to the ground. It crackled sharply on the silent, deserted street. Too large for one hand, he took the cracker in both hands and tried to break it. It was damp and soggy, and the sweet surface stuck to his hands. The more it bent the more it resisted. He was in the end unable to break it.

FLANNERY O'CONNOR
1925–1964

Flannery O'Connor, a Georgian, was born in Milledgeville and died in Savannah. For more than a decade she suffered from an incurable disease, a form of lupus. This misfortune and her Catholic faith, devoutly adhered to among the Fundamentalists who surrounded her, are two of the influences that set her apart and perhaps made her sensitive to misfits and outsiders.

However, Flannery O'Connor rejected the idea that she specialized in freaks: "When a child draws he doesn't try to be grotesque but to set down exactly what he sees." And again, in defense of what may seem to some an art of abnormality, she writes: "To the hard of hearing you shout, and for the almost blind you draw large startling figures."

Though her world is one of the submerged, even at times of the depraved, she never writes about it as a Northerner would. She does not look down on or askance at her characters. These poor whites and decayed gentility are her own, viewed without patronage, indignation, or sentimentality.

Many of her stories deal with the pain that comes of the inability of people to connect. Beneath this ordinary alienation, however, is a deeper concern with the varying capacities of human beings to achieve transcendence. One need not be a Catholic to be moved by her work, but one must accept the fact that a firmly held religious doctrine lies at its heart. In her preface for the second edition of her novel Wise Blood she makes this clear: "That belief in Christ is to some a matter of life and death has been a stumbling block for readers who would prefer to think it a matter of no great consequence."

"The Artificial Nigger" is a story, part tender, part grim, about the grandfather-grandson relationship. It is also about unevolved whites and the obsessive importance a differently pigmented people may assume in their minds. But it is really about Mr. Head's "denial" of Nelson, obviously meant to recall a more terrible denial. It is about grace, "the action of mercy" Mr. Head so grievously stands in need of.

The Artificial Nigger

MR. HEAD awakened to discover that the room was full of moonlight. He sat up and stared at the floor boards — the color of silver — and then at the ticking on his pillow, which might have been brocade, and after a second, he saw half of the moon five feet away in his shaving mirror, paused as if it were waiting for his permission to enter. It rolled forward and cast a dignifying light on everything. The straight chair against the wall looked stiff and attentive as if it were awaiting an order and Mr. Head's trousers, hanging to the back of it, had an almost noble air, like the garment some great man had just flung to his servant; but the face on the moon was a grave one. It gazed across the room and out the window where it floated over the horse stall and appeared to contemplate itself with the look of a young man who sees his old age before him.

Mr. Head could have said to it that age was a choice blessing and that only with years does a man enter into that calm understanding of life that makes him a suitable guide for the young. This, at least, had been his own experience.

He sat up and grasped the iron posts at the foot of his bed and raised himself until he could see the face on the alarm clock which sat on an overturned bucket beside the chair. The hour was two in the morning. The alarm on the clock did not work but he was not dependent on any mechanical means to awaken him. Sixty years had not dulled his responses; his physical reactions, like his moral ones, were guided by his will and strong character, and these could be seen plainly in his features. He had a long tube-like face with a long rounded open jaw and a long depressed nose. His eyes were alert but quiet, and in the miraculous moonlight they had a look of composure and of ancient wisdom as if they belonged to one of the great guides of men. He might have been Vergil summoned in the middle of the night to go to Dante, or better, Raphael, awakened by a blast of God's light to fly to the side of Tobias. The only dark spot in the room was Nelson's pallet, underneath the shadow of the window.

Nelson was hunched over on his side, his knees under his chin and his heels under his bottom. His new suit and hat were in the boxes that they had been sent in and these were on the floor at the foot of the pallet where he could get his hands on them as soon as he woke up. The slop jar, out of the shadow and made snow-white in the moonlight, appeared to stand guard over him like a small personal angel. Mr. Head lay back down, feeling entirely confident that he could carry out the moral mission of the coming day. He meant to be up before Nelson and to have the breakfast cooking by the time he awakened. The boy was always irked when Mr. Head was the first up. They would have to leave the house at four to get to the railroad junction by five-thirty. The train was to stop for them at five forty-five and they had to be there on time for this train was stopping merely to accommodate them.

This would be the boy's first trip to the city though he claimed it would be his second because he had been born there. Mr. Head had tried to point out to him that when he was born he didn't have the intelligence to determine his whereabouts but this had made no impression on the child at all and he continued to insist that this was to be his second trip. It would be Mr. Head's third trip. Nelson had said, "I will've already been there twict and I ain't but ten."

Mr. Head had contradicted him.

"If you ain't been there in fifteen years, how you know you'll be able to find your way about?" Nelson had asked. "How you know it hasn't changed some?"

"Have you ever," Mr. Head had asked, "seen me lost?"

Nelson certainly had not but he was a child who was never satisfied until he had given an impudent answer and he replied, "It's nowhere around here to get lost at."

"The day is going to come," Mr. Head prophesied, "when you'll find you ain't as smart as you think you are." He had been thinking about this trip for several months but it was for the most part in moral terms that he conceived it. It was to be a lesson that the boy would never forget. He was to find out from it that he had no cause for pride merely because he had been born in a city. He was to find out that the city is not a great place. Mr. Head meant him to see everything there is to see in a city so that he would be content to stay at home for the rest of his life. He fell asleep thinking how the boy would at last find out that he was not as smart as he thought he was.

He was awakened at three-thirty by the smell of fatback frying and he leaped off his cot. The pallet was empty and the clothes boxes had been thrown open. He put on his trousers and ran into the other room. The boy had a corn pone on cooking and had fried the meat. He was sitting in the half-dark at the table, drinking cold coffee out of a can. He had on his new suit and his new gray hat pulled low over his eyes. It was too big for him but they had ordered it a size large because they expected his head to grow. He didn't say anything but his entire figure suggested satisfaction at having arisen before Mr. Head.

Mr. Head went to the stove and brought the meat to the table in the skillet. "It's no hurry," he said. "You'll get there soon enough and it's no guarantee you'll like it when you do neither," and he sat down across from the boy whose hat teetered back slowly to reveal a fiercely expressionless face, very much the same shape as the old man's. They were grandfather and grandson but they looked enough alike to be brothers and brothers not too far apart in age, for Mr. Head had a youthful expression by daylight, while the boy's look was ancient, as if he knew everything already and would be pleased to forget it.

Mr. Head had once had a wife and daughter and when the wife died, the daughter ran away and returned after an interval with Nelson. Then one morning, without getting out of bed, she died and left Mr. Head with sole care of the year-old child. He had made the mistake of telling Nelson that he had been born in Atlanta. If he hadn't told him that, Nelson couldn't have insisted that this was going to be his second trip.

"You may not like it a bit," Mr. Head continued. "It'll be full of niggers."

The boy made a face as if he could handle a nigger.

"All right," Mr. Head said. "You ain't ever seen a nigger."

"You wasn't up very early," Nelson said.

"You ain't ever seen a nigger," Mr. Head repeated. "There hasn't been a nigger in this county since we run that one out twelve years ago and that was before you were born." He looked at the boy as if he were daring him to say he had ever seen a Negro.

"How you know I never saw a nigger when I lived there before?" Nelson asked. "I probably saw a lot of niggers."

"If you seen one you didn't know what he was," Mr. Head said, completely exasperated. "A six-month-old child don't know a nigger from anybody else."

"I reckon I'll know a nigger if I see one," the boy said and got up and straightened his slick sharply creased gray hat and went outside to the privy.

They reached the junction some time before the train was due to arrive and stood about two feet from the first set of tracks. Mr. Head carried a paper sack with some biscuits and a can of sardines in it for their lunch. A coarse-looking orange-colored sun coming up behind the east range of mountains was making the sky a dull red behind them, but in front of them it was still gray and they faced a gray transparent moon, hardly stronger than a thumbprint and completely without light. A small tin switch box and a black fuel tank were all there was to mark the place as a junction; the tracks were double and did not converge again until they were hidden behind the bends at either end of the clearing. Trains passing appeared to emerge from a tunnel of trees and, hit for a second by the cold sky, vanish terrified into the woods again. Mr. Head had had to make special arrangements with the ticket agent to have this train stop and he was secretly afraid it would not, in which case, he knew Nelson would say, "I never thought no train was going to stop for you."

Under the useless morning moon the tracks looked white and fragile. Both the old man and the child stared ahead as if they were awaiting an apparition.

Then suddenly, before Mr. Head could make up his mind to turn back, there was a deep warning bleat and the train appeared, gliding very slowly, almost silently around the bend of trees about two hundred yards down the track, with one yellow front light shining. Mr. Head was still not certain it would stop and he felt it would make an even bigger idiot of him if it went by slowly. Both he and Nelson, however, were prepared to ignore the train if it passed them.

The engine charged by, filling their noses with the smell of hot metal and then the second coach came to a stop exactly where they were standing. A conductor with the face of an ancient bloated bulldog was on the step as if he expected them, though he did not look as if it mattered one way or the other to him if they got on or not. "To the right," he said.

Their entry took only a fraction of a second and the train was already speeding on as they entered the quiet car. Most of the travelers were still sleeping, some with their heads hanging off the chair arms, some stretched across two seats, and some sprawled out with their feet in the aisle. Mr. Head saw two unoccupied seats and pushed Nelson toward them. "Get in there by the winder," he said in his normal voice which was very loud at this hour of the morning. "Nobody cares if you sit there because it's nobody in it. Sit right there."

"I heard you," the boy muttered. "It's no use in you yelling," and he sat down and turned his head to the glass. There he saw a pale ghost-like face scowling at him beneath the brim of a pale ghost-like hat. His grandfather, looking quickly too, saw a different ghost, pale but grinning, under a black hat.

Mr. Head sat down and settled himself and took out his ticket and started reading aloud everything that was printed on it. People began to stir. Several woke up and stared at him. "Take off your hat," he said to Nelson and took off his own and put it on his knee. He had a small amount of white hair that had turned tobacco-colored over the years and this lay flat across the back of his head. The front of his head was bald and creased. Nelson took off his hat and put it on his knee and they waited for the conductor to come ask for their tickets.

The man across the aisle from them was spread out over two seats, his feet propped on the window and his head jutting into the aisle. He had on a light blue suit and a yellow shirt unbuttoned at the neck. His eyes had just opened and Mr. Head was ready to introduce himself when the conductor came up from behind and growled, "Tickets."

When the conductor had gone, Mr. Head gave Nelson the return half of his ticket and said, "Now put that in your pocket and don't lose it or you'll have to stay in the city."

"Maybe I will," Nelson said as if this were a reasonable suggestion.

Mr. Head ignored him. "First time this boy has ever been on a train," he explained to the man across the aisle, who was sitting up now on the edge of his seat with both feet on the floor.

Nelson jerked his hat on again and turned angrily to the window.

"He's never seen anything before," Mr. Head continued. "Ignorant as the day he was born, but I mean for him to get his fill once and for all."

The boy leaned forward, across his grandfather and toward the stranger. "I was born in the city," he said. "I was born there. This is my second trip." He said it in a high positive voice but the man across the aisle didn't look as if he understood. There were heavy purple circles under his eyes.

Mr. Head reached across the aisle and tapped him on the arm. "The thing to do with a boy," he said sagely, "is to show him all it is to show. Don't hold nothing back."

"Yeah," the man said. He gazed down at his swollen feet and lifted the left one about ten inches from the floor. After a minute he put it down and lifted the other. All through the car people began to get up and move about and yawn and stretch. Separate voices could be heard here and there and then a general hum. Suddenly Mr. Head's serene expression changed. His mouth almost closed and a light, fierce and cautious both, came into his eyes. He was looking down the length of the car. Without turning, he caught Nelson by the arm and pulled him forward. "Look," he said.

A huge coffee-colored man was coming slowly forward. He had on a light suit and a yellow satin tie with a ruby pin in it. One of his hands rested on his stomach which rode majestically under his buttoned coat, and in the other he held the head of a black walking stick that he picked up and set down with a deliberate outward motion each time he took a step. He was proceeding very slowly, his large brown eyes gazing over the heads of the passengers. He had a small white mustache and white crinkly hair. Behind him there were two young women, both coffee-colored, one in a yellow dress and one in a green. Their progress was kept at the rate of his and they chatted in low throaty voices as they followed him.

Mr. Head's grip was tightening insistently on Nelson's arm. As the procession passed them, the light from a sapphire ring on the brown hand that picked up the cane reflected in Mr. Head's eye, but he did not look up nor did the tremendous man look at him. The group proceeded up the rest of the aisle and out of the car. Mr. Head's grip on Nelson's arm loosened. "What was that?" he asked.

"A man," the boy said and gave him an indignant look as if he were tired of having his intelligence insulted.

"What kind of a man?" Mr. Head persisted, his voice expressionless.

"A fat man," Nelson said. He was beginning to feel that he had better be cautious.

"You don't know what kind?" Mr. Head said in a final tone.

"An old man," the boy said and had a sudden foreboding that he was not going to enjoy the day.

"That was a nigger," Mr. Head said and sat back.

Nelson jumped up on the seat and stood looking backward to the end of the car but the Negro had gone.

"I'd of thought you'd know a nigger since you seen so many when you was in the city on your first visit," Mr. Head continued. "That's his first nigger," he said to the man across the aisle.

The boy slid down into the seat. "You said they were black," he said in an angry voice. "You never said they were tan. How do you expect me to know anything when you don't tell me right?"

"You're just ignorant is all," Mr. Head said and he got up and moved over in the vacant seat by the man across the aisle.

Nelson turned backward again and looked where the Negro had disappeared. He felt that the Negro had deliberately walked down the aisle in order to make a fool of him and he hated him with a fierce raw fresh hate; and also, he understood now why his grandfather disliked them. He looked toward the window and the face there seemed to suggest that he might be inadequate to the day's exactions. He wondered if he would even recognize the city when they came to it.

After he had told several stories, Mr. Head realized that the man he was talking to was asleep and he got up and suggested to Nelson that they walk over the train and see the parts of it. He particularly wanted the boy to see the toilet so they went first to the men's room and examined the plumbing. Mr. Head demonstrated the ice-water cooler as if he had invented it and showed Nelson the bowl with the single spigot where the travelers brushed their teeth. They went through several cars and came to the diner.

This was the most elegant car in the train. It was painted a rich egg-yellow and had a wine-colored carpet on the floor. There were wide windows over the tables and great spaces of the rolling view were caught in miniature in the sides of the coffee pots and in the glasses. Three very black Negroes in white suits and aprons were running up and down the aisle, swinging trays and bowing and bending over the travelers eating breakfast. One of them rushed up to Mr. Head and Nelson and said, holding up two fingers, "Space for two!" but Mr. Head replied in a loud voice, "We eaten before we left!"

The waiter wore large brown spectacles that increased the size of his eye whites. "Stan' aside then please," he said with an airy wave of the arm as if he were brushing aside flies.

Neither Nelson nor Mr. Head moved a fraction of an inch. "Look," Mr. Head said.

The near corner of the diner, containing two tables, was set off from the rest by a saffron-colored curtain. One table was set but empty but at the other, facing them, his back to the drape, sat the tremendous Negro. He was speaking in a soft voice to the two women while he buttered a muffin. He had a heavy sad face and his neck bulged over his white collar on either side. "They rope them off," Mr. Head explained. Then he said, "Let's go see the kitchen," and they walked the length of the diner but the black waiter was coming fast behind them.

"Passengers are not allowed in the kitchen!" he said in a haughty voice. "Passengers are NOT allowed in the kitchen!"

Mr. Head stopped where he was and turned. "And there's good reason for that," he shouted into the Negro's chest, "because the cockroaches would run the passengers out!"

All the travelers laughed and Mr. Head and Nelson walked out, grinning. Mr. Head was known at home for his quick wit and Nelson felt a sudden keen pride in him. He realized the old man would be his only support in the strange place they were approaching. He would be entirely alone in the world if he were ever lost from his grandfather. A terrible excitement shook him and he wanted to take hold of Mr. Head's coat and hold on like a child.

As they went back to their seats they could see through the passing windows that the countryside was becoming speckled with small houses and shacks and that a highway ran alongside the train. Cars sped by on it, very small and fast. Nelson felt that there was less breath in the air than there had been thirty minutes ago. The man across the aisle had left and there was no one near for Mr. Head to hold a conversation with so he looked out the window, through his own reflection, and read aloud the names of the buildings they were passing. "The Dixie Chemical Corp!" he announced. "Southern Maid Flour! Dixie Doors! Southern Belle Cotton Products! Patty's Peanut Butter! Southern Mammy Cane Syrup!"

"Hush up!" Nelson hissed.

All over the car people were beginning to get up and take their luggage off the overhead racks. Women were putting on their coats and hats. The conductor stuck his head in the car and snarled, "Firstoppppmry," and Nelson lunged out of his sitting position, trembling. Mr. Head pushed him down by the shoulder.

"Keep your seat," he said in dignified tones. "The first stop is on the edge of town. The second stop is at the main railroad station." He had come by this knowledge on his first trip when he had got off at the first stop and had had to pay a man fifteen cents to take him into the heart of town. Nelson sat back down, very pale. For the first time in his life, he understood that his grandfather was indispensable to him.

The train stopped and let off a few passengers and glided on as if it had never ceased moving. Outside, behind rows of brown rickety houses, a line of blue buildings stood up, and beyond them a pale rose-gray sky faded away to nothing. The train moved into the railroad yard.

Looking down, Nelson saw lines and lines of silver tracks multiplying and criss-crossing. Then before he could start counting them, the face in the window started out at him, gray but distinct, and he looked the other way. The train was in the station. Both he and Mr. Head jumped up and ran to the door. Neither noticed that they had left the paper sack with the lunch in it on the seat.

They walked stiffly through the small station and came out of a heavy door into the squall of traffic. Crowds were hurrying to work. Nelson didn't know where to look. Mr. Head leaned against the side of the building and glared in front of him.

Finally Nelson said, "Well, how do you see what all it is to see?"

Mr. Head didn't answer. Then as if the sight of people passing had given him the clue, he said, "You walk," and started off down the street. Nelson followed, steadying his hat. So many sights and sounds were flooding in on him that for the first block he hardly knew what he was seeing. At the second corner, Mr. Head turned and looked behind him at the station they had left, a putty-colored terminal with a concrete dome on top. He thought that if he could keep the dome always in sight, he would be able to get back in the afternoon to catch the train again.

As they walked along, Nelson began to distinguish details and take note of the store windows, jammed with every kind of equipment — hardware, drygoods, chicken feed, liquor. They passed one that Mr. Head called his particular attention to where you walked in and sat on a chair with your feet upon two rests and let a Negro polish your shoes. They walked slowly and stopped and stood at the entrances so he could see what went on in each place but they did not go into any of them. Mr. Head was determined not to go into any city store because on his first trip here, he had got lost in a large one and had found his way out only after many people had insulted him.

They came in the middle of the next block to a store that had a weighing machine in front of it and they both in turn stepped up on it and put in a penny and received a ticket. Mr. Head's ticket said, "You weigh 120 pounds. You are upright and brave and all your friends admire you." He put the ticket in his pocket, surprised that the machine should have got his character correct but his weight wrong, for he had weighed on a grain scale not long before and knew he weighed 110. Nelson's ticket said, "You weigh 98 pounds. You have a great destiny ahead of you but beware of dark women." Nelson did not know any women and he weighed only 68 pounds but Mr. Head pointed out that the machine had probably printed the number upside down, meaning the 9 for a 6.

They walked on and at the end of five blocks the dome of the terminal sank out of sight and Mr. Head turned to the left. Nelson could have stood in front of every store window for an hour if there had not been another more interesting one next to it. Suddenly he said, "I was born here!" Mr. Head turned and looked at him with horror. There was a sweaty brightness about his face. "This is where I come from!" he said.

Mr. Head was appalled. He saw the moment had come for drastic action. "Lemme show you one thing you ain't seen yet," he said and took him to the corner where there was a sewer entrance. " Squat down," he said, "and stick you head in there," and he held the back of the boy's coat while he got down and put his head in the sewer. He drew it back quickly, hearing a gurgling in the depths under the sidewalk. Then Mr. Head explained the sewer system, how the entire city was underlined with it, how it contained all the drainage and was full of rats and how a man could slide into it and be sucked along down endless pitchblack tunnels. At any minute any man in the city might be sucked into the sewer and never heard from again. He described it so well that Nelson was for some seconds shaken. He connected the sewer passages with the entrance to hell and understood for the first time how the world was put together in its lower parts. He drew away from the curb.

Then he said, "Yes, but you can stay away from the holes," and his face took on that stubborn look that was so exasperating to his grandfather. "This is where I come from!" he said.

Mr. Head was dismayed but he only muttered, "You'll get your fill," and they walked on. At the end of two more blocks he turned to the left, feeling that he was circling the dome; and he was correct for in a half-hour they passed in front of the railroad station again. At first Nelson did not notice that he was seeing the same stores twice but when they passed the one where you put your feet on the rests while the Negro polished your shoes, he perceived that they were walking in a circle.

"We done been here!" he shouted. "I don't believe you know where you're at!"

"The direction just slipped my mind for a minute," Mr. Head said and they turned down a different street. He still did not intend to let the dome get too far away and after two blocks in their new direction, he turned to the left. This street contained two- and three-story wooden dwellings. Anyone passing on the sidewalk could see into the rooms and Mr. Head, glancing through one window, saw a woman lying on an iron bed, looking out, with a sheet pulled over her. Her knowing expression shook him. A fierce-looking boy on a bicycle came driving down out of nowhere and he had to jump to the side to keep from being hit. "It's nothing to them if they knock you down," he said. "You better keep closer to me."

They walked on for some time on streets like this before he remembered to turn again. The houses they were passing now were all unpainted and the wood in them looked rotten; the street between was narrower. Nelson saw a colored man. Then another. Then another. "Niggers live in these houses," he observed.

"Well come on and we'll go somewheres else," Mr. Head said. "We didn't come to look at niggers," and they turned down another street but they continued to see Negroes everywhere. Nelson's skin began to prickle and they stepped along at a faster pace in order to leave the neighborhood as soon as possible. There were colored men in their undershirts standing in the doors and colored women rocking on the sagging porches. Colored children played in the gutters and stopped what they were doing to look at them. Before long they began to pass rows of stores with colored customers in them but they didn't pause at the entrances of these. Black eyes in black faces were watching them from every direction. "Yes," Mr. Head said, "this is where you were born — right here with all these niggers."

Nelson scowled. "I think you done got us lost," he said.

Mr. Head swung around sharply and looked for the dome. It was nowhere in sight. "I ain't got us lost either," he said. "You're just tired of walking."

"I ain't tired, I'm hungry," Nelson said. "Give me a biscuit."

They discovered then that they had lost the lunch.

"You were the one holding the sack," Nelson said. "I would have kepaholt of it."

"If you want to direct this trip, I'll go on by myself and leave you right here," Mr. Head said and was pleased to see the boy turn white. However, he realized they were lost and drifting farther every minute from the station. He was hungry himself and beginning to be thirsty and since they had been in the colored neighborhood, they had both begun to sweat. Nelson had on his shoes and he was unaccustomed to them. The concrete sidewalks were very hard. They both wanted to find a place to sit down but this was impossible and they kept on walking, the boy muttering under his breath, "First you lost the sack and then you lost the way," and Mr. Head growling from time to time, "Anybody wants to be from this nigger heaven can be from it!"

By now the sun was well forward in the sky. The odor of dinners cooking drifted out to them. The Negroes were all at their doors to see them pass. "Whyn't you ast one of these niggers the way?" Nelson said. "You got us lost."

"This is where you were born," Mr. Head said. "You can ast one yourself if you want to."

Nelson was afraid of the colored men and he didn't want to be laughed at by the colored children. Up ahead he saw a large colored woman leaning in a doorway that opened onto the sidewalk. Her hair stood straight out from her head for about four inches all around and she was resting on bare brown feet that turned pink at the sides. She had on a pink dress that showed her exact shape. As they came abreast of her, she lazily lifted one hand to her head and her fingers disappeared into her hair.

Nelson stopped. He felt his breath drawn up by the woman's dark eyes. "How do you get back to town?" he said in a voice that did not sound like his own.

After a minute she said, "You in town now," in a rich low tone that made Nelson feel as if a cool spray had been turned on him.

"How do you get back to the train?" he said in the same reedlike voice.

"You can catch you a car," she said.

He understood she was making fun of him but he was too paralyzed even to scowl. He stood drinking in every detail of her. His eyes traveled up from her great knees to her forehead and then made a triangular path from the glistening sweat on her neck down and across her tremendous bosom and over her bare arm back to where her fingers lay hidden in her hair. He suddenly wanted her to reach down and pick him up and draw him against her and then he wanted to feel her breath on his face. He wanted to look down and down into her eyes while she held him tighter and tighter. He had never had such a feeling before. He felt as if he were reeling down through a pitchblack tunnel.

"You can go a block down yonder and catch you a car take you to the railroad station, Sugarpie," she said.

Nelson would have collapsed at her feet if Mr. Head had not pulled him roughly away. "You act like you don't have any sense!" the old man growled.

They hurried down the street and Nelson did not look back at the woman. He pushed his hat sharply forward over his face which was already burning with shame. The sneering ghost he had seen in the train window and all the foreboding feelings he had on the way returned to him and he remembered that his ticket from the scale had said to beware of dark women and that his grandfather's had said he was upright and brave. He took hold of the old man's hand, a sign of dependence that he seldom showed.

They headed down the street toward the car tracks where a long yellow rattling trolley was coming. Mr. Head had never boarded a streetcar and he let that one pass. Nelson was silent. From time to time his mouth trembled slightly but his grandfather, occupied with his own problems, paid him no attention. They stood on the corner and neither looked at the Negroes who were passing, going about their business just as if they had been white, except that most of them stopped and eyed Mr. Head and Nelson. It occurred to Mr. Head that since the streetcar ran on tracks, they could simply follow the tracks. He gave Nelson a slight push and explained that they would follow the tracks on into the railroad station, walking, and they set off.

Presently to their great relief they began to see white people again and Nelson sat down on the sidewalk against the wall of a building. "I got to rest myself some," he said. "You lost the sack and the direction. You can just wait on me to rest myself."

"There's the tracks in front of us," Mr. Head said. "All we got to do is keep them in sight and you could have remembered the sack as good as me. This is where you were born. This is your old home town. This is your second trip. You ought to know how to do," and he squatted down and continued in this vein but the boy, easing his burning feet out of his shoes, did not answer.

"And standing there grinning like a chim-pan-zee while a nigger woman gives you direction. Great Gawd!" Mr. Head said.

"I never said I was nothing but born here," the boy said in a shaky voice. "I never said I would or wouldn't like it. I never said I wanted to come. I only said I was born here and I never had nothing to do with that. I want to go home. I never wanted to come in the first place. It was all your big idea. How you know you ain't following the tracks in the wrong direction?"

This last had occurred to Mr. Head too. "All these people are white," he said.

"We ain't passed here before," Nelson said. This was a neighborhood of brick buildings that might have been lived in or might not. A few empty automobiles were parked along the curb and there was an occasional passerby. The heat of the pavement came up through Nelson's thin suit. His eyelids began to droop, and after a few minutes his head tilted forward. His shoulders twitched once or twice and then he fell over on his side and lay sprawled in an exhausted fit of sleep.

Mr. Head watched him silently. He was very tired himself but they could not both sleep at the same time and he could not have slept anyway because he did not know where he was. In a few minutes Nelson would wake up, refreshed by his sleep and very cocky, and would begin complaining that he had lost the sack and the way. You'd have a mighty sorry time if I wasn't here, Mr. Head thought; and then another idea occurred to him. He looked at the sprawled figure for several minutes; presently he stood up. He justified what he was going to do on the grounds that it is sometimes necessary to teach a child a lesson he won't forget, particularly when the child is always reasserting his position with some new impudence. He walked without a sound to the corner about twenty feet away and sat down on a covered garbage can in the alley where he could look out and watch Nelson wake up alone.

The boy was dozing fitfully, half conscious of vague noises and black forms moving up from some dark part of him into the light. His face worked in his sleep and he had pulled his knees up under his chin. The sun shed a dull dry light on the narrow street; everything looked like exactly what it was. After a while Mr. Head, hunched like an old monkey on the garbage can lid, decided that if Nelson didn't wake up soon, he would make a loud noise by bamming his foot against the can. He looked at his watch and discovered that it was two o'clock. Their train left at six and the possibility of missing it was too awful for him to think of. He kicked his foot backwards on the can and a hollow boom reverberated in the alley.

Nelson shot up onto his feet with a shout. He looked where his grandfather should have been and stared. He seemed to whirl several times and then, picking up his feet and throwing his head back, he dashed down the street like a wild maddened pony. Mr. Head jumped off the can and galloped after but the child was almost out of sight. He saw a streak of gray disappearing diagonally a block ahead. He ran as fast as he could, looking both ways down every intersection, but without sight of him again. Then as he passed the third intersection, completely winded, he saw about half a block down the street a scene that stopped him altogether. He crouched behind a trash box to watch and get his bearings.

Nelson was sitting with both legs spread out and by his side lay an elderly woman, screaming. Groceries were scattered about the sidewalk. A crowd of women had already gathered to see justice done and Mr. Head distinctly heard the old woman on the pavement shout, "You've broken my ankle and your daddy'll pay for it! Every nickel! Police! Police!" Several of the women were plucking at Nelson's shoulder but the boy seemed too dazed to get up.

Something forced Mr. Head from behind the trash box and forward, but only at a creeping pace. He had never in his life been accosted by a policeman. The women were milling around Nelson as if they might suddenly all dive on him at once and tear him to pieces, and the old woman continued to scream that her ankle was broken and to call for an officer. Mr. Head came on so slowly that he could have been taking a backward step after each forward one, but when he was about ten feet away, Nelson saw him and sprang. The child caught him around the hips and clung panting against him.

The women all turned on Mr. Head. The injured one sat up and shouted, "You sir! You'll pay every penny of my doctor's bill that your boy has caused. He's a juve-nile deliquent! Where is an officer? Somebody take this man's name and address!"

Mr. Head was trying to detach Nelson's fingers from the flesh in the back of his legs. The old man's head had lowered itself into his collar like a turtle's; his eyes were glazed with fear and caution.

"Your boy has broken my ankle!" the old woman shouted. "Police!"

Mr. Head sensed the approach of the policeman from behind. He stared straight ahead at the women who were massed in their fury like a solid wall to block his escape, "This is not my boy," he said. "I never seen him before."

He felt Nelson's fingers fall out of his flesh.

The women dropped back, staring at him with horror, as if they were so repulsed by a man who would deny his own image and likeness that they could not bear to lay hands on him. Mr. Head walked on, through a space they silently cleared, and left Nelson behind. Ahead of him he saw nothing but a hollow tunnel that had once been the street.

The boy remained standing where he was, his neck craned forward and his hands hanging by his sides. His hat was jammed on his head so that there were no longer any creases in it. The injured woman got up and shook her first at him and the others gave him pitying looks, but he didn't notice any of them. There was no policeman in sight.

In a minute he began to move mechanically, making no effort to catch up with his grandfather but merely following at about twenty paces. They walked on for five blocks in this way. Mr. Head's shoulders were sagging and his neck hung forward at such an angle that it was not visible from behind. He was afraid to turn his head. Finally he cut a short hopeful glance over his shoulder. Twenty feet behind him, he saw two small eyes piercing into his back like pitchfork prongs.

The boy was not of a forgiving nature but this was the first time he had ever had anything to forgive. Mr. Head had never disgraced himself before. After two more blocks, he turned and called over his shoulder in a high desperately gay voice, "Let's us go get us a Co' Cola somewheres!"

Nelson, with a dignity he had never shown before, turned and stood with his back to his grandfather.

Mr. Head began to feel the depth of his denial. His face as they walked on became all hollows and bare ridges. He saw nothing they were passing but he perceived that they had lost the car tracks. There was no dome to be seen anywhere and the afternoon was advancing. He knew that if dark overtook them in the city, they would be beaten and robbed. The speed of God's justice was only what he expected for himself, but he could not stand to think that his sins would be visited upon Nelson and that even now, he was leading the boy to his doom.

They continued to walk on block after block through an endless section of small brick houses until Mr. Head almost fell over a water spigot sticking up about six inches off the edge of a grass plot. He had not had a drink of water since early morning but he felt he did not deserve it now. Then he thought that Nelson would be thirsty and they would both drink and be brought together. He squatted down and put his mouth to the nozzle and turned a cold stream of water into his throat. Then he called out in the high desperate voice, "Come on and getcher some water!"

This time the child stared through him for nearly sixty seconds. Mr. Head got up and walked on as if he had drunk poison. Nelson, though he had not had water since some he had drunk out of a paper cup on the train, passed by the spigot, disdaining to drink where his grandfather had. When Mr. Head realized this, he lost all hope. His face in the waning afternoon light looked ravaged and abandoned. He could feel the boy's steady hate, traveling at an even pace behind him and he knew that (if by some miracle they escaped being murdered in the city) it would continue just that way for the rest of his life. He knew that now he was wandering into a black strange place where nothing was like it had ever been before, a long old age without respect and an end that would be welcome because it would be the end.

As for Nelson, his mind had frozen around his grandfather's treachery as if he were trying to preserve it intact to present at the final judgment. He walked without looking to one side or the other, but every now and then his mouth would twitch and this was when he felt, from some remote place inside himself, a black mysterious form reach up as if it would melt his frozen vision in one hot grasp.

The sun dropped down behind a row of houses and hardly noticing, they passed into an elegant suburban section where mansions were set back from the road by lawns with birdbaths on them. Here everything was entirely deserted. For blocks they didn't pass even a dog. The big white houses were like partially submerged icebergs in the distance. There were no sidewalks, only drives, and these wound around and around in endless ridiculous circles. Nelson made no move to come nearer to Mr. Head. The old man felt that if he saw a sewer entrance he would drop down into it and let himself be carried away; and he could imagine the boy standing by, watching with only a slight interest, while he disappeared.

A loud bark jarred him to attention and he looked up to see a fat man approaching with two bulldogs. He waved both arms like someone shipwrecked on a desert island. "I'm lost!" he called. "I'm lost and can't find my way and me and this boy have got to catch this train and I can't find the station. Oh Gawd I'm lost! Oh hep me Gawd I'm lost!"

The man, who was bald-headed and had on golf knickers, asked him what train he was trying to catch and Mr. Head began to get out his tickets, trembling so violently he could hardly hold them. Nelson had come up to within fifteen feet and stood watching.

"Well," the fat man said, giving him back the tickets, "you won't have time to get back to town to make this but you can catch it at the suburb stop. That's three blocks from here," and he began explaining how to get there.

Mr. Head stared as if he were slowly returning from the dead and when the man had finished and gone off with the dogs jumping at his heels, he turned to Nelson and said breathlessly, "We're going to get home!"

The child was standing about ten feet away, his face bloodless under the gray hat. His eyes were triumphantly cold. There was no light in them, no feeling, no interest. He was merely there, a small figure, waiting. Home was nothing to him.

Mr. Head turned slowly. He felt he knew now what time would be like without seasons and what heat would be like without light and what man would be like without salvation. He didn't care if he never made the train and if it had not been for what suddenly caught his attention, like a cry out of the gathering dusk, he might have forgotten there was a station to go to.

He had not walked five hundred yards down the road when he saw, within reach of him, the plaster figure of a Negro sitting bent over on a low yellow brick fence that curved around a wide lawn. The Negro was about Nelson's size and he was pitched forward at an unsteady angle because the putty that held him to the wall had cracked. One of his eyes was entirely white and he held a piece of brown watermelon.

Mr. Head stood looking at him silently until Nelson stopped at a little distance. Then as the two of them stood there, Mr. Head breathed, "An artificial nigger!"

It was not possible to tell if the artificial Negro were meant to be young or old; he looked too miserable to be either. He was meant to look happy because his mouth was stretched up at the corners but the chipped eye and the angle he was cocked at gave him a wild look of misery instead.

"An artificial nigger!" Nelson repeated in Mr. Head's exact tone.

The two of them stood there with their necks forward at almost the same angle and their shoulders curved in almost exactly the same way and their hands trembling identically in their pockets. Mr. Head looked like an ancient child and Nelson like a miniature old man. They stood gazing at the artificial Negro as if they were faced with some great mystery, some monument to another's victory that brought them together in their common defeat. They could both feel it dissolving their differences like an action of mercy. Mr. Head had never known before what mercy felt like because he had been too good to deserve any, but he felt he knew now. He looked at Nelson and understood that he must say something to the child to show that he was still wise and in the look the boy returned he saw a hungry need for that assurance. Nelson's eyes seemed to implore him to explain once and for all the mystery of existence.

Mr. Head opened his lips to make a lofty statement and heard himself say, "They ain't got enough real ones here. They got to have an artificial one."

After a second, the boy nodded with a strange shivering about his mouth, and said, "Let's go home before we get ourselves lost again."

Their train glided into the suburb stop just as they reached the station and they boarded it together, and ten minutes before it was due to arrive at the junction, they went to the door and stood ready to jump off if it did not stop; but it did, just as the moon, restored to its full splendor, sprang from a cloud and flooded the clearing with light. As they stepped off, the sage grass was shivering gently in shades of silver and the clinkers under their feet glittered with a fresh black light. The treetops, fencing the junction like the protecting walls of a garden, were darker than the sky which was hung with gigantic white clouds illuminated like lanterns.

Mr. Head stood very still and felt the action of mercy touch him again but this time he knew that there were no words in the world that could name it. He understood that it grew out of agony, which is not denied to any man and which is given in strange ways to children. He understood it was all a man could carry into death to give his Maker and he suddenly burned with shame that he had so little of it to take with him. He stood appalled, judging himself with the thoroughness of God, while the action of mercy covered his pride like a flame and consumed it. He had never thought himself a great sinner before but he saw now that his true depravity had been hidden from him lest it cause him despair. He realized that he was forgiven for sins from the beginning of time, when he had conceived in his own heart the sin of Adam, until the present, when he had denied poor Nelson. He saw that no sin was too monstrous for him to claim as his own, and since God loved in proportion as He forgave, he felt ready at that instant to enter Paradise.

Nelson, composing his expression under the shadow of his hat brim, watched him with a mixture of fatigue and suspicion, but as the train glided past them and disappeared like a frightened serpent into the woods, even his face lightened and he muttered, "I'm glad I've went once, but I'll never go back again!"

Yuri Kazakov
1927–

Born in Moscow in 1927 of working-class parents, Kazakov played in jazz and symphony orchestras until his mid-twenties, then became a writer. He has spent much time in the remote regions east and north of the Urals stretching as far as the Barents Sea. A world of water and woods and weather, of animals, of hunters and fishers, is reflected in his greatly beloved stories.

The one that follows may not belong in this collection. The book in which I found it, Arcturus the Hunting Hound, was written for children. But I think it will speak to grown-up readers too, perhaps recalling for them, in its simpler way, Hemingway's early stories. Though an accepted Soviet writer, Kazakov seems to exist in an old-Russian, pantheistic climate of feeling unviolated by politics. In his work, to quote Nikishka's father's phrase, "everything is alive." It is good to be reminded by this songlike story that when we were children we too must have wondered what the stones think. Kazakov brings back the wonder.

Nikishka's Secrets

THE CABINS RAN out of the forest, ran out on the shore, and had nowhere else to run — they stopped, frightened, bunched up, and looked
out, bewitched, at the sea . . . The village stood all in a knot! In the
narrow alleys wooden bridges resonantly echoed every step. When
someone walked — you could hear it far away. The old women pressed
to the windows, looked, and listened: was somebody carrying salmon,
or going to the forest with a hunting bag, or just like that? . . . At night,
in the strange white night, if a chap hurried after a girl, again everything
was heard, and everybody knew who hurried after whom.

The village cabins with their high sheds were sensitive. They were
strongly built, and each had a long life — they remembered everything,
they knew everything. If a Pomor went away on a sailboat and it ran
over the waves, the village saw the broad dark sail and knew: he was
going to his fishery. If fishermen came in a motorboat from deep-sea
fishing, the village knew about them — what they brought and how the
fishing was. If an old man died, they prayed for him in their own fashion, read out of ancient books, laid him in the gloomy, sandy cemetery,
and again the village saw everything and sensitively accepted the weeping of the wives.

Everybody in the village loved Nikishka. Somehow he wasn't like the
rest — he was quiet and gentle, whereas all the children in the village
who helped the fishermen were lively and mischievous. He was about
eight years old, with a blond forelock, a pale, freckled face, big ears,
limp and thin, and eyes that didn't match: the left one was yellowish,
the right one turquoise. Sometimes he looked at you — and he was a
silly baby; he fixed his eyes on you another time — and he looked like
a wise old man.

Quiet and thoughtful was Nikishka. He kept away from children,
didn't play, liked to listen to conversation, spoke seldom and then with
questions: "And what's this?" "And why is that?" He was talkative only
with his father and mother. His voice was delicate and pleasant, like a
reed pipe, but he laughed in a deep voice like a person who is dumb:
"Hui-hui-hui!" The children teased him. The least thing and they'd run
and shout: "Nikishka-the-Silent! Silent One, laugh!" Then Nikishka
would be angry and feel hurt. He would hide in the shed, sit there alone,
rock his body, and whisper something. But it was nice in the shed: it
was dark, nobody went in there, you could think about different things,

and there was a strong smell of hay, and tar, and dry seaweed.

A horse stood saddled by Nikishka's porch. He was gnawing the wattle fence, chipping it with his big yellow teeth; he got tired of it, closed his eyes, hung his head, slumped down, bent one hind foot under, sighed deeply every other breath, and opened his nostrils wide. The horse stood, dozed, and the village already knew: Nikishka was going to his father at the fishery, eight miles away, along the shore, past mountains and forest.

Nikishka came out on the stoop with his mother. Over his shoulder was a sealskin knapsack, on his feet boots, on his head a cap, and around his thin neck a scarf: it was already cold — October outside.

"Keep going along the shore, all the way along the shore. Don't turn off to the side. You'll have mountains on the way. You'll pass those mountains, and then the path itself will show you. It's near from there. Don't lose your way. Look well . . . It's only eight miles; it's near!"

Nikishka stood mute, puffing softly, not listening very well to his mother. He climbed on the horse, got into the saddle, put his feet in the stirrups, and frowned:

"Giddap!"

The horse started off. On the way he woke up and put his ears back — he wanted to understand what kind of rider he had on him now. The cabins rocked past. "Tuk-tuk," the horse's shoes clattered on the bridge. The huts came to an end, and the bathhouses poured out to meet them. There were many bathhouses, every courtyard had its own — and all were different: if the master of the house was a good one, the bathhouse was good; if he was a poor master, the bathhouse was not so good. But now the bathhouses came to an end, too, the gardens of oats passed by, and the sea glistened on the left.

The horse crunched along the sand, over the damp seaweed. He looked askance at the sea, and his eyes rolled — he didn't like the sea — he wanted to go farther to the right, as far from the water as possible. But Nikishka knowingly jerked the left rein and kicked the horse with his heels. The horse submitted but went along on the very edge of the water, bending his neck and snorting.

Not far from the shore were stones. There were many of them, exposed by the ebb tide; they were black and wet. Over by the stones the waves broke into foam, boiled up into white surf, and rumbled impotently. Here, near the shore, it was altogether still — you could see the bright bottom where sparks of mother-of-pearl shells blazed up and disappeared. A transparent wave was licking the sand. Sea gulls sat on the stones and looked sleepily at the sea. When Nikishka rode up, they flew off quietly, glided headlong just over the water and suddenly — wings up, tail like a fan — they sat down on the water. The low sun shone brightly, the sea beneath glistened and seemed to bulge. Long capes of land floated in a blue haze, as if they hung over the sea.

Nikishka looked around. His unmatched eyes were radiant; he let his lips spread in a smile. He looked at the sun, at the bulging, fiery sea, and laughed:

"Hui-hui-hui! . . ."

Sandpipers were flying over the shore, calling sadly, clear as glass. They teetered on their tall legs beside the sea and ran right up to the water: the wave retreated — and they went after it along the wet; the wave returned — and they went back.

"Kuli-kuli . . ." murmured Nikishka. He stopped the horse and looked at how choice they were with their beaks like an awl.

And what will you not find in the sand by the sea! There were wet red jellyfish, left behind by the ebb tide, looking like bloody liver, and other kinds of jellyfish — with four little violet rings in the middle. There were starfish with purplish, twisted rays, and there were also the tracks of sea gulls, long and tangled, and right there, too, their lilac-and-white droppings. Seaweed lay in piles, touched by decay, giving out a heavy, damp smell. And the track of bare feet, too, stretched along right by the water, turned off to the forest, and trampled near a curious dark snag grown into the sand. Who walked there? Where did he go and what for?

Nikishka was enjoying himself. The horse kept crunching with his hoofs and snorting. Sometimes he stepped by chance on a jellyfish, and it would splatter over the sand like precious stones. It was empty in front, empty behind, empty to the left, empty to the right. On the left was the sea, on the right the forest. And what was in the forest? In the forest there was heather, and there were crooked pines, little ones, wicked ones, and the same kind of birches. There were also berries in the forest, sweet ones: cowberries and bilberries. And mushrooms: sticky boletus, firm saffron milkcaps, russulas with a little film and with pine needles sticking up on their caps. Bears walked in the forest and other animals, but there were no birds at all, only hazel hens calling delicately to one another. Grandfather Sozon said: "The birds have flown away for some reason. Time was you'd go to the forest with a hunting bag and you'd shoot a whole bag full. But now the birds have flown away for some reason, God be with them, they have gone away completely."

Rivers ran out of the forest to the sea, big ones and little ones. Over the big rivers wooden bridges had been built. The horse sniffed the logs and listened to the water sounding below. He would take a step, bend his neck, and look back.

"Giddap!" Nikishka would say quietly.

The horse would take another step. But the sound on such bridges is hollow, and the water below is dark as strong tea. All the rivers run from the marshes. There is no pure water, all of it is dark, and the sea near the river mouths casts yellow foam upon the sand.

That black thing grown into the sand over there was either a snag or maybe a dark, uneven stone. The horse would notice it from afar, prick up his ears, raise his head high, and try his best to get to the side — he was afraid.

"Don't you try and dive to the side," Nikishka said to the horse. "That's nothing. That's just a tree that was growing, and it rotted and got stuck in the sand. See, it's a snag? That's what it is, it's nothing to hurt you."

The horse listened carefully, quivered his hide, snorted, and carried Nikishka on, ever on and on. He listened to Nikishka. All the animals listened to him.

Now the mountains began. High and black, they fell in a sheer wall to the sea. Small pines and birches clung to the precipices — they looked at the sea and waited for trouble. And down below was stony scree: the stones were crawling down to the water to drink. There were many stones, piled one upon another. The horse walked more cautiously, sniffing, picking out where to put his feet. He walked and walked, got stubborn, stopped, and would go neither forward, nor back, nor to the side. Nowhere. Nikishka got down, took the horse by the bridle, and strode over the wet stones. The horse stretched out his neck, pressed his ears close, and stumbled after Nikishka, then cowered, shoes clicking, legs trembling. And the waves rolled noisily under his feet. "Shshshoo!" they ran up. "Ssss!" they ran back. "Shshshoo!" they ran up again.

No, the horse couldn't go on. It seemed to him that a watery abyss yawned on the left and that the sea was flowing in. It was making a lot of noise, while under his hoofs were stones — you couldn't escape, you couldn't run away! He stopped in terror, snorted, and showed his yellow teeth. Nikishka got angry. He jerked and pulled the bridle with all his strength. "Giddap!" he cried. The horse wouldn't go — he looked at Nikishka with quivering smoky violet eyes. Nikishka felt ashamed, came up, stroked the horse on the cheek, and whispered something gentle and caressing. The horse listened to Nikishka's whispering. He listened to the sound of the sea. He breathed heavily and swayed his sides. Where could he go? On the left was the sea, on the right the mountains, and there were stones before and behind. The horse gathered resolution, stumbled forward, and his shoes clicked anew.

At last they got out of the screes. Nikishka led the horse to a big stone, climbed into the saddle, and again the hoofs crunched along the sand and over the seaweed. And the land ahead kept putting capes out into the sea, like long, greedy fingers. Nikishka rode on — before him was a far-off blue cape. He rode up to it — interesting: and what lay over there, behind it? Behind it was another cape, extending still farther into the sea, and another, and another, and so on without end.

An imperceptible path was beginning, and the horse turned into it of his own accord. Nikishka fell to thinking. He looked around and wanted to understand this mystery, wanted everything he saw to reveal itself to him all at once. If you didn't understand this mystery, all you could do was look with longing, drink it in with your eyes, listen with your ears, and smell. And Nikishka looked around enchanted, lost in thought, while the path went ever farther from the sea and on through the forest. It grew still and golden. Under the horse's feet there were tongues — yellow, red, and orange. It smelled of moss. Everywhere there were mushrooms — saffron milkcaps and ruddy milkcaps. The whole forest was burning. Only the fir trees were green, and heather spread in flat little islands. The forest was clad in all its beauty, while from under the earth peered mossgrown stones, dark and brown, and standing separately were gray, disfigured, twisted firs and birches, looking strangely like apple trees.

If only he would meet someone! But nobody came; Nikishka was alone in the silent forest. Would he come to the dwelling soon? There was no one to ask, the pines and firs kept still, the stones looked mysteriously at Nikishka from under the ground. And suddenly in the midst of this speechlessness, of this dead silence and the sounds of inanimate things, there came a song. And you could hear someone tapping with an ax and could smell smoke. With ears perked up, the horse neighed loudly and trotted ahead. He smelled a dwelling. Nikishka rode out of the forest. Before him was a little cabin — his father's fishery. Everything was new, everything strong and in good order; smoke poured from the chimney; on a long barge-pole an antenna huddled; nets were drying on racks; it smelled of fish; and a sailboat lay on rollers, its black side greasy. On the stoop sat his father, tapping with an ax. He was making a stern oar and singing a song.

2

His father saw Nikishka and got up — a huge bearded man in high boots and tarpaulin tunic with a knife at his belt. His hands were red, his face brown, his beard fair, while his eyes under their heavy brows were sharp and intent.

"My little son has come!" the father said joyfully. "That's the dream I was dreaming . . . Well, how are things at home there? Everybody alive?"

"Alive!" answered Nikishka. He got off the horse, swayed, and stamped his feet. "The chairman gave the horse to Uncle Ivan, mamma sent me, and I went . . . I rode and rode, I got all worn out, and my back hurts."

"Ah, you're my fine lad!" the father said and caressed Nikishka, stroking his flaxen hair with his large hand. "I heard stamping but couldn't figure out who it was. And there was Nikishka! You weren't afraid to come?"

"No, it was all right. I saw birds, I saw mushrooms, and I talked to the horse. It's an intelligent horse. Here, this is for you — mamma put it on me," and Nikishka took off the knapsack. "But why did the stones look at me? Do they think, too? Doubtless those that lie in an awkward position roll over at night — your side can get all tired lying the whole day."

"Stones?" the father said and fell to thinking. "You have to suppose that stones are alive too. Everything is alive!"

"And do you understand what the birches talk about?"

"Why, doubtless they talk in their own language, birch language. You have to know their language. Else how can you understand!"

"But where is Uncle Ivan?"

"Uncle Ivan went to a neighboring fishery, to Kerzhenka. Recently some fishermen were going there in a motor sailboat, and they took him along — they've got a bathhouse there. We haven't any here, so that's why Uncle Ivan went."

"And when will he go to the village?"

"Tomorrow he'll go to the village, to get medical treatment. His legs, you see, are all broken down. He'll go on the horse, along the shore."

"And how will I go?"

"You will stay with me. You'll stay? We'll go salmon fishing."

"I'll stay!"

"Well, now! I'll go and unsaddle the horse."

The father went, caught the horse, and unsaddled him. Then he brought out a rope and tied the horse to a birch so he shouldn't go off to the forest. Nikishka went into the cabin: there was a strong smell of fish, the coals in the stove were smoldering, there was bread on the table and some bowls and spoons. The walls were pasted over with posters, and up on a shelf was a pile of newspapers. It was clean in the cabin, swept up. Gauntlets hung on a rope, foot-cloths and trousers were drying. Nikishka went out, walked all around the cabin and looked in the barn. The barn was open, it was never locked — there was nobody to lock out. Nikishka was about to go into the barn and sit there awhile and think about the day's happenings, when suddenly something alive showed up in the barn, something dark red, like a dim flame. Its eyes shone, a reddish gleam blazed in its eyes, like the sun before setting. A dog! A big, shaggy . . .

Nikishka squatted down and, all eyes, looked at the dog, then glanced around — his father couldn't see. Nikishka started talking to the dog:

"Adya . . . Ooorr! Hoo-hoorrr . . . hum!"

The dog was silent, sniffed and put his head to one side. One ear up, the other down, he thrashed his tail — he liked Nikishka. When Nikishka had had his fill of talking, he came out of the barn, and the dog ran behind him as if he had known him for ages. Nikishka looked at his father — how big and handsome he was, lit up by the sun, like a forest czar.

"Well, little son," his father said gaily, "we'll go after salmon right away! Just wait till I finish making the oar."

Nikishka went off a little and lay down on the warm sand. The dog ran up and lay down beside him, breathing fast. Nikishka closed his eyes. It seemed to him that he was still being rocked — that he was riding on the horse and that the sea gulls were endlessly flying over the sea, while the mountains and the forest went by. And someone was lightly singing a song, the voice now swelled, now died away. It was singing him to sleep, and the sun shone, while the sea kept saying: "Shshshoo!" as it rolled in, and "Ssss!" as it went back. The rotting seaweed smelled strong, it stupefied him, while clear as glass the sandpipers called: "Pee-peee! Pee-peee!"

Nikishka lay, neither sleeping nor dozing . . . The sand was warm, the dog was warm. He looked at Nikishka with fiery eyes and said: "Let's go to the forest, Nikishka!" "I'm going on the sea to watch for salmon!" Nikishka replied. But the dog kept on: "Let's go to the forest, I'll show you secrets. We'll hear what the birches whisper about, we'll find out what the stones think." Nikishka was curious about them. He was un-certain now whether to go on the sea or to the forest, but his father came up just at that moment with the new oar in his hand:

"Get up, little son, we'll go!"

Nikishka got up and went to the shore with his father. And the sea was glad: it blazed up, began to play, became blue, and seemed to beckon to them and spread out. The father leaned his chest against the sailboat and pushed it into the water. He seated Nikishka in the stern while he himself thumped along the water with his boots. But now he climbed into the sailboat, settled down between the oars, gave Nikishka a scull, and they pulled away from the shore and unfurled the sail. The shore rocked, the dog on the shore rocked . . . But the father rowed well, the waves slapped at the sailboat's ribs and flew up in spray. They sailed cautiously up to the trap, tied the sailboat to the pole, and the father rose and looked intently below, into the inmost recess — nothing there!

"Empty," the father whispered and sat down quite at peace.

Nikishka looked around. It was quiet roundabout, not a sound. A light breeze blew steadily, the sun shone, the sea blinded the eyes, the shore was far away, dark, going to either side. And it seemed to Nikishka that he had been here, had sat long ago, for years, watching for salmon and thinking about something. Or did he dream that?

"The tide has begun," said the father. "The water went away, and now it is coming back."

"It's fair weather," quietly answered Nikishka. "It's nice! You can see the bottom . . ."

"Of course! The salmon likes a bright bottom. It doesn't need stones or seaweed. It likes to move on the bottom, in the mid-tide. High water or low tide — that doesn't suit it, it doesn't like that, but moves, I say, in the mid-tide."

"And that's the beetle?"

"That? That's the beetle, little son. To beat the salmon with. It is big and strong, so you can't pull it out, you'll get in a sweat. So we beat it with the beetle."

"And what if the salmon jumps out?"

"Why, no. We've got a trap for that. You see that cloth? That's a net. Those are walls on necklaces with drawstrings, and down below . . . Take a look, take a look!"

Nikishka leaned over the side, shaded his unmatched eyes with his hands, looked into the water, into the depths, and saw greenish patches of light on the bottom, saw the meshes of the net.

"You see? Look, down below there's a net, too — that's the bottom — that's the trap now, and over there are two gates, over there where the two poles stick up side by side, the gates are there . . . The salmon goes along, enters the gates — and into the trap, and in the trap we beat it. When it goes through the gates, the way is barred, we lift up the bottom and we beat the fish."

"I know," said Nikishka, remembering something.

"That's what I say, too — you know," agreed the father. "You know everything."

"But why do the boys tease me?"

"They are little fools, don't listen to them. They are mischievous boys, everything is mischief with them, but you are a good boy, quiet and intelligent, so they tease you. Don't listen to them, you are cleverer than all of them."

"That's because I think a lot."

"But don't think a lot and don't think a little, but like this: if you want to — think; if you don't want to — don't think."

"But now here's what I am thinking: where does this water in the sea go to and afterwards flows back? The rivers — they run into the sea, but where does the sea run into?"

"The sea? Hm!" the father scratched his beard, looked to the horizon and imagined. "The sea, we have to think, goes into the throat, into the Arctic Ocean. And from the ocean it pours into other oceans."

"And are there lots of other oceans?"

"Lots of them, little son. And there are many countries on earth."

"And were you there?"

"I was! In Italy and France I've been, and in Norway when I was a sailor."

"And what's Italy like?"

"Italy? Italy, little son, is a nice country. It's warm there, lots of sun, all kinds of fruits grow there, sweet and delicious. Everybody there is suntanned, they go around undressed, and there's no winter at all."

"How — no winter?"

"Like that. There's no snow, no frost, nothing. Sun the year around."

"Nice!" sighed Nikishka. "I'd like to go there!"

"And you will," said the father. "You'll grow up, study to be a captain, they'll give you a big ship in Arkhangelsk, and you'll go past Norway, around the earth, right into the Mediterranean Sea."

"And were you a captain?"

"No, I was a sailor. I've been everything: woodcutter, hunter, fisherman, trapper . . ."

"Oh, look there, what's that?"

"Where?"

"Over there it seems . . ."

"Ah! That's a seal. A seal, little son, swam up to take a look at us."

"I know. But where does he live?"

"He lives in the sea. In the daytime he earns his living catching fish, and at night he swims to the shore and sleeps on the stones in remote places."

"And why do they kill him? People don't eat him, you know."

"His pelt is a good one and he has lots of fat. He's easy to kill, he's stupid; they steal up and shoot him with a rifle. And we go after him in all sorts of ways: sometimes on sailboats, sometimes on icebreakers. Now more and more on icebreakers."

"But if the weather is bad, is it scary on a sailboat?"

"Oh, it's scary. You'll grow up and then I'll take you hunting animals — in time you'll get to know our little northern sea. Over there where the sparkles are," the father said, pointing with his hand, "where the sun is, there's a nice little island, Zhizhgin it's called. The seals herd there. On this Zhizhgin, the Pomors always earn a living. There's a little cabin on remote rocks. The Pomors go there in their sailboats, live there, eat there, wait for the wind, for good weather, that is. In good weather they put out to sea, shoot seals, and at night sleep on an ice floe. Sometimes in bad weather they get carried so fast, so fast — you shout with all your might and say good-by to your life. If a man is lucky, it will let go of him soon, the wind will change, it will calm down. But him whom it carries into the throat, past Kanin's Nose, and into the ocean . . . there, only if they spot him from an airplane will they save him, otherwise . . ."

"Salmon!" Nakishka whispered suddenly.

"Let's go!" The father moved to the nose, got down on his knees, and leaned over the trap. "And it's true! Well, heaven bless us, I'm going to lift the bottom, and you hold the beetle . . ."

Quickly the father untied the sailboat and rowed sideways around the trap to the gates. The gates came in from the sides; the father leaned down and put his hands in the water. Nikishka held onto his perch. And in the depths something was silently rushing around — something big, strong, and alive — the poles quivered, the guy-ropes vibrated like the strings of a harp. The nylon net rustled, and the father drew it to the sailboat. Nikishka stretched out his neck and looked down. Now there was less and less room for the salmon. Twice already it had lashed the surface. The father held the bottom he had picked up in one hand; with the other he felt around for the beetle. He found it, raised his hand, and waited for the moment to strike, while the salmon fought ever more violently, ever harder, struck noisily against the bottom of the sailboat, would not yield, and doused the fishermen with water. Now the fish was in full view, as if in a bowl of foam. If the salmon could cry out, it would cry out in terror. The father struck it with all his might on the head, and at once everything was cut short — the salmon became limp and flopped on its side. The father seized the fish by the gills, with an effort drew it into the sailboat, and the salmon shuffled down under Nikishka's feet. Nikishka looked at it with steadfast gaze, but it was still alive, its gills still quivered, its scales still contracted — a huge silvery fish with dark back, with lower jaw bent upward, and with large smoke-colored eyes.

The father let the bottom drop, got the sailboat away from the trap, wiped his face on his sleeve, wiped his hands, smelling of fish, on his trousers, and looked merrily at the salmon and at Nikishka.

"That's how we got her!"

Nikishka was pale, amazed, and could not collect himself. And again the sailboat was tied to the pole and rocked up and down on the wave. The father was silent. Laying his powerful red hands on his knees, he rested. As for Nikishka, now that he had become a little used to the salmon, he brought to mind his father's words about seals.

"No, I'd rather be a captain! I don't want to kill seals: they don't bother anybody . . ."

"You could be a captain," agreed the father and looked at the sky: "Take a look, clouds are drawing over the sky, hiding the sun. We'll go home soon . . . You can be a captain or you can also be an engineer . . ."

"An engineer? What for?"

"What do you mean — what for? You'll build something, that's a business, too. Even for us, you know: you could build an asphalt road along the shore, construct landings, lights will burn, machines will whirr . . ."

Nikishka sank into thought. He looked at the distant shore: how dark it was, how uninhabited. . . .

"All right," he decided. "I'll be an engineer."

"Well, now. We'll sit a little longer — and then home. I've got some fish there. Recently in the morning I was examining the net on the sea-shore, and many little fish had got caught. We'll make a fish soup and boil up some tea — it'll be nice to sleep, too. But now let's be quiet . . . We have to watch for salmon."

Everything was still, the sea kept still, the sailboat rocked noiselessly, the shore kept still, not a sound was borne from there. The low sun had already disappeared in the clouds; everything roundabout had grown dark and sad. And there was nobody anywhere! Everywhere it was empty, uninhabited. Occasional sea gulls flew, hazel hens hid in the forest on the shore, and the two fishermen in the sailboat rocked, and with them rocked the sleeping salmon.

3

The stove droned and crackled. It was warm in the cabin, twilight outside. The father lit the lamp and set a pail of water between his feet — he was scaling small spotted cod and thin navaga for a fish soup. And Nikishka dozed. He had had his fill of talking for the day, his fill of looking, listening, and rocking. He was tired — he was dozing and thinking goodness-knows-what.

The weather was changing sharply. An up-river dinner wind was blowing, you could hear the noise of the sea, in the west the sky grew greener and greener, a bluish tint showed, and the air became glassy: an evening of unusual purity began to come on, with stars and a lackluster heavenly light.

The red-haired dog was lying by the stove, sleeping and quivering in his sleep. Nikishka started up and listened with half an ear — his father was talking about something peaceful, long familiar, close: he was talking about fish, about the sea, about boats, about the village, about winds — midnight wind, shore wind, prankster wind, dinner wind . . . His father was big; he was bending low over the pail; his hair, flaxen like Nikishka's, hung down over his eyes; his beard was fluffed up. He himself was motionless, only his hands moved. The knife glittered, the fish fell in the pail with a splash, and his father's shadow on the wall gave a start. His father talked on and on in a low voice. Nikishka closed his eyes and saw his native land with its sea, its forests and its lakes, saw the sun, the silent birds, the strange animals. It seemed to him that he was just on the verge of learning some secret known to nobody else, that he would utter a mysterious word and the silence would be broken, and everything would start talking to Nikishka, and everything would all at once become comprehensible to him. But the word didn't come; the secret was not revealed. Nikishka heard his father's even voice and heard and saw much more besides.

He saw what the red-haired dog was dreaming about. He was dreaming about the forest, about terrible, unknown beasts who were attacking him from all sides. The dog ran and barked with fear, his only rescue was Nikishka. Nikishka heard — the stones beginning to whisper, the sea resounding, the trees in the forest rustling, someone about to call out . . . He saw — his father rocking on an ice floe in a storm and shouting; he saw, besides, a huge, angry salmon approaching the shore, swimming on the bottom, on the clear bottom, while behind it were others — they were looking for the hiding place of fathers.

The wood in the stove droned and crackled . . . Nikishka's father went out of the cabin to pour water from the pail; you could hear him walking behind the wall, getting wood, then entering the cabin. The wood dropped with a crash by the stove. The red-haired dog jumped up. Nikishka gave a start and opened his eyes.

"Are you asleep, little son?" his father said, bending over him. "Did you see what's going on in the open? Such a clear night! Take a look, go take a look . . ."

Nikishka went out — it was dark, cold, and a raw wind was blowing. The sun had long set, the forest couldn't be seen, but up above, among the stars, an oblong-shaped spot shone like a gem. It was as if a little cloud was floating at a terrible height, lit up by the last light of the sun. But now the little cloud slowly and uncertainly drew out in length, puffed up in the middle, and bent like a rainbow arch between west and east. Nikishka looked, his head tossed back. The door slammed, the dog ran up to Nikishka, and after the dog the father came out and also lifted up his head.

Vague shadows began to pass over the cloud. The colors kept changing, getting bluer, deeper — from milky to blue. It seemed to Nikishka that the cloud was straining, was trying to burn with a ruby-colored flame, trying to take over the place of the vanished sun. Stronger and stronger glimmered the colors, more and more light poured from above. But its efforts were vain: everything faded, and again great vague shadows moved sadly over the arch of light.

Nikishka looked; his father looked and was silent; the dog looked and was also silent; the horse was silent — he had fallen asleep by the birch. Everything was silent. Only the sea was brightened by the heavenly fire and sounded and resounded.

Now the light went out entirely. Nikishka went into the warm cabin and got on the bed, feet and all. The dog lay down by the stove. The father set the fish soup on the fire and put on the tea kettle.

Presently Nikishka would go to bed and dream extraordinary dreams. The village would stand around him, the cabins with their window-eyes and the forest would come close, the stones and mountains, the horse and the red-haired dog would appear, the sea gulls would come flying, the sandpipers would run together on their thin legs, the salmon would rise out of the sea — all of them would come to Nikishka. They would begin to look at him and wait silently for Nikishka's hidden word — so they could reveal to him all together the secrets of their dumb souls.

GABRIEL GARCÍA MÁRQUEZ
1928–

*Winner of the Nobel Prize for literature in 1982, the Colombian García
Márquez in 1970 took the Western literary world by storm with his realistic-
fantastic* One Hundred Years of Solitude. *"The Great American Novel" has
become a cliché to smile at, but García Márquez's epic narrative may indeed
amount to something like the Great Latin American Novel.*

*It is useful to remember that the writer, who seems often to be forcing
the imagination beyond its natural limits, spent many of his first forty years
as a working journalist in Colombia, Paris, Rome, Caracas, Havana, New
York, and Mexico City. His "myths" float up from an infrastructure of relentlessly scrutinized reality, that of his unhappy native land and by extension all of Latin America. His magic and his realism exist together. His
Macondo (the setting of* One Hundred Years *and many of his stories) is no
Erewhon. It is there.*

*Somewhere he speaks of "the mistaken and absurd world of rational crea-
tures." The phrase locates him. His fallen angels and charismatic dead and
submarine cities and corpses that double for men are not the mere self-
indulgences of a lively — or deadly — fantasy. They are cautionary metaphors intended to remind us of the mistakes we commit, the absurdities into
which we fall, when we persist in our exclusive trust in reason. Behind his
approach lies Latin America's nightmare history. As we more fortunate
North Americans begin to acknowledge this nightmare we also begin to
enter García Márquez's world of wonders and brutality.*

*"Death Constant Beyond Love" is partly about his obsessive theme, "the
erosion of death." But it is also about political corruption and the straits
that constrict the human soul in a community where love has no chance
against terror.*

Death Constant Beyond Love

SENATOR ONÉSIMO SÁNCHEZ had six months and eleven days to go
before his death when he found the woman of his life. He met her in
Rosal del Virrey, an illusory village which by night was the furtive wharf
for smugglers' ships; and on the other hand, in broad daylight looked
like the most useless inlet on the desert, facing a sea that was arid and
without direction and so far from everything no one would have suspected that someone capable of changing the destiny of anyone lived
there. Even its name was a kind of joke, because the only rose in that
village was being worn by Senator Onésimo Sánchez himself on the
same afternoon when he met Laura Farina.

It was an unavoidable stop in the electoral campaign he made every
four years. The carnival wagons had arrived in the morning. Then came
the trucks with the rented Indians who were carried into the towns in
order to enlarge the crowds at public ceremonies. A short time before
eleven o'clock, along with the music and rockets and jeeps of the retinue,
the ministerial automobile, the color of strawberry soda, arrived. Senator Onésimo Sánchez was placid and weatherless inside the air-condi-
tioned car, but as soon as he opened the door he was shaken by a gust
of fire and his shirt of pure silk was soaked in a kind of light-colored
soup and he felt many years older and more alone than ever. In real
life he had just turned forty-two, had been graduated from Göttingen
with honors as a metallurgical engineer, and was an avid reader, although without much reward, of badly translated Latin classics. He was
married to a radiant German woman who had given him five children
and they were all happy in their home, he the happiest of all until they
told him, three months before, that he would be dead forever by next
Christmas.

While the preparations for the public rally were being completed, the
senator managed to have an hour alone in the house they had set aside
for him to rest in. Before he lay down he put in a glass of drinking water
the rose he had kept alive all across the desert, lunched on the diet cere-
als that he took with him so as to avoid the repeated portions of fried
goat that were waiting for him during the rest of the day, and he took
several analgesic pills before the time prescribed so that he would have
the remedy ahead of the pain. Then he put the electric fan close to the
hammock and stretched out naked for fifteen minutes in the shadow of

the rose, making a great effort at mental distraction so as not to think about death while he dozed. Except for the doctors, no one knew that he had been sentenced to a fixed term, for he had decided to endure his secret all alone, with no change in his life, not because of pride but out of shame.

He felt in full control of his will when he appeared in public again at three in the afternoon, rested and clean, wearing a pair of coarse linen slacks and a floral shirt, and with his soul sustained by the anti-pain pills. Nevertheless, the erosion of death was much more pernicious than he had supposed, for as he went up onto the platform he felt a strange disdain for those who were fighting for the good luck to shake his hand, and he didn't feel sorry as he had at other times for the groups of bare-foot Indians who could scarcely bear the hot saltpeter coals of the sterile little square. He silenced the applause with a wave of his hand, almost with rage, and he began to speak without gestures, his eyes fixed on the sea, which was sighing with heat. His measured, deep voice had the quality of calm water, but the speech that had been memorized and ground out so many times had not occurred to him in the nature of telling the truth, but, rather, as the opposite of a fatalistic pronounce-ment by Marcus Aurelius in the fourth book of his *Meditations*.

"We are here for the purpose of defeating nature," he began, against all his convictions. "We will no longer be foundlings in our own country, orphans of God in a realm of thirst and bad climate, exiles in our own land. We will be different people, ladies and gentlemen, we will be a great and happy people."

There was a pattern to his circus. As he spoke his aides threw clusters of paper birds into the air and the artificial creatures took on life, flew about the platform of planks, and went out to sea. At the same time, other men took some prop trees with felt leaves out of the wagons and planted them in the saltpeter soil behind the crowd. They finished by setting up a cardboard façade with make-believe houses of red brick that had glass windows, and with it they covered the miserable real-life shacks.

The senator prolonged his speech with two quotations in Latin in or-der to give the farce more time. He promised rainmaking machines, portable breeders for table animals, the oils of happiness which would make vegetables grow in the saltpeter and clumps of pansies in the win-dow boxes. When he saw that his fictional world was all set up, he pointed to it. "That's the way it will be for us, ladies and gentlemen," he shouted. "Look! That's the way it will be for us."

The audience turned around. An ocean liner made of painted paper was passing behind the houses and it was taller than the tallest houses in the artificial city. Only the senator himself noticed that since it had been set up and taken down and carried from one place to another the superimposed cardboard town had been eaten away by the terrible climate and that it was almost as poor and dusty as Rosal del Virrey.

For the first time in twelve years, Nelson Farina didn't go to greet the senator. He listened to the speech from his hammock amidst the remains of his siesta, under the cool bower of a house of unplaned boards which he had built with the same pharmacist's hands with which he had drawn and quartered his first wife. He had escaped from Devil's Island and appeared in Rosal del Virrey on a ship loaded with innocent macaws, with a beautiful and blasphemous black woman he had found in Paramaribo and by whom he had a daughter. The woman died of natural causes a short while later and she didn't suffer the fate of the other, whose pieces had fertilized her own cauliflower patch, but was buried whole and with her Dutch name in the local cemetery. The daughter had inherited her color and her figure along with her father's yellow and astonished eyes, and he had good reason to imagine that he was rearing the most beautiful woman in the world.

Ever since he had met Senator Onésimo Sánchez during his first electoral campaign, Nelson Farina had begged for his help in getting a false identity card which would place him beyond the reach of the law. The senator, in a friendly but firm way, had refused. Nelson Farina never gave up, and for several years, every time he found the chance, he would repeat his request with a different recourse. But this time he stayed in his hammock, condemned to rot alive in that burning den of buccaneers. When he heard the final applause, he lifted his head, and looking over the boards of the fence, he saw the back side of the farce: the props for the buildings, the framework of the trees, the hidden illusionists who were pushing the ocean liner along. He spat without rancor.

"*Merde,*" he said. "*C'est le Blacamén de la politique.*"

After the speech, as was customary, the senator took a walk through the streets of the town in the midst of the music and the rockets and was besieged by the townspeople, who told him their troubles. The senator listened to them good-naturedly and he always found some way to console everybody without having to do them any difficult favors. A woman up on the roof of a house with her six youngest children managed to make herself heard over the uproar and the fireworks.

"I'm not asking for much, Senator," she said. "Just a donkey to haul water from Hanged Man's Well."

The senator noticed the six thin children. "What became of your husband?" he asked.

"He went to find his fortune on the island of Aruba," the woman answered good-humoredly, "and what he found was a foreign woman, the kind that put diamonds on their teeth."

The answer brought on a roar of laughter.

"All right," the senator decided, "you'll get your donkey."

A short while later an aide of his brought a good pack donkey to the woman's house and on the rump it had a campaign slogan written in indelible paint so that no one would ever forget that it was a gift from the senator.

Along the short stretch of street he made other, smaller gestures, and he even gave a spoonful of medicine to a sick man who had had his bed brought to the door of his house so he could see him pass. At the last corner, through the boards of the fence, he saw Nelson Farina in his hammock, looking ashen and gloomy, but nonetheless the senator greeted him, with no show of affection.

"Hello, how are you?"

Nelson Farina turned in his hammock and soaked him in the sad amber of his look.

"*Moi, vous savez,*" he said.

His daughter came out into the yard when she heard the greeting. She was wearing a cheap, faded Guajiro Indian robe, her head was decorated with colored bows, and her face was painted as protection against the sun, but even in that state of disrepair it was possible to imagine that there had never been another so beautiful in the whole world. The senator was left breathless. "I'll be damned!" he breathed in surprise. "The Lord does the craziest things!"

That night Nelson Farina dressed his daughter up in her best clothes and sent her to the senator. Two guards armed with rifles who were nodding from the heat in the borrowed house ordered her to wait on the only chair in the vestibule.

The senator was in the next room meeting with the important people of Rosal del Virrey, whom he had gathered together in order to sing for them the truths he had left out of his speeches. They looked so much like all the ones he always met in all the towns in the desert that even the senator himself was sick and tired of that perpetual nightly session. His shirt was soaked with sweat and he was trying to dry it on his body with the hot breeze from an electric fan that was buzzing like a horse fly in the heavy heat of the room.

"We, of course, can't eat paper birds," he said. "You and I know that the day there are trees and flowers in this heap of goat dung, the day there are shad instead of worms in the water holes, that day neither you nor I will have anything to do here, do I make myself clear?"

No one answered. While he was speaking, the senator had torn a sheet off the calendar and fashioned a paper butterfly out of it with his hands. He tossed it with no particular aim into the air current coming from the fan and the butterfly flew about the room and then went out through the half-open door. The senator went on speaking with a control aided by the complicity of death.

"Therefore," he said, "I don't have to repeat to you what you already know too well: that my reelection is a better piece of business for you than it is for me, because I'm fed up with stagnant water and Indian sweat, while you people, on the other hand, make your living from it."

Laura Farina saw the paper butterfly come out. Only she saw it because the guards in the vestibule had fallen asleep on the steps, hugging their rifles. After a few turns, the large lithographed butterfly unfolded completely, flattened against the wall, and remained stuck there. Laura Farina tried to pull it off with her nails. One of the guards, who woke up with the applause from the next room, noticed her vain attempt.

"It won't come off," he said sleepily. "It's painted on the wall."

Laura Farina sat down again when the men began to come out of the meeting. The senator stood in the doorway of the room with his hand on the latch, and he only noticed Laura Farina when the vestibule was empty.

"What are you doing here?"

"*C'est de la part de mon père,*" she said.

The senator understood. He scrutinized the sleeping guards, then he scrutinized Laura Farina, whose unusual beauty was even more demanding than his pain, and he resolved then that death had made his decision for him.

"Come in," he told her.

Laura Farina was struck dumb standing in the doorway to the room: thousands of bank notes were floating in the air, flapping like the butterfly. But the senator turned off the fan and the bills were left without air and alighted on the objects in the room.

"You see," he said, smiling, "even shit can fly."

Laura Farina sat down on a schoolboy's stool. Her skin was smooth and firm, with the same color and the same solar density as crude oil, her hair was the mane of a young mare, and her huge eyes were brighter than the light. The senator followed the thread of her look and finally found the rose, which had been tarnished by the saltpeter.

"It's a rose," he said.

"Yes," she said with a trace of perplexity. "I learned what they were in Riohacha."

The senator sat down on an army cot, talking about roses as he unbuttoned his shirt. On the side where he imagined his heart to be inside his chest he had a corsair's tattoo of a heart pierced by an arrow. He threw the soaked shirt to the floor and asked Laura Farina to help him off with his boots.

She knelt down facing the cot. The senator continued to scrutinize her, thoughtfully, and while she was untying the laces he wondered which one of them would end up with the bad luck of that encounter.

"You're just a child," he said.

"Don't you believe it," she said. "I'll be nineteen in April."

The senator became interested.

"What day?"

"The eleventh," she said.

The senator felt better. "We're both Aries," he said. And smiling, he added:

"It's the sign of solitude."

Laura Farina wasn't paying attention because she didn't know what to do with the boots. The senator, for his part, didn't know what to do with Laura Farina, because he wasn't used to sudden love affairs and, besides, he knew that the one at hand had its origins in indignity. Just to have some time to think, he held Laura Farina tightly between his knees, embraced her about the waist, and lay down on his back on the cot. Then he realized that she was naked under her dress, for her body gave off the dark fragrance of an animal of the woods, but her heart was frightened and her skin disturbed by a glacial sweat.

"No one loves us," he sighed.

Laura Farina tried to say something, but there was only enough air for her to breathe. He laid her down beside him to help her, he put out the light and the room was in the shadow of the rose. She abandoned herself to the mercies of her fate. The senator caressed her slowly, seeking her with his hand, barely touching her, but where he expected to find her, he came across something iron that was in the way.

"What have you got there?"

"A padlock," she said.

"What in hell!" the senator said furiously and asked what he knew only too well. "Where's the key?"

Laura Farina gave a breath of relief.

"My papa has it," she answered. "He told me to tell you to send one of your people to get it and to send along with him a written promise that you'll straighten out his situation."

The senator grew tense. "Frog bastard," he murmured indignantly. Then he closed his eyes in order to relax and he met himself in the darkness. *Remember,* he remembered, *that whether it's you or someone else, it won't be long before you'll be dead and it won't be long before your name won't even be left.*

He waited for the shudder to pass.

"Tell me one thing," he asked then. "What have you heard about me?"

"Do you want the honest-to-God truth?"

"The honest-to-God truth."

"Well," Laura Farina ventured, "they say you're worse than the rest because you're different."

The senator didn't get upset. He remained silent for a long time with his eyes closed, and when he opened them again he seemed to have returned from his most hidden instincts.

"Oh, what the hell," he decided. "Tell your son of a bitch of a father that I'll straighten out his situation."

"If you want, I can go get the key myself," Laura Farina said.

The senator held her back.

"Forget about the key," he said, "and sleep awhile with me. It's good to be with someone when you're so alone."

Then she laid his head on her shoulder with her eyes fixed on the rose. The senator held her about the waist, sank his face into woods-animal armpit, and gave in to terror. Six months and eleven days later he would die in that same position, debased and repudiated because of the public scandal with Laura Farina and weeping with rage at dying without her.

CYNTHIA OZICK

1928–

The intimidatingly intelligent Cynthia Ozick is a respected essayist, critic, translator, and novelist. It is her short stories and novellas, however, that have won her her high reputation. She uses a profound knowledge of Jewish tradition and an un-self-conscious feeling for Yiddish rhythms to shape, in language ranging from the vernacular to the baroque, fictions in which the comic and the mystical are often blended. Her view of life is unconcessive; she is not a comfortable writer.

"The Shawl" will endure as one of the few literary masterpieces directly inspired by that great technological achievement of the Germans, the gas chamber. Its two thousand words of almost intolerable intensity develop, with the shawl as symbol, the basic theme of the human — indeed animal — will to survive.

But always at a cost. That cost is described in a remarkable sequel, a novella whose length prevents inclusion in this collection. Called "Rosa," it deals with Rosa's later life in Miami. Madness, whose inception we witness in "The Shawl," is its real subject, the special madness peculiar to our period, so increasingly efficient in the production of displaced minds as well as bodies.

The Shawl

STELLA, COLD, COLD the coldness of hell. How they walked on the roads together, Rosa with Magda curled up between sore breasts, Magda wound up in the shawl. Sometimes Stella carried Magda. But she was jealous of Magda. A thin girl of fourteen, too small, with thin breasts of her own, Stella wanted to be wrapped in a shawl, hidden away, asleep, rocked by the march, a baby, a round infant in arms. Magda took Rosa's nipple, and Rosa never stopped walking, a walking cradle. There was not enough milk; sometimes Magda sucked air; then she screamed. Stella was ravenous. Her knees were tumors on sticks, her elbows chicken bones.

Rosa did not feel hunger; she felt light, not like someone walking but like someone in a faint, in trance, arrested in a fit, someone who is already a floating angel, alert and seeing everything, but in the air, not there, not touching the road. As if teetering on the tips of her fingernails. She looked into Magda's face through a gap in the shawl: a squirrel in a nest, safe, no one could reach her inside the little house of the shawl's windings. The face, very round, a pocket mirror of a face: but it was not Rosa's bleak complexion, dark like cholera, it was another kind of face altogether, eyes blue as air, smooth feathers of hair nearly as yellow as the Star sewn into Rosa's coat. You could think she was one of *their* babies.

Rosa, floating, dreamed of giving Magda away in one of the villages. She could leave the line for a minute and push Magda into the hands of any woman on the side of the road. But if she moved out of line they might shoot. And even if she fled the line for half a second and pushed the shawl-bundle at a stranger, would the woman take it? She might be surprised, or afraid; she might drop the shawl, and Magda would fall out and strike her head and die. The little round head. Such a good child, she gave up screaming, and sucked now only for the taste of the drying nipple itself. The neat grip of the tiny gums. One mite of a tooth tip sticking up in the bottom gum, how shining, an elfin tombstone of white marble gleaming there. Without complaining, Magda relinquished Rosa's teats, first the left, then the right; both were cracked, not a sniff of milk. The duct crevice extinct, a dead volcano, blind eye, chill hole, so Magda took the corner of the shawl and milked it instead. She sucked and sucked, flooding the threads with wetness. The shawl's good flavor, milk of linen.

It was a magic shawl, it could nourish an infant for three days and three nights. Magda did not die, she stayed alive, although very quiet. A peculiar smell, of cinnamon and almonds, lifted out of her mouth. She held her eyes open every moment, forgetting how to blink or nap, and Rosa and sometimes Stella studied their blueness. On the road they raised one burden of a leg after another and studied Magda's face. "Aryan," Stella said, in a voice grown as thin as a string; and Rosa thought how Stella gazed at Magda like a young cannibal. And the time that Stella said "Aryan," it sounded to Rosa as if Stella had really said "Let us devour her."

But Magda lived to walk. She lived that long, but she did not walk very well, partly because she was only fifteen months old, and partly because the spindles of her legs could not hold up her fat belly. It was fat with air, full and round. Rosa gave almost all her food to Magda, Stella gave nothing; Stella was ravenous, a growing child herself, but not growing much. Stella did not menstruate. Rosa did not menstruate. Rosa was ravenous, but also not; she learned from Magda how to drink the taste of a finger in one's mouth. They were in a place without pity, all pity was annihilated in Rosa, she looked at Stella's bones without pity. She was sure that Stella was waiting for Magda to die so she could put her teeth into the little thighs.

Rosa knew Magda was going to die very soon; she should have been dead already, but she had been buried away deep inside the magic shawl, mistaken there for the shivering mound of Rosa's breasts; Rosa clung to the shawl as if it covered only herself. No one took it away from her. Magda was mute. She never cried. Rosa hid her in the barracks, under the shawl, but she knew that one day someone would inform; or one day someone, not even Stella, would steal Magda to eat her. When Magda began to walk Rosa knew that Magda was going to die very soon, something would happen. She was afraid to fall asleep; she slept with the weight of her thigh on Magda's body; she was afraid she would smother Magda under her thigh. The weight of Rosa was becoming less and less; Rosa and Stella were slowly turning into air.

Magda was quiet, but her eyes were horribly alive, like blue tigers. She watched. Sometimes she laughed — it seemed a laugh, but how could it be? Magda had never seen anyone laugh. Still, Magda laughed at her shawl when the wind blew its corners, the bad wind with pieces of black in it, that made Stella's and Rosa's eyes tear. Magda's eyes were always clear and tearless. She watched like a tiger. She guarded her shawl. No one could touch it; only Rosa could touch it. Stella was not allowed. The shawl was Magda's own baby, her pet, her little sister. She tangled herself up in it and sucked on one of the corners when she wanted to be very still.

Then Stella took the shawl away and made Magda die.

Afterward Stella said: "I was cold."

And afterward she was always cold, always. The cold went into her heart: Rosa saw that Stella's heart was cold. Magda flopped onward with her little pencil legs scribbling this way and that, in search of the shawl; the pencils faltered at the barracks opening, where the light began. Rosa saw and pursued. But already Magda was in the square outside the barracks, in the jolly light. It was the roll-call arena. Every morning Rosa had to conceal Magda under the shawl against a wall of the barracks and go out and stand in the arena with Stella and hundreds of others, sometimes for hours, and Magda, deserted, was quiet under the shawl, sucking on her corner. Every day Magda was silent, and so she did not die. Rosa saw that today Magda was going to die, and at the same time a fearful joy ran in Rosa's two palms, her fingers were on fire, she was astonished, febrile: Magda, in the sunlight, swaying on her pencil legs, was howling. Ever since the drying up of Rosa's nipples, ever since Magda's last scream on the road, Magda had been devoid of any syllable; Magda was a mute. Rosa believed that something had gone wrong with her vocal cords, with her windpipe, with the cave of her larynx; Magda was defective, without a voice; perhaps she was deaf; there might be something amiss with her intelligence; Magda was dumb. Even the laugh that came when the ash-stippled wind made a clown out of Magda's shawl was only the air-blown showing of her teeth. Even when the lice, head lice and body lice, crazed her so that she became as wild as one of the big rats that plundered the barracks at daybreak looking for carrion, she rubbed and scratched and kicked and bit and rolled without a whimper. But now Magda's mouth was spilling a long viscous rope of clamor.

"Maaaa —"

It was the first noise Magda had ever sent out from her throat since the drying up of Rosa's nipples.

"Maaaa . . . aaa!"

Again! Magda was wavering in the perilous sunlight of the arena, scrabbling on such pitiful little bent shins. Rosa saw. She saw that Magda was grieving for the loss of her shawl, she saw that Magda was going to die. A tide of commands hammered in Rosa's nipples: Fetch, get, bring! But she did not know which to go after first, Magda or the shawl. If she jumped out into the arena to snatch Magda up, the howling would not stop, because Magda would still not have the shawl; but if she ran back into the barracks to find the shawl, and if she found it, and if she came after Magda holding it and shaking it, then she would get Magda back, Magda would put the shawl in her mouth and turn dumb again.

Rosa entered the dark. It was easy to discover the shawl. Stella was heaped under it, alseep in her thin bones. Rosa tore the shawl free and flew — she could fly, she was only air — into the arena. The sunheat murmured of another life, of butterflies in summer. The light was placid, mellow. On the other side of the steel fence, far away, there were green meadows speckled with dandelions and deep-colored violets; beyond them, even farther, innocent tiger lilies, tall, lifting their orange bonnets. In the barracks they spoke of "flowers," of "rain": excrement, thick turd-braids, and the slow stinking maroon waterfall that slunk down from the upper bunks, the stink mixed with a bitter fatty floating smoke that greased Rosa's skin. She stood for an instant at the margin of the arena. Sometimes the electricity inside the fence would seem to hum; even Stella said it was only an imagining, but Rosa heard real sounds in the wire: grainy sad voices. The farther she was from the fence, the more clearly the voices crowded at her. The lamenting voices strummed so convincingly, so passionately, it was impossible to suspect them of being phantoms. The voices told her to hold up the shawl, high; the voices told her to shake it, to whip with it, to unfurl it like a flag. Rosa lifted, shook, whipped, unfurled. Far off, very far, Magda leaned across her air-fed belly, reaching out with the rods of her arms. She was high up, elevated, riding someone's shoulder. But the shoulder that carried Magda was not coming toward Rosa and the shawl, it was drifting away, the speck of Magda was moving more and more into the smoky distance. Above the shoulder a helmet glinted. The light tapped the helmet and sparkled it into a goblet. Below the helmet a black body like a domino and a pair of black boots hurled themselves in the direction of the electrified fence. The electric voices began to chatter wildly. "Maa-maa, maaamaaa," they all hummed together. How far Magda was from Rosa now, across the whole square, past a dozen barracks, all the way on the other side! She was no bigger than a moth.

All at once Magda was swimming through the air. The whole of Magda traveled through loftiness. She looked like a butterfly touching a silver vine. And the moment Magda's feathered round head and her pencil legs and balloonish belly and zigzag arms splashed against the fence, the steel voices went mad in their growling, urging Rosa to run and run to the spot where Magda had fallen from her flight against the electrified fence; but of course Rosa did not obey them. She only stood, because if she ran they would shoot, and if she tried to pick up the sticks of Magda's body they would shoot, and if she let the wolf's screech ascending now through the ladder of her skeleton break out, they would shoot; so she took Magda's shawl and filled her own mouth with it, stuffed it in and stuffed it in, until she was swallowing up the wolf's screech and tasting the cinnamon and almond depth of Magda's saliva; and Rosa drank Magda's shawl until it dried.

WILLIAM TREVOR

1928–

*County Cork seems to specialize in producing short story writers of genius.
Trevor, like Sean O'Faolain and Frank O'Connor, was born there. Educated
at Trinity College, Dublin, he removed to England in 1960, when he began
his writing career. While many of his stories are set in Ireland (see also his
charming literary travelogue,* A Writer's Ireland), *many more are so English
in feeling and background that, as with other brilliant Irish emigrants, he is
often thought of as essentially English.*

*This collection has no business assigning grades, but its content cannot
avoid being in part influenced by the editor's predilections and limitations
of taste. For the record, then, I set down the confession that I think William
Trevor the finest short story writer currently using our language. One cannot come to this conviction, however arguable, unless one reads his entire
output, or at least the fifty-nine stories collected in* The Stories of William
Trevor. *It is only then that one is struck by the dazzling variety of social and
individual universes he effortlessly explores in a precise, undercharged
prose.*

*Trevor's vision of life, like Pritchett's, is seriocomic. If one were permitted
to apply only one adjective to his work, it might be "wise." He seems so
mature, so non-self-defensive. One gets from most of his work a deep satisfaction. He adds solid increments to our knowledge of human nature and
particularly of the dismaying chasms of misunderstanding that separate
beings of the same species.*

*Trevor often uses a rather well-worn technical ploy of the modern short
story — a scrutiny of the intersecting points of two themes or lines of narrative. That is the case with the complicated affair called "A Complicated
Nature." Attridge's failed marriage and the bizarre predicament into which
Mrs. Matara forces him are intricately intertwined. The last sentence opens
a door: it has the ring of an O. Henry surprise ending, but its psychological
reverberations are of an entirely different order.*

A Complicated Nature

AT A PARTY ONCE Attridge overheard a woman saying he gave her the shivers. "Vicious-tongued," this woman, a Mrs. de Paul, had said. "Forked like a serpent's."

It was true, and he admitted it to himself without apology, though "sharp" was how he preferred to describe the quality the woman had referred to. He couldn't help it if his quick eye had a way of rooting out other people's defects and didn't particularly bother to search for virtues.

Sharp about other people, he was sharp about himself as well: confessing his own defects, he found his virtues tedious. He was kind and generous to the people he chose as his friends, and took it for granted that he should be. He was a tidy man, but took no credit for that since being tidy was part of his nature. He was meticulous about his dress, and he was cultured, being particularly keen on opera — especially the operas of Wagner — and on Velasquez. He had developed his own good taste, and was proud of the job he had made of it.

A man of fifty, with hair that had greyed and spectacles with fine, colourless rims, he was given to slimming, for the weight he had gained in middle age rounded his face and made it pinker than he cared for: vanity was a weakness in him.

Attridge had once been married. In 1952 his parents had died, his father in February and his mother in November. Attridge had been their only child and had always lived with them. Disliking — or so he then considered — the solitude their death left him in, he married in 1953 a girl called Bernice Golder, but this most unfortunate conjunction had lasted only three months. "Nasty dry old thing," his ex-wife had screamed at him on their honeymoon in Siena, and he had enraged her further by pointing out that nasty and dry he might be but old he wasn't. "You were never young," she had replied more calmly than before. "Even as a child you must have been like dust." That wasn't so, he tried to explain; the truth was that he had a complicated nature. But she didn't listen to him.

Attridge lived alone now, existing comfortably on profits from the shares his parents had left him. He occupied a flat in a block, doing all his own cooking and taking pride in the small dinner parties he gave. His flat was just as his good taste wished it to be. The bathroom was tiled with blue Italian tiles, his bedroom severe and male, the hall warmly rust. His sitting-room, he privately judged, reflected a part of himself that did not come into the open, a mysterious element that even he knew little about and could only guess at. He'd saved up for the Egyptian rugs, scarlet and black and brown, on the waxed oak boards. He'd bought the first one in 1959 and each year subsequently had contrived to put aside his January and February Anglo-American Telegraph dividends until the floor was covered. He'd bought the last one a year ago.

On the walls of the room there was pale blue hessian, a background for his four tiny Velasquez drawings, and for the Toulouse-Lautrec drawing and the Degas, and the two brown charcoal studies, school of Michelangelo. There was a sofa and a sofa-table, authenticated Sheraton, and a Regency table in marble and gold that he had almost made up his mind to get rid of, and some Staffordshire figures. There was drama in the decoration and arrangement of the room, a quite flamboyant drama that Attridge felt was related to the latent element in himself, part of his complicated nature.

"I'm hopeless in an emergency," he said in this room one afternoon, speaking with off-putting asperity into his ivory-coloured telephone. A woman called Mrs. Matara, who lived in the flat above his, appeared not to hear him. "Something has gone wrong, you see," she explained in an upset voice, adding that she'd have to come down. She then abruptly replaced the receiver.

It was an afternoon in late November. It was raining, and already — at half-past three — twilight had settled in. From a window of his sitting-room Attridge had been gazing at all this when his telephone rang. He'd been looking at the rain dismally falling and lights going on in other windows and at a man, five storeys down, sweeping sodden leaves from the concrete forecourt of the block of flats. When the phone rang he'd thought it might be his friend, old Mrs. Harcourt-Egan. He and Mrs. Harcourt-Egan were to go together to Persepolis in a fortnight's time and there were still some minor arrangements to be made, although the essential booking had naturally been completed long since. It had been a considerable surprise to hear himself addressed by name in a voice he had been quite unable to place. He'd greeted Mrs. Matara once or twice in the lift and that was all: she and her husband had moved into the flats only a year ago.

"I do so apologize," Mrs. Matara said when he opened the door to her. Against his will he welcomed her into the hall and she, knowing the geography of the flat since it was the same as her own, made for the sitting-room. "It's really terrible of me," she said, "only I honestly don't know where to turn." She spoke in a rushed and agitated manner, and he sighed as he followed her, resolving to point out when she revealed what her trouble was that Chamberlain, the janitor, was employed to deal with tenants' difficulties. She was just the kind of woman to make a nuisance of herself with a neighbor, you could tell that by looking at her. It irritated him that he hadn't sized her up better when he'd met her in the lift.

She was a woman of about the same age as himself, he guessed, small and thin and black-haired, though the hair, he also guessed, was almost certainly dyed. He wondered if she might be Jewish, which would account for her emotional condition: she had a Jewish look, and the name was presumably foreign. Her husband, whom he had also only met in the lift, had a look about the eyes which Attridge now said to himself might well have been developed in the clothing business. Of Austrian origin, he hazarded, or possibly even Polish. Mrs. Matara had an accent of some kind, although her English appeared otherwise to be perfect. She was not out of the top drawer, but then people of the Jewish race rarely were. His own ex-wife, Jewish also, had most certainly not been.

Mrs. Matara sat on the edge of a chair he had bought for ninety guineas fifteen years ago. It was also certainly Sheraton, a high-back chair with slim arms in inlaid walnut. He'd had it resprung and upholstered and covered in striped pink, four different shades.

"A really ghastly thing," Mrs. Matara said, "a terrible thing has happened in my flat, Mr. Attridge."

She'd fused the whole place. She couldn't turn a tap off. The garbage disposal unit had failed. His ex-wife had made a ridiculous fuss when, because of her own stupidity, she'd broken her electric hair-curling apparatus on their honeymoon. Grotesque she'd looked with the plastic objects in her hair; he'd been relieved that they didn't work.

"I really can't mend anything," he said. "Chamberlain is there for that, you know."

She shook her head. She was like a small bird sitting there, a wren or an undersized sparrow. A Jewish sparrow, he said to himself, pleased with this analogy. She had a handkerchief between her fingers, a small piece of material, which she now raised to her face. She touched her eyes with it, one after the other. When she spoke again she said that a man had died in her flat.

"Good heavens!"

"It's terrible!" Mrs. Matara cried. "Oh, my God!"

He poured brandy from a Georgian decanter that Mrs. Harcourt-Egan had given him three Christmases ago, after their trip to Sicily. She'd given him a pair, in appreciation of what she called his kindness on that holiday. The gesture had been far too generous: the decanters were family heirlooms, and he'd done so little for her in Sicily apart from reading *Northanger Abbey* aloud when she'd had her stomach upset.

The man, he guessed, was not Mr. Matara. No woman would say that a man had died, meaning her husband. Attridge imagined that a window-cleaner had fallen off a step-ladder. Quite clearly, he saw in his mind's eye a step-ladder standing at a window and the body of a man in white overalls huddled on the ground. He even saw Mrs. Matara bending over the body, attempting to establish its condition.

"Drink it all," he said, placing the brandy glass in Mrs. Matara's right hand, hoping as he did so that she wasn't going to drop it.

She didn't drop it. She drank the brandy and then, to Attridge's surprise, held out the glass in a clear request for more.

"Oh, if only you would," she said as she poured it, and he realized that while he'd been pouring the first glass, while his mind had been wandering back to the occasion in Sicily and the gift of the decanters, his guest had made some demand of him.

"You could say he was a friend," Mrs. Matara said.

She went on talking. The man who had died had died of a heart attack. The presence of his body in her flat was an embarrassment. She told a story of a love affair that had begun six years ago. She went into details: she had met the man at a party given by people called Morton, the man had been married, what point was there in hurting a dead man's wife? what point was there in upsetting her own husband, when he need never know? She rose and crossed the room to the brandy decanter. The man, she said, had died in the bed that was her husband's as well as hers.

"I wouldn't have come here — oh God, I wouldn't have come here if I hadn't been desperate." Her voice was shrill. She was nearly hysterical. The brandy had brought out two patches of brightness in her cheeks. Her eyes were watering again, but she did not now touch them with the handkerchief. The water ran, over the bright patches, trailing mascara and other make-up with it.

"I sat for hours," she cried. "Well, it seemed like hours. I sat there looking at him. We were both without a stitch, Mr. Attridge."

"Good heavens!"

"I didn't feel anything at all. I didn't love him, you know. All I felt was, Oh God, what a thing to happen!"

Attridge poured himself some brandy, feeling the need for it. She reminded him quite strongly of his ex-wife, not just because of the Jewish thing or the nuisance she was making of herself but because of the way she had so casually said they'd been without a stitch. In Siena on their honeymoon his ex-wife had constantly been flaunting her nakedness, striding about their bedroom. "The trouble with you," she'd said, "you like your nudes on canvas."

"You could say he was a friend," Mrs. Matara said again. She wanted him to come with her to her flat. She wanted him to help her dress the man. In the name of humanity, she was suggesting, they should falsify the location of death.

He shook his head, outraged and considerably repelled. The images in his mind were most unpleasant. There was the naked male body, dead on a bed. There was Mrs. Matara and himself pulling the man's clothes on to his body, struggling because *rigor mortis* was setting in.

"Oh God, what can I do?" cried Mrs. Matara.

"I think you should telephone a doctor, Mrs. Matara."

"Oh, what use is a doctor, for God's sake? The man's dead."

"It's usual —"

"Look, one minute we're having lunch — an omelette, just as usual, and salad and Pouilly Fuissé — and the next minute the poor man's dead."

"I thought you said —"

"Oh, you know what I mean. 'Lovely, oh darling, lovely,' he said, and then he collapsed. Well, I didn't know he'd collapsed. I mean, I didn't know he was dead. He collapsed just like he always collapses. Post-coital —"

"I'd rather not hear —"

"Oh, for Jesus' sake!" She was shouting. She was on her feet, again approaching the decanter. Her hair had fallen out of the pins that held it and was now dishevelled. Her lipstick was blurred, some of it even smeared her chin. She looked most unattractive, he considered.

"I cannot help you in this matter, Mrs. Matara," he said as firmly as he could. "I can telephone a doctor —"

"Will you for God's sake stop about a doctor!"

"I cannot assist you with your friend, Mrs. Matara."

"All I want you to do is to help me put his clothes back on. He's too heavy, I can't do it myself —"

"I'm very sorry, Mrs. Matara."

"And slip him down here. The lift is only a few yards —"

"That's quite impossible."

She went close to him, with her glass considerably replenished. She pushed her face at his in a way that he considered predatory. He was aware of the smell of her scent, and of another smell that he couldn't prevent himself from thinking must be the smell of sexual intercourse: he had read of this odour in a book by Ernest Hemingway.

"My husband and I are a contentedly married couple," she said, with her lips so near to his that they almost touched. "That man upstairs has a wife who doesn't know a thing, an innocent woman. Don't you understand such things, Mr. Attridge? Don't you see what will happen if the dead body of my lover is discovered in my husband's bed? Can't you visualize the pain it'll cause?"

He moved away. It was a long time since he had felt so angry and yet he was determined to control his anger. The woman knew nothing of civilized behaviour or she wouldn't have come bursting into the privacy of a stranger like this, with preposterous and unlawful suggestions. The woman, for all he knew, was unbalanced.

"I'm sorry," he said in what he hoped was an icy voice. "I'm sorry, but for a start I do not see how you and your husband could possibly be a contentedly married couple."

"I'm telling you we are. I'm telling you my lover was contentedly married also. Listen, Mr. Attridge." She approached him again, closing in on him like an animal. "Listen, Mr. Attridge; we met for physical reasons, once a week at lunchtime. For five years, ever since the Mortons' party, we've been meeting once a week, for an omelette and Pouilly Fuissé, and sex. It had nothing to do with our two marriages. But it will now: that woman will see her marriage as a failure now. She'll mourn it for the rest of her days, when she should be mourning her husband. I'll be divorced."

"You should have thought of that —"

She hit him with her left hand. She hit him on the face, the palm of her hand stinging the pink, plump flesh.

"Mrs. Matara!"

He had meant to shout her name, but instead his protest came from him in a shrill whisper. Since his honeymoon no one had struck him, and he recalled the fear he'd felt when he'd been struck then, in the bedroom in Siena. "I could kill you," his ex-wife had shouted at him. "I'd kill you if you weren't dead already."

"I must ask you to go, Mrs. Matara," he said in the same shrill whisper. He cleared his throat. "At once," he said, in a more successful voice.

She shook her head. She said he had no right to tell her what she should have thought of. She was upset as few women can ever be upset: in all decency and humanity it wasn't fair to say she should have thought of that. She cried out noisily in his sitting-room and he felt that he was in a nightmare. It had all the horror and absurdity and violence of a nightmare: the woman standing in front of him with water coming out of her eyes, drinking his brandy and hitting him.

She spoke softly then, not in her violent way. She placed the brandy glass on the marble surface of the Regency table and stood there with her head down. He knew she was still weeping even though he couldn't see her face and couldn't hear any noise coming from her. She whispered that she was sorry.

"Please forgive me, Mr. Attridge. I'm very sorry."

He nodded, implying that he accepted this apology. It was all very nasty, but for the woman it was naturally an upsetting thing to happen. He imagined, when a little time had passed, telling the story to Mrs. Harcourt-Egan and to others, relating how a woman, to all intents and purposes a stranger to him, had telephoned him to say she was in need of assistance and then had come down from her flat with this awful tragedy to relate. He imagined himself describing Mrs. Matara, how at first she'd seemed quite smart and then had become dishevelled, how she'd helped herself to his brandy and had suddenly struck him. He imagined Mrs. Hartcourt-Egan and others gasping when he said that. He seemed to see his own slight smile as he went on to say that the woman could not be blamed. He heard himself saying that the end of the matter was that Mrs. Matara just went away.

But in fact Mrs. Matara did not go away. Mrs. Matara continued to stand, weeping quietly.

"I'm sorry, too," he said, feeling that the words, with the finality he'd slipped into them, would cause her to move to the door of the sitting-room.

"If you'd just help me," she said, with her head still bent. "Just to get his clothes on."

He began to reply. He made a noise in his throat.

"I can't manage," she said, "on my own."

She raised her head and looked across the room at him. Her face was blotched all over now, with make-up and tears. Her hair had fallen down a little more, and from where he stood Attridge thought he could see quite large areas of grey beneath the black. A rash of some kind, or it might have been flushing, had appeared on her neck.

"I wouldn't bother you," she said, "if I could manage on my own." She would have telephoned a friend, she said, except there wouldn't be time for a friend to get to the block of flats. "There's very little time, you see," she said.

It was then, while she spoke those words, that Attridge felt the first hint of excitement. It was the same kind of excitement that he experienced just before the final curtain of *Tannhäuser,* or whenever, in the Uffizi, he looked upon Credi's Annunciation. Mrs. Matara was a wretched, unattractive creature who had been conducting a typical hole-in-corner affair and had received her just rewards. It was hard to feel sorry for her, and yet for some reason it was harder not to. The man who had died had got off scot-free, leaving her to face the music miserably on her own. "You're inhuman," his ex-wife had said in Siena. "You're incapable of love. Or sympathy, or anything else." She'd stood there in her underclothes, taunting him.

"I'll manage," Mrs. Matara said, moving towards the door.

He did not move himself. She'd been so impatient, all the time in Siena. She didn't even want to sit in the square and watch the people. She'd been lethargic in the cathedral. All she'd ever wanted was to try again in bed. "You don't like women," she'd said, sitting up with a glass of Brolio in her hand, smoking a cigarette.

He followed Mrs. Matara into the hall, and an image entered his mind of the dead man's wife. He saw her as Mrs. Matara had described her, as an innocent woman who believed herself faithfully loved. He saw her as a woman with fair hair, in a garden, simply dressed. She had borne the children of the man who now lay obscenely dead, she had made a home for him and had entertained his tedious business friends, and now she was destined to suffer. It was a lie to say he didn't like women, it was absurd to say he was incapable of sympathy.

Once more he felt a hint of excitement. It was a confused feeling now, belonging as much in his body as in his mind. In a dim kind of way he seemed again to be telling the story to Mrs. Harcourt-Egan or to someone else. Telling it, his voice was quiet. It spoke of the compassion he had suddenly felt for the small unattractive Jewish woman and for another woman, a total stranger whom he'd never even seen. "A moment of truth," his voice explained to Mrs. Harcourt-Egan and others. "I could not pass these women by."

He knew it was true. The excitement he felt had to do with sympathy, and the compassion that had been engendered in it. His complicated nature worked in that way: there had to be drama, like the drama of a man dead in a bed, and the beauty of being unable to pass the women by, as real as the beauty of the Madonna of the Meadow. With her cigarette and her Brolio, his ex-wife wouldn't have understood that in a million years. In their bedroom in Siena she had expected something ordinary to take place, an act that rats performed.

Never in his entire life had Attridge felt as he felt now. It was the most extraordinary, and for all he knew the most important, occasion in his life. As though watching a play, he saw himself assisting the dead, naked man into his clothes. It would be enough to put his clothes on, no need to move the body from one flat to another, enough to move it from the bedroom. "We put it in the lift and left it there," his voice said, still telling the story. " 'No need,' I said to her, 'to involve my flat at all.' She agreed; she had no option. The man became a man who'd had a heart attack in a lift. A travelling salesman, God knows who he was."

The story was beautiful. It was extravagant and flamboyant, incredible almost, like all good art. Who really believed in the Madonna of the Meadow, until jolted by the genius of Bellini? *The Magic Flute* was an impossible occasion, until Mozart's music charged you like an electric current.

"Yes, Mr. Attridge?"

He moved towards her, fearing to speak lest his voice emerged from him in the shrill whisper that had possessed it before. He nodded at Mrs. Matara, agreeing in this way to assist her.

Hurrying through the hall and hurrying up the stairs because one flight of stairs was quicker than the lift, he felt the excitement continuing in his body. Actually it would be many months before he could tell Mrs. Harcourt-Egan or anyone else about any of it. It seemed, for the moment at least, to be entirely private.

"What was he?" he asked on the stairs in a whisper.

"Was?"

"Professionally." He was impatient, more urgent now than she. "Salesman or something, was he?"

She shook her head. Her friend had been a dealer in antiques, she said.

Another Jew, he thought. But he was pleased because the man could have been on his way to see him, since dealers in antiques did sometimes visit him. Mrs. Matara might have said to the man, at another party given by the Mortons or anywhere else you liked, that Mr. Attridge, a collector of pictures and Staffordshire china, lived in the flat below hers. She could have said to Attridge that she knew a man who might have stuff that would interest him and then the man might have telephoned him, and he'd have said come round one afternoon. And in the lift the man collapsed and died.

She had her latchkey in her hand, about to insert it into the lock of her flat door. Her hand was shaking. Surprising himself, he gripped her arm, preventing it from completing the action with the key.

"Will you promise me," he said, "to move away from these flats? As soon as you conveniently can?"

"Of course, of course! How could I stay?"

"I'd find it awkward, meeting you about the place, Mrs. Matara. Is that a bargain?"

"Yes, yes."

She turned the key in the lock. They entered a hall that was of the exact proportions of Attridge's but different in other ways. It was a most unpleasant hall, he considered, with bell chimes in it, and two oil paintings that appeared to be the work of some emergent African, one being of Negro children playing on crimson sand, the other of a Negro girl with a baby at her breast.

"Oh, God!" Mrs. Matara cried, turning suddenly, unable to proceed. She pushed herself at him, her sharp head embedding itself in his chest, her hands grasping the jacket of his grey suit.

"Don't worry," he said, dragging his eyes away from the painting of the children on the crimson sand. One of her hands had ceased to grasp his jacket and had fallen into one of his. It was cold and had a fleshless feel.

"We have to do it," he said, and for a second he saw himself again as he would see himself in retrospect: standing with the Jewish woman in her hall, holding her hand to comfort her.

While they still stood there, just as he was about to propel her forward, there was a noise.

"My God!" whispered Mrs. Matara.

He knew she was thinking that her husband had returned, and he thought the same himself. Her husband had come back sooner than he usually did. He had found a corpse and was about to find his wife holding hands with a neighbour in the hall.

"Hey!" a voice said.

"Oh no!" cried Mrs. Matara, rushing forward into the room that Attridge knew was her sitting-room.

There was the mumble of another voice, and then the sound of Mrs. Matara's tears. It was a man's voice, but the man was not her husband: the atmosphere which came from the scene wasn't right for that.

"There now," the other voice was saying in the sitting-room. "There now, there now."

The noise of Mrs. Matara's weeping continued, and the man appeared at the door of the sitting-room. He was fully dressed, a sallow man, tall and black-haired, with a beard. He'd guessed what had happened, he said, as soon as he heard voices in the hall: he'd guessed that Mrs. Matara had gone to get help. In an extremely casual way he said he was really quite all right, just a little groggy due to the silly blackout he'd had. Mrs. Matara was a customer of his, he explained, he was in the antique business. "I just passed out," he said. He smiled at Attridge. He'd had a few silly blackouts recently and despite what his doctor said about there being nothing to worry about he'd have to be more careful. Really embarrassing, it was, plopping out in a client's sitting-room.

Mrs. Matara appeared in the sitting-room doorway. She leaned against it, as though requiring its support. She giggled through her tears and the man spoke sharply to her, forgetting she was meant to be his client. He warned her against becoming hysterical.

"My God, you'd be hysterical," Mrs. Matara cried, "if you'd been through all that kerfuffle."

"Now, now —"

"For Christ's sake, I thought you were a goner. Didn't I?" she cried, addressing Attridge without looking at him and not waiting for him to reply. "I rushed downstairs to this man here. I was in a frightful state. Wasn't I?"

"Yes."

"We were going to put your clothes on and dump you in his flat."

Attridge shook his head, endeavouring to imply that that was not accurate, that he'd never have agreed to the use of his flat for this purpose. But neither of them was paying any attention to him. The man was looking embarrassed, Mrs. Matara was grim.

"You should damn well have told me if you were having blackouts."

"I'm sorry," the man said. "I'm sorry you were troubled," he said to Attridge. "Please forgive Mrs. Matara."

"Forgive *you*, you mean!" she cried. "Forgive you for being such a damn fool!"

"Do try to pull yourself together, Miriam."

"I tell you, I thought you were dead."

"Well, I'm not. I had a little blackout —"

"Oh, for Christ's sake, stop about your wretched blackout!"

The way she said that reminded Attridge very much of his ex-wife. He'd had a headache once, he remembered, and she'd protested in just the same impatient tone of voice, employing almost the same words. She'd married again, of course — a man called Saunders in ICI.

"At least be civil," the man said to Mrs. Matara.

They were two of the most unpleasant people Attridge had ever come across. It was a pity the man hadn't died. He'd run to fat and was oily, there was a shower of dandruff on his jacket. You could see his stomach straining his shirt, one of the shirt-buttons had actually given way.

"Well, thank you," Mrs. Matara said, approaching Attridge with her right hand held out. She said it gracelessly, as a duty. The same hand had struck him on the face and later had slipped for comfort into one of his. It was hard and cold when he shook it, with the same fleshless feel as before. "We still have a secret," Mrs. Matara said. She smiled at him in her dutiful way, without displaying interest in him.

The man had opened the hall-door of the flat. He stood by it, smiling also, anxious for Attridge to go.

"This afternoon's a secret," Mrs. Matara murmured, dropping her eyes in a girlish pretence. "All this," she said, indicating her friend. "I'm sorry I hit you."

"Hit him?"

"When we were upset. Downstairs. I hit him." She giggled, apparently unable to help herself.

"Great God!" The man giggled also.

"It doesn't matter," Attridge said.

But it did matter. The secret she spoke of wasn't worth having because it was sordid and nothing else. It was hardly the kind of thing he'd wish to mull over in private, and certainly not the kind he'd wish to tell Mrs. Harcourt-Egan or anyone else. Yet the other story might even have reached his ex-wife, it was not impossible. He imagined her hearing it, and her amazement that a man whom she'd once likened to dust had in the cause of compassion falsified the circumstances of a death. He couldn't imagine the man his ex-wife had married doing such a thing, or Mrs. Matara's husband, or the dandruffy man who now stood by the door of the flat. Such men would have been frightened out of their wits.

"Goodbye," she said.

"Goodbye," the man said, smiling at the door.

Attridge wanted to say something. He wanted to linger for a moment longer and to mention his ex-wife. He wanted to tell them what he had never told another soul, that his ex-wife had done terrible things to him. He disliked all Jewish people, he wanted to say, because of his ex-wife and her lack of understanding. Marriage repelled him because of her. It was she who had made him vicious-tongued. It was she who had em-bittered him.

He looked from one face to the other. They would not understand and they would not be capable of making an effort, as he had when faced with the woman's predicament. He had always been a little on the cold side, he knew that well. But his ex-wife might have drawn on the other aspects of his nature and dispelled the coldness. Instead of dis-playing all that impatience, she might have cosseted him and accepted his complications. The love she sought would have come in its own good time, as sympathy and compassion had eventually come that afternoon. Warmth was buried deep in some people, he wanted to say to the two faces in the hall, but he knew that, like his ex-wife, the faces would not understand.

As he went he heard the click of the door behind him and imagined a hushed giggling in the hall. He would be feeling like a prince if the man had really died.

MILAN KUNDERA
1929–

Born in Brno, Czechoslovakia, the now permanently exiled Kundera ranks as the most brilliant writer in his native language. Son of a famous pianist, he joined the Communist party in 1947 but soon got into trouble for "ideological differences." His successful first novel, The Joke, was banned after the Russians invaded Czechoslovakia in 1968. He also lost his job as a professor at the Prague Institute for Advanced Cinematographic Studies. In 1975, now "unemployable," the Kunderas left for France. In 1981 President Mitterand granted them French citizenship.

His most considerable work so far is probably the ferociously intelligent The Unbearable Lightness of Being. *His short stories, however, introduced to us through the invaluable efforts of Philip Roth, are more accessible to American readers. We have still to assimilate the contemporary Czech literary temperament, so complex in its wit, irony, and philosophical melancholy that no easy rubric such as "dissident" can summarize it. Indeed, Kundera, while of course antitotalitarian, is in essence apolitical. That is, he turns a sad though interested eye on all forms of the technostate and on the kitsch with which it is replacing traditional culture.*

We might suggest his acerbic view of sex by contrasting him with D. H. Lawrence. The theme pervades the work of both. Yet, could they meet, I think they would be quite unable to understand each other. Kundera would judge Lawrence hysterical and soft-headed. Lawrence would find Kundera anesthetic to the mystique of the blood.

Kundera's erotic stories are both funny and bleak. (One collection is titled Laughable Loves.) *For him sex has become a diminished thing, a game we are driven to play, and one in which there are no winners. The story that follows is about two lovers who, assuming changed, mock personalities, become in effect four. As they fall into and out of their perilous impersonations, they learn some disturbing things about love, hatred, jealousy, sensuality, and moral responsibility. Their fiction they find "suddenly making an assault upon real life." As citizens of a repressive state they vainly try through erotic gamesmanship to experience some kind of freedom, even the freedom of artifice. In another remarkable story ("Edward and God") Kundera remarks, "A man lives a sad life when he cannot take anything or anyone seriously."*

The Hitchhiking Game

I

THE NEEDLE on the gas gauge suddenly dipped toward empty and the young driver of the sports car declared that it was maddening how much gas the car ate up. "See that we don't run out of gas again," protested the girl (about twenty-two), and reminded the driver of several places where this had already happened to them. The young man replied that he wasn't worried, because whatever he went through with her had the charm of adventure for him. The girl objected; whenever they had run out of gas on the highway it had, she said, always been an adventure only for her. The young man had hidden and she had had to make ill use of her charms by thumbing a ride and letting herself be driven to the nearest gas station, then thumbing a ride back with a can of gas. The young man asked the girl whether the drivers who had given her a ride had been unpleasant, since she spoke as if her task had been a hardship. She replied (with awkward flirtatiousness) that sometimes they had been *very* pleasant but that it hadn't done her any good as she had been burdened with the can and had had to leave them before she could get anything going. "Pig," said the young man. The girl protested that she wasn't a pig, but that he really was. God knows how many girls stopped him on the highway, when he was driving the car alone! Still driving, the young man put his arm around the girl's shoulders and kissed her gently on the forehead. He knew that she loved him and that she was jealous. Jealousy isn't a pleasant quality, but if it isn't overdone (and if it's combined with modesty), apart from its inconvenience there's even something touching about it. At least that's what the young man thought. Because he was only twenty-eight, it seemed to him that he was old and knew everything that a man could know about women. In the girl sitting beside him he valued precisely what, until now, he had met with least in women: purity.

The needle was already on empty, when to the right the young man caught sight of a sign, announcing that the station was a quarter of a mile ahead. The girl hardly had time to say how relieved she was before the young man was signaling left and driving into a space in front of the pumps. However, he had to stop a little way off, because beside the pumps was a huge gasoline truck with a large metal tank and a bulky hose, which was refilling the pumps. "We'll have to wait," said the young man to the girl and got out of the car. "How long will it take?" he shouted to the man in overalls. "Only a moment," replied the attendant, and the young man said: "I've heard that one before." He wanted to go back and sit in the car, but he saw that the girl had gotten out the other side. "I'll take a little walk in the meantime," she said. "Where to?" the young man asked on purpose, wanting to see the girl's embarrassment. He had known her for a year now but she would still get shy in front of him. He enjoyed her moments of shyness, partly because they distinguished her from the women he'd met before, partly because he was aware of the law of universal transience, which made even his girl's shyness a precious thing to him.

2

The girl really didn't like it when during the trip (the young man would drive for several hours without stopping) she had to ask him to stop for a moment somewhere near a clump of trees. She always got angry when, with feigned surprise, he asked her why he should stop. She knew that her shyness was ridiculous and old-fashioned. Many times at work she had noticed that they laughed at her on account of it and deliberately provoked her. She always got shy in advance at the thought of how she was going to get shy. She often longed to feel free and easy about her body, the way most of the women around her did. She had even invented a special course in self-persuasion: she would repeat to herself that at birth every human being received one out of the millions of available bodies, as one would receive an allotted room out of the millions of rooms in an enormous hotel. Consequently, the body was fortuitous and impersonal, it was only a ready-made, borrowed thing. She would repeat this to herself in different ways, but she could never manage to feel it. This mind-body dualism was alien to her. She was too much one with her body; that is why she always felt such anxiety about it.

She experienced this same anxiety even in her relations with the young man, whom she had known for a year and with whom she was happy, perhaps because he never separated her body from her soul and she could live with him *wholly*. In this unity there was happiness, but right behind the happiness lurked suspicion, and the girl was full of that. For instance, it often occurred to her that the other women (those who weren't anxious) were more attractive and more seductive and that the young man, who did not conceal the fact that he knew this kind of woman well, would someday leave her for a woman like that. (True, the young man declared that he'd had enough of them to last his whole life, but she knew that he was still much younger than he thought.) She wanted him to be completely hers and she to be completely his, but it often seemed to her that the more she tried to give him everything, the more she denied him something: the very thing that a light and superficial love or a flirtation gives to a person. It worried her that she was not able to combine seriousness with lightheartedness.

But now she wasn't worrying and any such thoughts were far from her mind. She felt good. It was the first day of their vacation (of their two-week vacation, about which she had been dreaming for a whole year), the sky was blue (the whole year she had been worrying about whether the sky would really be blue), and he was beside her. At his, "Where to?" she blushed, and left the car without a word. She walked around the gas station, which was situated beside the highway in total isolation, surrounded by fields. About a hundred yards away (in the direction in which they were traveling), a wood began. She set off for it, vanished behind a little bush, and gave herself up to her good mood. (In solitude it was possible for her to get the greatest enjoyment from the presence of the man she loved. If his presence had been continuous, it would have kept on disappearing. Only when alone was she able to *hold on* to it.)

When she came out of the wood onto the highway, the gas station was visible. The large gasoline truck was already pulling out and the sports car moved forward toward the red turret of the pump. The girl walked on along the highway and only at times looked back to see if the sports car was coming. At last she caught sight of it. She stopped and began to wave at it like a hitchhiker waving at a stranger's car. The sports car slowed down and stopped close to the girl. The young man leaned toward the window, rolled it down, smiled, and asked, "Where are you headed, miss?" "Are you going to Bystritsa?" asked the girl, smiling flirtatiously at him. "Yes, please get in," said the young man, opening the door. The girl got in and the car took off.

3

The young man was always glad when his girl friend was gay. This didn't happen too often; she had a quite tiresome job in an unpleasant environment, many hours of overtime without compensatory leisure and, at home, a sick mother. So she often felt tired. She didn't have either particularly good nerves or self-confidence and easily fell into a state of anxiety and fear. For this reason he welcomed every manifestation of her gaiety with the tender solicitude of a foster parent. He smiled at her and said: "I'm lucky today. I've been driving for five years, but I've never given a ride to such a pretty hitchhiker."

The girl was grateful to the young man for every bit of flattery; she wanted to linger for a moment in its warmth and so she said, "You're very good at lying."

"Do I look like a liar?"

"You look like you enjoy lying to women," said the girl, and into her words there crept unawares a touch of the old anxiety, because she really did believe that her young man enjoyed lying to women.

The girl's jealousy often irritated the young man, but this time he could easily overlook it for, after all, her words didn't apply to him but to the unknown driver. And so he just casually inquired, "Does it bother you?"

"If I were going with you, then it would bother me," said the girl and her words contained a subtle, instructive message for the young man; but the end of her sentence applied only to the unknown driver, "but I don't know you, so it doesn't bother me."

"Things about her own man always bother a woman more than things about a stranger" (this was now the young man's subtle, instructive message to the girl), "so seeing that we are strangers, we could get on well together."

The girl purposely didn't want to understand the implied meaning of his message, and so she now addressed the unknown driver exclusively: "What does it matter, since we'll part company in a little while?"

"Why?" asked the young man.

"Well, I'm getting out at Bystritsa."

"And what if I get out with you?"

At these words the girl looked up at him and found that he looked exactly as she imagined him in her most agonizing hours of jealousy. She was alarmed at how he was flattering her and flirting with her (an unknown hitchhiker), and *how becoming it was to him*. Therefore she responded with defiant provocativeness, "What would *you* do with me, I wonder?"

"I wouldn't have to think too hard about what to do with such a beautiful woman," said the young man gallantly and at this moment he was once again speaking far more to his own girl than to the figure of the hitchhiker.

But this flattering sentence made the girl feel as if she had caught him at something, as if she had wheedled a confession out of him with a fraudulent trick. She felt toward him a brief flash of intense hatred and said, "Aren't you rather too sure of yourself?"

The young man looked at the girl. Her defiant face appeared to him to be completely convulsed. He felt sorry for her and longed for her usual, familiar expression (which he used to call childish and simple).

He leaned toward her, put his arm around her shoulders, and softly spoke the name with which he usually addressed her and with which he now wanted to stop the game.

But the girl released herself and said: "You're going a bit too fast!"

At this rebuff the young man said: "Excuse me, miss," and looked silently in front of him at the highway.

4

The girl's pitiful jealousy, however, left her as quickly as it had come over her. After all, she was sensible and knew perfectly well that all this was merely a game. Now it even struck her as a little ridiculous that she had repulsed her man out of jealous rage. It wouldn't be pleasant for her if he found out why she had done it. Fortunately women have the miraculous ability to change the meaning of their actions after the event. Using this ability, she decided that she had repulsed him not out of anger but so that she could go on with the game, which, with its whimsicality, so well suited the first day of their vacation.

So again she was the hitchhiker, who had just repulsed the overenterprising driver, but only so as to slow down his conquest and make it more exciting. She half turned toward the young man and said caressingly:

"I didn't mean to offend you, mister!"

"Excuse me, I won't touch you again," said the young man.

He was furious with the girl for not listening to him and refusing to be herself when that was what he wanted. And since the girl insisted on continuing in her role, he transferred his anger to the unknown hitchhiker whom she was portraying. And all at once he discovered the character of his own part: he stopped making the gallant remarks with which he had wanted to flatter his girl in a roundabout way, and began to play the tough guy who treats women to the coarser aspects of his masculinity: willfulness, sarcasm, self-assurance.

This role was a complete contradiction of the young man's habitually solicitous approach to the girl. True, before he had met her, he had in fact behaved roughly rather than gently toward women. But he had never resembled a heartless tough guy, because he had never demonstrated either a particularly strong will or ruthlessness. However, if he did not resemble such a man, nonetheless he had *longed* to at one time. Of course it was a quite naive desire, but there it was. Childish desires withstand all the snares of the adult mind and often survive into ripe old age. And this childish desire quickly took advantage of the opportunity to embody itself in the proffered role.

The young man's sarcastic reserve suited the girl very well — it freed her from herself. For she herself was, above all, the epitome of jealousy. The moment she stopped seeing the gallantly seductive young man beside her and saw only his inaccessible face, her jealousy subsided. The girl could forget herself and give herself up to her role.

Her role? What was her role? It was a role out of trashy literature. The hitchhiker stopped the car not to get a ride, but to seduce the man who was driving the car. She was an artful seductress, cleverly knowing how to use her charms. The girl slipped into this silly, romantic part with an ease that astonished her and held her spellbound.

5

There was nothing the young man missed in his life more than light-heartedness. The main road of his life was drawn with implacable precision. His job didn't use up merely eight hours a day, it also infiltrated the remaining time with the compulsory boredom of meetings and home study, and, by means of the attentiveness of his countless male and female colleagues, it infiltrated the wretchedly little time he had left for his private life as well. This private life never remained secret and sometimes even became the subject of gossip and public discussion. Even two weeks' vacation didn't give him a feeling of liberation and adventure; the gray shadow of precise planning lay even here. The scarcity of summer accommodations in our country compelled him to book a room in the Tatras six months in advance, and since for that he needed a recommendation from his office, its omnipresent brain thus did not cease knowing about him even for an instant.

He had become reconciled to all this, yet all the same from time to time the terrible thought of the straight road would overcome him — a road along which he was being pursued, where he was visible to everyone, and from which he could not turn aside. At this moment that thought returned to him. Through an odd and brief conjunction of ideas the figurative road became identified with the real highway along which he was driving — and this led him suddenly to do a crazy thing.

"Where did you say you wanted to go?" he asked the girl.

"To Banska Bystritsa," she replied.

"And what are you going to do there?"

"I have a date there."

"Who with?"

"With a ccrtain gentleman."

The car was just coming to a large crossroads. The driver slowed down so he could read the road signs, then turned off to the right.

"What will happen if you don't arrive for that date?"

"It would be your fault and you would have to take care of me."

"You obviously didn't notice that I turned off in the direction of Nove Zamky."

"Is that true? You've gone crazy!"

"Don't be afraid, I'll take care of you," said the young man.

So they drove and chatted thus — the driver and the hitchhiker who did not know each other.

The game all at once went into a higher gear. The sports car was moving away not only from the imaginary goal of Banska Bystritsa, but also from the real goal, toward which it had been heading in the morning: the Tatras and the room that had been booked. Fiction was suddenly making an assault upon real life. The young man was moving away from himself and from the implacable straight road, from which he had never strayed until now.

"But you said you were going to the Low Tatras!" The girl was surprised.

"I am going, miss, wherever I feel like going. I'm a free man and I do what I want and what it pleases me to do."

6

When they drove into Nove Zamky it was already getting dark.

The young man had never been here before and it took him a while to orient himself. Several times he stopped the car and asked the passersby directions to the hotel. Several streets had been dug up, so that the drive to the hotel, even though it was quite close by (as all those who had been asked asserted), necessitated so many detours and roundabout routes that it was almost a quarter of an hour before they finally stopped in front of it. The hotel looked unprepossessing, but it was the only one in town and the young man didn't feel like driving on. So he said to the girl, "Wait here," and got out of the car.

Out of the car he was, of course, himself again. And it was upsetting for him to find himself in the evening somewhere completely different from his intended destination — the more so because no one had forced him to do it and as a matter of fact he hadn't even really wanted to. He blamed himself for his piece of folly, but then became reconciled to it. The room in the Tatras could wait until tomorrow and it wouldn't do any harm if they celebrated the first day of their vacation with something unexpected.

He walked through the restaurant — smoky, noisy, and crowded —

and asked for the reception desk. They sent him to the back of the lobby near the staircase, where behind a glass panel a superannuated blonde was sitting beneath a board full of keys. With difficulty, he obtained the key to the only room left.

The girl, when she found herself alone, also threw off her role. She didn't feel ill-humored, though, at finding herself in an unexpected town. She was so devoted to the young man that she never had doubts about anything he did, and confidently entrusted every moment of her life to him. On the other hand the idea once again popped into her mind that perhaps — just as she was now doing — other women had waited for her man in his car, those women whom he met on business trips. But surprisingly enough this idea didn't upset her at all now. In fact, she smiled at the thought of how nice it was that today she was this other woman, this irresponsible, indecent other woman, one of those women of whom she was so jealous. It seemed to her that she was cutting them all out, that she had learned how to use their weapons; how to give the young man what until now she had not known how to give him: light-heartedness, shamelessness, and dissoluteness. A curious feeling of satisfaction filled her, because she alone had the ability to be all women and in this way (she alone) could completely captivate her lover and hold his interest.

The young man opened the car door and led the girl into the restaurant. Amid the din, the dirt, and the smoke he found a single, unoccupied table in a corner.

7

"So how are you going to take care of me now?" asked the girl provocatively.

"What would you like for an aperitif?"

The girl wasn't too fond of alcohol, still she drank a little wine and liked vermouth fairly well. Now, however, she purposely said: "Vodka."

"Fine," said the young man. "I hope you won't get drunk on me."

"And if I do?" said the girl.

The young man did not reply but called over a waiter and ordered two vodkas and two steak dinners. In a moment the waiter brought a tray with two small glasses and placed it in front of them.

The man raised his glass, "To you!"

"Can't you think of a wittier toast?"

Something was beginning to irritate him about the girl's game. Now sitting face to face with her, he realized that it wasn't just the *words* which were turning her into a stranger, but that her *whole persona* had changed, the movements of her body and her facial expression, and that she unpalatably and faithfully resembled that type of woman whom he knew so well and for whom he felt some aversion.

And so (holding his glass in his raised hand), he corrected his toast: "O.K., then I won't drink to you, but to your kind, in which are combined so successfully the better qualities of the animal and the worse aspects of the human being."

"By 'kind' do you mean all women?" asked the girl.

"No, I mean only those who are like you."

"Anyway it doesn't seem very witty to me to compare a woman with an animal."

"O.K.," the young man was still holding his glass aloft, "then I won't drink to your kind, but to your soul. Agreed? To your soul, which lights up when it descends from your head into your belly, and which goes out when it rises back up to your head."

The girl raised her glass. "O.K., to my soul, which descends into my belly."

"I'll correct myself once more," said the young man. "To your belly, into which your soul descends."

"To my belly," said the girl, and her belly (now that they had named it specifically), as it were, responded to the call; she felt every inch of it.

Then the waiter brought their steaks and the young man ordered them another vodka and some soda water (this time they drank to the girl's breasts), and the conversation continued in this peculiar, frivolous tone. It irritated the young man more and more how *well able* the girl was to become the lascivious miss. If she was able to do it so well, he thought, it meant that she really *was* like that. After all, no alien soul had entered into her from somewhere in space. What she was acting now was she herself; perhaps it was that part of her being which had formerly been locked up and which the pretext of the game had let out of its cage. Perhaps the girl supposed that by means of the game she was *disowning* herself, but wasn't it the other way around? Wasn't she becoming herself only through the game? Wasn't she freeing herself through the game? No, opposite him was not sitting a strange woman in his girl's body; it was his girl, herself, no one else. He looked at her and felt growing aversion toward her.

However, it was not only aversion. The more the girl withdrew from him *psychically*, the more he longed for her *physically*. The alien quality of her soul drew attention to her body, yes, as a matter of fact it turned her body into a body for *him* as if until now it had existed for the young man hidden within clouds of compassion, tenderness, concern, love, and emotion, as if it had been lost in these clouds (yes, as if this body had been lost!). It seemed to the young man that today he was seeing his girl's body for the first time.

After her third vodka and soda the girl got up and said flirtatiously, "Excuse me."

The young man said, "May I ask you where you are going, miss?"

"To piss, if you'll permit me," said the girl and walked off between the tables back toward the plush screen.

8

She was pleased with the way she had astounded the young man with this word, which — in spite of all its innocence — he had never heard from her. Nothing seemed to her truer to the character of the woman she was playing than this flirtatious emphasis placed on the word in question. Yes, she was pleased, she was in the best of moods. The game captivated her. It allowed her to feel what she had not felt till now: a *feeling* of *happy-go-lucky irresponsibility*.

She, who was always uneasy in advance about her every next step, suddenly felt completely relaxed. The alien life in which she had become involved was a life without shame, without biographical specifications, without past or future, without obligations. It was a life that was extraordinarily free. The girl, as a hitchhiker, could do anything, *everything was permitted her*. She could say, do, and feel whatever she liked.

She walked through the room and was aware that people were watching her from all the tables. It was a new sensation, one she didn't recognize: *indecent joy caused by her body*. Until now she had never been able to get rid of the fourteen-year-old girl within herself who was ashamed of her breasts and had the disagreeable feeling that she was indecent, because they stuck out from her body and were visible. Even though she was proud of being pretty and having a good figure, this feeling of pride was always immediately curtailed by shame. She rightly suspected that feminine beauty functioned above all as sexual provocation and she found this distasteful. She longed for her body to relate only to the man she loved. When men stared at her breasts in the street it seemed to her that they were invading a piece of her most secret privacy which should belong only to herself and her lover. But now she was the hitchhiker, the woman without a destiny. In this role she was relieved of the tender bonds of her love and began to be intensely aware of her body. And her body became more aroused the more alien the eyes watching it.

She was walking past the last table when an intoxicated man, wanting to show off his worldliness, addressed her in French: "*Combien, mademoiselle?*"

The girl understood. She thrust out her breasts and fully experienced every movement of her hips, then disappeared behind the screen.

9

It was a curious game. This curiousness was evidenced, for example, in the fact that the young man, even though he himself was playing the unknown driver remarkably well, did not for a moment stop seeing his girl in the hitchhiker. And it was precisely this that was tormenting. He saw his girl seducing a strange man, and had the bitter privilege of being present, of seeing at close quarters how she looked and of hearing what she said when she was cheating on him (when she had cheated on him, when she would cheat on him). He had the paradoxical honor of being himself the pretext for her unfaithfulness.

This was all the worse because he worshipped rather than loved her. It had always seemed to him that her inward nature was *real* only within the bounds of fidelity and purity, and that beyond these bounds it simply didn't exist. Beyond these bounds she would cease to be herself, as water ceases to be water beyond the boiling point. When he now saw her crossing this horrifying boundary with nonchalant elegance, he was filled with anger.

The girl came back from the rest room and complained: "A guy over there asked me: *Combien, mademoiselle?*"

"You shouldn't be surprised," said the young man, "after all, you look like a whore."

"Do you know that it doesn't bother me in the least?"

"Then you should go with the gentleman!"

"But I have you."

"You can go with him after me. Go and work out something with him."

"I don't find him attractive."

"But in principle you have nothing against it, having several men in one night."

"Why not, if they're good-looking."

"Do you prefer them one after the other or at the same time?"

"Either way," said the girl.

The conversation was proceeding to still greater extremes of rudeness; it shocked the girl slightly but she couldn't protest. Even in a game there lurks a lack of freedom; even a game is a trap for the players. If this had not been a game and they had really been two strangers, the hitchhiker could long ago have taken offense and left. But there's no escape from a game. A team cannot flee from the playing field before the end of the match, chess pieces cannot desert the chessboard: the boundaries of the playing field are fixed. The girl knew that she had to accept whatever form the game might take, just because it was a game. She knew that the more extreme the game became, the more it would be a game and the more obediently she would have to play it. And it was futile to evoke good sense and warn her dazed soul that she must keep her distance from the game and not take it seriously. Just because it was only a game her soul was not afraid, did not oppose the game, and narcotically sank deeper into it.

The young man called the waiter and paid. Then he got up and said to the girl, "We're going."

"Where to?" The girl feigned surprise.

"Don't ask, just come on," said the young man.

"What sort of way is that to talk to me?"

"The way I talk to whores," said the young man.

10

They went up the badly lit staircase. On the landing below the second floor a group of intoxicated men was standing near the rest room. The young man caught hold of the girl from behind so that he was holding her breast with his hand. The men by the rest room saw this and began to call out. The girl wanted to break away, but the young man yelled at her: "Keep still!" The men greeted this with general ribaldry and addressed several dirty remarks to the girl. The young man and the girl reached the second floor. He opened the door of their room and switched on the light.

It was a narrow room with two beds, a small table, a chair, and a washbasin. The young man locked the door and turned to the girl. She was standing facing him in a defiant pose with insolent sensuality in her eyes. He looked at her and tried to discover behind her lascivious expression the familiar features which he loved tenderly. It was as if he were looking at two images through the same lens, at two images superimposed one upon the other with the one showing through the other. These two images showing through each other were telling him that *everything* was in the girl, that her soul was terrifyingly amorphous, that it held faithfulness and unfaithfulness, treachery and innocence, flirtatiousness and chastity. This disorderly jumble seemed disgusting to him, like the variety to be found in a pile of garbage. Both images continued to show through each other and the young man understood that the girl differed only on the surface from other women, but deep down was the same as they: full of all possible thoughts, feelings, and vices, which justified all his secret misgivings and fits of jealousy. The impression that certain outlines delineated her as an individual was only a delusion to which the other person, the one who was looking, was subject — namely himself. It seemed to him that the girl he loved was a creation of his desire, his thoughts, and his faith and that the *real* girl now standing in front of him was hopelessly alien, hopelessly *ambiguous*. He hated her.

"What are you waiting for? Strip," he said.

The girl flirtatiously bent her head and said, "Is it necessary?"

The tone in which she said this seemed to him very familiar; it seemed to him that once long ago some other woman had said this to him, only he no longer knew which one. He longed to humiliate her. Not the hitchhiker, but his own girl. The game merged with life. The game of humiliating the hitchhiker became only a pretext for humiliating his girl. The young man had forgotten that he was playing a game. He simply hated the woman standing in front of him. He stared at her and took a fifty-crown bill from his wallet. He offered it to the girl. "Is that enough?"

The girl took the fifty crowns and said: "You don't think I'm worth much."

The young man said: "You aren't worth more."

The girl nestled up against the young man. "You can't get around me like that! You must try a different approach, you must work a little!"

She put her arms around him and moved her mouth toward his. He put his fingers on her mouth and gently pushed her away. He said: "I only kiss women I love."

"And you don't love me?"

"No."

"Whom do you love?"

"What's that got to do with you? Strip!"

11

She had never undressed like this before. The shyness, the feeling of inner panic, the dizziness, all that she had always felt when undressing in front of the young man (and she couldn't hide in the darkness), all this was gone. She was standing in front of him self-confident, insolent, bathed in light, and astonished at where she had all of a sudden discovered the gestures, heretofore unknown to her, of a slow, provocative striptease. She took in his glances, slipping off each piece of clothing with a caressing movement and enjoying each individual stage of this exposure.

But then suddenly she was standing in front of him completely naked and at this moment it flashed through her head that now the whole game would end, that, since she had stripped off her clothes, she had also stripped away her dissimulation, and that being naked meant that she was now herself and the young man ought to come up to her now and make a gesture with which he would wipe out everything and after which would follow only their most intimate lovemaking. So she stood naked in front of the young man and at this moment stopped playing the game. She felt embarrassed and on her face appeared the smile which really belonged to her — a shy and confused smile.

But the young man didn't come to her and didn't end the game. He didn't notice the familiar smile. He saw before him only the beautiful, alien body of his own girl, whom he hated. Hatred cleansed his sensuality of any sentimental coating. She wanted to come to him, but he said: "Stay where you are, I want to have a good look at you." Now he longed only to treat her as a whore. But the young man had never had a whore and the ideas he had about them came from literature and hearsay. So he turned to these ideas and the first thing he recalled was the image of a woman in black underwear (and black stockings) dancing on the shiny top of a piano. In the little hotel room there was no piano, there was only a small table covered with a linen cloth leaning against the wall. He ordered the girl to climb up on it. The girl made a pleading gesture, but the young man said, "You've been paid."

When she saw the look of unshakable obsession in the young man's eyes, she tried to go on with the game, even though she no longer could and no longer knew how. With tears in her eyes she climbed onto the table. The top was scarcely three feet square and one leg was a little bit shorter than the others so that standing on it the girl felt unsteady.

But the young man was pleased with the naked figure, now towering above him, and the girl's shy insecurity merely inflamed his imperiousness. He wanted to see her body in all positions and from all sides, as he imagined other men had seen it and would see it. He was vulgar and lascivious. He used words that she had never heard from him in her life. She wanted to refuse, she wanted to be released from the game. She called him by his first name, but he immediately yelled at her that she had no right to address him so intimately. And so eventually in confusion and on the verge of tears, she obeyed, she bent forward and squatted according to the young man's wishes, saluted, and then wiggled her hips as she did the Twist for him. During a slightly more violent movement, when the cloth slipped beneath her feet and she nearly fell, the young man caught her and dragged her to the bed.

He had intercourse with her. She was glad that at least now finally the unfortunate game would end and they would again be the two people they had been before and would love each other. She wanted to press her mouth against his. But the young man pushed her head away and repeated that he only kissed women he loved. She burst into loud sobs. But she wasn't even allowed to cry, because the young man's furious passion gradually won over her body, which then silenced the complaint of her soul. On the bed there were soon two bodies in perfect harmony, two sensual bodies, alien to each other. This was exactly what the girl had most dreaded all her life and had scrupulously avoided till now: love-making without emotion or love. She knew that she had crossed the forbidden boundary, but she proceeded across it without objections and as a full participant — only somewhere, far off in a corner of her consciousness, did she feel horror at the thought that she had never known such pleasure, never so much pleasure as at this moment — beyond that boundary.

12

Then it was all over. The young man got up off the girl and, reaching out for the long cord hanging over the bed, switched off the light. He didn't want to see the girl's face. He knew that the game was over, but didn't feel like returning to their customary relationship. He feared this return. He lay beside the girl in the dark in such a way that their bodies would not touch.

After a moment he heard her sobbing quietly. The girl's hand diffidently, childishly touched his. It touched, withdrew, then touched again, and then a pleading, sobbing voice broke the silence, calling him by his name and saying, "I am me, I am me . . ."

The young man was silent, he didn't move, and he was aware of the sad emptiness of the girl's assertion, in which the unknown was defined in terms of the same unknown quantity.

And the girl soon passed from sobbing to loud crying and went on endlessly repeating this pitiful tautology: "I am me, I am me, I am me . . ."

The young man began to call compassion to his aid (he had to call it from afar, because it was nowhere near at hand), so as to be able to calm the girl. There were still thirteen days' vacation before them.

DONALD BARTHELME
1931–

Our literary establishment should get brownie points for nonstuffiness. Of all our short story writers Donald Barthelme is perhaps the most experimental, the least compromising. Yet the establishment not only accepts him but has made him one of its luminaries: he has won a whole handful of book awards, held prestigious university posts, and earned recognition from the PEN American Center executive board, the American Academy and Institute of Arts and Letters, and the Guggenheim Foundation. Today any literary pioneer wishing to remain unrespectable is up against it. Long before an American Rimbaud could become a maudit, *Harvard would offer him a Chair.*

To put down Barthelme as "clever" or a cult object (though he is both) is unfair. He has been translated into ten languages or more. That argues the existence of a solid audience tuned to his wavelength.

As one only intermittently on that wavelength, I am often baffled by his far-out mental linkages and disjunctions. But perhaps bafflement is the fitting reaction. Perhaps his weird and ironical stories/fables/monologues are enigmatic because in our time so many matters, including the mere survival of the human race, appear enigmatic. In the portrayal of disintegration, clarity is not the highest desideratum. In "The Balloon" the author (or someone) says, "We have learned not to insist on meanings, and they are rarely looked for now, except in cases involving the simplest, safest phenomena." With meanings voided, only words are left. In "The Indian Uprising" he (or someone) says, "Strings of language extend in every direction to bind the world into a rushing, ribald whole."

Lest this nihilistic stance make for an overly portentous tone, he mitigates it via the elegant kidding and shrewd exploitation of the barren clichés of our pop culture. Here he is a master.

As for "Game," it may be, for all I know, about thermonuclear war or about our present human condition in which normal relations among people are becoming, it would seem, an irrelevance. Whatever it is about, "Game" propels me through a whole range of the anxiety-emotions that hallmark our lives. An achievement.

Game

SHOTWELL KEEPS THE JACKS and the rubber ball in his attaché case and will not allow me to play with them. He plays with them, alone, sitting on the floor near the console hour after hour, chanting "onesies, twosies, threesies, foursies" in a precise, well-modulated voice, not so loud as to be annoying, not so soft as to allow me to forget. I point out to Shotwell that two can derive more enjoyment from playing jacks than one, but he is not interested. I have asked repeatedly to be allowed to play by myself, but he simply shakes his head. "Why?" I ask. "They're mine," he says. And when he has finished, when he has sated himself, back they go into the attaché case.

It is unfair but there is nothing I can do about it. I am aching to get my hands on them.

Shotwell and I watch the console. Shotwell and I live under the ground and watch the console. If certain events take place upon the console, we are to insert our keys in the appropriate locks and turn our keys. Shotwell has a key and I have a key. If we turn our keys simultaneously the bird flies, certain switches are activated and the bird flies. But the bird never flies. In one hundred thirty-three days the bird has not flown. Meanwhile Shotwell and I watch each other. We each wear a .45 and if Shotwell behaves strangely I am supposed to shoot him. If I behave strangely Shotwell is supposed to shoot me. We watch the console and think about shooting each other and think about the bird. Shotwell's behavior with the jacks is strange. Is is strange? I do not know. Perhaps he is merely a selfish bastard, perhaps his character is flawed, perhaps his childhood was twisted. I do not know.

Each of us wears a .45 and each of us is supposed to shoot the other if the other is behaving strangely. How strangely is strangely? I do not know. In addition to the .45 I have a .38 which Shotwell does not know about concealed in my attaché case, and Shotwell has a .25 caliber Beretta which I do not know about strapped to his right calf. Sometimes instead of watching the console I pointedly watch Shotwell's .45, but this is simply a ruse, simply a maneuver, in reality I am watching his hand when it dangles in the vicinity of his right calf. If he decides I am behaving strangely he will shoot me not with the .45 but with the Beretta. Similarly Shotwell pretends to watch my .45 but he is really watching my hand resting idly atop my attaché case, my hand resting idly atop my attaché case, my hand. My hand resting idly atop my attaché case.

In the beginning I took care to behave normally. So did Shotwell. Our behavior was painfully normal. Norms of politeness, consideration, speech, and personal habits were scrupulously observed. But then it became apparent that an error had been made, that our relief was not going to arrive. Owing to an oversight. Owing to an oversight we have been here for one hundred thirty-three days. When it became clear that an error had been made, that we were not to be relieved, the norms were relaxed. Definitions of normality were redrawn in the agreement of January 1, called by us, The Agreement. Uniform regulations were relaxed, and mealtimes are no longer rigorously scheduled. We eat when we are hungry and sleep when we are tired. Considerations of rank and precedence were temporarily put aside, a handsome concession on the part of Shotwell, who is a captain, whereas I am only a first lieutenant. One of us watches the console at all times rather than two of us watching the console at all times, except when we are both on our feet. One of us watches the console at all times and if the bird flies then that one wakes the other and we turn our keys in the locks simultaneously and the bird flies. Our system involves a delay of perhaps twelve seconds but I do not care because I am not well, and Shotwell does not care because he is not himself. After the agreement was signed Shotwell produced the jacks and the rubber ball from his attaché case, and I began to write a series of descriptions of forms occurring in nature, such as a shell, a leaf, a stone, an animal. On the walls.

Shotwell plays jacks and I write descriptions of natural forms on the walls.

Shotwell is enrolled in a USAFI course which leads to a master's degree in business administration from the University of Wisconsin (although we are not in Wisconsin, we are in Utah, Montana or Idaho). When we went down it was in either Utah, Montana or Idaho, I don't remember. We have been here for one hundred thirty-three days owing to an oversight. The pale green reinforced concrete walls sweat and the air conditioning zips on and off erratically and Shotwell reads *Introduction to Marketing* by Lassiter and Munk, making notes with a blue ballpoint pen. Shotwell is not himself, but I do not know it, he presents a calm aspect and reads *Introduction to Marketing* and makes his exemplary notes with a blue ballpoint pen, meanwhile controlling the .38 in my attaché case with one-third of his attention. I am not well.

We have been here one hundred thirty-three days owing to an oversight. Although now we are not sure what is oversight, what is plan. Perhaps the plan is for us to stay here permanently, or if not permanently at least for a year, for three hundred sixty-five days. Or if not for a year for some number of days known to them and not known to us, such as two hundred days. Or perhaps they are observing our behavior in some way, sensors of some kind, perhaps our behavior determines the number of days. It may be that they are pleased with us, with our behavior, not in every detail but in sum. Perhaps the whole thing is very successful, perhaps the whole thing is an experiment and the experiment is very successful. I do not know. But I suspect that the only way they can persuade sun-loving creatures into their pale green sweating reinforced concrete rooms under the ground is to say that the system is twelve hours on, twelve hours off. And then lock us below for some number of days known to them and not known to us. We eat well although the frozen enchiladas are damp when defrosted and the frozen devil's food cake is sour and untasty. We sleep uneasily and acrimoniously. I hear Shotwell shouting in his sleep, objecting, denouncing, cursing sometimes, weeping sometimes, in his sleep. When Shotwell sleeps I try to pick the lock on his attaché case, so as to get at the jacks. Thus far I have been unsuccessful. Nor has Shotwell been successful in picking the locks on my attaché case so as to get at the .38. I have seen the marks on the shiny surface. I laughed, in the latrine, pale green walls sweating and the air conditioning whispering, in the latrine.

I write descriptions of natural forms on the walls, scratching them on the tile surface with a diamond. The diamond is a two and one-half carat solitaire I had in my attaché case when we went down. It was for Lucy. The south wall of the room containing the console is already covered. I have described a shell, a leaf, a stone, animals, a baseball bat. I am aware that the baseball bat is not a natural form. Yet I described it. "The baseball bat," I said, "is typically made of wood. It is typically one meter in length or a little longer, fat at one end, tapering to afford a comfortable grip at the other. The end with the handhold typically offers a slight rim, or lip, at the nether extremity, to prevent slippage." My description of the baseball bat ran to 4500 words, all scratched with a diamond on the south wall. Does Shotwell read what I have written? I do not know. I am aware that Shotwell regards my writing-behavior as a little strange. Yet it is no stranger than his jacks-behavior, or the day he appeared in black bathing trunks with the .25 caliber Beretta strapped to his right calf and stood over the console, trying to span with his two arms outstretched the distance between the locks. He could not do it, I had already tried, standing over the console with my two arms outstretched, the distance is too great. I was moved to comment but did not comment, comment would have provoked countercomment, comment would have led God knows where. They had in their infinite patience, in their infinite foresight, in their infinite wisdom already imagined a man standing over the console with his two arms outstretched, trying to span with his two arms outstretched the distance between the locks.

Shotwell is not himself. He has made certain overtures. The burden of his message is not clear. It has something to do with the keys, with the locks. Shotwell is a strange person. He appears to be less affected by our situation than I. He goes about his business stolidly, watching the console, studying *Introduction to Marketing,* bouncing his rubber ball on the floor in a steady, rhythmical, conscientious manner. He appears to be less affected by our situation than I am. He is stolid. He says nothing. But he has made certain overtures, certain overtures have been made. I am not sure that I understand them. They have something to do with the keys, with the locks. Shotwell has something in mind. Stolidly he shucks the shiny silver paper from the frozen enchiladas, stolidly he stuffs them into the electric oven. But he has something in mind. But there must be a quid pro quo. I insist on a quid pro quo. I have something in mind.

I am not well. I do not know our target. They do not tell us for which city the bird is targeted. I do not know. That is planning. That is not my responsibility. My responsibility is to watch the console and when certain events take place upon the console, turn my key in the lock. Shotwell bounces the rubber ball on the floor in a steady, stolid, rhythmical manner. I am aching to get my hands on the ball, on the jacks. We have been here one hundred thirty-three days owing to an oversight. I write on the walls. Shotwell chants "onesies, twosies, threesies, foursies" in a precise, well-modulated voice. Now he cups the jacks and the rubber ball in his hands and rattles them suggestively. I do not know for which city the bird is targeted. Shotwell is not himself.

Sometimes I cannot sleep. Sometimes Shotwell cannot sleep. Sometimes when Shotwell cradles me in his arms and rocks me to sleep, singing Brahms' "Guten Abend, gute Nacht," or I cradle Shotwell in my arms and rock him to sleep, singing, I understand what it is Shotwell wishes me to do. At such moments we are very close. But only if he will give me the jacks. That is fair. There is something he wants me to do with my key, while he does something with his key. But only if he will give me my turn. That is fair. I am not well.

ALICE MUNRO

1931–

Born, educated, and at present living in Ontario, Alice Munro is one of a small but impressive group of contemporary Canadian short story writers. She has published four collections.

Munro's sharp eyes fix themselves on the choices, the dilemmas, the failures and successes — whether sexual or familial — faced by women, often in early middle age, generally intelligent, keenly aware of the era they live in. A frequent theme is the desire of women to hitch their lives to men — and the frustration that comes after they have done so.

Her plain, hard realism opens up again and again to admit wise, quiet, often sorrowful insights into the relationship of the sexes. Many of her characters are "free spirits," sometimes a bit raffish, all closely observed. She does not tackle "big" themes but works with the small tensions and avoidances that give us away. Like Ring Lardner, she excels in the lively depiction of dull or at least "average" people.

"Bardon Bus" is a kind of torch song raised to the level of high craftsmanship.

Bardon Bus

I THINK OF BEING an old maid, in another generation. There were plenty of old maids in my family. I come of straitened people, madly secretive, tenacious, economical. Like them, I could make a little go a long way. A piece of Chinese silk folded in a drawer, worn by the touch of fingers in the dark. Or the one letter, hidden under maidenly garments, never needing to be opened or read because every word is known by heart, and a touch communicates the whole. Perhaps nothing so tangible, nothing but the memory of an ambiguous word, an intimate, casual tone of voice, a hard, helpless look. That could do. With no more than that I could manage, year after year as I scoured the milk pails, spit on the iron, followed the cows along the rough path among the alder and the black-eyed Susans, spread the clean wet overalls to dry on the fence, and the tea towels on the bushes. Who would the man be? He could be anybody. A soldier killed at the Somme or a farmer down the road with a rough-tongued wife and a crowd of children; a boy who went to Saskatchewan and promised to send for me, but never did, or the preacher who rouses me every Sunday with lashings of fear and promises of torment. No matter. I could fasten on any of them, in secret. A lifelong secret, lifelong dream-life. I could go round singing in the kitchen, polishing the stove, wiping the lamp chimneys, dipping water for the tea from the drinking-pail. The faintly sour smell of the scrubbed tin, the worn scrub-cloths. Upstairs my bed with the high headboard, the crocheted spread, and the rough, friendly-smelling flannelette sheets, the hot-water bottle to ease my cramps or be clenched between my legs. There I come back again and again to the center of my fantasy, to the moment when you give yourself up, give yourself over, to the assault which is guaranteed to finish off everything you've been before. A stubborn virgin's belief, this belief in perfect mastery; any broken-down wife could tell you there is no such thing.

Dipping the dipper in the pail, lapped in my harmless craziness, I'd sing hymns, and nobody would wonder.

> "He's the Lily of the Valley,
> The Bright and Morning Star.
> He's the Fairest of Ten Thousand to my Soul."

2

This summer I'm living in Toronto, in my friend Kay's apartment, finishing a book of family history which some rich people are paying me to write. Last spring, in connection with this book, I had to spend some time in Australia. There I met an anthropologist whom I had known slightly, years before, in Vancouver. He was then married to his first wife (he is now married to his third) and I was married to my first husband (I am now divorced). We both lived in Fort Camp, which was the married students' quarters, at the university.

The anthropologist had been investigating language groups in northern Queensland. He was going to spend a few weeks in the city, at a university, before joining his wife in India. She was there on a grant, studying Indian music. She is the new sort of wife with serious interests of her own. His first wife had been a girl with a job, who would help him get through the university, then stay home and have children.

We met at lunch on Saturday, and on Sunday we went up the river on an excursion boat, full of noisy families, to an animal preserve. There we looked at wombats curled up like blood puddings, and disgruntled, shoddy emus, and walked under an arbor of brilliant unfamiliar flowers and had our pictures taken with koala bears. We brought each other up-to-date on our lives, with jokes, sombre passages, buoyant sympathy. On the way back we drank gin from the bar on the boat, and kissed, and made a mild spectacle of ourselves. It was almost impossible to talk because of the noise of the engines, the crying babies, the children shrieking and chasing each other, but he said, "Please come and see my house. I've got a borrowed house. You'll like it. Please, I can't wait to ask you, please come and live with me in my house."

"Should I?"

"I'll get down on my knees," he said, and did.

"Get up, behave!" I said. "We're in a foreign country."

"That means we can do anything we like."

Some of the children had stopped their game to stare at us. They looked shocked and solemn.

3

I call him X, as if he were a character in an old-fashioned novel, that pretends to be true. X is a letter in his name, but I chose it also because it seems to suit him. The letter X seems to me expansive and secretive. And using just the letter, not needing a name, is in line with a system I often employ these days. I say to myself, "Bardon Bus, No. 144," and I see a whole succession of scenes. I see them in detail; streets and houses. LaTrobe Terrace, Paddington. Schools like large, pleasant bungalows, betting shops, frangipani trees dropping their waxy, easily bruised, and highly scented flowers. It was on this bus that we rode downtown, four or five times in all, carrying our string bags, to shop for groceries at Woolworths, meat at Coles, licorice and chocolate ginger at the candy store. Much of the city is built on ridges between gullies, so there was a sense of coming down through populous but half-wild hill villages into the central part of town, with its muddy river and pleasant colonial shabbiness. In such a short time everything seemed remarkably familiar and yet not to be confused with anything we had known in the past. We felt we knew the lives of the housewives in sun-hats riding with us on the bus, we knew the insides of the shuttered, sun-blistered houses set up on wooden posts over the gullies, we knew the streets we couldn't see. This familiarity was not oppressive but delightful, and there was a slight strangeness to it, as if we had come by it in a way we didn't understand. We moved through a leisurely domesticity with a feeling of perfect security — a security we hadn't felt, or so we told each other, in any of our legal domestic arrangements, or in any of the places where we more properly belonged. We had a holiday of lightness of spirit without the holiday feeling of being at loose ends. Every day X went off to the university and I went downtown to the research library, to look at old newspapers on the microfilm reader.

One day I went to the Toowong Cemetery to look for some graves. The cemetery was more magnificent and ill-kempt than cemeteries are in Canada. The inscriptions on some of the splendid white stones had a surprising informality. "Our Wonderful Mum," and "A Fine Fellow." I wondered what this meant, about Australians, and then I thought how we are always wondering what things mean, in another country, and I would talk this over with X.

The sexton came out of his little house, to help me. He was a young man in shorts, with a full-blown sailing ship tattooed on his chest. *Australia Felix* was its name. A harem girl on the underside of one arm, a painted warrior on top. The other arm decorated with dragons and banners. A map of Australia on the back of one hand; the Southern Cross on the back of the other. I didn't like to peer at his legs, but had an impression of complicated scenes like a vertical comic strip, and a chain of medallions wreathed in flowers, perhaps containing girls' names. I took care to get all these things straight, because of the pleasure of going home and telling X.

He too would bring things home: conversations on the bus; word derivations; connections he had found.

We were not afraid to use the word love. We lived without responsibility, without a future, in freedom, with generosity, in constant but not wearying celebration. We had no doubt that our happiness would last out the little time required. The only thing we reproached ourselves for was laziness. We wondered if we would later regret not going to the Botanical Gardens to see the lotus in bloom, not having seen one movie together; we were sure we would think of more things we wished we had told each other.

4

I dreamed that X wrote me a letter. It was all done in clumsy block printing and I thought, that's to disguise his handwriting, that's clever. But I had great trouble reading it. He said he wanted us to go on a trip to Cuba. He said the trip had been offered to him by a clergyman he met in a bar. I wondered if the clergyman might be a spy. He said we could go skiing in Vermont. He said he did not want to interfere with my life but he did want to shelter me. I loved that word. But the complications of the dream multiplied. The letter had been delayed. I tried to phone him and I couldn't get the telephone dial to work. Also it seemed I had the responsibility of a baby, asleep in a dresser drawer. Things got more and more tangled and dreary, until I woke. The word shelter was still in my head. I had to feel it shrivel. I was lying on a mattress on the floor of Kay's apartment at the corner of Queen and Bathurst streets at eight o'clock in the morning. The windows were open in the summer heat, the streets full of people going to work, the street-cars stopping and starting and creaking on the turn.

This is a cheap, pleasant apartment with high windows, white walls, unbleached cotton curtains, floorboards painted in a glossy gray. It has been a cheap temporary place for so long that nobody ever got around to changing it, so the wainscoting is still there, and the old-fashioned perforated screens over the radiators. Kay has some beautiful faded rugs, and the usual cushions and spreads, to make the mattresses on the floor look more like the divans and less like mattresses. A worn-out set of bedsprings is leaning against the wall, covered with shawls and scarves and pinned-up charcoal sketches by Kay's former lover, the artist. Nobody can figure a way to get the springs out of here, or imagine how they got up here in the first place.

Kay makes her living as a botanical illustrator, doing meticulous drawings of plants for textbooks and government handbooks. She lives on a farm, in a household of adults and children who come and go and one day are gone for good. She keeps this place in Toronto, and comes down for a day or so every couple of weeks. She likes this stretch of

Queen Street, with its taverns and secondhand stores and quiet derelicts. She doesn't stand much chance here of running into people who went to Branksome Hall with her, or danced at her wedding. When Kay married, her bridegroom wore a kilt, and his brother officers made an arch of swords. Her father was a brigadier-general; she made her debut at Government House. I often think that's why she never tires of a life of risk and improvisation, and isn't frightened by the sound of brawls late at night under these windows, or the drunks in the doorway downstairs. She doesn't feel the threat that I would feel, she never sees herself slipping under.

Kay doesn't own a kettle. She boils water in a saucepan. She is ten years younger than I am. Her hips are narrow, her hair long and straight and dark and streaked with gray. She usually wears a beret and charming, raggedy clothes from the secondhand stores. I have known her six or seven years and during that time she has often been in love. Her loves are daring, sometimes grotesque.

On the boat from Centre Island she met a paroled prisoner, a swarthy tall fellow with an embroidered headband, long gray-black hair blowing in the wind. He had been sent to jail for wrecking his ex-wife's house, or her lover's house; some crime of passion Kay boggled at, then forgave. He said he was part Indian and when he had cleared up some business in Toronto he would take her to his native island off the coast of British Columbia, where they would ride horses along the beach. She began to take riding lessons.

During her break-up with him she was afraid for her life. She found threatening, amorous notes pinned to her nightgowns and underwear. She changed her locks, she went to the police, but she didn't give up on love. Soon she was in love with the artist, who had never wrecked a house but was ruled by signs from the spirit world. He had gotten a message about her before they met, knew what she was going to say before she said it, and often saw an ominous blue fire around her neck, a yoke or a ring. One day he disappeared, leaving those sketches, and a lavish horrible book on anatomy which showed real sliced cadavers, with innards, skin, and body hair in their natural colors, injected dyes of red or blue illuminating a jungle of blood vessels. On Kay's shelves you can read a history of her love affairs: books on prison riots, autobiographies of prisoners, from the period of the parolee; this book on anatomy and others on occult phenomena, from the period of the artist; books on caves, books by Albert Speer, from the time of the wealthy German importer who taught her the word *spelunker;* books on revolution which date from the West Indian.

She takes up a man and his story wholeheartedly. She learns his language, figuratively or literally. At first she may try to disguise her condition, pretending to be prudent or ironic. "Last week I met a peculiar character —" or, "I had a funny conversation with a man at a party, did

I tell you?" Soon a tremor, a sly flutter, an apologetic but stubborn smile. "Actually I'm afraid I've fallen for him, isn't that terrible?" Next time you see her she'll be in deep, going to fortune-tellers, slipping his name into every other sentence; with this mention of the name there will be a mushy sound to her voice, a casting down of the eyes, an air of cherished helplessness, appalling to behold. Then comes the onset of gloom, the doubts and anguish, the struggle either to free herself or to keep him from freeing himself; the messages left with answering services. Once she disguised herself as an old woman, with a gray wig and a tattered fur coat; she walked up and down, in the cold, outside the house of the woman she thought to be her supplanter. She will talk coldly, sensibly, wittily, about her mistake, and tell discreditable things she has gleaned about her lover, then make desperate phone calls. She will get drunk, and sign up for rolfing, swim therapy, gymnastics.

In none of this is she so exceptional. She does what women do. Perhaps she does it more often, more openly, just a bit more ill-advisedly, and more fervently. Her powers of recovery, her faith, are never exhausted. I joke about her, everybody does, but I defend her too, saying that she is not condemned to living with reservations and withdrawals, long-drawn-out dissatisfactions, inarticulate wavering miseries. Her trust is total, her miseries are sharp, and she survives without visible damage. She doesn't allow for drift or stagnation and the spectacle of her life is not discouraging to me.

She is getting over someone now; the husband, the estranged husband, of another woman at the farm. His name is Roy; he too is an anthropologist.

"It's really a low ebb falling in love with somebody who's lived at the farm," she says. "Really low. Somebody you know all about."

I tell her I'm getting over somebody I met in Australia, and that I plan to be over him just about when I get the book done, and then I'll go and look for another job, a place to live.

"No rush, take it easy," she says.

I think about the words "getting over." They have an encouraging, crisp, everyday sound. They are in tune with Kay's present mood. When love is fresh and on the rise she grows mystical, tentative; in the time of love's decline, and past the worst of it, she is brisk and entertaining, straightforward, analytical.

"It's nothing but the desire to see yourself reflected," she says. "Love always comes back to self-love. The idiocy. You don't want them, you want what you can get from them. Obsession and self-delusion. Did you ever read those journals of Victor Hugo's daughter, I think that's who it was?"

"No."

"I never did either, but I read about them. The part I remember, the part I remember reading about, that struck me so, was where she goes out into the street after years and years of loving this man, obsessively loving him, and she meets him. She passes him in the street and she either doesn't recognize him or she does but she can't connect the real man any more with the person she loves, in her head. She can't connect him at all."

5

When I knew X in Vancouver he was a different person. A serious graduate student, still a Lutheran, stocky and resolute, rather a prig in some people's opinion. His wife was more scatterbrained; a physiotherapist named Mary, who liked sports and dancing. Of the two, you would have said she might be the one to run off. She had blonde hair, big teeth; her gums showed. I watched her play baseball at a picnic. I had to go off and sit in the bushes, to nurse my baby. I was twenty-one, a simple-looking girl, a nursing mother. Fat and pink on the outside; dark judgments and strenuous ambitions within. Sex had not begun for me, at all.

X came around the bushes and gave me a bottle of beer.

"What are you doing back here?"

"I'm feeding the baby."

"Why do you have to do it here? Nobody would care."

"My husband would have a fit."

"Oh. Well, drink up. Beer's supposed to be good for your milk, isn't it?"

That was the only time I talked to him, so far as I can remember. There was something about the direct approach, the slightly clumsy but determined courtesy, my own unexpected, lightened feeling of gratitude, that did connect with his attentions to women later, and his effect on them. I am sure he was always patient, unalarming; successful, appreciative, sincere.

6

I met Dennis in the Toronto Reference Library and he asked me out to dinner.

Dennis is a friend of X's, who came to visit us in Australia. He is a tall, slight, stiff, and brightly smiling young man — not so young either, he must be thirty-five — who has an elaborately courteous and didactic style.

I go to meet him thinking he may have a message for me. Isn't it odd, otherwise, that he would want to have dinner with an older woman he has met only once before? I think he may tell me whether X is back in Canada. X told me that they would probably come back in July. Then he was going to spend a year writing his book. They might live in Nova Scotia during that year. They might live in Ontario.

When Dennis came to see us in Australia, I made a curry. I was pleased with the idea of having a guest and glad that he arrived in time to see the brief evening light on the gully. Our house like the others was built out on posts, and from the window where we ate we looked out over a gully like an oval bowl, ringed with small houses and filled with jacaranda, poinciana, frangipani, cypress, and palm trees. Leaves like fans, whips, feathers, plates; every bright, light, dark, dusty, glossy shade of green. Guinea fowl lived down there, and flocks of rackety kookaburras took to the sky at dusk. We had to scramble down a steep dirt bank under the house to get to the wash-hut, and peg the clothes on a revolving clothesline. There we encountered spider-webs draped like tent-tops, matched like lids and basins with one above and one below. We had to watch out for the one little spider that weaves a conical web and has a poison for which there is no antidote.

We showed Dennis the gully and told him this was a typical old Queensland house with the high tongue-and-groove walls and the ventilation panels over the doors filled with graceful carved vines. He did not look at anything with much interest, but talked about China, where he had just been. X said afterwards that Dennis always talked about the last place he'd been and the last people he'd seen, and never seemed to notice anything, but that he would probably be talking about us, and describing this place, to the next people he had dinner with, in the next city. He said that Dennis spent most of his life travelling, and talking about it, and that he knew a lot of people just well enough that when he showed up somewhere he had to be asked to dinner.

Dennis told us that he had seen the recently excavated Army Camp at Sian, in China. He described the rows of life-sized soldiers, each of them so realistic and unique, some still bearing traces of the paint which had once covered them and individualized them still further. Away at their backs, he said, was a wall of earth. The terra-cotta soldiers looked as if they were marching out of the earth.

He said it reminded him of X's women. Row on row and always a new one appearing at the end of the line.

"The Army marches on," he said.

"Dennis, for God's sake," said X.

"But do they really come out of the earth like that?" I said to Dennis. "Are they intact?"

"Are which intact?" said Dennis with his harsh smile. "The soldiers or the women? The women aren't intact. Or not for long."

"Could we get off the subject?" said X.

"Certainly. Now to answer your question," said Dennis, turning to me. "They are very seldom found as whole figures. Or so I understand. Their legs and torsos and heads have to be matched up, usually. They have to be put together and stood on their feet."

"It's a lot of work, I can tell you," said X, with a large sigh.

"But it's not that way with the women," I said to Dennis. I spoke with a special, social charm, almost flirtatiously, as I often do when I detect malice. "I think the comparison's a bit off. Nobody has to dig the women out and stand them on their feet. Nobody put them there. They came along and joined up of their own free will and some day they'll leave. They're not a standing army. Most of them are probably on their way to someplace else anyway."

"Bravo," said X.

When we were washing the dishes, late at night, he said, "You didn't mind Dennis saying that, did you? You didn't mind if I went along with him a little bit? He has to have his legends."

I laid my head against his back, between the shoulder blades.

"Does he? No. I thought it was funny."

"I bet you didn't know that soap was first described by Pliny and was used by the Gauls. I bet you didn't know they boiled goat's tallow with the lye from the wood ashes."

"No. I didn't know that."

7

Dennis hasn't said a word about X, or about Australia. I wouldn't have thought his asking me to dinner strange, if I had remembered him better. He asked me so he would have somebody to talk to. Since Australia, he has been to Iceland, and the Faeroe Islands. I ask him questions. I am interested, and surprised, even shocked, when necessary. I took trouble with my makeup and washed my hair. I hope that if he does see X, he will say that I was charming.

Besides his travels Dennis has his theories. He develops theories about art and literature, history, life.

"I have a new theory about the life of women. I used to feel it was so unfair the way things happened to them."

"What things?"

"The way they have to live, compared to men. Specifically with aging.

Look at you. Think of the way your life would be, if you were a man. The choices you would have. I mean sexual choices. You could start all over. Men do. It's in all the novels and it's in life too. Men fall in love with younger women. Men want younger women. Men can get younger women. The new marriage, new babies, new families."

I wonder if he is going to tell me something about X's wife; perhaps that she is going to have a baby.

"It's such a coup for them, isn't it?" he says in his malicious, sympathetic way. "The fresh young wife, the new baby when other men their age are starting on grandchildren. All those men envying them and trying to figure out how to do the same. It's the style, isn't it? It must be hard to resist starting over and having that nice young mirror to look in, if you get the opportunity."

"I think I might resist it," I say cheerfully, not insistently. "I don't really think I'd want to have a baby, now."

"That's it, that's just it, though, you don't get the opportunity! You're a woman and life only goes in one direction for a woman. All this business about younger lovers, that's just froth, isn't it? Do you want a younger lover?"

"I guess not," I say, and pick my dessert from a tray. I pick a rich creamy pudding with pureed chestnuts at the bottom of it and fresh raspberries on top. I purposely ate a light dinner, leaving plenty of room for dessert. I did that so I could have something to look forward to, while listening to Dennis.

"A woman your age can't compete," says Dennis urgently. "You can't compete with younger women. I used to think that was so rottenly unfair."

"It's probably biologically correct for men to go after younger women. There's no use whining about it."

"So the men have this way of renewing themselves, they get this refill of vitality, while the women are you might say removed from life. I used to think that was terrible. But now my thinking has undergone a complete reversal. Do you know what I think now? I think women are the lucky ones! Do you know why?"

"Why?"

"Because they are forced to live in the world of loss and death! Oh, I know, there's face-lifting, but how does that really help? The uterus dries up. The vagina dries up."

I feel him watching me. I continue eating my pudding.

"I've seen so many parts of the world and so many strange things and so much suffering. It's my conclusion now that you won't get any happiness by playing tricks on life. It's only by natural renunciation and by accepting deprivation, that we prepare for death and therefore that we get any happiness. Maybe my ideas seem strange to you?"

I can't think of anything to say.

8

Often I have a few lines of a poem going through my head, and I won't
know what started it. It can be a poem or rhyme that I didn't even know
I knew, and it needn't be anything that conforms to what I think is my
taste. Sometimes I don't pay any attention to it, but if I do, I can usually
see that the poem, or the bit of it I've got hold of, has some relation to
what is going on in my life. And that may not be what seems to be going
on.

For instance last spring, last autumn in Australia, when I was happy,
the line that would go through my head, at a merry clip, was this:

"Even such is time, that takes in trust —"

I could not go on, though I knew trust rhymed with dust, and that
there was something further along about "and in the dark and silent
grave, shuts up the story of our days." I knew the poem was written by
Sir Walter Raleigh on the eve of his execution. My mood did not accord
with such a poem and I said it, in my head, as if it was something pretty
and lighthearted. I did not stop to wonder what it was doing in my head
in the first place.

And now that I'm trying to look at things soberly I should remember
what we said when our bags were packed and we were waiting for the
taxi. Inside the bags our clothes that had shared drawers and closet
space, tumbled together in the wash, and been pegged together on the
clothesline where the kookaburras sat, were all sorted and separated and
would not rub together any more.

"In a way I'm glad it's over and nothing spoiled it. Things are so often
spoiled."

"I know."

"As it is, it's been perfect."

I said that. And that was a lie. I had cried once, thought I was ugly,
thought he was bored.

But he said, "Perfect."

On the plane the words of the poem were going through my head
again, and I was still happy. I went to sleep thinking the bulk of X was
still beside me and when I woke I filled the space quickly with memories
of his voice, looks, warmth, our scenes together.

I was swimming in memories, at first. Those detailed, repetitive scenes
were what buoyed me up. I didn't try to escape them, didn't wish to.
Later I did wish to. They had become a plague. All they did was stir up
desire, and longing, and hopelessness, a trio of miserable caged wildcats
that had been installed in me without my permission, or at least without
my understanding how long they would live and how vicious they would
be. The images, the language, of pornography and romance are alike;
monotonous and mechanically seductive, quickly leading to despair.

That was what my mind dealt in; that is what it still can deal in. I have tried vigilance and reading serious books but I can still slide deep into some scene before I know where I am.

On the bed a woman lies in a yellow nightgown which has not been torn but has been pulled off her shoulders and twisted up around her waist so that it covers no more of her than a crumpled scarf would. A man bends over her, naked, offering a drink of water. The woman, who has almost lost consciousness, whose legs are open, arms flung out, head twisted to the side as if she has been struck down in the course of some natural disaster — this woman rouses herself and tries to hold the glass in her shaky hands. She slops water over her breast, drinks, shudders, falls back. The man's hands are trembling, too. He drinks out of the same glass, looks at her, and laughs. His laugh is rueful, apologetic, and kind, but it is also amazed, and his amazement is not far from horror. How are we capable of all this? his laugh says, what is the meaning of it?

He says, "We almost finished each other off."

The room seems still full of echoes of the recent commotion, the cries, pleas, brutal promises, the climactic sharp announcements and the long subsiding spasms.

The room is brimming with gratitude and pleasure, a rich broth of love, a golden twilight of love. Yes, yes, you can drink the air.

You see the sort of thing I mean, that is my torment.

9

This is the time of year when women are tired of sundresses, prints, sandals. It is already fall in the stores. Thick sweaters and skirts are pinned up against black or plum-colored velvet. The young salesgirls are made up like courtesans. I've become feverishly preoccupied with clothes. All the conversations in the stores make sense to me.

"The neckline doesn't work. It's too stark. I need a flutter. Do you know what I mean?"

"Yes. I know what you mean."

"I want something very classy and very provocative. Do you know what I mean?"

"Yes. I know exactly what you mean."

For years I've been wearing bleached-out colors which I suddenly can't bear. I buy a deep-red satin blouse, a purple shawl, a dark-blue skirt. I get my hair cut and pluck my eyebrows and try a lilac lipstick, a brownish rouge. I'm appalled to think of the way I went around in Australia, in a faded wraparound cotton skirt and T-shirt, my legs bare because of the heat, my face bare too and sweating under a cotton hat. My legs with the lumps of veins showing. I'm half convinced that a more artful getup would have made a more powerful impression, more dramatic clothes might have made me less discardable. I have fancies of meeting X unexpectedly at a party or on a Toronto street, and giving him a shock, devastating him with my altered looks and late-blooming splendor. But I do think you have to watch out, even in these garish times; you have to watch out for the point at which the splendor collapses into absurdity. Maybe they are all watching out, all the old women I see on Queen Street: the fat woman with pink hair; the eighty-year-old with painted-on black eyebrows; they may all be thinking they haven't gone too far yet, not quite yet. Even the buttercup woman I saw a few days ago on the streetcar, the little, stout, sixtyish woman in a frilly yellow dress well above the knees, a straw hat with yellow ribbons, yellow pumps dyed-to-match on her little fat feet — even she doesn't aim for comedy. She sees a flower in the mirror: the generous petals, the lovely buttery light.

I go looking for earrings. All day looking for earrings which I can see so clearly in my mind. I want little filigree balls of silver, of diminishing size, dangling. I want old and slightly tarnished silver. It's a style I well remember; you'd think the secondhand stores would be sure to have them. But I can't find them, I can't find anything resembling them, and they seem more and more necessary. I go into a little shop on a side street near College and Spadina. The shop is all done up in black paper with cheap, spooky effects — for instance a bald, naked mannequin sitting on a stepladder, dangling some beads. A dress such as I wore in the fifties, a dance dress of pink net and sequins, terribly scratchy under the arms, is displayed against the black paper in a way that makes it look sinister, and desirable.

I look around for the tray of jewelry. The salesgirls are busy dressing a customer hidden from me by a three-way mirror. One salesgirl is fat and gypsyish with a face warmly colored as an apricot. The other is spiky and has a crest of white hair surrounded by black hair, like a skunk. They are shrieking with pleasure as they bring hats and beads for the customer to try. Finally everybody is satisfied and a beautiful young lady, who is not a young lady at all but a pretty boy dressed up as a lady, emerges from the shelter of the mirror. He is wearing a black velvet dress with long sleeves and a black lace yoke; black pumps and gloves; a little black hat with a dotted veil. He is daintily and discreetly made up; he has a fringe of brown curls; he is the prettiest and most ladylike person I have seen all day. His smiling face is tense and tremulous. I remember how when I was ten or eleven years old I used to dress up as a bride in old curtains, or as a lady in rouge and a feathered hat. After all the effort and contriving and my own enchantment with the finished product there was a considerable letdown. What are you supposed to do now? Parade up and down on the sidewalk? There is a great fear and daring and disappointment in this kind of display.

He has a boyish, cracking voice. He is brash and timid.

"How do I look, momma?"

"You look very nice."

10

I am at a low point. I can recognize it. That must mean I will get past it.

I am at a low point, certainly. I cannot deal with all that assails me unless I get help and there is only one person I want help from and that is X. I can't continue to move my body along the streets unless I exist in his mind and in his eyes. People have this problem frequently, and we know it is their own fault and they have to change their way of thinking, that's all. It is not an honorable problem. Love is not serious though it may be fatal. I read that somewhere and I believe it. Thank God I don't know where he is. I can't telephone him, write letters to him, waylay him on the street.

A man I had broken with used to follow me. Finally he persuaded me to go into a café and have a cup of tea with him.

"I know what a spectacle I am," he said. "I know if you did have any love left for me this would destroy it."

I said nothing.

He beat the spoon against the sugar bowl.

"What do you think of, when you're with me?"

I meant to say, "I don't know," but instead I said, "I think of how much I want to get away."

He reared up trembling and dropped the spoon on the floor.

"You're free of me," he said in a choking voice.

This is the scene both comic and horrible, stagy and real. He was in desperate need, as I am now, and I didn't pity him, and I'm not sorry I didn't.

11

I have had a pleasant dream that seems far away from my waking state. X and I and some other people I didn't know or can't remember were wearing innocent athletic underwear outfits, which changed at some point into gauzy bright white clothes, and these turned out to be not just clothes but our substances, our flesh and bones and in a sense our souls. Embraces took place which started out with the usual urgency but were transformed, by the lightness and sweetness of our substance, into a rare state of content. I can't describe it very well, it sounds like a movie-dream of heaven, all banality and innocence. So I suppose it was. I can't apologize for the banality of my dreams.

12

I go along the street to Rooneem's Bakery and sit at one of their little tables with a cup of coffee. Rooneem's is an Estonian bakery where you can usually find a Mediterranean housewife in a black dress, a child looking at the cakes, and a man talking to himself.

I sit where I can watch the street. I have a feeling X is somewhere in the vicinity. Within a thousand miles, say, within a hundred miles, within this city. He doesn't know my address but he knows I am in Toronto. It would not be so difficult to find me.

At the same time I'm thinking that I have to let go. What you have to decide, really, is whether to be crazy or not, and I haven't the stamina, the pure, seething will, for prolonged craziness.

There is a limit to the amount of misery and disarray you will put up with, for love, just as there is a limit to the amount of mess you can stand around a house. You can't know the limit beforehand, but you will know when you've reached it. I believe this.

When you start really letting go this is what it's like. A lick of pain, furtive, darting up where you don't expect it. Then a lightness. The lightness is something to think about. It isn't just relief. There's a queer kind of pleasure in it, not a self-wounding or malicious pleasure, nothing personal at all. It's an uncalled-for pleasure in seeing how the design wouldn't fit and the structure wouldn't stand, a pleasure in taking into account, all over again, everything that is contradictory and persistent and unaccommodating about life. I think so. I think there's something in us wanting to be reassured about that, right alongside — and at war with — whatever there is that wants permanent vistas and a lot of fine talk.

I think about my white dream and how it seemed misplaced. It strikes me that misplacement is the clue, in love, the heart of the problem, but like somebody drunk or high I can't quite get a grasp on what I see.

What I need is a rest. A deliberate sort of rest, with new definitions of luck. Not the sort of luck Dennis was talking about. You're lucky to be sitting in Rooneem's drinking coffee, with people coming and going, eating and drinking, buying cakes, speaking Spanish, Portuguese, Chinese, and other languages that you can try to identify.

13

Kay is back from the country. She too had a new outfit, a dark-green schoolgirl's tunic worn without a blouse or brassiere. She has dark-green knee socks and saddle oxfords.

"Does it look kinky?"

"Yes it does."

"Does it make my arms look dusky? Remember in some old poem a woman had dusky arms?"

Her arms do look soft and brown.

"I meant to get down on Sunday but Roy came over with a friend and we all had a corn roast. It was lovely. You should come out there. You should."

"Some day I will."

"The kids ran around like beautiful demons and we drank up the mead. Roy knows how to make fertility dolls. Roy's friend is Alex Walther, the anthropologist. I felt I should have known about him but I didn't. He didn't mind. He's a nice man. Do you know what he did? After dark when we were sitting around the fire he came over to me and just sighed, and laid his head on my lap. I thought it was such a nice simple thing to do. Like a St. Bernard. I've never had anybody do that before."

John Updike
1932–

Born in Shillington, Pennsylvania (the "Olinger" of his stories), Updike attended Harvard College and the Ruskin School of Drawing and Fine Art in Oxford. His training as an artist is reflected in the visual acuteness of his imagery. Extraordinarily prolific, he has worked with equal ease in the fields of the novel, the short story, literary criticism, and poetry. He is an expert ventriloquist, his assortment of convincing voices including small-town car dealers, WASP exurbanites and suburbanites, young (and troubled) marrieds, adolescents, Jewish novelists, and modern witches and warlocks.

Adept at the exact registration of quotidian surface experience, he surprises us with his sudden subsurface descents, all recorded in a flexible prose that can be perfectly straightforward but is also often colored by the luxuriant, even the dandiacal. Elegance and the feathery touch distinguish much of his work. He is a virtuoso performer.

"Pigeon Feathers" modulates a traditional theme: the shock the trusting adolescent mind feels when suddenly faced with the great unanswerable questions — death, the immortality of the soul, the resurrection of the body, the truth or illusion of dogmatic faith. It is rich in the symbolic correspondences, crafty echoes and chimes that sound also in some of his novels. The elaborate pigeon metaphor works effectively to convey the confusion, the sense of "an ocean of horror," the desperate appeal for certainty, of a sensitive fourteen-year-old. One knows David is destined to become quite a good writer.

Pigeon Feathers

WHEN THEY MOVED to Firetown, things were upset, displaced, re-arranged. A red cane-back sofa that had been the chief piece in the living room at Olinger was here banished, too big for the narrow country parlor, to the barn, and shrouded under a tarpaulin. Never again would David lie on its length all afternoon eating raisins and reading mystery novels and science fiction and P. G. Wodehouse. The blue wing chair that had stood for years in the ghostly, immaculate guest bedroom, gazing through the windows curtained with dotted swiss toward the telephone wires and horse-chestnut trees and opposite houses, was here established importantly in front of the smutty little fireplace that supplied, in those first cold April days, their only heat. As a child, David had been afraid of the guest bedroom — it was there that he, lying sick with the measles, had seen a black rod the size of a yardstick jog along at a slight slant beside the edge of the bed and vanish when he screamed — and it was disquieting to have one of the elements of its haunted atmosphere basking by the fire, in the center of the family, growing sooty with use. The books that at home had gathered dust in the case beside the piano were here hastily stacked, all out of order, in the shelves that the carpenters had built along one wall below the deep-silled windows. David, at fourteen, had been more moved than a mover; like the furniture, he had to find a new place, and on the Saturday of the second week he tried to work off some of his disorientation by arranging the books.

It was a collection obscurely depressing to him, mostly books his mother had acquired when she was young: college anthologies of Greek plays and Romantic poetry, Will Durant's *Story of Philosophy*, a soft-leather set of Shakespeare with string bookmarks sewed to the bindings, *Green Mansions* boxed and illustrated with woodcuts, *I, the Tiger*, by Manuel Komroff, novels by names like Galsworthy and Ellen Glasgow and Irvin S. Cobb and Sinclair Lewis and "Elizabeth." The odor of faded taste made him feel the ominous gap between himself and his parents, the insulting gulf of time that existed before he was born. Suddenly he was tempted to dip into this time. From the heaps of books piled around him on the worn old floorboards, he picked up Volume II of a four-volume set of *The Outline of History*, by H. G. Wells. Once David had read *The Time Machine* in an anthology; this gave him a small grip on the author. The book's red binding had faded to orange-pink on the spine. When he lifted the cover, there was a sweetish, attic-like smell, and his mother's maiden name written in unfamiliar handwriting on the flyleaf — an upright, bold, yet careful signature, bearing a faint relation to the quick scrunched backslant that flowed with marvellous consistency across her shopping lists and budget accounts and Christmas cards to college friends from this same, vaguely menacing long ago.

He leafed through, pausing at drawings, done in an old-fashioned stippled style, of bas-reliefs, masks, Romans without pupils in their eyes, articles of ancient costume, fragments of pottery found in unearthed homes. He knew it would be interesting in a magazine, sandwiched between ads and jokes, but in this undiluted form history was somehow sour. The print was determinedly legible, and smug, like a lesson book. As he bent over the pages, yellow at the edges, they seemed rectangles of dusty glass through which he looked down into unreal and irrelevant worlds. He could see things sluggishly move, and an unpleasant fullness came into his throat. His mother and grandmother fussed in the kitchen; the puppy, which they had just acquired, for "protection in the country," was cowering, with a sporadic panicked scrabble of claws, under the dining table that in their old home had been reserved for special days but that here was used for every meal.

Then, before he could halt his eyes, David slipped into Wells's account of Jesus. He had been an obscure political agitator, a kind of hobo, in a minor colony of the Roman Empire. By an accident impossible to reconstruct, he (the small *h* horrified David) survived his own crucifixion and presumably died a few weeks later. A religion was founded on the freakish incident. The credulous imagination of the times retrospectively assigned miracles and supernatural pretensions to Jesus; a myth grew, and then a church, whose theology at most points was in direct contradiction of the simple, rather communistic teachings of the Galilean.

It was as if a stone that for weeks and even years had been gathering weight in the web of David's nerves snapped them and plunged through the page and a hundred layers of paper underneath. These fantastic falsehoods — plainly untrue; churches stood everywhere, the entire nation was founded "under God" — did not at first frighten him; it was the fact that they had been permitted to exist in an actual human brain. This was the initial impact — that at a definite spot in time and space a brain black with the denial of Christ's divinity had been suffered to exist; that the universe had not spit out this ball of tar but allowed it to continue in its blasphemy, to grow old, win honors, wear a hat, write books that, if true, collapsed everything into a jumble of horror. The world outside the deep-silled windows — a rutted lawn, a whitewashed barn, a walnut tree frothy with fresh green — seemed a haven from which he was forever sealed off. Hot washrags seemed pressed against his cheeks.

He read the account again. He tried to supply out of his ignorance objections that would defeat the complacent march of these black words, and found none. Survivals and misunderstandings more far-fetched were reported daily in the papers. But none of them caused churches to be built in every town. He tried to work backwards through the churches, from their brave high fronts through their shabby, ill-attended interiors back into the events at Jerusalem, and felt himself surrounded by shifting gray shadows, centuries of history, where he knew nothing. The thread dissolved in his hands. Had Christ ever come to him, David Kern, and said, "Here. Feel the wound in My side"? No; but prayers had been answered. What prayers? He had prayed that Rudy Mohn, whom he had purposely tripped so he cracked his head on their radiator, not die, and he had not died. But for all the blood, it was just a cut; Rudy came back the same day, wearing a bandage and repeating the same teasing words. He could never have died. Again, David had prayed for two separate war-effort posters he had sent away for to arrive tomorrow, and though they did not, they did arrive, some days later, together, popping through the clacking letter slot like a rebuke from God's mouth: *I answer your prayers in My way, in My time.* After that, he had made his prayers less definite, less susceptible of being twisted into a scolding. But what a tiny, ridiculous coincidence this was, after all, to throw into battle against H. G. Wells's engines of knowledge! Indeed, it proved the enemy's point: Hope bases vast premises on foolish accidents, and reads a word where in fact only a scribble exists.

His father came home. Though Saturday was a free day for him, he had been working. He taught school in Olinger and spent all his days performing, with a curious air of panic, needless errands. Also, a city boy by birth, he was frightened of the farm and seized any excuse to get away. The farm had been David's mother's birthplace; it had been her idea to buy it back. With an ingenuity and persistence unparalleled in her life, she had gained that end, and moved them all here — her son, her husband, her mother. Granmom, in her prime, had worked these fields alongside her husband, but now she dabbled around the kitchen futilely, her hands waggling with Parkinson's disease. She was always in the way. Strange, out in the country, amid eighty acres, they were crowded together. His father expressed his feelings of discomfort by conducting with Mother an endless argument about organic farming. All through dusk, all through supper, it rattled on.

"Elsie, I *know*, I know from my education, the earth is nothing but chemicals. It's the only damn thing I got out of four years of college, so don't tell me it's not true."

"George, if you'd just walk out on the farm you'd know it's not true. The land has a *soul*."

"Soil, has, no, soul," he said, enunciating stiffly, as if to a very stupid class. To David he said, "You can't argue with a femme. Your mother's a real femme. That's why I married her, and now I'm suffering for it."

"*This* soil has no soul," she said, "because it's been killed with super-phosphate. It's been burned bare by Boyer's tenant farmers." Boyer was the rich man they had bought the farm from. "It used to have a soul, didn't it, Mother? When you and Pop farmed it?"

"Ach, yes; I guess." Granmom was trying to bring a forkful of food to her mouth with her less severely afflicted hand. In her anxiety she brought the other hand up from her lap. The crippled fingers, dull red in the orange light of the kerosene lamp in the center of the table, were welded by paralysis into one knobbed hook.

"Only human indi-vidu-als have souls," his father went on, in the same mincing, lifeless voice. "Because the Bible tells us so." Done eating, he crossed his legs and dug into his ear with a match miserably; to get at the thing inside his head he tucked in his chin, and his voice came out low-pitched at David. "When God made your mother, He made a real femme."

"George, don't you read the papers? Don't you know that between the chemical fertilizers and the bug sprays we'll all be dead in ten years? Heart attacks are killing every man in the country over forty-five."

He sighed wearily; the yellow skin of his eyelids wrinkled as he hurt himself with the match. "There's no connection," he stated, spacing his words with pained patience, "between the heart — and chemical fertil-izers. It's alcohol that's doing it. Alcohol and milk. There is too much — cholesterol — in the tissues of the American heart. Don't tell me about chemistry, Elsie; I majored in the damn stuff for four years."

"Yes and I majored in Greek and I'm not a penny wiser. Mother, put your waggler *away!*" The old woman started, and the food dropped from her fork. For some reason, the sight of her bad hand at the table cruelly irritated her daughter. Granmom's eyes, worn bits of crazed crys-tal embedded in watery milk, widened behind her cockeyed spectacles. Circles of silver as fine as thread, they clung to the red notches they had carved over the years into her little white beak. In the orange flicker of the kerosene lamp her dazed misery seemed infernal. David's mother began, without noise, to cry. His father did not seem to have eyes at all; just jaundiced sockets of wrinkled skin. The steam of food clouded the scene. It was horrible but the horror was particular and familiar, and distracted David from the formless dread that worked, sticky and sore, within him, like a too large wound trying to heal.

He had to go to the bathroom, and took a flashlight down through the wet grass to the outhouse. For once, his fear of spiders there felt trivial. He set the flashlight, burning, beside him, and an insect alighted on its lens, a tiny insect, a mosquito or flea, made so fine that the weak light projected its X-ray onto the wall boards; the faint rim of its wings, the blurred strokes, magnified, of its long hinged legs, the dark cone at the heart of its anatomy. The tremor must be its heart beating. Without warning, David was visited by an exact vision of death: a long hole in the ground, no wider than your body, down which you are drawn while the white faces above recede. You try to reach them but your arms are pinned. Shovels pour dirt into your face. There you will be forever, in an upright position, blind and silent, and in time no one will remember you, and you will never be called. As strata of rock shift, your fingers elongate, and your teeth are distended sideways in a great underground grimace indistinguishable from a strip of chalk. And the earth tumbles on, and the sun expires, and unaltering darkness reigns where once there were stars.

Sweat broke out on his back. His mind seemed to rebound off a solidness. Such extinction was not another threat, a graver sort of danger, a kind of pain; it was qualitatively different. It was not even a conception that could be voluntarily pictured; it entered him from outside. His protesting nerves swarmed on its surface like lichen on a meteor. The skin of his chest was soaked with the effort of rejection. At the same time that the fear was dense and internal, it was dense and all around him; a tide of clay had swept up to the stars; space was crushed into a mass. When he stood up, automatically hunching his shoulders to keep his head away from the spider webs, it was with a numb sense of being cramped between two huge volumes of rigidity. That he had even this small freedom to move surprised him. In the narrow shelter of that rank shack, adjusting his pants, he felt — his first spark of comfort — too small to be crushed.

But in the open, as the beam of the flashlight skidded with frightened quickness across the remote surfaces of the barn and the grape arbor and the giant pine that stood by the path to the woods, the terror descended. He raced up through the clinging grass pursued, not by one of the wild animals the woods might hold, or one of the goblins his superstitious grandmother had communicated to his childhood, but by spectres out of science fiction, where gigantic cinder moons fill half the turquoise sky. As David ran, a gray planet rolled inches behind his neck. If he looked back, he would be buried. And in the momentum of his terror, hideous possibilities — the dilation of the sun, the triumph of the insects, the crabs on the shore in *The Time Machine* — wheeled out of the vacuum of make-believe and added their weight to his impending oblivion.

He wrenched the door open; the lamps within the house flared. The wicks burning here and there seemed to mirror one another. His mother was washing the dishes in a little pan of heated pump-water; Granmom fluttered near her elbow apprehensive. In the living room — the downstairs of the little square house was two long rooms — his father sat in front of the black fireplace restlessly folding and unfolding a newspaper as he sustained his half of the argument. "Nitrogen phosphorus, potash: these are the three replaceable constituents of the soil. One crop of corn carries away hundreds of pounds of" — he dropped the paper into his lap and ticked them off on three fingers — "nitrogen, phosphorus, potash."

"Boyer didn't grow corn."

"*Any* crop, Elsie. The human animal —"

"You're killing the *earth*worms, George!"

"The human animal, after thousands and *thou*sands of years, learned methods whereby the chemical balance of the soil may be maintained. Don't carry me back to the Dark Ages."

"When we moved to Olinger the ground in the garden was like slate. Just one summer of my cousin's chicken dung and the earthworms came back."

"I'm sure the Dark Ages were a fine place to the poor devils born in them, but I don't want to go there. They give me the creeps." Daddy stared into the cold pit of the fireplace and clung to the rolled newspaper in his lap as if it alone were keeping him from slipping backwards and down, down.

Mother came into the doorway brandishing a fistful of wet forks. "And thanks to your DDT there soon won't be a bee left in the country. When I was a girl here you could eat a peach without washing it."

"It's primitive, Elsie. It's Dark Age stuff."

"Oh what do *you* know about the Dark Ages?"

"I know I don't want to go back to them."

David took from the shelf, where he had placed it this afternoon, the great unabridged Webster's Dictionary that his grandfather had owned. He turned the big thin pages, floppy as cloth, to the entry he wanted, and read

> soul . . . 1. An entity conceived as the essence, substance, animating principle, or actuating cause of life, or of the individual life, esp. of life manifested in psychical activities; the vehicle of individual existence, separate in nature from the body and usually held to be separable in existence.

The definition went on, into Greek and Egyptian conceptions, but David stopped short on the treacherous edge of antiquity. He needed to read no further. The careful overlapping words shingled a temporary shelter for him. "Usually held to be separable in existence" — what could be fairer, more judicious, surer?

His father was saying, "The modern farmer can't go around sweeping up after his cows. The poor devil has thousands and *thou*sands of acres on his hands. Your modern farmer uses a scientifically-arrived-at mixture, like five-ten-five, or six-twelve-six, or *three*-twelve-six, and spreads it on with this wonderful modern machinery which of course we can't afford. Your modern farmer can't *afford* medieval methods."

Mother was quiet in the kitchen; her silence radiated waves of anger.

"Now now Elsie; don't play the femme with me. Let's discuss this calmly like two rational twentieth-century people. Your organic farming nuts aren't attacking five-ten-five; they're attacking the chemical fertilizer crooks. The monster firms."

A cup clinked in the kitchen. Mother's anger touched David's face; his cheeks burned guiltily. Just by being in the living room he was associated with his father. She appeared in the doorway with red hands and tears in her eyes, and said to the two of them, "I knew you didn't want to come here but I didn't know you'd torment me like this. You talked Pop into his grave and now you'll kill me. Go ahead, George, more power to you; at least I'll be buried in good ground." She tried to turn and met an obstacle and screamed, "Mother, stop hanging on my *back!* Why don't you go to *bed?*"

"Let's all go to bed," David's father said, rising from the blue wing chair and slapping his thigh with a newspaper. "This reminds me of death." It was a phrase of his that David had heard so often he never considered its sense.

Upstairs, he seemed to be lifted above his fears. The sheets on his bed were clean. Granmom had ironed them with a pair of flatirons saved from the Olinger attic; she plucked them hot off the stove alternately, with a wooden handle called a goose. It was a wonder, to see how she managed. In the next room, his parents grunted peaceably; they seemed to take their quarrels less seriously than he did. They made comfortable scratching noises as they carried a little lamp back and forth. Their door was open a crack, so he saw the light shift and swing. Surely there would be, in the last five minutes, in the last second, a crack of light, showing the door from the dark room to another, full of light. Thinking of it this vividly frightened him. His own dying, in a specific bed in a specific room, specific walls mottled with wallpaper, the dry whistle of his breathing, the murmuring doctors, the nervous relatives going in and out, but for him no way out but down into the funnel. *Never touch a doorknob again.* A whisper, and his parents' light was blown out. David prayed to be reassured. Though the experiment frightened him, he lifted his hands high into the darkness above his face and begged Christ to touch them. Not hard or long: the faintest, quickest grip would be final for a lifetime. His hands waited in the air, itself a substance, which seemed to move through his fingers; or was it the pressure of his pulse? He returned his hands to beneath the covers uncertain if they had been touched or not. For would not Christ's touch *be* infinitely gentle?

Through all the eddies of its aftermath, David clung to this thought about his revelation of extinction: that there, in the outhouse, he had struck a solidness qualitatively different, a rock of horror firm enough to support any height of construction. All he needed was a little help; a word, a gesture, a nod of certainty, and he would be sealed in, safe. The assurance from the dictionary had melted in the night. Today was Sunday, a hot fair day. Across a mile of clear air the church bells called, *Celebrate, celebrate.* Only Daddy went. He put on a coat over his rolled-up shirtsleeves and got into the little old black Plymouth parked by the barn and went off, with the same pained hurried grimness of all his actions. His churning wheels, as he shifted too hastily into second, raised plumes of red dust on the dirt road. Mother walked to the far field, to see what bushes needed cutting. David, though he usually preferred to stay in the house, went with her. The puppy followed at a distance, whining as it picked its way through the stubble but floundering off timidly if one of them went back to pick it up and carry it. When they reached the crest of the far field, his mother asked, "David, what's troubling you?"

"Nothing. Why?"

She looked at him sharply. The greening woods cross-hatched the space beyond her half-gray hair. Then she showed him her profile, and gestured toward the house, which they had left a half-mile behind them. "See how it sits in the land? They don't know how to build with the land any more. Pop always said the foundations were set with the compass. We must try to get a compass and see. It's supposed to face due south; but south feels a little more *that* way to me." From the side, as she said these things, she seemed handsome and young. The smooth sweep of her hair over her ear seemed white with a purity and calm that made her feel foreign to him. He had never regarded his parents as consolers of his troubles; from the beginning they had seemed to have more troubles than he. Their confusion had flattered him into an illusion of strength; so now on this high clear ridge he jealously guarded the menace all around them, blowing like a breeze on his fingertips, the possibility of all this wide scenery sinking into darkness. The strange fact that though she came to look at the brush she carried no clippers, for she had a fixed prejudice against working on Sundays, was the only consolation he allowed her to offer.

As they walked back, the puppy whimpering after them, the rising dust behind a distant line of trees announced that Daddy was speeding home from church. When they reached the house he was there. He had brought back the Sunday paper and the vehement remark, "Dobson's too intelligent for these farmers. They just sit there with their mouths open and don't hear a thing the poor devil's saying."

"What makes you think farmers are unintelligent? This country was made by farmers. George Washington was a farmer."

"They are, Elsie. They are unintelligent. George Washington's dead. In this day and age only the misfits stay on the farm. The lame, the halt, the blind. The morons with one arm. Human garbage. They remind me of death, sitting there with their mouths open."

"My *father* was a farmer."

"He was a frustrated man, Elsie. He never knew what hit him. The poor devil meant so well, and he never knew which end was up. Your mother'll bear me out. Isn't that right, Mom? Pop never knew what hit him?"

"Ach, I guess not," the old woman quavered, and the ambiguity for the moment silenced both sides.

David hid in the funny papers and sports section until one-thirty. At two, the catechetical class met at the Firetown church. He had transferred from the catechetical class of the Lutheran church in Olinger, a humiliating comedown. In Olinger they met on Wednesday nights, spiffy and spruce, in the atmosphere of a dance. Afterwards, blessed by the brick-faced minister from whose lips the word "Christ" fell like a burning stone, the more daring of them went with their Bibles to a luncheonette and smoked. Here in Firetown, the girls were dull white cows and the boys narrow-faced brown goats in old men's suits, herded on Sunday afternoons into a threadbare church basement that smelled of stale hay. Because his father had taken the car on one of his endless errands to Olinger, David walked, grateful for the open air and the silence. The catechetical class embarrassed him, but today he placed hope in it, as the source of the nod, the gesture, that was all he needed.

Reverend Dobson was a delicate young man with great dark eyes and small white shapely hands that flickered like protesting doves when he preached; he seemed a bit misplaced in the Lutheran ministry. This was his first call. It was a split parish; he served another rural church twelve miles away. His iridescent green Ford, new six months ago, was spattered to the windows with red mud and rattled from bouncing on the rude back roads, where he frequently got lost, to the malicious satisfaction of many. But David's mother liked him, and, more pertinent to his success, the Haiers, the sleek family of feed merchants and innkeepers and tractor salesmen who dominated the Firetown church, liked him. David liked him, and felt liked in turn; sometimes in class, after some special stupidity, Dobson directed toward him out of those wide black eyes a mild look of disbelief, a look that, though flattering, was also delicately disquieting.

Catechetical instruction consisted of reading aloud from a work booklet answers to problems prepared during the week, problems like, "I am the _____ , the _____ , and the _____ , saith the Lord." Then there was a question period in which no one ever asked any questions. Today's theme was the last third of the Apostles' Creed. When the time came for questions, David blushed and asked, "About the Resurrection of the Body — are we conscious between the time when we die and the Day of Judgment?"

Dobson blinked, and his fine little mouth pursed, suggesting that David was making difficult things more difficult. The faces of the other students went blank, as if an indiscretion had been committed.

"No, I suppose not," Reverend Dobson said.

"Well, where is our soul, then, in this gap?"

The sense grew, in the class, of a naughtiness occurring. Dobson's shy eyes watered, as if he were straining to keep up the formality of attention, and one of the girls, the fattest, simpered toward her twin, who was a little less fat. Their chairs were arranged in a rough circle. The current running around the circle panicked David. Did everybody know something he didn't know?

"I suppose you could say our souls are asleep," Dobson said.

"And then they wake up, and there is the earth like it always is, and all the people who have ever lived? Where will Heaven be?"

Anita Haier giggled. Dobson gazed at David intently, but with an awkward, puzzled flicker of forgiveness, as if there existed a secret between them that David was violating. But David knew of no secret. All he wanted was to hear Dobson repeat the words he said every Sunday morning. This he would not do. As if these words were unworthy of the conversational voice.

"David, you might think of Heaven this way: as the way the goodness Abraham Lincoln did lives after him."

"But is Lincoln conscious of it living on?" He blushed no longer with embarrassment but in anger; he had walked here in good faith and was being made a fool.

"Is he conscious now? I would have to say no; but I don't think it matters." His voice had a coward's firmness; he was hostile now.

"You don't."

"Not in the eyes of God, no." The unction, the stunning impudence, of this reply sprang tears of outrage in David's eyes. He bowed them to his book, where short words like Duty, Love, Obey, Honor, were stacked in the form of a cross.

"Were there any other questions, David?" Dobson asked with renewed gentleness. The others were rustling, collecting their books.

"No." He made his voice firm, though he could not bring up his eyes.

"Did I answer your question fully enough?"

"Yes."

In the minister's silence the shame that should have been his crept over David: the burden and fever of being a fraud were placed upon *him*, who was innocent, and it seemed, he knew, a confession of this guilt that on the way out he was unable to face Dobson's stirred gaze, though he felt it probing the side of his head.

Anita Haier's father gave him a ride down the highway as far as the dirt road. David said he wanted to walk the rest, and figured that his offer was accepted because Mr. Haier did not want to dirty his bright blue Buick with dust. This was all right; everything was all right, as long as it was clear. His indignation at being betrayed, at seeing Christianity betrayed, had hardened him. The straight dirt road reflected his hardness. Pink stones thrust up through its packed surface. The April sun beat down from the center of the afternoon half of the sky; already it had some of summer's heat. Already the fringes of weeds at the edges of the road were bedraggled with dust. From the reviving grass and scuff of the fields he walked between, insects were sending up a monotonous, automatic chant. In the distance a tiny figure in his father's coat was walking along the edge of the woods. His mother. He wondered what joy she found in such walks; to him the brown stretches of slowly rising and falling land expressed only a huge exhaustion.

Flushed with fresh air and happiness, she returned from her walk earlier than he had expected, and surprised him at his grandfather's Bible. It was a stumpy black book, the boards worn thin where the old man's fingers had held them; the spine hung by one weak hinge of fabric. David had been looking for the passage where Jesus says to the one thief on the cross, "Today shalt thou be with me in paradise." He had never tried reading the Bible for himself before. What was so embarrassing about being caught at it, was that he detested the apparatus of piety. Fusty churches, creaking hymns, ugly Sunday-school teachers and their stupid leaflets — he hated everything about them but the promise they held out, a promise that in the most perverse way, as if the homeliest crone in the kingdom were given the Prince's hand, made every good and real thing, ball games and jokes and pert-breasted girls, possible. He couldn't explain this to his mother. There was no time. Her solicitude was upon him.

"David, what are you doing?"

"Nothing."

"What are you doing at Grandpop's Bible?"

"Trying to read it. This is supposed to be a Christian country, isn't it?"

She sat down on the green sofa, which used to be in the sun parlor at Olinger, under the fancy mirror. A little smile still lingered on her face from the walk. "David, I wish you'd talk to me."

"What about?"

"About whatever it is that's troubling you. Your father and I have both noticed it."

"I asked Reverend Dobson about Heaven and he said it was like Abraham Lincoln's goodness living after him."

He waited for the shock to strike her. "Yes?" she said, expecting more.

"That's all."

"And why didn't you like it?"

"Well; don't you see? It amounts to saying there isn't any Heaven at all."

"I don't see that it amounts to that. What do you want Heaven to be?"

"Well, I don't know. I want it to be *something*. I thought he'd tell me what it was. I thought that was his job." He was becoming angry, sensing her surprise at him. She had assumed that Heaven had faded from his head years ago. She had imagined that he had already entered, in the secrecy of silence, the conspiracy that he now knew to be all around him.

"David," she asked gently, "don't you ever want to rest?"

"No. Not forever."

"David, you're so young. When you get older, you'll feel differently."

"Grandpa didn't. Look how tattered this book is."

"I never understood your grandfather."

"Well I don't understand ministers who say it's like Lincoln's goodness going on and on. Suppose you're not Lincoln?"

"I think Reverend Dobson made a mistake. You must try to forgive him."

"It's not a *question* of his making a mistake! It's a question of dying and never moving or seeing or hearing anything ever again."

"But" — in exasperation — "darling, it's so *greedy* of you to want more. When God has given us this wonderful April day, and given us this farm, and you have your whole life ahead of you —"

"You think, then, that there is God?"

"Of course I do" — with deep relief, that smoothed her features into a reposeful oval. He had risen and was standing too near her for his comfort. He was afraid she would reach out and touch him.

"He made everything? You feel that?"

"Yes."

"Then who made Him?"

"Why, Man. Man." The happiness of this answer lit up her face radiantly, until she saw his gesture of disgust. She was so simple, so illogical; such a femme.

"Well that amounts to saying there is none."

Her hand reached for his wrist but he backed away. "David, it's a mystery. A miracle. It's a miracle more beautiful than any Reverend Dobson could have told you about. You don't say houses don't exist because Man made them."

"No. God has to be different."

"But, David, you have the *evidence*. Look out the window at the sun; at the fields."

"Mother, good grief. Don't you see" — he rasped away the roughness in his throat — "if when we die there's nothing, all your sun and fields and what not are all, ah, *horror?* It's just an ocean of horror."

"But David, it's not. It's so clearly not that." And she made an urgent opening gesture with her hands that expressed, with its suggestion of a willingness to receive his helplessness, all her grace, her gentleness, her love of beauty, gathered into a passive intensity that made him intensely hate her. He would not be wooed away from the truth. *I am the Way, the Truth . . .*

"No," he told her. "Just let me alone."

He found his tennis ball behind the piano and went outside to throw it against the side of the house. There was a patch high up where the brown stucco that had been laid over the sandstone masonry was crumbling away; he kept trying with the tennis ball to chip more pieces off. Superimposed upon his deep ache was a smaller but more immediate worry; that he had hurt his mother. He heard his father's car rattling on the straightaway, and went into the house, to make peace before he arrived. To his relief, she was not giving off the stifling damp heat of her anger, but instead was cool, decisive, maternal. She handed him an old green book, her college text of Plato.

"I want you to read the Parable of the Cave," she said.

"All right," he said, though he knew it would do no good. Some story by a dead Greek just vague enough to please her. "Don't worry about it, Mother."

"I *am* worried. Honestly, David, I'm sure there will be something for us. As you get older, these things seem to matter a great deal less."

"That may be. It's a dismal thought, though."

His father bumped at the door. The locks and jambs stuck here. But before Granmom could totter to the latch and let him in, he had knocked it open. He had been in Olinger dithering with track meet tickets. Although Mother usually kept her talks with David a confidence, a treasure between them, she called instantly, "George, David is worried about death!"

He came to the doorway of the living room, his shirt pocket bristling with pencils, holding in one hand a pint box of melting ice cream and in the other the knife with which he was about to divide it into four sections, their Sunday treat. "Is the kid worried about death? Don't give it a thought, David. I'll be lucky if I live till tomorrow, and I'm not worried. If they'd taken a buckshot gun and shot me in the cradle I'd be better off. The *world*'d be better off. Hell, I think death is a wonderful thing. I look forward to it. Get the garbage out of the way. If I had the man here who invented death, I'd pin a medal on him."

"Hush, George. You'll frighten the child worse than he is."

This was not true; he never frightened David. There was no harm in his father, no harm at all. Indeed, in the man's steep self-disgust the boy felt a kind of ally. A distant ally. He saw his position with a certain strategic coldness. Nowhere in the world of other people would he find the hint, the nod, he needed to begin to build his fortress against death. They none of them believed. He was alone. In that deep hole.

In the months that followed, his position changed little. School was some comfort. All those sexy, perfumed people, wisecracking, chewing gum, all of them doomed to die, and none of them noticing. In their company David felt that they would carry him along into the bright, cheap paradise reserved for them. In any crowd, the fear ebbed a little;

he had reasoned that somewhere in the world there must exist a few people who believed what was necessary, and the larger the crowd, the greater the chance that he was near such a soul, within calling distance, if only he was not too ignorant, too ill-equipped, to spot him. The sight of clergymen cheered him; whatever they themselves thought, their collars were still a sign that somewhere, at some time, someone had recognized that we cannot, *cannot,* submit to death. The sermon topics posted outside churches, the flip, hurried pieties of disc jockeys, the cartoons in magazines showing angels or devils — on such scraps he kept alive the possibility of hope.

For the rest, he tried to drown his hopelessness in clatter and jostle. The pinball machine at the luncheonette was a merciful distraction; as he bent over its buzzing, flashing board of flippers and cushions, the weight and constriction in his chest lightened and loosened. He was grateful for all the time his father wasted in Olinger. Every delay postponed the moment when they must ride together down the dirt road into the heart of the dark farmland, where the only light was the kerosene lamp waiting on the dining-room table, a light that drowned their food in shadow and made it sinister.

He lost his appetite for reading. He was afraid of being ambushed again. In mystery novels people died like dolls being discarded; in science fiction enormities of space and time conspired to crush the humans; and even in P. G. Wodehouse he felt a hollowness, a turning away from reality that was implicitly bitter, and became explicit in the comic figures of futile clergymen. All gaiety seemed minced out on the skin of a void. All quiet hours seemed invitations to dread.

Even on weekends, he and his father contrived to escape the farm; and when, some Saturdays, they did stay home, it was to do something destructive — tear down an old henhouse or set huge brush fires that threatened, while Mother shouted and flapped her arms, to spread to the woods. Whenever his father worked, it was with rapt violence; when he chopped kindling, fragments of the old henhouse boards flew like shrapnel and the ax-head was always within a quarter of an inch of flying off the handle. He was exhilarating to watch, sweating and swearing and sucking bits of saliva back into his lips.

School stopped. His father took the car in the opposite direction, to a highway construction job where he had been hired for the summer as a timekeeper, and David was stranded in the middle of acres of heat and greenery and blowing pollen and the strange, mechanical humming that lay invisibly in the weeds and alfalfa and dry orchard grass.

For his fifteenth birthday his parents gave him, with jokes about him being a hillbilly now, a Remington .22. It was somewhat like a pinball machine to take it out to the old kiln in the woods where they dumped their trash, and set up tin cans on the kiln's sandstone shoulder and shoot them off one by one. He'd take the puppy, who had grown long legs and a rich coat of reddish fur — he was part chow. Copper hated the gun but loved the boy enough to accompany him. When the flat acrid crack rang out, he would race in terrified circles that would tighten and tighten until they brought him, shivering, against David's legs. Depending upon his mood, David would shoot again or drop to his knees and comfort the dog. Giving this comfort to a degree returned comfort to him. The dog's ears, laid flat against his skull in fear, were folded so intricately, so — he groped for the concept — *surely*. Where the dull-studded collar made the fur stand up, each hair showed a root of soft white under the length, black-tipped, of the metal-color that had lent the dog its name. In his agitation Copper panted through nostrils that were elegant slits, like two headed cuts, or like the keyholes of a dainty lock of black, grained wood. His whole whorling, knotted, jointed body was a wealth of such embellishments. And in the smell of the dog's hair David seemed to descend through many finely differentiated layers of earth: mulch, soil, sand, clay, and the glittering mineral base.

But when he returned to the house, and saw the books arranged on the low shelves, fear returned. The four adamant volumes of Wells like four thin bricks, the green Plato that had puzzled him with its queer softness and tangled purity, the dead Galsworthy and "Elizabeth," Grandpa's mammoth dictionary, Grandpa's Bible, the Bible that he himself had received on becoming a member of the Firetown Lutheran Church — at the sight of these, the memory of his fear reawakened and came around him. He had grown stiff and stupid in its embrace. His parents tried to think of ways to entertain him.

"David, I have a job for you to do," his mother said one evening at the table.

"What?"

"If you're going to take that tone perhaps we'd better not talk."

"What tone? I didn't take any tone."

"Your grandmother thinks there are too many pigeons in the barn."

"Why?" David turned to look at his grandmother, but she sat there staring at the burning lamp with her usual expression of bewilderment.

Mother shouted, "Mom, he wants to know why!"

Granmom made a jerky, irritable motion with her bad hand, as if generating the force for utterance, and said, "They foul the furniture."

"That's right," Mother said. "She's afraid for that old Olinger furniture that we'll never use. David, she's been after me for a month about those poor pigeons. She wants you to shoot them."

"I don't want to kill anything especially," David said.

Daddy said, "The kid's like you are, Elsie. He's too good for this world. Kill or be killed, that's my motto."

His mother said loudly, "Mother, he doesn't want to do it."

"Not?" The old lady's eyes distended as if in horror, and her claw descended slowly to her lap.

"Oh, I'll do it, I'll do it tomorrow," David snapped, and a pleasant crisp taste entered his mouth with the decision.

"And I had thought, when Boyer's men made the hay, it would be better if the barn doesn't look like a rookery," his mother added needlessly.

A barn, in day, is a small night. The splinters of light between the dry shingles pierce the high roof like stars, and the rafters and crossbeams and built-in ladders seem, until your eyes adjust, as mysterious as the branches of a haunted forest. David entered silently, the gun in one hand. Copper whined desperately at the door, too frightened to come in with the gun yet unwilling to leave the boy. David stealthily turned, said "Go away," shut the door on the dog, and slipped the bolt across. It was a door within a door; the double door for wagons and tractors was as high and wide as the face of a house.

The smell of old straw scratched his sinuses. The red sofa, half-hidden under its white-splotched tarpaulin, seemed assimilated into this smell, sunk in it, buried. The mouths of empty bins gaped like caves. Rusty oddments of farming — coils of baling wire, some spare tines for a harrow, a handleless shovel — hung on nails driven here and there in the thick wood. He stood stock-still a minute; it took a while to separate the cooing of the pigeons from the rustling in his ears. When he had focused on the cooing, it flooded the vast interior with its throaty, bubbling outpour: there seemed no other sound. They were up behind the beams. What light there was leaked through the shingles and the dirty glass windows at the far end and the small round holes, about as big as basketballs, high on the opposite stone side walls, under the ridge of the roof.

A pigeon appeared in one of these holes, on the side toward the house. It flew in, with a battering of wings, from the outside, and waited there, silhouetted against its pinched bit of sky, preening and cooing in a throbbing, thrilled, tentative way. David tiptoed four steps to the side, rested his gun against the lowest rung of a ladder pegged betwen two upright beams, and lowered the gunsight into the bird's tiny, jauntily cocked head. The slap of the report seemed to come off the stone wall behind him, and the pigeon did not fall. Neither did it fly. Instead it stuck in the round hole, pirouetting rapidly and nodding its head as if in frantic agreement. David shot the bolt back and forth and had aimed again before the spent cartridge had stopped jingling on the boards by his feet. He eased the tip of the sight a little lower, into the bird's breast, and took care to squeeze the trigger with perfect evenness. The slow contraction of his hand abruptly sprang the bullet; for a half-second there was doubt, and then the pigeon fell like a handful of rags, skimming down the barn wall into the layer of straw that coated the floor of the mow on this side.

Now others shook loose from the rafters, and whirled in the dim air with a great blurred hurtle of feathers and noise. They would go for the hole; he fixed his sight on the little moon of blue, and when a pigeon came to it, shot him as he was walking the ten inches of stone that would have carried him into the open air. This pigeon lay down in that tunnel of stone, unable to fall either one way or the other, although he was alive enough to lift one wing and cloud the light. It would sink back, and he would suddenly lift it again, the feathers flaring. His body blocked that exit. David raced to the other side of the barn's main aisle, where a similar ladder was symmetrically placed, and rested his gun on the same rung. Three birds came together to this hole; he got one, and two got through. The rest resettled in the rafters.

There was a shallow triangular space behind the cross beams supporting the roof. It was here they roosted and hid. But either the space was too small, or they were curious, for now that his eyes were at home in the dusty gloom David could see little dabs of gray popping in and out. The cooing was shriller now; its apprehensive tremolo made the whole volume of air seem liquid. He noticed one little smudge of a head that was especially persistent in peeking out; he marked the place, and fixed his gun on it, and when the head appeared again, had his finger tightened in advance on the trigger. A parcel of fluff slipped off the beam and fell the barn's height onto a canvas covering some Olinger furniture, and where its head had peeked out there was a fresh prick of light in the shingles.

Standing in the center of the floor, fully master now, disdaining to steady the barrel with anything but his arm, he killed two more that way. He felt like a beautiful avenger. Out of the shadowy ragged infinity of the vast barn roof these impudent things dared to thrust their heads, presumed to dirty its starred silence with their filthy timorous life, and he cut them off, tucked them back neatly into the silence. He had the sensation of a creator; these little smudges and flickers that he was clever to see and even cleverer to hit in the dim recesses of the rafters — out of each of them he was making a full bird. A tiny peek, probe, dab of life, when he hit it, blossomed into a dead enemy, falling with good, final weight.

The imperfection of the second pigeon he had shot, who was still lifting his wing now and then up in the round hole, nagged him. He put a new clip into the stock. Hugging the gun against his body, he climbed the ladder. The barrel sight scratched his ear; he had a sharp, garish vision, like a color slide, of shooting himself and being found tumbled on the barn floor among his prey. He locked his arm around the top rung — a fragile, gnawed rod braced between uprights — and shot into the bird's body from a flat angle. The wing folded but the impact did not, as he had hoped, push the bird out of the hole. He fired again, and again, and still the little body, lighter than air when alive, was too heavy to budge from its high grave. From up here he could see green trees and a brown corner of the house through the hole. Clammy with the cobwebs that gathered between the rungs, he pumped a full clip of eight bullets into the stubborn shadow, with no success. He climbed down, and was struck by the silence in the barn. The remaining pigeons must have escaped out the other hole. That was all right; he was tired of it.

He stepped with his rifle into the light. His mother was coming to meet him, and it tickled him to see her shy away from the carelessly held gun. "You took a chip out of the house," she said. "What were those last shots about?"

"One of them died up in that little round hole and I was trying to shoot it down."

"Copper's hiding behind the piano and won't come out. I had to leave him."

"Well don't blame me. *I* didn't want to shoot the poor devils."

"Don't smirk. You look like your father. How many did you get?"

"Six."

She went into the barn, and he followed. She listened to the silence. Her hair was scraggly, perhaps from tussling with the dog. "I don't suppose the others will be back," she said wearily. "Indeed, I don't know why I let Mother talk me into it. Their cooing was such a comforting noise." She began to gather up the dead pigeons. Though he didn't want to touch them, David went into the mow and picked up by its tepid, horny, coral-colored feet the first bird he had killed. Its wings unfolded disconcertingly, as if the creature had been held together by threads that now were slit. It did not weigh much. He retrieved the one on the other side of the barn; his mother got the three in the middle and led the way across the road to the little southern slope of land that went down toward the foundations of the vanished tobacco shed. The ground was too steep to plant and mow; wild strawberries grew in the tangled grass. She put her burden down and said, "We'll have to bury them. The dog will go wild."

He put his two down on her three; the slick feathers let the bodies slide liquidly on one another. He asked, "Shall I get you the shovel?"

"Get it for yourself; *you* bury them. They're your kill. And be sure to make the hole deep enough so he won't dig them up." While he went to the tool shed for the shovel, she went into the house. Unlike her, she did not look up, either at the orchard to the right of her or at the meadow on her left, but instead held her head rigidly, tilted a little, as if listening to the ground.

He dug the hole, in a spot where there were no strawberry plants, before he studied the pigeons. He had never seen a bird this close before. The feathers were more wonderful than dog's hair, for each filament was shaped within the shape of the feather, and the feathers in turn were trimmed to fit a pattern that flowed without error across the bird's body.

He lost himself in the geometrical tides as the feathers now broadened and stiffened to make an edge for flight, now softened and constricted to cup warmth around the mute flesh. And across the surface of the infinitely adjusted yet somehow effortless mechanics of the feathers played idle designs of color, no two alike, designs executed, it seemed, in a controlled rapture, with a joy that hung level in the air above and behind him. Yet these birds bred in the millions and were exterminated as pests. Into the fragrant open earth he dropped one broadly banded in slate shades of blue, and on top of it another, mottled all over in rhythms of lilac and gray. The next was almost wholly white, but for a salmon glaze at its throat. As he fitted the last two, still pliant, on the top, and stood up, crusty coverings were lifted from him, and with a feminine, slipping sensation along his nerves that seemed to give the air hands, he was robed in this certainty: that the God who had lavished such craft upon these worthless birds would not destroy His whole Creation by refusing to let David live forever.

PHILIP ROTH

1933–

It was with a collection of short stories, Goodbye Columbus, *that the twenty-six-year-old Philip Roth first impressed readers sharp-eared enough to detect a new voice. It was followed by a succession of novels, each surprising though not all equally successful.* Portnoy's Complaint *is still remembered for its classic portrait of the Jewish mother as well as the partly comic agony of its sex- and self-obsessed protagonist. The* Zuckerman Bound *trilogy is perhaps his most solid achievement, although its curious mixture of confessional and controlled art makes some readers squirm with embarrassment.*

The Jewish middle class, and particularly its intellectual fringes, are Roth's territory. He displays a cutting humor, a remarkable ear for dialogue, and dexterity in using fantasy to make us see reality afresh.

"Eli, the Fanatic" studies an excessive character, a type frequently encountered in his pages. In a way, for all its comic tone, it is akin to Cynthia Ozick's "The Shawl," included in this volume. A story about "a simple matter of zoning" turns out not to be so simple after all. Eli's irrationality, his wild rebellion against the frightened assimilationist conformism of his suburban fellow Jews, is a manifestation of guilt. But the guilt would never have expressed itself in quite this crazy way had Hitler's gas chambers never existed. Yet Roth never mentions them.

Even readers to whom Eli's "conversion" may seem strange beyond belief cannot fail to admire Roth's sheer energy, his satiric edge, the sparse efficiency with which he fastens to the page even his minor characters.

Eli, the Fanatic

LEO TZUREF stepped out from back of a white column to welcome Eli
Peck. Eli jumped back, surprised; then they shook hands and Tzuref
gestured him into the sagging old mansion. At the door Eli turned, and
down the slope of lawn, past the jungle of hedges, beyond the dark,
untrampled horse path, he saw the street lights blink on in Woodenton.
The stores along Coach House Road tossed up a burst of yellow — it
came to Eli as a secret signal from his townsmen: "Tell this Tzuref where
we stand, Eli. This is a modern community, Eli, we have our families,
we pay taxes . . ." Eli, burdened by the message, gave Tzuref a dumb,
weary stare.

"You must work a full day," Tzuref said, steering the attorney and his
briefcase into the chilly hall.

Eli's heels made a racket on the cracked marble floor, and he spoke
above it. "It's the commuting that's killing," he said, and entered the dim
room Tzuref waved open for him. "Three hours a day . . . I came right
from the train." He dwindled down into a harp-backed chair. He expected it would be deeper than it was and consequently jarred himself
on the sharp bones of his seat. It woke him, this shiver of the behind, to
his business. Tzuref, a bald shaggy-browed man who looked as if he'd
once been very fat, sat back of an empty desk, halfway hidden, as
though he were settled on the floor. Everything around him was empty.
There were no books in the bookshelves, no rugs on the floor, no draperies in the big casement windows. As Eli began to speak Tzuref got
up and swung a window back on one noisy hinge. "May and it's like
August," he said, and with his back to Eli, he revealed the black circle
on the back of his head. The crown of his head was missing! He returned
through the dimness — the lamps had no bulbs — and Eli realized all
he'd seen was a skullcap. Tzuref struck a match and lit a candle, just as
the half-dying shouts of children at play rolled in through the open window. It was as though Tzuref had opened it so Eli could hear them.

"Aah, now," he said. "I received your letter."

Eli poised, waiting for Tzuref to swish open a drawer and remove the
letter from his file. Instead the old man leaned forward onto his stomach,
worked his hand into his pants pocket, and withdrew what appeared to
be a week-old handkerchief. He uncrumpled it; he unfolded it; he ironed
it on the desk with the side of his hand. "So," he said.

Eli pointed to the grimy sheet which he'd gone over word-by-word with his partners, Lewis and McDonnell. "I expected an answer," Eli said. "It's a week."

"It was so important, Mr. Peck, I knew you would come."

Some children ran under the open window and their mysterious babble — not mysterious to Tzuref, who smiled — entered the room like a third person. Their noise caught up against Eli's flesh and he was unable to restrain a shudder. He wished he had gone home, showered and eaten dinner, before calling on Tzuref. He was not feeling as professional as usual — the place was too dim, it was too late. But down in Woodenton they would be waiting, his clients and neighbors. He spoke for the Jews of Woodenton, not just himself and his wife.

"You understood?" Eli said.

"It's not hard."

"It's a matter of zoning . . ." and when Tzuref did not answer, but only drummed his fingers on his lips, Eli said, "We didn't make the laws . . ."

"You respect them."

"They protect us . . . the community."

"The law is the law," Tzuref said.

"Exactly!" Eli had the urge to rise and walk about the room.

"And then of course" — Tzuref made a pair of scales in the air with his hands — "The law is not the law. When is the law that is the law not the law?" He jiggled the scales. "And vice versa."

"Simply," Eli said sharply. "You can't have a boarding school in a residential area." He would not allow Tzuref to cloud the issue with issues. "We thought it better to tell you before any action is undertaken."

"But a house in a residential area?"

"Yes. That's what residential means." The DP's English was perhaps not as good as it seemed at first. Tzuref spoke slowly, but till then Eli had mistaken it for craft — or even wisdom. "Residence means home," he added.

"So this is my residence."

"But the children?"

"It is their residence."

"*Seventeen* children?"

"Eighteen," Tzuref said.

"But you *teach* them here."

"The Talmud. That's illegal?"

"That makes it school."

Tzuref hung the scales again, tipping slowly the balance.

"Look, Mr. Tzuref, in America we call such a place a boarding school."

"Where they teach the Talmud?"

"Where they teach period. You are the headmaster, they are the students."

Tzuref placed his scales on the desk. "Mr. Peck," he said, "I don't believe it . . ." but he did not seem to be referring to anything Eli had said.

"Mr. Tzuref, that is the law. I came to ask what you intend to do."

"What I *must* do?"

"I hope they are the same."

"They are." Tzuref brought his stomach into the desk. "We stay." He smiled. "We are tired. The headmaster is tired. The students are tired."

Eli rose and lifted his briefcase. It felt so heavy packed with the grievances, vengeances, and schemes of his clients. There were days when he carried it like a feather — in Tzuref's office it weighed a ton.

"Goodbye, Mr. Tzuref."

"Sholom," Tzuref said.

Eli opened the door to the office and walked carefully down the dark tomb of a corridor to the door. He stepped out on the porch and, leaning against a pillar, looked down across the lawn to the children at play. Their voices whooped and rose and dropped as they chased each other round the old house. The dusk made the children's game look like a tribal dance. Eli straightened up, started off the porch, and suddenly the dance was ended. A long piercing scream trailed after. It was the first time in his life anyone had run at the sight of him. Keeping his eyes on the lights of Woodenton, he headed down the path.

And then, seated on a bench beneath a tree, Eli saw him. At first it seemed only a deep hollow of blackness — then the figure emerged. Eli recognized him from the description. There he was, wearing the hat, that hat which was the very cause of Eli's mission, the source of Woodenton's upset. The town's lights flashed their message once again: "Get the one with the hat. What a nerve, what a nerve . . ."

Eli started towards the man. Perhaps he was less stubborn than Tzuref, more reasonable. After all, it was the law. But when he was close enough to call out, he didn't. He was stopped by the sight of the black coat that fell down below the man's knees, and the hands which held each other in his lap. By the round-topped, wide-brimmed Talmudic hat, pushed onto the back of his head. And by the beard, which hid his neck and was so soft and thin it fluttered away and back again with each heavy breath he took. He was asleep, his sidelocks curled loose on his cheeks. His face was no older than Eli's.

Eli hurried towards the lights.

The note on the kitchen table unsettled him. Scribblings on bits of paper had made history this past week. This one, however, was unsigned. "Sweetie," it said, "I went to sleep. I had a sort of Oedipal experience with the baby today. Call Ted Heller."

She had left him a cold soggy dinner in the refrigerator. He hated cold soggy dinners, but would take one gladly in place of Miriam's presence.

He was ruffled, and she never helped that, not with her infernal analytic powers. He loved her when life was proceeding smoothly — and that was when she loved him. But sometimes Eli found being a lawyer surrounded him like quicksand — he couldn't get his breath. Too often he wished he were pleading for the other side; though if he were on the other side, then he'd wish he were on the side he was. The trouble was that sometimes the law didn't seem to be the answer, *law* didn't seem to have anything to do with what was aggravating everybody. And that, of course, made him feel foolish and unnecessary . . . Though that was not the situation here — the townsmen had a case. But not *exactly,* and if Miriam were awake to see Eli's upset, she would set about explaining his distress to him, understanding him, forgiving him, so as to get things back to Normal, for Normal was where they loved one another. The difficulty with Miriam's efforts was they only upset him more; not only did they explain little to him about himself or his predicament, but they convinced him of *her* weakness. Neither Eli nor Miriam, it turned out, was terribly strong. Twice before he'd faced this fact, and on both occasions had found solace in what his neighbors forgivingly referred to as "a nervous breakdown."

Eli ate his dinner with his briefcase beside him. Halfway through, he gave in to himself, removed Tzuref's notes, and put them on the table, beside Miriam's. From time to time he flipped through the notes, which had been carried into town by the one in the black hat. The first note, the incendiary:

To whom it may concern:
   Please give this gentleman the following: Boys shoes with rubber heels and soles.

> 5 prs size 6c
> 3 prs size 5c
> 3 prs size 5b
> 2 prs size 4a
> 3 prs size 4c
> 1 pr size 7b
> 1 pr size 7c

Total 18 prs. boys shoes. This gentleman has a check already signed. Please fill in correct amount.

> L. TZUREF
> Director, Yeshivah of
> Woodenton, N.Y.
> (5/8/48)

"Eli, a regular greenhorn," Ted Heller had said. "He didn't say a word. Just handed me the note and stood there, like in the Bronx the old guys who used to come around selling Hebrew trinkets."

"A Yeshivah!" Artie Berg had said. "Eli, in Woodenton, a Yeshivah! If I want to live in Brownsville, Eli, I'll live in Brownsville."

"Eli," Harry Shaw speaking now, "the old Puddington place. Old man Puddington'll roll over in his grave. Eli, when I left the city, Eli, I didn't plan the city should come to me."

Note number two:

Dear Grocer:

Please give this gentleman ten pounds of sugar. Charge it to our account, Yeshivah of Woodenton, NY — which we will now open with you and expect a bill each month. The gentleman will be in to see you once or twice a week.

L. Tzuref, Director
(5/10/48)

P.S. Do you carry kosher meat?

"He walked right by my window, the greenie," Ted had said, "and he nodded, Eli. He's my *friend* now."

"Eli," Artie Berg had said, "he handed the damn thing to a *clerk* at Stop N' Shop — and in that hat yet!"

"Eli," Harry Shaw again, "it's not funny. Someday, Eli, it's going to be a hundred little kids with little *yamalkahs* chanting their Hebrew lessons on Coach House Road, and then it's not going to strike you funny."

"Eli, what goes on up there — my kids hear strange sounds."

"Eli, this is a modern community."

"Eli, we pay taxes."

"Eli."

"Eli."

"*Eli!*"

At first it was only another townsman crying in his ear; but when he turned he saw Miriam, standing in the doorway, behind her belly.

"Eli, sweetheart, how was it?"

"He said no."

"Did you see the other one?" she asked.

"Sleeping, under a tree."

"Did you let him know how people feel?"

"He was sleeping."

"Why didn't you wake him up? Eli, this isn't an everyday thing."

"He was tired!"

"Don't shout, please," Miriam said.

" 'Don't shout. I'm pregnant. The baby is heavy.' " Eli found he was getting angry at nothing she'd said yet; it was what she was going to say.

"He's a very heavy baby the doctor says," Miriam told him.

"Then sit *down* and make my dinner." Now he found himself angry about her not being present at the dinner which he'd just been relieved

that she wasn't present at. It was as though he had a raw nerve for a
tail, that he kept stepping on. At last Miriam herself stepped on it.

"Eli, you're upset. I understand."

"You *don't* understand."

She left the room. From the stairs she called, "I do, sweetheart."

It was a trap! He would grow angry knowing she would be "understanding." She would in turn grow more understanding seeing his anger.
He would in turn grow angrier . . . The phone rang.

"Hello," Eli said.

"Eli, Ted. So?"

"So nothing."

"Who is Tzuref? He's an American guy?"

"No. A DP. German."

"And the kids?"

"DP's too. He teaches them."

"What? What subjects?" Ted asked.

"I don't know."

"And the guy with the hat, you saw the guy with the hat?"

"Yes. He was sleeping."

"Eli, he sleeps with the *hat?*"

"He sleeps with the hat."

"Goddamn fanatics," Ted said. "This is the twentieth century, Eli.
Now it's the guy with the hat. Pretty soon all the little Yeshivah boys'll
be spilling down into town."

"Next thing they'll be after our daughters."

"Michele and Debbie wouldn't look at them."

"Then," Eli mumbled, "you've got nothing to worry about, Teddie,"
and he hung up.

In a moment the phone rang. "Eli? We got cut off. We've got nothing
to worry about? You worked it out?"

"I have to see him again tomorrow. We can work something out."

"That's fine, Eli. I'll call Artie and Harry."

Eli hung up.

"I thought you said *nothing* worked out." It was Miriam.

"I did."

"Then why did you tell Ted *something* worked out?"

"It did."

"Eli, maybe you should get a little more therapy."

"That's enough of that, Miriam."

"You can't function as a lawyer by being neurotic. That's no answer."

"You're ingenious, Miriam."

She turned, frowning, and took her heavy baby to bed.

The phone rang.

"Eli, Artie. Ted called. You worked it out? No trouble?"

"Yes."

"When are they going?"

"Leave it to me, will you, Artie? I'm tired. I'm going to sleep."

In bed Eli kissed his wife's belly and laid his head upon it to think. He laid it lightly, for she was that day entering the second week of her ninth month. Still, when she slept, it was a good place to rest, to rise and fall with her breathing and figure things out. "If that guy would take off that crazy hat. I know it, what eats them. If he'd take off that crazy hat everything would be all right."

"What?" Miriam said.

"I'm talking to the baby."

Miriam pushed herself up in bed. "Eli, please, baby, shouldn't you maybe stop in to see Dr. Eckman, just for a little conversation?"

"I'm fine."

"Oh, sweetie!" she said, and put her head back on the pillow.

"You know what your mother brought to this marriage — a sling chair and a goddam New School enthusiasm for Sigmund Freud."

Miriam feigned sleep, he could tell by the breathing.

"I'm telling the kid the truth, aren't I, Miriam? A sling chair, three months to go on a *New Yorker* subscription, and *An Introduction to Psychoanalysis*. Isn't that right?"

"Eli, must you be aggressive?"

"That's all you worry about, is your insides. You stand in front of the mirror all day and look at yourself being pregnant."

"Pregnant mothers have a relationship with the fetus that fathers can't understand."

"Relationship my ass. What is my liver doing now? What is my small intestine doing now? Is my island of Langerhans on the blink?"

"Don't be jealous of a little fetus, Eli."

"I'm jealous of your island of Langerhans!"

"Eli, I can't argue with you when I know it's not me you're really angry with. Don't you see, sweetie, you're angry with yourself."

"You and Eckman."

"Maybe he could help, Eli."

"Maybe he could help you. You're practically lovers as it is."

"You're being hostile again," Miriam said.

"What do you care — it's only *me* I'm being hostile towards."

"Eli, we're going to have a beautiful baby, and I'm going to have a perfectly simple delivery, and you're going to make a fine father, and there's absolutely no reason to be obsessed with whatever is on your mind. All we have to worry about —" she smiled at him "— is a name."

Eli got out of bed and slid into his slippers. "We'll name the kid Eckman if it's a boy and Eckman if it's a girl."

"Eckman Peck sounds terrible."

"He'll have to live with it," Eli said, and he went down to his study where the latch on his briefcase glinted in the moonlight that came through the window.

He removed the Tzuref notes and read through them all again. It unnerved him to think of all the flashy reasons his wife could come up with for his reading and rereading the notes. "Eli, why are you so *preoccupied* with Tzuref?" "Eli, stop getting *involved*. Why do you think you're getting *involved*, Eli?" Sooner or later, everybody's wife finds their weak spot. His goddam luck he had to be neurotic! Why couldn't he have been born with a short leg.

He removed the cover from his typewriter, hating Miriam for the edge she had. All the time he wrote the letter, he could hear what she would be saying about his not being *able* to let the matter drop. Well, her trouble was that she wasn't *able* to face the matter. But he could hear her answer already: clearly, he was guilty of "a reaction formation." Still, all the fancy phrases didn't fool Eli: all she wanted really was for Eli to send Tzuref and family on their way, so that the community's temper would quiet, and the calm circumstances of their domestic happiness return. All she wanted were order and love in her private world. Was she so wrong? Let the world bat its brains out — in Woodenton there should be peace. He wrote the letter anyway:

Dear Mr. Tzuref:

Our meeting this evening seems to me inconclusive. I don't think there's any reason for us not to be able to come up with some sort of compromise that will satisfy the Jewish community of Woodenton and the Yeshivah and yourself. It seems to me that what most disturbs my neighbors are the visits to town by the gentleman in the black hat, suit, etc. Woodenton is a progressive suburban community whose members, both Jewish and Gentile, are anxious that their families live in comfort and beauty and serenity. This is, after all, the twentieth century, and we do not think it too much to ask that the members of our community dress in a manner appropriate to the time and place.

Woodenton, as you may not know, has long been the home of well-to-do Protestants. It is only since the war that Jews have been able to buy property here, and for Jews and Gentiles to live beside each other in amity. For this adjustment to be made, both Jews and Gentiles alike have had to give up some of their more extreme practices in order not to threaten or offend the other. Certainly such amity is to be desired. Perhaps if such conditions had existed in prewar Europe, the persecution of the Jewish people, of which you and those 18 children have been victims, could not have been carried out with such success — in fact, might not have been carried out at all.

Therefore, Mr. Tzuref, will you accept the following conditions? If you can, we will see fit not to carry out legal action against the Yeshivah for failure to comply with township Zoning ordinances No. 18 and No. 23. The conditions are simply:

1. The religious, educational, and social activities of the Yeshivah of Woodenton will be confined to the Yeshivah grounds.

2. Yeshivah personnel are welcomed in the streets and stores of Woodenton provided they are attired in clothing usually associated with American life in the 20th century.

If these conditions are met, we see no reason why the Yeshivah of Woodenton cannot live peacefully and satisfactorily with the Jews of Woodenton — as the Jews of Woodenton have come to live with the Gentiles of Woodenton. I would appreciate an immediate reply.

> Sincerely,
> ELI PECK, Attorney

Two days later Eli received his immediate reply:

Mr. Peck:
The suit the gentleman wears is all he's got.

> Sincerely,
> LEO TZUREF, Headmaster

Once again, as Eli swung around the dark trees and onto the lawn, the children fled. He reached out with his briefcase as if to stop them, but they were gone so fast all he saw moving was a flock of skullcaps.

"Come, come . . ." a voice called from the porch. Tzuref appeared from behind a pillar. Did he *live* behind those pillars? Was he just watching the children at play? Either way, when Eli appeared, Tzuref was ready, with no forewarning.

"Hello," Eli said.

"Sholom."

"I didn't mean to frighten them."

"They're scared, so they run."

"I didn't do anything."

Tzuref shrugged. The little movement seemed to Eli strong as an accusation. What he didn't get at home, he got here.

Inside the house they took their seats. Though it was lighter than a few evenings before, a bulb or two would have helped. Eli had to hold his briefcase towards the window for the last gleamings. He removed Tzuref's letter from a manila folder. Tzuref removed Eli's letter from his pants pocket. Eli removed the carbon of his own letter from another manila folder. Tzuref removed Eli's first letter from his back pocket. Eli removed the carbon from his briefcase. Tzuref raised his palms. ". . . It's all I've got . . ."

Those upraised palms, the mocking tone — another accusation. It was a crime to keep carbons! Everybody had an edge on him — Eli could do no right.

"I offered a compromise, Mr. Tzuref. You refused."

"Refused, Mr. Peck? What is, is."

"The man could get a new suit."

"That's all he's got."

"So you told me," Eli said.

"So I told you, so you know."

"It's not an insurmountable obstacle, Mr. Tzuref. We have stores."

"For that too?"

"On Route 12, a Robert Hall —"

"To take away the one thing a man's got?"

"Not take away, *replace*."

"But I tell you he has nothing. *Nothing*. You have that word in English? *Nicht? Gornisht?*"

"Yes, Mr. Tzuref, we have the word."

"A mother and a father?" Tzuref said. "No. A wife? No. A baby? A little ten-month-old baby? No! A village full of friends? A synagogue where you knew the feel of every seat under your pants? Where with your eyes closed you could smell the cloth of the Torah?" Tzuref pushed out of his chair, stirring a breeze that swept Eli's letter to the floor. At the window he leaned out, and looked, beyond Woodenton. When he turned he was shaking a finger at Eli. "And a medical experiment they performed on him yet! That leaves nothing, Mr. Peck. Absolutely nothing!"

"I misunderstood."

"No news reached Woodenton?"

"About the suit, Mr. Tzuref. I thought he couldn't afford another."

"He can't."

They were right where they'd begun. "Mr. Tzuref!" Eli demanded. "*Here?*" He smacked his hand to his billfold.

"Exactly!" Tzuref said, smacking his own breast.

"Then we'll buy him one!" Eli crossed to the window and taking Tzuref by the shoulders, pronounced each word slowly. "We-will-pay-for-it. All right?"

"Pay? What, diamonds!"

Eli raised a hand to his inside pocket, then let it drop. Oh stupid! Tzuref, father to eighteen, had smacked not what lay under his coat, but deeper, under the ribs.

"Oh . . ." Eli said. He moved away along the wall. "The suit is all he's got then."

"You got my letter," Tzuref said.

Eli stayed back in the shadow, and Tzuref turned to his chair. He swished Eli's letter from the floor, and held it up. "You say too much . . . all this reasoning . . . all these conditions . . ."

"What can I do?"

"You have the word 'suffer' in English?"

"We have the word suffer. We have the word law too."

"Stop with the law! You have the word suffer. Then try it. It's a little thing."

"They won't," Eli said.

"But you, Mr. Peck, how about you?"

"I am them, they are me, Mr. Tzuref."

"Aach! You are us, we are you!"

Eli shook and shook his head. In the dark he suddenly felt that Tzuref might put him under a spell. "Mr. Tzuref, a little light?"

Tzuref lit what tallow was left in the holders. Eli was afraid to ask if they couldn't afford electricity. Maybe candles were all they had left.

"Mr. Peck, who made the law, may I ask you that?"

"The people."

"No."

"Yes."

"Before the people."

"No one. Before the people there was no law." Eli didn't care for the conversation, but with only candlelight, he was being lulled into it.

"Wrong," Tzuref said.

"We make the law, Mr. Tzuref. It is our community. These are my neighbors. I am their attorney. They pay me. Without law there is chaos."

"What you call law, I call shame. The heart, Mr. Peck, the heart is law! God!" he announced.

"Look, Mr. Tzuref, I didn't come here to talk metaphysics. People use the law, it's a flexible thing. They protect what they value, their property, their well-being, their happiness —"

"Happiness? They hide their shame. And you, Mr. Peck, you are shameless?"

"We do it," Eli said, wearily, "for our children. This is the twentieth century . . ."

"For the goyim maybe. For me the Fifty-eighth." He pointed at Eli. "That is too old for shame."

Eli felt squashed. Everybody in the world had evil reasons for his actions. Everybody! With reasons so cheap, who buys bulbs. "Enough wisdom, Mr. Tzuref. Please. I'm exhausted."

"Who isn't?" Tzuref said.

He picked Eli's papers from his desk and reached up with them. "What do you intend for us to do?"

"What you must," Eli said. "I made the offer."

"So he must give up his suit?"

"Tzuref, Tzuref, leave me be with that suit! I'm not the only lawyer in the world. I'll drop the case, and you'll get somebody who won't talk compromise. Then you'll have no home, no children, nothing. Only a lousy black suit! Sacrifice what you want. I know what I would do."

To that Tzuref made no answer, but only handed Eli his letters.

"It's not me, Mr. Tzuref, it's them."

"They are you."

"No," Eli intoned, "I am me. They are them. You are you."

"You talk about leaves and branches. I'm dealing with under the dirt."

"Mr. Tzuref, you're driving me crazy with Talmudic wisdom. This is that, that is the other thing. Give me a straight answer."

"Only for straight questions."

"Oh, God!"

Eli returned to his chair and plunged his belongings into his case. "Then, that's all," he said angrily.

Tzuref gave him the shrug.

"Remember, Tzuref, you called this down on yourself."

"I did?"

Eli refused to be his victim again. Double-talk proved nothing. "Goodbye," he said.

But as he opened the door leading to the hall, he heard Tzuref.

"And your wife, how is she?"

"Fine, just fine." Eli kept going.

"And the baby is due when, any day?"

Eli turned. "That's right."

"Well," Tzuref said, rising. "Good luck."

"You know?"

Tzuref pointed out the window — then, with his hands, he drew upon himself a beard, a hat, a long, long coat. When his fingers formed the hem they touched the floor. "He shops two, three times a week, he gets to know them."

"He *talks* to them?"

"He sees them."

"And he can tell which is my wife?"

"They shop at the same stores. He says she is beautiful. She has a kind face. A woman capable of love . . . though who can be sure."

"*He* talks about *us*, to *you?*" demanded Eli.

"You talk about us, to her?"

"Goodbye, Mr. Tzuref."

Tzuref said, "Sholom. And good luck — I know what it is to have children. Sholom," Tzuref whispered, and with the whisper the candles went out. But the instant before, the flames leaped into Tzuref's eyes, and Eli saw it was not luck Tzuref wished him at all.

Outside the door, Eli waited. Down the lawn the children were holding hands and whirling around in a circle. At first he did not move. But he could not hide in the shadows all night. Slowly he began to slip along the front of the house. Under his hands he felt where bricks were out. He moved in the shadows until he reached the side. And then, clutching his briefcase to his chest, he broke across the darkest spots of the lawn. He aimed for a distant glade of woods, and when he reached it he did not stop, but ran through until he was so dizzied that the trees seemed to be running beside him, fleeing not towards Woodenton but away. His lungs were nearly ripping their seams as he burst into the yellow glow of the Gulf station at the edge of town.

"Eli, I had pains today. Where were you?"

"I went to Tzuref."

"Why didn't you call? I was worried."

He tossed his hat past the sofa and onto the floor. "Where are my winter suits?"

"In the hall closet. Eli, it's May."

"I need a strong suit." He left the room, Miriam behind him.

"Eli, talk to me. Sit down. Have dinner. Eli, what are you doing? You're going to get moth balls all over the carpet."

He peered out from the hall closet. Then he peered in again — there was a zipping noise, and suddenly he swept a greenish tweed suit before his wife's eyes.

"Eli, I love you in that suit. But not now. Have something to eat. I made dinner tonight — I'll warm it."

"You've got a box big enough for this suit?"

"I got a Bonwit's box, the other day. Eli, *why?*"

"Miriam, you see me doing something, let me do it."

"You haven't eaten."

"I'm *doing* something." He started up the stairs to the bedroom.

"Eli, would you please tell me what it is you want, and why?"

He turned and looked down at her. "Suppose this time you give me the reasons *before* I tell you what I'm doing. It'll probably work out the same anyway."

"Eli, I want to help."

"It doesn't concern you."

"But I want to help *you*," Miriam said.

"Just be quiet, then."

"But you're upset," she said, and she followed him up the stairs, heavily, breathing for two.

"Eli, what now?"

"A shirt." He yanked open all the drawers of their new teak dresser. He extracted a shirt.

"Eli, batiste? With a tweed suit?" she inquired.

He was at the closet now, on his knees. "Where are my cordovans?"

"Eli, why are you doing this so compulsively? You look like you *have* to do something."

"Oh, Miriam, you're supersubtle."

"Eli, stop this and talk to me. Stop it or I'll call Dr. Eckman."

Eli was kicking off the shoes he was wearing. "Where's the Bonwit box?"

"Eli, do you want me to have the baby right *here!*"

Eli walked over and sat down on the bed. He was draped not only with his own clothing, but also with the greenish tweed suit, the batiste shirt, and under each arm a shoe. He raised his arms and let the shoes drop onto the bed. Then he undid his necktie with one hand and his teeth and added that to the booty.

"Underwear," he said. "He'll need underwear."

"Who!"

He was slipping out of his socks.

Miriam kneeled down and helped him ease his left foot out of the sock. She sat with it on the floor. "Eli, just lie back. Please."

"Plaza 9-3103."

"What?"

"Eckman's number," he said. "It'll save you the trouble."

"Eli —"

"You've got that goddam tender 'You need help' look in your eyes, Miriam, don't tell me you don't."

"I don't."

"I'm not flipping," Eli said.

"I know, Eli."

"Last time I sat in the bottom of the closet and chewed on my bedroom slippers. That's what I did."

"I know."

"And I'm not doing that. This is not a nervous breakdown, Miriam, let's get that straight."

"Okay," Miriam said. She kissed the foot she held. Then, softly, she asked, "What *are* you doing?"

"Getting clothes for the guy in the hat. Don't tell me why, Miriam. Just let me do it."

"That's all?" she asked.

"That's all."

"You're not leaving?"

"No."

"Sometimes I think it gets too much for you, and you'll just leave."

"What gets too much?"

"I don't *know,* Eli. Something gets too much. Whenever everything's peaceful for a long time, and things are nice and pleasant, and we're expecting to be even happier. Like now. It's as if you don't think we *deserve* to be happy."

"Damn it, Miriam! I'm giving this guy a new suit, is that all right? From now on he comes into Woodenton like everybody else, is that all right with you?"

"And Tzuref moves?"

"I don't even know if he'll take the suit, Miriam! What do you have to bring up moving!"

"Eli, I didn't bring up moving. Everybody did. That's what everybody wants. Why make everybody un*happy*. It's even a law, Eli."

"Don't tell me what's the law."

"All right, sweetie. I'll get the box."

"*I'll* get the box. Where is it?"

"In the basement."

When he came up from the basement, he found all the clothes neatly folded and squared away on the sofa: shirt, tie, shoes, socks, underwear, belt, and old gray flannel suit. His wife sat on the end of the sofa, looking like an anchored balloon.

"Where's the green suit?" he said.

"Eli, it's your loveliest suit. It's my favorite suit. Whenever I think of you, Eli, it's in that suit."

"Get it out."

"Eli, it's a Brooks Brothers suit. You say yourself how much you love it."

"Get it out."

"But the gray flannel's more practical. For shopping."

"Get it out."

"You go overboard, Eli. That's your trouble. You won't do anything in moderation. That's how people destroy themselves."

"I do *everything* in moderation. That's my trouble. The suit's in the closet again?"

She nodded, and began to fill up with tears. "Why does it have to be *your* suit? Who are you even to decide to give a suit? What about the others?" She was crying openly, and holding her belly. "Eli, I'm going to have a baby. Do we need all *this?*" and she swept the clothes off the sofa to the floor.

At the closet Eli removed the green suit. "It's a J. Press," he said, looking at the lining.

"I hope to hell he's happy with it!" Miriam said, sobbing.

A half hour later the box was packed. The cord he'd found in the kitchen cabinet couldn't keep the outfit from popping through. The trouble was there was too much: the gray suit *and* the green suit, an oxford shirt as well as the batiste. But let him have two suits! Let him have three, four, if only this damn silliness would stop! And a hat — of course! God, he'd almost forgotten the hat. He took the stairs two at a time and in Miriam's closet yanked a hatbox from the top shelf. Scattering hat and tissue paper to the floor, he returned downstairs, where he packed away the hat he'd worn that day. Then he looked at his wife, who lay outstretched on the floor before the fireplace. For the third time in as many minutes she was saying, "Eli, this is the real thing."

"Where?"

"Right under the baby's head, like somebody's squeezing oranges."

Now that he'd stopped to listen he was stupefied. He said, "But you have two more weeks . . ." Somehow he'd really been expecting it was to go on not just another two weeks, but another nine months. This led him to suspect, suddenly, that his wife was feigning pain so as to get his mind off delivering the suit. And just as suddenly he resented himself for having such a thought. God, what had he become! He'd been an unending bastard towards her since this Tzuref business had come up — just when her pregnancy must have been most burdensome. He'd allowed her no access to him, but still, he was sure, for good reasons: she might tempt him out of his confusion with her easy answers. He could be tempted all right, it was why he fought so hard. But now a sweep of love came over him at the thought of her contracting womb, and his child. And yet he would not indicate it to her. Under such splendid marital conditions, who knows but she might extract some promise from him about his concern with the school on the hill.

Having packed his second bag of the evening, Eli sped his wife to Woodenton Memorial. There she proceeded not to have her baby, but to lie hour after hour through the night having at first oranges, then bowling balls, then basketballs, squeezed back of her pelvis. Eli sat in the waiting room, under the shattering African glare of a dozen rows of fluorescent bulbs, composing a letter to Tzuref.

Dear Mr. Tzuref:
    The clothes in this box are for the gentleman in the hat. In a life of sacrifice what is one more? But in a life of no sacrifices even one is impossible. Do you see what I'm saying, Mr. Tzuref? I am not a Nazi who would drive eighteen children, who are probably frightened at the sight of a firefly, into homelessness. But if you want a home here, you must accept what we have to offer. The world is the world, Mr. Tzuref. As you would say, what is, is. All we say to this man is change your clothes. Enclosed are two suits and two shirts, and everything else he'll need, including a new hat. When he needs new clothes let me know.
    We await his appearance in Woodenton, as we await friendly relations with the Yeshivah of Woodenton.

He signed his name and slid the note under a bursting flap and into the box. Then he went to the phone at the end of the room and dialed Ted Heller's number.
    "Hello."
    "Shirley, it's Eli."
    "Eli, we've been calling all night. The lights are on in your place, but nobody answers. We thought it was burglars."
    "Miriam's having the baby."
    "At home?" Shirley said. "Oh, Eli, what a fun idea!"
    "Shirley, let me speak to Ted."
    After the ear-shattering clatter of the phone whacking the floor, Eli

heard footsteps, breathing, throat-clearing, then Ted. "A boy or a girl?"

"Nothing yet."

"You've given Shirley the bug, Eli. Now she's going to have *our* next one at home."

"Good."

"That's a terrific way to bring the family together, Eli."

"Look, Ted, I've settled with Tzuref."

"What's the sad date of departure?"

"They're not leaving. But I settled it, Ted. You'll never know they're there."

"A guy dressed like the House of David, and I'll never know they're there! Eli, what do you call this?"

"He's changing his clothes."

"To what, another funeral suit?"

"Tzuref promised me. Next time he comes to town, he comes dressed like you and me."

"Somebody's kidding somebody, Eli."

Eli's voice shot up. "If he says he'll do it, he'll do it!"

"And he said it?"

"He said it."

"Suppose he doesn't change — just suppose. I mean that *might* happen, Eli. This might just be a stall, till he gets the UJA or somebody involved."

"No," Eli assured him.

"But, Eli, he changes. Okay. And they're still up there, aren't they, sitting on that lousy hill!"

"You'll never know it."

"Look, is this what we asked of you, Eli? Eli, did we put our faith and trust in you? You're a lawyer, Eli, you've got the gift of gab, nobody ever denied that. But is this what we asked of you that night? Did Artie or Herb or me ask for this guy to become a Beau Brummel? We don't think they should be living in a community like this, Eli. And we speak for the Jewish members of the community. Eli, they appointed us and we appointed you. What's happened?"

"What happened, happened," Eli heard himself say.

"And what is that supposed to mean! Eli, this is a simple matter of zoning. You don't abide by the ordinance you go. One two three."

"It's not that simple," Eli said, ". . . with people involved."

"People? You want to know something about those people, they're religious fanatics is what they are. Dressing like that. What goes on up there, Eli? That's what I'd really like to find out. I'm skeptical, Eli, I'm goddam skeptical. I don't even know about this Sunday School crap. Sunday mornings I have to drive my kid all the way to Scarsdale to learn Bible stories? And you know what she comes up with, Eli — that this Abraham in the Bible was going to kill his own kid for a *sacrifice!* You call that religion, Eli? I call it sick. Today a guy like that they'd lock him up. This is an age of science, Eli. They've disproved all that stuff and I refuse to sit by and watch it happening on my own front lawn."

"Nobody's sacrificing anything . . ."

"It's a goddam hideaway for people who can't face life, if you ask me. Take pork, for instance. It's clean now, government inspection, all kinds of special drugs they feed the goddam animals, everything scientifically done, but *they* won't eat it. What do you call that but superstition, Eli? And if you've got one superstition, Eli, you've got a thousand. It's a matter of *needs*. They invent this stuff Eli, because they can't take their place in society. I'll be damned if my kids are going to grow up in an environment like that!"

"Teddie, look at it the other way. We can convert them."

"What are you crazy, Eli — you think I want to make a bunch of Catholics out of them. There's peace in this town, Eli — and a good healthy relationship because it's modern Jews and Protestants. Last week, Eli, I've been wanting to tell you this — last week, Jimmy Knudson took a group from Kiwanis to the Unitarian Church, and I sat there, Eli, and I was impressed. Nobody wailing or crying or any of that stuff. Nobody making a damn *ritual* out of suffering. Everything was modern — even the plate glass window is made out of some kind of plastic, Jimmy said, so a hurricane can't blow it out or anything. And the priest, Eli, was dressed like you and me and he *talked* like you and me. Eli, in his sermon he quoted from the *Atlantic Monthly magazine,* for Christ sake. That's the difference, Eli, between superstition and religion."

"You can't beat those Unitarian priests for good plain sense."

"That's what I'm saying, Eli. I'm for common sense."

"Common sense says to make this guy change his clothes, Teddie."

"Common sense says get them out."

"Ted, give them a chance. *Introduce* them to common sense."

"Eli, you're dealing with *fanatics*. They're still observing holidays nobody even knows the reason for! I say get rid of them and get rid of them now, before feelings are hurt. I'll tell you, Eli, the town is hot about it. You know Jimmy Knudson, Eli — he's been at my house and me at his so many times I can't count it. But even he mentioned it to me. He says he wouldn't be at all surprised if a *Life* magazine guy came up here to take pictures. Wouldn't that be sweet, Eli — 'Life Goes to a Bar Mitzvah Party on Coach House Road.' "

"I think you're exaggerating, Ted. I don't think *Life*'s interested or anybody else."

"I'm interested, Eli. And you're *supposed* to be interested."

"I *am*. Let's see what happens if he changes his clothes. Let's just see, Teddie."

"He won't."

"Let's see."

"Jesus Christ, Eli."

"Let's see, Teddie. If he doesn't by . . . by tomorrow, then I get an injunction Monday morning."

"All right. All right. But tomorrow's the Judgment Day, Eli."

"I hear the trumpets," Eli said, and hung up. A few moments later he was told that Mrs. Peck would positively not be delivered of a child until the morning. He was to go home and get some rest, he looked like *he* was having the baby. The nurse winked and left.

But Eli did not go home. He carried the Bonwit box out into the street with him and put it in the car. The night was soft and starry, and he began to drive the streets of Woodenton. Square cool windows, apricot-colored, were all one could see beyond the long lawns that fronted the homes of the townsmen. The stars polished the permanent baggage carriers atop the station wagons in the driveways. He drove on, slowly, up, down, around. Only his tires could be heard taking the gentle curves in the road. What peace. What incredible peace. Have children ever been so safe in their beds? Parents so full in their stomachs? Water so warm in its boilers? Never — never in Rome, never in Greece, never even where Tigris and Euphrates swelled and met! Never even did walled cities have it so good! Was it any wonder then that they wanted to keep things as they were? This is what civilization has been working towards for centuries — peace and safety. All the caveman wanted in the cave was a safe warm place to love his wife and play with his children. For all his jerkiness, it was what Ted Heller wanted. It was what Ted Heller's parents had wanted in the Bronx. It was what his grandparents had wanted in Poland, and theirs in Russia, or wherever else they'd been driven from. It was what Miriam wanted. The world was at last a place for families, even Jewish families. At least Woodenton was — and that was so precious, so vulnerable a gift that perhaps there had to be a communal ruthlessness — or even numbness — to protect it. They *had* to be careful — any kind of bug might make a hole in such a frail expensive fabric. The greatest good for the greatest number . . . Eli was thinking as he drove on beyond the train station, and parked his car at the darkened Gulf sign. He stepped out, carrying his box.

At the top of the hill one window trembled with light. What was Tzuref doing up there in that office? Studying a language no one understood? Practicing customs whose origins were long forgotten? Suffering sufferings already suffered once too often? Why keep it up! However, if a man chose to be stubborn, then he couldn't expect to survive. The world is give-and-take. What sense to sit and brood over a suit. Eli would give him one last chance . . . He stopped at the top. No one was around. He walked slowly up the lawn, setting each foot into the grass, listening to the shh shh shh his shoes made as they bent the wetness into the sod. He looked around. Here there was nothing. Nothing! An old decaying house — and a suit . . .

On the porch he slid behind a pillar. He felt someone was watching him. But only the stars gleamed down. And at his feet, off and away, Woodenton glowed up. He set his package on the step of the great front door. Inside the cover of the box he felt to see if his letter was still there. When he touched it, he pushed it deeper into the green suit, which his fingers still remembered from winter. He should have included some light bulbs. Then he slid back by the pillar again, and this time there was something on the lawn. It was the second sight he had of him. He was facing Woodenton and barely moving across the open space towards the trees. His right fist was beating his chest. And then Eli heard a sound rising with each knock on the chest. What a moan! It could raise hair, stop hearts, water eyes. And it did all three to Eli, plus more. Some feeling crept into him for whose deepness he could find no word. It was strange. He listened — it did not hurt to hear this moan. But he wondered if it hurt to make it. And so, with only stars to hear, he tried. And it did hurt. Not the bumblebee of noise that turned at the back of his throat and winged out his nostrils. What hurt buzzed down. It stung and stung inside him, and in turn the moan sharpened. It became a scream, louder, a song, a crazy song that whined through the pillars and blew out to the grass, until the strange hatted creature on the lawn turned and threw his arms wide, and looked in the night like a scarecrow.

Eli ran, and when he reached the car the pain was only a bloody scratch across his neck where a branch had whipped back as he fled the greenie's arms.

The following day his son was born. But not till one in the afternoon, and by then a great deal had happened.

First, at nine-thirty the phone rang. Eli leaped from the sofa — where he'd dropped the night before — and picked it screaming from the cradle. He could practically smell the hospital as he shouted into the phone, "Hello, yes!"

"Eli, it's Ted. Eli, he *did* it. He just walked by the store. I was opening the door, Eli, and I turned around and I swear I thought it was you. But it was him. He still walks like he did, but the clothes, Eli, the clothes."

"Who?"

"The greenie. He has on man's regular clothes. And the suit, it's a beauty."

The suit barreled back into Eli's consciousness, pushing all else aside. "What color suit?"

"Green. He's just strolling in the green suit like it's a holiday. Eli . . . is it a Jewish holiday?"

"Where is he now?"

"He's walking straight up Coach House Road, in this damn tweed job. Eli, it worked. You were right."

"We'll see."

"What next?"

"We'll see."

He took off the underwear in which he'd slept and went into the kitchen where he turned the light under the coffee. When it began to perk he held his head over the pot so it would steam loose the knot back of his eyes. It still hadn't when the phone rang.

"Eli, Ted again. Eli, the guy's walking up and down every street in town. Really, he's on a tour or something. Artie called me, Herb called me. Now Shirley calls that he just walked by our house. Eli, go out on the porch you'll see."

Eli went to the window and peered out. He couldn't see past the bend in the road, and there was no one in sight.

"Eli?" He heard Ted from where he dangled over the telephone table. He dropped the phone into the hook, as a few last words floated up to him — "Eliyousawhim . . . ?" He threw on the pants and shirt he'd worn the night before and walked barefoot on to his front lawn. And sure enough, his apparition appeared around the bend: in a brown hat a little too far down on his head, a green suit too far back on the shoulders, an unbuttoned-down button-down shirt, a tie knotted so as to leave a two-inch tail, trousers that cascaded onto his shoes — he was shorter than that black hat had made him seem. And moving the clothes was that walk that was not a walk, the tiny-stepped shlumpy gait. He came round the bend, and for all his strangeness — it clung to his whiskers, signaled itself in his locomotion — he looked as if he belonged. Eccentric, maybe, but he belonged. He made no moan, nor did he invite Eli with wide-flung arms. But he did stop when he saw him. He stopped and put a hand to his hat. When he felt for its top, his hand went up too high. Then it found the level and fiddled with the brim. The fingers fiddled, fumbled, and when they'd finally made their greeting, they traveled down the fellow's face and in an instant seemed to have touched each one of his features. They dabbed the eyes, ran the length of the nose, swept over the hairy lip, until they found their home in the hair that hid a little of his collar. To Eli the fingers said, *I have a face, I have a face at least.* Then his hand came through the beard and when it stopped at his chest it was like a pointer — and the eyes asked a question as tides of water shifted over them. *The face is all right, I can keep it?* Such a look was in those eyes that Eli was still seeing them when he turned his head away. They were the hearts of his jonquils, that only last week had appeared — they were the leaves on his birch, the bulbs in his coach lamp, the droppings on his lawn: those eyes were the eyes in his head. They were his, he had made them. He turned and went into his house and when he peeked out the side of the window, between shade and molding, the green suit was gone.

The phone.

"Eli, Shirley."

"I saw him, Shirley," and he hung up.

He sat frozen for a long time. The sun moved around the windows. The coffee steam smelled up the house. The phone began to ring, stopped, began again. The mailman came, the cleaner, the bakery man, the gardener, the ice cream man, the League of Women Voters lady. A Negro woman spreading some strange gospel calling for the revision of the Food and Drug Act knocked at the front, rapped the windows, and finally scraped a half-dozen pamphlets under the back door. But Eli only sat, without underwear, in last night's suit. He answered no one.

Given his condition, it was strange that the trip and crash at the back door reached his inner ear. But in an instant he seemed to melt down into the crevices of the chair, then to splash up and out to where the clatter had been. At the door he waited. It was silent, but for a fluttering of damp little leaves on the trees. When he finally opened the door, there was no one there. He'd expected to see green, green, green, big as the doorway, topped by his hat, waiting for him with those eyes. But there was no one out there, except for the Bonwit's box which lay bulging at his feet. No string tied it and the top rode high on the bottom.

The coward! He couldn't do it! He couldn't!

The very glee of that idea pumped fuel to his legs. He tore out across his back lawn, past his new spray of forsythia, to catch a glimpse of the bearded one fleeing naked through yards, over hedges and fences, to the safety of his hermitage. In the distance a pile of pink and white stones — which Harriet Knudson had painted the previous day — tricked him. "Run," he shouted to the rocks. "Run, you . . ." but he caught his error before anyone else did, and though he peered and craned there was no hint anywhere of a man about his own size, with white, white, terribly white skin (how white must be the skin of his body!) in cowardly retreat. He came slowly, curiously, back to the door. And while the trees shimmered in the light wind, he removed the top from the box. The shock at first was the shock of having daylight turned off all at once. Inside the box was an eclipse. But black soon sorted from black, and shortly there was the glassy black of lining, the coarse black of trousers, the dead black of fraying threads, and in the center the mountain of black: the hat. He picked the box from the doorstep and carried it inside. For the first time in his life he *smelled* the color of blackness: a little stale, a little sour, a little old, but nothing that could overwhelm you. Still, he held the package at arm's length and deposited it on the dining room table.

Twenty rooms on a hill and they store their old clothes with me! What am I supposed to do with them? Give them to charity? That's where they came from. He picked up the hat by the edges and looked inside. The crown was smooth as an egg, the brim practically threadbare. There is nothing else to do with a hat in one's hands but put it on, so Eli dropped the thing on his head. He opened the door to the hall closet and looked at himself in the full-length mirror. The hat gave him bags under the eyes. Or perhaps he had not slept well. He pushed the brim lower till a shadow touched his lips. Now the bags under his eyes had inflated to become his face. Before the mirror he unbuttoned his shirt, unzipped his trousers, and then, shedding his clothes, he studied what he was. What a silly disappointment to see yourself naked in a hat. Especially in that hat. He sighed, but could not rid himself of the great weakness that suddenly set on his muscles and joints, beneath the terrible weight of the stranger's strange hat.

He returned to the dining room table and emptied the box of its contents: jacket, trousers, and vest (*it* smelled deeper than blackness). And under it all, sticking between the shoes that looked chopped and bitten, came the first gleam of white. A little fringed serape, a gray piece of semiunderwear, was crumpled at the bottom, its thready border twisted into itself. Eli removed it and let it hang free. What is it? For warmth? To wear beneath underwear in the event of a chest cold? He held it to his nose but it did not smell from Vick's or mustard plaster. It was something special, some Jewish thing. Special food, special language, special prayers, why not special BVD's? So fearful was he that he would be tempted back into wearing his traditional clothes — reasoned Eli — that he had carried and buried in Woodenton everything, including the special underwear. For that was how Eli now understood the box of clothes. The greenie was saying, Here, I give up. I refuse even to be tempted. We surrender. And that was how Eli continued to understand it until he found he'd slipped the white fringy surrender flag over his hat and felt it clinging to his chest. And now, looking at himself in the mirror, he was momentarily uncertain as to who was tempting who into what. Why *did* the greenie leave his clothes? Was it even the greenie? Then who was it? And why? But, Eli, for Christ's sake, in an age of science things don't happen like that. Even the goddam pigs take drugs . . .

Regardless of who was the source of the temptation, what was its end, not to mention its beginning, Eli, some moments later, stood draped in black, with a little white underneath, before the full-length mirror. He had to pull down on the trousers so they would not show the hollow of his ankle. The greenie, didn't he wear socks? Or had he forgotten them? The mystery was solved when Eli mustered enough courage to investigate the trouser pockets. He had expected some damp awful things to happen to his fingers should he slip them down and out of sight — but when at last he jammed bravely down he came up with a khaki army sock in each hand. As he slipped them over his toes, he invented a genesis: a G.I.'s present in 1945. Plus everything else lost between 1938 and 1945, he had also lost his socks. Not that he had lost the socks, but that he'd had to stoop to accepting these, made Eli almost cry. To calm himself he walked out the back door and stood looking at his lawn.

On the Knudson back lawn, Harriet Knudson was giving her stones a second coat of pink. She looked up just as Eli stepped out. Eli shot back in again and pressed himself against the back door. When he peeked between the curtain all he saw were paint bucket, brush, and rocks scattered on the Knudsons' pink-spattered grass. The phone rang. Who was it — Harriet Knudson? Eli, there's a Jew at your door. *That's me.* Nonsense, Eli, I saw him with my own eyes. *That's me, I saw you too, painting your rocks pink.* Eli, you're having a nervous breakdown again. Jimmy, Eli's having a nervous breakdown again. Eli, this is Jimmy, hear you're having a little breakdown, anything I can do, boy? Eli, this is Ted, Shirley says you need help. Eli, this is Artie, you need help. Eli, Harry, you need help you need help . . . The phone rattled its last and died.

"God helps them who help themselves," intoned Eli, and once again he stepped out the door. This time he walked to the center of his lawn and in full sight of the trees, the grass, the birds, and the sun, revealed that it was he, Eli, in the costume. But nature had nothing to say to him, and so stealthily he made his way to the hedge separating his property from the field beyond and he cut his way through, losing his hat twice in the underbrush. Then, clamping the hat to his head, he began to run, the threaded tassels jumping across his heart. He ran through the weeds and wild flowers, until on the old road that skirted the town he slowed up. He was walking when he approached the Gulf station from the back. He supported himself on a huge tireless truck rim, and among tubes, rusted engines, dozens of topless oil cans, he rested. With a kind of brainless cunning, he readied himself for the last mile of his journey.

"How are you, Pop?" It was the garage attendant, rubbing his greasy hands on his overalls, and hunting among the cans.

Eli's stomach lurched and he pulled the big black coat round his neck.

"Nice day," the attendant said and started around to the front.

"Sholom," Eli whispered and zoomed off towards the hill.

The sun was directly overhead when Eli reached the top. He had come by way of the woods, where it was cooler, but still he was perspiring beneath his new suit. The hat had no sweatband and the cloth clutched his head. The children were playing. The children were always playing, as if it was that alone that Tzuref had to teach them. In their shorts, they revealed such thin legs that beneath one could see the joints swiveling as they ran. Eli waited for them to disappear around a corner before he came into the open. But something would not let him wait — his green suit. It was on the porch, wrapped around the bearded fellow, who was painting the base of a pillar. His arm went up and down, up and down, and the pillar glowed like white fire. The very sight of him popped Eli out of the woods onto the lawn. He did not turn back, though his insides did. He walked up the lawn, but the children played on; tipping the black hat, he mumbled, "Shhh . . . shhhh," and they hardly seemed to notice.

At last he smelled paint.

He waited for the man to turn to him. He only painted. Eli felt suddenly that if he could pull the black hat down over his eyes, over his chest and belly and legs, if he could shut out all light, then a moment later he would be home in bed. But the hat wouldn't go past his forehead. He couldn't kid himself — he was there. No one he could think of had forced him to do this.

The greenie's arm flailed up and down on the pillar. Eli breathed loudly, cleared his throat, but the greenie wouldn't make life easier for him. At last, Eli had to say "Hello."

The arm swished up and down; it stopped — two fingers went out after a brush hair stuck to the pillar.

"Good day," Eli said.

The hair came away; the swishing resumed.

"Sholom," Eli whispered and the fellow turned.

The recognition took some time. He looked at what Eli wore. Up close, Eli looked at what he wore. And then Eli had the strange notion that he was two people. Or that he was one person wearing two suits. The greenie looked to be suffering from a similar confusion. They stared long at one another. Eli's heart shivered, and his brain was momentarily in such a mixed-up condition that his hands went out to button down the collar of his shirt that somebody else was wearing. What a mess! The greenie flung his arms over his face.

"What's the matter . . ." Eli said. The fellow had picked up his bucket and brush and was running away. Eli ran after him.

"I wasn't going to hit . . ." Eli called. "Stop . . ." Eli caught up and grabbed his sleeve. Once again, the greenie's hands flew up to his face. This time, in the violence, white paint spattered both of them.

"I only want to . . ." But in that outfit Eli didn't really know what he wanted. "To talk . . ." he said finally. "For you to look at me. Please, just *look* at me . . ."

The hands stayed put, as paint rolled off the brush onto the cuff of Eli's green suit.

"Please . . . please," Eli said, but he did not know what to do. "Say something, speak *English*," he pleaded.

The fellow pulled back against the wall, back, back, as though some arm would finally reach out and yank him to safety. He refused to uncover his face.

"Look," Eli said, pointing to himself. "It's your suit. I'll take care of it."

No answer — only a little shaking under the hands, which led Eli to speak as gently as he knew how.

"We'll . . . we'll moth-proof it. There's a button missing" — Eli pointed — "I'll have it fixed. I'll have a zipper put in . . . Please, please

— just look at me . . ." He was talking to himself, and yet how could he stop? Nothing he said made any sense — that alone made his heart swell. Yet somehow babbling on, he might babble something that would make things easier between them. "Look . . ." He reached inside his shirt to pull the frills of underwear into the light. "I'm wearing the special underwear, even . . . Please," he said, "*please, please, please*" he sang, as as if it were some sacred word. "Oh, *please* . . ."

Nothing twitched under the tweed suit — and if the eyes watered, or twinkled, or hated, he couldn't tell. It was driving him crazy. He had dressed like a fool, and for what? For this? He reached up and yanked the hands away.

"There!" he said — and in that first instant all he saw of the greenie's face were two white droplets stuck to each cheek.

"Tell me —" Eli clutched his hands down to his sides — "Tell me, what can I do for you, I'll do it . . ."

Stiffly, the greenie stood there, sporting his two white tears.

"Whatever I can do . . . Look, look, what I've done *already*." He grabbed his black hat and shook it in the man's face.

And in exchange, the greenie gave him an answer. He raised one hand to his chest, and then jammed it, finger first, towards the horizon. And with what a pained look! As though the air were full of razors! Eli followed the finger and saw beyond the knuckle, out past the nail, Woodenton.

"What do you want?" Eli said. "I'll bring it!"

Suddenly the greenie made a run for it. But then he stopped, wheeled, and jabbed that finger at the air again. It pointed the same way. Then he was gone.

And then, all alone, Eli had the revelation. He did not question his understanding, the substance or the source. But with a strange, dreamy elation, he started away.

On Coach House Road, they were double-parked. The Mayor's wife pushed a grocery cart full of dog food from Stop N' Shop to her station wagon. The President of the Lions Club, a napkin around his neck, was jamming pennies into the meter in front of the Bit-in-Teeth Restaurant. Ted Heller caught the sun as it glazed off the new Byzantine mosaic entrance to his shoe shop. In pinkened jeans, Mrs. Jimmy Knudson was leaving Halloway's Hardware, a paint bucket in each hand. Roger's Beauty Shoppe had its doors open — women's heads in silver bullets far as the eye could see. Over by the barbershop the pole spun, and Artie Berg's youngest sat on a red horse, having his hair cut; his mother flipped through *Look,* smiling: the greenie had changed his clothes.

And into this street, which seemed paved with chromium, came Eli Peck. It was not enough, he knew, to walk up one side of the street. That was not enough. Instead he walked ten paces up one side, then on an angle, crossed to the other side, where he walked ten more paces, and crossed back. Horns blew, traffic jerked, as Eli made his way up Coach House Road. He spun a moan high up in his nose as he walked. Outside no one could hear him, but he felt it vibrate the cartilage at the bridge of his nose.

Things slowed around him. The sun stopped rippling on spokes and hubcaps. It glowed steadily as everyone put on brakes to look at the man in black. They always paused and gaped, whenever he entered the town. Then in a minute, or two, or three, a light would change, a baby squawk, and the flow continue. Now, though lights changed, no one moved.

"He shaved his beard," Eric the barber said.

"Who?" asked Linda Berg.

"The . . . the guy in the suit. From the place there."

Linda looked out the window.

"It's Uncle Eli," little Kevin Berg said, spitting hair.

"Oh, God," Linda said, "Eli's having a nervous breakdown."

"A nervous breakdown!" Ted Heller said, but not immediately. Immediately he had said, "Hoooly . . ."

Shortly, everybody in Coach House Road was aware that Eli Peck, the nervous young attorney with the pretty wife, was having a breakdown. Everybody except Eli Peck. He knew what he did was not insane, though he felt every inch of its strangeness. He felt those black clothes as if they were the skin of his skin — the give and pull as they got used to where he bulged and buckled. And he felt eyes, every eye on Coach House Road. He saw headlights screech to within an inch of him, and stop. He saw mouths: first the bottom jaw slides forward, then the tongue hits the teeth, the lips explode, a little thunder in the throat, and they've said it: Eli Peck Eli Peck Eli Peck Eli Peck. He began to walk slowly, shifting his weight down and forward with each syllable: E–li–Peck–E–li–Peck– E–li–Peck. Heavily he trod, and as his neighbors uttered each syllable of his name, he felt each syllable shaking all his bones. He knew who he was down to his marrow — they were telling him. Eli Peck. He wanted them to say it a thousand times, a million times, he would walk forever in that black suit, as adults whispered of his strangeness and children made "Shame . . . shame" with their fingers.

"It's going to be all right, pal . . ." Ted Heller was motioning to Eli from his doorway. "C'mon, pal, it's going to be all right . . ."

Eli saw him, past the brim of his hat. Ted did not move from his doorway, but leaned forward and spoke with his hand over his mouth. Behind him, three customers peered through the doorway. "Eli, it's Ted, remember Ted . . ."

Eli crossed the street and found he was heading directly towards Harriet Knudson. He lifted his neck so she could see his whole face.

He saw her forehead melt down to her lashes. "Good morning, Mr. Peck."

"Sholom," Eli said, and crossed the street where he saw the President of the Lions.

"Twice before . . ." he heard someone say, and then he crossed again, mounted the curb, and was before the bakery, where a delivery man charged past with a tray of powdered cakes twirling above him. "Pardon me, Father," he said, and scooted into his truck. But he could not move it. Eli Peck had stopped traffic.

He passed the Rivoli Theater, Beekman Cleaners, Harris' Westinghouse, the Unitarian Church, and soon he was passing only trees. At Ireland Road he turned right and started through Woodenton's winding streets. Baby carriages stopped whizzing and creaked — "Isn't that . . ." Gardeners held their clipping. Children stepped from the sidewalk and tried the curb. And Eli greeted no one, but raised his face to all. He wished passionately that he had white tears to show them . . . And not till he reached his own front lawn, saw his house, his shutters, his new jonquils, did he remember his wife. And the child that must have been born to him. And it was then and there he had the awful moment. He could go inside and put on his clothes and go to his wife in the hospital. It was not irrevocable, even the walk wasn't. In Woodenton memories are long but fury short. Apathy works like forgiveness. Besides, when you've flipped, you've flipped — it's Mother Nature.

What gave Eli the awful moment was that he turned away. He knew exactly what he could do but he chose not to. To go inside would be to go halfway. There was more . . . So he turned and walked towards the hospital and all the time he quaked an eighth of an inch beneath his skin to think that perhaps he'd chosen the crazy way. To think that he'd *chosen* to be crazy! But if you chose to be crazy, then you weren't crazy! It's when you didn't choose. No, he wasn't flipping. He had a child to see.

"Name?"

"Peck."

"Fourth floor." He was given a little blue card.

In the elevator everybody stared. Eli watched his black shoes rise four floors.

"Four."

He tipped his hat, but knew he couldn't take it off.

"Peck," he said. He showed the card.

"Congratulations," the nurse said. ". . . the grandfather?"

"The father. Which room?"

She led him to 412. "A joke on the Mrs.?" she said, but he slipped in the door without her.

"Miriam?"

"Yes?"

"Eli."

She rolled her white face towards her husband. "Oh, Eli . . . Oh, Eli."

He raised his arms. "What could I do?"

"You have a son. They called all morning."

"I came to see him."

"Like *that!*" she whispered harshly. "Eli, you can't go around like that."

"I have a son. I want to see him."

"Eli, why are you doing this to me!" Red seeped back into her lips. "*He's* not your fault," she explained. "Oh, Eli, sweetheart, why do you feel guilty about everything. Eli, change your clothes. I forgive you."

"Stop forgiving me. Stop understanding me."

"But I love you."

"That's something else."

"But, sweetie, you *don't* have to dress like that. You didn't do anything. You don't have to feel guilty because . . . because everything's all right. Eli, can't you see that?"

"Miriam, enough reasons. Where's my son?"

"Oh, please, Eli, don't flip now. I need you now. Is that why you're flipping — because I need you?"

"In your selfish way, Miriam, you're very generous. I want my son."

"Don't flip now. I'm afraid, now that he's out." She was beginning to whimper. "I don't know if I love him, now that he's out. When I look in the mirror, Eli, he won't be there . . . Eli, Eli, you look like you're going to your own funeral. Please, can't you leave well enough *alone?* Can't we just have a family?"

"No."

In the corridor he asked the nurse to lead him to his son. The nurse walked on one side of him, Ted Heller on the other.

"Eli, do you want some help? I thought you might want some help."

"No."

Ted whispered something to the nurse; then to Eli he whispered, "Should you be walking around like this?"

"Yes."

In his ear Ted said, "You'll . . . you'll frighten the kid . . ."

"There," the nurse said. She pointed to the first crib in the second row and looked, puzzled, to Ted.

"Can I go in?"

"No," the nurse said. "She'll hold him up." She knocked on the enclosure full of babies, and when a face appeared behind the window she said, "Peck."

Ted grabbed his arm. "Eli, you're not thinking of doing something you'll be sorry for . . . are you, Eli? Eli — I mean you know you're still Eli, don't you?"

"What day is it?"

"The nineteenth, Eli, of May. Eli, you know what *year* it is, don't you?"

Eli saw a nurse before him, holding an infant in a bassinet.

"Oh, Christ . . ." Ted said. "Jesus, Eli, you don't think you're the guy in the Bible stories, do you?" And suddenly he said, "You wait right here, pal . . ." and was gone.

Eli leaned forward and spoke into the glass. It did not make any difference if the reddened ball before him understood. Even if it didn't see him, it made no difference.

"I'm your father," he said. "Eli Peck."

He moved closer to the window, and when he spoke left a foggy O before his mouth.

"I'm wearing a black hat and a black suit," he told the child, "and special underwear. In a little while Dr. Eckman'll make me take off the whole business . . ."

Down the corridor he saw a door open. There were two men in white standing with Ted Heller. They all stared at him.

"But I'll keep the suit at home," Eli continued, "and I'll wear it again. I promise. Every year on the nineteenth of May, I'll wear it. I promise. All day. I won't work, I won't talk, I won't do anything but walk around with this black suit. And when you're old enough, I'll get you one, and you'll walk with me . . ."

At the end of the hall the door shut, and Ted and the two men started towards him. The men wore white shoes, white gowns, white skullcaps; they smelled, but not like Eli's suit.

Ted spoke softly. "Eli, time is up, pal."

But Eli wasn't finished. "And when you move away, you'll wear it too. You can go some place that makes even Woodenton look like a slum, but you'll wear it. And you'll make your son wear it, wherever *he* goes . . ."

"How are you feeling, Mr. Peck? First child upsets everyone."

"And his son with him."

"Excuse me, rabbi," a clear deep voice said, "but you're wanted . . . in the temple."

"That's right, rabbi," Ted said, "someone's waiting for you in the temple. There's a service going on."

"And your son's son's son . . ."

"What's he mumbling?"

"And his son, and so on, and we'll never forget . . ."

"Okay, rabbi. Okay okay okay okay everything's going to be okay . . ." Clearly, he saw the white men surround him and then he felt himself being glided away from the window. "Okay easy does it everything's all right everything's all right —"

He cried back to his son. "*Remember!*"

And in a moment they tore off his jacket. The cloth gave in one yank. Then a needle slid under the skin. The drug calmed his soul, but did not touch it down where the blackness had reached.

Joyce Carol Oates
1938–

Joyce Carol Oates is a phenomenon. Though at this writing only forty-seven years old, she has already published more than twenty-five works of fiction, including some three hundred short stories — but not including those written at the age of three or four when her career began. She has also published numerous volumes of verse, plays, and critical essays; in her spare time she is a professor of English and an occasional itinerant cultural ambassador; and she is highly visible as a busy book reviewer. As a magnet is to iron filings so is Joyce Carol Oates to literary prizes.

It is easy to declare that she writes too much but hard to prove that she would write much better if she didn't. (Balzac also wrote too much — and we are glad of it.) Little of her work is casual or commercial. If some of it fails of final effect, that is not because her central, most passionate energies are not engaged. Indeed it is the very intensity of the engagement that at times defeats the reader.

She is not only prolific but versatile. Because many of her stories are composed in the Gothic mode and therefore stick in our memories like a nightmare, we forget that she has also written historical, feminist, and detective fiction. Furthermore, her A Bloodsmoor Romance stands out as one of the most relentlessly extended parodies in the language.

Oates is one of many contemporary American writers interested in abnormal states. Her stories often deal with characters in frenzied pursuit of their identities, schizophrenics, mutilators of their own souls. The story that follows is a controlled study of an uncontrollable mind. The adolescent girl who is its center represents a type familiar to us from the sixties ("How I Contemplated" was first published in 1969) but persists into our own decade.

What gives the story its special quality is the exact rendition of the unhappy girl's voice as she records, in the chilling form of notes for a classroom assignment, the incremental growth of hysteria. Fascinated, we watch the dark confusion resulting from the impossibility of reconciling a sleek suburban life with recollections of horror and degradation.

How I Contemplated the World
from the Detroit House of Correction
and Began My Life Over Again

*Notes for an Essay for an English Class at Baldwin Country
Day School; Poking Around in Debris; Disgust and Curiosity;
A Revelation of the Meaning of Life; A Happy Ending . . .*

I · EVENTS

1. The girl (myself) is walking through Branden's, that excellent store.
Suburb of a large famous city that is a symbol for large famous American cities. The event sneaks up on the girl, who believes she is herding
it along with a small fixed smile, a girl of fifteen, innocently experienced.
She dawdles in a certain style by a counter of costume jewelry. Rings,
earrings, necklaces. Prices from $5 to $50, all within reach. All ugly. She
eases over to the glove counter, where everything is ugly too. In her
close-fitted coat with its black fur collar she contemplates the luxury of
Branden's, which she has known for many years: its many mild pale
lights, easy on the eye and the soul, its elaborate tinkly decorations, its
women shoppers with their excellent shoes and coats and hairdos, all
dawdling gracefully, in no hurry.

Who was ever in a hurry here?

2. The girl seated at home. A small library, paneled walls of oak.
Someone is talking to me. An earnest, husky, female voice drives itself
against my ears, nervous, frightened, groping around my heart, saying,
"If you wanted gloves, why didn't you say so? Why didn't you ask for
them?" That store, Branden's, is owned by Raymond Forrest who lives
on Du Maurier Drive. We live on Sioux Drive. Raymond Forrest. A
handsome man? An ugly man? A man of fifty or sixty, with gray hair,
or a man of forty with earnest, courteous eyes, a good golf game; who
is Raymond Forrest, this man who is my salvation? Father has been
talking to him. Father is not his physician; Dr. Berg is his physician.
Father and Dr. Berg refer patients to each other. There is a connection.
Mother plays bridge with . . . On Mondays and Wednesdays our maid
Billie works at . . . The strings draw together in a cat's cradle, making a
net to save you when you fall . . .

3. *Harriet Arnold's.* A small shop, better than Branden's. Mother in her black coat, I in my close-fitted blue coat. Shopping. Now look at this, isn't this cute, do you want this, why don't you want this, try this on, take this with you to the fitting room, take this also, what's wrong with you, what can I do for you, why are you so strange . . . ? "I wanted to steal but not to buy," I don't tell her. The girl droops along in her coat and gloves and leather boots, her eyes scan the horizon, which is pastel pink and decorated like Branden's, tasteful walls and modern ceilings with graceful glimmering lights.

4. Weeks later, the girl at a bus stop. Two o'clock in the afternoon, a Tuesday; obviously she has walked out of school.

5. The girl stepping down from a bus. Afternoon, weather changing to colder. Detroit. Pavement and closed-up stores; grillwork over the windows of a pawnshop. What is a pawnshop, exactly?

II   CHARACTERS

1. The girl stands five feet five inches tall. An ordinary height. Baldwin Country Day School draws them up to that height. She dreams along the corridors and presses her face against the Thermoplex glass. No frost or steam can ever form on that glass. A smudge of grease from her forehead . . . could she be boiled down to grease? She wears her hair loose and long and straight in suburban teen-age style, 1968. Eyes smudged with pencil, dark brown. Brown hair. Vague green eyes. A pretty girl? An ugly girl? She sings to herself under her breath, idling in the corridor, thinking of her many secrets (the thirty dollars she once took from the purse of a friend's mother, just for fun, the basement window she smashed in her own house just for fun) and thinking of her brother who is at Susquehanna Boys' Academy, an excellent preparatory school in Maine, remembering him unclearly . . . he has long manic hair and a squeaking voice and he looks like one of the popular teen-age singers of 1968, one of those in a group, *The Certain Forces, The Way Out, The Maniacs Responsible.* The girl in her turn looks like one of those fieldsful of girls who listen to the boys' singing, dreaming and mooning restlessly, breaking into high sullen laughter, innocently experienced.

2. The mother. A Midwestern woman of Detroit and suburbs. Belongs to the Detroit Athletic Club. Also the Detroit Golf Club. Also the

Bloomfield Hills Country Club. The Village Women's Club at which lectures are given each winter on Genet and Sartre and James Baldwin, by the Director of the Adult Education Program at Wayne State University ... The Bloomfield Art Association. Also the Founders Society of the Detroit Institute of Arts. Also ... Oh, she is in perpetual motion, this lady, hair like blown-up gold and finer than gold, hair and fingers and body of inestimable grace. Heavy weighs the gold on the back of her hairbrush and hand mirror. Heavy heavy the candlesticks in the dining room. Very heavy is the big car, a Lincoln, long and black, that on one cool autumn day split a squirrel's body in two unequal parts.

3. The father. Dr.   . He belongs to the same clubs as #2. A player of squash and golf; he has a golfer's umbrella of stripes. Candy stripes. In his mouth nothing turns to sugar, however; saliva works no miracles here. His doctoring is of the slightly sick. The sick are sent elsewhere (to Dr. Berg?), the deathly sick are sent back for more tests and their bills are sent to their homes, the unsick are sent to Dr. Coronet (Isabel, a lady), an excellent psychiatrist for unsick people who angrily believe they are sick and want to do something about it. If they demand a male psychiatrist, the unsick are sent by Dr.   (my father) to Dr. Lowenstein, a male psychiatrist, excellent and expensive, with a limited practice.

4. Clarita. She is twenty, twenty-five, she is thirty or more? Pretty, ugly, what? She is a woman lounging by the side of a road, in jeans and a sweater, hitchhiking, or she is slouched on a stool at a counter in some roadside diner. A hard line of jaw. Curious eyes. Amused eyes. Behind her eyes processions move, funeral pageants, cartoons. She says, "I never can figure out why girls like you bum around down here. What are you looking for anyway?" An odor of tobacco about her. Unwashed underclothes, or no underclothes, unwashed skin, gritty toes, hair long and falling into strands, not recently washed.

5. Simon. In this city the weather changes abruptly, so Simon's weather changes abruptly. He sleeps through the afternoon. He sleeps through the morning. Rising, he gropes around for something to get him going, for a cigarette or a pill to drive him out to the street, where the temperature is hovering around 35°. Why doesn't it drop? Why, why doesn't the cold clean air come down from Canada; will he have to go up into Canada to get it? will he have to leave the Country of his Birth and sink into Canada's frosty fields ... ? Will the F.B.I. (which he dreams about constantly) chase him over the Canadian border on foot, hounded out in a blizzard of broken glass and horns ... ?

"Once I was Huckleberry Finn," Simon says, "but now I am Roderick Usher." Beset by frenzies and fears, this man who makes my spine go cold, he takes green pills, yellow pills, pills of white and capsules of dark blue and green . . . he takes other things I may not mention, for what if Simon seeks me out and climbs into my girl's bedroom here in Bloomfield Hills and strangles me, what then . . . ? (As I write this I begin to shiver. Why do I shiver? I am now sixteen and sixteen is not an age for shivering.) It comes from Simon, who is always cold.

III   WORLD EVENTS

Nothing.

IV   PEOPLE & CIRCUMSTANCES
CONTRIBUTING TO THIS DELINQUENCY

Nothing.

V   SIOUX DRIVE

George, Clyde G. 240 Sioux. A manufacturer's representative; children, a dog, a wife. Georgian with the usual columns. You think of the White House, then of Thomas Jefferson, then your mind goes blank on the white pillars and you think of nothing. Norris, Ralph W. 246 Sioux. Public relations. Colonial. Bay window, brick, stone, concrete, wood, green shutters, sidewalk, lantern, grass, trees, blacktop drive, two children, one of them my classmate Esther (Esther Norris) at Baldwin. Wife, cars. Ramsey, Michael D. 250 Sioux. Colonial. Big living room, thirty by twenty-five, fireplaces in living room, library, recreation room, paneled walls wet bar five bathrooms five bedrooms two lavatories central air conditioning automatic sprinkler automatic garage door three children one wife two cars a breakfast room a patio a large fenced lot fourteen trees a front door with a brass knocker never knocked. Next is our house. Classic contemporary. Traditional modern. Attached garage, attached Florida room, attached patio, attached pool and cabana, at-

tached roof. A front door mail slot through which pour *Time Magazine, Fortune, Life, Business Week*, the *Wall Street Journal*, the *New York Times*, the *New Yorker*, the *Saturday Review, M.D., Modern Medicine, Disease of the Month* . . . and also . . . And in addition to all this, a quiet sealed letter from Baldwin saying: *Your daughter is not doing work compatible with her performance on the Stanford-Binet* . . . And your son is not doing well, not well at all, very sad. Where is your son anyway? Once he stole trick-and-treat candy from some six-year-old kids, he himself being a robust ten. The beginning. Now your daughter steals. In the Village Pharmacy she made off with, yes she did, don't deny it, she made off with a copy of *Pageant Magazine* for no reason, she swiped a roll of Life Savers in a green wrapper and was in no need of saving her life or even in need of sucking candy; when she was no more than eight years old she stole, don't blush, she stole a package of Tums only because it was out on the counter and available, and the nice lady behind the counter (now dead) said nothing . . . Sioux Drive. Maples, oaks, elms. Diseased elms cut down. Sioux Drive runs into Roosevelt Drive. Slow, turning lanes, not streets, all drives and lanes and ways and passes. A private police force. Quiet private police, in unmarked cars. Cruising on Saturday evenings with paternal smiles for the residents who are streaming in and out of houses, going to and from parties, a thousand parties, slightly staggering, the women in their furs alighting from automobiles bought of Ford and General Motors and Chrysler, very heavy automobiles. No foreign cars. Detroit. In 275 Sioux, down the block in that magnificent French-Normandy mansion, lives
himself, who has the C   account itself, imagine that! Look at where he lives and look at the enormous trees and chimneys, imagine his many fireplaces, imagine his wife and children, imagine his wife's hair, imagine her fingernails, imagine her bathtub of smooth clean glowing pink, imagine their embraces, his trouser pockets filled with odd coins and keys and dust and peanuts, imagine their ecstasy on Sioux Drive, imagine their income tax returns, imagine their little boy's pride in his experimental car, a scaled-down C   , as he roars around the neighborhood on the sidewalks frightening dogs and Negro maids, oh imagine all these things, imagine everything, let your mind roar out all over Sioux Drive and Du Maurier Drive and Roosevelt Drive and Ticonderoga Pass and Burning Bush Way and Lincolnshire Pass and Lois Lane.

When spring comes, its winds blow nothing to Sioux Drive, no odors of hollyhocks or forsythia, nothing Sioux Drive doesn't already possess, everything is planted and performing. The weather vanes, had they weather vanes, don't have to turn with the wind, don't have to contend with the weather. There is no weather.

VI   DETROIT

There is always weather in Detroit. Detroit's temperature is always 32°. Fast-falling temperatures. Slow-rising temperatures. Wind from the north-northeast four to forty miles an hour, small-craft warnings, partly cloudy today and Wednesday changing to partly sunny through Thursday . . . small warnings of frost, soot warnings, traffic warnings, hazardous lake conditions for small craft and swimmers, restless Negro gangs, restless cloud formations, restless temperatures aching to fall out the very bottom of the thermometer or shoot up over the top and boil everything over in red mercury.

Detroit's temperature is 32°. Fast-falling temperatures. Slow-rising temperatures. Wind from the north-northeast four to forty miles an hour . . .

VII   EVENTS

1. The girl's heart is pounding. In her pocket is a pair of gloves! In a plastic bag! Airproof breathproof plastic bag, gloves selling for twenty-five dollars on Branden's counter! In her pocket! Shoplifted! . . . In her purse is a blue comb, not very clean. In her purse is a leather billfold (a birthday present from her grandmother in Philadelphia) with snapshots of the family in clean plastic windows, in the billfold are bills, she doesn't know how many bills . . . In her purse is an ominous note from her friend Tykie *What's this about Joe H. and the kids hanging around at Louise's Sat. night? You heard anything?* . . . passed in French class. In her purse is a lot of dirty yellow Kleenex, her mother's heart would break to see such very dirty Kleenex, and at the bottom of her purse are brown hairpins and safety pins and a broken pencil and a ballpoint pen (blue) stolen from somewhere forgotten and a purse-size compact of Cover Girl Make-Up, Ivory Rose . . . Her lipstick is Broken Heart, a corrupt pink; her fingers are trembling like crazy; her teeth are beginning to chatter; her insides are alive; her eyes glow in her head; she is saying to her mother's astonished face *I want to steal but not to buy.*

2. At Clarita's. Day or night? What room is this? A bed, a regular bed, and a mattress on the floor nearby. Wallpaper hanging in strips. Clarita says she tore it like that with her teeth. She was fighting a barbaric tribe that night, high from some pills; she was battling for her life with men wearing helmets of heavy iron and their faces no more than Christian crosses to breathe through, every one of those bastards looking

like her lover Simon, who seems to breathe with great difficulty through the slits of mouth and nostrils in his face. Clarita has never heard of Sioux Drive. Raymond Forrest cuts no ice with her, nor does the C account and its millions; Harvard Business School could be at the corner of Vernor and 12th Street for all she cares, and Vietnam might have sunk by now into the Dead Sea under its tons of debris, for all the amazement she could show ... her face is overworked, overwrought, at the age of twenty (thirty?) it is already exhausted but fanciful and ready for a laugh. Clarita says mournfully to me *Honey somebody is going to turn you out let me give you warning*. In a movie shown on late television Clarita is not a mess like this but a nurse, with short neat hair and a dedicated look, in love with her doctor and her doctor's patients and their diseases, enamored of needles and sponges and rubbing alcohol ... Or no: she is a private secretary. Robert Cummings is her boss. She helps him with fantastic plots, the canned audience laughs, no, the audience doesn't laugh because nothing is funny, instead her boss is Robert Taylor and they are not boss and secretary but husband and wife, she is threatened by a young starlet, she is grim, handsome, wifely, a good companion for a good man ... She is Claudette Colbert. Her sister too is Claudette Colbert. They are twins, identical. Her husband Charles Boyer is a very rich handsome man and her sister, Claudette Colbert, is plotting her death in order to take her place as the rich man's wife, no one will know because they are *twins* ... All these marvelous lives Clarita might have lived, but she fell out the bottom at the age of thirteen. At the age when I was packing my overnight case for a slumber party at Toni Deshield's she was tearing filthy sheets off a bed and scratching up a rash on her arms ... Thirteen is uncommonly young for a white girl in Detroit, Miss Brock of the Detroit House of Correction said in a sad newspaper interview for the *Detroit News;* fifteen and sixteen are more likely. Eleven, twelve, thirteen are not surprising in colored ... they are more precocious. What can we do? Taxes are rising and the tax base is falling. The temperature rises slowly but falls rapidly. Everything is falling out the bottom, Woodward Avenue is filthy, Livernois Avenue is filthy! Scraps of paper flutter in the air like pigeons, dirt flies up and hits you right in the eye, oh Detroit is breaking up into dangerous bits of newspaper and dirt, watch out ...

Clarita's apartment is over a restaurant. Simon her lover emerges from the cracks at dark. Mrs. Olesko, a neighbor of Clarita's, an aged white wisp of a woman, doesn't complain but sniffs with contentment at Clarita's noisy life and doesn't tell the cops, hating cops, when the cops arrive. I should give more fake names, more blanks, instead of telling all these secrets. I myself am a secret; I am a minor.

3. My father reads a paper at a medical convention in Los Angeles. There he is, on the edge of the North American continent, when the

unmarked detective put his hand so gently on my arm in the aisle of Branden's and said, "Miss, would you like to step over here for a minute?"

And where was he when Clarita put her hand on my arm, that wintry dark sulphurous aching day in Detroit, in the company of closed-down barber shops, closed-down diners, closed-down movie houses, homes, windows, basements, faces ... she put her hand on my arm and said, "Honey, are you looking for somebody down here?"

And was he home worrying about me, gone for two weeks solid, when they carried me off ... ? It took three of them to get me in the police cruiser, so they said, and they put more than their hands on my arm.

4. I work on this lesson. My English teacher is Mr. Forest, who is from Michigan State. Not handsome, Mr. Forest, and his name is plain, unlike Raymond Forrest's, but he is sweet and rodentlike, he has conferred with the principal and my parents, and everything is fixed ... treat her as if nothing has happened, a new start, begin again, only sixteen years old, what a shame, how did it happen? — nothing happened, nothing could have happened, a slight physiological modification known only to a gynecologist or to Dr. Coronet. I work on my lesson. I sit in my pink room. I look around the room with my sad pink eyes. I sigh, I dawdle, I pause, I eat up time, I am limp and happy to be home, I am sixteen years old suddenly, my head hangs heavy as a pumpkin on my shoulders, and my hair has just been cut by Mr. Faye at the Crystal Salon and is said to be very becoming.

(Simon too put his hand on my arm and said, "Honey, you have got to come with me," and in his six-by-six room we got to know each other. Would I go back to Simon again? Would I lie down with him in all that filth and craziness? Over and over again.)

a Clarita is being betrayed as in front of a Cunningham Drug Store she is nervously eying a colored man who may or may not have money, or a nervous white boy of twenty with sideburns and an Appalachian look, who may or may not have a knife hidden in his jacket pocket, or a husky red-faced man of friendly countenance who may or may not be a member of the Vice Squad out for an early twilight walk.)

I work on my lesson for Mr. Forest. I have filled up eleven pages. Words pour out of me and won't stop. I want to tell everything ... what was the song Simon was always humming, and who was Simon's friend in a very new trench coat with an old high school graduation ring on his finger ... ? Simon's bearded friend? When I was down too low for him, Simon kicked me out and gave me to him for three days, I think, on Fourteenth Street in Detroit, an airy room of cold cruel drafts with newspapers on the floor . . . Do I really remember that or am I piecing it together from what they told me? Did they tell the truth? Did they know much of the truth?

VIII　CHARACTERS

1. Wednesdays after school, at four; Saturday mornings at ten. Mother drives me to Dr. Coronet. Ferns in the office, plastic or real, they look the same. Dr. Coronet is queenly, an elegant nicotine-stained lady who would have studied with Freud had circumstances not prevented it, a bit of a Catholic, ready to offer you some mystery if your teeth will ache too much without it. Highly recommended by Father! Forty dollars an hour, Father's forty dollars! Progress! Looking up! Looking better! That new haircut is so becoming, says Dr. Coronet herself, showing how normal she is for a woman with an I.Q. of 180 and many advanced degrees.

2. Mother. A lady in a brown suede coat. Boots of shiny black material, black gloves, a black fur hat. She would be humiliated could she know that of all the people in the world it is my ex-lover Simon who walks most like her . . . self-conscious and unreal, listening to distant music, a little bowlegged with craftiness . . .

3. Father. Tying a necktie. In a hurry. On my first evening home he put his hand on my arm and said, "Honey, we're going to forget all about this."

4. Simon. Outside, a plane is crossing the sky, in here we're in a hurry. Morning. It must be morning. The girl is half out of her mind, whimpering and vague; Simon her dear friend is wretched this morning . . . he is wretched with morning itself . . . he forces her to give him an injection with that needle she knows is filthy, she has a dread of needles and surgical instruments and the odor of things that are to be sent into the blood, thinking somehow of her father . . . This is a bad morning, Simon says that his mind is being twisted out of shape, and so he submits to the needle that he usually scorns and bites his lip with his yellowish teeth, his face going very pale. *Ah baby!* he says in his soft mocking voice, which with all women is a mockery of love, *do it like this — Slowly* — And the girl, terrified, almost drops the precious needle but manages to turn it up to the light from the window . . . is it an extension of herself then? She can give him this gift then? *I wish you wouldn't do*

this to me, she says, wise in her terror, because it seems to her that Simon's danger — in a few minutes he may be dead — is a way of pressing her against him that is more powerful than any other embrace. She has to work over his arm, the knotted corded veins of his arm, her forehead wet with perspiration as she pushes and releases the needle, staring at that mixture of liquid now stained with Simon's bright blood . . . When the drug hits him she can feel it herself, she feels that magic that is more than any woman can give him, striking the back of his head and making his face stretch as if with the impact of a terrible sun . . . She tries to embrace him but he pushes her aside and stumbles to his feet. *Jesus Christ,* he says . . .

5. Princess, a Negro girl of eighteen. What is her charge? She is closed-mouthed about it, shrewd and silent, you know that no one had to wrestle her to the sidewalk to get her in here; she came with dignity. In the recreation room she sits reading *Nancy Drew and the Jewel Box Mystery,* which inspires in her face tiny wrinkles of alarm and interest: what a face! Light brown skin, heavy shaded eyes, heavy eyelashes, a serious sinister dark brow, graceful fingers, graceful wristbones, graceful legs, lips, tongue, a sugar-sweet voice, a leggy stride more masculine than Simon's and my mother's, decked out in a dirty white blouse and dirty white slacks; vaguely nautical is Princess' style . . . At breakfast she is in charge of clearing the table and leans over me, saying, *Honey you sure you ate enough?*

6. The girl lies sleepless, wondering. Why here, why not there? Why Bloomfield Hills and not jail? Why jail and not her pink room? Why downtown Detroit and not Sioux Drive? What is the difference? Is Simon all the difference? The girl's head is a parade of wonders. She is nearly sixteen, her breath is marvelous with wonders, not long ago she was coloring with crayons and now she is smearing the landscape with paints that won't come off and won't come off her fingers either. She says to the matron *I am not talking about anything,* not because everyone has warned her not to talk but because, because she will not talk; because she won't say anything about Simon, who is her secret. And she says to the matron, *I won't go home,* up until that night in the lavatory when everything was changed . . . "No, I won't go home I want to stay here," she says, listening to her own words with amazement, thinking that weeds might climb everywhere over that marvelous $180,000 house and dinosaurs might return to muddy the beige carpeting, but never never will she reconcile four o'clock in the morning in Detroit with eight o'clock breakfasts in Bloomfield Hills . . . oh, she aches still for Simon's hands and his caressing breath, though he gave her little pleasure, he took everything from her (five-dollar bills, ten-dollar bills, passed into her numb hands by men and taken out of her hands by Simon) until she

herself was passed into the hands of other men, police, when Simon evidently got tired of her and her hysteria . . . *No, I won't go home, I don't want to be bailed out.* The girl thinks as a *Stubborn and Wayward Child* (one of several charges lodged against her), and the matron understands her crazy white-rimmed eyes that are seeking out some new violence that will keep her in jail, should someone threaten to let her out. Such children try to strangle the matrons, the attendants, or one another . . . they want the locks locked forever, the doors nailed shut . . . and this girl is no different up until that night her mind is changed for her . . .

IX THAT NIGHT

Princess and Dolly, a little white girl of maybe fifteen, hardy however as a sergeant and in the House of Correction for armed robbery, corner her in the lavatory at the farthest sink and the other girls look away and file out to bed, leaving her. God, how she is beaten up! Why is she beaten up? Why do they pound her, why such hatred? Princess vents all the hatred of a thousand silent Detroit winters on her body, this girl whose body belongs to me, fiercely she rides across the Midwestern plains on this girl's tender bruised body . . . revenge on the oppressed minorities of America! revenge on the slaughtered Indians! revenge on the female sex, on the male sex, revenge on Bloomfield Hills, revenge revenge . . .

X DETROIT

In Detroit, weather weighs heavily upon everyone. The sky looms large. The horizon shimmers in smoke. Downtown the buildings are imprecise in the haze. Perpetual haze. Perpetual motion inside the haze. Across the choppy river is the city of Windsor, in Canada. Part of the continent has bunched up here and is bulging outward, at the tip of Detroit; a cold hard rain is forever falling on the expressways . . . Shoppers shop grimly, their cars are not parked in safe places, their windshields may be smashed and graceful ebony hands may drag them out through their shatterproof smashed windshields, crying, *Revenge for the Indians!* Ah, they all fear leaving Hudson's and being dragged to the very tip of the city and thrown off the parking roof of Cobo Hall, that expensive tomb, into the river . . .

XI   CHARACTERS WE ARE
FOREVER ENTWINED WITH

1. Simon drew me into his tender rotting arms and breathed gravity into me. Then I came to earth, weighed down. He said, *You are such a little girl,* and he weighed me down with his delight. In the palms of his hands were teeth marks from his previous life experiences. He was thirty-five, they said. Imagine Simon in this room, in my pink room: he is about six feet tall and stoops slightly, in a feline cautious way, always thinking, always on guard, with his scuffed light suede shoes and his clothes that are anyone's clothes, slightly rumpled ordinary clothes that ordinary men might wear to not-bad jobs. Simon has fair long hair, curly hair, spent languid curls that are like . . . exactly like the curls of wood shavings to the touch, I am trying to be exact . . . and he smells of un-heated mornings and coffee and too many pills coating his tongue with a faint green-white scum . . . Dear Simon, who would be panicked in this room and in this house (right now Billie is vacuuming next door in my parents' room; a vacuum cleaner's roar is a sign of all good things), Simon who is said to have come from a home not much different from this, years ago, fleeing all the carpeting and the polished banisters . . . Simon has a deathly face, only desperate people fall in love with it. His face is bony and cautious, the bones of his cheeks prominent as if with the rigidity of his ceaseless thinking, plotting, for he has to make money out of girls to whom money means nothing, they're so far gone they can hardly count it, and in a sense money means nothing to him either except as a way of keeping on with his life. *Each Day's Proud Struggle,* the title of a novel we could read at jail . . . Each day he needs a certain amount of money. He devours it. It wasn't love he uncoiled in me with his hollowed-out eyes and his courteous smile, that remnant of a prosperous past, but a dark terror that needed to press itself flat against him, or against another man . . . but he was the first, he came over to me and took my arm, a claim. We struggled on the stairs and I said, *Let me loose, you're hurting my neck, my face,* it was such a surprise that my skin hurt where he rubbed it, and afterward we lay face to face and he breathed everything into me. In the end I think he turned me in.

2. Raymond Forrest. I just read this morning that Raymond Forrest's father, the chairman of the board at   , died of a heart attack on a plane bound for London. I would like to write Raymond Forrest a note of sympathy. I would like to thank him for not pressing charges against me one hundred years ago, saving me, being so generous . . . well, men like Raymond Forrest are generous men, not like Simon. I would like to write him a letter telling of my love, or of some other emotion that is positive and healthy. Not like Simon and his poetry, which he scrawled down when he was high and never changed a word . . . but when I try

to think of something to say, it is Simon's language that comes back to me, caught in my head like a bad song, it is always Simon's language:

> There is no reality only dreams
> Your neck may get snapped when you wake
> My love is drawn to some violent end
> She keeps wanting to get away
> My love is heading downward
> And I am heading upward
> She is going to crash on the sidewalk
> And I am going to dissolve into the clouds

XII   EVENTS

1. Out of the hospital, bruised and saddened and converted, with Princess' grunts still tangled in my hair . . . and Father in his overcoat looking like a prince himself, come to carry me off. Up the expressway and out north to home. Jesus Christ, but the air is thinner and cleaner here. Monumental houses. Heartbreaking sidewalks, so clean.

2. Weeping in the living room. The ceiling is two stories high and two chandeliers hang from it. Weeping, weeping, though Billie the maid is *probably listening*. I will never leave home again. Never. Never leave home. Never leave this home again, never.

3. Sugar doughnuts for breakfast. The toaster is very shiny and my face is distorted in it. Is that my face?

4. The car is turning in the driveway. Father brings me home. Mother embraces me. Sunlight breaks in movieland patches on the roof of our traditional-contemporary home, which was designed for the famous automotive stylist whose identity, if I told you the name of the famous car he designed, you would all know, so I can't tell you because my teeth chatter at the thought of being sued . . . or having someone climb into my bedroom window with a rope to strangle me . . . The car turns up the blacktop drive. The house opens to me like a doll's house, so lovely in the sunlight, the big living room beckons to me with its walls falling away in a delirium of joy at my return, Billie the maid is *no doubt* listening from the kitchen as I burst into tears and the hysteria Simon got so sick of. Convulsed in Father's arms, I say I will never leave again, never, why did I leave, where did I go, what happened, my mind is gone wrong, my body is one big bruise, my backbone was sucked dry, it

wasn't the men who hurt me and Simon never hurt me but only those girls ... my God, how they hurt me ... I will never leave home again ... The car is perpetually turning up the drive and I am perpetually breaking down in the living room and we are perpetually taking the right exit from the expressway (Lahser Road) and the wall of the rest room is perpetually banging against my head and perpetually are Simon's hands moving across my body and adding everything up and so too are Father's hands on my shaking bruised back, far from the surface of my skin on the surface of my good blue cashmere coat (dry-cleaned for my release) ... I weep for all the money here, for God in gold and beige carpeting, for the beauty of chandeliers and the miracle of a clean polished gleaming toaster and faucets that run both hot and cold water, and I tell them, *I will never leave home, this is my home, I love everything here, I am in love with everything here* ...

I am home.

MARGARET ATWOOD

1939–

The continuing emergence of Canadian writers as a literary force has been marked by a small constellation of excellent short story writers, most of them women. Among these Margaret Atwood, born in Ottawa, is in some ways the most interesting. Esteemed as a poet, she has also gained a solid reputation for her novels, especially Surfacing (1972). Her short stories are contained in such collections as Dancing Girls (1977) and Bluebeard's Egg (1985).

While her stories incorporate a remarkable variety of themes, many are strongly feminist in tone, many vigorously affirm her Canadian heritage. Some explore the difficulty — because one must be either man or woman — that lies in being merely human. All demonstrate a tough, honest, unfoolable intelligence.

In "The Man from Mars" two quite ordinary lives intersect to generate a situation that grows in complexity until — though only for the moment — those lives cease to be ordinary. Margaret Atwood never raises her voice, yet the desired effect of mingled pathos and irony registers perfectly.

The Man from Mars

A LONG TIME AGO Christine was walking through the park. She was still wearing her tennis dress; she hadn't had time to shower and change, and her hair was held back with an elastic band. Her chunky reddish face, exposed with no softening fringe, looked like a Russian peasant's, but without the elastic band the hair got in her eyes. The afternoon was too hot for April; the indoor courts had been steaming, her skin felt poached.

The sun had brought the old men out from wherever they spent the winter: she had read a story recently about one who lived for three years in a manhole. They sat weedishly on the benches or lay on the grass with their heads on squares of used newspaper. As she passed, their wrinkled toadstool faces drifted towards her, drawn by the movement of her body, then floated away again, uninterested.

The squirrels were out, too, foraging; two or three of them moved towards her in darts and pauses, eyes fixed on her expectantly, mouths with the ratlike receding chins open to show the yellowed front teeth. Christine walked faster, she had nothing to give them. People shouldn't feed them, she thought; it makes them anxious and they get mangy.

Halfway across the park she stopped to take off her cardigan. As she bent over to pick up her tennis racquet again someone touched her on her freshly bared arm. Christine seldom screamed; she straightened up suddenly, gripping the handle of her racquet. It was not one of the old men, however: it was a dark-haired boy of twelve or so.

"Excuse me," he said, "I search for Economics Building. Is it there?" He motioned towards the west.

Christine looked at him more closely. She had been mistaken: he was not young, just short. He came a little above her shoulder, but then, she was above the average height; "statuesque," her mother called it when she was straining. He was also what was referred to in their family as "a person from another culture": oriental without a doubt, though perhaps not Chinese. Christine judged he must be a foreign student and gave him her official welcoming smile. In high school she had been president of the United Nations Club; that year her school had been picked to represent the Egyptian delegation at the Mock Assembly. It had been an unpopular assignment — nobody wanted to be the Arabs — but she had seen it through. She had made rather a good speech about the Palestinian refugees.

"Yes," she said, "that's it over there. The one with the flat roof. See it?"

The man had been smiling nervously at her the whole time. He was wearing glasses with transparent plastic rims, through which his eyes bulged up at her as though through a goldfish bowl. He had not followed where she was pointing. Instead he thrust towards her a small pad of green paper and a ballpoint pen.

"You make map," he said.

Christine set down her tennis racquet and drew a careful map. "We are here," she said, pronouncing distinctly. "You go this way. The building is here." She indicated the route with a dotted line and an X. The man leaned close to her, watching the progress of the map attentively; he smelled of cooked cauliflower and an unfamiliar brand of hair grease. When she had finished Christine handed the paper and pen back to him with a terminal smile.

"Wait," the man said. He tore the piece of paper with the map off the pad, folded it carefully and put it in his jacket pocket; the jacket sleeves came down over his wrists and had threads at the edges. He began to write something; she noticed with a slight feeling of revulsion that his nails and the ends of his fingers were so badly bitten they seemed almost deformed. Several of his fingers were blue from the leaky ballpoint.

"Here is my name," he said, holding the pad out to her.

Christine read an odd assemblage of g's, y's and n's, neatly printed in block letters. "Thank you," she said.

"You now write your name," he said, extending the pen.

Christine hesitated. If this had been a person from her own culture she would have thought he was trying to pick her up. But then, people from her own culture never tried to pick her up; she was too big. The only one who had made the attempt was the Moroccan waiter at the beer parlour where they sometimes went after meetings, and he had been direct. He had just intercepted her on the way to the Ladies' Room and asked and she said no; that had been that. This man was not a waiter though, but a student; she didn't want to offend him. In his culture, whatever it was, this exchange of names on pieces of paper was probably a formal politeness, like saying thank you. She took the pen from him.

"That is a very pleasant name," he said. He folded the paper and placed it in his jacket pocket with the map.

Christine felt she had done her duty. "Well, goodbye," she said. "It was nice to have met you." She bent for her tennis racquet but he had already stooped and retrieved it and was holding it with both hands in front of him, like a captured banner.

"I carry this for you."

"Oh no, please. Don't bother, I am in a hurry," she said, articulating clearly. Deprived of her tennis racquet she felt weaponless. He started to saunter along the path; he was not nervous at all now, he seemed completely at ease.

"*Vous parlez français?*" he asked conversationally.

"*Oui, un petit peu,*" she said. "Not very well." How am I going to get my racquet away from him without being rude? she was wondering.

"*Mais vous avez un bel accent.*" His eyes goggled at her through the glasses: was he being flirtatious? She was well aware that her accent was wretched.

"Look," she said, for the first time letting her impatience show, "I really have to go. Give me my racquet, please."

He quickened his pace but gave no sign of returning the racquet. "Where are you going?"

"Home," she said. "My house."

"I go with you now," he said hopefully.

"*No,*" she said: she would have to be firm with him. She made a lunge and got a grip on her racquet; after a brief tug of war it came free.

"Goodbye," she said, turning away from his puzzled face and setting off at what she hoped was a discouraging jog-trot. It was like walking away from a growling dog: you shouldn't let on you were frightened. Why should she be frightened anyway? He was only half her size and she had the tennis racquet, there was nothing he could do to her.

Although she did not look back she could tell he was still following. Let there be a streetcar, she thought, and there was one, but it was far down the line, stuck behind a red light. He appeared at her side, breathing audibly, a moment after she reached the stop. She gazed ahead, rigid.

"You are my friend," he said tentatively.

Christine relented: he hadn't been trying to pick her up after all, he was a stranger, he just wanted to meet some of the local people; in his place she would have wanted the same thing.

"Yes," she said, doling him out a smile.

"That is good," he said. "My country is very far."

Christine couldn't think of an apt reply. "That's interesting," she said. "*Très intéressant.*" The streetcar was coming at last; she opened her purse and got out a ticket.

"I go with you now," he said. His hand clamped on her arm above the elbow.

"You . . . stay . . . *here,*" Christine said, resisting the impulse to shout but pausing between each word as though for a deaf person. She detached his hand — his hold was quite feeble and could not compete with her tennis biceps — and leapt off the curb and up the streetcar steps, hearing with relief the doors grind shut behind her. Inside the car and a block away she permitted herself a glance out a side window. He was standing where she had left him; he seemed to be writing something on his little pad of paper.

When she reached home she had only time for a snack, and even then she was almost late for the Debating Society. The topic was, "Resolved: That War Is Obsolete." Her team took the affirmative and won.

Christine came out of her last examination feeling depressed. It was not the exam that depressed her but the fact that it was the last one: it meant the end of the school year. She dropped into the coffee shop as usual, then went home early because there didn't seem to be anything else to do.

"Is that you, dear?" her mother called from the livingroom. She must have heard the front door close. Christine went in and flopped on the sofa, disturbing the neat pattern of cushions.

"How was your exam, dear?" her mother asked.

"Fine," said Christine flatly. It had been fine; she had passed. She was not a brilliant student, she knew that, but she was conscientious. Her professors always wrote things like "A serious attempt" and "Well thought out but perhaps lacking in *élan*" on her term papers; they gave her *B*s, the occasional *B* +. She was taking Political Science and Economics, and hoped for a job with the Government after she graduated; with her father's connections she had a good chance.

"That's nice."

Christine felt, resentfully, that her mother had only a hazy idea of what an exam was. She was arranging gladioli in a vase; she had rubber gloves on to protect her hands as she always did when engaged in what she called "housework." As far as Christine could tell her housework consisted of arranging flowers in vases: daffodils and tulips and hyacinths through gladioli, irises and roses, all the way to asters and mums. Sometimes she cooked, elegantly and with chafing-dishes, but she thought of it as a hobby. The girl did everything else. Christine thought it faintly sinful to have a girl. The only ones available now were either foreign or pregnant; their expressions usually suggested they were being taken advantage of somehow. But her mother asked what they would do otherwise; they'd either have to go into a Home or stay in their own countries, and Christine had to agree this was probably true. It was hard, anyway, to argue with her mother. She was so delicate, so preserved-looking, a harsh breath would scratch the finish.

"An interesting young man phoned today," her mother said. She had finished the gladioli and was taking off her rubber gloves. "He asked to speak with you and when I said you weren't in we had quite a little chat. You didn't tell me about him, dear." She put on the glasses which she wore on a decorative chain around her neck, a signal that she was in her modern, intelligent mood rather than her old-fashioned whimsical one.

"Did he leave his name?" Christine asked. She knew a lot of young men but they didn't often call her; they conducted their business with her in the coffee shop or after meetings.

"He's a person from another culture. He said he would call back later."

Christine had to think a moment. She was vaguely acquainted with several people from other cultures, Britain mostly; they belonged to the Debating Society.

"He's studying Philosophy in Montreal," her mother prompted. "He sounded French."

Christine began to remember the man in the park. "I don't think he's French, exactly," she said.

Her mother had taken off her glasses again and was poking absent-mindedly at a bent gladiolus. "Well, he sounded French." She meditated, flowery sceptre in hand. "I think it would be nice if you had him to tea."

Christine's mother did her best. She had two other daughters, both of whom took after her. They were beautiful; one was well married already and the other would clearly have no trouble. Her friends consoled her about Christine by saying, "She's not fat, she's just big-boned, it's the father's side," and "Christine is so healthy." Her other daughters had never gotten involved in activities when they were at school, but since Christine could not possibly ever be beautiful even if she took off weight, it was just as well she was so athletic and political, it was a good thing she had interests. Christine's mother tried to encourage her interests whenever possible. Christine could tell when she was making an extra effort, there was a reproachful edge to her voice.

She knew her mother expected enthusiasm but she could not supply it. "I don't know, I'll have to see," she said dubiously.

"You look tired, darling," said her mother. "Perhaps you'd like a glass of milk."

Christine was in the bathtub when the phone rang. She was not prone to fantasy but when she was in the bathtub she often pretended she was a dolphin, a game left over from one of the girls who used to bathe her when she was small. Her mother was being bell-voiced and gracious in the hall; then there was a tap at the door.

"It's that nice young French student, Christine," her mother said.

"Tell him I'm in the bathtub," Christine said, louder than necessary. "He isn't French."

She could hear her mother frowning. "That wouldn't be very polite, Christine. I don't think he'd understand."

"Oh, all right," Christine said. She heaved herself out of the bathtub, swathed her pink bulk in a towel and splattered to the phone.

"Hello," she said gruffly. At a distance he was not pathetic, he was a nuisance. She could not imagine how he had tracked her down: most likely he went through the phone book, calling all the numbers with her last name until he hit on the right one.

"It is your friend."

"I know," she said. "How are you?"

"I am very fine." There was a long pause, during which Christine had a vicious urge to say, "Well, goodbye then," and hang up; but she was aware of her mother poised figurine-like in her bedroom doorway. Then he said, "I hope you also are very fine."

"Yes," said Christine. She wasn't going to participate.

"I come to tea," he said.

This took Christine by surprise. "You do?"

"Your pleasant mother ask me. I come Thursday, four o'clock."

"Oh," Christine said, ungraciously.

"See you then," he said, with the conscious pride of one who has mastered a difficult idiom.

Christine set down the phone and went along the hall. Her mother was in her study, sitting innocently at her writing desk.

"Did you ask him to tea on Thursday?"

"Not exactly, dear," her mother said. "I did mention he might come round to tea *some*time, though."

"Well, he's coming Thursday. Four o'clock."

"What's wrong with that?" her mother said serenely. "I think it's a very nice gesture for us to make. I do think you might try to be a little more co-operative." She was pleased with herself.

"Since you invited him," said Christine, "you can bloody well stick around and help me entertain him. I don't want to be left making nice gestures all by myself."

"Christine, *dear*," her mother said, above being shocked. "You ought to put on your dressing gown, you'll catch a chill."

After sulking for an hour Christine tried to think of the tea as a cross between an examination and an executive meeting: not enjoyable, certainly, but to be got through as tactfully as possible. And it *was* a nice gesture. When the cakes her mother had ordered arrived from *The Pâtisserie* on Thursday morning she began to feel slightly festive; she even resolved to put on a dress, a good one, instead of a skirt and blouse. After all, she had nothing against him, except the memory of the way he had grabbed her tennis racquet and then her arm. She suppressed a quick impossible vision of herself pursued around the livingroom, fending him off with thrown sofa cushions and vases of gladioli; nevertheless she told the girl they would have tea in the garden. It would be a treat for him, and there was more space outdoors.

She had suspected her mother would dodge the tea, would contrive to be going out just as he was arriving: that way she could size him up and then leave them alone together. She had done things like that to Christine before; the excuse this time was the Symphony Committee. Sure enough, her mother carefully mislaid her gloves and located them with a faked murmur of joy when the doorbell rang. Christine relished for weeks afterwards the image of her mother's dropped jaw and flawless recovery when he was introduced: he wasn't quite the foreign potentate her optimistic, veil-fragile mind had concocted.

He was prepared for celebration. He had slicked on so much hair cream that his head seemed to be covered with a tight black patent-leather cap, and he had cut the threads off his jacket sleeves. His orange tie was overpoweringly splendid. Christine noticed, however, as he shook her mother's suddenly-braced white glove that the ballpoint ink on his fingers was indelible. His face had broken out, possibly in anticipation of the delights in store for him; he had a tiny camera slung over his shoulder and was smoking an exotic-smelling cigarette.

Christine led him through the cool flowery softly-padded livingroom and out by the French doors into the garden. "You sit here," she said. "I will have the girl bring tea."

This girl was from the West Indies. Christine's parents had been enraptured with her when they were down at Christmas and had brought her back with them. Since that time she had become pregnant, but Christine's mother had not dismissed her. She said she was slightly disappointed but what could you expect, and she didn't see any real difference between a girl who was pregnant before you hired her and one who got that way afterwards. She prided herself on her tolerance; also there was a scarcity of girls. Strangely enough, the girl became progressively less easy to get along with. Either she did not share Christine's mother's view of her own generosity, or she felt she had gotten away with something and was therefore free to indulge in contempt. At first Christine had tried to treat her as an equal. "Don't call me 'Miss Christine,' " she had said with an imitation of light, comradely laughter. "What you want me to call you then?" the girl had said, scowling. They had begun to have brief, surly arguments in the kitchen, which Christine decided were like the arguments between one servant and another. Her mother's attitude towards each of them was similar; they were not altogether satisfactory but they would have to do.

The cakes, glossy with icing, were set out on a plate and the teapot was standing ready; on the counter the electric kettle boiled. Christine headed for it, but the girl, till then sitting with her elbows on the kitchen table and watching her expressionlessly, made a dash and intercepted her. Christine waited until she had poured the water into the pot. Then, "I'll carry it out, Elvira," she said. She had just decided she didn't want the girl to see her visitor's orange tie; already, she knew, her position in the girl's eyes had suffered because no one had yet attempted to get *her* pregnant.

"What you think they pay me for, Miss Christine?" the girl said insolently. She swung towards the garden with the tray; Christine trailed her, feeling lumpish and awkward. The girl was at least as big as she was but in a different way.

"Thank you, Elvira," Christine said when the tray was in place. The girl departed without a word, casting a disdainful backward glance at the frayed jacket sleeves, the stained fingers. Christine was now determined to be especially kind to him.

"You are very rich," he said.

"No," Christine protested, shaking her head, "we're not." She had never thought of her family as rich; it was one of her father's sayings that nobody made any money with the Government.

"Yes," he repeated, "you are very rich." He sat back in his lawn chair, gazing about him as though dazed.

Christine set his cup of tea in front of him. She wasn't in the habit of paying much attention to the house or the garden; they were nothing special, far from being the largest on the street; other people took care of them. But now she looked where he was looking, seeing it all as though from a different height: the long expanses, the border flowers blazing in the early-summer sunlight, the flagged patio and walks, the high walls and the silence.

He came back to her face, sighing a little. "My English is not good," he said, "but I improve."

"You do," Christine said, nodding encouragement.

He took sips of his tea, quickly and tenderly as though afraid of injuring the cup. "I like to stay here."

Christine passed him the cakes. He took only one, making a slight face as he ate it; but he had several more cups of tea while she finished the cakes. She managed to find out from him that he had come over on a church fellowship — she could not decode the denomination — and was studying Philosophy or Theology, or possibly both. She was feeling well-disposed towards him: he had behaved himself, he had caused her no inconvenience.

The teapot was at last empty. He sat up straight in his chair, as though alerted by a soundless gong. "You look this way, please," he said. Christine saw that he had placed his miniature camera on the stone sundial her mother had shipped back from England two years before. He wanted to take her picture. She was flattered, and settled herself to pose, smiling evenly.

He took off his glasses and laid them beside his plate. For a moment she saw his myopic, unprotected eyes turned towards her, with something tremulous and confiding in them she wanted to close herself off from knowing about. Then he went over and did something to the camera, his back to her. The next instant he was crouched beside her, his arm around her waist as far as it could reach, his other hand covering her own hands which she had folded in her lap, his cheek jammed up against hers. She was too startled to move. The camera clicked.

He stood up at once and replaced his glasses, which glittered now with a sad triumph. "Thank you, Miss," he said to her. "I go now." He slung the camera back over his shoulder, keeping his hand on it as though to hold the lid on and prevent escape. "I send to my family; they will like."

He was out the gate and gone before Christine had recovered; then she laughed. She had been afraid he would attack her, she could admit it now, and he had; but not in the usual way. He had raped, *rapeo, rapere, rapui, to seize and carry off,* not herself but her celluloid image, and incidentally that of the silver tea service, which glinted mockingly at her as the girl bore it away, carrying it regally, the insignia, the official jewels. Christine spent the summer as she had for the past three years: she was the sailing instructress at an expensive all-girls camp near Algonquin Park. She had been a camper there, everything was familiar to her; she sailed almost better than she played tennis.

The second week she got a letter from him, postmarked Montreal and forwarded from her home address. It was printed in block letters on a piece of the green paper, two or three sentences. It began, "I hope you are well," then described the weather in monosyllables and ended, "I am fine." It was signed, "Your friend." Each week she got another of these letters, more or less identical. In one of them a colour print was enclosed: himself, slightly crosseyed and grinning hilariously, even more spindly than she remembered him against her billowing draperies, flowers exploding around them like firecrackers, one of his hands an equivocal blur in her lap, the other out of sight; on her own face, astonishment and outrage, as though he was sticking her in the behind with his hidden thumb.

She answered the first letter, but after that the seniors were in training for the races. At the end of the summer, packing to go home, she threw all the letters away.

When she had been back for several weeks she received another of the green letters. This time there was a return address printed at the top which Christine noted with foreboding was in her own city. Every day she waited for the phone to ring; she was so certain his first attempt at contact would be a disembodied voice that when he came upon her abruptly in midcampus she was unprepared.

"How are you?"

His smile was the same, but everything else about him had deteriorated. He was, if possible, thinner; his jacket sleeves had sprouted a lush new crop of threads, as though to conceal hands now so badly bitten they appeared to have been gnawed by rodents. His hair fell over his eyes, uncut, ungreased; his eyes in the hollowed face, a delicate triangle of skin stretched on bone, jumped behind his glasses like hooked fish. He had the end of a cigarette in the corner of his mouth, and as they walked he lit a new one from it.

"I'm fine," Christine said. She was thinking, I'm not going to get involved again, enough is enough, I've done my bit for internationalism. "How are you?"

"I live here now," he said. "Maybe I study Economics."

"That's nice." He didn't sound as though he was enrolled anywhere.

"I come to see you."

Christine didn't know whether he meant he had left Montreal in order to be near her or just wanted to visit her at her house as he had done in the spring; either way she refused to be implicated. They were outside the Political Science building. "I have a class here," she said. "Goodbye." She was being callous, she realized that, but a quick chop was more merciful in the long run, that was what her beautiful sisters used to say.

Afterwards she decided it had been stupid of her to let him find out where her class was. Though a timetable was posted in each of the colleges: all he had to do was look her up and record her every probable movement in block letters on his green notepad. After that day he never left her alone.

Initially he waited outside the lecture rooms for her to come out. She said hello to him curtly at first and kept on going, but this didn't work; he followed her at a distance, smiling his changeless smile. Then she stopped speaking altogether and pretended to ignore him, but it made no difference, he followed her anyway. The fact that she was in some way afraid of him — or was it just embarrassment? — seemed only to encourage him. Her friends started to notice, asking her who he was and why he was tagging along behind her; she could hardly answer because she hardly knew.

As the weekdays passed and he showed no signs of letting up, she began to jog-trot between classes, finally to run. He was tireless, and had an amazing wind for one who smoked so heavily: he would speed along behind her, keeping the distance between them the same, as though he were a pull-toy attached to her by a string. She was aware of the ridiculous spectacle they must make, galloping across campus, something out of a cartoon short, a lumbering elephant stampeded by a smiling, emaciated mouse, both of them locked in the classic pattern of comic pursuit and flight; but she found that to race made her less nervous than to walk sedately, the skin on the back of her neck crawling with the feel of his eyes on it. At least she could use her muscles. She worked out routines, escapes: she would dash in the front door of the Ladies' Room in the coffee shop and out the back door, and he would lose the trail, until he discovered the other entrance. She would try to shake him by detours through baffling archways and corridors, but he seemed as familiar with the architectural mazes as she was herself. As a last refuge she could head for the women's dormitory and watch from safety as he was skidded to a halt by the receptionist's austere voice: men were not allowed past the entrance.

Lunch became difficult. She would be sitting, usually with other members of the Debating Society, just digging nicely into a sandwich, when he would appear suddenly as though he'd come up through an unseen manhole. She then had the choice of barging out through the crowded cafeteria, sandwich half-eaten, or finishing her lunch with him standing behind her chair, everyone at the table acutely aware of him, the conversation stilting and dwindling. Her friends learned to spot him from a distance; they posted lookouts. "Here he comes," they would whisper, helping her collect her belongings for the sprint they knew would follow.

Several times she got tired of running and turned to confront him. "What do you want?" she would ask, glowering belligerently down at him, almost clenching her fists; she felt like shaking him, hitting him.

"I wish to talk to you."

"Well, here I am," she would say. "What do you want to talk about?"

But he would say nothing; he would stand in front of her, shifting his feet, smiling perhaps apologetically (though she could never pinpoint the exact tone of that smile, chewed lips stretched apart over the nicotine-yellowed teeth, rising at the corners, flesh held stiffly in place for an invisible photographer), his eyes jerking from one part of her face to another as though he saw her in fragments.

Annoying and tedious though it was, his pursuit of her had an odd result: mysterious in itself, it rendered her equally mysterious. No one had ever found Christine mysterious before. To her parents she was a beefy heavyweight, a plodder, lacking in flair, ordinary as bread. To her sisters she was the plain one, treated with an indulgence they did not give to each other: they did not fear her as a rival. To her male friends she was the one who could be relied on. She was helpful and a hard worker, always good for a game of tennis with the athletes among them. They invited her along to drink beer with them so they could get into the cleaner, more desirable Ladies and Escorts side of the beer parlour, taking it for granted she would buy her share of the rounds. In moments of stress they confided to her their problems with women. There was nothing devious about her and nothing interesting.

Christine had always agreed with these estimates of herself. In childhood she had identified with the false bride or the ugly sister; whenever a story had begun, "Once there was a maiden as beautiful as she was good," she had known it wasn't her. That was just how it was, but it wasn't so bad. Her parents never expected her to be a brilliant social success and weren't overly disappointed when she wasn't. She was spared the manoeuvring and anxiety she witnessed among others her age, and she even had a kind of special position among men: she was an exception, she fitted none of the categories they commonly used when talking about girls; she wasn't a cock-teaser, a cold fish, an easy lay or a snarky bitch; she was an honorary person. She had grown to share their contempt for most women.

Now, however, there was something about her that could not be explained. A man was chasing her, a peculiar sort of man, granted, but still a man, and he was without doubt attracted to her, he couldn't leave her alone. Other men examined her more closely than they ever had, appraising her, trying to find out what it was those twitching bespectacled eyes saw in her. They started to ask her out, though they returned from these excursions with their curiosity unsatisfied, the secret of her charm still intact. Her opaque dumpling face, her solid bear-shaped body became for them parts of a riddle no one could solve. Christine sensed this. In the bathtub she no longer imagined she was a dolphin; instead she imagined she was an elusive water-nixie, or sometimes, in moments of audacity, Marilyn Monroe. The daily chase was becoming a habit; she even looked forward to it. In addition to its other benefits she was losing weight.

All these weeks he had never phoned her or turned up at the house. He must have decided however that his tactics were not having the desired result, or perhaps he sensed she was becoming bored. The phone began to ring in the early morning or late at night when he could be sure she would be there. Sometimes he would simply breathe (she could recognize, or thought she could, the quality of his breathing), in which case she would hang up. Occasionally he would say again that he wanted to talk to her, but even when she gave him lots of time nothing else would follow. Then he extended his range: she would see him on her streetcar, smiling at her silently from a seat never closer than three away; she could feel him tracking her down her own street, though when she would break her resolve to pay no attention and would glance back he would be invisible or in the act of hiding behind a tree or hedge.

Among crowds of people and in daylight she had not really been afraid of him; she was stronger than he was and he had made no recent attempt to touch her. But the days were growing shorter and colder, it was almost November, often she was arriving home in twilight or a darkness broken only by the feeble orange streetlamps. She brooded over the possibility of razors, knives, guns; by acquiring a weapon he could quickly turn the odds against her. She avoided wearing scarves, remembering the newspaper stories about girls who had been strangled by them. Putting on her nylons in the morning gave her a funny feeling. Her body seemed to have diminished, to have become smaller than his.

Was he deranged, was he a sex maniac? He seemed so harmless, yet it was that kind who often went berserk in the end. She pictured those ragged fingers at her throat, tearing at her clothes, though she could not think of herself as screaming. Parked cars, the shrubberies near her house, the driveways on either side of it, changed as she passed them from unnoticed background to sinister shadowed foreground, every detail distinct and harsh: they were places a man might crouch, leap out from. Yet every time she saw him in the clear light of morning or afternoon (for he still continued his old methods of pursuit), his aging jacket and jittery eyes convinced her that it was she herself who was the tormentor, the persecutor. She was in some sense responsible; from the folds and crevices of the body she had treated for so long as a reliable machine was emanating, against her will, some potent invisible odour, like a dog's in heat or a female moth's, that made him unable to stop following her.

Her mother, who had been too preoccupied with the unavoidable fall entertaining to pay much attention to the number of phone calls Christine was getting or to the hired girl's complaints of a man who hung up without speaking, announced that she was flying down to New York for the weekend; her father decided to go too. Christine panicked: she saw herself in the bathtub with her throat slit, the blood drooling out of her neck and running in a little spiral down the drain (for by this time she believed he could walk through walls, could be everywhere at once). The girl would do nothing to help; she might even stand in the bathroom door with her arms folded, watching. Christine arranged to spend the weekend at her married sister's.

When she arrived back Sunday evening she found the girl close to hysterics. She said that on Saturday she had gone to pull the curtains across the French doors at dusk and had found a strangely contorted face, a man's face, pressed against the glass, staring in at her from the garden. She claimed she had fainted and had almost had her baby a month too early right there on the livingroom carpet. Then she had called the police. He was gone by the time they got there but she had recognized him from the afternoon of the tea; she had informed them he was a friend of Christine's.

They called Monday evening to investigate, two of them. They were very polite, they knew who Christine's father was. Her father greeted them heartily; her mother hovered in the background, fidgeting with her porcelain hands, letting them see how frail and worried she was. She didn't like having them in the livingroom but they were necessary.

Christine had to admit he'd been following her around. She was relieved he'd been discovered, relieved also that she hadn't been the one to tell, though if he'd been a citizen of the country she would have called the police a long time ago. She insisted he was not dangerous, he had never hurt her.

"That kind don't hurt you," one of the policemen said. "They just kill you. You're lucky you aren't dead."

"Nut cases," the other one said.

Her mother volunteered that the thing about people from another culture was that you could never tell whether they were insane or not because their ways were so different. The policeman agreed with her, deferential but also condescending, as though she was a royal halfwit who had to be humoured.

"You know where he lives?" the first policeman asked. Christine had long ago torn up the letter with his address on it; she shook her head.

"We'll have to pick him up tomorrow then," he said. "Think you can keep him talking outside your class if he's waiting for you?"

After questioning her they held a murmured conversation with her father in the front hall. The girl, clearing away the coffee cups, said if they didn't lock him up she was leaving, she wasn't going to be scared half out of her skin like that again.

Next day when Christine came out of her Modern History lecture he was there, right on schedule. He seemed puzzled when she did not begin to run. She approached him, her heart thumping with treachery and the prospect of freedom. Her body was back to its usual size; she felt herself a giantess, self-controlled, invulnerable.

"How are you?" she asked, smiling brightly.

He looked at her with distrust.

"How have you been?" she ventured again. His own perennial smile faded; he took a step back from her.

"This the one?" said the policeman, popping out from behind a notice board like a Keystone Kop and laying a competent hand on the worn jacket shoulder. The other policeman lounged in the background; force would not be required.

"Don't *do* anything to him," she pleaded as they took him away. They nodded and grinned, respectful, scornful. He seemed to know perfectly well who they were and what they wanted.

The first policeman phoned that evening to make his report. Her father talked with him, jovial and managing. She herself was now out of the picture; she had been protected, her function was over.

"What did they *do* to him?" she asked anxiously as he came back into the livingroom. She was not sure what went on in police stations.

"They didn't do anything to him," he said, amused by her concern. "They could have booked him for Watching and Besetting, they wanted to know if I'd like to press charges. But it's not worth a court case: he's got a visa that says he's only allowed in the country as long as he studies in Montreal, so I told them to just ship him down there. If he turns up here again they'll deport him. They went around to his rooming house, his rent's two weeks overdue, the landlady said she was on the point of kicking him out. He seems happy enough to be getting his back rent paid and a free train ticket to Montreal." He paused. "They couldn't get anything out of him though."

"*Out* of him?" Christine asked.

"They tried to find out why he was doing it; following you, I mean." Her father's eyes swept her as though it was a riddle to him also. "They said when they asked him about that he just clammed up. Pretended he didn't understand English. He understood well enough, but he wasn't answering."

Christine thought this would be the end, but somehow between his arrest and the departure of the train he managed to elude his escort long enough for one more phone call.

"I see you again," he said. He didn't wait for her to hang up.

Now that he was no longer an embarrassing present reality, he could be talked about, he could become an amusing story. In fact, he was the only amusing story Christine had to tell, and telling it preserved both for herself and for others the aura of her strange allure. Her friends and the men who continued to ask her out speculated about his motives. One suggested he had wanted to marry her so he could remain in the country; another said that oriental men were fond of well-built women: "It's your Rubens quality."

Christine thought about him a lot. She had not been attracted to him, rather the reverse, but as an idea only he was a romantic figure, the one man who had found her irresistible; though she often wondered, inspecting her unchanged pink face and hefty body in her full-length mirror, just what it was about her that had done it. She avoided whenever it was proposed the theory of his insanity: it was only that there was more than one way of being sane.

But a new acquaintance, hearing the story for the first time, had a different explanation. "So he got you, too," he said, laughing. "That has to be the same guy who was hanging around our day camp a year ago this summer. He followed all the girls like that. A short guy, Japanese or something, glasses, smiling all the time."

"Maybe it was another one," Christine said.

"There couldn't be two of them, everything fits. This was a pretty weird guy."

"What . . . *kind* of girls did he follow?" Christine asked.

"Oh, just anyone who happened to be around. But if they paid any attention to him at first, if they were nice to him or anything, he was unshakable. He was a bit of a pest, but harmless."

Christine ceased to tell her amusing story. She had been one among many, then. She went back to playing tennis, she had been neglecting her game.

A few months later the policeman who had been in charge of the case telephoned her again.

"Like you to know, Miss, that fellow you were having the trouble with was sent back to his own country. Deported."

"What for?" Christine asked. "Did he try to come back here?" Maybe she had been special after all, maybe he had dared everything for her.

"Nothing like it," the policeman said. "He was up to the same tricks in Montreal but he really picked the wrong woman this time — a Mother Superior of a convent. They don't stand for things like that in Quebec — had him out of here before he knew what happened. I guess he'll be better off in his own place."

"How old was she?" Christine asked, after a silence.

"Oh, around sixty, I guess."

"Thank you very much for letting me know," Christine said in her best official manner. "It's such a relief." She wondered if the policeman had called to make fun of her.

She was almost crying when she put down the phone. What *had* he wanted from her then? A Mother Superior. Did she really look sixty, did she look like a mother? What did convents mean? Comfort, charity? Refuge? Was it that something had happened to him, some intolerable strain just from being in this country; her tennis dress and exposed legs too much for him, flesh and money seemingly available everywhere but withheld from him wherever he turned, the nun the symbol of some final distortion, the robe and veil reminiscent to his nearsighted eyes of the women of his homeland, the ones he was able to understand? But he was back in his own country, remote from her as another planet; she would never know.

He hadn't forgotten her though. In the spring she got a postcard with a foreign stamp and the familiar block-letter writing. On the front was a picture of a temple. He was fine, he hoped she was fine also, he was her friend. A month later another print of the picture he had taken in the garden arrived, in a sealed manila envelope otherwise empty.

Christine's aura of mystery soon faded; anyway, she herself no longer believed in it. Life became again what she had always expected. She graduated with mediocre grades and went into the Department of Health and Welfare; she did a good job, and was seldom discriminated against for being a woman because nobody thought of her as one. She could afford a pleasant-sized apartment, though she did not put much energy into decorating it. She played less and less tennis; what had been muscle with a light coating of fat turned gradually into fat with a thin substratum of muscle. She began to get headaches.

As the years were used up and the war began to fill the newspapers and magazines, she realized which eastern country he had actually been from. She had known the name but it hadn't registered at the time, it was such a minor place; she could never keep them separate in her mind.

But though she tried, she couldn't remember the name of the city, and the postcard was long gone — had he been from the North or the South, was he near the battle zone or safely far from it? Obsessively she bought magazines and pored over the available photographs, dead villagers, soldiers on the march, colour blowups of frightened or angry faces, spies being executed; she studied maps, she watched the late-night newscasts, the distant country and terrain becoming almost more familiar to her than her own. Once or twice she thought she could recognize him but it was no use, they all looked like him.

Finally she had to stop looking at the pictures. It bothered her too much, it was bad for her; she was beginning to have nightmares in which he was coming through the French doors of her mother's house in his shabby jacket, carrying a packsack and a rifle and a huge bouquet of richly coloured flowers. He was smiling in the same way but with blood streaked over his face, partly blotting out the features. She gave her television set away and took to reading nineteenth-century novels instead; Trollope and Galsworthy were her favourites. When, despite herself, she would think about him, she would tell herself that he had been crafty and agile-minded enough to survive, more or less, in her country, so surely he would be able to do it in his own, where he knew the language. She could not see him in the army, on either side; he wasn't the type, and to her knowledge he had not believed in any particular ideology. He would be something nondescript, something in the background, like herself. Perhaps he had become an interpreter.

RAYMOND CARVER
1939–1988

Frank Kermode and Irving Howe, two respected critics, have hailed Raymond Carver as a modern master of the American short story. "A Small, Good Thing" won first place in the 1983 Prize Stories: The O. Henry Awards edited by William Abrahams, an experienced judge of the form. On the other hand, Erich Eichman, reviewing a Carver collection in the November 1983 issue of New Criterion, condemns his "deadeningly sparse, stylized prose" and his "condescension." In allusion to a rather vacuous statement by Carver ("art is also a superior amusement"), he concludes: "Cathedral isn't art and it isn't very amusing either."

To be sure, Carver is never amusing, but to evoke such startlingly opposed reactions he must have something, and it may be art. I suggest that if you can take his Dick-and-Jane English prose, many of his stories do reflect, painfully but forcefully, the banality of a certain segment of American life. His people, sometimes but not always poor, are inarticulate, and Carver understands their inarticulacy. They are at the end of their rope, just hanging on, nearer despair than rebellion, except for the spurious rebellion of violence.

It is true that Carver's near-dead prose often borders on the monotonous. But just as often it seems suited to the job of exposing, without comment and almost without emotion, the littleness of some of our lives.

"A Small, Good Thing" has feeling, however stylishly repressed. Without the curious subplot supplied by the baker's blind intrusion into the pathetic story, it would have been a mere tear-jerker. As it stands, it seems to me validly moving, almost Chekhovian.

A Small, Good Thing

SATURDAY AFTERNOON she drove to the bakery in the shopping center. After looking through a loose-leaf binder with photographs of cakes taped onto the pages, she ordered chocolate, the child's favorite. The cake she chose was decorated with a space ship and launching pad under a sprinkling of white stars, and a planet made of red frosting at the other end. His name, SCOTTY, would be in green letters beneath the planet. The baker, who was an older man with a thick neck, listened without saying anything when she told him the child would be eight years old next Monday. The baker wore a white apron that looked like a smock. Straps cut under his arms, went around in back and then to the front again, where they were secured under his heavy waist. He wiped his hands on his apron as he listened to her. He kept his eyes down on the photographs and let her talk. He let her take her time. He'd just come to work and he'd be there all night, baking, and he was in no real hurry.

She gave the baker her name, Ann Weiss, and her telephone number. The cake would be ready on Monday morning, just out of the oven, in plenty of time for the child's party that afternoon. The baker was not jolly. There were no pleasantries between them, just the minimum exchange of words, the necessary information. He made her feel uncomfortable, and she didn't like that. While he was bent over the counter with the pencil in his hand, she studied his coarse features and wondered if he'd ever done anything else with his life besides be a baker. She was a mother and thirty-three years old, and it seemed to her that everyone, especially someone the baker's age — a man old enough to be her father — must have children who'd gone through this special time of cakes and birthday parties. There must be that between them, she thought. But he was abrupt with her — not rude, just abrupt. She gave up trying to make friends with him. She looked into the back of the bakery and could see a long, heavy wooden table with aluminum pie pans stacked at one end; and beside the table a metal container filled with empty racks. There was an enormous oven. A radio was playing country-Western music.

The baker finished printing the information on the special order card and closed up the binder. He looked at her and said, "Monday morning." She thanked him and drove home.

On Monday morning, the birthday boy was walking to school with another boy. They were passing a bag of potato chips back and forth and the birthday boy was trying to find out what his friend intended to give him for his birthday that afternoon. Without looking, the birthday boy stepped off the curb at an intersection and was immediately knocked down by a car. He fell on his side with his head in the gutter and his legs out in the road. His eyes were closed, but his legs moved back and forth as if he were trying to climb over something. His friend dropped the potato chips and started to cry. The car had gone a hundred feet or so and stopped in the middle of the road. The man in the driver's seat looked back over his shoulder. He waited until the boy got unsteadily to his feet. The boy wobbled a little. He looked dazed, but okay. The driver put the car into gear and drove away.

The birthday boy didn't cry, but he didn't have anything to say about anything either. He wouldn't answer when his friend asked him what it felt like to be hit by a car. He walked home, and his friend went on to school. But after the birthday boy was inside his house and was telling his mother about it — she sitting beside him on the sofa, holding his hands in her lap, saying, "Scotty, honey, are you sure you feel all right, baby?" thinking she would call the doctor anyway — he suddenly lay back on the sofa, closed his eyes, and went limp. When she couldn't wake him up, she hurried to the telephone and called her husband at work. Howard told her to remain calm, remain calm, and then he called an ambulance for the child and left for the hospital himself.

Of course, the birthday party was canceled. The child was in the hospital with a mild concussion and suffering from shock. There'd been vomiting, and his lungs had taken in fluid which needed pumping out that afternoon. Now he simply seemed to be in a very deep sleep — but no coma, Dr. Francis had emphasized, no coma, when he saw the alarm in the parents' eyes. At eleven o'clock that night, when the boy seemed to be resting comfortably enough after the many X-rays and the lab work, and it was just a matter of his waking up and coming around, Howard left the hospital. He and Ann had been at the hospital with the child since that afternoon, and he was going home for a short while to bathe and change clothes. "I'll be back in an hour," he said. She nodded. "It's fine," she said. "I'll be right here." He kissed her on the forehead, and they touched hands. She sat in the chair beside the bed and looked at the child. She was waiting for him to wake up and be all right. Then she could begin to relax.

Howard drove home from the hospital. He took the wet, dark streets very fast, then caught himself and slowed down. Until now, his life had gone smoothly and to his satisfaction — college, marriage, another year of college for the advanced degree in business, a junior partnership in an investment firm. Fatherhood. He was happy and, so far, lucky — he knew that. His parents were still living, his brothers and his sister were established, his friends from college had gone out to take their places in the world. So far, he had kept away from any real harm, from those forces he knew existed and that could cripple or bring down a man if the luck went bad, if things suddenly turned. He pulled into the driveway and parked. His left leg began to tremble. He sat in the car for a minute and tried to deal with the present situation in a rational manner. Scotty had been hit by a car and was in the hospital, but he was going to be all right. Howard closed his eyes and ran his hand over his face. He got out of the car and went up to the front door. The dog was barking inside the house. The telephone rang and rang while he unlocked the door and fumbled for the light switch. He shouldn't have left the hospital, he shouldn't have. "Goddamn it!" he said. He picked up the receiver and said, "I just walked in the door!"

"There's a cake here that wasn't picked up," the voice on the other end of the line said.

"What are you saying?" Howard asked.

"A cake," the voice said. "A sixteen-dollar cake."

Howard held the receiver against his ear, trying to understand. "I don't know anything about a cake," he said. "Jesus, what are you talking about?"

"Don't hand me that," the voice said.

Howard hung up the telephone. He went into the kitchen and poured himself some whiskey. He called the hospital. But the child's condition remained the same; he was still sleeping and nothing had changed there. While water poured into the tub, Howard lathered his face and shaved. He'd just stretched out in the tub and closed his eyes when the telephone rang again. He hauled himself out, grabbed a towel, and hurried through the house, saying, "Stupid, stupid," for having left the hospital. But when he picked up the receiver and shouted, "Hello!" there was no sound at the other end of the line. Then the caller hung up.

He arrived back at the hospital a little after midnight. Ann still sat in the chair beside the bed. She looked up at Howard, and then she looked back at the child. The child's eyes stayed closed, the head was still wrapped in bandages. His breathing was quiet and regular. From an apparatus over the bed hung a bottle of glucose with a tube running from the bottle to the boy's arm.

"How is he?" Howard said. "What's all this?" waving at the glucose and the tube.

"Dr. Francis's orders," she said. "He needs nourishment. He needs to keep up his strength. Why doesn't he wake up, Howard? I don't understand, if he's all right."

Howard put his hand against the back of her head. He ran his fingers through her hair. "He's going to be all right. He'll wake up in a little while. Dr. Francis knows what's what."

After a time, he said, "Maybe you should go home and get some rest. I'll stay here. Just don't put up with this creep who keeps calling. Hang up right away."

"Who's calling?" she asked.

"I don't know who, just somebody with nothing better to do than call up people. You go on now."

She shook her head. "No," she said, "I'm fine."

"Really," he said. "Go home for a while, and then come back and spell me in the morning. It'll be all right. What did Dr. Francis say? He said Scotty's going to be all right. We don't have to worry. He's just sleeping now, that's all."

A nurse pushed the door open. She nodded at them as she went to the bedside. She took the left arm out from under the covers and put her fingers on the wrist, found the pulse, then consulted her watch. In a little while, she put the arm back under the covers and moved to the foot of the bed, where she wrote something on a clipboard attached to the bed.

"How is he?" Ann said. Howard's hand was a weight on her shoulder. She was aware of the pressure from his fingers.

"He's stable," the nurse said. Then she said, "Doctor will be in again shortly. Doctor's back in the hospital. He's making rounds right now."

"I was saying maybe she'd want to go home and get a little rest," Howard said. "After the doctor comes," he said.

"She could do that," the nurse said. "I think you should both feel free to do that, if you wish." The nurse was a big Scandinavian woman with blond hair. There was the trace of an accent in her speech.

"We'll see what the doctor says," Ann said. "I want to talk to the doctor. I don't think he should keep sleeping like this. I don't think that's a good sign." She brought her hand up to her eyes and let her head come forward a little. Howard's grip tightened on her shoulder, and then his hand moved up to her neck, where his fingers began to knead the muscles there.

"Dr. Francis will be here in a few minutes," the nurse said. Then she left the room.

Howard gazed at his son for a time, the small chest quietly rising and falling under the covers. For the first time since the terrible minutes after Ann's telephone call to him at his office, he felt a genuine fear starting in his limbs. He began shaking his head. Scotty was fine, but instead of sleeping at home in his own bed, he was in a hospital bed with bandages around his head and a tube in his arm. But this help was what he needed right now.

Dr. Francis came in and shook hands with Howard, though they'd just seen each other a few hours before. Ann got up from the chair. "Doctor?"

"Ann," he said and nodded. "Let's just first see how he's doing," the doctor said. He moved to the side of the bed and took the boy's pulse. He peeled back one eyelid and then the other. Howard and Ann stood beside the doctor and watched. Then the doctor turned back the covers and listened to the boy's heart and lungs with his stethoscope. He pressed his fingers here and there on the abdomen. When he was finished, he went to the end of the bed and studied the chart. He noted the time, scribbled something on the chart, and then looked at Howard and Ann.

"Doctor, how is he?" Howard said. "What's the matter with him exactly?"

"Why doesn't he wake up?" Ann said.

The doctor was a handsome, big-shouldered man with a tanned face. He wore a three-piece blue suit, a striped tie, and ivory cufflinks. His gray hair was combed along the sides of his head, and he looked as if he had just come from a concert. "He's all right," the doctor said. "Nothing to shout about, he could be better, I think. But he's all right. Still, I wish he'd wake up. He should wake up pretty soon." The doctor looked at the boy again. "We'll know some more in a couple of hours, after the results of a few more tests are in. But he's all right, believe me, except for the hairline fracture of the skull. He does have that."

"Oh, no," Ann said.

"And a bit of a concussion, as I said before. Of course, you know he's in shock," the doctor said. "Sometimes you see this in shock cases. This sleeping."

"But he's out of any real danger?" Howard said. "You said before he's not in a coma. You wouldn't call this a coma, then — would you, doctor?" Howard waited. He looked at the doctor.

"No, I don't want to call it a coma," the doctor said and glanced over at the boy once more. "He's just in a very deep sleep. It's a restorative measure the body is taking on its own. He's out of any real danger, I'd say that for certain, yes. But we'll know more when he wakes up and the other tests are in," the doctor said.

"It's a coma," Ann said. "Of sorts."

"It's not a coma yet, not exactly," the doctor said. "I wouldn't want to call it coma. Not yet, anyway. He's suffered shock. In shock cases, this kind of reaction is common enough; it's a temporary reaction to bodily trauma. Coma. Well, coma is a deep, prolonged unconsciousness, something that could go on for days, or weeks even. Scotty's not in that area, not as far as we can tell. I'm certain his condition will show improvement by morning. I'm betting that it will. We'll know more when he wakes up, which shouldn't be long now. Of course, you may do as you like, stay here or go home for a time. But by all means feel free to leave the hospital for a while if you want. This is not easy, I know." The doctor gazed at the boy again, watching him, and then he turned to Ann and said, "You try not to worry, little mother. Believe me, we're doing all that can be done. It's just a question of a little more time now." He nodded at her, shook hands with Howard again, and then he left the room.

Ann put her hand over the child's forehead. "At least he doesn't have a fever," she said. Then she said, "My God, he feels so cold, though. Howard? Is he supposed to feel like this? Feel his head."

Howard touched the child's temples. His own breathing had slowed.

"I think he's supposed to feel this way right now," he said. "He's in shock, remember? That's what the doctor said. The doctor was just in here. He would have said something if Scotty wasn't okay."

Ann stood there a while longer, working her lip with her teeth. Then she moved over to her chair and sat down.

Howard sat in the chair next to her chair. They looked at each other. He wanted to say something else and reassure her, but he was afraid, too. He took her hand and put it in his lap, and this made him feel better, her hand being there. He picked up her hand and squeezed it. Then he just held her hand. They sat like that for a while, watching the boy and not talking. From time to time, he squeezed her hand. Finally, she took her hand away.

"I've been praying," she said.

He nodded.

She said, "I almost thought I'd forgotten how, but it came back to me. All I had to do was close my eyes and say, 'Please God, help us — help Scotty,' and then the rest was easy. The words were right there. Maybe if you prayed, too," she said to him.

"I've already prayed," he said. "I prayed this afternoon — yesterday afternoon, I mean — after you called, while I was driving to the hospital. I've been praying," he said.

"That's good," she said. For the first time, she felt they were together in it, this trouble. She realized with a start that, until now, it had only been happening to her and to Scotty. She hadn't let Howard into it, though he was there and needed all along. She felt glad to be his wife.

The same nurse came in and took the boy's pulse again and checked the flow from the bottle hanging above the bed.

In an hour, another doctor came in. He said his name was Parsons, from Radiology. He had a bushy mustache. He was wearing loafers, a Western shirt, and a pair of jeans.

"We're going to take him downstairs for more pictures," he told them. "We need to do some more pictures, and we want to do a scan."

"What's that?" Ann said. "A scan?" She stood between this new doctor and the bed. "I thought you'd already taken all your X-rays."

"I'm afraid we need some more," he said. "Nothing to be alarmed about. We just need some more pictures, and we want to do a brain scan on him."

"My God," Ann said.

"It's perfectly normal procedure in cases like this," this new doctor said. "We just need to find out for sure why he isn't back awake yet. It's normal medical procedure, and nothing to be alarmed about. We'll be taking him down in a few minutes," this doctor said.

In a little while, two orderlies came into the room with a gurney. They were black-haired, dark-complexioned men in white uniforms, and they said a few words to each other in a foreign tongue as they unhooked the boy from the tube and moved him from his bed to the gurney. Then they wheeled him from the room. Howard and Ann got on the same elevator. Ann gazed at the child. She closed her eyes as the elevator began its descent. The orderlies stood at either end of the gurney without saying anything, though once one of the men made a comment to the other in their own language, and the other man nodded slowly in response.

Later that morning, just as the sun was beginning to lighten the windows in the waiting room outside the X-ray department, they brought the boy out and moved him back up to his room. Howard and Ann rode up on the elevator with him once more, and once more they took up their places beside the bed.

They waited all day, but still the boy did not wake up. Occasionally, one of them would leave the room to go downstairs to the cafeteria to drink coffee and then, as if suddenly remembering and feeling guilty, get up from the table and hurry back to the room. Dr. Francis came again that afternoon and examined the boy once more and then left after telling them he was coming along and could wake up at any minute now. Nurses, different nurses from the night before, came in from time to time. Then a young woman from the lab knocked and entered the room. She wore white slacks and a white blouse and carried a little tray of things which she put on the stand beside the bed. Without a word to them, she took blood from the boy's arm. Howard closed his eyes as the woman found the right place on the boy's arm and pushed the needle in.

"I don't understand this," Ann said to the woman.

"Doctor's orders," the young woman said. "I do what I'm told. They say draw that one, I draw. What's wrong with him, anyway?" she said. "He's a sweetie."

"He was hit by a car," Howard said. "A hit-and-run."

The young woman shook her head and looked again at the boy. Then she took her tray and left the room.

"Why won't he wake up?" Ann said. "Howard? I want some answers from these people."

Howard didn't say anything. He sat down again in the chair and crossed one leg over the other. He rubbed his face. He looked at his son and then he settled back in the chair, closed his eyes, and went to sleep.

Ann walked to the window and looked out at the parking lot. It was night, and cars were driving into and out of the parking lot with their lights on. She stood at the window with her hands gripping the sill, and knew in her heart that they were into something now, something hard. She was afraid, and her teeth began to chatter until she tightened her jaws. She saw a big car stop in front of the hospital and someone, a woman in a long coat, get into the car. She wished she were that woman and somebody, anybody, was driving her away from here to somewhere else, a place where she would find Scotty waiting for her when she stepped out of the car, ready to say *Mom* and let her gather him in her arms.

In a little while, Howard woke up. He looked at the boy again. Then he got up from the chair, stretched, and went over to stand beside her at the window. They both stared out at the parking lot. They didn't say anything. But they seemed to feel each other's insides now, as though the worry had made them transparent in a perfectly natural way.

The door opened and Dr. Francis came in. He was wearing a different suit and tie this time. His gray hair was combed along the sides of his head, and he looked as if he had just shaved. He went straight to the bed and examined the boy. "He ought to have come around by now. There's just no good reason for this," he said. "But I can tell you we're all convinced he's out of any danger. We'll just feel better when he wakes up. There's no reason, absolutely none, why he shouldn't come around. Very soon. Oh; he'll have himself a dilly of a headache when he does, you can count on that. But all of his signs are fine. They're as normal as can be."

"It is a coma, then?" Ann said.

The doctor rubbed his smooth cheek. "We'll call it that for the time being, until he wakes up. But you must be worn out. This is hard. I know this is hard. Feel free to go out for a bite," he said. "It would do you good. I'll put a nurse in here while you're gone if you'll feel better about going. Go and have yourselves something to eat."

"I couldn't eat anything," Ann said.

"Do what you need to do, of course," the doctor said. "Anyway, I wanted to tell you that all the signs are good, the tests are negative, nothing showed up at all, and just as soon as he wakes up he'll be over the hill."

"Thank you, doctor," Howard said. He shook hands with the doctor again. The doctor patted Howard's shoulder and went out.

"I suppose one of us should go home and check on things," Howard said. "Slug needs to be fed, for one thing."

"Call one of the neighbors," Ann said. "Call the Morgans. Anyone will feed a dog if you ask them to."

"All right," Howard said. After a while, he said, "Honey, why don't *you* do it? Why don't you go home and check on things, and then come back? It'll do you good. I'll be right here with him. Seriously," he said. "We need to keep up our strength on this. We'll want to be here for a while even after he wakes up."

"Why don't *you* go?" she said. "Feed Slug. Feed yourself."

"I already went," he said. "I was gone for exactly an hour and fifteen minutes. You go home for an hour and freshen up. Then come back."

She tried to think about it, but she was too tired. She closed her eyes and tried to think about it again. After a time, she said, "Maybe I *will* go home for a few minutes. Maybe if I'm not just sitting right here watching him every second, he'll wake up and be all right. You know? Maybe he'll wake up if I'm not here. I'll go home and take a bath and put on clean clothes. I'll feed Slug. Then I'll come back."

"I'll be right here," he said. "You go on home, honey. I'll keep an eye on things here." His eyes were bloodshot and small, as if he'd been drinking for a long time. His clothes were rumpled. His beard had come out again. She touched his face, and then she took her hand back. She understood he wanted to be by himself for a while, not have to talk or share his worry for a time. She picked her purse up from the nightstand, and he helped her into her coat.

"I won't be gone long," she said.

"Just sit and rest for a little when you get home," he said. "Eat something. Take a bath. After you get out of the bath, just sit for a while and rest. It'll do you a world of good, you'll see. Then come back," he said. "Let's try not to worry. You heard what Dr. Francis said."

She stood in her coat for a minute trying to recall the doctor's exact words, looking for any nuances, any hint of something behind his words other than what he had said. She tried to remember if his expression had changed any when he bent over to examine the child. She remembered the way his features had composed themselves as he rolled back the child's eyelids and then listened to his breathing.

She went to the door, where she turned and looked back. She looked at the child, and then she looked at the father. Howard nodded. She stepped out of the room and pulled the door closed behind her.

She went past the nurses' station and down to the end of the corridor, looking for the elevator. At the end of the corridor, she turned to her right and entered a little waiting room where a Negro family sat in wicker chairs. There was a middle-aged man in a khaki shirt and pants, a baseball cap pushed back on his head. A large woman wearing a housedress and slippers was slumped in one of the chairs. A teenaged girl in jeans, hair done in dozens of little braids, lay stretched out in one of the chairs smoking a cigarette, her legs crossed at the ankles. The family swung their eyes to Ann as she entered the room. The little table was littered with hamburger wrappers and Styrofoam cups.

"Franklin," the large woman said as she roused herself. "Is it about Franklin?" Her eyes widened. "Tell me now, lady," the woman said. "Is it about Franklin?" She was trying to rise from her chair, but the man had closed his hand over her arm.

"Here, here," he said. "Evelyn."

"I'm sorry," Ann said. "I'm looking for the elevator. My son is in the hospital, and now I can't find the elevator."

"Elevator is down that way, turn left," the man said as he aimed a finger.

The girl drew on her cigarette and stared at Ann. Her eyes were narrowed to slits, and her broad lips parted slowly as she let the smoke escape. The Negro woman let her head fall on her shoulder and looked away from Ann, no longer interested.

"My son was hit by a car," Ann said to the man. She seemed to need to explain herself. "He has a concussion and a little skull fracture, but he's going to be all right. He's in shock now, but it might be some kind of coma, too. That's what really worries us, the coma part. I'm going out for a little while, but my husband is with him. Maybe he'll wake up while I'm gone."

"That's too bad," the man said and shifted in the chair. He shook his head. He looked down at the table, and then he looked back at Ann. She was still standing there. He said, "Our Franklin, he's on the operating table. Somebody cut him. Tried to kill him. There was a fight where he was at. At this party. They say he was just standing and watching. Not bothering nobody. But that don't mean nothing these days. Now he's on the operating table. We're just hoping and praying, that's all we can do now." He gazed at her steadily.

Ann looked at the girl again, who was still watching her, and at the older woman, who kept her head down, but whose eyes were now closed. Ann saw the lips moving silently, making words. She had an urge to ask what those words were. She wanted to talk more with these people who were in the same kind of waiting she was in. She was afraid, and they were afraid. They had that in common. She would have liked to have said something else about the accident, told them more about Scotty, that it had happened on the day of his birthday, Monday, and that he was still unconscious. Yet she didn't know how to begin. She stood looking at them without saying anything more.

She went down the corridor the man had indicated and found the elevator. She waited a minute in front of the closed doors, still wondering if she was doing the right thing. Then she put out her finger and touched the button.

She pulled into the driveway and cut the engine. She closed her eyes and leaned her head against the wheel for a minute. She listened to the ticking sounds the engine made as it began to cool. Then she got out of the car. She could hear the dog barking inside the house. She went to the front door, which was unlocked. She went inside and turned on lights and put on a kettle of water for tea. She opened some dogfood and fed Slug on the back porch. The dog ate in hungry little smacks. It kept running into the kitchen to see that she was going to stay. As she sat down on the sofa with her tea, the telephone rang.

"Yes!" she said as she answered. "Hello!"

"Mrs. Weiss," a man's voice said. It was five o'clock in the morning, and she thought she could hear machinery or equipment of some kind in the background.

"Yes, yes! What is it?" she said. "This is Mrs. Weiss. This is she. What is it, please?" She listened to whatever it was in the background. "Is it Scotty, for Christ's sake?"

"Scotty," the man's voice said. "It's about Scotty, yes. It has to do with Scotty, that problem. Have you forgotten about Scotty?" the man said. Then he hung up.

She dialed the hospital's number and asked for the third floor. She demanded information about her son from the nurse who answered the telephone. Then she asked to speak to her husband. It was, she said, an emergency.

She waited, turning the telephone cord in her fingers. She closed her eyes and felt sick at her stomach. She would have to make herself eat. Slug came in from the back porch and lay down near her feet. He wagged his tail. She pulled at his ear while he licked her fingers. Howard was on the line.

"Somebody just called here," she said. She twisted the telephone cord. "He said it was about Scotty," she cried.

"Scotty's fine," Howard told her. "I mean, he's still sleeping. There's been no change. The nurse has been in twice since you've been gone. A nurse or else a doctor. He's all right."

"This man called. He said it was about Scotty," she told him.

"Honey, you rest for a little while, you need the rest. It must be that same caller I had. Just forget it. Come back down here after you've rested. Then we'll have breakfast or something."

"Breakfast," she said. "I don't want any breakfast."

"You know what I mean," he said. "Juice, something. I don't know. I don't know anything, Ann. Jesus, I'm not hungry, either. Ann, it's hard to talk now. I'm standing here at the desk. Dr. Francis is coming again at eight o'clock this morning. He's going to have something to tell us then, something more definite. That's what one of the nurses said. She didn't know any more than that. Ann? Honey, maybe we'll know something more then. At eight o'clock. Come back here before eight. Meanwhile, I'm right here and Scotty's all right. He's still the same," he added.

"I was drinking a cup of tea," she said, "when the telephone rang. They said it was about Scotty. There was a noise in the background. Was there a noise in the background on that call you had, Howard?"

"I don't remember," he said. "Maybe the driver of the car, maybe he's a psychopath and found out about Scotty somehow. But I'm here with him. Just rest like you were going to do. Take a bath and come back by seven or so, and we'll talk to the doctor together when he gets here. It's going to be all right, honey. I'm here, and there are doctors and nurses around. They say his condition is stable."

"I'm scared to death," she said.

She ran water, undressed, and got into the tub. She washed and dried quickly, not taking the time to wash her hair. She put on clean underwear, wool slacks, and a sweater. She went into the living room, where the dog looked up at her and let its tail thump once against the floor. It was just starting to get light outside when she went out to the car.

She drove into the parking lot of the hospital and found a space close to the front door. She felt she was in some obscure way responsible for what had happened to the child. She let her thoughts move to the Negro family. She remembered the name Franklin and the table that was covered with hamburger papers, and the teenaged girl staring at her as she drew on her cigarette. "Don't have children," she told the girl's image as she entered the front door of the hospital. "For God's sake, don't."

She took the elevator up to the third floor with two nurses who were just going on duty. It was Wednesday morning, a few minutes before seven. There was a page for a Dr. Madison as the elevator doors slid open on the third floor. She got off behind the nurses, who turned in the other direction and continued the conversation she had interrupted when she'd gotten into the elevator. She walked down the corridor to the little alcove where the Negro family had been waiting. They were gone now, but the chairs were scattered in such a way that it looked as if people had just jumped up from them the minute before. The tabletop was cluttered with the same cups and papers, the ashtray was filled with cigarette butts.

She stopped at the nurses' station. A nurse was standing behind the counter, brushing her hair and yawning.

"There was a Negro boy in surgery last night," Ann said. "Franklin was his name. His family was in the waiting room. I'd like to inquire about his condition."

A nurse who was sitting at a desk behind the counter looked up from a chart in front of her. The telephone buzzed and she picked up the receiver, but she kept her eyes on Ann.

"He passed away," said the nurse at the counter. The nurse held the hairbrush and kept looking at her. "Are you a friend of the family or what?"

"I met the family last night," Ann said. "My own son is in the hospital. I guess he's in shock. We don't know for sure what's wrong. I just wondered about Franklin, that's all. Thank you." She moved down the corridor. Elevator doors the same color as the walls slid open and a gaunt, bald man in white pants and white canvas shoes pulled a heavy cart off the elevator. She hadn't noticed these doors last night. The man wheeled the cart out into the corridor and stopped in front of the room nearest the elevator and consulted a clipboard. Then he reached down and slid a tray out of the cart. He rapped lightly on the door and entered the room. She could smell the unpleasant odors of warm food as she passed the cart. She hurried on without looking at any of the nurses and pushed open the door to the child's room.

Howard was standing at the window with his hands behind his back. He turned around as she came in.

"How is he?" she said. She went over to the bed. She dropped her purse on the floor beside the nightstand. It seemed to her she had been gone a long time. She touched the child's face. "Howard?"

"Dr. Francis was here a little while ago," Howard said. She looked at him closely and thought his shoulders were bunched a little.

"I thought he wasn't coming until eight o'clock this morning," she said quickly.

"There was another doctor with him. A neurologist."

"A neurologist," she said.

Howard nodded. His shoulders were bunching, she could see that. "What'd they say, Howard? For Christ's sake, what'd they say? What is it?"

"They said they're going to take him down and run more tests on him, Ann. They think they're going to operate, honey. Honey, they *are* going to operate. They can't figure out why he won't wake up. It's more than just shock or concussion, they know that much now. It's in his skull, the fracture, it has something, something to do with that, they think. So they're going to operate. I tried to call you, but I guess you'd already left the house."

"Oh, God," she said. "Oh, please, Howard, please," she said, taking his arms.

"Look!" Howard said. "Scotty! Look, Ann!" He turned her toward the bed.

The boy had opened his eyes, then closed them. He opened them again now. The eyes stared straight ahead for a minute, then moved slowly in his head until they rested on Howard and Ann, then traveled away again.

"Scotty," his mother said, moving to the bed.

"Hey, Scott," his father said. "Hey, son."

They leaned over the bed. Howard took the child's hand in his hands and began to pat and squeeze the hand. Ann bent over the boy and kissed his forehead again and again. She put her hands on either side of his face. "Scotty, honey, it's Mommy and Daddy," she said. "Scotty?"

The boy looked at them, but without any sign of recognition. Then his mouth opened, his eyes scrunched closed, and he had no more air in his lungs. His face seemed to relax and soften then. His lips parted as his last breath was puffed through his throat and exhaled gently through the clenched teeth.

The doctors called it a hidden occlusion and said it was a one-in-a-million circumstance. Maybe if it could have been detected somehow and surgery undertaken immediately, they could have saved him. But more than likely not. In any case, what would they have been looking for? Nothing had shown up in the tests or in the X-rays.

Dr. Francis was shaken. "I can't tell you how badly I feel. I'm so very sorry, I can't tell you," he said as he led them into the doctors' lounge. There was a doctor sitting in a chair with his legs hooked over the back of another chair, watching an early-morning TV show. He was wearing a green delivery-room outfit, loose green pants and green blouse, and a green cap that covered his hair. He looked at Howard and Ann and then looked at Dr. Francis. He got to his feet and turned off the set and went out of the room. Dr. Francis guided Ann to the sofa, sat down beside her, and began to talk in a low, consoling voice. At one point, he leaned over and embraced her. She could feel his chest rising and falling evenly against her shoulder. She kept her eyes open and let him hold her. Howard went into the bathroom, but he left the door open. After a violent fit of weeping, he ran water and washed his face. Then he came out and sat down at the little table that held a telephone. He looked at the telephone as though deciding what to do first. He made some calls. After a time, Dr. Francis used the telephone.

"Is there anything else I can do for the moment?" he asked them.

Howard shook his head. Ann stared at Dr. Francis as if unable to comprehend his words.

The doctor walked them to the hospital's front door. People were entering and leaving the hospital. It was eleven o'clock in the morning. Ann was aware of how slowly, almost reluctantly, she moved her feet. It seemed to her that Dr. Francis was making them leave when she felt they should stay, when it would be more the right thing to do to stay. She gazed out into the parking lot and then turned around and looked back at the front of the hospital. She began shaking her head. "No, no," she said. "I can't leave him here, no." She heard herself say that and thought how unfair it was that the only words that came out were the sort of words used on TV shows where people were stunned by violent or sudden deaths. She wanted her words to be her own. "No," she said, and for some reason the memory of the Negro woman's head lolling on the woman's shoulder came to her. "No," she said again.

"I'll be talking to you later in the day," the doctor was saying to Howard. "There are still some things that have to be done, things that have to be cleared up to our satisfaction. Some things that need explaining."

"An autopsy," Howard said.

Dr. Francis nodded.

"I understand," Howard said. Then he said, "Oh, Jesus. No, I don't understand, doctor. I can't, I can't. I just can't."

Dr. Francis put his arm around Howard's shoulders. "I'm sorry. God, how I'm sorry." He let go of Howard's shoulders and held out his hand. Howard looked at the hand, and then he took it. Dr. Francis put his arms around Ann once more. He seemed full of some goodness she didn't understand. She let her head rest on his shoulder, but her eyes stayed open. She kept looking at the hospital. As they drove out of the parking lot, she looked back at the hospital.

At home, she sat on the sofa with her hands in her coat pockets. Howard closed the door to the child's room. He got the coffee-maker going and then he found an empty box. He had thought to pick up some of the child's things that were scattered around the living room. But instead he sat down beside her on the sofa, pushed the box to one side, and leaned forward, arms between his knees. He began to weep. She pulled his head over into her lap and patted his shoulder. "He's gone," she said. She kept patting his shoulder. Over his sobs, she could hear the coffee-maker hissing in the kitchen. "There, there," she said tenderly. "Howard, he's gone. He's gone and now we'll have to get used to that. To being alone."

In a little while, Howard got up and began moving aimlessly around the room with the box, not putting anything into it, but collecting some things together on the floor at one end of the sofa. She continued to sit with her hands in her coat pockets. Howard put the box down and brought coffee into the living room. Later, Ann made calls to relatives. After each call had been placed and the party had answered, Ann would blurt out a few words and cry for a minute. Then she would quietly explain, in a measured voice, what had happened and tell them about arrangements. Howard took the box out to the garage, where he saw the child's bicycle. He dropped the box and sat down on the pavement beside the bicycle. He took hold of the bicycle awkwardly so that it leaned against his chest. He held it, the rubber pedal sticking into his chest. He gave the wheel a turn.

Ann hung up the telephone after talking to her sister. She was looking up another number when the telephone rang. She picked it up on the first ring.

"Hello," she said, and she heard something in the background, a humming noise. "Hello!" she said. "For God's sake," she said. "Who is this? What is it you want?"

"Your Scotty, I got him ready for you," the man's voice said. "Did you forget him?"

"You evil bastard!" she shouted into the receiver. "How can you do this, you evil son of a bitch?"

"Scotty," the man said. "Have you forgotten about Scotty?" Then the man hung up on her.

Howard heard the shouting and came in to find her with her head on her arms over the table, weeping. He picked up the receiver and listened to the dial tone.

Much later, just before midnight, after they had dealt with many things, the telephone rang again.

"You answer it," she said. "Howard, it's him, I know." They were sitting at the kitchen table with coffee in front of them. Howard had a small glass of whiskey beside his cup. He answered on the third ring.

"Hello," he said. "Who is this? Hello! Hello!" The line went dead. "He hung up," Howard said. "Whoever it was."

"It was him," she said. "That bastard. I'd like to kill him," she said. "I'd like to shoot him and watch him kick," she said.

"Ann, my God," he said.

"Could you hear anything?" she said. "In the background? A noise, machinery, something humming?"

"Nothing, really. Nothing like that," he said. "There wasn't much time. I think there was some radio music. Yes, there was a radio going, that's all I could tell. I don't know what in God's name is going on," he said.

She shook her head. "If I could, could get my hands on him." It came to her then. She knew who it was. Scotty, the cake, the telephone number. She pushed the chair away from the table and got up. "Drive me down to the shopping center," she said. "Howard."

"What are you saying?"

"The shopping center. I know who it is who's calling. I know who it is. It's the baker, the son-of-a-bitching baker, Howard. I had him bake a cake for Scotty's birthday. That's who's calling. That's who has the number and keeps calling us. To harass us about the cake. The baker, that bastard."

They drove down to the shopping center. The sky was clear and stars were out. It was cold, and they ran the heater in the car. They parked in front of the bakery. All of the shops and stores were closed, but there were cars at the far end of the lot in front of the movie theater. The bakery windows were dark, but when they looked through the glass they could see a light in the back room and, now and then, a big man in an apron moving in and out of the white, even light. Through the glass, she could see the display cases and some little tables with chairs. She tried the door. She rapped on the glass. But if the baker heard them, he gave no sign. He didn't look in their direction.

They drove around behind the bakery and parked. They got out of the car. There was a lighted window too high up for them to see inside. A sign near the back door said THE PANTRY BAKERY, SPECIAL ORDERS. She could hear faintly a radio playing inside and something creak — an oven door as it was pulled down? She knocked on the door and waited. Then she knocked again, louder. The radio was turned down and there was a scraping sound now, the distinct sound of something, a drawer, being pulled open and then closed.

Someone unlocked the door and opened it. The baker stood in the light and peered out at them. "I'm closed for business," he said. "What do you want at this hour? It's midnight. Are you drunk or something?"

She stepped into the light that fell through the open door. He blinked his heavy eyelids as he recognized her. "It's you," he said.

"It's me," she said. "Scotty's mother. This is Scotty's father. We'd like to come in."

The baker said, "I'm busy now. I have work to do."

She had stepped inside the doorway anyway. Howard came in behind her. The baker moved back. "It smells like a bakery in here. Doesn't it smell like a bakery in here, Howard?"

"What do you want?" the baker said. "Maybe you want your cake? That's it, you decided you want your cake. You ordered a cake, didn't you?"

"You're pretty smart for a baker," she said. "Howard, this is the man who's been calling us." She clenched her fists. She stared at him fiercely. There was a deep burning inside her, an anger that made her feel larger than herself, larger than either of these men.

"Just a minute here," the baker said. "You want to pick up your three-day-old cake? That it? I don't want to argue with you, lady. There it sits over there, getting stale. I'll give it to you for half of what I quoted you. No. You want it? You can have it. It's no good to me, no good to anyone now. It cost me time and money to make that cake. If you want it, okay, if you don't, that's okay, too. I have to get back to work." He looked at them and rolled his tongue behind his teeth.

"More cakes," she said. She knew she was in control of it, of what was increasing in her. She was calm.

"Lady, I work sixteen hours a day in this place to earn a living," the baker said. He wiped his hands on his apron. "I work night and day in here, trying to make ends meet." A look crossed Ann's face that made the baker move back and say, "No trouble, now." He reached to the counter and picked up a rolling pin with his right hand and began to tap it against the palm of his other hand. "You want the cake or not? I have to get back to work. Bakers work at night," he said again. His eyes were small, mean-looking, she thought, nearly lost in the bristly flesh around his cheeks. His neck was thick with fat.

"I know bakers work at night," Ann said. "They make phone calls at night, too. You bastard," she said.

The baker continued to tap the rolling pin against his hand. He glanced at Howard. "Careful, careful," he said to Howard.

"My son's dead," she said with a cold, even finality. "He was hit by a car Monday morning. We've been waiting with him until he died. But, of course, you couldn't be expected to know that, could you? Bakers can't know everything — can they, Mr. Baker? But he's dead. He's dead, you bastard!" Just as suddenly as it had welled in her, the anger dwindled, gave way to something else, a dizzy feeling of nausea. She leaned against the wooden table that was sprinkled with flour, put her hands over her face, and began to cry, her shoulders rocking back and forth. "It isn't fair," she said. "It isn't, isn't fair."

Howard put his hand at the small of her back and looked at the baker. "Shame on you," Howard said to him. "Shame."

The baker put the rolling pin back on the counter. He undid his apron and threw it on the counter. He looked at them, and then he shook his head slowly. He pulled a chair out from under the card table that held papers and receipts, an adding machine, and a telephone directory. "Please sit down," he said. "Let me get you a chair," he said to Howard. "Sit down now, please." The baker went into the front of the shop and returned with two little wrought-iron chairs. "Please sit down, you people."

Ann wiped her eyes and looked at the baker. "I wanted to kill you," she said. "I wanted you dead."

The baker had cleared a space for them at the table. He shoved the adding machine to one side, along with the stacks of notepaper and receipts. He pushed the telephone directory onto the floor, where it landed with a thud. Howard and Ann sat down and pulled their chairs up to the table. The baker sat down, too.

"Let me say how sorry I am," the baker said, putting his elbows on the table. "God alone knows how sorry. Listen to me. I'm just a baker. I don't claim to be anything else. Maybe once, maybe years ago, I was a different kind of human being. I've forgotten, I don't know for sure. But I'm not any longer, if I ever was. Now I'm just a baker. That don't excuse my doing what I did, I know. But I'm deeply sorry. I'm sorry for your son, and sorry for my part in this," the baker said. He spread his hands out on the table and turned them over to reveal his palms. "I don't have any children myself, so I can only imagine what you must be feeling. All I can say to you now is that I'm sorry. Forgive me, if you can," the baker said. "I'm not an evil man, I don't think. Not evil, like you said on the phone. You got to understand what it comes down to is I don't know how to act anymore, it would seem. Please," the man said, "let me ask you if you can find it in your hearts to forgive me?"

It was warm inside the bakery. Howard stood up from the table and took off his coat. He helped Ann from her coat. The baker looked at them for a minute and then nodded and got up from the table. He went to the oven and turned off some switches. He found cups and poured coffee from an electric coffee-maker. He put a carton of cream on the table, and a bowl of sugar.

"You probably need to eat something," the baker said. "I hope you'll eat some of my hot rolls. You have to eat and keep going. Eating is a small, good thing in a time like this," he said.

He served them warm cinnamon rolls just out of the oven, the icing still runny. He put butter on the table and knives to spread the butter. Then the baker sat down at the table with them. He waited. He waited until they each took a roll from the platter and began to eat. "It's good to eat something," he said, watching them. "There's more. Eat up. Eat all you want. There's all the rolls in the world in here."

They ate rolls and drank coffee. Ann was suddenly hungry, and the rolls were warm and sweet. She ate three of them, which pleased the baker. Then he began to talk. They listened carefully. Although they were tired and in anguish, they listened to what the baker had to say. They nodded when the baker began to speak of loneliness, and of the sense of doubt and limitation that had come to him in his middle years. He told them what it was like to be childless all these years. To repeat the days with the ovens endlessly full and endlessly empty. The party food, the celebrations he'd worked over. Icing knuckle-deep. The tiny wedding couples stuck into cakes. Hundreds of them, no, thousands by now. Birthdays. Just imagine all those candles burning. He had a necessary trade. He was a baker. He was glad he wasn't a florist. It was better to be feeding people. This was a better smell anytime than flowers.

"Smell this," the baker said, breaking open a dark loaf. "It's a heavy bread, but rich." They smelled it, then he had them taste it. It had the taste of molasses and coarse grains. They listened to him. They ate what they could. They swallowed the dark bread. It was like daylight under the fluorescent trays of light. They talked on into the early morning, the high, pale cast of light in the windows, and they did not think of leaving.

Ann Beattie

1947–

Ann Beattie pins to her pages specimen after specimen of an American sub-culture now just starting to show signs of obsolescence. Her sec stories and novels deal largely with those legatees of the sixties who, having more or less "made it" economically, are still adrift emotionally. Beattie, aware that their dimensions are too small for tragedy, never tries for it. For her the depiction of depression, pointlessness, and rootlessness will do, and she is dead on target.

Her people, usually well educated, articulate, sensitive, are often also mal-adjusted, casual sharers of drugs and beds, sexually uncertain, ill matched as couples, alcoholics or on the way to alcoholism, divorced, separated, negative, failed artists, neurotically mod. We conventionally praise fiction writers for their ability to make characters come alive. We should praise Beattie for her ability to make them come half alive, for that is what they are.

She has contrived a style to match her world: designedly level-toned, bare of ornament, a bit invertebrate. She works not with plots but with situa-tions, small jams, bits and pieces of frustration.

A nonanecdotal painting is often labeled an Arrangement. She gives us Arrangements. The reader is led to follow casually dropped clues rather than a consecutive narrative. Her stories are not so much told as overheard.

Marital discord and a self-indulgent male (Beattie makes a pretty good case for her hard-eyed view of the masculine sex) lie at the center of "Week-end," a fair sample of her work. Taken as a whole, it might use as an um-brella title Hemingway's In Our Time.

Weekend

ON SATURDAY MORNING Lenore is up before the others. She carries her baby into the living room and puts him in George's favorite chair, which tilts because its back legs are missing, and covers him with a blanket. Then she lights a fire in the fireplace, putting fresh logs on a few embers that are still glowing from the night before. She sits down on the floor beside the chair and checks the baby, who has already gone back to sleep — a good thing, because there are guests in the house. George, the man she lives with, is very hospitable and impetuous; he extends invitations whenever old friends call, urging them to come spend the weekend. Most of the callers are his former students — he used to be an English professor — and when they come it seems to make things much worse. It makes *him* much worse, because he falls into smoking too much and drinking and not eating, and then his ulcer bothers him. When the guests leave, when the weekend is over, she has to cook bland food: apple-sauce, oatmeal, puddings. And his drinking does not taper off easily anymore; in the past he would stop cold when the guests left, but lately he only tapers down from Scotch to wine, and drinks wine well into the week — a lot of wine, perhaps a whole bottle with his meal — until his stomach is much worse. He is hard to live with. Once when a former student, a woman named Ruth, visited them — a lover, she suspected — she overheard George talking to her in his study, where he had taken her to see a photograph of their house before he began repairing it. George had told Ruth that she, Lenore, stayed with him because she was simple. It hurt her badly, made her actually dizzy with surprise and shame, and since then, no matter who the guests are, she never feels quite at ease on the weekends. In the past she enjoyed some of the things she and George did with their guests, but since overhearing what he said to Ruth she feels that all their visitors have been secretly told the same thing about her. To her, though, George is usually kind. But she is sure that is the reason he has not married her, and when he recently remarked on their daughter's intelligence (she is five years old, a girl named Maria) she found that she could no longer respond with simple pride; now she feels spite as well, feels that Maria exists as proof of her own good genes. She has begun to expect perfection of the child. She knows this is wrong, and she has tried hard not to communicate her anxiety to Maria, who is already, as her kindergarten teacher says, "untypical."

At first Lenore loved George because he was untypical, although after she had moved in with him and lived with him for a while she began to see that he was not exceptional but a variation on a type. She is proud of observing that, and she harbors the discovery — her silent response to his low opinion of her. She does not know why he found her attractive — in the beginning he did — because she does not resemble the pretty, articulate young women he likes to invite, with their lovers or girl friends, to their house for the weekend. None of these young women have husbands; when they bring a man with them at all they bring a lover, and they seem happy not to be married. Lenore, too, is happy to be single — not out of conviction that marriage is wrong but because she knows that it would be wrong to be married to George if he thinks she is simple. She thought at first to confront him with what she had overheard, to demand an explanation. But he can weasel out of any corner. At best, she can mildly fluster him, and later he will only blame it on Scotch. Of course she might ask why he has all these women come to visit, why he devotes so little time to her or the children. To that he would say that it was the quality of the time they spent together that mattered, not the quantity. He has already said that, in fact, without being asked. He says things over and over so that she will accept them as truths. And eventually she does. She does not like to think long and hard, and when there is an answer — even his answer — it is usually easier to accept it and go on with things. She goes on with what she has always done: tending the house and the children and George, when he needs her. She likes to bake and she collects art postcards. She is proud of their house, which was bought cheaply and improved by George when he was still interested in that kind of work, and she is happy to have visitors come there, even if she does not admire them or even like them.

Except for teaching a night course in photography at a junior college once a week, George has not worked since he left the university two years ago, after he was denied tenure. She cannot really tell if he is unhappy working so little, because he keeps busy in other ways. He listens to classical music in the morning, slowly sipping herbal teas, and on fair afternoons he lies outdoors in the sun, no matter how cold the day. He takes photographs, and walks alone in the woods. He does errands for her if they need to be done. Sometimes at night he goes to the library or goes to visit friends; he tells her that these people often ask her to come too, but he says she would not like them. This is true — she would not like them. Recently he has done some late-night cooking. He has always kept a journal, and he is a great letter writer. An aunt left him most of her estate, ten thousand dollars, and said in her will that he was the only one who really cared, who took the time, again and again, to write. He had not seen his aunt for five years before she died, but he wrote regularly. Sometimes Lenore finds notes that he has left for her. Once, on the refrigerator, there was a long note suggesting clever Christmas presents for her family that he had thought of while she was out. Last week he Scotch-taped a slip of paper to a casserole dish that contained leftover veal stew, saying: "This was delicious." He does not compliment her verbally, but he likes to let her know that he is pleased.

A few nights ago — the same night they got a call from Julie and Sarah, saying they were coming for a visit — she told him that she wished he would talk more, that he would confide in her.

"Confide what?" he said.

"You always take that attitude," she said. "You pretend that you have no thoughts. Why does there have to be so much silence?"

"I'm not a professor anymore," he said. "I don't have to spend every minute *thinking*."

But he loves to talk to the young women. He will talk to them on the phone for as much as an hour; he walks with them through the woods for most of the day when they visit. The lovers the young women bring with them always seem to fall behind; they give up and return to the house to sit and talk to her, or to help with the preparation of the meal, or to play with the children. The young woman and George come back refreshed, ready for another round of conversation at dinner.

A few weeks ago one of the young men said to her, "Why do you let it go on?" They had been talking lightly before that — about the weather, the children — and then, in the kitchen, where he was sitting shelling peas, he put his head on the table and said, barely audibly, "Why do you let it go on?" He did not raise his head, and she stared at him, thinking that she must have imagined his speaking. She was surprised — surprised to have heard it, and surprised that he said nothing after that, which made her doubt that he had spoken.

"Why do I let what go on?" she said.

There was a long silence. "Whatever this sick game is, I don't want to get involved in it," he said at last. "It was none of my business to ask. I understand that you don't want to talk about it."

"But it's really cold out there," she said. "What could happen when it's freezing out?"

He shook his head, the way George did, to indicate that she was beyond understanding. But she wasn't stupid, and she knew what might be going on. She had said the right thing, had been on the right track, but she had to say what she felt, which was that nothing very serious could be happening at that moment because they were walking in the woods. There wasn't even a barn on the property. She knew perfectly well that they were talking.

When George and the young woman had come back, he fixed hot apple juice, into which he trickled rum. Lenore was pleasant, because she was sure of what had not happened; the young man was not, because he did not think as she did. Still at the kitchen table, he ran his thumb across a pea pod as though it were a knife.

This weekend Sarah and Julie are visiting. They came on Friday evening. Sarah was one of George's students — the one who led the fight to have him rehired. She does not look like a troublemaker; she is pale and pretty, with freckles on her cheeks. She talks too much about the past, and this upsets him, disrupts the peace he has made with himself. She tells him that they fired him because he was "in touch" with everything, that they were afraid of him because he was so in touch. The more she tells him the more he remembers, and then it is necessary for Sarah to say the same things again and again; once she reminds him, he seems to need reassurance — needs to have her voice, to hear her bitterness against the members of the tenure committee. By evening they will both be drunk. Sarah will seem both agitating and consoling, Lenore and Julie and the children will be upstairs, in bed. Lenore suspects that she will not be the only one awake listening to them. She thinks that in spite of Julie's glazed look she is really very attentive. The night before, when they were all sitting around the fireplace talking, Sarah made a gesture and almost upset her wineglass, but Julie reached for it and stopped it from toppling over. George and Sarah were talking so energetically that they did not notice. Lenore's eyes met Julie's as Julie's hand shot out. Lenore feels that she is like Julie: Julie's face doesn't betray emotion, even when she is interested, even when she cares deeply. Being the same kind of person, Lenore can recognize this.

Before Sarah and Julie arrived Friday evening, Lenore asked George if Sarah was his lover.

"Don't be ridiculous," he said. "You think every student is my lover? Is Julie my lover?"

She said, "That wasn't what I said."

"Well, if you're going to be preposterous, go ahead and say that," he said. "If you think about it long enough, it would make a lot of sense, wouldn't it?"

He would not answer her question about Sarah. He kept throwing Julie's name into it. Some other woman might then think that he was protesting too strongly — that Julie really was his lover. She thought no such thing. She also stopped suspecting Sarah, because he wanted that, and it was her habit to oblige him.

He is twenty-one years older than Lenore. On his last birthday he was fifty-five. His daughter from his first marriage (his *only* marriage; she keeps reminding herself that they are not married, because it often seems that they might as well be) sent him an Irish country hat. The present made him irritable. He kept putting it on and putting it down hard on his head. "She wants to make me a laughable old man," he said. "She wants me to put this on and go around like a fool." He wore the hat all morning, complaining about it, frightening the children. Eventually, to calm him, she said, "She intended *nothing*." She said it with finality, her tone so insistent that he listened to her. But having lost his reason for bitterness, he said, "Just because you don't think doesn't mean others don't think." Is he getting old? She does not want to think of him getting old. In spite of his ulcer, his body is hard. He is tall and handsome, with a thick mustache and a thin black goatee, and there is very little gray in his kinky black hair. He dresses in tight-fitting blue jeans and black turtleneck sweaters in the winter, and old white shirts with the sleeves rolled up in the summer. He pretends not to care about his looks, but he does. He shaves carefully, scraping slowly down each side of his goatee. He orders his soft leather shoes from a store in California. After taking one of his long walks — even if he does it twice a day — he invariably takes a shower. He always looks refreshed, and very rarely admits any insecurity. A few times, at night in bed, he has asked, "Am I still the man of your dreams?" And when she says yes he always laughs, turning it into a joke, as if he didn't care. She knows he does. He pretends to have no feeling for clothing, but actually he cares so strongly about his turtlenecks and shirts (a few are Italian silk) and shoes that he will have no others. She has noticed that the young women who visit are always vain. When Sarah arrived, she was wearing a beautiful silk scarf, pale as conch shells.

Sitting on the floor on Saturday morning, Lenore watches the fire she has just lit. The baby, tucked in George's chair, smiles in his sleep, and Lenore thinks what a good companion he would be if only he were an adult. She gets up and goes into the kitchen and tears open a package of yeast and dissolves it, with sugar and salt, in hot water, slushing her fingers through it and shivering because it is so cold in the kitchen. She will bake bread for dinner — there is always a big meal in the early evening when they have guests. But what will she do for the rest of the day? George told the girls the night before that on Saturday they would walk in the woods, but she does not really enjoy hiking, and George will be irritated because of the discussion the night before, and she does not want to aggravate him. "You are unwilling to challenge anyone," her brother wrote her in a letter that came a few days ago. He has written her for years — all the years she has been with George — asking when she is going to end the relationship. She rarely writes back because she knows that her answers sound too simple. She has a comfortable house. She cooks. She keeps busy and she loves her two children. "It seems unkind to say *but*," her brother writes, "but . . ." It is true; she likes simple things. Her brother, who is a lawyer in Cambridge, cannot understand that.

Lenore rubs her hand down the side of her face and says good morning to Julie and Sarah, who have come downstairs. Sarah does not want orange juice; she already looks refreshed and ready for the day. Lenore pours a glass for Julie. George calls from the hallway, "Ready to roll?" Lenore is surprised that he wants to leave so early. She goes into the living room. George is wearing a denim jacket, his hands in the pockets.

"Morning," he says to Lenore. "You're not up for a hike, are you?"

Lenore looks at him, but does not answer. As she stands there, Sarah walks around her and joins George in the hallway and he holds the door open for her. "Let's walk to the store and get Hershey bars to give us energy for a long hike," George says to Sarah. They are gone. Lenore finds Julie still in the kitchen, waiting for the water to boil. Julie says that she had a bad night and she is happy not to be going with George and Sarah. Lenore fixes tea for them. Maria sits next to her on the sofa, sipping orange juice. The baby likes company, but Maria is a very private child; she would rather that she and her mother were always alone. She has given up being possessive about her father. Now she gets out a cardboard box and takes out her mother's collection of postcards, which she arranges on the floor in careful groups. Whenever she looks up, Julie smiles nervously at her; Maria does not smile, and Lenore doesn't prod her. Lenore goes into the kitchen to punch down the bread, and Maria follows. Maria has recently gotten over chicken pox, and there is a small new scar in the center of her forehead. Instead of looking at Maria's blue eyes, Lenore lately has found herself focusing on the imperfection.

As Lenore is stretching the loaves onto the cornmeal-covered baking sheet, she hears the rain start. It hits hard on the garage roof.

After a few minutes Julie comes into the kitchen. "They're caught in this downpour," Julie says. "If Sarah had left the car keys, I could go get them."

"Take my car and pick them up," Lenore says, pointing with her elbow to the keys hanging on a nail near the door.

"But I don't know where the store is."

"You must have passed it driving to our house last night. Just go out of the driveway and turn right. It's along the main road."

Julie gets her purple sweater and takes the car keys. "I'll be right back," she says.

Lenore can sense that she is glad to escape from the house, that she is happy the rain began.

In the living room Lenore turns the pages of a magazine, and Maria mutters a refrain of "Blue, blue, dark blue, green blue," noticing the color every time it appears. Lenore sips her tea. She puts a Michael Hurley record on George's stereo. Michael Hurley is good rainy-day music. George has hundreds of records. His students used to love to paw through them. Cleverly, he has never made any attempt to keep up with what is currently popular. Everything is jazz or eclectic: Michael Hurley, Keith Jarrett, Ry Cooder.

Julie comes back. "I couldn't find them," she says. She looks as if she expects to be punished.

Lenore is surprised. She is about to say something like "You certainly didn't look very hard, did you?" but she catches Julie's eye. She looks young and afraid, and perhaps even a little crazy.

"Well, we tried," Lenore says.

Julie stands in front of the fire, with her back to Lenore. Lenore knows she is thinking that she is dense — that she does not recognize the implications.

"They might have walked through the woods instead of along the road," Lenore says. "That's possible."

"But they would have gone out to the road to thumb when the rain began, wouldn't they?"

Perhaps she misunderstood what Julie was thinking. Perhaps it has never occurred to Julie until now what might be going on.

"Maybe they got lost," Julie says. "Maybe something happened to them."

"Nothing happened to them," Lenore says. Julie turns around and Lenore catches that small point of light in her eye again. "Maybe they took shelter under a tree," she says. "Maybe they're screwing. How should I know?"

It is not a word Lenore often uses. She usually tries not to think about that at all, but she can sense that Julie is very upset.

"Really?" Julie says. "Don't you care, Mrs. Anderson?"

Lenore is amused. There's a switch. All the students call her husband George and her Lenore; now one of them wants to think there's a real adult here to explain all this to her.

"What am I going to do?" Lenore says. She shrugs.

Julie does not answer.

"Would you like me to pour you tea?" Lenore asks.

"Yes," Julie says. "Please."

George and Sarah return in the middle of the afternoon. George says that they decided to go on a spree to the big city — it is really a small town he is talking about, but calling it the big city gives him an opportunity to speak ironically. They sat in a restaurant bar, waiting for the rain to stop, George says, and then they thumbed a ride home. "But I'm completely sober," George says, turning for the first time to Sarah. "What about you?" He is all smiles. Sarah lets him down. She looks embarrassed. Her eyes meet Lenore's quickly, and jump to Julie. The two girls stare at each other, and Lenore, left with only George to look at, looks at the fire and then gets up to pile on another log.

Gradually it becomes clear that they are trapped together by the rain. Maria undresses her paper doll and deliberately rips a feather off its hat. Then she takes the pieces to Lenore, almost in tears. The baby cries, and

Lenore takes him off the sofa, where he has been sleeping under his yellow blanket, and props him in the space between her legs as she leans back on her elbows to watch the fire. It's her fire, and she has the excuse of presiding over it.

"How's my boy?" George says. The baby looks, and looks away.

It gets dark early, because of the rain. At four-thirty George uncorks a bottle of Beaujolais and brings it into the living room, with four glasses pressed against his chest with his free arm. Julie rises nervously to extract the glasses, thanking him too profusely for the wine. She gives a glass to Sarah without looking at her.

They sit in a semicircle in front of the fire and drink the wine. Julie leafs through magazines — *New Times, National Geographic* — and Sarah holds a small white dish painted with gray-green leaves that she has taken from the coffee table; the dish contains a few shells and some acorn caps, a polished stone or two, and Sarah lets these objects run through her fingers. There are several such dishes in the house, assembled by George. He and Lenore gathered the shells long ago, the first time they went away together, at a beach in North Carolina. But the acorn caps, the shiny turquoise and amethyst stones — those are there, she knows, because George likes the effect they have on visitors; it is an expected unconventionality, really. He has also acquired a few small framed pictures, which he points out to guests who are more important than worshipful students — tiny oil paintings of fruit, prints with small details from the unicorn tapestries. He pretends to like small, elegant things. Actually, when they visit museums in New York he goes first to El Grecos and big Mark Rothko canvases. She could never get him to admit that what he said or did was sometimes false. Once, long ago, when he asked if he was still the man of her dreams, she said, "We don't get along well anymore." "Don't talk about it," he said — no denial, no protest. At best, she could say things and get away with them; she could never get him to continue such a conversation.

At the dinner table, lit with white candles burning in empty wine bottles, they eat off his grandmother's small flowery plates. Lenore looks out a window and sees, very faintly in the dark, their huge oak tree. The rain has stopped. A few stars have come out, and there are glints on the wet branches. The oak tree grows very close to the window. George loved it when her brother once suggested that some of the bushes and trees should be pruned away from the house so it would not always be so dark inside; it gave him a chance to rave about the beauty of nature, to say that he would never tamper with it. "It's like a tomb in here all day," her brother had said. Since moving here, George has learned the names of almost all the things that are growing on the land: he can point out abelia bushes, spirea, laurels. He subscribes to *National Geographic* (although she rarely sees him looking at it). He is at last in touch, he says, being in the country puts him in touch. He is saying it now to Sarah, who has put down her ivory-handled fork to listen to him. He gets up to change the record. Side two of the Telemann record begins softly.

Sarah is still very much on guard with Lenore; she makes polite conversation with her quickly when George is out of the room. "You people are so wonderful," she says. "I wish my parents could be like you."

"George would be pleased to hear that," Lenore says, lifting a small piece of pasta to her lips.

When George is seated again, Sarah, anxious to please, tells him, "If only my father could be like you."

"Your father," George says. "I won't have that analogy." He says it pleasantly, but barely disguises his dismay at the comparison.

"I mean, he cares about nothing but business," the girl stumbles on.

The music, in contrast, grows lovelier.

Lenore goes into the kitchen to get the salad and hears George say, "I simply won't let you girls leave. Nobody leaves on a Saturday."

There are polite protests, there are compliments to Lenore on the meal — there is too much talk. Lenore has trouble caring about what's going on. The food is warm and delicious. She pours more wine and lets them talk.

"Godard, yes, I know . . . panning that row of honking cars *so* slowly, that long line of cars stretching on and on."

She has picked up the end of George's conversation. His arm slowly waves out over the table, indicating the line of motionless cars in the movie.

"That's a lovely plant," Julie says to Lenore.

"It's Peruvian ivy," Lenore says. She smiles. She is supposed to smile. She will not offer to hack shoots off her plant for these girls.

Sarah asks for a Dylan record when the Telemann finishes playing. White wax drips onto the wood table. George waits for it to solidify slightly, then scrapes up the little circles and with thumb and index finger flicks them gently toward Sarah. He explains (although she asked for no particular Dylan record) that he has only Dylan before he went electric. And *Planet Waves* — "because it's so romantic. That's silly of me, but true." Sarah smiles at him. Julie smiles at Lenore. Julie is being polite, taking her cues from Sarah, really not understanding what's going on. Lenore does not smile back. She has done enough to put them at ease. She is tired now, brought down by the music, a full stomach, and again the sounds of rain outside. For dessert there is homemade vanilla ice cream, made by George, with small black vanilla-bean flecks in it. He is still drinking wine, though; another bottle has been opened. He sips wine and then taps his spoon on his ice cream, looking at Sarah. Sarah smiles, letting them all see the smile, then sucks the ice cream off her spoon. Julie is missing more and more of what's going on. Lenore watches as Julie strokes her hand absently on her napkin. She is wearing a thin silver choker and — Lenore notices for the first time — a thin silver ring on the third finger of her right hand.

"It's just terrible about Anna," George says, finishing his wine, his ice cream melting, looking at no one in particular, although Sarah was the one who brought up Anna the night before, when they had been in the house only a short time — Anna dead, hit by a car, hardly an accident at all. Anna was also a student of his. The driver of the car was drunk, but for some reason charges were not pressed. (Sarah and George have talked about this before, but Lenore blocks it out. What can she do about it? She met Anna once: a beautiful girl, with tiny, childlike hands, her hair thin and curly — wary, as beautiful people are wary.) Now the driver has been flipping out, Julie says, and calling Anna's parents, wanting to talk to them to find out why it has happened.

The baby begins to cry. Lenore goes upstairs, pulls up more covers, talks to him for a minute. He settles for this. She goes downstairs. The wine must have affected her more than she realizes; otherwise, why is she counting the number of steps?

In the candlelit dining room, Julie sits alone at the table. The girl has been left alone again; George and Sarah took the umbrellas, decided to go for a walk in the rain.

It is eight o'clock. Since helping Lenore load the dishes into the dishwasher, when she said what a beautiful house Lenore had, Julie has said very little. Lenore is tired, and does not want to make conversation. They sit in the living room and drink wine.

"Sarah is my best friend," Julie says. She seems apologetic about it. "I was so out of it when I came back to college. I was in Italy, with my husband, and suddenly I was back in the States. I couldn't make friends. But Sarah wasn't like the other people. She cared enough to be nice to me."

"How long have you been friends?"

"For two years. She's really the best friend I've ever had. We understand things — we don't always have to talk about them."

"Like her relationship with George," Lenore says.

Too direct. Too unexpected. Julie has no answer.

"You act as if you're to blame," Lenore says.

"I feel strange because you're such a nice lady."

A nice lady! What an odd way to speak. Has she been reading Henry James? Lenore has never known what to think of herself, but she certainly thinks of herself as being more complicated than a "lady."

"Why do you look that way?" Julie asks. "You *are* nice. I think you've been very nice to us. You've given up your whole weekend."

"I always give up my weekends. Weekends are the only time we socialize, really. In a way, it's good to have something to do."

"But to have it turn out like this . . ." Julie says. "I think I feel so strange because when my own marriage broke up I didn't even suspect. I mean, I couldn't act the way you do, anyway, but I —"

"For all I know, nothing's going on," Lenore says. "For all I know, your friend is flattering herself, and George is trying to make me jealous." She puts two more logs on the fire. When these are gone, she will either have to walk to the woodshed or give up and go to bed. "Is there something . . . *major* going on?" she asks.

Julie is sitting on the rug, by the fire, twirling her hair with her finger. "I didn't know it when I came out here," she says. "Sarah's put me in a very awkward position."

"But do you know how far it has gone?" Lenore asks, genuinely curious now.

"No," Julie says.

No way to know if she's telling the truth. Would Julie speak the truth to a lady? Probably not.

"Anyway," Lenore says with a shrug, "I don't want to think about it all the time."

"I'd never have the courage to live with a man and not marry," Julie says. "I mean, I wish I had, that we hadn't gotten married, but I just don't have that kind of . . . I'm not secure enough."

"You have to live somewhere," Lenore says.

Julie is looking at her as if she does not believe that she is sincere. Am I? Lenore wonders. She has lived with George for six years, and sometimes she thinks she has caught his way of playing games, along with his colds, his bad moods.

"I'll show you something," Lenore says. She gets up, and Julie follows. Lenore puts on the light in George's study, and they walk through it to a bathroom he has converted to a darkroom. Under a table, in a box behind another box, there is a stack of pictures. Lenore takes them out and hands them to Julie. They are pictures that Lenore found in his darkroom last summer; they were left out by mistake, no doubt, and she found them when she went in with some contact prints he had left in their bedroom. They are high-contrast photographs of George's face. In all of them he looks very serious and very sad; in some of them his eyes seem to be narrowed in pain. In one, his mouth is open. It is an excellent photograph of a man in agony, a man about to scream.

"What are they?" Julie whispers.

"Pictures he took of himself," Lenore says. She shrugs. "So I stay," she says.

Julie nods. Lenore nods, taking the pictures back. Lenore has not thought until this minute that this may be why she stays. In fact, it is not the only reason. It is just a very demonstrable, impressive reason. When she first saw the pictures, her own face had become as distorted as George's. She had simply not known what to do. She had been frightened and ashamed. Finally she put them in an empty box, and put the box behind another box. She did not even want him to see the horrible pictures again. She does not know if he has ever found them, pushed back against the wall in that other box. As George says, there can be too much communication between people.

Later, Sarah and George come back to the house. It is still raining. It turns out that they took a bottle of brandy with them, and they are both drenched and drunk. He holds Sarah's finger with one of his. Sarah, seeing Lenore, lets his finger go. But then he turns — they have not even said hello yet — and grabs her up, spins her around, stumbling into the living room, and says, "I am in love."

Julie and Lenore watch them in silence.

"See no evil," George says, gesturing with the empty brandy bottle to Julie. "Hear no evil," George says, pointing to Lenore. He hugs Sarah closer. "I speak no evil. I speak the truth. I am in love!"

Sarah squirms away from him, runs from the room and up the stairs in the dark.

George looks blankly after her, then sinks to the floor and smiles. He is going to pass it off as a joke. Julie looks at him in horror, and from upstairs Sarah can be heard sobbing. Her crying awakens the baby.

"Excuse me," Lenore says. She climbs the stairs and goes into her son's room, and picks him up. She talks gently to him, soothing him with lies. He is too sleepy to be alarmed for long. In a few minutes he is asleep again, and she puts him back in his crib. In the next room Sarah is crying more quietly now. Her crying is so awful that Lenore almost joins in, but instead she pats her son. She stands in the dark by the crib and then at last goes out and down the hallway to her bedroom. She takes off her clothes and gets into the cold bed. She concentrates on breathing normally. With the door closed and Sarah's door closed, she can hardly hear her. Someone taps lightly on her door.

"Mrs. Anderson," Julie whispers. "Is this your room?"

"Yes," Lenore says. She does not ask her in.

"We're going to leave. I'm going to get Sarah and leave. I didn't want to just walk out without saying anything."

Lenore just cannot think how to respond. It was really very kind of Julie to say something. She is very close to tears, so she says nothing.

"Okay," Julie says, to reassure herself. "Good night. We're going."

There is no more crying. Footsteps. Miraculously, the baby does not wake up again, and Maria has slept through all of it. She has always slept well. Lenore herself sleeps worse and worse, and she knows that George walks much of the night, most nights. She hasn't said anything about it. If he thinks she's simple, what good would her simple wisdom do him?

The oak tree scrapes against the window in the wind and rain. Here on the second floor, under the roof, the tinny tapping is very loud. If

Sarah and Julie say anything to George before they leave, she doesn't hear them. She hears the car start, then die out. It starts again — she is praying for the car to go — and after conking out once more it rolls slowly away, crunching gravel. The bed is no warmer; she shivers. She tries hard to fall asleep. The effort keeps her awake. She squints her eyes in concentration instead of closing them. The only sound in the house is the electric clock, humming by her bed. It is not even midnight.

She gets up, and without turning on the light, walks downstairs. George is still in the living room. The fire is nothing but ashes and glowing bits of wood. It is as cold there as it was in the bed.

"That damn bitch," George says. "I should have known she was a stupid little girl."

"You went too far," Lenore says. "I'm the only one you can go too far with."

"Damn it," he says, and pokes the fire. A few sparks shoot up. "Damn it," he repeats under his breath.

His sweater is still wet. His shoes are muddy and ruined. Sitting on the floor by the fire, his hair matted down on his head, he looks ugly, older, unfamiliar.

She thinks of another time, when it was warm. They were walking on the beach together, shortly after they met, gathering shells. Little waves were rolling in. The sun went behind the clouds and there was a momentary illusion that the clouds were still and the sun was racing ahead of them. "Catch me," he said, breaking away from her. They had been talking quietly, gathering shells. She was so surprised at him for breaking away that she ran with all her energy and did catch him, putting her hand out and taking hold of the band of his swimming trunks as he veered into the water. If she hadn't stopped him, would he really have run far out into the water, until she couldn't follow anymore? He turned on her, just as abruptly as he had run away, and grabbed her and hugged her hard, lifted her high. She had clung to him, held him close. He had tried the same thing when he came back from the walk with Sarah, and it hadn't worked.

"I wouldn't care if their car went off the road," he says bitterly.

"Don't say that," she says.

They sit in silence, listening to the rain. She slides over closer to him, puts her hand on his shoulder and leans her head there, as if he could protect her from the awful things he has wished into being.

MARK HELPRIN
1947–

Only thirty-nine at this writing, Mark Helprin has already lived at least two lives: that of a scholar and that of a man of action. An accomplished linguist (six languages), he holds degrees from Harvard College and Harvard's Center for Middle Eastern Studies. He has been a Guggenheim Fellow and a recipient of the Prix de Rome of the American Academy and Institute of Arts and Letters. On the other hand, he has served in the British merchant navy, the Israeli infantry, and the Israeli air force. He parachutes, climbs mountains, fools his friends with comic impersonations, and were he not a rigorously law-abiding citizen, could qualify as a cat burgler.

He would like to be a diplomat but will probably remain a writer. He is already more than a good one. His novels, Refiner's Fire and Winter's Tale, have been heatedly praised, especially the phenomenally successful latter title. The same is true of his two collections of short stories.

If there is such a Western Hemisphere movement as late-twentieth-century romanticism ("magic realism" is the current reviewers' shorthand), he may well epitomize its North American branch. He blends what he knows with what he can, with blinding ease, merely conceive. Taking over the fairy tale, he infuses it with a wild humor, an untethered fantasy, and a sophistication and elegance of style universes away from its folkish roots.

"The Schreuderspitze" seems to me one of his most beautiful tales. All fine works of fiction, whatever their ostensible subject, conceal the same subtext: the transforming power of the imagination. Here that power is levered so as to work as therapy. It can not only relieve the grief of tragic loss; it can annul it. Using mountain climbing as an extended metaphor, Helprin subtly counterpoints Franzen's world of practical reality and Wallich's world of visionary achievement.

The Schreuderspitze

IN MUNICH are many men who look like weasels. Whether by genetic accident, meticulous crossbreeding, an early and puzzling migration, coincidence, or a reason that we do not know, they exist in great numbers. Remarkably, they accentuate this unfortunate tendency by wearing mustaches, Alpine hats, and tweed. A man who resembles a rodent should never wear tweed.

One of these men, a commercial photographer named Franzen, had cause to be exceedingly happy. "Herr Wallich has disappeared," he said to Huebner, his supplier of paper and chemicals. "You needn't bother to send him bills. Just send them to the police. The police, you realize, were here on two separate occasions!"

"If the two occasions on which the police have been here had not been separate, Herr Franzen, they would have been here only once."

"What do you mean? Don't toy with me. I have no time for semantics. In view of the fact that I knew Wallich at school, and professionally, they sought my opinion on his disappearance. They wrote down everything I said, but I do not think that they will find him. He left his studio on the Neuhausstrasse just as it was when he was working, and the landlord has put a lien on the equipment. Let me tell you that he had some fine equipment — very fine. But he was not such a great photographer. He didn't have that killer's instinct. He was clearly not a hunter. His canine teeth were poorly developed; not like these," said Franzen, baring his canine teeth in a smile which made him look like an idiot with a mouth of miniature castle towers.

"But I am curious about Wallich."

"So is everyone. So is everyone. This is my theory. Wallich was never any good at school. At best, he did only middling well. And it was not because he had hidden passions, or a special genius for some field outside the curriculum. He tried hard but found it difficult to grasp several subjects; for him mathematics and physics were pure torture.

"As you know, he was not wealthy, and although he was a nice-looking fellow, he was terribly short. That inflicted upon him great scars — his confidence, I mean, because he had none. He could do things only gently. If he had to fight, he would fail. He was weak.

"For example, I will use the time when he and I were competing for the Heller account. This job meant a lot of money, and I was not about to lose. I went to the library and read all I could about turbine engines. What a bore! I took photographs of turbine blades and such things, and seeded them throughout my portfolio to make Herr Heller think that I had always been interested in turbines. Of course, I had not even known what they were. I thought that they were an Oriental hat. And now that I know them, I detest them.

"Naturally, I won. But do you know how Wallich approached the competition? He had some foolish ideas about mother-of-pearl nauti-luses and other seashells. He wanted to know how shapes of things me-chanical were echoes of shapes in nature. All very fine, but Herr Heller pointed out that if the public were to see photographs of mother-of-pearl shells contrasted with photographs of his engines, his engines would come out the worse. Wallich's photographs were very beautiful — the tones of white and silver were exceptional — but they were his undoing. In the end, he said, 'Perhaps, Herr Heller, you are right,' and lost the contract just like that.

"The thing that saved him was the prize for that picture he took in the Black Forest. You couldn't pick up a magazine in Germany and not see it. He obtained so many accounts that he began to do very well. But he was just not commercially-minded. He told me himself that he took only those assignments which pleased him. Mind you, his business vol-ume was only about two-thirds of mine.

"My theory is that he could not take the competition, and the de-mands of his various clients. After his wife and son were killed in the motorcar crash, he dropped assignments one after another. I suppose he thought that as a bachelor he could live like a bohemian, on very little money, and therefore did not have to work more than half the time. I'm not saying that this was wrong. (Those accounts came to me.) But it was another instance of his weakness and lassitude.

"My theory is that he has probably gone to South America, or thrown himself off a bridge — because he saw that there was no future for him if he were always to take pictures of shells and things. And he was weak. The weak can never face themselves, and so cannot see the practical side of the world, how things are laid out, and what sacrifices are required to survive and prosper. It is only in fairy tales that they rise to triumph."

Wallich could not afford to get to South America. He certainly would not have thrown himself off a bridge. He was excessively neat and or-derly, and the prospect of some poor fireman handling a swollen bloated body resounding with flies deterred him forever from such nonsense.

Perhaps if he had been a Gypsy he would have taken to the road. But he was no Gypsy, and had not the talent, skill, or taste for life outside Bavaria. Only once had he been away, to Paris. It was their honeymoon, when he and his wife did not need Paris or any city. They went by train and stayed for a week at a hotel by the Quai Voltaire. They walked in the gardens all day long, and in the May evenings they went to concerts where they heard the perfect music of their own country. Though they were away for just a week, and read the German papers, and went to a corner of the Luxembourg Gardens where there were pines and wildflowers like those in the greenbelt around Munich, this music made them sick for home. They returned two days early and never left again except for July and August, which each year they spent in the Black Forest, at a cabin inherited from her parents.

He dared not go back to that cabin. It was set like a trap. Were he to enter he would be enfiladed by the sight of their son's pictures and toys, his little boots and miniature fishing rod, and by her comb lying at the exact angle she had left it when she had last brushed her hair, and by the sweet smell of her clothing. No, someday he would have to burn the cabin. He dared not sell, for strangers then would handle roughly all those things which meant so much to him that he could not even gaze upon them. He left the little cabin to stand empty, perhaps the object of an occasional hiker's curiosity, or recipient of cheerful postcards from friends travelling or at the beach for the summer — friends who had not heard.

He sought instead a town far enough from Munich so that he would not encounter anything familiar, a place where he would be unrecognized and yet a place not entirely strange, where he would have to undergo no savage adjustments, where he could buy a Munich paper.

A search of the map brought his flying eye always southward to the borderlands, to Alpine country remarkable for the steepness of the brown contours, the depth of the valleys, and the paucity of settled places. Those few depicted towns appeared to be clean and well placed on high overlooks. Unlike the cities to the north — circles which clustered together on the flatlands or along rivers, like colonies of bacteria — the cities of the Alps stood alone, *in extremis,* near the border. Though he dared not cross the border, he thought perhaps to venture near its edge, to see what he would see. These isolated towns in the Alps promised shining clear air and deep-green trees. Perhaps they were above the tree line. In a number of cases it looked that way — and the circles were far from resembling clusters of bacteria. They seemed like untethered balloons.

He chose a town for its ridiculous name, reasoning that few of his friends would desire to travel to such a place. The world bypasses badly named towns as easily as it abandons ungainly children. It was called Garmisch-Partenkirchen. At the station in Munich, they did not even inscribe the full name on his ticket, writing merely "Garmisch-P."

"Do you live there?" the railroad agent had asked.

"No," answered Wallich.

"Are you visiting relatives, or going on business, or going to ski?"

"No."

"Then perhaps you are making a mistake. To go in October is not wise, if you do not ski. As unbelievable as it may seem, they have had much snow. Why go now?"

"I am a mountain climber," answered Wallich.

"In winter?" The railway agent was used to flushing out lies, and when little fat Austrian boys just old enough for adult tickets would bend their knees at his window as if at confession and say in squeaky voices, "Half fare to Salzburg!," he pounced upon them as if he were a leopard and they juicy ptarmigan or baby roebuck.

"Yes, in the winter," Wallich said. "Good mountain climbers thrive in difficult conditions. The more ice, the more storm, the greater the accomplishment. I am accumulating various winter records. In January, I go to America, where I will ascend their highest mountain, Mt. Independence, four thousand metres." He blushed so hard that the railway agent followed suit. Then Wallich backed away, insensibly mortified.

A mountain climber! He would close his eyes in fear when looking through Swiss calendars. He had not the stamina to rush up the stairs to his studio. He had failed miserably at sports. He was not a mountain climber, and had never even dreamed of being one.

Yet when his train pulled out of the vault of lacy ironwork and late-afternoon shadow, its steam exhalations were like those of a man puffing up a high meadow, speeding to reach the rock and ice, and Wallich felt as if he were embarking upon an ordeal of the type men experience on the precipitous rock walls of great cloud-swirled peaks. Why was he going to Garmisch-Partenkirchen anyway, if not for an ordeal through which to right himself? He was pulled so far over on one side by the death of his family, he was so bent and crippled by the pain of it, that he was going to Garmisch-Partenkirchen to suffer a parallel ordeal through which he would balance what had befallen him.

How wrong his parents and friends had been when they had offered help as his business faltered. A sensible, graceful man will have symmetry. He remembered the time at youth camp when a stream had changed course away from a once gushing sluice and the younger boys had had to carry buckets of water up a small hill, to fill a cistern. The skinny little boys had struggled up the hill. Their counsellor, sitting comfortably in the shade, would not let them go two to a bucket. At first they had tried to carry the pails in front of them, but this was nearly impossible. Then they surreptitiously spilled half the water on the way up, until the counsellor took up position at the cistern and inspected each cargo. It had been torture to carry the heavy bucket in one aching hand. Wallich finally decided to take two buckets. Though it was agony, it was a better agony than the one he had had, because he had retrieved his balance, could look ahead, and, by carrying a double burden, had strengthened himself and made the job that much shorter. Soon, all the boys carried two buckets. The cistern was filled in no time, and they had a victory over their surprised counsellor.

So, he thought as the train shuttled through chill half-harvested fields, I will be a hermit in Garmisch-Partenkirchen. I will know no one. I will be alone. I may even begin to climb mountains. Perhaps I will lose fingers and toes, and on the way gather a set of wounds which will allow me some peace.

He sensed the change of landscape before he actually came upon it. Then they began to climb, and the engine sweated steam from steel to carry the lumbering cars up terrifying grades on either side of which blue pines stood angled against the mountainside. They reached a level stretch which made the train curve like a dragon and led it through deep tunnels, and they sped along as if on a summer excursion, with views of valleys so distant that in them whole forests sat upon their meadows like birthmarks, and streams were little more than the grain in leather.

Wallich opened his window and leaned out, watching ahead for tunnels. The air was thick and cold. It was full of sunshine and greenery, and it flowed past as if it were a mountain river. When he pulled back, his cheeks were red and his face pounded from the frigid air. He was alone in the compartment. By the time the lights came on he had decided upon the course of an ideal. He was to become a mountain climber, after all — and in a singularly difficult, dangerous, and satisfying way.

A porter said in passing the compartment, "The dining car is open, sir." Service to the Alps was famed. Even though his journey was no more than two hours, he had arranged to eat on the train, and had paid for and ordered a meal to which he looked forward in pleasant anticipation, especially because he had selected French strawberries in cream for dessert. But then he saw his body in the gently lit half mirror. He was soft from a lifetime of near-happiness. The sight of his face in the blond light of the mirror made him decide to begin preparing for the mountains that very evening. The porter ate the strawberries.

Of the many ways to attempt an ordeal perhaps the most graceful and attractive is the Alpine. It is far more satisfying than Oriental starvation and abnegation precisely because the European ideal is to commit difficult acts amid richness and overflowing beauty. For that reason, the Alpine is as well the most demanding. It is hard to deny oneself, to pare oneself down, at the heart and base of a civilization so full.

Wallich rode to Garmisch-Partenkirchen in a thunder of proud Alps. The trees were tall and lively, the air crystalline, and radiating beams spoke through the train window from one glowing range to another. A world of high ice laughed. And yet ranks of competing images assaulted him. He had gasped at the sight of Bremen, a port stuffed with iron ships gushing wheat steam from their whistles as they prepared to sail. In the mountain dryness, he remembered humid ports from which these massive ships crossed a colorful world, bringing back on laden decks a catalogue of stuffs and curiosities.

Golden images of the north plains struck from the left. The salt-white plains nearly floated above the sea. All this was in Germany, though Germany was just a small part of the world, removed almost entirely from the deep source of things — from the high lakes where explorers touched the silvers which caught the world's images, from the Sahara where they found the fine glass which bent the light.

Arriving at Garmisch-Partenkirchen in the dark, he could hear bells chiming and water rushing. Cool currents of air flowed from the direction of this white tumbling sound. It was winter. He hailed a horse-drawn sledge and piled his baggage in the back. "Hotel Aufburg," he said authoritatively.

"Hotel Aufburg?" asked the driver.

"Yes, Hotel Aufburg. There is such a place, isn't there? It hasn't closed, has it?"

"No, sir, it hasn't closed." The driver touched his horse with the whip. The horse walked twenty feet and was reined to a stop. "Here we are," the driver said. "I trust you've had a pleasant journey. Time passes quickly up here in the mountains."

The sign for the hotel was so large and well lit that the street in front of it shone as in daylight. The driver was guffawing to himself; the little guffaws rumbled about in him like subterranean thunder. He could not wait to tell the other drivers.

Wallich did nothing properly in Garmisch-Partenkirchen. But it was a piece of luck that he felt too awkward and ill at ease to sit alone in restaurants while, nearby, families and lovers had self-centered raucous meals, sometimes even bursting into song. Winter took over the town and covered it in stiff white ice. The unresilient cold, the troikas jingling through the streets, the frequent snowfalls encouraged winter fat. But because Wallich ate cold food in his room or stopped occasionally at a counter for a steaming bowl of soup, he became a shadow.

The starvation was pleasant. It made him sleepy and its constant physical presence gave him companionship. He sat for hours watching the snow, feeling as if he were part of it, as if the diminution of his body were great progress, as if such lightening would lessen his sorrow and bring him to the high rim of things he had not seen before, things which would help him and show him what to do and make him proud just for coming upon them.

He began to exercise. Several times a day the hotel manager knocked like a woodpecker at Wallich's door. The angrier the manager, the faster the knocks. If he were really angry he spoke so rapidly that he sounded like a speeded-up record: "Herr Wallich, I must ask you on behalf of the other guests to stop immediately all the thumping and vibration! This is a quiet hotel, in a quiet town, in a quiet tourist region. Please!" Then the manager would bow and quickly withdraw.

Eventually they threw Wallich out, but not before he had spent October and November in concentrated maniacal pursuit of physical strength. He had started with five each, every waking hour, of pushups, pull-ups, sit-ups, toe-touches, and leg-raises. The pull-ups were deadly — he did one every twelve minutes. The thumping and bumping came from five minutes of running in place. At the end of the first day, the pain in his chest was so intense that he was certain he was not long for the world. The second day was worse. And so it went, until after ten days there was no pain at all. The weight he abandoned helped a great deal to expand his physical prowess. He was, after all, in his middle twenties, and had never eaten to excess. Nor did he smoke or drink, except for champagne at weddings and municipal celebrations. In fact, he had always had rather ascetic tendencies, and had thought it fitting to have spent his life in Munich — "Home of Monks."

By his fifteenth day in Garmisch-Partenkirchen he had increased his schedule to fifteen apiece of the exercises each hour, which meant, for example, that he did a pull-up every four minutes whenever he was awake. Late at night he ran aimlessly about the deserted streets for an hour or more, even though it sometimes snowed. Two policemen who huddled over a brazier in their tiny booth simply looked at one another and pointed to their heads, twirling their fingers and rolling their eyes every time he passed by. On the last day of November, he moved up the valley to a little village called Altenburg–St. Peter.

There it was worse in some ways and better in others. Altenburg–St. Peter was so tiny that no stranger could enter unobserved, and so still that no one could do anything without the knowledge of the entire community. Children stared at Wallich on the street. This made him walk on the little lanes and approach his few destinations from the rear, which led housewives to speculate that he was a burglar. There were few merchants, and, because they were cousins, they could with little effort determine exactly what Wallich ate. When one week they were positive that he had consumed only four bowls of soup, a pound of cheese, a pound of smoked meat, a quart of yogurt, and two loaves of bread, they were incredulous. They themselves ate this much in a day. They wondered how Wallich survived on so little. Finally they came up with an answer. He received packages from Munich several times a week and in these packages was food, they thought — and probably very great delicacies. Then as the winter got harder and the snows covered everything they stopped wondering about him. They did not see him as he ran out of his lodgings at midnight, and the snow muffled his tread. He ran up the road toward the Schreuderspitze, first for a kilometre, then two, then five, then ten, then twenty — when finally he had to stop because he had begun slipping in just before the farmers arose and would have seen him.

By the end of February the packages had ceased arriving, and he was a changed man. No one would have mistaken him for what he had been. In five months he had become lean and strong. He did two hundred and fifty sequential pushups at least four times a day. For the sheer pleasure of it, he would do a hundred and fifty pushups on his fingertips. Every day he did a hundred pull-ups in a row. His midnight run, sometimes in snow which had accumulated up to his knees, was four hours long.

The packages had contained only books on climbing, and equipment. At first the books had been terribly discouraging. Every elementary text had bold warnings in red or green ink: "It is extremely dangerous to attempt genuine ascents without proper training. This volume should be used in conjunction with a certified course on climbing, or with the advice of a registered guide. A book itself will not do!"

One manual had in bright-red ink, on the very last page: "Go back, you fool! Certain death awaits you!" Wallich imagined that, as the books said, there were many things he could not learn except by human example, and many mistakes he might make in interpreting the manuals, which would go uncorrected save for the critique of living practitioners. But it didn't matter. He was determined to learn for himself and accomplish his task alone. Besides, since the accident he had become a recluse, and could hardly speak. The thought of enrolling in a climbing school full of young people from all parts of the country paralyzed him. How could he reconcile his task with their enthusiasm? For them it was recreation, perhaps something aesthetic or spiritual, a way to meet new friends. For him it was one tight channel through which he would either burst on to a new life, or in which he would die.

Studying carefully, he soon worked his way to advanced treatises for those who had spent years in the Alps. He understood these well enough, having quickly learned the terminologies and the humor and the faults of those who write about the mountains. He was even convinced that he knew the spirit in which the treatises had been written, for though he had never climbed, he had only to look out his window to see high white mountains about which blue sky swirled like a banner. He felt that in seeing them he was one of them, and was greatly encouraged when he read in a French mountaineer's memoirs: "After years in the mountains, I learned to look upon a given range and feel as if I were the last peak in the line. Thus I felt the music of the empty spaces enwrapping me, and I became not an intruder on the cliffs, dangling only to drop away, but an equal in transit. I seldom looked at my own body but only at the mountains, and my eyes felt like the eyes of the mountains."

He lavished nearly all his dwindling money on fine equipment. He calculated that after his purchases he would have enough to live on through September. Then he would have nothing. He had expended large sums on the best tools, and he spent the intervals between his hours of reading and exercise holding and studying the shiny carabiners, pitons, slings, chocks, hammers, ice pitons, axes, étriers, crampons, ropes, and specialized hardware that he had either ordered or constructed himself from plans in the advanced books.

It was insane, he knew, to funnel all his preparation into a few months of agony and then without any experience whatever throw himself alone onto a Class VI ascent — the seldom climbed *Westgebirgsausläufer* of the Schreuderspitze. Not having driven one piton, he was going to attempt a five-day climb up the nearly sheer western counterfort. Even in late June, he would spend a third of his time on ice. But the sight of the ice in March, shining like a faraway sword over the cold and absolute distance, drove him on. He had long passed censure. Had anyone known what he was doing and tried to dissuade him, he would have told him to go to hell, and resumed preparations with the confidence of someone taken up by a new religion.

For he had always believed in great deeds, in fairy tales, in echoing trumpet lands, in wonders and wondrous accomplishments. But even as a boy he had never considered that such things would fall to him. As a good city child he had known that these adventures were not necessary. But suddenly he was alone and the things which occurred to him were great warlike deeds. His energy and discipline were boundless, as full and overflowing as a lake in the mountains. Like the heroes of his youth, he would try to approach the high cord of ruby light and bend it to his will, until he could feel rolling thunder. The small things, the gentle things, the good things he loved, and the flow of love itself were dead for him and would always be, unless he could liberate them in a crucible of high drama.

It took him many months to think these things, and though they might not seem consistent, they were so for him, and he often spent hours alone on a sunny snow-covered meadow, his elbows on his knees, imagining great deeds in the mountains, as he stared at the massive needle of the Schreuderspitze, at the hint of rich lands beyond, and at the tiny village where he had taken up position opposite the mountain.

Toward the end of May he had been walking through Altenburg–St. Peter and seen his reflection in a store window — a storm had arisen suddenly and made the glass as silver-black as the clouds. He had not liked what he had seen. His face had become too hard and too lean. There was not enough gentleness. He feared immediately for the success of his venture if only because he knew well that unmitigated extremes are a great cause of failure. And he was tired of his painful regimen.

He bought a large Telefunken radio, in one fell swoop wiping out his funds for August and September. He felt as if he were paying for the privilege of music with portions of his life and body. But it was well worth it. When the storekeeper offered to deliver the heavy console, Wallich declined politely, picked up the cabinet himself, hoisted it on his back, and walked out of the store bent under it as in classic illustrations for physics textbooks throughout the industrialized world. He did not put it down once. The storekeeper summoned his associates and they bet and counterbet on whether Wallich "would" or "would not" as he moved slowly up the steep hill, up the steps, around the white switchbacks, onto a grassy slope, and then finally up the precipitous stairs to the balcony outside his room. "How can he have done that?" they asked. "He is a small man, and the radio must weigh at least thirty kilos." The storekeeper trotted out with a catalogue. "It weighs fifty-five kilograms!" he said. "Fifty-five kilograms!" and they wondered what had made Wallich so strong.

Once, Wallich had taken his little son (a tiny, skeptical, silent child who had a riotous giggle which could last for an hour) to see the inflation of a great gas dirigible. It had been a disappointment, for a dirigible is rigid and maintains always the same shape. He had expected to see the silver of its sides expand into ribbed cliffs which would float over them on the green field and amaze his son. Now that silver rising, the sail-like expansion, the great crescendo of a glimmering weightless mass, finally reached him alone in his room, too late but well received, when a Berlin station played the Beethoven Violin Concerto, its first five timpanic D's like grace before a feast. After those notes, the music lifted him, and he riveted his gaze on the dark shapes of the mountains, where a lightning storm raged. The radio crackled after each near or distant flash, but it was as if the music had been designed for it. Wallich looked at the yellow light within a softly glowing numbered panel. It flickered gently, and he could hear cracks and flashes in the music as he saw them delineated across darkness. They looked and sounded like the bent riverine limbs of dead trees hanging majestically over rocky outcrops, destined to fall, but enjoying their grand suspension nonetheless. The music travelled effortlessly on anarchic beams, passed high over the plains, passed high the forests, seeding them plentifully, and came upon the Alps like waves which finally strike the shore after thousands of miles in open sea. It charged upward, mating with the electric storm, separating, and delivering.

To Wallich — alone in the mountains, surviving amid the dark massifs and clear air — came the closeted, nasal, cosmopolitan voice of the radio commentator. It was good to know that there was something other than the purity and magnificence of his mountains, that far to the north the balance reverted to less than moral catastrophe and death, and much stock was set in things of extraordinary inconsequence. Wallich could not help laughing when he thought of the formally dressed audience at the symphony, how they squirmed in their seats and heated the bottoms of their trousers and capes, how relieved and delighted they would be to step out into the cool evening and go to a restaurant. In the morning they would arise and take pleasure from the sweep of the drapes as sun danced by, from the gold rim around a white china cup. For them it was always too hot or too cold. But they certainly had their delights, about which sometimes he would think. How often he still dreamed, asleep or

and did not understand why these perfect dreams suddenly came to him. Surely they did not arise from within. He had never had the world so beautifully portrayed, had never seen as clearly and in such sure, gentle steps, had never risen so high and so smoothly in unfolding enlightenment, and he had seldom felt so well looked after. And yet, there was no visible presence. But it was as if the mountains and valleys were filled with loving families of which he was part.

Upon his return from the railroad platform, a storm had come suddenly from beyond the southern ridge. Though it had been warm and clear that day, he had seen from the sunny meadow before his house that a white storm billowed in higher and higher curves, pushing itself over the summits, finally to fall like an air avalanche on the valley. It snowed on the heights. The sun continued to strike the opaque frost and high clouds. It did not snow in the valley. The shock troops of the storm remained at the highest elevations, and only worn gray veterans came below — misty clouds and rain on cold wet air. Ragged clouds moved across the mountainsides and meadows, watering the trees and sometimes catching in low places. Even so, the air in the meadow was still horn-clear.

In his room that night Wallich rocked back and forth on the wicker chair (it was not a rocker and he knew that using it as such was to number its days). That night's crackling infusion from Berlin, rising warmly from the faintly lit dial, was Beethoven's Eighth. The familiar commentator, nicknamed by Wallich Mälzels Metronom because of his even monotone, discoursed upon the background of the work.

"For many years," he said, "no one except Beethoven liked this symphony. Beethoven's opinions, however — even regarding his own creations — are equal at least to the collective pronouncements of all the musicologists and critics alive in the West during any hundred-year period. Conscious of the merits of the F-Major Symphony, he resolutely determined to redeem and . . . ah . . . the conductor has arrived. He steps to the podium. We begin."

Wallich retired that night in perfect tranquillity but awoke at five in the morning soaked in his own sweat, his fists clenched, a terrible pain in his chest, and breathing heavily as if he had been running. In the dim unattended light of the early-morning storm, he lay with eyes wide open. His pulse subsided, but he was like an animal in a cave, like a creature who has just escaped an organized hunt. It was as if the whole village had come armed and in search of him, had by some miracle decided that he was not in, and had left to comb the wet woods. He had been dreaming, and he saw his dream in its exact form. It was, first, an emerald. Cut into an octagon with two long sides, it was shaped rather like the plaque at the bottom of a painting. Events within this emerald were circular and never-ending.

They were in Munich. Air and sun were refined as on the station plat-

form in the mountains. He was standing at a streetcar stop with his wife
and his two daughters, though he knew perfectly well in the dream that
these two daughters were meant to be his son. A streetcar arrived in
complete silence. Clouds of people began to embark. They were dressed
and muffled in heavy clothing of dull blue and gray. To his surprise, his
wife moved toward the door of the streetcar and started to board, the
daughters trailing after her. He could not see her feet, and she moved in
a glide. Though at first paralyzed, as in the instant before a crash, he did
manage to bound after her. As she stepped onto the first step and was
about to grasp a chrome pole within the doorway, he made for her arm
and caught it.

He pulled her back and spun her around, all very gently. Her presence
before him was so intense that it was as if he were trapped under the
weight of a fallen beam. She, too, wore a winter coat, but it was slim
and perfectly tailored. He remembered the perfect geometry of the lapels. Not on earth had such angles ever been seen. The coat was a most
intense liquid emerald color, a living light-infused green. She had always
looked best in green, for her hair was like shining gold. He stood before
her. He felt her delicacy. Her expression was neutral. "Where are you
going?" he asked incredulously.

"I must go," she said.

He put his arms around her. She returned his embrace, and he said,
"How can you leave me?"

"I have to," she answered.

And then she stepped onto the first step of the streetcar, and onto the
second step, and she was enfolded into darkness.

He awoke, feeling like an invalid. His strength served for naught. He
just stared at the clouds lifting higher and higher as the storm cleared.
By nightfall the sky was black and gentle, though very cold. He kept
thinking back to the emerald. It meant everything to him, for it was the
first time he realized that they were really dead. Silence followed. Time
passed thickly. He could not have imagined the sequence of dreams to
follow, and what they would do to him.

He began to fear sleep, thinking that he would again be subjected to the
lucidity of the emerald. But he had run that course and would never do
so again except by perfect conscious recollection. The night after he had
the dream of the emerald he fell asleep like someone letting go of a cliff
edge after many minutes alone without help or hope. He slid into sleep,
heart beating wildly. To his surprise, he found himself far indeed from
the trolley tracks in Munich.

Instead, he was alone in the center of a sunlit snowfield, walking on
the glacier in late June, bound for the summit of the Schreuderspitze.
The mass of his equipment sat lightly upon him. He was well drilled in
its use and positioning, in the subtleties of placement and rigging. The
things he carried seemed part of him, as if he had quickly evolved into

a new kind of animal suited for breathtaking travel in the steep heights.

His stride was light and long, like that of a man on the moon. He nearly floated, ever so slightly airborne, over the dazzling glacier. He leaped crevasses, sailing in slow motion against intense white and blue. He passed apple-fresh streams and opalescent melt pools of blue-green water as he progressed toward the Schreuderspitze. Its rocky horn was covered by nearly blue ice from which the wind blew a white corona in sines and cusps twirling about the sky.

Passing the bergschrund, he arrived at the first mass of rock. He turned to look back. There he saw the snowfield and the sun turning above it like a pinwheel, casting out a fog of golden light. He stood alone. The world had been reduced to the beauty of physics and the mystery of light. It had been rendered into a frozen state, a liquid state, a solid state, a gaseous state, mixtures, temperatures, and more varieties of light than fell on the speckled floor of a great cathedral. It was simple, and yet infinitely complex. The sun was warm. There was silence.

For several hours he climbed over great boulders and up a range of rocky escarpments. It grew more and more difficult, and he often had to lay in protection, driving a piton into a crack of the firm granite. His first piton was a surprise. It slowed halfway, and the ringing sound as he hammered grew higher in pitch. Finally, it would go in no farther. He had spent so much time in driving it that he thought it would be as steady as the Bank of England. But when he gave a gentle tug to test its hold, it came right out. This he thought extremely funny. He then remembered that he had either to drive it in all the way, to the eye, or to attach a sling along its shaft as near as possible to the rock. It was a question of avoiding leverage.

He bent carefully to his equipment sling, replaced the used piton, and took up a shorter one. The shorter piton went to its eye in five hammer strokes and he could do nothing to dislodge it. He clipped in and ascended a steep pitch, at the top of which he drove in two pitons, tied in to them, abseiled down to retrieve the first, and ascended quite easily to where he had left off. He made rapid progress over frightening pitches, places no one would dare go without assurance of a bolt in the rock and a line to the bolt — even if the bolt was just a small piece of metal driven in by dint of precariously balanced strength, arm, and Alpine hammer.

Within the sphere of utter concentration easily achieved during difficult ascents, his simple climbing evolved naturally into graceful technique, by which he went up completely vertical rock faces, suspended only by pitons and étriers. The different placements of which he had read and thought repeatedly were employed skillfully and with a proper sense of variety, though it was tempting to stay with one familiar pattern. Pounding metal into rock and hanging from his taut and colorful wires, he breathed hard, he concentrated, and he went up sheer walls.

At one point he came to the end of a subtle hairline crack in an otherwise smooth wall. The rock above was completely solid for a hundred feet. If he went down to the base of the crack he would be nowhere. The only thing to do was to make a swing traverse to a wall more amenable to climbing.

Anchoring two pitons into the rock as solidly as he could, he clipped an oval carabiner on the bottom piton, put a safety line on the top one, and lowered himself about sixty feet down the two ropes. Hanging perpendicular to the wall, he began to walk back and forth across the rock. He moved to and fro, faster and faster, until he was running. Finally he touched only in places and was swinging wildly like a pendulum. He feared that the piton to which he was anchored would not take the strain, and would pull out. But he kept swinging faster, until he gave one final push and, with a pathetic cry, went sailing over a drop which would have made a mountain goat swallow its heart. He caught an outcropping of rock on the other side, and pulled himself to it desperately. He hammered in, retrieved the ropes, glanced at the impassable wall, and began again to ascend.

As he approached great barricades of ice, he looked back. It gave him great pride and satisfaction to see the thousands of feet over which he had struggled. Much of the west counterfort was purely vertical. He could see now just how the glacier was riverine. He could see deep within the Tyrol and over the border to the Swiss lakes. Garmisch-Partenkirchen looked from here like a town on the board of a toy railroad or (if considered only two-dimensionally) like the cross-section of a kidney. Altenburg–St. Peter looked like a ladybug. The sun sent streamers of tan light through the valley, already three-quarters conquered by shadow, and the ice above took fire. Where the ice began, he came to a wide ledge and he stared upward at a sparkling ridge which looked like a great crystal spine. Inside, it was blue and cold.

He awoke, convinced that he had in fact climbed the counterfort. It was a strong feeling, as strong as the reality of the emerald. Sometimes dreams could be so real that they competed with the world, riding at even balance and calling for a decision. Sometimes, he imagined, when they are so real and so important, they easily tip the scale and the world buckles and dreams become real. Crossing the fragile barricades, one enters his dreams, thinking of his life as imagined.

He rejoiced at his bravery in climbing. It had been as real as anything he had ever experienced. He felt the pain, the exhaustion, and the reward, as well as the danger. But he could not wait to return to the mountain and the ice. He longed for evening and the enveloping darkness, believing that he belonged resting under great folds of ice on the wall of the Schreuderspitze. He had no patience with his wicker chair, the bent wood of the windowsill, the clear glass in the window, the green-sided hills he saw curving through it, or his brightly colored equipment hanging from pegs on the white wall.

. . .

Two weeks before, on one of the eastward roads from Altenburg–St. Peter — no more than a dirt track — he had seen a child turn and take a well-worn path toward a wood, a meadow, and a stream by which stood a house and a barn. The child walked slowly upward into the forest, disappearing into the dark close, as if he had been taken up by vapor. Wallich had been too far away to hear footsteps, and the last thing he saw was the back of the boy's bright blue-and-white sweater. Returning at dusk, Wallich had expected to see warmly lit windows, and smoke issuing efficiently from the straight chimney. But there were no lights, and there was no smoke. He made his way through the trees and past the meadow only to come upon a small farmhouse with boarded windows and no-trespassing signs tacked on the doors.

It was unsettling when he saw the same child making his way across the upper meadow, a flash of blue and white in the near darkness. Wallich screamed out to him, but he did not hear, and kept walking as if he were deaf or in another world, and he went over the crest of the hill. Wallich ran up the hill. When he reached the top he saw only a wide empty field and not a trace of the boy.

Then in the darkness and purity of the meadows he began to feel that the world had many secrets, that they were shattering even to glimpse or sense, and that they were not necessarily unpleasant. In certain states of light he could see, he could begin to sense, things most miraculous indeed. Although it seemed self-serving, he concluded nonetheless, after a lifetime of adhering to the diffuse principles of a science he did not know, that there was life after death, that the dead rose into a mischievous world of pure light, that something most mysterious lay beyond the enfolding darkness, something wonderful.

This idea had taken hold, and he refined it. For example, listening to the Beethoven symphonies broadcast from Berlin, he began to think that they were like a ladder of mountains, that they surpassed themselves and rose higher and higher until at certain points they seemed to break the warp itself and cross into a heaven of light and the dead. There were signs everywhere of temporal diffusion and mystery. It was as if continents existed, new worlds lying just off the coast, invisible and redolent, waiting for the grasp of one man suddenly to substantiate and light them, changing everything. Perhaps great mountains hundreds of times higher than the Alps would arise in the sea or on the flatlands. They might be purple or gold and shining in many states of refraction and reflection, transparent in places as vast as countries. Someday someone would come back from this place, or someone would by accident discover and illumine its remarkable physics.

He believed that the boy he had seen nearly glowing in the half-darkness of the high meadow had been his son, and that the child had been teasing his father in a way only he could know, that the child had been asking him to follow. Possibly he had come upon great secrets on the other side, and knew that his father would join him soon enough and that then they would laugh about the world.

When he next fell asleep in the silence of a clear windless night in the valley, Wallich was like a man disappearing into the warp of darkness. He wanted to go there, to be taken as far as he could be taken. He was not unlike a sailor who sets sail in the teeth of a great storm, delighted by his own abandon.

Throwing off the last wraps of impure light, he found himself again in the ice world. The word was all-encompassing — *Eiswelt*. There above him the blue spire rocketed upward as far as the eye could see. He touched it with his hand. It was indeed as cold as ice. It was dense and hard, like glass ten feet thick. He had doubted its strength, but its solidity told that it would not flake away and allow him to drop endlessly, far from it.

On ice he found firm holds both with his feet and with his hands, and hardly needed the ice pitons and étriers. For he had crampons tied firmly to his boots, and could spike his toe points into the ice and stand comfortably on a vertical. He proceeded with a surety of footing he had never had on the streets of Munich. Each step bolted him down to the surface. And in each hand he carried an ice hammer with which he made swinging cutting arcs that engaged the shining stainless-steel pick with the mirrorlike wall.

All the snow had blown away or had melted. There were no traps, no pitfalls, no ambiguities. He progressed toward the summit rapidly, climbing steep ice walls as if he had been going up a ladder. The air became purer and the light more direct. Looking out to right or left, or glancing sometimes over his shoulders, he saw that he was now truly in the world of mountains.

Above the few clouds he could see only equal peaks of ice, and the Schreuderspitze dropping away from him. It was not the world of rock. No longer could he make out individual features in the valley. Green had become a hazy dark blue appropriate to an ocean floor. Whole countries came into view. The landscape was a mass of winding glaciers and great mountains. At that height, all was separated and refined. Soft things vanished, and there remained only the white and the silver.

He did not reach the summit until dark. He did not see the stars because icy clouds covered the Schreuderspitze in a crystalline fog which flowed past, crackling and hissing. He was heartbroken to have come all the way to the summit and then be blinded by masses of clouds. Since he could not descend until light, he decided to stay firmly stationed until he could see clearly. Meanwhile, he lost patience and began to address a presence in the air — casually, not thinking it strange to do so, not thinking twice about talking to the void.

He awoke in his room in early morning, saying, "All these blinding clouds. Why all these blinding clouds?"

Though the air of the valley was as fresh as a flower, he detested it. He pulled the covers over his head and strove for unconsciousness, but he grew too hot and finally gave up, staring at the remnants of dawn light soaking about his room. The day brightened in the way that stage lights come up, suddenly brilliant upon a beam-washed platform. It was early June. He had lost track of the exact date, but he knew that sometime before he had crossed into June. He had lost them in early June. Two years had passed.

He packed his things. Though he had lived like a monk, much had accumulated, and this he put into suitcases, boxes, and bags. He packed his pens, paper, books, a chess set on which he sometimes played against an imaginary opponent named Herr Claub, the beautiful Swiss calendars upon which he had at one time been almost afraid to gaze, cooking equipment no more complex than a soldier's mess kit, his clothing, even the beautifully wrought climbing equipment, for, after all, he had another set, up there in the *Eiswelt*. Only his bedding remained unpacked. It was on the floor in the center of the room, where he slept. He put some banknotes in an envelope — the June rent — and tacked it to the doorpost. The room was empty, white, and it would have echoed had it been slightly larger. He would say something and then listen intently, his eyes flaring like those of a lunatic. He had not eaten in days, and was not disappointed that even the waking world began to seem like a dream.

He went to the pump. He had accustomed himself to bathing in streams so cold that they were too frightened to freeze. Clean and cleanly shaven, he returned to his room. He smelled the sweet pine scent he had brought back on his clothing after hundreds of trips through the woods and forests girdling the greater mountains. Even the bedding was snowy white. He opened the closet and caught a glimpse of himself in the mirror. He was dark from sun and wind; his hair shone; his face had thinned; his eyebrows were now gold and white. For several days he had had only cold pure water. Like soldiers who come from training toughened and healthy, he had about him the air of a small child. He noticed a certain wildness in the eye, and he lay on the hard floor, as was his habit, in perfect comfort. He thought nothing. He felt nothing. He wished nothing.

Time passed as if he could compress and cancel it. Early-evening darkness began to make the white walls blue. He heard a crackling fire in the kitchen of the rooms next door, and imagined the shadows dancing there. Then he slept, departing.

On the mountain it was dreadfully cold. He huddled into himself against the wet silver clouds, and yet he smiled, happy to be once again on the summit. He thought of making an igloo, but remembered that he hadn't an ice saw. The wind began to build. If the storm continued, he would die. It would whittle him into a brittle wire, and then he would snap. The best he could do was to dig a trench with his ice hammers.

He lay in the trench and closed his sleeves and hooded parka, drawing the shrouds tight. The wind came at him more and more fiercely. One gust was so powerful that it nearly lifted him out of the trench. He put in an ice piton, and attached his harness. Still the wind rose. It was difficult to breathe and nearly impossible to see. Any irregular surface whistled. The eye of the ice piton became a great siren. The zippers on his parka, the harness, the slings and equipment, all gave off musical tones, so that it was as if he were in a place with hundreds of tormented spirits.

The gray air fled past with breathtaking speed. Looking away from the wind, he had the impression of being propelled upward at unimaginable speed. Walls of gray sped by so fast that they glowed. He knew that if he were to look at the wind he would have the sense of hurtling forward in gravityless space.

And so he stared at the wind and its slowly pulsing gray glow. He did not know for how many hours he held that position. The rape of vision caused a host of delusions. He felt great momentum. He travelled until, eardrums throbbing with the sharpness of cold and wind, he was nearly dead, white as a candle, hardly able to breathe.

Then the acceleration ceased and the wind slowed. When, released from the great pressure, he fell back off the edge of the trench, he realized for the first time that he had been stretched tight on his line. He had never been so cold. But the wind was dying and the clouds were no longer a great corridor through which he was propelled. They were, rather, a gentle mist which did not know quite what to do with itself. How would it dissipate? Would it rise to the stars, or would it fall in compression down into the valley below?

It fell; it fell all around him, downward like a lowering curtain. It fell in lines and stripes, always downward as if on signal, by command, in league with a directive force.

At first he saw just a star or two straight on high. But as the mist departed a flood of stars burst through. Roads of them led into infinity. Starry wheels sat in fiery white coronas. Near the horizon were the few separate gentle stars, shining out and turning clearly, as wide and round as planets. The air grew mild and warm. He bathed in it. He trembled. As the air became all clear and the mist drained away completely, he saw something which stunned him.

The Schreuderspitze was far higher than he had thought. It was hundreds of times higher than the mountains represented on the map he had seen in Munich. The Alps were to it not even foothills, not even rills. Below him was the purple earth, and all the great cities lit by sparkling lamps in their millions. It was a clear summer dawn and the weather was excellent, certainly June.

He did not know enough about other cities to make them out from the shapes they cast in light, but his eye seized quite easily upon Munich.

He arose from his trench and unbuckled the harness, stepping a few paces higher on the rounded summit. There was Munich, shining and pulsing like a living thing, strung with lines of amber light — light which reverberated as if in crystals, light which played in many dimensions and moved about the course of the city, which was defined by darkness at its edge. He had come above time, above the world. The city of Munich existed before him with all its time compressed. As he watched, its history played out in repeating cycles. Nothing, not one movement, was lost from the crystal. The light of things danced and multiplied, again and again, and yet again. It was all there for him to claim. It was alive, and ever would be.

He knelt on one knee as in paintings he had seen of explorers claiming a coast of the New World. He dared close his eyes in the face of that miracle. He began to concentrate, to fashion according to will with the force of stilled time a vision of those he had loved. In all their bright colors, they began to appear before him.

He awoke as if shot out of a cannon. He went from lying on his back to a completely upright position in an instant, a flash, during which he slammed the floorboards energetically with a clenched fist and cursed the fact that he had returned from such a world. But by the time he stood straight, he was delighted to be doing so. He quickly dressed, packed his bedding, and began to shuttle down to the station and back. In three trips, his luggage was stacked on the platform.

He bought a ticket for Munich, where he had not been in many many long months. He hungered for it, for the city, for the boats on the river, the goods in the shops, newspapers, the pigeons on the square, trees, traffic, even arguments, even Herr Franzen. So much rushed into his mind that he hardly saw his train pull in.

He helped the conductor load his luggage into the baggage car, and he asked, "Will we change at Garmisch-Partenkirchen?"

"No. We go right through, direct to Munich," said the conductor.

"Do me a great favor. Let me ride in the baggage car."

"I can't. It's a violation."

"Please. I've been months in the mountains. I would like to ride alone, for the last time."

The conductor relented, and Wallich sat atop a pile of boxes, looking at the landscape through a Dutch door, the top of which was open. Trees and meadows, sunny and lush in June, sped by. As they descended, the vegetation thickened until he saw along the cinder bed slow-running black rivers, skeins and skeins of thorns darted with the red of early raspberries, and flowers which had sprung up on the paths. The air was warm and caressing — thick and full, like a swaying green sea at the end of August.

They closed on Munich, and the Alps appeared in a sweeping line of white cloud-touched peaks. As they pulled into the great station, as sooty as it had ever been, he remembered that he had climbed the Schreuderspitze, by its most difficult route. He had found freedom from grief in the great and heart-swelling sight he had seen from the summit. He felt its workings and he realized that soon enough he would come once more into the world of light. Soon enough he would be with his wife and son. But until then (and he knew that time would spark ahead), he would open himself to life in the city, return to his former profession, and struggle at his craft.

Acknowledgments

Max Beerbohm, "A. V. Laider": Reprinted by permission of Sir Rupert Hart-Davis.

Colette, "The Other Wife": From *The Collected Stories of Colette,* edited and with an introduction by Robert Phelps. Selection and Introduction copyright © 1983 by Farrar, Straus and Giroux, Inc. Translation copyright © 1957, 1966, 1983 by Farrar, Straus and Giroux, Inc. Reprinted by permission of Farrar, Straus and Giroux, Inc.

Somerset Maugham, "The Facts of Life": From *Complete Short Stories* by W. Somerset Maugham. Copyright 1939 by W. Somerset Maugham. Reprinted by permission of the Executors of the Estate of W. Somerset Maugham, Doubleday and Co., Inc., and William Heinemann, Ltd.

A. E. Coppard, "Dusky Ruth": Copyright 1948, © renewed 1976 by C. D. Coppard. Reprinted by permission of Harold Matson Co., Inc.

Horacio Quiroga, "The Dead Man": From *The Decapitated Chicken and Other Stories* by Horacio Quiroga, translated by Margaret Sayres Peden. Copyright © 1976 by the University of Texas Press. Reprinted by permission of the publisher.

Franz Kafka, "In the Penal Colony": From *The Penal Colony* by Franz Kafka, translated by Willa and Edwin Muir. Copyright 1948, © 1976 by Schocken Books, Inc. Reprinted by permission of Schocken Books, Inc., and Martin Secker and Warburg, Ltd.

D. H. Lawrence, "Odour of Chrysanthemums": From *The Complete Short Stories,* volume II, by D. H. Lawrence. Copyright 1934 by Frieda Lawrence. Copyright © renewed 1962 by Angelo Ravagli and C. Montague Weekley, Executors of the Estate of Frieda Lawrence Ravagli. All rights reserved. Reprinted by permission of the Estate of Mrs. Frieda Lawrence Ravagli, Viking Penguin, Inc., and Laurence Pollinger, Ltd.

Katherine Mansfield, "The Fly": From *The Short Stories of Katherine Mansfield.* Copyright 1922 by Alfred A. Knopf, Inc. Copyright renewed 1950 by John Middleton Murry. Reprinted by permission of Alfred A. Knopf, Inc.

Katherine Anne Porter, "He": From *Flowering Judas and Other Stories* by Katherine Anne Porter. Copyright 1930, © 1958 by Harcourt Brace Jovanovich, Inc. Reprinted by permission of Harcourt Brace Jovanovich, Inc., and Jonathan Cape, Ltd.

Ivo Andrić, "Thirst": From *The Kenyon Review,* Vol. XXVIII, No. 4 (1966). Translated by Aleksander Stefanovich. Reprinted by permission of the translator.

Isaac Babel, "My First Goose": From *The Collected Stories of Isaac Babel.* Copyright © 1955 by S. G. Phillips, Inc. Reprinted by permission of S. G. Phillips, Inc.

James Thurber, "The Greatest Man in the World": From *The Thurber Car-*

nival, published by Harper & Row. Copyright 1945 by James Thurber. Copyright © 1973 by Helen W. Thurber and Rosemary T. Sauers. From *Vintage Thurber* (2 vols.), collection copyright © 1963 by Hamish Hamilton, Ltd. Reprinted by permission of Helen W. Thurber and Hamish Hamilton, Ltd.

Aníbal Monteiro Machado, "The Piano": From *Modern Brazilian Short Stories,* translated by William Grossman. Reprinted by permission of the University of California Press.

F. Scott Fitzgerald, "Babylon Revisited": From *Taps at Reveille.* Copyright 1931 by Curtis Publishing Co. Copyright © renewed 1959 by Frances Scott Fitzgerald Lanahan. Reprinted by permission of Charles Scribner's Sons and The Bodley Head.

William Faulkner, "That Evening Sun": From *Collected Stories of William Faulkner.* Copyright 1931, © renewed 1959 by William Faulkner. Reprinted by permission of Random House, Inc., and Curtis Brown Group, Ltd.

Jorge Luis Borges, "Tlön, Uqbar, Orbis Tertius": From *Labyrinths* by Jorge Luis Borges. Copyright © 1962, 1964 by New Directions Publishing Corp. Reprinted by permission of New Directions, Laurence Pollinger, Ltd., and Penguin Books, Ltd.

Elizabeth Bowen, "Mysterious Kôr": From *The Collected Stories of Elizabeth Bowen.* Copyright 1946, © renewed 1974 by Elizabeth Bowen. Reprinted by permission of Alfred A. Knopf, Inc. Copyright 1944 by Elizabeth Bowen. Reprinted by permission of Curtis Brown Group, Ltd., and Jonathan Cape, Ltd.

Vladimir Nabokov, "First Love": Reprinted by permission of Mrs. Vladimir Nabokov.

Ernest Hemingway, "My Old Man": From *The Short Stories of Ernest Hemingway.* Copyright 1925 by Charles Scribner's Sons. Copyright renewed 1953 by Ernest Hemingway. Reprinted by permission of the Executors of the Estate of Ernest Hemingway and Charles Scribner's Sons.

E. B. White, "The Door": From *The Second Tree from the Corner* (Harper & Row). Copyright 1939, © 1967 by E. B. White. Originally appeared in *The New Yorker.*

Sean O'Faolain, "Lovers of the Lake": From *The Collected Stories of Sean O'Faolain.* Copyright © 1983 by Sean O'Faolain. Reprinted by permission of Little, Brown and Co. in association with the Atlantic Monthly Press and Curtis Brown, Ltd.

V. S. Pritchett, "The Camberwell Beauty": From *Collected Stories* by V. S. Pritchett. Reprinted by permission of V. S. Pritchett, Random House, Inc., and Chatto & Windus, Ltd.

Kay Boyle, "Men": From *Fifty Stories* by Kay Boyle. First appeared in *Harper's Bazaar.* Copyright 1941 by Hearst Magazines, Inc. Copyright © 1955, 1964, 1966, 1980 by Kay Boyle. Reprinted by permission of Doubleday and Co., Inc., and Penguin Books, Ltd.

Morley Callaghan, "A Cap for Steve": Copyright 1952, © renewed 1980 by Morley Callaghan. Reprinted by permission of Don Congdon Associates, Inc.

Frank O'Connor, "The Drunkard": From *Collected Stories* by Frank O'Connor. Copyright 1951 by Frank O'Connor. Reprinted by permission of Alfred A. Knopf, Inc., Joan Daves, and A. D. Peters and Co., Ltd. Originally appeared in *The New Yorker.*

Graham Greene, "Cheap in August": From *The Collected Stories of Graham Greene.* Copyright © 1964 by Graham Greene. Reprinted by permission of Viking Penguin, Inc., and William Heinemann, Ltd.

Isaac Bashevis Singer, "The Dead Fiddler": From *The Collected Stories of*

Isaac Bashevis Singer. Copyright © 1966, 1982 by Isaac Bashevis Singer. First appeared in *The New Yorker.* Reprinted by permission of Farrar, Straus and Geroux, Inc.

John O'Hara, "Flight": From *The O'Hara Generation* by John O'Hara. Copyright © 1964, 1965, 1966 by John O'Hara. Reprinted by permission of Random House, Inc., and U.S. Trust Company, Trustee of the Estate of John O'Hara.

Robert Penn Warren, "The Patented Gate and the Mean Hamburger": From *The Circus in the Attic and Other Stories* by Robert Penn Warren. Copyright 1947, © 1975 by Robert Penn Warren. Reprinted by permission of Harcourt Brace Jovanovich, Inc.

Dino Buzzati, "The End of the World": From *Restless Nights: Selected Stories of Dino Buzzati,* translated by Lawrence Venuti. Copyright © 1983 by Lawrence Venuti. Reprinted by permission of North Point Press. All rights reserved.

Eudora Welty, "Death of a Traveling Salesman": From *A Curtain of Green and Other Stories.* Copyright 1941, © 1969 by Eudora Welty. Reprinted by permission of Eudora Welty, Harcourt Brace Jovanovich, Inc., and A. M. Heath and Co., Ltd.

John Cheever, "The Five-Forty-Eight": From *The Stories of John Cheever.* Copyright 1954 by John Cheever. Reprinted by permission of Alfred A. Knopf, Inc., and International Creative Management.

Mary Lavin, "The Living": Reprinted by permission of the author.

William Sansom, "The Vertical Ladder": From *The Stories of William Sansom.* Copyright © 1960 by William Sansom. Reprinted by permission of Little, Brown and Co. in association with the Atlantic Monthly Press.

Irwin Shaw, "Medal from Jerusalem": From *Short Stories: Five Decades* by Irwin Shaw. Copyright 1937, 1938, 1939, 1940, 1941, 1942, 1943, 1944, 1945, 1946, 1947, 1949, 1950, 1952, 1953, 1954, 1955, 1956, 1957, 1958, 1961, 1963, 1964, 1967, 1968, 1969, 1971, 1973, 1977, 1978 by Irwin Shaw. Reprinted by permission of Arthur Greene, Trustee of the Estate of Irwin Shaw, and Delacorte Press.

Julio Cortázar, "The Southern Thruway": From *All Fires the Fire and Other Stories,* translated by Suzanne Jill Levine. Copyright © 1973 by Random House, Inc. Reprinted by permission of Pantheon Books, a division of Random House, Inc., and Marion Boyars Publishers, Ltd.

Bernard Malamud, "The Jewbird": From *Idiots First* by Bernard Malamud. Copyright © 1963 by Bernard Malamud. Reprinted by permission of Farrar, Straus and Giroux, Inc., A. M. Heath and Co., Ltd., and Chatto & Windus.

Saul Bellow, "A Silver Dish": From *Him with His Foot in His Mouth and Other Stories* by Saul Bellow. Copyright © 1974, 1978, 1982, 1984 by Saul Bellow, Ltd. Reprinted by permission of Harper & Row, Publishers, Inc., and Harriet Wasserman Literary Agency, Inc. Originally appeared in *The New Yorker.*

Jean Stafford, "The Interior Castle": From *The Collected Stories of Jean Stafford.* Copyright 1946, © renewed 1973 by Jean Stafford. Reprinted by permission of the Estate of Jean Stafford, Farrar, Straus and Giroux, Inc., and A. M. Heath and Co., Ltd.

Carson McCullers, "Madame Zilensky and the King of Finland": From *The Ballad of the Sad Café and Collected Short Stories* by Carson McCullers. Copyright 1936, 1941, 1942, 1943, 1950, 1951, 1955 by Carson McCullers. Reprinted by permission of Floria V. Lasky, Executrix of the Estate of Carson McCullers, and Houghton Mifflin Co.

John Updike, "Pigeon Feathers": From *Pigeon Feathers and Other Stories* by John Updike. Reprinted by permission of Alfred A. Knopf, Inc., and Andre Deutsch. Originally appeared in *The New Yorker*. Copyright © 1961 by John Updike.

Philip Roth, "Eli, the Fanatic": From *Goodbye Columbus* by Philip Roth. Copyright © 1959 by Philip Roth. Reprinted by permission of Houghton Mifflin Co.

Joyce Carol Oates, "How I Contemplated the World from the Detroit House of Correction and Began My Life Over Again": From *The Wheel of Love and Other Stories* by Joyce Carol Oates. Copyright © 1970, 1969, 1968, 1967, 1966, 1965 by Joyce Carol Oates. Reprinted by permission of Vanguard Press, Inc.

Margaret Atwood, "The Man from Mars": From *Dancing Girls* by Margaret Atwood. Reprinted by permission of Phoebe Larmore and McClelland & Stewart, Ltd.

Raymond Carver, "A Small, Good Thing": From *Cathedral* by Raymond Carver. Copyright © 1981, 1982, 1983 by Raymond Carver. Reprinted by permission of Random House, Inc., and Collins Publishers.

Ann Beattie, "Weekend": From *Secrets and Surprises* by Ann Beattie. Copyright © 1976, 1977, 1978 by Anne Beattie. Reprinted by permission of Random House, Inc., and International Creative Management.

Mark Helprin, "The Schreuderspitze": From *Ellis Island and Other Stories* by Mark Helprin. Copyright © 1977 by Mark Helprin. Reprinted by permission of Delacorte Press/Seymour Lawrence and Hamish Hamilton, Ltd. Originally published in *The New Yorker*.